A Woman of Substance
Act of Will

Barbara Taylor Bradford

Diamond Books
an imprint of HarperCollins*Publishers*,
77–85 Fulham Palace Road,
Hammersmith, London W6 8JB

This Diamond Books Omnibus edition first published 1993
9 8 7 6 5 4 3 2 1

A Woman of Substance © Barbara Taylor Bradford 1979
Act of Will © Barbara Taylor Bradford 1986

ISBN 1 85813 293 2 (UK)
ISBN Diamond Books 0 261 66167 1 (international edition)

Photoset in Linotron Ehrhardt by Rowland Phototypesetting Ltd,
Bury St Edmunds, Suffolk

Printed in Great Britain by Mackays of Chatham Ltd

Contents

A Woman of Substance

Contents

The value of life lies not in the length of days, but in the use we make of them; a man may live long, yet get little from life.

Whether you find satisfaction in life depends not on your tale of years, but on your will.

— MONTAIGNE, *Essays*

I have the heart of a man, not of a woman, and I am not afraid of anything . . .

— ELIZABETH I, Queen of England

ACKNOWLEDGEMENTS

Many people gave assistance to me during the writing of this book, but it is to Miss Carolyn Blakemore, senior editor of Doubleday & Company, New York, that I am most deeply indebted and whom I must thank first. For three years she gave unstintingly of her valuable advice and time, and her encouragement and belief sustained me at all times. But apart from her moral support, I am grateful to her for her technical skills as an editor, her good taste and sense of style.

I would also like gratefully to acknowledge invaluable help from the staff of the Reading Room of the British Museum, as well as the staffs of the following: Leeds Public Library; Bradford Public Library; Armley Public Library; the Newspaper Microfilm Division of Leeds Public Library; Bankfield Museum, Halifax; Kirkstall Abbey House Museum, Leeds; Fountains Hall, Studley Royal, Yorkshire; Temple Newsam House, Leeds; the Imperial War Museum, London; the New York Public Library. In particular I must thank Mr Ernest Hall of Leigh Mills, Stanningley Bottom, Leeds, for devoting hours to showing me around old portions of the mills and supplying pertinent information regarding conditions in the Yorkshire woollen mills at the turn of the century; my thanks also to Mr Ronald Jacobson, Export Liaison Manager of Marks and Spencer, Ltd, London, for providing old photographs of the original Marks and Spencer's Penny Bazaars in Leeds, and for information regarding the founding and development of that company.

I owe special thanks to Mrs Susan Watt, formerly London editor of Doubleday & Company, whose research was always meticulous and efficiently and promptly supplied, often on very short notice. I would also like to thank all of those friends who helped in a variety of ways: Mr Ronald M. Sumrie, chairman of Sumrie Clothes of Leeds, for introductions to woollen mills in Yorkshire; Mrs Frances Lyons Barish of New York, for giving me access to her father's World War I diaries, for generously typing and duplicating relevant parts; Miss Pauline V. Delli Carpini of New York, for general assistance with the preparation of the final manuscript which saved me untold hours; Mr Eugene H. Winick of Ernst, Cane, Berner & Gitlin, New York, for legal advice regarding wills, trusts, and estates; Mr Morton J. Mitosky of New York, for advice about the same; Mr and Mrs Eric Clarke of Ripon, who drove me across Yorkshire on numerous occasions and reacquainted me with old childhood haunts; Mr and Mrs Eric Fielding, my gracious hosts on my various research trips to London; Mr Peter W. McGill, chairman of AP Publishing, Sydney, who supplied me with detailed maps and vital research material about Australia; Mrs Joan Feeley of New York, for typing a long manuscript most meticulously; Mrs Charlotte Wendel, who helped to keep me physically fit; Mrs Janet Schiff of Chicago, who diligently proofread major portions of the finished manuscript. I would like to express my gratitude to Mrs Joy Klein of New York, not only for her friendship but also for her extraordinary understanding of my obsession with this book, which was expressed in countless ways. Also, my most sincere thanks to Mr Paul Gitlin of Ernst, Cane, Berner & Gitlin, New York, and to Mr

George Greenfield of John Farquharson Ltd, London, my literary representatives for many years and both dear friends whose confidence and support I deeply appreciate.

Finally, I owe a special debt to my parents, Mr and Mrs Winston Taylor of Leeds, for their encouragement and dedication to my project. They also spent many months seeking out old books and newspapers, and their vivid recollections of Yorkshire in the early 1900s provide much of the background for this novel. And my gratitude to my husband for his understanding and belief.

New York, 1979

Quotation from 'The Poems of Yurii Zhivago', Hamlet, from *Doctor Zhivago*, by Boris Pasternak, translated by Max Haywood and Manya Harari. Copyright © 1958. Reprinted by permission of William Collins Sons and Company Limited.

PART ONE

THE VALLEY
1968

He paweth in the valley and rejoiceth in his strength:
he goeth on to meet the armed men.

— JOB

ONE

Emma Harte leaned forward and looked out of the window. The private Lear jet, property of the Sitex Oil Corporation of America, had been climbing steadily up through a vaporous haze of cumulus clouds and was now streaking through a sky so penetratingly blue its shimmering clarity hurt the eyes. Momentarily dazzled by this early-morning brightness, Emma turned away from the window, rested her head against the seat, and closed her eyes. For a brief instant the vivid blueness was trapped beneath her lids and, in that instant, such a strong and unexpected feeling of nostalgia was evoked within her that she caught her breath in surprise. It's the sky from the Turner painting above the upstairs parlour fireplace at Pennistone Royal, she thought, a Yorkshire sky on a spring day when the wind has driven the fog from the moors.

A faint smile played around her mouth, curving the line of the lips with unfamiliar softness, as she thought with some pleasure of Pennistone Royal. That great house that grew up out of the stark and harsh landscape of the moors and which always appeared to her to be a force of nature engineered by some Almighty architect rather than a mere edifice erected by mortal man. The one place on this violent planet where she had found peace, limitless peace that soothed and refreshed her. Her home. She had been away far too long this time, almost six weeks, which was a prolonged absence indeed for her. But within the coming week she would be returning to London, and by the end of the month she would travel north to Pennistone. To peace, tranquillity, her gardens, and her grandchildren.

This thought cheered her immeasurably and she relaxed in her seat, the tension that had built up over the last few days diminishing until it had evaporated. She was bone tired from the raging battles that had punctuated these last few days of board meetings at the Sitex corporate headquarters in Odessa; she was supremely relieved to be leaving Texas and returning to the relative calmness of her own corporate offices in New York. It was not that she did not like Texas; in point of fact, she had always had a penchant for that great state, seeing in its rough sprawling power something akin to her native Yorkshire. But this last trip had exhausted her. I'm getting too old for gallivanting around on planes, she thought ruefully, and then dismissed that thought as unworthy. It was dishonest and she was never dishonest with herself. It saved so much time in the long run. And, in all truthfulness, she did not feel old. Only a trifle tired on occasion and especially when she became exasperated with fools; and Harry Marriott, president of Sitex, was a fool and inherently dangerous, like all fools.

Emma opened her eyes and sat up impatiently, her mind turning again to business, for she was tireless, sleepless, obsessive when it came to her vast business enterprises, which rarely left her thoughts. She straightened her back and crossed her legs, adopting her usual posture, a posture that was contained and regal. There was an imperiousness in the way she held her head and in her general demeanour, and her green eyes were full of enormous power. She lifted one of her small, strong

15

hands and automatically smoothed her silver hair, which did not need it, since it was as impeccable as always. As indeed she was herself, in her simple yet elegant dark grey worsted dress, its severeness softened by the milky whiteness of the matchless pearls around her neck and the fine emerald pin on her shoulder.

She glanced at her granddaughter sitting opposite, diligently making notes for the coming week's business in New York. She looks drawn this morning, Emma thought, I push her too hard. She felt an unaccustomed twinge of guilt but impatiently shrugged it off. She's young, she can take it, and it's the best training she could ever have, Emma reassured herself and said, 'Would you ask that nice young steward – John, isn't it? – to make some coffee please, Paula. I'm badly in need of it this morning.'

The girl looked up. Although she was not beautiful in the accepted sense of that word, she was so vital she gave the impression of beauty. Her vividness of colouring contributed to this effect. Her glossy hair was an ink-black coif around her head, coming to a striking widow's peak above a face so clear and luminous it might have been carved from pale polished marble. The rather elongated face, with its promi-nent cheekbones and wide brow, was alert and expressive and there was a hint of Emma's resoluteness in her chin, but her eyes were her most spectacular feature, large and intelligent and of a cornflower blue so deep they were almost violet.

She smiled at her grandmother and said, 'Of course, Grandy. I'd like some myself.' She left her seat, her tall slender body moving with grace. She's so thin, Emma commented to herself, too thin for my liking. But she always has been. I suppose it's the way she's made. A leggy colt as a child, a racehorse now. A mixture of love and pride illuminated Emma's stern face and her eyes were full of sudden warmth as she gazed after the girl, who was her favourite, the daughter of Emma's favourite daughter, Daisy.

Many of Emma's dreams and hopes were centred in Paula. Even when she had been only a little girl she had gravitated to her grandmother and had also been curiously attracted to the family business. Her biggest thrill had been to go with Emma to the office and sit with her as she worked. While she was still in her teens she had shown such an uncanny understanding of complex machinations that Emma had been truly amazed, for none of her own children had ever displayed quite the same aptitude for her business affairs. Emma had secretly been delighted, but she had watched and waited with a degree of trepidation, fearful that the youthful enthusiasm would be dissipated. But it had not waned, rather it had grown. At sixteen Paula scorned the suggestion of a finishing school in Switzerland and had gone immediately to work for her grandmother. Over the years Emma drove Paula relentlessly, more harsh and exacting with her than with any of her other employees, as she assiduously educated her in all aspects of Harte Enterprises. Paula was now twenty-three years old and she was so clever, so capable, and so much more mature than most girls of her age that Emma had recently moved her into a position of significance in the Harte organization. She had made Paula her personal assistant, much to the stupefaction and irritation of Emma's oldest son, Kit, who worked for the Harte organization. As Emma's right hand, Paula was privy to most of her corporate and private business and, when Emma deemed fit, she was her confidante in matters pertaining to the family, a situation Kit found intolerable.

The girl returned from the galley kitchen laughing. As she slid into her seat she said, 'He was already making tea for you, Grandy. I suppose, like everyone else, he thinks that's all the English drink. But I said we preferred coffee. You do, don't you?'

Emma nodded absently, preoccupied with her affairs. 'I certainly do, darling.' She turned to her briefcase on the seat next to her and took out her glasses and a sheaf of folders. She handed one to Paula and said, 'Please look at these figures for the New York store. I would be interested in what you think. I believe we are about to take a major step forward. Into the black.'

Paula looked at her alertly. 'That's sooner than you thought, isn't it? But then your reorganization has been very drastic. It should be paying off by now.' Paula opened the folder with interest, her concentration focused on the figures. She had Emma's talent for reading a balance sheet with rapidity and detecting, almost at a glance, its strengths and its weaknesses and, like her grandmother's, her business acumen was formidable.

Emma slipped on her horn-rimmed glasses and took up the large blue folder that pertained to Sitex Oil. As she quickly ran through the papers there was a gleam of satisfaction in her eyes. She had won. At last, after three years of the most despicable and manipulative fighting she had ever witnessed, Harry Marriott had been removed as president of Sitex and kicked upstairs to become chairman of the board.

Emma had recognized Marriott's shortcomings years ago. She knew that if he was not entirely venal he was undoubtedly exigent and specious, and dissimulation had become second nature to him. Over the years, success and the accumulation of great wealth had only served to reinforce these traits, so that now it was impossible to deal with him on any level of reason. As far as Emma was concerned, his judgement was crippled, he had lost the little foresight he had once had, and he certainly had no comprehension of the rapidly shifting inner worlds of international business.

As she made notations on the documents for future reference, she hoped there would be no more vicious confrontations at Sitex. Yesterday she had been mesmerized by the foolhardiness of Harry's actions, had watched in horrified fascination as he had so skilfully manoeuvred himself into a corner from which Emma knew there was no conceivable retreat. He had appealed to her friendship of some forty-odd years only once, floundering, helpless, lost; a babbling idiot in the face of his adversaries, of whom she was the most formidable. Emma had answered his pleas with total silence, an inexorable look in her pitiless eyes. *And she had won*. With the full support of the board. Harry was out. The new man, her man, was in and Sitex Oil was safe. But there was no joy in her victory, for to Emma there was nothing joyful in a man's downfall.

Satisfied that the papers were in order, Emma put the folder and her glasses in her briefcase, settled back in her seat, and sipped the cup of coffee. After a few seconds she addressed Paula. 'Now that you have been to several Sitex meetings, do you think you can cope alone soon?'

Paula glanced up from the balance sheets, a look of astonishment crossing her face. 'You wouldn't send me in there alone!' she exclaimed. 'It would be like sending a lamb to the slaughter. You wouldn't do that to me yet.' As she regarded her grandmother she recognized that familiar inscrutable expression for what it truly was, a mask to hide Emma's ruthless determination. My God, she *does* mean

17

it, Paula thought with a sinking feeling. 'You're not really serious, are you, Grandmother?'

'Of course I'm serious!' A flicker of annoyance crossed Emma's face. She was surprised at the girl's unexpected but unequivocal nervousness, for Paula was accustomed to high-powered negotiations and had always displayed nerve and shrewdness. 'Do I ever say anything I don't mean? You know better than that, Paula,' she said sternly.

Paula was silent and, in that split second of silence, Emma became conscious of her tenseness, the startled expression that lingered on her face. Is she afraid? Emma wondered. Surely not. She had never displayed fear before. She was not going to turn out like the others, was she? This chilling possibility penetrated Emma's brilliant mind like a blade and was so unacceptable she refused to contemplate it. She decided then that Paula had simply been disturbed by the meeting, perhaps more so than she had shown. It had not disturbed Emma; rather it had irritated her, since she had found the bloodletting unnecessary and a waste of precious time, and therefore all the more reprehensible. But *she* had seen it all before, had witnessed the rapacious pursuit of power all of her life, and she could take it in her stride. With her strength she was equipped to deal with it dispassionately. As Paula will have to learn to do, she told herself.

The severity of her expression did not change, but her voice softened as she said, 'However, I won't send you alone to Sitex until you know, as I already know, that you can handle it successfully.'

Paula was still holding the folder in her hands, delicate hands with tapering fingers. She put the folder down and sat back in her seat. She was regaining her composure and, gazing steadily at her grandmother, she said quietly, 'What makes you think they would listen to me the way they listen to you? I know what the board think of me. They regard me as the spoiled, pampered granddaughter of a rich and powerful woman. They dismiss me as empty-headed and silly, a brainless pretty face. They wouldn't treat me with the same deference they treat you, and why should they? I'm not you.'

Emma pursed her lips to hide a small amused smile, sensing injured pride rather than fear. 'Yes, I know what they think of you,' she said in a much milder tone, 'and we both know how wrong they are. And I do realize their attitude riles you, darling. I also know how easy it would be for you to disabuse them of their opinions of you. But I wonder, Paula, would you want to do that?'

She looked at her granddaughter quizzically, a shrewd glint in her eyes, and when the girl did not answer, she continued: 'Being underestimated by men is one of the biggest crosses I've had to bear all of my life, and it was particularly irritating to me when I was your age. However, it was also an advantage and one I learned to make great use of, I can assure you of that. You know, Paula, when men believe they are dealing with a foolish or stupid woman they lower their guard, become negligent and sometimes even downright reckless. Unwittingly they often hand you the advantage on a plate.'

'Yes, but . . .'

'No buts, Paula, please. And don't you underestimate me. Do you honestly think I would expose you to a dangerous situation?' She shook her head and smiled. 'I know what your capabilities are, my dear. I have always been sure of you. More

18

sure of you than any of my own children, apart from your mother, of course, and you've never let me down.'

'I appreciate your confidence, Grandmother,' Paula replied steadily, 'but I do find it hard to deal effectively with people who don't take me seriously and the Sitex board do not.' A stubborn look dulled the light in her eyes and her mouth became a thin tight line, an unconscious replica of her grandmother's.

'You know, you really surprise me. You have enormous self-assurance and have dealt with all manner of people, on all levels, since you were quite a young girl. It has never seemed to disturb you before.' Emma sighed heavily. 'And haven't I told you countless times that what people think about you in business is unimportant. The important thing is for you to know who you are and what you are. And frankly I always thought you did.'

'I do!' Paula cried, 'but I am not sure that I have your capacity for hard work, or your experience.'

Emma's face darkened. 'Yes, you do. Furthermore, you have all the advantages of education I never had, so don't let me hear you speak so negatively of yourself again! I'll concede experience to you, but only to a degree. And you are gaining more of that every day. I'll tell you in all honesty, Paula, I would have no compunction in sending you back to Sitex tomorrow – and without me. Because I know you would handle yourself brilliantly. After all, I raised you, I trained you. Don't you think I *know* what I created?'

A carbon copy of yourself and a copy is never quite as good as the original, Paula thought dryly, but said, 'Please don't be angry, Grandmother.' Her voice was gentle. 'You did a wonderful job. *But I am not you.* And the board are very aware of that. It's bound to affect their attitude!'

'Now listen to me!' Emma leaned forward and her narrowed eyes were like green glass slits underneath the old wrinkled lids. She spoke more slowly than was her custom, to give weight to her words.

'You seem to have forgotten one thing! When you walk into Sitex in my place, you walk in there with something they have to take seriously. Power! Whatever they think of your ability, that power is the one thing they cannot ignore. The day you take over from me, after my death, you will be representing your mother, who will have become the single largest stockholder of Sitex. With her power of attorney you will be controlling twenty-five per cent of the preferred stock and fifteen per cent of the common stock of a multi-million-dollar corporation.' She paused and stared intently at Paula, and then continued: 'That's not ordinary power, Paula. That's immense power, and especially so in one person's hands. And don't you ever forget that. Believe me, they won't when it comes to the crunch. They didn't yesterday. But in spite of their unparalleled behaviour – and I am beginning to realize just how much it did upset you – they were unable to ignore me and what I represent!' Emma sat back in her seat, but she kept her eyes focused on Paula, and her face was implacable.

The girl had been listening attentively to her grandmother, as she always did, and her nervousness was ebbing away. For she did have courage and spirit, and not a little of Emma's resoluteness. But the virulence of the fighting at Sitex had indeed appalled her, as Emma suspected. As she gazed at her grandmother, reflecting on her words, she marvelled at her again, as she had yesterday. Emma was seventy-eight years old. An old woman. Yet she had none of the infirmities of the aged, nor their loss of grace. She was vital and totally in command of her faculties. Paula had watched her grandmother's performance at Sitex with awe, had been amazed at her invincible strength, but most of all she had admired her integrity in the face of incredible pressure and opposition. Now Paula wondered, with a cold and calculating objectivity, whether she would ever have that sense of purpose, that icy tenacity to manipulate those men as astutely as her grandmother had. She was not sure. But then some of the nagging doubts were dispelled as she recognized the truth of her grandmother's words. Finally it was her own driving ambition that ultimately overcame the remnants of nervousness.

She spoke with renewed confidence. 'You're right, of course. Power is the most potent of weapons, probably more so than money. And I'm sure it is the only thing the Sitex board do understand.' She paused and looked at her grandmother directly. 'I'm not afraid of them! Don't think that, Grandy. Although I must admit they did disgust me. I suppose if I was afraid, I was afraid of failing you.' The smile she gave Emma was full of sureness and the troubled look had left her face.

Emma leaned forward and patted her hand reassuringly. 'Don't ever be afraid of failing, Paula. It's stopped more people achieving their goals than I care to think about. When I was your age I didn't have time to worry about failing. I *had* to succeed to survive. And always remember what you just said to me about power. It *is* the ultimate weapon. Power, not money, talks. Money is only important when you're truly poor, when you need it for a roof over your head, for food and clothes. Once you have these essentials taken care of and go beyond them, money is simply a unit, a tool to work with. And don't ever let anyone persuade you that power corrupts. It doesn't always, only when those with power will do anything to hold on to that power. Sometimes it can even be ennobling.' She smiled briefly and added with great positiveness. 'And you won't fail me, my dear.'

'I hope not, Grandy,' Paula said, and when she saw the challenging look that swept over Emma's face, she added quickly, 'I know I won't! But what about Harry Marriott? He's the chairman and he appears to hate me.'

'I don't think he hates you, Paula. Fears you perhaps.' Emma's voice was suddenly flat, but there was a dark gleam in her eyes. She had many memories of Harry Marriott, none of them very pleasant, for she had crossed swords with him innumerable times in the past.

'Fears me! Why?' Surprise made the girl's voice rise noticeably, and she leaned forward towards her grandmother.

A flicker of contempt touched Emma's face as she thought of Marriott. 'Because you remind him too much of your grandfather and that unnerves him. Harry was afraid of your grandfather from the very beginning, when they formed the original Sydney – Texas Oil Company and started drilling. Your grandfather always knew what Harry was and Harry instinctively knew that he knew. Hence his fear. When your grandfather left the Sitex stock to me it was with the understanding that I would never sell it as long as I lived. I was to hold it in trust for your mother and any children she might have. You see, your grandfather had great vision, Paula. He recognized years ago that Sitex would become the major company it is today and he wanted us to benefit from it. And he wanted Harry controlled. He wanted my rein on him always.'

'I don't think he can do any more damage at Sitex. He's been rendered virtually powerless, thanks to you. Grandfather would be proud of you, darling,' Paula said, and then asked with some curiosity, 'Do I really resemble him? Grandfather, I mean?'

Emma looked at Paula quickly. They were flying into the sun and a passage of light, very intense and golden, came in through the window. It centred on Paula as she was speaking. To Emma, her hair seemed shinier and blacker in this golden light, hanging in folds like swatches of velvet around the pale still face, and her eyes were bluer and more alive than ever. His eyes. His hair. She smiled gently, her eyes lighting up. 'Sometimes you do, like right now. But mostly I think it's something in your manner that flusters Harry Marriott. And you have no cause to worry about him, Paula. He won't be there for long.' She turned to the briefcase on the seat and began sorting her papers. After a few minutes she looked up and said, 'If you've finished with the balance sheets of the New York store I'll have them back. By the way, do you agree with me?'

'Yes, I do, Grandy. They've made a marvellous turnaround.'

'Let's hope we can keep *them* on the straight and narrow,' Emma said as she took the folder from Paula. She put on her glasses and began studying the figures from the Paris store, already calculating the changes that would have to be made there. Emma knew the store was running into trouble and her mouth tightened in aggravation as she concentrated on the damning figures, and considered the moves she would make on their return to England.

Paula poured herself another cup of coffee and, as she sipped it, regarded her grandmother carefully. This is the face I've seen all my life and loved all my life, she reflected, a wave of tenderness sweeping through her. And she doesn't look her age at all, in spite of what she thinks. She could easily pass for a woman in her early sixties. Paula knew that her grandmother's life had been hard and frequently painful, yet, surprisingly, her face was incredibly well preserved. Paula realized, as she looked at Emma, that this was due in no small measure to the excellence of her bone structure. She noted the webs of wrinkles etching lacy patterns around her grandmother's eyes and mouth, as well as the two deep lines scoring down from her nostrils to her chin. But she also saw that the cheeks above these lines were still firm, and the green eyes that turned flinty in anger were not the rheumy wavering eyes of an old woman. They were alert and knowing. And yet some of her troubled life *is* reflected in her face, she thought, observing the indomitable set of Emma's mouth and the pugnacious tilt of her chin. Paula acknowledged to herself that her grandmother *was* austere and somewhat stern of eye, to many the basilisk. Yet she was also aware that this autocratic bearing was often softened by a beguiling charm, a sense of humour, and an easy naturalness. And, now that her guard was down, it was a vulnerable face, open and fine and full of wisdom.

Paula had never been afraid of her grandmother, but she recognized that most of the family were, her Uncle Kit in particular. Paula remembered now how delighted she had been when her Uncle Kit had once likened her to Emma. 'You're as bad as your grandmother,' he had said when she was about six or seven years old. She had not fully understood what he had meant, or why he had said it, but she had guessed that it was a reprimand from the look on his face. She had been thrilled to be called 'as bad as your grandmother', because surely this meant that she, too, must be special like Grandy and everyone would be afraid of *her*, as they were afraid of her grandmother.

Emma looked up from the papers. 'Paula, how would you like to go to the Paris store when we leave New York? I really think I have to make some changes in the administration, from what I see in these balance sheets.'

'I'll go to Paris if you want, but to tell you the truth, I had thought of spending some time in Yorkshire, Grandy. I was going to suggest to you that I do a tour of the northern stores,' Paula remarked, keeping her voice casual and light.

Emma was thunderstruck and she did not attempt to disguise this. She took off her glasses slowly and regarded her granddaughter with a quickening interest. The girl flushed under this fixed scrutiny and her face turned pink. She looked away, dropped her eyes, and murmured, 'Well, you know I'll go where you think I'm most needed. Obviously it's Paris.' She sat very still, sensing her grandmother's surprised reaction.

'Why this sudden interest in Yorkshire?' Emma demanded. 'It strikes me there is some fatal fascination up there! Jim Fairley, I presume,' she added.

Paula shifted in her seat, avoiding her grandmother's unflickering stare. She smiled falteringly and the flush deepened as she said defensively, 'Don't be ridiculous! I just thought I ought to take inventory at the northern stores.'

'Inventory my eye and Peggy Martin!' Emma exclaimed. And she thought to herself: I can read Paula like a book. Of course it's Fairley. Aloud she said, 'I do know that you are seeing him, Paula.'

'Not any more!' Paula cried, her eyes flashing. 'I stopped seeing him months ago!' As she spoke she instantly recognized her mistake. Her grandmother had so easily trapped her into admitting the one thing she had vowed she would never admit to her.

Emma laughed softly, but her gaze was steely. 'Don't be so upset. I'm not angry. Actually I never was. I only wondered why you never told me. You usually tell me everything.'

'At first I didn't tell you because I know how you feel about the Fairleys. That vendetta of yours! And I didn't want to upset you. God knows, you've had enough trouble in your life, without me causing you any more. When I stopped seeing him there seemed to be no point in bringing up something that was finished. I didn't want to disturb you unnecessarily, that's all.'

'The Fairleys don't upset me,' Emma snapped. 'And in case you've forgotten, I employ Jim Fairley, my dear. I would hardly have him running the Yorkshire Consolidated Newspaper Company if I didn't trust him.' Emma gave Paula a searching glance and asked quickly, curiously, 'Why did you stop seeing him?'

'Because I ... we ... he ... because,' Paula began, and hesitated, wondering whether she dare go on. She did not want to hurt her grandmother. But in her crafty way she's known about our relationship all the time, Paula thought. The girl drew in her breath and, knowing herself to be trapped, said, 'I stopped seeing Jim because I found myself getting involved. I knew if I continued to see him it would only mean eventual heartache for me, and for him, and pain for you, too.' She paused and looked away and then continued with the utmost quiet: 'You know you wouldn't accept a Fairley in the family, Grandmother.'

'I'm not so sure about that,' Emma said in a voice that was hardly audible. So it went that far, she thought. She felt unutterably weary. Her cheekbones ached and her eyes were scratchy from fatigue. She longed to close her eyes, to be done with this silly and useless discussion. Emma tried to smile at Paula, but her mouth was parched and her lips would not move. Her heart constricted and she was filled with an aching sadness, a sadness she thought had been expunged years ago. The memory of him was there then, so clearly evoked that it bit like acid into her brain. And Emma saw Edwin Fairley as vividly as if he was standing before her. And in his shadow there was Jim Fairley, his spitting image. Edwin Fairley, usually so elusive in her memory, was caught and held and all the pain he had caused her was there, a living thing. A feeling of such oppression overcame her she could not speak.

Paula was watching her grandmother intently and she was afraid for her when she saw the sad expression on that severe face. There was an empty look in Emma's eyes and, as she stared into space, her mouth tightened into a harsh and bitter line. Damn the Fairleys, all of them, Paula cursed. She leaned forward and took hold of her grandmother's hand anxiously. 'It's over, Grandy. It wasn't important. Honestly. I'm not upset about it. And I *will* go to Paris, Grandy! Oh, Grandy darling, don't look like that, please. I can't bear it.' Paula smiled shakily, concerned, afraid, conciliatory. These mingled emotions ran together and underlying them all was a sickening fury with herself for permitting her grandmother to goad her into this ridiculous conversation, one she had been avoiding for months.

After a short time the haunted expression faded from Emma's face. She swallowed hard and took control of herself, exercising that formidable iron will that was the root of her power and her strength. 'Jim Fairley's a good man. Different from the others . . .' she began. She stopped and sucked in her breath. She wanted to proceed, to tell Paula she could resume the friendship with Jim Fairley. But she could not. *Yesterday was now. The past was immutable.*

'Don't let's talk about the Fairleys. I said I would go to Paris,' Paula cried, clinging to her grandmother's hand. 'You know best and perhaps I should look the store over anyway.'

'I think you *must* go over there, Paula, to see what's going on.'

'I'll go as soon as we get back to London,' Paula said swiftly.

'Yes, that's a good idea,' Emma agreed rather brusquely, as glad as Paula to change the subject, but also instinctively pressed for time, as she had been all of her life. Time was a precious commodity to Emma. Time had always been evaluated as money and she did not want to waste it now, dwelling on the past, resurrecting painful events that had taken place some sixty years ago.

Emma said, 'I think I must go directly to the office when we arrive in New York. Charles can take the luggage to the apartment, after he's dropped us off. I'm worried about Gaye, you see. Have you noticed anything peculiar when you've spoken to her on the phone?'

Paula was sitting back in her seat, relaxed and calm again, relieved that the subject of Jim Fairley had been dropped. 'No, I haven't. What do you mean?'

'I can't pin it down to anything specific,' Emma continued thoughtfully, 'but instinctively I know something is dreadfully wrong. She has sounded edgy during all of our conversations. I noticed it the day she arrived from London and called me at Sitex. Haven't you detected anything in her voice?'

'No. But then she has been speaking mostly to you, Grandmother. You don't think there is some trouble with the business in London, do you?' Paula asked, alarmed.

'I sincerely hope not,' Emma said, 'that's all I need after the Sitex situation.'

23

She drummed her fingers on the table for a few moments and then looked out of the window, her mind awash with thoughts of her business and her secretary, Gaye Sloane. In her sharp and calculating way she enumerated all of the things that could have gone wrong in London and then gave up. Anything might have happened and it was futile to speculate and hazard wild guesses. That, too, was a waste of time.

She turned to Paula and gave her a wry little smile. 'We'll know soon enough, my dear. We should be landing shortly.'

TWO

The American corporate offices of Harte Enterprises took up six floors in a modern office block on Park Avenue in the Fifties. If the English department-store chain Emma Harte had founded years ago was the visible symbol of her success, then Harte Enterprises was the living heart and sinew. An enormous octopus of an organization, with tentacles that stretched half around the world, it controlled clothing factories, woollen mills, real estate, a retail merchandise company, and newspapers in England, plus large blocks of shares in other major English companies.

As the original founder of this privately held corporation, Emma still owned 100 per cent of the shares of Harte Enterprises, and it operated solely under her aegis, as did the chain of department stores that bore her name, with branches in the north of England, London, Paris, and New York. Harte Stores was a public company, trading on the London Stock Exchange, although Emma was the majority shareholder and chairman of the board. The diversified holdings of Harte Enterprises in America included real estate, a Seventh Avenue dress-manufacturing company, and other stock investments in American industries.

Whilst Harte Stores and Harte Enterprises were worth millions of pounds, they represented only a portion of her fortune. Apart from owning 40 per cent of the stock in the Sitex Oil Corporation of America, she had vast holdings in Australia, including real estate, mining, coal fields, and one of the largest fully operating sheep stations in New South Wales. In London, a small but rich company called E.H. Incorporated controlled her personal investments and real estate.

It had been Emma's custom to travel to New York several times a year. She was actively involved in all areas of her business empire and although she was not particularly distrustful of those to whom she had given extraordinary executive powers, confident of her own shrewd judgement in these choices, there was a canny Yorkshire wariness about her. She was impelled to leave nothing to chance and she also believed that it was vital for her presence to be felt in New York from time to time.

Now, as the Cadillac that had brought them from Kennedy Airport pulled up in front of the skyscraper that housed her corporate offices, Emma's thoughts reverted to Gaye Sloane. Emma had instantly detected Gaye's nervousness during their first telephone conversation when she had arrived from London. Originally

Emma had thought this was due to tiredness after the long transatlantic flight, but the nervousness had accelerated rather than diminished over the last few days. Emma had noted the tremulous quality in Gaye's voice, her clipped manner, her obvious desire to terminate their talks as quickly as possible. This not only baffled Emma but disturbed her, for Gaye was behaving totally out of character. Emma contemplated the possibility that personal problems might be upsetting Gaye, but her inclination was to dismiss this idea, knowing Gaye as well as she did. Intuitively Emma knew that Gaye was troubled by a business problem, one which was of some import and one which ultimately affected her. She resolved to make her talk with Gaye the priority of the day's business.

Emma shivered as they alighted from the car. It was a raw January day, and although the sun was bright in a clear sky, the wind was sharp with frost and Atlantic rain. She could barely remember a time when she had not felt icy cold all over and sometimes it seemed to her that her bones were frozen into solid blocks of ice, as if frostbite had crept into her entire being and petrified her very blood. That numbing excruciating coldness that had first invaded her body in childhood had rarely left her since, not under the heat of tropical sun nor in front of blazing fires nor in the central heating of New York, which she usually found suffocating. She coughed as she and Paula hurried towards the building. She had caught a cold before they had left for Texas and it had settled on her chest, leaving her with this hacking cough that flared up constantly. As they swung through the doors into the building, Emma was for once thankful for that furnace-like heating in her offices.

They took the elevator up to the thirtieth floor, where their own offices were located. 'I think I had better see Gaye at once, and alone,' Emma said as they stepped out. 'Why don't you go over the balance sheets of the New York store with Johnston and I'll see you later,' she suggested.

Paula nodded. 'Fine. Call me if you need me, Grandmother. And I do hope everything is all right.' Paula veered to the left as Emma continued on to her own office, moving through the reception area quickly and with agility. Emma smiled at the receptionist, and exchanged cordial greetings with her as she swept through the double doors that led to her private domain. She closed the doors firmly behind her, for she did not subscribe to this American custom of open doors in executive offices. She thought it peculiar and distracting, addicted as she was to total privacy. She threw her tweed coat and her handbag carelessly on to one of the sofas and, still holding the briefcase, she crossed the room to the desk. This was a gargantuan slab of heavy glass on a simple base of polished steel, a dramatic focal point in the highly dramatic office. It was angled across a corner, looking out into the vast and lovely room, facing towards a plate-glass window. This covered the whole of one wall and rose to the ceiling in a glittering sweep that presented a panoramic view of the city skyline, which Emma always thought of as a living painting of enormous power and wealth and the heartbeat of American industry.

She enjoyed her New York office, different as it was from her executive suite in the London store, which was filled with the mellow Georgian antiques she preferred. Here the ambiance was modern and sleek, for Emma had a great sense of style and she had decided that as much as she loved period furniture, it would be unfitting when juxtaposed against the slick architecture of this great steel-and-glass structure that pushed its way up into the sky. And so she had assembled the best in modern furniture design. Mies van der Rohe chairs were mingled with long,

25

slender Italian sofas, all of them upholstered in dark leather as soft and as supple as silk. There were tall steel-and-glass étagères filled with books, cabinets of rich polished rosewood, and small tables made of slabs of Italian marble balanced on polished chrome bases. Yet for all of its modern overtones there was nothing austere or cold about the office, which had a classical elegance and was the epitome of superior taste. It had, in fact, a tranquil beauty, a softness, filled as it was with a misty mélange of intermingled blues and greys, these subdued tones washing over the walls and the floor, enlivened here and there by rafts of more vivid colours in the cushions on the sofas and in the priceless French Impressionist paintings which graced the walls. Emma's love of art was also evidenced in the Henry Moore and Brancusi sculptures and the temple heads from Angkor Wat, which were displayed on black marble pedestals around the room. The great soaring window was sheathed in sheer bluish-grey curtains which fell like a heavy mist from the ceiling, and when they were open, as they were now, the room seemed to be part of the sky, as if it was suspended in space above the towering concrete monoliths of Manhattan.

Emma smiled as she sat down at the desk, for Gaye's handiwork was apparent. The long sweep of glass was neat and uncluttered, just the way she liked it, bare except for the telephones, the silver mug of pens, the yellow legal pad she favoured for notes, and the practical metal extension lamp that flooded the desk with light. Her correspondence, interoffice memos, and a large number of telexes were arranged in respective files, while a number of telephone messages were clipped together next to the telephones. She took out her glasses and read the telephone messages and the telexes, making various notations on these, and then she buzzed for Gaye. The minute she entered the room Emma knew that her fears had not been unfounded. Gaye was haggard and she had dark smudges under her eyes and seemed to vibrate with tension. Gaye Sloane was a woman of about thirty-eight and she had been Emma's executive secretary for six years, although she had been in her actual employ for twelve years. She was a model of diligence and efficiency and was devoted to Emma, whom she not only admired but held in considerable affection. A tall well-built woman with an attractive appearance, she was always self-contained, usually in command of herself.

But as she walked across the room Emma detected raw nerves barely controlled. They exchanged pleasantries and Gaye sat down in the chair opposite Emma's desk, her pad in her hand.

Emma sat back in her chair, consciously adopting a relaxed attitude in an effort to make Gaye feel as much at ease as possible. She glanced at her secretary kindly and asked quietly, 'What's wrong, Gaye?'

Gaye hesitated momentarily and then said rather hurriedly, feigning surprise, 'Why, nothing, Mrs Harte. Truly, I'm just tired. Jet lag, I think.'

'Let's forget about jet lag, Gaye. I believe you are extremely upset and have been since you arrived in New York. Now come along, my dear, tell me what's bothering you. Is it something here or is there a problem with business in London?'

'No. Of course not!' Gaye exclaimed, but she paled slightly and looked away, avoiding Emma's steady gaze.

Emma leaned forward, her arms on the desk, her eyes glittering behind her glasses. She became increasingly conscious of the woman's suppressed emotions and sensed that Gaye was troubled by something of the most extreme seriousness. As she continued to study her she thought Gaye seemed close to total collapse.

'Are you ill, Gaye?'

'No, Mrs Harte. I'm perfectly well, thank you.'

'Is something in your personal life disturbing you?' Emma now asked as patiently as she could, determined to get to the root of the problem.

'No, Mrs Harte.' Her voice was a whisper.

Emma took off her glasses and gave Gaye a long, piercing look and said briskly, 'Come, come, my dear! I know you too well. There is something weighing on your mind and I can't understand why you won't tell me about it. Have you made some sort of mistake and are afraid to explain? Surely not after all these years. Nobody is infallible and I'm not the ogre I'm supposed to be. You, of all people, should know that by now.'

'Oh, I do, Mrs Harte . . .' The girl broke off. Her voice was shaking and she was close to tears.

The woman sitting opposite Gaye was composed and in absolute control of herself. She was no weakling, Gaye knew that only too well. She was tough and resilient, an indomitable woman who had achieved her phenomenal success because of her formidable character and her strength of will, plus her resourcefulness and brilliance in business. To Gaye, Emma Harte was as indestructible as the coldest steel that could not be twisted or broken. But I am about to break her now, she thought, panic taking hold of her again.

Emma had seen, with gathering disquiet, the twitching muscles and the fear in her eyes. She stood up decisively and crossed the room to the rosewood bar, shaking her head in perplexity. She opened the bar, poured a measure of cognac into a small glass, and brought it back to Gaye.

'Drink this, my dear. It will make you feel better,' she said, patting the woman's arm affectionately.

Tears sprang into Gaye's eyes and her throat ached. The brandy was harsh and it stung her throat but she was suddenly glad of its rough taste. She sipped it slowly and remembered Emma's kindnesses to her over the years. At that precise moment she wished, with great fervency, that she was not the one who had to impart this news. Gaye realized that there were those, who had dealt with Emma as a formidable adversary, who considered her to be cynical, rapacious, cunning, and ruthless. On the other hand, Gaye knew that she was generous of her time and money and understanding of heart. As she was being understanding now. Perhaps Emma *was* wilful and imperious and even power-ridden. But surely life had made her so. Gaye had always said to Emma's critics, and with the utmost veracity, that above all the other tycoons of her calibre and stature, Emma Harte had compassion, and was just and charitable and infinitely kind.

Gaye eventually became aware of this prolonged silence between them, of Emma's fixed stare. She put the glass down on the edge of the desk and smiled weakly at Emma. 'Thank you, Mrs Harte. I do feel better.'

'Good. Now Gaye, why don't you confide in me? It can't be all that terrible.'

Gaye was paralysed, unable to speak.

Emma shifted in her seat and leaned forward urgently. 'Look here, is this something to do with me, Gaye?' Her voice was calm and strong.

It seemed to give Gaye a degree of confidence. She nodded her head and was about to speak, but when she saw the look of concern enter Emma's eyes, her

27

courage deserted her again. She put her hands up to her face and cried involuntarily, 'Oh God! How can I tell you!'

'Let's get it out in the open, Gaye. If you don't know where to begin, then begin in the middle. Just blurt it out. It's often the best way to talk about something unpleasant, which I presume this is.'

Gaye nodded and began hesitatingly, choking back her tears, her hands twitching nervously, her eyes staring and wide. She spoke rapidly in bursts, wanting to tell it all now, and get it over as quickly as possible. It would be a relief, for it had preyed on her mind for days.

'It was the door . . . I remembered . . . I went back . . . I heard them talking . . . No, shouting . . . they were angry . . . arguing . . . they were saying . . .'

'Just a minute, Gaye.' Emma held up her hand to stop the incoherent flow of words. 'I don't want to interrupt you, but can you try to be a little more explicit. I know you're upset, but slow down and take it calmly. What door?'

'Sorry.' Gaye drew a deep breath. 'The door of the filing room that opens on to the boardroom in London. I'd forgotten to lock it last Friday night. I was leaving the office and I remembered I had forgotten to turn off the tape machine, and *that* reminded me of the door. I went back to my office, because I was leaving on Saturday night for New York. I unlocked the door at my side and walked through the filing room to lock the door at the other end.'

As Gaye had been speaking Emma had a mental image of the filing room in the executive suite of offices in the London store. It was a long narrow room with filing cabinets banked on either side and rising to the ceiling. A year ago, Emma had broken through the back wall of the filing room into the adjoining boardroom and added a door. This measure had been to facilitate easy access to documents that might be needed at board meetings, but it had also turned out to be a useful little artery that linked the boardroom and the executive offices and so saved a great deal of time.

Innumerable questions ran through Emma's mind, but she reserved them for later. She nodded for her secretary to continue.

'I know how particular you are about that door being locked, Mrs Harte. As I walked through the filing room from my office I noticed that the door was not simply unlocked but actually open . . . ajar. That's when I heard them . . . through the crack in the door. I didn't know what to do. I was afraid they would hear me closing and locking the door. I didn't want anyone to think I was eavesdropping. So I stopped for a moment, and then I turned off the light, so they wouldn't know I was in the filing room. Mrs Harte, I . . .' Gaye paused and swallowed, momentarily unable to continue.

'Go on, Gaye, it's all right.'

'I wasn't eavesdropping, I really wasn't, Mrs Harte. You know I'm not like that. It was purely accidental . . . that I heard them, I mean. I heard them say . . . say . . .'

Gaye stopped again, shaking all over. She looked at Emma, who was sitting perfectly rigid in her chair, her face an unreadable mask.

'I heard them say, no, *one* of them said that you were getting too old to run the business. That it would be hard to prove that you were senile or incompetent, but that you would agree to step down to avoid a scandal, to prevent a catastrophe with the Harte shares on the Stock Exchange. They argued about this. And then he, that is, the one who had been doing most of the talking, said that the stores had to be sold to a conglomerate and that this would be easy as several companies would be interested in a take-over. He then said that Harte Enterprises could be sold off in pieces . . .' Gaye hesitated, and looked closely at Emma in an attempt to discern her reactions. But Emma's face was still inscrutable.

The sun came out from behind a bank of grey clouds and streamed into the room, a great cataract of brilliant light that was harsh and unrelenting, flooding that vast space with a white brilliance that made the room look alien, unreal, and frightful to Emma. She blinked and shielded her eyes against it.

'Could you close the curtains please, Gaye,' she murmured, her voice a hoarse whisper.

Gaye flew across the room and pushed the automatic button that operated the curtains. They swept across the soaring window with a faint swishing sound and the penetrating radiance in the room was softly diffused. She returned to her chair in front of the desk and, gazing at Emma, she asked with some concern, 'Are you all right, Mrs Harte?'

Emma had been staring at the papers on her desk. She lifted her head slowly and looked across at Gaye with blank eyes. 'Yes. Please go on. I want to know all of it. And I am perfectly sure there *is* more.'

'Yes, there is. The other one said it was futile to battle with you now, either personally or legally, that you couldn't live much longer, that you were getting old, very old, almost eighty. And the other one said you were so tough they would have to shoot you in the end.' Gaye covered her mouth with her hand to stifle a sob and tears pricked her eyes. 'Oh, Mrs Harte, I'm so sorry.'

Emma was so still she might have turned to stone. Her eyes were suddenly cold and calculating. 'Are you going to tell me who these two gentlemen were, Gaye? Mind you, I use that term loosely,' she said with biting sarcasm. Before Gaye had a chance to reply Emma knew deep within herself, deep down in the very marrow of her bones, exactly whom Gaye would condemn when she opened her mouth. And yet part of her was still disbelieving, still hopeful, and she must hear it from Gaye's own mouth to truly believe it. To accept her own damning suspicions as fact.

'Oh God, Mrs Harte! I wish I didn't have to tell you this!' She took a deep breath. 'It was Mr Ainsley and Mr Lowther. They started to quarrel again, and Mr Lowther said that they needed the girls with them. Mr Ainsley said the girls *were* with them, that he already talked to them. But that he had not talked to Mrs Amory, since she would never agree. He said she must not be told anything, under any circumstances, because she would immediately run and tell you. Mr Lowther then said again that there was nothing they could do about taking over the business whilst you were still alive. He told Mr Ainsley that they would never get away with it, because they did not have the power, or enough shares between them, to gain control. He said they would just have to wait until you were dead. He was adamant about this. He also told Mr Ainsley that he himself was entitled to the controlling shares of the Harte chain and that he was certain you would leave them these shares. He then informed Mr Ainsley that he intended to run the Harte chain and that he would never agree to sell the stores to a conglomerate. Mr Ainsley was furious, almost hysterical, and started to scream the most terrible things at Mr Lowther. But Mr Lowther eventually calmed him down, and he said he *would* agree to the sale of Harte Enterprises, and that would bring Mr Ainsley all the millions he wanted. Mr Ainsley then asked if Mr Lowther knew what was in your will. Mr Lowther told him he didn't know, but that he thought you would be fair with them all. He did express some concern about Miss Paula, because she was so close to you. He said he didn't know what she had been able to wheedle out of you. This upset Mr Ainsley, and he grew very excited again and said that they must formulate a plan of action now, one which they could put into operation after your death, in the event that your will did not favour them.'

Gaye paused breathlessly, poised on the edge of her chair.

Emma could not speak or move or think, so stunned and shaken was she now. As she reflected on Gaye's words the blood rushed to her head and a faintness settled over her. Every bone in her body felt weighted down by the most dreadful fatigue, a fatigue that was leaden and stupefying.

Her heart shifted within her, and it seemed to Emma that in that instant it withered and turned into a cold, hard little pebble. An immense pain flooded her entire being. It was the pain of despair. The pain of betrayal. Her two sons were plotting against her. Robin and Kit. Half brothers who had never been close were now hand in glove, partners in treachery. She was incredulous as she thought: God Almighty! It's not possible. It can't be possible. Not Kit. Not Robin. They could never be so venal. Never. Not my boys! Yet somewhere in the recesses of her mind, in her innermost soul, she knew that it was true. And that anguish of heart and soul and body was displaced by an anger of such icy ferocity that it cleared her brain and propelled her to her feet. Dimly, distantly, she heard Gaye's voice coming to her as if from a cavernous depth.

'Mrs Harte! Mrs Harte! Are you ill?'

Emma leaned forward across the desk, which she gripped tightly to steady herself, and her face was drawn and pinched. Her voice was low as she said, 'Are you sure of all this, Gaye? I don't doubt you, but are you certain you heard everything correctly? You realize the seriousness of what you have recounted, I'm sure, so think very carefully.'

'Mrs Harte, I am absolutely sure of everything I've said,' Gaye answered quietly. 'Furthermore, I have not added or subtracted anything, and I haven't exaggerated either.'

'Is that all?'

'No, there's more.' Gaye bent down and picked up her handbag. She opened it and took out a tape, which she placed on the desk in front of Emma.

Emma regarded the tape, her eyes narrowing. 'What is this?'

'It's a tape of everything that was said, Mrs Harte. Except for whatever occurred before I went into the filing room. And the first few sentences I heard. They are missing.'

Emma looked at her uncomprehendingly, her eyebrows lifting, questions on the tip of her tongue. But before she could ask them, Gaye proceeded to explain more fully.

'Mrs Harte, the tape machine was on. That's why I went back to the office in the first place. When I went into the filing room, and heard them shouting, I was distracted for a minute. I turned off the filing-room light so they wouldn't come in and see me. It was then that I saw the red light on the machine flickering and I went to turn this off, too. But it suddenly occurred to me to record their conversation, since I was getting the general drift of it, and realized its importance. So I pressed the record button. Everything they said after that moment is on here, even the things which were said after I closed the door and couldn't hear clearly.'

Emma had the irresistible desire to laugh out loud, a bitter, hollow laugh. She resisted the impulse, lest Gaye think her raving mad and out of her senses, or hysterical at the most. The fools, the utter fools! she thought. And the irony of it! They had chosen her own boardroom in which to plot against her. That was their first and most crucial mistake. An irrevocable mistake. Kit and Robin were directors of Harte Enterprises, but they were not on the board of the department-store chain. They did not come to board meetings at the store, and so they did not know that she had recently installed sophisticated equipment to record the minutes, another time-saving device. It liberated Gaye for other duties and she simply typed up the minutes from the tapes when it was convenient. The microphones were hooked up under the boardroom table, hidden for aesthetics rather than for any reasons of secrecy in the elegant Georgian room with its fine antiques and paintings of great worth. Emma looked down at the tape on the glass desk, and to her it was an evil thing, lying there like a coiled and venomous snake.

'I assume you have listened to this, Gaye?'

'Yes, Mrs Harte. I waited until they left and then I played it back, I took it home with me on Friday and it hasn't been out of my sight since then.'

'Is there much more on it? More than you have already told me?'

'About another ten minutes or so. They were discussing . . .'

Emma held up her hand, utterly exhausted, unable to hear any more. 'Never mind, Gaye. I'll play it later. I know quite enough already!'

She stood up and walked across the room to the window, erect and composed, though her steps were slow and dragged wearily across the thick carpet. She moved the curtains slightly. It had started to snow. The crystal flakes fell in glittering white flurries, swirling and eddying in the wind, brushing up against the window and coating it with a light film as delicate and as fine as white lace. But the flakes were rapidly melting under the bright sun, running in rivulets down the glass and turning into drizzle before they reached the ground. Emma looked down. Far below her the traffic moved in slow unending lines up and down Park Avenue and the scene was strangely remote. And everything was hushed in the room, as if the entire world had stopped and was silent, stilled for ever.

She pressed her aching head against the window and closed her eyes and thought of her two sons, of all her children, but mostly of her adored Robin, her favourite son. Robin, who had become her antagonist after they had clashed a few years before about a take-over bid for the chain of stores. A bid which came from out of the blue and which she did not want to even discuss, never mind consider. When she had refused to talk to the conglomerate involved, he had been vociferous in his condemnation of her, exclaiming angrily that she did not want to sell because she did not want to relinquish her power. She had met resentment from him in such virulent proportions that she was at first incredulous and then truly infuriated. What nerve, what gall, she had thought at the time, that he would dare to dictate to her about her business. One in which he did not have the slightest interest, except for the money it brought him. Robin the handsome, the dashing, the brilliant Member of Parliament. Robin with his long-suffering wife, his mistresses, his rather questionable male friends, and his taste for high living. Yes, Robin was the instigator of this deadly little plot, of that she was quite sure.

Kit, her eldest son, did not have the imagination or the nerve to promulgate so nefarious a scheme. But what he lacked in imagination he made up for in plodding diligence and stubbornness and he was uncommonly patient. Kit could wait years for anything he truly wanted, and she had always known he wanted the stores. But he had never had any aptitude for retailing, and long ago, when he was still young, she had manoeuvred him into Harte Enterprises, steered him towards the woollen mills in Yorkshire, which he ran with a degree of efficiency. Yes, Kit could always be manoeuvred, and no doubt Robin is doing just that, she thought contemptuously.

She contemplated her three daughters and her mouth twisted into a grim smile as she considered Edwina, the eldest, the first born of all her children. She had worked like a drudge and fought like a tigress for Edwina when she was still only a girl herself, for she had loved Edwina with all her heart. And yet she had always known that Edwina had never truly felt the same way about her, oddly distant as a little girl, remote in her youth, and that remoteness had turned into real coldness in later years. Edwina had allied herself with Robin at the time of the take-over bid, backing him to the hilt. Undoubtedly she was now his chief ally in this perfidious scheme. She found it hard to believe that Elizabeth, Robin's twin, would go along with them, and yet perhaps she would. Beautiful, wild, untameable Elizabeth, with her exquisite features and beguiling charm and her penchant for expensive husbands, expensive clothes, and expensive travel. No amount of money was ever enough to satisfy her and she needed it as constantly and as desperately as Robin.

Daisy was the only one of whom she was sure, because she knew that of all her children Daisy truly loved her. Daisy was not involved in this scheme of things, because she would never be a party to a conspiracy engineered by her brothers and sisters to slice up the Harte holdings. Apart from her love and her loyalty, Daisy had the utmost respect for her and faith in her judgement. Daisy never questioned her motives or decisions, because she recognized that they were generated by a sense of fair play, and were based entirely on judicious planning.

Daisy was her youngest child, and as different in looks and character from Emma as the others were, but she was closely bound to her mother and they cared for each other with a deep and powerful love that bordered on adoration. Daisy was all sweetness and gentleness, fine and honourable and good. At times, in the past, Emma had mused on Daisy's intrinsic purity and honesty and worried about it, believing her to be too open and soft for her own safety. Emma had reasoned that her goodness could only make her dangerously vulnerable. But, eventually, she had begun to comprehend that there was a deep and strong inner core in Daisy that was tenacious. In her own way she could be as implacable as Emma, and she was unshakeable in her beliefs, brave and courageous in her actions, and steadfast in her loyalties. Emma had finally recognized that it was Daisy's very goodness that protected her. It enfolded her like a shining and impenetrable sheath of chain mail and so made her incorruptible and inviolate against all.

And the others know that, Emma thought, as she continued to gaze out at the skyline of Manhattan, her heart flooded with despair. She was still shaken; however, the stunned feeling that she had been bludgeoned about her head and her body was slowly dissipating. She discovered, too, that although she had been thunder-struck initially, this reaction was also a passing thing. She actually felt no sense of surprise now at Gaye's story. It was not that she had ever anticipated these actions of her children, for in all truth she had not. But few things came as a surprise to Emma any more and in her wisdom, understanding, and experience of life, family treachery was not surprising to her at all.

Emma had come to believe long ago that ties of blood did not assure fidelity or love. It's not true that blood is thicker than water, she thought, except in Daisy's case. She really is part of me. She remembered a conversation she had once had with her banker, Henry Rossiter. It was years ago now, but it came back to her quite strongly, each nuance so clear it might have taken place only yesterday. He had said grimly that Daisy was like a dove that had been flung into a nest of vipers. Emma had shuddered with revulsion at his savage analogy. To dispel the hideous image he had conjured up before her eyes, she had told him that he was being melodramatic and overimaginative, and she had laughed, so that he would not observe her true reactions. Now on this January day, in her seventy-ninth year, she recalled Henry's words, which had been so ominous, as she contemplated the first four children she had borne and raised, and who had turned on her. A nest of vipers indeed, she thought.

She turned away from the window abruptly and went back to her desk. She sat down and her unflickering eyes rested on that vile tape for a moment, and then she lifted her briefcase on to the desk, opened it, and dropped the tape into it without further comment.

Gaye had been watching with some consternation, her face grave. She was disturbed by Emma's appearance. Her countenance was now glazed over by a kind of hard grimness, and she looked haggard and drawn. The fine bones of her face, always very prominent, were so gaunt and close to the surface of her skin they appeared almost fleshless. Her naturally pale face was ashen. The spots of rouge stood out like raw smudges on her cheeks, and her lips had turned livid under the gloss of the red lipstick. Emma's wide-set green eyes, usually so clear and so brilliant and so comprehending, were now clouded with dark pain and disillusionment and the agony of fully acknowledged betrayal. To Gaye her face had taken on the overtones of a death mask.

There was something fragile and vulnerable about Emma at this moment and she looked so very old that Gaye had the desire to run and put her arms around her. But she refrained, afraid Emma would think of it as an intrusion, for she knew that there was an unremitting self-reliance and intense pride in Emma's nature, which was forbidding, and she had an innate sense of privateness about her personal affairs.

She asked quietly and with some tenderness, 'Do you feel ill, Mrs Harte? Can I get you anything?'

'I'll be all right in a few minutes, Gaye.' Emma attempted a smile. She bent her head and she felt the prick of tears behind her eyes. Eventually she looked up and said, 'I think I would like to be alone for a little while, Gaye. To think. Would you make me a cup of tea and bring it in shortly, in about ten minutes, please?'

'Of course, Mrs Harte. As long as you are sure you will be all right alone.' She stood up and moved towards the door, hesitating briefly.

Emma smiled. 'Yes, I will, Gaye. Don't worry.' Gaye left the room and Emma leaned back in her chair and closed her eyes, relaxing her rigid muscles. First Sitex and now this, she thought wearily, and then there is Paula and her lingering interest in Jim Fairley. Always the past coming back to haunt me, she reflected sadly, although she knew deep within herself that no one ever escaped the past. It was the burden of the present and of the future and you carried it with you always.

Years ago, when Emma had been a young woman and had seen traits developing in her children which alarmed her, she had thought: It's *my* fault. I have made them what they are. Some I've neglected, others I've loved too well and too hard, all of them I've indulged and spoiled for the most part. But as she had grown older and wiser, her guilt was diluted as she came to believe that each man was responsible for his own character. Eventually she had been able to acknowledge to herself that if character did determine a man's destiny then every man and woman created their own heaven or hell. It was then that she had truly understood what Paul McGill had meant when he had once said to her, 'We are each the authors of our own lives, Emma. We live in what we have created. There is no way to shift the blame and no one else to accept the accolades.' From that moment on she had been able to come to grips with her mixed and frequently turbulent emotions about her children. She had refrained from agonizing over them and she had stopped blaming herself for their weaknesses and their faults. They alone were responsible for what they had made of their lives, and she was enabled to shake off the feeling that she was culpable.

All this came back to her now as she remembered Paul's words and she thought: *No, I'm not guilty. They are motivated by their own greed, their own vaunting and misplaced ambitions.* She rose again and crossed to the window, a degree of firmness returning to her step, the resolute expression settling on her face. She looked out absently. It had stopped snowing and the sun was shining in a clear sky. After a few moments of contemplation she returned to her desk. She knew what her course of action must be. She buzzed for Gaye, who responded immediately and came into the room carrying the tea tray. She set it down on the desk in front of Emma, who thanked her, and then went and sat in the chair opposite the desk. She *is* dauntless, Gaye said to herself as she gazed at Emma, noting the calm expression in her eyes, the steady hand that poured the tea.

After a moment Emma smiled at her. 'I'm feeling better, Gaye. I think you had better make three reservations on any plane leaving for London tonight. I know several airlines have early evening flights. I don't care which one it is, just get us on a flight.'

'Yes, Mrs Harte. I'll start calling right away.' She stood up to take her leave.

'By the way, Gaye dear, I am quite certain Paula will wonder why we are returning to London sooner than expected. I shall tell her I have urgent business that needs my attention. I would prefer her not to know anything about this . . .' She paused, searching for the appropriate word, and laughed bitterly. 'This plot I suppose we should call it.'

'I wouldn't dream of mentioning it to Miss Paula or anyone!' Gaye exclaimed vehemently.

'And Gaye . . .'

'Yes, Mrs Harte?'

'Thank you. You did the right thing. I am very grateful to you.'

'Oh, Mrs Harte, please . . . what else could I do? I was simply afraid to tell you because I knew how much it would distress you.'

Emma smiled. 'I know. Now see if you can get us on a plane.'

Gaye nodded and left the room. Emma sipped the tea, her mind crowded with thoughts. Thoughts of her business, her children and her grandchildren. The family she had raised, the dynasty she had created. She knew what must be done to preserve it all. But could she do it? Her heart fluttered as she envisioned the days ahead. But she knew she would find the strength somehow. It struck her then how ironical life was. Her sons had made an irrevocable mistake by plotting in her own boardroom. Admittedly they had chosen what they thought was a propitious time, early evening on a Friday, when everyone had left. Even so, she was aghast at their utter stupidity. There was another flaw in their plot and it was a flaw that was fatal. *They had underestimated her.* And, finally, by a twist of fate, she had been forewarned of their treachery. Now that she was prepared, she could handle the situation most effectively, anticipate their next moves and forestall them. She smiled grimly to herself. She had always been something of a gambler in her business, in life in general, and once again she was holding the equivalent of a straight flush. Her luck was holding. She prayed that it would hold long enough.

THREE

Henry Rossiter pressed the telephone closer to his ear, as if better to hear the woman's voice, concentrating on her words, straining and attentive, for although Emma Harte's voice was well modulated as always, she spoke more softly than usual.

'And so, Henry, I would appreciate it if you would come over to the store at about eleven-thirty this morning. I thought we could chat for about an hour and then have lunch here in the boardroom. If you are free, of course.'

He hesitated and it was almost imperceptible, but he knew Emma had caught it and he said quickly, 'That's fine, my dear, I shall be glad to come over.'

'Do you have another appointment, Henry? I would hate to inconvenience you.'

He did, and it was an important luncheon date that had been arranged for some time, but he was hardly going to offend his most important client, who also happened to be one of the richest women in England, possibly in the world, since it was hard to truly estimate her real worth. He knew that she was astute enough to realize he would have a previous appointment, so he refrained from the tiny white lie and, clearing his throat, he said, 'Yes, I do, but it is easy for me to cancel it, if you wish, my dear.'

'Good. I appreciate it, Henry. I will see you at eleven-thirty then. Goodbye, Henry.'

'Goodbye, Emma,' he murmured, but she had already hung up.

Henry had known Emma Harte for almost forty years, long enough to fully understand that there was always an imperious demand beneath her soft-spoken requests, that they were really commands uttered in the most dulcet of tones and the most charming manner. That inbred charm had carried her a long way, as Henry was the first to acknowledge.

She had said nothing unusual and he had been unable to detect any undertones

35

of disquiet or anger in her voice, and yet a peculiar sense of foreboding had descended upon him as they talked. Henry was not without perception, and, being the ultimate banker, he was always carefully attuned to his clients, fully conscious of their basic characteristics, the quirks and foibles of their personalities. He had to be, since he was handling their money and usually much of their business, and he had come to realize years ago that the very rich could also be very difficult, especially about their money.

It struck him suddenly that it was Emma's unexpected invitation to lunch which puzzled him. It was unprecedented and therefore, to him, somewhat alarming. Emma, as he knew only too well, was a creature of habit. She rarely had luncheon dates and when she did they were carefully planned days before. This digression from her normal routine was decidedly odd and the more he pondered on this, the more Henry was convinced something was amiss. And yet he had spoken to her three times since her return from New York a week ago and she had been her usual self, brisk and businesslike and, on the surface, seemingly untroubled.

He took off his glasses, leaned back in his chair, and wondered if she was dissatisfied about the way the bank was handling her business. Henry had always been predisposed to worry, especially about the bank, and lately this had developed into a chronic condition. 'There's probably a simple explanation for the invitation. I'm just imagining something is wrong,' he muttered aloud with a degree of irritation; none the less, he pressed the intercom and told his secretary to ask Osborne to come in and see him immediately.

Tony Osborne, and two other officers of the private bank, supervised Emma Harte's business affairs in England, both corporate and personal. All of them were answerable to him and he reviewed Emma's affairs twice and sometimes three times a week. Osborne often chided him for using so much physical manpower and was continually insisting they should use computers to deal with the Harte holdings. But Henry did not trust computers, being conservative, even old-fashioned, in his ways. Furthermore, he thought that the supervision of something in the region of three hundred million pounds, give or take a few million, was worth any amount of manpower it might cost the bank. Emma was demanding and she was shrewd, probably shrewder, in fact, than any banker he knew, including himself. Henry needed to be absolutely sure they could answer any questions at any time, which is why the accounts were under daily surveillance. Henry wanted all that salient information right at his fingertips, night as well as day, if necessary.

Osborne interrupted his thoughts as he knocked on the door and glided into the room. Conceited young pup, he's too egotistical and ambitious by far, and too smooth, Henry thought, regarding the immaculately tailored young man before him. But what can you expect from scholarship Eton.

'Good morning, Henry.'

'Morning, Osborne.'

'Quite a beautiful day, isn't it? I think spring is going to be early this year, Henry. Don't you agree?'

'I'm not a weather vane,' Henry murmured.

Osborne missed the snub or chose to ignore it. However, his manner became a little more businesslike and his voice was a shade cooler. 'I want to talk to you about the Rowe account –' Tony began.

Henry held up his hand and shook his head. 'Not now, Osborne. I called you in because I have just spoken to Mrs Harte. She asked me to go over to the store later this morning. Is everything in order? No problems?'

'Absolutely not!' Osborne was emphatic in his surprise. 'Everything is under control.'

'I assume you have been keeping an eye on her foreign holdings. Did you go over them yesterday?' Henry played with the pen on his desk, still somewhat beset by worry.

'We always do on Monday. We checked her American and Australian interests, and all are steady. Sitex is doing well. There's actually been a rise in the price since the new president went in there. Look here, Henry, is something wrong? What's up?' he asked.

Henry shook his head. 'Nothing that I am aware of, Osborne. But I do like to be completely current and informed before I see her. I think I'll take a look at her accounts with you. Let's go to your office.'

After an hour and a half of concentrating on the most pertinent of the Harte accounts, Henry was totally satisfied that Osborne and his assistants had been both precise and diligent in their work. All of the English figures were current and the figures for the foreign Harte holdings were as up-to-date as they could be with the changing world markets, the different time zones, and the rise and fall of stock prices. At eleven sharp, for he was punctilious about time, Henry put on his black overcoat, picked up his bowler hat and umbrella, and left the office. He stood on the steps of the bank, sniffing the air for a moment. It was cold but crisp and sunny. Osborne was right, it was a beautiful day for January, spring-like in its clear freshness. He walked swiftly down the street, swinging his umbrella jauntily, a tall, handsome man in his early sixties, whose serious and dignified demeanour belied a sharp sense of humour and a flirtatious nature.

Henry Rossiter had a cool mind, which was also quite brilliant. A cultured man, he was an art connoisseur, a collector of rare first editions, a devotee of drama and music. He could also ride and shoot like the gentleman he was, and he was Master of the Hunt of the county where his ancestral home was located. The product of a rich and old Establishment family, landed gentry, in fact, he was today a curious amalgam of upper-class English conservative principles and international sophistication. He had been married twice and was currently divorced, which made him one of London's most eligible bachelors, much in demand by chic hostesses, for he was entertaining, charming, and adept in all the social graces, and something of a bon vivant. In short, he was attractive and lethal, a success both in business and in society.

Henry hailed a cab at the corner and got in. Leaning forward, he said, 'Harte's, please,' and sat back, relaxed and confident that Emma could have no complaints about the bank. Absolutely none whatsoever. He still could not fathom the reason for her sudden invitation, but he had shed his incipient worry. Women, he thought with fond exasperation, unpredictable creatures at the best of times! He truly believed all women were quite impossible, having been baffled, confused, and bewitched by them all of his life. But now he felt compelled to readjust his thinking, as far as Emma was concerned. He simply could not, in all honesty, label her unpredictable or even impossible. Headstrong, yes, and sometimes even stubborn to the point of rigidity. But mostly he knew Emma to be prudent and levelheaded, and circumspection was undoubtedly her most basic characteristic. No, 'unpredictable' was not a word he would ever associate with Emma.

As the cab pushed its way through the congested traffic towards Knightsbridge, Henry's thoughts stayed with Emma Harte. They had been friends and business associates for many years and had enjoyed a compatible and mutually rewarding relationship. He had always found Emma easy to work with, for her mind was logical and direct. She did not think in that convoluted female way, nor was her mind cluttered up with the usual womanish nonsense. He smiled to himself. Once he had told her that she did not have a mind like a woman at all, that it was more like a man's. 'Oh, is there a difference!' she had retorted with some asperity, but there had been an amused smile on her face. At the time he had been a trifle hurt, for he had meant it as a great compliment, in view of his disparaging opinions of women, or rather, their intellectual capacities.

He had been entranced by Emma from the first day they had met. Then he had thought her to be the most fascinating woman he had ever encountered and he still did. Once, long ago, he had even believed himself to be in love with her, although she had never been aware of his feelings. He had been twenty-four and she had been thirty-nine and that most desirable of all creatures, the experienced older woman. She had been extraordinarily striking in her appearance, with her luxuriant hair coming dramatically to a widow's peak above a broad forehead and enormous vividly green eyes that were bright and alive. She was filled with a tremendous energy, a robust vitality that was infectious, and he was always buoyed up by her vivacity and her incredible optimism. She was a refreshing change from the insipid and constrained women he had been surrounded by all his life. Emma had a sardonic wit, a capacity for laughing both at herself and at her troubles, and an innate gaiety and zest for living that Henry found remarkable. From then, until this very day, he had been continually staggered by her intelligence, her prescience, and her unconquerable determination. And he had always been susceptible to that natural charm of hers, a charm which Henry knew had been consciously distilled over the years, and which she had learned to use with consummate skill, carefully exploiting its effects to the fullest for the most propitious results.

For almost thirty years he had been her financial adviser. She always listened to him carefully and appreciated his suggestions and they had never quarrelled in all of this time. In a peculiar sort of proprietary way he was inordinately proud of Emma and what she had become. A great lady. An unparalleled business success. It was a well-established fact that Emma Harte's London store surpassed any other in the world, not only in size but in the quality and variety of its merchandise. Not without reason was she known as one of the great merchant princes, although few knew, as Henry did, the enormous and crippling price she had paid for her success. He had always felt that the foundations of her immense retailing empire were compounded of her own self-sacrifice and dogged will power, her genius for selling, her instinctive understanding of the public's whims, an unerring eye for recognizing trends, and nerve enough to gamble when necessary. He had once told Tony Osborne that the bricks and mortar of the store were wrought from her great vision, her amazing facility for finance, and her uncanny ability to rise from the most impossible situations to triumph. And he had meant it. As far as Henry was concerned, she had done it all alone, and the London store, of all the stores she owned, was a towering testimony to her invincible strength.

''Ere we are,' the cab-driver said cheerily. Henry got out, paid the fare, and hurried down the side street to the staff entrance and the elevator that would take him to the top floor and Emma's executive offices.

Gaye Sloane was talking to one of the secretaries in the outer reception office when Henry walked in. She greeted him warmly. 'Mrs Harte is waiting for you,' she said as she opened the door to Emma's office and ushered him inside.

Emma was sitting at her desk, which was covered with papers. He thought she looked oddly frail behind it. She glanced up as he came in, took off her glasses, and stood up. He realized that her frailty had only been an illusion created by the large heavy desk, for she moved towards him swiftly, lightly, full of vitality, her face wreathed in smiles. She was elegantly dressed in a dark bottle-green velvet suit, with something white and silky at the throat caught in an emerald pin, and emerald earrings glittered at her ears.

'Henry darling, how lovely to see you,' she said as she took hold of his arm affectionately. He smiled and bent down to kiss her on the cheek and thought: She seems well enough. But he detected a drawn look around her eyes and she was paler than usual.

'Let me look at you, Emma dear,' he said, holding her away from him so that he could regard her more fully. He laughed and shook his head in mock bewilderment. 'You'll have to tell me your secret, darling. I don't know how you do it, but you look positively blooming.'

Emma smiled. 'Hard work, a clean life, and a clear conscience. And you shouldn't complain, Henry. You look marvellous yourself. Come on, darling, let's have a sherry and a chat.' She led him over to the comfortable arrangement of chairs and a sofa in front of the fireplace, where a roaring fire blazed. They sat down opposite each other and Emma poured sherry into two crystal glasses.

'Here's to that great man whose name is Emma,' he said, lifting his glass to touch hers before taking a sip.

Emma threw him a quick, surprised glance and laughed gaily. 'Why, Henry!' She laughed again and then said with some amusement, 'With all due respect, I am not Catherine the Great and you're not Voltaire. But thank you, anyway. I assume you meant that as a compliment.'

Henry smiled broadly. 'Is there anything you don't know, my dear? And yes, of course I meant it as a compliment.'

Emma was still laughing. 'There's a lot I don't know, Henry. But one of my gallant grandsons got here before you. He said exactly the same thing to me yesterday. And when I complimented him on *his* compliment, he had the good grace to tell me the source. You're a day too late, darling!'

Henry chuckled with her. 'Well, we obviously think alike. And which grandson was it?' he asked, always curious about Emma's large and unorthodox family.

'I do have a few, don't I?' Emma said with a fond smile. 'It must get confusing. It was Alexander, Elizabeth's son. He was here yesterday afternoon, down from Yorkshire and in a real uproar about his Uncle Kit, who was being extremely stubborn about putting new machinery into one of the mills. It is a costly move, but eventually it will save us a lot of money and step up production. Alexander was quite right and I sorted it out in the end, without too much of a bloodbath.'

'He's a bright boy and devoted to you, Emma. Incidentally, talking of Christopher . . .' He paused and smiled. 'Excuse me, Emma, I never could call him Kit. Anyway, to continue, I ran into Christopher a few weeks ago and I was somewhat surprised to see him with Edwina and Robin. They were dining at the Savoy.'

Emma had been relaxed, regarding Henry with affection, amused at his gallantry. Now she tensed, but she kept her face open and bland. 'Oh, really. I'm glad to see my children are getting along together at last,' she said lightly, while carefully storing that piece of information at the back of her mind.

Henry lit a cigarette and went on, 'I was surprised because I didn't realize Christopher was friendly with the other two. And frankly I didn't know Robin was still thick with Edwina. I thought that was a temporary situation created when there was all that trouble about the take-over bid a few years back. Actually, I never did understand that liaison, Emma. I always thought those two detested each other until they became so chummy. Obviously it's lasted.'

Emma smiled thinly. 'You say you don't understand their friendship, Henry, yet I discovered long ago that dark and desperate plots make for very peculiar bedmates. You're right. Of course, they did dislike each other intensely, but they haven't been out of each other's pockets since that trouble with the conglomerate.'

'Mmmm. It was a funny business, wasn't it? But thank God it all blew over. Well, as I said, I thought it rather odd to see the three of them together,' he finished, and sipped his sherry, totally oblivious of the disturbing thoughts he had stirred up in Emma.

She regarded him carefully, and said with great casualness, 'Oh, I don't think it's so odd, Henry. To tell you the truth, I've heard on the family grapevine that the three of them are planning a gathering of the clan for my birthday,' she lied blandly. 'I suspect they were meeting to discuss the arrangements.'

'I thought your birthday was at the end of April.'

'It is, darling. But that's only a couple of months away.'

'I hope I get an invitation,' he said. 'After all, you'll need an escort and I have been your most constant admirer for nigh on forty years.'

'You will, darling,' Emma replied, relieved that the awkward moment had been so easily bridged. 'But I didn't ask you here to chat about my offspring. I wanted to talk to you about a couple of things . . .'

The telephone rang and Emma stood up abruptly. 'Excuse me, Henry. It must be Paula calling from Paris. That is the only call I told Gaye she could put through.'

'Of course, my dear,' he said, standing up also. She crossed the room to her desk and he sat down, relaxing in front of the fire, enjoying his sherry and his cigarette, his mind at ease. Emma looked tired, yet he could not detect any outward signs that she was troubled. In fact, he thought she seemed rather gay. He glanced around the room as she continued her telephone conversation. He envied Emma this office, which was more like a library in a stately home than a place of business. With its panelled walls, soaring shelves of books, magnificent English paintings, and handsome Georgian antiques it was a gracious retreat, one which he would have liked to own and work in himself.

Emma finished her call and he stood up as she rejoined him by the fire. She had a folder of papers in her hand which Henry could not fail to notice. She placed the folder on the table next to her chair and sat down. Henry settled back in his chair and lit another cigarette.

'Paula sends her love, Henry. She's in Paris, taking care of a few things at the store for me.'

'Delightful girl,' Henry responded, a note of admiration in his voice. 'She's so like Daisy, sweet and open and uncomplicated. When is she returning?'

Emma did not think Paula was uncomplicated at all, but she resisted any comment about her granddaughter. 'On Thursday. Another sherry, Henry?' she asked as she started to pour it into his glass.

'Yes, thank you, darling. You said you wanted to talk to me about a few things, before you took Paula's call.' He eyed the folder curiously. 'Anything serious?'

'No, not at all. I would like to liquidate some of my personal assets and I thought you could handle it for me,' Emma replied, her voice casual, her face relaxed. She sipped her drink slowly and waited, regarding Henry intently, knowing only too well how he would react.

In spite of his anxiety earlier, he was taken by surprise. He had not expected this at all. He put down his glass and leaned forward, a worried pucker creasing his brow. 'Do you have problems, Emma?' he asked quietly.

Emma met his gaze directly. 'No, Henry. I told you I want to liquidate some of my own assets. For personal reasons. There are no problems. You should know that, darling. After all, you handle most of my banking business.'

Henry reflected for an instant, his mind rapidly reassembling all those figures he had seen that morning. Had he inadvertently missed something of vital importance? No. That was not possible. He breathed a little more easily, and cleared his throat. 'Well, yes, that's true,' he said thoughtfully. 'In fact, I looked over all of your accounts before I came over. Everything is in good order. Very good order. As a matter of fact, things have never looked better,' he finished in all truthfulness.

'I need a little cash, Henry. Ready cash. For personal reasons, as I said. So, rather than sell any shares, I thought I would get rid of some real estate, jewellery, and part of my art collection.'

Henry was so flabbergasted he was momentarily rendered speechless. Before he recovered sufficiently to make a comment she handed him the folder. He took out his glasses, put them on, and looked at the lists inside, startled and apprehensive. As his eyes ran down the assets he remembered his foreboding earlier in the morning. Perhaps his instincts had been correct.

'Emma! All this doesn't represent a little cash, as you casually call it. These assets represent millions of pounds!'

'Oh, I know. I figured about seven or eight million pounds. What do you think, Henry dear?' she asked calmly.

'Good God! Emma! Why do you suddenly need seven or eight million pounds? And what do *I* think? you ask me. *I* think there is something wrong and that you are not telling me. You *must* have problems I can have no way of knowing about!' His grey transparent eyes blazed as he endeavoured to control his anger. He was certain she was hiding something, and it annoyed him.

'Oh, come on, Henry,' Emma clucked. 'Don't get so excited. Nothing's wrong. Actually, I only need about six million for my . . . shall we call it my personal project? I prefer to sell these things, since I don't need them anyway. I never wear that jewellery. You know I'm not overly fond of diamonds. And even when it's sold I'll still have more than enough that is decent for a woman of my age. The real estate is cumbersome. I don't want that either, and I feel this is the perfect time

41

to sell and make a profit. I'm being rather clever really,' she finished on a self-congratulatory note, smiling pleasantly at Henry.

He gazed at her in astonishment. She had the knack of making all of her actions sound admirably pragmatic and it generally maddened him. 'But the art collection, Emma! My dear, you put so much love and time and care into gathering these . . . these masterpieces. Are you sure you want to let them go?' His voice had taken on a saddened, wistful tone. He glanced at the list in his hand. 'Look what you're listing here. Sisleys, Chagalls, Monets, Manets, Dalis, Renoirs, and Pissarros, and a Degas. *Two*, in fact. It's a fabulous collection.'

'Which you so generously helped me to acquire over the years, through your contacts in the art world. I am grateful to you for that, Henry. More than you will ever know. But I want to liquidate. As you say, it's a fabulous collection and so it should bring a fabulous price,' she said crisply.

'Oh, indeed it will!' Henry asserted, the banker in him suddenly taking over. 'If you are absolutely certain you want me to sell the collection I can do so very easily.' His voice became enthusiastic. 'Actually I have a client in New York who would love to get his hands on these paintings. And he'll pay the right price, too, my dear. But, Emma, really! I don't know what to say. It seems such a shame . . .' His voice trailed off weakly, for he suddenly recognized that she had manipulated him rather cleverly, and turned his attention away from her reasons for selling.

'Good,' Emma said hurriedly, seizing the opportunity to further promote Henry's enthusiasm, his banker's instincts. 'What about the real estate in Leeds and London? I think the block of flats in Hampstead and the East End factory property will go for a good price.'

'Yes, they will. So will the office block in the West End. You're right, of course, it is a good time to sell.' He concentrated on the various lists she had given him, making swift mental calculations. She had underestimated the overall worth, he decided. The paintings, the real estate, and the jewellery would bring about nine million pounds. He put the folder down, and lit a cigarette as his anxiety accelerated.

'Emma, dear. You must tell me if you have problems. Who else is there to help you but me?' He smiled at her and reached over and patted her arm fondly. He had never been able to remain angry with her for very long.

'Henry, my darling Henry. I don't have problems,' Emma replied in her most conciliatory and reassuring manner. 'You know I don't. You said yourself things have never looked better.' She went over and sat next to him on the sofa and took his hand. 'Look here, Henry, I need this money for a personal reason. It has nothing to do with a problem. I promise you. Please believe me, Henry, I *would* tell you. We've been friends for so many years, and I've always trusted you, haven't I?' She smiled up at him, using the full force of her charm, her eyes crinkling with affection.

He returned her smile and tightened his hand over hers. 'Yes. We have always trusted each other, in fact. As your banker, I realize you have no business or money problems as such, Emma. But I simply cannot understand why you need six million pounds and why you won't tell me what it's for. Can't you, my dear?'

Her face became enigmatic. She shook her head. 'No. I can't tell you. Will you handle the liquidation of these assets for me?' she asked in her most businesslike manner.

Henry sighed. 'Of course, Emma. There was never any question about that, was there?'

She smiled. 'Thank you, Henry. How long will it take to liquidate?'

He shrugged. 'I don't really know. Probably several weeks. I am sure I can sell the art collection within the next week. I also think I have a client who would buy the jewellery privately, so we avoid a public sale. The real estate should move fairly easily, too. Yes, I would say a month at the most.'

'Excellent!' Emma exclaimed. She jumped up and moved over to the fireplace, standing with her back towards it. 'Don't look so miserable, darling. The bank is going to make money, too, you know. And the government, with all the taxes I shall have to pay!'

He laughed. 'Sometimes I think you're quite incorrigible, Emma Harte.'

'I am! I'm the most incorrigible woman I know. Now, let's go into the boardroom and have lunch, and you can tell me about all your latest lady friends and the exciting parties you've been to whilst I have been in New York.'

'Splendid idea,' he said, although he was still riddled by that strange apprehension as he followed her across the office.

The following day Emma began to feel unwell. The cough she had developed in New York still troubled her and there was a tightness in her chest. But it was a whole week before she succumbed, and for that entire week she assiduously refused to admit there was anything wrong with her normally robust health. Imperiously, she brushed aside the fussing of Gaye Sloane and her daughter Daisy. She refused to deviate from her usual work schedule and religiously went to the office at seven-thirty every morning, returning to her house in Belgrave Square at seven in the evening. Since she was accustomed to working in her executive suite at the store until eight-thirty and sometimes nine o'clock at night, she felt this relatively early departure was a great concession on her part. But it was her only one.

Sometimes, at the end of a day, as she pored over the mountainous pile of balance sheets, stock reports, dividend sheets, and legal documents, she was wracked by coughing that exhausted her and left her weak and listless for a while. To Emma, the rasping cough was ominous; nevertheless, she carried on, pressed by a feeling of tremendous urgency. It was not the routine business matters that troubled her, for these she dealt with quickly, precisely, and with her own brand of shrewdness. It was the pile of legal documents, prepared by her solicitors at her bidding, that were her gravest concern. With them spread out before her on the huge desk, illuminated by the shaded lamp, she would sometimes balk at the enormity of the work still to be accomplished. She would think: I won't finish! There's not enough time left. And her mind would be frozen by momentary panic. But this mental paralysis was a passing emotion and she would continue to work again, reading and making notations for her solicitors. As she worked one thought would run through her head: The documents must be irreversible, irrevocable! They must be watertight. I must be sure, absolutely sure that they can never be contested in a court of law.

Often the pains in her chest and rib cage became razor sharp and almost unbearable. It was then that she was forced to stop working for a while. She would get up and cross the luxuriously appointed office, so wracked by pain that she was temporarily unaware of its gracious, timeless beauty, a beauty she had patiently created, and which normally gave her a great satisfaction. She would open the tiny bar and with trembling hands pour herself a brandy and then rest for a short time on the sofa in front of the fire. She did not especially like the taste of brandy, but since it warmed her and also seemed to deaden the pain briefly, she thought it the lesser of two evils. More importantly, it enabled her to go back to her desk and continue working on the legal papers. As she pushed herself beyond physical endurance, she would fume inwardly and curse the treachery of her body, which had so betrayed her at this most crucial time.

One night, towards the end of the week, she was working feverishly at her desk when she had a sudden and quite irresistible urge to go down into the store. At first she dismissed the idea as the silly whim of an old woman who was feeling vulnerable, but the thought so persisted that she could not ignore it. She was literally overcome with an inexplicable desire, a *need*, to walk through those vast, great halls below, as if to reassure herself of their very existence. She rose slowly. Her bones were afflicted with an ague and the pain in her chest was ever present. After descending in the lift and speaking to the security guard on duty, she walked through the foyer that led to the ground-floor departments. She hesitated on the threshold of the haberdashery department, regarding the hushed and ghostlike scene that spread itself out before her. By day it glittered under the blaze of huge chandeliers, with their globes and blades of crystal that threw off rays of prismatic light. Now, in the shadows and stillness of the night, the area appeared to her as a petrified forest, suspended in time and space, inanimate, frozen and lifeless. The vaulted ceiling, cathedral-like in its dimensions, was filled with bluish lacy patterns, eerie and mysterious, while the panelled walls had taken on a dark purple glaze under the soft, diffused glow which emanated from the wall sconces. She moved noiselessly across the richly carpeted floor until she arrived at the food halls, a series of immense, rectangular rooms flowing into each other through high-flung arches faintly reminiscent of medieval monastic architecture.

To Emma, the food halls would always be the nucleus of the store, for in essence they had been the beginning of it all, the tiny seed from which the Harte chain had grown and flowered to become the mighty business empire it was today. In contrast to the other areas of the store, here at night, as by day, the full supplement of chandeliers shone in icy splendour, dropping down from the domed ceilings like giant stalactites that filled the adjoining halls with a pristine and glistening luminosity. Light bounced back from the blue and white tiled walls, the marble counter tops, the glass cases, the gleaming steel refrigerators, the white tiled floor. Emma thought they were as clean and as beautiful and as pure as vast and silent snowscapes sparkling under hard, brilliant sun. She walked from hall to hall, surveying the innumerable and imaginative displays of foodstuffs, gourmet products, delicacies imported from all over the world, good wholesome English fare, and an astonishing array of wines and liquors, and she was inordinately proud of all she observed. Emma knew there were no other food halls, in any store anywhere in the world, which could challenge these, and she smiled to herself with a profound and complete satisfaction. Each one was an extension of her instinctive good taste, her inspired planning and diligent purchasing; in the whole hierarchy of Harte Enterprises, no one could lay claim to their creation but she herself. Indeed, she was so filled with a sense of gratification and well-being that the pains in her chest virtually disappeared.

When she came to the charcuterie department, a sudden mental image of her first shop in Leeds flitted before her, at once stark and realistic in every detail. It was so compelling it brought her to a standstill. That little shop from which all this had issued forth; how unpretentious and insignificant it had been in comparison to this elegant establishment that exuded refinement and wealth! She stood quite still, alert, straining, listening, as if she could hear sounds from long ago in the silence of this night. Forgotten memories, nostalgic and poignant, rushed back to her with force and clarity. Images, no longer nebulous and abandoned, took living form. As she ran her hands over the rich polished oak counter it seemed to her that her fingers touched the scrubbed deal surface of the counter in the old shop. She could smell the acrid odour of the carbolic soap she had used to scrub the shop every day; she could hear the tinny, rattling clink of the old-fashioned second-hand cash register as she joyfully rang up her meagre sales.

Oh, how she had loved that poor, cramped little shop, filled to overflowing with her own homemade foods and jams, bottles of peppermints, and stone jars of pickles and spices.

'Who would have thought it would become *this*?' Emma said aloud, and her voice echoed back to her in the silence of the empty hall where she stood. 'Where did I find the energy?' She was momentarily baffled. She had not thought of her achievements for so many years now, always too preoccupied with business to fritter away her time ruminating on her success. She had long ago relegated that task to her competitors and adversaries. Because of their own duplicity and ruthlessness they would never be able to comprehend that the Harte chain had been built on something as fundamental as honesty, spirited courage, patience, and sacrifice.

Sacrifice. That word was held in her brain like a fly caught in amber. For indeed she had made tremendous sacrifices to achieve her unparalleled success, her great wealth, and her undeniable power in the world of international business. *She had given up her youth, her family, her family life, much of her personal happiness, all of her free time, and countless other small, frivolous yet necessary pleasures enjoyed by most women.* With great comprehension she recognized the magnitude of her loss, as a woman, a wife, and a mother. Emma let the tears flow unchecked and in their flowing a measure of her agony was assuaged.

Slowly the tears subsided. As she gathered her senses, in an attempt to calm herself, it did not occur to Emma that she had willingly renounced all the things for which she now grieved, through her driving ambition and overriding desire for security, a security that always seemed beyond her grasp, however rich she became. There was a dichotomy in her character which she had never been able to come to grips with. But such thoughts evaded her this night, as she struggled with an unaccustomed sense of loss, feelings of loneliness and despair mingled with remorse.

Within a short time she was totally in command of herself again, and she was mortified that she had given way to such negative feelings, such self pity; she despised weakness in others and it was an emotion she was not familiar with in herself. She thought angrily: I am living what I alone created. I cannot change anything now. I simply have to go on to the end.

She pulled herself up, erect and straight-backed and proud. She thought: Too much of me has gone into this. I will not let it pass into the wrong hands, unworthy, careless hands that will tear it down. I am right to plot and scheme and manipulate. Not only for the past and for what it has cost *me*, but for the future and for all those who work here and take pride in this store just as I do.

The events of the past few weeks had proved to her that great dissension about the control of the business and the distribution of her wealth would arise within her family after her death, unless she circumvented the dissident members of her family before she died. Now she would finish the last of the legal documents which would prevent the dissolution of this store and her vast business empire; documents carefully drawn which would unalterably preserve all of this and her great personal wealth as well, ensuring its passing into the right hands, the hands of *her* choice.

The following Monday morning, the pains in her chest were so intense and her breathing so impaired Emma was unable to leave her bed. It was then that she allowed Paula to call Dr Rogers, her London physician. The preceding weekend, most of the documents had been signed, witnessed, and sealed, and now Emma felt she could allow herself the indulgence of being ill. After Dr Rogers had examined her, he and Paula had been huddled at one end of her bedroom, their voices muffled and barely audible. She overheard a few words, but she did not have to eavesdrop; she had suspected for the last few days that she had again contracted pneumonia, and what she overheard only served to confirm her own diagnosis. Later that morning, they took her by ambulance to the London Clinic, but not before she had elicited a promise from Paula to bring Henry Rossiter to see her that same day. Henry arrived in the late afternoon, aghast to find her in an oxygen tent, surrounded by all manner of equipment and fussed over by starchy, antiseptic nurses and concerned doctors. She smiled inwardly at the sight of Henry's white face and worried eyes that betrayed him so easily, since she was aware of Henry's dependency on her or, rather more accurately, her business. He clasped her hand and told her that she would soon be well again. She had tried to return the pressure of his clasp, but she felt so weak her hand hardly moved in his. With a stupendous effort she asked him in a whisper if everything would be all right. But he misunderstood, believing her to be referring to herself, when in fact she was asking him about the liquidation of her assets which he was handling. He kept up his soothing talk, reassuring her over and over again that she would soon be home, until she was indignant and fuming with impotent rage.

It was then that Emma realized that she was utterly alone, just as she had always been alone when portentous matters arose. Through all the vicissitudes of her life, whenever she had faced the gravest problems imaginable, she had been totally abandoned and so forced to depend entirely on her own resources. And she knew that she could only rely on herself now to accomplish the few remaining tasks which would preserve her empire and her dynasty. To do that she had to live, and she determined then not to succumb to this ridiculous sickness invading her weak, old woman's body; she would live and breathe if it took all of her strength. Every ounce of her will power would be brought to bear. It would undoubtedly be the greatest effort of will she had ever exercised, but she would *force* herself to live.

She was tired though now, so very tired. Dimly in the distance she heard the nurses asking Henry Rossiter to leave. She was given some medication and the oxygen tent was placed around her again. She closed her eyes. She was falling asleep and as she drifted off she felt herself growing younger and younger. She

46

was a young girl again, just sixteen, back in Yorkshire, running on her beloved moors high above Fairley village, to the Top of the World. The heather and the bracken brushed against her feet, the wind caught at her long skirts so that they billowed out and her hair was a stream of silk ribbons flying behind her as she ran. The sky was as blue as speedwells and the larks wheeled and turned against the face of the sun. She could see Edwin Fairley now, standing by the huge rocks just under the shadow of the crags above Ramsden Ghyll. When he saw her he waved and went on climbing upwards towards the ledge where they always sat protected from the wind, surveying the world far below. He did not look back but went on climbing. 'Edwin! Edwin! Wait for me!' she called, but her voice was blown away by the wind and he did not hear. When she reached Ramsden Crags she was out of breath and her pale face was flushed from the exertion. 'I ran so hard, I thought I would die,' she gasped as he helped her up on to the ledge. He smiled. 'You will never die, Emma. We are both going to live for ever and ever, here at the Top of the World.' The dream fragmented into hundreds of infinitesimal pieces and slowly began to fade as she fell into a profound sleep.

FOUR

Emma lived. Everyone said it was a miracle that a woman of seventy-eight years of age could survive yet another attack of bronchial pneumonia and the varied complications that had accompanied it this time. They also expressed amazement at her incredible recuperative ability which had enabled her to leave the London Clinic at the end of three weeks. Emma, when these comments were repeated to her, said nothing. She simply smiled enigmatically and thought to herself: Ah, but they don't realize that the will to live is the strongest force in the world.

After two days of enforced rest at her house in Belgravia she impatiently left her bed and, disregarding the advice of her doctors, went to the store. This was not such a foolish act of defiance as it seemed on the surface, for although she could be empirical she was not reckless and she also knew her own body intimately, could gauge her strength with accuracy, and now she knew herself to be fully recovered. She was greeted warmly by her employees, who for the most part held her in affection. They took her sudden return for granted. It was Paula who hovered nervously around her, cosseting, worried and concerned.

'I do wish you would stop fussing, darling,' Emma said crisply as Paula followed her into her office, murmuring something about endangering her health. Emma took off her fur-lined tweed coat. She stood for a few moments warming her hands by the fire and then she walked across the room in her usual energetic way, a buoyant springiness in her step, her carriage perfectly straight and autocratic.

The black waves of shock and despair which had engulfed her after Gaye's revelations of her children's plotting had subsided, admittedly slowly and painfully, but they had subsided. The sinister imputations that could be drawn from that damning conversation on the tape, and her acceptance of their treachery, had only served to anneal her mind. She saw things with a cold and clear objectivity, exactly as they were, unclouded by needless emotion. During her illness, as she had drawn upon her iron will, ruthlessly fighting to live, she had come to terms with herself. And a great peace came flowing into her one day like a flood of warm bright light and it gave her solace and renewed inner strength. It was as if her brush with death had reinforced her spirit and her dauntless courage. Her vitality had returned, accompanied now by a quiet calm that surrounded her like a protective shell.

She took up her position behind the great carved Georgian desk, back in command of her domain. She smiled lovingly at Paula. 'I'm quite recovered, you know,' she said brightly and reassuringly. And indeed she looked it, although this was partially due to the illusion she had rather cleverly contrived that morning. Noting her pallor and the tired lines around her eyes and mouth as she dressed, she had shunned the dark sombre colours she generally favoured and had selected a bright coral dress from her wardrobe. This was made of fine wool, softly cut with a draped cowl collar that fell in feminine folds around the neck. She was fully aware that the warm colour and the softness of the neckline against her face was flattering, and with a few carefully applied cosmetics she had completed the effect. There was a robust healthy glow about her which Paula did not fail to notice.

Paula realized this was created by artifice to some degree, conscious always of her grandmother's numerous and varied devices when she wanted to delude. She smiled to herself. Her grandmother could be so crafty sometimes. Yet Paula also sensed true vibrancy in Emma, a new energy and purpose. As she scrutinized her carefully she had to admit that Emma appeared to be her old self. Only more so, she thought, as if she had been totally rejuvenated.

She smiled at her grandmother and said gently, although a little reprovingly, 'I know *you*, Grandy. You'll do far too much. You mustn't overtax yourself the first day.'

Emma leaned back in her chair, thankful to be alive and on her feet again and capable of returning to her business. She was quite willing to acquiesce to anything at that moment. 'Oh, I won't, darling,' she said quickly. 'I have a few phone calls to make and some dictation to give Gaye, and that's about it. I shall be easy on myself. I promise!'

'All right,' Paula said slowly, wondering if she really meant what she said. Her grandmother could get caught up in the rush of the day's activities at the store without thinking. 'I trust you to keep your promise,' Paula added, a sober expression on her face. 'Now I have to go to a meeting with the fashion buyer for the couture department. I'll pop in and see you later, Grandy.'

'By the way, Paula, I thought I would go to Pennistone Royal the weekend after next. I hope you can come with me,' Emma called to her across the room.

Paula stopped at the door and looked back. 'Of course! I'd love to,' she cried, her eyes lighting up. 'When do you intend to leave, Grandy?'

'A week from tomorrow. Early on Friday morning. But we'll discuss it later.'

'Wonderful. After my meeting I'll clear my desk and cancel my appointments for that day. I have nothing on my schedule that is very important, so I can drive up with you.'

'Good. Come and have tea with me this afternoon at four o'clock and we can make our plans.'

Paula nodded and left the office, a radiant smile on her face as she thought of the prospects of a weekend in Yorkshire. She was also greatly relieved that her grandmother was being wise enough to prolong her recuperation by going to her country house in the North.

Emma was true to her word. She attended to some of her urgent correspondence, had a brief session with Gaye and also one with David Amory, Daisy's husband and Paula's father, who was also the joint managing director of the Harte chain of stores. David was a man Emma admired and trusted implicitly, and who carried the heavy burden of the day-to-day running of the stores. She was making her last telephone call of the afternoon when Paula came into the office carrying the tea tray. She hovered near the door and gave Emma an inquiring look, mouthing silently: 'Can I come in?'

Emma nodded, motioned for her to enter with an impatient gesture of one hand, and went on talking. 'Very well, it's settled then. You will arrive on Saturday. Goodbye.' She hung up and walked across the room to the fireplace, where Paula was sitting in front of the low table pouring tea.

Emma leaned forward to warm her hands and said, 'She's the most bolshy of them all and I wasn't certain she would accept. But she did.' Her green eyes gleamed darkly in the firelight and the faint smile on her face was scornful. 'She had no choice really,' she murmured to herself as she sat down.

'Who, Grandy? Who were you talking to?' Paula asked, passing a cup of tea to her.

'Thank you, dear. Your Aunt Edwina. She wasn't sure at first whether or not she could rearrange her plans.' Emma laughed cynically. 'However, she thought better of it and decided to come to Pennistone Royal after all. It will be quite a family gathering. They're all coming.'

Paula's head was bent over the tea tray. 'Who, Grandy? What do you mean?' she asked, momentarily puzzled.

'Everybody's coming. Your aunts and uncles and cousins.'

A shadow flitted across Paula's face. 'Why?' she cried with surprise. 'Why do *they* all have to come? You know they will make trouble. They always do!' Her eyes opened widely and real horror registered on her face.

Emma was surprised at Paula's reaction. She regarded her calmly, but said in a sharp tone, 'I doubt that! I'm quite positive, in fact, that they are all going to be on their best behaviour.' An expression resembling a smirk played briefly around Emma's mouth. She sat back, crossed her legs decisively, and sipped her tea, looking nonchalant and unconcerned. 'Oh yes, I am absolutely *certain* of that, Paula,' she finished firmly, the smirk expanding into a self-confident smile.

'Oh, Grandy, how could you!' Paula cried, and the look she gave Emma was reproving. 'I thought we could look forward to a pleasant, restful weekend.' She paused and bit her lip. 'Now it's all spoiled,' she went on in an accusatory tone. 'I don't mind the cousins, but the others. Ugh! Kit and Robin and the rest of them are almost too much to bear all together.' She grimaced as she contemplated a weekend with her aunts and uncles.

'Please trust me, darling,' Emma said in a soft voice which was so convincing Paula's disquiet began to subside.

'Well, all right, if you are happy about it. But it's so soon after your illness. Do you think you can stand a house full of . . . of . . . people? . . .' Her voice trailed off lamely and she looked woebegone and suddenly helpless.

'They're not *people*, are they, darling? Surely not. We can't dismiss them like that. They are my family after all.'

Paula had been staring at the teapot, vaguely disturbed. Now she flashed Emma a swift look, for she had detected that edge of cynicism in her voice. But Emma's face was bland, revealing nothing. She's concocting something, Paula thought with some alarm. But she quickly dismissed the idea, chiding herself for being so suspicious. She arranged a sunny smile on her face and said, 'Well, I'm glad Mummy and Daddy are coming. I don't seem to have seen much of them for ages, with all my travelling.' She hesitated, stared at Emma curiously, and then asked hurriedly, 'Why have you invited all of the family, Grandmother?'

'I thought it would be pleasant to see all of my children and grandchildren after my illness. I don't see enough of them, darling,' she suggested mildly and asked, 'Now do I?'

As Paula returned her grandmother's steady gaze she realized, with an unexpected shock, that in spite of her soft voice her grandmother's eyes were as cold and as hard as the great McGill emerald that glittered on her finger. A flicker of real fear touched Paula's heart, for she recognized that look. It was obdurate, and also dangerous.

'No, I don't suppose you do see much of them, Grandy,' Paula said, so quietly it was almost a whisper, not daring to probe further and also reluctant to have her suspicions confirmed. And there the conversation was terminated.

A week later, at dawn on Friday morning, they left London for Yorkshire, driving out of the city in a cold drizzling rain. But as the Rolls-Royce roared up the modern motorway that had replaced the old Great North Road they began hitting brighter weather. The rain had stopped and the sun was beginning to filter through the grey clouds. Smithers, Emma's driver for some fifteen years, knew the road like the palm of his hand, anticipating the bad patches, the twists and the bumps, slowing when necessary, picking up speed when there was a clear smooth stretch of road before them. Emma and Paula chatted desultorily part of the way, but mostly Emma dozed and Paula worried about the forthcoming weekend, which, in spite of her grandmother's assurances to the contrary, loomed ahead like a nightmare. She gazed dully out of the window, troubled as she reflected on her aunts and uncles.

Kit. Pompous, patronizing and, to Paula, a devious, ambitious man whose ineffable hatred for her was thinly disguised beneath a veneer of assumed cordiality. And he would be accompanied by June, his cold and frigid wife, whom she and her cousin Alexander had gleefully nicknamed 'December' when they were children. A chilly, utterly humourless woman who over the years had become an insipid reflection of Kit. And then there was Uncle Robin, a different kettle of fish indeed. Handsome, caustic, smooth-talking, and strangely decadent. She always thought of him as reptilian and dangerous and for all of his charm and polish he repelled her. She particularly disliked him because he treated his rather nice wife, Valerie, with an icy scorn, a contempt that bordered on real cruelty. Her Aunt Edwina was something of an unknown quantity to her, for Edwina spent most of her time knee deep in the bogs of Ireland with her horses. Paula remembered her as a forbidding woman, snobbish and dull and sour. Aunt Elizabeth was beautiful, and amusing in a brittle sort of way, yet she could be unpredictable and her skittishness grated on Paula's nerves.

Paula sighed. A picture of Pennistone Royal formed in her mind's eye, that lovely old house so full of beauty and warmth which she loved as much as Emma did. She imagined herself riding her horse up on the moors in the brisk clean air, and then quite unexpectedly she saw Jim Fairley's face. She closed her eyes and her heart clenched. She dare not think of him. She must not think of him. She steeled herself against those turbulent, distressing emotions that whipped through her whenever the memory of him came rushing back.

Paula opened her eyes and looked out of the window, determinedly closing her mind to Jim Fairley. Her love. Her only love. Forbidden to her because of her grandmother's past. A little later she glanced at her watch. They were already well beyond Grantham heading towards Doncaster, and were making excellent time. The traffic was relatively light because of the early hour. She settled back in her seat and closed her eyes.

Half an hour later Emma stirred and sat up, wide awake and fresh. She moved slightly to look out of the window, smiling quietly to herself. She always knew when she was in Yorkshire. This was where her roots were and her bones responded with that atavistic knowledge and sense of place. Her place. The one place where she truly belonged.

They drove quickly along the motorway, bypassing all the familiar towns. Doncaster, Wakefield, and Pontefract. And finally they were in Leeds. Grey, brooding Leeds, yet powerful and rich, pulsating with vibrant energy, one of the great industrial centres of England with its clothing factories, woollen mills, iron foundries, engineering companies, cement works, and great printing plants. Her city. The seat of her power, the foundation of her success and her great wealth. They passed buildings and factories she owned and the enormous department store that bore her name, slowing down as they threaded their way through the busy morning traffic in the city centre, and then they were out on the open road again heading towards the country.

Within the hour they were pulling up in the cobbled courtyard of Pennistone Royal. Emma practically leapt out of the car. It was bitterly cold and a penetrating wind was blowing down from the moors, yet the sun was a golden orb in a clear cobalt sky and, under the sweep of the wind, the early March daffodils were rippling rafts of bright yellow against the clipped green lawns that rolled down to the lily pond far below the long flagged terrace. Emma drew in a breath of air. It was pungent with the peaty brackenish smell of the moors, the damp earth, and a budding greenness that heralded spring after a hard winter. It had rained the night before and, even though it was noon, dew still clung to the trees and the shrubs, giving them an iridescent quality in the cool northern light.

As she always did, Emma looked up at the house as she and Paula walked towards it. And once more she was deeply moved by its imposing beauty, a beauty that was singularly English, for nowhere else could such a house have flowered so magnificently and so attuned to the surrounding landscape. Its beginnings rooted in the seventeenth century, there was a majestic dignity to the mixture of Renaissance and Jacobean architecture, indestructible and everlasting with its ancient crenellated towers and mullioned leaded windows that glimmered darkly against the time-worn grey stones. But there was a softness to the grandeur and even the protruding gargoyles, weathered by the centuries, were now bereft of their frightening countenances. They did not linger long on the terrace. In spite of the clear bright radiance there was no warmth in the sun, and the wind that blew in across the Dales from the North Sea was tinged with rawness. For all its beauty and spring freshness it was a treacherous day. Emma and Paula moved quickly up the steps, past the topiary hedges silhouetted against the edge of the velvet lawns like proud sentinels from a bygone age.

Before they reached the great oak door, it was flung open. Hilda, the house-keeper, was on the stone steps, her face wreathed in smiles. 'Oh, madame!' she cried excitedly, rushing forward to clasp Emma's outstretched hand. 'We've been so worried about you. Thank goodness you're better. It's lovely to have you back. And you, too, Miss Paula.' She broke into more smiles again and hurried them into the house. 'Come in, come in, out of the cold.'

'I can't tell you how glad I am to be home,' Emma said as they went into the house. 'How have you been, Hilda?'

'Very well, madame. Just worried about you. We all have. Everything is running smoothly here. I'm all prepared for the family. Is Smithers bringing the luggage, madame? I can send Joe down to the car if you think he needs help.' Words tumbled out of her in her excitement.

'No, thank you, Hilda. I'm sure Smithers can manage,' Emma replied. She walked into the middle of the great stone entrance hall and looked around, smiling to herself with pleasure. Her eyes rested on the fine old oak furniture, the tapestries that lined the walls, the huge copper bowl of daffodils and pussy willow on the refectory table.

'The house looks beautiful, Hilda,' she said with a warm smile. 'You've done a good job as always.'

Hilda glowed. 'I have coffee ready, madame, or I can make some tea. But perhaps you'd prefer a sherry before lunch,' she volunteered. 'I put your favourite out in the upstairs parlour, madame.'

'That's a good idea, Hilda. We'll go up now. Lunch about one o'clock. Is that all right?' Emma asked, her foot already on the first step.

'Of course, madame.' She hurried off to her duties in the kitchen, humming under her breath, and Paula followed Emma up the soaring staircase, marvelling once more at her grandmother's vitality.

'I'll join you in a moment, Grandy,' Paula said as they walked down the long corridor leading to various bedrooms and the upstairs parlour. 'I'd like to freshen up before lunch.'

Emma nodded. 'So would I, darling. I'll see you shortly.' She went into her own room and Paula continued down the corridor to hers. Later, after she had changed her travelling suit for a light wool dress and had attended to her face and hair, Emma went through into the parlour which adjoined her bedroom. This was her favourite room at Pennistone Royal. A fire blazed in the hearth and Hilda had turned on several of the silk-shaded lamps, so that the room was filled with soft light. Emma's swift glance was approving as she crossed to the fireplace to warm herself in her habitual way.

The upstairs parlour of this ancient house was distinguished by a gentle beauty, refinement, and good taste. It was understated and unpretentious, yet this very simplicity was deceptive to any but the most experienced eye. It was the kind of understatement that could only be achieved by great expenditure of money and the most patient and skilful acquisition of the very best in furniture and furnishings.

The dark polished floor gleamed against the exquisite Savonnerie carpet that splashed faded pastel colours into the centre of the room. The palest of yellows washed over the walls and gave the whole room a sunny, airy feeling and everywhere sparkling silver and crystal gleamed richly against the mellow patinas of the handsome Georgian tables, consoles, and cabinets and the large elegant desk.

Two long sofas, facing each other across a butler's tray table in front of the fireplace, were as enveloping and as comfortable as deep feather beds. They were covered in a romantic chintz ablaze with clear vivid flowers of bright pink, yellow, blue, and red entwined amongst trailing green vines on a white ground. The Pembroke tables and small consoles all held rare porcelain bowls and vases filled with fresh spring hyacinths, jonquils, tulips, daffodils, and imported mimosa. The warmth of the fire had opened them up so that the air was aromatic with their mingled scents. A Chippendale cabinet, of great elegance and beauty, was filled with matchless Rose Medallion china, whilst side tables held priceless crystal and carved jade lamps with pale cream shades of the finest silk. In front of one of the soaring leaded windows, a Georgian rent table held a selection of the very latest books and a library table behind one of the sofas was piled high with all the current newspapers and magazines.

The bleached oak fireplace, where Emma stood regarding the room, was ornately carved and upon it reposed lovely old silver candlesticks holding white candles and in the centre rested a seventeenth-century carriage clock. The Turner landscape dominated the wall above the fireplace. Redolent with misty greens and clear blues, its romantic bucolic setting was evocative and poignant to Emma and it never failed to stir a nostalgic longing in her heart, as it did now as she turned to admire it.

Portraits of a young nobleman and his wife, by Reynolds, flanked the Chippendale cabinet and a collection of exquisitely rendered miniatures was grouped on the wall behind the desk. Emma's unerring eye for colour and form and her skill at placing and arranging furniture were in evidence everywhere and yet this was not an overly feminine room, being devoid of useless clutter and bric-à-brac. It was a handsome and gracious parlour where a man could also feel at ease in the softly diffused beauty and great comfort.

When she felt warmed throughout, Emma went over to the small console that held a silver tray of drinks and crystal glasses. She poured out two sherries and carried them back to the fireplace. As she waited for Paula she glanced at the morning newspapers. Her own paper, the *Yorkshire Morning Gazette*, was looking much better since she had brought Jim Fairley in as managing editor. He had made a great number of changes, all of which had improved the paper. He had revamped the format and the layout looked brighter and more modern, as did her evening paper, the *Yorkshire Evening Standard*, which was also under Jim's control. Advertising revenue had increased, as had the circulation of both papers. He had done an excellent job and Emma was more than satisfied. Jim Fairley . . . Paula . . . She could no longer think of him without thinking of Paula, too. In Emma's mind the girl was always fatefully in his shadow. She sighed. The door opened and Emma turned away from her introspection. She looked at Paula with fondness as she walked across the room. 'I have a sherry here for you, my dear,' she said, gesturing towards the table.

Paula was smiling cheerfully, having decided in the privacy of her own room to be her most charming self to every one of her unpleasant relatives this weekend.

It was the only thing she could do, and under the circumstances her grandmother needed as much support as she could get with the leeches around, as Paula called them, although this was mostly said to herself or her cousins Alexander and Emily, who shared her views.

'I thought I would go riding this afternoon, if you don't mind, Grandy,' she said as she joined Emma by the fire. 'It's such a beautiful day even though it is cold.'

Emma nodded, delighted. She wanted to be alone after lunch and she had contemplated sending Paula into Leeds on some invented errand. Now that was not necessary. 'Yes, you should, darling. It will do you good. But wrap up warmly. I intend to take it easy myself. I have to plan the seating arrangement for the family dinner tomorrow night and then I shall rest.'

'When are the others coming?' Paula asked, keeping her voice purposely light and casual.

'I expect some of them will come tonight. The others tomorrow.' Emma's tone was as mild as Paula's, for she had sensed the girl's unhappiness about the weekend and she did not want her to be more distressed than she already was.

'It will be quite a houseful, Grandy. We haven't all been gathered here for years.'

'That's true.'

'Is Aunt Elizabeth bringing her husband?'

'Does she have one at the moment?' Emma asked with not a little malice.

'Oh you are terrible, Grandy!' Paula laughed. 'You know very well she does. The Italian count. Gianni.'

'Humph! He's as much a count as I'm the Pope,' Emma retorted disparagingly. 'More like an Italian waiter to my mind.' She sipped her sherry. Her green eyes glittered above the glass.

'Grandy! He's very nice. Much too nice to cope with Aunt Elizabeth.'

'You're right! This one has lasted longer than the others, come to think of it. I'm surprised she hasn't done a bolt before now. Isn't it about time?'

Paula laughed again. 'I don't know. Who does with her? Anyway, perhaps this marriage will work better than the last.'

'And all the others before the last,' Emma commented dryly.

Paula was amused. 'You've had several husbands yourself, Grandmother.'

'Not as many as Elizabeth and furthermore I didn't divorce them one after the other. Nor did mine get younger and younger as I got older,' Emma pointed out. But she had the good grace to laugh. 'Poor Elizabeth. She has such an idealistic attitude towards love and marriage. She's as romantic now as she was when she was sixteen. I just wish she'd settle down.'

'And grow up, Grandy. Anyway, I suppose she will bring Gianni and the twins with her. Emily was at the Bradford store this past week, so I guess she will drive over tonight.'

'Yes, she's going to do that. I spoke to her yesterday and she . . .'

Hilda knocked on the door and bounced into the room. 'Lunch is ready, madame,' she announced, and added proudly. 'Cook has made all your favourite dishes, madame.'

Emma smiled. 'We'll be right down, Hilda.' She was fond of the housekeeper who had been with her for thirty years and with whom, in all that time, she had never exchanged one cross word. Most of Hilda's life had been devoted to running

Pennistone Royal, which she did unobtrusively and with great efficiency, pride, and love.

'What were you saying about Emily, Grandmother?' Paula asked as they followed Hilda out of the room.

'Oh, yes, I spoke to her yesterday and she said she would drive over in time to have dinner with us, and that perhaps Alexander would come with her. Otherwise he will drive over later.'

Hilda was standing in the hall, outside the dining-room door. She held it open for them and followed them into the room. 'Cook has made that fresh vegetable soup you like, madame, and done a lovely fried plaice.' She bustled over to the sideboard to serve them, adding, 'Chips, too. I know you said no more fried food because of your diet, but just this once won't hurt, madame,' she said, ladling out the soup into Royal Worcester bowls.

'If you say so, Hilda.' Emma laughed, and winked at Paula, who was so startled by this unexpected facial movement in her grandmother she almost dropped the glass of water she was holding.

That afternoon, whilst Paula went riding on the moors, Emma sat upstairs in her parlour, where she always worked and went over all the legal documents which had been prepared by her solicitors before she was taken ill. She spent some time studying them thoughtfully and when she had finished she called Henry Rossiter in London.

She dispensed with the preliminary greetings quickly, as she always did, and said briskly, 'Henry, where do we now stand on the liquidation of those personal assets of mine?'

'I have all the papers in front of me, Emma. I was just going over them,' he replied, clearing his throat.

To Emma his voice sounded suddenly quavering and tired. My dear old friend is getting old, she thought sadly. I shall miss him when he retires. Emma herself had no intention of retiring. She would die upright, sitting behind her desk.

'Ah, yes. I have them all now, Emma. Everything has been sold and the prices were very good. Excellent, in fact. We realized just under nine million pounds. Not bad, eh?'

'That's marvellous, Henry! Where is the money?'

'Why, right here in the bank. Where did you think it was, my dear?' He sounded startled, even a little affronted, and Emma smiled to herself.

'I know it's in the bank, Henry, but which account is it deposited in?' she asked patiently.

'I placed it in your own private business account, E.H. Incorporated.'

'Please transfer it today, Henry. To my current account. My *personal* current account.'

It was obvious to Emma that Henry was astounded. There was a silence for a few seconds and she heard him sucking in his breath. When he found his voice at last he said, 'Emma, that's ridiculous! Nobody puts nearly nine million pounds in a personal current account. You've got about two hundred thousand pounds in that account anyway. Look here, I know you said you needed about six million pounds

55

for some personal project, but the remainder of the money from the sales should be working for you.'

'I don't want it working for me, Henry. I want it in my current account.' She laughed and could not resist teasing him a little. 'I might want to go shopping, Henry.'

'Shopping!' he exploded. 'Come now, Emma! Not even *you* can spend that amount shopping! That's the most ridiculous thing I've heard you say in all the years I've known you.' He was furious.

'I certainly can spend that amount of money shopping, Henry, depending, of course, on what *exactly* I'm buying,' Emma said acidly, thinking to herself that Henry's marvellous sense of humour always seemed to evaporate into thin air when he was discussing money. 'Please, Henry, no more discussion. Deduct the bank's fee for handling the sales, and the taxes to be paid, and put the rest in my personal current account.'

He sighed in exasperation. 'Very well. I suppose you know what you're doing. After all, it is your money, Emma.'

You're damn right it is, Emma thought.

Emma worked on her seating plan for the family dinner on Saturday night and prepared a suggested menu for Hilda. Then, after locking the legal documents in her briefcase, she went into her bedroom to rest. It was going to be an extremely difficult weekend, of that she was absolutely sure. Yet she felt no apprehension or the slightest twinge of anxiety, simply a cold detachment and a natural distaste as she envisioned the scenes which were bound to ensue after the family dinner on Saturday night.

She had an abhorrence of scenes, which in their inherent violence and futility both repelled and irritated her, and she tried to avoid them at all cost, particularly with her children. In spite of her reassurances to Paula, she knew that a few altercations would be an inevitability during the next few days. She accepted this fact with resignation and steeled herself in preparation. She was not sure whether any of her children, other than Daisy, had lately developed enough inner strength to help them withstand a sudden crisis with a degree of fortitude. If they had, it would be a staggering surprise to her, but she would welcome this development because it might conceivably alleviate some of the unpleasantness. At the same time, she did not have to speculate on how they would at first respond to her news.

Emma understood all of them well enough to anticipate and gauge their reactions. Apart from Daisy, who was not involved, each one of them would, in turn, be shocked and infuriated by the news she would impart. She realized she was going to strike a swift and terrible blow, a blow which would affect all of their lives. But she felt no disquiet or pity, for it would be a blow from the sword they had forced her to take up and wield in defence, through their own foolhardy self-interest and avariciousness.

Neither did she suffer feelings of guilt about the innumerable plans she had made for the future. And she certainly did not have one iota of compassion for those who would be the most badly affected. There was only a heartbreaking sadness buried deeply inside her that at times felt like a constricting steel band around her chest. It was a sadness that sprang from her hurt and her disappointment in her children, and from a chilling horror at the knowledge that they had cold-bloodedly plotted against her. Years ago Emma had ceased to expect their love and she no longer sought their approbation but, in spite of that, she had never imagined she would have reason to question their loyalty at any time. The devastating implications of their scheming had at first left her thunderstruck, but this initial reaction had rapidly been replaced by a numbing anger and finally she had felt only pure contempt. She smiled grimly as she reflected on their duplicity, a duplicity so ill-conceived and lacking in skill and imagination that she had known about it from its very inception.

At least she could have had a degree of respect for them if they had been less transparent and a little more adroit in their plotting. Emma had always had the ability to stand back and admire a strong and cunning adversary, however grudging that admiration was. As far as her children were concerned, she was appalled at their lack of judgement, and their ingenuousness, which had precipitated their reckless and fatal actions and which had apparently led them to underestimate her.

She frowned and turned her thoughts away from the dissident members of her family, focusing her love on Daisy, Paula, and all of her other grandchildren. Eventually the quiet calm was restored and she slept, a deep untroubled sleep.

Afternoon tea had been a ritual at Pennistone Royal for years. It was a ritual Emma enjoyed, but even if she had not, Hilda would have not permitted it to be abandoned. 'Over my dead body, madame,' she had cried when Emma had suggested forgoing it a few years ago. Emma had shrugged and laughed helplessly. Hilda was a local woman who had come to work for Emma just after she had bought and restored Pennistone Royal and she was more like a member of the family than a paid servant. She was devoted to Emma, whom she described to anyone who would listen as 'a good simple woman, with no fancy ideas', adding with typical bluntness, 'and a real lady whatever her beginnings were. More so than many who were born such, I can tell you!' Emma was already a legend in the area, not only because of her power and wealth but for the many charitable deeds she had performed, quietly, with no fanfare and no desire for accolades, as was her way. But whenever Hilda had the opportunity she would proudly enumerate all of Emma's good works yet again like a litany, not forgetting to mention that her Madame had put *her* own son Peter through university and had created a series of scholarships for the talented children of Pennistone and Fairley. 'And what about her Foundation,' she would continue, with a sniff, arching her neck and narrowing her eyes shrewdly. 'Now, the Foundation gives away more money than *I* care to mention. Millions! Yes, millions. There is nothing tight-fisted about Emma Harte, that's the truth. Which is more than I can say about some of the other rich folk around here. They wouldn't give a blind man a light on a rainy night, never mind part with a few coppers for the needy.' And when she wasn't singing the praises of Emma she was proclaiming the virtues of Paula, whom she had helped to raise and whom she loved just as much as if she were her own daughter.

And so, promptly at four o'clock, Hilda came sailing into the parlour, carrying before her a great silver tea tray set with a beautiful Georgian silver tea service of exquisite design and delicate china which was translucent when held to the light. Following in her wake was one of the two young maids who came daily to work at the house, who also carried another gargantuan tray, this one laden with food painstakingly prepared by the cook.

'Put that on the desk for a minute, Brenda,' Hilda instructed, 'and bring one of the small tables over here by the fire to hold it.' She put her own tray down on the butler's table and, puffing and blowing from exertion, she paused to catch her breath, motioning to Brenda where to position the second table for convenience. The two women carefully arranged the trays in front of the fire and then Brenda slipped out of the room, leaving Hilda to make the finishing touches. She surveyed Cook's handiwork critically and then a smile of gratification slowly spread itself across her plump rosy face. There were hot buttered scones, thin slices of bread and butter, homemade strawberry jam, clotted cream, wafer-like sandwiches of cucumber, tomatoes, and smoked salmon, sweet biscuits, and a fruit cake decorated on the top with almonds. It was a real old-fashioned Yorkshire tea. Hilda carefully folded the fine lawn serviettes, put one on each plate with a small pearlhandled silver knife and fork, threw logs on to the fire, plumped the cushions, and then looked around. When she had reassured herself that everything was to her satisfaction she knocked on Emma's bedroom door.

'Are you awake, madame?'

'Yes, Hilda. Come in,' Emma called.

Hilda opened the door and poked her head around it, smiling. 'Tea is ready!' she announced. 'And Miss Paula is back from her ride. She said to tell you she'll be here in a few minutes. She's changing out of her riding clothes.'

'Thank you, Hilda. I'll be there shortly.'

'Ring if you need anything, madame,' Hilda added, and then went down to the kitchen to have her own tea and give a word of praise to Cook.

When Paula came in a little while later she stood in the doorway and caught her breath, unexpectedly moved by the beauty of the parlour. It was hushed and still, as if time had passed it by. The only sound was the crackling of the fire that burned in the huge hearth. Sunshine filtered in through the tall leaded windows, dusky and golden, bathing the furniture and paintings in a mellow light, and the air, heavy with the perfume of hyacinths and spring flowers, flowed around her, enveloping her in its heady fragrance. There was something poignant about this great old room. Memories stirred within her, faintly elusive and nostalgic. She glided silently across the floor, almost afraid to move within that stillness, fearful that the rustling of her dress might disrupt and destroy that gentle peace. She sank on to one of the sofas and her eyes roamed around the room. Here it was easy to forget that there was a world outside, a world full of pain and ugliness and despair. She drifted gently on the edge of memory, recalling her childhood in this ancient place, the happy times she had spent here with her mother and father, her cousins and her young friends. And Grandy. Always Grandy. Her grandmother was never far away, always there to wipe away her tears, laugh at her childish pranks, admire her small achievements and to scold and cosset and love her. Her grandmother had made her what she was. It was Grandy who had told her she was clever and beautiful and special. Unique, she had said. It was Grandy who had given her inner security and confidence and strength, who had taught her to face the truth without fear and with a courageous heart . . .

She did not hear Emma come in, so soft was her step. Emma, too, paused to admire, but her attention was focused solely on Paula. How lovely she looks, Emma thought, like a figure from some old painting, remote and wistful, the maiden with the unicorn.

'There you are, darling!' Emma exclaimed. 'You're looking beautiful and refreshed after your ride.'

Paula glanced up swiftly, momentarily startled. 'Oh, Grandy, you made me jump. I was miles away.'

As Emma seated herself opposite Paula her eyes lighted on the tea tray. 'My goodness, look at all this food. Hilda is too much,' she murmured, shaking her head in mild exasperation. 'How can we eat all this! It's only a few hours to dinner.'

Paula laughed. 'I know! Perhaps she feels you need building up. You know how she fusses over you. But she's really gone to town today. It's like the nursery teas she used to make when I was small.'

'I'm not hungry at all,' Emma murmured, 'and she's going to be so hurt if we don't eat anything.'

'I'm ravenous, so don't worry,' Paula remarked, picking up a sandwich. 'It was cold up there on the moors and I rode for miles. It's given me quite an appetite.' She bit into the sandwich as Emma looked on approvingly.

'I'm glad to see you eating for once. You always seem to pick at your food. No wonder you're so thin . . .'

The telephone on Emma's desk rang. Paula jumped up. 'Don't disturb yourself, darling,' she said, dashing across the room, 'it's probably only one of the family.' She picked up the phone. 'Yes, Hilda, I'll take it. Hello? It's Paula. Do you want to speak to Grandmother?' She listened briefly and said, 'Oh, all right. Yes. Fine. Goodbye.' Paula came back to her place on the sofa. 'It was Aunt Elizabeth. She's coming tomorrow morning and bringing the twins . . . and the husband.'

'So now we know,' Emma remarked with a chuckle. The telephone rang again. 'Oh dear, I do hope they're not all going to call and tell us when they are arriving. This could go on for the rest of the day,' Emma exclaimed impatiently.

Paula hurried across the room and took the call, which as always was monitored first by Hilda. 'Emily! How are you?' she cried when she heard her cousin's voice. They were close friends. 'Yes, of course you can. She's right here.' Paula put the phone down on the desk and motioned to Emma. 'It's Emily, Grandy, she wants to talk to you.'

'Knowing Emily, this could be quite an involved conversation,' Emma said with a smile, and picking up her cup of tea, she took it with her to the desk. Sitting down, she lifted the phone and said briskly, 'Hello, darling. How are . . .'

'I'm fine, Grandmother,' Emily interrupted in her young breathy voice, in a tremendous rush as always. 'I can't talk long. I'm in a frightful hurry! But I just wanted to tell you that Sarah is flying up from London this afternoon. I'm going to pick her up at Yeadon airport at six-thirty, so we'll definitely be there for dinner. Oh, and Alexander said to tell you he might be late. Uncle Kit's being truculent about that machinery. He's had Alexander going over all the figures again. Alexander's furious! Well, anyway, he thinks he can be at Pennistone by eight o'clock, if that isn't too late. Also, Jonathan is taking the train up from London to Leeds. But he said not to send Smithers. He'll get a taxi.'

All of this had issued forth in a steady uninterrupted stream, in Emily's typical fashion, which Emma was quite accustomed to. She sat back comfortably, an amused glint in her eyes, listening attentively, occasionally sipping her tea. Emily was always pressed for time, even more so than she was herself, and it often occurred to Emma that her voluble and volatile young granddaughter seemed to speak in a series of exclamation marks. Now she said teasingly, 'For someone in a rush this seems to be a very long conversation, Emily dear.'

'Grandy! Don't be mean! I can't help it if all your idiot grandchildren make me the repository of their messages. Ooh! I've one more. Philip is going to try and come with me; if not, he'll drive over with Alexander. Grandy dear . . .' Emily paused and her voice dropped, was suddenly soft and full of lilting charm. 'Can I ask a favour?'

'Of course, darling,' Emma replied, repressing an amused but loving smile. She knew that cajoling tone of Emily's only too well, adopted whenever she wanted something.

'Could I borrow one of your evening dresses, please? I only brought a few things when I came up to Bradford last week. I didn't know you would be giving a big family party. I've nothing to wear. I looked through the store here today and everything is so *dowdy*! And I simply don't have time to go over to the Leeds store.'

Emma laughed. 'If you think the clothes in the store are dowdy, I don't know what you'll find here, dear,' she remarked, wondering what on earth a pretty twenty-one-year-old blonde dynamo could possibly find suitable in *her* wardrobe.

'That red chiffon dress! The one from Paris! It fits me. So do the red silk shoes,' Emily rushed on excitedly. 'I knew you wouldn't mind me trying it on, so I did last weekend when I was at Pennistone. It looks super on me, Grandy. Please, can I borrow it? I'll be careful.'

'I'd forgotten about that dress, Emily. Of course you can wear it, if you wish. I don't know why I ever bought it in the first place. Perhaps you'd like to keep it,' Emma suggested generously.

Emily sucked in her breath in delighted surprise but said, 'Oh, Grandy darling, I couldn't do that!' There was another little pause. 'Don't you *want* it, Grandmother?'

Emma smiled to herself. 'Not really, Emily. It's far too dashing for me. It's yours.'

'Oh, Grandy! Goodness! Oh, thank you, darling! You're an angel. Grandy? . . .'

'Yes, Emily? What else?'

'Would it be an imposition to ask you to lend me your *old* diamond earrings. That dress needs a little . . . well . . . it needs a little something, doesn't it?' Emily cried enthusiastically. 'It needs good jewellery, don't you think?'

Emma burst out laughing. 'Really, Emily, you're so funny. I don't know what you mean by *old* diamond earrings. Do I have such a thing?'

'Yes! Those drops. The teardrops. You never wear them! Maybe you've forgotten them,' Emily volunteered, her voice rising hopefully.

'Oh, those. Yes. You can wear them and anything else you want. In the meantime, how are things at the Bradford store?'

'Thank you, Grandy, for the earrings, I mean. And things here are very good. I'll tell you about some of the changes I've made when I see you. Otherwise it's all sort of quiet and dull.'

'Well, you'll be in Leeds next week, which isn't so bad,' Emma pointed out. 'And we'll talk about your changes tonight. By the way, it doesn't matter if the boys are late. Hilda always makes a cold supper on Fridays,' Emma explained, and went on, 'Your mother just called. She's coming tomorrow wi . . .'

'Grandmother! Gosh! I forgot!' Emily broke in. 'I wanted to alert you to something *awful*. Mummy has had a furious row with the twins! Something about a statue they've made for you. They're insisting on bringing it and Mummy says it's simply hideous and won't fit into the car. But that's not surprising, with all the luggage *she* drags around with her. Anyway there's been a terrible fuss and the twins are upset and they want to move in and live with you! I just thought *you* should know exactly what to *expect*!' She sighed dramatically. 'What a family!'

'Thank you for telling me,' Emma said thoughtfully. 'But let's not worry about all that now. I'm sure by the time Elizabeth arrives the twins will be calm again. They can stay with me for a while if they wish. Is that all, Emily?' Emma asked patiently.

'Yes. Gosh! I must rush, Grandy. I'm way behind. Goodbye. See you tonight.'

'Goodbye . . .' Emma stared at the telephone and then she laughed. Emily had already hung up. She leaned back in her chair and shook her head, still laughing. 'It doesn't surprise me at all that the store managers tremble when Emily arrives on the scene. She's a whirlwind.'

Paula smiled at Emma, nodding her head in agreement. 'I know. But she's awfully good at her job, Grandy. I think you ought to consider sending her to the Paris store for a while. She would be terrific.'

Emma raised an eyebrow in surprise. 'But she doesn't speak French,' she said, 'otherwise I might consider it.'

'She does, Grandy.' Paula sat up. 'She's been taking lessons,' Paula explained, cautiously feeling her way. 'She would love to go and I think she might be the answer you've been looking for.'

'Well, I'll think about it,' Emma remarked, rather pleased at Paula's information. Emily was diligent, she knew that. Perhaps it *was* the solution. Emily, like all of her other grandchildren who were old enough, worked within the Harte companies and had proved herself to be tireless and assiduous in her work. She would consider it later. Now she turned her mind to more immediate problems. 'I have made the seating plan for dinner,' Emma began, and poured herself another cup of tea.

Paula looked at her with interest. 'Yes, you told me you were going to, Grandy.' Paula waited expectantly.

Emma cleared her throat. 'I think I have seated everyone appropriately. I've tried to separate the ones who don't get along too well, although, as I said, I am sure everyone will be on their best behaviour.' She put her hand in her pocket and her fingers curled around the paper. She was still reluctant to bring it out and show it to Paula.

'I hope so, Grandy! It's such a crowd and you know how difficult some of them can be.' She laughed sardonically. 'Impossible, wouldn't you say?'

'Oh yes, indeed,' Emma replied. She leaned back against the sofa and stared at Paula intently, questioningly. 'I suppose they all thought I was drawing my last breath these last few weeks, didn't they?'

The unexpected question surprised Paula. 'I don't know,' she began thoughtfully. 'Perhaps . . .' She hesitated and then her exasperation with her aunts and uncles got the better of her. 'Oh, they're such leeches, Grandy!' she exclaimed angrily. 'I don't know why you bother with them! I'm sorry. I know they're your children, but I just get furious every time I think of them.'

'You don't have to apologize to me, dear. I know only too well what they are.' Emma smiled thinly. 'I don't delude myself that they are coming to see me out of concern. They accepted my invitation out of curiosity. Vultures come to regard the carcass. But I'm not dead yet and I have made no immediate plans for dying,' she finished, a note of triumph in her voice.

Paula leaned forward quickly, staring at Emma fixedly. 'Then why did you invite them, Grandy, if you know what they are?' she asked in a deliberate voice.

Emma smiled enigmatically and her eyes turned cold. 'I wanted to see them all together for one last time.'

'Don't say that, Grandy! You're better and we are going to take care of you properly this time. To hell with the stores and business,' Paula cried passionately.

'By the "last time", I meant the last time I will invite them here for this kind of weekend,' Emma declared. 'I have a little family business to attend to, and as they are involved, they should be here. All of them. Together.' Her mouth tightened into the familiar resolute line and her eyes gleamed darkly.

Concern clouded Paula's eyes. 'You must promise me you won't let them upset you,' she said, noting the expression on Emma's face. 'And you shouldn't be worrying about family business this weekend. Is it *so* important it can't wait?' she demanded fiercely.

'Oh, it's nothing all that vital,' Emma said dismissively with a shrug. 'Just a few details regarding the trust funds. It won't take long, and of course I won't let them disturb me.' A half smile flickered across her face. 'Actually, I'm rather looking forward to it.'

'I'm not sure that I am,' Paula said carefully. 'May I see the seating plan?'

'Of course, darling.' Emma moved her position slightly and put her hand in her pocket. She felt the paper and hesitated, and then, taking a deep breath, she pulled it out. 'Here you are.' She handed the paper to Paula, waiting expectantly, holding herself perfectly still, hardly daring now to breathe at all.

Paula's eyes travelled quickly over the paper. Emma was watching her intently. Paula's eyes stopped. Opened wide. Moved on. Returned again to the previous spot. A look of total disbelief spread itself across her face. 'Why, Grandy? Why?' Her voice rose sharply in anger and the paper fluttered to the floor. Emma was silent, waiting for the initial surprise to disappear, for Paula to calm down.

'*Why?*' Paula demanded, jumping up, her face white, her mouth trembling. 'You have no right to invite Jim Fairley tomorrow night. He's not family. I don't want him here! I won't have him here! I won't! I won't! *How could you, Grandmother!*'

She ran to the window and Emma could see she was fighting to control herself. Her thin shoulders hunched over as she pressed her forehead against the pane of glass, her narrow shoulder blades sharp and protruding under the silk dress. Emma's heart ached with love for her and she felt her pain as deeply as if it were her own. 'Come here and sit down. I want to talk to you, darling,' Emma said softly.

Paula swung around quickly, her eyes now so dark they looked navy blue. 'I don't want to talk to you, Grandmother. At least not about Jim Fairley!' She stood poised by the window, defiant, reproachful, filled with rage. She trembled and clasped and unclasped her hands in agitation. How could her grandmother have been so thoughtless. To ask Jim Fairley to the dinner was cruel and unfair, and she had never known her grandmother to be either of these things. She turned her back on Emma and laid her head against the window again, looking out at the green treetops yet seeing nothing, pushing back the tears that rushed into her eyes.

To Emma she looked suddenly pathetically young and vulnerable and hurt. She is the one thing of value that I cherish, Emma thought, her heart contracting with love. Of all my grandchildren, she is the one I love the most. My hard and terrible life has been worth it just for the joy of her. This girl. This strong, dauntless, courageous, loyal girl who would put my desires before her own happiness.

'Come here, darling. I have something I must tell you.'

Paula stared at Emma abstractedly as if she were in shock. With reluctance she came back to the fireplace, moving like a sleepwalker, her face blank. She was still fuming, but the shaking had ceased. Her eyes were flat and dull, like hard stones of lapis lazuli in her ashen face. She sat down erect and rigid on the sofa. There was something contained, unyielding about her that was frightening to Emma, who knew she must quickly explain, so that look would leave her granddaughter for ever. Emma had chosen an oblique way of informing Paula that she had invited Jim Fairley to the dinner, because she did not trust herself to do it verbally. But now she must speak. Explain. Put the girl out of her terrible torment.

'I have invited Jim Fairley tomorrow, Paula, because he is indirectly involved in the family business matters I mentioned to you earlier.' She paused and sucked in her breath and then continued more firmly, looking at Paula closely. 'But that is not the only reason. I also invited him for you. And I might add he was delighted to accept.'

Paula was transfixed, incredulous. A deep flush rose up from her neck, filling her face with dark colour and her mouth shook again. 'I don't understand . . . invited him for me . . .' She was flustered and confused. Her hair had somehow worked loose from the hair slide in her agitation and she moved it away from her face impatiently. She shook her head in bewilderment. 'What are you saying, Grandmother? You have always hated the Fairleys. I don't understand.'

Emma pushed herself on to her feet and went and sat on the sofa. She took one of Paula's beautiful tapered hands in her own small sturdy ones. She gazed at Paula and her heart tightened when she looked into her eyes, vast caverns in the paleness of her face and full of pain. Emma touched that wan face, smiling gently, and then she said in a hoarse whisper, 'I am an old woman, Paula. A tough old woman who has fought every inch of the way for everything I have. Strong, yes, but also tired. Bitter? Perhaps I was. But I have acquired *some* wisdom in my struggle with life, my struggle to survive, and I wondered to myself the other day why the silly pride of a tough old woman should stand in the way of the one person I love the most in the whole world. It struck me I was being selfish, and foolish, to let events of sixty years ago cloud my judgement now.'

'I still don't understand,' Paula murmured, bafflement in her eyes.

'I am trying to tell you that I no longer have any objections to you seeing Jim Fairley. I had a long conversation with him yesterday, during which I gathered he still feels the same way about you. That he has always had very serious intentions. I told him this afternoon that if he wishes to marry you, he not only has my permission, but my blessing as well. I bless both of you, with all my love.'

Paula was speechless. Her mind would not accept her grandmother's words. For months she had cautioned herself not to think of Jim, had finally accepted that there was no possible future for them. She had been hard on herself, ruthlessly pushing aside all emotion, all feelings, pouring her energy into her work in her abject misery. Through the blur of her tears she saw Emma's face, that face she had seen and loved all of her life. That face she trusted. Emma was smiling fondly, waiting, and her eyes were wise and understanding and full of love. The tears slid silently down Paula's cheeks and she shook her head. 'I can't believe you would change your mind,' she said, her voice choked.

'I did.'

These two simple words, uttered with firmness and conviction, finally penetrated Paula's aching brain, her battered heart. She began to sob, her whole body heaving as the smothered and pent-up emotions of months were released. She slumped forward, blindly reaching for Emma, who cradled her in her arms like a child, stroking her hair and murmuring softly to her in the way she had done when she was a little girl. 'It's all right. Hush, darling. It's all right. I promise you it's all right.'

Eventually the heaving sobs subsided and Paula looked up at Emma, a tremulous smile on her face. Emma wiped the tears from her face with one hand, stared intently at her and said, 'I never want to see you unhappy again as long as I live. I've had enough unhappiness for both of us.'

'I don't know what to say. I'm numb. I can't believe it,' Paula replied quietly. Jim. *Jim!*

Emma nodded. 'I know how you feel,' she said, and her tired eyes brightened. 'Now, why don't you do me a favour. Go and call Jim. He's still at the paper. He's waiting for you, in fact. Invite him for dinner tonight, if you wish. Or better still, drive into Leeds and have dinner with him alone. I'll have Emily and Sarah for company, and perhaps Alexander and the others will arrive in time for supper.' She laughed, her eyes shining. 'I do have other grandchildren, you know.' Paula hugged her and kissed her, and then she was gone, flying out of the room without another word.

Wings on her feet, Emma thought, going to her love. She sat for a while on the sofa, preoccupied with thoughts of Paula and Jim and so many other things. Then she stood up suddenly, abruptly, and walked to the window, stretching her stiffened limbs, smoothing her dress with her hands, patting her silver hair into place. She opened one of the leaded windows and looked out.

Below her in the garden the trees glistened in the cool evening air, and everything was dark green and perfectly still. Not a blade of grass, not a leaf stirred, and the birds were silent. She could see the daffodils rapidly losing their brilliant colour, bleaching palely to white now that the sun had set, and the topiary hedges were slowly turning black. She stood there for a long time in the gloaming, watching the dusk descend as the crystalline northern light faded behind the low hump line of hills on the horizon. The mist was drifting into the garden, wrapping everything before it in a vaporous, opal-tinted shawl, rising suddenly to obscure the trees and the shrubs and the old flagged terrace, until all these images were fused together.

Emma shivered and closed the window, turning back into the welcoming warmth and comfort of the room. She walked across the faded Savonnerie carpet, still shivering slightly from the cold damp air that had blown in through the window. She picked up the poker and energetically pushed the burning logs around, throwing on more of them to build the huge roaring fire she loved.

She sat by the fireside staring into the flames, content and at peace, forgotten memories of her youth invading her mind as she waited for her other grandchildren to arrive. She thought of the Fairleys. All of them were gone now, except for James Arthur Fairley, the last of the line. 'Why should he suffer, and Paula, for the mistakes of a dead generation?' she asked herself aloud, and then thought: I was right to do this. It is my gift to her. To both of them.

It was growing darker outside and in the dimly lit room the firelight cast its strange and mysterious shadows across the walls and the ceiling and in amongst them she saw so many old and familiar faces. Her friends. Her enemies. All of them dead long ago. Ghosts ... just ghosts that could no longer touch her or hers.

Life is like a circle, she mused. My life began with the Fairleys and it will end with them. The two points have now joined to make the full circle.

PART TWO

THE ABYSS
1904–5

Long is the way
And hard, that out
of hell leads up to light.

– JOHN MILTON, *Paradise Lost*

FIVE

'Mam . . . Mam . . . Are yer awake?' Emma called softly from the doorway. There was no answer.

She hovered uncertainly near the door, her ears straining for the slightest sound, but the room was as still as the grave. Nervously she pulled the meagre shawl more tightly around her slender shoulders, shivering in the thin nightgown in the bitter cold before the dawn, her pale face a ghostly beacon in the murky darkness.

'Mam! Mam!' she cried in an urgent whisper, and crept further into the room, moving cautiously, feeling her way around the few mean pieces of furniture, her eyes not yet adjusted to the gloom. She could scarcely breathe, so dank and stale was the malodorous air. She shuddered, momentarily repelled by the mingled odours of musty walls, soiled bedclothes, and cloying sweat. It was the unmistakable stench of poverty and sickness. She sucked in her breath and edged forward.

When she reached the iron bedstead her heart missed a beat as she peered down at the sick woman who lay inert underneath the bedclothes, which were thrown about in disarray. *Her mother was dying. Perhaps she was already dead.* Panic and fear sent shudders through her thin little body, so that she shook uncontrollably. She bent forward and pressed her face to her mother's body, straining towards that fragile form, as if to imbue it with renewed vigour, to give it life. She screwed her eyes tightly shut and uttered a silent prayer, passionate and beseeching, every ounce of her concentration pouring into it. Please, God, don't let me mam die! I'll be good for the rest of me life. I'll do anything Yer want, God. I will, God, I will! Just don't let me mam die. Emma believed that God was good. Her mother had told her that God was Goodness. That He was understanding and forgiving. Emma did not believe in a wrathful God, the God of retribution and revenge that the Methodist minister warned about in his sermons on Sundays. Her mother had said God was Inconceivable Love and her mam knew best. Emma's God was compassionate. He *would* answer her prayer.

She opened her eyes and began to stroke the woman's feverish brow gently. 'Mam! Mam! Can yer hear me? Are yer all right?' she asked again in a voice quavering with dread. There was still no visible response.

In the wavering light from the tiny candle flame the woman's face was clearly in focus. Usually pale, it had taken on an ashen cast and beads of sweat coated it with a glistening film that looked ghastly in the weak light. The once luxuriant brown hair fell in limp and listless fronds across the damp brow and lay in a tangled mass on the sodden pillow behind her. There was a sweetness in the face, which the pain and suffering had not completely obliterated, but all the traces of the gentle beauty of her youth had been dissipated by the ravages of grim poverty, by the years of punishing struggle for survival, and finally by this deadly and virulent sickness. An aureole of death was around Elizabeth Harte and she would not live to see these last few months of winter move forward into spring. She was suffering from the wasting disease which was consuming her little by little every day, leaving her a withered and wraith-like old woman. She was not quite thirty-four years old.

Hers was a grim sickroom, for it contained few elements of comfort or beauty, none of the amenities of life. The bed was the dominant piece of furniture and it took up most of the space under the sloping eaves. Apart from the bed there were few scant furnishings. The rickety table, made of bamboo, was wedged in the corner, between the bed and the small window, and upon this reposed a worn black Bible, a pottery mug, and the medicine Dr Malcolm had prescribed. Near the door there was a crude wooden chest, whilst the mahogany washstand, with its cracked white marble top, rested against the wall on the far side of the window. The cottage was built into the side of the moorland and this made it cruelly damp and unhealthy through all the seasons of the year, but especially so in these harsh northern winters when rain-soaked gales and driving snow blew ferociously across the fells. Yet in spite of the dampness, the spartan frugality, and the dreary ambiance, the room was spotlessly clean. Freshly washed and starched cotton curtains hung at the window, and the few pieces of rustic furniture gleamed brightly with beeswax and Emma's constant care. Not a speck of dust marred the worn wooden floor, which was covered in part with clipped rugs, homemade from pieces of gaily coloured rags hooked into sacking. Only the bed was unkempt and neglected, for Emma could change the bed linen but once a week, when she came home from Fairley Hall, where she was in service.

Elizabeth moved uneasily and with some agitation. 'Is that our Emma?' The voice was so feeble with fatigue it was barely audible.

'Yes, Mam, it's me,' the girl cried, clutching her mother's hand.

'What time is it, Emma?'

'Just turned four o'clock. Old Willy knocked us up early this morning. I'm sorry if I waked yer, Mam, but I wanted ter make sure yer were all right, afore I went up yonder ter the Hall.'

Elizabeth sighed. 'Aye, lass. I'm not so badly. Don't fret so. I'll get up later and –' She began to cough violently and pressed her fragile hands to her chest trying to contain the tremors that shook her. Emma poured medicine into the pot mug on the table and, slipping her arms around her mother, she propped her up so that she could drink from the pot. 'Try this, Mam. It's the stuff from Dr Mac, and it seems ter do yer good,' she exclaimed, in the most cheerful voice she could summon. Elizabeth attempted to sip from the pot between bouts of the persistent coughing that racked her body. Slowly the obstinate rattle in her chest abated and eventually she was able to take a long draught of the medicine. Although she was suffering from shortness of breath and exertion she managed to speak.

'Yer'd best go down and see ter yer father and the lads, luv. I'll rest a while and perhaps afore yer go ter work yer'll bring me up some tea.' The febrile light in her eyes was dimming and she seemed more conscious of her surroundings, more aware of the girl who stood beside the bed.

Emma bent down and kissed the woman's lined cheek with tenderness and pulled the blankets up around the wasted shoulders protectively. 'Aye, I will.' She slipped out of the room and closed the door softly. As she ran down the narrow stone staircase, ignoring its high perilous slant in her haste, raised voices wafted up to meet her halfway. Emma stood quite still and drew in her breath sharply, her heart sinking into the pit of her stomach. A feeling of nausea swept over her as she envisioned the ugly scene awaiting her. Winston, her brother, and her father were quarrelling again and the violence of their confrontation was only too evident from their angrily raised voices. The chilling thought that they would disturb her mother caused Emma to cry out involuntarily. She stifled the frightened half cry, pressing her roughened hands to her mouth, and sat down heavily on the cold stone steps, wondering helplessly how she could stop them fighting. If her mam heard them she would crawl out of bed to make peace between them, even if it took her last ounce of strength. Elizabeth Harte had always been the buffer between her son Winston and her husband. In these last few weeks she had been too debilitated to leave her bed, a virtual prisoner in the mean little room under the eaves. But when she heard their violent disagreements, she cried a lot and the fever accelerated and became more virulent and she coughed until she was worn out with coughing.

'Fools!' Emma said out loud. Grown men acting like bairns and them too selfish ter think of me poor mam. This thought galvanized her. She jumped up quickly, the sinking sickness replaced by a cold anger that grew in magnitude as Emma continued her descent down the staircase. She pushed open the kitchen door and stood rigid and tense on the threshold, her hand tightly gripping the doorframe. As she regarded the scene her green eyes took on a flinty look.

Unlike the damp and cheerless room upstairs, this was a cosy, heartwarming place. A fire blazed in the grate and a large iron kettle was hissing on the hob. The giant-sized cabbage roses on the wallpaper had long since lost their summer glory, but the smudged pink outlines left behind added a warming mellow cast to the walls. Pieces of polished horse brass gleamed around the fireplace, twinkling in the soft light with the lustre of freshly minted gold sovereigns. Two comfortable high-backed wooden chairs stood on either side of the fireplace and there was a tall Welsh dresser opposite, filled with blue and white willow-patterned dishes. In the very centre of the room, a large scrubbed wood table took pride of place and was surrounded by six rush-seated chairs. White lace curtains graced the windows and the red brick floor sparkled. The room had a robust, rosy glow, a glow enhanced by the roaring fire that blazed up the chimney and the trembling flicker of the paraffin lamp that stood on the mantelshelf.

It was a scene that Emma carried with her, especially when she was at Fairley Hall, for it engendered a sense of well-being within her and comforted her when she was alone. Now her cherished image was shattered. Everything was in its place, nothing had been moved, but the atmosphere was charged, and ugly and angry words reverberated and bounced off the walls. The two men, her father and her brother, faced each other like animals, oblivious to her, oblivious to everything except this deadly hatred between them.

John 'Big Jack' Harte was a large man, as his nickname implied. Without his boots, in his stocking feet, he stood six foot two and was ramrod straight. He had fought the Boers in Africa in 1900, a sergeant in the Seaforth Highlanders, and it was said of him that he could fell a man with one blow from his massive fist. He had a powerfully built frame, a handsome roughhewn face, a ruddy complexion, and a splendid head of wavy hair the colour of polished jet.

He stood towering over his son Winston, his fist raised in anger and ready to bring down hard on the boy. His face was livid with volcanic wrath and his eyes flared dangerously. 'Thee's not going into no navy and that's last I'll hear of it in this house, me lad! Thee's under age and no permission will thee get from me.

71

Now drop it once and for all, our Winston, or thee'll feel me strap across thee back. Thee's not too old yet for a good hiding, me lad, and don't thee forget it!'

Winston glowered back at his father, his unusually beautiful face flushed and contorted with frustration and anger, his blue eyes icy. 'If I want ter go, I'll go,' he screamed passionately. 'Yer can't stop me if I runs away and run away I will, out of this godforsaken hole, where there's nowt but misery and poverty and dying –'

'Little monkey! Talk back ter me, would thee! We'll soon see about that!'

The boy could not move for a split second and then, as the bubble of rage burst in his head, he stepped forward and lifted his arm as if to strike his father. But through the dizzying haze of his blinding anger he saw something menacing in those eyes and he paled and backed away, faltering, mortally afraid of his father's strength. Although he was not as tall and as muscular as his father, Winston was well built and strong, but he was made of finer stuff, more like his mother. And he knew he was no physical match for Big Jack Harte. Winston had strong instincts for self-preservation and especially so when it applied to his person, for the fifteen-year-old boy was increasingly conscious of his striking looks and he knew them to be his most powerful asset.

'Don't think I didn't see that, our Winston! I'll teach thee ter raise thee hand ter me, lad! That I will. I'm going ter give thee a good hiding thee won't forget as long as thee lives. And it's long overdue!' As he spoke he began to unbuckle the black leather belt around his trousers, pulling it off hurriedly in his excitement. He wrapped it around his right hand, buckle first, moving towards Winston threateningly and with immense power.

'Ah, yer can't scare me!' Winston cried shrilly, nonetheless retreating to the Welsh dresser, putting the table safely between them. 'Yer wouldn't dare hit *me*! Me mam won't never forgive yer, if yer puts that strap on me!' he warned.

Big Jack Harte appeared not to hear. He moved forward rapidly and with agility, the black leather strap dangling ominously in his tightened fist. He lifted his arm and would have brought the strap down across the boy's head if Emma had not rushed across the room at this moment and jumped in front of her father. She grabbed his arm and held it with both hands, using all of her strength. Her face was gaunt in the firelight and she shook with rage. She stood before her father unflinchingly. She was the only one who dared defy him, who had the nerve to stand up to him. And she could usually quell his wrath, subdue him into docility.

Although her voice was quiet when she spoke there was vehemence in her words. 'Shut up, Dad! What's got in ter yer? Shouting and bawling at this hour and our mam lying badly upstairs. Yer should know better, our dad. And yer should be ashamed of yerself! Now sit down and drink yer tea, or I'll be the one that runs away, and then where would yer all be, eh?' She held tightly on to his raised arm, which she could not move. 'Come on, Dad,' she cajoled in a softer tone, 'don't be stubborn. Our Winston won't run off ter the navy. That's all big talk on his part.'

'That's what yer think, is it, Miss Nosy Parker?' Winston interjected furiously from the safety of his corner on the other side of the room. 'Well, yer wrong for once in yer short life, our Emma. I mean it. Yes, I do.'

Emma swung around to face her brother. She strove to control herself. 'Stop it, Winston,' she hissed. 'Yer'll have me mam downstairs next and her so poorly. And stop this stupid talk of joining the Royal Navy. Me dad's right, yer are too young. And yer'll break our mam's heart if yer runs away. So stop it. And now!'

Winston's eyes gleamed with unfamiliar resentment and hostility. 'Miss Bossy Knickers, that's what yer are,' he cried derisively. 'Mind yer own business, Miss Bossy. Always interfering. Yer make me sick. Yer nowt but a slip of a lass and what do yer knows about owt, Emma Harte!' There was a tinge of venom in his voice, but he recoiled under her piercing gaze, which was full of coldness. Her expression was one of indifference as she turned her back on him with deliberateness. Winston was vaguely conscious that he was afraid of his sister. Not afraid in the sense that he was afraid of his father's brute force, but in another, wholly different way which he did not fully comprehend. As if to belie his feelings, he sucked in his breath and cried, 'Too big for yer boots, Emma Harte. That's what yer are!' Emma ignored this last outburst and pressed her lips together, willing herself not to respond.

Jack had been dimly aware of this heated exchange between his two eldest children and he had used the few seconds to cool his rage. Now he turned his leonine head slowly and regarded his son with penetrating intensity. 'Enough's enough, Winston,' he said in a voice still roughened with the residue of anger, yet controlled. 'Leave thee sister alone. Thee's done plenty of damage for one day, and I won't be forgetting it for a hell of a long time.'

'She's always poking her nose inter me business –' Winston retorted, but stopped short when he saw the irate glint in his father's eyes, the flush rising on his neck to suffuse his face. Jack moved restlessly under Emma's loosening grip and Winston thought better of arousing his father again. He slid with catlike grace to the far end of the kitchen, towards their younger brother Frank, who had been cowering against the set pot shaking with fear and whimpering during the uproar.

Emma was seething at his stupidity and inability to gauge their father's moods, to know when to hold his tongue. Watching him whispering to Frank and consoling him, she wished he *would* run away and then perhaps they would have some peace. This disloyal thought so paralysed her she let go of her father's arm. Winston's presence had always been necessary to her and they were inseparable. He was her ally, her only friend, and as such she had considered him to be indispensable. The realization that perhaps he was not stunned her. She turned back quickly to her father, took his arm, and, somewhat shaken, said quietly, 'Come on, Dad, sit down now.'

For a moment Jack Harte would not yield under the determined but light pressure of her hands on his muscular body. He looked down at the girl and thought how thin she was and he knew how easy it would be to free himself from her grip. With a flick of his wrist he could send her frail body hurtling across the room. But he had never struck Emma and he never would. He relaxed and allowed her to manoeuvre him into the chair. He gazed at the pale face, usually so grave and thoughtful, which still slightly twitched with aggravation, and he was moved as only she, of all his children, could move him. And as he contemplated his daughter, the only one who dared to challenge him, Big Jack had a rare and sudden flash of insight. He recognized with great clarity of vision that he was facing implacable will. A will wrought of iron and, in one so young, frightening and shocking. That unyielding little countenance filled him with a mixture of emotions, new emotions for him, compounded of pride and fear. He was proud of Emma's strength, yet afraid for her because of it. It would get her into trouble one day, of that he felt sure. She was independent of spirit and there was no room for independent spirits in their world. Their class was inevitably ground under the heels of the bosses.

Emma's fierce will would be broken and he dreaded that day. He prayed then that he would not be around to see it, for it would break his heart, just as surely as it would break hers.

As he continued to stare at her, he saw the girl clearly for the first time in years. He saw the undernourished body, the thin neck, and the scrawny shoulders underneath the shabby little nightgown. But he also saw something else. He saw the transparency of the skin, as white as the snow that lingered still on the highest fells. He saw the sparkling eyes full of emerald fire, twin reflections of his own. He saw the richness of the russet hair that came to a widow's peak above the proud brow. He saw in that undeveloped childish body the beginning of prettiness, but would it ever come to flower? His heart shifted and seemed to move imperceptibly with an unbearable ache and he was filled with profound anger and grief when he thought of the life of drudgery that lay ahead of her. She was a drudge already, here and at Fairley Hall, and she was so young.

Her light, girlish voice brought him out of his reverie. 'Dad, Dad, don't yer feel well?' She was bending over him.

'There's nowt wrong with me, lass. Have thee looked in on thee mam? How is she?'

'She was a bit poorly afore I came down, but she's resting easy like now. I'm going ter take her some tea in a minute.'

She started to move away from him and he smiled at her, white teeth flashing, eyes loving, but she did not respond in her usual affectionate way, the way he had anticipated. She simply patted his arm and gave him a long careful look and he felt curiously reproached and shamed by his own child, as if he were the child and she the parent. And it bothered him enormously, for Emma was his favourite and he understood her and had the most profound love for her. He did not want to be diminished in her eyes. Her esteem was very necessary to him. Mechanically he leaned over and lifted his boots from the hearth. It was getting late and he would have to leave soon for the Fairley brickyard, where he and Winston worked. It was on the Pudsey road and it took them a full hour to walk there.

Emma crossed the kitchen with a burst of energy and renewed purpose. She wanted to dispel the mood, return things to normal, for although their thoughtlessness still rankled, she was not one to bear a grudge for long. She spied Frank at the set pot. He was calm again and with great concentration was preparing the sandwiches for their lunch and tea breaks, which they took to work with them in their jock boxes. She hurried over to join him, rolling up her sleeves purposefully, the air crackling with her vitality.

'Frank, lad, whatever do yer think yer doing!' she cried when she reached the boy, her eyes widening in surprise, her head bobbing from side to side in her excitement. 'Lathering that dripping on like there's no termorrow!' She grabbed the knife from the startled boy's hand and, clucking in mild irritation, she began to scrape some of the dripping off the bread. These scrapings she thriftily returned to the brown stone jar that stood on the wooden chopping board which covered the set pot opening. 'We're not gentry yet, our Frank,' she went on, and expertly finished making the sandwiches herself, folding the bread cakes over and cutting them in half decisively and with a little flourish.

Frank shrank from Emma, his lower lip trembling, his hazel eyes brimming with hot tears, his small face pinched and scared. Frank was twelve and small for his age. He had a head of fair hair as soft as duck's down, a milky skin, and a gentle face, almost girlish in its prettiness. Much to his humiliation, his sweet appearance had earned him the nicknames of 'Sissy' and 'Nancy' at the Fairley mill, where he worked as a bobbin ligger. Under Winston's expert tuition he had learned to fight back with his fists, but his preference was to walk away from the taunts and jibes, his head held high, ignoring them. And that was the way he would be all of his life, always sensitive and thin-skinned, but capable of turning the other cheek, proudly and with disdain.

His fair hair fell over his eyes and he pushed it away nervously, turning pathetically to Winston, his defender, who had just finished washing at the sink. 'I didn't mean no harm, Winston,' he said, and the tears slid down his freckled cheeks.

Winston had witnessed this scene at first with astonishment and then with amusement, aware that Emma's brisk manner was her way of reasserting her motherly authority over them, and also of restoring their usual morning routine. He knew that her clucking and spluttering about the dripping was harmless. He put down the towel he had been using and pulled the younger boy to him, holding him comfortingly in the crook of his arm.

'Well, I'll go ter hell and back!' he exclaimed, feigning horror, as he addressed his father. He bit his lip to hide a smile and continued, 'I never thought I'd live ter see the day our Emma turned inter a nip scrape. I think some of old man Fairley's habits have rubbed off on yon lass.' He spoke mildly, all the hostility washed out of his eyes.

Emma whirled on them, her face flushed in the firelight that blazed up the chimney and filled her hair full of golden lights. She brandished the knife before her. 'That's not fair! I'm not a nip scrape! Am I, Dad?' she appealed, and rushed on breathlessly before he could answer, 'Anyway, old man Fairley's that well off he's bowlegged with brass and do yer know why? Because he wouldn't nip a currant in two and give yer half. So there!' She spoke heatedly, although not with anger, and there was an embarrassed expression on her crimson face. Winston knew his teasing had hit its mark, for Emma loathed stinginess and it was the worst accusation anyone could level at her, even in jest.

Bridling and tossing her head, she said huffily, 'That dripping was two inches thick. Yer couldn't have eaten them sandwiches. Yer would've been sick, that yer would.'

Winston started to laugh, unable to suppress his amusement any longer. Jack threw him a startled glance, his thick black brows puckering together in a jagged line across his brow as he gazed at the boy mystified. But he saw at once that Winston's laughter was not malicious and he saw, too, Emma's increasing confusion and humiliation. As he looked from one to the other the boy's mirth infected him. He chuckled and slapped his knee.

Emma glared at them and slowly a sheepish grin spread itself across her face. She was laughing herself. 'What a fuss over a ha'porth of dripping,' she muttered through her laughter, shaking her head as she put down the knife. Frank looked in bewilderment at them all, at first uncomprehending, and as he realized their merriment was real he laughed, too, wiping away his tears on the sleeve of his grey shirt. Emma hugged him to her. 'Don't take on so, Frank luv. I meant no harm, yer silly duck nut. And don't wipe yer nose on yer sleeve,' she scolded gruffly as she stroked back his hair and kissed the top of his head with tenderness.

A feeling of friendliness and genuine family affection was miraculously restored. Emma sighed with relief and began her managerial bustling again. 'We'll all have ter look sharp and get a move on, or we'll be late for work,' she cried, catching sight of the clock on the mantel. It had just turned a quarter to five and her father and Winston had to leave at five o'clock to reach the brickyard by six, when they had to clock in. She felt the teapot under the cosy. The pot was still hot. 'Come on, Frank, take this tea up ter our mam for me,' she said, pouring tea into a mug and adding generous portions of milk and sugar. 'And, Dad, mend the fire for me, will yer, please. Bank it up so that it lasts till me Aunt Lily comes in. And, Winston, wash the pots whilst I finish making yer jock. And, Dad, don't forget the fireguard.'

She handed the mug of tea to Frank. 'And ask me mam if she wants some bread and jam, and hurry up about it, me lad, there's still a lot of chores ter be done afore I go ter the Hall.' Frank took the tea carefully in both of his small hands and hurried across the room, his boots ringing hollowly on the brick floor as he headed for the staircase. Whistling under his breath, Winston gathered the dirty mugs and plates from the table and carried them over to the sink, whilst Jack turned to the fireplace and began stacking on the logs. Emma smiled to herself. Peace was restored. She moved to the set pot and began to wrap the sandwiches in the cotton serviettes her mother had so carefully hemmed, dampening them first so that the sandwiches would stay fresh.

Jack devoted his attention to the fire, interspersing the logs with treasured pieces of coal and then heaping on coal dust so that the fire would last until his sister Lily came in to tend to Elizabeth later in the morning. As he swung his great body around to reach for the fireguard he glanced surreptitiously at Winston, who was mechanically washing the pots at the kitchen sink. He regretted his outburst of anger earlier. There was no deep-rooted hatred between them, only this irritation that was increasingly difficult to repress in them both. He did not even blame the boy for wanting to leave Fairley; nevertheless, he could not permit him to go. Dr Malcolm had said nothing specific about Elizabeth's health, but Jack did not require a medical opinion to confirm what he already suspected. She was dying. Winston's departure at this time would be the last nail in her coffin. He was her favourite child. She loved all of her children, but Winston was special, being the eldest and so like her in looks. Jack dare not let him leave and yet he could not tell the boy his reasons. 'And he always picks the wrong time ter discuss it,' Jack muttered to himself as he put the fireguard around the grate. He rested for a moment against the guard, staring into the fire, blinded by searing grief and overwhelming despair. It was grief for Elizabeth, who had been so brutalized by life, despair for his young children, who would be motherless before the last of the snows melted into spring.

He felt a light touch on his arm and he knew it was Emma. He swallowed hard, his throat constricted. He coughed hoarsely and straightened himself to his full height, attempting a smile. 'Yes, luv, what is it?'

'Yer'll be late, Dad. Yer best go and see me mam now, afore yer leave.'

'Aye, lass. I'll just wash this coal dust off me hands.' Jack moved to the sink, where Winston was drying the pots. 'Go up and see thee mam, lad, and I'll be up in a minute. Thee knows how upset she gets if we don't all see her afore we leaves.' Winston nodded, wiped the last of the mugs quickly, and left the kitchen, still nervously whistling between his teeth.

Jack looked over at Emma, who was standing at the set pot, the tea caddy in her hands. She was measuring out their mashings of tea and sugar into small pieces of paper, screwing the ends together securely so nothing would be spilled. 'Thee'll be catching thee death in that nightgown, Emma, and there's no warmth in that shawl. Thee best get dressed lass, now everything's in order down here.'

'Yes, I will, Dad. I've finished putting up yer mashings,' she said with a sunny smile that illuminated her serious face with sudden radiance. Her eyes, so unusually deep and vividly green, were bright and shining, and Jack knew that her affection for him was intact. She ran across the kitchen to her father. He was smiling down at her. Emma stood on tiptoe and, putting her thin arms around his neck, she pulled his face down to hers. She kissed his cheek and said, 'I'll see yer next Saturday, Dad.' Jack held her for a brief moment longer, his sinewy arms tightening around her protectively as a surge of tenderness swept through him. 'Aye, luv, and take care of theeself up yonder at the Hall,' he mumbled in a tight voice. She was gone before he could catch his breath, slipping out of his arms and streaking across the room like a flash of lightning, and Jack was alone in the kitchen.

He sighed and reached for his coat on the peg behind the door. He felt around in the pockets for the small leather straps he fastened around his corduroy trousers to prevent the dust from the bricks rising up his legs. He sat down at the table and buckled them on, wondering as he did whether he should tell Elizabeth he had given in his notice at the brickyard. He frowned, his large hands expertly tightening the straps until he had just the right pressure. It had been a hard decision for Jack to make, since jobs were scarce and so many men were out of work, and also he liked working in the fresh air, even though slinging wet clay up onto a gantry for ten hours a day was killing work for any man. He did not object to the hard work, he did object to the pay it brought him and he had said so to Stan, the gaffer, last Friday. 'Eighteen shillings and tenpence is nowt much ter take home at the end of the week, Stan. And me a married man with three kids. I'm not blaming me kids on anybody but meself, mind thee, but bloody old man Fairley's paying starvation wages. That he is, Stan, and thee knows it,' he had said with a quiet vehemence.

Stan had shaken his head, and even though he had spoken with some sympathy he had not been able to meet Jack's fixed stare. 'Aye, Jack, there's summat in what thee says. It's a bloody crime, it is. But there's gaffers walking around that only get twenty bob a week. I don't get much more meself. Nowt I can do about it, though. Take it or leave it, lad.' He had told Stan he would leave it, in no uncertain terms, and he had reluctantly gone to the Fairley mill on Saturday morning, cap in hand, swallowing his pride. He had seen Eddie, the foreman, his friend since boyhood, who had signed him on to start in a week's time at twenty shillings a week, which was an improvement if not much of one. He pondered the question of telling Elizabeth and abruptly decided against it. She knew he loathed mill work and it would only grieve her and aggravate her condition. No, he would not tell her until he was already working at the mill next week. He had one consolation, small though it was. The mill was down at the bottom of the village, in the valley on the banks of the river Aire, and it was only ten minutes away from the cottage. He was close at hand if Elizabeth needed him, if there was an emergency, and this thought cheered him so enormously it made the mill work seem that much less unpalatable to him.

The church clock in the village struck five and he sprang up, striding across the room swiftly with that easy grace many tall men have quite unconsciously. He took the stairs two at a time, his heavy hobnail boots hitting the stone steps with a harsh metallic ring that was an oddly mournful echo in the silence of the cottage.

Emma was dressed and standing with Winston and Frank by the side of the bed. They seemed a woebegone little trio in their drab and shabby clothes, which were also patched and darned. But these clothes were scrupulously clean and neat, as they were themselves with their scrubbed faces and carefully combed hair. And each child, as disparate as they were in appearance, had a sort of refinement that stood out so strikingly that those poor, threadbare garments became insignificant. They had a curious dignity as they stood there so solemn-faced and quiet. The children parted and stepped back to make way for Jack as he bounded into the room, bristling with energy, a cheerful smile carefully arranged on his face.

Elizabeth lay back against the mound of pillows, pale and piteously depleted, but the feverish glaze on her face had vanished and she appeared more tranquil. Emma had washed her face and brushed her hair, and the blue shawl she had wrapped around her mother's shoulders intensified the blueness of Elizabeth's uncommonly lovely eyes; her hair fanned out across the pillows like skeins of soft spun silk. Not a spot of colour stained the whiteness of her face and to Jack, in the candlelight, it was like the carved ivory he had seen in Africa, the contours and planes sharp and finely chiselled, devoid of any crudity of form. She had the appearance of a small and very delicate figurine. Her face lit up when she saw Jack. She stretched out her thin arms weakly towards him and when he reached the bed he pulled her to him almost fiercely, holding her feeble body against his own strong virile one as if to never let her go.

'Thee looks worlds better, Elizabeth luv,' he said in a voice so gentle it seemed to stroke the air delicately. And it was hardly recognizable as his own.

'I am, John,' she asserted bravely. 'I'll be up tonight when yer gets home, and I'll have a good sheep's-head broth boiling for yer, luv, and dumplings, too, and fresh bread cakes.'

He released her tenderly and placed her back on the pillows, and as he gazed at that pitifully wasted face he did not see it as it truly was at all. He saw only the beautiful girl he had known all of his life. She looked at him with such trust and adoration his heart clenched with sorrow and there was nothing he could do to save her. And that strange impulse came over him again, an impulse which was occurring with increasing frequency and compelling urgency, in reality a compulsion to pick her up bodily in his arms and take her out of this mean room and run with her to the top of the moors, which she longed for always. There on the high fells the air was pure and bracing and the sky was a vast reflection of her eyes, and he felt in some inexplicable and mysterious way that on that high ground this disease would be blown out of her, that she would be miraculously revived and filled with life.

But the lavender tints and pale vaporous mists of the long summer days were now swept away by northern gales. If only it was summer he *would* take her up there, the Top of the World she called it, and he would lay her down against a knoll of heather amongst green ferns and tender young bilberry leaves, and they would sit together in contentment in the shelter of Ramsden Crags, warmed by the sun, alone except for the linnets and larks fluttering by in the hazy golden light.

78

It was not possible. The earth was hard with black February frost and the sweeping moorland was savage and desolate under a sky bleak and rain-filled.

'John luv, did yer hear what I said? I'll be up tonight and we can all have our suppers together, in front of the fire, like we used ter afore I was sick.' There was a new vividness in Elizabeth's voice, an excitement unquestionably created by Jack's presence.

'Thee mustn't get out of bed, luv,' he cautioned hoarsely. 'Doctor says thee must have complete rest, Elizabeth. Our Lily will come in later and tend to thee, and make the supper for us. Now thee must promise me thee won't do owt foolish, lass. Now promise me.'

'Oh, yer do fret so, John Harte. But I promise, if that's what pleases yer. I'll stay abed.'

He leaned forward so that only she could hear. 'I love thee, Elizabeth, I do that,' he whispered.

She looked deeply into his eyes and she saw that love so clearly reflected, changeless and everlasting, and she said, 'I love thee, too, John, till the day I die and even after that.'

He kissed her quickly, hardly daring to look at her again, and as he got up off the bed his movements were jerky and disjointed, almost as if he had relinquished command of his great body. He crossed the bedroom in three quick strides. 'Come on, Winston, kiss thee mam and let's be off. We're running late, lad,' he called brusquely.

Winston and Frank each kissed their mother and moved away from the bed to the door with the utmost quiet. Winston had not addressed a remark to Emma since his teasing in the kitchen earlier, and now he gave her one of his most charming and breezy smiles, and said from the top of the stairs, 'See yer Saturday, Emma. Ta'rar, luv.'

She waved and smiled. 'Ta'rar, Winston,' adding as an afterthought, 'Frank, yer'd best finish getting ready for work. I'll be down right sharpish and we can leave together.' Frank nodded, his little head bobbing up and down, his pale face serious. 'Yes, Emma,' he cried, and clattered noisily down the steps after Winston.

Emma sat down on the edge of the bed. 'Do yer need owt afore I go, Mam?' Elizabeth shook her head. 'The tea was good, luv. It's all I need till yer Aunt Lily comes, and I'm not hungry.'

She's never hungry. How will she ever be well if she never eats? Emma asked herself, and said with a cheerfulness she did not feel, 'All right, Mam, but yer must eat the food me Aunt Lily brings when she comes. Yer must keep up yer strength.'

Elizabeth smiled faintly. 'I will, luv.'

'Shall I blow out the candle?' Emma asked, preparing to leave.

Elizabeth looked lovingly at the girl. 'Aye, yer can when yer go. I'll rest a while. Yer a good lass, Emma. I don't know what I'd do without yer. Now get yerself off ter the Hall. I don't want yer ter be late, when Mrs Turner let yer come home ter see me in the middle of the week. And be a good lass. Mrs Fairley's a real lady, that she is.'

'Yes, Mam,' Emma whispered, blinking back the tears. She kissed her mother with great tenderness and rearranged the bedclothes, patting the pillows and straightening the sheet and quilt with her usual efficiency. As she pulled the bedclothes up around Elizabeth she said, 'I'll try and find a sprig of heather on me way home on Saturday, Mam. Perhaps there's a bit the frost didn't get, under the crags.'

SIX

Jack and Winston had gone to the brickyard and Frank was alone in the kitchen, which was now dimly lit, for Jack had turned out the paraffin lamp as he always did when he left for work. The only illumination came from a candle on the table and the fire, which occasionally flared and momentarily filled the room with a sudden lambent light. Dusky shadows lurked eerily on the perimeters of the kitchen and the air was hushed, except for the intermittent crackling of the logs, which hissed and spurted from time to time.

Frank sat in one of the high-backed chairs by the fireside and the chair dwarfed him, so enormous was it, and he appeared much smaller and more fragile than he actually was. The boy was small-boned and delicate, yet for all that he was surprisingly wiry and tough, like a little terrier.

This morning he seemed forlorn in his grey work shirt and baggy trousers, hand-me-downs from Winston, and his legs in their carefully darned grey socks, dangling over the edge of the chair, looked pathetic and far too weak to lift the great boots, which were too large and ugly and had also once belonged to Winston. But in reality, and in spite of his appearance, there was nothing forlorn about Frank Harte, for he occupied an inner world so filled with beautiful images and soaring dreams and expectations, it made his day-to-day existence seem totally inconsequential. And this perfect world protected him from the harshness of their poverty-stricken life, nourished him so completely he was, for the most part, quite oblivious to the deprivations and spartan conditions in which they lived.

Essentially Frank was a happy little boy, content to retreat into his imagination, one that was vivid and fertile, and the only time he had been truly dismayed and saddened was when he had left the church school in the village last summer. It was with a degree of resignation that he had stoically accepted the fact that he had to work in the mill with the other young boys, collecting empty yarn bobbins. His father had told him regretfully yet firmly that they needed the few shillings he would bring home every week and so he had left school when he had reached twelve years. He had been an astonishingly acute and avid pupil, soaking up knowledge with a rapidity and understanding that had utterly amazed the teacher. She thought he was unique and was distressed to discover his fate was to be the mill. She knew he was capable of so much more if only he was given the chance; she also knew he was doomed by the circumstances of his birth.

Although Frank no longer went to school, he continued his studies as best he could on his own. He read and reread the meagre collection of threadbare books his mother owned and anything else he could get his hands on. Words were somehow awesome and yet magical to Frank, and he loved them with a deep intensity that bordered on veneration. He would form and re-form sentences in his head and continually wrote little snatches of prose on the precious bits of paper

80

that Emma brought home for him from the Hall. He was constantly caught up in abstract ideas, although he did not yet comprehend they were abstract ideas, and these ideas puzzled and challenged him. For Frank Harte had a truly genuine intellect, one that was to develop with great brilliance later in his life.

Now he sat staring steadily into the fire, a mug of tea in his small hands, a rapt expression on his face, and his eyes, so dreamy and faraway, saw endless and incredible visions amongst the flickering flames.

The door creaked and startled him and he lifted his head sharply and looked about. Emma came into the room, silent and preoccupied. Frank began to sip his tea, his hazel eyes peering over the rim of the mug, following her progress around the room. She stopped at the window, moved the curtain, and, looking out, said, without turning to him, 'It's still dark outside, but we don't have ter leave yet. We can wait a bit longer until it's lighter and I'll run part of the way ter the Hall, so I won't be late.'

Frank put the mug down on the hearth and said, 'Me dad filled the teapot with hot water and he told me ter make yer a sandwich. It's there, on the set pot.'

She eyed the sandwich warily, and noticing the expression on her face, Frank exclaimed defensively, 'I didn't lather it with dripping. I put it on and scraped it off, just like yer said, our Emma.' There was a hidden smile on Emma's face and her eyes crinkled with amusement as she poured herself a mug of tea and put the sandwich on the plate. She carried them both over to the fireplace and sat down opposite Frank. She munched on her sandwich abstractedly, still worrying about her mother.

Her little brother regarded her thoughtfully and with some curiosity, for he was extremely susceptible to Emma, whom he adored. He constantly sought her approbation, but in his anxiety to please he usually did something ridiculously foolish which irritated her and so incurred her disfavour. However, this was usually short-lived. There was not a little admiration in his pale eyes as he leaned forward and said confidingly, and with great solemnity, 'I'm glad yer stopped 'em fighting. I'm scared when they shout. I am that, Emma.'

She looked at him absently, lost in her thoughts, as she put the plate down on the hearth. 'I knows. But it's always over nowt, lad.'

'Well, it still scares me,' he went on quickly, 'that's why I was lathering the dripping on too thick afore, yer knows. I was nervous,' he finished, trying to completely exonerate himself with her.

Emma laughed. 'Oooh! What a whopper that is, our Frankie!' she chided.

The boy bristled. His thin body tensed and his mild eyes were suddenly fierce as he cried with unaccustomed passion, 'Me mam says yer not ter call me Frankie, our Emma!'

Emma saw how serious he was and said with a smile, 'Sorry, luv. Yer right, our mam does hate nicknames.'

Frank straightened himself in the chair, assuming a dignified and important air. 'Me mam says I'm a great lad and Frankie is a baby name!' he exclaimed in his squeaky boy's voice, which nonetheless was surprisingly firm.

'That's true, yer are,' Emma replied, giving him a loving smile. 'Well, we'd best get ready.' She took the dishes they had been using to the sink, washed and dried them quickly, and then returned to the fireplace. Emma picked up her boots from the hearth, where her father had placed them to warm, and pulled them on decisively. As she was lacing up her boots, Emma stole a glance at Frank and thought impatiently: There he is, daydreaming again. A lot of good his dreams will do him! *She* rarely had time to indulge herself in fantasies, but when she did they were unromantically solid and practical. Her dreams were of warm coats for them all. Lots of beautiful black coal in the cellar. A larder stuffed to overflowing with smoked hams and wheels of cheese, hunks of beef, and row upon row of bottled fruits and vegetables, just like the pantry at the Hall. And gold sovereigns jingling in her purse, enough to buy all these necessities and luxuries for her mother and new boots for her father. She sighed. Frank dreamed of books and visiting London and riding in fine cabs and going to the theatre, dreams that were fed by the illustrated magazines she sometimes brought home from the Hall. And Winston dreamed of joining the navy and sailing around the world and having an adventurous life in exotic places. Frank and Winston dreamed of pleasure and glory. Emma, when she had the time to dream, dreamed of survival.

She sighed again. She would willingly settle for a few extra shillings a week to help them along, never mind gold sovereigns. She stood up purposefully and went and put on her coat, calling to Frank, 'Don't sit there gawping like a sucking duck, lad. Get yer coat on. It's twenty ter six and I'll be late if I don't hurry now.'

She handed Frank his coat and scarf, which he tied around his neck. Emma, clucking and shaking her head, immediately untied the scarf and wrapped it around his small fair head, fastening it tightly under his chin. She picked up his flat cap and slapped it firmly on top of the scarf, ignoring his wriggling and his protestations.

'Oh, Emma, I don't like me scarf this way,' he cried defiantly. 'The other lads laugh at me and say I'm a sissy.'

'It won't keep yer ears warm around yer neck and I've told yer afore, Frank, don't pay no heed to what folks say. Now come on and look sharp about it.'

She tied on her own scarf, handed Frank his jock box, glanced around the room once more, and then blew out the candle. Gripping Frank's hand tightly in hers, she pulled him out of the cottage.

They emerged into a black dawn and the cold hit them in an icy blast, moisture-laden and full of frost. The two children hurried down the flagged path, past the shrivelled and frozen elder and lilac bushes in the meagre little garden, its bleak inhospitable soil as hard and unrelenting as iron. The only sound was the whining of the wind and the sharp slap of their boots against the cold stones, as they made their way down Top Fold. This small cul-de-sac of cottages where they lived was set high up in Fairley village. Behind it was the higher background of the sweeping moors and it was an isolated spot, desolate and uninviting, and only the pale lights that gleamed in some of the cottage windows gave credence to the idea that it was inhabited. When they finally reached the top of the street, Frank lifted his cold little face to Emma and said, 'Shall I stop at me Aunt Lily's then?'

'Yes, luv. And tell her ter go ter see me mam early this morning. Tell her she's been rambling a bit but was resting quiet when we left. And don't stop chattering ter me Aunt Lily for long. Yer knows the gaffer closes the mill gates at six o'clock sharp. If yer gets locked out yer'll have ter wait 'til eight o'clock and they'll dock yer wages. And be a good lad!' She kissed his face and pulled his cap down more tightly on his head.

'Will yer wait and watch me till I gets to Aunt Lily's?' Frank asked, trying hard not to show that he was frightened at this hour. Emma nodded. 'Yes, luv. Go on then.'

Frank ran off into the mist, occasionally sliding on the cobblestones, which were slippery and glazed over with hoary frost. She watched his little figure streaking down the street until he was just a faint outline in the murky light. But she could hear his boots hitting the cobbles and when they stopped she knew he had reached their aunt's house, a small cottage on this main street that slanted down to the village and the river Aire. His loud banging on the door with his tin jock box reassured her that he had indeed reached his destination. He'll waken the dead as well as me Aunt Lily, she thought wryly, and then she wished she had not thought of the dead. Emma shivered as she turned in the opposite direction and headed towards the moors.

She was a solitary yet gallant figure, in her long black skirt and shabby coat, which was far too small, as she trudged doggedly and bravely on towards Fairley Hall, her eyes occasionally lifting to scan the leaden sky and the bleak dark moors that stretched in an unending line before her.

SEVEN

The hills that rise up in an undulating sweep to dominate Fairley village and the stretch of the Aire Valley below it are always dark and brooding in the most clement of weather. But when the winter sets in for its long and deadly siege the landscape is brushstroked in grisaille beneath ashen clouds and the moors take on a savage desolateness, the stark fells and bare hillsides drained of all colour and bereft of life. The rain and snow drive down endlessly and the wind that blows in from the North Sea is fierce and raw. These gritstone hills, infinitely more sombre than the green moors of the nearby limestone dale country, sweep through vast silences broken only by the mournful wailing of the wind, for even the numerous little becks, those tumbling, dappled streams that relieve the monotony in spring and summer, are frozen and stilled.

This great plateau of moorland stretches across countless untenanted miles towards Shipley and the vigorous industrial city of Leeds beyond. It is amazingly featureless, except for occasional soaring crags, a few blackened trees, shrivelled thorns, and abandoned ruined cottages that barely punctuate its cold and empty spaces. Perpetual mists, pervasive and thick, float over the rugged landscape, obscuring the highest peaks and demolishing the foothills, so that land and sky merge in an endless mass of grey that is dank and enveloping, and everything is diffused, without motion, wrapped in unearthly solitude. There is little evidence here of humanity, little to invite man into this inhospitable land at this time of year, and few venture out into its stark and lonely reaches.

But it was towards this harsh moorland that Emma so stoically marched on this icy February morning in 1904. The narrow winding road that snaked its way across the hills was the quickest route to Fairley Hall and Emma had to brave the moors in all seasons of the year and at all hours.

She shivered as she hurried along, and huddled further into her coat, which was a castoff from the Hall and offered as much protection as paper, threadbare and patched as it was. It had already been a sorry, worn-out bit of clothing when Cook had given it to her in the summer, but Emma had received it gratefully and she had patiently darned the holes and lengthened the hem and sewn on new buttons. She had outgrown it all too quickly, and it stretched across her back tightly. The sleeves were too short and her thin arms poked out pathetically in scarecrow fashion, exposing childish wrists to the elements. The wind bit treacherously through the meagre coat and the damp air drenched her, penetrating into her bones, so that her legs felt numbed and without life. She pulled her scarf more securely around her head and then thrust her chapped hands back into her pockets quickly. Her teeth chattered and her eyes watered from the icy blasts and she fervently wished she was already at the Hall, as much as she disliked that place.

By the time Emma reached the stone-walled field that led out to the moors she was breathless. She rested against the stile for a moment, her breathing still laboured, her heart thundering in her chest. She looked down the steep road she had just traversed. Below her the fog was patchy, clearing in parts, and in the distance she could see the twinkling lights now burning brightly in all the cottages, as the village awakened. Beyond, in the valley, there was a faint dim glow that told her that the Fairley mill was preparing for its daily business. Soon the shrill mill whistle would start to hoot, breaking the silence with its strident tones, announcing the opening of the gates. In a short time, the men and women of Fairley would be hurrying down to clock in and start another day of drudgery, combing the raw wool, spinning the fine woollens and worsted cloths that were shipped all over the world.

Emma looked lingeringly at the village where her mother lay, and which was also the last sign of life until she reached the Hall, and then she turned abruptly. She had rested long enough and now she must hurry if she was to reach the Hall by six o'clock, which was when Cook expected her. Emma hitched up her skirts, climbed over the stile, and jumped down into the field with agility. The ground under her feet was unyielding with frost and the mist floated and rolled in front of her, obliterating the dead gorse bushes and the few paltry, frostbitten trees as it drifted over the landscape. Now and then banks of snow became visible, the fantastic glistening shapes illusory in the vaporous air, and to Emma there was something fearful, almost menacing about the moors at this hour. She shuddered but she pressed on bravely. She could hardly see the path, but she had been working at the Hall for two years now, and she knew it well, and her feet followed it with a degree of sureness. The crunching of her footsteps on the frosty earth was the only sound in the early-morning air.

Her thoughts turned to her father as she tramped along. Emma loved her father and understood the nature of him, but he had disturbed her not a little in the last few months. Her dad just wasn't the same since he had returned from the Boer War. It seemed to Emma that all the spirit had ebbed out of him, and he was given to quiet withdrawn moods, yet conversely, he would often erupt into sudden almost uncontrollable anger, when Winston, or anyone other than herself or her mother, exasperated him.

These inconsistencies in her father's behaviour and his wildly contrasting moods baffled Emma, and when he stared at her vacantly he seemed like a lost child.

Sometimes she wanted to grab hold of him and shake him vigorously, in an effort to rouse him to renewed life. She was too small and fragile for that, so instead she would attempt to shake him out of his dejection with her questions, badgering him about money, reminding him of her mother's sickness. His face always remained immobile and closed, but his eyes filled with pain. It was Elizabeth's sickness and his sorrow for his wife that had changed Jack Harte and petrified his spirit, and rendered him virtually useless; it was not the war which had wrought the drastic upheaval in his nature.

But Emma, in her youthful naïveté, did not fully comprehend this. Passionately devoted to one singular pursuit, that of changing the constrained circumstances in which they lived, she was solely concerned with their survival, and this blinded her to anything else. All she knew was that her dad had no answers for her, no solutions to their problems. In an effort to placate her he would resort to the same old phrase he employed so often lately. 'Things'll get better soon, luv,' he would say. Her brother Winston was always duped by this confident and optimistic mood of their father's and his eyes would instantly shine with anticipation of better days. He would ask excitedly, 'When, Dad? When?' Emma's pragmatic brain would scream, 'How, Dad? How?' although she never uttered a word. She was afraid to throw out this challenge when her father was attempting to reassure Winston and she also knew, unquestioningly and from past experience, that there would be no genuine response and that no practical ideas would be proffered. Emma, realist that she was, had acknowledged this inevitability months ago and she had come to accept it with resignation, since she did not know how to combat her father's inertia and impotence, his procrastination and his lack of enterprise.

'Nowt ever happens ter change our lot because me dad never does owt ter change it!' Emma said aloud and with vehemence, as she scrambled over the low wall and out on to the moorland path beyond the field. Emma had not yet come to understand that when hope is taken away from a man he is left with nothing, sometimes not even the will to live. And all the hope had been kicked out of Jack Harte long ago.

She blew on her frozen hands and then pushed them back into her pockets, as she began her ascent up the lower slope that would lead her to Ramsden Ghyll and then on upwards, to the top of the moors and the road to Fairley Hall. Emma had not mentioned money to her father lately, but it never left her thoughts. They must have more money if they were to survive, if her mother was to regain her strength and her health. Emma knew that without money you were nothing, just a powerless and oppressed victim of the ruling class, a yoked and shackled beast of burden destined to a life of mindless drudgery, and an existence so wretched and so without hope, so filled with terror and despair that it was hardly worth the contemplation let alone the living. Without money you were susceptible to all the capricious whims and moods and fancies of the careless, thoughtless rich, to all the vicissitudes of life. Without money you were vulnerable to the world.

Since she had worked at Fairley Hall, Emma had come to understand many things. Blessed with acute observation, she was also innately shrewd and amazingly perceptive for her years. She had quickly seen and noted the outrageous and monstrous discrepancies between life at Fairley Hall and life in the village. The Fairleys lived in luxury, even splendour, pampered and totally isolated from the harsh realities of the lives of the workers, whose pitiless and endless toil financed their velvet-lined world of ease and privilege.

Observing the Fairleys and the way they lived, Emma had begun to comprehend that money did not only buy necessities, but so much else as well. She had come to realize that the possessor of money also possessed power, a most desirable asset to Emma, because she knew now that power made you invulnerable. It made you safe. By the same token, Emma had come to bitterly accept the fact that there was no justice or liberty for the poor. But she suspected, with the beginning of cynicism, that you could *buy* both quite easily. Just as easily as you could buy the medicines and nourishing food they needed for her mother, providing you had the right amount of shillings to place on the counter. Yes, she thought, money *is* the answer to everything.

There must be a way for me to earn more money, she decided as she made her way up the path. There were poor people and there were rich people in the world, and if some people could be rich then obviously so could others, she reasoned. Her father always said it was a question of birth and of luck. Emma was scornful of these ready answers, for she doubted their veracity, and so she refused to accept them. If a person came up with a brilliant plan and worked hard, harder than anyone else, then surely that person could earn money. Lots of it. A fortune perhaps. Emma had kept her eye on this goal for some time, never wavering, never truly discouraged, for what she lacked in experience of life she made up for with traits perhaps of greater value – intuition, imagination, and ambition. Instinctively Emma understood many things, and one of these was the cold hard fact that money was not necessarily always inherited or acquired by chance. She knew, in spite of what her father said, that there were other ways to amass a fortune. She sighed. It seemed to Emma, as she hurried along, chilled to the bone and full of despair about her mother, that she was all alone and friendless, battling the world without a helping hand or an encouraging word from anyone. But she had determined months ago that she would not let this defeat her. She would find a way to make money, lots of it, for only then would they be safe.

Her feet followed the narrow path and in spite of the denseness of the fog, she knew she was reaching the top of the lower slope, for she was panting and her legs were aching from climbing. She shivered under the rising wind that whistled down from the high fells, and pulled up the collar of her coat. Her hands were frozen stiff, but her feet were warm. Her father had repaired her boots just the week before, buying strong leather from the tannery and thick felt for the inner soles. She had stood by him and watched as he had cut the soles and hammered them firmly on to the worn uppers, cobbling the boots on the old iron last in the kitchen. She thought, too, of the steaming hot broth Cook would have waiting for her, and the warmth of the huge kitchen at the Hall, and these incentives made her hurry.

A few skeletal trees loomed up in front of her in the relentless environment, stark and spectral against the glassy green sky. Her heart began to pound rapidly, partially from exertion, but also from dread, for beyond these lone trees the path plummeted down into Ramsden Ghyll, a dell between the hills. The Ghyll was the spot Emma hated most on her journey to the Hall, for it was an eerie place, filled with grotesque rock formations and blasted tree stumps. The mist, trapped as it was between the twin peaks that soared above the dell, gathered and coagulated into heavy grey darkness that was almost impassable.

Emma was nervous of this place, but nonetheless she hurried on, chiding herself for her nervousness as she plunged down the path into the Ghyll. She was afraid

of the beasties and the goblins and the spectres of the moor which seemed to float
vapour-like, yet so threateningly, amongst these great rocks formed of millstone
grit. She was afraid, too, of the lost souls the villagers superstitiously said haunted
the Ghyll. To block out the images of goblins and monsters and lost souls, she
began to sing in her head. She never sang aloud at this hour on the moors, for
fear of waking the dead. She did not know many songs, except for the few they
had all learned at school, and she found these insipid and childish. So instead she
sang 'Onward, Christian Soldiers', forming the words silently and marching bravely
along to the rhythmic beat that ran through her head.

She was halfway across the Ghyll when the words were suddenly swept away.
Emma stopped tramping and stood perfectly still. She was transfixed, listening
acutely. Just below the level of the wind she heard it, a low lumbering sound as if
something huge and powerful, and propelled by immense force, was coming down
the path from the other side of the Ghyll. She shrank back against a formation of
rocks and held her breath, fear trickling through her like icy water. And then he
was standing there before her, not an inchoate monster like a rock or a tree, but
a wholly formed monster, a man, who was enormously tall and who peered down
to stare at her through the swirling fog.

Emma sucked in her breath and clenched her fists in her pockets. She wondered
frantically whether she should dart out in front of him and run back along the path,
but she was so paralysed with terror she could not move. And then the monster
spoke and terrified her even more.

'Faith and if it's not me good fortune, to be sure, to be meeting a spry young
colleen on these blasted moors at this ungodly hour. 'Tis the Divil's own place, I
am thinking, and no fit land to be a-wandering in, on this cold morning.'

Emma was speechless. She looked up at the man who towered above her, but
she was unable to distinguish his features in the murky light. She pressed herself
closer into a crevice between the rocks, wishing she could dissolve into it, her eyes
starting out of her head in alarm.

The man spoke again, his voice ghostly and disembodied coming to her through
the mist. 'Ah, and 'tis afeared the little colleen is, and no wonder, a startling ye
like I did. But it's only a stupid man that I am to be sure, that has lost himself in
this blasted fog on his way to Fairley Hall. Can ye be pointing me in the right
direction and I'll be on me way?'

Her heart beat less frenziedly, but Emma was still trembling and afraid, for a
stranger on these moors – and he was indeed a stranger – could be just as dangerous
as any monster. Her father had warned her never to talk to anyone she did not
know, who was not from the valley, and who was therefore a 'foreigner' in the
parts, and suspect. She flattened herself against the rocks, wishing he would go
away, pressing her lips firmly together. Perhaps if she did not respond to his
questions he would disappear as suddenly as he had appeared.

'Faith and I am thinking that the cat's got her tongue. Sure and that's it,' the
man continued, as if addressing a third person. Emma bit her lip and looked about
her anxiously. There seemed to be no one else there, although it was hard to tell
in the greying light.

'I won't be harming ye, little colleen,' the strange voice went on. 'Just show me
the way to Fairley Hall and I'll be on me way, to be sure I will.'

Emma still could not see the man's face, for it was lost in the mist that engulfed

87

them both. She looked down. She could make out his great feet encased in hobnail boots and the bottoms of his trousers. He had not moved a fraction from the spot where he had first stopped, but had remained stationary, as if he sensed that any sudden movement on his part would send her scurrying out of her hiding place, such as it was, and off into the fog in terror.

He cleared his throat and said again, more softly, 'I won't be a-harming ye, little one. Don't be afeared of me.'

There was something in the tone of his voice that made Emma relax her taut muscles. Slowly the quivering in her limbs began to subside. He had a strange voice, but it was lovely, musical and lilting, and different from any voice she had ever heard before. And then Emma, listening acutely, and with all of her senses alerted in anticipation of trouble, realized how gentle his voice was, recognized with a sudden rush of clarity that it was filled with kindness and warmth. Still, he *was* a stranger. Then much to her horror and with some surprise, Emma found herself asking involuntarily, 'Why do yer want ter go ter the Hall then?' She was so angry with herself she could have bitten her tongue off.

'I be going there to repair the chimneys and the flues. It was himself who came to see me last week. Squire Fairley. Yes, indeed, himself came to visit me in Leeds and was kind enough and generous, too, he was, I might be adding, to be offering me the job.'

Emma eyed the man suspiciously, lifting her damp face to peer at him through the mist. He was the tallest man she had ever seen and he was roughly dressed in workman's clothes and he had a sack slung over his shoulder.

'Are yer a navvy then?' she now asked with some caution, for she had just remembered that Cook had told her that a navvy had been engaged to do repair work and bricklaying at the Hall.

The man roared with laughter, a deep belly laugh that shook his whole vast frame. 'I am that, to be sure. Shane O'Neill's the name, but the whole world calls me Blackie.'

Emma squinted up at him again, trying to examine his face in the dim and vaporous air. 'Yer not a blackamoor, are yer?' she asked tremulously, and then rebuked herself for her stupidity. O'Neill was an Irish name and that explained his singsong speech, which was so unfamiliar to her. But she had heard of the Irish brogue and surely this was it.

Her question seemed to tickle this giant even more and he laughed again, saying, 'No, I'm not a blackamoor. Just a black Irishman. And what might yer be called?'

She hesitated again. Emma believed that the less people knew about you, the better off you were, the safer you were, for if they knew nothing they could do you no harm. But to her fresh amazement she found herself telling him, 'Emma. Emma Harte's me name.'

'Pleased to be a meeting ye, Emma Harte. Well then, now as we are acquainted, so to speak, will ye be kind enough to put me on the road to Fairley Hall, please?'

'It's the way yer came, back yonder,' Emma said, shivering, now thoroughly chilled from lingering in the damp and icy dell. Then once again, much to her annoyance but before she could stop herself, she explained, 'I'm going ter the Hall. Yer can walk with me if yer wants.'

'Why, thank ye, Emma. So, let us be a-marching! 'Tis divilish cold and damp out here. Worse than the bogs of the ould sod in winter!' the man declared, stamping his feet on the frozen earth in an effort to warm them.

Emma slipped out from her hiding place amongst the rocks, and led the way up the track that would take them out of Ramsden Ghyll and on to the flat plateau of moors that stretched all the way to Fairley Hall. It was a narrow and somewhat precarious track, rising steeply upwards, and they had to walk in single file. Emma hurried in front of the Irishman, scrambling and sliding about in her haste to be out of the dell. They did not speak, for it was a steep hill and strenuous to traverse. Also, the path itself was rough, and scattered as it was with rocks and gnarled tree roots embedded in the frozen ground, it was exceedingly treacherous and dangerous in winter.

When they came up out of the Ghyll and on to the flat plateau the mist had dispersed, blown away by the gusting wind that roared down from the soaring fells. The morning air was tinged with opal and the livid sky was filling with incandescent light, a light that seemed to emanate from some hidden source below the horizon, a light peculiar to these northern climes that blazed with the most intense clarity. It was flooding the hump line of hills with sudden bright radiance, so that they were as burnished and shimmering as molten brass.

Emma stopped, panting for breath, and turned to look towards Ramsden Crags in the distance, as she always did. 'Look at the horses,' she said, pointing to the huge crags that were poised in solitary splendour against the horizon.

Blackie O'Neill followed her gaze and caught his breath. The girl was right. The rocks did look like great horses rearing up against the skyline, their roughhewn shapes suddenly taking on life, as if they were giant mythical steeds galloping across the heavens and glimmering like struck gold in the radiant light.

'Why, 'tis a beautiful sight. What is that place?' Blackie asked.

'Ramsden Crags, but the villagers sometimes call it Flying Horses. Me mam calls it the Top of the World,' Emma confided.

'And indeed it looks as if it is just that, to be sure it does,' Blackie murmured, dumping his sack on the ground and breathing deeply of the fresh air, now that they were out of the misty Ghyll.

Emma had not yet really looked fully at Blackie O'Neill. He had been behind her on the path leading out of the dell and he stood behind her now at the edge of the Ghyll. Her mother had always instilled good manners in her, and had told her that it was rude to stare, but now Emma's curiosity got the better of her and she permitted herself to turn slowly. She looked up at the man who had so scared her initially and she was startled to see that he was young, perhaps no more than eighteen. And he was quite the most extraordinary man she had ever set eyes upon.

Blackie returned her gaze, smiling broadly, and in a flash of insight the girl knew why she had so inexplicably lost her fear of him in the Ghyll. In spite of his size, and his roughness of dress, there was something ineffably gentle and fine about this man, both in his expression and in his general demeanour. His face was open, friendly, and quite guileless, and his wide smile was warm, and sunny and somewhat mischievous, while his dark eyes were kind and understanding. Emma found herself smiling back at him unabashedly, warming to him in a way that was unprecedented for her, as wary and suspicious of strangers as she always was.

'Yer can't see the Hall from here,' Emma explained, 'but it's not far now, just over the crest of the moors yonder. Come on, I'll show yer the way, Blackie!' she cried enthusiastically, much taken with her new friend.

Blackie nodded and lifting the large sack, he slung it over one shoulder with apparent ease, as if it were a small and insignificant bundle in his large strong hands. He fell into step with Emma, who was already marching briskly along the top road, and began to whistle nonchalantly, his head thrown back, his vibrant curls blowing in the breeze.

From time to time, Emma looked up at him surreptitiously. She had never met anyone like him before and he fascinated her. Blackie, in turn, was not unconscious of this scrutiny; in fact, he was very much aware of it and it amused him. He had sized up the girl in a flash, for he was quick and had a perceptive eye. He guessed she must be about fourteen, or thereabouts, and a local girl going on an errand to Fairley Hall. She was such a small sprite. No wonder he had frightened her in the fog. As they traversed the road together he smiled, admiring the stalwart way she stepped out, endeavouring to keep up with his long strides. He slowed down considerably when he saw how breathless she was becoming.

Shane Patrick Desmond O'Neill, commonly known to the world as Blackie, was about six feet three inches tall, but he appeared to be so much bigger in stature because of the largeness of his frame, his broad sweeping back and his powerful shoulders. He was brawny and well built, but there was no excess flesh on him. He was all muscle and sinew. He exuded virility, a ruddy health, and indomitable strength. He had long legs and a surprisingly narrow and well-defined waist below an expansive chest. It was easy to understand why the world called him Blackie. His thick and heavy hair, which flowed back from a clear brow, was as black as ebony and just as shiny, and his eyes, of a brown so deep they also looked black, resembled great chunks of glittering coal. Set widely apart, under thick curving brows, these eyes were large and soft and very often wise, although they could gleam and flash with anger when Blackie's temper was aroused. Likewise they could just as easily turn mournful and tragic when his Celtic soul was troubled by melancholy thoughts. But, for the most part, they were filled with merriment.

His skin was dark, yet not swarthy; rather, it was a nut brown and tinged with ruddiness across his high cheekbones, a sort of light mahogany colour that undoubtedly came from long exposure to the elements. His nose was straight and fairly narrow, although it broadened slightly at the tip, and his nostrils were flaring. His wide mouth and long Irish upper lip betrayed his Celtic origins. He had a cleft in his strongly moulded chin and when he laughed, which was often, his cheeks dimpled and his face took on an amazing vitality.

Blackie O'Neill was, in fact, an exceptionally handsome young man. But it was his manner and his attitude that were most intriguing and which, in many ways, set Blackie apart from other men. He exuded liveliness and gaiety. His face was full of vivacity, and it had great mobility and not a little wit. An easy, careless charm was second nature to him, and he was buoyant of spirit, as if he accepted life for what it was, and was constantly entertained by it. There was a lighthearted self-confidence inherent in him, and to Emma, observing him, he seemed untouched by the weariness and the fear and the hopelessness that haunted the men of the village, bowing them down and ageing them prematurely.

For the first time in her young life Emma had met someone with an unquenchable spirit and a soul that was joyous and without rancour, a man who loved his life and lived it to the fullest, and she had a vague glimmering of all this, and it intrigued and mystified and impressed her.

As she hurried along next to this handsome young giant her eyes turned to him often, and she found she was filled with an intense and voracious inquisitiveness about him. He was a cheerful companion, who in the oddest and most inexplicable way made her feel safe as he tramped by her side, saying little, smiling his vivid smile, sometimes whistling merrily, his bright eyes scanning the crest of the moors expectantly, anticipating the sight of the spires of Fairley Hall. And something of his light and genial good humour seemed to mysteriously transfer itself to Emma, and her face, so unremittingly stern and intent for one so young, was softened by a hint of hidden gaiety.

She was taken by surprise when Blackie opened his mouth and began to sing, his rich baritone filling the silent air with the most melodious sweet sounds that startled her, so beautiful were they.

> 'The Minstrel Boy to the war is gone,
> In the ranks of death you'll find him.
> His father's sword he has girded on,
> And his wild harp slung behind him . . .'

As she listened to Blackie singing, Emma was filled with a swift and piercing pain, and tears rushed to her eyes, for she was touched in a way she had never been before. There was something hauntingly sad yet bittersweet about the words and the poignant melody, and her throat ached with the tears, so sudden, so unexpected, which she tried to choke back, afraid of appearing childish, and even a little foolish, to this man as he finished the ballad of the Minstrel Boy.

Blackie looked at her, and observing the glistening tears that trembled on her lashes, asked softly, 'Did ye not like me song then, little one?'

Emma swallowed deeply and cleared her throat several times. Finally she was able to speak. 'Oh yes, I did, Blackie. I really did. It's just that it's so sad.' She brushed her hand across her eyes, wiping away the tears quickly, and noting the look of concern clouding his face, she added hurriedly, 'But yer have a luvely voice, yer do that.' She smiled, hoping her tears had not offended him.

Blackie had been surprised by the girl's sensitive and emotional reaction to his singing, and he returned her smile and said with great gentleness, 'Aye, 'tis a sad song to be sure, but a beautiful one, Emma. Still and all, 'tis only an old ballad. Ye must not be upset. And since ye are kind enough to say ye like me voice, such as it is, I'll be singing ye a song that will surely make ye laugh, I am thinking.'

And he did. His rich and splendid voice formed the most merry sounds now, the lively words of an Irish jig tripping lightly from his facile tongue. He had purposely selected an amusing bit of nonsense, filled with tongue-twisting clan names, and soon Emma was laughing delightedly, the momentary sadness of the ballad forgotten in her newly found merriment.

When he had finished she cried gaily, 'That *was* funny. Yer'll have ter sing it for Mrs Turner, the cook at the Hall. She'll like it, I bet she will, and I bet it'll make her laugh.'

'Sure and will I not be happy to, Emma,' Blackie replied kindly, and then he said curiously, 'And why are ye off to Fairley Hall so early in the day, might I be asking?'

'I'm in service there,' Emma answered solemnly, returning his friendly gaze with unflickering, steady eyes.

'Indeed ye are, are ye! And what can a little snippet like ye do to earn ye keep?' he asked.

'I'm the kitchen maid.' Seeing her half-averted eyes, the downcast drooping of her mouth, and the grim expression that swept across her face, Blackie decided she did not savour her work at the Hall. She volunteered no more information, and retreated behind the mask-like expression which had settled on her small countenance. Sensing her discomfort, he did not question her further and they walked on in silence, something of the gaiety they had so recently shared washed away in the wake of her mood, which had so abruptly changed.

She was a funny little thing to Blackie, this colleen of the moors whom he had come upon so unexpectedly, a shabby starveling creature, all skin and bone. This Emma Harte looked to him as if she needed a good meal, several good meals, for many months to come. Indeed she did. She was a poverty-stricken child who should be at home and in bed, and not wandering these moors, so godforsaken and lifeless, at the crack of dawn in the midst of a bitter winter.

In spite of her shabbiness, her clothes were tidy and neatly patched, and he could see that her face was scrubbed and shining clean. Not that too much of that face was visible, swathed as it was in the thick black woollen scarf. But her eyes, whenever she turned them on him, were of incredible beauty. They were large and luminous and vividly green, just about the greenest eyes he had ever seen.

Emma cut into Blackie's thoughts when she asked, 'Yer said afore yer were a black Irishman. What's that, then?' Blackie turned to Emma and saw that the stark strained look had disappeared from her face.

His eyes held a mischievous glint as he said, 'Well, mavourneen, not a blackamoor from Africa, as ye suspected, but a man with my colouring, the black hair and the black eyes 'tis said we inherited from the Spanish.'

She had been about to ask him what 'mavourneen' meant, but this last statement so astounded her the question was swept out of her mind. 'Spanish! There aren't no Spanish in Ireland. I knows better'n that!' Emma scoffed with a degree of fierceness, her eyes flashing. 'I've been ter school, yer knows,' she informed Blackie as an afterthought, and proudly, wondering if he thought she was a fool.

Blackie was amused by her reaction, but he kept a straight face. 'Then, being as how ye are such an ejicated young colleen, ye must be a knowing that King Philip of Spain sent a great Armada to invade England in the time of Queen Elizabeth. 'Tis said that some of the galleons foundered and sank off the coast of Ireland and that the survivors, Spaniards all, settled in the Emerald Isle. 'Tis them, they say, the black Irish are descended from, and maybe that's the God's truth, I am thinking.'

'I knows about Spain and that Armada, but I didn't know owt about the Spaniards living in Ireland,' said Emma, looking up at him carefully.

There was such scepticism in her eyes that Blackie slapped his leg and roared with laughter. 'Faith and it's doubting me that she is! But 'tis the truth I be telling ye, Emma. On the heads of the Blessed Saints I do swear it's the truth I am speaking, mavourneen.'

Emma now said challengingly, 'Hey, what does that mean, that word "mavourneen"? Yer keep calling me that, Blackie. I never did hear such a word afore. It's not rude, is it?'

Blackie shook his head, his vital curls rippling and dancing as he did, the perpetual laughter flickering in his eyes and across his wide mouth. 'It's the Irish word for dear or darlin', Emma. Like the word "luv" the Yorkshire folk are always using. It ain't no rude word, little colleen. Affectionate is the best way of describing it, I am thinking. Besides, who would be rude to a spry young ejicated lady like ye?' he finished, adopting his most serious voice, his most gallant manner.

'Oh, aye,' Emma said, a flick of that hard Yorkshire scepticism noticeable in her voice.

There was a small silence and then, half turning and touching his arm impulsively, she asked, 'Do yer live in Leeds then, Blackie?' Her face was suddenly animated and interested and he sensed a new excitement in her.

'I do. I do. Sure and it's a grand town. Have ye ever been there, Emma?' Her face fell. 'No. But I will go one day! Me dad promised ter take me on a day trip, and I knows he will when he can spare the time like.'

And the money for the fares, Blackie thought astutely. But detecting the lack of conviction in her voice, and sensing her dejection, he said vigorously and with some positiveness, 'Sure and he will, Emma! Faith and ye will find it the most exciting place. Aye, 'tis exceedingly exciting. And busy! A virtual metropolis, I am thinking. It has great arcades with the most wondrous shops filled with grand finery for the ladies, and the gents, too. Yes, finery like a queen would wear, Emma. Silk and satin gowns beyond description. Beautiful hats with great feathery plumes and veils, fancy stockings and soft leather buttoned boots and parasols and reticules. All ye little heart could be desiring. And silk cravats for the gents as can afford 'em. Aye, and diamond stickpins, too, and ebony walking canes with silver knobs and sleek top hats. Such finery like ye never did see in ye whole life, I am thinking, Emma.'

Blackie paused, and then observing the wonderment in her eyes, the vibrancy now illuminating her face, and acutely aware of her eagerness to hear more, he continued his description of Leeds. 'There are elegant restaurants serving the most incredible delicacies to tempt ye palate, Emma. And dance halls, and a music hall called the City Varieties and plush theatres where they put on plays that come all the way up from London town. Why, I've seen Vesta Tilley and Marie Lloyd on the stage in Leeds meself, with me own eyes, mavourneen. Then there are the new tramcars. Amazing vehicles, to be sure, that run on tracks without the need for horses to pull 'em any more. They go from the Corn Exchange to all parts of town. I have ridden on one, sure and I have. I sat on the top deck, that's open to the world and the weather, viewing the town like a real gent. Faith and there are many wonders to see in Leeds, yes indeed.'

Emma's eyes glowed, all the weariness and worry which had enveloped her earlier that morning miraculously dissipated, her imagination inflamed, and her emotions stirred most palpably by Blackie's recital. She attempted, as always, to contain herself, but in her anxiousness for further information about this most extraordinary place, her voice rose and became shrill. 'Why did yer go ter live in Leeds then, Blackie? Tell me more about it!'

'I went to live in Leeds because there was no work in me native Ireland.' His voice dropped, was low now and sad, yet there was no disgruntlement or rancour in it, only dim resignation.

'It was me Uncle Pat, settled in Leeds for this many a year, who did bid me come over to be a working by his side as a navvy. Lots of work in Leeds, being as how it's a growing metropolis, as I told ye afore, Emma. When I saw all the new manufactories going up and the mills and the foundries, as well as the handsome carriages and the elegant houses of the gentry, I thought to meself: Sure and this is the place for a boyo like ye, Blackie O'Neill, a spalpeen that's not afeared of hard work, strong and brawny and a match for any man. This is indeed the place to be a-staying, faith and it is, for the streets are surely paved with gold! A man can make a fortune in Leeds, I was believing, so stay I did. That was five years ago. Now me Uncle Pat and me have our own business going. We do repair work and building for the millowners and the gentry. Doing well, sure and we are, little colleen. Small it is now, but I know it will be growing. Ye see, I aim to be rich one day. I am going to make meself a pile and be a millionaire!'

He tossed his head cockily and laughed, his face full of youthful optimism. He put his arm around her shoulders and said confidentially and with the utmost self-assurance, 'I aim to get me a diamond stickpin and be an elegant gent, a real toff, that I do, mavourneen. On the Blessed Heads of the Saints, I swear I do!'

Emma had listened attentively. Blackie's account had been thrilling and it had held her spellbound, had aroused all manner of longings within her. But it was that magical word 'fortune' that had made the most profound impact on her. Thoughts of fancy clothes and theatres were swept away. Those things were insignificant in comparison to Blackie's revelations about the opportunities for making a fortune in Leeds. Here was someone after her own heart, who knew that money could be earned as well as inherited. Emma's heart was pounding so hard she thought her chest would burst, and now it took all of her strength for her to retain her composure. She felt she could not speak and then, at last, 'Can a girl like *me* make a fortune in Leeds?' she asked, breathless in her anticipation of his answer.

This was the last thing Blackie had expected. He was dumbfounded. He stared down at Emma and saw the starveling girl who reached only up to his chest, so fragile and wan and undernourished, and his heart clenched with feelings of pity and protectiveness. Poor little mavourneen, he thought, I should have held me tongue. Fool that I am, filling her head with dreams of a better life, a world she'll never see. He was about to answer her negatively when, with a terrible clarity, he recognized the gleam in her eyes for what it was – ambition, raw and inexorable. He took in the face, now suddenly stern in its fixity, the eyes blazing hard green light. It was the most implacable face he had ever seen and he was shocked by what he saw. Blackie felt a cold chill on the back of his neck and his Celtic intuition told him that she was in deadly earnest. He could not encourage the preposterous idea of her running off to Leeds, yet he must attempt to pacify her.

And so Blackie bit back the 'no' he had been about to utter, drew in a deep breath, smiled, and said with all the gallantry he could summon, 'Faith, and to be sure ye could. But not now, Emma. Ye are but a little colleen. Ye can't be going off to Leeds until ye are older, I am thinking. 'Tis a fine city, sure and it is, full of prospects, but awesome and dangerous, too, for a little snippet like ye.'

Emma appeared not to hear this. At least she ignored it. 'Where would I work to make this fortune?' she rushed on, undaunted. 'What would I do?'

Blackie realized she was not going to be easily appeased. He pretended to consider the question seriously, for he was only humouring her, in spite of his initial response. She did not look as if she would make it to Fairley Hall, let alone Leeds, and had he not imagined that relentless expression on her face? Anything was possible on these ghostly moors, at this hour, in the depth of winter.

'Well, let me be thinking this one out,' he said cautiously. 'Perhaps ye could work in one of the manufactories making the fine dresses or maybe in one of the elegant shops selling the finery to the ladies. Many things there are ye could do, but as I said afore, I must be thinking on it careful. That's important, sure and it is. We must find ye the right occupation. That's the secret of success, ye knows, Emma. Least, so I've heard tell.'

She nodded, realizing the truth of what he said, and debated whether to confide further in Blackie, but her canniness, that inbred wariness, made her hold her tongue. She decided she had said enough for the moment. But she did have one more question and it was of crucial importance to her. 'If I comes ter Leeds one day, when I'm growed up like yer say I should be, will yer help ter show me the ropes like, Blackie?' She was gazing up at him and he saw that her face was the face of a child again and he breathed a sigh of relief, although he was not certain why.

'Faith and sure I will, Emma. It will be me pleasure. I live at Mrs Riley's boardinghouse on the "ham and shank", but ye can always find me at the Mucky Duck.'

'What's that then? The "ham and shank"?' Her brows puckered in bewilderment.

He laughed, amused at her puzzlement. 'What rhymes with "ham and shank"?'

'Lots of things!' she exclaimed pithily, and threw him a scathing look.

'The Bank, that's what. Ham and shank. The Bank. See? It rhymes. Rhyming slang we calls it in Leeds. 'Tis the railway bank though, not the riverbank, near the Leylands. But that ain't such a good neighbourhood, full of roughs and toughs it is! Not the place for a colleen to be a-wandering in alone, I am thinking. So if ye wants to find me, just go to the Mucky Duck in York Road and ask for Rosie. She's the barmaid and she'll know where I am, if I ain't in the pub. Ye see, I might be at the Golden Fleece in Briggate. Ye can be leaving a message with Rosie, to be sure ye can, and she'll get it to me or me Uncle Pat the same day.'

'Thank yer, Blackie, ever so much,' said Emma, mentally repeating with the greatest of care the names he had reeled off, so that she would remember them. For she did intend to go to Leeds and make her fortune.

She fell silent. They walked along not speaking, both of them lost in their own thoughts, yet it was a harmonious silence, without unease or awkwardness. Strangers though they were, they had taken to each other and a kind of understanding had sprung up between them, brief as their acquaintance was.

Blackie looked about him, thinking how grand it was to be alive, to have a job of work to do, a few shillings warming his pocket, and most importantly, the prospect of lots more to come. Even the moors had a strange compelling beauty now that he could see them properly. The fog had lifted long before and the air was no longer damp and moisture-laden. It was a brisk day, with a light wind that imbued the naked trees, so rigid and lifeless at this season, with a new and graceful mobility as they waved in the breeze. And the sky was no longer the colour of dull lead. It leaked a hard metallic blue.

They had almost reached the end of the flat plateau of moorland, and Blackie was beginning to wonder when they would arrive at Fairley Hall, when Emma announced, 'The Hall is yonder, Blackie,' as if she had read his thoughts. She was pointing straight ahead.

His eyes followed the direction of her outstretched arm. He could see nothing but the empty moorland. 'Where? I must be the blind one, Emma. I can't see no spires and chimneys, like himself described to me last week.'

'Yer will when we gets ter the top of the ridge over yonder,' she asserted, 'then it's downhill all the way. In a couple of ticks we'll be in the Baptist Field and that's right next ter the Hall.'

EIGHT

Emma and Blackie were now standing on top of the ridge she had indicated. Behind them, sweeping into the cloudless sky, were the high fells where the last of the snow shimmered here and there like uneven swatches of white satin rippling in the watery sunlight. Below them was a small valley, typical of the West Riding, cradled in the arms of the encircling moors that extended to the rim of the horizon.

And in this dun-coloured valley, all dim greys, dusty charcoals, and earthy browns, stood Fairley Hall. Only the tops of the spires and the chimneys were visible to the eye from where they were standing, for the house itself was obscured by a copse of trees. Unlike the stunted trees that intermittently broke the barrenness of the moors, these trees were tall and stately oaks, their widely splayed branches intertwining to form an intricate pattern. Plumes of smoke from the chimneys twisted upward behind the trees, filling the chill blue sky with wispy grey question marks. Suddenly, a flock of rooks fluttered out of the copse, winding up and out in a long wavy line like a coil of thick black rope flung carelessly into the air. Otherwise there was no sign of life in this neat little valley which slumbered undisturbed at this early hour, serene and peaceful in the infinite silence.

Surprisingly, the ridge on which Emma and Blackie stood did not drop down precipitously as Blackie had anticipated, but fell away into a short gentle slope that rolled towards the edge of a small field. Drystone walls, built long ago by the crofters, surrounded this field and others in the distance, cutting out a patchwork design on the floor of the valley, a design that to Blackie seemed extraordinarily orderly and tidy, juxtaposed as it was against the wild and sprawling moors. It looked as though a giant hand had neatly carved up the land most precisely and then enclosed each portion with the old and rugged walls.

Emma ran ahead, calling to Blackie as she did, 'Come on then, I'll race yer ter the gate!' She flew off down the slope at such a speed he was momentarily taken aback, both by her incredible swiftness and her unexpected burst of energy. She was wiry, this one. Gripping the sack tightly in one hand, Blackie leaped after her, at first at a goodly pace. With his great physical strength and long legs he could have outstripped her easily, but when he had almost caught up with her he fell back, slackening his speed, so that she could win her race.

Emma stood triumphantly by the gate. 'Yer'll have ter look more sharpish and get a move on if yer wants ter beat *me*,' she proclaimed with a small swagger. 'I'm a good runner, yer knows,' she added, panting.

Blackie grinned at this tiny display of vanity and then adopted an admiring attitude. 'Indeed, so I can see, mavourneen! Ye are as fast as a greyhound at the dog tracks, I am thinking. I'd put me money on ye any day, sure and I would.'

Emma bestowed a gratified smile on him and a gleam of satisfaction flickered across her face briefly. Then she turned quickly, unlatched the gate, pushed it slightly, and jumped on to the first rung, clinging to it fiercely as the gate swung forward into the field, carrying her with it. Glancing back at Blackie over her shoulder, she called, 'I always have a swing on this gate here, even though I'm not supposed ter.' When the gate groaned to a quivering standstill she stepped off briskly and pulled it back, apparently intending to repeat the operation, her face slightly flushed, her eyes merry.

Blackie threw down his sack. 'Here let me give ye a push, Emma.'

Nodding excitedly, she climbed on to the first rung again and clutched the gate tightly with her small chapped hands, as Blackie sent it flying into the field much faster than before. Her worn coat billowed out behind her and laughter washed over her face. Blackie watched her, enjoying her delight in this simple pleasure. Why, she's only a bairn at that, he thought, a rush of warmth filling his throat. How could I have imagined otherwise? Sure and it's stupid that I am.

Emma dropped off the gate and beckoned to him. 'Come on! Let's be going. I'm ever so late and I'll be copping it from Mrs Turner.'

Blackie picked up his sack and joined her. He put his arm around her in a brotherly fashion and fell into step with her as they proceeded to the bottom of the field. 'I have to be confessing to ye that I'm mighty curious about the folk at Fairley Hall. What are they like, mavourneen?'

There was a tiny silence.

'Yer'll see in a minute.' Emma smiled oddly. 'We're almost there now.' Freeing herself from him, she ran ahead without another word.

Blackie looked after her, frowning, puzzled by that curious smile. She was such a small figure on the path in front of him, skipping along almost with a carefree air. He had to admit she baffled him. One minute she was a child, her face soft and laughing; the next she seemed like an old woman, her face cast in bronze. Yet they were all queer, these Yorkshire folk, with their flat harsh accents, their self-reliant characters, their dour and opinionated natures, their rabid suspicion of strangers, their shrewdness and lightning perception of character. And their veneration of money. Still, he had discovered they could be generous-spirited and hospitable, and they had a sense of humour, even if it was somewhat blunt and pithy at times. Indeed, they were funny folk, and perhaps the very peculiarities he had discerned in Emma were simply vestiges of these Yorkshire traits. Yes, that must be it, he thought, and he quickened his steps to catch up with her.

Emma was waiting for him at the copse of trees which skirted the end of the field. 'There's the Hall, Blackie,' she said in a voice totally devoid of emotion.

Blackie stopped dead in his tracks and let out a long low whistle in stunned astonishment. Fairley Hall was in their direct line of vision and it bore no resemblance to the images he had conjured up in his head after his recent talk with Squire Fairley in Leeds.

'Mary, Mother of Jesus!' he cried, his eyes opening wide in disbelief. 'It's not possible, mavourneen. Nobody could have built a house like that!' He closed his eyes convulsively and when he opened them again he discovered he was not only disappointed in what he saw, but utterly appalled as well.

'The Hall's the grandest house for miles around. Nowt as big as it by here,' Emma pointed out in the same toneless voice. 'Me dad calls it Fairley's Folly.' He did not notice the faint bitter smile on her lips.

'I can see why,' Blackie murmured, thinking that it was the most grotesque house he had ever seen. As he stared at it, his jaw slack and his mouth drooping open, he recognized with dismay that it had no redeeming features at all. For Blackie O'Neill had an unusually accurate eye for perspective and line and, in fact, his one dream in life had been to study architecture. This had not been possible, but encouraged by his Parish priest, Father O'Donovan, when a boy, he had taught himself as much as he could from a few books, and because of his desire to learn and his very natural talent, he had become exceedingly knowledgeable about design and construction.

Now he scanned the house with keen and critical eyes. The closer they drew to it, the more Blackie perceived what a monstrosity it was. It appeared to crouch like an implacable monster amidst carefully planned yet oddly incongruous gardens, its blackened stone walls grim and unwelcoming. Gothic-like spires leapt up from the four corners of the central building, which was square and dominating and was crowned with a bizarre cupola. It struck him that this central building was the oldest part, probably dating back to the late 1790s, and if it had been left alone it would have had a semblance of dignity, perhaps even a touch of grandeur. But other wings had obviously been added over the years, seemingly with little thought, and they sprouted off on both sides without regard to form or design. He could now see that they were bastardized interpretations of Regency and Victorian styles, and all of them mingled together to create a chaotic effect.

In essence, Fairley Hall was a hodgepodge of diverse periods that competed with each other to create a façade that was without proportion, symmetry, or beauty. The house was large, solid, and rich, a veritable mansion, in fact, but its architectural inconsistencies made it hideous. Blackie sighed. He loved simplicity and he thought wistfully of the lovely old Georgian houses in Ireland, with their fluid lines and classical proportions that gave them such perfect balance. He had not expected to find such a house on these rough Yorkshire moors, but not unaware of the standing and importance of the Fairley family, and their great wealth, he had anticipated a structure that had more taste and refinement than this.

They had almost reached the house when Emma cut into his thoughts as she said, 'What do yer think ter it then?' She looked up at him curiously, tugging at his arm.

'Not much! 'Tis a Folly to be sure, just as ye dad says. It may be the grandest house in these parts, but it ain't to the tastes of me.'

'Won't yer have a house like the Hall then, when yer gets ter be this toff, this millionaire yer said yer'd be one day?' she probed, scrutinizing him shrewdly. 'I thought *all* millionaires lived in grand houses like Fairley.'

'True! True!' he said quickly. 'They do live in grand houses, but not always ones as ugly as Fairley Hall, Emma. I would never want such a house for meself. It offends me eyes, sure and it does, for it has no beauty or harmony or style.'

Blackie glanced ahead and grimaced at the thought of occupying such a grotesque mausoleum.

That bitter smile played around Emma's mouth again and there was a tiny gleam of malicious satisfaction in her eyes. Although she lacked exposure to the world beyond the moors, and so had no basis for comparison, she had always instinctively known that the Hall was an eyesore without grace or beauty. Her dad and the villagers might sarcastically call it Fairley's Folly, but, nonetheless, they were still impressed. She laughed to herself, a little spitefully. Blackie had just confirmed her own opinions of Fairley Hall and this pleased her.

Now she turned to Blackie, who had risen even more in her esteem, and said inquisitively, 'What kind of a house will yer live in then, when yer gets ter be this rich millionaire?'

The gloomy expression on his face lifted and was instantly replaced with a throbbing vibrancy. His black eyes shone as he exclaimed, 'It will be in the Georgian style, built of pure white stone, with a handsome portico and great soaring columns and wide front steps. There will be many tall shining windows, looking out on to fine green lawns and gardens. It will have lots of spacious rooms, with lofty ceilings, and they will all be full of light and airiness. The floors will be made of polished oak and the fireplaces will all be in the Robert Adam style. In the entrance hall, which will be huge, I am going to have a floor made of white marble and a great curving staircase will lead to the upper floors. In every room I will use pastel colours, the light blues and pale greens that are soft and restful to the eyes, and I intend to purchase excellent furniture for all of these rooms. Yes, indeed! I shall select the best styles of Sheraton and Hepplewhite and maybe a little Chippendale. Paintings, too, I shall have, and many other fine and beautiful things. Ah, mavourneen, it will be a house to take ye breath away, faith and it will. I promise ye that. I aim to build it meself, to me own design, sure and I do!'

'Build it yerself, ter yer own design,' she repeated in a hushed tone, her face full of wonder. 'Do yer know how ter design houses then, Blackie?'

'Aye, to be sure I do,' he responded proudly. 'I go to the night school in Leeds to be learning draftsmanship, and that's the next best thing to architecture. Ye'll see, Emma, I'll build that house one day and ye'll come and visit me when ye are a grand lady.'

Emma looked at Blackie in awe. 'Can anybody go ter this night school ter learn things?' she asked, thinking of her brother Frank.

Blackie looked down at her expectant face, so filled with hope, and told her confidently, 'Sure and they can. At the night school they teach ye everything ye might want to be learning.'

His answer delighted Emma and she stored the information at the back of her mind to tell Frank later, and asked, with her usual avid curiosity, 'Who's this Robert Adam then, and them others yer mentioned? Yer knows, Sheraton and Hepplewhite and Chippendale?'

Blackie's face glowed, for they were embarking on a subject close to his heart. 'Robert Adam was the great architect of the eighteenth century, Emma. He built many grand and beautiful houses for the gentry that are wondrous to behold. Ah, but Adam was more than that, I am thinking, for he furnished them, too, with style and taste. Nobody has ever bettered him, mavourneen. The others I spoke about,' he went on enthusiastically, 'were the three greatest furniture makers of the Georgian period, sure and they were. Master craftsmen who made the furniture for the Quality folk.'

He grinned and winked at her. 'Ye see, I aim to have nothing but the best when I'm a rich boyo. For I often says to meself, "What's the point of having money, Blackie O'Neill, if ye don't get the pleasure from it?" So I aim to be spending it. That's what it's for, I am thinking. Are ye not after agreeing with me?'

Emma regarded him soberly. Mostly when she thought of money it was in terms of the necessities of life. Blackie had presented new possibilities to her. 'Aye, I suppose so,' she said cautiously. 'As long as yer've got enough money ter spare, ter buy all them fine things.'

He roared with laughter. So much so that tears of merriment squeezed out of the corners of his eyes. 'Ye are a canny Yorkshire colleen, I can see that,' he said through his laughter. 'But what's *enough*, Emma? I've heard tell of some men who never have enough money to satisfy them.'

Like Squire Fairley, she thought sourly, but said, 'And where will yer build yer beautiful house, Blackie? Will it be in Leeds then?'

He wiped his eyes on the back of his sleeve, his merriment subsiding, and shook his head. 'No, I don't think it will. I am considering building it in Harrogate, where all the toffs live,' he said importantly. 'Aye, that will be the place, I am thinking,' he continued, the certainty in his voice more pronounced. ''Tis a fine town. A spa. Just the place for a spalpeen like me. Have ye heard of it, Emma?'

'Yes, me mam has been ter Harrogate, a long time ago, when she went ter visit her cousin Freda in Ripon. She told me about it once. She said it's a real posh place.'

He laughed. 'It is, it is! And tell me, Emma, do ye like the sound of me house, that I shall be building for meself one of these fine days?'

'Ooh, I do, Blackie! Yer house'll be luvely, I just knows it will. Not like this place. Yer should see this house at night. It frightens me more than when I have ter walk past the cemetery,' she confided.

Blackie frowned and looked swiftly at her small face, which was childlike and trusting, and he smiled reassuringly. 'Ah, 'tis only a house, little colleen. A house can't harm ye.'

She did not respond to this comment but compressed her lips and quickened her steps, as they were suddenly engulfed by the giant blue-grey shadows cast by Fairley Hall. Now that they were close to it, Blackie became conscious of another aspect of the house and it was one which instantly disturbed him. It seemed to Blackie, as he regarded it, that the great mansion was strangely brooding and hostile, as if it had never known life or laughter or gaiety. He had the oddest feeling that all those who crossed its threshold were held captive forever.

He looked up. Immense windows gazed down at them, heavily draped against the world, and to Blackie they were like the eyes of blind men, empty, hollow, and dead. A shaft of sunlight struck the blackened walls and those dim and mysterious windows, and this light, hard and full of clarity, appeared to emphasize the impregnability and bleakness of Fairley Hall. Blackie told himself he was being ridiculous and over-imaginative, but these emotions did not diminish as Emma led him around the corner of the house and out of the shadows. They headed across a cobbled stable yard, full of sunlight and blue sky, towards the servants' entrance. Automatically he put his arm around her shoulders and then he grinned at the absurdity of his action. She had been coming here far longer than he had and was surely without need of his protection. And protection against what? he wondered, mystified at himself.

Emma looked up at him and smiled, as if once again she had read his thoughts. But as they mounted the steps that smile faltered and the light in her eyes dulled. A watchful expression settled on her face as she turned the iron handle of the door and walked into the kitchen.

NINE

'And what time do yer think this is then, ter be strolling in like there's no termorrow? And looking as if yer don't have a care in the world as well! Aay, lass, I'd about given thee up. I had that!'

The sharp voice echoing around the kitchen emanated from a little dumpling of a woman who was as broad of beam as she was short in stature. Birdlike brown eyes, peeping out above apple-rosy cheeks, flashed with indignation, and the starched white cap, perched like a crown on top of her greying auburn hair, bobbed about as she tossed her head.

'And don't stand there gawping at me like a sucking duck!' she went on crossly, waving the ladle at Emma. 'Get a move on with yer, now that yer are here, lass! We've no time ter be wasting today.'

'I'm ever so sorry, Mrs Turner,' Emma cried as she ran across the room, pulling off her scarf and struggling out of her coat. Bundling them up in a roll, she went on quickly in an apologetic tone, 'I set off in time, I did really, Mrs Turner. But it was ever so foggy on the moors and in the Ghyll and –'

'Aye, and I expect yer stopped ter laik on yon gate as usual,' Cook interrupted with some impatience. 'Yer'll be copping it, lass, one of these fine days, yer will that!'

Emma had disappeared into a cupboard, under the stairs which led up to the family's living quarters, and her voice was muffled when she called out, 'I'll catch up with me work, Mrs Turner. Yer knows I will.'

'Yer'll have ter, that's a certainty,' Cook retorted with asperity. 'I can see we'll have an uproar on our hands today. What with Mrs Hardcastle in Bradford and company coming up from London town and Polly right badly.' She shook her head, sighed heavily at the thought of her burdens, adjusted her cap, and banged the ladle down on the table. Then she swung around and stared at Blackie, whom she had so far ignored. Placing her hands on her hips, she looked him over appraisingly, her beady eyes suspicious. 'And what's this the cat's dragged in then? Lochinvar,' she said acidly.

Blackie took a step forward and opened his mouth, but before he could speak, Emma's voice floated out from the cupboard. 'It's the navvy, Mrs Turner. The one yer were expecting ter mend the flues and all. His name's Shane O'Neill, but the whole world calls him Blackie.'

101

'Top of the morning to ye,' Blackie cried, flashing her a cheery smile and bowing elaborately.

Cook ignored this friendly greeting and said, 'Irish, eh? Well, I can't say as I hold that against yer. I can see yer a strong lad. No room for weaklings in this house!' She paused and her eyes now lighted on the sack he had placed on the floor next to him, which was old and very grimy. 'And what's in that mucky *thing*?' she asked.

'Just me tools and a few er ... er ... personal items,' Blackie said, shuffling his feet in embarrassment.

'Well, don't be dragging it over me clean floor!' she admonished. 'Put it in that there corner, where it's out of the way.' She then marched to the stove, saying in a gentler tone, 'Yer'd best come ter the fire and get yerself warm, lad.'

Mrs Turner bustled around the stove, clattering pan lids, peering at the contents of her bubbling pots, muttering under her breath. Her temper had abated. This was mostly irritation rather than real anger, and it was chiefly engendered by anxiety for Emma crossing the lonely moors rather than the girl's tardiness, which was not so important. What was half an hour, after all? She smiled to herself. Emma was a good lass, which was more than you could say for most in this dreadful day and age.

Blackie dumped his sack in the corner and loped over to the enormous fireplace that covered almost the whole of one wall. As he warmed his hands in front of the fire he became conscious of two things. He was frozen stiff and he was hungry. These sensations were precipitated by the steaming warmth of the room and the delicious smells pervading the air. He sniffed and his mouth watered as he inhaled the pungent smell of smoky country bacon frying, the warm, sweet fragrance of freshly baked bread, and wafting over these tempting odours he detected the rich savoury tang of a vegetable broth boiling. His stomach growled and he licked his lips hungrily.

Slowly his body began to thaw and he stretched luxuriously like a great cat, his eyes sweeping quickly over the room, and what he saw cheered Blackie immensely, helped to dissipate his foreboding of earlier. For there was nothing brooding or menacing about this kitchen. It was a splendid, warming, cheerful place and spanking clean. All manner of copper pots and pans sparkled lustrously on the white-washed walls, and the flagged stone floor shone whitely in the bright light of the gas jets and the crackling fire that leapt and roared up the big chimney. Strong oak furniture, highly waxed, gleamed softly in this roseate glow.

Blackie heard the click of a door and he looked up as Emma emerged from the cupboard. She had changed into a dark blue serge dress, obviously cut from the same cloth as Cook's, and she was fastening on a large blue-and-white-striped cotton apron. 'Did yer say Polly was poorly again, Mrs Turner?' she asked, moving hurriedly in the direction of the stove.

'Aye, lass. Bad cough she has. Summat terrible. I made her stay abed this morning. Yer might look in on her later, ter see if she wants owt.' There was true warmth in Cook's voice and her face softened as she regarded the girl. Blackie looked at her and recognized there was no real animosity in her. It was apparent, from the loving expression now flooding her face, that Mrs Turner was inordinately fond of Emma.

'Yes, I'll pop up after breakfast is served and take her some broth,' Emma agreed, trying not to look overly concerned about Polly. Emma was convinced she had the same sickness as her mother, for Emma had detected all the telltale signs: the weakness, the fever, and the terrible coughing.

Mrs Turner nodded, 'Aye, that's a good lass.' She frowned and peered at Emma through the steam. 'Yer'll have ter do Polly's work today, as well as yer own, yer knows, luv. Can't be helped! Murgatroyd tells me Mrs Wainright arrives for a visit this afternoon and with Mrs Hardcastle still away we're really shorthanded.' She exhaled a loud sigh of exasperation and banged the spoon against the side of the pot furiously. 'Aye, I wish I was the housekeeper here, I do that! It's a right cushy job Nellie Hardcastle's got and no mistake. Always tripping off, that she is!'

Emma repressed a smile. This was an old bone of contention. 'Yer right, Mrs Turner, but we'll manage somehow,' she said reassuringly. She liked Cook, who was the only one who showed her any kindness at the Hall, and she always tried to please her. Emma ran back to the cupboard under the stairs and pulled out a large basket containing brushes, cloths, polishes, and black lead, and headed for the staircase. 'I'll make a start,' she called, beginning to mount the stairs, waving to Blackie as she did.

Mrs Turner's head jerked up quickly. 'Nay, lass, I'm not that heartless! Yer looks nithered ter death. Go ter the fire and warm up, and drink a cup of this broth afore yer goes up yonder.' She lifted the lid off the large iron pot, stirred it vigorously, clucked with satisfaction, and began to ladle broth into a large mug. 'Will yer have a cup, lad?' she called to Blackie, already filling a second mug.

'To be sure I will and it's thanking ye I am,' Blackie cried.

'Come on, lass, give Blackie this mug and take yer own,' Cook said, and went on briskly, 'And how about a bacon buttie, lad? It goes down well with me broth.'

'Thanks. I don't mind if I do. It's famished that I am.'

'Can yer eat one, Emma luv?'

'No, thanks, Mrs Turner,' Emma replied as she took the mugs from Cook. 'I'm not hungry.' Cook gave her a sharp look. 'Aay, lass, yer don't eat enough. Yer'll never get fat on broth and tea.'

Emma carried the mugs carefully to the fireplace and handed one to Blackie without a word, but as she sat down on the other stool and looked up at him a sweet smile drifted over her face, the wariness abating. 'Thank ye,' he said, returning her smile, and then his eyes narrowed as he became aware of her for the first time since they had met on the moors.

As they sipped the broth in silence, Blackie regarded Emma surreptitiously, endeavouring to conceal the surprise he was feeling. He was stunned really. Now that she had removed the camouflaging scarf and shed the tight old coat, he could see her more clearly and he noted that the girl was not such a starveling creature as he had originally thought. He could not call her beautiful, if he was to measure her by the popular picture-postcard standards of the day. She was no typical Edwardian beauty, all pink marshmallow softness and swooning femininity; neither was she fluffily pretty or pert. But she was arresting and there was something indefinable about her that captured his imagination, held his attention, and made him catch his breath as he studied her. Her face was a perfect oval, with high, rather prominent cheekbones, a straight and slender nose, and a delicately curved mouth that dimpled at the corners when she smiled. Her teeth were small, even, and very white between her pale pink lips, which he noticed held a suggestion of sweetness and vulnerability when she was unguarded. If her smooth forehead was a little too broad it was by no means unattractive, and it was balanced by the widow's-peak hairline that cut into her clear skin so dramatically, and by the exquisitely shaped brows that were sweeping golden-brown arcs above her wide-set eyes. These eyes, which had struck him so forcibly earlier, were indeed as shining and as green as emeralds, set below thick and curling golden-brown lashes that cast gentle dusky shadows on her skin. This was like pale cream silk and as smooth, and without blemish. Her luxuriant russet-brown hair was simply dressed, pulled back smoothly to reveal her face most strikingly. The gleaming hair was plaited and then twisted into a bun that nestled in the nape of her neck and, in the dancing firelight, it seemed like a rich velvet cap threaded through with golden strands.

She is thin and still small, he thought. But he also knew she had some growing to do in the next few years. Blackie could tell from her build that she would be tall and slender when she matured into young womanhood. She was already beginning to flower, for he saw the swell of tender young breasts and shapely hips under the voluminous apron, and long legs that contributed much to her easy gracefulness.

Blackie's innate sense of beauty and fineness was not solely restricted to architecture, art, and artefacts, but extended to women and horses as well. His ardour for women was almost, but not quite, surpassed by his predilection for horses and the races, and he particularly prided himself on his ability to judge horseflesh and single out a thoroughbred when he saw one. Now as he looked at Emma more fully he thought: That's it! She has the look of a thoroughbred! He knew she was a poor girl from the working class, yet her face was that of an aristocrat, for it contained breeding and refinement. It was these aspects that combined to create that indefinable quality he had detected earlier. She was patrician and she had an inbred dignity that was unique. He saw only one feature that betrayed her station in life – her hands. They were small and sturdy, but also chapped and reddened, and the nails were broken and rough. He knew only too well that their ugly condition was caused by the hard work she performed.

He wondered what would become of Emma, and he was filled with a sadness alien to his nature as he contemplated her future. What was there for her in this house and this bleak mill village on the desolate moors? Perhaps she was right to want to try her luck in Leeds. Maybe there she had a chance of living and not merely surviving.

Mrs Turner interrupted his musings as she bounced over to the fireplace and thrust a plate of sandwiches at him in her bustling manner. 'Here's yer bacon butties, lad. Eat 'em now afore Murgatroyd comes down. He's a real nip scrape and likes ter keep us all on a starvation diet. Mean old bug –' She bit back the last word and looked with a degree of apprehension at the door at the top of the stairs.

Turning to Emma, she went on, 'Yer don't have ter black-lead the grates this morning. They'll do till tomorrow. But light the fire in the morning room, dust the furniture, run the carpet sweeper over the rug, and set the table for breakfast, like Polly showed yer afore. Then come back and help me with the breakfast. Later yer can clean the dining room, the drawing room, and the library – oh! and pay attention when yer dust that there panelling in the library, lass, straight across with the duster and then down, so that the dust falls along the edge of the moulding – and do all the carpets as well. Then yer'll have ter clean Mrs Fairley's upstairs parlour. When yer've finished that it should be just the right time for yer ter take her breakfast up. Yer can make the beds afore lunch and dust the children's room. This afternoon yer can start on the remainder of the ironing. There's the silver ter polish and the best china ter wash . . .' Mrs Turner paused, somewhat breathless, and drew a piece of crumpled paper from her pocket. She straightened it out and pursed her lips in concentration as she read it.

'Yes, Mrs Turner,' Emma murmured softly, and jumped off the stool. She smoothed down her large apron and waited for further instructions, wondering how she would cope with these multitudinous duties.

Blackie looked at Emma carefully, a small knot of anger twisting in his stomach. He had listened to Cook's recital at first with amusement, but now he was outraged. Nobody could do so much work in one day, least of all Emma, who was only a child. Yet Emma seemed unconcerned as she stood patiently at Mrs Turner's side. Observing her more closely, Blackie realized that a certain geniality concealed the anxiety in her dark eyes, and her mouth had tightened unconsciously. He glanced quickly at Cook. He knew she was not trying to exploit Emma, for basically she was a kind woman, but he was still appalled. She was using Emma as a workhorse and this truly dismayed him, and he could not resist saying, 'That's a heavy load for a little colleen, I am thinking.'

Mrs Turner stared at him with surprise, and flushed. 'Aye, lad, it is. But Polly's right badly and there's nowt I can do about it, what with company coming and all. That reminds me, Emma,' she went on hurriedly, looking embarrassed, 'yer'll have ter prepare the guest room for Mrs Wainright.'

Emma turned to Mrs Turner, who was studying the piece of paper attentively. 'Shall I go upstairs, then?' she asked. Emma was no fool, and whilst she had listened to Cook's allocation of the work without complaint, she was, nonetheless, dismayed. She wouldn't have time to stop for breath if she was to finish by suppertime and she was anxious to get started on her chores.

'Aye, in a tick, lass,' Cook said distractedly. 'Just let me read these here menus. Maybe I can manage the breakfast meself, after all.' She screwed up her eyes and peered at the paper. 'Now, let's see. Scrambled eggs and bacon for Master Edwin. Kidneys, bacon, sausages, and fried potatoes for Master Gerald. A kipper for the Squire. Tea, toast, fresh bread, butter, jam, marmalade. That's it and it's enough!' Her head moved violently on her short plump neck and she grumbled, 'I don't know why they can't all eat the same thing in this family!'

After a short pause, Mrs Turner asserted, 'Well, I believe I can cope with breakfast, luv. And lunch is simple. Just cold ham, Madeira sauce, mashed potatoes, and apple pie with custard.' She turned the paper over and clucked to herself. 'I'm thinking yer'll have ter give me a hand with dinner though, lass. Murgatroyd's got some menu suggested. Mmm! He has indeed. Clear chicken soup, saddle of mutton with caper sauce, roasted potatoes and cauliflower with a cheese sauce. Trifle. Wensleydale cheese and biscuits. And a Welsh rarebit for Master Gerald –' She stopped and blinked and glared at the paper. 'A Welsh rarebit for Master Gerald indeed!' she repeated in disbelief. 'As if he doesn't eat enough all day long as it is. He's getting to be a real little pig, our Master Gerald is. If there's owt I can't stand it's greediness!' she declared to the room at large. Bristling, she pushed the paper into her pocket. 'Yer can go up then, luv, and be careful when yer dusting,' she cautioned.

'Yes, Mrs Turner,' Emma said evenly, her face devoid of expression. 'I expect I'll see yer later, Blackie,' she cried, and flashed him a small smile.

'To be sure ye will, mavourneen, for I shall be here for a few days, I am thinking.'

'Aye, that's true,' Mrs Turner interjected. 'Squire has neglected things around here of late, what with Master Edwin sick since Christmas and the missis so frail these days – I'm glad Mrs Wainright's coming, she always cheers things up around here – yes, the missis has been out of sorts –' Mrs Turner stopped midsentence and clamped her mouth shut.

Blackie and Emma followed her gaze, which was directed towards the door at the top of the stairs. A man had entered and was ponderously descending the stairs. Blackie assumed it was the butler.

Murgatroyd was a tall, scrawny man. He had a cadaverous face etched with bitter lines which made his countenance forbidding. Small eyes, so pale they were almost colourless, were set closely together in deep hollow sockets. These porcine eyes appeared to be even smaller than they really were, since they were partially obscured by bushy black brows that sprouted like bristles in a heavy unbroken line across his forehead. He wore black trousers, a black-striped white shirt with a high collar, and a green baize butler's apron. His sleeves were rolled up to reveal long gangling arms, corded with bluish veins.

There was a mournful expression on his face and his eyes gleamed with hostility. 'What's all this? What's all this?' he cried in a high-pitched voice as he paused at the bottom of the stairs. 'No wonder we're behind today. Gabbing like a lot of magpies. I can see yer in dereliction of yer duty, Cook,' he continued pompously. 'That lazy, good-for-nowt lass should've been up yonder a good half hour ago, she should that! The Squire's not in the charity business, yer knows. She does little enough work as it is, for what she gets paid. Overly generous the Squire is. Three shillings a week indeed. A princely sum for doing nowt.' He scowled at Emma, who was standing near the cupboard under the staircase. 'What are yer waiting for? Get up yonder at once!' he snarled.

Emma nodded mutely and picked up the basket, the dustpan, and the carpet sweeper, and made for the stairs. As she edged past Murgatroyd some of the utensils fell out of the basket, including the black-lead powder. The tin rolled across the floor and the lid flew off, spilling the black powder at Murgatroyd's feet. Emma gasped with horror and bent to pick it up. As she did, Murgatroyd swung his arm and struck her hard across her head with the back of his hand.

'Yer stupid little sod!' he screamed. 'Can't yer do owt right? Look at the mess yer've made on the clean floor.'

Emma reeled from the unexpected and violent blow and she staggered back, dropping the carpet sweeper and dustpan. Blackie jumped off the stool in horror. Anger bubbled up in him. He clenched his fists and stepped towards the butler. I'll kill him! he thought. I'll kill the bastard!

Cook was already halfway across the kitchen, and as she passed Blackie she pressed him back and shook her head warningly, hissing, 'Yer'd best stay out of this, lad. Leave him ter me.'

Mrs Turner faced Murgatroyd like a bantam fighting cock. Her face was purple with rage and the look in her eyes was murderous. She raised her small fist and shook it at him, full of spunk. 'Yer nasty bugger!' she cried passionately. 'It was only an accident. The lass didn't do it on purpose.' She regarded Murgatroyd through blazing eyes. 'If I ever sees yer strike that lass again, yer life won't be worth living. I promise yer that. I won't go ter the Squire. Indeed I won't! I'll tell her bloody father! And yer knows what's in store for yer if Big Jack Harte gets his hands on yer. He'll make bloody mashed potatoes out of yer!'

Murgatroyd glowered at Mrs Turner, but refrained from any response. Blackie, whose eyes had been riveted on Murgatroyd like a hawk's, detected sudden apprehension in him. Why, he's a coward, thought Blackie. He's a blustering poltroon, lily-livered, and full of hot air!

Cook swung away from Murgatroyd with disgust and turned to Emma, who was kneeling on the floor neatly replacing all the items which had fallen from the basket. 'Are yer all right, luv?' she asked with concern. Emma lifted her head and nodded slowly. Her face was like carved white marble and just as immobile. Only her eyes had life, for they burned with an intense hatred for Murgatroyd. 'I'll get a wet cloth and clean up the black lead,' she said softly, sheathing her anger.

Murgatroyd now turned his attention to Blackie. He proceeded into the room smoothly as if nothing had happened. 'O 'Neill, right? The navvy from Leeds. The Squire said ter expect yer this morning.' He weighed Blackie with those cold eyes and nodded approvingly. 'Well, yer looks like a strong bloke. I hopes yer not afraid of work, lad.'

It was a considerable effort for Blackie to speak civilly to the butler, but he knew he had no alternative. He swallowed hard and said in the most matter-of-fact tone he could summon, 'That's me, to be sure. If ye gives me the details of the work I'll get to it.'

Murgatroyd pulled a scrap of paper from his pocket and handed it to Blackie. 'It's all written down here. Yer *can* read, I suppose?'

'I can that.'

'Good. Now, as ter yer wages. Fifteen shillings for a week's work and yer board and lodgings while yer here. That's what the Squire instructed.' His eyes were full of cunning.

Blackie bit back a knowing smile. Why, he's trying to swindle me, the crafty divil, he thought, but said, 'No, sir! One guinea was the price that the Squire arranged with me in Leeds. And one guinea it is, *Mister* Murgatroyd.'

The butler's eyes opened wide in surprise. 'Yer don't expect me ter believe that the Squire himself came ter see yer, do yer, lad? His agent in Leeds always deals with such trifling matters,' he declared.

Regarding Murgatroyd acutely, Blackie recognized immediately that the man's amazement was genuine. His handsome Irish face broke into a broad smile. 'Faith, and sure it was himself that came to see me and me Uncle Pat. We own a small building business, ye see. He engaged me to do the repairs here, and me Uncle Pat to work at the mills and the newspaper offices in Leeds. And I am certain about the price, to be sure I am. Perhaps ye should be after asking the Squire again. There's been a mistake, I am thinking.' Blackie chuckled inwardly, for the butler was obviously not only flustered but vexed by the turn of events.

'Indeed, I will speak ter the Squire!' Murgatroyd snapped. 'He must have forgotten what he arranged with yer. He's more important matters ter be thinking about! Well, get on with yer, lad. The yardman's in the stables. He'll show yer where everything is, and yer room above the stables, where yer'll be sleeping.'

Murgatroyd dismissed Blackie with a curt nod and sat down at the kitchen table.

'I'll be having me tea and a bacon buttie,' he called to Cook, who threw him a nasty glance. She picked up the knife and began to attack the loaf of bread with great ferocity and from the expression on her face it was apparent that she wished it was Murgatroyd she was demolishing.

Blackie strode over to his sack and hoisted it on his shoulder. Emma was collecting her cleaning materials together at the foot of the stairs. 'I'll see ye tonight, mavourneen,' he said softly, and smiled.

'Aye, if I've finished me work by then,' she responded glumly. Seeing the disturbed look that flashed onto his face, she smiled. 'Oh, I'll be finished. Don't worry about me. Ta'rar, Blackie.' He watched her disappear up the stairs before he opened the kitchen door and went out into the cold morning air, his mind full of disturbing thoughts about the occupants of Fairley Hall, and most especially Emma, who was so defenceless in this strange house.

Emma paused in the small upstairs lobby that adjoined the kitchen staircase and put down the cleaning utensils she was carrying. She eased the basket on her arm and leaned against the wall. Her face was drawn and her head ached from the stunning blow, and she was seething with resentment. Murgatroyd never lost an opportunity to mistreat her. It seemed to her that he enjoyed cuffing her, and even though he continually snarled at Polly, he was not as brutal with her. His reprehensible display of temper a few minutes ago had been nothing unusual and she knew he would have walloped her again if Cook had not interceded. He'll hit me once too often, she thought grimly, and then I'll show him.

She adjusted the heavy basket on her arm, picked up the other items, and walked slowly down the corridor, her senses alert, listening acutely for any untoward noises in the house. But there were no sounds, for the family were still asleep. The corridor was filled with murky light and smelled faintly of wax and dry dust and a peculiar mustiness that bespoke windows long shuttered and cloistered, airless rooms. She wished she was back in the kitchen, which was the only cheerful spot in Fairley Hall.

In spite of its grandness and rich furnishings, the house filled Emma with a nameless terror from which she wanted always to flee. There was something fearful and oppressive about the chill dark rooms with their lofty ceilings and heavy furniture, the immense halls, and the winding corridors that drifted endlessly through the house. It was a place of hushed silences, seclusion, and hidden mysteries, a secretive house redolent of unhappiness and decay. And yet for all that quiescence there was a sheathed turbulence everywhere, contained but ominous and stealthily waiting to break loose.

Emma was shivering as she glided across the rich Turkey carpet in the vast front entrance hall and pushed open the double doors of the morning room. She stood on the threshold and nervously glanced around. Meagre fingers of gauzy sunlight fought their way into the room through the tall windows, heavily curtained in white silk and draped with thick blue velvet hangings. Dark portraits gazed down from the dim blue flocked-velvet walls and Emma imagined, absurdly, that their ancient eyes followed her as she crept towards the fireplace, squeezing past the many pieces of ponderous Victorian furniture made of mahogany so dark they looked black in the gloomy light. The only sound was the plaintive ticking of the clock on the carved black marble mantelshelf.

Emma deposited the cleaning equipment on the floor and knelt down in front of the fireplace. She dusted off the traces of ash and filled it with the paper spills and chips of wood Murgatroyd had placed in a pile on the hearth, along with the matches. She lit the paper and when the chips took hold she opened the brass scuttle and lifted out small pieces of coal. These she gingerly placed on the burning wood. The coal did not catch light immediately, so she lifted her apron and fanned the fire until it began to blaze.

The monotonous ticking of the clock reminded Emma she had little time to waste. She cleaned the room with efficiency and speed, in spite of the cumbersome and cluttered arrangements of furniture. When she had accomplished this, she took a fine white Irish linen tablecloth from the sideboard drawer and placed it over the great circular table. She arranged four place settings of silver and ran back to the sideboard for the dishes. As she was taking out four blue-and-white Crown Derby plates she tensed and held herself very still. Her neck prickled and gooseflesh sprang up on her arms, for she knew she was no longer alone. She sensed rather than heard another presence in the room. She turned slowly on her haunches. Squire Fairley was standing in the doorway watching her intently.

She stood up quickly and dropped a small curtsy. 'Good morning, Squire,' she mumbled timorously, clutching the plates firmly to her breast, so that they would not rattle in her trembling hands. Her legs shook, although more from surprise than fear.

'Morning. Where's Polly?'
'She's badly, Squire.'
'I see,' he said laconically.

His eyes bored into her as he regarded her with the utmost concentration. He frowned and a puzzled expression settled on his face. After a prolonged silence, during which Emma stared at him mesmerized, he nodded tersely, turned smartly on his heels, and left. The banging of the library door as he slammed it harshly behind him made her start in surprise. It was only then that she breathed with relief and finished setting the table for the family's breakfast.

TEN

Adam Fairley stood in the middle of the library and pressed his hands to his face. He was tired, exhausted, in fact, for he had slept badly yet again. His insomnia was nothing new. He seemed to be cursed with it these days, or rather these interminable nights. Even when he resorted to drinking five, sometimes six large ports after dinner, and vintage port at that, the wine did not act as a sedative. He would sleep for several hours, a drugged and heavy stupor descending upon him, but then he would awaken suddenly in the early hours, perspiring or shivering, depending on his nightmares, his mind a turmoil of painfully dredged-up memories and analytical assessments of his life, which did not please him. It had not for a long time.

He walked up and down the room slowly, lost in contemplation, a compact, trimly built man of about six feet, with an attractive, intelligent face, well modelled and sensitive, which was pale and drawn today, and etched with fatigue. His fine eyes were greyish blue in colour and intensely brilliant, almost incandescent, and extraordinarily lucid, filled with hidden depths and the suggestion of spirituality. But today they were red-rimmed and the light in them was dimmed. The most surprising feature in his somewhat ascetic face was his mouth, which was exceedingly sensual, although the sensuality was generally repressed and disguised by the austere expression that constantly played around his lips. His light brown hair had a blondish cast to it, was straight and finely textured. He wore it brushed loosely across his shapely head, slightly longer than was the vogue. He had an aversion to the pomaded hairstyles that were currently the mode for gentlemen of fashion. Consequently, a forelock of hair continually fell down over his wide brow, and he had developed a nervous habit of pushing it back quickly. He did this now as he paced the floor.

Oddly enough, this impatient gesture never seemed to create dishevelment in him, for Adam Fairley was one of those men who looked eternally well groomed, no matter what the circumstance or whatever activity occupied him. His appearance was faultless. He was always superbly attired, befitting the occasion, with the flair usually attributed to a dandy, and yet he was not flashy in the least.

His Savile Row suits were so impeccably cut, so beautifully styled and made with such perfect precision and unerring tailoring, they were the envy of his cohorts in London and his colleagues in the wool trade in Leeds and Bradford. For the most part, they were of fine cloths from his own mills, or from those of his friends – woollens and worsteds from the great looms of Yorkshire, undisputed centre of the world's woollen business and of which Adam Fairley was the undisputed king. All in all, Adam Fairley was the quintessence of sartorial elegance. He disliked anything shoddy or crude, and his weakness for fine clothes was one of his few indulgences. Conversely, it never occurred to him that the house in which he lived was singularly lacking in beauty. He rarely noticed it.

After a few minutes, he ceased pacing and walked across the room to the enormous carved ebony desk. He sat down in the dark wine-red leather chair and stared dully at his engagement diary. His eyes were scratchy and burning from lack of sleep, his body ached, and his head was throbbing not only from fatigue but from the wearisome thoughts that beset him. He felt there was nothing in his life of any worth. No joy, no love, no warmth, no companionship, not even any interests into which he could channel his energies. There was nothing ... nothing but endless lonely days stretching slowly and inexorably into endless lonelier nights, day after day, year after year.

All animation slipped away and his face took on gauntness. Violet smudges bruised his cheeks below his eyes, were strong evidence of the ravages of the night before, of the countless hours he had paced his bedroom, racked with an anguish he found unendurable. And yet it was a boyish face, sorrowful and weary as it was. Adam Fairley looked much younger than his forty-four years.

My life is a damnable mess, he thought with dissatisfaction. *What's the point of living? I have nothing to live for. I wish I had the courage to put a bullet through my head and end it all forever.*

This thought so shocked him he sat bolt upright in the chair and gripped its arms. He looked at his hands. They were shaking. Even in his worst moments, which had been not infrequent lately, he had never before thought of taking his

110

own life. In the past he had always equated suicide with cowardice, yet now he admitted to himself that perhaps, in an oblique way, this act did take a kind of courage. It occurred to him that only the stupid never contemplated suicide. *Surely most men of intelligence have considered it at some time or other?* he asked himself. For he realized, with a sickening sense of futility, that knowledge of life and the human condition inevitably brought disillusionment and despair. For him it had also brought a sense of helplessness, which he found increasingly intolerable.

In spite of his wealth and position, Adam Fairley was a tormented man who had been bitterly disappointed in life. He no longer expected happiness, but he did crave contentment and, at the very least, peace of mind. And yet he could find no respite from his bitter loneliness and the desolation in his heart, all the more unbearable because it was, to a great extent, of his own creation. Adam's dissatisfaction and searing disillusionment sprang from his betrayal of himself, his ambitions, his dreams, and his ideals. It was the failure of intellect and of moral conviction.

Adam lifted his head wearily and looked around the library slowly, as if seeing it after a long journey. This was a baronial and impressive room, with its immense high-flung ceiling and grand proportions, its panelled walls of bleached oak, its collection of scholarly books, and its handsome antiques. Fine Persian rugs threw rafts of vibrant red and dark blue jewel tones across the polished wood floor, and a selection of rare hunting prints graced the walls not covered with the many bookshelves. A comfortable Chesterfield sofa, upholstered in a leather the colour of tawny ruby wine, was positioned next to the intricately carved oak fireplace, along with several deep wing chairs of dark wine velvet. Nearby, an ebony library table was heaped with newspapers, journals, and illustrated magazines, and in one corner a black-walnut chest held a silver tray of crystal decanters filled with port, brandy, sherry, whisky, and gin, as well as leaded crystal Waterford glasses that glittered in the faint grey light.

The library had never been quite as ponderous as the other rooms in Fairley Hall, and Adam had always fought his wife's desire to overload it with bric-à-brac and 'folderols', as he disdainfully called her other decorative trinkets. In consequence, the room had a degree of graciousness and dignity, albeit a dignity that was masculine. Like his bedroom, which was somewhat more austere, it perfectly reflected his character and his tastes. Adam spent most of his time in the library, unless they were entertaining guests, which was rare these days, and it had become his haven, where he thankfully retreated to read and meditate, undisturbed in his solitariness.

He took out his pocket watch and looked at the time. It was almost seven-thirty and he had seen no sign of the servants, except for the forlorn maid cleaning the morning room. Cursing the housekeeper's absence, he tugged on the bell pull and glared with irritation at the cold and empty grate. As he waited for Murgatroyd to appear, the photogravure of himself in the dress uniform of the Fourth Hussars caught his eye. He turned and bent to look at it more fully, pursing his lips as he scrutinized it intently. He smiled ruefully. What a face! So full of anticipation, expectation, and yes, even happiness. He hardly recognized it as himself.

Murgatroyd knocked on the door and entered the room, interrupting Adam's thoughts. 'Good morning, Murgatroyd,' he said in his cool voice.

The butler advanced towards him smoothly, adjusting his black jacket. 'Good morning, Squire. I trust yer slept well, sir. Fine day it is today, for yer journey ter Leeds. Sunny and dry and hardly no wind at all. Cook'll be ready with yer breakfast shortly. She's preparing yer a kipper, sir.' This was said with such obsequiousness Adam winced and averted his face, so that Murgatroyd would not see the look of disgust in his eyes.

When Adam made no response, the butler went on, 'Is there owt else yer'll be wanting, sir, besides the kipper, I mean?'

Unctuous fool, Adam thought, now looking at Murgatroyd fully. 'A fire would be desirable, I think.'

'Begging yer pardon, sir?' Murgatroyd seemed flustered. He glanced swiftly at the empty grate and condemned Emma under his breath.

'A fire, Murgatroyd!' Adam repeated. 'It's cold enough in here to freeze the balls off a brass monkey –' Adam stopped and coughed behind his hand, a flicker of amusement touching his eyes as he noted Murgatroyd's discomfort. 'Ahem! Well, let me put it this way. The atmosphere in this room is comparable only to the Arctic this morning. It seems to me that I employ enough servants to run a battleship and yet it appears that I cannot get a few simple amenities.' Annoyed as he was, this was said in Adam's usual self-contained way, for he rarely displayed temperament with anyone, least of all the servants.

Bloody hell! He's in a right proper mood this morning, Murgatroyd thought, and said in an oily voice, 'I'm ever so sorry, sir, I am indeed. Polly's badly and the other lass was late. I don't know, if I'm not standing over 'em every minute of the day these lasses do nowt. I told yon lass ter light the fire in here ages ago, I did th –'

'What's wrong with you, man? Are you crippled?' Adam interjected softly, but his eyes were like icy pools.

A startled expression flashed across Murgatroyd's dolorous face. 'No! No, of course not, sir. I'll attend ter it right sharpish, Squire,' he said hurriedly, bowing subserviently several times in a jerky fashion.

'Yes. Do!'

'Right away, Squire.' He bowed again and backed out of the room.

'Oh, Murgatroyd!'

'Yes, sir?'

'Did the navvy arrive from Leeds? Young O'Neill.'

'Yes, sir. Came by this morning, early, he did. I've given him the list of repairs.'

'Good. See he has everything he needs to do the job right. And make sure he has the facilities of the kitchen. Plenty of food and the like.'

Murgatroyd nodded, surprised at the Squire's concern about a mere labourer. It both baffled and interested him. 'Yes, sir. Yer can rely on me, as always. I'll handle it. By the by, Squire, what shall I be paying him for his week's work?' His crafty eyes did not leave Adam's face.

Adam frowned. 'I told you last night he was to receive one guinea for his work. Is your memory failing you, man?'

'No, sir. It must've slipped me mind, that's all.'

'I see. Well, no harm done. In the meantime, I would appreciate it if you would attend to the fire immediately. I am rapidly turning into a block of ice. And I would like a cup of hot tea, Murgatroyd, if that's not too difficult to accomplish.'

The edge to Adam's voice did not go unnoticed by the butler. 'Right away, sir,' he said, bowing. He turned and scurried out, full of venom for Cook and the maids, and not so kindly disposed towards the Squire either. All that there tippling in the dead of night, that's what makes *him* liverish, he mumbled under his breath as he closed the door softly behind him.

Adam gazed at the door. Murgatroyd was developing a peculiar tendency to forget conversations about money, especially when related to wages for the outside workers, who came to the Hall from time to time. The butler was too parsimonious by far and it bothered him. Also, Adam, who thought Murgatroyd was an ignorant man, suspected that the butler was a tyrant in his own domain downstairs.

He shook his head and turned again to his youthful portrait. He did not need to see that face to be reminded of his abandoned military career. It had been much on his mind recently. He had come to believe that his life would have been so very different if he had followed his lodestar, and not turned away from it, out of loyalty to his father. It was too late for regrets, but, nevertheless, he had them.

As he stood there in the dark cold room a mental image of himself as a youth flashed into his mind's eye. He saw the thin intense boy he had been, home from Eton for the holidays, announcing to his father, with a fervency bordering on fanaticism, his intention of entering the army. His father had not only been flabbergasted but strongly, and vehemently, opposed to the idea, which he refused to countenance.

Adam recalled how unwavering his determination had been, how his dogged persistence and all manner of persuasive tactics had eventually convinced his father that he was sincere. The old Squire had finally succumbed and grudgingly agreed to let him take the entrance examination for Sandhurst, which he had passed with no problem. The old man really behaved quite decently, Adam now thought, and with a certain fondness, as he remembered his father.

The old Squire, Richard Fairley, had been a hearty, blustering Yorkshireman, one of the most powerful and richest industrialists in the North of England, with a gambler's instinct for the main chance, a shrewd eye for business, and a mind as sharp as a steel blade. Once Adam had proved himself to be an exemplary cadet at the military academy, he had thrown all of his power and money behind his son. When Adam expressed a desire to join a cavalry regiment, being an incomparable horseman, Richard Fairley had left no stone unturned to accomplish this end. Through his wealth and his political connections he had obtained a place for Adam in the Fourth Hussars. He could easily afford the expense of two hundred pounds a year a commission in the cavalry entailed, along with the cost and upkeep of two horses and a string of polo ponies, which he had bought for his younger son. Being an astute observer of human nature, the old Squire had come to recognize that Adam had all the natural attributes of character a soldier required. He was ideally suited to military life, for he had a keen mind, great discipline, a sense of honour, and courage. Something of a romantic, Adam thirsted for adventure in foreign parts and, as an imperialist devoted to the goals and ambitions of Queen Victoria, he longed to serve his country, and his Queen, in the rapidly expanding Empire.

Adam had just gained his commission in the Fourth Hussars when his elder brother Edward had been tragically drowned in a boating accident. The old Squire had been brokenhearted. He also believed that the touchstone of a man's character was dedication to duty. In no uncertain terms, and in spite of his understanding of Adam's basic temperament, he had informed his younger son that his duty was to return to Yorkshire and take Edward's place in the family business enterprises, which were huge.

This morning Adam could remember his father's voice. 'No more gallivanting around on horses in fancy uniforms, quelling the natives in godforsaken foreign regions,' he had blustered, valiantly striving to subdue and disguise his raw grief for Edward. It was a grief that had been painfully apparent to Adam, who had been reluctantly compelled to resign his commission. He was bitterly disappointed, but he had behaved in the only way he knew how, as an officer and a gentleman, bound by codes of honour and obligation to family. He had accepted his filial duty with grace, not recognizing at the time that his ready acquiescence to his father's command was a mistake that was irrevocable. He knew it now. It was a fact that haunted him. As he walked back to his desk Murgatroyd knocked on the door and hurried in carrying a coal scuttle. 'Yer tea'll be coming up in a minute, sir,' he said.

'Thank you, Murgatroyd. I would appreciate it if you would light the lamps at that end of the room.' As he spoke Adam struck a match and lit the lamp on his desk and then pulled his engagement diary towards him. He looked over his appointments with boredom. He had a board meeting at the *Yorkshire Morning Gazette* in Leeds, the newspaper company of which he was the controlling shareholder. Later there was luncheon with a cloth buyer from London, one of his most important customers. Not such a heavy day after all. He would have time to stop at the mill in Fairley on his way to Leeds, to speak to Wilson, the manager, about his son Gerald's progress. He stifled a sigh. Business was beginning to pall on him. There were no challenges anymore. Now that he thought about it, there never had been really. He had no interest in the pursuit of money; in fact, he had never harboured any ambitions for great wealth or power. His success was his father's success, and his grandfather's before him, and he had only reaped the rewards.

Certainly Adam Fairley had increased the fortune he had inherited, but to him it seemed as if this had happened through fortuitous accidents rather than any true brilliance on his part. In this he did himself an injustice, for he was not without a certain business acumen that, although it was less obvious than his father's, was, none the less, just as trenchant. He was known to be a tough negotiator in spite of his gentle soft-spoken manner, and some of his associates even considered him to be as calculating an opportunist as his father.

He pushed the diary away. The fire was now burning brightly, and although its warmth had not yet fully permeated the vast room, the sight of the blazing flames flying up the chimney cheered him and the chilled feeling that had previously enveloped him was beginning to ebb away. The library lost its shadowy gloominess. Although its style was basically severe and there was a paucity of bric-à-brac, the room had a comfortable ambiance that denoted masculinity, solidness, lineage, and old money rather than wealth newly acquired.

Murgatroyd had busied himself at the fireplace, then paused at Adam's desk. He cleared his throat. Adam looked up from the newspaper company's annual balance sheet he was perusing. 'Yes, Murgatroyd, what is it?'

'I was wondering, sir, should I have the maid prepare the same room for Mrs Wainright? The Grey Room in the main wing? She likes that there room, Squire, I knows that. And I always wants Mrs Wainright ter be real comfortable like.'

For once, the butler's fawning attitude failed to irritate Adam. He scarcely noticed it in his surprise. He stared at Murgatroyd, for a moment nonplussed. And then he remembered. In his preoccupation with his own problems he had completely forgotten that his sister-in-law was arriving this afternoon. 'Yes, yes, that will be fine, Murgatroyd,' Adam conceded, and added quickly, 'And please find out what happened to my tea, and let me know when the children come down for breakfast. I will wait for them this morning.' Adam dismissed the butler with a curt nod.

'Certainly, sir.' A vengeful look settled on Murgatroyd's face the moment he left the library, and he hurried down to the kitchen to give Emma a piece of his mind and the back of his hand. She was undermining him, dillydallying with that tea.

Adam opened the centre drawer of his desk and frantically searched for Olivia's letter to Adele, realizing that his introspection was making him extremely forgetful. He must pull himself out of his mental dejection, which was becoming a permanent condition, or he would drive himself insane. *As insane as that woman upstairs.*

Mostly, Adam resisted the temptation to conjecture about his wife's mental stability, dismissing her odd behaviour of the last few years as a combination of female vapours, general depression, hypochondria, and the peculiar vagueness that had always been predominant in her character. She was full of strange fears and delusions, but these, too, he had concluded to be mere female imaginings. He wondered now, with a small stab of guilt, if his attitude had been engendered by a sense of self-protection, for he never wanted to admit to himself that Adele might conceivably be losing her mind. As long as he did not think about it, he did not have to face that reality.

Now he faced it, recognizing that at times she had been like mad Ophelia, wandering dazedly around the upstairs corridors in bewilderment, a glazed expression on her face, her hair in disarray, the floating chiffon peignoir she favoured enveloping her like a nimbus. Some months ago, on a business trip to London, he had described her behaviour to his friend Andrew Melton, a doctor of some renown, who had listened patiently, and had suggested that Adele be examined by a doctor in Leeds or, better still, himself. Adam had been prepared to take Adele to London at once. But on his return to Fairley he had been astonished and relieved to find that her strangeness had evaporated and she seemed perfectly normal ever since. Frail, yes, but not suffering from delusions. But he knew instinctively, and with a crushing sense of dread, that the fragile cocoon of sanity that surrounded her might shatter at any moment.

Now he obstinately pushed away this disturbing thought and glanced at Olivia Wainright's letter. She would arrive at Leeds station on the three-thirty train from London. He would be able to meet her train immediately after his luncheon. He turned his attention to the balance sheet and made a few notations on the side, and then went through other business documents he had neglected and which needed his immediate attention.

As he worked on the papers Adam was unaware that his face had changed quite perceptibly. The haggard look had miraculously disappeared, and his eyes had brightened. All Adam knew, as he worked, was that his spirits had lifted unexpectedly, and quite inexplicably. There was a diffident tapping on the door. Adam lifted his head and called, 'Come in,' shifting slightly in his chair to observe the door. It opened slowly and Emma entered. She was carrying a cup of tea on a small silver tray and she hesitated in the doorway.

'It's yer tea, Squire,' she murmured. Her voice was hardly audible. She dropped a half curtsy as she spoke and almost spilled the tea. Her solemn green eyes

115

regarded him steadily, but she made no move to bring him the tea and Adam thought she appeared afraid to approach the desk.

He smiled at her faintly. 'Put it over there, on the table by the fireplace,' he said quietly. She did as she was told, deposited the tray, and hurried back to the door. She dropped a curtsy again and turned to leave.

'Who told you to do that? To curtsy every time you see me.'

Emma looked back at him, a startled expression crossing her face, and her eyes, widening, betrayed what seemed to him to be sheer fright.

She swallowed and said timidly, 'Murgatroyd, Squire.' She paused and looked at him with great directness and asked in a stronger voice, 'Don't I do it proper like?'

He bit back a smile. 'Yes, you do. But it irritates me enormously to have you all bobbing up and down constantly. You don't have to curtsy to me. I'm not King Edward, you know. I told Polly to refrain from doing it, and I assumed she had informed Murgatroyd of my wishes. Obviously she did not. You may tell Murgatroyd what I have said and don't do it again.'

'Yes, Squire.'

'What's your name, girl?'

'Emma, Squire.'

He nodded thoughtfully. 'You may go, Emma, and thank you again for the tea.'

Emma started to curtsy automatically, but corrected herself quickly and flew out of the room. As she descended the stairs to the kitchen she laughed softly to herself, and it was a grim laugh. Did he think she was daft, trying to soft-soap her like that! Telling her she didn't have to curtsy. It was no skin off her nose either way and, whatever he did, she would never change her mind about him. Never. As long as she lived.

Adam crossed the floor to the fireplace and Emma's face stayed with him. It struck a chord in his memory, as it had done when he first noticed her earlier that morning, but one so hazy he could not grasp it. She must be from the village, yet she did not resemble any of the villagers and he had known every family all of his life. The puzzled frown returned to his handsome face as he probed around in his mind, attempting to revive the memory to full consciousness. It remained fleeting and elusive. There was a purity and innocence and nobility in the girl's young face, and those eyes, filled with a piercing and brilliant Arctic greenness, were the most dazzling eyes he had ever seen. She reminded him of someone but he was damned if he could remember who it was.

He picked up the cup and saucer and drank the tea quickly before it became cold. He was warming himself in front of the fire when there was another knock on the door, the same light tapping as before, but this time it was much firmer. At his bidding the door opened and Emma was standing there once more. She seemed less hesitant, and Adam looked at her intently, as the memory became strangely alive again, yet still unformed.

For a brief instant their eyes met and locked and neither of them seemed able to look away, and Adam thought with amazement and sudden comprehension: Why, the girl's not afraid of me. She hates me! He recoiled from her gaze. Emma thought: He's a mean and wicked man, living off the toil of others, and her young and trembling heart hardened against him more resolutely.

Her voice was strong and cold as she said, 'Murgatroyd said ter tell yer the

116

children are waiting for yer in the morning room, Squire.' She gripped the side of the door tightly to steady herself, for she was dizzy from the second punishing blow she had just received from Murgatroyd's cruel hand.

Adam nodded, aware that he had an inflexible enemy in this strange yet attractive girl, although he could not conceive why this should be so. She retreated quietly without another glance. Adam noticed that she had not had to correct herself from curtsying.

ELEVEN

A few moments later, Adam strode into the morning room, his manner brisk, his face composed. As he entered the room he collided with one of the fragile tables. He grabbed it, along with the Meissen shepherdess that reclined on its surface, just before both crashed to the floor, and as he righted them he swore under his breath with mingled irritation and frustration.

Glancing at the butler, who was standing by the sideboard waiting to serve them breakfast, he said in a quiet voice, 'Please remove this table later, Murgatroyd. Find another place for it. I don't care where, just get it out of the way. I'm always tripping over it.'

'Yes, sir,' Murgatroyd said, arranging the lids on the numerous silver chafing dishes.

Adam sat down and regarded his two children, who were already seated. 'Good morning,' he said pleasantly. Gerald made a mumbled response, but Edwin pushed his chair back, stood up swiftly, and came to Adam's chair. He kissed him lightly on the cheek and said with the sunniest of smiles, 'Good morning, Father.'

Adam returned his younger son's smile and patted his shoulder affectionately. His disillusionment with his life and his marriage was equalled only by his disappointment in his children, although he did have a genuine fondness for Edwin, who was the nicer of the two. He also bore a striking physical resemblance to his father.

'How are you, old chap?' Adam asked gently. 'Feeling better, I hope.' Observing Edwin's pale face, he went on quickly, 'But we have to get some colour into those cheeks, Edwin. I think you should go riding this afternoon, or at least take a walk on the moors. Blow the cobwebs away. Right?'

'Yes, Father,' Edwin said, sitting down and shaking out his linen serviette carefully. 'I wanted to go out yesterday, but Mother said it was too cold for me.' His face, surprisingly mature for a fifteen-year-old, lit up in anticipation. 'Shall I tell Mother *you* said I could go out today?'

'Don't worry about that, Edwin. I will tell your mother myself,' Adam answered crisply, thinking that Adele would turn the boy into a hypochondriac like herself if he did not watch her. Adam now felt he had been remiss of late, in neglecting Edwin as he had. He resolved to keep a tighter rein on him and remove the boy from his mother's sickly and sickening influence.

Murgatroyd meanwhile had carried a silver platter to the table. He was standing by Adam's side and he presented the kipper to him with an ostentatious flourish. 'It looks right delicious, Squire. I'm sure yer'll enjoy it. Shall I serve it now, sir?'

Adam gave his assent and repressed a feeling of rising nausea as he looked at the platter. The strong odour of the smoked fish made his stomach lurch, and he regretted the port he had drunk so conscientiously the night before. While Murgatroyd served the fish, Adam picked up the silver teapot and poured himself a cup of tea, adding sugar and milk absently, hoping desperately the tea would quell his biliousness into submission. He turned to Murgatroyd. 'Thank you. The boys can serve themselves this morning, since you are short of help. You can go about your other duties, Murgatroyd.'

'Thank yer, Squire.' The butler returned the platter to the sideboard and backed out of the room. Gerald scraped back his ornate Victorian chair unceremoniously and rushed to the sideboard, followed more slowly and sedately by Edwin.

When they returned to the table Adam stared with enormous distaste at the large portions of food piled upon Gerald's plate, and the nausea swamped through him again, so that he felt faint and slightly dizzy. Why, the boy had become a positive glutton. He decided to have a word with Gerald privately later. His seventeen-year-old son was far too gross, and his appearance, in combination with his crude and raucous manner, affronted Adam whenever he set eyes on him. For Gerald's body was a mass of blubber, totally devoid of any sharp contrasts or hard angles, a roly-poly body thickly covered with layer upon layer of fat, as dense as a whale's. A dollop of lard, thought Adam grimly. He corrected himself. A mountain of lard. He winced.

'How are you progressing at the mill, Gerald? It is still going well?' Adam waited impatiently as his elder son masticated his food laboriously, eventually swallowing it in one gulp after what seemed like an interminable time to Adam.

Gerald wiped his epicene mouth on his serviette unhurriedly, and said finally, 'Yes, it is, Father. Wilson is very pleased with my progress. He says I have a real aptitude for the wool business, and I'm enjoying it. He says there's no sense keeping me on the mill floor, learning all the different processes. He thinks I know enough and he's moving me into his office today.' Gerald's round ruddy face was bland enough, but his dark brown eyes betrayed a shifty cunning.

'That is good news, Gerald. I'm delighted,' Adam said, although he was not especially surprised. Gerald had always been predisposed to entering the business and he had tremendous energy and a capacity for hard work, in spite of all that monstrous weight he carried around. He was also exceedingly avaricious, which Adam found deplorable. In fact, he had lately come to believe that money was Gerald's most consuming passion, even taking precedence over food. He considered both to be regrettable.

Adam cleared his throat and continued thoughtfully, 'I shall be talking to Wilson myself later. I intend to stop at the mill on my way to Leeds. I have quite a few appointments to keep there today, before I meet your Aunt Olivia's train. You do know she is coming to stay with us for several months, don't you?'

'Yes, Father,' Gerald said, patently uninterested in his aunt's arrival. He attacked the remainder of his breakfast with renewed and unrestrained vigour.

But Edwin's face immediately lost the forlorn look which had so recently washed over it. 'I'm so glad Aunt Olivia is coming to stay, Father,' he announced excitedly. 'She's a real sport!'

Adam smiled. He picked up *The Times*, which was folded next to his plate, and opened it, the pages rustling as he began to read the day's news.

Silence descended upon the room. The only sounds were the crackling of the logs, the faintly hissing gas jets, and the gentle tinkling of silver against china as the boys ate their breakfasts. They knew better than to chatter needlessly when their father was engrossed in *The Times*. This presented no problems since Gerald had little in common with Edwin, who had long been alienated from him.

'A damnable mess! A damnable mess!' Adam suddenly exploded behind his paper, his voice echoing around the room and breaking the silence. Unaccustomed to seeing their father angry, or hearing him raise his voice, his sons stared at him in startled surprise.

Finally Edwin ventured a question. 'What's wrong, Father? Has something in the paper disturbed you?' he asked.

'The Free Trade Question! Parliament has only just reassembled and they are already off to a running start with that one. It's going to be a damnable mess, you mark my words. It will bring Balfour down, I am sure. And his government. Maybe not now, but certainly in the not too distant future, if this ridiculous nonsense continues.'

Edwin cleared his throat. His light grey-blue eyes, so like his father's, were alive with intelligence in his gentle face. He said, 'Yes, I think you are absolutely right, Father. I read in yesterday's paper that Winston Churchill is strongly opposed to the Free Trade Bill, and you know how shrewd he is. He is fighting it hard and I am sure it will be a troublesome time for the government, just as you say.'

Adam's surprise was apparent. 'I didn't know you were interested in politics, Edwin. This is something new, isn't it?'

Edwin opened his mouth to speak, but Gerald sniggered and interjected scornfully, 'Churchill! Who cares what he thinks. He's only Member for Oldham anyway. A Lancashire mill town. If he follows in his father's footsteps his political career will be as short-lived as Lord Randolph's. Churchill is a braggart and a flash in the pan!'

Adam coughed behind his hand. When he spoke his voice was cold but quiet. 'I don't agree with you, Gerald. And I think Edwin is quite right. Winston Churchill is a keen young politician who knows what the issues are all about. You know, he made quite a name for himself in the South African war, with that escape of his from the Boers. Became a hero to the public, in fact, and when he entered politics his maiden speech was well received. He's been doing extremely well ever since, and I have a sneaking suspicion that we have not heard the last of young Winston. I believe he is going to be an important man in this country one day. But really, all that is irrelevant. You attacked Churchill in the most spurious way, but carefully ignored Edwin's actual point, which is that the government is going to be in serious trouble over the Free Trade Bill. Edwin was echoing my own sentiments.'

Gerald, who had been listening acutely, looked as if he was about to make a caustic retort. But he thought better of it, stood up, and took his plate to the sideboard to serve himself more food. A malicious gleam entered his dark brown eyes and his posture was arrogant as he moved ponderously from dish to dish.

Edwin's face was radiant as he turned his shining eyes on his father and smiled. He had been vindicated for once and he had found an unexpected ally in his father.

119

Adam smiled kindly at his younger son. 'Do you understand what the Free Trade Question is all about, Edwin?' Adam asked.

'I think so, Father. Isn't it about taxing food and other goods?'

'Yes. But it's also a little more complicated than that. You see, the Protectionists, led by Chamberlain, are trying to persuade the government to abandon the system of Free Trade and cheap food which this country has thrived upon for so long. They want to impose tariffs and taxation on all goods to protect the English manufacturers against so-called foreign competition.' Adam paused, and then continued, 'It might make some sense if we were in a slump, but our industries are enjoying a ruddy health right now. That's one reason why Chamberlain's bill is preposterous, as a great majority of us realize. It would be disastrous for the country. First of all, everyone fears it would mean dearer food. That would not affect us, of course, or people of our station in life. However, it is a very real fear to the working-class housewife, who sees the price of meat and bread increasing. Apart from this, there is a general belief, especially among Liberals, that free trade is the only way to preserve international peace and understanding. There's an old saying that comes to mind, Edwin, "If goods do not cross frontiers, armies will." Churchill understands these essential points. He has said time and time again that the Protectionists are wrong in economics, wrong in political conceptions, and most frighteningly wrong in their estimate of public opinion. He's right, my boy.'

'What will happen, Father?' Edwin queried.

'I think we are going to witness a bitter and bloody battle between the Tariff Reform League, which supports Joe Chamberlain, and the Unionist Free Food League created by the Unionist Free-Traders, who oppose him. The Duke of Devonshire is the president of the latter group and he's gathered many distinguished Conservatives around him, including Churchill.'

'Do you think they will win? Churchill's group?'

'I certainly hope so, Edwin, for the sake of the country.'

'But the House *is* divided, isn't it, Father?'

'Indeed it is. And the Tory Party. That's why I said I felt trouble was brewing. Arthur Balfour is attempting to sit on the fence, but that won't do him much good. He may well find himself out of 10 Downing Street sooner than he expects.'

Gerald returned to the table noisily and he sat down so abruptly and so heavily the table rocked, the china and silver rattled, and tea splashed out of his cup, staining the white tablecloth with an ugly dark patch. Adam observed Gerald with immense coldness, and glared at him, his annoyance mounting. 'Really, Gerald! Do try to be a little more mannerly at the table. And don't you think you ought to curb yourself? This unrestrained gorging of food is not good for your health. It's also perfectly disgusting!'

The boy chose to ignore this mild chastisement, reached for the pepper pot, and generously seasoned his food. 'Mother says I have a normal appetite for a growing boy,' he remarked smugly. Adam bit back an acerbic comment and sipped his tea.

As he ate, Gerald glanced at his father cagily. 'To return to our earlier discussion, Father. I'm sure you'll agree that as gentlemen we can have differences of opinion without resorting to quarrels.' Adam flinched at this pretentiousness as Gerald went on talking. 'I just wanted to say that I still don't think much of Churchill, in spite of your comments to the contrary. After all, who does he represent? A lot of cotton spinners in clogs and shawls!'

'That's not strictly true, Gerald. And don't be too hasty to dismiss the working classes. Times are changing.'

'You sound like one of the new socialists, Father. Bathtubs for the workers? You know they would only put coal in them.'

'That's a snide and ridiculous story which has gone around lately, Gerald, put out by those antiquated diehards who are afraid of changes in this country,' Adam said cuttingly. 'But it is only a story and I'm dismayed you would give it dignity by repeating it. I had expected better of you, Gerald.'

Gerald grinned fatuously, but his narrowed eyes were hostile. 'Don't tell me you're intending to give the Fairley workers bathtubs, Father.'

Adam looked at his son icily. 'No, I'm not. But I've always tried to improve conditions at the mill, as you well know, and I shall certainly continue to do so.'

'Well, don't bother,' Gerald exclaimed heatedly. 'The men are restless enough as it is. Keep 'em down and working hard and hungry. It keeps 'em out of trouble and under our control.'

'That's not a very admirable motto, Gerald, or a very farsighted policy either,' Adam snapped. 'But we shall discuss the mill later. In the meantime, I would like to point out that you've a lot to learn about human nature and the workers, my boy. They've been treated abominably in the past. More reform has to come, and I hope it does so without too much bloodshed.'

'You'd better not let your friends in the wool trade hear you talking like that, or they'll castigate you as a traitor to your class, sir,' Gerald responded.

'Don't be impertinent!' his father exclaimed, his eyes flashing with chilly silvery lights. Adam, who rarely lost his temper, was in danger of doing so now. But he took control of himself and poured another cup of tea. Because of his fatigue and mental weariness his patience was worn threadbare, and his nerves were far too close to the surface for his own comfort.

Gerald grinned and winked at Edwin, who was gazing at him in astonishment after this exceptional display of insolence. He was horrified at Gerald's effrontery, and he looked from his father to Gerald, and then dropped his eyes.

Infuriated, but in command of himself, Adam opened the newspaper and was about to disappear behind it, when Edwin, conscious of his father's disquiet and in an effort to distract him, said, 'Did you know Kitchener when you were in the army, Father?'

'No, I didn't, Edwin. Why do you ask?' Adam queried with impatience. He put the paper down, staring at Edwin curiously.

'I read a story yesterday about him clashing with Lord Curzon in India. Did you see the story in *The Times*, Father? I wondered exactly why they are always at loggerheads? Do you know, sir?'

'Yes, I did see the story, Edwin, and the chief reason those two are always arguing is because when Kitchener went to India as Commander in Chief of the British army he took it upon himself to redistribute the troops. He rapidly gained greater administrative control of the army and the Viceroy was opposed to that, and still opposes it, I might add. Curzon's met his match there, I'm afraid. Kitchener's not a man to be thwarted. He'll have his way, come hell or high water.'

'You don't like Kitchener, do you, Father?' Edwin suggested.

'I wouldn't say that, my boy. But why do you assume such a thing?'

'You once told me, when I was little, that it was Kitchener's fault that Gordon was killed at Khartoum.'

Adam gave Edwin a penetrating look. 'You have a prodigious memory. But I didn't quite say that. If I recall correctly, I said that Kitchener's relief expedition arrived too late to save General Gordon. Khartoum had already been stormed by the Mahdists, who had brutally murdered Gordon. It wasn't Kitchener's fault exactly. In reality, it was Gladstone's, because he delayed in sending relief to Gordon for too long. It caused quite a furore at the time. In fact, public indignation at Gordon's abandonment actually contributed to the downfall of Gladstone's government. But no, I don't blame Kitchener for Gordon's death, to answer your question. And Kitchener's a good soldier, my boy, and devoted to duty.'

'I see,' Edwin said thoughtfully, vastly relieved that his father was calmer.

'Are you interested in the army, or is it going to be politics for you, Edwin? I can see you are interested in both,' Adam said. Not one to remain irritated for long, his anger with Gerald was beginning to lessen.

'Oh no, Father. I think I would like to be a barrister.' Edwin announced this with enthusiasm. But then his face fell as he noticed the fixed frown on Adam's face. 'Do you not approve, Father?'

Adam smiled quickly, sensing his son's sudden disappointment. 'Of course I approve. Anything you want, old chap. I was rather taken aback, that's all. It didn't occur to me that you would be interested in the law. However, I have always known you were not really cut out for the business. And anyway, Gerald seems to be at home at the mill.' He threw a swift look at his elder son and his voice hardened as he went on, 'Correct, Gerald?'

Gerald nodded and said, 'Absolutely! I know Wilson will give you a good report on me.' He paused and glanced at his brother slyly. 'Anyway, Edwin would not like working in the mill and he's far too delicate in health for the harsh conditions. I thought at one time he might be interested in the newspaper, but since he's not, I heartily endorse his ambition to study law. And why not? It's quite a good idea to have a legal brain in the family.'

This was uttered in the most dulcet of tones, the words artfully couched to hide Gerald's cunning. He was inordinately jealous of his younger brother and the last thing he wanted was Edwin interfering in the business. By rights it was his, as the eldest son and heir, and he aimed to keep it for himself and himself alone.

Adam was not deceived. Gerald's guile was all too apparent to him, and under the circumstances it was probably fortuitous that Edwin did not nurture any ambitions to enter the family business. Adam suspected Gerald could be a ruthless adversary when necessary. 'Well, that seems to be settled then, Edwin,' he said slowly, drumming his fingers lightly on the table. 'It appears you have Gerald's good wishes, too.'

Edwin beamed, first at Gerald, and then at his father. 'I'm so glad you approve and that I have your consent, Father,' he cried jubilantly. 'I thought you might object, sir.'

'Of course I don't.' Adam picked up the *Yorkshire Morning Gazette* and turned to the Bradford Wool Market. He perused the section quickly and said to Gerald, 'Good. Wool prices are relatively steady and exports well up. We're still cornering the world market. England's cloth exports are averaging something like twenty-seven million running yards a year, the same as last year and the year before. Not bad at all.'

Gerald's avaricious eyes glittered darkly in his flaccid face. 'Wilson told me yesterday that we would have an excellent year ourselves. Business is booming. By the way, are you going to see that wool man from Australia this morning? Bruce McGill. You do know he's coming to the mill.'

'Damnation! I'd forgotten,' Adam exclaimed with exasperation. 'I can't see him, I'm afraid. Wilson will have to deal with him.'

'Yes, Father. Well, I'd better be going to the mill.' Gerald rose and clattered out noisily.

Adam frowned at his retreating figure and then turned to Edwin. 'I'll have a word with my solicitor about you, my boy, when I see him next week. Perhaps he will have some ideas about your further education after public school. We'll have to decide which university you will go to, Edwin.'

'Yes, Father, and thank you so much. I do appreciate your interest in me, I really do, sir.' He loved and respected his father.

At this moment Emma knocked and came into the room, carrying a large tray. She stared at Adam coldly and then glanced away quickly, fixing her eyes on the silver teapot. 'Murgatroyd sent me up ter start clearing away, if yer've finished, Squire,' she said in a hard voice, clutching the tray tightly and holding herself very still.

'Yes, we have finished, thank you, Emma. You can take everything away, but leave the teapot. I may want another cup before I leave.' Adam's eyes were gentle and he smiled at her kindly.

Emma, who had partially turned to listen to him, had averted her head again and she did not see the kindness and compassion that illuminated his sensitive face. 'Yes, sir,' she said stonily, and went to the sideboard. She propped the tray against it and returned to the table to collect the dirty dishes.

Adam sighed and continued his conversation with Edwin.

Emma moved around the circular table quietly, gathering the used silver and the plates with as little fuss and noise as possible. This was protection in itself, for she believed the less people noticed your existence, the easier it was to get along without trouble. Unfortunately, and to her constant dismay, Master Gerald always noticed her and took great pleasure in picking on her, just as he had in the hall a few moments ago. He had jostled against her and pinched her viciously on the thigh, so that she had almost dropped the tray. Her heart filled with anger and humiliation at the remembrance.

She carried the dishes to the sideboard and began to stack them on the tray, wondering how long she could tolerate living in this house, and the terrible people who occupied it. She wished she could run away with Winston, but she knew that was not possible. They did not take girls in the Royal Navy and there was certainly no other place she could go. And anyway, her mam needed her, and her dad, and little Frankie. Panic gripped her and a fine sweat broke out on her forehead and ran down between her breasts. She must get away from this house. From Fairley. Before something dreadful happened. She was powerless in this house, and she knew, with sinking dread, that all sorts of wicked acts could be committed against the poor by the rich. Money. She must get money. Not just a few extra shillings for sewing and mending clothes in the village, but lots of money. Yes, that was the answer. She had always known it was. She must find a way to make a fortune. But how? Where? It was then that she remembered Blackie O'Neill and his tales of Leeds, the city whose streets were paved with gold. That was the key, and there she would find the secret of making money, so much money she would never be afraid or powerless ever again. And then the tables would be turned on the Fairleys. Slowly the fear began to slip away.

The tray was filled to overflowing and Emma picked it up, almost staggering under its weight. She gritted her teeth and glided out of the room in silence, her head held high, a proud look on her face, rigid determination in the set of her shoulders. And for all of her youth and inexperience there was a certain regality in her carriage.

Edwin had begun to fidget in his chair. Eventually he said, 'May I be excused, Father? I have to keep up with my schoolwork, otherwise I will be behind when I return to Worksop.'

Adam's glance was approving. 'Why, that's very diligent of you. Go ahead, old chap. But do get some fresh air this afternoon.'

'Yes, sir.' Edwin stood up and went to the door with his usual grace.

'Oh, Edwin.'

'Yes, Father?' The boy stopped, his hand on the doorknob.

'I think it would be nice if you dined with your Aunt Olivia and myself this evening.'

'Gosh! Thank you, sir. I'd enjoy that!' Excited by this unexpected invitation, Edwin forgot himself and exuberantly slammed the door behind him so hard that the gas fixtures on the wall rattled and trembled precariously.

His father smiled. Edwin was growing up to be a nice boy and Adam was delighted he was beginning to show a little independence of spirit. Perhaps his mother's sickly influence had not been so damaging after all. Adele. He should go up and see her. He had many matters to discuss with her, which, as usual, he had been avoiding for weeks. If he was honest with himself he had to admit that he was avoiding it now. He thought of his wife. Fragile, pretty, vain, brittle Adele. Smiling her sweet smile. That perpetual smile that had begun to horrify him. Adele with her iridescent blonde beauty that had so captivated him years ago. How quickly he had discovered it was a chilly beauty that camouflaged selfishness and a heart that was as cold as marble. It also apparently disguised mental instability as well. They had not had any real contact or communication for years. Ten years to be exact, when Adele had retreated gratefully into a shell of vapourish semi-invalidism. Smiling sweetly, as ingenuous as always, she had closed her bedroom door firmly, locking it pointedly against him. At the time Adam had been startled to find that he accepted her termination of her connubial duties with a resignation that bespoke his own profound relief.

Long ago, Adam Fairley had come to accept that his lifeless and loveless marriage was by no means unique. Many of his friends were bound in similar bleak and fruitless unions, although he doubted that they had to contend with disorders of the mind as well. With abandon, and without a second thought, his friends took solace in other comforting feminine arms. Adam's fastidiousness, and his innate sense of taste, precluded casual affairs with women of easy virtue. For in spite of his sensuous nature, Adam Fairley was not essentially carnal or given to fleshly pursuits, and he required other attributes in a woman as well as a beautiful face and body. And so, over the years, he had learned to accept celibacy as a permanent condition, and it bordered now on asceticism. He did not understand that this was a state of being that held its own attractions for the women he came into contact with socially, who found him irresistible. In his misery with his life he was blind to the flurry he created, and if he had noticed he would not have cared.

Adam went to the window, parted the curtains, and looked out. The dark rain clouds had scurried away, leaving a sky that was a vivid light blue, and so sharp and polished it was like the inside of an upturned enamelled bowl, and the pale yet bright sun intensified the cold lucency of the northern light. The black hills were as stark and barren as always, but for Adam they held an overpowering and enigmatic beauty. They had been there for eons before he was born and they would be there long after he was dead. Always the land remained, changeless and everlasting, the source of the Fairleys' power and their strength. In the scheme of things, he was just a droplet in the vast universe and suddenly his problems seemed of little significance, and even petty, for he was just a transitory being on this rich and splendid earth and, being mortal like all men, he would die one day. And what would it matter then? What would it have all been about? And who would care?

His reflective mood was shattered by the sound of horses' hooves, as Gerald drove rapidly across the stable yard in the trap on his way to the mill. Adam thought then of Gerald and Edwin. He had become aware of so many things this morning, not only about himself but also about his sons. By reason of primogeniture, Gerald would inherit the Fairley lands, the Hall, the mill, and all the other Fairley holdings, with the understanding that he would take care of his brother for his lifetime. But Edwin would receive nothing of real worth and would have to rely solely on the bounty of Gerald. Not a very pleasant prospect, Adam thought. He now recognized that it was imperative that he make proper provision for his younger son in his will. He determined to see his solicitor at the first opportunity. *He did not trust Gerald. No, he did not trust Gerald at all.*

TWELVE

The Fairley family fortune, now controlled by Adam Fairley, was founded on two sound principles – the acquisition of land and the making of cloth.

The land came first.

Adam Fairley could trace his lineage back to the twelfth century and one Hubert Fairley. A document drawn in 1155, and still in existence in the vault at Fairley Hall, states that Hubert was given the lands of Arkwith and Ramsden in the West Riding of Yorkshire by the Crown. The document was drawn in the presence of Henry II and signed by fourteen witnesses at Pontefract Castle, where the King used to stay on his visits to Yorkshire. With Hubert's continuing prosperity and growing renown as a 'King's man', Arkwith eventually came to be known as Fairley. It was Hubert who built the original Fairley Manor on the site where the present Hall now stands.

Succeeding Fairleys received more land and favours from their grateful sovereigns. Staunchly Royalist, many of them took up arms in defence of their Crown and country and were admirably rewarded. It was Henry VIII who granted to John Fairley the adjoining land of Ramsden Moors at the time of the Dissolution of the Monasteries, for services to Henry during the King's ecclesiastical reforms. Later Henry's daughter Elizabeth Tudor sold 'the valley of Kirkton on the banks of the river Aire to William Fairley, Squire of Fairley Manor and Hamlet'. Elizabeth I, always desperately striving to replenish the royal coffers, had long resorted to selling off Crown lands. She looked with a degree of favour on William Fairley, for his son Robert was a sea captain who had sailed with Drake to the Indies. Later his ship was part of the great English fleet, led by the intrepid Drake, which sailed into Cádiz harbour and defeated the Armada in 1588. Consequently, the Queen sold the Kirkton land at a fair price. It was the procurement of this particular parcel of land on the river Aire that was a decisive factor in the development of the Fairley fortunes, for the river was to be the source of power for the original mill.

Robert's son Francis, named after Drake, had no seafaring or military ambitions and, in fact, from this time on there were no more military men in the family until Adam became, for a brief period, a cavalry officer in the Fourth Hussars. Francis, plodding, diligent, but not too imaginative by nature, at least had enough of the merchant's instinct to foresee the growing importance of so basic and essential a product as cloth. He started a small domestic industry for the weaving of wool at the end of the sixteenth century. The local villagers continued to spin and weave in their cottages, but what had formerly been woven for personal use was now made for sale. It was from this modest beginning that the great Fairley enterprises flowered, and which were to make Francis' descendants not only rich but the most powerful woollen kings in the West Riding. By the beginning of the seventeenth century, Fairley was already a flourishing wool-manufacturing hamlet with a cropping shop, a fulling mill on the river, and a breached reservoir.

Francis Fairley had joined the cloth to the land.

But without the land there could have been no cloth. Fairley's location in the West Riding, its geology, and its climate all contributed greatly to the success of the family's wool-manufacturing business.

Fairley village is situated in the foothills of the Pennine Chain, that great range of interlocking spurs of hills that roll down the centre of England from the Cheviots on the Scottish border to the Peak in Derbyshire, and which is called 'the backbone of England' by those who live in its regions. The geology of the Pennine Chain varies. In the north of Yorkshire the hills are of white limestone rock on which grows sweet grass. But there are few springs in limestone country, and these abound with limestone, and limestone water is particularly harsh to fibres. Further down the Chain there is a sudden break called the Aire Gap, through which the river Aire flows towards Leeds. It is just south of Skipton and the Aire Gap that the West Riding begins. Here the Pennine Hills are now composed of dark and hard millstone grit, with a fringe of coal measure and coatings of peat or clay. Very little grows on millstone grit. Oats and coarse grass are its only crops. However, these are the crops that short-haired sheep feed and thrive on best. Also, coal and grit country has numerous streams which rarely fail, for the moisture-heavy winds that sweep in across the hills from the Atlantic provide abundant rain the year round. The water in these rocky little becks contains no lime. It is soft and kind to fibres.

Sheep's wool and soft water are the two necessities for the making of cloth, and both are plentiful in the West Riding.

And so with these natural elements in their favour the Fairleys' wool business grew, and especially so in the eighteenth century. But this amazing growth was also due to the enterprise and progressiveness of three Fairleys, father, son, and grandson – Joshua, Percival, and David. All were pioneers in the wool business and, being astute, they recognized the importance of the new inventions coming into being, which would help increase production in the most efficient manner. Whilst some rival manufacturers in the West Riding at first resisted these technological innovations that were to change the social and economic structure of England, the Fairleys did not. They enthusiastically purchased these 'newfangled machines', as they were scathingly called by less progressive cloth merchants, and at once put them to advantageous use.

Gerald, heir presumptive to the immense fortune presently in the hands of Adam Fairley, had inherited one singular trait from his forebears, a trait totally lacking in Adam. And this was their love for the wool business. It elicited in Gerald the same intense passion evoked by money and food. When Gerald was on the mill floor, amidst the clattering machinery, he too was in his natural element. He felt completely alive, was filled with a pulsating strength. The strident noise of the rattling machines, which deafened Adam, were not at all discordant to Gerald, who thought they made the most beautiful music he had ever heard. And the malodorous stink of the oily wool, so noxious to his father, was for Gerald an intoxicating perfume. When Gerald saw the great stacks of hundreds upon hundreds of bolts of Fairley cloth, he thrilled with an excitement incomparable to anything he had ever felt in the seventeen years of his young life.

This morning, as Gerald drove down the lower road that cut across the valley from the Hall, he was thinking about the mill; or, more precisely, his father and Edwin in relation to the mill. He did not see the landscape or notice the weather or feel the biting cold. He was lost in the labyrinths of his own convoluted thoughts. Edwin had been neatly disposed of at breakfast. Very neatly indeed. And more precipitously than he had ever imagined possible in his wildest and most exigent dreams. Not that Edwin was a real threat. After all, he, Gerald, was the heir and by birthright everything was his under the law. Yet it had often occurred to him recently that Edwin might conceivably want to enter the woollen business and that he could not have prevented. It would have been an unnecessary nuisance. Now there was no longer any need for him to worry about Edwin. His brother was rendered powerless, and of his own volition. As for his father ... well! There was something corrupt in Gerald and he was riven by an immense hatred for his father. Insensitive as he was, Gerald had only a vague glimmering that this feeling sprang from a terrible and consuming envy. He constantly tried to diminish his father in his own mind. He picked on a few of Adam's traits, which in reality were insignificant and irrelevant, and blew them out of all proportion until they became damning and unforgivable faults. Parsimonious to a point of being miserly, narrow-minded, and parochial, Gerald fumed internally about the money his father spent on his clothes, his trips to London and abroad, and he became enraged and even violent when he contemplated the good hard cash his father was pouring into the newspaper.

Gerald was pondering on all of this as he drove down to the mill. Suddenly he

127

laughed out loud as it struck him that his father's lack of interest in the business and his attitude in general paved the way for him, and sooner than he had anticipated.

Now that he thought about it, he really had no alternative but to take matters into his own hands, considering the way his father was behaving. He determined to talk to the Australian wool man himself this morning. Wilson had told him yesterday that Bruce McGill wanted to sell them Australian wool. The way orders were pouring in for their cloth they might be in need of it and, in any event, it was surely worthwhile striking up a friendship with McGill, who was one of the most powerful and wealthiest sheep ranchers in Australia.

He also decided it would be a good idea to encourage his father's penchant for protracted absences, instead of fighting it. Those disappearing acts would suit his own ends now. He could not wait for the day his father retired. It would not be soon enough for him.

THIRTEEN

Adele Fairley's upstairs sitting room at Fairley Hall contained many individually beautiful objects, and yet, in spite of that, it was not a beautiful room. It was lifeless and oddly empty in feeling, a feeling that sprang from an all-pervading ambiance of bleakness, of utter desolation. Certainly this feeling did not emanate from a need for furnishings, for, on the contrary, it was teeming with possessions.

The sitting room was vast, large and square in its dimensions, with a vaulted ceiling that appeared to float up and beyond into infinity. This was lavishly embellished with plaster cornices and mouldings, and panels inset with oval plaques and cherubim, and entwining flowers and acanthus leaves, the whole expanse painted a stark and pristine white and from the centre of which dropped a gigantic and magnificent chandelier of shimmering crystal. Many windows, tall and majestic, intersected the walls, and an eighteenth-century Gothic fireplace of glacial white marble was an imposing counterpoint with its huge mantel and great carved columns and soaring proportions.

Almost everything in the room was blue: Pale blue damask sheathed the walls, rippled at the windows, slithered across the sofas and fragile gilt chairs, and even the antique carpet was a sweep of glistening blue on the dark oak floor. Mirrors, crystal ornaments, glass domes covering dried flowers and wax fruit, pieces of finely wrought silver, and priceless porcelain were all charged and glittered with cold reflected light that only served to underscore the icy sterility of the room. A fire blazed continually in the hearth, costly jade and porcelain lamps threw out rays of softening light, the antique furniture gleamed as pools of ripe dark colour, yet these did nothing to diminish the gelid atmosphere, and there was a sense of abandonment hanging in the air.

Weighted down as it was with possessions, it betrayed the pathetic efforts of a lonely and disturbed woman to find some solace in material wealth, an attempt to restore her damaged psyche by surrounding herself with things rather than people, as if they could give her the illusion of life. Few people who entered this room ever felt truly comfortable or at ease, and even Adele herself, the sole perpetrator of this monument of dubious taste, now seemed lost and adrift, a ghostly presence moving abstractedly through the multitudinous paraphernalia she had accumulated so acquisitively, so assiduously, and which she no longer seemed to notice.

This morning she came into the room tentatively, pausing cautiously on the threshold of her adjoining bedroom. Her eyes, large and beautiful but now filled with pinpoints of apprehension, flicked around the room hurriedly, and her aristocratic fingers clutched nervously at the silver-streaked white silk peignoir she was wearing. She pulled the filmy fabric closer to her body protectively, glancing around quickly, yet again, to reassure herself she was absolutely alone, that no servant was skulking in a dim corner, dusting or cleaning and intruding on her privacy.

Adele Fairley was tall and graceful, but so tempered of movement that at times she appeared to do everything in slow motion. This was the effect she gave now as she left the safety of the shadowy doorway and glided into the room. Her pale blonde hair was almost silver in tone, and it fell about her face in soft curls and delicate tendrils, and cascaded down her back in undulating waves to blend into the silvered snowy silk enveloping her body, so that the two seemed almost indistinguishable. She paused at one of the windows and turned to gaze out across the valley, a remote unseeing look in her eyes. The landscape had changed in the past few weeks. The dusty greys and sombre blacks had given way to the first signs of spring greenness. But Adele saw this only dimly, as if through a veil, lost as she was in her own thoughts and preoccupations. An inverted woman, isolated within herself, she lived quite separate and apart from the world around her, and she was curiously detached, curiously oblivious to externals. Her internal life had become her only reality.

As she stood, motionless, at the window, the sunlight struck her face, illuminating the smooth contours. In spite of her thirty-seven years there was a girlishness and a purity about Adele Fairley, but it was the purity of a perfectly sculptured marble statue that had been immured for years behind glass; which had never been warmed by love or pained by sorrow or moved to compassion at another's suffering.

Unexpectedly, and with an abruptness that was most unnatural for her, Adele swung away from the window, suddenly intent in her purpose. She glided swiftly to a display cabinet on the far wall, her eyes glittering. The cabinet, a French vitrine, contained many exquisite objects that Adele had collected on her travels with Adam over the years. These had once been Adele's pride, and she had found constant pleasure in them, but now they no longer interested her.

She stood in front of the cabinet and looked about her anxiously before taking a small key from her pocket. As she unlocked the cabinet her lovely eyes narrowed and a sly and secretive expression slipped on to her face, distorting it into a mask that blurred her stunning beauty. She reached inside the cabinet and carefully lifted out a decanter. This was of dark red Venetian glass, intricately chased with silver, very old and priceless. It glinted in the sun and threw off a myriad of fiery prisms, but Adele did not stop to admire it as once she had. Instead, she removed the stopper hastily and, with trembling hands, lifted the decanter to her pale cold lips. She drank urgently, greedily, like one dying of thirst, tossing back several swift draughts with a seasoned hand, and then, hugging the decanter to her possessively, she closed her eyes thankfully, breathing deeply. As the liquid trickled slowly through her, warming her, the profound terror that perpetually worked inside her began to subside, and the fundamental anxiety that was ever present when she first awakened to a new day gradually began to ebb away. A sense of well-being, of euphoria, washed over her as the alcohol permeated her system. She looked around the room. It now appeared less hostile and frightening to her and she became aware of the soft sunlight pouring in, of the brightly burning fire, of the spring flowers in the vases.

She smiled to herself and lifted the decanter to her lips again. Only a trickle of liquid touched her tongue and she held the decanter away from her, shaking it impatiently, glaring at it with anger and disbelief. It was empty.

'Damn! Damn! Damn!' she cried out vehemently, her voice fuming with rage. She looked at the decanter again. Her hands began to shake and her body was suddenly besieged by cold tremors. Did I drink so much last night? she asked herself. She was aghast to discover she could not remember. Then the rising panic truly took hold of her, and it was with an awful sense of dread that she comprehended her predicament. *There was no more alcohol in her suite of rooms.* This scared her to a point of paralysis. Even if she did not succumb to the temptation of taking another drink during the day, she always needed to know it was available, for her own sense of security. But there was not a drop left now.

Half staggering, she groped her way blindly to a chair and fell into it, her mind blank. Still clutching the decanter to her body, she wrapped her arms around herself and rocked to and fro, whimpering and moaning, held in the clutches of an unbearable anguish. Oh God! Oh God! What will I do? What will I do? She shivered, and closed her eyes, as always fleeing reality.

Her face had paled to ashy white, and in repose, with her head thrown back limply against the chair and her hair hanging loosely over her shoulders, she looked wan and childlike.

Eventually she opened her eyes. 'My sweet little baby,' she said, gazing down at the object in her arms. 'Sweet darling baby. Darling Gerald.' She paused and stared down at her arms again, confusion registering on her face. 'Or is it Edwin?' She nodded her head slowly. 'Of course it's not Gerald. It *is* Edwin.' She began to coo and murmur unintelligible words to herself as she rocked frantically in the chair.

About an hour later Adele Fairley underwent a transfiguration. The agitation that had held her in its grip fell away, and her demeanour became composed. She glanced out of the window and noticed it was raining. Not the typical light shower so common in Yorkshire at this time of year, but a heavy downpour. Torrents of water, driven against the windows by the high wind that had sprung up, slashed furiously at the glass, which quivered and rattled under the onslaught. The trees lashed the air and the gardens appeared to vibrate under the force of the gale. Only the moors were unaffected by the tumult, implacable and sombre, a line of black monoliths flung defiantly into the bleached-out sky. Adele shuddered as she gazed at them. They had always seemed grim to her southern eye, accustomed as it was to the bucolic green gentleness of her native Sussex, and she thought of them as an imprisoning wall that encompassed this house and the village, shutting her off from the world. She was an alien in this alien land.

She shivered. She was cold. Her hands and feet were like icicles. She pulled the thin robe closer to her, but it offered no warmth. She saw, with dismay, that the fire had dwindled down to a few burning embers. As she stood up and moved

130

into the room her foot struck the decanter which had slipped unnoticed to the floor. Puzzled, she picked it up, wondering what it was doing there. Why was it on the floor? She examined it carefully for any cracks. Then it came to her. She had been looking for a drink earlier and had taken the decanter out of the vitrine. When was that? An hour, two hours ago? She could not remember. She did recall her behaviour. She laughed softly. How foolish she had been, to become so panic-stricken. She was mistress of this house, and all she had to do was to ring for Murgatroyd and instruct him to bring her a bottle of whisky, and one of brandy, surreptitiously, as he always did, so Adam would not know.

The clatter of china in the corridor outside the sitting room alerted her that the maid was approaching with her breakfast. Hastily, Adele returned the decanter to the vitrine, locked it, and swept out of the room with unusual swiftness, the silver-streaked white peignoir billowing out behind her like iridescent wings, her hair streaming down her back in rivulets of silver.

She closed the bedroom door quietly and leaned back against it, a satisfied smile on her face. She must select a morning dress, a becoming one, and after breakfast she would attend to her hair and her face. Then she would send for Murgatroyd. As she went to the wardrobe she told herself she must try to remember that *she* was the mistress of Fairley Hall, and no one else. She must assert herself. This very day. Her sister Olivia had been kind in taking over so many managerial duties, since her arrival in February, but now she would have to relinquish them.

'I am well enough to assume them myself,' Adele said aloud, and she truly believed her words. Yes, that will please Adam, she decided. And then her throat tightened at the thought of her husband. She frowned. But would it please him? He thought her a fool, and quite unlike her sister, whom he considered to be a paragon of every virtue under the sun. Lately she had come to think of Adam as a man surrounded by a wall of great reserve. She shivered. In recent weeks she had also been frighteningly aware of the menace in his eyes. Not only that, he was always watching her with his pale eyes. So was Olivia. They didn't know it, but she watched them watching her avidly, and whispering together in corners. They were in league. They were plotting against her. As long as she was fully conscious of their plotting they could not harm her. She must be on guard against them at all times. Adam. Olivia. Her enemies.

She began to pull out dress after dress, frenetically and with a superhuman energy, flinging them carelessly on to the floor. She was searching for one dress in particular. It was a special dress with special powers. Once she put it on she would automatically become mistress of this house again, of that she was quite certain. She knew the dress was there. It must be there ... unless ... unless Olivia had stolen it ... just as she had stolen her role as mistress of Fairley Hall. She continued to pull out dresses and other clothes frantically, tossing them on to the floor until the wardrobe was completely empty. She stared at it for a prolonged moment, and then distractedly looked down at the piles of silks and satins, georgettes and chiffons, and velvets and wools that swirled in a mass of intense colour at her feet.

Why were her peignoirs and morning dresses and day suits and evening gowns lying on the floor? What had she been looking for? She could not remember. She stepped over them, and walked across the floor to the cheval mirror near the window. She stood in front of it, playing with her hair absently, lifting it above her

131

head and then letting it fall down slowly to catch the light, repeating the gesture time after time. Her face was blank, utterly without emotion, but her eyes blazed with delirium.

FOURTEEN

Emma entered Adele Fairley's sitting room so hurriedly she was almost running. Her feet, in their new black button boots that shone like glittering mirrors, barely seemed to touch the floor, and the starched white petticoat underneath her long blue woollen dress crackled and rustled in the silence. She gripped the heavy silver tray tightly in her work-roughened hands, holding it out in front of her, and high, to avoid contact with the furniture, and to prevent any accidents.

Her face, just visible above the outsized tray, was scrubbed to shining cleanliness and glowed with youthful health, as did her green eyes that were brilliant with intelligence beneath the thick lashes. Her russet hair, brushed and gleaming, was pulled back severely into a thick bun in the nape of her neck, and today the widow's peak was more pronounced than ever, accentuated as it was by the maid's cap that framed her face like a little halo. This was as glistening white and as stiffly starched as her large apron and the collar and cuffs on her dress, all recently purchased for her in Leeds by Olivia Wainright. The dress, too, was new, but this Emma had made herself from a length of cloth from the Fairley mill, which had also been given to her by Mrs Wainright. Emma's delight in the new dress was surpassed only by her pride in Olivia Wainright's smiling approval of her dexterity with the scissors and her skill with a needle and thread.

These new clothes, simple though they were, not only helped to dispel the starveling appearance that had given Emma the downtrodden air which had so appalled Blackie, but they also considerably enhanced her naturally arresting good looks. The combination of blue and white was crisp and immaculate, and the tailored style of the uniform, and the smart little cap, brought her finely articulated features into focus and made her seem older than she really was. But more important than the clothes was the subtle change in her demeanour, which had occurred over the last two months. Although she was still internally apprehensive about being in such close proximity to some members of the Fairley family, and indeed of working at Fairley Hall at all, that apprehension was more controlled than it had ever been in her two years of service there. Also, her initial timidness about being suddenly propelled into the upstairs quarters had lessened. Her diffidence was now disguised by a rigid self-containment that manifested itself in an exterior composure so austere and so dignified it bordered on hauteur, and which in anyone else of her age would have seemed ridiculous yet was somehow perfectly natural in Emma. She was beginning to acquire a measure of self-confidence, and tentative as this still was, it gave her a kind of naïve poise.

This change in Emma's manner had been wrought by a number of circumstances, and the most obvious, although in reality of lesser consequence in the overall scheme of things, was the radical developments in the domestic scene at Fairley

Hall, precipitated by Olivia Wainright's arrival. Olivia Wainright was a woman of impeccable character, high principles, and down-to-earth common sense. Although she was innately fine and good, had a well-developed moral sense of right and wrong, and was constantly infuriated and moved to compassion by the blatant lack of humanity in this Edwardian era, she was by no means a bleeding heart. Neither was she easily persuaded, or manipulated, by importuning or sentimental appeals to her charity, generosity, and intrinsic decency. In fact, she could be exceedingly severe with those she considered to be malingerers or professional beggars, and was sternly disapproving of certain so-called worthy charitable organizations which she considered did more harm than good, and, as often as not, foolishly squandered the monetary donations they received. Yet she had a fierce abhorrence of injustice and mindless cruelty and brutality, most especially when directed at those with no means of retaliation. If her dealings with staff were exacting, strict, and firm, they were, nevertheless, tempered by a quiet sympathy and a considered benevolence, for she recognized the dignity of honest toil and respected it. She was a lady in the truest sense of that word, educated, honourable, refined, well-bred, dignified, and courteous to everyone.

Olivia's very presence in the house, her keen interest in all aspects of its management, her daily involvement with the servants, and her redoubtable character had all had the most profound effect. The atmosphere at the Hall in general, and especially downstairs, had improved vastly. It was less fraught with antipathy and intrigue. Olivia had become, quite automatically, a natural buffer between Murgatroyd and the other servants, in particular Emma. From the first moment she had become aware of the girl's existence, Olivia had taken a most particular and uncommon liking to her, and had shown her both kindness and consideration. Even though Emma still worked hard, she was treated with less abuse and in a more humane fashion. The butler continued to verbally castigate her on occasion, but he had not struck her once since the advent of Olivia, and Emma knew he would not dare. Cook's threats to expose his mistreatment of her to her father might not intimidate him for long, but certainly Olivia Wainright did, of that Emma was positive.

Emma felt a degree of gratitude to Olivia Wainright, yet in spite of that she was curiously ambivalent in her feelings about the older woman. Suspicious, cautious, and wary though she was with everyone, she sometimes found herself admiring Olivia, much against her will. This emotion continually surprised Emma and also vexed her, for her fundamental distrust of the gentry, and the Fairleys in particular, had not abated in the least. So she endeavoured always to suppress the rush of reluctant warmth and friendliness that surfaced whenever she came into contact with Mrs Wainright. And yet, because of Olivia Wainright's singular and most apparent interest in her, Emma was taking a new pride in her work, and much of the time she was less fearful and resentful than she had been in the past.

Apart from this, when Polly became sick Emma had been given Polly's duties of attending to Adele Fairley. This close and more familiar contact with her mistress had, in itself, been an influence on Emma, and had also helped to change her life at the Hall to some extent, and for the better. As for Adele, Emma found her spoiled, self-indulgent, extremely demanding of her time and attention, but her unfailing and profound gentleness with the girl outweighed these other characteristics. Then again, Adele's chronic vagueness, and her perverse disregard of the stringent domestic rules quite common in such a large house, gave Emma autonomy to care for Mrs Fairley as they both deemed fit, and without too much interference from anyone else in the establishment. This new independence, meagre as it actually was, engendered in Emma a sense of freedom, and even a degree of authority that she had not experienced at the Hall before, and it certainly removed her from Murgatroyd's jurisdiction and foul temper for much of the time.

If Emma looked up to Olivia Wainright, thought her the more superior woman, and, against her volition, secretly adored her, she could not help liking Adele Fairley in spite of what she was. Mainly she felt sorry for her. To Emma she could be forgiven her carelessness and her strange lapses, since Emma considered her to be childlike and, oddly enough, in need of protection in that strange household. Sometimes, to her astonishment, Emma found herself actually excusing Mrs Fairley's patent obliviousness to the suffering of others less fortunate, for Emma knew instinctively this was not caused by conscious malice or cruelty, but simply emanated from sheer thoughtlessness and lack of exposure to the lives of the working class. Her attitude towards Mrs Fairley was much the same attitude she adopted at home. She took charge. She was even a little bossy at times. But Adele did not seem to notice this, and if she did, she apparently did not mind. Emma alone now took care of her and attended to all her daily needs and comforts. Adele had come to depend on her, and she found Emma indispensable in much the same way Murgatroyd was indispensable, because of the secret supplies of drink he provided.

Between them the two sisters had, in their different ways, shown Emma a degree of kindness and understanding. And whilst this did not entirely assuage the hurt she felt at the humiliations inflicted on her by other members of the family, it made her life at the Hall all that more bearable. But it was one other element, fundamental, cogent, and therefore of crucial importance, that had done the most to bring about the change in Emma's personality. And this was the consolidation of several natural traits that were becoming the determinative factors in her life – her fierce ambition and her formidable will. Both had converged and hardened into a fanatical sense of purpose that was the driving force behind everything she did. Blackie's initial stories about Leeds had originally fired her imagination, and on his subsequent visits to the Hall she had assiduously questioned him, and minutely so, about prospects of work there. Constrained, circumspect, and even negative as he was at times, he had unwittingly fostered her youthful dreams of glory, of money, of a better life, and, inevitably, of escape from the village.

And so Emma had come finally to the realization that her life at Fairley Hall was just a brief sojourn to be patiently endured, since it would end one day. She now believed, with a sure and thrusting knowledge, that she would leave when the time was right, and she felt certain this was in the not too distant future. Until then she was not merely marking time, but learning everything she could to prepare herself for the world outside, which did not frighten her in the least.

Emma also had a secret she had shared with no one, not even Blackie. It was a plan, really. But a plan so grand it left no room for doubt, and it filled her days with that most wonderful of all human feelings – hope. It was a hope that foreshadowed all else in her cheerless young life. It gave added meaning to her days and made every hour of punishing toil totally irrelevant. It was this blind belief, this absolute faith in herself and her future, that often put a lively spring into her step, brought an occasional smile to her normally solemn young face, and sustained her at all times.

On this particular morning, filled with all that hope, wearing her new pristine uniform, and with her cheerfully shining face, she looked as bright and as sparkling as a brand-new penny. As she moved purposefully across the rich carpet she was like a gust of fresh spring air in that cloistered and overstuffed room. Squeezing gingerly between a whatnot and a console overflowing with all that preposterous bric-à-brac, Emma shook her head in mock horror. All this blinking junk! she thought, and with mild exasperation, as she remembered how long it always took her to dust everything. Although she was not afraid of hard work, she hated dusting, and this room in particular.

'Half of it could be thrown out inter the midden and nobody'd miss owt,' she exclaimed aloud, and then clamped her mouth tightly shut self-consciously and peered ahead, fully expecting to see Mrs Fairley sitting in the wing chair she favoured near the fireplace, for traces of her perfume permeated the air. But the room was deserted and Emma breathed a sigh of relief. She wrinkled her nose and sniffed several times, and with not a little pleasure. She had grown used to the pungent floral scent pervading the suite of rooms and had actually come to like it. In fact, somewhat to her surprise, for she was not one given to frivolities, Emma had discovered that she was most partial to the smell of expensive perfumes, the touch of good linens and supple silks, and the sparkle of brilliant jewels. She smiled secretively to herself. When she was a grand lady, like Blackie said she would be one day, and when she had made the fortune she intended to make, she would buy herself some of that perfume. Jasmine, it was. She had read the label on the bottle on Mrs Fairley's dressing table. It came all the way from London, from a shop called Floris, where Mrs Fairley bought all of her perfumes and soaps and potpourri for the bowls, and the little bags of lavender for the chests of drawers that held her delicate lawn and silk undergarments. Yes, she would have a bottle of that Jasmine scent and a bar of French Fern soap and even some little bags of lavender for her underclothes. And if she had enough money to spare they would be just as silky and as soft as Mrs Fairley's fine garments.

But she did not have time to indulge herself in thoughts of such fanciful things right now, and she put them firmly out of her mind as she hurried to the fireplace with the tray. There was too much to be done this morning and she was already late. Cook had overloaded her with extra chores in the kitchen, which had delayed her considerably, and consequently she was irritated. Not so much about the extra chores, but the delay they had caused. Punctuality had taken on a new and special significance to Emma and had become of major importance to her in the past few months. She hated to be late with Mrs Fairley's breakfast, or with anything else for that matter, for since being elevated to the position of parlourmaid she took her new responsibilities very seriously.

She placed the breakfast tray carefully on the small Queen Anne tea table next to the wing chair, in readiness for Mrs Fairley, who liked to have her breakfast in front of the fire. She looked over the tray to be sure it was perfect, rearranged some of the china more attractively, plumped up the cushions on the wing chair, and turned her attention to the dying fire. She knelt in front of the fireplace and began to rekindle it with paper spills, chips of wood, and small pieces of coal, handling them cautiously with the fire tongs in an effort to keep her hands clean.

She clucked impatiently. Mrs Turner with her extra chores was a real nuisance sometimes! If she had been up to the sitting room on time she would not have been faced with the task of making the fire again. This annoyed her because it ate into her precious time, and Emma, so rigid and relentless with herself, hated any deviation from her normal routine. It put her out of sorts because it ruined her timetable for the entire day. This timetable, Emma's own recent creation, was her Bible and she lived by it. She knew that without it she would be hopelessly lost.

She picked up the bellows and worked them in front of the meagre fire. Under the force of the small but strong gusts of air, the smouldering chips of wood spurted and spluttered, finally ignited and began to burn rapidly. In the sudden conflagration her face was illuminated. A small frown now creased her brow and her cheerful expression was obliterated, as she remembered with clarity and bitterness what her life had been like without that timetable.

On that day, early in February, when Polly had been struck down and forced to take to her bed, Emma had resignedly accepted the fact that she had to do Polly's work as well as her own. She knew she had no alternative. Strong of constitution and basically optimistic of nature, she had scurried about the Hall like a demon and with immense energy, telling herself that Polly would be up and about the next day and well enough to do her own work again. But this had not happened. Emma was suddenly burdened with the whole load of domestic chores, seemingly for an indefinite period. She soon became overwhelmed by her innumerable duties and acutely nervous about completing them efficiently.

Those first few days she had been bone tired at the end of every day, for she started working at six o'clock in the morning and barely stopped for breath, let alone a rest, until she finished at seven in the evening. By then she was almost always too weary to eat her supper and, in fact, it had usually taken a supreme effort of will and the last ounce of her strength to crawl up the attic stairs to her room. White and shaking and speechless with exhaustion, she had hardly had the energy to undress, and she invariably dropped on to the uncomfortable little bed in a dim and mindless stupor. She would fall into a heavy and stupefied sleep at once, and yet she never felt refreshed when she awakened the next day. Her back and shoulders still ached, her eyes were red-rimmed with fatigue, her arms and legs were like leaden weights, and her hands were sore and raw.

As she had shiveringly dressed in the cold attic room and washed in the icy water from the washbowl, she had seethed with a fulminating anger she found hard to quell. Yet she did not dare to complain for fear of reprisals from Murgatroyd or, even worse, dismissal. Daily, she dragged her weary body through that mausoleum of a house, up and down the many stairs, along the winding corridors, across the great halls and larger rooms, dusting, polishing, sweeping, black-leading grates, stoking fires, making beds, cleaning silver, ironing linens, and taking care of Adele Fairley's needs as well. And as she did, she often wondered how long she could continue without collapsing. This thought terrified her even more and made her grit her teeth and marshal her diminishing energies, for the money she earned was so desperately needed at home. She could not afford to collapse, for the sake of her family, and so she pushed herself almost beyond endurance, propelled by sheer force of will power and sustained by the icy terror of losing her job.

One morning, after about a week of this backbreaking toil, Emma was cleaning the carpet in the drawing room, rushing up and down and across the immense expanse of florid flowers and arabesques entwined in oriental convolutions, the carpet sweeper a dangerous weapon in her hands as she handled it with force and a certain abandon. As she had raced to and fro, a staggering thought entered her mind and it so amazed Emma it brought her to a standstill in the middle of a clump of purple rosettes. She leaned on the carpet sweeper, totally absorbed in her thoughts, and slowly a look of absolute comprehension crossed her face. Emma had just realized that the cleaning and care of Fairley Hall was difficult to manage because it not only was badly planned but was downright muddled. At that moment, it also struck her that this was due to Murgatroyd's poor organization and his haphazard distribution of the work. Lots of minor jobs were repeated daily, and unnecessarily so, and too much time was wasted on them because of Murgatroyd's pernickety fussing about trivialities. Then again, major jobs such as cleaning the silver, ironing the mountains of washing, and dusting the panelling in the library were all jammed together to be completed in one day. It was not possible for one person to accomplish all of this work properly, and also attend to the general chores which had to be done the same day. But there was a solution and it had come to Emma in a flash, as she had stood poised with the carpet sweeper in the centre of the drawing room floor. It was a solution so simple she was surprised no one else had ever thought of it. *The solution was planning.* She suddenly knew that if the work was planned properly and systematically, in a sensible way, and distributed more intelligently, it would be easier to manage. Of this she was absolutely confident, and the more she thought about it, the more convinced she had become.

In an effort to make some sense out of this muddled daily routine, Emma began to time herself at each job, and then scribbled down the amount of time each one took on a scrap of paper culled from the wastepaper basket in the library. She next made a list of all the daily chores, plus the major tasks for the entire week. For several nights thereafter, as exhausted as she was, Emma had forced herself to stay awake as she wrestled with the problem. She had studied her piece of paper assiduously, pondered over each chore and the time involved, and then she had set about creating her own special work plan. She first distributed the heavier work more evenly, staggering the jobs that were complicated or time-consuming over the whole week, so that they were easier to handle along with the daily routine. She also allocated a given amount of time to each specific chore, ruthlessly cutting corners with the less important ones for expediency's sake. Satisfied at last that she had made a semblance of sense out of what had previously been a hopeless muddle, she had copied her makeshift plan on a less grubby piece of paper and had hurried excitedly to show it to Cook, well pleased with herself and also vastly relieved. If the new routine was followed precisely the work could be accomplished in a more orderly and practical fashion, to the benefit of everyone.

To Emma's amazement Cook had not only been thunderstruck but had thrown a temperamental fit that was unprecedented, and had gone on to warn her, in the most dire terms, of Murgatroyd's most certain and deadly wrath at such unthinkable and unwarranted cheekiness, her plump red face clouded with worry and also alarm. Only then did Emma recognize the magnitude of what she was proposing and she had trembled at the thought of Murgatroyd's bellicose temper, his strident invectives and stinging blows.

But Mrs Turner had not reckoned with that streak of stubbornness in Emma, that implacable will. Almost at once, both of these characteristics overcame the girl's initial misgivings and she firmly resolved, in her doggedly wilful way, to be neither thwarted nor forestalled in her efforts to bring a little ease and orderliness to her work. As she listened impatiently to Mrs Turner's continued and overly ominous rantings, it occurred to Emma, now coldly calculating, that she could not permit herself to be deterred by Cook, whom she had just decided was a fool. She determined there and then that the only way to accomplish her purpose was to circumvent Murgatroyd altogether.

'I'm going upstairs ter show this plan of mine ter Mrs Wainright,' Emma had announced in a hard, firm voice, her face sternly set. 'We'll see what she has ter say about it all. She's already been planning them there menus since she's been here, and I bet she's going ter start running this house afore long. And about time somebody did!' she had finished defiantly, and, as was later proven, quite prophetically. Without another word to Cook she had turned and marched up the kitchen stairs, before her nerve failed her, leaving Cook aghast at her temerity. For a split second, the usually verbose Mrs Turner was rendered speechless, flabbergasted at this unexpected display of vociferous rebellion on the part of Emma.

She finally found her voice. 'Going up ter see Mrs W. won't be doing yer no good, lass,' she had cried vehemently as Emma continued to climb the stairs without looking back. 'Yer stepping out of yer station in life, my girl and that'll get yer nowt but the sack!' she continued as the door had banged loudly behind a silent and determined Emma.

Emma had barely spoken more than two words to Olivia Wainright in the short week she had been visiting at Fairley, and she had felt shy and awkward as she had tapped on the library door. At Olivia's bidding she had entered the room and had stood nervously in the doorway, hesitating, her hands clenched tightly at her sides, paralysed by unanticipated fright. Olivia Wainright was sitting behind Adam's desk, attending to the sadly neglected household accounts he had asked her to look into, and which previously had been handled by Murgatroyd. In her tailored dark serge skirt and white lace blouse, with its high neck and leg-of-mutton sleeves, she looked the epitome of aristocratic elegance. A large and exquisite cameo brooch relieved the severity of the high neckline and a long strand of rosy pearls gleamed lustrously against the guipure lace bodice, and there were matching pearl studs at her ears. Her dark hair was swept up into an elaborate pompadour and it gave her face a fragile appearance, like a lovely flower on a long and slender stem.

Emma, timorous and quaking, was rooted to the spot. She gazed at Olivia, mesmerized by her beauty, grace, and sophisticated stylishness, and as she had continued to stare in awe she became painfully conscious of her own old patched blue dress and the stained and greying striped pinny that had seen better days. She ran her hands down her rumpled skirt and across the creased pinafore in an effort to smooth out the wrinkles, but it was a vain effort. She had looked down at her old boots with their worn cracked uppers and then flushed with embarrassment, and she felt shame for the first time in her life. It was a shame that made her heart clench in a way she had not experienced before, and it filled her with the most intense feelings of inferiority and worthlessness, feelings she was not to forget as long as she lived. Emma knew that poverty was not a crime, even if the world treated it as such, yet she felt like a criminal as she hovered, shamefaced, anxious, and tongue-tied, on the edge of the luxurious carpet, acutely aware of the picture she made. Why should this rich and elegant lady take what she had to say seriously? she wondered.

But Emma, for all her intelligence and precocious perception, had no way of knowing that Olivia Wainright was an exceptional woman, understanding of heart and generous of spirit, who put great store in justice, fair play, and compassion, and was only too willing to help the deserving better themselves if they so desired. Nor did Emma realize that Olivia was not regarding her critically or with derision or the self-serving pity of the patronizing dogooder, but with enormous curiosity and a most genuine interest. Preoccupied as she had been with her sister's poor health and Adam's depressed state since her arrival, she had not as yet had time to delve into the domestic situation at the Hall. And whilst she had noticed the little maid flitting about the house, this was the first opportunity she had had to observe her so closely. From the moment Emma had entered the library Olivia had been struck by her refined good looks, which were not at all diminished or obscured by the disreputable uniform and the grimy cap that so dismayed Olivia, whose own servants were dressed attractively and decently, albeit in plain utilitarian attire. Returning Emma's steady gaze, she noticed that the girl's face and hair were scrupulously clean and she had an aura of neatness and grooming about her, in spite of that dreadful clothing, and this Olivia found commendable.

Emma meanwhile had taken a diffident step forward. Her boots creaked horribly in the quiet room, much to her mortification, and she stopped, abashed and self-conscious, a look of discomfiture on her face.

Olivia had paid no attention to the squeaking, if she heard it at all, and had smiled kindly and said in a gentle voice, 'What is it? Do you have a problem you wish to discuss with me?' Olivia Wainright had been blessed since girlhood with an extraordinary ability to make everyone, and especially servants, feel comfortable in her presence. This inherent quality quite obviously transmitted itself to Emma, who now approached the desk more confidently, praying her boots wouldn't squeak again. They did. Emma winced and cleared her throat loudly, hoping to counteract the sound. She stood in front of Olivia, swallowed hard, remembered to curtsy, and said with a kind of shaking firmness, 'Yes, I do have a problem, so ter speak, ma'am.'

'First, tell me your name, child,' said Olivia, smiling again.

'It's Emma, ma'am,' said Emma nervously.

'Well then, Emma, what is this problem you have? The only way we will solve it is to talk about it. Isn't that so?' asked Olivia.

Emma had nodded, and in a voice that was almost a whisper, she had explained the domestic routine, its basic difficulties, and her own problems of coping with them because of the poor organization. Olivia had listened patiently, a warm smile on her calm and lovely face, a thoughtful expression in her lucent blue eyes. But as Emma continued her doleful recital, Olivia had become quietly enraged, and her blood had boiled at the inequity of the situation and the execrable management of her brother-in-law's home, an establishment of some standing and enormous wealth, where matters should not have been allowed to deteriorate so disgracefully, as they most apparently had, and nearly beyond redemption from the sound of it.

When Emma had finished speaking, Olivia studied her intently, somewhat surprised by the girl's sweet and melodious voice and her concise explanation. This had been perfectly lucid, despite her limited vocabulary and her idiomatic speech

139

pattern, which fortunately was not so broad in dialect as Olivia had expected it to be. Olivia had instinctively perceived that the girl was neither exaggerating nor embellishing, and she knew she had listened to a veracious witness to the prevailing circumstances at the Hall, and she was shocked.

'Do you mean to tell me, Emma, that at this moment you are the only maid employed in this house?' Olivia had asked.

'Er, no, not exactly, ma'am,' Emma had replied quickly. 'There's a girl that sometimes helps Cook. And Polly. But she's still badly as I said afore. *She's* really the parlourmaid.'

'And since Polly's sickness you alone have been doing Polly's work as well as your own? Cleaning this entire house and looking after Mrs Fairley as well? Am I correct, Emma?'

'Yes, ma'am,' Emma said, shuffling her feet nervously.

'I see,' Olivia had responded quietly, and she was further outraged. Olivia Wainright was accustomed to order and tranquillity in her own homes, and being an able and proficient administrator of her London house, her country estate, and her business affairs, she was, not unnaturally, astounded at the preposterousness of conditions at Fairley. 'Inexcusable and utterly ridiculous,' murmured Olivia, almost to herself, straightening up in the chair.

Misunderstanding these words and detecting the edge of annoyance in Olivia Wainright's voice, Emma became alarmed. 'I'm not trying ter get out of owt I'm supposed ter do, ma'am,' said Emma, fearful that she might be dismissed for her boldness and presumption, which conceivably could be taken for shirking. 'I'm not afraid of hard work, I'm not that! It's just that Murgatroyd's got it – got it planned bad, ma'am.'

'So it would appear, from what you tell me, Emma,' Olivia had responded, the thoughtful expression lingering in her eyes. Emma looked at her carefully, and encouraged by the woman's outwardly tranquil appearance, she had finally pulled out the crumpled bit of paper and smoothed it out.

'I made this here plan, ma'am. Well, anyways, I think it'll be easier for me to do me chores this way. I worked it out proper like.' Emma stepped closer to the desk and handed Olivia the paper. As she did, Olivia noticed the girl's terribly chapped and sore hands and was appalled. She looked into the solemn face hovering before her and saw the dark smudges under her enormous eyes, became aware of the tired droop of the painfully thin shoulders, and she was so unexpectedly moved her heart ached with the most genuine sorrow. Olivia was seized with a sudden sense of shame for Adam, even though she was perfectly sure that he was not cognizant of the facts. She sighed and looked down at the grubby bit of paper. Olivia studied it carefully and was both newly amazed and impressed. The girl was obviously above average intelligence and most certainly had an efficient and practical turn of mind. The household routine had been worked out precisely and in an organized manner, and Olivia decided she herself could not have improved upon it.

'Well, Emma, I see exactly what you mean. Seemingly you devoted a lot of thought to this timetable and I must compliment you. Indeed I must.'

'Yer mean yer think it's more – more better my way?' asked Emma, relieved and not a little elated.

'More efficient, I believe you mean, Emma,' Olivia had responded suppressing

140

a smile. 'I think we should put your timetable into operation immediately, Emma. I certainly approve of it and I am confident Murgatroyd will recognize the sense of it as well,' she had said, pronouncing the butler's name with coldness. Observing the worried expression that flickered in Emma's eyes, she had added reassuringly, 'I will speak to him about it myself. I shall also instruct him to engage another girl from the village to assist you with the heavier work. It is still rather a lot for you to cope with single-handedly, Emma, in spite of your most practical timetable.'

'Yes, ma'am. Thank yer, ma'am,' said Emma, bobbing a curtsy and smiling for the first time in days.

'Well then, run along, Emma. And please tell Murgatroyd I wish to see him. At once,' said Olivia.

'Yes, ma'am. Please, ma'am, can I have my plan back? Me *timetable*, I mean. So as I knows what I'm doing.'

Olivia concealed another smile. 'Of course. Here it is. By the way, Emma, is that the only uniform you have?' asked Olivia.

Emma flushed and bit her lip and looked down at the crumpled dress and pinafore with dismay and great embarrassment. 'Yes, ma'am. For winter, that is. I've got a cotton one for summer,' Emma had mumbled self-consciously.

'We must rectify that at once. If you tell me your size I shall attend to it myself, when I go to Leeds later this week,' Olivia announced, and had added, 'I shall buy you several uniforms, for winter and summer, Emma. One of each is simply not enough.'

'Ooh! Thank yer, ma'am, ever so much!' cried Emma. A thought struck her and she had said respectfully, 'Begging yer pardon, Mrs Wainright, ma'am, but I could make 'em meself, if I had the cloth. Me mam taught me how ter sew, ever so good like.'

'Did she indeed? That's excellent. I shall ask the Squire for some lengths of cloth from the mill and I shall purchase the cotton for the summer uniforms in Leeds. You may go now, Emma, and incidentally, I am glad you came to see me with your problems. You must always do that, for as long as I am staying here at Fairley.'

'Yes, ma'am. Thank yer, ma'am. And I will come ter see yer if owt else bothers me,' Emma had promised. She bobbed a curtsy and hurried out of the library, clutching her timetable as if it were the crown jewels. She did not see the look of compassion mingled with admiration on Olivia Wainright's face; nor was she aware that she had set in motion a chain of events that were to change everybody's life at Fairley Hall.

There was no ugly uproar or altercation in the kitchen about Emma's unprecedented display of independence. Murgatroyd tactically ignored it, since it suited his own purpose admirably. In fact, he paid little attention to Emma's activities, and Emma knew this was because he was too preoccupied maintaining his own position in the household to care about her. Now that he was under the eagle eye of Mrs Wainright he had to watch his step and, undoubtedly, whatever she had said to him had been effective. Observing Murgatroyd out of the corner of her eye, as he scurried to and fro, bowed and scraped, and pulled his weight in the household for once, Emma would often smile to herself and there was both irony and a flicker of smugness in the smile that flitted across her young face. Emma had begun to comprehend that Murgatroyd had met his match in Olivia Wainright.

Gentle of manner though she was, Emma knew that the courteous demeanour disguised a strong will and an exacting but fair nature.

However, as the weeks passed, the timetable and Emma's rigid adherence to it had begun to amuse Cook, who had long forgotten her own objections to it. She had never witnessed anything like it in all her years of service. It sent her into gales of loud, though kindly, laughter. She would slap her pendulous thighs and shake her head and say, between gusting peals of mirth, 'Aye, lass, yer a rum 'un, yer are that. Whoever heard of a blinking timetable, 'cept at the railway station. And yer tek yerself so serious, yer do that, Emma lass. Yer run about this 'ere house like the Devil himself is after yer, slaving yer fingers ter the bone. And where's it all going ter get yer, when all's said and done? I'll tell yer summat, and yer should mark me words, lass. The more yer do in life, the less yer gets thought of. I knows, aye, that I do.'

At these raucous but genial outbursts, Emma would look at Cook with large eyes, but said nothing. She did not have time to explain her reasons. Time now meant money to Emma, and she would not waste her precious time chattering. And anyway, Emma was sure Cook would not understand. How could she know that the timetable was, in a sense, a kind of protection for her? It enabled her to work in a more efficient and orderly manner. She could ease the work load on various days and conserve her strength. Not only that, because of it, Emma was able to steal a little time for herself and this stolen time was of vital importance to her. Several afternoons a week, and early most evenings, she retreated to her attic room and worked on the dresses and other clothes she altered or repaired for Mrs Wainright and Mrs Fairley. She was paid separately for this work, at Olivia Wainright's insistence, and her little tobacco box of shillings and sixpences was slowly growing. Nothing was going to deter her from making this money, her own secret money, even if she had to occasionally skimp on some of her chores to make time for the sewing. It was with a grim determination that she sewed diligently into the middle of the night, by the light of three candles, her eyes scratchy, her fingertips sore, her shoulders aching as she hunched over the elaborate gowns and blouses and skirts and dresses and fine undergarments, plying her exquisite stitches. For the money she earned from this sewing was being acquired, most methodically and religiously, to finance Emma's Plan, which she always thought of with a capital *P*.

Cook knew about the sewing, but not about the late hours Emma kept, and had she known she would have been annoyed, for she was fond of the girl and had her welfare at heart. So Emma did not enlighten her about this either, preferring to keep her own counsel.

Although Mrs Turner was a woman with a degree of native shrewdness, she was not blessed with great intelligence or perception, and she did not understand Emma's character in the least. Nor did she have the foresight to recognize that the girl was displaying the first youthful glimmering of an amazing organizing ability that was to prove formidable; or that her punctuality, diligence, and unrelenting efficiency were the first outward signs of an immense self-discipline and the driving ambition that would grow to monstrous proportions, and which would prove to be the very roots of her success later.

At this moment in her life, Emma certainly did not understand this either, and the future was far from her mind as she remembered the events of the past few months whilst attending to the fire. She sighed softly. Those days had been bad days, but they had passed now. She visibly brightened. Things *had* improved. Her timetable worked successfully and her life was a lot easier. Mrs Wainright had kept her word and had hired another girl, Annie Stead, from the village, whom Emma was patiently, and sometimes vociferously, training as the betweenmaid. The domestic routine was running as smoothly as clockwork, so much so it was like a miracle and one that Emma prayed would last. But apart from this, and most importantly, Mrs Wainright had increased Emma's wages by two shillings a week, a welcome addition to the family income.

Emma lifted a large log with the tongs and dropped it on to the fire, which was now burning merrily and throwing off so much heat Emma's face was warm and flushed. She stood up, smoothed her pinafore, adjusted her dainty cap, and straightened her cuffs, for she took exceptional pride in her appearance ever since Blackie had told her she looked 'fetching' and was the prettiest colleen in the whole county of Yorkshire. She glanced around the sitting room and scowled. The thunderstorm had ceased as abruptly as it had begun, but the sky was still overcast and it filled the room with gloomy shadows. It's ever so dark in here, she said to herself, and turned up the lamps on the black lacquered chinoiserie tables flanking the fireplace. The room was immediately suffused with brighter light, warm and glowing, which counteracted the dismal atmosphere and the chilliness produced by the preponderance of blue furnishings.

Emma stepped back and regarded the mantelpiece, her head on one side, her eyes thoughtful as she appraised the objects aligned along the marble shelf. There were a pair of silver candlesticks, beautiful Georgian pieces holding white candles, an elaborate porcelain clock, supported in the paws of two lions rampant on either side, and which chimed like a tinkling bell on the half hour, and Dresden figurines of a lady and gentleman in old-fashioned dress. Emma, by herself, had rearranged all of these objects in a more harmonious way, as she had done with numerous other pieces elsewhere in the room. Sometimes she was sorely tempted to hide half of the bric-à-brac in various cupboards and drawers, since she considered it to be superfluous, but she did not dare go that far. Occasionally she wondered where she had found the courage to regroup most of it without permission, not that Mrs Fairley seemed to notice, or anyone else for that matter. She was still contemplating the mantelpiece, congratulating herself on the attractive effect she had created, when a slight rustling sound caught her attention. She turned swiftly to see Adele Fairley standing in the doorway of her adjoining bedroom.

'Oh, Mrs Fairley! Good morning, ma'am,' Emma said, and dropped a curtsy. Although the Squire had told her weeks ago not to curtsy to him, because it annoyed him, Emma felt obliged to do so in the presence of her mistress and Mrs Wainright.

Adele nodded and smiled weakly, and then she seemed to sway and stagger, as if she was ill, and she clutched at the door jamb to steady herself, and closed her eyes.

Emma rushed across the room to her side. 'Mrs Fairley, are yer all right? Do yer feel badly?' Emma inquired solicitously, taking her arm.

Adele opened her eyes. 'I felt faint for a moment. But it's nothing. I didn't sleep very well.'

Emma scrutinized her through narrowed eyes. Mrs Fairley looked paler than ever, and her hair, normally so beautifully groomed, was uncombed and she looked dishevelled, which was also unusual. Emma noticed that Adele's eyes were red and swollen.

'Come ter the fire and get yerself warm, ma'am, and have some of this nice hot tea,' Emma said sympathetically, and led her firmly across the floor. Adele, swaying and leaning heavily on Emma, drifted into the room on a cloud of Jasmine scent that was momentarily overpowering, her silvered robe dragging limply behind her.

Emma settled her in the wing chair, glanced at her anxiously, and said briskly, 'I made scrambled eggs for yer this morning, Mrs Fairley. I knows yer enjoys 'em, and yer didn't eat much of yer dinner last night, I noticed.' As she spoke she removed the lid from the silver dish and pushed it forward, drawing her mistress's attention to it.

Adele Fairley brought her distant gaze from the fire and looked at the eggs without interest, an absent expression on her face as pale as death. 'Thank you, Polly,' she said, and her voice was listless and without any emotion. She lifted her head slowly and stared at Emma, a puzzled expression flickering on to her face. She blinked in bewilderment and shook her head. 'Oh, it's you, Emma. Of course, I'd forgotten, Polly is sick. Is she any better? When is she coming back to work?'

Emma was so completely unnerved by these remarks she stepped back involuntarily and stared with disbelief at Adele, her eyes widening, the silver lid in her hand poised in mid-air. In an effort to disguise her alarm, she plopped the lid back on the dish with a loud clatter and cleared her throat nervously. And then she said in a voice that quivered, 'But, Mrs Fairley, don't yer remember?' She paused and gulped and continued tremulously, 'Polly's – Polly's –' She stopped again and then blurted out quickly, 'Polly's dead, Mrs Fairley. She died last week and they buried her on Thursday –' Her voice, so low now it was almost a whisper, trailed off, as she stared at Adele with growing disquietude.

Adele Fairley passed her hand over her brow wearily and covered her eyes and then, after a second, she forced herself to look directly at Emma. 'Yes, I do remember, Emma. Forgive me. These headaches, you know. They are quite dreadful and leave me utterly exhausted. Sometimes I am inclined to be forgetful, I am afraid. Oh dear! Yes, poor Polly. So young.' Adele's face, only briefly lucid, glazed over and she turned to the fire in a trance.

Emma, who had grown accustomed to Adele's chronic absentmindedness, was, nevertheless, appalled at this particular lapse of memory, which was shocking to her, and unforgivable. How could Mrs Fairley forget someone's death so quickly and apparently with such ease? Emma asked herself, horrified. Especially Polly, who had worked like a little Trojan for her for five years, and had been devoted. Until this moment Emma had, for the most part, been able to excuse Adele's heedless indifference to the troubled lives of others, ascribing it to her pampered life and her unrealistic and even childish view of the world. But this incident she found hard to overlook. Emma did not attempt to conceal the contemptuous expression that slid on to her face and her mouth tightened into a stern and unyielding line. Why, she's no different from the rest, she thought condemningly. They're all the same, the rich.

Emma looked at Adele staring so unconcernedly into the fire and she was outraged and also disgusted, and it occurred to her that Adele was not only shallow and selfish but heartless. In Emma's opinion, even Adele's gentleness no longer seemed a redeeming characteristic. But after a long moment, Emma pushed the

144

anger down, controlling it with steely determination until it was finally quelled into partial submission, for she knew it was a wasted emotion. Emma also knew that it was ridiculous to dwell on the natures of the gentry. Where would that get the likes of her in the long run? What would it achieve? Nothing! Neither could she afford to squander her valuable time trying to understand the rich, whose ways were so mysterious to her. She needed her time and energy to make things easier for her mam and dad and Frankie, who was only just recovering from the whooping cough.

Emma began to busy herself around the Queen Anne tea table, concealing her feelings behind a show of efficiency, her composure restored to its usual quiet containment, her face so inscrutable it was like pale stone. But as she poured the tea, buttered the toast, and served the eggs, Emma kept seeing Polly's pathetically dwindled face and her dark eyes burning feverishly in their hollow sockets and her heart lurched with a terrible sadness, and the pity she had felt for Adele only a short while before was diluted.

'Eat this afore it gets cold, Mrs Fairley,' said Emma stonily.

Adele looked up at Emma with her silvery eyes and smiled her deliquescent smile, that melting smile that lighted up her face, and it was as if the conversation about Polly had never taken place at all. Tranquillity dwelt in her face and her eyes were clear and comprehending.

'Thank you, Emma. I am a little hungry. And I must say, you do take good care of me.' She sipped the tea and went on chattily, 'How is your mother, Emma? Is she still improving in health?'

So sudden and incredible was the change in Adele that Emma stared at her in puzzlement. And then she said quickly, 'Yes, ma'am, thank yer. She's not half as badly as she was, being as the weather's improved, and it's easier on me dad now that he's working down at yon mill.'

Adele inclined her head. 'The eggs are good, Emma,' she said, finishing a forkful.

Emma understood that the brief moment of friendly discourse was over and she reached into her pocket and fished around for the menu for dinner, which Cook had given to her. Although Adele had long ago relinquished her control of the household affairs to Murgatroyd, and more recently to her sister, Cook persisted in sending up the menus daily for her approval. Mrs Turner had worked for Adele since she had come to Fairley as Adam's bride and she was always deferential to Adele, and would brook no interference with this ritual of the menus, and made no bones about the fact that, to her way of thinking, Mrs Fairley was still the mistress of Fairley Hall, and nobody else. And so she treated her as such and with the utmost consideration and respect. It never occurred to the loyal Mrs Turner that Adele paid little attention to the menus, nor did it seem to disturb her that no comment, favourable or otherwise, was ever forthcoming.

Emma pulled the menu from her pocket and held it out to Adele. 'Cook says will yer please look over this here menu for dinner, Mrs Fairley,' she said.

Adele made a little moue and laughed lightly. 'I can't be bothered with that this morning, Emma. You know very well I trust Mrs Hardcastle to plan suitable menus and she always does. I am quite sure today is no exception.'

Emma shifted on her feet nervously, the paper fluttering in her hand. She gave Adele a curious look. What's wrong with Mrs Fairley? she asked herself, her heart pounding unreasonably. She's worse this morning than she's ever been. Emma bit her lip, as a most disturbing thought struck her. Was Mrs Fairley touched? It had not occurred to her before that the rich could be daft in the head. She had always thought that such a terrible affliction was the prerogative of the poor, but perhaps she was wrong. And Mrs Fairley was acting so peculiar it was enough to make anybody wonder. First she had forgotten Polly was dead, and now she was talking about Mrs Hardcastle as if she didn't know she had been relieved of her duties as housekeeper weeks ago.

Emma hesitated, uncertain how to respond. Mrs Fairley might be offended if she kept referring to her forgetfulness. So she said slowly, choosing her words with care, 'Didn't I tell yer afore, Mrs Fairley, that Mrs Hardcastle left? It must've slipped me mind. It was when yer were badly in bed. Mrs Wainright gave her the sack. She said Mrs Hardcastle had a bad habit of tekking a holiday when it wasn't no holiday.'

Adele stared down at the breakfast tray. Of course! Olivia had sent Hardcastle packing in a flurry of disfavour. Olivia had stood here in this very room and told her she had let Hardcastle go. She had been infuriated at her sister's presumption, but she had been unable to countermand her orders. She had been too ill, and anyway Adam had backed Olivia to the hilt and it would have been useless to oppose them. Now she must watch herself. Pay more attention to the things she said, even to Emma, otherwise the girl might become suspicious of her, just as Olivia and Adam were suspicious. Yes, she must be more careful. She lifted her head and smiled warmly, her face a picture of innocence.

There was a clever and deadly cunning in Adele. She had the uncanny ability to dissimulate, and to disguise her bizarre foibles when she so chose, slipping easily behind a façade that simulated rationality, and her behaviour at times could appear very normal, as it did now.

'Perhaps you told me, Emma. I know Mrs Wainright mentioned it. But I *was* very sick and so worried about Master Edwin at the time, and it obviously did not register. Well, let us not worry about that now. And let me see the menu.' She held out her hand and took the paper. She gave it only a cursory glance, as always, and handed it back to Emma.

'Excellent! A repast for royalty, I would say,' declared Adele smilingly. And for once, she added, 'Give Cook my compliments and tell her she has outdone herself, Emma.'

'Yes, ma'am,' said Emma, replacing the menu in her pocket, tactfully not bothering to point out that it was not Cook who had planned the menu but Olivia Wainright. 'Here's the *Gazette*, Mrs Fairley,' Emma went on, passing the newspaper to her mistress. 'I'll go and do the bedroom now,' she finished, bobbing a small curtsy.

'Thank you, Emma. And when you have finished you can draw my bath, so that I can bathe and dress after breakfast.'

'Yes, ma'am,' Emma said, and hurried into the bedroom.

Emma stifled a cry of amazement when she entered the room and saw the clothes Adele had pulled out of the wardrobe strewn all over the floor in chaotic heaps. She clamped her hand over her mouth, horror-struck, and stood perfectly still, glaring at the dresses and gowns and robes and other beautiful garments lying in tangled disarray. Whatever's got in ter her? she muttered under her breath, gaping at the clothes incredulously, and then added inwardly: She might not be touched, but she's acting as daft as a brush, she is that! As she stepped carefully around the clothes, a feeling of anger mingled with acute frustration made a tight knot in Emma's stomach. She realized furiously it would take her some time to bring order to the clothes and return them to the wardrobe and their former neatness. Her timetable would really be ruined now! Methodically she began picking them up, slipping each garment on to a coat hanger and placing it in the wardrobe, working with efficiency and her usual swiftness, in a concentrated effort to save as much of her precious time as possible.

Meanwhile, Adele continued to peck at her breakfast delicately and after a few mouthfuls she pushed the plate away, feeling revolted by the food. She shook her head violently from side to side, as if to clear it of cobwebs. As she did, she told herself she must try to be more alert and cease her perpetual daydreaming; otherwise she would never reinstate herself as mistress of the house. She would ring for Murgatroyd later, who at least recognized her authority, and order him to bring her the whisky.

There was a sharp knock on the door and it was flung open with a certain abruptness. Engrossed as she was in her musings about the butler, Adele half expected to see Murgatroyd standing there, and she opened her eyes, sat up smartly, and turned to the door, smiling her melting smile, ready to greet the butler. She was therefore astonished to meet the cool and contemplative gaze of her husband. The smile congealed and she froze in the chair. He rarely came to her room.

Adam noticed her fearful reaction and, although it dismayed him, he wisely disregarded it.

'Good morning, Adele. I trust you slept well,' he said.

Adele looked at him carefully, filled with antagonism and the most virulent resentment. In her present disturbed state of mind, feelings of fear and doubt were paramount within her, and she viewed everything he said and did with unwarranted mistrust. Consequently, she had become guarded with him.

Finally she spoke. 'No, I did not sleep very well,' she said coldly.

'I'm sorry to hear that, my dear. Perhaps you can take a rest this afternoon,' he suggested kindly.

'Perhaps,' said Adele, looking at him in stupefaction and with some consternation, wondering what had precipitated this unexpected visit.

Adam remained standing in the doorway, leaning against it with his usual inbred elegance. He had not crossed the threshold of this room in ten long years and he had no intention of doing so ever again. It had always appalled and embarrassed him, with its clutter and frigid blueness and delicacy and overriding femininity. Now it sickened him.

Of late, conversations with Adele were extraordinarily painful to Adam. He always started out with the kindest of intentions, but she invariably managed to brush him the wrong way, and he found himself growing irritated with her, and increasingly impatient. He was therefore anxious to conclude what he had come to say as peaceably and as swiftly as possible, and so he said quickly, 'I want to talk to you about Edwin, Adele.' He eyed her warily, for he fully recognized he was embarking on a sensitive subject.

She sat bolt upright in the chair and clutched the arms. 'What about him?' she cried, her eyes flaring with apprehension. Edwin was her favourite, and she adored him.

147

Conscious of her growing alarm, he said gently, 'It's time he went back to boarding school, wouldn't you say? Even though it is almost half term, I think he should return immediately. I would like him to have the next couple of weeks catching up with his studies. He has quite a lot of ground to cover, you know. After all, he has been at home since Christmas. Far too long, in my opinion.'

'It's perfectly ridiculous to send him back now, it's hardly worth it! He can return after Easter!' cried Adele with growing perturbation. She paused and took several deep breaths to steady herself. 'Anyway, he's still in delicate health, Adam,' she added, adopting a more cajoling tone and giving him the benefit of her sweetest smile that no longer made any impression on him.

'Nonsense!' admonished Adam firmly. 'His health is fine. He's a robust boy and he has quite recovered from the pneumonia. You pamper Edwin, Adele. It's not good for him. And however well-intentioned your motives are, you are smothering him. He should be with boys of his own age, in more disciplined and rigorous surroundings. You treat him like a baby.'

'I do not!' exclaimed Adele defensively, her voice rising to a shriek, and the smouldering resentment against her husband turned into instant hatred.

'I have no intention of quarrelling with you about this matter, Adele,' said Adam icily. 'I have quite made up my mind and nothing will persuade me to change it, most particularly your abnormal desire to cling to the boy. I have also spoken to Edwin and he wishes to return to school as soon as possible.'

Adam looked at Adele pointedly. 'At least *he* sees the sense of it. And I must say, he has been most diligent under the circumstances, trying to continue his studies on his own. But that's hardly good enough for me, Adele.' Adam cleared his throat and softened his tone. 'You must consider Edwin, my dear. He misses school and his friends, which is only natural. And so' – Adam hesitated and then went on softly – 'and so, I came to inform you that I intend to drive him to Worksop myself. Tomorrow.'

Adele smothered a small gasp. So soon, she thought, and tears sprang into her eyes. She turned her head so Adam would not see. Her hand shook as she brushed away the tears surreptitiously. Adam was doing this to thwart her. It was not for Edwin's sake at all. He was jealous that Edwin preferred to stay at home with her. She had a sudden physical compulsion to jump up and fly at him with her hands, to strike him, to tell him he was cruelly taking away the only person who loved her and whom she loved.

But she looked back at Adam and at once saw the implacability etched across his sternly handsome face and she knew then, with a sinking feeling, that she would not achieve anything by fighting him. He was inexorable. 'Very well, Adam, whatever you say,' said Adele, her voice still quavering and filled with incipient tears. Gathering a little more strength, she continued, 'But I wish you to know that I am only agreeing to this – this – ridiculous decision of yours because you say Edwin himself has expressed a desire to return to school. Although I am not so sure he's such a reliable judge of his fitness to return so quickly. Personally, I think it's preposterous when half term is imminent. He'll hardly get there before it's time for him to come home. All that travelling back and forth is debilitating, especially to a little boy who has been so sick. I think you are very hard on Edwin, Adam. I really do.'

Adam could not resist the impulse of retorting caustically, 'Edwin's no longer a little boy. Furthermore, I don't want him growing up to be a sissy, Adele, and he will if he remains tied to his mother's apron strings. You've always tended to spoil and pamper him, and it's a miracle that he's turned out so well. So far.'

Adele gasped and her pale face flushed with deep colour. 'You are most unfair, Adam. Edwin's never been tied to my apron strings, as you so vulgarly put it. How could he have been? You sent him away to school when he was only –' Her voice was so filled with emotion she could not continue, but after a moment she went on tearfully, 'Only twelve. And if I've spoiled him a little it's simply because he is sensitive and has always been put upon by Gerald.'

Adam stared at her, taken aback, and then he smiled sardonically. 'Well, well, my dear, you are more observant than I believed you to be. I am glad to know you realize Gerald hectors him incessantly and behaves most churlishly towards poor Edwin. That's another reason I want him out of this house – to remove him from his brother's taunting. He will be much happier at school, until he's old enough to defend himself on Gerald's level. Although personally I hope he'll rise above it. Not a very admirable offspring, our eldest son,' he finished softly, but with enormous scorn.

This comment went over Adele's head. A weary look settled on her face. She sighed deeply, and passed her hand over her brow. A rising feeling of nausea was making her dizzy and she fervently wished Adam would go away and leave her in peace. This effort to maintain her sense of balance and appear coherent was sapping what little vitality she had left. She felt enervated. 'The matter is settled then, Adam,' said Adele quietly, fighting the pressing need to retreat into her inner world where nothing could touch her. 'I have a splitting headache,' she whined, 'and I'm sure you have other urgent matters to attend to yourself.'

'Yes, I have.' He scrutinized her thoughtfully, and a strange sadness enveloped him. There was sympathy in his voice as he said, 'I hope you feel better, my dear. I am sorry this conversation has been painful for you, but you know I am only thinking of Edwin.'

Considering the conversation to be concluded, Adam inclined his head courteously and turned on his heel. Something made him pause and he looked back at her frowning, suddenly conscious of the obscure expression in her eyes, the glassy sheen coating her face.

'I can assume that you will be well enough to grace us with your company at dinner this evening, can't I? You know we are expecting guests,' said Adam.

She sat up startled. 'Tonight!'

'Yes, tonight. Don't tell me you have forgotten the dinner party Olivia has planned for Bruce McGill, the Australian sheep rancher. She mentioned it to you earlier in the week,' Adam said sharply, holding his irritation in check.

'But that is on Saturday, Adam. Olivia told me it was Saturday. I know she did. I wouldn't make a mistake like that,' she cried peevishly.

Oh, wouldn't you, Adam thought, and stared at her with coldness. 'Today *is* Saturday, Adele.'

Flustered, she touched her forehead nervously. 'Of course. How silly of me,' she murmured hurriedly. 'Yes, I am sure I will feel well enough to come down for dinner.'

'Good.' He half smiled. 'Please excuse me, Adele. I have to see Wilson at the mill, and then I am going into Leeds. I look forward to seeing you this evening, my dear.'

'Yes, Adam,' Adele said, and fell back into the chair, feeling faint, and also great alarm at the prospect of facing people, and in particular a stranger.

Adam closed the door softly behind him. He was considerably surprised. It was a major achievement for him to have wrested Edwin from her clinging hands with so little opposition. In a way, even her momentary show of spirit had been a relief to him. Usually her entreaties to keep Edwin at her side were accompanied by floods of tears, vapourish swoonings, and the most irrational display of hysterics that he always found himself incapable of dealing with. The scenes in the past had been insupportable and had mortified him.

Emma, working in the bedroom, had not been able to avoid overhearing this conversation, even though she never consciously eavesdropped, as the other servants often did. She finished making the bed and pursed her lips and thought: Poor woman. He's such a bully, and so mean ter her. Like he is ter everybody.

Although Emma's hatred for Adam Fairley was unreasonable and without any foundation, it was quite real. So was her enormous dislike for Gerald, who never lost an opportunity to torment her. But she held no grudge against Edwin, who was always sweet with her, and she did respect Olivia Wainright. Now she wondered if she had been uncharitable about Mrs Fairley earlier, and she paused, clutching a silk pillow to her chest, and thought hard about this. Perhaps it's him that makes her act queer, she said to herself. He gets her ever so flustered and upset. Maybe that's why she's always forgetting stuff and things, and walks around in a flipping daze. Emma replaced the silk pillow, smoothed it over, and pulled up the eau-de-Nil green coverlet made of heavy satin, her mind still lingering on Adele Fairley's strange ways. A rush of sympathy for Adele flowed through her and quenched the feelings of anger mixed with animosity she had been harbouring, and for some reason, quite unknown to herself, Emma felt decidedly happier about this change of heart.

Emma was dusting the Venetian glass-and-mirrored dressing table in front of the oriel window, humming to herself, when Adele walked into the room. Her face was tense with concern and her cheekbones stood out starkly, sharp ridges under her eyes, which were clouded with misery. Her anxiety about the impending dinner party had forced her to push aside both the desperate desire to retreat into herself and her longing for the soothing whisky. In his present unrelenting mood, Adam struck terror in her heart, and it was imperative that she made an appearance that evening and behaved with decorum and dignity. Whatever it cost her in effort, she must be controlled and at ease and charming, and no one must have the slightest inkling of her emotional turmoil.

Then the cunning in Adele surfaced and she smiled to herself. She had a card up her sleeve and it was always a winning card. Her beauty. Adele knew that her incredible looks never failed to stun people. So much so that their attention was deflected from the idiosyncrasies of her personality, which otherwise might be quickly detected. She decided she must look absolutely breathtaking at the dinner. She would hide behind the façade of her beauty.

She hurried to the wardrobe, which Emma had just restored to order, and opened the huge double doors impatiently. Emma's heart sank into her boots. She had an instant picture of Adele scattering the clothes all over the room again, and she looked up and said quickly, 'I put all yer clothes away, proper like, Mrs Fairley. Is there summat yer looking for? Summat in particular like?' Startled, Adele turned

150

around abruptly. She had forgotten Emma was in the bedroom. 'Oh! Emma. Yes. I am wondering what to wear for the dinner party tonight. Quite important people have been invited, you know.' She rustled through the gowns and went on in a querulous tone, 'You will be here to help me dress, won't you, Emma? You know I can't possibly manage without you.'

'Yes, ma'am. Mrs Wainright asked me ter work over the weekend,'stead of having me time off as usual, 'cos of the dinner,' said Emma quietly.

'Thank goodness!' Adele cried with relief, and continued her search for an appropriate gown. The fact that Emma had been forced to forgo her weekend at home with her family failed to register or make the slightest impression on Adele. She was only concerned with herself. Finally her hands lighted on a gown and she pulled it out, holding it up to show Emma. Lately, Adele had found it difficult to make decisions without conferring with Emma, and she now elicited her advice about the dress she was holding.

'Do you think this is beautiful enough?' she asked, pressing the gown against her body. 'I must look my best tonight – outstanding, in fact.'

Emma moved away from the dressing table and stood in front of Adele. She cocked her head on one side and screwed up her eyes, looking at the dress carefully and critically. She knew the gown was expensive and that it had come from Worth. Mrs Fairley had told her that before. And it was beautiful, all rippling white satin and delicate lace. Yet Emma did not really like it. She thought it was too fussy and not at all flattering to Mrs Fairley.

After a few moments' thoughtful consideration, Emma said, 'Well, it is beautiful, ma'am. But I think it's a bit – a bit pale for yer, if yer don't mind me saying so. Yes, that's it, Mrs Fairley. It makes yer look ever so washed out, so ter speak, next ter yer pale skin and with yer blonde hair.'

The pleasant expression on Adele's face dissolved and she glared at Emma. 'But what will I wear? This is a new gown, Emma. I have nothing else that is at all appropriate.'

Emma smiled faintly. There must be at least a hundred gowns Adele could choose from and all of them very beautiful.

'What yer need is summat more – more –' Emma paused, searching her mind for a word. She thought of the illustrated magazines she had read that showed photographs of the latest fashions, and the word she needed instantly flashed into her mind. 'Yer need summat more *elegant*, that'll make heads turn. Yes, that's it, Mrs Fairley, and I knows just the right dress.' She ran to the wardrobe and pulled out a gown made of black velvet. It was the ideal colour to show off Adele's beautiful ivory complexion and the lustrous silvery-gold hair. Then Emma frowned as she looked at it again. It was trimmed with blood-red roses that swathed one shoulder and fell down the side of the gown in a long trail.

'This is the one,' she exclaimed with absolute sureness, and added, 'If I tek them there roses off.'

Adele stared at her in horror and disbelief. 'Remove the roses! You can't possibly do that. You'll ruin the dress. And anyway, without the roses it will look too drab.'

'No, it won't, Mrs Fairley, ma'am. Honest, it won't. It'll look more *elegant*. It will. I just knows it will. And yer can wear that luvely necklet, the sparkling one, and them there earbobs. And I'll put yer hair up in that pompadour style I copied

151

for yer, from the picture in the magazine yer showed me last week. Oh, yer'll look ever so luvely in this dress, Mrs Fairley, yer will really.'

Adele seemed doubtful and sat down heavily on the green satin chaise, frowning and biting her lip. Emma flew to the dressing table, picked up a pair of nail scissors, and, undeterred by Adele's cry of protest, she expertly cut the stitches holding the roses in place.

'Look, now it's really *elegant*, Mrs Fairley,' exclaimed Emma excitedly, pulling off the roses unceremoniously. She held up the gown with a triumphant flourish.

Adele was furious. 'You've ruined it!' she gasped, her voice shrill. 'And it *is* drab! Just as I said it would be.' For once she was angry with Emma and her eyes blazed.

'It won't be drab when yer gets it on, and with yer beautiful jewels,' Emma said firmly, ignoring the small burst of anger. 'And if yer wants, I'll sew them blinking roses back on later. But first we'll try it this way, Mrs Fairley. Please,' she pleaded.

Adele was silent, her face like a thundercloud, and she gave Emma a petulant look as she twisted her hands nervously together in her lap.

'I can put them roses back on in two shakes of a lamb's tail, when I helps yer ter get ready. So don't worry about it, Mrs Fairley,' said Emma reassuringly.

'Well – all right,' said Adele reluctantly, somewhat pacified, although still pouting.

Emma smiled confidently. 'I'll pop it back in the wardrobe for now. Don't worry, Mrs Fairley, yer'll look luvely tonight, yer will that. I promise. Now I'll go and draw yer bath for yer, ma'am.'

'Thank you, Emma,' said Adele dully, still worrying about the dinner. Emma returned the gown to the wardrobe and hurried into the bathroom.

Adele went to her dressing table and took out the red velvet case that contained her diamond necklace, bracelets, and matching earrings. She lifted out the necklace and held it up to her throat. Its shimmering brilliance caused her to draw in her breath in surprise. She had forgotten how magnificent it was and, now that she thought about it, the black velvet gown would set it off perfectly. Perhaps Emma had been right, after all, in her choice. Adele smiled with delight. She would look so ravishing tonight even Adam would be speechless.

FIFTEEN

Later that day, when Emma finished her general chores, she returned to the upstairs sitting room with afternoon tea for Adele Fairley. Adele had declined to come down for lunch, claiming a headache and fatigue, and so Emma had taken great care with the tea, being determined to make Mrs Fairley eat something to keep up her strength for the important evening that lay ahead. Having overheard the conversation between Adele and Adam, and later witnessing Adele's concern over her gown, Emma had intuitively sensed her apprehension about the dinner party. She felt protective of Adele, now that her sympathetic feelings were restored, and she wanted to assuage Adele's nervousness as best she could. Pampering her a little was the only way Emma knew how to do this.

152

For these reasons, even though she was more overworked than usual because of the dinner party, Emma had painstakingly prepared some of the things Adele enjoyed for tea, hoping to tempt her jaded appetite. There were tiny cucumber sandwiches and others filled with egg, cream crackers spread with shrimp paste, hot buttered scones, home-made cherry jam, Cook's delicious shortbread biscuits and Eccles cakes. She had also made a huge pot of the tea Mrs Fairley preferred, although Emma didn't know how she could drink it. To Emma it tasted funny, like smoky water, and not at all like real tea, even if it was expensive and was specially ordered from Fortnum and Mason in London. But there was no accounting for the tastes of the rich, Emma decided, as she trudged up the staircase with the tea tray. They ate and drank the strangest things, to her way of thinking. She liked good plain food herself, and didn't hold with fancy dishes and rich sauces and peculiar delicacies, which never tempted her. She also believed the gentry ate too many meals with too many courses. To Emma it was disgusting the way they gorged themselves gluttonously like ravenous pigs. No wonder they suffered from indigestion and were liverish and bad-tempered. It was all that food and drink that did it. Even when I make me fortune, I'll still eat simple, she commented to herself as she went into Mrs Fairley's suite of rooms.

Adele had been resting all afternoon. She was still lying in the great four-poster bed, propped up against the pile of pale green pillows, reading the *Yorkshire Morning Gazette*, when Emma entered the room and carried the tray over to the bed. Adele looked up from the newspaper and smiled sweetly.

'I'm glad you suggested I take a rest,' said Adele, adjusting her position against the pillows. 'I slept for quite a long time and I do feel more rested and refreshed for tonight, just as you said I would, Emma.' She smiled again and there was a hint of gratitude in her eyes.

Emma stared at Adele intently. The tense lines that had etched her mouth with anxiousness that morning had vanished. Her face was relaxed and calm, and her eyes were so clear and bright they were almost merry. Even the badly swollen lids had lost their red puffiness and the deathly pallor had been replaced by a delicate glow that perfectly reflected the pale pink satin nightgown she wore.

Why, she looks ever so beautiful, Emma thought, and said, 'I've brought yer summat ter eat, Mrs Fairley. Yer must be right famished, seeing as how yer didn't have owt since breakfast. Try and get summat down yer, even if it's only a few mouthfuls.' She placed the tray next to Adele on the bed and continued, 'I even made that funny tea yer like.'

Adele laughed and for once there was gaiety in her voice. 'You mean the Lapsang Souchong, Emma. Thank you.'

'Yes, that's it. Lapsang Souchong –' Emma repeated slowly, and hesitated. Then she said questioningly, 'Do I say it proper like, ma'am?'

'You do indeed,' asserted Adele, somewhat amused, as she poured a cup for herself.

Emma smiled slightly. She liked to learn things, for future reference. She would need to know a lot when she went to Leeds to make her fortune. Now she cleared her throat and said, 'Begging yer pardon, Mrs Fairley, but I'd like ter look at yer dress again, if yer don't mind. I wants ter be sure that there's nowt wrong with it. That there's nowt that needs fixing. I wants it ter be perfect for the dinner. Will I be in yer way?'

'Of course not, Emma. And if it does need anything done to it, you may stay here and work. You don't have to go up to your room. But I'm sure it's not damaged. I've hardly worn it, you know,' said Adele.

Whilst Adele had her tea, Emma took out the black velvet gown and examined it minutely for any defects. It was in beautiful condition, except for a loose hook and a few torn stitches on the hemline of the train where Mrs Fairley had obviously caught her heel. Emma also noticed there were lots of dangling threads visible down the side of the gown, where she had cut off the roses. She would have to pull the threads out gently, she realized, in order not to damage the expensive black velvet.

Emma carried the gown to the chaise and began to work on it with great care, for she was a perfectionist and gave every task her undivided attention. She was glad to sit down for a while. She had been run off her feet all day and she was facing a long and arduous evening, since she was to help Murgatroyd serve the dinner. She relaxed as she worked and the tiredness she had been experiencing earlier gradually began to evaporate.

A certain kind of compatibility had developed between Emma and Mrs Fairley in the last few months. Disparate as they were in background and age, they were curiously at ease with each other, and although this understanding was unexpressed, it was, none the less, valid. The girl intuitively sensed the older woman's terrible anguish, and despite her youth and inexperience, she recognized the tragedy of Adele's life. Quite automatically and without much forethought, Emma knew how to behave properly around her and without underscoring or feeding Adele's extreme anxiety in any way. On her part, Adele had grown to like Emma, whom she found patient, kind, and unobtrusive when she worked in the suite of rooms. Adele also thought Emma was pretty and this pleased her, for she could not abide ugliness. And so an aura of peace enveloped them as they sat together in the room, the young girl passively sewing, the older woman partaking of her afternoon tea.

The bedroom was filled with the mellowest of lights that flooded through the tall windows, and the fire crackled and blazed in the grate, giving off a cheery glow that was both warming and comforting. The pale watery apple-green silk that covered the walls, swathed the windows, and fell down in rippling cascades from the four corners of the carved oak bed created a cool and restful effect, one that gave Emma a sense of tranquillity and, since the bedroom was not as cluttered with bric-à-brac as the adjoining sitting room, she also found it less overpowering and irritating to be in.

And it was certainly more restful than the kitchen she had just left, which was full of hot bustle, flying tempers, and all manner of frantic goings-on. Annie, the betweenmaid, was assisting Cook with the preparation of the food for the dinner, which was such an elaborate meal even Annie's mother had been engaged to help out for the evening. Mrs Wainright had planned a wonderful menu, they all agreed on that, even though Cook kept grumbling that things were getting a little too fancy for her liking. Emma suspected that Mrs Turner's little tantrums, temperamental outbursts, and complaining sprang from her extreme nervousness about coping with such an intricate meal. Although Mrs Turner always claimed that good solid Yorkshire cooking was her great speciality, Emma had long comprehended that it was her entire repertoire.

As she pulled out the threads, Emma thought about that menu and laughed to herself quietly, as she recalled Mrs Turner's face when she had read it that morning. Her eyes had stood out on stalks and she had huffed and puffed for a full hour. She could just imagine her flustered rantings and ravings downstairs right now. Poor Cook had never prepared a dinner quite like this in all her years at Fairley. The guests were first to be served chilled caviar garnished with chopped hard-boiled eggs, chopped raw onions, and wedges of lemon with melba toast. After that came the lobster soufflé with a lobster sauce, followed by turtle soup flavoured with sherry. 'Not too much sherry,' Mrs Wainright had warned, 'just the right amount to add a dash of piquancy.' Then there would be Dover sole cooked in a creamy white wine sauce containing slices of mushrooms and shallots. The main course was roast beef with horseradish sauce, potatoes roasted in the pan with the meat, carrots and peas, and a thick gravy made of the juices from the beef. There was to be a cheese board of Stilton, Cheshire, and Wensleydale cheeses with a selection of crackers and digestive biscuits. Finally, three desserts would be served as a finale to the meal, which Cook kept referring to as 'a blinking banquet'. These were a compote of mixed fruits, made from Cook's pantry supplies bottled last summer, and currently soaking in Kirsch, a fresh lemon pie with thick whipped cream, and a chocolate mousse, which Mrs Wainright had said must be light and fluffy to be really perfect.

Emma knew that some of these dishes had definitely strained Cook's talents, which had never been put to such a test, and, in fact, Emma herself had been pressed into hurried service earlier. She had made the soup and the sauces for the fish and meat dishes, prepared the mousse, and covered the fruit compote with the liqueur, scrupulously following Mrs Wainright's instructions.

Emma was decidedly happy to have escaped for a while. The hubbub had increased with great rapidity in the last hour and Cook was so harassed she was getting truculent with the maids, and Annie's mother as well. Emma smiled again. She knew only too well how easily rattled Cook became when there was any change in the kitchen routine. Not only that, this was the first big dinner party the Squire had given in several years and it had sent everyone into a flurry, except Mrs Wainright. And me, Emma thought then, preening a little inside, remembering Mrs Wainright's compliments about her cool head, her efficiency, and her light hand with the sauces and the mousse.

Although she had no taste for rich and elaborate dishes herself, Emma liked cooking and had begun to find it a challenge to prepare interesting meals. With Olivia's arrival, the menus in general had become a little fancier than was normal at Fairley, and Emma had been helping Mrs Turner with the cooking lately. She was also learning a lot from Mrs Wainright, who wrote out explicit instructions for every new dish and usually came down to the kitchen to supervise. Emma had kept the menus and the instructions and had pasted them into an old school exercise book. Her intuition had automatically told her they would come in useful one day. Now she reminded herself to copy down the name of the peculiar tea, Lapsang Souchong, in her book, and the names of the wines Mrs Wainright had selected from the cellar with Murgatroyd, each one for a different dish. Emma had listened carefully to Mrs Wainright that morning and had learned for the first time that red wine was always served with meat, white wine with fish, and champagne with dessert. The names on the bottles were funny. 'Frenchy names,' Mrs Turner had told her with a huffy grimace. Murgatroyd had glared. 'But the very best, you ignorant woman,' he had snapped. 'Vintage wines the old Squire himself put down years ago. Can't be bettered hereabouts, not even in fancy London town,' he had finished pompously.

Yes. I must remember to copy the wine names proper like, and ask Mrs Turner for the dinner menu and them there recipes, Emma said to herself. She pulled off a length of black cotton from the reel, licked the end, threaded the needle, and began to sew the hemline of the dress, her mind on her exercise book. Everything that might be of some value went into it. She didn't know what information she might require in Leeds when she put her Plan with a capital *P* into operation, and she must be absolutely prepared in every way. The tattered old book contained menus for all kinds of meals, innumerable recipes, household hints, sewing instructions, little sketches for dresses and hats Emma had designed herself, and some of Mrs Fairley's special and most secret beauty hints. Now it'll have a wine list, Emma thought, and was pleased. Emma sewed patiently, thinking her ambitious thoughts, glancing up from time to time to observe Mrs Fairley. She must keep a close eye on her, to be sure she didn't get nervous or upset before the dinner, which was a long way off yet. The guests were coming at eight-fifteen and dinner was to be served at eight-thirty sharp, Murgatroyd had told her, warning her in a snooty voice to be dressed and ready in a fresh uniform. As if she didn't know that.

Adele Fairley was unusually calm as she finished her tea, picked up the newspaper, and continued to read it. Sheer fear of Adam's wrath, if she appeared in any way strange that night, had made her control her impulse, her very need, to send for Murgatroyd and ask for the drink, the only thing that could blunt the sharp edges of her pain these days. She had resorted to alcohol as an anodyne for her ills only in the last year and was still able to resist it, when circumstances forced her to do so. As yet she was not sodden with it, nor had she become a confirmed alcoholic. That afternoon she had assiduously removed the temptation of drinking by taking to her bed. Cowardly though this stratagem was, it had served its purpose. Also, Adele had not realized just how worn out she was, and she had fallen into a numbed and exhausted sleep immediately. When she awakened she discovered she felt better, and more importantly, and much to her amazement, she was less riddled with anxiety.

She concentrated on the newspaper, another ruse to keep her mind occupied and prevent her from dwelling on either the need for a drink or the impending evening that loomed ominously ahead. She turned the page and glanced at the Court Circular, which gave items of news from Buckingham Palace. As she scanned the column of fine black print she learned that the Russian and French ambassadors had been received by King Edward yesterday; the Marquess of Londonderry had had an audience with His Majesty after the Council; the Queen and Princess Victoria had visited an exhibition of drawings. Bored, she rustled through the paper to the back pages. Her eyes caught the words Bradford Market. She passed on hurriedly. That was all she needed! More about wool. She knew enough about that to last her a lifetime. As her eyes lighted on the advertisement for John Smith and Tadcaster ales, Adele thought longingly of the whisky and her mouth felt suddenly dry. She moistened her lips and her eyes flew nervously to the other page. She folded the paper in half and began to wade through a long story about Lord Fitzwilliam's Hunt at Clifton near Doncaster. She concentrated all of her attention on this, attempting to block out the persistent image of the glass of amber liquid that floated before her eyes and settled enticingly on the centre of the page.

The sound of clattering hooves, whinnying horses, and the clamour of raised voices floated up from outside and broke the gentle mood and silence of the bedroom.

'What on earth is that dreadful fuss? All that shouting?' Adele cried, her eyes flaring with surprise, as the voices grew more voluble and angry in tone.

Emma shook her head, equally mystified. She put down the gown she was still working on and ran to the window. She parted the curtains and looked down into the courtyard below.

'It's the children, ma'am,' she said quietly, biting her lip, and turning back to face Mrs Fairley. 'It's Master Gerald. He's shouting and bawling at Master Edwin summat terrible like.' Emma hesitated, almost afraid to go on. Adele looked at her expectantly. Emma gulped. 'Mrs Fairley, I think he's crying, poor Master Edwin is.'

'Edwin!' shrieked Adele, and she pushed aside the tray so vigorously Emma thought there would be an accident. Adele leapt out of the bed and flew across the room like a Valkyrie in flight, her hair streaming down her back. She moved with such unaccustomed velocity, Emma stepped aside hurriedly when Adele reached the window and violently jerked the white lace curtains apart and looked out. The scene being enacted below made Adele's throat tighten and her face took on a ghastly pallor.

The two boys were still mounted, after their ride, and Gerald was berating Edwin, his blubbery face swollen and red with temper. Edwin, in spite of his tears, was valiantly trying to defend himself against this verbal onslaught. Adele threw open the window with great force, about to intervene. At this precise moment, Gerald moved his horse closer to Edwin's, and Adele cringed, hardly daring to breathe. She watched Gerald deliberately kick his booted foot into the lower rib cage of Russet Dawn, Edwin's chestnut stallion. As the boot struck, the startled horse reared up on its hind legs, crazed and afraid, its nostrils flaring as it leapt forward violently. Edwin would have been thrown on to the rough cobblestones if he had not been an excellent equestrian like his father. He kept his head, and consequently his seat, and with superb horsemanship brought Russet Dawn under control.

Adele was so horrified, so sickened, so angered by this malicious act, her whole body began to shake and for a moment her throat was constricted. Long ago Adele had admitted to herself she was actually afraid of Gerald. He was a bully. But now her terrible rage and her concern for Edwin enabled her to overcome this inherent and often paralysing fear.

The courtyard was suddenly deathly quiet. Gerald was actually grinning. Edwin was wiping his tear-stained cheeks with the back of his hand. Adele seized the moment. She leaned out of the window and cried in an uncommonly harsh tone, 'What is the meaning of this commotion, Gerald? What is this dreadful altercation all about? You are behaving in the most deplorable manner, which I will not tolerate.'

Gerald looked up and blinked, taken aback at his mother's unanticipated appearance at the window, and also by the firmness of her tone. Gerald had always despised his mother, even as a little boy. He thought her foolish and vain, and he sniggered at her behind her back.

Now he moved restlessly in the saddle and cleared his throat. 'It's nothing of any importance, Mother. Your precious darling is perfectly capable of taking care of himself, even though he is a big baby, thanks to your pampering,' he said with rude disdain. 'Go back to bed, Mother. We don't want you interfering with us, or as an arbitrator, for that matter.'

'How dare you speak to me with such insolence,' exclaimed Adele with enormous coldness, shocked at Gerald's audacity. 'I want, no *demand*, an explanation about this matter or you will answer to your father. Come to the library at once. And remove your filthy riding boots before doing so!'

Gerald was so flabbergasted at this extraordinary reversal in his mother's mien, which was normally meek and abstracted, he gaped at her openmouthed, his usual scornful retorts unuttered. Edwin was not at all surprised, but he was afraid for his mother, and a worried look flashed across his sensitive face.

'But there's nothi –' Gerald began.

'At once, I said!' Adele snapped, and closed the window in his face with a loud bang, a grim expression ringing her mouth. Then she began to tremble, almost convulsively, although this was more from anger than any other emotion. She clutched the green silk draperies to steady herself.

Emma moved closer to her and took her arm. 'Oh, Mrs Fairley, don't upset yerself so. Please. Remember the dinner. Yer must keep yerself calm for tonight. Pay no mind ter Master Gerald, Mrs Fairley. Yer knows what boys are like, always bickering and squabbling amongst 'emselves.'

Indeed I do know what boys are like, especially that horrid little monster, Adele thought, but said, rather shakily, 'Yes, Emma, you are right to some extent. But occasionally children must be chastised when they have misbehaved, and taught the difference between right and wrong. Now, where is my dressing gown?'

'It's here, ma'am,' said Emma, picking up the purple velvet robe faced and trimmed with pink satin that matched the nightgown, which was lying across the chair in front of the dressing table. 'And here are yer slippers,' she went on, reaching for the purple velvet mules decorated with pink osprey feathers. She took them to Adele.

'Thank you. Where is the Squire?' asked Adele as she struggled hurriedly into her dressing gown and slipped her feet into the mules.

'He went ter Leeds, Mrs Fairley. And I knows he won't be back till six. I heard him telling Murgatroyd that,' said Emma.

'I see. Where is Mrs Wainright? Perhaps you can find her, Emma, and ask her to join me in the library,' said Adele.

'She's not here either, ma'am. She went to the village ter see the Reverend Martin about summat to do with the church,' Emma explained, wondering how Mrs Fairley would cope with Gerald alone. He could be a real devil when he wanted, and mean. She knew that only too well.

Adele sighed heavily and looked at Emma, but made no comment, her silvery eyes thoughtful. Resolutely she pushed aside the panic that was beginning to take hold of her. For once in her life it seemed she would have to deal with an unpleasant situation on her own. She had resolved earlier to assert herself in the household, and now the opportunity had apparently presented itself. However difficult it might

158

prove to be, she must handle it at all costs. That despicable little fiend is not going to get away with this as easily as he imagined, she decided. She took several deep breaths and then looked at herself in the ornate Venetian mirror on the dressing table. She wound her hair into a chignon and secured it with several tortoiseshell combs. Satisfied with her appearance, she threw her shoulders back and moved across the room with sureness, coldly imperious in her bearing.

But she faltered at the door and looked back at the speechless Emma, who was astonished at this quite phenomenal show of strength.

'Perhaps you had better accompany me to the library, Emma,' said Adele softly. Though her heart was beating with great rapidity and she felt physically weak, her steely determination to confront Gerald was intact. Nevertheless, she believed Emma's reassuring presence would bolster her courage even more.

'Yes, Mrs Fairley, ma'am, course I'll come with yer,' said Emma, vastly relieved that she had been asked. If there was trouble she could always run for Murgatroyd. He might be a tyrant downstairs in the kitchen, but he was devoted to Mrs Fairley.

SIXTEEN

Together they made their way down the long and dusky corridor and slowly descended the first flight of the grand staircase richly carpeted in red. Adele held on to the polished oak banister to steady herself and Emma supported her other arm under the elbow. When they reached the central landing, where the two upper left and right flights converged to join the main staircase, Adele paused to catch her breath, clinging tightly to the intricately carved newel post.

An immense stained-glass window floated high above this landing and the staircase, and it blazed with brilliant jewel colours and threw off rafts of awesome fiery light that washed over the white walls and spilled into the cavernous hall below. Emma glanced down and she shivered unexpectedly. The deserted hall looked gruesome, even frightening, in the unearthly bluish-red radiance that made crouching beasties and grotesqueries of the dark wood furniture and the huge potted palms. Once again terror trickled through her veins and she wanted, as always, to flee from this oppressive house full of secrets and concealed violence.

Don't be daft, she told herself firmly, but she held on to Mrs Fairley's arm more tightly, as much to quell her own fears as give support to Adele.

When they finally reached the hall, Adele looked around swiftly and then she also shivered and drew her robe about her. It seemed she echoed Emma's own sentiments when she said, 'It's awfully gloomy and unwelcoming in here, Emma. Please turn up the gaslights.'

Emma did as she was bid and hastened after Adele, who was already sweeping grandly into the library, her back stiff, her head lifted proudly on her tense shoulders, her face as unmoving as white onyx. Murgatroyd was busy polishing the crystal glasses on the black-walnut chest, in readiness for the evening, when Adele entered with Emma close on her heels. He straightened up quickly and looked in some amazement at Mrs Fairley, who rarely appeared downstairs during the day, if at all.

'Why, madame, how nice ter see yer looking so well. Can I get yer owt, Mrs Fairley?' he asked deferentially.

'No, thank you, Murgatroyd,' Adele said, trying to smile.

'There's nowt wrong, is there, Mrs Fairley?' he asked, peering at her closely.

Adele, walking across the floor with Emma in her wake, said quickly, 'No, no, of course not, Murgatroyd. I wish to speak to the children about a certain matter, that's all. But thank you for your concern.'

'Not at all, madame,' said Murgatroyd. His curiosity aroused, the butler hovered solicitously around Adele, who declined the chair he proffered and stood in front of the fireplace. Emma retreated into the background, her face grim, her eyes watchful.

Adele turned to him. 'If I need anything I will ring for you, Murgatroyd,' she said, dismissing him with a slight nod.

'Certainly, madame,' said the butler, bowing servilely. He picked up his cloths and backed out of the room. As he left he threw an ugly look at Emma. The way that lass has wormed her way in with the missis and Mrs Wainright is summat ter fair tek yer breath away, he mumbled enviously. He closed the door sharply behind him.

Adele remained standing, one hand gripping the edge of the mantelpiece, the other in the pocket of her robe, clenched in such a tight ball her nails dug into the palm. Her instinct was to run upstairs and retreat behind locked doors. Only her solicitude for Edwin kept her firmly rooted to the spot and prepared to face Gerald, whom she knew to be vicious.

The door opened and Gerald came in, followed closely by Edwin, who took up a position next to his father's desk. His face was a picture of dismay, and he trembled.

Gerald rolled ponderously across the room, his obese body bulging in his tight riding jacket and breeches. The sly Gerald had just decided it was infinitely preferable to deal with his mother, rather than his father. In his opinion that vain and vacuous woman could easily be manipulated. He knew his father could not.

You stupid bitch, he thought, smiling at Adele lovingly. He came to a standstill and positioned himself directly in front of her. He arranged a bland look on his face and said with unfamiliar pleasantness, 'Mother, please excuse me for being so rude to you. It was quite unpardonable, I know. But we were a little excited, I'm afraid. However, I didn't mean to be impertinent or hurtful to you in any way. I hope you can forgive me, Mother dearest.'

Having anticipated an angry and abusive display or, at the most, further insolence, Adele was momentarily startled. A little surge of relief flooded through her and she was about to relax her taut muscles. She instinctively checked herself. Despite Gerald's low opinion of her, she had more insight than he credited her with, and she knew what he was and she did not trust him. She also recognized that, like all bullies, he was a coward.

She held herself perfectly still and rigid. And she was unbending. She knew if she relented she would not only lose face but would expose Edwin to further mistreatment at Gerald's hands.

'You did behave with the most appalling rudeness, Gerald,' said Adele. 'I will overlook it this time, but I expect more respectful and gentlemanly conduct in future.' Her voice was steady. She looked him right in the eye unflinchingly, and went on, 'You will now give me an explanation of your abominable behaviour in the courtyard. I wish to know why you –' Adele paused and glanced coldly at her son. 'Why you were treating Edwin so unspeakably. I think it is quite reprehensible the way you continually pick on him. Your own brother, indeed. I will not permit it to continue, Gerald.'

Gerald, shifting about impatiently, realized this was not going to be as simple as he had thought. Moreover, he was confounded by his mother's control. Now understanding that a mere apology would not suffice, as he had misguidedly imagined, he took a deep breath and began to explain, in a conciliatory tone. 'It was really all a storm in a teacup, Mother dear. Please believe me, that's the absolute truth. It was unfortunate I became so – er – er ruffled.' He paused and flashed her a falsely loving smile. 'We were out riding on the moors, as you know. On our way back we came across a dog, probably from the village, caught in one of those traps Father has had put down for the rabbits and other vermin. Edwin became upset about this, excessively so, I would say, and actually wanted to release the dog. I wouldn't let him. We argued about this, Mother, mainly because I didn't want Edwin injuring himself. Those traps are extremely dangerous, you know. I persuaded Edwin to ride on, and for some reason, quite unknown to me, he became more tearful as we reached the house. That's all there is to it, Mother dearest.'

'I see,' said Adele thoughtfully. She gave Gerald a penetrating look and he flinched slightly under this fixed examination, but said blandly enough, 'I have told you the truth, Mother. Ask Edwin.'

'Oh, I fully intend to,' said Adele grimly. Her legs had turned to water and a pulse in her temple was beginning to pound. She forced herself to continue, and she turned to regard Edwin. 'I would now like you to tell me your side of this – this – ghastly tale, dear.'

'Yes, Mother,' Edwin said, joining her by the fireplace. His face was still chalk white and his alarm was patently obvious, although this was caused by consternation for his mother's health, rather than fear of his brother. In spite of his sensitive nature, Edwin could stand up to him most of the time.

He coughed behind his hand and then said softly, 'Gerald did tell you the truth. At least, most of it. He simply omitted the fact that the dog was still alive and writhing in the most terrible pain. When Gerald wouldn't let me attempt to release it, I suggested we sent the yardman out to set it free. Or if that was not feasible, to shoot it and put it out of its suffering. That seemed to me to be the only merciful thing to do.' Edwin stopped and stared accusingly at Gerald, who quickly averted his eyes.

Edwin's voice rose in anger. 'But he laughed at me. Actually laughed, and said I was being childish and hysterical. Gerald even went so far as to suggest that it would be a waste of time and also of the bullet. That's why I became so heated.' He pushed his hand through his fair hair agitatedly. 'It was his cruelty that maddened me. And when I said I would tell Father about the dog Gerald became terribly abusive.'

Adele swallowed, attempting to subdue the feeling of revulsion that swamped her. 'How disgusting you are. To let a poor helpless animal suffer like that and not try to put it out of its torment. Why, you are not even –' Her furious gaze stabbed at Gerald, who did not budge but merely returned his mother's condemning gaze steadily.

'Please, Mother, don't *distress* yourself so. You'll make yourself ill again,' said Gerald in a gentle voice that sheathed his deceitfulness. 'The dog was on its last legs. It's probably dead by now, anyway.' He shrugged. Gerald knew he must dispense with this matter before his father returned from Leeds, otherwise there would be an uproar of no small proportions. So he said, again with fraudulent gentleness, 'What would you like me to do, Mother, to make amends? I do so hate to see you in such a disturbed state.'

Adele had been staring right through the bulbous Gerald, an inscrutable look on her face. 'I would like you to bring the yardman to me immediately, Gerald,' said Adele.

Gerald blinked and his jaw dropped open stupidly. 'You mean bring him here, into the house? Into Father's library?' he said, balking at this idea.

'Yes, Gerald, into the house. I certainly have no intention whatsoever of going to the stables.'

'But, Mother, perhaps –'

'Don't argue, Gerald.'

'Yes, Mother. As you wish,' he said grudgingly.

Adele's eyes searched out Emma, who was standing in a shadowy corner, her face as ashen and as perturbed as Edwin's. 'Emma, please run down to the kitchen and get me a glass of water. This horrendous story has made me feel quite queasy.'

'Yes, ma'am,' said Emma, bobbing.

'And you, Edwin,' Adele continued, 'will be doing me a great service if you will be kind enough to get me the smelling salts from my bedroom. They're on the dressing table, dear.' Edwin nodded and slipped out after Emma.

Adele now focused her blazing eyes and all of her attention on her elder son. He was edging towards the door. 'Gerald, before you go for the yardman I wish to speak to you.' Adele's voice was sweet and she smiled brilliantly.

Gerald was instantly confused by this radical change. 'What about?' he said rudely.

'A matter of some importance. Come back here, Gerald.' Adele beckoned.

Gerald reluctantly moved forward and it occurred to him too late that his mother's voice had not been sweet at all. It had oozed acid and that smile had been a dangerous smile. He wavered, and, quailing, held back.

Adele took a sudden step forward and in a lightning movement grabbed the boy's wrist. They were only a few inches apart and Adele lifted her other hand and struck him savagely across the cheek.

Gerald recoiled and tried to break free. Adele held him in a vice-like grip that was surprisingly strong, and she leaned forward urgently. She stared deep into his eyes, and with loathing.

'If I see you endanger Edwin's life in any way, ever again, or hear that you have done so, I won't answer for the consequences!'

A quick denial sprang to Gerald's facile tongue, but when he saw the knowing gleam in his mother's eyes he thought better of it. For the first time in his life he was cowed by this woman who, in her towering rage, appeared more beautiful than she had ever been, and was awesome.

'I *saw* you kick Russet Dawn,' Adele continued in the same venomous hiss. 'And in the rib cage. You know as well as I do that when a highly strung hunter is struck unexpectedly, and with force, it is guaranteed to bolt. That's why you did it, of course! Edwin could easily have been killed. You know what they do to murderers in England, don't you, Gerald? They hang them by the neck until they are dead! Need I say more? Do you understand me?'

Gerald had blanched. His mother's long nails bit into his flesh and red weals were appearing on his blubbery face. 'Yes, I understand you,' he mumbled.

'Good. You are fortunate I have decided not to reveal your wickedness to your father. But I warn you now, I will do so if anything like this ever happens in the future.' Adele regarded Gerald for a long moment and then released her hold, flinging her son's hand away violently, as if it were contaminated. 'Get out of my sight! Now! Before I strike you again!' she shrieked. Gerald fled.

The door slammed and Adele covered her jerking mouth with her hands. She was shaking. This was the first time she had ever struck one of her children, or anyone else for that matter, and her own violence appalled her. Adele leaned back on the sofa and closed her eyes. After a short time she heard Emma's voice.

'Are yer feeling a bit faint, then, Mrs Fairley? Here's the water.' Opening her eyes, Adele saw Emma and Edwin standing before her. She drank the water gratefully and gave the empty glass back to Emma. 'Thank you.'

Edwin knelt down at his mother's feet and waved the smelling salts under her nose several times. Adele grimaced and drew back. 'Thank you, dear. But that's quite enough. I'm perfectly recovered.'

In spite of this assurance, Edwin continued to frown anxiously. 'Are you certain? You look frightfully pale.'

'Yes, Edwin.' Adele smiled at him and patted his head. 'You're a good boy.' She glanced at Emma. 'But I would like another glass of water, please.'

'Yes, ma'am. I brought a jug of it up.' Emma ran to the walnut chest where she had left the water and poured a second glass.

'Perhaps you should take a brandy, Mother. It might give you a little strength.'

'No!' cried Adele.

This was uttered with such fierceness that Edwin shrank back. He seemed hurt as he said, 'I'm sorry, Mother. I just thought it would revive you.'

'I know, dear, and at any other time I would take a small glass, for medicinal purposes only, of course. But I must keep a clear head for tonight's dinner party, Edwin. It will be a long evening and various wines will be served. I don't want to start drinking too early in the day.' In fact, Adele needed a drink desperately, but she fought the desire. She threw him a tender look. 'I didn't mean to sound so sharp. Do forgive me, my dearest.'

'There's nothing to forgive,' said Edwin, returning her loving glance. 'I know how wearisome this has been for you. I'm sorry you had to get involved.'

The door opened to admit Gerald, accompanied by the yardman. 'On our way over from the stables I took the opportunity to explain about the poor trapped dog and your grave concern about it, Mother dearest,' said Gerald with a hint of sarcasm, his cocky manner fully restored.

Adele rose and regarded them both with coldness. 'I see.' She eyed the yardman. 'I assume you know how to handle these traps and can release the dog easily. I want you to go and do that immediately.'

'Aay, I don't knows abart that,' the man muttered. 'T'maister won't think owt much o' this. Women laiking abart in t'men's business. Mind yer, I allos told 'im yon traps were right dangerous. I know'd there'd be trouble, I did that. I told t'maister summat bad'd 'appen. Newfangled junk, that's wot yon traps are.'

'Quite so. But since you are apparently the only person here who can manipulate them, please go and do as I say. I will take full responsibility with the master,' Adele said. 'We cannot be certain the dog is dead. In fact, it is probably alive and suffering. Go and attend to the matter at once. If it is dead, bury it. Should it be alive, and if it has some chance of surviving, bring it back here and care for it. Otherwise, if the poor thing is beyond hope, shoot it and bury it out on the moors.'

She glared at the man shuffling in the doorway. 'What are you waiting for? Go at once! Master Gerald will accompany you, so that he can report back to me on his return,' she snapped, her nerves jangling.

'But, Mother!' said Gerald fractiously. 'There's no reason for me to go. He's perfectly capable of handling this by himself.'

'Don't quibble! Do as I say,' commanded Adele.

Seeing the obdurate look in his mother's eyes, Gerald shrugged and said, 'Let's get on with it then, man.' They left together, Gerald in a high dudgeon.

Adele sat down and stared into the fire. Although she was oddly oblivious to the suffering of people, paradoxically the thought of an animal injured and in pain always moved her.

Emma brought her the water. 'They'll do as yer've told them,' she said. 'Don't worry so, Mrs Fairley.'

'Shall I assist you upstairs, Mother?' Edwin suggested. 'You should rest for a while, before dressing for dinner.'

'Yes, Edwin, that is a good idea,' said Adele thankfully. She was drained. Dealing with Gerald had taken its toll and vitiated her energy. The impending evening would be a further strain, and she wanted to gather her diminishing strength in readiness for it. At this moment she fervently wished she could retreat to her comfortable enveloping bed with a bottle and lose herself in her inner world. She stood up abruptly and Edwin took her arm and led her out of the library.

They mounted the stairs slowly and Emma followed dutifully behind. As Edwin shepherded his mother into the bedroom with great gentleness, Emma caught Edwin's attention and motioned for him to follow her. He excused himself to his mother and hurried after Emma, who was waiting in the sitting room.

'What is it, Emma?' he asked with misgiving, conscious of the worried expression on her face.

'Don't leave yer mother alone, Master Edwin,' Emma cautioned softly. 'Can yer stop a bit and read ter her, or chat with her, till I changes me uniform and comes back ter help her get ready?'

'Why, of course I can, Emma. But wouldn't it be wiser if she slept for a while?' he asked. 'Why shouldn't she be left alone?'

'Because she frets about things and she's ever so nervous about this blinking dinner party. And I knows she won't sleep, 'cos she had a long rest this afternoon. Just sit with her and keep her company. Help ter get her mind off the dinner. I'll be back in a tick, ter start doing her hair,' said Emma.

Edwin nodded in agreement. 'Yes, you are quite correct, Emma. She does worry and easily becomes distracted.' He reached out impulsively and touched Emma's arm lightly. 'Thank you so much, Emma, for taking care of my mother with such

164

kindness. I do appreciate it, really and truly I do,' he said with warm sincerity, his eyes soft and gentle.

Emma looked up at Edwin, who was tall for his age, surprised but delighted at this show of gratitude. 'That's ever so nice of yer ter say that, Master Edwin. I do me best, yer knows,' she answered sweetly, glowing with genuine pleasure. And then she smiled. It was the most dazzling of smiles, one that illuminated her face with such radiance it actually appeared to shimmer in the dying afternoon light, and her eyes, widely open and tilted upward, were so spectacularly green and brilliant they were breathtaking.

Why, she's beautiful, Edwin thought, momentarily staggered and blinded by her radiance and that beguiling smile and those incredible emerald eyes full of vivid intelligence, honesty, and innocence that gazed at him unwaveringly and with perfect trust. How odd that I never noticed her beauty before, he thought in wonderment, unable to tear his eyes away from hers. Imperceptibly, Edwin's young heart shifted and tightened and he was besieged by an overpowering emotion, one he had not previously ever felt and which he did not understand. They continued to gaze at each other, as if mesmerized, locked in a prolonged moment of silence so intense the air seemed to vibrate around them, and they were like two figures isolated and petrified by time. Edwin's naked face was bleached, the bones stark and pronounced. His limpid eyes were registering every plane and angle and smooth contour of that face before him, as if he felt compelled to commit it to memory for ever. A light flush began to permeate Emma's neck and cheeks, and her pale pink lips parted slightly. She was puzzled by that strained and staring look in Edwin's eyes and concern flooded her face, extinguishing the radiance. It was then that Edwin recognized obtusely, just below the level of his conscious, that something of tremendous importance had happened to him, although he was not sure what this was. He did not comprehend, in his youthfulness, that he was now beholding the only woman he would ever truly love. The woman who would tragically haunt him for all the days of his life, and whose name he would cry out, and with yearning, as he drew his last breath.

Quite unexpectedly tears pricked the back of Edwin's eyes and he was forced to turn his head. He swallowed hard, coughing behind his hand with embarrassment, humbled and oddly shy in front of this girl who had wrought such sudden upheaval within him. 'Excuse me,' he said, coughing again, hardly daring to look at her, but he could not resist and his eyes swept back to hers. Emma smiled gently and with kindness, and her face was so exquisite, so fragile, so tender, Edwin had to curb the strongest impulse to reach out and take it between his hands and touch it reverently. Eventually he managed to say in a strangled voice, 'You are a fine girl, Emma. And I *will* stay with Mother, as you suggest, until you can come back.'

He turned on his heel and went towards the bedroom. As he crossed the floor, with that easy gracefulness inherited from his father, he experienced a peculiar sense of loss, a sensation of such profound loneliness it overwhelmed him and brought him to a standstill. Shaken, he swung around with involuntary force and Emma was startled. He stared at her with great intensity and his eyes were questioning and perplexed. Emma studied him gravely, and with a new understanding remarkably mature in its perception. She smiled faintly, and before he could say anything else she hastened out of the room with the tea tray, the dishes rattling noisily.

Miraculously, the hubbub in the kitchen had abated, and although Mrs Turner was flushed and perspiring, she seemed less irritable and anxious about the dinner. She was presiding over the steaming pots and pans with a certain bombastic pride, a self-congratulatory smile on her plum-coloured face, the ladle hooked on to her apron pocket, her hands on her hips.

Emma placed the tray near the sink and said, 'If yer don't need me for owt, Mrs Turner, I think I'd best go and get ready for tonight.'

'Aye, luv, yer had, and right sharpish,' responded Cook, looking at the clock on the mantel. 'Everything's under control here. It's plain sailing from now on, I'd say.' She bestowed a complacent smile on Emma. 'There's nowt much ter them there fancy recipes, once yer get the hang of 'em,' she continued in a satisfied tone. 'Next time we have a big dinner, I'll be able ter do 'em with me eyes closed!'

Annie, who was polishing a large silver meat dish in the corner, looked up and grinned. She winked at Emma, who turned away, bit back an amused smile, and said, 'I'm sure yer will, Mrs Turner. I'll see yer later.'

Emma climbed the steep and twisting narrow stairs that led to her room in the attic. She shivered as she entered it. The window was wide open, and the blue curtains were billowing out wildly in the cool evening breeze from the moors. Emma ran to the window and closed it, and then quickly undressed. She stood at the washstand in front of the small leaded window and scrubbed her face with cold water and a flannel until it shone with rosy freshness. She brushed out her long hair, deftly twisted it into a thick bun, and then put on the evening uniform she had recently made. This was a black wool dress with long tight sleeves and a long straight skirt, and it was considerably more severe than her daytime uniform. But a white silk collar and cuffs relieved the starkness of the black, as did the frilled organdie apron she now tied around her slender waist.

Emma stared at her reflection in the mirror and was suddenly pleased with what she saw. She secured the jaunty white organdie cap on top of her head, smiling happily to herself. It had just occurred to her that she looked pretty. Blackie was always telling her that she was fetching, and Master Edwin obviously thought the same thing. She knew *that*, if only from the way he had looked at her earlier. She dwelt on Edwin. He was not a bit like the other Fairleys. She shuddered, thinking then of Gerald and the horrifying story of the dog. He was cruel and full of malice, whereas Edwin was kind and good. In fact, he did not seem to belong to Fairley Hall at all. She wondered if he had been stolen away from some other house by the gypsies, and sold to the Squire for a lot of money. She laughed out loud at her vivid imaginings which she knew were foolish. Things like that only happened in the tales her brother Frank made up on his bits of paper, and then read to her when she had the time to listen. She sighed suddenly. She would be sorry when Edwin returned to school. Tomorrow, she had heard the Squire say. She would miss his friendly smiles and his daily pleasantries and his thoughtfulness. His mother will miss him, too, she thought, overcome by a feeling of deep sadness for Adele. Intuitively Emma realized that Edwin was the only person who could give a measure of comfort to that troubled and haunted woman.

Now, in a hurry as always, Emma turned away from the mirror, hung up her day uniform on a peg behind the door, and hurried downstairs. She must help Mrs Fairley to dress for dinner. The sitting room was empty and when Emma went through into the bedroom she was surprised to find Edwin alone. 'Where's yer mother, Master Edwin?'

Edwin looked up from the book he was reading and stifled a small gasp at the sight of her. Emma was even more beautiful, if that were possible, and he gazed at her in entrancement. The black dress made her look much taller, and willowy, and it gave her a certain elegance that was striking. Also, the black enhanced her ivory complexion, which had taken on the appearance of lustrous porcelain, creamy and rich and tinted with the palest of apricots. The white cap, perched provocatively atop her shapely head, set off her tawny russet-brown hair, and her eyes glowed with intense colour and were brilliantly alive. Cat's eyes, he thought. Yes, there was something decidedly feline about Emma at this moment and it was highly arresting.

'Excuse me, Master Edwin, but where's Mrs Fairley?' Emma said with a hint of impatience mingled with concern.

Edwin was interrupted from his contemplation of her. 'She's bathing, Emma,' he answered quickly.

Emma frowned. 'But she usually waits for me ter draw her bath for her,' she said, biting her lip. She eyed the clock. 'And I'm not late! It's only just six o'clock.'

'Please don't worry, Emma. Mother's not upset. She simply wanted to start dressing earlier than usual. In fact, I went in and drew the bath for her,' he explained.

'Yer should've rung for me, Master Edwin,' Emma pointed out reprovingly, her mouth sternly set.

Edwin laughed gaily. 'For heaven's sake, Emma, don't look so cross. No harm has been done. And don't you think you have enough to do tonight? It was no bother for me to run Mother's bath.'

'If yer say so, Master Edwin. And thank yer,' said Emma politely. She then asked quietly, 'How is yer mam? She's not gone and got herself all worked up again, has she?'

'Not at all, Emma. I read to her, as you suggested, and we chatted for a while. I made her laugh, in fact, telling her about the boys at school and their antics. She's in good spirits, Emma, truly she is.'

'Thank goodness for that,' said Emma with some relief. She gave him a tentative smile and began to busy herself in the bedroom. As she continued her small tasks, Emma chatted unselfconsciously to Edwin, who was observing her every movement studiously and with admiration. 'So what happened to the dog, then, Master Edwin? Did Master Gerald come back and report about it, as Mrs Fairley told him ter do?'

'Yes, Emma. Gerald was here a little while ago. The dog was still alive. But the injuries were so bad there was little hope for it. They shot it and dug a grave out on the moors.' He sighed heavily. 'Well, now it's out of its suffering. That's the most important thing. I cannot abide cruelty, Emma,' he finished on a confiding note.

'Aye, I knows that, Master Edwin,' said Emma. 'What a shame the poor little dog got caught,' she murmured sympathetically. 'Them traps are right dangerous, yer knows.'

Before Edwin had a chance to comment further, Adele came into the bedroom, wrapped in a thick woollen bathrobe. 'There you are, Emma.' She glanced at Edwin. 'Would you excuse me now, my dearest boy. I have to dress, you know.'

'Yes, Mother,' said Edwin, as respectful as always. He ran over and kissed her. 'Have a lovely evening, darling,' he added, smiling at her.

'Thank you, Edwin. I am sure I will,' said Adele, not sure at all that she would. But she determined not to give one thought to the forthcoming evening, or she would become hysterical and quite incapable of leaving her room at all. After Adele had dressed herself in her underclothes, Emma laced her into her corset. 'Tighter, Emma,' cried Adele, with a small gasp, gripping the bedpost to steady herself.

'Nay, Mrs Fairley, ma'am, if I makes the laces any tighter yer won't be able ter eat owt,' Emma pointed out. 'Come ter think of it, yer won't be able ter breathe either!'

'Of course I will! Don't be foolish, Emma.' said Adele crisply. 'I like a tiny waist.'

'Well, tiny waist or no, yer don't want ter be fainting away at the dinner, now do yer, Mrs Fairley?'

Adele paled slightly as she recognized the truth of this. It would be a catastrophe if she passed out during the evening. Adam would never believe it was actually from lack of breath, and for no other reason. 'Well, perhaps you are right,' she conceded reluctantly. 'Don't make the laces any tighter then, but don't loosen them either, Emma. They are perfect just as they are. And please tie them in a strong double bow, so they won't work open.'

'Yes, ma'am,' said Emma, finishing the task quickly. 'Now we'd best start on yer hair, Mrs Fairley. Yer knows it takes me ages.'

Adele sat down at the glittering mirrored dressing table, studying her face admiringly and with loving self-absorption, whilst Emma brushed out the long shimmering hair and started the tortuous procedure of shaping it into a magnificent coiffure. This was an elegant pompadour, currently the height of fashion, which Adele had noticed in an illustrated magazine showing the latest London and Paris haute couture. The previous week, when Emma had copied it for Adele, she had taken a degree of licence and had elaborated upon it, adding her own special touches and adapting the original style so that it was more flattering to Adele's fragile looks. To Adele's astonishment the finished results had been not only quite outstanding and distinctly original but extraordinarily professional as well.

Now Emma swept the masses of hair up and away from Adele's face, working the great lengths into the basic pompadour that was the foundation of the style. She rolled and folded the hair all around Adele's head, so that it framed her exquisite features dramatically, anchoring it securely with hairpins. Emma worked patiently and skilfully in silent concentration, and at one moment she actually stood back to admire her handiwork, nodding her head with satisfaction, her eyes glowing. She had almost finished when she realized she had exhausted her supply of hairpins.

Emma clucked to herself with annoyance. Adele stared at her through the mirror, frowning. 'What is it? No problems, I hope, Emma! My hair must be beautifully dressed tonight.'

'Oh, it will be, ma'am,' Emma reassured her. 'It is already. But I need a few more hairpins, for the top curls. I'll just pop along ter see Mrs Wainright, and ask ter borrow some. Excuse me, ma'am.' Emma put the silver, monogrammed hairbrush on the dressing table, bobbed a curtsy, and flitted out.

The corridor was gloomy and wreathed in amorphous shadows, and the pieces of ornate Victorian furniture that punctuated its long expanse were like nebulous phantoms in the cold murky light emanating from the gas fixtures on the walls. Emma had to traverse the entire length of the shadowy corridor to reach Olivia Wainright's room and, since it was deserted, she ran all the way, although this was prompted not so much by nervousness or fear as by her pressing need to save time, as usual. She was panting when she tapped on the door.

'Come in,' Olivia called out in a light melodious voice. Emma opened the door and stood politely on the threshold, as always surveying the room with grudging approval. It was the only one that appealed to her at Fairley Hall, apart from the cheerful kitchen.

Olivia Wainright was sitting at the carved oak dressing table with her back to the door. She swivelled around quickly. 'Yes, Emma, do you need me for something?' she asked with her usual courtesy.

Emma had taken a step forward, smiling in return, but she suddenly stiffened and stopped short. Olivia's face was unnaturally pale, denuded as it was of the French rouges and powders and the other cosmetics she normally favoured. This intense pallor gave her a wan and exhausted look, as did her very white lips. Her aquamarine eyes were glittering and appeared larger and bluer in the paleness of her delicate face, their almost supernatural colour emphasized even more by the sky-blue silk robe she wore. Her dark brown hair, usually beautifully groomed and upswept in a fashionable style, fell around her shoulders like a glossy velvet cowl in the refracted light from the dressing-table lamps.

Emma knew she was gaping at Olivia Wainright and that this was the height of rudeness. But she could not help herself, and she could not turn away, so stupefied was she. That pallor, the tumbling hair, those brilliant eyes, all merged to form a face that overflowed with gentleness and poignancy, a luminous, haunting face with which Emma was only too familiar.

Olivia, meanwhile, had immediately perceived Emma's strong reaction. She was mystified and regarded the girl at first curiously, and then with mounting nervousness, the powder puff dangling in her hand.

'Good gracious, Emma, whatever is it? Why, you look as if you have seen a ghost, child. Are you feeling ill?' she cried in a voice unusually vehement for her.

Emma shook her head. Finally she spoke. 'No, no, Mrs Wainright. Nowt's wrong. Please don't fret yerself, ma'am. Excuse me, if I looked a bit funny like –' Emma paused, uncertain of how to correctly explain her behaviour, which she knew must have seemed queer and was also improper. She coughed behind her hand. 'I felt a bit faint for a second,' she lied, and continued more truthfully and in a stronger voice, 'I ran ever so fast down the corridor. Yes, that was it.'

Olivia relaxed, but she continued to frown. 'You are always running, Emma. One of these days you will have an accident. But never mind that now. Are you sure you are perfectly all right? You are very white indeed. Perhaps you should lie down until the guests arrive,' Olivia suggested with obvious concern.

'Thank yer, ever so much, ma'am. But I'm better. *Honest*. I was just puffed. And I can't rest now, Mrs Wainright. I've got ter finish getting Mrs Fairley ready. That's why I came. Ter borrow some hairpins, if yer can spare a few,' Emma explained in a rush of words to camouflage her considerable embarrassment. 'Of course. You may have these,' Olivia said, gathering up a handful.

Emma took them from her and attempted a smile. 'Thank yer, Mrs Wainright.'

Olivia's perceptive eyes contemplated Emma thoughtfully. She was not at all certain she believed the girl's explanation. However, since she could not imagine any other logical reason for her ashen face and her apparent distress, she had no alternative but to accept it.

'You do look a little peaked to me, Emma,' she said slowly. 'After the guests have arrived, and when you have attended to the ladies' wraps, I want you to rest in the kitchen until it is time to serve dinner at eight-thirty. I don't want you collapsing from fatigue. Inform Murgatroyd that is my wish.'

'Yes, ma'am. That's kind of yer,' said Emma. She felt guilty and ashamed for pretending to feel faint, and also for having lied to Mrs Wainright.

Olivia reached out and patted Emma's shoulder. She shook her head in fond exasperation. 'Sometimes I think you are much too diligent for your own good, Emma. You know I am more than satisfied with your work. Try and take things at a slower pace, child,' she said with the utmost kindness.

Emma, staring up at her fixedly, felt her throat tighten with emotion and tears stung her eyes. She cleared her throat. 'Yes, ma'am.' She bobbed a curtsy and left the room as sedately as she could. Once she was safely in the corridor, Emma exhaled deeply and with enormous relief. She leaned against a small carved table to steady herself. Her legs felt wobbly and her heart was hammering. She looked back at the door, shaking her head from side to side in total disbelief. *Olivia Wainright looked like her own mother.* As incredible as that seemed, Emma had just seen it with her own eyes. She's the spitting image of me mam, she whispered to herself with awe, and still disbelieving.

Emma then wondered why she had never noticed this likeness before. Instantly she understood. It was very simple really. In all of the time Olivia had been staying at Fairley Hall, Emma had never seen her so intimately revealed, undressed and ungroomed in the privacy of her room, until a few moments ago. Sitting at the dressing table in the diffused light, so informally attired, her face naked of cosmetics, she looked a different woman from the one Emma was accustomed to seeing moving around the house so elegantly and with cool authority. In her naturalness Olivia was still stunningly lovely, but without the stylish clothes, the elaborate hairdos, and the other artifices of fashion, she appeared ingenuous and vulnerable, and there was a sweet simplicity about her that was girlish and even innocent.

And Emma was not mistaken. Olivia Wainright, stripped of the outer trappings of the chic society woman, did resemble Elizabeth Harte. In fact, the resemblance was so extraordinary as to be uncanny. They might have been created from the same mould, except that Elizabeth's beauty was now only a faint echo of Olivia's. Worn out as she was by the struggle to survive, riddled with consumption, undernourished, and in constant pain, her fine looks had blurred and slowly begun to fade. Yet Emma had seen in Olivia her mother's beauty as it had once been, and this had not only startled her but moved her as well. Emma was not the only one to have noticed the strong likeness between these two women from such different worlds. Another occupant of Fairley Hall had also detected it and, like Emma, had been rocked to the core at this discovery.

But Emma was unaware of this as she stood staring at Olivia Wainright's door, still shaking her head. She regained some of her composure and for once in her life she did not run. She walked down the corridor, and slowly, benumbed by this odd coincidence. As she made her way back to Adele's bedroom, it did not occur to Emma that perhaps she had unconsciously recognized the similarity earlier, and that this might partially explain her secret adoration of Olivia. Only years later did this thought strike her, and quite forcibly so.

In Emma's absence, Adele had attended to her face. For once she had decided it was necessary to resort to her jars of French cosmetics. She had applied a little rouge, just enough to highlight her cheekbones and dispel the paleness of her skin, and had also touched her lips with it. She was lightly powdering her nose when Emma entered.

'Here I am then, Mrs Fairley,' said Emma in a low voice, hurrying to the dressing table, and the waiting Adele.

Normally too preoccupied with self to be conscious of anyone else, Adele was particularly keyed up and alert tonight, in readiness for the important and perhaps trying evening that lay ahead. She was so acutely aware, in fact, she noticed the subdued note in Emma's voice, which was always so cheerful, and she gave her a piercing look.

'Did Mrs Wainright give you the hairpins? Was there a problem?' she asked quickly.

'Oh no, ma'am,' responded Emma, already starting to work on the remaining curls. 'She had plenty ter spare.'

'What is Mrs Wainright wearing tonight, Emma?' Adele continued curiously, watching Emma carefully through the mirror.

'I didn't see her dress, Mrs Fairley,' said Emma quietly, her face closed and still.

Adele pursed her lips in frustration and disappointment. She had been longing to know which one of her many exquisite gowns Olivia had selected. Adele had always been highly competitive with her older sister, and this was now more pronounced and consuming than ever. Adele was filled with mortification, and infuriated by the fact that Olivia managed to appear elegant and arresting on every occasion. She smiled, and not a little smugly. *She* would outshine everyone tonight. Olivia will be dowdy in comparison to me, she thought gloatingly.

'There we are, ma'am, all finished!' exclaimed Emma with a triumphant flourish of the brush, stepping back to regard Adele's hair. She gave Adele the small silver hand mirror. 'See if yer like the back, Mrs Fairley.'

Adele moved and twisted and swivelled in the chair, viewing her pompadour from all angles. 'Why, Emma, it's positively divine,' she cried with delight. She laughed gaily. 'It's a work of art. A masterpiece. And so flattering to me. You *are* a clever girl.'

Adele put on her evening slippers and then stepped into the gown Emma was holding for her. She stood in front of the cheval mirror, and Emma patiently fastened the long line of buttons up the back, praying Adele wouldn't remember the roses she had removed earlier. They were ugly, and Emma was convinced they ruined the gown, which was elegant and dramatic in its basic simplicity. As she did up the last button, Emma said hurriedly, hoping to divert her attention, 'All we need for the finishing touch are yer jewels, Mrs Fairley.'

'In a moment, Emma,' said Adele, stepping back to view herself. She was ecstatic at the vision she made. The black velvet gown stunningly emphasized her tall, lissom figure and its excellent cut drew attention to her tiny waist. It had a low neckline that was draped adroitly across the shoulders, and a tightly moulded bodice that hugged her figure deliciously. She decided it was her most becoming gown as, intoxicated with herself, she swirled around on her elegantly shod feet that peeped out beneath her skirt. Emma was quite right about the roses. They were ghastly, she thought, marvelling that her young maid had such an innate sense of taste.

She sat down and took the diamond chandelier earrings out of the red velvet case and put them on. She added two bracelets and several rings, and then Emma placed the diamond necklace around her throat, securing it carefully. It was a glittering lacy web of brilliant, perfectly cut and mounted stones. The diamonds had such fire, such life, such matchless beauty, Emma gasped.

'It is exquisite, is it not?' remarked Adele. 'The Squire gave it to me,' she went on, and sighed. 'He used to give me so many lovely jewels,' she confided softly.

'It fair takes me breath away, Mrs Fairley, it does that,' Emma said in awe, wondering what it had cost. A fortune, no doubt. Bought from the toil of others, she thought with a stab of bitterness, thinking of Frankie and her dad labouring at the mill.

Adele did not see the scowl on Emma's face, and she threw her a gratified smile and opened another velvet case. She lifted out a large diamond brooch and commenced to pin it on the small draped sleeve that barely covered the top of her left arm.

Emma compressed her mouth. 'Er – er – Mrs Fairley, ma'am, I don't knows that yer needs that there brooch, if yer don't mind me saying so –'

'It was my mother's,' said Adele peremptorily.

'Oh! Then please excuse me, Mrs Fairley. I understand. Yer wants ter wear it for sentimental reasons,' said Emma with the utmost politeness. But she was dismayed. The brooch was unnecessary, and it ruined the whole effect she had been striving for.

Sentimental reasons, repeated Adele inwardly, gazing into the mirror. Her eyes, narrowing perceptibly, were as cold and as glittering as the diamonds she wore. She looked down at the brooch absently and thought of her mother and then slowly lifted her head.

Vaguely, Adele removed the brooch and returned it to its case. She wanted no reminders of her mother. Nor did she want Olivia to be reminded either. Olivia thought she was mad, just like their mother had been mad. So did Adam. They were plotting against her. Oh yes, they were. Adam and Olivia. She saw them, whispering in corners of this hideous house.

Her eyes fixed on Emma, who was closing the jewel cases, and she grabbed hold of her arm tightly. Taken by surprise, Emma flinched. But noting the sudden glazed and febrile expression, she did not struggle or attempt to free herself. 'Yes, Mrs Fairley? What is it?' she asked gently.

'You must get away from this place, Emma! Away from this house. Before it's too late. It's pernicious,' Adele whispered.

Emma looked at Adele, baffled by this statement. 'Per – per – what? I don't know what that word means, Mrs Fairley.'

Adele laughed her shrill laugh, and it sent an icy chill through Emma. 'It means wicked. Wicked! Wicked! Wicked!' she shrieked, her voice almost a scream.

'Hush, hush, Mrs Fairley,' said Emma as calmly as she could. She was shaking and gooseflesh made prickles up and down her arms. What a queer thing for her

172

ter say, she thought fearfully. But she didn't have time to think about that now. She had something more important to worry about: Mrs Fairley herself. Emma freed her arm carefully and peered at the clock. Her heart sank. The guests would soon be arriving, and in her present state Mrs Fairley was hardly in a fit condition to go downstairs and join them.

Emma looked around helplessly, considering the best course of action to take, her face white and tense. She wondered if she should run and fetch Mrs Wainright, or perhaps Master Edwin. And then some instinct warned her to avoid involving them. She alone would have to pull Mrs Fairley out of this distracted mood. Emma knelt on the floor and took hold of Adele's slender, aristocratic hands with her own small scarred ones. They were as cold as death. Emma squeezed them so tightly she thought they would snap in half from the pressure. 'Mrs Fairley! Mrs Fairley! Listen ter me,' Emma said urgently, making her voice strong and compelling. 'Yer *must* listen ter me. The guests'll be here any minute. Yer must pull yerself together and go down ter meet 'em. Yer must, for yer own sake!' she exclaimed fiercely, passionate in her determination to reach Adele.

Adele appeared not to hear. Her opaque eyes regarded Emma blindly. Emma tightened her grasp on Adele's hands, even though ugly red marks were beginning to appear. She gripped them so strenuously her own fingers hurt. 'Please, Mrs Fairley! Get a hold of yerself. At once, do yer hear! At *once*!' Emma's voice was now enormously cold, and commanding, and all of her stubborn will rose up in her. It surfaced on her face, stern in its fixity of purpose, as she forced Adele to listen to her. The older woman's expression remained closed. Emma contemplated slapping her cheek, to rouse her from this stupor. She changed her mind. She did not dare. She was not afraid of the consequences. She simply did not want to mar Adele's fragile skin.

Finally Adele's eyes flickered with a hint of life, and her pale lips parted. Emma took a deep breath and gripped her by the shoulders. 'Yer must go downstairs, Mrs Fairley. Now! Afore it's too late! Yer're the Squire's wife. The mistress of this house. The Squire's waiting for yer, Mrs Fairley.'

Emma shook her more forcefully. 'Look at me, Mrs Fairley. *Look at me.*' Emma's eyes blazed hard green light. 'Yer must get control of yerself. If yer don't, there's bound ter be trouble. There'll be a right scandal, Mrs Fairley!'

Adele heard her dimly, above the sound of splintering crystal that reverberated in her head. Slowly the shattering and tinkling began to ebb away, and she saw Emma more clearly as her eyes became focused and lost their cloudiness. Now Emma's voice was penetrating her tired mind. It was strong. 'I'll be there, if yer needs me, ma'am. All yer have ter do is signal me during dinner, if yer needs owt. Or ring for me later. I'll see yer all right. I will! I'll look after yer, Mrs Fairley. I promise!' Emma said, her tone cajoling yet firm.

Adele blinked and sat up with an abruptness that was almost violent. What had Emma been saying? That she was the mistress of this house . . . the Squire's wife. Yes, that was what she had said. And it was true. Adele passed her hand over her brow and it was a gesture that bespoke her confusion and weariness and despair.

'Shall I fetch yer a drink of water, Mrs Fairley?' asked Emma, relieved that a semblance of comprehension, of normality, was returning to Adele's face.

'No, thank you, Emma,' Adele whispered, looking directly at her. 'I don't know what happened. My head began to ache again. Yes, that was it, Emma. Another of my dreadful headaches. They are so debilitating, you know.' She smiled faintly. 'But it has passed, thank goodness.'

'Are yer sure, ma'am?' Emma inquired solicitously, studying her closely.

'Yes, yes. And I must go downstairs!' She stood up shakily and moved to the cheval mirror. Emma hurried after her.

'Now just look at yerself, Mrs Fairley. See how beautiful yer are,' Emma pointed out, adopting an admiring and reassuring voice, in an effort to bolster Adele's self-confidence. 'The Squire will be right proud of yer, ma'am. He will that.'

Oh! My God! Adam! She must go down there and conduct herself with propriety and dignity and grace and charm; otherwise Adam's wrath would come tumbling about her head, and that she could not survive. She regarded her own image in the glass, and suddenly she saw it objectively, as one views a stranger. That image was of a stunningly beautiful woman. Then she remembered. She was supposed to hide behind the mask of her beauty, so that everyone would be deluded, including Adam.

Her smile wreathed her face with loveliness and her luminous eyes sparkled with silvery lights. She smoothed the skirt of her gown and swung around lightly. 'I'm ready, Emma,' she said sweetly.

'Shall I come with yer, Mrs Fairley?'

'No, thank you. I can manage on my own,' Adele answered with absolute sureness. She glided through the adjoining sitting room and out into the corridor, just as the porcelain lions' clock on the mantelshelf struck the hour.

SEVENTEEN

The dinner had been a tremendous success so far, much to Adam Fairley's profound relief and satisfaction. He leaned back in his chair at the head of the table, smiling inwardly, and surveyed his guests and the glittering scene that spread out before his eyes.

The atmosphere was relaxed and friendly, almost jovial, and everyone appeared to be at ease. It had been a long time since Adam had heard the murmurous sounds of genial chatter and gaiety reverberating against these old walls, and it filled him with a sense of such gratification he was positively startled. At the beginning of the evening he had been suffering from extreme nervousness. It was not unnatural for Adam to feel apprehensive, in view of Adele's past performances, and whilst he had been able to conceal his fears, he had been uneasy, all of his senses alerted for trouble. But as the dinner progressed without incident, these feelings were lessening and he had started to unbend. From time to time he would marvel that the malaise of his spirit, which had slowly been diminishing in the last few weeks, had now, this night, miraculously disappeared. It was as if a great burden had been lifted from his shoulders and he felt unfettered and even carefree.

He lifted the crystal glass of champagne Murgatroyd had just refilled and sipped it slowly, savouring its sparkling iciness. The food had been delicious, the wines excellent, and Murgatroyd and Emma had executed their duties with aplomb, as though they were a seasoned team accustomed to handling such a complicated and elaborate dinner every night of the week. He realized this achievement was no accident. It had been accomplished only with Olivia's expert planning, and her perfect taste was apparent everywhere.

Adam looked down the long expanse of white linen, until Adele was in his direct line of vision. He had watched her closely all night and her behaviour had astounded him. She was charming and attentive to their guests and, on the surface at least, she seemed like the woman she had been years ago. And she looked magnificent. She was flirting outrageously with Bruce McGill, who appeared to be fascinated, much to Adam's wry amusement. He suspected there was something of the actress in Adele. Certainly she had made a grand enough entrance. Bruce had arrived earlier than the other guests, in order to conclude their business, and they had been strolling across the hall when she had materialized at the top of the staircase. Aware that they had noticed her, she had paused histrionically at the central landing, clinging for a second to the newel post, and then she had floated down the main staircase like Aphrodite descending from the heavens. Bruce, his mouth slightly agape, had been momentarily speechless and, to Adam, he had looked like a stage-struck schoolboy. That expression still lingered on the Australian's face. Seated at Adele's left, he was giving his rapt attention to her and Adele's tinkling laughter drifted down to Adam on the warm air. He narrowed his eyes, observing her closely. For all of her beauty there was something oddly removed about her. The Snow Queen. Never to be touched.

Adam's eyes swivelled to Olivia, who was seated at the centre of the table. She had that special self-assurance so often found in upper-class English women, who were always at ease and in command of themselves and the situation, whether seated on a horse or at a dinner table. She looked just as magnificent as Adele, but in a less brittle way. Her kingfisher-blue silk gown was elegant, and provocatively low-cut, although not quite as daringly so as Adele's. A choker of sapphires made a ring of blue fire around her neck, the same stones cascaded in linked drops from her small ears, and matching bracelets entwined those superb arms. She was listening quietly to her dinner partner, and in repose her face was serene. Sleeping Beauty. Waiting to be awakened, Adam said to himself, instantly astonished that such an extraordinary thought should have entered his mind.

He caught Olivia's eye. She was smiling at him warmly and she inclined her head towards the dining-room door. He nodded, understanding that she thought the meal should now be terminated.

Adam gestured to Murgatroyd, who hastened to his side. 'I assume you have put out liqueurs and cigars in the library, Murgatroyd.'

'Oh, yes, Squire. The best French cognacs, port, and Bénédictine. Also the usual Scotch and Irish. Mrs Wainright instructed me to put a tray of drinks in the drawing room for the ladies as well.'

'Excellent, Murgatroyd.' Adam turned to the female guests seated nearest to him. 'I know you will excuse us if we gentlemen leave you to your own devices for a short while,' he said with a smile. He pushed back his chair and looked around the table. 'Shall we adjourn, gentlemen?' he continued, standing up. With murmured assents the other men followed suit and filed out of the dining room, chatting amongst themselves.

Upon entering the library, Bruce McGill took a whisky and soda from Murgatroyd and made his way to the fireside. Bruce was in his late forties, tall and spare, and with the rolling gait of a man who has spent his whole life on a horse. He had thick and curling brown hair above a craggy face, one that automatically inspired confidence, especially in women, and his eyes were merry. His manner was masculine and there was a dashing air about him that was most engaging.

He joined Adam and said, 'Here's to your health, laddie, and a long and successful business relationship.' He smiled broadly and his eyes twinkled 'I think it goes without saying that we will have a most rewarding friendship.' He clinked glasses with Adam.

'And to you, too, Bruce.' Adam had taken a strong liking to Bruce McGill, for all of his toughness and penchant for striking a hard bargain. The man was straightforward and honest, and Adam appreciated these qualities since they were also inherent in his own nature. Now he said, 'So you're going up to town next week, now that you've finished your business in Yorkshire. How long will you be staying in London?'

'A fortnight. I sail for Sydney early in May.' Bruce's face lit up eagerly. 'Any chance of seeing you in town, Adam? Can you come up for a few days? We could dine, take in a few theatres, have a little fun. I have some very nice friends I am sure you would enjoy meeting.' He paused and winked. 'Delectable friends, in fact, even though I do say so myself.'

Adam chuckled and shook his head. 'As tempting as it sounds, I don't think I should be absent from the mill right now. We have a lot of pressing orders to fill, and I can't leave all of the administrative burdens to Wilson. He needs me. Sorry, but I must decline, Bruce. Next time you're here, perhaps.'

'You have been a very good host to me, Adam, on my various trips to Yorkshire in the last few months. And talking of hospitality, if I can't persuade you to be my guest in London, can I inveigle you into coming to Australia later in the year? I would really like you to visit Dunoon.'

'That's very kind of you, old chap,' said Adam. His eyes brightened at the idea. 'I might just do that. Indeed I might.'

'You would enjoy it. I promise you that. There's only me and my boy, Paul, out at the sheep station in Coonamble, except for the hands, of course. My wife died three years ago. But I have a good housekeeper, and we would make you very comfortable. We could also spend a wee while in Sydney. It's an interesting city, if not as sophisticated as London,' he finished with a rueful laugh. Now he grasped Adam's arm as he said, 'Look here. I have another idea. Why don't you consider buying land in Australia, Adam? You know, it would be a good investment. You might even think about starting a small sheep station of your own. I could find you the right hands, and I'd even supervise it in your absence. Become your own supplier, eh?'

Adam looked at Bruce speculatively. 'You've got a good point there, Bruce. It's worth considering, and I will think seriously about taking the trip. I'll let you know about that later this year.' Adam took out his pocket watch and glanced at it. 'Let's have another drink and then perhaps we should join the ladies in the drawing room, before they get too restless.'

'Good idea. Incidentally, I must compliment you on your wife, Adam. She is beautiful and most entertaining. You are a lucky man.'

'Aren't I just,' said Adam, smiling faintly. If only you knew. If only you knew, he thought with raw bitterness, as they made their way across the library.

EIGHTEEN

'Will there be owt else then, Squire?' Murgatroyd asked. The guests had long since departed, Adele and Olivia had retired, and Adam was alone in the library.

'No, thank you, Murgatroyd. Oh, and by the way, I must commend you on the way you executed your duties tonight. I was most pleased, and also with Emma. Please tell her so, and give her my thanks.'

Murgatroyd, who had absolutely no intention of doing this, said, 'Right ho, Squire. That I will. And thank yer, sir, ever so much.'

Adam picked up the brandy and soda Murgatroyd had just prepared for him, and with a friendly nod he left the butler to his late-night duties. When Adam entered his bedroom a few moments later he was delighted to see that the fire had been lit in the grate. Its blaze was cheerful, and he hurried over to it. Adam stood, as always, with his back to the fire, his long legs spread wide apart, enjoying the warmth from the rapidly burning logs. He stared ahead, somewhat absently, his face serious, the drink in his hand untouched, his mind awash with innumerable thoughts.

His bedroom was spartan in its austereness. The walls were white and unadorned, the high ceiling punctuated with dark beams, and the polished floor was bare. Apart from the heavy wine-coloured draperies at the windows and the handsomely framed portrait of his father above the fireplace, it was devoid of luxury and the usual trappings of wealth. It had the character of an officer's quarters. The few personal items, such as the ivory brushes on the dressing table and the writing materials on the desk, were laid out with such military precision and neatness they looked as if they were awaiting inspection by a superior. Adam's only concession to comfort was the large black leather chair positioned next to the fireplace. However, it was this very simplicity that appealed to him, for it was a relief after the emphatically decorated rooms downstairs. Like his library, he found his bedroom tranquil and relaxing, a quiet inner sanctum where he could shed the burdens of the day, undisturbed in his preferred solitude.

Yet, for some reason, tonight the room appeared alien to him and even desolate, in spite of the warm blaze of the firelight and the diffused glow from the old oil lamp on the table by his narrow bed. He peered about him fretfully, frowning intently. He was suddenly uncommonly restless. Adam began to pace the floor, keyed up in a way he had not been in years. He was beside himself and he did not know why. And he was now so damned warm. He pulled at the velvet cravat around his neck and hastily untied it. He strode backward and forward urgently, but after ten minutes of this frantic pacing, he paused finally at the fireplace, grabbed the glass, and drank down the brandy and soda in several swift gulps.

Adam looked around the room. He ran his hand through his hair distractedly. He was hemmed in, constrained by these four walls. He thought condemningly: But you were your own willing prisoner, Adam Fairley. Were you not? He had built his own sarcophagus. The walls appeared to advance on him menacingly. He must escape. He leapt for the door and wrenched it open. He stepped out into the dimly lit corridor and proceeded swiftly down the staircase. He pushed open the door of the library. Moonlight was streaming into the room and it was so bright he did not bother to light a lamp. He hurried to the walnut chest and poured himself a large brandy. His hands shook. He drank the brandy neat, slopping some on his ruffled cuff in his haste. He poured another one. His hands continued to shake uncontrollably.

Adam stood by the walnut chest, endeavouring to calm himself. Eventually he started to breathe more normally, the pounding in his heart subsided, and the sense of oppression slowly began to lift. Why am I so agitated tonight? What in God's name is wrong with me? He felt unutterably lonely and despairing. He had a desperate need to talk to someone. To a friend who would understand. But he had no friends in this cheerless and godforsaken house. Except Olivia. Of course! Olivia! She was compassionate and wise. He would go and talk to her. She would listen to his troubles, intelligently and with patience. He would go to her at once. Now. Adam left the library. He took the stairs two at a time, bursting with renewed energy mingled with relief at the thought of talking to Olivia, of unburdening himself. He had reached the central landing when the grandfather clock in the hall struck twelve. It brought him to an abrupt standstill. 'Fool,' he muttered. He could not go to Olivia's room this late. It would be an unpardonable intrusion. She was probably in bed and asleep by now. He continued to mount the stairs more slowly. The spring had left his step and his shoulders sagged.

Adam paused at the door of his bedroom, his hand on the knob, and then, against his volition but with great deliberateness, he continued on down the corridor to Olivia's room, propelled by some force infinitely stronger than himself. A sliver of light showed under her door. His spirits lifted. It gave him the encouragement he needed. Before he could knock, the door flew open and a stream of light flooded out into the darkened corridor. Adam was momentarily startled and blinded, and he blinked several times. Olivia stood silhouetted against the bright radiance from the lamps behind her. Her slender body looked ethereal, almost unreal. He could not see the expression on her face, for she stood in her own shadow.

Adam stared at her, unable to speak.

Olivia opened the door wider, and, without uttering one word, she moved aside to let him pass. He took several long strides into the room and, in spite of his natural polish and inbred charm, Adam discovered, much to his chagrin, that he was utterly tongue-tied. He had no idea what he would say to her. All previous thoughts were swept entirely out of his head. Olivia closed the door softly behind her and leaned against it, a gentle expression on her face. Adam hovered nervously, towering above her, his mouth dry. She looked up at him expectantly.

Finally Adam cleared his throat in embarrassment. 'I'm sorry to intrude so late, Olivia,' he began, racking his brains for a plausible explanation. He took a deep breath. 'But I – I – couldn't sleep, and so I went downstairs for a drink.' He indicated the glass in his hand, smiling ruefully. 'On my way back to my room, I remembered I had not thanked you for arranging the dinner party so beautifully. I do appreciate everything you did to make it such a tremendous success.'

'Oh, Adam, please,' Olivia exclaimed warmly. 'You know how much I love entertaining. I enjoyed it enormously.'

178

'Nevertheless, it would have been most ungrateful of me not to have expressed my appreciation to you,' said Adam. He was beginning to breathe more easily. He was also vastly relieved to have handled this presumptuous invasion of her privacy with a degree of adeptness.

Olivia did not answer. She continued to look up at him questioningly. A tiny frown wrinkled her smooth brow, and her eyes, very blue and perceptive, did not leave his face. He's had a lot to drink, but he's not drunk, she thought. He's in absolute command of himself. The perfect gentleman, as always.

Under her steady gaze Adam became fully conscious of his dishevelment. He realized, to his considerable discomfiture, that he was not only without his coat, but his shirt was open halfway down his chest and his cravat dangled loosely around his neck. He was acutely embarrassed again, and he fumbled with the front of his shirt, attempting, unsuccessfully, to pull it together. He smiled weakly. 'Well, I had better leave you, my dear. I don't want to disturb you further. I would not have ventured to intrude if I had not seen your light.'

'I thought I heard someone outside in the corridor,' she said, not adding she had known that it was he.

Adam took a tentative step towards the door. Olivia made no effort to open it. She remained leaning against it, her face tranquil, her outward composure intact, but her heart was fluttering and unaccustomed waves of panic shot through her. After a long moment of silence she looked up at him and said softly, 'Don't go, Adam. Please stay and chat for a while. I am not at all tired. I was reading, as you can see.' She gestured to the newspaper on the table near the sofa. 'Your own illustrious journal at that,' she added, hoping she sounded nonchalant enough. When he made no response, she said hastily, 'Unless you want to retire yourself –'

'No. No. I don't,' he interrupted peremptorily. Realizing his anxiety had made him excessively vehement, he softened his tone. 'Actually, I would enjoy talking to you, Olivia. I'm wide awake myself. All that stimulating conversation tonight, I've no doubt,' he muttered with a small nervous laugh. 'Provided you are certain I am not keeping you out of bed.'

'No, really you are not. Please, come to the fire, Adam, and make yourself comfortable,' Olivia said, moving gracefully into the room, her panic subsiding. She brushed so close to him he caught the faintest whiff of her perfume, something light and evocative. Its name eluded him but the scent lingered in his nostrils tantalizingly.

Adam followed her to the fireplace slowly. Olivia sat down on the sofa in front of the fire. It would have been the most natural thing for Adam to have seated himself next to her, but he did not. He carefully avoided the sofa and lowered himself into a nearby chair.

Olivia settled back against the cushions, smoothed her skirt, and then she looked across at Adam and smiled. It was such a loving smile Adam experienced a peculiar plunging sensation near his heart, and he stared at her transfixed. She had changed her evening gown for a soft and flowing blue silk robe of oriental design; otherwise she looked exactly the same as she had at the dinner. He had never seen her looking more beautiful in all of the twenty years he had known her.

He lowered his head as he became conscious he was staring at her far too intently. He compressed his mouth and peered into his drink, and then he lifted the glass to his mouth automatically. He was mortified to see that his hand trembled.

Observing him from her position on the sofa, Olivia thought: He is very nervous. If only I can make him feel relaxed, and at ease, perhaps he will stay. And so she said, 'It was a lovely evening, Adam.'

Adam stiffened. 'What did you make of Adele tonight?' he asked rather brusquely, and went on in the same tone, 'I was delighted to see her so controlled. But then it occurred to me, in the drawing room after dinner, that she was so normal she was – well – almost abnormal.'

Olivia looked at Adam alertly. 'I'm sure she was playing one of her roles, Adam. She sometimes does that, you know, when she is confronted with a situation she finds difficult. I think it's probably the only way she can deal with people. She retreats in a sense and dons a mask to conceal her real feelings.'

Adam was thoughtful as he digested her words. 'Why, I think you are right, Olivia,' he said. 'That's exactly it. And it's remarkably astute of you to recognize it.'

A faint smile flickered in Olivia's eyes. 'She is my sister, after all.' She sighed and shook her head. Her face was tinged with sadness. She had long been aware of Adele's deep-seated inner conflicts, her inability to create a stable relationship with anyone, least of all Adam, and she sighed again. 'I have really tried to help her since I have been at Fairley, but she is so wary and truculent at times it is quite a difficult task.' Olivia leaned forward with some intensity and continued, 'Do you know, Adam, as strange as this might sound, I feel she is suspicious of me.'

'It doesn't seem strange at all. She is the same with me, these days,' he said. 'In a way, I am sorry I did not discuss Adele's health with you when you first arrived in February. But I didn't want to worry you unduly. I must confess, though, I was a bit concerned about her last year. Her behaviour was so extraordinary it was –'

Adam paused, seeking the appropriate word, and finally he said, 'Her behaviour was actually rather irrational. There is no other way of describing it. However, she has improved enormously in the past six months, and so I hesitated to alarm you unnecessarily.' He smiled faintly, looking shamefaced. 'And you have had your hands full with this mismanaged household since you arrived.'

Olivia shifted her position on the sofa and crossed her legs. Her heart went out to him. He looked so boyish and vulnerable. 'You could have spoken to me, Adam. A burden shared is often so much easier to carry,' she said sympathetically. 'Of course, I know Andrew Melton has been a great help to you. He told me you have discussed Adele with him, from time to time. When I last saw him he sounded most encouraged, and very optimistic about her –' Olivia's voice wavered, and stopped.

Adam discovered he was unable to meet her gaze. He said, 'When did you have occasion to see Andrew Melton?'

He spoke with such harshness, Olivia was further startled. 'Why, he has been to a number of my dinner parties in London, and he has taken me to the opera and concerts on several occasions,' she said quietly, baffled by his manner. 'He naturally asked me about Adele. I hope you don't think Andrew betrayed a confidence.' When he did not reply, she said in a more insistent tone, 'You don't, do you?'

Adam ignored this question. The anger he was now experiencing was overwhelming. 'So you have been seeing quite a lot of Andrew,' he said at last in a tight voice.

'There is nothing improper in that, is there, Adam? My being friendly with Andrew? After all, you introduced us. Now you look most disapproving.'

'No, of course there is nothing wrong in your seeing him. And I am not disapproving,' he said, his voice low.

Oh, yes, you are, Olivia thought, although she still could not conceive the reason for his attitude. He and Andrew were the closest and oldest of friends. She sat back on the sofa and folded her hands in her lap, saying nothing. She did not want to upset him further.

Adam could no longer bear to keep his face averted. He was compelled to look at her. Their eyes met. He saw the questions in hers, the confusion and hurt on her face. Her lips parted as if to speak, but no words were forthcoming. She is so incredibly lovely, he thought. Yet there is something frail about her at this moment, something so very vulnerable. His heart shifted, and as he continued to look into her eyes, those eyes as blue as speedwells, the most curious longing swept through him. He ached to put his arms around her, to hold her close to him, to beg her forgiveness for his curtness, to expunge the sadness on her face with his kisses. *With his kisses.* He was appalled.

And then he knew. Adam Fairley recognized, with the most stunning clarity, what his agitation and tension and restlessness were all about. He stood up abruptly and gripped the mantelshelf. You bloody fool, he thought. You utter bloody fool. You are jealous. You were jealous of Bruce McGill earlier, when he was hovering around Olivia. And you are jealous of Andrew Melton because he is infinitely more eligible. You would be jealous of any man who so much as looked at her. *You are jealous because you want her for yourself*.

He felt the blood rushing up into his face. He had a sick feeling in the pit of his stomach and he thought he would never be able to look at her again without betraying his feelings. Staring broodingly into the grate he became aware of the glass in his hand. Dazedly he lifted it to his cold lips and tossed the brandy down in one gulp.

Olivia sensed, rather than saw, his disquiet, for his face was hidden from her. She sat very still, and waited, hoping he would confide in her. She glanced at him surreptitiously out of the corner of her eye, and she curbed the impulse to reach out and rest her hand on his arm comfortingly. He moved his head imperceptibly, and his face was starkly revealed to her. It was rigidly set and his lips were so pale they were almost white. He gripped the mantel with one hand, and a muscle in his face began to work.

'Adam! Adam! You look strange. What on earth's the matter?' she cried.

Vaguely he heard her voice. He shut his eyes tightly and then opened them quickly. 'Nothing's wrong. I'm perfectly all right,' he said curtly. He had to get out of here. At once. Before he behaved dishonourably. Disgraced his name. Made a fool of himself. He did not move, and he admitted to himself, with a terrible sinking feeling, that he could not move. Yet in all good conscience he had to leave. He could not abuse her position in his house, take advantage of her vulnerability under his roof. Like a sleepwalker he moved across the floor.

'Adam! Where are you going?' Olivia called after him. She stood up. Her face

181

was ashen. Her voice shook as she cried, 'Have I done something to offend you, Adam?'

Slowly he turned on his heels and looked directly at her. He noted the concern in her face, the alarm in her eyes, and he was moved in a way he had not been moved for years. How could you ever offend me, my love? he thought. Once more he had that crushing urge to reach out for her, to pull her into his arms. He swallowed hard. 'You have not done or said anything to upset me, Olivia,' he answered as evenly as possible, striving for normality.

He hesitated, and in that moment of hesitation he weakened. And Adam Fairley was undone.

'I was simply going down to the library to get myself another brandy and a cigar,' he lied. As he spoke he knew he could not leave her. He could not leave her here alone as long as that look compounded of fright and perplexity remained in her eyes.

'I have a decanter of brandy here,' she said, gesturing to the console table.

'But no cigars, I'm afraid. There are plenty of cigarettes, of course.' Without waiting for him to answer, Olivia picked up the glass he had left on the mantel shelf and took a step in the direction of the console in front of the window.

He strode across the room and took the glass from her. His hand brushed hers and he felt small shock waves running up his arm. 'Please, Olivia, sit down. I will fix it myself,' he said firmly. He pressed her gently on to the sofa. It seemed to him that her flesh burned his fingers through the thin silk of the robe she was wearing.

Adam stood at the console with his back to her, his hand clutching the neck of the crystal decanter. He closed his eyes. Oh, my God. My God. *I love her.* I've loved her for years, he thought. How could I not have realized that before? I want her. Oh God, how I want her. I want her more than I have ever wanted any other woman. But you cannot have her, a small voice answered in the back of his mind. His hand tightened on the decanter. He must take command of himself and of his emotions. He must not embarrass her, or frighten her. He must behave as normally as he always had in her presence and as a gentleman of honour.

'Do you mind if I open the window, Olivia? It's frightfully hot in here,' Adam said at last.

'No, please do,' Olivia said quietly. Her panic had been allayed, but she was still bewildered by his behaviour.

Olivia's eyes had followed Adam across the room, her gaze preoccupied, her face wreathed with concern. But suddenly her full attention was riveted on him. He was reaching across the table to open the window, and his body was at an oblique angle. The silk shirt stretched tautly across his broad back and shoulders and forearms, his exceptional physique apparent through the fine fabric, his muscles rippling as he moved with his usual litheness. My darling, she thought. My love.

Adam breathed deeply at the window. After several seconds he picked up the decanter and two glasses, and brought them back to the sofa. He looked down at Olivia and smiled. 'I thought you might join me, Olivia,' he said, his voice steady. 'It's not much fun drinking alone.' He poured two brandies, and handed her one.

'Thank you,' she said, returning his smile.

'Forgive me for behaving so rudely before,' Adam said, settling in the chair. 'It was churlish of me to let my worries get the better of me, when you were putting

182

up with me at this late hour.' He stretched out his long and elegant legs and leaned back in the chair, relaxing. The hammering in his head had receded and the tight pain in his chest had all but disappeared. His only thought was to exonerate himself with her and put her at ease.

'You don't have to apologize, Adam. And if you need a shoulder to lean on, I'm always here,' she said softly. She gazed at him with enormous gentleness.

'Yes, I know that, Olivia,' he responded. He bent forward and picked up the drink from the table. His shirt sagged open to reveal his chest and the mat of fair hair that covered it. Olivia, regarding him keenly over the rim of her glass, felt herself flushing unexpectedly. Her heart missed a beat. She dropped her eyes quickly.

'Well, I'm certainly not going to bore you with my problems tonight,' Adam went on quietly. 'Especially after such a pleasant evening. You know, this house was getting to be a veritable tomb until tonight. No laughter, no fun, no gaiety anymore. Things are going to be different from now on,' he exclaimed. He lit a cigarette, feeling unexpectedly elated.

Olivia observed him thoughtfully. She found in Adam every quality she most admired and respected. His intellect and his cultivation were a constant revelation. Her eyes lingered on his handsome face. He has such distinction and grace, she thought. And such beautiful eyes. Large and widely set and lucent. So different from her husband's eyes. His had been small, black, and deeply socketed. Charles had always been considered a handsome man. She herself had thought him rather too stockily built and glowering to be truly handsome. She had not loved Charles at all. Poor dead Charles. Her father had arranged the marriage.

'Penny for your thoughts,' said Adam, watching her intently, fully conscious of her introspection.

Olivia jumped, startled from her reverie, and, taken off guard, she said. 'I was thinking about Charles.'

'Oh. I see.' So that was it. Adam concentrated on the tip of his shoe, so she would not notice the expression on his face. If he were honest with himself he had to admit he had also been jealous of Charles.

Now he said in a gentle voice, 'Are you happy, Olivia? I have often wondered about that lately.'

'Of course I'm happy,' she cried. Did he imagine – could he possibly believe she was grieving for Charles? 'Why would you think I am not happy?'

A faint smile played on his lips. 'I don't know, really. I suppose because you are alone. No one wants to be alone. You are still a young woman, and a beautiful one at that. I'm sure you must have other suitors, as well as Andrew Melton.' He tried to laugh. 'Why, I saw a decided gleam in Bruce McGill's eye tonight, and I don't doubt there are other gentlemen with expectations.'

Olivia sipped the brandy. Her eyes were brilliant and they did not leave his face. 'Andrew is not a suitor,' she said. 'He is a good friend, that's all. Nor am I interested in Bruce McGill.' She gave him a long look. 'Actually, I'm not interested in any man,' she exclaimed more strongly. And thought: Only in you, my darling, but you are my sister's husband and therefore you will never know.

Adam ran his hand through his hair impatiently. 'Do you mean you have not considered the idea of remarrying?' he pressed.

'No, I haven't, because I have no intention of remarrying. Ever.' Olivia hesitated and then said, 'Adam, I am a little cold. Would you mind closing the window, please?'

'At once,' he said, leaping up.

When he returned, Olivia edged to the end of the sofa. 'Please sit here, by my side, Adam. There is something I must ask you.'

He had no alternative but to lower himself on the sofa. He did this with a certain grimness, avoiding the merest contact with her.

'Yes, Olivia? What is it, my dear?'

'I am troubled because you are, or rather were, so upset earlier. I know you said you did not wish to talk about your problems tonight. But can't you confide in me?' She gave him the most tender of smiles. 'It does help to talk to a friend on occasion, and I hate to see you distressed.'

Adam wondered how to extricate himself. He certainly could not tell her the real reasons for his disquiet earlier. 'There is nothing to discuss, Olivia,' he said finally. 'I suppose I worry about the children, the mill, and the newspaper. Just the usual everyday worries of a man in my position. But not too serious,' he lied expertly.

'And you worry about Adele, don't you?' she prompted.

'To a certain degree,' admitted Adam, reluctant to think about his wife. 'Please try to relax about her health. She *is* better. You told me that yourself, and Andrew agrees. And I am here to help you. To make things easier for you,' Olivia said in her most reassuring tone.

'But you will be leaving in a few months. You said you had to return to London in July.'

'Oh, Adam, you know I will stay as long as I am needed.'

'Will you really?' Adam felt his spirits lifting.

She smiled. 'Yes. Was that worrying you? You know I love being here. And I am quite lonely in London, in spite of my busy life and all of my friends. Adele, the children, and you, why, you are the only family I have now.' Impulsively, she reached out and placed her hand on his knee in a consoling way. 'I will stay in Yorkshire as long as you think I am needed.'

Adam could not answer. He could only stare down at her hand. It lay there on his knee, soft and cool and white, like an immobile dove. But it scorched through the cloth of his trousers like hot steel. He felt the flush rising on his neck to suffuse his face. His heart began to beat more rapidly and he had to bite his inner lip to control himself. He picked up her hand, intending to place it safely in her lap. But, as he held it, he found his fingers slowly tightening on hers and he felt her tremble. He looked into her face. Her eyes were so dark they were almost black. And they were filled with that strange sadness he had noticed so often lately.

Olivia returned his gaze steadily, and then, with a small shock, she became conscious of the naked desire on Adam's face, saw the sensuality on those partially opened lips, heard his rapid breathing, and she was afraid. Not of Adam Fairley. Of herself. She extracted her hand gently, and moved away from him slowly.

A look of suffering flashed into Adam's eyes, and, before he could stop himself, he reached out and took her hand and brought it up to his lips. He uncurled her fingers and kissed the palm, pressing it to his mouth. He closed his eyes. He thought he would explode.

Olivia's head lay back on the sofa and her mouth was quivering. A small muscle

184

leapt on her slender white neck, and her breasts rose and fell under the robe. Adam moved closer to her. He looked deeply into her eyes, which hovered so close to his, and at last he recognized that sad expression for what it truly was. It was not sadness at all. It was an aching longing, an undisguised yearning – and it was for him. He knew this unquestionably. Joy surged through him. He bent over her and kissed her, crushing her mouth under his so fiercely her teeth grazed his lips. Her arms were around his neck. Her hands touched the back of his head, his shoulders, his spine, pressing him closer to her. Adam could hear her heart banging against his own and she trembled as violently as he did himself.

Olivia moved slightly within his arms and now he felt the cool insistent touch of her hands against his bare chest. He kissed her hair and her face and her throat, all the while murmuring her name, calling her his love, his darling, his only love, saying things to her he had never said to any woman. And she answered him with the same endearments, her voice vibrating with such love and desire it further thrilled him.

Abruptly, Adam pulled away from Olivia and stood up. He looked down at her. Her eyes were wide and questioning.

Olivia stared back at Adam. His face was congested, his eyes blazed, and his entire body throbbed with unbridled passion as he towered above her. Mesmerized, she was unable to tear her eyes away from him.

In the terrible grip of his own onrushing desire, pushed beyond endurance by the sensuality flaring in him after years of self-imposed celibacy, further aroused by Olivia's responsive ardour that fully matched his own, and inflamed by drink, Adam Fairley could no longer hold himself in check. Without uttering a word, he picked her up in his arms and carried her across the floor.

Olivia clung to him, her arms wound tightly around him, her face buried in the soft tendrils of hair that curled on the back of his neck. She could hear his heart thudding as loudly as her own. She tightened her grip on him.

At this moment the vestiges of her principles disintegrated and the stringent rules she had lived by were abandoned. All were swept away by the force of their passion and yearning for each other. Emotions repressed for years finally tore loose, for she no longer had the will to restrain them, and she could not think rationally any more. She was in the arms of the only man she had ever loved. The man to whom she had irrevocably belonged from the first day she had met him. And that was all that mattered now.

Adam's legs shook as he strode to the bed. I shouldn't be doing this, he thought. She is my wife's sister. It is against all the precepts of my religion, my upbringing, my code of honour. I should not be doing this. It's wrong, he told himself. And then he thought: *But I don't give a damn.*

Adam put Olivia down gently on the bed. She lay back against the pillows, looking up at him, her face still white and strained, her breathing hurried. Adam sat down on the edge of the bed and leaned over her. He put his hands around her neck and unclasped the necklace and carefully removed the sapphires from her ears. He placed them on the bedside table and took her face in his hands with great tenderness. He kissed her long and deeply. Then, half smiling, he stood up and walked swiftly to the bedroom door. He heard her gasp. He turned and looked back at her. He took in the pain and bewilderment on her face, the stark terror flooding her eyes.

'I've waited for you for twenty years,' Olivia whispered in a voice so low it was a moan. 'That's half my life, Adam Fairley. You're not going to leave me now?'

Adam shook his head. 'No, I'm not going to leave you, my darling. Never. Ever again.'

His eyes did not leave her face. With one hand he locked the door and with the other he began to unfasten the rest of the sapphire studs on his ruffled silk shirt.

NINETEEN

Emma sat at the table in the kitchen of Fairley Hall, sewing a white lace collar on to a silk blouse which Olivia Wainright had given to her as a gift, along with a dark green cotton dress and a thick woollen shawl of the brightest red.

It was warm and snug in the large kitchen. The fire burned merrily in the hearth, the sun poured in through the sparkling windows, and the whole room gleamed in the bright afternoon light, which bounced off the shining copper and polished brass and struck the flagstone floor sharply, so that this, too, looked golden. The atmosphere was exceptionally tranquil, it being Sunday. Murgatroyd had just departed for Pudsey to visit his sister, and Annie, the betweenmaid, was upstairs in the dining room, following Emma's instructions and setting the table for dinner. The roaring fire spurted and crackled almost in unison with the little whistles and snores that issued forth from Mrs Turner's spherical body. The cook was sprawled in a chair, dozing in front of the fire, her cap askew, her ample bosom rising and falling contentedly as she slumbered on, dreaming her untroubled dreams. The only other sounds were the ticking of the clock and the occasional roar of the wind as it rattled against the windows. Although it was sunny, and the sky was a clear cerulean blue, it was a blustering April day outside.

Emma smoothed out the silk and held the blouse up in front of her, gazing at it appraisingly. With her innate sense of taste and her keen eyes she was quick to recognize its elegance. It was almost new, and such a lovely blue. Like the sky outside, Emma thought, glancing out of the window. Like me mam's eyes, she said to herself, and decided she would give it to her mother when she went home later in the week. The idea of being able to give her mother something so beautiful filled Emma with immense pleasure, and her usually sober face was suddenly illuminated by a most joyful smile. She picked up a lace cuff and started to stitch it neatly on to one of the long, full sleeves, her mind turning with thoughts of Leeds, and her Plan with a capital *P*.

Just then the outside kitchen door flew open so violently, and with such rattlings and bangings, Emma was startled. She looked at the door expectantly, and decided it had been blown open by the force of the gale which was raging outside. She was about to go and close it when a cheery face appeared around the door jamb. Vibrant black curls blew in the wind, bright black eyes danced merrily above tanned cheeks, and the wide mouth broke into a mischievous grin.

'Sure and I hope ye won't be turning a cold spalpeen away on this bitter day.'

The voice was full of lilting brogue and laughter and love of life. ''Tis a cup of tea I hope ye'll be offering me.'

'Blackie!' shrieked Emma, totally forgetting the sleeping Mrs Turner in her delight, and she leapt up and ran across the room, her skirts swishing around her long legs, her face wreathed in smiles. Blackie eased his great frame through the door, and came down the steps in three swift jumps. He swept Emma up into his brawny arms, swung her around several times until the room whirled before her eyes, and then he put her down carefully. He steadied her gently and held her at arms' length, scrutinizing her intently.

'Ye get to look more fetching every time I be seeing ye, mavourneen,' he exclaimed. 'I do believe ye are the prettiest colleen in the whole of England, and that's the God's truth, I am thinking.'

Emma blushed prettily. 'Aay, Blackie, yer a real tease. Don't be so silly.' This was said somewhat scathingly, but nevertheless she beamed with pleasure.

The noise and bustle and sudden flurry had awakened Cook, who sat up with a start and rubbed her eyes. She blinked, momentarily confused. 'Now, lass, what's going on?' she shouted, glowering at Emma. 'Yer making enough noise ter waken t'dead!'

Before Emma could announce the arrival of their unexpected visitor, Blackie was striding across the kitchen to pacify Cook. 'Faith and are ye not a sight for sore eyes, Mrs Turner me luv,' Blackie said. ''Tis only me, come to pay me compliments and give ye this.' He paused at her chair and, with a small flourish, pulled a brown paper bag out of his coat pocket, which he gave to her, bowing elaborately. Mrs Turner's irascibility instantly evaporated at the sight of Blackie O'Neill, of whom she had grown very fond.

'Why, Blackie, aren't yer the one,' said Cook, positively glowing. She peeped into the bag and her birdlike brown eyes lit up. 'Ooh, Blackie, me favourite toffees and humbugs. Thank yer, lad. That's right thoughtful of yer. It is that. And have yer heard our news? We don't have ter worry no more about the likes of Murgatroyd. No, by gum, we don't.' A gloating look settled on Cook's face as she confided. 'He's had his wings clipped, Blackie lad. He has that. Things have changed around here since Mrs Wainright came.' Cook gave him the benefit of a gratified smile and went on, 'Mrs Wainright is ever so good to us all. Yes, she is indeed. Why, that woman's an angel.'

'From all I be hearing she must be an angel,' said Blackie, his eyes merry. 'And can I not see with me own eyes that things have improved, Mrs Turner? To be sure they have, thank God.' Blackie stole a quick look at Emma, and was further impressed. She was blossoming into a truly lovely young woman. She looked cared for and beautiful, with her glowing face and silky hair, wearing her crisp blue dress and starched white apron.

'Yes, indeed, it warms the cockles of me heart to see the colleen so well fed, and dressed in a bit of decent clothing.' Blackie added, nodding his head approvingly. Cook clucked her agreement and leaned back in the chair. She popped a humbug into her mouth and propped her feet up on the hearth, toasting her toes.

Now Blackie sat down at the table opposite Emma. He fished around inside his coat and brought out a small package. 'And *this* is for ye, mavourneen,' he said importantly, placing it on the table in front of her. His gay black eyes regarded her fondly.

Emma stared at the package and then she looked up at Blackie with large eyes. 'What is it?' she asked, her voice hushed.

'Just a little bit o' nonsense. A birthday present for ye,' said Blackie. His mouth twitched with pleasure as he observed her growing curiosity mingled with anticipation.

'But it's not me birthday till the end of April,' said Emma. She picked up the package and turned it over in her hands, examining it with mounting interest. She had never received a present like this before. A present wrapped in silver paper and tied with a silver ribbon. Never in her whole life. It looked almost too beautiful to open.

'Yes, I know when it is,' Blackie told her. 'But me Uncle Pat's sending me to Harrogate, to do a big building job, and I'll be gone for three weeks or more. I didn't want to be missing the special occasion of ye birthday. That's why I brought it for ye today, me bonny mavourneen.'

Emma looked down at the gift in her hands. Her face was flushed and her vivid eyes sparkled with shimmering green light. 'Can I open it now then?' she asked, unable to contain her excitement. 'I don't have ter wait, do I?'

'Sure and ye don't, Emma. Open it this minute,' said Blackie, enjoying the scene enormously.

Emma untied the silver ribbon and removed the silver paper with the greatest of care. A small black box was revealed, which Emma stared at wide-eyed, her heart fluttering. Slowly she lifted the lid. 'Oh, Blackie, it's lovely,' she gasped, her eyes growing larger. With trembling hands she took out a small brooch designed in the shape of a bow and decorated with bright green stones. She held it up to the light. The cheap little brooch glittered with such radiance in the sunlight its tawdriness was diminished and, in her hands, it seemed to take on a special kind of beauty, and even Blackie was amazed.

'Look, Mrs Turner,' Emma shrieked, running to show her. Cook said, 'Well, aren't you a lucky lass. That was right kind of Blackie ter remember yer fifteenth birthday.'

'It's only glass,' Blackie said in an apologetic tone. 'But when I saw it in the shop in Leeds, in one of them grand arcades, I said to meself, "Why, 'tis the colour of Emma's emerald eyes, sure and it is." So buy it I did, without another minute's hesitation.' Blackie grinned in his engaging way. 'When I'm a toff, that millionaire I'm planning to be one day, I shall be buying ye a brooch exactly like this one, mavourneen. But it will be made of the real emeralds, I can promise ye that,' he announced with the utmost confidence.

'Yer don't have ter do that,' Emma exclaimed quickly. 'This is the most beautiful brooch I've ever seen. Why, I shall keep it *always*. I don't want no emeralds, Blackie. This is perfect. Thank yer, ever so much.' She smiled at him radiantly and kissed him on the cheek.

He hugged her to him and said, 'I am glad ye be liking it, Emma.'

Emma sat down, the smile lingering on her face, and after a few seconds she returned the brooch safely to its box, but she left the lid off, so that she could admire it.

'Well now, how about a nice cup of tea, lad?' said Cook, heaving herself up out of the chair with a great deal of huffing and puffing. She straightened her cap, smoothed down her apron, and went on, 'The kettle's on t 'hob and I'll have a pot mashed in two shakes of a lamb's tail.' As she spoke the cook padded over to the dresser, took down a brown pot and a tea caddy, and began to busy herself at the dresser.

'Thank ye, Mrs Turner, I don't mind if I do,' said Blackie, crossing his great legs and sitting back comfortably in the chair. He gave his full attention to Emma. 'And what are ye doing here on Sunday, might I be asking?' he queried, frowning. 'I thought ye would be having the day off, as ye always do. I was going to stop off at ye dad's and leave ye the present, after I'd dropped in for a little visit with Mrs Turner here.'

'The Squire gave a dinner party last night and Mrs Wainright asked me ter work over the weekend, seeing as how there was a right lot of clearing up ter do,' explained Emma. 'I won't be going home till Thursday, but Mrs Wainright's ever so kind, Blackie, and she's given me four whole days off. Two ter make up for this weekend, and next Saturday and Sunday as well.'

'I am glad to be hearing that,' said Blackie. 'So, the Squire had a dinner party, did he? I bet it was real posh, Emma, eh? Lots of toffs here, I am thinking.' Blackie grinned 'I've no doubt about that, at all, at all. Ah, yes, the money is a wonderful thing to be having.'

Emma nodded solemnly, her eyes glittering. 'Yer right, Blackie, anybody can be a toff with money.' She eyed him appraisingly and continued, 'Yer don't look so bad yerself. Is that a new suit, then?'

Blackie beamed and sat up straighter, smoothing down his sombre black jacket made of good broadcloth. 'It is indeed. And a new tie,' he said, touching the dark blue cravat proudly. He winked. 'Sure and I'm all in me Sunday best today. Ye don't think I'd come visiting an ejicated young lady in me working clothes, do ye now?'

Emma smiled and, ignoring this comment, said, 'Yer should've seen Mrs Fairley and Mrs Wainright. They looked ever so beautiful. Like the pictures from the illustrated magazines. Real *elegant*.'

'I can just imagine,' said Blackie. He gazed at Emma affectionately and added, 'And that's the way ye'll be looking one day, me spry young colleen, when ye are the grand lady.'

Emma blushed. 'Oh, I don't knows about that,' she murmured, suddenly bashful. 'But tell me, what's happening in Leeds? Tell me some more about Leeds, Blackie. What've yer been doing there lately?'

'Not much news,' said Blackie cautiously, his eyes wary as he became conscious of that look on her face, that look which always appeared when she mentioned the city. 'Things are just the same, I am thinking. I have nothing exciting to be telling ye, mavourneen, sure and that's the God's truth. And all I've been doing, since I last saw ye in March, is work hard. Me and me Uncle Pat, why, we've more jobs than we can handle these days. Thanks to the Squire. Sure and it is himself who has helped us to prosper. Giving us the recommendations and all.' Now unable to conceal his jubilation, he added exuberantly, and without stopping to consider the effect it might have on her, 'I not be telling ye a lie, Emma, when I say that business is booming in Leeds.'

Emma looked at Blackie intently. She thought: Then I must go there soon, but said, 'And what's in it for the Squire? Recommending yer for all this work?'

Blackie threw back his great head and roared with laughter. 'There be nothing in it for himself,' he said. 'Whyever should ye be thinking such a thing, mavourneen?' Blackie pulled a red kerchief out of his pocket, wiped his eyes, and blew his nose.

''Cos I knows the Squire, and *he* would never do owt for nowt,' she said pithily, contempt curving her mouth. 'Talk about hard-faced, yer could straighten nails on his.'

Blackie laughed again and slapped his knee. 'Emma! Emma! Not everybody's on the take or on the make,' he remonstrated gently. 'Especially a fine gent like the Squire. He recommends us because he is acquainted with our work. He knows we are good bricklayers and builders, me and me Uncle Pat. Sure and he does.' He paused and said with a degree of certitude, 'He also recommends us because he likes us, I am thinking.'

'Oh, aye,' remarked Emma dryly, her eyes doubtful. She found this hard to believe.

Blackie leaned forward across the table, and said confidingly, 'Well, it is more than the *liking* of us. Ye see, mavourneen, me Uncle Pat saved the Squire's life three years ago, and himself has been grateful ever since.'

'Saved the Squire's life,' Emma echoed coldly. 'And how did he do that, then?'

'The Squire was driving through Leeds in his gig. Down Briggate, I believe it was, and the horse bolted. Sure and it did. Me Uncle Pat saw it happening, and with the great presence of mind he leapt on the horse and brought it to a standstill, after a great struggle, terrifying to behold, so I understand,' said Blackie, unconsciously throwing back his shoulders. 'He's a big man and strong, me Uncle Pat is, but it took all of his great strength, indeed it did! The Squire could have been killed, sure and he could, if it hadn't been for me Uncle Pat. And mighty dangerous it was. Why, me Uncle Pat was almost trampled under the horse and maimed for life.'

Blackie gave Emma a knowing look. 'Anyway, mavourneen, the Squire was grateful, as I said, and impressed with me Uncle Pat's bravery and he wanted to reward him –' Blackie shook his head and went on scoffingly, 'Me Uncle Pat, well, *he* wouldn't be taking the money. "Only a heathen takes money for the saving of a man's life," so says me Uncle Pat to the Squire. So, the Squire, out of his eternal gratitude, gives us the work and recommends us,' Blackie finished triumphantly, nodding his head. 'And glad we are to be getting it, mavourneen.'

'Yer Uncle Pat *must* be very brave,' said Emma. She pondered for a moment and then her mouth compressed into a thin line. 'Well, I hope yer charge the Squire plenty, and *them* that he recommends,' she commented with acerbity.

'Why, Emma Harte! What a thing to be saying,' cried Blackie, feigning horror. He concealed his amusement and exclaimed, 'I can see ye are growing up to be a real hardheaded Yorkshire lass.'

'The tea's ready,' announced Cook, interrupting their conversation. 'Emma, get out the best cups and saucers, and put the best lace cloth on the table, being as it's Sunday and we've got company.' Cook waddled over with the tea tray. 'What can I do to be helping ye, Mrs Turner?' asked Blackie, standing up.

'Nowt, lad. Sit yerself down. We'll have it all ready in two ticks.' She bustled away, returning a few seconds later with another tea tray laden with plates of thick ham sandwiches, slices of delicious veal-and-ham pie, hot sausage rolls, small dishes of pickled onions, beetroot, and piccalilli, warm buttered scones, blackberry jam, and a giant-sized caraway-seed cake.

'I swear I've never set eyes on a tea party like this, Mrs Turner. Faith and that's the truth,' said Blackie. 'Ye have outdone yeself, Mrs Turner, me darlin'. Sure and it's the finest spread I've ever seen.'

'Sounds ter me as if yer kissed the Blarney stone afore yer left Ireland,' said Cook, but her eyes were laughing and full of fun. She glanced at Blackie warmly and slapped him on the shoulder. 'Aay, get on with yer, lad. There's nowt ter be gained from flattering an old body like me.'

At this moment, Annie, the betweenmaid, came down the steps from the upstairs quarters. Tall and robust, with a creamy pink-and-white complexion, flaxen hair, and pale blue eyes, Annie looked for all the world like the typical buxom milkmaid and her manner was also decidedly bovine. Emma, putting out the cups and saucers, looked up. 'Did yer finish upstairs, Annie? Is everything all right, luv?' Annie nodded slowly, but her usually placid expression had disappeared, which Emma noticed instantly. 'Come ter the sink and wash yer hands then, luv, and we'll be having our teas,' Emma went on hurriedly, manoeuvring Annie across the kitchen, and out of Cook's earshot. 'Did yer break summat, luv?' asked Emma.

'No, Emma. I was ever so careful, like yer told me ter be,' said Annie.

'Well, what's wrong, then? Yer looked worried ter death. I can see yer not yerself.'

'It's Mrs Fairley,' Annie whispered conspiratorially. 'She fair give me a right turn, she did that, Emma.'

'What happened?' Emma turned on the tap and made a show of washing her hands to drown out their voices.

'I went up ter see the missis, like yer told me ter, after I'd finished setting the table. But when I knocked on her door she didn't answer. Anyroads, I went in ter the sitting room, and there she was, sitting in the dark, talking a mile a minute –'

'So what's wrong with that?' interrupted Emma impatiently.

'Yer don't understand, Emma! There was nobody there with her. She was talking ter the empty chair,' whispered Annie, her eyes like saucers.

'Nay, Annie luv. That can't be so. Maybe Mrs Wainright was there. Perhaps she was somewhere in the room and yer didn't notice,' countered Emma with a deep frown, although she guessed, as she spoke, that this was probably not the case.

'Mrs Wainright's not back from Kirkend,' murmured Annie. 'Anyroads, when Mrs Fairley sees me, she stops talking ter the chair. I asked her if she wanted her tea, ever so polite like, as yer told me ter be. She said she didn't, but ter tell yer she'll have her dinner in her room later,' said Annie. She began to breathe a little more easily, now that she was safely back in the kitchen.

'I'd best go up ter see her,' said Emma worriedly.

'No, yer don't have ter, Emma. The missis told me she was tired, so I helped her ter bed. She laid herself down and was off in a few minutes –' Annie stopped and took hold of Emma's arm. 'Emma –' she began hesitatingly, and paused again.

'Yes, luv, what is it now?' asked Emma.

'Mrs Fairley smelled ever so funny. She smelled of *whisky*. Least I think it was,' confided Annie.

Emma's eyes narrowed, but she adopted a sceptical tone. 'Oh, Annie, yer must be imagining things.'

'No, I'm *not*. Honest, Emma!'

Emma glared at Annie. 'First of all, how do yer knows what whisky smells like, Annie Stead? All yer dad sups is beer.' She gave Annie a penetrating look, and added protectively, 'Mrs Fairley has a special medicine that she takes. That's what yer smelled, Annie Stead.'

'If yer say so,' said Annie, for she was in awe of Emma, and also afraid of her. Nonetheless, she found the courage to add, 'Still, the missis *was* talking ter herself. Make no mistake about that!'

Emma, who felt compelled to defend Adele Fairley, thought quickly, and said with a small, knowing smile, 'Come ter think of it, Mrs Fairley often reads aloud ter herself. That's probably what she was doing when yer went in ter see her. Yer just didn't notice the book, that's all.' She gave Annie such a threatening look the girl blanched and shrank away. 'But if yer that concerned, I'll go up and see her right now,' remarked Emma coolly.

Annie shook her head. 'No! No! Leave her be, Emma. She was fast asleep when I left her a few minutes ago.'

'Now, there, lasses! What's all this 'ere whispering by the sink. Yer knows I don't like that sort of thing,' cried Mrs Turner crossly. She clapped her hands. 'Emma! Annie! Come 'ere at once and get yer teas. I won't have that there whispering!'

'Don't say owt ter Cook,' Emma cautioned. She turned off the tap, dried her hands, and attempted to look unconcerned. So Annie has smelled the drink, too, Emma thought with dismay. But, as she sat down at the table, she acknowledged to herself that there was no point in going upstairs, if Mrs Fairley was sleeping. That's the best thing for her right now, Emma decided, with her usual common sense.

Under Blackie's ebullient influence Emma soon cheered up. He was a marvellous raconteur and he kept them laughing during tea with his amusing stories and teasings. Emma found she was able to put Adele Fairley out of her mind completely, and she began to enjoy herself as much as the others. She laughed a great deal, much to Blackie's satisfaction. In his opinion, Emma was always too serious by far, so that he derived great pleasure from her gaiety.

The atmosphere was frivolous, and the kitchen rang with Blackie's boisterous laughter, the girls' high-pitched giggles and squeals of delight, and Cook's occasional reprimands 'ter keep the noise down', uttered good-naturedly enough through her own pealing laughter.

When they had finished eating, Emma said, 'Sing us a song, Blackie. Will yer, please?'

'Sure and I will, mavourneen. And what will ye pleasure be?'

'Would yer sing "Danny Boy", Blackie? Mrs Turner likes t –' Emma broke off and looked at the kitchen door, which had burst open wildly and was swinging on its hinges in the wind. She was flabbergasted to see her brother Frank standing on the threshold. He banged the door shut furiously, and hurtled down the stone steps, his boots clattering loudly, his small face white and cold, his thin body shivering in his threadbare jacket.

'Good gracious me! What's all this, then?' cried Mrs Turner, looking perturbed.

Emma jumped up and flew across the room. 'Frank lad, what's wrong?' she asked, pulling him to her protectively. Frank was gasping for breath, his eyes were wide with fright, and the freckles stood out on his drawn face. Emma led him to the fire gently, clucking to him in her motherly way and patting his shoulder soothingly. The boy's breathing was laboured, for he had run all the way from the village, and, as yet, he was unable to speak. Finally he managed to gasp, 'Me dad says yer've got ter come right sharpish, our Emma. Now!'

'Whatever's the matter?' said Emma, staring into his face with alarm, her mind racing. Frank's eyes filled with tears and before he spoke Emma knew instinctively exactly what he was going to say. She held her breath and prayed to God she was wrong.

'It's our mam, Emma. Me dad says ter tell yer she's right badly. And Dr Mac's there. Come on!' he yelled, frantically tugging at her arm.

Emma's face went chalk white and fear darkened her eyes, so that they took on the colour of malachite. She pulled off her apron, ran to the kitchen cupboard, and grabbed her coat and scarf without uttering a word. Blackie and Mrs Turner exchanged worried glances. Mrs Turner said, 'Now, lass, I'm sure it's nowt serious. Don't be fretting yerself. Yer knows yer mam has been a lot better lately.' Her tone was reassuring, but her plump face was the picture of concern.

Blackie had risen and solicitously helped Emma into her coat. He squeezed her arm and said consolingly, 'Mrs Turner's right. To be sure she is, Emma. Don't be afeared now. Ye mam's in good hands with the doctor.' He paused and looked into her stricken face. 'Would ye like me to come with ye?'

Emma looked up at him and shook her head. 'But if Dr Mac's with her it must be summat serious.' Emma's voice quavered and her eyes brimmed with tears.

'Now, don't be jumping to the conclusions,' Blackie said with great gentleness, endeavouring to calm her fears. 'Ye mam will be fine, mavourneen. Sure and she will.' Emma looked up at him sorrowfully and she did not answer. Blackie put his strong arms around her and hugged her to him. After a few seconds he released her and touched her face tenderly. 'Ye must have faith,' he whispered softly, gazing into her eyes.

'Yes, Blackie,' she whispered, tying on her scarf. Then she grabbed Frank's hand and hurried him across the room. 'I don't think I'll get back in time ter help yer with dinner, Mrs Turner,' she called, running up the steps. 'But I'll try. Ta'rar.' The door slammed behind Emma and Frank.

Mrs Turner sat down heavily in the chair. 'It seemed too good ter be true. The way her mam improved in the last few weeks. The calm before the storm, if yer asks me,' she muttered dourly. 'Poor bairn, and she was having such a good time for once.'

'Let's not look on the black side, Mrs Turner. Her mam might be having a small attack, that's all. It could be a false alarm,' said Blackie with a show of cheeriness, but his heart was heavy and a melancholy look clouded his black eyes.

Once they were outside, Emma did not attempt to question Frank at all. She knew, deep in the marrow of her bones, that it was imperative for her to get home as quickly as possible, without wasting a minute of precious time. Her father would not have sent for her unless her mother had taken a turn for the worse. In spite of the confident reassurances Blackie and Mrs Turner had given her, Emma was quite positive of this, and she trembled as her alarm flared into cold terror.

Hand in hand, Emma and Frank ran across the stable yard, down the path by the copse of great oaks, and through the Baptist Field. Together, they struggled up the small slope rising to the plateau of moorland and the wide track that led to the village. By this time, Frank was fighting for breath and he found it difficult to keep up with Emma's increasing pace. She gripped his hand tighter and pulled him along after her relentlessly, ignoring his protestations and little gurgling cries.

He tripped and fell, but Emma did not stop, nor did she pay any attention to him. With an almost superhuman strength she dragged him along in her wake, his little body trailing limply in the dirt behind her. His wailing cries and ear-piercing screams finally registered, and pulled her up short.

'Frank! For heaven's sake,' she yelled wildly, staring down at him furiously. 'Get up, lad! This minute!' She attempted to pull him to his feet, but Frank lay inertly on the path.

'I can't keep up with yer, our Emma.'

Emma, who was not a naturally cruel person, was now disturbed almost to the point of hysteria. Her only thought was to get home to her mother, who needed her. 'Then yer'll have ter follow me,' she shouted with coldness.

Emma set off along the rough moorland track, her iron will pushing her forward with a preternatural energy. She gathered speed as she ran, her skirts flying out behind her in the wind. And one thought filled her mind as she ran: Don't let me mam die. It was a prayer really, and she repeated it over and over again. *Please, God, don't let me mam die.*

When she reached Ramsden Ghyll, Emma stopped and looked back. She could see Frank following on behind. But she could not wait for him, and she plunged down into the Ghyll without slowing her pace. At one moment she stumbled and almost fell, but she recovered herself quickly, and flew on. It was dark in the Ghyll, where the overhanging rocks cast giant shadows and excluded all light, but Emma did not notice the eeriness or the gloom. She was soon scrambling up the path on the other side of the Ghyll, and out into the bright sunlight. She was panting excessively and her breathing was impaired. Yet she did not stop. She hurtled forward along the top path, stones and bits of dirt flying out behind her, until, sobbing and breathless, she staggered up to Ramsden Crags. She rested against a rock, trying to regain her breath. The sound of pounding horse's hooves thundering along the path suddenly broke the silence. Emma looked back, startled. She was surprised to see Blackie galloping towards her on one of the Squire's horses. He held Frank in front of him.

Blackie brought the horse to a standstill and Emma recognized Russet Dawn, Master Edwin's chestnut. Blackie leaned down and gave her his large hand. He stuck out his foot and said, 'Jump up, Emma. Use me foot to mount.' Emma did as he instructed and pulled herself up on to the horse behind him. 'Hang on,' he cried as they set off again at a brisk canter. Soon they were in sight of the church spire and within minutes they were pulling up at Top Fold.

TWENTY

The kitchen of the Harte cottage was deserted when Emma entered and closed the door softly behind her. It was gloomy in the late-afternoon light, and desolate. The fire had burned out and the grate was filled with cold ashes and there was a smell in the air of cabbage and fried onions and burnt pots. Me dad spoilt the Sunday dinner again, Emma thought absently, as she took off her coat and scarf and looked around. The cottage was ominously silent and Emma shivered as she crept up the stone steps to her mother's room, her heart beating rapidly as her alarm increased.

Her father was alone, bending over Elizabeth. He was gently wiping her sweating face with a flannel and he stroked her damp and tangled hair lovingly. He looked up as Emma tiptoed in. His eyes were dark and brooding and filled with sorrow, and his face was harshly set and the colour of dull lead in the twilight.

'Me mam – what happened?' Emma whispered hoarsely.

Jack shook his head wearily. 'Dr Mac says it's a relapse. She's been growing weaker and weaker these last few days. She's no fight left in her,' he mumbled in a strangled voice. 'Doctor just left. No hope –' His voice cracked and he looked away swiftly, biting down his grief, swallowing hard on the incipient tears aching in his throat.

'Don't say that, Dad,' Emma cried softly but with great vehemence. She glanced around. 'Where's our Winston?'

'I sent him ter get Aunt Lily.' Elizabeth stirred restlessly. Jack turned back to her quickly and sponged her face again, and with tenderness. 'Thee can come over ter the bed, Emma. But don't make a noise. Thee mam must rest quiet like,' Jack said, his voice low and sorrowing. He stepped back, so Emma could sit on the small stool, and he touched her shoulder gently. 'Thee mam's been asking for thee,' he murmured.

Emma took hold of her mother's wasted hand. It was icy and lifeless. Elizabeth opened her eyes slowly, as if the effort to lift her lids was almost too enormous. She stared blankly at Emma. 'Mam, it's me,' Emma said quietly, tears brimming into her eyes. Her mother's face was utterly without colour and there was a peculiar sheen to it. Faint purple smudges stained the skin around her eyes, and her delicate lips were as white as the bedsheet. She continued to look at Emma dazedly. Emma clutched her mother's hand more tightly and fear rose in her like a fierce wave. She said again, and more insistently, 'Mam! Mam! It's me, Emma.'

Elizabeth smiled faintly and recognition illuminated her eyes, which suddenly lost their cloudiness and became more comprehending. 'Emma luv,' she said weakly. She attempted to touch her daughter's face, but she was too exhausted and her hand dropped limply on to the bed. 'I waited for yer ter come, Emma.' Her voice was a fluttering whisper. Her breath came in small, rapid pants, and she shivered under the blankets.

'Mam! Mam! Yer'll be all right, won't yer?' Emma said, her voice urgent with apprehension. 'Yer'll get better, won't yer, Mam?'

'I am better, luv,' Elizabeth said. A gentle smile played around her lips. She sighed deeply. 'Yer a good lass, Emma.' She paused and her breathing became belaboured. 'Promise me yer'll look after Winston and Frank. And yer dad.' Her voice was now so faint it was hardly audible.

'Don't talk like that, Mam,' cried Emma, her voice quavering.

'Promise me!' Elizabeth's eyes stretched wide with mute appeal.

'Yes, I promise, Mam,' Emma said chokingly. The tears rolled down her cheeks silently. She leaned forward and touched her mother's dwindled face and kissed her lips, and laid her face next to her mother's. 'Fetch yer dad,' cried Elizabeth, with a little panting gasp, and the last of her rapidly diminishing strength.

Emma turned and motioned to her father, who was standing by the window. He strode over to the bed and sat down, and took Elizabeth in his arms and held her to him desperately. He felt as if a scythe was ripping at his insides, tearing out his heart. He did not know how he could endure the pain, the agony of her dying. She lay back on the pillows. Her face was waxy and turning grey. She opened her eyes and he saw they were filled with a new and radiant light. She tried to clutch at his arm, but she was far too weak and her hand fell away, trembling. He bent towards her. She whispered to him and he nodded, unable to speak in his searing grief.

Jack pulled back the bedclothes and lifted Elizabeth in his strong arms, carrying her carefully to the window. She was so light, as light as a fallen leaf, and she barely stirred in his arms. The window was open and the curtains billowed out in the evening breeze, and her dark hair was blown around her face. He looked down at her. She had the most rapturous expression on her face and her eyes were shining. She breathed deeply of the fresh air, and he felt her whole body stretch tautly in his arms as she lifted her head and looked out longingly towards the moors.

'The Top of the World,' she said, and her voice was so clear and so strong and so young at that moment, he was momentarily startled. It echoed around the room with a vibrancy that was almost abnormal. She fell back in his arms. A tender smile flickered briefly on her lips. She sighed several times, long deep sighs that rippled through her whole body. And then she was still.

'Elizabeth!' Jack cried, his voice raw with emotion, and he cradled her body in his arms, rocking her to him, and his tears drenched her face.

'Me mam!' Emma screamed, and flew across the room. Jack turned and looked at Emma blindly, tears coursing down his cheeks. He shook his head. 'She's gone, lass,' he said, and he carried Elizabeth back to the bed and covered her body with the bedclothes. He crossed her hands on her breasts and smoothed her hair away from her face, so tranquil in death, and touched her eyelids. He bent down and kissed her icy lips, and his own shook with his pain and despair.

Emma was sobbing by his side. 'Dad, oh, Dad,' she cried, clinging to him. He straightened up and looked down into her streaming face. Then he put his arms around her and pulled her to him comfortingly. 'She's free now, Emma. Free at last of the terrible suffering.' He choked back his own sobs and held Emma closer to him. He stroked her hair and consoled her, and they were locked together for a long time in their mutual anguish.

At last Jack said, 'It's God's will,' and he sighed.

Emma moved away from him and lifted her tear-stained face. 'God's will!' she repeated slowly, and her young voice was excessively harsh and unremitting. 'There's no such thing as God!' she cried, her eyes blazing. 'I knows that now. Because if there was a God, He wouldn't have let me mam suffer all these years, and He wouldn't have let her die!'

Jack stared at her aghast and before he could respond she was running out of the bedroom. He heard her feet hammering on the stairs and the front door banging behind her. He turned wearily, his great body sagging, and he looked down at his dead wife and a sob rose in him again, and he was engulfed by a terrible darkness. He stumbled like a sleepwalker to the window and looked out. Dimly, through his pain, he saw Emma running up Top Fold towards the moors. The sky was saffron bleeding into scarlet as the sun fluttered down below the bleak hills. Its last shimmering rays were streaking across Ramsden Crags, just visible in the gloaming.

'If Elizabeth is anywhere, that's where she is now,' he said. 'At the Top of the World.'

TWENTY-ONE

When Adam Fairley returned from Worksop, early on Sunday evening, he found Olivia sitting alone in the library. He hurried over to her, smiling with delight, his eyes lighting up with love. He was still overwhelmed by the emotions of the night before, and this showed in his glowing face, which had lost its ascetic gauntness, in the buoyancy of his step, in the joyfulness of his whole demeanour.

But when Olivia looked up at him, he drew in his breath sharply and stared at her, his intelligent eyes sweeping over her face swiftly. She was excessively pale and she seemed burdened by a certain weariness, and he saw at once, and to his enormous dismay, that she was greatly disturbed.

Adam took hold of her hands and pulled her up from the Chesterfield, without speaking. He kissed her cheek and took her into his arms, embracing her warmly. She clung to him and buried her head on his shoulder, and he felt her body trembling against his own. After a few seconds she drew away gently, and looked up at him. Her gaze was penetrating, and in her lovely aquamarine eyes Adam detected confusion and misery.

'What is it, Olivia?' he asked softly. 'You are troubled and that sorely grieves me.'

Olivia shook her head and sat down. Her face was etched with sadness and her shoulders drooped dejectedly. She folded her hands in her lap, staring at them studiously, and still she did not speak. Adam joined her on the sofa and picked up one of her hands. He held it tightly in both of his own, pressing it lovingly.

'Come, come, my dear, this won't do,' he exclaimed in a falsely cheerful voice. 'Did something happen to upset you?' Adam knew, as he spoke, that this was the most ridiculous question. She was obviously disturbed about the development in their relationship, and this both alarmed and frightened him.

Olivia cleared her throat and finally lifted her head slowly. Her eyes shone with tears. 'I think I must leave here, Adam. At once. Tomorrow, in fact.'

Adam's heart sank into the pit of his stomach and he was filled with dread. 'But why?' he cried, leaning closer. He tightened his grip on her hand.

'You *know* why, Adam. I cannot remain here after – after last night. I am in an untenable position.'

'But you said you loved me,' he protested.

Olivia smiled faintly. 'I do love you. I've loved you for years. And I will always love you. But I cannot stay here, Adam, in the same house as my sister, your wife, and conduct a clandestine love affair. I cannot!'

'Olivia, Olivia, let us not be hasty. Surely, if we are discreet –'

'It's not only that,' she interrupted quickly. 'What we did last night was wrong. We committed a terrible sin.'

Adam said, almost roughly, 'Because I committed adultery. Is that what you're saying, Olivia? It was not you, but I, who committed a sin, in the eyes of the law. That is a matter for my conscience, not yours. So let me worry about that.'

'We both committed a sin – in the eyes of God,' she answered very softly. Observing the grave look on her face, he knew, with an awful sense of foreboding, that she was in deadly earnest. He did not want her conscience to drive her away from him. He could not let her go. Not now. Not ever again. Not when they had found each other at last, after all the years of loneliness and unhappiness they had both endured, trapped in their worthless marriages.

Adam spoke urgently. 'Olivia, I understand the way you feel. Believe me, I do. You are a good and honest person. Duplicity and intrigue are not in your nature. I know, too, that you have a strong sense of personal honour. As I do myself. I fought my emotions, my desire for you, very hard last night.'

He paused and gazed deeply into her eyes. He touched her face tenderly. 'I suppose it *was* wrong, in a way. But we didn't hurt anyone, least of all Adele. And I certainly don't feel any remorse or guilt. You shouldn't either. That would be pointless, for we cannot undo what we did, not can we alter the fact that we love each other. And I do love you. More than I have ever loved any other woman.'

'I know,' she murmured sadly. 'Nevertheless, we cannot think of ourselves, selfishly. We must put duty first.' Her eyes filled with the tears she had been trying to withhold, and her face overflowed with her love for him. 'I know it is not in you to behave shoddily, Adam.'

'Everything you say is true, of course. But I cannot live the rest of my life without you, my love.' He shook his head. 'I cannot!' His luminous eyes implored her. 'Please stay with me, at least until July, as you planned, and as you promised last night. For my part, I promise I will never intrude on you, or force myself upon you.' Adam took her hands in his again. 'Such a thing would be irremissible, in view of the circumstances and your feelings about Adele, and your position in this house. But please, Olivia, stay with me for a few months,' he beseeched her, his voice low and hoarse with his desperation. 'I *swear* I will not attempt to make love to you. Please, please don't abandon me to life in this mausoleum. To life alone in this loveless house.'

Olivia's heart went out to him. She did love him, so very much, and life had dealt him a cruel blow, saddling him with her sick and disturbed sister. He who was so vital, so full of life, and so fine and good. As she studied that strained and suffering face before her, Olivia felt her resolution wavering, her determination to leave Yorkshire dissolving. Slowly she began to weaken, for she found it hard to deny him. And what he asked was really not all that unreasonable. 'All right, I will stay,' she said at last, in the gentlest of voices. 'But it must be on the conditions you have just mentioned.' She moved closer to him on the sofa, took his agonized face in her hands, and kissed his cheek. 'It's not that I don't desire you, my darling. Because I do,' she murmured. 'However, we cannot be lovers in this house.'

Adam exhaled a long and deep sigh. 'Thank God!' he exclaimed. That deadening coldness that had afflicted his body gradually seeped out of him, and his sense of relief was so enormous it was almost euphoric. Now he took her in his arms and pressed her head against his shoulder, stroking her hair. 'I need you so very much, my love. Your presence is as vital to me as breathing. But I swear I will not lay a finger on you, or compromise you in any way. I am happy just to be with you, to have your companionship, to know you love me. You feel the same way, don't you?'

'Yes, I do,' Olivia responded. 'We must be discreet, though, and not display our affection for each other so readily, or so openly.' She looked into his face, so close to hers, and smiled for the first time. 'Like this. It would be most embarrassing if Gerald, or one of the servants, walked in now.' As she finished speaking she extracted herself from his embrace.

'Quite right,' Adam remarked with a small dry laugh. He was ready to acquiesce to anything she wanted, if it meant keeping her by his side. 'Well, my love, if we are going to be circumspect, perhaps we had better have a sherry, and sit on opposite sides of the room, and chat about inconsequential things.' He made his voice light and he was able, at last, to laugh. 'Would you like a drink before dinner, my sweet?'

'Yes, that would be lovely, Adam. And most natural-looking wouldn't you say, should we be surprised by any member of the household.' Her eyes were suddenly merry and she found herself laughing with him.

Adam grinned at her and stood up. Her eyes followed him across the room. She felt an unexpected ache in the region of her heart, and she wondered if they would have the strength to control their emotions, to deny each other. *We must*, she said firmly to herself.

Adam returned with the sherries. He handed her one, clinking her glass. 'Cheers, my dear.' He smiled wryly and, very pointedly, sat in the chair opposite. 'Is this a discreet enough distance?' he asked, his eyes twinkling.

'I should say so,' she said, laughing again. She sat back on the Chesterfield and relaxed, her usual equanimity fully restored. She trusted Adam implicitly. He would keep his word, and his distance, and that in itself would give her the necessary strength to do the same thing.

'There is just one thing more,' Adam began cautiously. 'You said we could not be lovers in this house. However, if I saw you in London, might it – could it be – different? We would be free there,' he asserted.

Olivia's pretty mouth curved into a small smile. 'Oh, Adam, darling, you are impossible,' she said, shaking her head. Then her eyes became quiet and grave. 'I don't know how to answer that. We would still be committing a sin, wouldn't we?' She blushed and dropped her eyes. 'I don't know what to say. I must think.'

'Please, don't get upset again, my love,' Adam cried, conscious of her discomfiture. 'We will not discuss that side of our relationship again. Not until you wish to discuss it. Could I ask one favour of you, though?'

'Of course, Adam,' said Olivia.

'When I am in town, you will dine with me, won't you? And accompany me to the theatre? You will *see* me, won't you?' he asked, his desperation again apparent in his voice.

'You know very well I will. We have always spent time together when you have been in London. Why should it change now, Adam? We have even more reasons to see each other – socially,' she declared in a positive voice that was also calm.

This reassured him. 'Good. Then it's all settled.' Adam stood up and threw a log on to the fire, pushing back the memory of their mutual passion of the night before.

'Was Edwin glad to be back at school?' Olivia asked.

Adam was lighting a cigarette. He drew on it and said, 'Yes, he was delighted to be back. Poor Edwin has been quite frustrated, cooped up with Adele all these months.' He sighed. 'She does coddle him so.' Adam rested an arm on the mantel-shelf and lifted one of his highly polished brown boots on to the hearth. He threw Olivia a swift glance, and, leaning closer to her, went on, in a lower voice, 'I do hope you are aware that Adele and I have not lived together as man and wife for over ten years.'

'Yes, I had assumed that,' said Olivia. She stood up and went to him. She kissed his face and stroked his hair. 'Everything will be all right. I know it will. Now, let me get you another sherry.'

She took the glass from him, and he smiled at her, thankful she was with him, and that now she intended to stay at Fairley through the summer. He watched her gliding across the floor of the library, graceful and elegant and self-assured, and he realized, with a sudden flash of perception, that without her his life would sink into darkness again. She *was* his life, and he resolved never to be apart from her ever again, as long as he lived.

TWENTY-TWO

'I just don't understand how our Winston could do a thing like that,' Big Jack Harte said to Emma. 'Running away so soon after thee mam died, without so much as a ta'rar.'

'But he did leave yer a note, Dad,' Emma said quickly. When he made no response, she went on, 'Don't worry, Dad. He'll come ter no harm in the navy. He's a big lad, and he can take care of himself.' She leaned across the table and squeezed his arm in a reassuring way.

'Aye, I knows that, lass. Still an' all, it was right deceitful of him ter do a moonlight flit, packing his stuff and creeping out in t'middle of t'night. It weren't like our Winston at all,' Jack grumbled, his disgruntlement obvious. He shook his head. 'And there's summat else – *I'd* like ter know how he managed ter get inter the Royal Navy without me signature on his papers. He's under age, thee knows, Emma, and he would've had to have me signature on 'em.'

Emma sighed. This conversation had been going on endlessly and repetitively for the last three days, since she had come home from the Hall, and it was beginning to irritate her.

But before she could answer, Frank piped up, 'He forged yer signature, Dad. Yes, I *bet* that's what he did! He had ter do that, ter get the recruiting officer ter accept him.'

Emma threw Frank the most furious glance, and said harshly, 'Hush up, Frank. Yer just a little tiddler. Yer don't know owt about such things.'

Frank was sitting at the other side of the kitchen, scribbling away, as was usual these days. He said, in a matter-of-fact tone, 'I knows all sorts of things, our Emma. From them there illustrated magazines and newspapers yer brings home from the Hall. I reads every line, yer knows.'

'Then I'll have ter stop bringing 'em,' she snapped, 'if they're going ter make yer so big-headed and cheeky. Yer getting ter be a right know-it-all, our Frank.'

'Oh, Emma, leave the bairn alone,' Jack muttered. He sucked on his pipe, engrossed in his thoughts, and then he said, 'Frank's right, yer knows. Our Winston must've forged me signature. No two ways about it, that's what he did. Sure as eggs is eggs.'

'I expect he did,' said Emma, 'since that's the only way he could've joined up. But what's done is done, and there's nowt we can do about it now. He's more than likely well on his way – to wherever they're sending him.'

'Aye, lass,' Jack said, settling back in the chair.

Emma was silent. She regarded her father intently, a worried frown slicing across her smooth wide brow. Her mother had been dead almost five months, and whilst Jack strived always to conceal his agonizing grief, Emma knew it was eating away at him inside. He had lost weight, for he hardly ate, and his great powerful body seemed to have shrunk. He was frighteningly contained, and, sometimes, when he was unaware of Emma's close scrutiny, his eyes would fill with tears, and his sorrow was most shockingly revealed on his drawn face. Emma would turn away helplessly, her own grief rising up in her so rabidly she found it hard to conquer. But she had to control herself. Someone had to hold the family together, and that apathy which had assailed her father months before her mother's death was even more apparent. Emma feared for her dad, and as the days went by her worry increased. Now this fresh problem of Winston's stealthy departure last week had imbued in Jack a new despondency.

Emma sighed. She had temporarily postponed her Plan with a capital *P*. She could not bring herself to leave for Leeds just yet, in view of Winston's scarpering off, even though she had saved quite a lot of shillings. She had over five pounds, a princely sum with which to finance the initial stages of her plan to make her fortune. But now was not the time to leave. And anyway, she had promised her mam she would look after the family. It was a promise that Emma felt honour-bound to keep. For the moment.

She picked up one of Olivia Wainright's recipes, coated the back of it with paste she had made from flour and water, and stuck it carefully into her exercise book for future reference. She looked at Olivia Wainright's handwriting. It was so beautiful. Rounded and elegant and flowing. Emma was striving to copy it. She was also paying strict attention to the way Olivia spoke, for she was endeavouring to imitate the way she pronounced her words. Blackie kept telling Emma she would be a grand lady one day, and she knew grand ladies had to speak proper like. She corrected herself silently. Yer didn't say 'proper like'. You said 'properly', or 'correctly'.

Suddenly, the silence in the small kitchen was broken, as Frank cried excitedly, 'Hey, Dad, I just thought of summat. If our Winston forged yer signature, then his papers aren't legal like, are they?'

Jack looked startled at this mature comment from Frank, which he himself had not even thought of. He contemplated his youngest child in wonderment. Frank continually amazed him these days. Eventually, Big Jack said, 'There's summat in that, Frank. Aye, there is, lad.' He was nothing short of impressed, for Frank was becoming a fountain of information, and all manner of intelligent comments fell from his lips when Jack least expected them.

'So what?' said Emma, glaring at Frank with open hostility, which was unparalleled for her, as protective as she was of Frank. But she wanted the subject of Winston's running away dropped. She knew that prolonging the discussion would only upset her dad further.

'If the papers aren't legal, our Emma, then me dad can get him out of the navy. Don't yer understand? They'd have ter – ter – discharge him! For falsifying the papers. Yes, that's it,' shouted the triumphant Frank, delighted with his shrewd deduction.

'He's right, Emma,' Jack said, his voice more positive, quite visibly cheering up.

'Our Frank might be right, but how are yer going ter go about getting Winston out, Dad?' Emma asked with her usual bluntness. 'Are yer going ter write ter the Royal Navy then? And who would yer write ter, anyroads?' She frowned at Frank, who had a pleased smile on his pale, freckled face. The boy was intelligent, Emma could not deny that, but he annoyed her when he created additional unrest in the house with his comments, which were sometimes far too clever for her liking.

'Yer could ask the Squire what ter do, Dad,' suggested Frank.

Jack mused on this, but Emma shrieked, 'Ask the Squire what ter do? I wouldn't ask him for owt. Why, he wouldn't give yer ha 'porth of spit without charging yer for it!' Her voice was icy and dripped scorn.

Jack ignored her remarks, and now said, 'Well, I could go inter Leeds and call at the recruiting office, and ask about our Winston. Find out where they sent him. What barracks he was shipped ter. They must've got records. And I could tell 'em what he did. Thee knows – forging me signature an' all.'

Emma sat bolt upright in the chair, her face formidable, and said in her firmest tone, 'Now listen ter me, our Dad. Yer not going ter do owt. Our Winston's always wanted ter go inter the Royal Navy, and now he's gone and done it. And think on one thing, our Dad. Winston's better off in the navy than slogging long hours at the Fairley brickyard, working in all that dust and muck. Leave him be, Dad.'

She paused and gave her father a long look that was also loving, and she softened her voice considerably. 'He'll write, our Winston will, when he gets settled in. So just leave him be, as I said afore.'

Jack nodded, for he respected Emma's judgement. 'Yes, luv, there's common sense in what thee says. He always did want ter get away from Fairley.' Jack sighed.

'I can't say as I blame him for that, mind thee. It was just the way he did it, sneaking off like.'

Emma couldn't help smiling. 'Well, Dad, I expect he knew if he asked yer permission yer'd have said no, and that's why he ran off, afore yer could stop him.' She stood up and went over and hugged her father. 'Come on, Dad luv, cheer up. Why don't yer go ter the pub, and have yerself a pint, and enjoy a bit of company with the lads,' she suggested. Fully expecting him to dismiss this suggestion, as he always did of late, she was amazed when he said, 'Aye, I thinks I will, lass.'

Later, after her father had left for the White Horse, Emma turned to Frank. 'I wish yer hadn't said that, Frank, about Winston forging me dad's signature and it not being legal, and getting Winston out of the navy. It only upsets our dad more. Now listen ter me, luvey –' She shook her forefinger at Frank, her face grave. 'I don't want no more talk about our Winston when I've gone back ter the Hall. Do yer hear, our Frankie?'

'Yes, Emma,' said Frank, biting his lip. 'I'm sorry, Emma. I didn't mean owt wrong. I didn't think owt of it. Don't be cross with me.'

'I'm not, luv. But just think on what I said, when yer alone with our dad.'

'I will. And, Emma.'

'Yes, luvey?'

'Please don't call me Frankie.'

Emma concealed a smile of amusement. He was so serious and adopting such a grown-up air. 'All right, *Frank*. Now, I thinks yer'd best be getting yerself ready for bed. It's eight o'clock and we all have ter be up early for work termorrow. And don't sit up half the night reading yer newspapers and books.' She clucked and shook her head. 'No wonder we never have any candles! Off yer go, lad. And I'll be up in a minute ter tuck yer in. And I'll bring yer a glass of milk, and an apple, as a special treat.'

He scowled at her. 'What do yer think I am, Emma Harte? A big baby? I don't wants yer ter tuck me in,' he cried as he picked up his notebook and newspapers. He turned when he went out of the kitchen door. 'But I'd like the apple,' he said with a small grin.

After she had washed up the dirty supper dishes stacked in the sink, Emma went upstairs. Frank was sitting up in bed, writing in his notebook. Emma put the apple and the milk on the table and sat down on the bed. 'And what's this yer writing now, our Frank?' she asked curiously. Like her father, she was constantly astonished by Frank's superior intelligence and his fertile brain. He also had an amazingly retentive memory.

'It's a g-g-h-o-s-t s-t-o-r-y,' he told her in a moaning voice. He looked at her solemnly and made his eyes large. 'A ghost story! All about haunted houses, and the spirits of the dead rising from their graves, and walking around. Ooooooohhh!' he whispered, his voice low and ominous. He fluttered the sheet at her. 'Shall I read it for yer, our Emma? It'll scare yer ter death,' he warned.

'No! Thanks very much! And don't be so daft,' she cried, straightening the sheet. Then she shivered involuntarily, at the same time chiding herself for being foolish, for she knew Frank was teasing her. But the grim superstitions of the North were ingrained in her, and gooseflesh rose on her arms. Emma cleared her throat and assumed a superior expression. 'And where's all this scribbling going ter get yer, our Frank? It's a waste of the good paper I brings home from the Hall, if yer asks me. Yer can't make no money, scribbling this junk.'

'Yes, yer can!' he cried with such extraordinary violence she was startled. 'And I'll tell yer where it's going ter get me. On to a newspaper when I'm a big lad. Maybe even the *Yorkshire Morning Gazette*. That's what!' He outstared her, and finished, 'Stick that in yer pipe and smoke it, Emma Harte.'

Laughter bubbled in Emma's throat, but comprehending he was in earnest, she kept her face straight. 'I see,' she remarked coolly. 'But not till yer grown up. In a few years perhaps we'll think about it.'

'Yes, Emma,' he said, and bit into the apple. 'Ooh, Emma, this is luvely. Thank yer.'

Emma smiled and smoothed his rumpled hair and kissed him in her motherly fashion. His small skinny arms went around her neck and he nuzzled against her affectionately, and with yearning. 'I luv yer, Emma. Ever so much,' he whispered.

'I luv yer, too, Frankie,' she answered, hugging him tightly. And on this occasion he did not reprimand her for using the diminutive.

'Don't stay up all night now, luv,' Emma told him as she quietly closed the door of his room.

'No, I won't. I promise, Emma.'

It was dark on the cold stone-flagged landing, and Emma edged her way into her own bedroom and carefully felt her way to the stand by the narrow bed. She groped for the matches and lit the stub of candle in the brass candle holder. The wick flickered tenuously, illuminating the blackness with a pale light. The tiny room was so frugally furnished it was virtually empty, but, like the rest of the cottage, it was scrupulously clean. Emma carried the candle over to a large wooden trunk in one corner of the room. She placed it on the window ledge nearby, and, kneeling down, she lifted the heavy lid of the trunk. A strong odour of camphor balls and dried lavender floated up out of the trunk. This had belonged to her mother and all of the things in it were Emma's now. Her dad had told her that had been her mother's wish. Emma had only looked once in the trunk, and hurriedly at that, since her mother's death. Until tonight she had been too emotional and grief-stricken to sort through her mother's treasured possessions.

She lifted out a black silk dress, old but hardly ever worn, and therefore still in good condition. She would try it on next weekend. She was quite sure it would fit her, with a few alterations. Underneath the black dress was her mother's simple white wedding gown. Emma touched it tenderly. The lace on it was yellowed with age. Wrapped in a piece of faded blue silk she found a small bouquet of flowers, dried and withered and falling apart. They had that sweet and sickly smell of dead roses. She wondered why her mother had kept them, what significance they had. But she would never know the answer to that now. There were some pieces of fine lawn underwear, obviously part of her mother's meagre trousseau, a black shawl embroidered with red roses, and a straw bonnet trimmed with flowers.

At the very bottom of the trunk was a small wooden box. Emma had seen the box many times before, when her mother had taken it out to select a piece of jewellery on very special and important occasions. Emma opened it with the small key sticking out of the lock. There was not very much jewellery in the box, and what there was had practically no value at all. She took out the garnet brooch and earrings her mother had always worn at Christmas and weddings and christenings, and on other such special days. It occurred to Emma, as she looked at them lying in her hands, that the stones were like dark rubies shimmering in the candlelight. Her mother had favoured the garnets above everything else she owned.

'I'll never part with these,' Emma said aloud, swallowing hard as her eyes misted over. She laid them on the floor and poked around in the box. There was a small cameo brooch and a silver ring, both of which she examined with interest. She tried on the ring. It fitted her perfectly. Her hand went back into the box and her fingers lighted on the gold cross and chain her mother had almost always worn. Emma grimaced. She wanted no reminders of God, who no longer existed for her. That was why she refused to go to Sunday school, even though her truancy annoyed her dad. She dropped the cross and chain on the floor next to the garnets, and lifted out a string of amber beads that were large and cool to her touch. They glowed with a deep golden colour, and to Emma's eye they had distinction. They had been a gift from a very grand lady, so her mam had told her several years ago.

After studying her new possessions for a few minutes longer, Emma began to replace them in the wooden box. It was at this moment that she felt something lumpy underneath the velvet which lined the bottom. She ran her fingers around the edge of the box. The velvet was loose and she was able to lift it up very easily. Its removal revealed a locket and a pin. Emma took out the locket and looked at it with curiosity. She did not remember ever noticing her mother wearing it. In fact, she had never seen it before. It was old, and beautifully worked, and made of real gold that glinted brightly in the light. She tried to open it, without success. She stood up, and hurried to find the scissors in her sewing box. After a few seconds, and with a little pressure, she was able to prize it open. There was a photograph of her mother on one side, taken when she was a girl. The other side was empty. Or was it? Emma looked more closely and saw that in place of a photograph there was a small lock of fair hair.

I wonder whose hair it is, she thought, trying to lift the glass covering it. But this was so firmly embedded in the locket she knew that if she prized at it too hard with the scissors it could easily shatter. Emma closed the locket and turned it over in her hands inquisitively. It was then that she saw the engraving on the back. It was indistinct and almost worn away by time. She could hardly make it out. She looked at it again, screwing up her eyes. Finally she brought the candle over to the trunk, and held the locket under the flickering flame.

The letters were very faint indeed. Slowly she read aloud, 'A to E – 1885.' Emma repeated the date to herself. That was nineteen years ago. Her mother had been fifteen in 1885. Did E stand for Elizabeth? It must, she decided. And who was A? She could not remember her mother ever mentioning anyone in the family with a name beginning with A. She decided she would ask her father when he came back from the pub later. Emma now placed the gold locket most carefully on top of the black dress, and fingered the pin, peering at it closely. How odd that her mother should have owned such a pin. She frowned. This was the kind of stickpin a gentleman wore in his cravat or stock, most probably with riding clothes, since it depicted a miniature riding crop with a tiny horseshoe set in the centre. It was also made of gold, she could tell that, and it was obviously valuable. It had certainly never belonged to her father.

Emma shook her head and sighed, rather mystified, and she automatically placed the locket and pin where they had reposed before, covered them with the velvet lining, and then put the remainder of the jewellery away in the wooden box. Methodically she returned all of the other items to the trunk and closed the lid, still shaking her head in bafflement. There was no doubt in Emma's sharp mind that the locket and the pin had been hidden by her mother, for some unknown reason, and this both puzzled and intrigued her. She decided then not to mention them to her father after all, although she was not quite sure what prompted this decision. She picked up her sewing box, blew out the candle, and went downstairs.

The kitchen was shadowy in the dim light emanating from the two candles on the table. Emma lit the paraffin lamps on the mantelshelf and the dresser, and carried the basket of mending she had brought home from the Hall over to the table, where she sat down to do her sewing. She worked first on a blouse belonging to Mrs Wainright, and then began to repair the hem on a petticoat of Mrs Fairley's. Poor Mrs Fairley, Emma thought, as she plied her stitches, she's as strange as ever. Quiet and sullen one minute, gay and chattering away the next. Emma would be relieved when Mrs Wainright returned from Scotland, where she was visiting friends. She had only been away for a fortnight, but it seemed like months. The Hall was not the same without her presence, and a peculiar nervousness was beginning to invade Emma with increasing regularity, and it bothered her not a little, since she found this acute edginess incomprehensible.

The Squire had also gone away, for the grouse shooting, so Cook had told her. He wouldn't be returning until the end of the week, far too soon to suit Emma's tastes. Things were quiet enough at the Hall, and, with Mrs Wainright and the Squire absent, Emma's duties had lessened. That was why Mrs Turner had let her have Friday off, as well as Saturday and Sunday. 'Spend a bit of time with yer dad, luv,' Mrs Turner had said, adding sympathetically, 'He needs yer right now, Emma.' And so she had spent three whole days at home this weekend, cleaning and washing and cooking for her dad and Frank. The only thing that had spoiled it was the fuss about Winston's disappearance earlier in the week. In Emma's mind, the interminable discussions were ridiculous, since there was no apparent solution to the problem.

Emma smiled suddenly to herself. Because there was less supervision at the Hall, she had been able to slip up to the moors on some sunny afternoons, to sit under the crags at the Top of the World, with Master Edwin. They had become firm friends during his summer holidays from boarding school.

Emma had become the recipient of many of Edwin's confidences. He told her all sorts of things, about his school, and the family, and most of them were special secrets she had promised never to reveal to a single soul. When Edwin had walked her across the moors on Thursday afternoon, he had told her that a great friend of his father's was arriving in a week's time, as a weekend guest. He was coming all the way from London, and he was a very important man, according to Edwin. A Dr Andrew Melton. Edwin was excited about the impending visit, because the doctor had just returned from America, and Edwin wanted to know all about New York. Not even Cook had been informed yet, or even Murgatroyd. Edwin had made her swear not to tell, and she had even had to say, 'Cross me heart and hope ter die,' as a reassurance to Edwin, making the appropriate gestures as well, crossing her heart and raising her right hand solemnly.

Emma's thoughts of Fairley Hall, and, more particularly, of Edwin, ceased abruptly as her father came in from the pub, just as the church clock was striking ten o'clock. She recognized at once that he had been drinking more than usual. He was unsteady on his feet, and his eyes were glazed. When he took off his jacket to hang it on the peg behind the front door he missed the peg, and the jacket dropped to the floor.

'I'll get it, Dad. Come and sit down, and I'll make yer some tea,' Emma said, putting aside the petticoat and rising quickly.

Jack picked up the coat himself, and this time he managed to hook it on to the peg. 'I don't want owt,' he mumbled, turning into the room. He took several jerky steps towards Emma and stopped. He stared at her for a long moment, astonishment flickering on to his face. 'Thee has such a look of thee mam sometimes,' he muttered.

Emma was surprised by this unexpected remark. She did not think she looked like her mother at all. 'I do?' she said questioningly. 'But me mam had blue eyes and darker hair –'

'Thee mother didn't have no widow's peak either, like thee does,' Jack interjected. 'That thee inherited from me mother, thee grandma. But still an' all, thee bears a striking resemblance ter thee mam, right this minute. When she was a girl. It's the shape of thee face, and thee features mostly. And thee mouth. Aye, thee's getting ter look powerfully like thee mam as thee gets older. Thee is that, lass.'

'But me mam was beautiful,' Emma began, and hesitated.

Jack steadied himself against the chair. 'Aye, she was that. Most beautiful lass by here thee ever did see. Weren't a man in Fairley didn't have his eye on thee mam at one time or t'other. Bar none. Aye, thee'd be right surprised if thee knew –' He bit off the rest of this sentence, and mumbled something unintelligible under his breath.

'What did yer say, Dad? I didn't hear yer?'

'Nowt, lass. Nowt that matters now.' Jack regarded Emma through his bleary eyes, which were, none the less, still quite discerning, and he half smiled 'Thee's also beautiful. Like thee mam was. But, thank God, thee's made of sterner stuff. Elizabeth was very delicate. Not strong like thee.' He shook his head sadly and moved uncertainly across the floor. He kissed her on the forehead and muttered his goodnight, and then he mounted the stone stairs, looking so much more pathetically diminished in size Emma wondered if he would be called *Big* Jack ever again. She sat down on the chair, gazing absently at the candle flame that flared so brightly before her eyes. She wondered what would become of her father. He was like a lost soul without her mother, and she knew he would never be the same. This realization filled her with a terrible sadness, for she was also aware there was nothing she could do to ease his acute pain, or the burden of his grief, which was total. He would mourn her mother until the day he himself died.

Eventually Emma roused herself from her reflections, picked up the petticoat, and continued sewing. She worked late into the night, doggedly determined to finish the repairs and alterations of the clothes from the Hall. Mrs Wainright paid her extra for this work, and Emma's crucial need for money enabled her to ignore her tired eyes, her aching fingers, and the general fatigue that gradually settled over her as the hours ticked by. It was well turned one o'clock in the morning when she folded away the last of the garments and crept upstairs to bed, avidly calculating the exact amount of money Mrs Wainright now owed her.

Once a year the grim and savage moors of the West Riding lose their blackened and colourless aspects. At the end of August a momentary transformation takes place practically overnight, when the heather blooms in such a burst of riotous colour the dun-tinted hills blaze with a sudden and glorious splendour. Wave upon wave of purple and magenta roll across the Pennines, crowning the dark industrial valleys below with a stunning beauty that is breathtaking even to the most jaundiced eye.

The vast plateau of moorland that sweeps up above Fairley village, and which is part of that great Pennine Chain, is no exception. Here, too, the sombre harshness is obliterated through September and into October. It is almost as if an immense bolt of local cloth has been flung generously across the hills, the weft and the warp of the weave a mixture of royal purple and blues and twists of green. For on the heathery slopes grow harebells and fern and bilberry, and even the scant gnarled trees are agleam with the freshest and smallest of fluttering leaves.

Larks and linnets glide up into the lucent air, and the sky, so often weighted down with rain-filled clouds, is dazzlingly blue and blazing with that incredible clarity of light so peculiar to the North of England. Not only is the relentless environment gentled and softened at this time of year, but the awesome silence of the winter is suddenly broken by the liveliest of sounds. The hillsides are all seamed by deep and narrow valleys and dells, each with its own tumbling little beck of clear water rushing down over polished brown stones, or sparkling with shimmering waterfalls that drop, unexpectedly, from the perilous rocky crags. Consequently, the sound of falling water is ever present on the Yorkshire moors in the summer months, accompanied by the sweet piercing trilling of the birds, the scurrying of the rabbits amongst the bilberry and bracken, the occasional bleat of the sheep that wander aimlessly over the heather-coloured hills seeking sustenance.

Emma Harte had a particular love of the moors, even in those grim and bitter winters when they became so brutal and frightening. Like her mother before her, she was at home there, up in that solitary hill country where, in her stark solitude, she never felt lonely or alone. She found in their vastness, in their very emptiness, a certain solace for whatever ailed her, drew a strange yet reassuring comfort from that imposing landscape. To Emma it was always beautiful through the ever-changing seasons, and most especially so in the late summer when the heather bloomed so profusely and with incredible brilliance.

On this Monday morning in August her spirits lifted considerably as she climbed over the stile into the long meadow, vividly green and speckled with daisies. She hurried along the narrow path, occasionally looking up, her deep-green eyes scanning the rising hills, lilac-tinted and running into purple beneath a sky that was china blue and without a single cloud. The sun was already seeping through the faint bluish haze on the horizon, staining it to golden, and she knew it would be another scorching hot day, as it had been all month.

For once she was glad to leave the cottage in Top Fold. Her father's distress about Winston's rapid departure had depressed her all weekend, and it was with a sense of relief that she had closed the cottage door and headed for the Top of the World. In that powerful and compelling wilderness, up there in that bright air, so purely bracing at this early hour, she felt free and unfettered, for Emma was a true child of the moors. Born and bred among them, it was as though their very characteristics had long ago penetrated her own soul, for she was as untameable and as relentless, and they were as much a part of her nature as the very breath she drew.

As a small child she had run unchecked over the high ridges and through the narrow valleys and little dells, her only companions the birds and the small timid creatures that inhabited the region. There was not a spot she did not know, and know well. She had her favourite places, well-guarded secret places, hidden in the crevices of the rocks and the folds of those wild hills, where all manner of pretty flowers blossomed when least expected and larks made their nests and crystal water tumbled over rocky slopes, scintillating icily in the sunlight, cool to drink and paddle in barefooted, toes curling deliciously on the dappled stones.

Now, as Emma escaped to her beloved moors, the oppressed feeling she had experienced for the last few days was lessening rapidly. She quickened her steps, following the familiar winding path that snaked upward, and she thought of Winston as she climbed on steadily. She would miss him, for they had always been close and dear companions, but she was happy for him. He had found the necessary courage to leave, to escape from the village and the Fairley brickyard, before it was too late. Her only regret was that her brother had been afraid to confide in her, believing, quite mistakenly, that she would tell their father or, at worst, attempt to persuade him to change his mind. She smiled to herself. How faulty Winston's judgement of her was. She would have readily encouraged him to pursue his dream, for she understood the nature of him, knew only too well how hemmed in and frustrated he had grown, with nothing much to look forward to in Fairley, except drudgery and boredom, and nights of drinking at the pub with his cloddish mates.

Emma paused to catch her breath as she came up on to the crest of the first ridge. She fanned her face, and took several deep breaths, before commencing her ascent of the slope to Ramsden Crags. They reared above her, huge granite horses dramatically outlined against the sky, ringed in sunshine, rivulets of which trickled down over their dark and ancient surfaces like running liquid gold. In winter, coated with ice and snow and sleet, their ghastly sheen could appal, but now in the soft summer air they appeared quite benign and welcoming. Emma looked about her, devouring the scenery with her eyes, as always drawing strength from those familiar surroundings. The haze was evaporating and, in spite of the gentle breeze blowing down from the high fells, she was already beginning to feel the heat. She was thankful she was wearing the dark green cotton dress Mrs Wainright had given her. It was light and cool against her bare legs.

Within minutes Emma was under the shadow of Ramsden Crags. She put down the heavy basket of clothes she was carrying, and seated herself on a flat rock. These days she always lingered for a moment at the Top of the World, for here she felt her mother's presence more assuredly than she did in the little cottage. To Emma, her mother still lived and breathed in this quiet sheltered spot, so well loved by them both. Emma saw her adored face in the pale shadows and vaporous moorland tints, heard her tinkling laughter echoing around the time-worn crags, communed with her in the gentle silence that was unbroken, except for the occasional bird call or the faint buzzing of a bee.

Emma rested her head against the rocks behind her and closed her eyes, conjuring up her mother's face. She opened them almost immediately and it seemed to her that her mother stood before her, radiant and smiling, the beloved image wholly formed. 'Oh, Mam, Mam, I do miss yer,' she said aloud, and she was filled with a longing, a yearning that was almost unbearable and brought an ache to her throat. She held out her arms, straining towards that nebulous image, which quickly faded. Emma sat quite still for a little while longer, leaning against the cool rocks, her eyes closed, pushing down the sadness that was still so near to the surface, and then, when she was contained, she picked up the basket and set off resolutely in the direction of Ramsden Ghyll.

Hurrying now, she shifted the heavy basket on to her other arm and descended into the Ghyll, all green darkness, shadowy and cool, where only thimblefuls of sunlight trickled in through the overhanging rocky ledges and ancient trees, whose crooked boughs knotted together like an old man's rheumatic gnarly fingers. A rabbit skittered across her path and disappeared behind a soaring boulder coated with mats of moss that were dark and velvety in the dim light. When she reached the middle of the dell, where all sunlight was totally obliterated, she began to sing, as she always did here, her light soprano echoing sweetly in the perfect stillness 'Oh, Danny Boy, the pipes, the pipes are calling. From glen to glen, and down the mountainside. The summer's gone, and all the roses falling. It's you, it's you must go, and I must bide.'

She stopped singing and smiled to herself, thinking warmly of Blackie. That was his favourite song and he had taught her the words. He had not been to the Hall for over a month. He had finished all of his work there for the moment. But sometimes he stopped by to see her, when he was in the district, and she wondered when he would be coming back. She missed him. Within minutes Emma was up and out of the chilly dell and in the bright air again, under the wide and shining sky, heading for the ridge that dropped down to the Hall. She began to walk more swiftly, to make up time, for she was later than usual this morning, well over an hour late, and Cook would already be grousing about her tardiness, of that she was certain. She ran down the slope and opened the old rickety wooden gate at the edge of the Baptist Field, closing it carefully behind her, dropping the heavy iron latch into place.

Emma no longer swung on the gate. She thought she was too grown-up to indulge in such a childish game. After all, she was fifteen and four months, already in her sixteenth year. A young lady almost, and young ladies, who intended to be grand ladies one day, did not do such frivolous things.

Entering the cobbled stable yard, Emma was somewhat taken aback to see Dr Malcolm's horse and trap tethered at the mounting block. The yard was deserted and unnaturally quiet, and there was no sign of Tom Hardy, the stableboy, who normally was busily currying the Squire's horses and polishing the brass on the harnesses at this hour. She frowned, wondering why Dr Mac was visiting the Hall at seven o'clock in the morning. Somebody must be badly, she surmised, and immediately thought of Edwin, who had taken a chill the week before. He was prone to chest colds, so Mrs Fairley had told her. Emma's feet flew up the stone steps leading to the back door, but not so quickly that her keen eyes did not notice the steps had not yet been scoured. That there Annie's getting neglectful of her duties, she thought with a flash of irritation.

The moment she entered the house Emma knew that something was dreadfully amiss. She quietly closed the door behind her and went down into the kitchen.

The fire blazed as always, the copper kettle hissed on the hob, but the delicious smell of breakfast cooking was noticeably absent. Cook sat in her chair near the fireplace, rocking to and fro, stifling her sobs and wiping her streaming eyes with the end of her apron, which was already sodden with her copious tears. Annie appeared to be reasonably controlled, and Emma strode rapidly across the flagged floor to her, hoping to elicit some information. But she perceived at once that Annie was as distraught as Cook, and she sat so rigidly in the chair she might have turned to a pillar of salt. Like Lot's wife, Emma thought.

Emma flung the basket down on the floor hastily. 'What's wrong?' she cried, looking from one to the other. 'Why is Dr Mac here? It's Master Edwin, isn't it? He's sick!' Neither Cook nor Annie appeared to hear her words. Certainly they paid no attention to her. And the dysphoria and apprehension in the air instantly communicated itself to Emma, so sharply that she quaked inside. The overwrought Mrs Turner now looked up, an anguished expression on her apple-dumpling face, her eyes red-rimmed. She gazed at Emma mutely, obviously unable to speak, and then she burst into further paroxysms of tears, rocking herself more violently than ever, moaning loudly between her sobs.

Emma was frantic. She reached out and touched Annie gently on the shoulder. The petrified girl jumped nervously, as if Emma's fingers had scourged her. She returned Emma's questioning look with a mindless stare. Annie blinked several times, very rapidly, and her mouth jerked, but she remained silent. And then she began to quiver. Emma took hold of her firmly with her small strong hands, attempting to calm her, filled with a mixture of impatience, and the beginnings of real panic.

Emma now realized she must go and find Murgatroyd immediately, but at that very moment the butler appeared at the top of the stairs leading to the family's living quarters. Emma's eyes flew urgently to his face. It was more dolorous than ever. He was wearing his black butler's coat, which was also unprecedented at this hour, when he was generally in his shirt sleeves and green baize apron, engaged in his pantry chores. On reaching the bottom of the stairs he leaned against the newel post and passed his hand over his brow in a futile gesture. His arrogant manner had been replaced by a deflated air, and this also registered most forcibly with Emma.

The bewildered girl took a few steps closer to him. 'Summat serious has happened. It's Master Edwin, isn't it?' she whispered. It was a statement rather than a question.

Murgatroyd looked down at her mournfully. 'No, it's the missis,' he said.

'She's badly then, is she? That's why Dr Mac's here –'

'She's dead,' interrupted Murgatroyd roughly, in a low harsh voice.

Emma took an involuntary step backward. She felt as if she had been struck across her face with great force. It seemed to her that all of the blood was draining out of her, and her legs trembled. Her voice was unsteady as she cried, 'Dead!'

'Aye, dead as a doornail,' Murgatroyd muttered tersely, his darkening face revealing his distress, which was most genuine.

For a split second Emma lost all power of speech. Her mouth opened and closed stupidly in her extreme nervousness and shock. Finally, she managed to say, 'But she wasn't badly when I left on Thursday afternoon.'

'No, and she weren't poorly yesterday either,' intoned Murgatroyd in a woebegone voice. He looked at Emma with gravity, and for once there was no hostility in his manner towards her. 'She tummeled down t'stairs during t'night. Broke her neck, so Dr Mac says.'

Emma gasped, and, reeling, she gripped the edge of the table to steady herself. Her eyes, wide and dazed, were riveted on the butler.

Murgatroyd inclined his head in Annie's direction. 'Yon lass found her at five-thirty this morning, when she went up ter take t'ashes out of the grates. Stiff as a board the missis was. Lying at the bottom of the front staircase in the entrance hall. That she was, and in her nightclothes. Fair scared the living daylights out of yon Annie, who come running ter fetch me like the Divil himself was after her.'

'It just can't be so,' Emma groaned, pressing her knuckles to her blanched mouth. Her eyes welled with tears.

'Aye, horrible it was, ter see her lying there, her eyes wide and open and all starey like, and glazed. And her head dangling loose like a broken doll's. I knows when I touched her she'd been dead for hours. Cold as marble, she was.'

Murgatroyd paused in his harrowing litany, and then went on, 'I carried her upstairs, fair gentle like, and laid her on her bed. And she might not have been dead at all. She looked ever so beautiful, just like she always was, with all that golden hair strewn about the pillow. Except for her staring eyes. I tried ter close 'em. But they just wouldn't shut. I had ter put two pennies on 'em, till Dr Mac got here. The poor, poor missis.'

The shaken and stupefied Emma dropped heavily into one of the chairs at the table. Tears were rolling down her cheeks, and she fished around in her pocket for the bit of clean rag that served as a handkerchief, and wiped her face. She hunched in the chair, so stunned and appalled she could hardly think. But gradually her composure returned, and it was then that she recognized she had grown extremely fond of Adele Fairley. She was doomed, Emma said to herself. And then she thought: I knew summat awful would happen here, in this terrible house, one day.

The silence in the sun-filled kitchen was leaden, broken only by the muffled sobs of the weeping Cook. After a few minutes, the butler emerged from his pantry and said, with sour bluntness, 'All this 'ere weeping and wailing like a lot of banshees has ter stop, yer knows.' He spoke to the room at large, his eyes sweeping over them all. 'We have our duties ter attend ter. There's the family ter consider.'

Emma looked at him alertly, thinking compassionately of Edwin and the grief he must be experiencing at the news of his mother's untimely and shocking death. 'The children,' she said, through her subsiding tears, and blew her nose. 'Do they know?'

'Dr Mac's talking ter Master Edwin in the library right this minute,' Murgatroyd informed her. 'I told Master Gerald meself, after I'd got the missis upstairs ter her room, and afore I sent Tom ter the village for the doctor. Master Gerald waited for Dr Mac, who dispatched him posthaste ter Newby Hall ter fetch the Squire home.'

'What about Mrs Wainright?' Emma ventured.

Murgatroyd threw her a scathing look. 'Do yer think I'm a gormless fool, lass? I already thought of that. Dr Mac wrote out a telegram, and Master Gerald is ter send it ter her in Scotland, from t'first post office he comes ter that's open.' The butler cleared his throat, and went on, 'Now, lass, let's get a move on down 'ere.

For a start, mash a pot of tea. The doctor needs a cup –' He glanced around the room and his beady eyes settled on Mrs Turner. 'So does Cook by the looks of it.'

Emma nodded, and hurried off to do as he had told her. Murgatroyd now addressed Cook in a louder voice. 'Come on, Mrs Turner. Pull yerself together, woman. There's a lot ter be done. We can't all collapse, yer knows.'

Cook lifted her sorrowful face and regarded Murgatroyd fretfully. Her ample bosom was still heaving, but her sobbing had ceased. She pushed herself up out of the chair, nodding her head. 'Aye, there's the bairns ter think about, and the Squire.' She wiped her damp and streaked face on her apron again, and then looked down at it, still shaking her head. 'Let me change me pinny, and then I'll start on breakfast. Not that I thinks anybody'll want owt.'

'Dr Mac might want a bite,' Murgatroyd said. 'I'm off up ter see him now. And ter draw the curtains. We must show the proper respect for the dead.'

Cook, who was changing her pinafore, said quickly, 'Did yer send Tom ter the village ter get Mrs Stead? Ter lay the missis out? She's the best by here for that job.'

'Aye, I did that.'

At the mention of her mother's name a flicker of comprehension entered Annie's deadened eyes. 'Yer've sent for me mam,' she said slowly, rousing herself from the stupor that had enveloped her for the last few hours.

'I did, Annie,' Murgatroyd asserted. 'She should be here any minute, and yer'd best look a bit more lively, afore she does arrive. She's got enough on her hands with the laying out. She don't needs ter be worrying about thee, lass.'

The cook shuffled over to Annie and put her arms around her, looking down into the girl's pale face. 'Do yer feel a bit better, luv?' she asked solicitously.

'Aye, I thinks so,' Annie mumbled. 'It gave me a right fright,' she gasped, 'finding the missis like that.' Her shaky voice cracked with emotion, and finally the tears suppressed by shock flowed unchecked.

'Have a good cry, luv. Get it out of yer system, afore yer mam gets here. Yer don't want ter be upsetting her, now do yer, luv?' Annie buried her head against Cook's comforting body, sobbing softly. Mrs Turner patted her shoulder and stroked her hair, murmuring kindly to her, and with motherly concern.

Satisfied that a degree of order had been restored, Murgatroyd turned on his heels and swiftly mounted the stairs. First he would consult with Dr Mac, to see if he had any further instructions, and then he must go around the house, drawing all the curtains, shutting out the light until after the funeral, as was the custom in the North after a death in the family.

Emma made the tea and they sat drinking it in silence, all of them subdued and sorrowing. It was Annie who finally spoke first. She looked at Emma across the table and said, 'I wish yer'd been here this weekend, Emma. Then yer'd have found the missis instead of me.' Annie's eyes widened. 'I'll never forget that look on the missis's face. Like she'd seen summat horrible afore she fell.'

Emma stared at Annie through narrowed eyes. 'What on earth do yer mean?'

Annie gulped. 'It was like she'd seen – seen one of them there abominations me mam says walks over t'moors at night,' Annie said, dropping her voice.

'Now, Annie, shut thee gob, lass. By gum, I won't have no fanciful talk about the spirits of the dead in this 'ere house,' Mrs Turner snapped. 'All them silly village superstitions. Stuff and nonsense, if yer asks me.'

Emma scowled. 'I wonder what Mrs Fairley was doing? Coming downstairs in the middle of the night. Murgatroyd said she's been dead for hours. She must've been wandering around at two or three o'clock in the morning.'

Annie volunteered quietly, 'I knows what she was doing.'

Both Mrs Turner and Emma stared at her in surprise, and with expectancy. 'And *how* do yer knows, Annie Stead?' asked Cook imperiously. 'Unless I'm mistaken, yer were fast asleep in yer room in the attic. Or yer should've been.'

'Aye, I was. But it *was* me that found her. And there was broken glass all around her body. From one of the best wine goblets, it was. She was still clutching part of t'stem, and there was dried blood on her hand, like rust, where she'd cut herself.' Annie shivered at the remembrance, and whispered, 'I bet she was coming down ter the library ter get herself a nip, 'cos I've sme –'

'Murgatroyd didn't mention no broken goblet ter me,' interjected Cook peremptorily, glaring at Annie.

'No, *he* wouldn't. But I saw him sweeping it up, ever so quick like,' Annie replied. 'He thought I hadn't seen it 'cos I was scared stiff.'

Cook continued to glare at Annie speechlessly, but Emma sucked in her breath, recognizing instantly the veracity of everything Annie had said. It was the most obvious explanation. 'Yer not ter repeat that ter anybody, Annie. Yer hear what I say? Not even ter the Squire,' Emma cautioned gravely. 'What's done is done, and the less said, the better.'

'Emma's right, luv,' said Cook, recovering herself. 'We don't wants no nasty gossip in the village. Let the poor missis rest in peace.'

Annie nodded. 'I promise not ter tell owt.'

Emma sighed and was thoughtful. Then she looked pointedly at Cook and said, 'It's right funny, when yer think about it. First Polly died, then me mam, and now Mrs Fairley. All in just a few months of each other.'

Cook returned Emma's concentrated stare. 'It's said, in these parts, that everything goes in threes.'

The funeral of Adele Fairley took place later that week. The Fairley mill was closed for the day, and all of the workers were in attendance, along with the servants from the Hall. The small cemetery adjoining Fairley Church overflowed with the villagers, the local gentry, and friends of the family from all over the county.

Two days after the funeral, Olivia Wainright left for London, accompanied by Edwin. Exactly one week later Adam Fairley departed himself, journeying south to join his youngest son at his sister-in-law's Mayfair town house.

Ernest Wilson was left in charge of the mill, much to Gerald Fairley's secret delight. For the callous, brainless, and irresponsible Gerald, quite unmoved by his mother's death, thought only of the infinite opportunities which now presented themselves. He fully intended to assert himself at the mill, and stringently so, in his father's absence, which he fervently hoped would be prolonged.

TWENTY-THREE

On a warm Sunday afternoon, in June of the following year, Edwin Fairley set out from Fairley Hall for the moors. He carried a picnic basket in one hand, laden with all sorts of delicious tidbits from Cook's groaning pantry, and in the other a sack containing some gardening implements and a few necessary items.

He and Emma had some hard work to do at Ramsden Crags, a task they had been planning for several weeks. Because of the inclement and frequently rainy weather, they had had to postpone this venture several times. On Friday, when Emma went home for her weekend off, Edwin had walked with her as far as the Crags. They had made an assignation to meet there at three o'clock today, the weather permitting.

And the weather does permit, Edwin thought. He glanced up. The pale sun was continually flitting in and out from behind the patchwork of grey and white clouds that littered the powder-blue sky, but there was no hint of rain. Even the light wind barely rustled the trees and the translucent air was so mild it was almost balmy.

Edwin purposely avoided the stables. A few minutes earlier, when he had gone down to the kitchen to collect the picnic basket, he had observed Annie Stead and Tom Hardy chatting and laughing together in the yard. They were courting, so Emma had informed him, and it was more than likely they would have paid no attention to him whatsoever, as immersed in each other as they appeared to be. On the other hand, he did not want to put them to the test, for he had no particular desire to arouse even their mildest curiosity. Not that it was unusual for him to picnic on the moors, but the sack might create a flicker of interest. He walked swiftly through the walled rose garden and out under the clump of old oaks. In a short time he was across the Baptist Field and mounting the slope rising on to the flat plateau of moorland and the narrow track that ran all the way to the Ghyll, and Ramsden Crags beyond.

Edwin breathed deeply, filling his lungs with the pure air, which was so much more bracing on this higher ground. His health was now fully restored and he felt vital again. At the beginning of May he had caught a summer cold, which had settled on his chest and developed into a bronchial condition. After two weeks in the school sanatorium he had been sent home to recuperate at the insistence of the school doctor.

Tom Hardy had driven the carriage over to Worksop to collect him, since his father was away, not an unusual circumstance these days. As far as Edwin could ascertain, his father made only periodic trips to Fairley, when absolutely necessary, and was often in London, or travelling on the Continent attending to unspecified business. However, his father had engaged a tutor for him, so that he would not fall behind in his studies. Although Edwin was a disciplined student, and perfectly capable of working alone, his father had wanted to be certain he sustained his brilliant scholastic record. It had been decided he would go to Cambridge when he was eighteen, to study for the bar under the Downing Professor of English Law at Downing College. Edwin and the tutor were alone at the Hall, except for Gerald and the servants. Edwin did not mind. Actually, he rather relished it. He was pretty much left to his own devices, except for the mornings of intense study with the tutor. Gerald ignored his existence, and barely addressed a remark to him. *He* was far too busy. Because the mill in Fairley, and the other two in Stanningley Bottom and Armley, took up most of Gerald's time, the two brothers only saw each other at meals, and not always then. Sometimes Gerald took one of Cook's packed lunches to the Fairley mill and ate there, an idea so unpalatable to Edwin it positively nauseated him.

Edwin began to whistle merrily as he headed along the ridge to Ramsden Crags, striding out at a brisk pace, his fair hair blowing in the breeze. He was looking forward to seeing Emma, and also to their impending project. Emma had challenged a theory he had about the Crags, and for some reason he felt compelled to prove his point. He wondered if he was being juvenile. Perhaps.

Edwin Fairley, who had just celebrated his seventeenth birthday, now considered himself to be quite grown-up, and he did appear much older than his actual years. This was due, not unnaturally, to the events that had taken place in the past year, not the least of which was his mother's death, so sudden and tragic. Her passing away had had a more profound effect on him than on his brother, for he had been so much closer and more intimately involved with his mother than Gerald. Edwin's sorrow was, at first, overwhelming, but being of a scholastic nature and a voracious reader like his father, he had inevitably buried himself in his studies. This intense dedication to learning prevented him from dwelling morbidly on her death, and its appalling circumstances. He had thrown himself, and with a vengeance, into innumerable other school activities, and all manner of sports, and these too had helped him to assuage his grief. They kept him busy from early morning until late at night. Eventually he had been enabled to adopt a more philosophical attitude, and now, finally, he accepted her loss with considerably less heartbreak.

Olivia Wainright had also played a crucial role in Edwin's development, albeit indirectly but, none the less, most effectively. When he visited her in London, for a portion of the school holidays, he was exposed to a wide circle of her friends – politicians, writers, journalists, and artists, many of them celebrated and outstanding men in their fields. These privileged encounters, in a society that was gay, pleasure-loving, and sophisticated, always had a tremendous impact on him. Olivia, aware of his charming manners and acutely attuned to his intelligent mind, made a point of including him at many of her soirées, which he thoroughly enjoyed and at which he executed himself admirably. Consequently, he had matured and had acquired a measure of polish and self-confidence. In certain subtle ways he was quite a different boy from the pampered 'mummy's darling' he had been when Adele was alive.

But, apart from the changes in his personality and attitudes, Edwin had also undergone an amazing physical transformation, due in no small measure to his newly acquired interest in sports. He had grown in height and filled out, and he was a strikingly handsome youth whose marked resemblance to his father was becoming more pronounced. He had inherited Adam Fairley's expressive bluish-grey eyes, his sensitive mouth with its hint of sensuality, and his intelligent, well-articulated face, although Edwin's was much less ascetic than his father's. He was now almost as tall and as broad as Adam. His physique, which was already quite splendid, and his rather classically handsome face, had earned him the nickname of 'Adonis' at Worksop, much to his irritation. He was constantly embarrassed by the flurry his looks created with the sisters and cousins of his school friends.

Edwin considered them twittering, insipid, and callow creatures. He loathed their vapid attentions, which flustered him. He much preferred to be in the company of Emma, who had been such a consolation to him during his bereavement. Not one of those young ladies of Quality, or the rich debutantes his father foisted on him, could compare to *his* Emma in beauty and grace, wit and spirit. And by God, she was beautiful. Every time he returned to Fairley she delighted him even more. At sixteen she was fully and exquisitely developed. Her shapely and feminine figure was that of a young woman and her face was sublime.

Edwin smiled happily. It would be grand to be with Emma, away from the prying eyes of the other servants. She made him laugh with her quick wit and her penchant for striking at the heart of the matter. He chuckled to himself. Murgatroyd came in for a great deal of her acerbity. She called him 'Frozen Face' behind his back, but only to Edwin. His brother Gerald had been dubbed 'Skinny Ribs', which made him laugh uproariously, since the obese Gerald was disgustingly fatter. These thoughts of Emma made him increase his pace and he was soon at the Crags. He put down the picnic basket and the sack and stepping forward, he shaded his eyes with his hand, scanning the landscape.

Emma, climbing up over the last crest, saw Edwin before he saw her. She began to run. The heather and bracken brushed against her feet, the wind caught at her long skirts so that they billowed out like puffy clouds, and her hair was a stream of russet-brown silk ribbons flying behind her as she ran. The sky was as blue as speedwells and the larks wheeled and turned against the face of the sun. She could see Edwin quite clearly now, standing by the huge rocks just under the shadow of the Crags above Ramsden Ghyll. When he saw her he waved, and began to climb upwards towards the ledge where they always sat protected from the wind, surveying the world far below. He did not look back, but went on climbing.

'Edwin! Edwin! Wait for me,' she called, but her voice was blown away by the wind and he did not hear. When she reached Ramsden Crags she was out of breath and her usually pale face was flushed from exertion.

'I ran so hard I thought I would die,' she gasped as he helped her up on to the ledge.

He smiled at her. 'You will never die, Emma. We are both going to live for ever and ever at the Top of the World.'

Emma glanced at him out of the corner of her eye, and laughed. Then she looked down and said, 'I see yer brought the sack.'

'Of course. And a picnic, too, for later.'

'I thinks we'll be needing it, after all the hard work we've got ter do.'

'It's not going to be as difficult as you think, Emma, and I'll be doing most of the work.' He scrambled down over the small boulders that were like roughhewn steppingstones, and dropped to the ground. He opened the sack, removed a hammer, a chisel, and a large nail. These he stowed away in his pocket.

Looking up at Emma on the ledge above him, Edwin said, 'I'm going to prove to you that this central rock is not part of the actual formation of the Crags, but is quite separate. And also that it can be moved.' As he spoke, Edwin kicked the base of a rock about four feet high and two feet wide. This was wedged between the larger boulders that soared up well beyond the ledge and into the sky.

'Well, maybe it can,' Emma said, glancing down at him. 'But I still thinks that even if yer moves it yer won't find owt behind it. Only more rocks.'

Edwin shook his head. 'No, Emma, I disagree. I am convinced there is a hollow space behind the rock.' He climbed back up on to the ledge, edged past her carefully, and positioned himself next to the peak of the rock in question. This was adjacent to the ledge, but a few inches lower, and it protruded slightly. Edwin knelt down on the ledge and took out the hammer and chisel. He moved closer to the rock and leaned over it.

'What are yer going ter do, Edwin?' Emma asked curiously, and cautioned quickly, 'Be careful yer don't topple over.'

'I'm quite safe,' he responded, and went on, 'You remember the crevice where I lost that shilling weeks ago. I heard it rattling as it fell, even though you say *you* didn't. I am going to make this crevice larger, into a hole, so that I can look down and see what's there, below the rock.'

'Yer'll see nowt but more rocks,' she said bluntly.

Edwin chuckled, and began to chip away at the crevice. Emma watched him patiently, shaking her head. She was quite certain Edwin was wasting his time, but she had decided to humour him when he had first lost his shilling. After ten minutes of constant chipping he had made a hole in the crevice about two inches in diameter. He lowered his head and pressed one eye to the hole, gripping the sides of the rock to balance himself.

'Can yer see owt, then?' asked Emma.

Edwin straightened up and shook his head. 'No, it's all black.' He pulled the nail out of his pocket, and half turned his head so he could see Emma. 'Edge closer to me, Emma, and listen very carefully.' She did as he told her, shuffling along the ledge and squeezing up to him. They both bent towards the hole and he dropped the nail into it. There was no sound at all for a few seconds and then they heard a distinct tinkle as it landed.

'Now! Did you hear that, Emma?'

'Yes, I did. But it might have dropped on another rock, that's all.'

'No, I don't think it did. It took too long to fall. It's on the ground,' Edwin cried firmly. He returned the implements to his jacket pocket. 'Move back along the ledge and climb down, but go slowly, so you don't slip. I'll follow you.'

Emma lowered herself on to the boulders below the ledge, backed down them cautiously, and jumped to the ground. Edwin was right behind her. He took off his jacket, threw it carelessly on one side, and rolled up his sleeves. Emma stood watching him as he fished around in the sack, a sceptical look on her face. 'What are yer going ter do now?' she asked.

'I'm going to remove all the moss and bits of heather and weeds growing here,' he exclaimed, indicating the base and lower sides of the rock. 'And you can help me.' He handed her a garden trowel and took up a small spade himself. 'You work at that side, and I'll work here.'

Emma thought this whole idea was a waste of time and energy; nevertheless, she began to work vigorously, digging out clumps of heather and moss which had crusted the rock for years. After a while she began to perspire. She put down the trowel, rolled up her sleeves, and opened the collar of her dress. Feeling more comfortable, she began to dig again. After about twenty minutes of hard toil they had accomplished a remarkable job of cleaning up the face and base of the rock.

Edwin stepped back and regarded it thoughtfully. 'Look, Emma,' he said. He took hold of her hand and pulled her to him. He pointed to the rock. 'Do you see how the rock itself is more clearly outlined, now that we've removed all the overgrowth. It's not part of the entire formation of the Crags at all. See how it has been wedged in between the great boulders. No rock could fall so accurately, Emma. I am certain it was placed there.'

Emma nodded her head. She had to agree. He was right, and she said so, adding, 'But, Edwin, it's still a fair size. How do yer think we're going ter shift it?'

He strode over to the rock and said, with absolute self-confidence, 'I am going to make this crevice here larger.' He tapped the central rock, and pointed out a small space at the base, between the rock itself and the soaring Crags rising up behind it. 'Then I am going to use a crowbar and a wedge to push the rock away from the Crags.'

'It'll never work, Edwin. And yer might hurt yerself.'

'No, I won't, Emma. And I've thought it all out very carefully.'

Working with the hammer and chisel, Edwin had soon made the space big enough to take the crowbar. He put the crowbar into the hole and wedged a small but strong log behind it, placing this on the ground to the left of the rock. 'Stand back, Emma,' he warned, 'go over there by the trees. The rock will fall forward, and I don't want you standing in its path.' Using all of his strength, Edwin pressed on the crowbar, pushing the protruding end of it on to the log, using it as a lever to force the rock away from the Crags. But it did not move. Edwin began to sweat profusely, and his arms ached, but he forced himself against the crowbar determinedly.

Emma held her breath, clasping her hands together. Edwin was wrong. It would not work. She had no sooner thought this than she saw it moving.

'Edwin! Edwin! I think I saw it coming away,' she shouted.

'I know,' he gasped, 'I felt it myself.' With a final thrust of energy he pressed against the crowbar, and, as he did, the rock toppled forward as he had predicted it would. A small aperture on the face of Ramsden Crags was revealed. This was about eighteen inches wide and two feet high. Edwin could not conceal his excitement. He swung around.

'Look, Emma! There's a hole here,' he cried triumphantly. He knelt down and peered into it, and then he inched his head inside. 'It's like a little tunnel. And here's the shilling and the nail!' He picked them up and pulled back. He held them out to show her, his face wreathed in smiles.

'Where do yer think it goes?' Emma asked, running to join him at the aperture.

'I don't know. Under the Crags, I suspect. They do stretch back for miles, you know. I'm going in.'

'Oh, Edwin, do yer think yer should?' A worried look settled on her face. 'It might be dangerous. What if yer started a rockslide and got stuck in there?'

Edwin stood up and pulled out his handkerchief. He mopped his damp face and brushed his hair back. 'I'll only go in a little way. And I brought candles and matches. They're in the sack. Would you get them for me, Emma, and that length of rope, please.'

'Yes, course I will.' She brought him the items he had requested. 'I'm going in with yer,' she announced.

He stared at her and frowned. 'I don't think so. Not at first. Let me go and investigate, and then I'll come back for you.'

She compressed her lips and said stoutly, 'I'm not afraid, yer knows.'

'Yes, I know that. But I think you should stay here, just in case I need something.' As he spoke Edwin tied the rope around his waist. He handed her the other end. 'Hold on to this. There could be a labyrinth of tunnels in there. I've been reading up on rock climbing and potholing, and potholers always tie a rope around themselves, for safety.'

Emma, who was now visibly impressed that Edwin's deductions had been accurate, immediately saw the sense of this. 'Well, just be careful –' She looked at Edwin, so tall and muscular, and then at the aperture. 'How are yer going ter get in there? That's what I wants ter knows. It's ever so tiny.'

'I'll have to squeeze in, and then crawl along.'

'Yer'll get yerself all mucky, Edwin Fairley. Cook'll wonder what yer've been up ter. Yer'll cop it!'

Edwin's mouth twitched and he burst out laughing. 'Emma, do stop worrying so much, and about trivialities. Cook's not going to say anything. We've come this far. Let's at least complete the project.'

Emma sighed. 'All right. But go ever so slow like, and if yer needs me, tug on the rope. Promise?'

'I promise.'

It was with a certain amount of trepidation that Emma watched Edwin disappear into the aperture. Slowly the length of rope unwound itself, as he moved further into the tunnel, until she was finally clinging to the very end of it, straining against the outer wall of the Crags. A flicker of anxiety crossed her face, and she lowered her head and called into the tunnel. 'Edwin! Are yer safe?'

'Yes,' came back his voice, echoing hollowly as if from a long distance. 'Yer've used up all the rope,' she cried, her voice rising shrilly.

'I know. Let go of it.'

'No! I won't!'

'Emma, let go of it!' he shouted in a commanding tone. She did so, much against her better judgement, and knelt down, looking into the aperture, suddenly afraid for Edwin. It seemed ominous in there.

But within minutes she heard a small scuffling sound, and to her great relief she saw the top of Edwin's fair head. She moved away from the opening so that he could squeeze out. His shirt and trousers were covered with dirt and his face was smudged with grime. He straightened up, grinning broadly. 'What's in there?' she asked, with mounting curiosity.

'A cave, Emma! A fantastic cave!' he cried, his light eyes shining. 'You see, I was right after all. Come on, I'll show you. And we don't need the rope. The tunnel is fairly straight and leads right into the cave.'

'A real cave. Fancy that!' Emma said, and then she smiled a little shamefacedly. 'I'm sorry I was doubting yer, Edwin.'

He laughed. 'That doesn't matter. If you hadn't doubted me I might not have felt obliged to prove myself right. Come on. Let's go.' He collected additional candles, and continued, 'You follow me. Keep your head down at first. The tunnel is very low at the outset.'

Edwin entered the hole and Emma wriggled in behind him, blinking her eyes as she adjusted to the darkness after the bright sunlight. They crawled along at first, but the deeper they went the higher and wider the tunnel became and they were able to walk in a crouching fashion the rest of the way. Soon Emma could see the faint flickering of the candle Edwin had left in the cave, and a few seconds later he was helping her to her feet in the cave itself.

Edwin began to light the extra candles and arrange them neatly in a line along a narrow ledge near the entrance. Whilst he was engaged in this task, Emma looked around with enormous interest. As the candles flared and illuminated the darkness, she saw that the cave was indeed fantastic, as Edwin had said. It was a large cavern with a ceiling that soared up into a weird conical shape. There were flat little ledges extending out from some of the rocky walls, while other portions had great indentations juxtaposed next to flat areas that were so perfectly smooth they looked as if they had been polished by a giant hand. There was a breathtaking grandeur about this ancient and spectacular interior, which was as old as time itself perhaps. It was cool and dry and absolutely silent. Emma felt a sense of awe.

Edwin handed her a candle and took one himself. 'Let's investigate,' he announced. He moved ahead and his foot struck something on the floor of the cave. He looked down, lowering the candle so that he could see better. 'Emma, look at this! It's the remnants of a fire!' He kicked the blackened and charred wood, which instantly crumbled. 'For heaven's sake, somebody discovered the cave before we did.'

'Yer right,' Emma asserted, staring at the charred wood. Then she caught a glimpse of what looked like a heap of sacks in the far corner. 'Over there, Edwin. Sacks, I thinks.'

He followed the direction of her pointing finger and strode rapidly across the cave. 'They are, indeed. And on this ledge above them there is an old piece of tallow candle. Oh, come on! Let's see what else we can find. You go around that side, and I'll poke about here,' he finished, his voice vibrating with eagerness.

Emma walked slowly, holding the candle out in front of her. She looked from side to side alertly as she moved, glancing down at the hard earth floor, scanning the high-flung walls. To her immense disappointment the far side of the cavern appeared to be quite empty. She was about to turn back and rejoin Edwin when the frail light from the candle illuminated a patch of smooth wall. She was certain she could make out faint markings on the wall, like writing scratched on to the surface. She ran over and held the candle close to it. It *was* writing. How interesting.

And then Emma sucked in her breath in amazement, for the first word she read was *Elizabeth*. She moved the candle. Written underneath was *Elizabetta*. And below, *Isabella*. Slowly, Emma's eyes followed the column running down the wall of the cave. *Lilibeth. Beth. Betty. Bess. Eliza. Liza. Lisa.* Next to this column was one single word, carved in giant capital letters. *ADAM*. She swallowed. Under the name was a small heart with an arrow piercing it, and inside the heart were the simple initials A. E.

Emma's eyes were pinned to the wall and those initials. A coldness settled over her, as she remembered the locket she had found in her mother's wooden box. Not me mam and *him*!

'Emma! Emma! Where are you? Cooee! Cooee!'

She pulled herself together as Edwin's footsteps drew closer, echoing on the hard ground. She opened her mouth and closed it at once, for a moment not trusting herself to speak coherently. Finally she called, 'Over here.'

'What did you find?' Edwin asked, rushing to her side. She pointed to the writing on the wall mutely. Edwin's eyes lighted on his father's name at once. 'Adam!' he read wonderingly, staring at the giant letters. 'Why, my father must have found this cave years ago!' He sounded jubilant. 'And look, here's every derivation of the name Elizabeth, even in Italian and Spanish. This is very intriguing, indeed. Who do you think Elizabeth was, or is?'

Emma was silent. Edwin appeared not to notice her lack of response, or her utter stillness, for she was as rigid as stone standing next to him. 'Well, I don't suppose I can very well ask Father. However, let's search around a bit more.' Edwin was buoyed up with enthusiasm. He left Emma standing in front of the scratchings on the wall, still staggered at their dreadful implications.

'Come here, Emma. I've found something else,' Edwin shouted after a few seconds had elapsed. Emma stifled the desire to run out of the cavern and it was with considerable reluctance that she joined him in the corner where the sacks were stacked. Edwin was holding a flat oval pebble, about three inches long and two inches wide. He handed it to her and held the candle over it. 'Do you see, Emma? The pebble has been painted on. It's a miniature, in oils, of a woman. See! I think it's Aunt Olivia. Yes, I'm positive it's her.'

Emma said nothing, but thought grimly: *No, it's not. It's me mam.*

'Don't you think it's Aunt Olivia?'

'Yes,' Emma responded dully.

Edwin put the stone in his pocket. 'I think I shall keep this,' he said.

Emma shivered and the candle wavered about in her hand. Edwin did not fail to notice this. 'Emma, you're cold.' He clucked sympathetically, and put his arm around her. Emma tried hard not to shrink away from him.

'Yes, I am. Let's get out of here. It's warmer in the sun.' Without waiting for him to reply, she extracted herself and ran to the opening of the cave. She blew out the candle and placed it on the ledge, and crouching, and then crawling, she moved with incredible speed along the tunnel until she was out in the fresh air. She heaved a sigh of relief. She would never go back in there. Never.

Edwin emerged a few moments later. His eyes sought out Emma. She stood under the shadow of Ramsden Crags, shaking her dress free of the dirt and dust, her hair blowing about her in the wind, her face inscrutable. As he continued to gaze at her he recognized that the strange coldness which sometimes invaded her face had crept back on to it. Sensitive as he was by nature, and especially to Emma, he at once detected a change in her mood, and a change that was radical. It distressed him.

He walked over to her and took her arm. 'Emma, is something wrong?' She did not answer, and averted her face. 'Is something wrong?' he said again, and more loudly.

She shook his hand off. 'No, nowt's wrong.'

'But you look peculiar. And you fled like a frightened rabbit out of the cave.'

'No, I didn't. I was cold, that's all.'

Edwin turned away, realizing he would not make any headway with her at this

222

moment. He brushed the dirt off his trousers, and began to busy himself collecting the tools. He felt suddenly deflated. Emma had seated herself on the flat rock where she always sat. He watched her as she lifted her long hair and moved it back over her shoulders gracefully. Then she folded her hands in her lap and sat staring ahead, looking out across the moors, and to the valley far beyond. He smiled to himself. She looked so prim and curiously dignified. No, regal, he told himself; it's the way she holds her head so high, and keeps her back so straight.

He wandered over to Emma, attempting a show of casualness. He sat down on the ground at her feet and looked up at her. 'Do you feel better now? Out here in the sunshine,' he ventured gently.

'Yes, thanks,' Emma said quietly, without so much as glancing at him.

Edwin winced. She sounded so cold and remote. He rested his head against the flat rock and closed his eyes, wondering why she was adopting this stern attitude. She had shut him out most purposefully, he recognized that. He felt a twinge in his chest, and that sense of loss he had experienced before.

Meanwhile, Emma's fertile brain was racing. How could her sweet and gentle mother have been friendly with Adam Fairley? *That terrible man.* And anyway, her mother had spent part of her girlhood in Ripon with Cousin Freda. It struck her then, and quite forcibly, that Elizabeth was not a very unusual name. Might it not be some other Elizabeth whose name was carved on the wall? A girl from the gentry perhaps, who had known Adam Fairley when he was young. There was more likelihood of *him* being friends with a girl of Quality than with one from the working class. But there was the stone Edwin had found. Still, that might really be a painting of Olivia Wainright, just as Edwin believed. It certainly looked like her. She thought then of the locket. Yet even that didn't mean anything significant. Lots of people had names beginning with an A. Anybody could have given it to her mother. Emma now found all of these conclusions quite irresistible. And because the idea of a friendship between her mother and Adam Fairley was intolerable and unacceptable to her, for it would besmirch her mother's memory, Emma slowly convinced herself that her mother was not the Elizabeth of the cave.

In no time at all she felt more cheerful. She looked down at Edwin resting peacefully at her feet. Poor Edwin. She had been mean to him and unfair, when he was always so nice to her. She tapped him lightly on the shoulder, almost playfully.

Edwin opened his eyes and glanced up, not without apprehension, uncertain of her mood. To his delight Emma was smiling at him, that lovely and most radiant smile, and her emerald eyes danced with the brightest of lights.

'I feel like it's teatime. Are yer hungry, Edwin?'

'I'm absolutely famished!' He was overjoyed to see her good humour fully restored. He jumped up and strode over to his jacket. He pulled out his small gold pocket watch. 'Why, Emma, it's already four-thirty. I'll unpack the picnic basket at once.'

Emma began to laugh, shaking her head. Edwin stared at her nonplussed. 'What is it?' he asked.

'I wish yer could see yerself, Edwin Fairley. Yer looks like a chimney sweep. Yer face is all mucky, and yer hands, and just look at mine.' She held up her hands, palms outward, to show him. He joined in her laughter.

'I'll race yer ter the beck down yonder,' she cried. She leapt up and flew down the adjacent hillside. Edwin raced after her. He caught up with her and snatched at her belt. She laughed and struggled, but he held on to the belt tightly. They tripped and fell, and rolled down over the moorland, still laughing with hilarity. They landed at the edge of the beck, and Emma would have fallen in if Edwin had not held her tightly in his arms.

'Now look what yer've gone and done, Edwin Fairley,' Emma remonstrated with mock annoyance through her laughter. 'Yer've got me frock all wet in the beck.'

Edwin released his grip on her and sat up, impatiently pushing the lock of hair away from his forehead. 'I am sorry, Emma. But it's only the hem. It will dry quickly in the sun.'

'Aye, I hopes it will.'

'You mean, "yes, I hope it will", Emma,' Edwin corrected her.

She threw him a knowing look and said in a mimicking tone, 'Yes, Edwin, you are quite right. I was not speaking properly.' She pronounced the words very carefully and her voice, always sweet and melodious, was now so cultivated he gaped.

Emma poked him in the ribs. 'I can speak like you if I want to,' she said, and then confided, 'I used to listen to your aunt. She has a lovely voice.'

'So do you, Emma, when you pronounce your words correctly and don't lapse into the Yorkshire dialect.' He smiled at her fondly. 'I hope you don't mind when I point out mistakes in your speech. But you did ask me to do that.'

'Yes, I did. And I am grateful.' She smiled to herself. She knew she had surprised him and this tickled her tremendously. She leaned over and washed the dirt off her hands in the beck, then cupped them and splashed water on to her face.

Edwin took out his handkerchief and gave it to her with a boyishly gallant gesture. 'Dry yourself on this.'

When Emma had finished her toilet, Edwin also washed himself, and then they sat at the edge of the beck that tumbled down over the rocky hillside, talking happily, enjoying being together as they always did. Edwin chattered enthusiastically about going to Cambridge to study for the bar, and explained in great detail what a barrister actually was. In turn, Emma spoke proudly of Winston and how handsome he had looked in his uniform, when he had come home on leave from the Royal Navy.

'He's been back ter Fairley twice now,' Emma said, 'and me dad's much better. More settled about Winston being away –' She sat up abruptly and looked at the sky. 'That's funny, I just felt a splash of rain.'

Edwin lifted his head. 'But the sky's blue and there are only a few grey clouds.'

'We'd best get the picnic basket and hurry back ter the Hall,' Emma announced quickly.

'Oh, don't be silly. It's only a summer shower. It will pass in a few minutes.'

But as he spoke the pale sun was doused by bloated clouds moving up over the rim of the moors with gathering speed. There was a loud blast of thunder. It appeared to crack the sky wide open, releasing searing blades of brilliant white lightning and then an eerie greyness that flooded out swiftly, staining the sky as effectively as black dye colours cloth, and obliterating the light.

'Come on!' Edwin cried. He pulled Emma up to her feet and with urgency.

'The weather is so unpredictable on these wretched moors. You never know when a storm will blow up.'

Together they scrambled up the hill. The rain came down in lashing torrents. It was heavy driving rain that fell like a relentless waterfall. By the time they reached Ramsden Crags almost all of the light had vanished and the only illumination came from the staccato flashes of lightning charging the sky with electricity, and the thunder boomed, echoing and reverberating against the towering structure of Ramsden Crags. Edwin and Emma were drenched to the skin, their clothes, faces, and hair streaming with water.

Edwin grabbed the sack and his wet jacket and tossed them over to Emma. 'Take these,' he shouted, and pushed her towards the opening of the cave.

'Don't yer think we should make a dash in for the Hall?' she protested.

'We'll never make it, Emma. We're in for a real thunderstorm. Look at the sky. It's as black as night. Don't argue! Into the cave, my girl. We'll be safe there, and dry.'

Although Emma was decidedly disinclined to return to the cave, she had to admit that Edwin's suggestion was sound. They had no alternative, really. The moors could be extremely dangerous in this kind of stormy weather. She clutched the sack and his jacket to her, and, with her lips grimly tightening, she crawled into the aperture. Edwin followed, pushing the picnic basket in front of him.

Once they were inside the cave, Emma stood at the entrance, trying to get her bearings. Edwin pulled out his handkerchief, wiped his hands, and gave it to Emma. Then he immediately took charge, and with such a burst of energy and efficiency Emma was momentarily startled. He lit the candles on the ledge at the entrance and opened the picnic basket.

'Here's the Sunday *Gazette*,' he called. 'I brought it to read, in case you were late. Good thing, too. Make some paper spills with it.' He dropped it at her feet, and went on, 'I saw a pile of logs and twigs over by the sacks earlier. They were perfectly dry. We'll soon have a fire going.' He picked up a candle, took Emma by the hand, and led her to a far corner.

'We'll make the fire about here,' Edwin said, scuffing the earth with the toe of his boot. 'It's about the best spot, since it gets the cross-ventilation from the tunnel to the outside and that one back there.' He gestured to another aperture Emma had not noticed before.

'Where does that go, Edwin?'

'I'm not really sure. It was too small for me to crawl into when I investigated earlier. But there are currents of air coming in from the moors. Now, come on, Emma. Let's hurry. Then we can sit on the sacks and attempt to dry ourselves. I'm freezing, and I'm sure you are.'

'Yes, I am.'

It did not take them long to get the fire started. The paper and the twigs caught hold at once, and when they were burning Edwin placed a couple of small logs on top of them. He began to busy himself with the empty sacks. There were about a dozen of them and these he arranged on the floor, rolling others into bolster-like shapes which he propped against the wall. 'It will be quite comfortable, Emma,' he said, turning and smiling at her reassuringly.

Emma was standing by the fire, shivering and shaking with cold. Her face still glistened with water and her wet hair streamed down her back. She was trying to wring out her dress, which was thoroughly soaked.

Edwin hurried to the fire, shivering himself. He began to cough. Emma looked across the flames at him and frowned. 'Oh, Edwin, I hopes yer don't catch another cold, just when yer better.'

'So do I,' he gasped, coughing behind his hand. After a moment the rasping subsided, and he said, 'I think you had better take off your dress, Emma. We can then spread it out to dry.'

She stared at him askance. 'Take me frock off!' she echoed disbelievingly. 'Oh, Edwin, I couldn't do that.'

'Don't be so ridiculous. You're wearing petticoats and – and – *things* underneath, are you not?'

'Yes,' she muttered between her teeth, which were now chattering.

'So, please do as I say,' he insisted in a brisk tone. 'I am going to take my shirt off. It's absolutely sopping, and if we sit around in our wet clothes we will *both* catch pneumonia.'

'I suppose yer right,' she replied grudgingly. Emma turned her back to him and began to unbutton her dress, feeling shy and awkward.

'Give me the dress,' Edwin ordered in the same firm voice, after she had stepped out of it. She handed it to him behind her back, without looking around. It was then that she decided she was being silly. After all, she *was* wearing a petticoat and a camisole top which completely covered her body, except for her arms.

She peeped over her shoulder and then slowly wheeled. Edwin was hanging her frock on a ledge, next to his shirt and undervest, anchoring them down with some small stones he had obviously found on the floor of the cave. Adopting a nonchalant air, Emma returned to the fire. She warmed her hands and face in front of the flames, and then tried to dry her long hair, squeezing the rain out of it and rubbing it between her hands. Edwin, who seemed quite oblivious to her state of partial undress, and also unperturbed, picked up the picnic basket and carried it over to the sacks. He knelt down and lifted out the stone jug of elderberry wine, and unpacked all of the food, which Cook had carefully wrapped in serviettes. Suddenly he let out a long low whistle of surprise.

Emma glanced at him. 'What is it?'

'Good old Mrs Turner,' he exclaimed with a wide grin as he continued to rummage about in the bottom of the basket. 'By Jove, she thinks of everything. She not only put in a serviette and tablecloth for my picnic, but a carriage blanket as well. What luck. The blanket, at least, will help to keep us warm.' He looked up, showing them to her triumphantly, and then his face fell. Water was dripping from her petticoat, making a puddle under her feet. 'Good Lord, Emma. You're really quite thoroughly soaked and still shivering. Don't you feel warmer?'

'A bit. But me legs are cold from me petticoat. It's as wet as me dress was.' She stepped nearer to the fire. Her boots squelched. She began to wring out the hem of the petticoat, striving to control her shivering.

Edwin stood up and looked down at his trousers, frowning. 'I am afraid my trousers are in the same condition.' He grimaced and joined her at the fire and they hovered together in front of the flames, hoping to dry their clothes. But this was to no avail, since the fire was really quite meagre and was therefore throwing off insufficient heat, and the atmosphere in the immense cavern was cold.

'This is futile!' Edwin declared after a short while. His legs were turning into blocks of ice and the coldness was now beginning to permeate his whole system. He began to cough, almost convulsively.

Emma looked at him with alarm, thinking how prone he was to taking chills. 'Are yer all right?'

'I'm freezing. I hope I don't come down with bronchitis again.' He shivered. 'It's these wet clothes.' He hesitated. 'I'm afraid there's only one thing to do, Emma. I think I must take off my trousers, and you must take off your petticoat and –'

'Take off all our clothes!' she gasped, shrinking back against the wall of the cave, a look of horror on her face. 'Edwin! We can't! It wouldn't be proper like,' she finished, and with fierceness.

A faint half smile glanced across his lips. He shrugged. 'Well, you may do as you wish, Miss Harte. But I have decided to undress, and hang my trousers and underclothes on the ledge to dry out. I am not going to catch my death because of any false modesty on my part.'

Emma positively glared at him. 'I thinks that would be very rude of yer, Edwin,' she said tartly. 'By gum, I do. It wouldn't be – be – gentlemanly.'

Chagrin crossed his face. 'Emma, I don't mean to offend you.' He thought hard, wondering what to do, fully understanding her feelings. His eye caught the tartan carriage rug and a solution instantly occurred to him. 'I have an idea. I shall wrap the carriage blanket around myself – like a kilt. It will cover me completely,' he reassured her. 'But I do think I must remove these wet things. We could be in here for hours.'

Emma bit her lip. What he said was sensible, but it did not diminish her embarrassment at the thought of him undressing in front of her. On the other hand, she did not want to be responsible for him getting sick. It also struck her that she herself did not necessarily have to take her clothes off. She could still try to dry herself in front of the fire. After a moment, she said slowly, 'Well, afore yer do take yer trousers off, crawl back ter the opening and see what the weather's like,' she insisted, and sharply. 'Maybe the storm's passed over and we can leave.'

'That is a possibility,' Edwin agreed, and hurried off to follow her instructions. Arriving at the end of the tunnel, Edwin was utterly dismayed when he poked his head out through the aperture. The rain was still falling in a deluge. A gale had blown up and was acting as a powerful lash against the rain. This was being driven in sheets on to the Crags. Bolts of lightning ripped through the blackened sky and thunder rolled down the hilly slopes like unceasing cannon fire. They were undoubtedly in for a long siege. He pulled his head back in quickly. It was then Edwin realized, and to his fury, that to return along the tunnel he would have to either crawl outside and re-enter, or shuffle backwards. He decided the former was the most feasible way and he edged himself out of the opening. He turned quickly on his knees and pushed back through the aperture, but not without getting drenched. When he finally crawled back into the cave he was shaking with cold and dripping rain.

Emma looked at him aghast. 'Now why did yer go outside?' she demanded. 'That was a daft thing ter do!'

He sighed, and explained. He picked up the serviette and dried his face and hair. Then he took the blanket and strode to the far side of the cave. He turned. 'My apologies, Emma. But my trousers are wetter than ever. I have no alternative but to take them off now.'

During Edwin's absence, Emma put another small log on to the fire and sat

227

huddled in front of it, continuing to squeeze the water from her petticoat, her face set in obdurate lines. And she was resolute in her determination not to undress, even though she was feeling the cold more intensely. Within a few seconds, Edwin was hanging up his trousers, underpants, and socks on the ledge, weighting them down with more small stones. Then he carried his boots over to the fire, where he deposited them to dry. Emma kept her face down, unable to look at him.

Observing her closely, Edwin began to laugh at the ridiculousness of the situation. 'It's all right, Emma. I am quite decent. I can assure you of that.'

Slowly, but with some unwillingness, Emma raised her head and she couldn't help smiling. Edwin had wrapped the carriage blanket around his waist and knotted it. It fell well below his knees, revealing only his bare ankles. 'It does look a bit like a kilt,' she said, adding with relief, 'and it does cover yer proper like.'

Edwin lowered himself next to her, and picked up the bottom of her petticoat, shaking his head sadly. 'You are being foolish. You'll take a chill, Emma. Why, you've only managed to dry the hem of this. The rest is soaking.' He dropped the skirt with an impatient gesture. Suddenly his face brightened and he reached for the tablecloth.

'Look here, Emma. You can wrap this around you. Like the saris the Indian maharanees wear.' He jumped up and shook it out. 'See, it's quite large.' Edwin gave her a small demonstration. He wound the tablecloth around his chest and knotted the two ends together. Then he slipped his left arm down under the cloth, pulling the knotted ends up on to his left shoulder. 'It does work remarkably well!' He smiled, glancing down at himself. 'Of course, I think it's more like a Roman toga than a sari,' he conceded in a serious voice.

'But it's one of Cook's best tablecloths!' Emma cried with consternation. 'I'd really cop it if I messed it up. I would that!'

Edwin concealed an amused smile. 'Under the circumstances, I don't think that is a matter worthy of our consideration. Now, is it?' He stretched out his hand to her. 'Come along, you silly girl,' he continued in a gentler tone, pulling her to her feet. 'Go to the other side of the cave and do as I say.' He shrugged himself out of the tablecloth and handed it to her.

Emma took it from him in a tentative way, and with such a show of nervousness her manner brought a smile to Edwin's face. He watched her as she scrutinized it carefully, a diffident expression flickering into her eyes.

Now laughter bubbled up in Edwin. 'Emma, you are behaving so fearfully I do believe you think I am some scurrilous reprobate who has dishonourable intentions,' he said, still laughing, and continued, 'and that I am endeavouring to manoeuvre you into a situation, so that I can take advantage of you. Please be reassured I have no lascivious motives.'

'I don't think that at all,' said Emma, scowling darkly, not truly understanding all of his long words, yet intuitively grasping what he meant. 'I knows yer wouldn't do owt – owt wrong, Edwin. I knows yer'd never harm me.'

He patted her shoulder and looked down at her, smiling with tenderness. 'Of course I wouldn't, Emma. Why, you are my best friend. My dearest friend, in fact.'

'Am I really?' she cried, her eyes lighting up with pleasure.

'Yes, you are. Now, run along and change into the' – Edwin paused and chuckled – 'the sari, such as it is. There are plenty of stones over there, and you can hang your things up to dry with mine. Meanwhile, I will prepare our picnic.' Edwin watched her retreating figure and thought: She is so sweet and so very endearing. She *is* my best friend. I am truly most fond of her. It did not occur to him that he actually loved her.

The candles on the ledge in the corner had burned down and Edwin took two more out of the sack. As he lit them he was thankful he had had the foresight to bring a plentiful supply. He was arranging the food on the serviettes when Emma returned to the fire. She dropped her boots next to his.

Looking up, Edwin saw at once that she approached the corner somewhat timidly, with an air of bashfulness and extreme modesty and rectitude. The tablecloth surrounded her like swaddling clothes and she held it tightly to her, arms criss-crossed over her breasts. It draped her lithe body more than adequately, but he was startled to see that it came only to her knees, revealing shapely calves and the slenderest of ankles. He had not known she had such long legs or such pretty feet. Still hugging the tablecloth to her, Emma sat down and looked up shyly, not speaking.

'Don't you feel better, being out of your wet underclothes?' he asked, his manner purposely insouciant, which he hoped would alleviate her timorousness, as well as the awkwardness he knew she was feeling.

'Yes, I do,' she muttered with a certain nervousness. She half smiled and glanced at the food spread out before them. 'I'm ever so hungry,' she announced, attempting to sound normal.

'So am I. I'm sorry there's only one plate and one mug. We'll have to share them.' He poured some of the elderberry wine and handed it to her.

'Thank yer, Edwin.'

'Now we're drier and warmer, this is quite a lark, isn't it?'

'Yes,' she responded softly, sipping the elderberry wine. 'My goodness, Cook did yer right proud!' Her eyes swept over the appetizing selection of sandwiches and other food. 'She must think yer've now got an appetite like "Skinny Ribs", packing up all this stuff.'

'Well, you know what Cook is like. Flapping around me like a mother hen. She thinks I need building up.' He gestured to the food. 'Take your pick first, Emma. There's bacon and egg pie, crab and tomato sandwiches, fruit cake and apples.'

Emma selected a piece of the pie, which she herself had made. But she did not bother to mention this. They munched hungrily on the food, sharing the mug of elderberry wine, which Edwin kept refilling. He chattered gaily to her and gradually Emma's embarrassment began to slip away. Edwin seemed unaware of her semi-naked state, much to her intense relief. In point of fact, he was diligently ignoring it. When they had finished eating they sat back against the rolled sacks, warming their feet in front of the fire. Emma said carefully, without looking at Edwin, 'What do yer think ter the writing on the wall, then? Do yer think yer dad made the carvings of the names?'

Edwin nodded his head vigorously. 'Yes, I do. In fact, I've been giving some considerable thought to the matter, particularly to all those derivations of the name Elizabeth, and I do believe I've guessed the identity of the lady in question.' He looked at her, his eyes brightly gleaming in the firelight. Emma held her breath. He continued, 'It occurred to me that it must be Lord Sydney's sister. Her name was Elizabeth, and my father and the Sydneys grew up together. I am certain they all played up here as children.'

'I didn't know Lord Sydney had a sister,' Emma said, with a little intake of breath. Her eyes fastened on Edwin's face. 'I've never seen her hereabouts, or heard mention of her.'

'She died about ten years ago in India, where her husband was in the Diplomatic Service. I have heard Father speak of her with great affection, on many occasions. She was about his age. The more I think about it, I am sure that's the truth.'

There was such a lessening of tension in Emma, such an alleviation of the painful thoughts in her troubled mind, her body sagged. How misguided she had been, jumping to such an unworthy conclusion about her mother and *him*. Of course Edwin was right, as he always was.

'That's got to be it!' she exclaimed, and smiled. After a small silence she said, 'I wonder what time it is.'

'I'll look at my watch.' Edwin went to the entrance, where he had carelessly thrown his jacket when they had rushed in from the storm. 'It's six o'clock,' he called, carrying the jacket back to the fire. 'This is very damp. I'd better spread it out on the floor to dry.' He glanced at her, a concerned look crossing his face as he said, 'Will your father be worrying about you, Emma?'

She shook her head. 'No. He knew Cook wanted me ter come back this afternoon, instead of termorrow, ter help her with the jam making. She expected me at five-thirty.'

'Oh dear, then *she* must be worrying about you,' Edwin cried.

'She probably thinks I'm still at home, what with the storm and all. She knows me dad wouldn't let me come over the moors in this weather,' Emma explained. 'But I bet she's fretting about yer, Edwin. Wondering where yer are.'

'Most probably. But she may conceivably think I made a dash for the village, which is closer than the house.' He sighed. 'Oh, well, it can't be helped.'

'Do yer think it's stopped raining yet, Edwin?'

'Would you like me to crawl along the tunnel and see?'

'Yes, perhaps yer'd better. But don't go outside and get yerself all wet again!' said Emma a little dictatorially.

He picked up a candle and left. He was back in a matter of seconds. 'It's still pouring and the thunder is cracking and booming,' he announced as he deposited the candle on the ledge. 'We can't leave just yet.' He sat down cross-legged on the sacks, carefully covering his knees with the carriage blanket. 'You know what these thunderstorms are like, Emma. They can last for hours.'

'Aye, I knows.' She stood up. 'I'd best see if our clothes are dry, so that we can get dressed.'

Emma glided lightly across the floor of the cave in her bare feet, her hair flowing down her back. She felt the clothes in her expert way, and said in a distraught voice, 'Oh, Edwin, they're still ever so damp. We'll have ter leave 'em a bit longer.' She swung around as she spoke and stared at him with the utmost dismay.

'We have to stay in here until the deluge subsides anyway,' he answered. 'Perhaps in half an hour they will be drier and by then the storm might have passed.'

'I hopes so,' she said, hurrying back.

They sat in the corner shivering, for the air in the huge cavern was now considerably colder and the fire was low. Edwin threw on another log and told her, 'The supplies are diminishing. We must be frugal with these last few logs.' They huddled together, attempting to draw warmth from each other. Edwin put his arm around

230

her and pulled her closer to him. Emma looked up, her eyes wide. 'Yer don't think we'll get trapped in here, do yer?' she asked tremulously.

He smiled reassuringly and his light eyes were soft and filled with the tenderest lights. 'Of course not! Don't be silly,' he exclaimed cheerfully. 'And don't be afraid. I am here to protect you Emma. Look, as soon as the clothes are in a better condition, we'll get dressed and see what it's like outside. If necessary we'll just have to brave the weather, depending on the time. We can't get back too late.'

'All right, Edwin,' she said, crouching closer to him.

Edwin put his other arm around Emma and began to rub one hand up and down her arm briskly, trying to warm her. 'There, is that better?' he asked gently.

'Yes, thank yer, Edwin.'

It all began perfectly innocently on Edwin's part. Slowly the brisk rubbing turned to slower stroking, the stroking into languorous caressing of her face and neck and shoulders. Emma did not demur. It was only when Edwin's hand accidentally brushed against her breast that she flinched and drew back, staring at him with surprise tinged with apprehension. She quickly moved away from his embrace and settled herself against the rolled-up sacks, putting distance between them.

'I'm sorry, Emma. I really didn't do that on purpose. Truly. Come back here. You'll soon be shivering over there,' he warned, irritated with himself and his carelessness, and also worried about her.

'I'm all right here. Thank yer,' she said coolly, leaning back and adopting a dignified posture that repudiated him.

'Please yourself,' Edwin muttered in dismay, drawing his legs up to his chest and wrapping his arms around his knees.

A long silence developed between them. Emma gazed into the fire, striving to control her shaking limbs, hoping he would not notice how cold she was growing. Edwin rested his head on his knees and stole a surreptitious look at her. At this precise moment the log blazed into sudden flames and his eyes started open in surprise. In the brighter firelight her figure was extraordinarily revealed to him. He had not realized before how flimsy the cotton table cloth was, since she had hitherto hugged it so tightly to her. He could now clearly see her firm and voluptuous breasts pressing tautly against the fabric, the outline of her thighs, the long column of her legs, and that triangular smudge, faintly dark, just above them. He could not tear his eyes away from her. As he gazed at her with yearning, he felt a thrill rushing through him.

This was not the first time Edwin had been excited. Like most youths of his age, he had been sexually stimulated before, in the usual boyish ways. But he had never actually been aroused by a girl in such a potent manner, for he had never seen one in dishabille and been in such close proximity to one so scantily dressed. Consequently, he was shaken by the intensity of his emotions. He was breathless, almost panting, and his throat felt tight. After a few seconds he managed to drag his spellbound eyes away from her tantalizing figure, staring at the wall in front of him. Flickering shadows floated about there in the soft firelight, creating amorphous little shapes, resembling animals and trees. There's a rabbit and that's a great old oak, he told himself, inventing living forms for those dancing images. He concentrated hard on that wall, pushing his desire down, turning his mind away from Emma, striving to ignore his throbbing excitement.

It was Emma who broke the silence. Eventually she said in a small voice, 'Edwin,

'I'm ever so cold.' Immediately he swung his head to look at her. She was curled up, shuddering uncontrollably and her teeth were beginning to chatter.

'Shall I come over there and help to keep you warm, Emma?' he asked diffidently, almost afraid of suggesting this for fear of her anger or her rejection.

To his surprise she whispered, 'Yes, please.' She looked at him shyly through her thick lashes and added, 'I'm sorry I got cross with yer, Edwin.'

Without answering he scrambled over to her. He wrapped his arms around her and, with one hand, pushed down her knees. Very gently he eased her on to the sacks until they were both supine and reclining on them full length. He partially covered her shivering slender body with his own broader one.

'This is the only way we'll keep warm,' he said. She edged closer to him, drawing comfort from him, cradled like a small child in his arms. 'Yes, I knows,' she murmured softly.

'Look at the dancing shadows,' he pointed out, 'and all the strange shapes they make. Animals and trees and mountains.'

Emma smiled, following his gaze. Miraculously, the cave had been transformed before her eyes. She was no longer intimidated by it and she no longer associated it with her mother and Adam Fairley. It had become a magical and wondrous place. Their very special enchanted, secret place. Hers and Edwin's.

Edwin began to rub her arm and shoulders, which were icy. Soon the goose pimples began to disappear and it seemed to him that her skin now felt like the smoothest of satins. It was not long before the caressing started afresh, for Edwin could not resist the feel of her. Emma looked up at him, her large eyes spilling green fire, her pink lips slightly parted so that he could see her small white teeth. He moved his hand up and brushed the russet-brown hair away from her face, running his fingers lightly over her rounded cheeks and down her throat so whitely vulnerable in the candles' glow.

'You are so beautiful, Emma,' he said in a low hoarse voice echoing with awe. 'Please let me kiss you. Just once. Please,' he begged.

She did not reply, but continued to gaze up at him. And there was so much trust and innocence and undisguised love in that pure face he was excessively moved. He bent towards her. He thought he would drown in the shimmering greenness of her eyes. His lips touched hers lightly. Her mouth was moist and sweet and so inviting one kiss did not suffice for Edwin Fairley. He kissed Emma again and again and again, with mounting intensity, allowing her no opportunity to protest.

When Edwin finally raised his head and looked down at her he saw that her eyes were closed. He stroked her face and her shoulders and his hand travelled down lingeringly until it was covering her breast. Only then did her eyes fly open wildly. 'Oh, Edwin, no! You mustn't!'

'Please, Emma. I won't do anything wrong. Just let me hold you for a moment,' he implored.

She hesitated, and he pressed his mouth to hers before she could refuse him, and he continued to fondle and stroke her. Almost without his conscious knowledge and quite unable to control himself, Edwin slipped his hand under the tablecloth which was draping her. He ran his fingers over her satin-smooth skin, his touch delicate but lightly quivering in his spiralling excitement. Emma pulled away from him with a small cry, a blush rising on her face, but he took hold of her and lovingly enfolded her in his arms, kissing her forehead.

'I love you, Emma,' he whispered, his face close to hers.

'But it's not right, ter be together like this,' she whispered back, trembling and afraid, her mind awash with dire thoughts of wickedness and temptations of the flesh that sent you to hell.

'Hush, my sweet Emma,' Edwin said consolingly, his voice reassuring. 'I am not going to do anything improper. I only want to feel you close to me. I won't harm you in any way. One never harms the person one loves the most in the whole world.'

His words filled her with sudden joy and she drew closer to him, searching his face hovering above hers, that sensitive face she knew so well. It appeared to shine with radiance in the candlelight. His eyes were widely open and full of adoration.

'Do yer really luv me, Edwin?' she asked in the softest of voices.

'I *do*, Emma. Oh, how I love you! Don't you love me?'

'Yes, Edwin. Oh, yes!'

Emma sighed, aware of his hands fluttering over her again, smoothing and patting and feeling every part of her, but so soothingly she began to relax, enjoying his warm and affectionate caresses. Suddenly his fingers touched that most forbidden place of all, insistent but as light as a feather. She was hardly conscious of what he was doing at first. And she could no longer protest or stop him, for she was overwhelmed by unexpected and strange but delicious sensations that sent small tremors through her, and made her heart pound. His mouth, his hands, his body, all enveloped her and he drew her closer and closer until she felt as if she was melting into Edwin. A lassitude settled over her as he continued to fondle her, arousing her to the pitch he himself was aroused to.

Edwin paused and looked at Emma. Her eyes were closed and he saw that she trembled slightly. He slipped out of the carriage blanket and, with the lightest of movements, he parted the tablecloth that still half covered her.

She did not stir, although her eyelids fluttered and her eyes opened, became wider, as she stared at him kneeling over her. Edwin Fairley's not a boy, he's a man, she thought, with a flash of amazement, and a trickle of fear, for that masculinity was now fully revealed. Edwin sucked in his breath, gazing at her wonderingly, filled with a yearning desire to possess her completely. And he marvelled at her loveliness. Her skin had a floral pallor to it, but it was dappled golden, here and there, from the candlelight and the fire's rosy glow. She resembled a perfectly sculptured marble statue.

Slowly and with great tenderness and delicacy Edwin helped Emma to overcome her terror, her reticence, and her inherent shyness. In spite of their mutual virginity, Edwin began to make love to Emma, and eventually she to him, under his softly whispered guidance. His desire flared into a passion he could no longer check, and it was this passion that imbued in him a finesse that was unconscious yet remarkable in its expertise. Only once did she stiffen, and he heard a small cry strangled in her throat as she bit it back. But he was so exquisitely gentle with her and adoring, this moment instantly passed, and soon he was carrying her along with him on a mounting wave of ecstasy. They were clinging together, moving now in perfect unison, engulfed by the sweet warmness of their fresh young bodies. Emma thought she was slowly dissolving under Edwin, becoming part of him.

Becoming him. They were one person now. She *was* Edwin. She moaned and moved her hands down to the small of his back which vibrated under her touch. It was then that Edwin experienced such a sensation of joy he thought he would scream out loud. As he rushed headlong into the very core of her he did not know that he shouted her name and begged her never to leave him.

TWENTY-FOUR

Some hours later the thunderstorm died as instantly as it had erupted into life, the torrential rain easing into a light drizzle that finally ceased with an eerie abruptness. The gusting high-powered gale that had ventilated those quiet hills had dropped away and an awesome stillness suffused the air.

The remote and cloudless sky was a darkling bitter green, almost black in its depth of colour, yet glassy and clear and filled with a curious luminosity, as if lit from within. A full moon was out, hard in its metallic whiteness, a perfect orb pitched high in the cold wide sky, illuminating the moors and the fellsides with the clarity and brilliance of a noonday sun. Its sharp radiance fell upon the terrible devastation, bringing it into stark focus. The fulminating storm had ravaged the landscape.

The immense fells, poised in precarious leaning angles above the moorland, were towering precipitous cliffs and from them the unceasing torrents of rain had rushed down in streaming cataracts, inflating the natural waterfalls so that they had become liquid avalanches, bloating the becks and streams until they were swollen and spilling over their banks, which were already bursting under the pressure. The cloudburst had swept over the moors like a gigantic tidal wave, its force and speed uprooting trees and shrubs and heath, dislodging rocks and boulders, hurling all before it on its relentless downward journey. The small glens and hollows between the hills that punctuated sections of the moorland were completely flooded. Animal life not swift enough to escape had been trapped in the onslaught. Stray sheep had been drowned in the flood, their stiffened bodies floating grotesquely in the murky waters of these newly made but unnatural ponds. Battered birds littered the ground, mangled bits of broken bones and bloodied feathers, their trilling songs stilled for ever.

And lightning had left its stamp everywhere. It had struck trees, slicing them apart sharply and cleanly, and charring their scant foliage to blackened ashes. A horse tethered in the long meadow near Top Fold had been knocked down by a bolt, dying instantaneously before its owner could reach it, mane singed, grey coat dappled red and black. Not even the village was unscarred. Slates had been ripped off roofs, windows broken, plaster torn from interior walls, flaking off like minute sprinkles of snow, and one cottage was almost completely wrecked. A stained-glass window in Fairley Church had been shattered into hundreds of rainbow-tinted slivers. It was the memorial window recently endowed by Adam Fairley in commemoration of Adele Fairley's death.

Up at Ramsden Crags, water sluiced over the great elevation of rocks and the ground was so muddy it was like running oil, a veritable bog, mucid and slippery. The two lone trees that had stood there for years, solitary sentinels to the left of the Crags, had toppled over in toy-soldier fashion, also demolished by the incessant flashes of violent lightning. Edwin crept out of the cave first and gave his hand to Emma, who was closely following him. They ducked away from the water that tumbled unchecked from the Crags relatively close to the aperture, their feet sinking ankle deep into the mire that oozed under them. Edwin placed the picnic basket on a boulder and helped Emma up on to the drier rocks, swiftly climbing after her. They gasped, almost in unison, and exchanged alarmed glances, dismay washing over their faces as they viewed the destruction so appalling to behold.

'We were lucky to find the cave when we did,' said Edwin to the gaping Emma by his side. He looked about him, shaken by the riven and shattered landscape. 'Do you realize we could have been killed out here! Either by lightning or by drowning in the flood!' Emma nodded and shuddered at their narrow escape, not speaking.

'Look at the waterfall up on Dimerton Fell,' Edwin then exclaimed. 'I've never seen it so full or raging before. It's incredible.'

Emma followed the direction his finger pointed, and caught her breath. The usually gentle waterfall, clearly visible in the moonlight and icily shimmering, had been transformed into a phenomenal spumescent cascade that was magnificent yet uncanny in its magnitude. Emma had to admit it was beautiful and said so, but her worry about returning to Fairley Hall was increasing by the minute. 'Edwin, don't yer think we should try and make it back ter the Hall. Cook's going ter play pop with yer, and me as well.'

'Yes, I do believe we should make tracks immediately,' Edwin agreed. 'Thank goodness the moon is so bright. At least we can see where we're walking. Shall we go?'

He made to leave and Emma tugged at his arm. 'But what about the opening ter the cave?' She inclined her head towards the aperture. 'The rock that covered it up before looks ter me as if it's sunk right inter the mud.'

'You're right, it has.' Edwin swung around, his eyes searching. He spotted the ruptured trees. 'I'll use some of those branches to cover the hole, and come back another day to put the rock in place.' He left the rocks, plodding through the slime doggedly, and dragged one of the trees over to the cavern's entrance. He stuck it deeply and securely into the muddy earth. The gnarled branches camouflaged the opening effectively.

Uncertain of what other disasters awaited them, they nonetheless set off bravely, their feet sinking into the glutinous mud, boots squelching, as they hurried away from the Top of the World, heading directly for Ramsden Ghyll. Emma slipped once as they scrambled over a ridge, slithering on the sodden ground. Edwin caught her immediately, and put his arm around her protectively, helping her to maintain her balance until they reached the narrow track. They had to manoeuvre their way with deliberation, stepping over disrupted rocks and splintered branches that had been flung haphazardly on to the path during one of the landslides. Upon reaching the Ghyll they stood hovering at the edge, staring in stupefaction. The bright moonlight illuminated part of the deep gully, enough for them to see that it was brimming with bubbling water seemingly about to seep over the top at any moment. Dead birds, rabbits, and a sheep wobbled misshapenly among the debris on its ghastly black surface, gruesome reminders of the fury so recently unleashed. Emma shuddered and pressed her face against Edwin's broad shoulder.

Edwin, holding her comfortingly, turned away. 'I should have realized the Ghyll would fill up. We'll have to turn back and go down over the ridge to the beck, cross it, and make for the lower road to the Hall.'

'But won't the beck be flooded as well?' Emma suggested, biting her lip.

'Most probably. But at least it's a bit narrower and not a ravine like the Ghyll. It shouldn't be too deep. We can swim across.'

'I can't swim,' Emma wailed.

'Don't worry. I'll look after you, Emma. I told you before, you will always be safe with me. I'll never let any harm come to you. Ever.' He hugged her to him affectionately, hoping to allay her nervousness, took her by the hand, led her back along the track and down an incline, reassuring her gently all the way. Unfortunately, Emma's prediction was correct. The little beck, where they had washed earlier that afternoon, had become a fully fledged and gushing stream, water spewing over the rocky hillside with remarkable swiftness, an eddying whirlpool foaming whitely against the banks. Edwin threw the picnic basket on the ground, gritted his teeth, and lowered himself cautiously down the bank and into the whirling depths. The water rose up to his chest. 'Leave the sack, Emma,' he shouted, 'and get on to my back. Put your arms around my neck, and hang on for dear life. I'll swim us both across.'

Emma hesitated. This girl, who was not, in reality, afraid of anything, had a strange and incomprehensible fear of water. Even as a small child, when her mother had washed her hair, she had always screamed, 'Don't get the water on me face, Mam,' the panic rising in her inexplicably.

'Emma, come along!' Edwin called. 'This water's freezing.'

Quelling her apprehension, Emma followed his instructions and tremblingly climbed on to his back. Edwin struck out across the beck, but he had misjudged the force of the water and several times he thought they would be dragged downstream, as if there were a rapid current sucking at his legs like a vortex. Yet he knew this could not be so. They went under once, but he valiantly struggled to the surface, spluttering, and pushed forward, swimming with all of his strength. It was an exhausting battle for Edwin, and a terrorizing experience for Emma, who clung to him tenaciously. Finally they reached the opposite bank. Edwin panted and gasped and spat out water, catching hold of a small shrub miraculously intact on the side of the bank. He paused to regain his breath, grasping the roots of the shrub, and then he hauled them both up out of the swirling beck, stumbling and sliding in the process. They fell on to the ground and lay there for several minutes, chests heaving, coughing and rasping and wiping the water from their faces.

At last Emma said, 'Thank yer, Edwin. I thought we'd drown once. I did, really. But yer a good swimmer.'

Edwin's chest was congested and tight, and he was unable to speak, but he gave her a lopsided smile and shook his head wearily.

'Do yer feel all right?' Emma regarded him with some misgiving. In the moonlight he looked extraordinarily pale and depleted, and he shivered more violently than she herself did.

'Yes.' He groaned, sitting up. 'Let's get going. It's cold, Emma.' He grinned ruefully as he looked at her dripping hair and face and clothes. 'We're like a couple of drowned rats again.'

'But we're safe and we'll soon be at the Hall,' she responded, adopting a cheerful tone.

The lower road had turned to mire and was also strewn here and there with rocks and branches. In spite of its slimy surface, and the various obstructions, they managed to walk at a brisk pace, and once Edwin's breathing was more normally restored they began to run, holding hands tightly, only slowing their pace when they had to skirt boulders and dismembered trees, arriving at the main entrance to Fairley Hall much sooner than they had anticipated. One of the great iron gates, bearing the Fairley family crest in polished bronze, had been half ripped off its hinges, and dangled precariously from the high brick wall surrounding the grounds. Walking up the gravel path, they saw that even here the storm had wreaked its havoc. Flower beds had been flattened, bushes shredded, hedges crushed, and some of the box and yew topiary specimens, clipped into fantastic shapes, had been smashed beyond recognition.

To Edwin's immense distress one of the great oaks had been struck by lightning, split asunder, a monument to time finally felled by God's wrath and nature's unpredictability. It was here that Edwin paused and took Emma in his arms. He pushed back her dripping hair and gazed down into her face, its loveliness unmarred by the water and mud streaking it, palely gleaming in the moonlight shafting through the bower of green oak leaves drifting above them. He bent down and kissed her fully on the mouth and with passion, but it was a passion tempered now by tenderness. They clung together, swaying gently. After a moment of silent communion, Edwin said, 'I love you, Emma. You love me, too, don't you?'

Her green eyes, iridescent with light and glittering catlike in the darkness, swept over his face, and a swift pain shot through her, piercing and poignant and she was filled with a strange emotion she had not experienced before. It was a sweet emotion, yet one tinged with sadness and a vague and curious yearning she did not understand. 'Yes, I do,' she answered softly.

He touched her face lightly, returning that penetrating look concentrated so ardently upon him. 'Then you will meet me up at the cave at the Top of the World, later in the week when the weather has improved, won't you?'

She was silent. Up until this moment Edwin had not contemplated the possibility that she might refuse, but now the idea struck him so forcibly he was filled with panic. 'Please, please say you will,' he entreated, conscious of the protracted silence, her hesitation. He pressed his body closer to hers and cajoled, 'We can have a picnic again.'

Still she remained silent. 'Oh, Emma, please, please don't spurn me.' His whisper was hoarse and a new desperation had crept into his voice. Edwin held her away from him and examined her face, so pale and inscrutable. There was a look in her eyes that baffled him, one he was quite incapable of interpreting. 'You're not upset about – about – what happened? What we did, are you?' he asked gently, wondering with rising alarm if this was indeed the reason for her unexpected and sudden unresponsiveness to him. Then in the faint moonlight sifting through the trees he saw the deep flush rising to her neck to flood her face with dark colour, and his heart sank. She *was* angry with him.

Emma turned away. But Edwin's harsh breathing stabbed at her and she quickly brought her face back to his, peering deeply into his bluish-grey eyes, and what she saw there made her heart lift on a crest that was joyous and it overwhelmed her. His eyes were full of love and longing but, hovering behind these mingled feelings so clearly apparent, she saw a flicker of fear. Emma knew then with the utmost certainty that Edwin Fairley did truly love her, just as he had said he did. And she loved him. He was part of her now. She marvelled that this one person in the whole world could suddenly mean so much to her, could have become, within a few hours, so necessary, taking precedence above all else. It was a possibility she had neither anticipated nor bargained for. She could no longer bear to witness the pain in his eyes. 'Yes, Edwin, I will meet yer up at the cave, and I'm not angry about what we did.' She smiled and it was that same smile that always suffused her face with radiance.

Edwin's facial muscles, tight and intense with apprehension, relaxed, and he too smiled, taking her into his arms with a rush of relief and happiness. 'Oh, Emma, Emma, my sweet Emma. You're everything to me.'

Poised under the old oaks, locked in an embrace that was further sealing their destinies, they were oblivious to their dripping clothes, their shivering limbs, the cold night air. They were conscious only of each other and their fierce and flaring emotions, not realizing, in their euphoria, that emotions could wreak devastation as horrendous as the ripped and shattered landscape surrounding them. Eventually they drew apart, searching each other's face for confirmation of their love. Edwin nodded, his eyes awash with tender lights, and Emma smiled, and then silently they went up to the house, hand in hand. Edwin was jaunty and seemingly untroubled, but Emma, pragmatist that she was, had suddenly begun to consider the welcome they would receive. She was patently aware that it would be far from cordial and certainly one of furious reprimands.

When they turned into the cobbled stable yard they saw that the kitchen door was wide open, spilling light. Standing in this corridor of light was a distraught Mrs Turner. She was perfectly still, watching, waiting, her arms akimbo, her plump face a stony mask, yet she gave the impression, in her very quietness, of wringing hands and doom and dire consequences. Emma slipped her hand out of Edwin's and hung back, allowing him to walk ahead of her.

Mrs Turner was utterly relieved and overjoyed to see Edwin, but her anxiety had been so pronounced, and she had been so overwrought for hours, this relief quickly manifested itself in a flash of intense anger. It was only because Edwin was the young master of the house, and therefore entitled to proper respect, that Cook controlled that anger, but her voice was shrill as she stared down at him.

'Master Edwin! Where have yer been? Yer gave me a right turn when yer didn't come home. Why, it's almost ten o'clock. I thought yer were lost on the moors, or dead, with this raging storm. Aye, I did that!' She shook her head energetically and her eyes sparked. 'By gum, Master Edwin, it's a good job the Squire's away, and Master Gerald is in Bradford for the weekend, or yer'd be copping it, yer would indeed. Scared me half ter death, yer did. Why, I've had Tom out twice with the lantern, searching for yer up yonder!'

The cook heaved a great sigh that rippled her vast bosom. 'Well, young man, don't dawdle about there, come inter the kitchen at once!' She turned and hurried inside, followed by Edwin, who was mounting the stone steps. She had not noticed Emma, who was reluctantly loitering in the shadows. Edwin stopped at the kitchen door and beckoned. 'Come on, it's all right, Emma. I'll handle Mrs Turner,' he whispered.

'I've got water boiling in the set pot in the washhouse,' Cook announced from the centre of the kitchen, her eyes roving swiftly over Edwin's filthy clothes that dripped water, and his mud-splattered face. 'Well, aren't yer a right sight, Master Edwin!' she snorted. 'Yer look as if yer've been dragged through a hedge backwards, yer do that.'

It was then that Mrs Turner saw Emma slipping through the door and down the kitchen stairs. She was incredulous and her jaw sagged. 'Aay, lass, what are yer doing here? I thought yer were safe at home with yer dad. I never dreamt yer were out in this weather.'

Emma did not answer. Mrs Turner looked from Emma to Edwin, staring at them open-mouthed. Her voice was brusque when she found it. 'Yer haven't told me yet what yer doing trailing in at this hour, with Master Edwin, looking like a drowned rat. Come on, lass, speak up!' She glared at Emma, and tapped her foot impatiently, hands on her hips.

Before Emma could reply, Edwin stepped forward and said with a show of self-confidence, and just enough superiority to remind Cook who he was, 'I came across Emma on the moors, during the storm, Mrs Turner. She told me she was due back this afternoon, to help you with the jam making, or some such other domestic task. We tried to make it back together, but *I* decided the thunderstorm was too dangerous. We sheltered up at Ramsden Crags as best we could, waiting for the tempest to abate.' He paused and fixed his cool eyes on the roiling cook. 'It was rather difficult getting back, even when the rain ceased. The Ghyll is flooded and the beck by the lower road is dangerously high. But, here we are, safe if a little bedraggled.' He smiled engagingly, displaying that irresistible charm of his father's, which was so inherent in him.

'Bedraggled! I thinks that's the blinking understatement of the year, Master Edwin, I do that!' Mrs Turner cried scathingly. 'Yer looks like a couple of mudlarks, nay, guttersnipes!' Her head rolled again and her eyes flew open. 'Thank heaven Murgatroyd's in Shipley. He wouldn't take kindly ter the fuss yer disappearance has caused around here, Master Edwin. Mark my words, he wouldn't, he wouldn't.'

'I didn't disappear, Mrs Turner,' Edwin responded quietly but with firmness. 'I got stranded on those wretched moors, through no fault of my own.'

'Aye, what yer say is true enough,' she muttered. She glared at them suddenly. 'Look at yer both, dripping mucky water and mud all over me clean floor. Upstairs at once, Master Edwin, and inter the bathtub. I don't want yer getting badly again. And take yer filthy boots off. I can't be having yer tracking mud all over t'carpet upstairs,' she admonished, but not unkindly.

Mrs Turner turned to Annie, who had remained silent but wide-eyed and agog with curiosity during this discourse. 'Annie, run ter the washhouse and get two big pails of water, and hurry upstairs ter Master Edwin's bathroom with 'em. And then bring two buckets in here for Emma.'

Cook now gave Emma her total attention. 'Yer shouldn't have stayed up on the moors, lass, with Master Edwin. Yer should've turned back. Fact is, yer could have both made it back ter the village in no time at all,' she remonstrated, her irascibility in evidence. She shook her head and looked from one to the other penetratingly. 'I thought yer'd have had more sense than that, lass, and Master Edwin as well.

239

Anyroads, inter the servants' bathroom, me lass. Yer need a hot tub afore yer catch yer death.'

Emma forced a smile on to her face. 'Yes, Mrs Turner.' She hurried to the servants' bathroom behind the kitchen without looking at Edwin.

Edwin had removed his boots and went up the stairs. He swung around at the top and said sweetly, with a warm smile, 'I do apologize, Mrs Turner, for causing you grief and worry. It was not intentional, you know.'

'Aye, Master Edwin, I knows.'

'Oh, by the way, I'm afraid I had to abandon the picnic basket. But I'll retrieve it for you another day.'

'Aye, I expects yer will, if there's owt left of it,' she mumbled. There was such chagrin on his face she softened, for Edwin was her favourite. 'When yer've had yer bath, get straight inter yer bed, and I'll bring yer up a nice plate of cold lamb and some bubble-and-squeak. I knows how much yer enjoys that,' she said, indicating the pan of leftover vegetables frying gently on the stove. 'I've kept the bubble-and-squeak warm for hours for yer, Master Edwin.'

'Thank you, Mrs Turner.' He smiled and was gone.

Cook gazed after his retreating figure and then sat down with a loud thump in the chair, her face creased with worry. She had seen the two of them, whispering and laughing together in corners of the house, when they were unaware of her keen but silent observation. She had also noticed them in the garden together, too many times for her liking of late. She pondered on Edwin's story, for a moment doubting it. She frowned. Yet it had a ring of truth to it, and she had never caught Master Edwin out in lies, or deceitfulness, since the day he was born. He wasn't like Gerald, who was cunning and devious.

Still . . . small suspicions crept into her mind, which was now awash with perplexed and troubled thoughts. It's not right, servants and gentry mixing, she said inwardly. Stepping out of her class, that lass is. She pondered further on this. 'That's bad. It makes for real trouble. We have ter know our place,' she said aloud to the empty room. Elsie Turner shuddered unexpectedly and goose pimples ran up her fat arms, as long-forgotten memories rushed back, so clear and vividly alive they brought her up in her chair with a start. Not again, she thought, and shivered. It can't be happening again.

TWENTY-FIVE

Emma walked across the terrace and down the path leading to the rose garden, carrying the flower basket on her arm, the garden shears in her hand. Lord and Lady Sydney were coming to luncheon, and Cook had sent her out to cut some blooms for the Waterford crystal vases in the dining and drawing rooms. Emma had a great love of flowers, in particular roses, and this garden was devoted to them, as its name implied. It was her favourite spot in the whole of the vast grounds of Fairley Hall and, to Emma, it seemed oddly out of character with the house, which she found ugly and depressing, for the garden was filled with an enveloping tranquillity that gave her a sense of peacefulness, and its beauty enriched her soul.

The lovely old garden was surrounded on all sides by stone walls hundreds of years old, covered with climbers that had been diligently trained over them, and which also scrambled up into two ancient trees at the far end, their blossoms shining amongst the darker foliage of the branches like fragile fragments of spun silk of the purest white. Wide borders under the walls flourished with floribunda roses, chosen especially for their large flowers and long blooming period, and they washed the garden with rafts of flaming colour the summer through. They were planted in large blocks, thickly clustered together, each one of a different variety, a riotous mingling of candescent hues. Blood red faded into deep coral, which in turn edged into blush and paler dusty pinks, with white and yellow adding their delicately fresh tints to this lavish interplay of roseate shades, coils of velvet set amidst the verdant leaves.

In the centre, surrounded by gravel paths, was the display area of the garden. This parterre, with its ornamental arrangement of flower beds of different shapes and sizes, was a stunning formal counterpoint to those wild and abundant borders rambling naturally in their informality, but which had been precisely planned for this striking contrasting effect. In the parterre, the rose beds of hybrid tea varieties were encircled by box, cut in triangles and diamonds and squares, the box clipped flat-topped, resembling moulded slabs as though meticulously carved out of polished stone. Like the rest of the grounds, the rose garden had suffered severe damage in the violent storm that had torn up the district in June. But Adam Fairley had brought in expert gardeners, including a rose specialist and a landscape artist, to assist his own gardener, and with an enormous expenditure of money and time, and superb skill, they had miraculously restored it to its former glory.

In the shining stillness of this blazing August morning, the garden had an enthralling and poignant beauty that caused Emma to catch her breath and pause to admire its exquisiteness. The sun floated high in a cloudless cornflower sky and the air was limpid and heavy with the heady scent of the fragrant roses that drifted all around her. Not a leaf moved and the only sound was the faint flutter of rushing wings as a lone bird soared up into the pellucid light, its warbling a faintly retreating echo. Emma sighed, marvelling at the loveliness all around her, and then moved on, intent in her purpose.

Since the roses in the parterre were never cut, Emma headed for the wilder borders under the walls. She perspired a little as she hurried down the gravel path and was grateful to reach the trees whose lush bowers, thickly green and low-hanging, offered cool refreshing shade. She knelt down and began to clip the stems, moving from shrub to shrub, selecting her blossoms carefully. The gardener had taught her how to cut only a few blooms from each bush, so that the overall appearance of the magnificent floribunda was never ruined by bare patches. She handled the roses gently, for their heads were fully opened, almost overblown, paying infinite attention to colour and variety, filling the basket slowly.

Emma smiled to herself as she worked. Edwin had returned to Fairley last night with the Squire, who always came back to Yorkshire for the start of the grouse-shooting season. Edwin had been visiting Olivia Wainright at her country house in the South for the last two weeks. To Emma it seemed like two years. The Hall was a desolate place at the best of times, but especially so with only Gerald Fairley in residence, and it had begun to oppress her even more than usual.

The lofty rooms, so vast and shadowy, were lifeless and eerily silent, and she always fled from them as soon as her work was finished. Now Edwin had returned everything would be different. She had missed his smiles, his tender endearments and his adoration, and their picnics on the moors, which had continued through June into July until he had left.

Sometimes Emma had gone up to the Top of the World and sat alone on her flat rock under the shadow of Ramsden Crags, daydreaming, lost in a multitude of thoughts. She never went into the cave without Edwin. Before he had departed for his holidays he had instructed her firmly never to attempt to move the rock without him, for it would be dangerous and she might easily hurt herself.

But now he was back and her loneliness had already been dispelled. Earlier that morning, when they had bumped into each other in the upstairs corridor, they had whisperingly arranged to meet in the rose garden for a few minutes before he went riding. She could hardly bear the agony of waiting for him. She fervently wished he would hurry. Her basket was filled to overflowing; also, Cook would be wondering where she was. A few moments later Emma heard his footsteps crunching on the gravel and looked up expectantly. She felt a quickening of her heart, unreasonably so, and a rush of happiness surged through her, bringing that vibrant light into her eyes, a smile to her face.

Edwin strode swiftly down the path with a nonchalant and carefree air, blithely swinging his crop in his hand. He was wearing a white shirt with a yellow silk ascot at his throat, buff breeches, and highly polished brown riding boots that glinted in the sunlight. He looked taller, broader, more grown-up than ever. How handsome he is, thought Emma, and her throat tightened. She felt a sharp stab of pain, and she recognized it fully as the bittersweet pain of love.

Edwin's face lit up when he saw her and he increased his pace. Then he was standing over her, smiling widely, his greyish-blue eyes reflecting his own obvious delight at being back again. Emma thought her heart would burst. He stretched out his hand and helped her up, walking her to a corner out of view of the house. He seized her in his arms and kissed her passionately, running a suntanned hand down her back caressingly. Then he stood away, his strong fingers gripping her shoulders, and he gazed deeply into her face as if seeing it for the first time. By God, she is a beauty, he thought, excitement trickling through him.

'I've missed you, Emma,' he said vehemently, his ardour apparent on his face. 'I couldn't wait to get back. Did you miss me?'

'Oh, yes, Edwin, I did. It was lonely with yer gone.' She smiled. 'Did yer enjoy yer holidays, then?'

He laughed and made a face. 'Well, yes, in some ways. But it was all a little too social for my liking. Aunt Olivia had tons of other guests coming and going interminably. She also gave two dances, which I could well have done without. Those silly debutante daughters of her friends do so get on my nerves.'

Emma held herself very still under his hands gripping her so tightly. Jealousy flicked into her mind at the thought of Edwin holding other girls in his arms, if only to dance with them. She found herself quite unable to speak.

Observing the pained look which crossed her face, he chided himself for his thoughtlessness, and then he grinned engagingly. 'I much prefer to be with you, Emma, my sweet one. Surely you know that.' He relaxed his hold. 'Let's go and sit over there,' he suggested, nodding to the old rustic seat made of knotted branches resting under a shady tree in a dim far corner of the garden.

He carried the flower basket for her, and when they were settled on the seat he said, 'Can we meet at the Top of the World on Sunday for a picnic? It is your weekend off, is it not?'

'Yes, it's me weekend off,' said Emma.

'You will meet me then, won't you?'

Emma looked at him, her eyes serious as they searched his face, now so dear to her and rarely out of her mind's eye, day or night.

Edwin smiled lovingly. 'You look very pensive all of a sudden. Don't tell me you've changed your mind about our trysts? It can't be that you don't love me any more.'

'Of course I love yer,' she exclaimed. 'Edwin –' Emma hesitated and swallowed. The words she knew must be said were lodged in her throat.

Edwin touched her shoulder fondly. 'Well then, why are you hesitating about meeting me?'

'Edwin, I'm going ter have a baby!' she blurted out harshly, not knowing how to tell him more gently, no longer able to carry this worrisome burden alone.

As Emma spoke her eyes did not leave his face, and she clasped her hands together to stop them trembling. In that tortuous moment of silence that hung between them like a lead curtain Emma's heart dropped. She was acutely aware of the stiffening of Edwin's body, the imperceptible drawing away from her, the look of disbelief that wiped the smile off his face, the dawning horror that followed swiftly and settled there, a frozen mask that bespoke his shock.

'Oh, my God!' he cried, slumping back against the bench. He gaped at her, his face now pale and twitching. Edwin felt as if he had been dealt a violent and crippling blow in his stomach. He was utterly devastated. He vainly endeavoured to still the shaking sensation that seized him, but with little success. At last he managed to speak. 'Emma, are you absolutely certain of this?'

She bit her lip, eyeing him, trying to assess his attitude. 'Yes, Edwin, I am.'

'Jesus bloody Christ!' he cried, forgetting his manners in his anxiety. He gazed into space, a spasm working on his face. A smothering feeling enveloped him. He thought he couldn't breathe. Eventually he turned and stared at her, his eyes wide with apprehension. 'My father will kill me,' he gasped, envisioning his father's towering wrath.

Emma threw him a swift and knowing glance. 'If yours doesn't, mine will,' she informed him bluntly, her voice low and hoarse.

'What in God's name are you going to do?' he asked.

'Don't yer mean what are *we* going ter do, Edwin?' This was asked mildly enough, but Emma was conscious of the alarm rising up into her already constricted throat. Not for one moment in the past few weeks had she anticipated such a reaction from him. She had known he would be disturbed and upset and worried at her news, just as she was herself. But she had not thought he would act as if this was her responsibility, and hers alone. It frightened her.

'Yes, of course I mean *we*,' he answered hastily. 'Emma, are you really and truly certain? Couldn't you just be – be – late?'

'No, Edwin. I'm positive.'

Edwin was silent, his mind floundering, a thousand thoughts pounding in his head. He had never contemplated this eventuality in his entrancement with her beauty, and the flaring passion she aroused in him. What an imbecile he had been not to have considered such an inevitability, the most obvious natural consequence of their lovemaking.

Emma broke the silence. '*Please*, Edwin, talk ter me! Help me! I've been ever so worried while yer've been away, knowing about the baby, not knowing what ter do. I couldn't tell anybody else. It's been summat terrible for me, it really has, waiting for yer ter get back ter Fairley.'

Edwin racked his brains. Eventually he cleared his throat, somewhat nervously. His voice was shaky. 'Look, Emma, I've heard there are doctors – doctors who take care of such matters, in the early stages of pregnancy, for a goodly sum of money. Maybe there would be one willing to do it. In Leeds or Bradford. Perhaps we can find one. I could sell my watch.'

Emma was flabbergasted. His words were like daggers plunging into her flesh. Their very cold-bloodedness was so shocking and repugnant to her she went cold all over. 'Go ter some quack!' she cried angrily and with increasing amazement, her eyes widening. 'Some charlatan who'll butcher me up with a knife and maybe kill me! Is that what yer suggesting, Edwin?' Her eyes were now immensely cold and darkly green and watchful. She could hardly believe he had uttered those dreadful words.

'But, Emma, I don't know what else to suggest! This is an absolute disaster. A catastrophe. You can't have the baby.'

Edwin continued to gaze at her in stupefaction, his mind in chaos. The decent thing to do would be to marry her. They could elope. To Gretna Green in Scotland. He had read about couples being married there. It was legal if you resided twenty-one days. He opened his mouth, about to say this, and then clamped it shut. But then what? The thought of his father's fury paralysed him. Of course, his father wouldn't kill him. He would do much worse. He would disown him. Cut him off with nothing. Edwin thought then of Cambridge, his future as a barrister. He couldn't be saddled with a wife now, at his age, at this most crucial time of his life. His eyes roved over her. She *was* a beautiful girl. This morning her russet-brown hair was swept up and away from her face, plaits forming a circle on top of her shapely head like a crown. The oval face, paler than usual, was like gleaming porcelain, exquisite and refined. The widow's peak protruding on to her wide brow, and those large emerald eyes lifted her beauty out of the ordinary. She was startling, there was no question about that. The right clothes ... elocution lessons ... an invented background. Such things were possible, and the proper tutoring could work miracles. Perhaps there was a way to solve this. *No, there is not. It would never work*, a small voice insisted at the back of his mind. He would be ruined. He could clearly evaluate his father's reaction. He would be infuriated to a point of madness. She was a girl from the village. Edwin's eyes rested on Emma and he thought of her with calculated objectivity, and for a split second her beauty dimmed. *She was a servant, after all*. The class differences between them were too enormous to be bridged.

And so Edwin swallowed hard and remained silent, biting back the words he had originally been ready to utter. And that was a mistake he would live to regret, for had he spoken up, claimed her as his own, braved his father and the world, Edwin's life would have been so very different.

Emma now saw with unmistakable clarity the renunciation on his face, was bitterly aware of the repudiation in his eyes. She straightened her back and her head flew up sharply on her slender neck. It took all of her self-control to speak normally, for she was shaking and her anger, hurt, and disgust were living organisms in her heart. 'I won't go ter one of them doctors, and yer silence tells me that yer not prepared ter marry me, Edwin.' She laughed lightly, but it was a cynical laugh. 'It wouldn't be proper, would it, *Master* Edwin? The gentry and the working class going so far as ter actually *marry*,' she pointed out with her usual stringent perception, her voice icily biting.

Edwin flinched. He had the peculiar sensation that she had just read his mind, and he flushed deeply. 'Emma, it's not that. It's not that I don't love you. But we're too young to marry,' he equivocated. 'I'm about to go to Cambridge. My father –'

'Aye, I knows,' she cut in, 'he'll kill yer.' Her brilliant eyes narrowed as she spoke, resting on his face with great intensity.

Edwin recoiled, and he knew then that he would never forget that piercing stare which condemned him so ferociously and with such loathing. He would never be able to eradicate it from his mind.

'Emma, I – I – I'm s-s-sorry,' he stammered, becoming scarlet, 'but it –'

She interrupted him again with stinging sharpness. 'I shall have ter leave Fairley. I can't stay here. I can't answer for what me dad would do. He couldn't stand the shame, for one thing, and he has a real violent temper.'

'When will you go?' he asked awkwardly, not meeting her eyes.

A look of total disdain slipped on to Emma's face. He couldn't wait for her to leave. That was most patently obvious to her. Her disillusionment was complete. 'As soon as I can,' she snapped.

Edwin dropped his head into his hands, pondering on what she had just said. Perhaps that was the ideal solution. For her to run away. He felt a little surge of relief and looked up. 'Do you have any money?' he asked.

Emma was reeling with nausea. The shock of Edwin's betrayal, of his weak and contemptible behaviour had stunned her. She thought she was going to keel over and fall off the seat on to the ground. Pain bent against pain, twisting together to form an iron band so crushing it was almost unbearable. Hurt, anger, humiliation, disappointment, and sudden panic merged into one immense heartbreaking ache that suffused her whole body. The scent of the roses lifted on the air in suffocating waves, overwhelmingly sweet and cloying, and it made her feel faint. Their perfume was choking her. She wanted to run far away from this garden, from him. Finally she said in a small, toneless voice, 'Yes, I have a bit of money saved up.'

'Well, I only have five pounds to my name. But naturally I will give it to you. It will be of some help, Emma.'

Emma's fierce pride rose up in her, commanding her not to accept, to refuse his offer, but for some reason, unknown to her at that precise instant, she changed her mind. 'Thank yer, Edwin.' She fixed him with that penetrating glare. 'There's one other thing yer can do for me.'

'Yes, Emma, anything. You know I'll do anything to help.'

Anything, she thought wonderingly. But he wouldn't do *anything*, only whatever was convenient for him, only what would absolve him of his responsibility in this matter.

'I'll be needing a suitcase,' she returned coldly, unable to conceal her bitterness.

'I'll put one in your room this afternoon, with the five pounds inside.'

'Thank you, Edwin. That is very kind of you.'

He did not miss the acidity, or the cultured tone she had unexpectedly adopted. He winced. 'Emma, please, please try to understand.'

'Oh, I do, Edwin. Oh, *how* I do!'

He stood up, shifting nervously on his feet, flustered and obviously anxious to be gone, to be done with all this. She looked at him standing there, so tall and handsome, the epitome of a gentleman on the outside. But what was he inside? she asked herself. A weakling. A terrified boy with only the physical attributes of a man. That was all. He was nothing. He was less than the dirt under her feet.

Emma herself now stood up and lifted the flower basket on to her arm. The strong fragrance of the roses invaded her nostrils, making her dizzy and sick again. She stared at him, poised near the bench.

'I won't be able to return the suitcase, since I won't ever be seeing you again, Edwin Fairley. Never, as long as I live.'

She walked away slowly, erect and proud and with great dignity, a dignity that masked the terrible desolation in her soul. The silence in the garden was a tangible thing she could reach out and touch. Everything looked unreal, attenuated and fading, then piercingly brilliant, stabbing at her eyes aching in their sockets. The air went dark around her and her eyes misted over. It was as if the clinging fog that shrouded the moors had descended. A deadening coldness seeped into her and her insides were shrivelling into nothing. Eroding. Eroding. Her heart fluttered in a rapid burst and then was still. And it hardened into stone. She placed one foot before the other, automatically moving them. They were like dead weights. She wondered if she had really expected Edwin to marry her. She was not sure. But she did know she had not expected him to behave with such a lack of concern for her predicament, her well-being, and nor such an abject display of cringing fear it was despicable. He had not even shown any concern for the child she was expecting. His child. What a pitiful specimen of humanity he was. She smiled with irony. Imagine him only having five pounds to his name. She had more than that herself. Fifteen pounds, to be exact. Plus her iron will. And her resoluteness.

Edwin watched her retreating figure soberly and with increasing unease, and then on an impulse he went after her. 'Emma,' he called. She ignored him. 'Emma, please wait,' he called again. She stopped and he held his breath, hoping she would turn back. But he realized she had paused because she had caught her dress on a shrub. She disentangled herself and went on up the steps to the terrace, without once looking back.

Edwin stood rigidly on the gravel path, clutching his riding crop so tightly his knuckles were sharp and pointed in the brilliant sunshine. Panic assailed him as she disappeared into the house. His legs were watery, his mind was swimming with confusion, and then the oddest sensation took hold of him, settling in the pit of his stomach. He felt as though something vital was draining out of him, and a strange aching emptiness engulfed him, sweeping away all other emotions. Standing there in that ancient rose garden, Edwin Fairley, at seventeen, did not know that this sickening, all-enveloping emptiness, this hollowness in his heart and soul, was a feeling which would never desert him as long as he lived. He would take it with him to his grave.

Emma carried the roses into the plant room next to the greenhouse and put the basket down on the table. She latched the door behind her firmly and rushed to the sink. She retched until she thought she would die, her eyes watering, her insides heaving. After a few seconds the nausea subsided and she wiped her face with her hands, resting against the old zinc sink, breathing deeply. Then she turned automatically to the roses and began to clip off some of the leaves, arranging the blooms carefully in the crystal vases, concentrating all of her attention on them. She could not stand the scent of the roses now. In fact, she would detest their pervasive perfume for ever, but she did have her work to do and this diligent effort on her part helped to calm her troubled mind, her quivering limbs.

It occurred to her, as she worked, that Edwin had not even asked her where she was going. Only when. Where would she go? She was not certain. But she would leave tomorrow. Her father and Frank worked at the mill on Saturday mornings, as did some of the other workers who wanted to make overtime. As soon as they had departed she herself would disappear. She would leave her father a note, just as Winston had done. She did not know what she would say in that note. She would think about that later.

Emma cursed herself under her breath as she worked. What a fool she had been. She felt no remorse or even regrets about their trysts at the cave. What had been done could not be undone, and to have regrets was a waste of valuable time. She was a fool for a different reason: she had allowed Edwin to distract her from her purpose, to interfere with her Plan with a capital *P*, in the same way she had permitted her mother's death, Winston's scarpering off, and her father's desperate need of her to make her waver in her determination to leave Fairley.

A faint hollow echo of a voice came back to her from the past. They were words said to her over a year ago, that night of the dinner party, that night before her mother's death, words long forgotten but remembered now. It was Adele Fairley's voice saying to her, 'You must get away from this place, Emma. Away from this house. Before it's too late.' Mrs Fairley was not as daft as everybody thought, Emma said to herself. *She* had known. Somehow *she* had known that doom and disorder and danger lurked within these walls.

Emma paused in her work and stood perfectly still, lost in thought. She gripped the table as a sudden tremor swept through her, and closed her eyes, concentrating on her thoughts. After a few moments she opened her eyes, staring blindly at the roses. Emma did not realize that a wholly new and dangerous light had entered those remarkable emerald eyes. It was a terrible awareness compounded of her bitter comprehension and the most unremitting calculation. It was then that she made a vow to herself, a vow intensely pledged with every fibre of her being, every ounce of her strength. *It would never happen again.* She would never allow anyone or anything to dissuade her from her course, to stand in her way, to thwart her, or weaken her determination. She would, from this day on, be single-minded of purpose to the exclusion of all else. The purpose: money. Vast amounts of it. For money was power. She would become so rich and powerful she would be invulnerable to the world. And after that? Revenge. She smiled and it was a smile that was both unyielding and vindictive.

Emma unlatched the door and picked up one of the vases, carrying it through into the dining room. She must get through her work today without the slightest show of emotion or panic, and she must avoid Edwin at all costs. She could never look on that face again, for her contempt had turned to bitter hatred; a hatred so consuming, so virulent it filled her mind absolutely, obliterating all else. She did not even think of the child she was carrying or the overwhelming problems facing her. This deadly hatred for Edwin Fairley, born in her that day, only served to reinforce the loathing she had always held for Adam Fairley, and it was a dreadful living force within her, lingering in her heart for almost all the days of her life. In essence it became a motivating factor, coalescing with her inherent ambition, her drive, her energy, and her shrewdness to propel her to heights not even she, at that moment, dreamed possible.

TWENTY-SIX

The following morning Edwin Fairley strolled across the mill yard, a disconsolate expression on his face. From time to time he glanced up at the village on the hill, wondering miserably about Emma.

He knew she would leave Fairley this weekend, if she had not already gone. He was quite positive about that. Very late last night, unable to sleep, beset by worry and twinges of guilt, he had crept up to her attic room. The suitcase he had deposited there that afternoon had disappeared, along with her clothes from the closet and the other small and pitiful things she kept at the Hall, such as the small vase of dried heather on the windowsill and bits of jewellery, including her prized possession, a horrid little green-glass brooch.

Edwin sighed. He was feeling wretched. He had behaved like an unspeakable cad. If only she had told him less abruptly, had waited until his head had cleared after the terrible shock of her disastrous news. Perhaps then he would have been able to think more intelligently, could have been more helpful. How? nagged a small voice. If he were honest with himself he had to admit he would not have married her. That was out of the question. But – Oh, God, stop driving yourself crazy, he told himself furiously, unable to cope with the turbulent thoughts racing through his head.

Emma had gone. And that was that. Under the circumstances, maybe she had been wise to leave immediately. Had she stayed she might have dragged him into the situation, albeit unwittingly, and there would have been a scandal the likes of which he did not dare to contemplate. That's unfair and unworthy of you to think that, Edwin Fairley, he chided himself with a stab of shame and a flash of rare insight into himself and Emma. She would never have claimed him as the father of her child. He knew her well enough to recognize that somehow she would have protected him. Sickeningly, he wondered how she would manage on her own, what she would do, where she had gone, or was going. In his state of panic, and stunned disbelief yesterday, he had not even bothered to find out her intended destination and now it haunted him.

He stopped his pacing when he reached the horses tethered near the mill gates. He stroked Russet Dawn, trying to still those distressing feelings so paramount within him. A brisk ride over the moors would do him good. He looked up. Not that it was a very good day. It was excessively gloomy. The sky was overcast and heavy and there was a strong wind. On the other hand, the visit to Kirkend would certainly preoccupy his mind and might conceivably prevent him from dwelling on the problem of Emma, and also alleviate the discomfort he was feeling within himself.

Edwin stared into space, his eyes vacant, and so at first he did not notice the little trickles of smoke eddying out from under the doors of the great warehouse nearby. It was only when Russet Dawn suddenly whinnied and pranced that he looked about quickly and spotted the smoke, which was becoming increasingly more obvious. Edwin caught his breath, soothed the horses, and ran towards the warehouse apprehensively.

As Edwin sped across the yard Jack Harte was coming around the corner from the weaving shed, carrying a pile of empty sacks. The side window of the warehouse was in his direct line of vision and his eyes flared open as he saw the red glow inside. He also saw Edwin Fairley tugging at the latch on the heavy doors. Jack started to run, fear flickering across his face, calling to Edwin to get away from the doors. 'Don't open 'em, lad,' he screamed, 'it's the worst thing thee can do. Get away from there, lad!' Edwin glanced at him, but ignored his words and continued his fumbling efforts to open the doors. He finally managed this and went inside, just as Jack reached the warehouse. Jack dumped the sacks on the ground and rushed in after Edwin, still crying out his warnings of imminent danger.

At the far end of the vast warehouse several wooden skips used for transporting the wool and the bobbins had somehow caught fire. Flying embers from these had embedded themselves in the bales of raw wool packed in sacks, and which were stacked on top of each other. They were blazing furiously, other stacks adjacent to them catching light in rapid succession. The warehouse itself, as well as the enormous quantities of wool stored there, was going up in flames like a tinder box, sparks and embers flying, smoke billowing, beams and wooden walls cracking and splintering away as tongues of fire rose up to the ceiling and spread out in all directions. In a few minutes it would be a conflagration of terrifying proportions, for the wind coming in through the open doors was fanning the flames into a molten furnace and the heat was sweltering, the smoke overpowering.

'Get out of 'ere, Master Edwin,' Big Jack yelled above the roar of the flames devouring the wooden building.

'We must do something at once!' gasped Edwin, who was staring at the blazing scene as if mesmerized.

'Aye, I knows that, lad. But this is no fit place for thee!' Jack grabbed his arm with a show of force and pulled him away. 'Come on, out of 'ere this minute. We'll have ter get the steam engine and the pumps going right fast if we're ter stop this spreading.'

They turned together, Jack leading the way through the heavy smoke swirling like a maelstrom in the warehouse, choking and blinking their watering eyes as they groped their way outside. Because of the density of the smoke, which was increasing by the second, Edwin did not see the iron ring attached to a trapdoor in the floor and he caught his foot in it, falling flat on his face. He tried to free himself, shouting to Jack, who was ahead of him. Jack pivoted swiftly and ran back. Dismay flashed across his face when he saw the toe of Edwin's riding boot wedged in the ring. He knelt down, endeavouring to release it.

'Can thee get thee leg out of thee boot, lad?' Jack cried.

'Not in this position.' Nevertheless, he wriggled and twisted his leg, but to no avail.

'This ring's a bit loose. I'll try and wrench it out of t'floor,' Jack spluttered, coughing harshly and wafting the smoke out of his face. Using all of his strength, he pulled on the iron ring and to his relief, after several strong tugs, it began to tear away from the wooden trapdoor.

At this moment, the wide platform running around the warehouse, just below ceiling level, began to glow as the fire rolled along it unchecked, a river of white-hot roaring flames. Bales of burning wool were being released as the platform sagged, disintegrated, and collapsed. Jack looked up with horror, a cry strangled in his throat. Huge bales were plummeting haphazardly from the platform just above them, like fiery meteors intent on destruction, and Edwin was trapped immediately below. Without hesitation or thought for himself, Jack threw himself on top of the boy protectively, shielding Edwin's body with his own. One of the flaming bales landed on top of Jack's back. Jack bit down on the scream that bubbled in his throat. Pain tore through him from the crushing weight of the bale and the fire that immediately ignited his clothes and began to sear his flesh. He struggled violently to throw off the bale, heaving his great shoulders and kicking with his legs. With a burst of energy he managed to thrust it partially away from his shoulders, and with one final desperate heave that took all of his diminishing strength it rolled over to one side. Jack leapt up, choking on the smoke he had inhaled. He ignored his excruciating pain and his burning clothes, and wrenched again on the ring with both of his powerful hands. Mercifully, because he had managed to loosen it before, it came away at once, and Edwin scrambled to his feet, his face livid with fear as well as distress for the man who had so selflessly and valiantly saved him.

Coughing and spluttering, the two of them stumbled out of the warehouse as a central portion of the roof crumbled. Jack staggered and fell convulsively on to the ground, twisting and writhing in agony, chest heaving, unable to breathe. Coughing himself, but inhaling the fresher air, Edwin ripped off his jacket and began to beat out Jack's burning clothes with it.

Adam Fairley was racing across the yard with Wilson, shouting orders to the couple of dozen mill hands close on his heels. He was aghast when he saw Jack Harte's blazing clothes and Edwin's vain efforts to smother the flames. Shrugging out of his jacket, he cried to Wilson, 'Bring buckets of water and get me those sacks over there.'

With speed and efficiency and great presence of mind, Adam threw his jacket on to Jack's burning shirt, grabbed Edwin's jacket from him and wrapped it around Jack's legs. He added the sacks Wilson had flung to him and rolled Jack on the ground in them, unconscious of the flames which singed his own hands. Wilson panted up with two buckets of water, followed by other workers carrying extra pails. Adam and Wilson threw water over Jack to cool the heat and deaden the flames until they were entirely extinguished, leaving behind charred clothes and sacks clinging to Jack, who lay inert and seemingly lifeless.

Adam knelt down and felt Jack's pulse. It was faint but there was a beat. Jack looked up at Adam, a glazed expression in his bloodshot eyes. He blinked. A small groan escaped his lips before he passed out from shock and the pains of his extensive burns.

Adam stood up, shaking his head worriedly. 'Carry him into my office, and gently!' Adam barked at two of the workers. He glanced swiftly at Edwin hovering by his side. 'Are you hurt?'

'No, Father. My clothes are a bit scorched,' Edwin answered between the coughing that racked him, 'and I'm full of this rotten smoke. But that's all.'

'Then you're fit enough to ride up to Clive Malcolm's. Tell him Jack Harte has been badly burned. Tell him to get here at once!'

Edwin was rooted to the spot. He gaped at his father speechlessly, sudden comprehension trickling into his mind.

'Confound it, Edwin! Don't stand there like an idiot!' Adam screamed angrily. 'Get going, boy. The man's life is in danger. He needs medical attention at once.'

'Yes, Father.' He stared at Adam again and then his eyes swivelled after Jack's body being carried into the offices. 'He saved my life,' he said quietly. 'The bale would have fallen on me if he hadn't thrown himself over me.'

'All right, Edwin, all right! I understand!' Adam snapped impatiently. 'I *understand* what you're saying. But we'll discuss that later. Now for God's sake do as I say. Go to Clive and ride like the very devil. Time is of the essence. Tell Clive this is extremely urgent.'

'Yes, Father.' Edwin swung himself up into the saddle and galloped out of the mill yard, one thought piercing into his brain with the most penetrating clarity: Emma's father had saved his life.

Adam now turned his attention to the burning warehouse. Fortunately, he had had the foresight to buy one of the new small steam-powered fire engines several years before, for just such an emergency. Ten of the men had already dragged it out of the shed where it was stored. The coal to power it was burning and the men were expertly coupling two hoses to the hydrants. Other mill hands from one of the back buildings were swelling into the yard, including the bully boys and little bobbin liggers. Amongst them was Frank Harte, who had not witnessed his father's accident in the fire. Under Wilson's organization, this group was formed into a chain between the mill yard and the river Aire, passing the brimming buckets of water up to their mates, returning the empty ones down the line to be filled and refilled again and again, until their arms ached. Issuing orders, fully in command of the situation, Adam worked alongside the mill hands grateful for these tough and hardy Yorkshiremen who were going about their duties with cool heads and extraordinary courage in this unexpected and dangerous emergency.

Suddenly the wind shifted. Adam sighed with relief and then he groaned, dismay flooding his face when he saw that part of the burning roof had toppled on to a patch of shrubs adjoining a small copse of trees which edged right up to the main street of the village. Now, with the change in the direction of the wind, the copse was in danger.

'Wilson, send some of the other men over to me,' Adam yelled. 'They've got to handle that copse at once! The trees will go next, if we're not careful. The wind's blowing the fire that way.'

'But the mill itself –' Wilson began.

'Damn it, man! Do as I say. I can always rebuild the mill. But there are women and children in those cottages. If the trees catch, the fire will spread up into the village itself in no time at all.'

Wilson dispatched five men to consult with Adam, who took them aside urgently. He spoke rapidly but concisely. 'Grab some axes from the shed and get over to the copse. Chop down small trees and bushes in front of those shrubs burning at the edge of the copse. Cut right down to the soil, clearing a narrow strip in front of the fire, so that any embers flying as it encroaches will fall into the strip and can be quickly extinguished. Then get buckets of water and start dousing all of the trees. We must prevent the fire taking hold in the copse at all costs.'

The five men nodded their understanding and silently scattered to fetch the axes and buckets of water. They set to work in the copse at once. Meanwhile, Adam hurried back to Wilson, who was supervising the spraying of the warehouse. Under the force of the water from the hoses and the buckets the fire was beginning to die down, and with the change in the wind it was now relatively well under control.

Adam took out his handkerchief and wiped his sweating, smoke-streaked face. Then he swung around as he heard wheels turning into the yard. Clive Malcolm leapt out with his bag almost before the trap drew to a standstill. He threw the reins to his wife, Violet, who had accompanied him. Edwin cantered into the yard, just behind the trap.

Adam pointed grimly at the offices. 'Harte's in a bad way, Clive. Do the best you can.'

'Any other casualties?' Clive cried as he raced across the yard.

'A few men have small burns and one was struck by a piece of falling roof. But nothing too serious, as far as I can ascertain. Get to Harte first. Edwin, go along with the doctor and Mrs Malcolm. See if there is anything you can do to assist them.'

Adam coughed. His lungs were filled with smoke and he felt nauseous from it. He looked over at the copse anxiously. The men had already made progress and were preventing the fire from spreading and, although the shrubs were still burning, the trees leading up to the village were unharmed. Embers flying up into the air were falling into the narrow strip which had been cleared, just as Adam had predicted they would. They were being rapidly dampened and put out with water from the continuous supply of buckets being passed along.

As he looked about him, surveying the damage to the warehouse, Adam slowly became conscious that the wind had dropped unexpectedly. He looked up at the sky. Damnation, why doesn't it rain? he muttered. He glanced yet again at the overcast sky, praying silently. Wilson hurried to him. 'I thinks we've about got it under control, Squire. I don't believe the mill's in any danger now.' As he spoke Wilson stared at Adam and a smile spread itself across his grimy face. 'By God, sir, I thinks it's going ter rain. Do yer knows, I just felt a drop.'

And Wilson was right. Rain it did. For once in his life, Adam Fairley welcomed the deluge that began to pour out of the sky, rippling down in heavy sheets, drenching them all and slaking the smouldering warehouse and the bushes in the copse. The mill hands stopped working and all of them turned to Adam, their voices rising in one single triumphant cheer.

'We're allus grumbling and grousing abart the blinking weather on t'moors, Squire, but this bloody rain's a gift from 'eaven,' shouted Eddie, one of the foremen.

Adam grinned. 'I couldn't have said it better myself, Eddie.'

Eddie now approached Adam standing with Wilson. 'Do yer mind if I goes up ter see me mate, Jack Harte, sir? There just might be summat I can do for t'doctor.'

'Yes, Eddie, please do so. I'm coming in myself.' Adam rested his hand on

252

Wilson's shoulder. 'I think you can manage down here now. By the look of the sky this is no light summer shower.'

'I agree, sir. I'll get the men organized with grappling hooks and ladders. We can start clearing up a bit of this mess.' Wilson glanced at the blackened and charred ruins of the warehouse, still smouldering and steaming under the rain falling in torrents. 'We was lucky, Squire. We was that!'

Adam nodded. 'I'll talk to you later about this, Wilson.' His eyes narrowed. 'It baffles me how the damn thing started in the first place.' Wilson returned Adam's steely gaze but was silent.

Before he went into the offices Adam called the men together in front of the wreckage. 'I want to thank you, lads, for pitching in the way you did, with such efficiency and coolness. And also with such bravery. There will be bonuses for all of you in your pay next week, as an expression of my very sincere gratitude. You saved the mill, and incidentally, the village as well. I won't forget this.'

Some of the men grinned, others touched their foreheads with brief little salutes, yet others nodded. All murmured their thanks. One of the men stepped forward and said, 'There weren't owt else we could do, Squire, now was there? It being our mill as well, so ter speak like. And yer didn't do so bad yerself, Squire, if yer don't mind me saying so. I thinks I speak for all t'lads when I say yer were a right trooper, sir.'

A half smile flickered in Adam's eyes. 'Thank you, Alfie.' He nodded cordially and left. Adam found Clive Malcolm in his office attending to Jack Harte. Eddie was standing near the window, talking quietly to Edwin.

'How is he?' Adam asked from the doorway. Clive looked around and frowned. 'Not good. But I think he's going to be all right, Adam. He's suffering from shock, of course, and bad burns on his back, shoulders, and thighs. Third-degree burns. I'm trying to make him as comfortable as possible, and then I must move him down to the valley hospital as quickly as possible. I shall need your big carriage, Adam, so I can keep him flat. I thought Edwin could ride up to the Hall and send Tom Hardy back with it right away. This is a real emergency with Harte. I just don't have the equipment and the medicines I need to treat him efficiently. I've got to get him into that hospital.'

'I'll send Edwin at once.' Adam inclined his head towards his son. 'Off you go, my boy, and make it fast. We have no time to lose apparently.'

'Yes, sir,' Edwin said, and left.

'Where are the other men, Clive? And how are they?

'Violet's patching them up in Wilson's office. They're not too badly hurt. First-degree burns, that's all. They will all be fine in a day or so.'

'Will Jack Harte live?' asked Adam, sitting down behind his desk wearily, a serious expression clouding his face.

'Yes, I think so. But to be honest with you, Adam, it's hard to tell. I don't know if there are any internal injuries yet. Edwin told me that one of the large bales fell on Harte. He also inhaled a lot of smoke and the heat from that scorches the lungs. I think one lung has possibly already collapsed.'

'Oh, my God!' Adam exclaimed, and passed his hand over his eyes. 'You don't sound too hopeful.'

'He's a strong man, Adam. I'm hoping we can pull him through.' Clive gave

Adam a sympathetic smile. 'Try not to worry, old chap. After all, it wasn't your fault. You're lucky the casualties are so few.'

Adam sighed. 'I know. But that could easily have been Edwin lying there in that condition, Clive. He did save Edwin's life, you know. And at the risk of his own. Jack Harte performed an act of such dauntless courage I'll never forget it. He was fearless and unselfish.' Adam's grey-blue eyes narrowed, and he shook his head. 'You don't find many men like Jack Harte in this world.'

Clive straightened up and his gaze rested on Adam, quietly intense. 'I know. He was always a bit different, wasn't he? But we'll fight for him, Adam. I promise you that.'

'All medical bills to me, Clive, for Harte and the other men. And instruct the hospital he has to have the very best of care. Spare no expense and don't put him in a general ward. I want a private room for him, and whatever else he needs he's to have.'

There was a light tapping on the door. 'Come in,' Adam called. The door opened and one of the bobbin liggers, covered in grime and dirt, stood in the entrance nervously. Adam looked at him in surprise.

'Yes, son, what is it?'

The boy hesitated. 'It's about me dad,' he said, looking over at Jack, his lips trembling. 'Is he – is he?' he began tremulously, tears brimming into his eyes.

Adam leapt up and strode across the floor. He brought the boy into the room gently, putting his arm around his shoulders.

'It's Frank, Jack's son, sir,' Eddie volunteered from his stance at the window.

'Come along, Frank,' Adam said softly, his arm still encircling the boy's shoulders. Tears rolled down Frank's face as he stood staring at his father. 'Is he dead?' he finally managed to say in a choked voice.

'Of course he isn't, Frank,' Adam reassured him with the utmost gentleness. 'He has been badly injured, I won't lie to you about that. But Dr Mac has made him comfortable and as soon as my carriage arrives we are going to transport him to the hospital in the valley. He will get the very best of medical care there.'

Adam pulled out his handkerchief and wiped the tears from Frank's face. 'Now, you must be a brave boy, and you mustn't worry. Your father will be better in no time at all.'

Frank looked up at Adam anxiously. 'Are yer sure, Squire? Yer wouldn't fib ter me, would yer?'

Adam smiled kindly. 'No, I wouldn't, Frank. I am telling you the truth, son.'

'Your father is resting comfortably,' Clive interjected, 'and as soon as I get him to the hospital we'll be able to treat him properly.'

Frank looked from Adam to Clive doubtfully, sniffling and suppressing his tears. He was silent and thoughtful for a moment and then he addressed Eddie. 'He will get better, Eddie, won't he?' he whispered.

Eddie stepped forward, forcing a cheerful smile on to his drawn face. 'Aye, lad, he will that! Yer father's a strong 'un. Now, don't yer fret yerself, lad. Come on, I'll take yer ter yer Aunt Lily's.' Eddie threw a swift glance at Adam, who nodded acquiescently. Adam patted Frank's shoulder. 'Run along with Eddie, Frank. And the doctor will stop by to see you later.' Adam's eyes examined Frank, sudden concern in them. 'Are you all right, son? You weren't hurt, were you?'

'No, Squire,' said Frank, still sniffling.

'All right, then, off you go. And thank you, Eddie, for all your help. I appreciate it.'

'I just did me best, sir,' said Eddie, smiling briefly. 'I'll be taking the lad ter his aunt's. She'll look after him.' Eddie grasped Frank's hand, squeezing it reassuringly, and the two of them left, Eddie murmuring consoling words to Frank.

'I think I had better go into Wilson's office and see the other men, Clive. I want to thank them and make sure they are comfortable,' Adam remarked.

'Let Violet take a look at those hands of yours, Adam,' Clive ordered firmly. 'They look a little raw to me.'

Later that afternoon Adam strode up and down the library at Fairley Hall, a brandy and soda in his bandaged hand, a thoughtful expression on his face. Wilson, who had just arrived, sat on the Chesterfield, watching him closely, quietly nursing his whisky.

Adam finally stopped his incessant pacing and sat down in the chair opposite. He lit a cigarette, drew on it, and said, 'How do you think the fire started in the warehouse, Wilson? It went up very suddenly and burned rather rapidly for my liking. I questioned Edwin earlier, and he said the wooden skips were blazing furiously when he opened the door, and that the first stack of bales was already flaring. I suppose the flying embers could have ignited the wool, and the draught from the door obviously fanned the flames, but it's still a mystery to me. Any ideas?'

Wilson was silent, his mouth tight and drawn, his face a picture of gravity. He sighed and looked directly at Adam. 'I could hazard a guess, Squire, but it's not a very palatable one.'

Adam leaned forward and stared at Wilson, fixing him intently. 'Speak up, Wilson. You've obviously given this some thought, just as I have myself all afternoon.'

Wilson scowled. 'Arson maybe.'

'Arson!' Adam was so flabbergasted he sat up with a start and banged his drink down on the table with a crash. 'Oh, come, come, Wilson, that's not possible. Surely it isn't!'

'Well, sir, raw wool doesn't burn that easily. But wood does. I also spoke ter Master Edwin and he told me the same thing – them there skips were going like wildfire. A bit of paraffin on one of the bales, soaking through the sacking inter the wool –' Wilson stopped and looked down into his drink, sighing. 'Yer knows, Squire, that could have been a bloody holocaust down there this morning, but for the wind changing and the rain starting when it did. We only had the fire in the warehouse partially under control, yer knows.'

'But why?' Adam demanded, still stunned and aghast at Wilson's words.

Wilson hesitated and sipped his whisky. Then he looked Adam squarely in the eye. 'Retaliation.'

'Retaliation! Retaliation for what? Against whom? I've been more than decent with the men in the last few years, for God's sake. You can't be serious, man.'

Wilson, who had been pondering on the cause of the fire for several hours, picked his words with care. He knew what had to be said, but he felt he must couch his opinions in the most diplomatic terms possible. He cleared his throat. 'Yer haven't been at yon mill much in the past year, sir, what with yer travelling

255

an' all. The men are a bit out of touch with yer, so ter speak. And when yer have been 'ere, yer visits have been brief –'

'Get to the point, Wilson. You said retaliation. I want to know what you mean by that,' Adam snapped.

Wilson drew in his breath. 'I thinks the fire might have been started on purpose like, because of Master Gerald.'

Adam stiffened, his eyes widening. 'Master Gerald! What's he been up to in my absence? By God, Wilson, I'll have his hide if he's responsible for this. I'll skin him alive!'

Wilson cleared his throat nervously. 'Look, Squire, Master Gerald's a hard worker. I'm the first ter say that. And he luvs the mill, like yer father did. But Master Gerald – well, sir, he just doesn't know how ter handle the men. Most of 'em just grin and turn away like, pay no attention ter him and get on with their work. But there's a little extremist group down at yon mill. Troublemakers ter some extent, yer might say. Labourites, yer knows, Squire. Well, they have come ter resent Master Gerald's way of dealing with 'em.'

'Out with it all, Wilson,' Adam said sternly, his anger most apparent.

'It's his manner, like I said,' Wilson replied, lighting a Woodbine. 'He's allus pushing the lads around, goading 'em on, cracking t'whip like. And when they come ter him for a few simple concessions, like a longer tea break for one thing, he just wafts 'em away –'

'You can't be serious! You don't expect me to believe a fire was started simply because Master Gerald refused to give the men a longer tea break. That's preposterous and damned ridiculous, Wilson!' Adam exploded, his usual self-control slipping momentarily.

'No, Squire, not for that one thing only, but for lots of things that have mounted up like, over these last months. Small things admittedly, but I knows some of the lads have been boiling lately at Master Gerald's harshness, his bullying, his temper an' all –' Wilson's voice trailed off.

Adam sighed heavily and leaned back in the chair, his eyes resting on Wilson contemplatively. 'And so you think some of them started a fire to get even.' Adam now moved forward, his gaze more penetrating than ever. 'But that's a futile gesture, Wilson, since the mill itself could have gone up, and they would have been laid off for weeks on half pay.'

'Aye, I knows. I've considered that fact meself,' Wilson conceded wearily. 'But I thinks a small fire was started ter make a point like. I don't think them as might have started it expected it ter get out of hand the way it did. I don't, really. Yer knows what I'm getting at, sir. Start a little blaze, destroy a few bales of wool. As I said, make a point. Slow down production, cause a bit of trouble. Make us sit up and take notice.'

'The culprits?' Adam demanded, glaring at Wilson.

'That's it, Squire, I can't be pointing any fingers. That group of men I mentioned were all at t'mill this morning, and they all pitched in like hell, that they did.' Wilson refrained from adding that three of the most violent agitators against Gerald Fairley were, in fact, noticeably and fortuitously absent that day. He himself would deal with them later. For he did believe arson was involved and he was fairly certain the absentees were the arsonists. He would put the fear of God into them. He prayed Adam Fairley would do the same with his son.

Adam was thoughtful, reflecting on Wilson's words, and then he said, 'What you're saying doesn't really make any sense. Why would they start a fire and then expose themselves to it? That would be most foolhardy.'

'I told yer, sir, I thinks them as started it intended it as a bit of a scare, that's all, never expecting it ter blaze the way it did, ter get out of control.'

Now Adam was silent, his wrath with Gerald fulminating inside him. He attempted to calm himself, to think clearly. What Wilson said did make sense – to a degree. Raw wool, because it was oily, smouldered rather than blazed at first. Conceivably, paraffin might well have been poured over one of the bales. Whoever had started the fire probably thought only a portion of the warehouse and a few bales would be damaged. Fools, he thought angrily. The stupid bloody fools. The warehouse was highly inflammable because it was built of wood. They had not considered that aspect or the ultimate consequences of their irresponsible actions. They had not realized the danger to all the mill buildings and the village.

'Very well, Wilson, I accept your explanation. You could be correct in your assumptions,' Adam said at last, his face tensely set. 'And, since the members of that radical group you mentioned were working this morning, we cannot make any accusations, I suppose, can we?'

'No, sir!' responded Wilson vehemently. 'We can't. We *daren't*. We've no evidence for one thing, and the way the men worked ter help extinguish the fire – by God, sir, they'd take right exception ter it, they would that. Also, the men'd stick together. We'd have a strike on our hands, I guarantee that, if we start talking about arson.' Wilson nodded gravely and cleared his throat. 'Perhaps yer could have a word with Master Gerald when he gets back from Shipley tomorrow, sir, if yer don't mind me suggesting it. Caution him ter temper his manner, his rough ways with the lads.'

'Oh, I intend to, Wilson. In fact, he'll get a dressing down the likes of which he's never had. Believe me, he will!' Adam declared, his fury rising to the surface again. 'I never dreamt he would so wilfully defy my instructions about treating the men decently.' After a short pause he softened his tone. 'In the meantime, we have a vital problem to contend with – supplies. All the bales in the warehouse were totally destroyed, as you know. How much raw wool do we have in the other warehouse?'

'Enough ter carry us through this month, I'd say, sir,' Wilson responded, his mind working rapidly, evaluating their supplies and their orders. He puffed on his Woodbine. 'We've got a shipment due in from McGill, from Australia, in two or three weeks, thank God. I thinks we'll be able to manage till then.'

'Do your best, Wilson. Get on to it first thing on Monday morning. I will come in early myself and we can make our assessments. And you had better build a new warehouse immediately. Use bricks, not wood. And also order another small fire engine. I don't anticipate a repetition of this disaster, but it's always wise to be prepared for any contingencies. As you said, we were lucky this time because of the change in the weather.'

'No, I don't expect it will happen again, Squire,' Wilson said, so sharply and with such conviction Adam glanced at him swiftly but made no comment. Wilson did not miss Adam's reaction and went on in a more even voice, 'But yer right, it's allus best ter have plenty of fire-fighting apparatus on 'and, just in case. I was thinking, sir, if yer likes I'll go down ter yon mill termorrow and start taking stock. It'll save time.'

'That's an excellent thought, Wilson, if you don't mind working on Sunday. I shall be there myself and we can do it together.'

'Right ho, sir.' Wilson paused, his eyes glinting shrewdly behind his steel spectacles. 'And yer will have a talk ter Master Gerald, won't yer?' he pressed.

'Rest assured I will, and in no uncertain terms.' Adam stood up. 'Let me freshen your drink, Wilson.'

'Thank yer, Squire. I wouldn't say no ter one for t'road.'

As Adam poured the whisky a sudden thought struck him most cogently: Wilson knew who the guilty parties were, but he was obviously not prepared to reveal their identities, for his own reasons, undoubtedly very sound reasons. So be it, Adam said to himself. He trusted Wilson to deal with them appropriately. He would deal with Gerald. His mouth tightened as he considered his elder son. The young idiot, he's undone all the good I strove so hard to achieve. Antagonizing the men was not only a rank display of poor judgement, it was an act of sheer folly. But it's also my fault, he admitted. I've given him far too much rope and my continuing absences have not helped. I shall have to spend more time in Fairley, he decided. But there was Olivia. He found it intolerable to be apart from her. She had become the whole reason for his existence. The rock on which his life was built. It was with sadness that he then acknowledged he had to pay more attention to the mill. That was, without question, an imperative taking precedence over everything else. Perhaps he could persuade Olivia to come to Fairley. She would understand. Damn that boy! A look of utter distaste crossed his face as he contemplated Gerald and the measures he would have to take with him. Gerald was a bully and therefore a coward. He would toe the line. *By God, he will*, Adam muttered under his breath.

He composed himself and carried the drinks back to Wilson. 'I wish Dr Mac would get here. I am extremely worried about Jack Harte,' Adam said, handing Wilson the glass of whisky.

'Aye, Squire, so am I. But Harte's a fighter. He'll pull through. He's got them bairns ter think about, yer knows.'

Adam sighed. 'I hope you're right, Wilson. I sincerely do. I can never repay the debt I owe him for saving Edwin's life.'

PART THREE

THE SLOPE
1905–10

'Tis a common proof,
That lowliness is young ambition's ladder,
Whereto the climber-upward turns
his face . . .

– WILLIAM SHAKESPEARE, *Julius Caesar*

TWENTY-SEVEN

'There's the Mucky Duck, luv,' said the tinker, drawing his horse and cart to a standstill in York Road and pointing a stubby and none too clean finger at the public house.

'But it says "Black Swan",' exclaimed Emma, reading the name on the sign swinging in the breeze. Confirming the lettering was a picture of a white pond upon which floated a somewhat primitive painting of an ebony swan, neck arched in such an ungainly fashion it was hardly a lifelike rendition of that elegant bird.

The tinker's wife, all Romany-dark curls and wrinkled tanned face, cackled uproariously at Emma's astonishment. 'Aye, lass, that's wot they calls the Black Swan in Leeds. The Mucky Duck. Don't yer get it?' She cackled again, displaying several gold teeth that glittered as brightly as the golden rings looped through her ears and which dropped below the red-and-white-checkered scarf draped on top of her gypsy hair.

'Yes, I do,' said Emma with an amused smile. She clutched her reticule to her and climbed down carefully from the cart. The tinker handed her the large leather suitcase which Edwin had deposited in her room yesterday with the five pounds. She looked up at the tinker and his gypsy wife and said gravely, and with enormous politeness, 'Thank you very much for giving me the ride all the way from Shipley. It was very kind of you.'

'Nay, lass, it weren't no trouble,' said the tinker kindly. 'Glad ter be of service ter a fine young lady like thee.' He flicked the reins and the dilapidated cart moved off, pots and pans strung on the sides rattling and banging merrily as the old wheels turned in rickety rhythm. The tinker's wife looked back, shouting, 'Lots o' luck in Leeds, me pretty 'un.'

'Thank you,' Emma called, waving at the retreating cart. She stood outside the pub for a moment and then picked up the suitcase, took a deep breath, and pushed open the swinging doors made of heavy wood, the upper panels inset with opaque glass embellished with engraved lilies and swans. She immediately found herself in a narrow and gloomy passage that smelled strongly of stale beer, tobacco smoke, and the faint reek of gas from the jets on the walls. The latter were lined with a dull brown wallpaper that only reinforced the forbidding atmosphere, which prevailed in spite of the burning gas jets and was not very inviting.

Emma looked about curiously. There was a carefully printed notice pinned on one wall which declared in large letters: *Women in shawls not allowed in here!* It seemed to her like an ominous warning. The opposite wall sported a repulsive painting of a charging bull in an equally ugly ornate gilt frame. Emma shuddered, her critical eye offended by its hideousness. Ahead of her was another set of double swinging doors, also inset with opaque glass, and she hurried forward and went through them. Emma stood in the entrance of what was obviously the main bar. It was brightly illuminated and infinitely more cheerful, with its colourful wallpaper and attractive sepia prints, and there was a piano in one corner. The bar was empty, except for two men leaning against the back wall drinking their frothing pints and chatting amiably together. Emma's sharp eyes scanned the surroundings, missing nothing. Two other rooms opened off the main bar. The sign hanging above the archway leading into one proclaimed it to be the Saloon Bar, while the other was labelled Tap Room. In the Tap Room she could see a lone workman playing darts, and two old men were seated at a table absorbed in a game of dominoes, clay pipes firmly clenched between their individual sets of nicotine-stained teeth, smoke swirling fuggily around them.

Emma now glanced towards the bar itself. Several large mirrors hung on the wall behind it, each one extolling the virtues of Tetley's pale ale and other local beers in black and gold lettering. There were innumerable bottles of spirits glittering against the mirrored backdrop and below them great kegs of beer. The long and expansive mahogany counter was polished to a sheen as glassy and almost as shimmering a surface as the mirrors themselves, and just visible above the mahogany bar was a mop of blonde hair. Emma walked sedately across the room, her boots tip-tapping lightly on the wooden floor. Out of the corner of her eye she was aware of the two men regarding her, but she paid no attention and kept her glance fixed unwaveringly ahead.

When she reached the bar she put down the suitcase, but gripped the reticule in her hands. The blonde head bobbed about below the bar. Emma cleared her throat. 'Excuse me,' she said.

The blonde head swivelled to reveal a cheerful face that was open and honest. It was a pink and white face, and extremely pretty, with full cheeks and dimples and merry brown eyes that danced under shapely blonde brows. 'Yes, luv?' said the blonde lady, rising slowly and somewhat ponderously from her crouching position, holding a glass tankard and a cloth in her hands.

Emma had to stifle a gasp, for that face, so sweet and dimpling and extraordinarily pretty, and that blonde head with its array of elaborately dressed curls, sat atop an enormously fat body that was also amazingly tall. Her incredible body was tightly encased in a bright yellow cotton dress with a low square neckline and short puffed sleeves. Gargantuan bosom, portions of wide shoulders, and long plumpish arms were in striking evidence and were also white and pinkly tinted and soft.

The lady was looking at her questioningly and Emma said courteously, 'I'm looking for a Miss Rosie. I was told she was the barmaid here.'

The pink face broke into a wide and friendly smile that was also highly engaging and full of the most natural charm. 'Well, yer've found her, luv. That's me. I'm Rosie. What can I do for yer, miss?'

Emma's taut body relaxed and she found herself automatically smiling back at the beaming Rosie. 'I'm a friend of Blackie O'Neill's. He told me that you would take a message for him. Get it to him quickly, or to his Uncle Pat.'

Ho! Ho! thought Rosie, concealing a knowing look. So Blackie was up to his tricks again with the lasses, was he! Well, he certainly knows how ter pick 'em, commented Rosie to herself. This one's a real looker. Rosie planted the glass and the cloth on the bar and said, 'Yes, luv, I can get a message ter Blackie. Trouble is, it won't do yer any good. He's not in Leeds, yer see. He went off yesterday. Yer've just missed him. Aye, he went ter Liverpool ter get the boat ter Ireland. Summat about going ter see an old priest who was very badly, mebbe dying, so Blackie was telling me afore he left.'

'Oh, dear,' said Emma, and distress registered on her face so acutely Rosie could not fail to notice it. The Junoesque barmaid stretched out her plump arm and rested plump fingers on Emma's hand gently. 'Are yer all right, luv? Yer look a bit faintish ter me. How about a brandy or a rum and pep, mebbe? Do yer good, yer knows.'

Emma shook her head, endeavouring to quell the anxiety flaring within her. 'No, thank you, Miss Rosie. I don't drink spirits,' she murmured. The possibility that Blackie would be away had never occurred to her. She was so shaken she found it difficult to speak.

'Then how about a nice glass of lemon pop?' went on Rosie, regarding Emma carefully. 'It's refreshing and yer looks ever so peaked ter me.' Without waiting for a response, Rosie uncorked a bottle of lemonade and poured a glass. Emma did not want to spend the money for the lemon drink. Every penny was precious to her; yet, then again, she did not want to offend Rosie either, who was being so kind and friendly.

'Thank you,' Emma said softly, and opened her handbag. 'How much is it, please?'

'Nay, lass, it's nowt. This one's on the 'ouse. On Rosie,' she said, placing the brimming glass in front of Emma. 'Go on, 'ave a sip. It won't kill yer,' she added jocularly, and laughed. Then her merry face sobered. The girl had turned as white as chalk and Rosie immediately noticed that the small hand in the white crotcheted glove trembled as it picked up the glass.

''Ere, 'Arry! Fetch me one of them there stools from out of the Tap Room, will yer, please?' called Rosie to one of the men at the far end of the bar. 'This 'ere young lady looks a bit wobbly on her pins ter me.'

'Right, Rosie,' said the man named Harry. He returned instantly, carrying a tall stool. ''Ere yer are, luv, sit yerself down,' he said, and gave Emma a warm smile before he rejoined his mate.

'Thank you.' Emma perched on the stool gratefully. She felt weak and her head was swimming at the alarming news Rosie had imparted about Blackie. Rosie leaned her elbows on the bar and looked at Emma intently, a concerned expression on her face, her jolliness dissipated. 'Look, luv, I knows it's none of me business, but do yer have troubles? Yer seems ever so upset ter me.'

Emma hesitated. Distrustful by nature, she also firmly believed in the old north-country adage, 'a still tongue and a wise head', and she was therefore not given to confiding anything in anyone. Now her mind worked rapidly and with its usual shrewdness. She was in a strange place. An enormous city. She did not know her way around. With Blackie in Ireland she had no one to turn to for help. And so she came to a swift decision. She would trust Rosie – but only to a certain extent. She had no choice, really. But first she had one other question and it was of vital importance.

She returned Rosie's steady gaze and instead of spilling out her troubles, as the barmaid probably expected, she said, 'What about Blackie's Uncle Pat? Could I go and see him and perhaps find out when Blackie is returning? He is, isn't he?'

'Oh, yes, luv. Blackie'll be back in a couple of weeks or so. A fortnight he said he was going for. But it won't do yer any good going ter see Pat either. He's in Doncaster doing a right big building job. He's gone for a bit, I expects.'

Emma sighed and stared fixedly at the lemonade. Rosie waited patiently, not

263

wanting to appear nosy but, riddled with curiosity, she insisted, 'Why don't yer tell me yer troubles, luv? Perhaps I can help.'

After only a moment's further hesitation, Emma said, 'Yes, I do have a problem. I have to find a place to stay. A boarding-house. Perhaps you can advise me, Miss Rosie. That's why I wanted to see Blackie.'

''Ere, lass, what's all this *Miss* Rosie? We don't stand on ceremony around 'ere. Everybody calls me Rosie. Just Rosie, plain and simple like. And why don't yer tell me yer name, being as how yer a friend of a friend.'

Emma thought of her father and the possibility of him searching for her. But from the note she had left he would believe she had gone to Bradford and he did not know about the Mucky Duck or Blackie's last name. She was safe. 'It's Emma Harte,' she said, and added, to her own amazement, 'Mrs Harte.'

Rosie's eyes widened. 'Are yer married, then?' she asked, thinking: And where's the husband? but refrained from prying. Emma nodded, not trusting herself to say anything else for the moment. She had surprised herself more than she had surprised Rosie.

'Well, seeing as we're properly acquainted, so ter speak, and now that I knows yer problem, let's get down ter brass tacks. Yer looking for a place ter park yerself. Mmmmm. Let me think on that.' Rosie frowned, her eyes thoughtful.

'What about that boarding-house where Blackie lives? Couldn't I go there?' Emma volunteered. She was feeling a little calmer, thinking more clearly.

'By gum, no lass!' exclaimed Rosie with such vehemence Emma was startled. 'I couldn't be letting a luvely young lady like thee go down there, ter the blinking "ham and shank" – that's the Bank, yer knows, near the Leylands. Full of toughs, it is. No, luv, that wouldn't be fitting like.' Rosie scowled and seriously pondered this problem, wanting to help the girl. After a moment her face resumed its usual jolly expression and she smiled. 'I 'ave it. Yer can go ter see Mrs Daniel. She rents out rooms in her 'ouse. It's not far from 'ere. Yer can walk it easy. I'll write down the address for yer. Tell her Rosie from the Mucky Duck sent yer. Yer'll be safe there. She's a bit of a gruff 'un, Mrs Daniel is, but kindly enough.'

'How much will a room cost?' Emma asked quietly.

Rosie looked at her sharply. 'Don't yer have much brass, luv?' she probed but not without sympathy. The girl looked visibly troubled again and her consternation at not finding Blackie had been more than apparent. What's that young boyo been up ter? Rosie wondered, staring at Emma. Yet the girl had said she was married. Still, there's more ter this than meets the eye, decided the shrewd Rosie.

Emma was conscious of Rosie's scrutiny. She cleared her throat and adopted a calm expression, 'Oh, yes, I do have a few pounds,' she said confidently, quite unconsciously tightening her grip on the bag, which had not left her hands since she had departed from Fairley early that morning. It contained every penny she had and her few bits of jewellery.

Rosie flashed Emma a reassuring smile. 'Well, then, that's not so bad, is it! And Mrs Daniel is fair and square like. She won't sting yer. I expects she'll charge yer a few shillings a week for a room, that's all. I don't thinks she gives yer any grub for that. But yer can buy yer own. There's a fish-and-chip shop at the end of her street, and there's allus a man with a cart selling pies and peas and roamin' around by her.'

'I'll manage,' said Emma, swallowing hard again. The mere thought of food nauseated her these days. The sickness she was now experiencing every morning seemed to last all day sometimes. She said, 'I'm grateful, Rosie, for your help. Really I am. And I'm sure Mrs Daniel's room will be fine.'

'Aye, it will, luv. And she's clean and honest. Look, sit and rest yerself. I'll go ter the back parlour and get a bit of paper and write down Mrs Daniel's address for yer.' Rosie paused and added, 'Yer a stranger in Leeds, aren't yer, Emma?'

'Yes, I am, Rosie.'

'Then I'll put it all down for yer. How ter get there like. I'll only be a tick.'

'Thank you, Rosie, you are kind.'

Rosie bustled off to the parlour, numerous thoughts running through her head. She was much taken with this girl who had appeared from nowhere. In point of fact, she was intrigued by her. Emma Harte had such – Rosie paused in the middle of the parlour, seeking the appropriate word to describe Emma. Dignity! Yes, that was it. She was good-looking, too. That face! thought Rosie with not a little wonder. Why, she had never seen so striking a face in all her life before. She was a beauty, really, even if it was a different sort of beauty. Uncommon like.

'This is no ordinary girl, or a lass from the working class. And that's a certainty!' Rosie announced aloud to the empty room. Rosie Miller, who considered herself to be a sound judge of people, since she came into contact with all types and classes in the pub, knew *she* could never be deceived by anybody. Aye, she's a real lady, Rosie decided. There was the way Emma spoke, for instance. No dialect or local slang in her speech and only the faintest hint of a Yorkshire accent in her cultured voice. Not only that, there was her bearing and fine manners. Breeding, said Rosie knowingly. And her clothes, thought the barmaid, as she searched for a piece of paper and a pencil. Well, the black dress was a bit old-fashioned, Rosie had to admit, but it was made of good stuff and was elegantly cut. And the cream bonnet was definitely real Leghorn straw and the flowers trimming it were of pure silk. Rosie knew things about clothes. She did indeed, and she had only ever seen Quality ladies wearing a bonnet like that one. London town it was. And what about the crocheted gloves and the smart leather bag with its tortoiseshell frame? Those were certainly the possessions of a proper lady, as were the amber beads. Rosie considered the suitcase she had observed on the floor. Costly, it was, and made of *real* leather. Yes, she's gentry all right, Rosie concluded. She licked the pencil and began to carefully print Mrs Daniel's address. As Rosie wrote she became further intrigued, considering that this Emma Harte had come seeking out Blackie O'Neill, the Irish navvy. He was a handsome hunk of a man, no doubt about that. Still, he was a common labourer. Now what can the connection between them be? Rosie asked herself, mystified.

' 'Ere I am,' exclaimed Rosie, sailing up behind the bar. She looks ever so sad, thought Rosie, glancing at Emma. Emma jumped. She had been lost in her thoughts. 'This is the address, and I've wrote down the directions as ter how yer get ter Mrs Daniel's 'ouse,' Rosie went on, handing the paper to Emma.

'Thank you, Rosie.' Emma read the paper. The directions were quite clear.

Rosie leaned over the bar, adopting a more confidential air 'I said afore, I don't want ter seem like a Nosy Parker, but yer still seem upset, luv. Can I help yer in any other way? Blackie's been a right good friend ter me. I'd like ter repay his kindness by helping a friend of his, 'specially a friend in need, so ter speak.'

Emma remained silent. She had no intention of confiding her real troubles in

265

Rosie; on the other hand, she was a kindhearted woman and was evidently a native of Leeds. It occurred to Emma she might be able to offer some advice on another matter. Emma turned her eyes on Rosie. 'Yes, I do have one other problem. I have to find a job,' Emma explained.

'Ooh, luv, I don't know where a fine young lady like thee could get work in Leeds.' Rosie leaned closer and dropped her voice and she could not resist asking, 'Where's yer husband, luv?'

Emma was not caught unawares. She had prepared herself for this obvious question during Rosie's absence, since she had told her she was married. 'He's in the Royal Navy. At the moment he's on Mediterranean duty. For the next six months.' This was said so coolly, with such sureness and confidence Rosie believed her.

'And don't yer have any other family, then?'

'No, I don't,' Emma lied.

'But where were yer living afore?' Rosie questioned, keen eyes peering. Fully conscious of Rosie's growing interest in her, Emma said, 'With his grandmother. Near Ripon. My husband is an orphan, as I am. His grandmother died recently and now I am alone, since Winston is away at sea. That is, I'm alone until he comes home on leave.' Although she had embarked upon a pack of lies, unintentionally and somewhat to her chagrin, Emma was endeavouring to stick to the truth as much as possible. It was simpler and, more importantly, easier to remember in the future.

'I see,' said Rosie, nodding. 'And how did yer meet Blackie, then?' She was no longer able to control her avid curiosity.

'Blackie came to do some work for – for my husband's grandmother,' Emma improvised swiftly. 'He was always kind, doing extra jobs for us, for very little money. He liked the old lady, you see. He also knew she was not long for this world. I had told him that when she died I wanted to come to Leeds to find work. Blackie said I should look him up.' Emma paused and sipped the lemonade to gain time. She was rather astounded at her aptitude for deception, and also her suavity at telling such a tall tale. On the other hand, she must now continue and make it convincing. 'Blackie suggested I might find work in one of the new shops, selling finery to the ladies. He thought a well-educated person like me would be useful in a shop. I can also sew and do alterations.'

'Aye, that's an idea,' said Rosie, feeling extremely pleased with herself. She had been right about this girl coming from Quality folk. It had been patently obvious to her all along that Emma could only have met Blackie in his capacity as a workman, doing repairs at her home. Impoverished gentry, that's what this Emma Harte was. 'I'll tell yer what yer should do, luv,' went on Rosie helpfully. 'Monday morning, bright and early, pop along ter Briggate. Yer'll find it easy enough. It's a big street. There are lots of new shops in them there fancy arcades. Yer might find just the right opening –' Rosie stopped short. A group of men had entered the pub and were heading towards the bar. She sighed and then smiled kindly at Emma. 'Sit a while, if yer wants, Emma. But it's going ter get busy now. I won't be having much time ter chat with yer, luv.'

'Thank you, but I had better go and see Mrs Daniel and settle the matter about the room.' Emma stood up. She smiled brightly. 'Thank you again, Rosie, for all your help. I appreciate it.'

Rosie nodded. 'Aay, lass, I've done nowt, really. Hey, keep in touch with me, yer hear! Let me know if yer moves from Mrs Daniel's 'ouse. So as I can tell Blackie where yer are. And pop in and see me, if yer gets lonely, or if yer needs owt else, luv.'

'Yes, I will, Rosie. Thank you again. Goodbye.' Emma picked up the suitcase and with another flashing smile she left the pub.

Rosie's soft doe-like eyes followed her thoughtfully. By gum, I hopes she's all right, she said to herself. Such a luvely girl. And all alone in the world. It's a right shame, it is, really. Rosie hoped she would see her again. There was something special about Emma Harte.

Once she was outside the pub Emma studied the paper Rosie had given her, pushed it into her pocket, and set off determinedly to find Mrs Daniel's house. There were, in actuality, many rooms for rent in the vicinity of the Mucky Duck, but Rosie had purposely selected Mrs Daniel's boarding-house for Emma, even though it was much farther away than she had indicated. Rosie had wanted the girl out of this dreadful area of Leeds, for York Road was bordered on all sides by tough neighbourhoods where grown men were not safe, let alone a defenceless girl. And so Rosie's own fear of the district had reached out like a protective arm to shield Emma.

Most of the streets stretching beyond and away from these devastating slum areas were safe, but they were narrow and ugly, with dark, mean-looking back-to-back houses pressing against each other, a cruel inheritance from the Victorian era, wretched dwellings for the working classes. Emma concentrated on the street names, hurrying as fast as she could, for this great city, full of bustling people, carts and horses, carriages and tram-cars, was confusing and strange to her after the quietness of Fairley village. Yet, conversely, she was not intimidated. However, she did not stop to consider these new and diverse sights, or gaze at them in wonder. Emma occupied herself fundamentally with one problem at a time, and at this very moment her aim was to install herself in a room, find a job, and wait for Blackie's return, in that order. She dare not think of anything else, and most especially the baby. She kept her eyes ahead but alert, noting the names as she sped along, one hand clutching her reticule in a fierce grip, the other grasping the leather suitcase.

After thirty minutes of fast walking, without a pause for breath, she sighed with relief. There in front of her was the street where Mrs Daniel's house was located. Rosie's directions had been explicit. Now, for the first time, Emma stopped and put down the suitcase and pulled the paper from her pocket – Mrs Daniel's house was number five. This street, too, was dark, with a poverty-stricken air, but Emma cheered considerably when she reached number five. It was a taller house than she had expected, and narrow, wedged in between others, its Victorian walls blackened by factory soot and years of industrial grime. But the lace curtains at the sparkling windows were crisp and white and the door knocker gleamed brightly in the faint afternoon sunlight. The three steps in front of the house had been scrubbed to silvery whiteness over the years and the edges were brilliantly yellow from the scouring stone obviously used daily to outline the worn rims.

Emma practically flew up the steps and banged the brass knocker several times. After a short delay the door was opened. A thin woman with grey hair and a sour expression on her lined and sallow face glared down at Emma.

'Yes, what do yer want?' she asked peremptorily.

'I would like to speak to Mrs Daniel, please?'

'That's me,' said the woman curtly.

The indomitable Emma was neither unnerved nor daunted by the woman's nasty tone and inhospitable manner. She had to get a room here at all costs. Today. She did not have time to roam Leeds looking any further. And so she smiled her most radiant smile and instinctively adopted a charming manner, one which she herself had not known she possessed until that very instant. 'I'm pleased to meet you, Mrs Daniel. My name is Emma Harte. Rosie from the Mucky Duck sent me to see you. She thought you would be willing to rent a room to me.'

'I only takes gentlemen boarders,' snapped Mrs Daniel, 'less trouble. Besides, I'm full.'

'Oh, dear me,' said Emma softly, riveting her enormous eyes on the woman. 'And Rosie was so sure you would have a room available. Even a small one would do.' Emma glanced up. 'It's quite a large house, isn't it?'

'Aye, it is, but me two best bedrooms are let. There's only the second attic and I never rents that.'

Emma's heart sank but the smile did not waver. 'Perhaps you might consider renting that other attic to me, Mrs Daniel. And I certainly wouldn't be any trouble. Rosie will give me a reference if –'

'It's not that,' the woman interrupted in a snappish tone. 'I'm full up, as I said.' She glared at Emma. 'I can only cope with two lodgers and I've got them already.' She made to close the door.

Emma smiled again, and winsomely. 'Please, Mrs Daniel, don't be hasty. It would be a great help to me if you would rent me the attic for a few weeks. Just as long as it is convenient for you. It would give me a chance to find somewhere else. Rosie was so sure you would be obliging. She spoke so well of you and recommended you highly. She told me you ran a clean and proper house, and that I would be safe here. Rosie said you were a good and honest woman.'

Mrs Daniel made no comment, but she was listening intently. 'You see, I'm not from Leeds,' Emma rushed on, determined to keep the woman engaged. She also wanted to convince her that she would be no trouble and dispel the apparent hostility the landlady had for women boarders. 'I was living near Ripon, with my husband's grandmother, and she died recently.' Emma noted the look of amazement on Mrs Daniel's face at the mention of a husband, but before she had a chance to say anything, Emma explained, 'My husband is in the Royal Navy. On the high seas for six months. I would be grateful if I could stay with you, for only a few weeks. It would give me time to find a place of our own, for when my dear husband comes back on leave.'

The woman was silent, obviously ruminating on Emma's story. Emma's mind raced. Persuasion, flattery, and charm were having no effect at all. Perhaps she should appeal to her greed. 'I can pay you a month in advance, Mrs Daniel. After all, a little extra money is always useful, isn't it? For that attic you never rent,' Emma said pointedly, and began to open her purse.

Gertrude Daniel, widow woman and childless, was not as surly as she appeared on the surface. In fact, her dour manner and grim face actually belied a rather kind heart and a pithy sense of humour. However, she had the strongest desire to close the door in the girl's face. She wasn't interested in the money. And she didn't like women boarders. Troublemakers, they were. Yet there was something about this particular girl that held her attention, and she *had* said she was married. Involuntarily, and to her enormous astonishment, she found herself saying, 'We'd best go inside. I don't want ter be discussing this on the front steps, with all the neighbours watching from behind their blinking curtains. Not that I can rent yer the attic, mind yer. But perhaps I can suggest another place yer can try.'

With this statement she opened the door wider and admitted Emma into the tiny hall and led the way to the front parlour. Gertrude Daniel was now considerably confused. She did not know for the life of her why she had let the girl into the house. Broken her own rule, she had. Her husband, Bert, had run off with their woman boarder years before. Still, Bert was kicking up daisies now. Nevertheless, she had never rented a room to a woman since then, and she had no intention of doing so now.

The front parlour was a shrine to Victorian bad taste. It was bursting with black horsehair sofas and chairs and mahogany whatnots. Purple chenille cloths covered a table, a piano, and a large stand. There were potted aspidistras on various other surfaces not crowded with bric-à-brac and the most revolting copies of famous oil paintings virtually jumped off the walls, which in turn were covered with bright red flocked-velvet wallpaper that stung the eyes.

'Sit down, then,' said Mrs Daniel, her voice still harsh.

Emma placed the suitcase on the violent red-and-purple Turkey carpet, and perched on the edge of a horsehair chair, clutching her bag. She was desperately trying to think of something infinitely more persuasive and ingratiating to say, when Mrs Daniel cut into her thoughts.

'This is the best parlour,' said the landlady, preening. 'Nice, isn't it?'

'Oh, yes, indeed. It's beautiful,' responded Emma swiftly, adopting her most sincere tone, whilst thinking how horrid it was.

'Do yer really like it?' asked Mrs Daniel, her voice suddenly an octave gentler.

'I do! *Very much.*' Emma glanced around. 'Why, it's one of the most elegant rooms I've ever seen. It's superb. You have excellent taste, Mrs Daniel,' gushed Emma, remembering words she had heard Olivia Wainright use so often in the past. She bestowed a glowing and admiring smile on Mrs Daniel.

'Well, fancy that. Thank yer very much.' Mrs Daniel was inordinately proud of her front parlour and for the first time her face softened.

Emma did not fail to notice this and grasped the opportunity. She opened her bag deliberately. 'Mrs Daniel, won't you rent me the attic, please? I said I would pay in advance. If you're worried about the money I –'

'No, that's not it,' interjected Mrs Daniel. 'If Rosie recommended yer, I knows yer all right for the brass –' Gertrude Daniel now hesitated, her eyes resting appraisingly on Emma. She had been scrutinizing her from the moment she had opened the door. Like Rosie earlier, she had noticed the girl's clothes at once. The frock was a bit dated, but good. She had also become increasingly aware of the girl's manners, her air of rectitude and refinement, her cultivated voice. This is Quality, she thought, and before she could stop herself, she said, 'Well, I don't know whether me second attic would be suitable for yer, seeing as how yer such a fine young lady. But, since yer've nowhere ter go at the minute, I'll show it ter yer. Mind yer, it can only be for a few weeks.'

Emma wanted to fling her arms around the woman's neck from sheer relief, but she kept herself perfectly still. 'That is very kind of you, Mrs Daniel. I do appreciate it,' she said in her most dignified voice, imitating Olivia Wainright yet again.

'Let's go up, then,' said the landlady, rising. She turned and threw Emma a quizzical look, eyebrows arched. 'And how come a fine young lady like thee knows Rosie at the Mucky Duck?' she asked, suddenly puzzled by the odd association.

Stick to the truth, such as it is, a small voice warned Emma. She said, without the slightest hesitation, 'A workman, who used to come to Grandmother's to do repairs to the house, knew she was not long for this world. I had explained to him I hoped to come to Leeds one day, to make a home for Winston, that's my dear husband, and myself, and perhaps find work in one of the shops. He was a friendly sort and he told me to visit Rosie when I did come to Leeds. He felt she would be helpful.'

Gertrude Daniel had listened attentively, assessing the girl's story. She spoke so sincerely and with such directness it was certainly a truthful statement. And it did make sense. She nodded, satisfied the girl was above board. 'Yes, I understand. And Rosie's a good lass. Help anybody, she would that. Providing they was worthy like.' She nodded again and motioned for Emma to follow her.

The attic was indeed small, but it was neatly furnished with a few simple pieces, including a single bed, a wardrobe, a washstand under the tiny window in the eaves, a chest, a chair, and a small table. It was also spotlessly clean. Emma could see that from the most cursory of glances. 'I'll take it,' she said.

'It's three shillings a week,' intoned Mrs Daniel defensively. 'It might seem a lot, but it's the fairest price I can give yer.'

'Yes, it *is* fair,' Emma agreed, and opened her reticule. She counted out a month's rent. She wanted to be certain she had a roof over her head until Blackie returned to Leeds.

Mrs Daniel looked at the money Emma had placed on the table. She saw immediately that the girl had paid a full month in advance. She was not sure she wanted her here in the house for that length of time. It was almost against her volition that she picked up the twelve shillings and pocketed them. 'Thank yer. I'll go and get yer case.'

'Oh, please, don't bother. I'll bring it up –' Emma began.

'No trouble,' said Mrs Daniel, already thumping down the stairs. She returned almost immediately with the suitcase and placed it inside the attic. She had recognized that it was made of real leather and, in fact, she had examined it carefully and another thought had struck her as she had climbed the stairs.

Now she fixed Emma with a fierce stare and said, 'There's one other thing I forgot ter tell yer. Since I can only manage ter take care of the two gentlemen's rooms, yer'll have ter make yer own bed and clean the attic.' Her eyes swept over Emma standing in front of her, so tall and beautiful and refined in appearance. Her eyes narrowed. 'Yer looks ter me like yer've led a lady's life, an easy life, since the day yer was born, if yer don't mind me saying so. Do yer knows how ter do housework?'

Emma kept her face straight. 'I can easily learn,' she remarked, not trusting herself to say another word for fear of laughter breaking loose.

'I'm glad ter hear that,' said the landlady bluntly. 'And by the by, I don't provide grub, yer knows. Not for only three shillings a week, prices being what they are these days.' Mrs Daniel continued to study the silent girl who was surrounded by an aura of calm and dignity and, for some reason she could not fathom, she added, 'But yer can use me kitchen if yer wants, as long as yer clean up after yerself. And I'll find a spot in one of me cupboards, so yer can store yer groceries if yer wants.'

'Thank you,' said Emma, almost choking with the suppressed laughter.

'Well then, I'll leave yer be, Mrs Harte, so yer can unpack.' Mrs Daniel nodded more cordially and closed the door behind her.

Emma pressed her hand to her mouth, listening to Mrs Daniel's thudding footsteps retreating until they finally ceased. She flew across the attic to the bed and pushed her face into the pillow, now permitting herself to laugh unchecked, until the tears rolled down her cheeks. *Do I know how to do housework!* she kept thinking, and the peals of laughter would start all over again. But eventually her merriment subsided and she sat up, wiping her eyes. She pulled off her crocheted gloves. She looked down at her hands and grinned with amusement. They might not be as work-roughened red as they used to be, but they were hardly the hands of a lady. Not yet. It's a good thing I kept my gloves on all day, she thought, or my hands would have probably given me away.

Now Emma stood up and walked over to the washstand. She stared at her reflection in the swingback mirror. The black dress and the cream bonnet were discards from Olivia Wainright's wardrobe and their quality was unmistakable. Her punctilious mimicry of Olivia's voice had not been difficult to accomplish, once she had commenced. In point of fact, speaking in a genteel fashion had come quite naturally to her, for she had a good ear and had practised with Edwin. The tinker and his gypsy wife, Rosie, and Mrs Daniel all believed her to be a fine young lady of Quality, albeit a trifle impoverished. And it was no accident. This was the precise impression she had strived to create, had hoped to establish immediately.

Before leaving Fairley, Emma had determined to start out in Leeds as she intended to continue – as a young lady who would become a grand lady. And a rich one. She smiled again, but now the smile was cynical and her eyes, turning dark with calculation, seemed, for a moment, as hard as the emeralds they so strikingly resembled. She would *show* the Fairleys but she could not dwell on that now. Her time was precious and must be planned with exactitude and used to the fullest. Every minute must be made to count. She would work eighteen hours a day, seven days a week, if necessary, to achieve her goal – to become somebody. To become a woman of substance.

Abruptly she turned away from the mirror, untied her bonnet, placed it on the chest, and hurried to the bed. Emma had such an abhorrence of dirt it was almost an obsession, and whilst the room itself appeared to be meticulously clean, she was impelled to examine the bed linen. The quilt was old but not badly worn. She pulled it off and looked at the sheets with her keen eyes. They were not new; in fact, they were neatly darned in places, but they were spotless and freshly laundered. To pacify herself completely, she stripped the bed down to the mattress, scrutinized it closely, turned it over, and with sigh of satisfaction she remade the bed swiftly and with her usual expertise.

As tired as she was, she unpacked her suitcase and put her clothes neatly away in the wardrobe and the chest. In the bottom drawer of the chest she found two clean face towels. As she took them out her eyes lighted on several books lying in the drawer. Her curiosity aroused, she picked one up. It was a volume of poems by William Blake, bound in dark red leather and beautifully illustrated with engravings. She opened it and looked at the flyleaf. Slowly she read out loud, 'Albert H. Daniel. His book.' She put it back and regarded the other volumes, also expensively bound. Her mouth formed the unfamiliar names: 'Spinoza. Plato. Aristotle.' She returned them carefully to the drawer, wondering who Albert H. Daniel was, and thinking how much Frank would love to get his hands on books like these.

Frank. Little Frankie. She caught her breath and sat down heavily on the chair, her heart beating rapidly. She thought of her father and she was filled with sorrow tinged with a deep yearning, and then a feeling of guilt flooded through her, leaving her weak and vitiated. She sagged against the back of the chair. That morning she had left him a note, telling him she had gone to Bradford to look for a better position in one of the big mansions. She had explained she had a few savings to keep herself for several weeks. She had urged him not to worry and had promised to return quickly, if she did not find a suitable post, adding that should she be fortunate enough to secure a good place she would write to him with her address.

And what will I write? she asked herself worriedly. She did not know. And she had more important things to think about for the next few days. Survival. That above all else.

TWENTY-EIGHT

Emma had been in Leeds for almost a week and so far had been unable to find work. For the past four days she had diligently visited every shop in Briggate and the adjoining streets, seeking any kind of position, prepared to take even the most menial. But to her growing dismay and alarm there were no openings at all. Doggedly, from early morning until dusk, she tramped the pavements, those pavements Blackie had said were paved with gold, but which seemed to her to get harder and dustier by the minute.

In these four days Emma had come to know the central areas of the city well, for she had a remarkable memory and a good sense of direction. In spite of an occasional attack of severe anxiety that would momentarily hold her in its grip, she found Leeds exciting, thrilling, in fact. She had also discovered, much to her own astonishment, that she had no fear of this enormous metropolis, so accurately described to her by Blackie well over a year ago. The great buildings, awesome in their incredible proportions, had seemed slightly overpowering on Monday morning when she had valiantly set out from Mrs Daniel's boarding-house, intent and relentless in her determination to secure a job. But she had quickly adjusted to the surroundings, which might easily have struck terror in one of weaker character, for Emma saw those immense structures for what they truly were: institutions of industry and progress, symbols of money and, inevitably, of power. And her staunch heart invariably quickened at the opportunities they offered, and her burning ambition was reinforced in her imaginative and optimistic mind, for Emma truly believed anything was possible.

The stores and factories, warehouses and iron foundries, printing works and office buildings towering above her, grim of architecture and pitted and blackened by the city's dirt, reminded her, in a curious way, of the moors, for these monoliths to commerce were just as implacable and indomitable and everlasting. As she had drawn an inexplicable and uncommon strength from those wild hills, so now she drew encouragement and hope from the soaring edifices starkly outlined against the skyline of Leeds, which was the fifth-largest city in England. Instinctively she recognized that here her future lay. In her youthfulness, she was determined it would be one of untold wealth, plus that irresistible power she longed so desperately to seize and hold for ever in her own small but tenacious hands.

This morning as she trudged along, Emma unexpectedly found herself in front of Leeds Town Hall and stopped to stare at it, gasping at its austere grandeur. Many wide steps led up to the imposing south façade, where four giant-sized white stone lions guarded its portals in front of Corinthian columns that floated up to dizzying heights. It was a square building, surmounted by a most amazing tower supported by additional columns echoing those on the south façade. There were clocks on four sides and the tower itself was topped by a strange bold cupola. It was a massive building of great weightiness, black and Victorian, and Gothic in its inspiration, yet it was not ugly. Emma decided it had a handsome and even graceful exterior and it was undoubtedly the most astounding landmark she had seen in Leeds so far. As she gaped at it, her eyes flaring open with wonder, it was not possible for Emma to know that its architect, Cuthbert Broderick, had also been in love with money and power, and his Town Hall, opened by Queen Victoria in 1858, had been the ultimate expression of that love. However, with her rare perception, Emma intuitively understood it was a personification of all the city stood for. As she continued to regard the Town Hall a most vivid and compelling thought flitted into her mind: *This city can either conquer you, or you can conquer it.* With her usual self-confidence she decided at once, and with no hesitation whatsoever. that it would be the latter.

Emma walked away from the Town Hall, glancing up at other structures and thinking: They are only buildings after all, filled with people just like you. She immediately corrected herself. No, not like you, Emma Harte. *You* are different. And *you* will be *very* different. *You* will be somebody of importance one day, and so fervently did she believe this it sustained her, fortified her courage, and spurred her on.

She ventured into a few more stores, only to be told the same thing time and again – no vacancies. Sighing to herself, she walked along Boar Lane, occasionally pausing to gaze into some of the windows, continually fascinated by the array of finery on display: dresses and bonnets, shoes, reticules and jewellery, furniture and ornaments, and so many other necessities as well as luxuries. And as she viewed these elegant establishments, her Plan with a capital *P* to make her fortune began to evolve. Always a potent idea, it had hitherto been vague, nebulous, undefined. Now suddenly she knew with great certainty what she would eventually do – what the Plan with a capital *P* would be. *She would have a shop.* Her own shop. A shop selling those essentials which people needed in their daily lives. That was it. Trade! She would go into trade. Obviously it would have to be a small shop at first. But it would grow. She would ensure that. She became excited. She would have more than one shop, two, maybe three, and she would be rich. Buoyed up by this idea, she increased her pace, propelled by her decision. Her perspicacious, inventive, and fertile brain raced, planning and scheming for the future tirelessly, as it always would.

Leeds was then, and still is, a lusty and vital city, and the streets on this busy Friday were, as usual, crowded with people rushing about their business. Tram-cars rumbled out from the Corn Exchange to all parts of the town and outlying districts. Fine carriages with prancing horses carried elegant ladies and gentlemen of distinction to their destinations. Prosperity, that sense of self-help and independence, nonconformity, hardheaded Yorkshire shrewdness and industriousness, were endemic, were communicated most vibrantly to Emma, so that she was instantly infected. And the rhythm and power of the city only served to consolidate and buttress these very same characteristics so intrinsic in her, for with her energy, tenacity, and zest, her obstinate will and driving ambition, she was, without knowing it, the very embodiment of Leeds. This was undoubtedly the place for her. She had always felt that to be true and now she was absolutely convinced.

She made her way decisively to Leeds Market in Kirkgate, an enormous, sprawling covered hall composed of an incredible conglomeration of stalls selling all manner of merchandise imaginable – pots and pans, kitchen utensils, china, fabrics, clothes, foodstuffs to be bought and taken home or eaten there, including jellied eels, meat pies, mussels, cockles, cartloads of fruit, fancy cakes, and toffee apples. She stopped at the Marks and Spencer Penny Bazaar, her attention riveted on the sign: *Don't ask the price, it's a penny!* Her eyes roved over the goods on display, so easy to view, open to inspection, so well organized in categories and so cheaply priced. She tucked the information at the back of her mind, her eyes keenly thoughtful. The idea of this Penny Bazaar is simple, yet it is exceedingly clever, she said to herself. Emma lingered for a moment longer, inspecting the goods, which included almost everything from wax candles and cleaning products to toys, stationery, and haberdashery, and then, still reflecting about the bazaar, she moved on. It was well turned two o'clock and she was conscious of a growing hunger gnawing at her. She bought a plate of winkles and mussels from the fishman's stall, lavished them with vinegar and pepper, ate them with her fingers, dried her hands on her handkerchief, and set out for North Street, where the tailoring shops were located. That morning one of the salesgirls in a dress shop in Thornton's Arcade had suggested she try her luck there. 'But go when it's daylight. It's a bit of a tough neighbourhood,' the girl had cautioned.

It was a boiling hot day. The sky was sullen and there seemed to be no air in the muggy, crowded streets. Emma fanned her face and opened the collar of her green cotton dress, feeling hot and overcome by the intense heat bouncing up in waves from the pavement. She leaned against a building in the shade, and when she was a little cooler she set out again. She had to find a job to support herself until the baby was born. After that she would work night and day if necessary, to get the money for the first shop. She smiled and with a degree of unfamiliar exultation. Her tired feet were forgotten, the exhaustion dissipated, and she stepped out surely and with confidence, secure in the knowledge that she would succeed. She had no alternative. She could not afford to fail.

Before long, following the salesgirl's instructions, she was entering North Street. The tailoring shops, in reality small factories, were not too difficult to find, their names being clearly indicated on the outside. Three sorties into three shops and three turndowns. 'Try Cohen's,' one of the men in the last workshop called after

274

her. 'It's in a side alley, off the top of North Street.' Emma thanked him and left. She found Cohen's within minutes, but again was told, 'Sorry, luv, no openings.' She paused at the end of this alley and looked back down North Street. She decided to keep walking straight ahead until she came to York Road. It was now getting late and she felt it would be wiser to return to Mrs Daniel's house as quickly as possible. She would rest tonight and start all over again tomorrow, looking for that job which was so crucial.

Panting, Emma continued up the street, which was rather steeply built. She was almost at the top when she felt something sharp strike her shoulder blade and a stone dropped at her feet. She turned swiftly, startled. Further down the street two scruffy-looking youths were grinning at her inanely. She shook her fist at them. 'Wicked boys!' she shouted. They laughed derisively and picked up handfuls of stones. Stiffening, Emma was poised to flee, but she instantly realized that the stones were not intended for her, were not being aimed in her direction. To Emma's immense horror she saw the boys bombarding a middle-aged man who had slipped and fallen. He attempted to rise, but stumbled, and then under the onslaught he huddled against the wall of a building, making a vain effort to shield his face. The louts were whooping and yelling and pitching stones furiously and in an unending stream. The man's parcel had rolled away, his spectacles were on the ground, and Emma could see that his cheek was bloodied where it had been struck by one of the stones.

Emma was outraged and revolted by this despicable display of needless cruelty and she leapt forward and ran down the street, her anger a raging force within her, and her face was grim and unremitting.

'Get going or I'll fetch a bobby!' she yelled, shaking her fist again. She was totally without fear in her fury. 'Little hooligans!' she continued, her voice rising sharply. 'Go on, get off with you, or I *will* fetch a policeman! The law will know how to deal with the likes of you, and it won't be very kindly.'

The two boys laughed at her insolently and stuck out their tongues, making ugly grimaces and shouting foul words, but at least their attention was diverted from the man. Emma, who was dauntless at all times was now so completely enraged she was invincible. She picked up a rock and said threateningly, 'How about a bit of your own medicine?' She raised her arm and was about to hurl the rock when to her surprise, and considerable relief, the boys backed off, thumbing their noses at her as they slunk away, their vile curses echoing in the air. Emma ran across to the man, who was struggling to his knees. She took hold of his arm reassuringly and helped him up. He was a small, spry man, sturdily built and wiry. He had wavy black hair greying at the temples and receding on top, sharply defined features, and bright black eyes.

Compassion had eradicated her grim expression and Emma said with concern, 'Are you hurt, sir?'

He shook his head, pulled a handkerchief from his pocket, and wiped the blood from his grazed cheek. 'No, I am not hurt,' he answered, blinking. 'Thank you, young lady. You have been very kind.' He blinked again and peered hard at the ground. 'Do you see my spectacles? They fell off in this unfortunate little skirmish.'

Emma found his glasses, examined them carefully, and handed them to him. 'Well, at least they're not broken,' she informed him with an encouraging smile.

The man thanked her and put on his spectacles. 'There, that is much better. Now I can see,' he said.

Emma bent down and picked up his parcel, actually a large paper bag. A loaf of bread had fallen out of it and rolled in the dirt. Emma held it away from her and blew on it, and tried to clean it with her hands, dusting off the dirt. 'It's not too grimy,' she explained, putting the loaf into the paper bag, which contained a number of other items, and giving it to him.

The man had retrieved a small black skullcap which he placed on his head and now he regarded Emma thoughtfully and with increasing interest. His voice was full of gratitude as he said, 'Thank you once again, young lady. It was brave of you to come to my defence. To my rescue.' He smiled and his eyes shone with appreciation. 'Not many men would intervene in these parts, let alone a young lady like you. Yes, indeed, you are of the good heart and the great courage. Quite a remarkable feat you performed. Very commendable!' He gazed at her with undisguised admiration, not a little impressed.

Even though the man spoke the most precise English and enunciated his words clearly, Emma detected a slight accent she could not place. He must certainly be from foreign parts, she decided, and then said, with a frown, 'Why were those horrid boys throwing stones at you?'

'Because I am a Jew.'

Emma was not actually sure what a Jew was but, always reluctant to display her ignorance on any matter, she chose to disregard his explanation, repeating again, 'But why would that make them want to throw stones at you?'

The man returned her questioning look steadily. 'Because people are always afraid of what they do not know, what they do not understand, the unfamiliar or the different, and that fear invariably turns to hate. Unreasoned hatred that makes no sense. In these parts the Jews are hated and defiled.' He shook his head. 'Ah, the human condition is strange, is it not? There are some people who hate for no reason at all. They just simply hate. They do not realize that their unjustified hatred inevitably turns inward to destroy them. Yes, it is self-destructive in the long run.'

His words, spoken so sadly and without rancour, pierced Emma's brain and touched her so profoundly she felt a sharp stab of pain near her heart. Was her hatred for Edwin wrong? No, a small voice insisted. It is not unreasoned hatred, the kind this man speaks about. You have every reason to feel the way you do. Edwin Fairley was treacherous and he betrayed you. She cleared her throat and touched the man's arm lightly. 'I am sorry people hate you and try to hurt you. How terrible for you to have to live with such – such –' She stopped, searching for the right word.

'Persecution,' the man volunteered. His dark eyes were clouded briefly by a haunting sorrow that was ancient, and then a faint and rueful smile touched his generous mouth. 'Ah, but then this little flurry was nothing in comparison to some of the debacles that occur. When the roughs and toughs really run amok they become excessively violent. Unmerciful. Attacking us and our homes. We suffer not only sneers, but blows and broken windows and many cruelties.' He shook his head wearily and then his face brightened. 'But then, these are not your problems, young lady. I must not burden you with them.'

Emma was aghast and perturbed by the things he had said and she was also baffled by his oddly calm acceptance of such a terrible situation. 'But can't the bobbies – the police – do anything to stop it?' she cried, her voice unaccustomedly harsh with anger.

The man smiled wryly. 'Not really. Occasionally they try to stop it, but mostly they turn a blind eye. Leeds is not such a law-abiding city in this day and age. We fend for ourselves, as best we can. Keep to ourselves. Go about our business quietly. Avoid confrontations that could easily provoke dangerous incidents.' He was becoming patently aware of the growing expression of horror in the girl's eyes and also of the bewilderment etched on her face, and with sudden insight he said, 'You do not know what a Jew is, young lady, do you?'

'Not exactly,' Emma began, and hesitated self-consciously, acutely ashamed of seeming so uninformed.

Observing her embarrassment, the man said softly, 'Would you like to know?'

'Yes, please. I like to know of many things.'

'Then I shall tell you,' he announced with a gentle smile. 'The Jews are a people descended from the Hebrews and the Israelites, from the tribes of Israel. Our religion is called Judaism. It is founded on the Old Testament and the Torah both.' Emma was listening intently and the man beheld the quickening interest on her face, the intelligence in her fine eyes. He was also fully conscious of her sympathetic attitude and so he continued patiently, 'Do you know your Bible, young lady?'

'Some of it,' said Emma.

'Then you have perhaps read the Book of Exodus. You certainly must know the Ten Commandments?' She nodded affirmatively, and he expounded further: 'The Ten Commandments were given to our people by Moses, when he led us out of Egypt and created the Jewish nation. Christianity itself is based on Judaism. Did you not know that?'

Although she loathed to appear illiterate, Emma had to say in all truthfulness, 'No, I didn't.'

The man's bright black eyes searched hers thoughtfully. 'Jesus Christ was a Jew and Jesus, too, was persecuted.' He sighed and it was a long, wearisome sigh. 'I suppose we Jews seem strange to some people, because our customs and dietary laws and form of worship are not the same as the Gentile ways.' He smiled to himself and remarked so softly it was practically a whisper, 'But perhaps we are not so different after all, when you stop to think.'

'Of course you are not! But people can be stupid and ignorant,' Emma exclaimed with some vehemence, recognizing the sense of what he said, and instantly comparing the rabid class differences in England that also bred cruelty and terrible inequities. She gave him a swift look. 'So you come from the land of the Jews, do you sir?' she asked, thinking of the accent that tinged his speech.

'No, I do not. You see, the Jews scattered throughout the world over the centuries. To Spain, Germany, Russia, Poland, and many other countries. I myself come from Kiev, in Russia. Most of the Jews in Leeds also come from Russia, or from Poland. We came here to escape the terror and harassment of the pogroms directed against us. I had my baptism of fire in my own country and so, as difficult as things here can be sometimes, they are not as terrible as they were in Russia. It is good to be in England. We have freedom here, thank God.'

The man was mindful of her listening to his recital so seriously and with infinite patience and another thought struck him. 'You cannot be from Leeds, or you would

277

know that there are many Jewish immigrants such as myself living here, and that we are despised by most.'

'I didn't know,' said Emma, adding, 'I come from Ripon.'

'Ah, from the rural area. That explains it!' He chuckled and his sad eyes unexpectedly twinkled. 'Well, young lady, I will not detain you any longer with my discourse on the Jews. My most grateful thanks again to you. And may the good Lord bless and protect you all of the days of your life.'

Emma flinched inside at this reference to the God she no longer acknowledged or believed in but, knowing the man meant well, she returned his friendly smile. 'It was nothing. Really it wasn't. I was glad to help you, sir.'

The man inclined his head courteously and started to walk away. However, after only a few steps he faltered and staggered against the wall, clutching his chest. Emma ran to him immediately. 'Are you all right?' She noticed his face was now as white as cotton, and drawn, and his lips were faintly blue and perspiration had broken out on his forehead.

'Yes, I am perfectly well,' he answered in a strangled voice, struggling for breath. After a moment he whispered, 'It was only a twinge. The indigestion maybe.'

Emma did not like the look of him. He appeared to be quite ill and in considerable discomfort. 'Do you live far away from here?' she asked urgently. 'I will take you to your home.'

'No! No! You have already done enough for me. Please. Please. I am all right. Do not worry yourself.'

'Where do you live?' Emma insisted firmly.

'In Imperial Street.' He could not resist smiling through his pain. 'A most unfortunate name for that poor little street, considering it is hardly royal in any sense of that word It's located in the Leylands, about ten minutes away from here.'

Emma's heart dropped at the mention of this area, since she had heard it was dangerous, the ghetto, but nevertheless, she kept her face calm and endeavoured to appear untroubled. 'Come along! I shall take you home. I don't think you are well at all, and besides, you might need me to protect you against another assault,' she pointed out. The man was utterly amazed at her consideration and her willingness to assist him yet again, and not wanting to be a nuisance, he tried hard to dissuade her, but in spite of his protestations Emma took command purposefully. Clutching her reticule tightly, she relieved him of his parcel, gripped his arm, and together they walked slowly up the street.

The man's acute chest pains were diminishing and as his breathing improved he began to feel better. He scrutinized the girl who was being so solicitous of him, helping him along so generously. Such kindness from a stranger he had never received. He coughed, pushing down the rush of emotion, saying quietly, 'You are being most thoughtful and kind. I do appreciate it.' He stopped, turned to her, and thrust out his hand. 'My name is Abraham Kallinski. May I have the honour of knowing yours?'

Emma tucked the parcel under her arm and took his hand. His grip was firm. 'It's Emma Harte.' He noticed the silver ring on her left hand. 'Mrs Harte, I assume?' Emma nodded, but did not elucidate. Being a courteous and civilized man, Abraham Kallinski respected the privacy of others and he therefore refrained from asking any more questions.

They walked at a steady, even pace, Emma supporting Abraham Kallinski under his elbow, and as they walked he told her more about himself, for he was gregarious, an outgoing and articulate individual. Emma, with her inquiring mind and fierce desire to learn, listened alertly, giving him her full attention. She soon discovered he had left Kiev in 1880, making his way to Rotterdam and thence to Hull, Yorkshire's greatest seaport. 'Like many of the other Jews from Russia and Poland, I came to Leeds intending to go to Liverpool and from there across to America,' he explained. 'However, I had to stay in Leeds for a period, to make the money for my ticket to America. Where Jews are, other Jews must go, and when I arrived I came immediately to the Leylands, where most of the Jewish immigrants live, seeking a *Landsmann*, that is, a man from my own country who spoke my language. I found work easily, for there is kinship and charity amongst Jews. We try to help each other.' He laughed as he reminisced. 'Ach, but I was young then. Twenty years old. When I was twenty-one I had the good fortune to meet the young lady who was to become my wife. She was born in Leeds. Her parents had fled Russia years before. And so, Mrs Harte, I stayed in Leeds. I never did go to America in the end. Well, here we are!' he gestured to the surroundings. 'This is where I have lived for the past twenty-five years, although not always in the same house.'

Emma looked about, her eyes darting from side to side with unconcealed curiosity as they entered the Leylands. It was a huddle of mean streets, dark courtyards, and sly alleys, the houses clustered together as if seeking protection from each other. Emma shuddered inside at the obvious signs of wretchedness and poverty as they wended their way through Byron Street and into the heart of the ghetto. A group of barefooted children in patched clothing were playing in the middle of Imperial Street and several men were hurrying home, their steps purposeful, their heads bent, eyes furtive. They are strange-looking men, Emma thought, with their beards and large round hats and long coats. They are quite different in appearance from Mr Kallinski, who seems so English. Emma smiled at this thought, having just been told he was Russian-born.

Abraham Kallinski stopped in front of a house at the far end of Imperial Street. To Emma's surprise it was larger and a bit grander than the others and was extremely well kept, with starched white curtains at the windows which were flanked by wooden shutters. 'This is my home,' he said, his face suddenly illuminated with such an expression of joy Emma was touched. His shoulders went back and there was pride in his voice.

'Then you will be all right now,' said Emma. 'I enjoyed listening to you, Mr Kallinski. It was very interesting. I do hope you feel better. Goodbye, Mr Kallinski.' She handed him his parcel, the smile still lingering on her face.

Abraham Kallinski stared at this lovely girl, this Gentile girl, who had been so helpful and who had devoted so much of her time to him and with a compassion that was rare, and he put out his hand and clutched her arm, detaining her. 'Please, please, come in for a moment. I wish my wife to meet you, Mrs Harte. She will want to thank you. She will be most grateful for the aid you have given me today and so selflessly. Please!'

'Oh, really Mr Kallinski, that's not necessary. And I should be getting along.'

'Please, just for a moment,' he begged, his eyes soft and imploring. 'It is hot. You are tired. Let us offer you a little hospitality. A glass of tea perhaps. A short rest.'

Emma did feel tired and thirsty, but she did not wish to intrude. Furthermore, she did not relish the idea of being stranded in the Leylands alone, especially in the late afternoon. 'Well, I really shouldn't,' Emma began, wavering. She was longing for a glass of water.

Aware of her hesitation, Abraham Kallinski was the one who now took charge. He manoeuvred Emma towards the door and opened it. 'Come. We will go inside,' he persisted, 'a little refreshment will indeed fortify you.'

Abraham Kallinski led her inside the house, which opened directly into a large kitchen that also seemed to Emma to be an all-purpose room. The woman standing at the stove turned as the door opened. Her eyes widened. 'Abraham! Abraham! Whatever has happened to you?' she cried, rushing across the floor, the spoon she had been using still clutched in her hand. 'Your clothes are all dirty, and look at your face! Oh, Abraham, you have been hurt!' She took his arm, her face a picture of distress mingled with fear.

'Now, Janessa, don't get excited,' he said in his most gentle voice and with a tender look, for Abraham adored his wife. 'I am not hurt. Just a little dishevelled. A small incident, that is all. I stumbled and fell in North Street and two young hooligans threw stones at me. You know how they are.' He brought Emma forward, his arm under her elbow. 'This is Mrs Harte, Janessa. Emma Harte. She came to my rescue. Sent the boys scurrying off with their tails between their legs and then she kindly brought me home. She insisted, in fact.'

Janessa Kallinski put down the spoon and grasped both of Emma's hands in her own, squeezing them tightly. 'I am delighted to meet you, Mrs Harte. Thank you! Thank you for helping my husband! That was most charitable of you and courageous. You could easily have been hurt yourself'She smiled at Emma with genuine gratefulness and went on in a warm tone, 'Please, come! Sit down. Let me offer you some refreshment. You look tired and hot.'

'I am happy to meet you, too,' Emma said politely. 'And thank you, Mrs Kallinski, I would appreciate a glass of water, please.' Janessa led Emma to a chair and pressed her into it 'The water you can have with pleasure. But also you must take a glass of lemon tea with us. Now, please, rest yourself.'

Mrs Kallinski was back in a second with the water, which Emma accepted eagerly, and she was suddenly quite relieved to be seated after her long day tramping the streets. She had not fully realized just how tired and depleted she was beginning to feel.

Abraham followed his wife to the other side of the kitchen, where she had been preparing the evening meal. He gave her the parcel. 'Here is the challah, Janessa. I am afraid it fell in the street, when I fell, but I do not think it is damaged.' His eyes twinkled. 'Not even bruised.' He looked at Emma. 'Please, excuse me for a moment.' He inclined his head with that grave courtesy of his and went upstairs.

Emma's eyes scanned the kitchen. It was large and pleasant and more than adequately furnished with a sofa and several comfortable chairs, a sideboard, and a large table surrounded by six chairs. The table was covered with a fresh white cloth that gleamed brightly in the fading afternoon light and was set for four people. The wallpaper was attractive and conservative and the rug on the floor was of good quality, as were the other appointments. Emma now observed Janessa as she made the tea and filled the glasses. She was taller than her husband and slender, with an attractive figure. Her fresh-complexioned face was handsome rather than pretty, wide and Slavic in its features, and her mouth was full and soft. Her glossy straight black hair was pulled back and coiled on her neck and she had large pale blue eyes under well-defined black brows. She wore a black cotton dress and a crisp white apron that added to the rather stately and even regal impression she gave. Emma guessed she must be in her late thirties.

Within minutes Mr Kallinski returned. He had removed the dust from his trousers, changed his jacket, brushed his hair, and attended to his bruised cheek. He washed his hands at the sink and then he spoke to his wife quietly before joining Emma. Janessa followed with the tea on a small tray. She handed a glass to Emma. 'I know this will revive you more than the water did, Mrs Harte,' she murmured and sat down opposite Emma.

Emma thanked her and sipped the tea. It was delicious. Lemon-flavoured with a piece of lemon floating in it, and it was sweet and hot. Emma had never had lemon tea before, but she refrained from mentioning this, as always wanting to appear both experienced and a young lady of Quality.

Mrs Kallinski gave her undivided attention to her husband. 'Are you sure you feel all right, Abraham? No twinges? No pains in your chest again?' She was unable to conceal her worry.

Mr Kallinski threw Emma a warning glance and said quickly, 'No! No! Nothing like that, Janessa. Please do not worry. I am completely recovered from the fall.'

Janessa looked doubtful, a frown scoring her brow, but she appeared to accept his statement in good faith. Abraham took a sip of tea and then regarded Emma. 'Do you live far from the Leylands, Mrs Harte?'

'Quite a little way. Do you know where the Mucky Duck is in York Road?' asked Emma. Mr Kallinski nodded. 'Well, I live about half an hour's walk from there, at the other end of York Road, in the opposite direction from the Leylands.'

'Ah, I see,' responded Mr Kallinski. He peered at the clock. 'It is getting later than I realized. When my sons return, which should be very soon, I will have them escort you home. It is not safe, this area, for a young lady alone.'

Emma was about to decline this offer, but immediately saw the common sense of it. She did not want to be exposed to danger in the ghetto and the adjoining districts, and so she said, 'Thank you. I think that *would* be a good idea.'

'It is the least we can do,' interjected Mrs Kallinski. 'We don't want your husband worrying about you, now do we?' Then she continued in her good-hearted way, 'And no doubt you are anxious to be getting home, to prepare your evening meal.'

Emma cleared her throat, not responding, forever cautious about confiding in strangers, but under Mrs Kallinski's affable gaze, she found herself saying, 'No, I don't have to prepare supper for my husband. He is in the Royal Navy. When he is at sea, as he is at present, I live alone.'

'Alone!' cried Mrs Kallinski, her dismay dousing the lambent light in her eyes. 'Do you not have any family?' The thought of this young girl being on her own in Leeds appalled Janessa, who came from a large, close-knit, and loving clan who were always there to protect and help each other.

Emma shook her head. 'No, my husband's grandmother died recently. We have no one else between us.' She saw the grieved expression on Mrs Kallinski's face and remarked hurriedly, 'Except each other, of course. But I am all right. Really. I live in a nice boarding-house in a decent area, with a good woman, who rents me a room.'

The Kallinskis exchanged swift and percipient glances. Abraham nodded his head in answer to his wife's unspoken question, which in her usual way she had communicated to him with her expressive eyes. Mrs Kallinski now leaned forward, clasping her hands together, her wide face shining with benevolence. 'If you do not have to go home immediately, if you have no other pressing reason to leave, will you not stay and partake of our Sabbath dinner with us? It would be our very great pleasure to welcome you.'

'Oh, no, I couldn't. Really, I couldn't,' Emma protested. 'It's very kind of you. But I just couldn't.' She flushed, wondering if the Kallinskis thought she had been trying to wangle an invitation to stay. 'Thank you. It's very kind of you. But I couldn't intrude.'

'Nonsense!' exclaimed Abraham. 'You would not be intruding. Good gracious, after what you did for me today!' He lifted his hands in the air, palms outward, and made several small upward gestures and went on, 'How can we ever thank you enough? Now, please, stay for the Sabbath dinner. It will be an honour to have you.' Seeing the baffled look on Emma's face, he explained, '*Our* Sabbath day is on Saturday. It commences at sundown on Friday, when we always celebrate the beginning of the holy day with the Friday dinner.'

'I see,' Emma said. A worried glint crept into her eyes and they wandered to the clock on the mantelpiece. Abraham followed her glance and nodded, understanding at once what was in her mind. 'Don't worry! Don't worry! Our sons will escort you home after supper.' His voice was reassuring. 'You will be safe with them, even if it is dark.'

'But I –' Emma began.

'It is settled, Mrs Harte,' Janessa interrupted graciously yet with an air of decision. 'You look tired, undoubtedly because of the trouble with those hooligans. The food will nourish you. Give you strength. You will enjoy it.' She reached over and patted Emma's arm. 'We have plenty. More than enough for an extra person, an honoured guest. Please, relax, and when David and Victor arrive they, too, will welcome you. And thank you for assisting their father today. Yes, they will be delighted to have you share our Sabbath dinner.'

Emma gave in under Mrs Kallinski's persuasive and good-natured pressure. Also, she was feeling hungry again and she had nothing very appetizing to eat at Mrs Daniel's, and the pots bubbling on the stove were emitting deliciously tempting odours. 'Thank you. I will be happy to join you, as long as it is no trouble.'

The Kallinskis beamed and Janessa leapt up, gliding to the stove to attend to the boiling pans. She spoke to Emma as she peeped at their contents. 'You have not eaten Jewish food before, I think, but you will like it.' She turned, the pan lid in her hand, and nodded positively. 'Yes, I know you will enjoy it. First we will have the chicken soup with matzo balls – those are similar to Yorkshire dumplings but smaller – and then a crisply roasted chicken all golden brown and moist, with carrots and other vegetables from the soup. We will finish with honey cakes and lemon tea. Yes, it is good, you will see –' Janessa stopped midsentence and swung around. The door had opened, and her face lit up with pleasure and pride as her two sons entered the house. Seeing Emma seated near the fireplace, they both paused and looked at her with interest and considerable surprise.

'David! Victor! Come, meet our guest. An honoured guest, for she helped your father out of trouble in the most admirable way today. A fine girl,' said Janessa, plopping the lid back on to the pan. She wiped her hands on a tea towel and hurried over to her two sons, drawing them into the room. 'Come along, boys, this is Emma Harte. Mrs Harte.' She led them to Emma, her face radiant. 'This is David,' she said, introducing the taller boy, 'and this is Victor.' The Kallinski boys shook hands with Emma, extended their greetings, and thanked her for coming to their father's aid. They crossed the room to the sofa and sat down together.

It was David who addressed Abraham, his eyes narrowing as he noticed the ugly black-and-blue bruise now most obvious on his father's cheek, which was puffy and swollen. 'What happened, Father?' he asked quietly and with deference, but there was a fierce glint in his eyes and he was striving to control his flaring anger. He knew it was the work of the Jew-baiters again.

Slowly Abraham explained about the incident, not leaving out the minutest detail and extolling Emma's brave participation in the matter in the most glowing terms. As he spoke, Emma looked at the boys with growing interest, endeavouring to evaluate them.

David and Victor Kallinski were as different in every way as two brothers could be. David, who was the elder at nineteen, was tall like his mother and well built. He had been blessed with her lovely blue eyes, although his were much deeper in tone and his face, handsome and open, had a suggestion of her Slavic bone structure in its width and overall shape. He had the same head of black wavy hair his father's had once been and he had also inherited the older man's outward-going manner, yet essentially David Kallinski was even more gregarious, vital, and energetic than Abraham. David was a mover, a doer, ambitious, clever and driven. If there was a faint hint of cynicism in his alert blue eyes it was somewhat counteracted by the generosity of his wide mouth and his friendly demeanour. David was intelligent, intuitive, and excessively motivated towards one goal: success. And, as he knew only too well the true nature of man, he therefore lived by one rule and one rule alone – the survival of the fittest. He not only intended to survive, but to survive in style and with wealth.

Victor, who was sixteen, was small, almost birdlike, and in this he resembled his father to some extent. He had his mother's straight shiny black hair, but otherwise he did not appear to physically favour either of them. His large eyes were soft and hazel in colour and his face was smooth and bland without any emphatic features, but he was pleasant-looking. His sober face mirrored his character, for Victor Kallinski was a gentle and reflective boy; and in one way his temperament was similar to his father's, in that Victor had, as did Abraham, a great forbearance and a deep understanding of human frailties, an understanding that was mature and remarkable in one so young. He was a thinker and a dreamer, and he had the soul of a poet. Victor was happiest when he was alone reading, or gazing at great paintings in the museum, or listening to the music of Mahler and Beethoven. He was reserved of nature to a point of shyness and not given to conversing easily with anyone, especially strangers. Victor was looking at Emma surreptitiously from under his long dark lashes, a quiet smile playing around his mouth, thinking what a compassionate girl she must be, and how her actions today only reinforced his inherent belief that essentially mankind was good. Like his father, Victor was utterly without bitterness.

David, the bolder and more self-assured of the two brothers, spoke to Emma first. 'That was very spunky of you, to stand up to those boys and help my father. And you're not even Jewish, are you?' he commented with his usual forthrightness.

His piercing blue eyes swept over her in a quick, all-encompassing inspection and he was impressed with the image she made, sitting there in the chair, her hands calmly folded in her lap.

'No, I am not Jewish,' said Emma. 'But I fail to see what difference that makes. I would help anyone in distress, and certainly somebody being assaulted the way your father was.'

David nodded. 'Not many people would, though,' he remarked succinctly, wondering what a refined girl was doing in the neighbourhood anyway. He opened his mouth to ask, when Janessa said, 'Mrs Harte, come and wash your hands, before the boys clean up, and then we will eat. It is almost sundown.' Janessa swept across the floor and set another place for Emma at the table, hovering near it until Emma and then the boys had completed their toilets.

They all stood around the large table, which was beautifully arranged, the four Kallinskis and Emma. 'Mother will bless the candles first,' David whispered. Emma stood perfectly still and watched and listened carefully, taking everything in. Janessa lit the two white candles and murmured a prayer over them in a strange language Emma did not understand, then they all sat down, David courteously pulling the chair out for Emma, Victor for his mother. Noting that all of the Kallinskis were bowing their heads, Emma followed suit. Out of the corner of her eye she saw Abraham bless the red wine in a small cup, again in that curious foreign tongue which she did not know was Hebrew. He took a sip of the wine and said another prayer over the twisted loaf of bread she herself had rescued from the street.

'Father just recited the kiddush and now we can eat, after the breaking of the bread,' David further informed her. The bread was broken by Abraham Kallinski and passed around, and Janessa brought steaming bowls of soup to the table that smelled delicious, and so the meal commenced. As she ate, Emma became aware of the harmony and immeasurable love that existed in this family. She began to relax, for the atmosphere was warm and congenial and she was made to feel so at ease and so welcome she was overwhelmed with gratitude at one moment, and her throat thickened with unexpected emotion. And she kept thinking: *Why are the Jews hated? They are loving and gentle people and kind and considerate. It is despicable the way they are treated.* And this was the way Emma Harte was to feel all of her life, staunchly defending her Jewish friends, constantly shocked and grieved by the excesses of naked racism that infected Leeds like the blight for many years.

The roasted chicken, like the soup before it, was cooked to perfection and was delectable, and for the first time since she had left Fairley, Emma felt both nourished and replete. She realized she had eaten very little in the week she had been in Leeds. She decided to correct that, for she was wise enough to understand that she must keep up her strength.

There was much conversation at the table, about many diverse subjects which fascinated Emma, most of it conducted by the garrulous David and his slightly less garrulous father. Janessa would make a quiet comment occasionally and nod in agreement or shake her head at Emma, all the time smiling benignly, content to be in her home with those she loved, basking in the palpable love that flowed around her, and the festive mood of the Friday-evening dinner. Victor hardly volunteered a word, but he smiled sometimes at Emma, his hazel eyes soft and shyly friendly. A short while later, when she served the honey cakes and tea, Janessa looked down at Emma, her blue eyes twinkling. 'I think you enjoyed our Jewish food, didn't you, Mrs Harte?'

Emma's own eyes were dancing. 'Oh, yes, I did, Mrs Kallinski. It was delicious. And please, call me Emma.' Her glance swept around the entire table. 'I would like everyone to call me Emma.' The Kallinski family nodded in unison and returned her smiles. 'We would be honoured,' said Abraham in his gravely courteous way.

They were drinking their tea when David's eyes swivelled to Emma sitting by his side. Like the others, David had noticed Emma's well-bred air, her good manners, and the quality of her dress, for even though it was cotton it was well cut. He was curious about her. Now he said, 'I don't want to seem nosy or rude, but what on earth were *you* doing in North Street this afternoon? Thank goodness you were, mind you. But it's not such a nice area for anyone to be wandering around in.'

Emma returned his piercing glance with one equally brilliant. 'I was looking for a job,' she said calmly.

Total silence descended and four pairs of Kallinski eyes centred on Emma.

It was Janessa who broke that silence. 'A girl like you! Looking for work in that terrible district!' she gasped, utterly thunderstruck.

'Yes,' said Emma softly. Since they were all gazing at her in amazement, she felt obliged to explain and she embarked on the same story she had invented for Rosie and repeated to Mrs Daniel, finishing, 'And in the past week I have been to every fancy store in Leeds, looking for work as a salesgirl without any success. So today I decided to try my luck in North Street, at the tailoring shops. But I didn't find anything there either. I had just been to Cohen's and was making my way home when I saw the boys assaulting Mr Kallinski.'

Three pairs of Kallinski eyes immediately swung away from Emma and lighted on Abraham, and again it was Janessa who spoke. 'Abraham! Abraham! *You* must do something for Emma.'

'Of course I must and I will,' he replied, beaming at Emma sitting next to him. He patted her arm. 'You do not have to worry about looking further. On Monday morning, at eight o'clock sharp, come to my tailoring shop and I will give you a job, Emma. I am sure we can find something suitable.' He glanced at David. 'Don't you agree, son?'

'Yes, Dad. We can start Emma off as a buttonholer. That's not so hard,' responded David.

Emma was so surprised she was almost rendered speechless, but she quickly found her voice. 'Why, thank you, Mr Kallinski! That would be wonderful.' She gave him an intent look. 'I learn very fast and I will work hard.' She paused and shook her head. 'I didn't know you had a tailoring shop.'

Abraham chuckled. 'How could you have known? Anyway, it is in Rockingham Street near Camp Road. David will write down the exact address for you. It is not a very large workshop. We have about twenty people. But we do well enough, making up.'

'What does "making up" mean?' asked Emma, baffled by this expression but, as always, anxious to clarify anything she did not understand.

Abraham gave her an avuncular smile. 'Ah, yes, of course you are not familiar with the term, since you do not know the tailoring trade. It means that we do work for larger clothiers, like Barran's and others, as do most of the Jewish tailoring shops in Leeds. We are an outside contractor.'

'I see,' said Emma. 'So you make suits for the big clothiers and they go and sell them. Am I right?'

'Not exactly, but I will let David explain. He is the one who lives, breathes, eats, and sleeps the tailoring trade in this family.'

David laughed engagingly. 'That's not quite true, Dad.' He leaned back in his chair and partially turned to Emma. 'We don't turn out an entire suit. We "make up" a particular section of a suit, maybe the sleeves, or jacket fronts and lapels, or the jacket backs, or sometimes trousers. We "make up" whatever the big factories decide to send us any given week.'

Emma, alert as usual, said, 'But why? That seems a funny way to do it. Isn't it more complicated than just making the whole suit in one place?'

David grinned. 'No, strangely enough, it isn't, because it's very well organized. It's also cheaper and faster. The big manufacturers can produce more finished suits by utilizing this method. They simply assemble all of the different parts at their own factories. It was an idea conceived by a little Jewish tailor called Herman Friend. It revolutionized the ready-made clothing industry and helped to put Leeds on the map as the biggest centre of ready-made clothing in the world. And the trade is growing more enormous every year.' An excited gleam entered his eyes. 'I tell you, Emma, the tailoring trade is going to make Leeds even more famous one day and immensely rich. It is indeed and I intend to be part of it all.'

'Such ideas he has, this son of mine,' murmured Abraham, shaking his head wonderingly, a hint of disbelief in his eyes.

Emma was vastly intrigued, as she always was at the mention of money and new ideas. 'This man, this Herman Friend, where did he get such an idea? Tell me more about him, David.'

'Who knows what gave him the idea,' he said with a shrug. 'But it was certainly an idea that worked. Anyway, Herman Friend had his own little workshop and was "making-up" for the John Barran factory, the first ready-made clothiers to start in Leeds after Singer invented the sewing machine. They're the biggest, and also non-Jewish, by the way. Friend invented the method of the divisional labour system when he was an outside contractor for Barran's, dividing the making of one single suit into five or six different operations. This immediately reduced the cost of producing ready-made suits and, as I said before, increased output. It also meant that Barran's, and the other big clothiers who adopted the system, could sell the suits at cheaper prices. Volume was the key and it put the price of a suit within the reach of the working man. Friend started to give out work to other small Jewish tailoring shops and the whole idea just snowballed.'

Emma said, 'A simple idea, but like so many simple ideas, it was very clever.'

David nodded his agreement, somewhat taken aback by this observation. He was even further surprised when Emma continued, 'Like the Marks and Spencer Penny Bazaar in Leeds Market. Now that is also a brilliant idea. Putting all the goods in different sections, showing them off so everyone can see them easily, examine them, and help themselves. And pricing them so cheaply. Don't you think *that* is clever, David?'

'I certainly do!' He smiled. 'Did you know that Michael Marks is also a Jewish immigrant who came to Leeds from Poland? He started with that one stall in Leeds

Market ten years ago. He recently went into partnership with Tom Spencer and now they have Penny Bazaars all over Leeds, and are expanding to other cities. They'll be a national chain one day. You'll see.'

Emma's eyes were fixed on David, her mouth slightly open with amazement, excitement bringing a flush to her pale face. She *was* right. Leeds *was* the place to make a fortune. Now she said, 'I believe anything is possible, if you have a good idea and are prepared to work hard.'

'You're absolutely correct, Emma,' responded David. He launched into another success story, which Emma ate up.

David and Emma could have talked all night, for they were both bursting with ambition, drive, and, most surprisingly, had an incredible vision quite remarkable for their years; and they intuitively began to recognize this and were drawn to each other instinctively. But Abraham glanced at the clock at this precise moment and said, 'I think it is time for you boys to escort Emma home. I am enjoying her company, too, but it is getting late and I do not like the idea of you being on the streets when the public houses are turning out. Dangerous, I think.'

'Yes, I must be getting along,' Emma said, pushing back her chair. 'But first I must help Mrs Kallinski to clear the table and wash the dishes.'

'No, no, that is not necessary, Emma. My husband is right. The boys must take you home immediately. David, don't forget to write out the address of the workshop for Emma, and then you must leave,' said Janessa.

Emma thanked the elder Kallinskis for their hospitality and the lovely dinner, and even more profusely for the job, which was so vital to her survival. She promised to be at the workshop on Monday morning at eight o'clock, and carefully tucked the paper into her handbag.

It was a relatively long walk back to Mrs Daniel's house, but Emma felt safe, flanked on either side by the silent Victor and the voluble David. They did not run into any street gangs, and for Emma the time passed quickly with David chattering about all manner of things, but mostly about the tailoring trade. They insisted on taking her right to Mrs Daniel's front door. In the gaslight from the streetlamp a few feet away, David and Victor were clearly illuminated. Emma looked from the solemn Victor to the laughing David and thought: They are so different but they are both very genuine. She gave her hand to Victor. 'Thank you for bringing me home. Goodbye,' she said.

Victor gripped her hand with firmness. 'Good night, Emma. And thank you for helping Father. It was good of you.'

'Yes, it was!' exclaimed David, who now grasped her hand in his. 'See you Monday morning, bright and early. Good night, Emma.'

They turned and began to walk away as she fitted the door key into the lock, but David stopped abruptly and ran back. 'We think alike, Emma,' he said, his voice vibrating confidently in the stillness. 'I know we are going to be friends. Good friends.'

Emma's face was serious and she believed him. She nodded. 'I think so, too, David.' He opened the door for her, and when she was safely inside he ran lightly down the steps and raced after Victor, who was waiting for him at the end of the street.

He was not aware of it then, but never had David Kallinski made a more prophetic pronouncement. They were indeed alike, for both were imbued with the will to

287

succeed. And on that hot August night in 1905 a friendship had begun that was to last over half a century. Together they would climb, in their own individualistic ways, struggling up out of grim poverty, fighting all manner of prejudices, reaching for bigger and better things, and in their rising and their reaching they would carry the city with them. They would put their indelible imprint on Leeds, not only in their outstanding achievements as business magnates, but in their vast philanthropies. It was Emma Harte and David Kallinski, plus a handful of other conscientious, driven, and visionary Jews and Gentiles, who were to give birth to a city's greatness.

TWENTY-NINE

The days slipped into weeks. August became September and then suddenly September had vanished. It was already the middle of October and Blackie had not returned to Leeds.

Emma constantly wondered what was detaining him in Ireland, worrying excessively when she was alone in the solitude of her little attic room, hoping he was not in some kind of trouble. She longed for Blackie to return because he was her closest friend and, although she was not aware of it, because he was associated with her past. Blackie O'Neill was the only emotional link to her background and so to her family, whom she loved and sorely missed. But essentially, the worry she periodically experienced was sincere concern for Blackie's well-being, rather than her own, for she was not given to self-pity. And she was managing reasonably well by herself. She had her job at Kallinski's tailoring shop and her room at Mrs Daniel's house and, tentative and even tenuous as these were, they gave her a certain degree of security that was comforting.

The landlady, growing less fractious and more cordial every day, had announced unexpectedly that Emma could continue to rent the room indefinitely. It had not taken the sharp-eyed Mrs Daniel long to note that Emma was fastidious, honest, and quietly reserved. She kept to herself, merely nodding politely to the two gentlemen boarders when she ran into them in the hall, moving swiftly upstairs to her own room in well-bred dignity. She was not a troublemaker, Gertrude Daniel had decided, and had told Emma, 'Yer can stay as long as yer want ter, lass. Yer no bother. None at all,' and with this utterance Mrs Daniel's dour face had broken into a beaming smile and she had patted Emma's arm almost affectionately.

Emma was earning enough money at Kallinski's to keep herself adequately and, most importantly, without having to dip into her precious savings. She was careful with her money to a point of frugality, spending it only for necessities, walking everywhere even when she was dropping from exhaustion and tempted to take a tram-car. But thrifty as she was, she did buy nourishing food. She was sensible enough to recognize she must fortify her strength and preserve her energy at all costs. If she neglected herself she might easily get sick and be unable to work, a thought that filled her with dread. There was the baby to think about, after all.

The job at the little workshop kept her busy from eight in the morning until six, sometimes seven o'clock, at night. Emma actually enjoyed working there and had done so since the first day. Abraham Kallinski ran his Rockingham Street tailoring shop with efficiency, but he was no tyrant, and because he was just, no one ever thought of abusing his kindness. The workers did not have to clock in and there were no stringent rules about talking, or the length of time taken for tea and lunch breaks. The employees were paid by the piece and it was up to them to make a living wage; and providing Abraham met his obligations to the big clothiers on time, he was satisfied, and he did not believe in cracking the whip on principle.

The girls were mostly Gentiles, but all of the men were Jewish. There was a wonderful feeling of camaraderie in the air, with much friendly bantering rising above the clack-clack-clacking of the treadle sewing machines. Emma sat at the long wooden worktable, up to her calves in clippings and bits of padding, working nimbly and at a pace that astounded the most seasoned of the girls. They were a gregarious bunch, all of them Leeds born and bred, blunt, pithily humorous but kindly. They spoke in the odd vernacular particular to Leeds, abbreviating words, slurring others together, dropping *h*'s and adding them where they should not have been. Emma understood the girls easily enough, for the patois of Leeds was basically a bastardization of the Yorkshire dialect spoken in the rural areas. She herself continued to speak correctly, always conscious of Olivia Wainright's melodious voice, always parroting it, never permitting herself to fall into the rough speech patterns of her fellow workers. Emma knew that bad habits were easy to acquire and hard to break. At first the girls had teased her about her cultivated voice. 'Talking like cut glass,' they called it. Emma simply smiled and took their ribbing in such a good-natured way they soon ceased and accepted her as one of them. But none of the girls at Kallinski's ever quite became accustomed to her beauty or her air of breeding. They were forever stealing looks at her and they stood in awe of her, although she did not know this.

Abraham kept a watchful eye on Emma, for he would never forget her compassion and rare courage, but he did so without showing her any favouritism, even though he was inordinately fond of her. Emma was always aware of Victor's hovering presence, particularly when she hit a small problem with her work. Her involvement so preoccupied her she never once noticed the adoration that shone in his gentle eyes whenever they lighted on her. David was her champion. He had taken her under his wing that first Monday morning when he had set her to buttonholing. He was not surprised when she mastered this technique within a few days and became one of the speediest and most adept workers. Conscious of her superior intelligence and her amazing facility for learning with rapidity, he started her cutting sleeves one day when a regular cutter was absent. David had rolled out the long bolt of fine Yorkshire cloth on the wooden trestle table, chalking on the pattern from a paper form and wielding the scissors with a dexterity that was enviable, explaining in detail to Emma as he went along.

Under David's training Emma soon learned to cut sleeves, lapels, then jacket fronts and backs, and finally trousers, always willing to pitch in and help when they were running behind with orders. By the middle of September she could easily have cut and sewn an entire suit on her own, without assistance from David. Abraham was stunned at her enormous capacity for work and impressed by her quick understanding of all aspects of tailoring. In fact, he was speechless at her skill, her single-mindedness, and her unflagging energy. Victor was silently admiring. David simply grinned like a Cheshire cat. He had perceived the nature of her character at their first meeting, an occasion he would always consider auspicious, if not indeed fortuitous. Emma Harte was a girl who was going places. He would bet his last shilling on that. He had his plans and she was part of them.

Janessa Kallinski continually extended invitations to Friday-night Sabbath dinner, for she had also grown fond of Emma and was as captivated as the rest of the family. Emma regulated her visits scrupulously, displaying an innate sense of social grace. She enjoyed her evenings in this warm and loving Jewish home, but she did not want to take advantage of their hospitality or appear to be forward and opportunistic. And when she did accept an invitation she always arrived with a small gift. A bunch of flowers bought in Leeds Market, a pot of jam she had made in Mrs Daniel's kitchen, and once a chocolate mousse, painstakingly prepared from Olivia Wainright's recipe and carried most carefully to the house in the Leylands in one of Mrs Daniel's best cut-glass bowls. The mousse had been a triumph and had sent the whole of the Kallinski family into gurglings of delight; and they were lavish with their praise of her culinary expertise, which Mrs Daniel had also commented on favourably.

Mostly, however, Emma's free time was spent alone. She was not always tired at the end of the working day but, since she had no friends in Leeds, other than the Kallinskis, she made her supper in the back kitchen and then retired to her attic. Sometimes she sewed at night, spending endless hours patiently altering the castoffs from Olivia Wainright's wardrobe. These had been given to her before Mrs Wainright had departed for London, following Adele Fairley's funeral. If the clothing had seen better days, none of it was so badly worn that it could not be fixed by Emma's ingenuity and her deftness with a needle. The basic quality and elegance of the clothes was unmistakable, and so she turned frayed cuffs and collars, patched and darned holes, and let out seams. She worked on a grey woollen suit, a red silk dress, various skirts and blouses, and a black woollen coat, as well as the black dress that had been her mother's, constantly endeavouring to keep her limited wardrobe in the best of condition and neat. She had no intention of buying anything new in the next few years. Occasionally she read the books she had found in the bottom drawer of the chest. She did not always understand the philosophical works, but they intrigued her and she would read sentences over and over again, digesting the words with thoughtfulness, filled with an immense gratification when the true meaning of the books became clear to her. She had a thirst for learning and acquiring knowledge and one of her few purchases had been a dictionary. But her favourite book of all was the volume of William Blake's poems and she pored over this regularly, reciting the verses aloud, enunciating the difficult words precisely, making a supreme effort to develop and perfect her speaking voice. In point of fact, Emma Harte never wasted a minute of her time, continually striving to better herself.

The first few weeks she had been in Leeds she had lain awake almost every night fretting about the baby. One day it struck her most forcibly that worrying about an event not due to take place until the following March was perfectly ridiculous. Also, it was a waste of time, that most precious of all commodities to Emma. She would think about the baby the day it was born and not before. Then, and only then, would she decide what her next step would be. Emma hoped the baby would be a girl. She was afraid that if it was a boy it would look like Edwin Fairley and that she would hate it for this reason. The poor baby isn't to blame, she would think, and every day she said to herself: I *know* it will be a girl, and this invariably cheered her up.

Emma had been to visit Rosie at the Mucky Duck twice, and on the last occasion she had left a note sealed in an envelope for Blackie, telling him where she lived and worked. She had also written to her father. She had told him she had not found a suitable position in Bradford, but that she was staying on in the hopes of doing so. She promised to be in touch soon. The letter had been most purposefully posted in Bradford. Although Emma begrudged spending the money for the railway ticket, she was too terrified to post the letter in Leeds for fear of discovery. And so, with that sense of self-preservation uppermost in her mind, she had trailed all the way to Bradford, posted the letter at the main post office, and taken the next train back to Leeds.

Now, on a Saturday morning in October, Emma sat at the table in the attic penning another note in her meticulously neat handwriting. For obvious reasons, this letter had to be full of lies; lies that at first bothered her enormously, until she told herself they were really white lies; and because they were meant to protect her father from knowing the terrible truth, which would shame him, and were intended to assuage his anxiety, they did not actually count. However, she decided to keep her story as simple as possible.

Emma wrote carefully: *Dear Dad: I am sorry I have not written since September. I have been looking hard for work. I am glad to tell you I have obtained a position with* . . . Emma stopped, conjuring up a name that was so common it would therefore be difficult to isolate and trace, continuing: *a Mrs John Smith. I am to be her personal maid. We are leaving for London today, returning in one month. When I get back to Bradford I will come and see you. Don't worry about me, Dad. I am fine. Love to you and Frank and Winston. Always your loving daughter, Emma.* She added a postscript. *PS. Here's a pound to help out.* Emma wrapped the pound note inside the letter, put it in the envelope, sealed it firmly, addressed it, and stuck on the stamp.

She hurried to get dressed, selecting the black frock that had been her evening uniform at Fairley Hall and which now boasted a frothy white lace collar and cuffs. She had wondered whether she ought to take her uniforms when she had left Fairley Hall. Wasn't that stealing? she had asked herself. But in the end she had had no compunction about packing them in Edwin's suitcase. The Fairleys had had their pound of flesh and the uniforms certainly wouldn't fit the bovine Annie.

Once she was outside the house Emma's spirits lifted. It was an Indian-summer day, with a polished blue sky, white candy-floss clouds, and radiant sunshine. It's a shimmering sort of day, Emma decided, breathing in the fresh air that was balmy for October. She walked smartly to City Square and crossed it to reach City Station, where she bought a ticket for Bradford. Luckily the train was standing on the platform and she boarded it immediately. When the train eventually chugged into Bradford, Emma leapt out of the carriage, dashed to the post office and back to the railway station with such speed she was able to catch the return train to Leeds.

Emma felt easier now that the letter to her father had been mailed, and she relaxed against the carriage seat as the train rumbled along the tracks. She did not have to write to her father again for a month. That gave her sufficient time to think up another story. Although there was no natural deceit in her character, Emma knew she must resort to subterfuge to appease her father, until after the baby was born. He might still worry about her, but not as much as he would if there was total silence on her part. She must be in touch with him on a regular basis and then perhaps he would not attempt to find her. He did not know where to look anyway. He believed her to be in Bradford, and there must be hundreds of Mrs John Smiths in that city. As always, she felt a sharp twinge of guilt when she thought of her father.

The trip to Bradford and back to Leeds had taken several hours and Emma was assailed by hunger pains when she stepped off the train in City Station. In fact, the hunger was so acute it was making her feel dizzy. She went directly to Leeds Market, where she bought herself a large portion of mussels and drowned them in pepper and vinegar, having lately developed a craving for spicy things. When these had been devoured with relish, she went to the pie stand and bought a meat pie, all fluffy, flaky pastry and piping hot and deliciously moist and tender inside. She strolled around the market for a short while, eating the pie unselfconsciously and looking at the diverse stalls, and then she wended her way to Briggate. On Saturday afternoons Emma made a point of wandering around the main streets of Leeds, gazing in the store windows, making mental notes of displays and the type of merchandise on sale. She went into several of the fine shops, eyeing the interior displays and observing what people were buying, conscious of that thrilling sensation growing inside her, as it always did when she entered a shop. She loved the bustle, the bright colours, the array of merchandise and its often ingenious presentation, the clink of the cash registers, the interesting faces of the shoppers, the elegant women in their smart clothes. She could not wait until she had her own shop. *Shops*, she corrected herself, as she stared at a collection of winter bonnets, none of which was to her taste; nor did she like the way they were presented.

After several hours of browsing, Emma decided she ought to go home. She had mending and other tasks to do and her feet ached. She had barely walked in through the front door when Mrs Daniel was upon her, sweeping down the narrow corridor from the back kitchen. Her eyes glinted sharply in the dim light and she threw Emma a quizzical look as she exclaimed, 'Yer've had a gentleman caller!'

Emma stood stock-still, her heart pounding unreasonably. Her father? Winston? They had somehow managed to find her! Don't be stupid, she told herself firmly. It was more than likely David Kallinski. He had been once before, delivering a message from his mother, but Mrs Daniel had been out and so she had never met him. Yes, it must have been David, Emma decided. She kept her voice steady, 'Oh, really. Did he leave his name, Mrs Daniel?'

'No, but he left yer this.' Mrs Daniel pulled an envelope out of her apron pocket.

'Thank you, Mrs Daniel,' said Emma, placing one foot on the stairs purposefully.

'Aren't yer going ter open it, then?' Mrs Daniel asked, her disappointment registering so apparently Emma was amused.

'Yes, of course I am,' Emma replied with a cool smile. She inclined her head to the landlady graciously. 'Please excuse me, Mrs Daniel.' Without giving her another glance, Emma mounted the stairs, her heart lifting. She had recognized the handwriting. It was Blackie's, and she certainly wasn't going to give Mrs Daniel the satisfaction of seeing her jubilation at receiving a note from a man who was obviously not her 'husband' of Royal Navy fame, the much-talked-about Winston.

Once she was in her room, Emma tore open the envelope with trembling fingers, her eyes seeking the signature immediately. It *was* from Blackie. He would be waiting for her at the Mucky Duck at five o'clock today. Emma dropped on to the bed and leaned her head against the pillow, closing her eyes, filled with the most overwhelming sense of relief and happiness.

At exactly four, when the grandfather clock in the front hall struck the hour, Emma sailed downstairs and out of the house before Mrs Daniel could waylay her with her prying questions and unconcealed curiosity. Outwardly, she was as contained as always, but inside she was bursting with a breathless anticipation at the idea of seeing Blackie O'Neill again. Oh, how she had missed him! It was only now that Emma realized the amount of discipline and self-control she had exercised, so as not to become depressed or feel utterly alone in Leeds, and she was astonished that she had been able to command her emotions so successfully.

So intent was Emma on reaching her destination, so involved was she with these inner thoughts, she was quite oblivious to the heads, both male and female, that turned to look after her as she swept along the pavement, heading for York Road and the Mucky Duck. She cut quite a swath in the grey woollen suit which she had skilfully repaired so that the worn parts would not show. It was of excellent cut and elegant in its basic simplicity. The long skirt was straight to the calf and from there it fell to her ankles in a small flare on either side. Topping the skirt was a tailored jacket, tightly fitted over the bodice, with rounded shoulders and narrow sleeves. Deep revers and a peplum from the waist to just below the hip gave it an undeniable chic not commonly seen in the neighbourhood; it was five years old and dated for London, but not for Leeds, and it *was* by Worth. With it Emma wore the blue silk blouse discarded long ago by Olivia Wainright, and its dainty white lace collar and cuffs were just visible. She had pinned Blackie's green-glass brooch on to one of the lapels, but this was her only piece of jewellery, other than her mother's plain silver ring on the third finger of her left hand. The white crocheted gloves and the black leather reticule with the tortoiseshell frame completed her outfit.

Emma was now five months pregnant. She herself was conscious of a thickening around her waist and hips, but her condition was not yet obvious to anyone else. The suit emphasized her willowy figure and enhanced her natural gracefulness. Her burnished hair, full of golden lights in the late-afternoon sunshine, was swept back from her oval face and brought the striking widow's peak into focus. That afternoon she had piled those glossy tresses on top of her head in a modified pompadour, experimenting with a style she had not previously worn, and it not only made her appear taller than her five feet six inches but also gave her a sophisticated air. There was a decided spring to her light step. She was feeling revitalized and her exhilaration was apparent to every passer-by.

Emma knew she had set out far too soon. She slowed her pace, not wanting to reach the pub before Blackie did. On arriving in Leeds in August, she had already worked out the story she would tell him. At this time in her life there was little duplicity in Emma. However, now that she was pregnant she was more self-protective than ever and her inbred wariness was increasing daily. The last thing she wanted was her father or Adam Fairley swooping down on her, a situation quite likely to arise if Blackie knew the facts and sprang gallantly to her defence. And so she had concocted a story within the realm of truth yet deceptive enough to dupe Blackie whilst being eminently plausible. She rehearsed the story as she walked, although she had committed it to memory weeks ago.

A small troop of Salvation Army ladies, resplendent in their long black uniforms, their bonnets bobbing, were marching down York Road from the opposite direction, singing lustily and thumping a drum. Rather than hang around outside and expose herself to the ritualistic Saturday-night dissertation of the evils of drink, Emma went immediately into the public house. She could always chat with Rosie if Blackie was not already there. She pushed open the heavy front doors and moved along the narrow corridor rank with the smell of stale beer and smoke. She paused briefly before going through the inner swinging doors. Blackie had beat her to it. His voice was distinguishable over the hum of the noise inside. Emma stepped through the doors and stood to one side.

There he was in all his glorious Irish splendour, vibrant black curls rippling back from tanned face, black eyes dancing, white teeth flashing between rosy lips, his superb looks prominently highlighted in the glare from the burning gas lamps. The pianist was banging out 'Danny Boy', and Blackie stood next to him, erect and proud, one hand on the piano top, his marvellous baritone ringing out above the clink of glasses and the subdued murmur of conversation. Emma put a gloved hand to her mouth to hide the laughter springing automatically to her lips. She had never seen *this* Blackie O'Neill before. But then she had never seen him in a pub either. What a performance he's giving, she thought in amazement, mesmerized by his theatrical stance.

In point of fact, Blackie O'Neill would have made a splendid actor. He certainly had all the necessary attributes required for that histrionic art – outstanding looks, natural charm, an instinctive sense of timing, emotional depth, and an animal magnetism that was spellbinding when projected to the fullest, and it was being decidedly projected at this very moment. There was not a little of the ham in Blackie and he was now playing outrageously to the crowd, who were electrified. He had come to the last verse of the old Irish air, and he stepped away from the piano, leaned forward, almost bowing, and then drew himself up to his full height of six feet three inches, expanding his broad chest. One great arm swept out and he finished triumphantly:

'And I shall hear, though soft ye tread above me,
And all my grave will warmer, sweeter be,
And you will bend and tell me that you love me,
And I shall sleep in peace until ye come to me!'

His voice struck at Emma's heart as it always did, and as the fading echoes of it washed over her in all-enveloping waves, her throat became tight with that bittersweet sadness she experienced whenever he sang. She blinked and looked around. There wasn't a dry eye in the place and she saw the flutter of white as handkerchiefs came out to wipe other moist eyes. The crowd was clapping spontaneously and she heard diverse voices shouting out requests: 'Give us another, Blackie, lad!' ... 'How about "The Minstrel Boy"!' ... 'Sing us "Cockles and Mussels", lad!' Blackie was bowing and grinning and bowing again, obviously enjoying every minute of the approval. He seemed about to oblige with another rendition when he spotted Emma.

'Later, mates,' he cried above the din, and crossed the floor in several quick strides, pushing his way through the group surrounding the piano. Emma stood shyly near the door, clutching her reticule. Blackie was towering above her, his eyes sweeping over her in one swift but appraising glance. His surprise at the radical change in her appearance was evident, even though he tried to conceal it. He recovered instantly and said, with his usual enthusiasm, 'Emma! It's wonderful to see ye, sure and it is, mavourneen.'

Blackie pulled her into his arms and hugged her. Then he stood her away, as was his habit, still holding her arms and gazing into her upturned face. 'Why, ye be looking more fetching than I ever did see ye, Emma. And quite the young lady. Yes, indeed!'

Emma laughed. 'Thank you, Blackie, and it's lovely to see you, too.' He grinned at her, his delight as obvious as hers. 'Come on, mavourneen. Let's be going into the Saloon Bar. It will be quieter in there, I am thinking, and we can talk better. It is also a more *suitable* spot for a fine young lady like ye.' He winked as he said this and asked, 'And what will ye be having to drink?'

'A lemonade, please,' she responded.

'Wait here,' Blackie ordered, and headed for the bar. Emma's eyes followed him. She had not seen him since the spring, almost nine months, and he, too, had changed. He seemed somehow more mature and, in spite of that natural exuberance that always bubbled to the surface, there was an air of containment about him, and she thought she also detected a certain sadness. Rosie, her vast body encased in startling orange satin, was beaming from ear to ear and waving at Emma, who returned her greeting. Blackie was back within seconds, carrying the drinks. 'Follow me,' he said, shouldering his way through the throng that filled the main room.

The Saloon Bar was relatively empty and certainly quieter, and Emma at once felt less uncomfortable here than in the public bar. She glanced around curiously. It was quite sedate, in fact rather elegant for a pub. Blackie found them a table in the corner, put down the drinks, pulled out a chair for her with a gentlemanly flourish, and seated himself opposite. He took a sip of the frothing pint and regarded her over the rim of the glass attentively. Then he placed it on the table and, leaning forward, said in a sober tone, 'And what's all this about, then? What are ye doing in Leeds? A little snippet like ye. I thought I told ye a long time ago this was no place for ye, until ye were older. Sure and I did, Emma Harte.'

Emma threw him a quick glance. 'I'm doing all right.'

'Aye, so I can see, by the looks of ye. But ye might not have been so lucky, I am thinking. Come on, out with it! What made ye leave Fairley?'

Emma was not ready to confide in him just yet and she ignored the question. 'Yes, I *was* lucky,' she conceded and, changing the subject, continued, 'I didn't know you would be away. I missed you, Blackie. Why were you in Ireland so long? I thought you were never coming back.'

His face became sorrowful. 'Ah, mavourneen, mavourneen,' he said through a deep sigh. 'It was me good friend Father O'Donovan, who was dying. An old priest I truly loved, who taught me everything I know. That is, what bit of learning I do have. I stayed with him till the end. Sad it was, oh, very sad indeed.' He shook his head and his Celtic soul seemed to be mourning afresh, for his eyes were dimming at the memory.

Emma stretched out her small hand and patted his arm. 'I am sorry, Blackie.

Really very sorry. I know how upset you must be.' She was silent for a moment, commiserating with him, and then she murmured softly, 'So that's why you stayed in Ireland all these months.'

'No, mavourneen. Father O'Donovan, God rest his soul, died within a couple of weeks. But I did stay on for a bit of a holiday with me cousins, Michael and Siobhan, who I hadn't seen in many a year. Then me Uncle Pat did write to me and told me I must get meself back to England quick like. I got back to Leeds yesterday. Naturally, it being Friday night, I came in for a pint. And what a surprise I did get when Rosie gave me ye letter. I was thunderstruck, if the truth be known.' He looked at her quizzically and finished, 'Out with it, colleen. Why did ye decide to leave Fairley?'

Emma eyed him a little charily and said quietly, 'Before I tell you the reason, Blackie, you must promise me something.'

Blackie stared at her, amazed more by the seriousness of her tone rather than her request. 'And what might that be?'

Emma met his direct gaze calmly. 'You must promise me you won't tell my father, or *anyone*, where I am.'

'And why all the secrecy?' Blackie demanded. 'Does not ye dad know where ye be?'

'He thinks I'm working in Bradford,' Emma explained.

'Ah, Emma, that's not right. Now why would ye not be telling ye dad where ye are?'

'Blackie, you haven't promised me yet,' she insisted in her coolest voice.

He sighed. 'All right, then, if that's the way ye be wanting it. I swear on the heads of the Blessed Saints that I won't be telling a living soul where ye be.'

'Thank you, Blackie.' There was a dignified expression on her face and she was not at all nervous or apprehensive as she said, 'I had to leave Fairley because I am going to have a baby!'

'Jaysus!' Blackie exploded in stunned disbelief. 'A baby!' he repeated, mouthing the word as if it were foreign to his tongue.

'Yes, in March,' Emma informed him calmly, 'and I had to leave because the boy, that is the father, well, he let me down.'

'He did what!' Blackie bellowed, his face growing scarlet. 'By God, I'll thrash the living daylights out of him! I will that. We will go to Fairley tomorrow and see ye dad and his dad. And by God he'll marry ye if I've got to beat him to a pulp to get him to the church!'

'Hush, Blackie,' Emma said. She could see he was in the grip of a terrible fury. 'It's no use, Blackie. When I told the boy the way it was, he said he *would* marry me. That I shouldn't worry. But then do you know what he did, that very night?'

'No, mavourneen, I cannot be imagining,' muttered Blackie through clenched teeth. For the first time in his life he felt the desire to kill. The idea that anyone would abuse Emma enraged him to a point of madness.

Emma had been watching Blackie very carefully and she said softly, 'He did a terrible thing, Blackie. *He ran away*. To join the Royal Navy. Fancy that!' Her eyes were large and her voice was low. 'He took a leaf out of my *own* brother's notebook,' she went on. 'He copied Winston and did a moonlight flit. Just like that. When he didn't come to the Hall to see me, as he had promised, I went down to the village to see him. It was then his dad told me that he had run off. He even showed me the note the boy had left.' She shook her head. 'What could I do, Blackie? I couldn't tell his dad. And I certainly couldn't tell mine. So I ran away to Leeds.'

'But perhaps ye dad would be understanding –' Blackie began, endeavouring to keep his voice steady.

'No, he wouldn't!' Emma cried with alarm, her face paling. She had known he might take this attitude and she must convince him she had to stay in Leeds. 'He would be angry and hurt! It would kill him, coming on top of my mother's death. I don't want to take any trouble to my father's doorstep. It's better this way.' Emma now softened her voice. 'Honestly, Blackie, it is. I know my father. He has a terrible temper and there would be a dreadful scandal in the village. It would ruin my life and the baby's. And my dad's, too. It's best he doesn't know. He couldn't stand the shame.'

'Aye, mavourneen, I can see ye point.' He stared at her, his face thoughtful. As she had so accurately assessed, he was not at all shocked by her revelation. Surprised, of course. And infuriated with the cowardice of the boy who had got her into trouble and then deserted her. But Blackie was familiar with human weaknesses, especially of the flesh, and he was not one to pass judgement. And yet, as he continued to observe her, he was immensely disturbed. It occurred to him that her story did not sit too well on his shoulders. His native intuition told him there was something terribly wrong with it, although he was not exactly sure what this was. He gave her the most penetrating look. There seemed to be no deception in her face. She was regarding him openly, her eyes innocent, and her lovely face overflowed with sweetness. Blackie pushed back the feelings of disquiet he was experiencing and said, in a controlled tone, 'And what will ye do when the baby comes? What will ye do with the baby, Emma?'

'I don't know yet, Blackie. I'll think of something. For the moment I must protect my father – let him continue to believe that I ran away to better myself, that I'm working in Bradford. After the baby's born, of course I shall go and see him, so that he knows I'm really all right. In the meantime I will keep writing to him, and then he won't worry so much.' Before Blackie had a chance to make any comment, Emma rushed on to explain about the letters she had sent from Bradford, and also told him everything else that had happened to her in Leeds. She painted a picture that was a trifle rosier than reality.

He gave her all of his attention and, as he listened, Blackie O'Neill began to realize that the change in her ran deeper than her outward appearance. Indefinable and subtle though this difference was, it *was* there, and it had not been wrought simply by the sophisticated upswept hairdo and the elegant clothes, undoubtedly castoffs from the Hall. There was a profound alteration in Emma herself. But that's to be expected, he decided. She's about to become a mother and her experiences of the last few months most certainly would affect her. Then it hit him. Emma was no longer the starveling child of the moors. She was a young woman and a beautiful one at that, and somehow she had managed to transform herself into a lady overnight. No, not overnight. It had been happening gradually over the past year and a half. He recognized that now. He himself had detected the thoroughbred strain in her the day they had met and now it was apparent for all to see. He smiled wryly. That explained Rosie's glowing description of her.

Her musical voice intruded on his thoughts. 'The Kallinskis are very nice, and so kind, Blackie. I hope you'll meet them. And I like working in the tailoring trade.

I'm doing very well, you know.' Emma was saying. 'I will be fine in Leeds, Blackie. I know I will.'

'Yes, I suppose ye will, Emma. But ye are not looking ahead,' he pointed out. 'How will ye look after the baby and work as well?' he demanded with fierceness.

Emma gave him a sharp look. 'I told you before, I'll think about that problem later! Right now, I have to make money. To keep myself and to save up for the baby coming.' She leaned forward and took his hand, squeezing it, hoping to reassure him. 'Please don't worry. There's always a solution to everything,' she said in a positive voice.

She smiled and her face, so close to his, bewitched him, and once again he became conscious of her as a woman, and his heart beat all that faster. He saw her in a different light than he had ever seen her before.

Without a second thought Blackie said urgently, 'I have a solution, Emma! Marry me! Then ye will be safe and secure. I'll take care of ye and the baby, too. Marry me, mavourneen!'

Emma was utterly astounded. She stared at Blackie, quite unable to speak, and for the first time since she had left Fairley she broke down, so moved was she by this loving and unselfish gesture on his part. She lowered her head and the tears spilled down her cheeks and dropped on to her hands fumbling in her bag for her handkerchief. She wiped her eyes and, through her tears, she said tremulously, 'Oh, Blackie, how wonderful of you to ask me to marry you! What a *lovely* thing for you to do.' She paused and gazed into his burning eyes. 'But I couldn't do that. It just wouldn't be fair to hamstring you with a wife, and another man's child. You have your plans, after all. You're going to be that toff, that millionaire. You don't need the responsibility of a family. I couldn't do that to you, Blackie.'

Blackie had spoken impulsively, not even certain of his real emotions or his true feelings for Emma, and yet, although he recognized the veracity of what she said, he felt a peculiar stab of disappointment at her refusal. 'But ye cannot be by yeself,' he persisted, grasping her small hand in his. 'Ye would be better off with me, mavourneen. Sure and ye would.'

'And what about you, Blackie O'Neill? Would you be better off with me?' She smiled a little timorously, the tears still glistening on her lashes. 'No, I think not. I won't do that to you, Blackie. The answer is no. I won't marry you. But thank you anyway. I'm honoured and flattered that you would ask me. Really I am, Blackie.'

He could see that she was adamant and he was not fully certain whether he was relieved or not. He was filled with a variety of emotions. Nevertheless, he felt compelled to say, 'Very well, mavourneen, we won't be discussing it further. At least for the time being. Let's just say me offer is open – indefinitely!'

Emma could not help laughing through her subsiding tears. She shook her head. 'Oh, Blackie, what will I do with you!'

His anger was slowly dissipating, his doubts about her story were temporarily forgotten, and he joined in her laughter. After a few moments he said, 'I'll tell ye what ye'll do with me, mavourneen mine. Ye'll come and have a bite of supper with me, at one of them fancy cafés I told ye about, and then I'll be taking ye to the City Varieties. Vesta Tilley is appearing tonight and ye'll enjoy the show, I am thinking. Would ye be liking that, Emma? Sure and it'll be grand to be having a bit of fun for a change. What do ye say? Will ye be accepting me invitation, then?'

'Yes, I'd love to come with you. Thank you. Blackie – I –' Emma hesitated and then confessed almost shyly, 'I'm glad you're back in Leeds. I feel ever so much better knowing you're around, knowing you're my friend.'

Blackie's long Irish upper lip drew back in a warm smile and his white teeth gleamed. 'Aye, I am ye friend, Emma,' he asserted. 'And I'm glad ye confided in me. Now that I be knowing what ye are facing in the next few months I can do a bit of planning, make sure to be around when ye need me. But we won't be talking about ye problems any more tonight. Sure, and we'll face things one by one, as they come along. Now we are going out on the town! I aim to be showing ye off, Emma, me darlin'.'

Emma smiled up at him, her face animated. Thankfully her problems were miraculously retreating now that she was with Blackie. She had felt safe with him from the very first day they had met on the moors and she knew instinctively he would always protect her.

Blackie followed her out of the Saloon Bar and into the main room, which was teeming with people. He could hardly help noticing the masculine heads swivelling to stare, the admiring glances thrown in her direction. He drew himself up to his full height and lifted his head higher. She's a looker, all right, he thought. Why, there isn't a man breathing that wouldn't be proud and delighted to have her by his side. Sure and that's the truth, Blackie decided.

Then Blackie O'Neill stopped dead in his tracks, staring fixedly at her straight back, her delicately tilted head. With a sudden flash of comprehension he perceived why her story had so bothered him earlier. This transformed Emma Harte, gliding ahead of him so gracefully, would never have become involved with one of the loutish boys from the village. *Never.* Such an idea was not only inconceivable but preposterous. Then who is the father of her child? he wondered, completely baffled. He realized it would be unwise to question her tonight. Pushing this new and disturbing thought out of his mind, Blackie arranged a pleasant smile on his face and caught up with Emma. He took her arm and shepherded her out into the street, chatting to her in his vivacious way, striving for a semblance of normality. But his eyes held a reflective light.

THIRTY

Blackie and Emma sat on the tram-car going to Armley. It was a bitter-cold Sunday afternoon early in January of 1906. Emma was huddled in the corner of her seat, her altogether beautiful profile turned to him in chilly silence.

Jesus, Mary, and Joseph! Blackie thought in exasperation. She's so stubborn at times she's positively rigid. He glanced at her out of the corner of his eye and turned away, further dismayed by the obdurate look on her face. He knew better than to utter one word. She had been obstinate in her refusal to take this trip from the first day he had mentioned it two weeks ago. It had taken all of his powers of persuasion and his smooth Irish tongue to get her to agree, and then her acquiescence had been grudging. Sometimes he did not understand Emma at all, and he had long realized that she was an extremely complex young woman with the most pertinacious will it had ever been his misfortune to encounter. On the other hand, he had to acknowledge that she was amazingly intelligent, even brilliant, and gifted in so many ways. And in most instances she was flexible and open to suggestions, thank the Almighty Lord.

Blackie peered at her again. Surprisingly, that stern expression did nothing to mar her beauty. In fact, it seemed to give her a curiously imperious air that was arresting. Today her hair was drawn back and plaited, the plaits forming loops that hung low on her neck, anchored by a large black taffeta bow in the nape. She wore the green-and-black tartan tam-o'-shanter and the matching scarf he had given her for Christmas; the tam-o'-shanter was perched at a jaunty angle, the long scarf wound around her neck and thrown casually over the shoulders of her black wool coat. Her hands, as always clinging tightly to the black reticule, were encased in bottle-green mittens knitted for her by the devoted Rosie. The dark green tones of the scarf and hat suited her admirably and brought out the greenness of her incredible eyes and the alabaster pallor of her flawless complexion. There was no doubt about it. Emma, in these last months of her pregnancy, looked extraordinarily healthy and well cared for, and as immaculately groomed as always.

The tram rumbled out of the city centre, heading for Whingate Junction in Armley, a picturesque village perched on a hill, about half an hour's ride away. Blackie sat lost in contemplation, patiently waiting for Emma's mood to change, praying that it would do so before they reached their destination. He would be glad when the baby was born and she could visit Fairley. Although she accepted her pregnancy philosophically and with little visible show of anxiety, Blackie knew she worried excessively about her father and Frank. She had even pressed him into service with the mailing of those all-important letters to her dad, badgering him to seek out any of his friends, who might be going to London. She was determined to keep up the pretence that she was travelling with her non-existent Mrs John Smith, which readily explained her absence from Bradford. As luck would have it, he had been able to oblige her in November and December, when some of his mates from the pub were going south to find work on London's East End docks. They had willingly agreed to post Emma's letters to her father, without asking any embarrassing questions. Blackie had commented to Emma, though. 'Ye dad will be wondering why ye don't give him an address, so's he can write to ye,' he had pointed out. 'No, he won't,' Emma had asserted sharply. 'In the November letter I told him I was going to Paris with my lady, and in the December letter I told him I was accompanying her to Italy. As long as he hears from *me*, that's all that matters.' Blackie eyed her, utterly astonished at the machinations of her mind. 'It seems ye've thought of everything,' he said dryly. To this remark she had not deigned to respond and the conversation had been terminated.

Blackie stole another look at her, moved closer, and put his arm around her shoulders, easing himself up to her on the seat. 'I hope ye'll consider moving to Armley,' he said carefully, steeling himself for her strong reaction, which, surprisingly, was not forthcoming. She remained perfectly still, her face staring ahead.

Encouraged, Blackie went on, 'Ye'll be happier living with Laura Spencer. Sure and ye will, mavourneen. Now that her widowed mother is dead she is looking for a paying guest, someone to share the expense of the house with her. A nice house it is, too. Small, of course, but cosy and well set up. Her late father was a foreman at the printing works, and her mother was a weaver. They had a bit of money and a decent going-on. It shows in the house, the furnishings and all, and Laura keeps it beautifully.' He paused and searched her face, proceeding in a cheery tone, 'Ye'll be real comfortable there. And as I told ye afore, Laura can get ye a job at Thompson's mill in Armley, where she works. I don't know why ye are being so stubborn about it, Emma.'

She swung her head unexpectedly and looked at him intensely, her green eyes flashing. 'Because I don't like being uprooted! I've just learned the tailoring trade and now you want me to leave Kallinski's and start working at the mill, learning to weave. It doesn't make sense, Blackie. And besides, I like it at Mrs Daniel's. She is very kindly these days and I do have the use of her kitchen.'

Blackie groaned. 'But, Emma, ye'll be having a whole house to share with Laura. Not only that, she lives just ten minutes way from Thompson's mill. At present ye spend three quarters of an hour walking to Kallinski's in the morning and the same amount of time to be getting home at night. It's a lot of walking in this raw weather. Even the Kallinskis see the sense of what I be suggesting, and David told me the other day that they will be happy to take ye back, after the bairn is born. So what do you have to lose? Nothing, I am thinking.' He sighed wearily. 'Ye are a wilful, headstrong girl, Emma, and all I am wanting is what's best for ye.'

Emma recognized the practicality of what he was suggesting, but for once in her life she was indecisive. 'I just don't know –'

Blackie now saw that wavering and he grabbed the opportunity, saying in a positive tone, 'Look, all I be asking is that ye *consider* it carefully, and that ye weigh all the odds before ye make a hasty decision not to move in with Laura.' He took hold of her sturdy hand and squeezed it. 'And please be nice with Laura. She's a good friend and I don't want ye to be acting rude or stuck-up.'

Emma flushed and glared at him. 'Rude! I'm never rude to anyone! You know better than that. And I'm not stuck-up either, Blackie O'Neill.'

He realized his mistake too late and, hoping to rectify it, said in the suavest of voices, 'I know ye don't mean to be snooty, Emma, me darlin'. But sometimes – well, sometimes ye do give the impression of being – let's say, a bit hoity-toity.'

'I do?' she said wonderingly, frowning and biting her lip. Emma was flabbergasted at this statement, for she truly did not know she could be formidable at times. Invariably her distant manner was engendered by her total preoccupation with her problems and her numerous plans, and nothing else. She remained silent, ruminating on what he had said, feeling mortified.

Sensing that she might be hurt, Blackie remarked gently, 'Ye'll be liking Laura. She's a sweet girl, that she is indeed. And I know she will be liking ye, Emma. Sure and she will, mavourneen.'

'*I'm* not so sure about that, in view of what you've just said,' Emma countered.

Blackie laughed a little shamefacedly. 'Now let's be forgetting that. All ye have to be doing is exercise a bit of that remarkable charm ye be possessing in such abundance, and everything will be fine.' He squeezed her hand again and went on, 'Armley is a grand little spot and very safe. 'Tis especially pretty in summer when the trees and flowers are blooming. There's Armley Park where the brass band plays every Sunday and other pleasant lanes and thoroughfares where ye can be taking a stroll. Also, St Mary's Hospital is nearby, and ye could be having the bairn there, when ye time comes. And there are plenty of shops, so ye won't be having to venture into Leeds for owt. Why, ye have everything ye be needing in Armley.'

Emma looked at him alertly. 'Shops,' she said thoughtfully. 'But I thought Armley was a tiny village. There can't be *that* many shops, Blackie.'

'Oh, aye, there are, mavourneen. Ye see, Armley is spread out, so to speak. It be quite large really. There are a lot of fine homes. Mansions, in fact, where the posh folk live. Millowners and the like. There are a number of good shops in Town Street catering to the Quality trade. I've seen 'em, when I've been visiting Laura afore. Ye'll have a chance to look at 'em yeself, when we walk down the main street to get to Laura's house.'

'What sort of shops?' Emma pressed, her eyes turned on him with fierce interest.

Aware that he had now captured her complete attention and observing the change in her attitude, Blackie spoke excitedly, hoping to sway her further. 'Well, let me be thinking. There be grocers, butchers, and greengrocers, all on Town Street, along with a pork butcher's shop, an off-licence, a fishmonger's, Keene's dairy, a chemist, and a newsagent. I've also noticed a draper's, a haberdasher's, a shoe store, and a fine ladies' dress establishment as well, mavourneen. It is quite an active thoroughfare, almost as busy as Briggate, indeed it is. Why, I think there are shops selling practically everything, Emma.'

Emma had listened carefully and she was rapidly reversing her preconceived ideas about sharing Laura Spencer's house. 'Tell me more about the village,' she said. 'For instance, how big is it? How many people live there?'

'Ah, Emma, me love, now ye have me. I must be confessing I don't know its exact size, or how many people reside in Armley. But it must be a goodly number, I am thinking, for the shops do a brisk business. Then again, there are several churches and chapels and quite a few schools, so there must be plenty of folk in the vicinity. Yes, it is a thriving place, sure and it is. Laura told me there is a public library and Liberal, Conservative and Workingmen's clubs. Why, there is even a jail in Armley. Horrible dungeon of a place, it is, by the looks of it.' Blackie winked at her. 'There are lots of pubs, too. I meself know at least six personally.'

Emma laughed for the first time since they had set out. '*You* would know that.'

'And what's wrong with a young spalpeen liking a pint of bitter now and then and an occasional noggin of good Irish?' Blackie asked jestingly, adopting an injured air. Then he tugged on her arm urgently. 'Come on, mavourneen! Here we are, Ye can be seeing Armley for yeself.'

The tram had stopped at the terminus halfway up the hill. Blackie jumped down agilely and helped Emma to alight. 'Careful now, love. It's pretty bad underfoot. I don't want ye to be having a spill and upsetting Tinker Bell,' he said, clasping her hands tightly in his.

'Tinker Bell?'

'Aye, Tinker Bell. That's what I be calling the baby, to meself of course. Ye know, after Tinker Bell in *Peter Pan*. Don't ye approve of me name for her?'

She laughed. 'Yes, I do, Blackie. But how do you *know* it will be a girl?'

'Because ye keep telling me it will be.' Blackie tucked her arm through his, pushed his hands into the pockets of his new navy-blue overcoat, and said, 'That's the Towers up there, where the rich folk live.' He inclined his head toward a splendid driveway lined with trees. And Town Street is just ahead of us. Now watch ye step. It's slippery today.'

'Yes, I will, Blackie.' She drew closer to him, shivering. The north wind gusting down the hill was laden with frost and biting. Emma looked up. The sky was a frozen canopy soaring above them, icily white, and the pale winter sun was hardly visible, a tiny silver coin thrown negligently up into the far corner of that vast and hollow firmament. It was oddly silent now that the tram had stopped, for there were no carriages out or people abroad on this bleak and cheerless Sunday.

'There's Charley Cake Park,' Blackie informed her, his head swivelling to the triangular-shaped plot on the opposite side of the road. 'It'll be a nice little place for ye to sit in the summer with Tinker Bell watching the passers-by.'

'I won't have any time to sit anywhere with any Tinker Bell,' Emma retorted, although this was said in a mild tone. She looked up at him sceptically. 'Charley Cake Park! What kind of name is that? I bet you made it up.'

'Now, why is it ye always challenge everything I be saying? I shall have to call ye Doubting Emma if ye are not careful, me lass. Anyway, that's the name, sure and it is. Laura told me that years ago a man called Charley hawked cakes there and that's how it –'

'Got its name,' Emma finished for him, her eyes full of merriment. 'I believe you, Blackie. Nobody could invent a name like that.'

He grinned, but said nothing, and they walked on in silence. Emma glanced about her with considerable interest. They were now passing a neat row of houses facing onto Town Street. It reminded her of a scene from a fairy tale. Immense pie-like wedges of powdery snow slid across the red rooftops and hung precariously at the edges, and dripping from the gutters were countless icicles, shimmering scintillas of spun sugar in that pellucid air. Magically, the snow and ice had turned the mundane little dwellings into quaint gingerbread houses. The fences and the gates and the bare black trees were also encrusted with frozen snowflakes that, to Emma, resembled the silvery decorations on top of a magnificent Christmas cake. Paraffin lamps and firelight glowed through the windows and eddying whiffs of smoke drifted out of the chimneys, but these were the only signs of life on Town Street. The houses looked snug and inviting, and Emma imagined a happy family in each one; parents lazily warming themselves in front of the lambent flames, rosy-cheeked children at their feet, eating apples and oranges and roasting chestnuts, all of them laughing and enjoying a peaceful afternoon together, surrounded by love. She thought with a terrible yearning of her father and Frank and she wished with fervency that she was sitting with them in front of the fire in the little cottage in Fairley.

'Now, Emma, here are the first of the shops,' Blackie announced, his voice booming out in the stillness. 'They go all the way down Town Street to Branch Road. Look, mavourneen, did I not tell ye the truth?'

Emma followed the direction of his gaze, her eyes wide with excitement, her sadness pushed to one side. 'Yes, you did,' she conceded. They passed the fishmonger's, the haberdasher's, the chemist's, and the grand ladies' dress establishment, and Emma recognized that this was indeed a fine shopping area. She was enormously intrigued and an idea was germinating. It will be easier to get a shop here. Rents will be cheaper than in Leeds, she reasoned logically. Maybe I can open my first shop in Armley, after the baby comes. And it would be a start. She was so enthusiastic about this idea that by the time they reached the street where Laura Spencer lived she already had the shop and was envisioning its diverse merchandise. Blackie might call her Doubting Emma, but she certainly had no doubts about one thing – her ultimate success. Her first shop *would* be in Armley and she would assiduously court the carriage trade. That was where the money was. Blackie had said so himself.

They walked along the street of terraced houses, all of them neat and respectable with their green painted doors, shining windows, trim gardens, and black iron gates. Just before they reached Laura Spencer's house a thought struck Emma. She stopped and grabbed Blackie's arm. 'What have you told Laura about me?' she asked.

Blackie gazed down at her, a faintly surprised look on his face. 'Why, exactly what ye told me to tell her,' he responded quietly. 'The same story ye told everybody, right down to the last detail, *Mrs* Harte, sailor's wife, expectant mother, dear friend of Blackie O'Neill.' Emma smiled with relief and nodded, and they went up the garden path together. She wondered what Laura was like, but in a sense that hardly mattered to her. The important thing was that *she* made a good impression on Laura.

Emma now realized that Blackie had confided very little about his friend and she did not know what to expect as they stood on the front step. She certainly wasn't prepared for the girl who opened the door and greeted them so charmingly, and with undisguised delight. Laura Spencer had the shining and tranquil face of a Madonna, and there was an expression of such trust in her eyes, and her smile was so loving, and so sweet, it was at once apparent to Emma that she was confronting someone who was unquestionably different from anyone else she had ever met.

Laura ushered them into the house, exclaiming on the rawness of the weather, sympathizing about the long cold journey they had just endured, her genuine concern for their well-being obvious. She took their coats, scarves, and Emma's tam-o'-shanter and hung them on the hat-stand near the door, and then drew them into the parlour, moving with infinite grace as she led them to chairs grouped around a roaring fire.

Now Laura took hold of Emma's hands as she said, 'I'm so happy to meet you, Emma. Blackie has told me such lovely things about you. Goodness, your hands are cold! Sit here and get the chill out of your bones, dear.'

Emma said, 'I'm glad to meet you, too, Laura.' Without appearing to rudely scrutinize the room Emma swiftly took in the subdued blue-and-white-striped wallpaper, the heavy blue velvet curtains at the windows, the few pieces of mahogany furniture, scant but gleaming with beeswax, and the attractiveness of the other furnishings. The room was small but neat, and not at all cluttered like Mrs Daniel's hideous front parlour. An air of solidness and comfort prevailed.

Laura said to them both apologetically, 'I am so sorry I wasn't all prepared for you, but I had to visit a sick friend and I was delayed longer than I anticipated. I just got in a little while before you arrived. Anyway, the tea will be ready shortly, and the kettle's boiling.'

Blackie said, 'That's all right, Laura. Don't fuss yeself. We're in no hurry, so take ye time, love.' This was uttered so softly and so temperately Emma's eyes flew to Blackie with quickening interest. She discerned a marked difference in his demeanour, which was restrained, and there was a look of mingled gentleness and respect on his face. This did not surprise Emma. She had already perceived that Laura's refined manner was bound to bring out the best in other people.

'Please excuse me for a moment or two,' Laura continued in her soft voice, placing the remainder of the china on the table. 'I have a few last-minute things to do in the kitchen.'

Blackie and Emma murmured their assent and Blackie said, 'Do ye mind if I smoke me pipe, Laura?' She was halfway across the floor and she turned and shook her head, her eyes filling with laughter. 'No, of course not. Please make yourself at home, and you too, Emma.'

From her vantage point near the fireplace, Emma could see Laura in the small kitchen that adjoined the parlour. She was wearing a pale blue woollen dress with a full skirt, long sleeves, and a large white Quaker collar, and although the dress was a little worn and darned in places, its simplicity and pristine colours added to the impression of immaculateness and virtue she conveyed. She's beautiful, Emma thought, intrigued by the tall, slender girl who appeared to be surrounded by an aura of spirituality.

Laura Spencer's features were so classically drawn, so fragile, and the bones were so fine, her face seemed attenuated at times. There were those, who were undiscerning, who considered her plain and faded and they would not have agreed with Emma at all. But Emma saw the Dresden china-like delicacy of the features that contributed so much to her exquisiteness, saw the golden lights in her honey-coloured hair that gave it a shimmering iridescence, saw the tenderness and wisdom that filled the enormous hazel eyes with a radiant luminosity. And she recognized Laura's loveliness for what it truly was – an outward reflection of purity.

Emma was not wrong in these assessments. There *was* indeed something special about Laura Spencer. Very simply, she refused to countenance evil. Laura was a Roman Catholic and unwavering in her faith; her religion, which she never discussed or inflicted on her friends, was the mainspring of her life. To Laura, God was neither nebulous nor remote. His presence was constant, eternal and everlasting.

Sitting there in that cosy parlour, listening to Laura's light voice echoing out from the kitchen, Emma was not yet entirely aware of all of this. But somehow, in some curious fashion, Laura's inner grace had mysteriously communicated itself to her, and she was experiencing a sense of peace so profound she was startled. Emma continued to gaze at Laura and she thought: *I want her to be my friend. I want her to like me. I want to share this house with her.*

'Ye are very quiet, mavourneen,' Blackie said. 'That's a bit unusual for ye, I am thinking. Ye are generally such a chatterbox.'

Emma jumped. He had startled her. 'I was just thinking,' she responded. Blackie smiled and puffed on his pipe. Emma was just as captivated by Laura as he had anticipated, and he was delighted.

'Could you bring the kettle into the kitchen, please, Blackie,' Laura called, 'so I can mash the tea.'

'Sure and I can, mavourneen,' he exclaimed. He lifted the steaming copper kettle off the hob and strode across the room, a towering bulk in that small space.

'Can I do anything?' Emma inquired eagerly, also rising.

Laura looked around the kitchen door. 'No, thank you, Emma. It's all ready now.' Within seconds she came into the parlour carrying a large tray containing plates of food and Blackie followed with the teapot.

As she sat down, Emma thought how nicely Laura had arranged the table. 'You are very artistic, Laura. The table looks lovely,' Emma volunteered. She smiled at Laura, who seemed pleased at this shyly offered compliment.

'Aye, 'tis a feast fit for kings, sure and it is,' Blackie said, also regarding the table. 'But ye shouldn't have made such a spread or gone to all this trouble, Laura. Ye have enough to do with all ye church work and charities.'

'It was no bother, Blackie. You know I like cooking. And I enjoy having visitors. Now, come along. Help yourselves. You must both be hungry after that chilly trip from Leeds. I'm sure you've worked up an appetite, Blackie.'

'Aye, I have that,' he responded, and helped himself to a sandwich. Something of Blackie's natural exuberance flowed to the surface during the tea and he kept the girls giggling at his stories, as was his artful way when he wanted to be entertaining. The actor in him could never be suppressed for long, and he became so volatile neither Emma nor Laura could get a word in edgewise. Laura, however, did respond swiftly to some of his more outrageous pronouncements, and Emma realized this gentle girl was blessed with a sense of humour in spite of her basic seriousness, and that mild manner belied a stringent wit.

For her part, Laura Spencer was impressed with Emma. She had been initially startled by her striking beauty, but while she had prepared the tea, Laura had observed her discreetly, and she had quickly become aware of the younger girl's pleasant yet dignified manner. She had also detected the intelligence in those matchless green eyes and the refinement in the oval face. Blackie had told her that Emma lived in a small uncomfortable attic and spent hours walking to and from work. He was worried about her health. And no wonder, Laura thought. She needs a little mothering at a time like this: seven months pregnant and utterly alone. She was filled with a rush of sisterly warmth for Emma.

As the tea progressed, Blackie pondered about the two girls who flanked him at the tea table. He loved them both, albeit in wholly different ways, and he was gratified that they had taken a liking to each other. He had known they would, even though they were exact opposites physically, and in temperament. He stole a look at Laura, who was wiping her vulnerable mouth with her serviette. There she was, all porcelain fragility, retiring, spiritual Laura, who was utterly selfless in so many ways. He glanced at Emma out of the corner of his eye. Next to Laura's gentle loveliness, Emma's beauty seemed fierce and wild; there was something frightening about her, and he had long suspected she might turn out to be ruthless and expedient, if that was ever necessary. And yet, in spite of their intrinsic difference, they shared several common traits – integrity, courage, and compassion. Perhaps those things will bind them in friendship, he thought. Also, even though Laura, at twenty-one, was only a few years older than Emma, Blackie believed she would look after her in an affectionate and motherly way. Likewise, he sensed that Emma's spirited and vivacious presence in the house would help to assuage the loneliness Laura had felt since her mother's death four months ago. He hoped so.

Emma was talking enthusiastically to Laura about the tailoring trade and Kallinski's workshop, and her vibrant voice caught his attention. Blackie turned to look at Emma. In the roseate glow of the parlour her animated face blazed with life. Her looks would blind any man, he said to himself. Then he wondered, as he had so often lately, who it was she had blinded seven or eight months ago. He still had not dared to ask her who the father of her child really was. He crushed down on that disturbing thought and turned his attention to the matter at hand – how to broach the subject of Emma moving in with Laura, and going to work at Thompson's mill.

Almost as if she had read his mind, he heard Laura say, 'You sound as if you really love the tailoring trade, Emma. And you've certainly mastered it quickly, from what I hear. I'm sure you would have no trouble learning to weave –' Laura paused, as always not wanting to appear presumptuous or forward.

'Is weaving very difficult?' Emma asked cautiously.

'No not really. Not when you've got the hang of it and understand the process. I don't think *you* would find it hard, Emma. Honestly I don't.'

Emma glanced swiftly at Blackie and then turned back to Laura and said, 'Can you get me a job at Thompson's? Are you *sure*?'

'Yes, I am positive!' Laura exclaimed. 'I spoke to the foreman the other day, and you can start any time you want. They are looking for new girls to train. You'd go on the looms right away, as a learner, of course.'

Emma pondered this for a split second and made up her mind. She plunged right in. 'Would you be willing to let me share the house with you, Laura? I won't be any trouble and I'll pay my way.' Her gaze did not stray from Laura.

Laura's angelic face broke into a delighted smile and her fine hazel eyes lit up. 'Of course, Emma. I would love to have you. Anyway, I can't really afford to keep this house on alone, but I am reluctant to give it up. I've lived here most of my life. Apart from that, you would be wonderful company for me. I've been looking for someone congenial and pleasant like you.' She leaned forward and squeezed Emma's arm affectionately, and in a reassuring way. 'And also, I think you would be better off here with me, what with the baby due in two months. I can look after you, Emma. And I know Blackie agrees –'

'I do that!' interjected Blackie, pleased with the turn of events.

'Do let me show you the rest of the house, and the room you would have, Emma,' Laura suggested. She led the way up the steep and narrow staircase. Laura opened a door on the landing. 'This would be yours, Emma,' she announced with a bright smile. She swept in ahead of them and lighted a candle on the dresser.

'Now, isn't this nice and comfy!' Blackie stated, hovering in the doorway. He pushed Emma forward.

Emma looked back at him. 'Yes, it is,' she said. Taking up most of the space was a large brass bed covered with a patchwork quilt. The walls were white, and there was even a clipped rug on the floor by the bed.

'This was my parents' room,' Laura said. She then added, rather shyly, 'I thought you would like it, Emma. Since it's large, and has a double bed, your husband could stay here when he's home on leave.' Emma opened her mouth and instantly shut it when she saw Blackie's face.

Blackie said, 'Er – er – well, he's not due to come home for a long while yet. A *very* long while. He's at sea. So, we don't have to be worrying about that!' He looked around, desperately wondering how to change the subject, and continued rapidly, in a rush of words, 'Now, Emma, do ye not see that space over there by the window? Between the wardrobe and the washstand? Ye could be fixing up a sewing table there and making the dresses for the ladies, like ye said ye wanted to. Laura wouldn't be minding. Would ye, Laura, me love?' He hoped he had managed to avert an awkward discussion about that damned imaginary husband of Emma's.

'No, not at all. It won't disturb me.' Laura glanced at Emma, who was surveying the room, a crease still puckering her smooth brow. Laura thought with dismay: Oh, dear. She doesn't like the house. But being unwilling to influence Emma in any way, she was prompted to say, 'It's a bit cold up here. Shall we go downstairs? You can let me know later, Emma. You don't have to make up your mind now.'

Emma saw the flicker of consternation on Laura's face and she grasped her arm. 'I like the room! Really I do! I would love to share the house with you. That is, if I can afford it, Laura.'

The three of them trooped back to the parlour. Blackie threw logs on to the fire and Laura got out her housekeeping accounts book. She joined Blackie and Emma in front of the hearth. 'The rent is four shillings a week, so your half would be two shillings, Emma. Then there is the cost of the logs and the coal in winter and the paraffin for the lamps. If you could split that with me I would be most grateful. Altogether, it will come to about five shillings a week in winter. But it will be less in summer.'

'Five shillings!' Emma exclaimed.

Laura stared at her, a worried expression flooding her eyes again. 'Oh, dear. Is that too much? Perhaps I can –'

'No, it's not too much,' Emma interrupted. 'I expected it to be more. It's certainly very fair. Why, I pay three shillings a week for the attic at Mrs Daniel's.'

Laura looked at Emma askance, and Blackie roared, 'I always told ye that bloody woman was robbing ye blind, and ye wouldn't pay no mind to me! Ah, Emma! Ye should have moved in with Laura weeks ago, like I was begging ye to.'

'Hush, Blackie. Don't get so excited,' Laura said lightly but with firmness. She handed the housekeeping book to Emma. 'You can see all the figures for yourself. I want you to know what everything costs.'

Emma did not want to take the book, but Laura forced it on her. She gave it the most cursory of glances, for she knew this girl would not attempt to make money out of her. After a moment she handed it back. 'Laura, please! I don't have to go through all these figures. I know you are scrupulous. In fact, maybe you are not charging me enough. I don't want you to be out of pocket.'

Laura said, 'Yes, it is enough. Really it is.' She returned the accounts book to the sideboard drawer and went on, 'Did Blackie tell you that you're not paid for the first month, while you are learning to weave?' Emma nodded. Laura cleared her throat and looked at Emma carefully, then she said, 'Well, for that first month you don't have to pay me anything.'

'No, I can't do that. It wouldn't be right,' Emma cried.

Laura was adamant. 'I will not take money from you when you're not earning, Emma.' The older girl saw the immense pride flaring on Emma's face and, understanding that she did not want to accept charity, and not wishing to embarrass her further, Laura remarked quietly, 'Just give me the two shillings for the rent. That's a happy medium.' Emma reluctantly agreed, so as not to offend Laura, although she was determined to pay her the whole of the five shillings. She would take it out of her savings.

'It's all settled, then. Emma will move in next Saturday. I shall bring her meself, sure and I will!' declared Blackie, now taking charge. He beamed at them both. 'Ye see, I was right all along. I knew it would work out and that ye would be liking each other.'

Emma smiled but made no comment. She was happy she had made the decision

308

to move to Armley, to share Laura Spencer's house. A strange pervading sense of peace settled over her again, and she relaxed in the chair, feeling suddenly at ease and more sure of the future than she had been for a long time. Everything was going to be all right. She knew that now. Emma was not aware of it at that moment, but she was never to forget that first encounter with Laura Spencer as long as she lived. Over the years she grew to realize that Laura was the only truly good person she had ever known, and she loved her deeply.

The following Friday Emma said a sad farewell to her fellow workers at the tailoring shop, who were sorry to see her leave, and to all of the Kallinskis, with whom she had Sabbath dinner at Janessa's insistence. After dinner Janessa took Emma to one side. 'I want you to promise me that you will come to me if you need anything in the next few months,' she said. 'Armley is not so far away and I can soon be there.'

'Oh, Mrs Kallinski, that's lovely of you. Thank you. I promise I will.'

It was a tearful parting and only David seemed undismayed. He knew their paths would cross again. He intended to make sure of that. Emma gave him her address in Armley and he extracted a faithful promise from her to write as soon as she was settled. Even Mrs Daniel had tears in her eyes when Emma left and she, too, asked her to stay in touch.

On Monday morning Laura took her to Thompson's mill. From the moment she entered it, Emma hated that place as fiercely as she had loved Abraham Kallinski's little factory. No camaraderie here. No jokes and laughter. Rigid discipline reigned, and the gaffers were harsh and demanding as they walked up and down between the looms. Emma instantly loathed the stench of the oily raw wool and was deafened by the unceasing rattling of the shuttles; on her third day there she was totally unnerved when she witnessed a shuttle fly off and strike a girl in the face, scarring her for life, an accident that was not unusual.

Laura was a good teacher, patient and explicit in her instructions; nevertheless, Emma found the weaving process difficult and she was terrified of getting a 'trap', which occurred when a hundred or so threads broke on the loom. A 'trap' took hours to repair. These were precious hours lost, and the weaver had to work furiously to make up the lost time. But Emma was careful and she never did have a 'trap' as long as she worked at the mill.

In her diligent way she persevered, for she was determined that nothing was going to get the better of her; she also knew she had no alternative but to prove herself a competent weaver in order to earn a living. With her singlemindedness, her fast mind and nimble fingers, she mastered the craft of weaving within the month, as Laura had predicted she would. Her self-confidence grew as her expertise increased, yet she still disliked working in that cheerless and rigidly controlled environment.

She and Laura started at six o'clock in the morning and finished at six at night, interminable and dreary days to Emma. As the weeks dragged on she grew heavier with child and increasingly weary and exhausted. To her dismay, her legs continually swelled up from standing long hours at the loom, and she often thought that the baby would be born right there at her feet on the mill floor. However, Laura was a great comfort to her and Emma constantly marvelled at her good humour, and she never ceased to wonder what she would have done without Laura's staunch support and her devotion.

One Tuesday evening, towards the end of March, Emma knew the baby was coming and Laura took her into St Mary's Hospital at Hill Top. After ten hours in labour she gave birth to her child, exactly one month to the day before her own seventeenth birthday. To Emma's joy it was a girl.

THIRTY-ONE

Emma sat in front of the fire in the parlour of Laura's house, staring morosely into space, her mind weighted down with a problem; a problem that pushed all else to one side. She had lived with it for the last few days, ever since the baby had been born. Now she knew it must be solved, and imminently. Emma had many imperatives, but taking precedence was her concern for her child. It was essential that she make a decision about the baby's immediate future. She could not afford to procrastinate.

Emma shivered, suddenly aware of a coldness in her legs, a numbing aching in her bones. She bestirred herself heavily, not as swift of movement as usual, picked up the poker and drove it into the logs in the fireplace, angrily as if to ventilate her sense of helplessness. The logs fell apart, sputtered, and flooded the room with the brightest of lights that illuminated its shining neatness, its cosy comfort.

The light glanced across the child lying at her feet in the makeshift cot, which Laura had fashioned out of a drawer and had lined with thick blankets and downy pillows. The baby lay on her side, her fluff of silver-blonde hair shimmering in the firelight, her round pink face turned to Emma, her tiny hand curled in a miniature fist next to her delicate mouth. She slept in perfect peace. This child was hers. *Part of her*. How could she ever give her up? Quite unexpectedly, a fierce sense of protectiveness invaded Emma and that single-mindedness of purpose to succeed, to rise above her circumstances, was strongly reinforced. 'I won't let anything happen to you!' she whispered softly but with vehemence to the sleeping child. 'I won't! And you'll have the best that money can buy. I promise you that!'

Emma continued to observe her daughter, now four days old, for a few moments longer and then she turned back to the fire. *No sacrifice she could ever make would be too great if it ensured the security and well-being of her baby*. Eventually she picked up the flannel nightgown she was making, determined not to dwell on the future. She began to sew. One step at a time. One day at a time. Slowly. Slowly. Building as you go along. That is the only way.

As she continued to ply her perfect stitches, an aura of total dejection, abnormal for Emma, enveloped her. She knew she could not keep the baby with her, even though she longed to do so. She had to work at the mill to earn a living and there was no one available to care for the child during the day. Emma would not countenance the idea of adoption or an orphanage. There was only one other solution. Emma was not particularly happy about this alternative; however, she had come to the realization, after several sleepless nights, that she really had no choice.

She turned the problem of the baby over in her mind yet again, wrestling with the advantages and disadvantages of the scheme she had concocted, diverse thoughts racing through her head as swiftly as her needle flew along the hem of the nightgown.

'Hello! Hello! Anybody home?'

Startled, Emma looked up quickly. The door had opened to admit Blackie O'Neill. It was a brisk March day outside and the wind had whipped the rosiest of tints into his perennially tanned cheeks and ruffled his black hair into a mass of dancing curls. He had a happy-go-lucky air about him and, to Emma, he seemed considerably pleased with himself. He was carrying several packages.

'Blackie! I didn't expect you so soon!' Emma exclaimed in surprise. She put down the sewing and stood up, automatically smoothing her immaculate hair.

Blackie grinned and deposited the parcels on the table. He pulled Emma to him and wrapped his huge arms around her, hugging her tightly, and with a show of great affection. 'Well, ye be looking the picture of health and beauty after ye confinement,' he remarked, staring at her appraisingly. Emma forced a smile, attempting to conceal her disquiet, but she said nothing. Seemingly unconscious of her dispirited mood, Blackie went on enthusiastically, 'I brought a few presents for the bairn. Trifles ye might be liking.' He indicated the items on the table.

'Oh, Blackie, you're too generous! You *mustn't* spend all your money on the baby. You bought the shawl only the other week.'

'That's what money is for, I am thinking. To be spent.' He shrugged out of his topcoat and went to hang it on the stand in the doorway. 'Me and me Uncle Pat are doing better than ever. We got three important jobs this week, and we'll be having to take on more men. Aye, success is in the air for the O'Neills.' He turned and winked at Emma. 'Anyway, I had a bit of a windfall yesterday, so to speak. Backed the winner at Doncaster races. That I did, mavourneen. I had a pound each way, at twenty to one, and made quite a bundle. So, this morning, I thought to meself: Since ye are a flush, boyo, this week, with a bit of extra money in ye pocket, Blackie O'Neill, ye must be sharing ye good fortune with Emma. And I took meself off at once to Briggate and bought a few things for me darlin' Tinker Bell.'

'I'm glad you won, Blackie. But shouldn't you be saving your money so you can build that grand house you're always talking about?' suggested the pragmatic Emma.

Blackie was amused. He shrugged. 'I'll be having me Georgian house one day, Emma. And the few shillings I've spent today won't be making all that much difference.' He lowered his enormous frame and knelt on the floor next to the cot. He peeped at the baby. 'And isn't she the most darlin' thing!' He smoothed the cot blanket with infinite care. 'A little cherub, sure and she is.' The baby moved and opened her eyes, blinking her long silvery lashes. She gurgled and kicked her legs under the coverlet. Blackie's eyes lit up. 'Look, mavourneen! I do believe she be recognizing her Uncle Blackie already. Sure and she does!'

'It seems she does. And she is a sweet baby, Blackie, and good, too. She hasn't cried at all since I've been home from the hospital.' Emma now glanced at the table. 'Thank you for the presents, Blackie.'

'Hush!' cried Blackie, straightening up. 'Come on, Emma. Open them. Start with this.' He handed her the largest package. Emma sat down in the chair, and unwrapped it. 'Why, Blackie, this is just lovely,' she exclaimed, lifting out a pink knitted coat trimmed with pink ribbons.

Blackie beamed. 'Here's the bonnet and a pair of booties to match,' he said, offering her another parcel. 'I hope they will all be fitting her. I had to be guessing the size, since I'm not accustomed to buying things for such a wee mite.' He looked at Emma anxiously. 'Do you think they are all right then?'

'They are perfect. *Really perfect*. Thank you, Blackie.'

'Unwrap this. It's the last,' he said. 'Not as practical as the coat and bonnet, I am thinking. But necessary, in a way. Tinker Bell has to have a few toys, ye know, mavourneen.'

Emma pulled the paper off excitedly and held up the fluffy white lamb which sported a large pink bow and a bell at its neck. 'Oh, isn't it sweet! And you bought a rattle as well.' She shook the polished bone ring, which also had a bell attached, and then placed the lamb and the rattle in the cot next to the baby. She stood up and kissed Blackie. 'Thank you, Blackie. You're so good to us.' Emma was touched by his thoughtfulness and the obvious care he had taken in selecting the clothes and the toys.

'Aay, it's nothing at all, me love,' he said, and glanced around. 'And where might Laura be?'

'There's a jumble sale at the Catholic church this afternoon and she's looking after one of the stalls. She'll be back in time for tea. You are staying, aren't you? We expected you to.'

'Sure and I am.' He settled himself in the chair opposite Emma and fished around in his pocket for his cigarettes. After he had lit one he said, 'And when do ye have to go back to the mill, mavourneen?'

Emma did not answer for a moment and then she lifted her head slowly. 'I can please myself. The foreman told Laura I could have the whole week off, after I came out of hospital. We're not so busy right now, and it doesn't matter to the mill either way, since I'm paid by the piece. They don't have to pay my wage when I'm not working.'

'Are ye going to take next week off? I think ye should,' Blackie remarked, eyeing her closely.

'So does Laura. She worries about my health. But I feel very well. I do really, Blackie. I could go back on Monday but –' Her voice trailed off and she examined the sewing, finishing thoughtfully, 'I don't think I will, though. I've things to do next week.' Emma dropped her eyes, not elucidating further. Blackie did not want to pry, knowing this would irritate her. Emma was not always given to making confidences, and he had learned not to question her unduly.

After a moment Emma said, 'So business is good, is it?'

'Aye, it is, colleen! And do ye know, I am drawing up me first plans for me first house, one of me own design.' He laughed wryly. 'Well, it's not a *whole* house, just a wing we are to build on to an existing house for a customer in Headingley. The gentleman that owns it, a real toff I might be adding, liked me ideas, and he told me to go ahead and to be making me plans. Them night-school classes in draftsmanship are going to be paying off. Ye'll see, mavourneen.'

'That's wonderful, Blackie.'

This was said somewhat listlessly, and Blackie was at once aware of her closed face, her obvious lack of interest. He studied her carefully and saw the dark glint in her green eyes, the grim expression on her lips. No, not grim. Miserable, he decided. He wondered what was disturbing her, but again refrained from asking any questions. As he continued to expound about the wing of the house he was to design and build, Blackie continued to watch her out of the corner of his eye. Finally he could not prevent himself saying, 'Why are ye looking so gloomy, me love? That's not like ye.' She did not respond. 'Nay, Emma, ye've got a face like a wet week. What's upsetting ye?'

'Oh, nothing, really –' She hesitated and then blurted out against her will. 'I'm a bit concerned about the baby not being christened.'

Blackie was flabbergasted. He stared at her uncomprehendingly and threw back his head and roared with laughter. Emma looked hurt, but he could not help it. 'Concerned about the baby not being christened!' he echoed, trying to swallow the last of his merriment. 'I can't believe me own ears, Emma. Why should that matter to ye? After all, ye've been telling me for months that ye are an atheist.'

'I am! I haven't changed my mind about *that*,' Emma cried. 'But I don't feel right about it. Not having her christened. The baby might believe in God when she grows up, and then she might hold it against me if she ever finds out she wasn't baptized.'

He could see she was in real earnest and so he said, 'Why don't ye go to see the vicar of Christ Church and arrange –'

'Oh, I couldn't do that,' Emma interjected harshly, fixing him with a cold stare. 'The vicar would want her birth certificate, that's customary, and he'd see straight-away that the baby is – is – illegitimate, and then he wouldn't do it. Besides, I don't want him, or anyone else, knowing my business.'

'Well, Emma, if ye don't go to Christ Church, I don't know what ye can do. There's no solution I can think of. Ye can't have her christened, and that's that!'

'Yes, I know. I wouldn't have mentioned it to you if you hadn't asked me why I was gloomy. And you're right, there's nothing to be done. I shall just have to hope the baby isn't angry with me one day.'

If the child's ever angry it will be about her illegitimacy and not her baptism, or rather lack of it, Blackie thought. But he said, 'Ye are such a contradiction, mavourneen mine. But look here, Emma, if it's that important to ye, why don't we take the baby to a church in another part of Leeds? One where ye are not likely to be knowing anybody, and have her christened there. Then it won't matter about anybody seeing the birth certificate.'

'No! No! I don't want a soul to know she's illegitimate,' Emma snapped. Suddenly an idea occurred to Blackie. A marvellous idea. 'I've got it! We'll have our own christening! Right here and now!' He leapt up and strode purposefully to the sink in the kitchen. 'Leeds Corporation water is as good as any for a baptism, I am thinking,' he shouted gaily. 'Bring me a bowl.'

'What do you mean by "have our own christening"? I don't understand.' Her brow puckered into a frown.

'Since ye are so troubled about the bairn not being baptized, I meself am going to it. *Now*. Bring her over to the sink. Come on,' he urged, standing in the kitchen doorway.

Total disbelief flickered on to Emma's face. 'You do it! But would it be proper? Would it be a *real* christening, I mean?'

'Sure and it would. Do as I say,' Blackie commanded. 'I can do just as good a

313

job as a vicar, or a priest, for that matter. Even though I am a lapsed Catholic I still believe in God, ye know. I might not be going to the church, Emma, but I never lost me faith. *Never.* Be sure of that. And God lives within all of us. That is my true belief. I feel Him in me heart, and that's what's most important. To feel His love and His presence eternally with us.'

Although Emma was astonished, she knew that he meant every word he said.

Blackie continued in a tender voice, 'I don't think He will be angry that I am taking matters into me own hands, in this emergency. And He will accept her as one of His blessed children, Emma. Sure and He will. His own son, Jesus, said, "Suffer little children to come unto me, and forbid them not; for of such is the kingdom of God." Please, believe me, it's the baptism and the spirit of love behind it that counts, and not the man that does it, or where it's done. We need neither a church nor a font, Emma.'

'I believe you, Blackie. I want you to christen the baby.'

'That's my Emma,' said Blackie. 'Now, pick up the baby and bring her over here.' Blackie occupied himself at the sink, preparing the bowl of tepid water, and then he hurried across to the sideboard and pulled open a drawer, searching for a towel.

Emma now lifted the baby out of the makeshift cot and cradled her in her arms, stroking her small face and cooing to her. 'Oh, my sweet little girl,' Emma exclaimed, entranced with the child. Unexpectedly Edwin Fairley's face flashed before her eyes. If only Edwin had not been so cruel. If only Edwin could see the baby now, he would love her as I do. To her horror, Emma found she could not expunge his face, or his name. She had not thought of him for weeks and then only with the most intense hatred. He had barely crossed her mind when the baby was born. Emma was so involved with these unparalleled thoughts of Edwin Fairley that she became distracted and her guard was lowered.

Blackie was calling from the other side of the room, 'And what will ye be calling Tinker Bell, then? Have ye thought of a name?'

So preoccupied was Emma, she did not think twice. Edwin's name was on the tip of her tongue and she said automatically, thoughtlessly, 'Edwina –' As that name fell from her lips Emma froze by the sink, so aghast was she at her own carelessness. What made me say that name? she wondered, furious with herself. She had never had any intention of calling the baby after Edwin. She had decided to name the baby Laura weeks ago. Emma felt as if the blood was draining out of her.

Blackie's jaw had dropped open and he was staring at her back. He could see that she held herself tensely and her shoulder blades were protruding through the thin silk of the white blouse she was wearing. He repeated the name Edwina to himself and then, without having to give it a second thought, he knew who the father of her child was. Edwin Fairley. There was no doubt in his mind about that. Everything fell neatly into place. Why had he not thought of Edwin before? It was so obvious. And he had been suspicious of her story for months, convinced that the fastidious Emma would not have entangled herself with a village yokel. Blackie's heart ached for Emma and he longed to console her. But he held himself in check. Although her face was turned away from him, Blackie was now acutely conscious of her embarrassment and he guessed that she had just made a dreadful slip of the tongue. He was positive she had never meant to call the child Edwina. Why

314

would she so blatantly spell it out for him? No, the canny Emma would never do that. It had been a mistake she could not now gracefully correct.

And so Blackie adopted an unconcerned tone and said, with a show of gaiety, 'And where did ye find such an *elegant* name, mavourneen? In one of them illustrated magazines, I am thinking. Sure and it is real fancy, but very fitting for me darlin' Tinker Bell. I like it. Sure and I do.'

Emma nodded, not trusting herself to speak. Blackie fussed with the towel, draping it over his arm, and then he tested the water, taking his time so that she could regain her composure. 'Now then, I'm ready,' he said with a bright smile. 'Hold the babe forward, Emma . . . Yes, that's right. Good, mavourneen.'

Somewhat recovered, Emma said, 'Her full name is to be Ed – Edwina.' She almost faltered, then swallowed and went on more steadily, 'Laura Shane –'

'Shane!' interrupted Blackie, his surprise evident.

'Yes, after you. I can't very well call her Desmond or Patrick, and Blackie would seem odd, now wouldn't it?'

Blackie chuckled. 'True! True! Well, 'tis flattered that I am and right pleased, Emma. So, let's commence.' He dipped his fingers in the bowl of water with a flourish and made the sign of the cross on the baby's forehead.

'Wait a minute,' Emma exclaimed, her eyes stretching widely. 'I'm not a Roman Catholic and neither is the baby. In the Church of England the vicar just sprinkles the water on in drips. He doesn't make a cross. We must do it properly. Start again, please.'

Blackie bit back a smile. For a so-called atheist she was being mighty particular. 'Sure and I understand, Emma.' He wiped the cross off the baby's brow with the towel and resumed. Once again he dipped his large brown fingers in the water and ceremoniously sprinkled a few drops on the child, who stared up at him unblinkingly.

'I christen thee Edwina Laura Shane Harte. In the name of God the Father, the Son, and the Holy Ghost.' Blackie crossed himself and then he bent down and kissed the baby. He smiled at Emma, and kissed her, too. 'There ye are, mavourneen. The baby is christened. Does that make ye feel happier?'

'Yes, Blackie. Thank you. It was beautiful. And just look at the baby. She's smiling again and she didn't even cry when you dropped the water on her. I'm going to make sure she has a good life. The best of everything, Blackie.' She turned her face to his and her gaze was solemn. 'She'll have the most beautiful clothes and go to the best schools and she'll be a real lady. I'm going to make sure of that. Nothing is going to stop me.' The serious expression eased into a tender smile. 'I wonder what she'll look like when she's older, Blackie. What do you think?'

A Fairley, that's a certainty, Blackie mused, regarding the child objectively. The signs were already there, as young as she was. He said, 'She'll be lovely, Emma. Aye, she will indeed. But put her back in the cot, and get out Laura's bottle of port wine. I think the least we can do is to be drinking a toast to the baby.'

'Oh, Blackie, do you think that's all right? Laura might be annoyed if we dip into her –'

'Don't be silly, Emma,' Blackie cried through his laughter. 'She won't care. And anyway, I'll go out later to the off-licence and buy another bottle. We have to be toasting Edwina, ye know. It's the custom.'

Emma nodded and did as he asked. They toasted the baby with the ruby port, which Emma had poured into two small glasses. 'May she be healthy, wealthy, and wise,' pronounced Blackie, taking a sip, 'and I won't be adding beautiful, for we know she'll be taking after her mother!'

Emma smiled at him with great fondness, and they sat down in front of the fire, drinking the wine, lost in their own thoughts. After a short while Emma said, 'We can't tell Laura about the christening. She wouldn't approve. She wouldn't think it proper. She'd also wonder why I didn't go to the church.'

Blackie nodded and frowned. 'Aye, ye are right about that. Still, what are ye going to be telling her, Emma? After all, she doesn't know the truth. She'll be thinking it funny if ye don't have the bairn baptized.'

'I'll tell her I'm having it done in Ripon,' said Emma, recognizing as she spoke that she had finally made her decision about the baby's immediate future.

'Ripon! Why there?' Blackie threw her a curious glance.

Emma looked at him carefully, cleared her throat, and said softly, 'Because that's where I'm going next week with the baby. I'm taking her to my cousin Freda's.' Blackie seemed baffled and Emma explained quickly. 'She will live there with my cousin. You know I can't keep the baby with me when I have to work. You said that yourself months ago.'

Blackie's eyes narrowed. 'Have ye been in touch with ye cousin, then? Has she agreed to take Edwina in?'

'No. I was afraid to write, in case she turned me down. But if I arrive there with the baby I know she won't do that,' Emma said, speaking in the most assured voice she could summon. 'Freda's a good woman, Blackie, and she was very close to my mother, even though she is much younger. She's a motherly sort and she loves children. She has two little ones of her own. I just know she won't refuse me when she sees the baby. And I shall pay her for looking after Edwina.'

Blackie sighed. 'Aye, I see the practical side of the idea, but won't ye be missing the child, Emma?'

'Oh yes, I will, Blackie. I will! But as soon as I'm on my feet, I shall bring Edwina back to live with me. In the meantime, I shall go to see her once or twice a month.'

Blackie shook his head, looking sorrowful, and his Celtic soul ached that she had to be separated from her child. But he said cheerfully, 'And when do ye intend to be going to Ripon?'

Emma bit her lip. 'I shall take the baby over there next week, before I go back to work. On Thursday. I'll stay with Freda that night and all day on Friday, to be with the baby a bit longer.' She saw the dismay on his face and cried, 'I have to do it! I have no choice!' Tears were imminent and her voice shook.

'I know, Emma, I know. Don't be getting yeself upset,' Blackie responded sympathetically. He leaned forward and squeezed her arm. 'It's the wisest course under the circumstances.'

'At least she will be with a member of my family and she'll be in the fresh country air,' Emma pointed out firmly, as if to convince herself, as well as Blackie, of the wisdom of her decision.

Blackie said, 'But what about ye dad? Won't ye cousin be telling him about the baby?'

'No, she won't, if I ask her not to,' Emma countered in a confident tone, hoping she was right. 'She knows what he's like, and she'll protect me for my mother's sake. They were like sisters.' Emma looked him right in the eye and went on, 'I shall tell her the whole truth, Blackie, about the boy from the village letting me down and running off to the navy. I'll have to.'

'Aye, I expect ye will,' remarked Blackie, now convinced that the truth had been slightly bent. Then another thought struck him forcibly, and he reflected for a minute, before saying, 'Emma, ye mentioned the birth certificate before. Ye will have to go and register the bairn's birth with the registrar in Leeds, to get the certificate. And ye'll have to give the father's name. It's the law.'

Emma's face darkened with distress. She had already thought of this herself and it bothered her not a little. She held herself very still, not answering.

'I can guess what ye are thinking, mavourneen. When the registrar asks ye for the name, ye are going to say "father unknown", are ye not?'

'Yes,' she acknowledged softly.

'Aye, I knew it. Well, I think ye should be putting *me* down as the father,' he said emphatically.

Emma was thunderstruck. 'Oh, Blackie, I can't! I won't! Why should you have that responsibility?'

His piercing stare was unwavering. 'Do ye want to give the name of the *real* father, Emma?' he asked pointedly.

'No!' she exclaimed, her eyes flaring.

'Well, then, wouldn't it be better to have *my* name on the certificate? The paper will still show that she's illegitimate, I realize that. But at least a name, such as it is, would look better than "father unknown". Think on that one, mavourneen.'

'But, Blackie –'

He held up his hand to silence her and there was a reproving look on his face. 'Do ye know how often ye say "But, Blackie"? Always disagreeing with me, ye are. It's settled,' he announced in a voice that forbade argument. 'And I shall come with ye to the registrar's office, just to make sure ye be doing as I say.' He stretched out his hand and patted her arm again. 'Ye'll see, it will be fine, Emma. And I am happy to take the responsibility, as ye call it, for Tinker Bell.' He grinned crookedly. 'I mean Edwina Laura Shane. Me darlin' godchild, so to speak.'

Emma's eyes filled up. She fumbled for her handkerchief and blew her nose, striving to curb her emotions. 'You're so good, Blackie. I don't know why you do so much for me.'

'Because I care about ye, Emma, and the wee one. Somebody's got to look out for ye both in this hard world, I am thinking,' he remarked softly, his affection reflected in his bright black eyes.

'You might regret it later. I mean, regret putting your name on the birth certificate.'

Blackie laughed dismissively. 'I never regret anything I be doing, mavourneen mine. I've found regrets to be a sinful waste of time.'

A brief smile touched Emma's lips. She knew it was fruitless to attempt to dissuade him once his mind was made up. He, too, could be very stubborn. She stared into the fire reflectively. 'I must keep the birth certificate in a safe place. Locked up. Laura must never see it,' she said. Her voice was so quiet it was almost inaudible.

Blackie was not certain he had heard correctly. He leaned forward and asked, 'What was that?'

She gave him the benefit of a long knowing look. 'I said, Laura must never see the birth certificate. Because *your* name will be on it.'

'I don't care about that,' exclaimed Blackie. 'But she shouldn't see it, for the simple reason that she'd know then ye are single, and that the babe's illegitimate. Did I not tell Laura ye were married to a sailor called Winston Harte? Pack of lies I told that poor girl. Ye are forgetting things, Emma.' He sighed heavily. 'That's the trouble with lying.'

Emma flushed. 'They were only white lies. I told them for the baby's sake, and you agreed all along that I was right,' she retorted fiercely. 'And I'm not forgetting anything. I was only thinking that I must protect *you*. And I don't want Laura to be hurt. She would be, if she saw your name on the birth certificate. She might believe you really were the father.'

'So what?' Blackie demanded, further bewildered.

'Laura loves you, Blackie.'

'Loves me! Laura! That's a lot of cod's wallop, mavourneen.' He burst out laughing and shook his head disbelievingly. 'Hell could freeze over before Laura would look at *me* twice. I don't have to tell ye that she's a staunch Roman Catholic, and devout, and she knows I'm lapsed. Come on, Emma. That's a daft idea. Loves me, indeed! On the heads of the Blessed Saints I do swear ye have lost ye mind.'

Emma threw him a fond but impatient look. 'You are a great fool, Blackie O'Neill. You can't see what's staring you in the face. Of course she loves you. Very much.'

'Did she tell ye that?' he cried, his glance quizzical.

'No, she didn't. But I know she does.' Observing his sceptical expression, Emma added vehemently, 'I just *know*, deep down inside, that she does!'

Blackie could not help laughing again. 'Ye are very imaginative, Emma. Sure and ye are. I don't believe it at all, at all.'

Emma shrugged resignedly. 'You don't have to, but it's true,' she asserted strongly. 'I can tell by the way she looks at you, and talks about you sometimes. I bet if you asked her, she'd marry you.'

Blackie was stunned. A peculiar look settled on his face, one Emma could not read. Emma said hurriedly, 'You mustn't tell her I've said anything, though. She'd be upset if she thought we'd been talking about her, behind her back. And anyway, she's never actually *told* me she loves you. That's just my opinion.'

Still Blackie did not answer. Emma rose and went over to him. She touched his massive shoulder lightly and he looked up at her, his eyes suddenly twinkling. 'Promise me you won't mention it to Laura, Blackie. *Please.*'

'I promise I won't mention it to a living breathing soul,' he said, patting the small hand resting on his shoulder. Satisfied that he would keep his word, Emma nodded and glided into the kitchen. 'I've got to start preparing things for tea,' she called over her shoulder.

'Aye, mavourneen,' he said, and threw another log on the fire. Blackie settled comfortably in the wing chair and lit a cigarette, chuckling to himself from time to time, vastly amused at Emma's words and not at all convinced of their veracity. 'Tis romantic girlish notions Emma is harbouring, he thought, and drew deeply on his Woodbine. None the less, he discovered she had given him something disturbing to think about. He sat dwelling on the possibility of Laura loving him; an idea that previously had never entered his mind and one so staggering he was shaken. Slowly, numerous things Laura had said and done in the past few years came back to him with vividness; things he had considered irrelevant but which now assumed significance in the light of Emma's comments. Was Emma correct in her conjectures about Laura's involvement with him? For the life of him he did not know. Yet Emma was nobody's fool. She was perceptive and, in fact, he had often been startled at her insight into people. Bemused, he ruminated on Laura Spencer and he discovered he found it quite difficult to gauge the depth and extent of his own feelings for her. Oh, he loved her. There was no doubt about that. It was virtually impossible not to love that gentle and tenderhearted girl. But how did he love her? Was he in love with her? Did he want her for his wife, as the mother of his children? Did he want to share the rest of his life, and his bed, with her? Was it she who was the object of his masculine desire and passion? He shook his head, nonplussed, unable to isolate and understand his true feelings for Laura. And what about Emma? He loved her, too. He had always believed this had been merely a fraternal interest; now he wondered if he had unconsciously deluded himself. He remembered the night in the Mucky Duck when he had asked her to marry him, out of a sense of protectiveness; yet that night he had seen that she was a highly alluring young woman. Blackie found he was jolted into annoyance with himself. Could it be, was it conceivable, that he actually loved Emma in the way a virile man loves a woman, with all his heart and his very soul? He strove to examine, with objectivity, his emotional involvement with both girls, only to find that he was even more perplexed and confused than ever, on the horns of a dilemma. How can a man love two women at the same time? he asked himself with mounting irritation. He ran his hand through his hair distractedly. This is a fine kettle of fish, Blackie O'Neill, he said to himself. The gaze in his black and brilliant eyes was inward and contemplative, as he endeavoured to answer these disquieting questions which Emma's conversation had posed. But the answers eluded him maddeningly, and they would continue to do so for some considerable length of time.

THIRTY-TWO

The main street of Fairley village was deserted, it being two o'clock on Sunday afternoon. It was a cool April day and, as was normal at this time of year, the sky was heavy with cinereous clouds that rolled in a gathering mass along the crest of those black implacable moors which stretched in eerie silence towards the smudged horizon. The watery sun had retreated hours ago and the village looked inhospitable, the grey stone walls and slate rooftops of the cottages fusing into the forbidding semi-industrial landscape, an unrelieved etching of monotones beneath that sullen metallic sky. The wind blowing in from the nearby limestone dale country was tinged with North Sea rain and a shower was imminent. It had already poured earlier, and the roofs and cobblestones held a silvery sheen that was glassy and stark in the dismal environment.

To Emma, climbing the steep hill, the village appeared smaller than she remembered, oddly diminished, but she had broader comparisons to draw upon now, and she recognized that her eyes had become accustomed to the imposing buildings of Leeds, the fine establishments of Armley. The depressing aspects of her surroundings were dimmed, became irrelevant, for she was filled with happiness. She smiled to herself. She was looking forward to seeing her father and Frank, and this reunion, so yearningly longed for, was uppermost in her thoughts, as it had been for days. They did not know she was coming today; she had not written to announce her impending visit, wanting to give them a lovely surprise. Her anticipation was fully revealed on her eager and shining face. Frank must have grown in the past ten months, she thought. She wondered how they would look, little Frank, now thirteen, and her father. She herself had taken great pains with her appearance, before setting out that morning, determined to look her very best. This was partially prompted by her sense of pride, but also to prove to her father that she had been successful out on her own in the world. She was wearing the red silk dress and the black wool coat which had formerly belonged to Olivia Wainright, and new black button boots purchased only last week. The shopping bag she carried contained thoughtfully selected presents: socks, a shirt, and a tie for her dad, plus his favourite pipe tobacco; socks, a shirt, and writing materials for Frank, along with an edition of *David Copperfield*. And, carefully placed on top of these things there was a bunch of spring flowers for her mother's grave. She had dipped into her precious savings to buy everything, but she had done so joyfully and with love; and in her black reticule there were three crisp pound notes for her father, to help with the family expenses.

The hill was steep, but Emma climbed it easily. There was a decided bounce to her step and she felt wonderfully alive. Optimistic as she was by nature, Emma was now inordinately confident of the future.

The baby was comfortably settled with her cousin Freda in Ripon. As Emma had predicted to Blackie, Freda had been more than willing to take Edwina in, and for as long as Emma wished. If she had been surprised at Emma's unexpected arrival on her doorstep, or shocked at her story, the loving and compassionate Freda had not betrayed this at all. She had taken everything in her stride. Her welcome had been genuine and she had fussed over Emma and commented ecstatically on Edwina's prettiness and her docile temper. She had promised to care for the child as if she were her own, and had faithfully pledged to keep Emma's circumstances a secret from Jack Harte, with whom she was not on very good terms, and whom, she explained, she had not heard from since Elizabeth's death in 1904. When Emma had left Ripon to return to Armley she was in a calmer frame of mind and, although she was saddened to leave the child, her confidence in Freda, who was so like her mother, had helped to assuage her wistfulness considerably. She knew Edwina was in capable hands, and that she would be looked after and cherished with complete devotion.

Now, as she passed the White Horse halfway up the hill, Emma quickened her steps, not wishing to encounter any of the men or boys from the village, those perennial stragglers who indulged in a last pint and never left the pub before two o'clock. They might appear at any moment on their way home for a late Sunday lunch. She was only a few steps past the pub when she heard the door open and the sound of raucous voices echoing in the chilly air, as a handful of men staggered out into the street, vociferously merry with the vast amounts of beer they had consumed. Emma hurried faster.

'Emma!'

Her heart dropped and she had the urge to run, reluctant to become embroiled in a conversation or to expose herself to curious questions from the locals. She increased her pace, without looking back. Drunken louts, she thought disdainfully.

'Emma! For God's sake wait. It's *me. Winston*!'

She stopped abruptly and swung around, her face lighting up. Her elder brother, resplendent in his naval uniform, was chasing up the street after her, waving his white sailor hat in his hand, his mates forgotten. They were staring after Winston, mouths agape, ogling Emma poised on the hill. Winston panted up to her. He threw his arms around her and hugged her to him, showering her face and her hair with kisses. A warm flush of happiness swept through her and she clung to him tightly, her love for him as fierce and as real as ever. With a sharp stab she realized how much she had missed him.

After a few seconds clutched in this tight embrace, they pulled away and automatically stared at each other, their eyes searching, questioning. Emma caught her breath as she looked up at Winston. His face had always been beautiful, but in an almost girlish way. Now it was extraordinarily and staggeringly handsome. Since she had last seen him he had matured. The high cheekbones, the wide brow, the straight nose, the generous mouth, and the well-shaped chin were all as finely drawn as ever, and yet they appeared much less delicate. There was strength in his face that bespoke his enormous masculinity. And those cornflower-blue eyes, widely set below the arched black brows and fringed with thick and curling black lashes, were brighter than she remembered, positively blinding in the cold northern light. His black hair was blowing in the breeze and his perfect white teeth flashed in his fresh-complexioned face as he smiled at her. He had grown and filled out. He was practically as tall as their father, and wide-shouldered and muscular. He's too handsome for his own good, Emma thought. Women must adore him but men must surely hate him, she decided, and then wondered how many girls had already fallen at his feet, how many broken hearts lay scattered in his ports of call. He would be irresistible to the opposite sex, she saw that only too clearly. She marvelled to herself that this incredible specimen of manhood was her brother; the skinny, hot-tempered boy who had teased her unmercifully, pulled her hair, quarrelled with her and fought her, but who had always been her staunch ally when necessary, and whom she had never ceased to secretly worship.

Winston, gazing back at Emma, was thinking: She's changed enormously. There's something very different about her. She's more self-assured, even worldly. By God, she's a stunning girl. He corrected himself. No, Emma is a woman now, and ripe for the plucking. A feeling of jealous possessiveness raced through him, was so powerful, so searing he was shaken at the intensity of his feelings. The brightest man breathing is not good enough for my sister. And he recognized then that he truly adored her. In point of fact, that was to be the major problem all of his life. No other woman would ever measure up to his sister in his eyes.

'You look wonderful,' Emma said at last, breaking the silence, her eyes overflowing with the tenderest of lights.

'So do you, little sister,' Winston said. 'Quite grown-up, too.' He smiled at her lovingly and with pride, and then the smile congealed. His joy was dampened when he remembered how poor little Frank had grieved for Emma, was still grieving for her, and a furious glint entered those startling eyes. He grabbed her arm roughly.

'Hey, our Emma, where the hell have you been all these months? We've been worried to death! How could you run off like that?'

There was a hidden smile on Emma's face. 'Oh, the pot's calling the kettle black, is it?'

Winston glared. 'I'm a man. That's different. You'd no business sneaking off that way. You were needed at home.'

'Don't shout, Winston,' said Emma. 'Dad knows where I've been. I've written to him regularly, and sent him money.'

Winston was scrutinizing her closely and scowling darkly. 'Yes, but you never put an address on those letters – where we could write back. That was wrong of you, Emma.'

'Dad knows I've been travelling with my lady, Mrs John Smith of Bradford. Please, Winston, don't look so angry, and let go of my arm. You're hurting me.'

'Sorry,' Winston muttered, and released his powerful grip. He took hold of her hand. 'Come on, don't let's stand here, making a spectacle of ourselves. I can see half a dozen lace curtains twitching.' He almost dragged her up to Top Fold.

'I expect you have a ship now, don't you, Winston?' asked Emma warmly, hoping to dispel her brother's belligerent mood.

'Yes,' said the laconic Winston.

Undismayed by his curtness, Emma persisted, 'Where are you stationed, Winston?'

'Scapa Flow.'

'Well, you must give me your address, so that I can write to you every week. Would you like me to?'

'If you want.'

'Yes, I do. And I'll give you my address. You'll write back to me, won't you, Winston?'

'Yes.'

Emma sighed inside. However, she knew him well enough not to be discouraged by his gruff answers. The evasiveness in her letters about her whereabouts over the past months obviously still rankled with him. She hoped her father would not have the same attitude, that *he* was not harbouring any grudges. Now she said gaily, 'It must be exciting, being in the navy. Seeing different places. I'm ever so glad you joined up, Winston, really I am. Why, you can see the world, just like you always dreamed about doing when you were little.' He did not respond, but Emma saw a softening on his face, and she pressed, 'It *is* exciting, isn't it?'

Winston was incapable of remaining angry with his beloved Emma for long. Also, he knew his brusqueness with her was really caused by his own growing apprehension. He must not upset her unduly. Not now when within minutes she was about to suffer a terrible shock. And so he adopted a cheeriness he did not feel, and said, 'Yes, you're right. It is exciting. I love the navy, Emma. I'm learning a lot. Not just about life at sea, but many other things, educational things. It's fascinating. I aim to do well in the navy, Emma.'

His last statement filled her with pleasure. She opened her mouth, but before she could comment, he rushed on, 'I'll tell you something I've never told anybody else, Emma. I was a bit scared at first.'

Emma's eyes flew open. '*You* scared? I don't believe it.'

Winston was relieved he had managed to divert her from asking any trying questions about the family. He cleared his throat. 'Well, I was,' he confided, a wry smile playing on his mouth. 'It was the night I boarded my ship for the first time. It was a cold night, and dark and raining, and they moved us from Shotley Barracks, opposite Harwich, to Sheerness. The picket boat drew up to the battleship, and I was going up the accommodation ladder to the quarterdeck when I saw these giant brass letters on the bulkhead shining in the faint light. "Fear God, Honour the King", they said. I got a funny sensation in the pit of my stomach. I was awed, Emma, and fearful. Those words were so – so – meaningful, so serious. Powerful, really. I suddenly understood about the great traditions of the British navy and all they stood for. The honour, the courage, and the glory inherited from men like Drake and Raleigh and Nelson. I realized I was in the service of my King and country. I felt a pride, a sense of duty. That night I think I began to take the navy seriously. It was no longer simply an escape route from Fairley, or a lark.'

Emma was both impressed and moved by his words. 'I'm proud of you, Winston. I bet Dad is, too.'

This remark wiped the smile off his face. 'Hurry up,' he said, striding out.

Emma had to run to keep up with him. 'Well, Dad is, isn't he?' she asked cheerfully, ignoring his glum expression, smiling widely.

'I don't know,' mumbled Winston, and he kept his head averted.

'Did you tell him all that? About the traditions of the navy and the way you felt? It would please him, Winston. It really would. He was a good soldier himself when he was in the Boer War and he's very patriotic, you know.'

Attempting to circumvent any discussion about their father, Winston said, 'And what about you, Emma? How have you been? I notice you are talking very fancy, for one thing.'

Amused, she peeked at him out of the corner of her eye and said in a jocular tone, 'So are you, Winston Harte. Do you think I'm deaf?'

'No, I don't. I've been paying attention to myself, Emma. In every way. And I don't just mean by speaking properly either. I am going in for promotion,' he announced. 'You don't think I want to stay a rating, do you? I'm moving up the ladder. I'll be an able seaman next, then a leading seaman. Eventually, I intend to be a petty officer, maybe even a chief petty officer one day.'

'Not an admiral?' Emma teased.

'I know my limitations,' he retorted, but his voice was kind. He put his arm around her shoulder protectively, in the way he had done when they were children. She was immediately aware of his unspoken love. Emma smiled inside, thinking how wonderful it was to be with Winston again, and in a few seconds she would be hugging her father, and little Frank, and it would be like old times.

They hurried down Top Fold in silence, and when they reached the garden gate leading to the cottage Emma's heart lifted with happiness and she extracted herself from Winston's embrace and flew up the flagged path, propelled by her mounting excitement. She did not see the heartsick expression clouding Winston's face.

Frank had his back to the door, and he was peering into the oven set to one side of the fireplace, when Emma walked in. 'Yer late again, our Winston. Me Aunty Lily'll play pop if she knows. I've tried ter keep yer dinner warm, but it looks a bit funny now. Still, here it is, Winston.' The younger boy straightened up and swung around. He almost dropped the plate he was holding the moment he saw Emma. His mouth sagged and his eyes became so huge they filled his narrow face like liquid pools of grey light. He was dumbfounded. Then he banged the plate down on to the table negligently and sped across the room. He flung himself into Emma's outstretched arms with such velocity he almost knocked her over. She held him close to her, stroking his hair. He began to cry, sobbing as if his heart would break. She was at once startled and baffled, and she tried to soothe him.

'Frank, lovey, don't cry so. I'm here, safe and well, and with presents for you, too. Presents you'll like, Frank.'

He raised his freckled and damp face to hers and said, with a snuffle, 'I've missed yer, Emma. Ever so much. I thought yer'd never come back. Never ever again.'

'Don't be silly. I'll always come back to see you. I've missed you, too, Frank. Now, come along, stop crying and let me take off my coat.'

Winston had thrown his cap on to a chair, and unable to look at Emma in his anxiety, he stared with distaste at the food on the plate. It had long ago coagulated into a mass of limp Yorkshire pudding, frizzled roast beef, mashed potatoes, and Brussels sprouts, all running together in a rapidly drying gravy. 'I don't feel very hungry,' he muttered in a low voice. Winston discovered to his dismay that he had lost his nerve. How could he tell her? All the right words had fled, leaving his mind empty.

'Me Aunt Lily'll be mad if yer don't eat yer dinner,' warned Frank.

Emma hung up her coat behind the door and returned to the fireplace with the shopping bag. She placed the flowers in the sink and pulled out the presents for Frank, hoping to bring a smile to that cheerless little face. 'These are for you, love,' she said with a bright smile, and then addressed her older brother. 'I'm sorry, Winston, I didn't bring you anything. I didn't know you'd be home on leave. But never mind, this will come in useful, I'm sure.' As she spoke she opened her reticule and took out one of the new pound notes. 'Take this, Winston. You can buy yourself some cigarettes and a pint or two.'

She carried the presents over to Frank, who accepted them from her silently. Then his eyes lit up. 'Thank yer, Emma. Just what I needed.' His pleasure was undisguised.

Now Emma busied herself at the Welsh dresser, taking out the other items. 'These are for Dad,' she said, her voice light. 'Where is he?' She glanced from Winston to Frank, a look of joyous expectation on her face.

Winston put the knife and fork down on the plate with a loud clatter, and Frank stood gazing at her vacantly, clutching his presents. Neither of them spoke.

'Where's our dad?' asked Emma. They still did not reply and Winston dropped his eyes again but looked up quickly, flashing a warning to Frank, who had blanched.

'What's wrong? Why are you both so quiet?' This was a fierce demand and fear began to trickle through her veins. She grabbed hold of Winston's arm urgently and brought her face closer to his, peering into his eyes, 'Where is he, Winston?'

Winston cleared his throat nervously. 'He's with our mam, Emma.'

Emma experienced a little burst of relief. 'Oh, you mean he's gone to visit her grave. I wish I'd been a bit sooner and I could have gone with him. I think I'll run up there now, and catch him before he –'

'No, Emma, you can't do that,' Winston cried, jumping up. He put his arm around her and led her to a chair. 'Sit down a minute, Emma.'

Winston lowered himself into the chair opposite her. He took her hand in his and held it tightly. 'You didn't understand me, love,' Winston began in a tiny voice that was so faint she could hardly hear it. 'I didn't mean our dad had gone to visit Mam's grave. I meant he was there with her. Lying next to her in the graveyard.'

Winston watched her attentively, ready to move towards her if necessary, the desire to insulate her pain uppermost in his mind. But she seemed uncomprehending.

'Our dad's dead,' said Frank, with his usual childlike bluntness. His voice was leaden with sorrow.

'Dead,' whispered Emma, incredulous. 'He can't be dead. It's not possible. I would have known if he had died. I would have known inside. In my heart. I just know I would.' As she uttered these words she realized from their grim expressions that it was true. Emma's face crumpled. Tears welled into her eyes and spilled out over the rims and rolled down her cheeks silently, falling on to the front of the red silk dress in small splashes.

Winston's eyes were blurred and he wept as he had wept when his father had died. Now his tears were for Emma. She had been so much closer to their father than either he or Frank. He brushed his hand across his eyes resolutely, resolving to be stalwart. He must try to console her, to alleviate her grief. He knelt at Emma's feet and wrapped his arms around her body. She fell against him, sobs wracking her. 'Oh, Winston! Oh, Winston! I never saw him again. I never saw him again!' she wailed.

'There, there, love,' Winston said, stroking her hair, murmuring softly to her, pressing her to his chest, comforting and tender. After a long time her sobbing began to diminish and slowly subsided altogether.

Frank was making tea at the sink, swallowing his own tears. He had to be brave, a big boy. Winston had told him that. But Emma's terrible distress had infected him and his shoulders jerked in silent misery. Winston became conscious of the boy's wretchedness and he beckoned to Frank, stretching out one arm. Frank skittered across the floor and buried his head against Winston, who encircled his sister and brother in his arms, lovingly, and with great devotion. He was the head of the family now and responsible for them both. The three of them stayed huddled together in silent commiseration, drawing solace from their closeness, until eventually all of their tears were used up.

The kitchen was full of gently shifting shadows, the greying light outside intruding bleakly through the glass panes, the flames in the grate meagre as the logs burned low. There was no sound except the sibilant hissing of the kettle on the hob, the murmurous ticking of the old clock, the pattering of spring rain as it hit the windows. Winston's voice sounded hollow in this dolorous silence. 'It's just the three of us now. We've got to stick together. We've got to be a family. That's what Dad and Mam would want. We must look after each other. Emma, Frank, do you both hear me?'

'Yes, Winston,' whispered Frank.

Dazed and sorrowing, Emma drew herself up and wiped her face with one hand. She was white with anguish. Her eyes were swollen and red-rimmed, and her mouth quivered, but she took steely control of herself, smiling at Winston weakly. She nodded her understanding of his words. She could not speak.

'Frank, please bring the tea over to the table,' Winston said, rising wearily. He sat in the chair opposite Emma and took out a cigarette. He looked at the packet of Woodbines and remembered, with a nostalgic twinge of sadness, how his father had always complained about his tab ends.

Emma pulled herself fully upright. She faced Winston. 'Why didn't you tell me straightaway, when I ran into you outside the White Horse?' she murmured.

'How could I, Emma? In the middle of the village street. I was so relieved to see you, I could only think how glad I was that you were safe and well. I was happy for a split second. And then I became afraid. That's why I chattered on about the navy, and rushed you home the way I did. I knew you'd break down. I wanted you here, in this house, when you heard the bad news.'

'Yes, you were right. You did the best thing. When did – did – our dad –' She pressed her handkerchief to her face and endeavoured to suppress the sobs. She had been grief-stricken at her mother's death, yet in a sense that had been anticipated for months. The news of her father's passing away had been so unexpected she was devastated, in a state of awful shock.

'He died five days after you left, last August,' said Winston dully, dragging on his cigarette, his face a picture of despondency.

Emma turned a ghastly putty colour and her face was so rigid, so unmoving it might have been cut from stone. I never knew, she thought. All these months I've been writing to him. Writing terrible lies. And all the time he was dead, and buried in the cold earth. She clapped her hand over her mouth, choking back a sob, heaving in silence.

Winston eventually calmed her down again and Frank brought the tea. She took hold of the cup. Her hand shook so badly she had to put it down. She stared into space and finally managed to ask, 'How did he die?' Her voice was drained. She looked at Frank and then at Winston.

'There was an accident,' Winston said. 'I was at Scapa Flow. Aunt Lily sent me a telegram and they let me come home on compassionate leave. We didn't know where to find you, Emma. We kept thinking you'd be back in a few days. Hoping against hope. But –'

Emma was silent. She had no excuses. A sick dismay lodged in her stomach, and guilt mingled with her grief, which was absolute. After a few seconds she asked tremulously, 'What kind of accident?' She was determined to know everything now, however heartrending it was. She turned to Frank, who had seated himself next to her. 'You were here before Winston arrived. Can you explain it to me? Would it be too hard for you, Frankie? Too painful, lovey?'

'No, Emma. I can tell you.' He gulped. 'Winston said I have to be brave and strong and accept life's hard knocks,' he intoned in that serious voice he sometimes adopted. Her heart went out to him. He was such a little boy and he was trying to be so courageous.

'You're a good, brave boy, Frank. Tell me all about it. But take your time.' She squeezed his hand reassuringly.

'Well, yer see, Emma, that Saturday yer left, me and me dad was working at t'mill, as yer knows. Anyways, there was a fire and me dad got burned. On his back and his shoulders and legs. Third-degree burns, so Dr Mac said. And he breathed a lot of smoke.'

Emma's blood ran cold as he was speaking. She shuddered, and her heart tightened as she imagined her father's pain, the suffering he must undoubtedly have endured from his tortuous injuries. She tried to steady herself, not wishing to disturb Frank, who was on the verge of tears again.

'Are yer all right, our Emma?' he asked solicitously.

'Yes, Frank. Finish telling me.'

Speaking gravely, he gave her the precise details of the injuries their father had sustained, the care and attention he had received, the concern of Adam Fairley, the devotion of Dr Mac and his wife, and the doctors at the valley hospital.

When he had finished, Emma said in a choked voice, 'How horrible for Dad to die like that, in such pain. I can't bear to think about it. How awful it must have been for him.'

Frank eyed her carefully. 'Me Aunty Lily said he didn't want to live any more.' His tone was hushed and his face was all bone and freckles, and he looked like a little old man to Emma.

She stared at him stupefied, her brows puckering. 'What a weird and terrible thing for her to say about our dad. What did she mean, lovey?'

Frank looked at Winston, who nodded his assent. 'We went ter see me dad every day,' Frank explained. 'Tom Hardy took us in the Squire's carriage. Me dad didn't seem ter get any better, Emma. On the Wednesday after the accident, when we was there, me Aunt Lily said ter him, "Now, Jack, yer can't go on like this yer knows, lad. Yer've got ter make an effort. Or yer'll be where poor Elizabeth is, in the cemetery." And me dad, well, he stared at her ever so funny like, with a faraway look in his eyes. Then he said, "I wish I *was* with Elizabeth, Lily." And when we was leaving, I kissed him and he said, "Goodbye, Frankie. Always be a good lad." Just like that. Final like. And when he kissed Winston –' Frank's eyes flew to his brother. 'Tell her what he said ter yer, Winston.'

Winston ran his hand through his hair. 'Dad said to me, "Look after the young 'uns, Winston. Stick together. And when Emma comes back from Bradford, tell her ter pick a sprig of heather for me and thee mam, up at the Top of the World, and keep it by her always for remembrance." And then –' Winston's voice cracked at the memory. He took a deep breath, and continued softly, 'Dad tried to get hold of my hand, Emma, but his were all burned and bandaged, so I brought my face down to his and he kissed me again, and he said, "I love thee all, Winston. But I love Elizabeth the best and I can't live without her." I began to cry, but Dad just smiled, and he had such a bright light in his eyes. They were as vivid as yours, Emma, and he looked happy. Really happy. He said I shouldn't be sad, because he had me mam to go to. I thought he was a bit delirious, to tell you the truth. The doctor came in then and asked us to leave. It was on the way back to Fairley that Aunt Lily said he'd die of a broken heart and not his burns. That he'd never stopped grieving for our mam. He died that same night, Emma. Peacefully, in his sleep. It was as if he had wanted to die, like Aunt Lily said.' Emma said, with a strangled sob, 'Did he understand that I hadn't returned from Bradford, and that's why I wasn't there, Winston?'

Her brother nodded. 'Yes, and he wasn't upset, Emma. He said he didn't have to see you, because you were locked in his heart for ever.'

Emma closed her burning eyes and leaned back against the chair. My father needed me and I wasn't here, she thought. If only I had waited a few days longer. She dreaded to hear more, but she could not stop herself probing for additional details. 'It must have been a terrible fire. Obviously you weren't hurt, Frank, thank heaven. Were many of the men injured? Who else died?'

'No, I wasn't hurt at all,' Frank reassured her. 'A few of the men had minor burns, but not serious. Only me dad died, Emma.'

Emma looked at him in puzzlement. 'But if there was a fire at the mill, surely –'

'The fire wasn't in the mill building. It was in the big warehouse,' Frank interrupted. 'Me dad was crossing the yard and he spotted the flames raging. If he hadn't gone inter the warehouse he wouldn't have been hurt at all. Yer see, Master Edwin was down in the mill yard that day, and he was struggling ter open the door of the warehouse. He went inside. Me dad ran in after him, warning him it was ever so dangerous. A blazing bale was falling from the gantry, near Master Edwin. Me dad threw himself on top of Master Edwin, ter protect him. The bale hit me dad, and he saved Master Edwin's life, and with selfless courage, so the Squire said.'

Emma went icy cold all over. 'My father saved Edwin Fairley's life!' she cried with such ferocity even Winston was brought up sharply, aghast at her tone. 'He died to save a Fairley! My father sacrificed himself for one of *them*!' She spat out the words venomously. 'I can't believe it!' she shouted. She began to laugh hysterically, and her bitterness rose up in her.

Her brothers were gaping at her incredulously. Frank cringed and drew away from her. Winston said, 'But Emma, anybody would have done the same thing –'

'Would they really!' she stormed, leaping out of the chair. She stood in the centre of the kitchen, her volcanic rage a stupendous force in her slender body. 'Would *Squire* Fairley? Or *Master* Gerald? Or *Master* Edwin?' Again she spat out the names and with a complete and virulent loathing. 'Would they have risked their lives to save our father's? Never. Never, I tell you. Not in a million years. Oh God! I can't stand it,' she screamed, and her whole body vibrated with her fulminating fury.

'Calm down. Calm down, Emma. You'll make yourself sick. It happened, and nothing will change that,' Winston said, shaken at her violent reaction, and afraid for her.

'The Squire has been ever so decent,' interposed Frank, also trying to mollify her. 'He pays us me dad's wages. A pound a week, we get. And he's going to pay it until I'm fifteen –'

'That's mighty big of him!' snarled Emma, her eyes threatening and ugly.

'That's forty-eight pounds a year.' She laughed caustically. 'He's paid it for the past ten months, I suppose. And he'll pay it for another two years. Very decent of him indeed!' Her tone dripped acid. 'Is that all my father's life was worth to the Fairleys? Approximately one hundred and fifty pounds, give or take a few shillings. It's a joke. A disgusting joke!' She caught her breath, her chest heaving. '*Is that all he was worth?*' she demanded once more.

Winston cleared his throat and said in his gentlest voice, 'Well, he does a bit more than that. The Squire, I mean. He moved Frank into the mill offices and he's being trained as a clerk. And every Sunday Aunt Lily goes up to the Hall and Cook gives her a basket of food. Enough for the whole week. For her and Frank. You see, Aunt Lily moved in here, Emma, to look after Frank. She gave up her cottage when Dad died. She's gone up to the Hall now, Emma, to get the food. It helps a lot.'

'A basket of food,' she repeated scathingly, and laughed nastily. 'Well, well, well.

328

The Squire *is* being generous.' She swung her head sharply and glowered at Frank. 'I'm surprised you don't choke on it, our Frank. I know I would!'

She turned on her heels and walked across the room, her head held high. Frank and Winston gazed at her stiff back and they exchanged worried glances. She put on her coat and took the flowers from the sink. She paused in the doorway and looked around. 'I'm going to the cemetery,' she said, her voice steely. 'And then I shall go up to the Top of the World. I doubt there's any heather there at this time of year, but I shall look. Anyway, I want to be by myself for a bit. I'll be back later, and we can talk some more. Make some plans for Frank's future. I'd like to see Aunty Lily as well.'

'I'll come with you,' said Winston. 'We'll both come, won't we, Frank?' The younger boy nodded his acquiescence.

'No!' exclaimed Emma. 'I told you I want to be alone. To think for a while.'

She closed the door softly behind her, before they had a chance to protest. She walked slowly up Top Fold, her feet dragging, a feeling of exhaustion swamping her. She headed for the small graveyard next to the church, aware of nothing except her overwhelming grief. Her face tightened and darkened, and there was a chilly light in her eyes as she looked ahead unwaveringly. And then her consummate hatred for the Fairleys, so close to the surface, rose up again and took hold of her, jostling against the grief for prominence in her mind. Was there no end to the pain that family would cause her? Was she to be cursed with them all the days of her life? Damn the Fairleys. All of them. Damn them! Damn them! Damn them! May they rot in hell!

THIRTY-THREE

And so it began: the most relentless pursuit of money ever embarked upon, the most grinding and merciless work schedule ever conceived and willingly undertaken by a seventeen-year-old girl.

By day, Emma worked at the mill; at night, after a hastily eaten light tea, she retreated to her bedroom at Laura's and designed and cut and sewed: clothes for a rapidly increasing clientele, local women informed by the devoted Laura of her flair with a needle, and her reasonable prices.

On Sundays, Emma baked fruit pies, bacon-and-egg pies, meat pies, and all manner of fancy pastries and cakes; she cooked mousses, jellies, custards, and trifles, using Olivia Wainright's recipes, catering for parties and special occasions for the neighbours and, before long, the local gentry. When she was not engaged in her culinary endeavours for her growing number of customers, she bottled fresh fruits and vegetables; pickled onions, red cabbage, and walnuts; made chutneys and relishes and jams, which were painstakingly labelled and dated in her meticulous script, supplies being hoarded in Laura's cellar to be sold later in her shop. Emma scrupulously lived on the weekly wage she earned at the mill as a weaver, and every penny she made from her dressmaking and catering was poured back into 'the business', as she called it, to purchase the necessary sewing materials and foodstuffs.

This worried Laura, but Emma pointed out, 'You've got to spend money to make money,' and she refused to listen to warnings about 'getting in over your head'. However, it was not long before Emma began to show a small profit, much to her satisfaction, and Laura's great relief.

Emma was dogged, ruthless with herself, scraping, saving, and working seven days a week and seven nights as well. She had no time to lose now. Her first goal – the first shop. And after that, more shops until she had a chain of shops just as Michael Marks had a chain of Penny Bazaars. But hers would be elegant stores which would cater to the carriage trade. That was where the real money was, where great quantities of money could be made by an astute retailer. To get that first shop Emma herself needed money. Money for the rent. Money for the fixtures and fittings and display stands. Money to purchase the stocks. Somehow she had to get that money and she determined that nothing and nobody would stop her. Emma had no doubts about her ultimate success. 'Failure' and 'defeat' were words now entirely erased from her vocabulary, for her belief in herself was absolute, and she knew, also, that she had one essential and most vital characteristic – an enormous capacity for work.

For a whole year, after she had learned of her father's death, Emma took no time off whatsoever, except to visit Edwina one day every month. She regretted she did not have time to go to Ripon more often, as she had promised Freda, but she assuaged her terrible feelings of guilt and worry by reminding herself she was working for Edwina's future.

Emma made only one trip to Fairley to see Frank during this time, and that was when Winston was home on leave again. They had decided, she and her elder brother, on that devastating April Sunday, that Frank should remain in Fairley with their Aunt Lily. It seemed to them both to be the best solution. He would continue to work in the mill offices until he was fifteen. At that time, they agreed, Frank could determine for himself whether or not he wished to pursue a writing career. If he did, Emma and Winston would somehow find a way for him to do this; perhaps working in Leeds, as a copy boy on one of the newspapers, learning the journalistic profession and attending night school; or perhaps they would have enough money between them to send him away to school.

'Frank has been given a brain, Winston. A marvellous brain. And he has a talent for words. It's a gift, really. It must not be wasted,' Emma had proclaimed. 'We must give him every chance, no matter what.' Winston had nodded his concurrence. Emma had also made another decision that afternoon. She had informed Winston, and in no uncertain terms, that he must send Frank writing materials on a continuing basis. 'Even if you have to forgo a few pints and cigarettes,' she had ordered. She herself would undertake to supply Frank with a good dictionary and other books of her choice. He ought to be exposed to literature, such as the plays of Shakespeare, the novels of Dickens, Trollope, and Thackeray, philosophical works and histories. Victor Kallinski knew all about books and he would help her to select the most appropriate ones. Frank had been given his orders, too. He must study diligently, reading every night and in all of his free time, in order to further his education on his own. Aunt Lily was instructed to enforce this programme.

'There will be no shirking, Frank, since Winston and I are making a special effort for you,' Emma had warned in her sternest tone. Frank had been only too delighted to accept her offer, and he was not at all appalled by the rigid timetable she had worked out for him. He could not wait for the first books to arrive and he knew, too, that he would not change his mind about writing.

Emma had told Winston, Frank, and her Aunt Lily, only partial truths when she had given them her address in Armley. She had explained that she called herself *Mrs* Harte, and had invented a husband in the navy, simply as protection against unwanted and bothersome young men who might otherwise come courting. Winston had smiled at this ruse. He had actually congratulated her on her sense of self-preservation and told her she was being practical. Emma did not breathe a word about Edwina.

With Winston's career in the navy progressing, Frank's future temporarily settled, and Edwina safe in Ripon, Emma felt she was free to embark on her Plan with a capital *P* and devote herself solely to her own ambitions. She was unflagging and intensely involved in her work schedule, one that would have felled anyone else. She was oblivious to the passing of the days, her surroundings, and anything else that would intrude on the average girl's thoughts.

Sometimes Emma was even oblivious to her friends. At first, Blackie had believed Emma would not be able to sustain the exhausting grind, and so he had quietly cautioned Laura not to interfere. But as the months dragged on and Emma persisted in her endless toil, they both became concerned. In particular, David Kallinski was worried to such an extent that one night he sought out Blackie at the Mucky Duck.

David had been tense, and without preamble had launched into the reason for his visit. 'Emma won't listen to me, Blackie. When I last spoke to her I suggested she should be a little kinder to herself, that she should only work during the week, like everyone else with any sense, and take the weekends off. I said something about doing everything in moderation, and do you know what she replied?'

Blackie had shaken his head, his own worry a reflection of David's. 'I've no idea, lad. She comes out with all sorts of strange remarks these days.'

'She said to me, "In my opinion, moderation is a vastly overrated virtue, particularly when applied to work, David." Can you believe it?'

'Aye, I can. She's stubborn, Emma is, David. And what ye be telling me doesn't surprise me. I've tried talking to her meself lately, without success. She just won't pay no mind to anybody,' Blackie had grumbled.

'Try talking to her again, Blackie. *Please*,' David had implored. 'Get her to take this Sunday off. I'll come up to Armley, and we'll go for a walk in the park, and listen to the band. Blackie, promise me you'll at least *try*.'

'By God, I'm going to do it, David! I shall be real forceful with her. I shall tell her how she is worrying us all. That ought to do the trick, I bet. I'm going to bring Emma to the park with Laura and me, even if I have to drag her there by the scruff of her neck!'

Now on the designated Sunday, a brilliantly sunny July afternoon, David Kallinski walked along Stanningley Road to the entrance of Armley Park. He was dressed in his best suit and a sparkling white shirt, set off by a deep wine-coloured cravat neatly knotted above his waistcoat, and fastened with an imitation-pearl pin. With his carefully pressed clothes, and his black boots shined to perfection, he had a well-groomed immaculate look about him. His thick black hair gleamed like jet and his handsome face, freshly barbered and smelling faintly of bay rum, was vibrant with pleasure at the thought of seeing Emma.

He entered the park through handsome iron gates, surmounted by the city's coat of arms, and strolled down the principal approach, a wide carriageway leading to a large classically designed fountain. He stood at ease, his hands in his pockets, watching the soaring jets of water being discharged high into the air and cascading back down into the fountain, scintillating like hundreds of strings of tiny diamonds as they caught and held the sunlight. Fascinated by the intricately constructed fountain, he moved closer and read the inscription.

Erected by William Gott of Armley House
In Commemoration of the Sixtieth Year of
the Reign of Her Majesty Queen Victoria
1837 to 1897

The Gott family were immensely wealthy millowners and had endowed many statues to the city of Leeds. When he could afford it, David decided, he would make philanthropic donations that would help people, rather than building statues and fountains, which, however beautiful, were essentially useless.

He turned away and traversed the exquisitely landscaped gardens, laid out in Italian style and flanked by pathways avenued by young limes and elms and poplars, all offering shade on this scorching day. The gardens blazed with glorious colour. Stylized flower beds were awash with the abundant reds and pinks of the gay geranium, the deep purples and sharp yellows of the velvet-petalled pansy, the whites and pinks and mauves of the tall and graceful foxglove. Variegated greens, lushly inviting, sloped away into the distance and were highlighted with patches of pink and white thrifts, and the cheerful little nasturtium leapt like fire alongside the cool blues of the iris. Skirting the gardens were all manner of shrubs and trees, for Armley Park contained more specimens than any other park in Leeds; various hollies moved darkly polished branches towards the softer weigela with its apple-like blossoms, while copper beeches, their leaves trembling with a burnished radiance in the warm breeze, towered majestically above mock orange blossom trees, festooned and dripping with the palest of blush pinks. Rockeried paths and open spaces of grass, as smooth as emerald satin, were enclosed by additional shrubs and trees, and richly planted borders of the vivid zinnia ranged down the flagged and gravelled walks.

Along these pathways moved starchly uniformed nannies pushing perambulators; courting couples; prettily gowned ladies accompanied by stiffly tailored husbands. David mingled amongst them, thinking how idyllic the scene was on this splendid day. He was glad to be alive with his future ahead of him and so many things to see and do, so much to achieve. Success beckoned and he was as positive as Emma that his own business enterprises would prosper.

And why not? This was the year of 1907, when King Edward's reign was at its zenith and his popularity with his people unchallenged; a year when society flirted and danced and hunted and sailed and laughed away the days under King Bertie's outgoing and benevolent rule; a year when the aristocracy made pleasure the god and gave no thought to the grim realities of life, or of war, for the African debacle was forgotten and peace in Europe was assured. In short, 1907 was a year when the ruling classes lived their carefree lives to the full, not considering the stony-faced world beyond the shores of their glorious and invincible England. And every Englishman, David Kallinski included, was lulled into a sense of false security by their debonair example. The years ahead were full of promise. Change was ripe in the air. Things could only get better. The future, for all, was bright with hope.

Consequently, David's step was lively as he headed for the bandstand. This pagoda-like structure, a dubious tribute to England's far-flung empire, added a touch of the exotic and the oriental to this typical English park, appeared oddly incongruous in that peaceful and gentle setting. Particularly so this afternoon, since it housed the visiting military band of the Grenadier Guards, bedazzling in their magnificent uniforms and shining from head to toe with the proverbial 'spit and polish' of the British army, and curiously out of place in that somewhat outlandish and whimsical replica of a mandarin's teahouse.

He scanned the seats in front of the bandstand and, seeing no sight of his friends, settled himself in one of the small wrought-iron chairs. The band finished warming up and, after a few flourishes, they commenced their programme with the national anthem. As the concert continued thoughts of Emma drifted into David's head and took complete hold of him. She was rarely out of his mind these days, and he realized his interest in her was not solely as a business associate, but as a woman. The tender but also passionate feelings he now harboured for her had crept up on him so stealthily he had been taken by surprise. And how did she feel about him? he wondered. Anything at all, other than affection and friendship? Was she too preoccupied with her work to give him a solitary thought? And she was married, a circumstance he had to face. The prospects were bleak for any man who had the bad luck to fall in love with a married woman. But love her he did. Where *is* that damned husband of hers? David asked himself. The missing husband had not appeared on the scene at all, not even when the baby was born. Sailors came home on leave, didn't they? It was a mystery, but David had not, as yet, ventured to ask Emma about her husband, or whether she still loved him. David suspected that she did not. Emma never mentioned him, nor did she appear to miss him. David sighed. He had to admit that his hands were tied. He could not, in all conscience, proclaim himself to her, in view of her marital status.

David, lost in his reverie, was startled by Blackie's voice at his shoulder. 'There ye are, me boyo!' David looked up quickly and was disappointed to see that only Laura Spencer accompanied Blackie. David stood and took Blackie's outstretched hand. He bent down and kissed Laura affectionately on the cheek, and flashed her a gay smile that belied his real feelings. However, he was unable to keep the dejection out of his voice when he asked, 'What happened to Emma? Where is she?'

'Ah, David, 'tis sorry I am to be telling ye that Emma declined the invitation. I tried, sure and I did, to persuade her to join us. But she was obstinate as always. She's finishing a blasted frock for a lady at the Towers, and she wouldn't budge an inch,' explained Blackie with a little grimace. 'Still an' all, she did say she'd be right delighted to see ye for supper at Laura's later.' Blackie continued in a cheery tone, 'Now, me lad, don't look so downcast! We'll go back to the house in a few hours. She'll be finished by then.' He swung his head to Laura. 'And what about ye, love? What would ye like to be doing?'

333

'Let's go for a walk, if David doesn't mind,' Laura murmured softly.

'Yes, let's do that,' David said.

The three of them wandered away from the bandstand and the rousing strains of 'Land of Hope and Glory'. David glanced at Laura. She looked radiant. She was wearing a simple dress made of an inexpensive muslin of the palest yellow, patterned with daisies and sprigs of green, and the gauzy fabric floated around her like a cloud of hazy sunny colour, emphasizing her willowy figure and her grace of movement. A large-brimmed straw hat, trimmed with yellow and pink tea roses, shaded her face and there was something ethereal about her today. Under the brim of the hat her face looked incandescent, framed by her golden hair and illuminated by her liquid eyes.

'You *are* looking lovely, Laura,' David said gallantly. 'And I like your dress. It's very becoming to you, love.'

'Thank you, David,' she said. 'Emma made it for me. She also trimmed this old hat and turned it into a brand new one. She's so talented, isn't she?'

David nodded and Blackie grunted. 'Aye, but her talent won't be doing her much good in the graveyard, I am thinking.'

'Blackie! What a terrible thing to say!' Laura cried. She gave David a lightning glance. He was silent, but she noticed then that he was biting his lip and looked worried. Laura wisely made no further remarks, but she threw a rather cold glare at Blackie, who had the grace to look chagrined.

They walked around the park slowly. Blackie and Laura talked amiably together about things in general; the usually gregarious David was silent and brooding. Eventually they found themselves at the top of a steep ridge where steps led down to the river Aire. Laura complained of the heat, and so they sat down on a bench under the shade of a weeping willow. David gazed morosely across the river, his eyes resting reflectively on the ruins of the grand Cistercian Abbey of Kirkstall on the opposite shore. Then they flitted across the tranquil scenery that stretched towards the horizon, taking in Horsforth Woods beyond the ruins, which were capped further by Rawdon village and Wharfedale's Reach. He sighed and took out his packet of cigarettes. He offered one to Blackie, who accepted it and murmured his thanks. Finally, David could not hold back any longer. He faced Blackie and said, 'I don't understand it, Blackie. What is it that drives Emma so hard?'

'Hatred, pure and simple,' Blackie replied automatically, and he could have bitten off his tongue. Furious with himself, he turned away.

Laura gasped and covered her mouth with her hand. She said, 'Oh, Blackie, surely not!'

David was equally disturbed by this statement. 'Hatred!' he said sharply. 'Not Emma. She is loving and sweet. And hatred for who?'

Blackie did not answer for a moment. He cursed himself instead. He was a big-mouthed fool. A stupid boyo. He was that, indeed. In Blackie's opinion Emma's hatred was for the Fairleys. But he was not about to divulge this to David or Laura.

'Come on, Blackie. Give me an answer,' David pressed. 'Don't sit there looking so mysterious.'

Blackie roused himself. 'I don't really know, David. I shouldn't have spoken so rashly, lad. But ye know what the Irish are like, always blabbering on. Anyroads, I didn't mean anybody specific.' Blackie paused, his face a picture of assumed innocence. 'I think perhaps it is hatred for the circumstances of her life,' he suggested, trying to cover his error. 'And hatred for poverty. That's what drives Emma. Her terrible need for money.'

David looked a bit sceptical and he frowned. 'I know Emma wants money. But then, so do you, Blackie. So do I. On the other hand, we don't devote our lives to its accumulation to the exclusion of all else.'

Blackie leaned forward, his black eyes intense. 'Aye, lad, but we be wanting money for different reasons than Emma. It occurs to me ye be desirous of it to buy yeself a better life. Sure and why not? 'Tis the fine house ye be wanting, David, and the smart carriage and the elegant clothes. A few of the beautiful things, I am thinking, just like me. And a bit of security for the future, eh?'

David nodded, for Blackie did indeed speak the truth. 'But you said Emma wants money for a different reason. What does she want it for?'

Blackie smiled a small, odd smile. 'As a weapon.'

'A weapon! Against whom?' Laura demanded.

Blackie took her hand gently. 'Don't be upsetting yeself, Laura. Ye be misunderstanding me, love.' He regretted having embarked on this discussion and he was loath to continue, but they had him cornered. Two pairs of questioning eyes pinned him down. He had to explain his statements as best he could. Blackie cleared his throat. 'I mean that Emma *herself* believes that money is a weapon –'

'Against who?' David cried, interrupting him abruptly. 'You still haven't answered Laura.'

'Not *against* anyone in particular, David.' He shrugged. 'Maybe against the world. Yes, I am thinking she will use her money, when she has it, against the world. Or rather, them in it that might try to do her wrong. Ye see. Emma wants money to protect herself and Edwina. She aims to build a fortress around herself and that child, so that nothing can hurt them. Ever. That's all I meant, lad.'

David was not only disbelieving but shocked. 'You are painting a very strange picture, Blackie. That's not the Emma I know.'

'Aye, lad, but I know her better than ye and for much longer. And I think I understand what drives her,' Blackie murmured, remembering that exigent look in Emma's eyes the first day they had met on the moors. 'I know for a fact she won't rest until she gets that shop. And then it'll be another shop, and another, and another, Emma aims to be a very rich woman one day. You know something, David? She'll succeed. Sure and she will.'

'But at what cost?' asked David. 'Look at her now. She's as thin as a rail and worn out. She has black rings under her eyes far too often these days.' His eyes rested on Laura. '*You* live with her. *You* must admit I'm right.'

Laura confessed, 'Yes, you are correct to some extent, David, but, in all fairness to Emma, she does eat properly and takes care of herself.'

'Except that she never sleeps.'

'Oh, she does, David!' Laura countered in defence of her friend. 'At least five hours. She doesn't seem to need as much rest as other people. But, of course, to be truthful, I am worried about her, too.' Laura touched Blackie's arm lightly. 'Maybe you should speak to her again. I mean, about taking it more easily.'

'How little ye be knowing her, Laura, if ye think anything I say would do any good. She won't listen,' said Blackie regretfully.

'You mean we just have to stand by and watch her kill herself with work!' cried David heatedly.

Blackie could not resist chortling. 'Don't let Emma hear ye say that,' he said through his laughter. 'She doesn't believe hard work killed anybody. Sloth, maybe. And ye know yeself what she said about moderation, David.' Blackie shook his head, his eyes still merry. 'Aye, she's unique, Emma is.'

David gazed at him for a moment and then he turned away and sat puffing on his cigarette, attempting to evaluate Blackie's words.

'You know, I thought Emma's idea about having a shop was foolish at first, Blackie,' Laura ventured, 'but now I am beginning to think it might be the best thing. It would get her out of the mill. She hates that place.'

David said, 'I had hoped she would come into partnership with me. By this time next year I will have saved up enough to start my own factory. I intend to make a line of women's clothes, as well as take on outside contracting, like my father does. Emma has already designed a line for me.' His face lit up. 'Have you seen it, Laura?'

'Yes, Emma showed me her sketches. Her ideas are marvellous. I think. Why, that coat with the detachable cape, and the reversible jacket are brilliant and her maternity clothes – well – they are revolutionary, wouldn't you say? I don't know of anyone making those wraparound skirts, blouses, and dresses that expand to fit the figure as it gets larger. Do you, David?'

'No. She's far ahead of her time as far as styling is concerned.'

'I can't argue with ye about that,' interjected Blackie. 'Listen, both of ye, don't let's be looking on the black side. Emma will be all right in the long run. She's a real survivor. But if it makes ye both feel better, why don't we *all* talk to her tonight. Careful like, so we don't upset her. Perhaps we can get her to slow down for a bit. The three of us together might be able to make some headway.' Blackie was not convinced Emma would pay any attention to them, but he wanted to alleviate their worry, Laura's in particular.

'Yes, let's do that,' agreed David. He now looked at Blackie guardedly before commencing in a cautious voice, 'Look here, Blackie, I know this is none of my business, but where the hell is that husband of Emma's? It seems a bit queer to me that he hasn't been home on leave. Emma came to work for Dad in August of 1905. That's almost two years ago and her husband has been noticeably absent all that time.'

Blackie had been anticipating this question, dreading it, in fact, for months. He had warned Emma time and again to prepare a plausible story. Last week she had told him she was soon going to announce that her sailor husband had deserted her. Taking a deep breath, Blackie now decided to save her the trouble. 'Ah, David, I'm glad ye asked me, sure and I am.' He turned swiftly to Laura and took her hand in his. 'And ye might as well be knowing, too, me love. Emma has been a trifle embarrassed, not knowing how to be telling ye both her news. Ye see, that bleeding husband –' He stopped short and squeezed Laura's hand apologetically. 'Sorry, love, I know ye don't like me to be swearing. Anyroads, that rascally husband of hers has done a bunk, ye might say. He deserted Emma some time ago.' Blackie, praying he was being convincing, went on, 'Seems he wants a big naval career, sure and he does. He told Emma he didn't want to be tied down by a wife. I don't expect we'll see hide nor hair of him in these parts. No, he won't ever be back. That's my guess.'

'Oh, Blackie, how terrible for poor Emma and the baby,' Laura cried, and he felt her hand tremble in his.

Blackie put his arm around her. 'Now, mavourneen, there's no reason for ye to be getting all worked up. Emma isn't that bothered, not at all, at all. 'Tis glad, she is, I am thinking. Sure and did she not say to me, "Good riddance", after she be telling me all the details,' he lied smoothly.

David was utterly still, but his heart was beating rapidly and a tingling excitement surged through his veins. 'I'm sorry to hear that,' he remarked in an even voice that did not betray the jubilance he was feeling. 'Still, if Emma is not unhappy, then perhaps it is for the best.' He wondered, as he spoke, how much a divorce cost.

Blackie nodded. 'Aye, ye are right.'

David sprang up. His despondency had vanished. 'Shall we make our way back and then listen to the music for a while, before going on to the house?'

'Sure and why not,' agreed Blackie. He helped Laura up off the bench and they walked slowly in the direction of the bandstand. And Blackie thought: I must warn Emma I've neatly disposed of that sailor husband of hers.

Whilst these discussions had been taking place in Armley Park, Emma was not at home sewing, as her friends believed. She was on her way to see Joe Lowther, who lived in another part of Armley.

The minute Laura and Blackie had departed, Emma had quickly changed into her black silk dress, donned her Leghorn straw bonnet, and taken sixty pounds out of the black tin box that contained her savings. She had rushed out of the house, close on the heels of her friends, a look of resolve on her face.

Quite by accident, when she had been shopping for groceries yesterday, she had seen *it*. The shop. *Her shop*. It was one of three that adjoined each other in a small block that fronted on to Town Street, and it was vacant. Emma had stopped abruptly, gazing at it hypnotized. It appeared exactly right for her in every way. The timing was perfect; she now had the money required for the rent and the stocks. The large empty window had been whitewashed, but there was a small clear space in the centre, where a notice had been neatly stuck on the inside. TO LET, it had read, and underneath was printed the name of the landlord, Mr Joe Lowther, and his address. Emma had memorized the details and hurried home late on Saturday afternoon, determined to be the first applicant the following day. She did not care that this was Sunday, a day when business was not normally conducted, since she was prepared to do business any day of the week.

Now as she walked briskly through the labyrinth of streets, almost breathless with mounting excitement, she half regretted selecting the black dress. It was really too warm for this scorching day. But in spite of the heat and the warmth of the dress, Emma did not slow her pace, and within fifteen minutes she was approaching the street where Joe Lowther lived. She found the house and marched up the stone steps resolutely. She knocked soundly three times and waited. A few moments elapsed before the door was opened by a tall, sturdily built young man. He was fair, with large grey eyes and light brown hair, and his pleasant face was open and honest. He was in his shirt sleeves and his hair was rumpled.

He stared down at Emma, obviously surprised to see a visitor. 'Yes, miss, what can I do for you?' he asked gruffly.

'I'd like to see your father, please,' Emma said politely, and proffered a tentative smile.

'My father? I think you must have the wrong house, miss. My father's been dead these past six years.'

'Oh dear, perhaps I've made a mistake. I was looking for the home of a Mr Joe Lowther.'

'Then you've found it, miss. I'm Joe Lowther.'

Emma was surprised. 'Oh! Well, please excuse me, but I thought you seemed a bit young to be the landlord of the shop on Town Street. The shop that's to let,' Emma said with her usual forthrightness. She saw at once that the young man was bristling and she rushed on, 'Are *you* that Mr Lowther?'

'That's me, all right,' said the young man. His eyes narrowed. 'Are you interested in the shop, then? For your *mother?*'

'No,' Emma said, faintly amused. He was apparently stinging from her reference to his youthful appearance, and so she smiled that radiant smile and her unwavering green gaze, warm and self-assured, did not leave his face. 'Actually, I want to rent the shop for myself.'

Joe Lowther said, 'Oh, you do, do you! Aren't you a bit *young?* What experience of retailing do you have, miss?'

Emma considered this to be none of his business, but refrained from telling him so, being canny enough not to brush him the wrong way again. Instead she said, 'I have some experience, and I've also done a lot of dressmaking and catering here in Armley. I have a nice business going, and now I want a shop so I can conduct it from there.' Her voice vibrated with enormous confidence as she added, 'And I'm certainly not too young, Mr Lowther.'

Joe shook his head. 'No. No. It wouldn't work. I can't say I'd be willing to rent the shop to you, miss,' he said with a certain brusqueness.

Emma ignored his blunt retort. 'But I am willing to take the shop off your hands now, Mr Lowther. At once. Today.' Emma climbed up two steps until she was on a level with Joe Lowther. She stared at him, exercising all of her considerable charm, smiling beguilingly. 'Can't we go inside and discuss this, Mr Lowther?' she asked in a voice as smooth as silk.

'I can't see the sense in that, since I won't change my mind,' he declared stubbornly. Her proximity was distracting him and as he looked into her face, only a few inches away from his, Joe felt himself growing hot around the collar.

Emma opened her purse, resorting to the one stratagem in which she had absolute belief. 'I can pay in advance, Mr Lowther.'

Joe reluctantly brought his gaze up to meet Emma's and he discovered he was mesmerized by those brilliant eyes observing him with such cool concentration. Whatever will the neighbours think if I invite her in? he asked himself. But since he was not generally discourteous, Joe was now ashamed of his rudeness and he found himself saying in a kinder voice, 'Well, you're right about one thing, we had better go inside.' This was really prompted by his concern for the gossips in the street and, so she would not think he had changed his mind about the shop, Joe felt obliged to add, 'It's not very fitting to discuss business on the doorstep at the best of times, and especially on Sunday. I don't usually do business on *Sundays*, miss.'

'Well, there's always a first time for everything, Mr Lowther,' said Emma, eyeing him with amusement from under her thick lashes. She was aware that Joe was ill at ease and she intended to use this to her advantage.

Why, she's as bold as brass, Joe thought, seething with combined annoyance and exasperation. Never the less, he opened the door wider and ushered her into the house. He showed her into the parlour. 'Excuse me. I'll be back in a minute. Please sit down,' said Joe. He closed the door behind him and retreated.

Emma stood in the middle of the room, blinking in the dim light. She grimaced as her eyes adjusted to the dolorous gloom. The room reminded her of Mrs Daniel's front parlour, all Victorian folderols and a preponderance of overstuffed furniture. But the furniture is good, she thought. There's just too much of it. She seated herself on an uncomfortable horsehair chair to wait.

Emma had discovered three important things since she had been in Leeds:. Money talked in the most persuasive voice. Put cold hard cash down on a table and few people could resist picking it up; payment in advance was another irresistible temptation and the more advance you paid, the stronger you were; and finally, opportunity had to be seized firmly the instant it presented itself, because it did not come knocking on the same door twice in one week. Emma considered all of these things, but mostly she wondered if Joe Lowther could be swayed by money. For some reason she was not positive of this. She frowned, ruminating on Joe, endeavouring to assess him. He was certainly bashful. She also knew she had unnerved him on the doorstep and, in her shrewd opinion, this gave her the upper hand. Still, that did not mean he would agree to rent her the shop. Apparently he believed her youth to be a disadvantage, and yet he did not appear to be much older than she was. He was perhaps twenty or twenty-one. None the less, it was imperative that she convince him she was capable and experienced at retailing, and that she would therefore be a responsible tenant. Perhaps three months' rent would be a suitable inducement. It would not only reassure him of her serious intentions, but would also illustrate her business acumen over the past year. It then struck Emma that she must be her most charming self. Joe Lowther would succumb to sweetness. Sweetness and money. An unbeatable combination. Emma smoothed her dress, feeling calm as the door opened.

Joe had put on his tie and jacket and his hair was now combed back neatly. Emma could see the water glistening on it. She dropped her head quickly so he would not detect the smile on her face. Joe Lowther had become quite transparent to her. There would be a bit of a tussle between them, but the shop would be hers when she left this house.

Joe sat down opposite Emma and, adopting his brusquest tone, he commenced, 'Now, about the shop, miss. I've been thinking it over, and I have definitely decided I can't rent it to you.'

'Why ever not?' Emma asked in her most dulcet voice.

'Because two people have failed in it this year, and they'd had a lot more experience than *you*. I don't want to sound harsh, miss, but you must understand I can't take a chance on renting to somebody who's a novice. I'm seeking a tenant that really knows retailing, who'll make a go of the shop, so I don't have to be worrying about it being vacant half the time. I've better things to do than play nursemaid.'

Emma gave Joe a smile that would have melted half the ice in the Arctic Circle and made her eyes wide but serious. 'Oh, I do realize that, Mr Lowther,' she answered. 'And, in some ways, I understand your reluctance because of my youth. However, it's not really of great consequence when you consider that I have been running a business from my home. I have been dealing with people, *selling* to them. My business has been highly profitable. I've made a lot of money with my dressmaking and homemade foodstuffs. I have good steady customers, mostly the carriage trade, and they would certainly give me their patronage if I had a shop.' Emma paused and flashed a brilliant smile. 'Why, they have assured me of that,' she fibbed adroitly. 'So you see, I'm not really as inexperienced as you believe, and I do have expectations.'

'Carriage trade, you say,' remarked Joe, not unimpressed. 'And how long have you been running this little business from your home?'

'About a year,' said Emma, leaning forward, eagerness washing over her face. 'And it's not so *little* either.'

Joe regarded her intently. She was direct and sounded businesslike and certainly she was not lacking in assurance. In fact, he had never met a girl as self-possessed as she was. Her spirit and enthusiasm were refreshing, almost infectious, and his doubts about her youth, and ability were rapidly diminishing. However, she disconcerted him, but then he had always been awkward around girls and one as beautiful as she was bound to make him feel insecure. Still, she only wanted to rent a shop from him and that was all. 'Well, I don't really know what to say,' he began hesitatingly.

Conscious that he was wavering, Emma held up her hand. 'Just a minute, Mr Lowther,' she said authoritatively. 'I said earlier I would pay you in advance.' She opened her black reticule and brought out a thick roll of bank notes. 'As you can see, Mr Lowther, I don't make idle claims. I am a woman of some substance, albeit a young one, and indeed I can pay you *well* in advance. I know I can make a go of the shop, Mr Lowther. I expect it to be a success within *six months*.'

Joe stared at her incredulously. 'Oh, come on! That's a bit far-fetched. Do you think I fell off a banana boat? I'm not green, you know.'

Emma decided these comments were unworthy of a reply. Instead she stretched out her hand. 'I have been so rude, Mr Lowther. I haven't introduced myself. My name is Emma Harte.'

He took her hand tentatively. He felt its dry coolness through the crocheted glove and her grip was firm, strong like a man's. 'Pleased to meet you, Miss Harte,' he said.

'It's *Mrs* Harte,' said Emma.

'Oh, excuse me,' said Joe, assailed by unexpected disappointment.

Emma grabbed the moment to drive her point home. 'I don't know what the rent is, Mr Lowther, but I would be prepared to pay you several months in advance.' She must make the offer so tempting he would not be able to refuse. 'Shall we say *six months* in advance? Surely that shows you my good faith and also my belief in myself.'

Joe was floundering, his resolve crumbling under the force of her compelling and winning personality. He recognized he was drawn to her. Dangerously attracted to her. The unworldly Joe was horrified. A married woman! Then it came to him in a rush. That was the real reason he did not want her as a tenant. He was afraid of falling under her spell.

Emma knew she was holding all the cards and she made her final move. She leaned forward and touched his arm gently. Joe jumped as if bitten by a snake. 'Look here, Mr Lowther,' Emma said firmly. 'I have another idea. Apart from paying you the rent in advance, I'm also prepared to give you a letter of agreement stating that should my business fail I will not vacate the premises until you find another tenant. In other words, I will guarantee to give you sufficient warning before leaving. Shall we say three months' notice?' she suggested in a guileless voice.

Joe found it impossible to argue with this girl. Not only were her terms sound, they were all in his favour. He would look like an imbecile if he refused such an offer. 'Well,' he said at last, 'you are certainly confident of your success in the shop, Mrs Harte. Otherwise you wouldn't suggest such an arrangement. But it's fair enough, I suppose. Don't you want to look over the shop first, before going into this venture?'

'I know the shop, Mr Lowther,' Emma said with an airy wave of her hand. 'I went into it several times. Your previous tenant was badly organized, the stock was shoddy and far too expensive for its quality, and she was obviously not a very clever buyer. Not only that, she didn't know her customers!'

'Oh,' said Joe, dumbfounded.

'I presume it's settled, Mr Lowther,' said Emma briskly.

'Er, yes, of course. I'll rent the shop to you,' he said. 'For a guinea a week. That makes it four guineas a month. There are living quarters attached to the shop. A large kitchen-parlour, a bedroom, and a huge cellar for storage. You could live there, behind the shop, and very comfortably, if you had a mind to.'

Emma nodded. 'Yes, I probably will live there. It makes sense. Now, four guineas a month is around forty-eight guineas a year, give or take a few shillings, isn't it?' She began to peel off the notes, doing some fast mental arithmetic. 'Could I have a receipt, please?' she asked politely, handing over the cash.

'Naturally,' said Joe. 'And I will get you the key and the rent book. I'll mark the book paid for six months. Should it be in your name or your husband's?'

'Mine, please. My husband is in the navy, Mr Lowther. In foreign parts.'

'Is he really!' said Joe.

Emma nodded and went on, 'I'll write you the letter of agreement about the three months' notice. I'll bring it around tomorrow evening. Is that convenient? You can show it to your solicitor, if you want.'

'No. No. That's not necessary. And tomorrow night is perfectly convenient,' said Joe. He stood up. 'I'll go and get the key and the rent book. I'll be back in a jiffy.'

'Aren't you going to count the money?' Emma asked, nodding at the pounds in his hand.

'I trust you,' Joe said. 'Please excuse me, Mrs Harte.'

Emma heard him whistling as he went through into the kitchen. A wide smile of self-congratulation mingled with exultation flew on to her face. She could hardly contain herself.

She now had her first shop.

THIRTY-FOUR

Joe Lowther shrugged into his black overcoat and dug his hands into his pockets, shivering as he strode along at a brisk pace. A fierce wind was whistling down the lane and it blew the sleet and snow against his body in swirling flurries. He was drenched again, as he had been every night this week. December had ushered in the foulest weather, which now at the end of the first week appeared to have settled in for a long siege. He was later than ever tonight. Once again he had been inveigled into staying at the foundry to finish the books as a special favour to Mr Ramsbotham, who had lately acquired the annoying habit of piling extra work on him. His tardiness irritated him for another, more significant reason. Usually on Friday evening, after his supper, he went to Emma Harte's to look over the books for her. Tonight he would not be able to get there until almost ten o'clock, and Joe, the product of a lower-middle-class upbringing, was rigid in his observance of the proprieties. It did not seem correct to go calling on a young woman who lived alone at such a late hour. Still, he had promised and he felt honour-bound to keep his word.

Joe had taught Emma bookkeeping, and supervising her ledgers was a practice he considered unnecessary these days. Nevertheless, it was one he did willingly and, if he was honest with himself, he looked forward to doing it. Emma had a staggering aptitude for figures and kept meticulous books. It had struck him recently that she actually enjoyed toiling over those endless columns of figures in a way he did not. If the truth be known, he did not like bookkeeping at all. It was hardly his vocation. However, he had been apprenticed in the accounting office at the foundry when he was fifteen, and after nine years it had become a way of life for him. It never occurred to Joe to seek a more congenial employer. He was too set in his ways and, since he was not ambitious and lacked the drive to strike out in new directions, he remained shackled to Ramsbotham's dreary books. Nor did it ever occur to the stolid Joe that he did not have to work at all, if he chose not to. He detested idleness and, more importantly, he harboured a palpable fear of boredom. His job at the foundry filled his days and helped to counteract the empty evenings of solitude that yawned inexorably before him month after month, year after year.

But Joe Lowther could have stopped working when his mother had died four years ago. It was then that Frederick Ainsley, the family solicitor, had sent for him to hear the will read and Joe had discovered, to his profound astonishment, that his mother had left him not only in comfortable circumstances but extremely well off. 'It is An Inheritance, my boy,' Mr Ainsley had said, speaking in capitals as befitted the occasion and the size of the estate. 'A tribute to your poor departed mother's prodigious and most commendable efforts over the years, and to your grandmother's before her,' the solicitor had intoned. Frederick Ainsley had then gone on to enumerate the number of properties Joe now owned, thanks to the unflagging industriousness of those two women on the maternal side of the family. The Inheritance, which Joe immediately felt obliged to think of in Mr Ainsley's large letters, included eight shops in Town Street, a row of cottages in Armley, several terrace houses in nearby Wortley, and, to Joe's further incredulity, two large plots of land near St Paul's Street in Leeds itself. 'Better hang on to those, Joe,' Ainsley had instructed. 'They will increase in value. Lots of building going on in Leeds. When you do sell it should be for a high price.' Finally, the speechless Joe had learned that his mother had left him fifty-five thousand pounds in cash in the Midland Bank. Joe had staggered out of the solicitor's office reeling from shock on that awesome day. Later, sitting on the tram on his way home to Armley, a cold anger had settled over him. His mother had never ceased her querulous warnings of financial disaster looming on the horizon. His sweet-tempered and henpecked father had been mercilessly driven into an early grave from overwork and lack of nourishing food and proper medical attention. Why had his mother been so cruel when they had had so much? he had asked himself, and his resentment of her had not lessened with time.

Joe had not touched that capital during these past few years. He had simply added to it, paying the revenue from the properties into the bank every month. Unlike his avaricious mother, there was little cupidity in Joe and as long as he had sufficient for his daily needs that was good enough for him. Most of the time money never crossed his mind at all.

However, he thought about it this night as he trudged through the dark wet streets. Two weeks earlier Emma had mentioned that she was investing in David Kallinski's first clothing factory in York Road. She had already designed a line of ladies' clothes for David and her enthusiasm was infectious. When Emma had suggested David might let him invest as well, Joe had been surprised. 'Money should be made to work, Joe,' Emma had pronounced, and she informed him that she hoped to double her money in no time at all.

Although Joe was cautious by nature, this was chiefly engendered by shyness, rather than any particular canniness. His laissez-faire attitude about finances had prompted him to shrug nonchalantly and agree to invest, if David wanted him to do so. Emma had said she would arrange it. 'I think two thousand pounds would be just the right amount,' she had gone on. 'If you can afford it. As a financial man, you should know, without me telling you, that money is a tool to be used to make more money, Joe. What good is it doing in the bank?'

I don't really need to make more money, Joe now said to himself. He was settled for life. On the other hand, he did not particularly want to lose two thousand pounds. He dismissed this negative thought. Joe had an infallible belief in Emma's innate shrewdness, having witnessed it at first hand, and he had long recognized her brilliance in business matters, amazing for a twenty-year-old girl. He trusted her judgement. Also, Joe was intelligent enough to acknowledge that he was really investing in the clothing factory for the fun of it. He liked David and Emma, and because he had few friends and was miserably lonely, he longed to be involved in their lives, to be part of this exciting venture.

So caught up was he in his diverse thoughts Joe found himself on his own doorstep in no time at all. He knocked the snow off his boots as he climbed the steps. Delicious aromas of food cooking greeted him, and the warmth of the sparkling kitchen dispelled his lonely feelings.

Mrs Hewitt was setting the table for his supper. 'There yer are, Joe,' she cried, her face beaming. 'By gum, yer look nithered ter death, luvey. Come ter the fire and get yerself warmed up.'

'Hello, Mrs Hewitt,' Joe said, taking off his cap and struggling out of his coat. He hurried over to the sink, rubbing his hands to dispel their iciness. He dried his hair and face, washed his hands, and then sat down by the fire. 'It's a blustery night, Mrs Hewitt, and very cold. I think there'll be a hard frost.'

Mrs Hewitt nodded. 'Aye, yer probably right, lad.' She glanced at him and frowned, 'Nay, Joe, don't sit there in yer wet boots, luv. Take 'em off at once. That's how yer get toothache, yer knows, luvey, sitting in wet boots.'

Joe smiled at this old wives' tale, but he unlaced his boots and placed them on the hearth to please her. She was a nice old body and looked after him far better than his mother ever had, and three nights a week she helped to transform this depressing house into a home.

'Look at this custard flan,' Mrs Hewitt exclaimed, pointing to the dessert on the table. 'Have yer ever seen owt as luvely? I bought it as pudding for yer, at Mrs Harte's. By gum, Joe, no wonder she does a roaring trade. And the way she's trained them two lasses of Mrs Long's to be her helpers, why, it fair takes me breath away.'

Joe smiled at her. 'I never thought she'd make such a go of it when she took that first shop. But she proved *me* wrong, and a lot of others as well.'

'Aye, lad, she's a right good tenant for yer,' Mrs Hewitt conceded.

'What's for supper?' Joe asked, warming his hands. 'It smells good.'

'I can't be taking no credit for yer dinner tonight, Joe,' the old woman replied. 'I bought yer a steak-and-kidney pie from Mrs Harte's, being as how yer liked the last one.'

'It sounds grand, Mrs Hewitt.'

'I was talking to Laura Spencer today, in the haberdashery, and do yer know, that wedding dress they're making for me cousin's lass is one of Mrs Harte's own designs. Miss Spencer told me that Mrs Harte is going to be designing clothes for one of them big factory places in Leeds.'

'So I understand,' said Joe.

'Fancy that and yer never told me, Joe.'

'It didn't occur to me, Mrs Hewitt. Is it so important?'

'Of course it is, Joe. Anything ter do with Emma Harte is important. Why, everybody thinks she's a right luvely young woman. So polite and dignified. The talk of Town Street with her fancy shops. And such a bonny lass.' She carried the bowl of turnips to the oven and continued, 'Would yer like a beer, Joe? I've got one cooling on the cellar head.'

'I wouldn't say no, Mrs Hewitt. Thank you.' Joe lit his pipe and settled back in the chair, warming his damp feet.

'Well, it's all ready now, Joe,' Mrs Hewitt proclaimed. 'I've finished the pots and yer supper'll stay nice and warm in the oven, luvey. Drink yer beer first, and then yer can help yerself later. I'll have ter be off. Ta'rar.'

Later, after he had read the paper, Joe took out the meat pie and vegetables and settled down to his supper. He had just finished eating when a loud banging on the door brought him up with a start. The door burst open to admit a flurry of snowflakes along with Mrs Minton, one of his tenants. Her face was purple and from the furious glint in her eyes Joe knew this was not caused by the icy wind but rather by her roiling temper.

'Good heavens, Mrs Minton –' he began.

'Don't Mrs Minton me, Joe Lowther!' she yelled. 'It's a crime! A bloody crime. *I just knew it!* Ever since she moved in I knew she was after me shop. And when yer rented her that other one on t'corner I told me husband it wouldn't be long before she had me out. There I am, plonk in the middle, between her food shop and her haberdashery, and she's aiming ter squeeze and squeeze till she get's me out inter the middle of Town Street. Yer can't deny I'm right!' The enraged Mrs Minton paused for breath, her hands on her hips, her stance defiant.

'Please, Mrs Minton, calm down. I don't know what on earth you're talking about.'

'I'm talking about Emma Harte, that's what! She wants me shop! I don't need a crystal bloody ball ter tell me that. She wants ter expand inter me shop. The shop I've had for ten years. The commercial travellers think she's no good, hoity-toity stuck-up Mrs Harte. Lady Muck, they calls her. Cutting 'em out, she is, going ter the manufacturers and warehouses herself and buying directly, instead of from the travellers. Then she slashes her prices so's nobody else in Town Street can get a sale in edgewise. Aye, she's a crafty cunning bitch, that Emma Harte is.'

'Mrs Minton!' Joe bellowed. 'Emma Harte is a nice girl and she works hard. She isn't trying to squeeze you out. She's simply running her shops in a businesslike manner.' Joe stared with distaste at the slovenly woman in her filthy coat and grimy scarf. She was a living reflection of her dirty shop, which was a triumph of confusion and run in the most slipshod manner imaginable.

'Aye, I bloody expected yer ter defend her,' Mrs Minton shouted. 'I told me husband I wouldn't be getting nowheres with yer. Stands ter reason yer'd watch out for yer fancy woman! Aye, and don't look like that. We all knows what's going on between the both of yer!' She took a step nearer to Joe and peered into his face, hissing, 'Yer fancy woman, that's what Emma bloody Harte is, and she a married woman! I'm surprised yer haven't put a bun in her oven already. But time will tell, me lad.'

Joe had blanched. 'Why, you foul-mouthed, despicable old woman. There is nothing between Mrs Harte and myself, other than a business relationship. And you'd better watch your words, Mrs Minton, or you'll find yourself the recipient of a writ for slander. I will not tolerate this kind of disgusting talk!'

Mrs Minton leaned forward and waved the rent book she was clutching under his nose. Joe thought she was going to strike him with it. 'I think you had better leave, Mrs Minton,' he said icily. 'Before I really lose my temper. I've just about had enough of you.'

With a toss of her head she swung on her heels and marched to the door. She looked back, her eyes blazing with animosity, and she shouted, 'Well, she's not going ter have the satisfaction of squeezing me out, because I'm leaving on me own account! And yer can take yer bloody rent book and shove it!' She flung the rent book across the room at Joe and it landed in the custard flan.

The door banged behind her. Joe stared at the rent book floating in the custard, fished it out, and carried it to the sink, wiping it clean with the dishcloth. He looked inside. Miserable old battle-axe, he thought, she owes me a month's rent. He knew he would have to whistle for that. He did not care.

Joe was horrified at the things Mrs Minton had said about Emma and himself. Surely they must have been uttered out of her consuming spite. Or did everyone in the neighbourhood really believe there was something between them? 'Fancy

345

woman' was not a prestigious name to pin on a woman. It was just another way of saying tart. He might have guessed some people would talk, if only the likes of Mrs Minton. But he had never laid a finger on Emma, and he felt a flush rising to flood his face. It was with a rush of guilt that he recalled those nights when he lay awake in his chaste bed, hardly able to breathe, his desire for Emma blazing until he could not bear it. For desire her he did. On those terrible nights he envisioned himself running his hands over Emma's beautiful body, pressing his mouth to hers, stroking her firm breasts, and ultimately taking her to him passionately. He shivered and closed his eyes, trying to obliterate those erotic images, those lustful and sensuous fantasies that haunted him.

After a few moments Joe felt calmer. Wanting a woman and craving to possess her was one thing, but it was scarcely a reality, and he resented the ghastly implications of Mrs Minton's words. Joe sighed wearily, recognizing that Emma had ruined the harridan's business, albeit unintentionally. She made sure her products and the shops themselves were more appealing and attractive than others in the vicinity. Her specialities, such as her delicious homemade foodstuffs, were renowned, as was her dressmaking, and she had captured the carriage trade for miles around. With her audacity and her superior merchandising, her two shops had become the busiest in Town Street in just under three years, and her profits were high. Joe was aware of that from his weekly inspection of her ledgers. So enormously high, in fact, she could now afford to invest two thousand pounds in David's business, as he himself intended to do. That kind of success was guaranteed to provoke jealousy and vicious talk.

Joe stood up, determined not to dwell on Mrs Minton's accusations. He would go and see Emma right away and tell her that Mrs Minton was about to vacate the premises. Emma could now have her third shop. Although she had never said a word to Joe, he knew that she had been angling for it for some time. It made sense, he had to admit that. With Mrs Minton gone Emma could indeed expand and the three adjoining shops would be like the department store she envisioned owning one day. He caught sight of the clock. It was well turned nine. He shrugged. To hell with the neighbours. I don't care what they believe. He went upstairs to put on a clean shirt.

Emma stood in the middle of the food shop and surveyed her handiwork with satisfaction. Everything looked beautiful, she decided, and it certainly had been well worth getting up at four-thirty that morning to create her special displays for Christmas. Her keen eyes spotted a particle of dust on one of the glass cabinets and she flew over with a cloth. She flicked it off and stood back, scanning the cabinets that sparkled in the bright light from the gas fixtures on the walls. Now they were absolutely perfect and nothing marred their pristine glitter. The food inside looked delectable. There were Christmas cakes topped with almonds; round fat plum puddings wrapped in fresh muslin, each one tied with a gay red ribbon; a selection of mince pies of various sizes; and yule logs made of sponge cake, thickly coated with rich dark chocolate and decorated with sprigs of marzipan mistletoe. Emma, assisted by the Long girls, had spent endless hours baking all of this seasonal fare but she knew her industriousness would be rewarded. Every item would be sold, along with the additional supplies stored in large tins in the cool cellar.

Emma smoothed the fresh white cloth on the table in front of the glass food cabinets and regarded her arrangement of foreign imports, delicacies she had purchased for the holiday season and which no other shop in Armley carried. She moved a blue-and-white china crock of crystallized ginger so that the French glazed fruits and the Turkish delight were easily visible, and deftly straightened the boxes of Egyptian dates and figs from Greece. She then hurried behind the counter and returned with a tray of small straw baskets containing marzipan fruits and jolly little pigs, which had arrived yesterday from Germany. The night before, Emma had lined the baskets with strips of crinkled green paper, and tied red bows on the handles. She was heavily stocked, but she anticipated a brisk business in the next few days. This was her third Christmas in the shop, and she was now so well established in the district she had no qualms about sales. She was convinced she would be inundated with customers, both her regulars and new ones.

Emma gave the shop a final glance, her eyes critically seeking out the tiniest imperfection. Not one was visible. The innumerable shelves, running around the walls and soaring up to the ceiling, held tins of ham, pork, and game, great black-and-gold canisters of varied teas, all manner of other staples, and her own bottled fruits, vegetables, and jams. Ranged below were jars of candied peel, glazed cherries, mincemeat, and cranberry and apple sauces for the Christmas turkeys and geese. Three huge barrels, to the right of the side counter, were filled to overflowing with nuts, apples, and oranges for the children's traditional Christmas stockings, and the faint aroma of fruit wafted sweetly on the air to blend with the mingled scents of the pungent herbs and spices from the Indies, the fragrance of the newly baked confectionery, and the mouth-watering smells of cheeses and cooked meats. Oh, how she loved her shop! Here she was secure, far away from the Fairleys and protected from them. She thought, too, and with enormous pleasure, of the forthcoming sales and her spiraling profits, and her face immediately broke into a smile.

Now Emma crossed to the door, pulled up the blinds, and drew back the bolts in readiness for her first customers. These would undoubtedly be the cooks and housekeepers from the fine mansions, who usually came trooping in early in the day to place their orders. Emma hoped their shopping lists would be longer than ever this week.

As the clock struck eight Emma took up her usual position behind the counter, seating herself on a stool next to the paraffin stove. She bent down and opened a cupboard, taking out the ledger for the haberdashery. In the year she had been renting Joe Lowther's second shop business had far exceeded her wildest dreams. Laura, whom she had persuaded to manage it for her, had proved to be both capable and efficient, and sales had doubled in the first six months. Emma perused the columns of those beautiful figures and sighed in gratification and relief. Edwina's future and her own were now assured.

The tinkling of the bell brought Emma's head up sharply and she put the ledger away and locked the cupboard. She stood up, smiling at the woman entering. It was the housekeeper from one of the fine residences in the elegant and exclusive row known as the Towers. 'Good morning, Mrs Jackson,' Emma said. 'You're out bright and early.'

347

'Morning to you, Mrs Harte. By gum, it's nippy today. I'm glad to be in in your lovely warm shop. I don't know why the other shopkeepers don't follow your example and heat up their premises.' Mrs Jackson shivered as she approached the counter with two large baskets. 'I thought I'd best get my order in first thing, though I won't be sending the gardener's lad for it till later in the week.' She handed over the baskets and sat down on the stool at the other side of the counter.

Emma stowed the baskets away and said, 'Can I offer you a cup of nice hot tea, Mrs Jackson?'

The woman's face, white and pinched from the freezing weather, lit up. 'You can that, luv, if it's no trouble. It was a right frosty walk down Town Street, I can tell you.'

Emma always kept a huge pot of tea prepared in the cold weather, which she dispensed generously to her clientele. She had discovered that a little hospitality cost nothing and paid enormous dividends. She lifted the pot from the table next to the stove, adjusted the tea cosy and poured the tea. 'Milk and sugar, isn't it, Mrs Jackson? And how's your little Freddy doing? Has he recovered from the measles?' Emma asked. She made a point of knowing about her customers' children and husbands, and their aches and pains, and she was always ready to offer a sympathetic ear.

Mrs Jackson accepted the tea, beaming with delight. 'Well, isn't that nice of you to remember Freddy. He'll be up and about for Christmas.' She opened her handbag and took out a piece of paper. 'Here's my list, Mrs Harte. I think it's complete, but I'll have a look round, if you don't mind and –' Mrs Jackson paused midsentence. The bell was tinkling and the door opened.

Emma's face broke into a surprised but delighted smile. 'Blackie!' she exclaimed, 'I didn't expect you until tonight.'

'Top of the morning to ye, Emma, and to ye, ma'am,' Blackie responded cheerily, inclining his head in Mrs Jackson's direction. 'I hope I'm not disturbing ye, Emma.'

'No, not at all. Come around the counter and help yourself to some tea, while I finish with Mrs Jackson,' said Emma, turning her attention to her customer. She looked over the list quickly. 'Yes, everything seems clear, Mrs Jackson. Still, perhaps you should –' Emma paused and gave the housekeeper a thoughtful look. 'I wonder if you should take some extra mince pies and yule logs. You know how the children love them, and it *is* a long holiday season this year. To be honest with you, I have a large number of orders to meet. I can't promise there will be much left at the end of the week, if you did decide you wanted more.'

'Ooh, I hadn't thought of that. Well, perhaps you'd better increase it. I don't want the missis upset with me. Make it three more of each and pop in another Christmas cake as well,' said Mrs Jackson. Her eyes caught the display of imports and she walked over to the table, carrying her mug of tea. 'By gum, these look real fancy.' She examined a box of Turkish delight and read out Emma's carefully lettered card. 'Exclusive to Harte's. Supply limited.'

Emma pretended to check the shopping list, watching Mrs Jackson from beneath her lashes. She had chosen those words deliberately last night, knowing they would appeal to her customers' snobbishness.

Mrs Jackson continued to look over the foreign sweetmeats and then said, 'I'm not so sure about any of these. They look interesting, but maybe they're just a bit too fancy for my missis.'

'Oh, do you think so, Mrs Jackson? I've always found the gentry to be partial to such delicacies,' Emma said pointedly. 'Actually, I'm sorry I didn't order more. Those items are going like wildfire. Why, only yesterday, one of the cooks from the Towers asked me to save her two of everything,' she improvised swiftly. 'Still, I realize they are a little expensive.'

Mrs Jackson gave Emma a sharp look. 'My missis isn't concerned about the price of anything, Mrs Harte,' she said defensively. 'I'll take *three* of everything!'

Emma smiled. She had learned to take advantage of the competitiveness between the local cooks and housekeepers, who were always trying to better each other. 'Very good, Mrs Jackson. I'll make a note and put them away immediately.'

Mrs Jackson's eyes roved over the shelves behind Emma. 'While you're at it, you'd best add a tin of that imported ham and four bottles of your chutney to my list. *My* lady's expecting a lot of *posh* guests over the holidays. It's wise to be prepared.'

'Yes, that's true. And you can always send the gardener's boy down later in the week, if there's anything else you've forgotten. You know I'll always do my best for *you*, Mrs Jackson.'

The housekeeper preened. 'It's nice to know I'm a favoured customer, Mrs Harte. I know I can rely on you. Now, do you think I've missed anything off the list, being as how you know so much about catering? I do want the missis to be pleased with my menus for the holidays.'

Emma made a show of thinking hard. 'I would add two tins of pork and three jars of apple sauce, if I were you. For emergencies. And perhaps a selection of cheeses to go with the Christmas cakes. Leave it to me, Mrs Jackson. I'll pick out the very best of my cheeses, and perhaps a couple of other items.'

Mrs Jackson placed the mug on the counter, looking as if Emma had just done her an enormous favour. 'Thank you, Mrs Harte. It's thoughtful of you to take so much trouble for me. I must say, you've made my life easier since you've been in Town Street. I don't have to do so much cooking these days. Well, I must be on me way. Merry Christmas to you, luv.' She paused at the door and waved.

'Merry Christmas, Mrs Jackson. And remember, don't you worry about a thing. I'll see your order is filled exactly,' Emma called after her.

'I bet you will,' Blackie said with a grin as he came around the counter and lowered himself on to the stool Mrs Jackson had vacated. 'Ye could sell coal to the natives in darkest Africa. I've never seen anything like it, Emma. Why, ye must have doubled that poor woman's order.'

'Tripled it,' said Emma with a smug little smile.

Blackie shook his head and adopted a serious expression. 'Well, Emma, I just stopped by to pay me condolences to ye.'

'Condolences?'

'Aye, I understand ye sailor husband passed away unexpectedly a few weeks ago. Died of typhoid fever in the Indian Ocean, so I be hearing. How very sad.' He threw back that great head and roared. Emma laughed with him. 'My God, Emma, what an imagination ye have. It's ye who should be an aspiring writer and not Frank. Typhoid fever in the Indian Ocean indeed!'

'Well, I had to kill him off,' Emma said. 'It was becoming a real nuisance – having a husband. Even one who had deserted me. I thought it was best to have him die far away and be buried at sea.'

349

Blackie chuckled. 'True. True.' He eyed her red wool dress. 'I can see ye are not in mourning.'

'My friends wouldn't expect me to wear black for a man who deserted me, now would they? I suppose Laura told you.'

'That she did. She said ye had received a letter from the Admiralty the other morning. Ye certainly lay it on thick, don't ye?'

'I had to make it sound authentic, Blackie. They were only white lies. I can tell the truth from now on.'

'Oh, ye can, can ye?'

'Yes, of course,' Emma said firmly. 'But not about Edwina. We have to protect her at all costs. Nobody must know that she's illegitimate, Blackie.'

'I won't be betraying ye, mavourneen. Ye know that. By the way, I saw David Kallinski yesterday. I went to look over the factory, so I can make me plans for the alterations. I hope ye don't mind, but I told him about ye husband passing on.'

'Oh! What did he say?' she asked cautiously.

'He said he was sorry. But to me he looked like a man who'd just inherited a million pounds.' Blackie scrutinized her carefully. 'What's going on between the two of ye, Emma?'

'Why, nothing,' she said evenly. 'I'm his business partner, that's all.'

'Oh, aye,' said Blackie thoughtfully. 'Well, it strikes me he thinks other wise.'

'Stuff and nonsense. It's your Celtic imagination getting the better of you. Yours is a sight more vivid than even Frank's.'

Blackie did not reply. He reached into his overcoat, pulled out a sheaf of papers, and handed them to Emma. 'Here are the plans for renovating the middle shop and then joining all three together like ye wanted, mavourneen. I aim to go into Mrs Minton's on either side. That is, from the haberdashery and through that wall over there. I'll make a sort of passage that links all three. How does that sound?'

'Wonderful, Blackie! You know I trust your judgement. I'll look at the plans tonight. When will you start?' she asked eagerly.

'Knowing ye, I suppose ye'd like me to start immediately, but it'll have to be after Christmas, Emma. We'll do a fast job, though, and ye'll be in the shop by the middle of January.'

THIRTY-FIVE

David Kallinski leaned back against the sofa in the kitchen-parlour behind Emma's food shop and thoughtfully regarded the last of her sketches. He held it away from him, his eyes narrowing perceptively.

As he continued to gaze at it David experienced a flash of excitement and his hands tightened on the drawing. If anything, her designs for their winter collection were even more striking than her summer outfits. They were superb, in fact. The lines were understated and elegant, balanced by fine detailing, and she had cleverly combined the colours for wholly different effects. Her colour sense was extraordinary, even if it was a little daring. Only Emma could have conceived of such unusual mixtures – burgundy trimmed with bright pink, navy blue highlighted with apple green, vivid cyclamen. flashed with lilac, and, on the other side of the spectrum, a mélange of rich autumnal tones enlivened by pure white, misty greys, and blues combined with violet, plus fir green sparked with rose. And they all worked beautifully together. Not only that, because of the simplicity of their basic construction, their clean lines and general lack of fussiness, her creations were ideal for the mass-manufacturing techniques he was employing at the factory.

David smiled with pleasure and pride in Emma. He did not know where her artistic gifts sprang from, but they were indisputable and her taste was matchless, her flair unrivalled. He had long come to recognize, and with not a little wonder, that Emma possessed natural genius. There was no other term appropriate to describe her incredible talent and, coupled with her prodigious energy, it made her formidable. Apart from her brilliance as a designer, she had an innate understanding of the public's whims, an uncanny knack of discerning ahead of time what they wanted and, more importantly, what they would buy. It was as if she had a daemon telling her things, and all of her ventures were instantaneous successes. David suspected that Emma Harte would make money at whatever she decided to turn her hand to, for her touch was golden. Both he and his father had been staggered at her total grasp of financial matters and her capacity for structuring complex monetary schemes, all of which stood up to their accountant's scrutiny and won his astonished approval. She read a balance sheet the way other people read a newspaper and she could pinpoint its flaws and its virtues in a matter of minutes. She was only just twenty-one and already she was scaling ambition's ladder with the swiftest and most determined of steps. It seemed to David that nothing could hold her back – it would have been like trying to harness lightning, he had long ago decided. She continually managed to amaze him and he dare not speculate where she would be in ten years' time. At the top of that ladder, he conjectured, and the prospects were dizzying.

David placed the sketch with the others and lit a cigarette. Things were proceeding on schedule and exactly as he had planned. He had been in business for four months, with Emma and Joe Lowther as his partners. Emma also acted as the designer and stylist, and his brother, Victor, was the factory manager. In one month David would be twenty-five, and he had no doubts whatsoever about the future of the Kallinski Clothing Company, or his own destiny. He intended to be a rich and important member of the community; and the whole of Leeds, indeed if not Yorkshire, would take notice of him one day. That was a promise he had made to himself years ago and he had every intention of keeping that promise.

David had launched into business on his own with flair, assurance, and aggressiveness and it had been a fortuitous start. At the initial showing of the summer collection, the first samples had been received with enthusiasm by the buyers from the big emporiums in Leeds, Bradford, Sheffield, and Manchester, who had fortunately followed up their accolades with surprisingly large orders. The tremendous energy that Emma, Victor, and he had expended, and the long hours they had put in to get the first collection under way, had certainly been justified.

David could not resist shuffling through the sketches once more. He spread them out on the floor and his excitement was barely contained. Yes, by God, she had done it again! This new line could not be bettered by any other manufacturer in Leeds, or even London for that matter. He was absolutely confident that after the winter showing the orders would be huge. He had heady visions of tripling the amount of business he would do in the next few months, for, like Emma, David Kallinski was a born salesman – charming, suave, and utterly dedicated to business.

Emma interrupted his thoughts as she came into the room carrying a steak-and-kidney pie from the storage cellar. David looked up and caught his breath. She had changed into one of their samples and it was enormously becoming to her. Although the style of the dress was not particularly revealing, being tailored and dignified, the fine wool clung to her lovely figure, gently outlining the high curve of her breasts, the rounded smoothness of her thighs, and the length of her graceful legs. The dress was of a dark bottle green and this colour served to emphasize the brilliance of her eyes and the translucency of her skin. He noticed she had done something different with that magnificent and abundant hair. It was pulled back as always, so that the widow's peak was highly visible, but she had brushed it loose for once and then captured the thick tresses in a dark green net, a sort of snood topped by a small green velvet bow. The netted russet hair fell to her shoulders and framed her incomparable face and it gave her an innocent look. She's the the most alluring creature in the world, David thought wonderingly.

Uncomfortably aware of his prolonged examination of her, Emma halted, frowning. 'Don't you like the designs, David?' she asked, misunderstanding the expression on his face.

'Good God, yes!' he cried. 'They're excellent, Emma. No, that's an understatement. They're outstanding. You've done a fantastic job. Truly.'

Emma smiled. 'Don't exaggerate,' she demurred, but she sighed with relief. After she had placed the pie in the oven, she glided over and sat on the floor at his feet, her back to the fire. She sorted through the sketches, expounding quickly on each one, her face revealing her zeal. She suggested minor changes to some of the designs, explained her ideas on the cutting and manufacturing processes most suitable, and volunteered her thoughts about costing. When they had first started, Emma had applied strict cost accounting to every phase of manufacturing and because of this they would be able to produce more for less than their competitors. She reiterated those points and David leaned forward, eagerness washing over his fine young face. He listened carefully, making mental notes of everything she said. Her advice had proved to be sound, and he always followed it.

When Emma had finished, David said, 'There's only one thing we didn't think about – a name for the line. We must come up with one immediately, because I've already put the summer collection into production and I must order the labels. I don't think Kallinski Clothes is a very exciting name, do you?'

Emma looked up quickly. Not wanting to hurt his feelings, she hesitated before saying, 'Not really. It's not – well – it's not very feminine, David. But I don't have any ideas. Why don't you ask Victor? He's very bright about such things.'

David broke into a grin. 'I guessed you'd suggest that and so I did already. Victor came up with one name this afternoon. I sort of like it, though I'm not sure that you will approve. He suggested we use the name of your famous namesake.'

'My famous namesake? Who on earth does he mean? I didn't know I had one.'

'I didn't know either, I'm ashamed to admit. Just goes to show how ignorant we are. He meant the first Emma Hart. That's Hart without the *e*.'

Undisguised curiosity flickered on to Emma's face. 'The first Emma Hart,' she echoed. 'Who is she?'

'The first Emma Hart was quite a famous lady, or infamous, depending on how you look at it. Let me explain. Your namesake married Sir William Hamilton and became Lady Hamilton. *That's* the name Victor suggested we adopt.' David laughed at her bewilderment. 'Emma Hart was Nelson's Lady Hamilton. His great love. His mistress. His bequest to the nation in his renowned will, so Victor tells me. Don't you remember your history books, my girl?' he teased.

'Oh, *that* Lady Hamilton! Mmmmm. It's not a bad name actually. Not bad at all,' she mused. 'Rather distinguished, when you think about it. Lady Hamilton Dresses. No, since we are making suits and coats as well, it would have to be Lady Hamilton Clothes, wouldn't it?'

'Yes, it would. Do you really like it, Emma? To be honest with you, I took to it at once, but I wanted to discuss it with you before I had the labels made. What do you say?'

Emma pondered, repeating the name in her head. It did have a catchy ring to it and it was rather classy. She remembered that Nelson was Winston's great naval hero. Perhaps this was a good omen. Maybe the name would be lucky. 'Yes, I do like it! Let's use it, David.'

'What about Joe? Shouldn't we ask his opinion?'

'Good heavens, David, surely you know Joe will approve of anything we suggest. You don't have to worry about *him*.' She laughed. 'What would we do without Victor? We're such a couple of illiterates, aren't we?'

'Perhaps we are, but we know how to make money. Anyway, how about a spot of sherry to celebrate selecting the name?' David stood up, bending over Emma. He offered her his outstretched hands and helped her up off the floor.

As Emma rose she lifted her head and smiled into David's face. Their eyes met and held. They stared at each other for a suspended moment, unable to look away, bright blue gaze impaled on one of vivid green. Emma felt an internal quivering, as she always did these days whenever David touched her. A flush rose to her face, and her heart began to pound unreasonably. She continued to stare into his adoring face, hypnotized by that sapphire blaze so full of yearning.

Long aware of her hesitancy and reserve, David moved swiftly. He pulled her into his arms, his mouth seeking hers. His lips touched her lips and he parted them gently but firmly. Emma felt the warm sweetness of his tongue and her senses overwhelmed her. Her fingers flew to the back of his head involuntarily and ran through his crisp black hair, and it was as if her touch was a firebrand. David held her closer to him, his strong hands sliding down over her shoulders to the small of her back. His palms pressed her slender body into his own muscular one and, as his embrace tightened, Emma felt the rise of his own desire against her thigh. It had been like this for several weeks now – the kissing, the touching, the ardent glances. Every time they were alone together they were both engulfed by a consciousness of their bodies straining for fulfilment in each other.

David assaulted Emma's emotions in a way that made her breathless and reeling. Her latent ardour, only tentatively and fleetingly awakened years before and then submerged, was surfacing with increasing persistency when David kissed her and held her in his arms. Emma trembled with a mixture of apprehension and alarm, old familiars that constantly assailed her in his presence. She tried to fight her clamouring feelings, but her mind floundered and she gave herself up to his sensual kisses.

They gravitated to the sofa without releasing their hold on each other and fell on to it. David bent over Emma, his eyes locked on hers and brimming with longing. His image filled her vision until she was lost in it, and she closed her eyes. David stroked her face and kissed her eyelids, her forehead, and her lips. Very carefully, he untied the green velvet bow and removed the net so that her hair was released in a cascade over her shoulders. He ran his hand through it, marvelling at her beauty and the fervency of the passion she aroused in him. He burned to possess her fully, and he knew he would never let her go.

David's vivid eyes roved over her body, lying so languorous on the sofa, and he was unable to restrain himself further. He began to caress her face, her neck, her shoulders, and her breasts, and a choking sensation filled his throat when her nipples hardened under his touch through the fine fabric of the dress. His desire spiralled into an exquisite pain that was almost unendurable.

Emma opened her eyes and she saw a fleeting flash of anguish smudge out the blueness of his eyes so that they became dark and intense. David moved closer to her and gripped her shoulders, and his mouth was demanding and hard on hers. He covered her body with his own, pressing down on her, and Emma rejoiced in the weight of him.

His voice was rasping in the hollow of her neck. 'Oh, Emma! Emma, darling! I can't stand this!'

'I know, David, I know,' she murmured. She smoothed his darkly curling hair and held his head against her breast, cradling him in her arms. Her hand stroked his broad shoulders and a cry of longing trembled on her lips. She bent her head and rested it on his and her hair drifted down around them like a silken veil. A long sigh rippled through her and she acknowledged that she loved David Kallinski and wanted him for herself, for the rest of her life, but her natural rectitude, coupled with her terrible fear of the consequences of sexual intimacy out of wedlock, would not permit her to succumb to her overwhelming emotions. It was not that she did not trust David. She did. She knew he would never betray her. He was no Edwin Fairley. And yet she bit down on those insistent desires, stifling them, and finally she denied him in her mind if not in her heart.

Very quietly Emma whispered into his hair, 'We have to stop this, David. It's getting worse every time, and it's not fair to you. We must not let the situation get out of hand.' She pushed him away from her with the utmost gentleness and sat up, dizzy and shaking.

David leaned back against the sofa and picked up a strand of her hair. He kissed it and then let it fall. He half smiled. 'Emma, I love you so much. Don't be afraid of me. I won't hurt you. Ever.'

Emma flinched at this deadly echo from the past. 'I'm not afraid of you, David,' she answered quietly. 'I'm afraid of myself when I'm with you like this and what might happen when we get so – so –'

'Please don't.' He placed a finger on her lips. 'I agree with you. We can't go on like this. It's insanity. But we must be together, Emma. I can't bear this torment for much longer.' He grasped her hand, his face earnest. 'Marry me, Emma. As soon as possible,' he implored. 'We must get married, you know that.'

'Married!' she cried.

David smiled. 'Yes, married. Don't sound so shocked. I've wanted to marry you for the last few years. I've only held myself in check because of your circumstances.'

He chuckled. 'Did you think I had dishonourable intentions, Emma? I would never attempt to compromise you. I love you far too much –' David stopped abruptly, staring at her, his eyes wide with surprise. 'Emma, what's wrong? You're as white as a sheet!'

'I cannot marry you, David,' Emma said in a low strangled voice.

'But why not? Don't be ridiculous!' He actually laughed, so disbelieving was he of her words. 'I told you I love you and I know you love me. It's the most natural outcome, isn't it? For us to get married. That's what people do when they love each other, Emma.'

Emma stood up unsteadily and moved across the floor. She looked out of the window and her eyes filled with tears. She discovered she was unable to answer him.

David gaped at her stiff back, her tensely set shoulders, baffled by her behaviour. 'What is it, Emma? For God's sake answer me!' he demanded.

'I cannot marry you, David. Please, let's leave it at that,' Emma said blinking back her tears.

'Of course you can!' David asserted fiercely. 'There is nothing to stop you now. Your husband is dead. You are free.' David paused, and when he spoke again it was with quiet intensity. 'Emma, I love you more than anyone or anything on this earth. I want to cherish and protect you with my life, for the rest of my life. We belong together, Emma. I know that deep in my heart. And so do you. There is something very special between us – an unbreakable bond.' Still she did not respond and another thought occurred to David. 'Is it because of Edwina?' he asked quickly. 'You don't have to worry about her. I'm not afraid of responsibility. I will adopt her, Emma, and the three of us can live together. We'll be happy and I –'

'It's not because of Edwina.'

'Then give me a good reason why you won't marry me!' he commanded, his face pale and washed with anxiety.

'David, I cannot marry you because your mother would never accept me. She would never approve of you marrying out of the faith. Surely I don't have to point that out to you. She wants you to marry a Jewish girl who will give her Jewish grandchildren –'

'To hell with all that!' David interrupted, his voice rising angrily. 'I don't care what my *mother* wants, Emma. *I* want *you* for my wife and that's all that counts.'

'I can't hurt your mother,' Emma whispered. 'She's been wonderful to me, almost like a second mother. I love her and I won't betray her. You're her eldest son, David. It would kill her if we married. I admit she's very fond of me, but it would not be quite the same thing – welcoming me as a daughter-in-law. Me a Gentile and she so Orthodox. Please listen to what I say, David. It's the truth and you must face it.'

David leaned forward on the sofa, his hands tightly clenched. 'I want you to look me in the eye and tell me you do not love me, Emma. Turn around and tell me that.'

'I can't,' Emma said quietly.

'Why not?' he shouted, his voice breaking.

'Because I do love you, David. Just as much as you love me.' Emma swung around slowly and crossed the floor. She knelt down at his feet and stared up into his face. She touched it fleetingly.

He clasped her tightly in his arms, smoothing her hair, kissing her tearstained cheeks. 'Then that's all that matters, my darling. That's all that matters.'

'No, David.' Emma pulled away and rose, seating herself next to him. 'Other things matter in life. I am not going to be responsible for creating heartache and pain for your parents. I will not divide your family. They have been too good to me. Besides, I couldn't live with myself.' She searched his obdurate face. 'David, don't you understand that it's not possible to build happiness on other people's misery? It might be all right at first, if we did marry, but eventually their anguish and disappointment would come between us. It would chip away at what we have, and finally destroy it.'

David had been staring at her capable little hand clasping his tightly. It was so small and curiously defenceless. At last he raised his eyes and saw the candour in her green gaze and he knew she had meant every word. But he could not prevent himself from crying, 'Are you trying to tell me that you are willing to sacrifice our happiness, mine and yours, just because of some religious beliefs that are not only outdated but utterly ridiculous! I can't believe it. Not *you*. Not *my* Emma. The stalwart Emma who would fight the world for anything she wanted!'

'Yes, I suppose I am. But it's not really like that, David. Please, try and understand –' She broke off. She had hurt him profoundly and she could not bear it.

David extracted his hand from hers and moved it across his face. He felt horribly faint to a point of nausea and an intolerable pain moved across his chest. It seemed that his life was draining away. It was as if someone had suddenly snatched his hopes and dreams and the promise of the future from his grasp. But he knew what Emma said was indeed true. He knew, too, that she would not change her mind, just as his mother would not.

David leapt up and paced in front of the fire. Finally, after a few minutes, he stopped and turned to Emma, staring at her. 'Is that your last word?' he asked so quietly she could scarcely hear him.

'Yes, David. I'm sorry, but I can't destroy your mother.'

'I understand, Emma. You must excuse me. I have to leave. Sorry about the dinner, but I seem to have lost my appetite.' He strode out before she could see the tears swimming in his eyes.

Emma stood up swiftly. 'David! Wait! Please wait!' The door slammed behind him and she was alone. She gazed at the door for a long moment and then picked up the sketches and placed them in the cupboard. Vaguely she thought of the dinner spoiling in the oven, but such intense feelings of dejection and misery overcame her she did not have the strength to remove the food. Her thoughts centred on David and not on herself, for unconsciously she had always known their relationship was doomed. They could be friends and business partners, but that was all. She had spent enough time with Janessa Kallinski to understand that David's mother would not tolerate anything else. Emma sat for a long time looking into the empty room and David's face swam before her. She would never forget that awful look of hurt on his face as long as she lived.

About an hour later Emma was roused from her stupor by a loud banging on the door. David had come back! She flew out into the small hallway, her heart leaping, his name on her lips. She flung open the door with eagerness and found herself staring into the bulbous face of Gerald Fairley.

Emma was so dumbfounded she momentarily lost all power of speech. But immediately her hand tightened on the knob and she stiffened, alerted for trouble. She tried to close the door but he had anticipated her. He pushed himself inside and closed the door firmly behind him.

Emma found her voice. 'What do you want?' she asked coldly. How had he managed to find her?

Gerald grinned. 'Aren't you going to invite me in, Emma?' he asked.

'No. I have nothing to say to you. Please leave immediately,' she said, summoning all of her courage and adopting her iciest tone.

Gerald, after all the years of gorging himself, was revolting in his incredible obesity, a mountain of flesh and powerfully strong. There was a derisive expression on his blubbery face. 'Not on your life! I have a few words to say to *you, Mrs* Harte,' he exclaimed with disdain.

'I repeat, I have nothing to say to you. Please leave.'

'Where's the child?' countered Gerald, his sly eyes full of malicious intent.

'What child?' said Emma coolly, but her legs shook and she longed for help, for David to return.

Gerald laughed in her face. 'Come on, don't give me that! I know you had Edwin's child. There's no use denying it. He confessed it to me this weekend. You see, I told him I had found you. Quite by accident, of course, since I wasn't looking for you. The silly fool wanted to come and see you, wanted to help you and his child. But I couldn't permit that.' Gerald brought his bloated face closer. Emma drew back against the wall, hardly breathing. Gerald smiled. 'It's a small world, Emma. We bought Thompson's mill last week. Imagine my surprise when I saw your name on the old books. You used to work there as a weaver, before you came up in the world. Went into trade, I see,' he said disparagingly. 'Now, where's the baby?'

'I did not have a child,' Emma insisted, clenching her hands by her sides.

'Don't lie to me. It would be very easy for me to check it out. Remember one thing, *Mrs* Harte. I have money and power. I can go to the local hospital – St Mary's, isn't it? – and after a few pounds have changed hands in the right quarters I can look at the records any time I want.'

Emma's heart sank. She knew he spoke the truth. Despite this, she was determined not to admit anything. '*I did not have a child,*' she repeated, her gaze unflickering.

'Oh, come on, Emma, tie one on the other leg and pull it. Edwin wouldn't confess such a thing if it were not true, especially since he is about to become engaged to Lady Jane Stansby.' Gerald grabbed her arm. 'I have the feeling you might use this child to blackmail Edwin later. That's common practice with tramps from the working class. But I aim to circumvent that. The Fairleys cannot afford a scandal. So come on, out with it. Where's the little bastard? And was it a girl or a boy?'

Emma glared at him. 'I told you, I did not have Edwin's child,' she said harshly, and her eyes blazed with intense hatred. She pulled her arm away. 'And if you ever lay a finger on me again, Gerald Fairley, I will kill you!'

He laughed and then his eyes shifted to the stairs illuminated by the dim glow from the bedroom lamp. He shoved her out of the way abruptly and bounded up the steps. Emma recovered her balance and flew up after him. 'How dare you push your way into my home. I shall go and fetch the police!' she cried.

Gerald had disappeared into the bedroom, and when Emma hurried in she found him pulling out drawers and flinging their contents all over the room. 'What do you think you're doing?' she shouted, shaking with rage.

'Looking for some evidence of the child you say you never had. I want to know where it is and who has it. I want to get to the bottom of this before you can cause any trouble.'

Emma stood rigidly still in the middle of the room, and her eyes held a dangerous gleam. Gerald Fairley was a bumbling fool. He would find nothing here that would lead him to Edwina.

Gerald turned, glaring, his great body swaying hideously as he lumbered across the floor. He grabbed her shoulders and began to shake her with such violence her head flew backwards and forwards. 'Bitch! You're nothing but a whoring bitch! Out with it! Where's the child?'

Spots of bright colour stained her pale cheeks, but nasty insinuations slid over her, leaving no real impression, for Gerald Fairley was beneath her scorn. 'There is no child,' Emma said through gritted teeth. 'And let go of me, you foul monstrosity.'

Gerald continued to shake her harder than ever, his huge hands biting into her shoulders until she winced with pain. Suddenly he released her unexpectedly and threw her away from him so forcibly Emma staggered and fell back on to the bed.

Gerald took in the richness of her tumbling hair, her ravishing face, the provocativeness of her shapely figure, and something stirred in him. He began to laugh as he eyed her lasciviously. 'How about a little of what you so willingly gave to my baby brother, Emma Harte? Women like you are usually ready for it any time of day or night. How about a bit of loving, *Mrs* Harte? Edwin always did have a sharp eye for a looker. I don't mind baby brother's leavings.'

Emma gaped at him, so stupefied she found she was paralysed. He advanced towards her and she saw, to her revulsion, that he was unbuttoning his trousers. She shrank back against the pillows, and then she tried to scramble off the bed. But it was too late. He was on her, his great weight crushing her back. He struggled with her skirt, attempting to lift it. Emma began to kick her legs, and Gerald grinned, holding her down with one arm. His face drew closer and he lowered his lips to her face. Emma moved her head from side to side, fighting with him, pushing him off, but although she was physically strong he was too much for her. He began to roll on top of her, grunting and moaning, pressing his horrendous body against hers, trying to pull up her skirts, without success, for he was hampered by his enormous weight. The grunting and the moaning and the rolling became more violent and then, with a final shudder, he went limp next to her and lay back on the bed depleted. Emma pushed herself up and sprang on to the floor, her breath coming in short, rapid pants. As she moved away from him her hand caught the side of her dress. It was horribly wet. A feeling of repugnance rose up in her throat, and she thought she would vomit. She flew to the tangled mass of clothes and linens scattered on the floor and grabbed a towel. She wiped her dress clean and then leapt to the sewing table. Her fingers curled around the scissors and she picked them up, and swung on Gerald, her eyes filled with murderous lights.

'Get up and get out, before I kill you!' she gasped with such venom he looked at her startled and taken unawares. She moved across the floor, the scissors raised in her hand like a dagger. Gerald's face blanched. She hovered over him. 'I tell you, I will kill you, Gerald Fairley, if you don't move that obscene body out of here at once!'

Gerald laughed mockingly. 'I don't think you would be foolish enough to do that,' he said. He sat up and buttoned his trousers, insolently taking his time.

'Don't tempt me!' she hissed.

Gerald heaved himself off the bed. 'I must say, I like a tiger, Emma. Makes it more exciting. I'll be back, my girl. And next time you'll be more cooperative.' He nonchalantly flicked the collar of her dress. 'This will be off and everything else. You'll be ready and waiting for me. I want to savour that beautiful body of yours, enjoy a bit of working-class rutting. I hear you're all like rabbits.' He grinned. 'What's good enough for the handsome Edwin is certainly good enough for me!'

Emma had the most overwhelming impulse to spit in his face, but she exercised restraint, not wishing to lower herself to his level. 'Leave my house immediately, Gerald Fairley, and don't ever come back – unless you want to encounter real trouble.'

He swung around, stumbling down the stairs, laughing raucously. Emma followed him, her rage fulminating. She stood at the top of the stairs and watched him descend, ponderously dragging his immense weight. She flung the scissors after him angrily and they rattled on the stone steps, landing at his feet. He looked up, leering at her. 'That's not polite,' he said.

'You're not worth swinging for, Gerald Fairley!' she screamed. Emma now sped down the stairs, propelled by her mounting fury. When she reached the bottom step she stared up at him, utterly fearless and totally in command of herself, her hatred blazing on her face.

She took a step nearer and said with deadly coldness, 'But I will ruin you! All of you! The Fairleys will rue the day they ever heard the name Emma Harte. Do you hear me? I will ruin you! I swear I will!'

'You ruin us! You? A whoring little tramp? Fat chance you have.' Gerald chucked her under the chin lightly and, infuriated, Emma struck out at him. Her nails clawed his face and brought blood.

'Why, you bloody little bitch!' Gerald shouted, and then he threw back his hideous head and laughed. 'I like a tiger, *Mrs* Harte, as I said before. Don't forget, I'll be back. I'm always in the vicinity. I'll pop in one afternoon for a bit of fun.'

'Get out! Get out!'

The moment the door banged behind him Emma turned the key and drew the bolts hurriedly. She went into the parlour and closed the curtains and washed the disgusting stain off her dress, scrubbing it with a cloth until it was spotless. Then she sat down in front of the fire, her body convulsed by dry heaving sobs. She felt sick and shaken and apprehensive. For the first time in years she was once again afraid of the Fairleys. Thank God Edwina was in Ripon. Gerald would never find her there. But he was just stupid enough to come back here and the idea petrified her.

The world's a jungle, she said, shivering in a huddle before the dying fire. And I'm still vulnerable to the animals in it. I do not have enough money yet with which to build a wall around Edwina and myself. We are painfully exposed. I need protection. She thought then of David with longing and despair. What she needed was a husband. That was most palpably obvious to her now. But David, her darling David, was forbidden to her. As much as they loved each other the objections of his family would drive a wedge between them. Her mind raced. Where could she find a husband who would protect her and Edwina? Whom could she marry? It came to her in a flash. Joe Lowther! She knew he loved her. The problem was, *she* did not love Joe. She liked him. How could she not? He was decent and kind and dependable. If she married Joe she would be cheating him of that most important of all things in a marriage – love. She also had to face the fact that she would have to share his bed, submit to his sexual advances, and bear his children. She went cold at this prospect. How could she willingly give herself to another man when David filled her heart and her soul? And yet she had no alternative. Emma began to weep, her sobs reverberating in the stillness of the little parlour.

'Forgive me, David,' she cried. 'Forgive me for what I'm about to do, my darling.'

PART FOUR

THE PLATEAU
1914–17

Life always gets harder towards the summit –
the cold increases, responsibility increases.
– Friedrich Nietzsche

THIRTY-SIX

The boardroom of the *Yorkshire Morning Gazette*, oak-panelled walls hung with antique engravings of renowned English authors, mahogany furniture polished to a ferocious glassy sheen, was smoke-filled and vibrating with tension. Adam Fairley and Lord Jocelyn Sydney sat opposite each other on either side of the immense conference table, their faces morose, their eyes grave as they chain-smoked in brooding silence, the crystal ashtrays in front of them littered with stubbed-out butts that bespoke hours of waiting and strain.

Adam, impeccably tailored in a dark blue suit, shifted restlessly in the black leather chair and ran his hand through his silver-streaked fair hair. His mouth, ringed with fatigue, suddenly tightened and his grey-blue eyes fixedly regarded the clock ticking with relentless precision in the leaden stillness.

'Damn it all!' he exclaimed, no longer able to control his temper. He swung to face Jocelyn. 'It's almost one o'clock. If Parker doesn't hurry up we'll miss the first edition. He's been fiddling with that lead story for a good twenty minutes. What on earth can the fool be doing, for Christ's sake!'

Jocelyn peered at Adam through the smoke. 'Pondering every word, shouldn't doubt! You ought to know that by now, old boy.'

'I'll give Parker five more minutes and then I'm going up to see him –' Adam broke off as a copy boy burst in. The heavy oak door swung back on its hinges and the activity and noise of a newspaper in the heat of production rolled into the quiet boardroom.

'Here's the proof of the front page, sir. And the editor says ter tell yer he's starting the presses in five minutes.' The boy slapped the damp newsprint dripping with wet ink on to the table in front of Adam and disappeared. The door banged behind him and silence was fully restored. Jocelyn hurried across the room. Placing one hand on Adam's broad shoulder, he bent down and looked at the proof. The banner headline, set in giant-sized type, was black and stark and it leapt across the page.

BRITAIN DECLARES WAR ON GERMANY

Two pairs of eyes quickly scanned the smaller crossheads on the broadsheet: *The Great Conflict Begun. British Minelayer Sunk. Belgium Invaded. Two New Battleships for Our Navy. Government Takes Control of Railways. Securing Food Supply. State Guarantee War Risk at Sea.*

Jocelyn tapped the lead story with one finger. 'How has Parker handled this, Adam? In my haste to get here tonight I forgot my spectacles and I can't read the small print.'

Adam read the proof quickly and said, 'I think Parker covered everything of importance.' He looked up at Jocelyn. 'I've dreaded and feared this war for years. But we're in the conflict now and there's no turning back.'

Jocelyn fixed Adam with a glassy stare. 'Did you really mean what you said earlier this evening – that it will be a prolonged war?'

'Indeed I did,' said Adam tersely. 'Contrary to what some of the experts in London are saying, I believe it will last several years. Two at least.'

Jocelyn's jaw sagged. 'As long as that!'

Adam nodded, his face grim. 'Yes. And it will be a war of attrition. A bloody holocaust the likes of which the world has never seen. Mark my words, Jocelyn.'

'Oh God, Adam, I pray you are wrong! I sincerely do!'

Adam did not answer. He lit a cigarette and gazed reflectively into space, envisioning the terrible consequences of Britain's entry into the war.

'We both need a stiff drink,' Jocelyn announced after a few moments. He hurried to the sideboard and his hands trembled as he prepared two brandy-and-sodas and carried them to the table. He handed one to Adam and sat down heavily in the next chair. Neither man bothered to toast the other on this sombre occasion, and they sipped their drinks in silence, preoccupied with their own thoughts.

Adam Fairley, newly appointed chairman of the board of the *Yorkshire Morning Gazette*, had kept up a tireless vigil at the newspaper for the past four days, sifting through the stories pouring in from the London office and Reuters, studying the grave news, watching Britain being inexorably drawn into the European crisis. His old friend Jocelyn Sydney had been a constant visitor, prowling up and down the boardroom yet insisting that as long as peace lasted the folly of war could be avoided. Adam had met Jocelyn's inherent optimism with an absolute pessimism that reflected his clarity of vision and an understanding of the facts, pronouncing that it was far too late to avert onrushing disaster.

That pessimism was apparent in Adam's voice as he suddenly roused himself and said, 'We're not as well prepared for this war as the Government would have us believe, Jocelyn.'

Astonishment mingled with alarm spread across Jocelyn's face. He opened his mouth, but before he could speak Adam said hurriedly, in an effort to assuage Jocelyn's burgeoning fears, 'Except for the navy, of course. Thank God Winston Churchill has been First Lord of the Admiralty for the past three years. Only he and a few other enlightened men saw the menace of approaching war and tried to make ready for it.' Adam's tone became guarded as he continued, 'I know Churchill has never been a favourite of yours, Jocelyn, but you must admit he had the foresight to recognize the increasing threat of German sea power as early as 1911, when he set about reorganizing the Fleet. Good job, too. By withdrawing our ships from China and the Mediterranean and concentrating the Home Fleet and the Battle Fleet in the North Sea, he has increased our strength immeasurably.'

'Yes, that's quite true,' Jocelyn conceded. 'And Churchill has had one aim I've always found most worthy – reinforcing the invincibility of the Royal Navy.'

'Yes, the navy is strong, but that's the only service that is, Jocelyn. The army is not at all well organized and our air power is minimal, even though Churchill has endeavoured to boost it lately.' Adam paused, drew on his cigarette, and concluded. 'The War Office has always been grossly inefficient. Actually, what we need now is a new Secretary of State for War!'

'Do you think Asquith will appoint one?' Jocelyn asked.

'I'm positive he will have to,' Adam responded firmly. 'He cannot function as Prime Minister and run the War Office as well, not in a time of crisis such as this.

I'm certain, knowing Asquith the way I do, that he will have the good sense to recognize that. And I hope he will have the wisdom to pick Lord Kitchener for the job. That's the man we need in our hour of peril. Not only for his tremendous ability but for the uplifting effect on public morale his appointment will have.'

'Yes, I see what you mean,' Jocelyn agreed. 'After all, Kitchener is a national hero.'

'He's more than that, Jocelyn. He's a national institution. He symbolizes success to the public. Every military engagement he undertakes comes off beautifully.' Adam swirled his drink, pondering. 'He will have to raise new armies, of course. The Territorial Army is not very large. In point of fact, whoever is appointed Secretary of State for War will have to embark on a campaign immediately to recruit single men to go to the front.'

Jocelyn's pale face had greyed. 'A campaign to recruit single men,' he repeated shakily. 'I hadn't thought of that.'

'Since we don't have a compulsory draft system, the country has to rely on volunteers – usually single men between the ages of eighteen and thirty.' Adam stopped, aware of the sick expression on Jocelyn's face. 'Are you all right, old chap? You look positively ghastly.'

'The boys,' Jocelyn said in a whisper. 'I'm not going to be able to restrain them, Adam. They'll both volunteer immediately. You're lucky, Adam. Gerald would never pass the physical and Edwin is married. Also, *he* has a sense of responsibility to you, and to Jane.'

'I'm not so sure about Edwin, to be very honest with you. He's also impulsive at times. Don't think being a married man will stop him if he makes up his mind to go to war. Edwin will consider his responsibility is to his King and country and not the family, or even to Jane. I have a sneaking suspicion they will take precedence over everything else.'

Jocelyn bit his lip nervously. 'This is a bloody foul mess-up, isn't it? Who would have thought a few years ago that we would be plunged into this disastrous situation, Adam.'

'Bruce McGill warned me ten years ago that there would be a great war,' Adam said quietly, his eyes brooding. 'He was right. That was in 1904 –'

'Was it, by Jove!' Jocelyn interjected. 'I didn't know old Bruce was a political pundit.'

'I'm not sure that he is,' Adam remarked. 'But he does happen to be a tremendously rich and powerful man, and he has friends in high places. When Bruce was in London last year with his son Paul he was full of foreboding, and I ignored him. I'm beginning to think I'm an ostrich like everyone else.' Adam stood up. 'I presume you're cancelling the shoot, Jocelyn.'

'Naturally. I don't expect anyone will be interested in grouse at a time like this,' Jocelyn replied with a weak smile. 'Thanks for inviting me down to the newspaper. I really appreciate it, old chap.'

'I've been glad to have your company, Jocelyn. Now let's be off. This room is beginning to suffocate me.'

An hour and a half later Adam's new Daimler motorcar was pulling into the driveway of Fairley Hall. Adam bade the chauffeur a crisp good-night and bounded up the steps.

Murgatroyd was hovering in the dimly lit entrance hall. He hurried forward when he saw Adam, as obsequious as always. 'Mrs Fairley came down ter the kitchen ter tell me and Cook that we was at war. Aye, it's horrible news.'

Adam cleared his throat. 'Yes, indeed it is, Murgatroyd. The days ahead are going to be difficult for us all. But we must pull together and be strong in the country's hour of need.' He noticed the light streaming out from the library. 'Has Mrs Fairley not retired yet, Murgatroyd?'

'No, sir. She's been waiting for yer. I built up the fire and made her some hot chocolate a bit ago, being as how it's a right nippy night.'

'I see.' Adam strode across the hall.

Olivia had heard Adam's voice and she was halfway across the floor when he entered the library. 'Oh, Adam, this is all quite dreadful,' she cried as she flew into his arms.

He held her close for a moment, stroking her hair. 'Yes, it is, my dear. However, we've been expecting it and we must be courageous.' He moved away from her and looked down into her face. 'You shouldn't have waited up for me. It's awfully late, darling.'

She returned his smile. 'I was terribly anxious to see you.'

'I'm afraid I am a little done in.'

'Perhaps a drink will help,' she suggested.

'It might indeed. I'll have a nightcap before we go to bed. A brandy, please.'

Olivia gave him a soft loving look. Adam watched her gliding across the floor, his spirits lifting as they always did when he was with her, the war momentarily forgotten. She was wearing a deep blue crêpe de chine evening dress which flattered her lissom figure and reflected the colour of her eyes. Her face was still unlined and the white streak that shot through her dark luxuriant hair was most arresting. At fifty-four she was a striking woman, and in Adam's opinion she grew more beautiful with age. They had been married for six years. In 1907 the Deceased Wife's Sister Marriage Act, legalizing a man's marriage to his sister-in-law, had been finally passed by Parliament after its defeat in 1901. Adam had convinced Olivia to become his wife in 1908, and they were so completely happy, so perfectly compatible no one else existed for them.

'Incidentally, Edwin telephoned earlier. I told him about the grim developments,' Olivia said, returning to the fireplace with the brandy.

Adam stiffened. 'How did he react?'

'With surprising mildness, I thought. He and Jane are driving over from Kirkby Malzeard tomorrow, to stay with us for a week as we had planned.'

'Well, that is good news,' Adam said. 'Knowing Edwin, I had visions of him careering back to town to be in the thick of things. I'm glad they are coming. At least you will have some congenial company when I'm absent during the day.'

'Do you think they are happy, Adam?'

'I'm damned if I know. Why do you ask?' It struck him then that perhaps Olivia had also noticed the curious lack of warmth between his son and daughter-in-law.

'I can't really put my finger on it,' Olivia said thoughtfully. 'There's a distance between them. Oh, Edwin is outwardly charming and most considerate. But not very affectionate. They don't seem like a couple to me. And sometimes I have noticed the most awful empty look in Edwin's eyes.' Olivia paused and stared at Adam. When he made no response, she pressed, 'Haven't you noticed it, darling?'

Wary though he was of embarking on this discussion, Adam admitted, 'Well, yes, I have, to be truthful. If there *is* anything wrong there it's definitely to do with Edwin. He's changed radically in the past few years. He devotes twenty-four hours a day to the law, or so it seems to me. He has no other interests and appears to be determined to become the most outstanding young barrister in England before he's reached thirty. And I feel he neglects Jane frightfully.'

'Yes, he does,' Olivia agreed.

'And yet he has every reason to be happy with her. Jane is charming and pretty and comports herself in the most mature and dignified manner. Pity they haven't had a child. I must say, I was rather looking forward to having a grandchild. Expected one by now. After all, they've been married three years.'

Olivia stared into the fire and after a long moment turned to Adam. 'Did you believe that nasty story Gerald told you a few years ago? The story about Edwin and Emma Harte?'

'Certainly not!' Adam exclaimed, wishing he meant his words. Intensely protective of Olivia, he did not wish to upset her tonight by dragging out old skeletons. And so for once in his life he lied to her. 'Gerald has no regard for the truth. His story was not only preposterous but quite unfounded. It was undoubtedly engendered by his desire to denigrate Edwin in my eyes. You know Gerald has always been inordinately jealous of his brother.'

Olivia was not entirely placated. 'I remember you made discreet inquiries at the time, about Emma and the child, but are you sure your information was correct, Adam?'

'Of course I am!' He put down the brandy balloon and took Olivia's hand. 'Now, why are you suddenly worrying about that old story? It's long forgotten.'

'I really don't know, darling. I suppose because we began to talk about Edwin's marriage and his happiness. If you say the story is not true, then Edwin can't have anything on his conscience.' Her eyes roved over Adam's face searchingly. 'And yet it has often crossed my mind that he does. Perhaps it's the peculiar look in his eyes that troubles me, Adam.'

Adam frowned. 'Now, come, my darling,' he said softly. 'You are being imaginative. Gerald told a pack of lies. I'm absolutely convinced of that. As for that look in Edwin's eyes, well, maybe it simply springs from his disappointment in his marriage. You should know as well as I do that not all marriages are as happy as ours.'

'Yes, that's true,' she murmured, and sighed. 'Poor Edwin. How terrible for him if he does not love Jane. It must be painful for her, too.'

Adam wanted to terminate the discussion and so he said firmly, 'It's very late, my darling. Let us go up to bed.'

As they left the library Adam acknowledged to himself that the state of Edwin's marriage did not particularly concern him at this precise moment. His consuming worry was that Edwin would volunteer for the army, for Adam knew that the boy no longer put much store in personal safety. Tragically, that most human of all instincts had died in Edwin the day Jack Harte had died. Adam believed that his younger son did not care whether he lived or not, and this attitude, coupled with his strong sense of patriotic duty, would propel Edwin into military service.

THIRTY-SEVEN

Emma clutched the telephone tighter, and her heart began to beat more rapidly than usual. 'I don't want you to do this, Frank! You're putting yourself in danger needlessly. It's foolish and –'

'No, it's not,' Frank interrupted, his voice echoing hollowly over the long-distance wire. 'Look Emma, I'd even toyed with the idea of joining up, but I know the army would never take me. Not with my poor eyesight and weak chest. But somebody's got to report the war over there. I *must* go, Emma.'

'But not *you*, Frank. You're only a boy!' Emma cried heatedly.

'No, I'm not. I'll be twenty-three next month.' His tone became intense. '*I want to go*. Please try to understand, Emma. Also, the editor wants me to go. In a way, it's a kind of honour.'

'*An honour!*' she gasped incredulously. 'Well, in my opinion it's an honour you can easily do without! You'll be in the trenches. In the thick of the fighting. The conditions will be terrible, and you said yourself you're not strong physically. Please, Frank, reconsider this. Think more carefully before you make a final decision!' Emma implored.

'I've already made up my mind,' her brother said firmly. 'Anyway, it's too late. That's why I'm ringing you now. I'm leaving for the front at five this morning.'

'Oh, Frank! I wish you hadn't done this without talking to me first,' she remonstrated.

'I'll be fine, Emma. Honestly, I will. Don't make it harder for me,' he pleaded. 'Now, take care of yourself and give my love to everyone. I'll be in touch, when and if I can. You'll know where I am from my dispatches in the *Chronicle*. Keep them for me, Emma, and try not to worry about me. Goodbye, love.'

'Oh, Frank! Frankie!' Her voice broke and she had to swallow hard to regain her control. 'Goodbye, Frank. And take a raincoat and strong boots –' She stopped, unable to continue.

'I will. Bye.'

The telephone went dead. Her mind froze at the idea of Frank hurtling across the battlefields of Flanders. This development was the last thing she had anticipated and she was stunned by her brother's news, and afraid for him. It was bad enough that Winston was somewhere with the Battle Fleet without Frank flinging himself into the fray. For the past few weeks she had consistently reassured herself that if England did go to war at least her younger brother was in no danger because of his frail constitution. And that would have been so if he had not made such a name for himself as a journalist. Frank, already a rising star in the newspaper firmament, was the type of young reporter editors sought out. He had an enormous command of the English language, was incisive and perceptive, a master of the descriptive phrase and matchless at capturing mood and atmosphere. Not only that, by nature he was romantic, adventurous, and oblivious to danger. She might have guessed he would want to be a war correspondent and now, as she reflected, she realized he had actually sounded excited about going.

Suddenly and quite irrationally, Emma wished that Frank was not so talented and then he would have been a failure. And safe. Indirectly perhaps it was all her fault, and if Frank was killed she would never forgive herself. I should have left him where he was – working on that nothing of a weekly newspaper in Shipley, where he would have stagnated, she said to herself angrily. But I had to go and interfere, because I was impressed with his ability, and ambitious for him. Too ambitious by far, she decided. She chided herself, but after a moment her natural pragmatism rose to the surface, as it generally did, for at twenty-five Emma was nothing if not practical, a characteristic that had been magnified in her over the years. You're being ridiculous, she told herself firmly, recognizing that Frank would have been just as successful without her help. His kind of incandescent talent could never be held back for long; furthermore, he had always been perfectly sure of his own destiny. She had merely propelled him to the top a little faster and that was all. Her role had been of minor importance. She had simply engineered a job for him as a junior reporter on the Leeds *Mercury*, through her friendship with the assistant editor, Archie Clegg. There had been no holding Frank back after that. He had risen with meteoric swiftness, astonishing her as much as Archie and his colleagues. Of course, there was the matter of the book. If she was honest with herself, she had to admit that she had been instrumental in bringing it to the attention of the right people. But if she had not, Frank would have done so himself eventually. When he was twenty he had shown her a novel he had been working on for two years, shyly requesting that she read it and mumbling that it was 'not very good, really'.

As busy as she was, Emma had stayed up all night reading it and had swooped down on Frank at the newspaper the following morning. 'Why do you say it's no good?' she had cried, barely able to contain her excitement. 'It's marvellous! And it's going to be published. *Leave it to me*.' She had swept Archie Clegg off to an expensive lunch at the Metropole in Leeds and thereafter had badgered him relentlessly, and on a daily basis, until he had undertaken to send the book to a publisher friend in London. It was accepted by Hollis and Blake immediately and she herself had negotiated a favourable contract for Frank. When they brought it out some months later it was received with critical acclaim. More importantly, to Emma at least, the novel was also a resounding success commercially. Frank had become a celebrity overnight and several months after the book's publication he had been offered a position on the *Daily Chronicle* and had departed for Fleet Street with Emma's blessing. Today he was considered one of the most brilliant young writers in English journalism and his future was assured. Or rather, it had been until tonight.

'Damn this rotten war!' Emma cried aloud, filled with a helpless fury. She viewed it as a terrible inconvenience, for it had disrupted her most carefully made plans. Yet in spite of her single-minded preoccupation with her business, she was wise enough to recognize that it had graver consequences. The war would throw the world into a turmoil and shatter thousands of lives, a prospect that filled her with dread.

Abruptly she stood up. Reflecting on the past and morbidly anticipating the future was a waste of time, that most deplorable of sins to Emma. There was

369

nothing she could do to change what had happened or control impending events obviously beyond her control. She pulled her blue silk dressing gown around her, shivering slightly, although the night was warm, and walked across the hall, her slippers clicking with a metallic ring against the marble floor, the sounds fading as she mounted the carpeted staircase. The grandfather clock, positioned at the turn of the stairs, struck two, its musical chimes reverberating loudly in the stillness of the sleeping house. Emma tiptoed into the bedroom, shrugged out of her dressing gown, and slipped into the great four-poster bed.

Joe stirred. 'Emma?'

'I'm sorry, Joe. Did I wake you?' she whispered, pulling the covers over her.

'No, the telephone did. Who was it?' he asked in a sleep-filled voice.

'Frank. He's going to the front as a war correspondent. He's leaving in a few hours. I couldn't persuade him not to go, Joe. I'm so afraid for him,' Emma said in a low voice.

'It's a bit soon, isn't it? We've only been at war a few days. Couldn't he have waited?'

'I begged him to change his mind but he wouldn't listen. Now I have the two of them to worry about –' She shivered and clutched the pillow, pressing back her incipient tears.

Joe became aware of her shivering. He moved closer to her. 'Don't worry, Emma,' he murmured. 'They'll be all right. Anyhow, this mess will be over in a few months.'

Emma groaned, suppressing the anger that flared in her. Joe had no conception of the facts. She had been predicting the war for months. Her words had fallen on stony ground and she no longer bothered to argue with him. Joe touched her shoulder tentatively. His pressure increased and he pulled her over on her back. He raised himself on one elbow, peering into her face in the dim light. Emma felt his warm breath against her cheek and she instantly stiffened. He smelled faintly of onions, beer, and stale tobacco and she moved her head away from him, filled with distaste. Joe began to kiss her face and his free hand slid under the bedclothes to grasp her breast.

'Joe, *please*. Not now!'

'Don't be cold to me, Emma,' he muttered thickly.

'I'm not being cold. I just don't feel up to –'

'You never do,' he snapped.

'That's unfair and you know it,' she said, bristling. 'It's been a long day and I'm upset about Frank. How can you be so inconsiderate? Anyway, you aren't very careful these days. I don't want to get pregnant again.'

'I'll be careful, Emma. I promise,' he said in a wheedling tone. 'Please, love. It's been weeks.'

'Ten days,' Emma said flatly, infuriated by his insensitivity and selfishness.

'But I want you,' he moaned, and ignoring her protestations, he pulled her into his arms. 'Please, Emma, don't turn me away.'

Emma did not answer. Mistaking her silence for acquiescence, Joe fumbled with her silk nightgown, his breathing now rapid and belaboured. He began to explore her body, his hands roughly insistent as they roamed over her legs and thighs and breasts. Emma averted her head, avoiding his kisses. She closed her eyes, crushing down on the impulse to push him away. In the four years they had been married Emma had made a tremendous effort to accommodate Joe Lowther's physical demands, and she knew she would yield yet again. It was easier than repulsing him and prevented violent quarrels later. Also, she had made a bargain with herself, to be a good wife to Joe, and she never reneged on a bargain. She had not reckoned with Joe's unflagging sexual aggressiveness and his voracious appetite, which seemed to increase rather than lessen with time.

It was too late to pull away without creating an explosive scene and so Emma automatically let her body go limp. And then she detached her mind, thinking of other things, fleeing into her private world. She began to do complicated mathematical calculations pertaining to her latest financial ventures, seeking refuge in her business to block out the reality of the moment.

Joe rolled on top of her, panting, his pounding against her relentlessly sustained. Her body was his anvil. His momentum increased and rudely shattered her self-induced detachment, and just as she had known he would, he lost all restraint, became utterly unconscious of her in his wild abandonment. He grasped her legs and roughly pushed them up against her chest and at that moment Emma thought her control would snap. She swallowed a scream of unexpected pain and rage and revulsion as he lunged at her time and time again, a charging bull mindlessly intent on its purpose.

He was still. Thank God he was finally still. Depleted, Joe fell against her, his breathing harsh but returning to normal slowly. Emma stretched out her cramped legs and moved her head wearily on the pillows, tears of humiliation seeping out of the corners, the taste of blood bitter in her mouth where she had bitten her inner lip. Unwanted sex was nauseating, was becoming unendurable, for Joe did not attract her physically and he aroused neither desire nor passion in her. Furthermore, he had never even tried to do so. Despite his own preoccupation with sex, or perhaps because of it, he was oblivious to her unresponsiveness. Perhaps if he had shown more consideration, had been sensitive and understanding of her female needs, the situation might have improved. As it was, Emma believed it was inexorably disintegrating. She did not truly know how long she could continue to tolerate his unremitting assaults on her body as she had done for so long. Joe seemed to be in a perpetual state of heightened potency and this frightened her.

Joe put his arms around her and buried his head against her bosom. 'That was wonderful, love,' he said quietly in a voice that was oddly shy. 'You're too much for any man. I can't get enough of it with you.'

Don't I know, she thought angrily but made no comment. Joe moved away from her, turned his back, and within minutes was fast asleep. Why, he didn't even say good night, Emma thought with a flare of irritation and she was mortified. She slid carefully out of bed and glided across the floor to the bathroom, her bare feet sinking into the thick pile of the fine Wilton carpet. She locked the door firmly behind her, threw off her crumpled nightgown, pinned up her hair, and stepped into the bath. Crouching in front of the taps she ran the water until it was steaming hot, almost too hot to bear, soaping her body generously, scrubbing energetically at her delicate white skin until it was bright red. And then she lay back in the water, hoping to soothe her aching body and calm her jangled nerves. After a while she began to feel relaxed and she climbed out of the bath and towelled herself dry. Moving across the elegantly appointed bathroom, Emma caught sight of herself in the mirror. She paused and looked at her face. There was not a trace of anguish or despair on that pale oval, but then there never was. Blackie was forever telling her she had the inscrutable face of an Oriental and she was beginning to believe him. But then my inscrutability serves my purpose most admirably, she said to herself. She took a clean nightgown out of a chest of drawers, slipped it over her head, picked up her slippers, and hurried downstairs.

Emma went immediately into the small study next to the drawing room, intending to work for an hour. She was wide awake and restless, and she always retreated into work when she wanted to avoid dwelling on unpleasant matters. But moonlight was pouring in through the french doors and she stood staring at the garden, admiring its beauty.

Impulsively Emma pushed open the doors and stepped out on to the long flagged terrace that ran the entire length of this side of the house. It was a lovely August night, so still and balmy the soft air seemed to enfold her. Emma breathed deeply, feeling a sudden sense of release, an easing of her worries. She looked up. The sky was soaring and hollow, a deep pavonian blue, clear and without cloud, and the new moon was a perfect sphere whose glassy surface was unmarred, and its sharp radiance cast a silvery sheen on the trees and shrubs, the rolling lawn and the glorious flower beds that punctuated the perimeters of the garden in the dusky shadows of old stone walls matted with ivy.

Emma swept along the terrace and stood poised at the top of the flight of stone steps that led down into the garden, her hand resting on one of the great urns positioned at their edge. Her eyes roved over her garden, so typically English, pastoral in its gentle beauty and filled with tranquillity. It was hard to believe there was a war raging on the other side of the Channel or to accept the fact that thousands of young Englishmen were preparing to enter that grim and bloody battle.

Emma proceeded slowly to the bottom of the garden, heading for her own special spot, the sheltered corner she loved the most. Here, near an old sun dial, magnificent rhododendron bushes and great clutches of peonies spilled forth their translucent pinks and mauves and whites. Joe had wanted to grow roses in this area, but Emma had objected in the strongest possible terms, not permitting one single bush to be planted anywhere in the garden. She had never told Joe that she could not abide that particular flower or that its perfume sickened her to the point of violent nausea.

A splendid beech tree, huge and spreading with its branches dipping down to touch the ground, was a protective arch of interwoven greens above an old garden seat. 'Mummy's seat', the children called it, for it was here that she always came when she wanted to escape the activities of her busy household, to think and to relax, and they had learned never to trespass on her solitude in this private place. Thoughts of Joe intruded into her mind, piercing her recently acquired composure. She stiffened as she recalled with dismay his arduous lovemaking. And then she found herself thinking: Poor Joe. He really can't help himself. Her anger was evaporating so unexpectedly Emma was astonished at this change in her emotions.

Earlier, pinned under Joe and raging with resentment, Emma had contemplated leaving him. Now she reviewed this idea and faltered. A separation was unthinkable, not only because of the children and their loving attachment to Joe and his to them, but because she herself needed Joe for a number of good reasons. Furthermore, Joe would never let her go. He loved her to a point of distraction. Sometimes she wished Joe was a philanderer and that when she spurned him, on those rare occasions, he would seek solace in more responsive arms. She had come to realize this was perfectly ridiculous. Joe wanted only her. No other woman could satisfy his urgent needs because she was the sole object of his desire.

Emma sat back on the seat and considered her marriage with objectivity, finally admitting that she had no intentions of changing the circumstances of her life. The alternatives did not appeal to her, and whatever else Joe was, he *was* a buffer between her and those who might wish to hurt her or Edwina. Also, she had to acknowledge that despite her basic unhappiness in her marriage, she was fond of Joe. He was considerate most of the time and he had never interfered with her business enterprises. Of course, he was phlegmatic and opinionated, and often flew into tantrums if she thwarted him, or sulked for days about inconsequential things. Yet despite these traits, which singularly irritated her, he was not a bad man.

Emma was too big a woman to harbour grudges and she acknowledged anew that Joe Lowther had been a good husband in a variety of other ways. She remembered some of his generous gestures now. He had bought her this house, for one thing, in December of 1910. That had been four months after her marriage, when she was carrying their child. In the preceding June, just before their wedding, Joe had come into another unexpected inheritance, one far more impressive than his mother's legacy. His ancient great-aunt, on the maternal side of the family, had died at the age of ninety-one. Since she was childless and without any other relatives, Joe had been the sole beneficiary in her will. Apart from the one-hundred-and-fifty-thousand pounds in cash and her large house in Old Farnley, he had become the new owner of four commercial properties in the centre of Leeds. These were operating factory buildings permanently rented to a tanner, a shoe manufacturer, a printer, and a wholesaler of dry goods. The annual income from these properties so far exceeded Joe's expectations he was astounded. He had weighed his financial situation and decided he could easily afford to buy the vacant house in the Towers, and maintain its upkeep on a comfortable scale.

The house stood in a private and secluded little park in Upper Armley that was surrounded by high walls and fronted by great iron gates. A circular driveway led up to the eight fine mansions situated within the park's precincts, each one self-contained, encircled by low walls and boasting a lavish garden. The moment Emma had walked into the house on that cold December day she had wanted it, marvelling at its grandness and delighted with its charming outlook over the garden and the park itself. There were numerous airy and well-proportioned reception rooms on the main floor, including a formal drawing room, an impressive dining room, a parlour, and a small study. At the back of the house there was a huge kitchen, a butler's pantry, servants' quarters, and a washhouse. Upstairs eight bedrooms of various dimensions and three bathrooms provided ample space for Joe's family, soon to be increased with the impending arrival of the baby. The third floor, under the eaves of the old grey stone house, was composed of two attics and a cedar-lined room for storage.

Because of its size, and Emma's insistence that she continue to run her business after the child's birth, Joe had eventually agreed to engage a small staff. Mrs Fenton, a local widow, had been installed as the housekeeper-cook, and Mrs Hewitt, Joe's former charwoman, came daily to clean. Mrs Hewitt's niece, Clara, originally engaged as nursemaid for Edwina, had remained with them to take care of Christopher, born in June of 1911.

The day Emma, Edwina, and Joe moved into the house Emma had experienced such a profound sense of security she had relaxed for the first time in years. In this fine mansion, so elegant and secluded, Emma was at last convinced she was absolutely protected from the Fairleys, and in particular Gerald Fairley. Emma shivered, recalling his unanticipated and violent intrusion into her life four years ago. That hideous April evening was still vividly etched on her mind and Emma knew she would never forget it. She had lived in a state of burgeoning anxiety for months after that visit.

It had taken Emma several weeks to convince David Kallinski that she would not reverse her decision. Eventually he accepted it with sorrow, and although they remained friends and partners, David wisely limited their association to business. Understanding his motives, whilst yearning for him, Emma had disguised her feelings, displaying no emotions, hoping this would help to ease his pain.

And then with calculation and consummate feminine wiles, she had set out to inveigle Joe Lowther into marriage. Already in love with her, overwhelmed by her beauty and impressed with her industriousness and business acumen, Joe had been an easy and willing target. As their friendship had developed he had grown bolder in his courtship. Receiving no rebuff, he had nervously proposed one month later and had been overjoyed when she accepted him, not recognizing that it was he who had been courted and manoeuvred.

The night he had proposed and after she had accepted him, Emma had told Joe that Edwina was illegitimate. She had done so with absolute candour, at the same time sagaciously omitting the identity of the father. She had simply repeated the story she had invented for Blackie O'Neill years before. Joe, impressed with her honesty, had been admiring of her stoicism at carrying such a burden alone. He had told her that her past did not interest him, and it truly did not. He was so besotted with Emma the only thing that mattered was her acceptance of him for a husband.

Emma, who had not wanted to start their marriage with deception about her circumstances or her child, was, nevertheless, aware that she had no choice but to tell Joe the truth. Joe believed she was the widow of a sailor called Winston Harte. How then could she conceivably explain her brother to him – also a sailor with the same name as her deceased nonexistent husband? For this reason, she had confided those same half-truths to Laura, and eventually to David, some weeks after her marriage. Neither one had appeared to be shocked and they accepted her explanation with understanding.

Emma's worst moment had been her confrontation with Winston and Frank, for it was also necessary to explain to her brothers the existence of a three-year-old daughter, who was obviously not Joe's offspring. Frank, still in awe of Emma, had not dared to offer one word of criticism. Winston, on the other hand, had placed Emma on a pedestal, and he had flown into a rage, disappointed in her and full of recriminations. After he had calmed down, he managed to convince himself she had been duped and unwilling, so that he could absolve Emma of all blame and keep her image untarnished. He had cursed the scoundrel who had violated his innocent sister in naval-barracks language so colourful both Emma and Joe had been flabbergasted.

Conscious of her brothers' intelligence and perception, Emma had coloured her story for their benefit, inventing a nebulous gentleman of doubtful background as the father of her child, whom she said she had met in Leeds. She had alerted Joe in advance, saying that she dare not tell them a boy from Fairley had taken advantage of her. There would be reprisals in the village if she did so. Joe had agreed there was sense in this and was her ally. For her part, Emma was relieved that she no longer had to fabricate stories about her past, for by nature she was not a liar.

Yes, Joe has been decent, Emma said to herself. He had insisted on adopting Edwina after their marriage and he had given her his name. And he loved Edwina as much as he loved his own child, if not more, Emma sometimes suspected.

As these wandering thoughts sifted through Emma's head she felt an unprecedented stab of guilt about her anger with Joe. He had behaved like a gentleman and had shown a degree of generosity towards her, and Emma reproached herself. The gift of her body and wifely devotion was a small price to pay when she considered everything dispassionately.

It would not be easy, Emma knew, when she thought of his wanton lust in the privacy of their bedroom. But she took hold of herself with cold determination, and resolved to be more understanding and warmly attentive to her husband in the future.

THIRTY-EIGHT

The following morning found Emma at her desk in her department store earlier than usual. Elegantly dressed in a severely tailored black silk dress and pearls – 'the Harte uniform', Joe called it – she sat studying two fat ledgers. Her deep absorption in those minute black figures running in punctilious columns down the wide pages was so complete she was only dimly aware of the store coming to life and of the sounds of traffic outside.

Emma's attention was riveted on the books for the department store, which she had bought in the latter part of 1912, renovated and modernized with Blackie O'Neill's assistance, and opened with fanfare in January of 1913.

The store had been an instantaneous success. Brilliant advertising, personally conceived by Emma, attracted the public to its doors. They came in droves to scrutinize and criticize this lavish and exotic emporium that had flowered within the hallowed precincts of Lister's, formerly the most conservative of stores, which had been taken over by some parvenu, an ambitious young woman with newfangled ideas. To their incredulity they were captivated by the glamorous ambiance and the air of exclusivity that pervaded every floor. Lulled into a state of euphoria by the elegant interiors with their glittering mirrors, plush carpeting, harmonious lighting effects, and the specially perfumed air, they remained to browse, to exclaim and admire, and were inevitably induced into buying, unaware that they had been cajoled by the tasteful and tranquil surroundings into spending money through a psychological approach far ahead of its time.

Emma's skilful displays of all her products attracted marvelling eyes to its quality, its stylishness, and the reasonable prices. The merchandise was the *dernier cri*, so elegant that the ladies of Leeds and other nearby towns found themselves unable to resist temptation, dipping into their purses with enthusiasm, under the gentle encouragement of the charming and pleasant-mannered salesgirls, rigorously trained by Emma in what she termed 'the art of the understated sell', and which in later years she was to call 'the soft sell'.

Another contributory factor to the store's popularity was the café Emma had opened on the second floor. She had decorated it in the style of an English country garden, utilizing pastoral scenic wallpaper, white-painted trellises, artificial topiary, and birdcages housing exquisitely rendered copies of colourful birds. She named it the Elizabethan Gazebo and dressed the waitresses in simple pale green uniforms, frilled white organdy aprons and caps. The enchanting setting, a refreshing change from the overblown pomposity of Victorian décor, the serene atmosphere, superior service, and the simple but tasty dishes made the Elizabethan Gazebo all the rage. It became the chic gathering place for morning coffee, light luncheons, and afternoon tea. Smart women took to rendezvousing there and few left the store without making some kind of purchase, just as Emma had shrewdly anticipated. This innovation, a wholly unique departure for a department store, immediately started a trend in Leeds. It prompted her envious competitors to follow suit, but their rococo imitations were tasteless in comparison, and her stylish café was so well established its business was unaffected.

The gift wrapping of merchandise was another idea dreamed up by Emma, who remembered her own excitement at receiving that brightly wrapped gift from Blackie on her fifteenth birthday. This small service was not performed by other local stores and it gave her yet another sales advantage. With her unerring understanding of the public, Emma was convinced this token gesture, costing relatively little in time, effort, and money, would delight her customers, especially since she made no charge for it, and she was proven right. A gift wrapped in silver paper, tied with silver ribbon, and decorated with a tiny spray of silk violets became the cachet of Harte's. So did the courtesy and helpfulness of the doorman who assisted with packages, opened carriage and motorcar doors, and performed other gallant little duties, and in his splendid gold-braided uniform of deep royal blue he added a touch of distinction to the main entrance. Finally, in an effort to persuade her customers to buy everything they needed from Harte's, and in greater quantity, Emma offered door-to-door delivery of goods three times a week. Her customers came to rely on this service, and it boosted sales to such a staggering extent she had to revise her timetable and send out her royal-blue vans five and sometimes even six days a week to fulfil the orders.

On this Saturday morning, twenty months after the store had opened its doors, Emma Harte was in the black and profits were soaring. She had more than sufficient cash in hand to carry her for several years, she decided, as she reviewed the figures. None the less, she was loath to pull fifty thousand pounds out of the store's bank account at this moment, even though it was hefty with deposits. The country had only been at war for four days, but with her prescience Emma knew they could be in for a long siege, and she might suffer serious setbacks if trade fell off because of the public's depressed mood, and their reluctance to buy in the grim days ahead. She recognized that she must not endanger the stability of the store by making rash moves or by over-extending herself.

Emma turned to the ledger for the Gregson Warehouse, a wholesale supply company she owned. Her eyes swept over the figures and she did some swift mental arithmetic. Her cash reserves for this company were considerably higher than the store's bank balance, chiefly because she had owned it for a longer period, was selling products in bulk to the mass market, and had virtually no overheads. Moreover, she was heavily stocked and she would not need to buy new merchandise from the manufacturers for a year, and so she did not anticipate heavy cash expenditures.

She turned the page. Her glance settled on the Accounts Receivable columns. A quick tabulation of the figures reminded Emma that she was owed almost one-hundred-and-eighty-thousand pounds by the various stores in London, Manchester, and Scotland who bought from the wholesale warehouse on a regular basis. She was not worried. The money would start trickling in within the next thirty days. However, she had been aware for some weeks that a number of stores were tardy in their payments. She jotted down the names of those customers whose accounts were overdue and running into the ninety-day period, determining that pressure must be exerted on the delinquent companies immediately. Her terms were thirty to sixty days, although she often extended credit for longer periods to old and valued customers. Now that practice will have to cease, she concluded with detachment. Emma, who could be understanding of problems on a personal level, was hard-headed and without sentiment when it came to business. Joe had once accused her of having ice water in her veins and she had responded, 'Yes, that's true. Just like a banker.'

Emma sat back in her chair, tapping her teeth with the end of the pencil, lost in thought, and then she leaned forward and picked up the clipping from the *Financial Times*, which had been on her desk for the past week. The story in question detailed the closing of the London Stock Exchange and the raising of the bank rate from 4 per cent to 8 per cent on Friday, July 31. Both measures had been sensational, and to Emma they were indicative of the grave view of the crisis taken in financial circles. Emma had realized that the first action was simply intended to avoid panic in the City, by giving dealers time to steady themselves before being called upon to settle their disorganized Stock Exchange accounts. But she was aware that the raising of the bank rate was meant to hinder the drain of gold out of the country. To Emma, watchful and weighing all the odds, this had been the most ominous sign of all. Whatever the politicians said, war was imminent.

These developments had prompted her to take action regarding a business venture she had been contemplating. Rather than intimidating her into abandoning this new enterprise, it had actually encouraged her to plunge ahead with it. At the same time, the rise in the bank rate had induced her to reject the idea of borrowing from the bank to finance the project, as she had originally intended, and despite the fact that she had never been reluctant to use the bank's money in the past.

In point of fact, when Emma began to extend her business in 1910, she had entered the arena of high finance with many powerful psychological advantages. By nature she was an optimist and totally unafraid of taking chances, believing she could make her own luck in business. Her risks were calculated risks and in a sense she was a guided gambler, as she was to be all of her life. David Kallinski understood her, being cast from the same mould himself.

Emma also had nerves of steel, and these characteristics set her apart from many of her male contemporaries and competitors who were unimaginative and fearful of losing what they had patiently accumulated. Emma was not at all inhibited by these fears, for she was dauntless, and responsive to all manner of business opportunities, which she seized with tenacious hands. Neither was she bothered by paper transactions or long-term borrowing. She had used all to her advantage in the past four years and would do so again if necessary.

But not at this moment, she said to herself, thinking of that 8 per cent bank rate. It was outrageous interest to pay. She had all that cash in the Gregson account and was owed a vast amount from the stores. She could easily take the fifty thousand pounds she needed without endangering the warehouse business. Removing the chequebook for the Gregson Warehouse from the drawer of her desk, she wrote out a cheque, put it in an envelope, addressed it to Frederick Ainsley, and returned the chequebook to the drawer. She looked at her watch, picked up the telephone, and dialled the warehouse.

Her manager, Vince Hartley, answered, as she had known he would. 'Good morning, Vince. I've been going over the ledger and I notice that a number of our customers are behind in payment,' she said.

'Morning, Mrs Harte. Yes, I know. I was going to talk to you about them –'

'I want you to start pulling that money in, Vince. First thing on Monday morning,' Emma interrupted. 'And don't write the usual dunning letters. Telephone and follow up with telegrams. I want immediate results. If they can't pay in full, insist on part payments. And you might point out to the stores whose accounts are outstanding for sixty days or longer that I intend to start charging interest. At once. Bank rates of 8 per cent.'

Vince Hartley sucked in his breath. 'Mrs Harte, that's a bit stiff, isn't it? I don't think they'll like it. They might not buy from us again –'

'I don't give a damn whether they like it or not. And I certainly couldn't care less if they don't buy from us.'

'But we're bursting at the seams with stocks. We'll have it on our hands if we're not careful.'

'No, we won't,' Emma said firmly. 'There's a war on now. Merchandise is going to be in short supply and hard to come by. I can use up those stocks in the store if necessary. In fact, I'll probably need them. Many of the manufacturers we buy from will be turning their factories over to the production of government supplies. Uniforms and such, and so I'm not at all concerned about the stocks in the warehouse. In a sense, they're a godsend.'

'Yes, I see your point,' Hartley conceded, wishing he had thought of that himself. But Emma Harte was always three jumps ahead of everyone else. Now he said, 'There's another problem I wanted to mention. Two of our commercial travellers, the ones covering Scotland, have given notice. They're joining up today. That leaves us short-staffed. Shall I take on some new men to replace them?'

'No, don't bother. The two working Manchester and London will be sufficient. As I said, I may well need that merchandise for the store and I don't want the warehouse to be completely depleted. Get on to those overdue accounts on Monday and let me know the results at the end of the day. I expect you to be tough about this, Vince. I don't have time to deal with it myself, but I will if necessary.'

'Please, Mrs Harte, don't worry. You can rely on me,' Hartley said nervously, knowing she meant every word.

'Until Monday, Vince. Goodbye.' Emma sat back in the chair, wondering if she should let the two remaining travellers go and cease all selling to other retailers, to reserve the stocks for herself in case of shortages. A knock on the door interrupted her musings. Emma looked up as Gladys Barnes, her young secretary, poked her head around the door.

'Mr Ainsley has arrived, Mrs Harte.'

'Show him in, Gladys, please.'

'Yes, Mrs Harte.'

Emma stood up, smoothed her skirt, and automatically patted her hair, walking across the floor to welcome her solicitor, whom she had been expecting. She was therefore taken aback, and also irritated, when Ainsley's son, Arthur, appeared on the threshold.

Arthur Ainsley, tall, slender, and with the blond good looks of a juvenile lead, was conscious of his physical attributes and the effect they had on most women. Elegantly dressed in a somewhat dandified manner, he played the part of the dashing young buck to the hilt and now he sauntered in with debonair aplomb.

He's forgotten his tennis racquet, Emma thought disparagingly, but she proffered him a charming smile. 'Good morning, Mr Ainsley.'

'Good morning, Mrs Harte. You look as splendid as always.' Ainsley flashed his perfect teeth and took her outstretched hand, his clasp lingering too long for Emma's comfort.

'Why, thank you, Mr Ainsley. Please, do sit down.' She glided to her desk and sat behind it, still smiling, sheathing her annoyance. In her opinion, Arthur Ainsley was a fop and she regarded him as his father's errand boy, even though he was a junior partner with the law firm. 'Is your father joining us?' she asked in an even tone.

'No, I'm afraid he can't. He came down with a frightful cold last night. Hence my presence instead of his,' Arthur replied, suavely apologetic.

'I am sorry,' Emma murmured.

'However,' Arthur went on quickly, 'he did ask me to tell you that you may telephone him at home, if you consider it necessary after our meeting. That is, if you feel I am not able to help you with your – er – er – problem.'

'I don't have a problem, Mr Ainsley,' Emma said coolly. 'I merely wished to bring to conclusion a certain matter I have been discussing with your father. I think you will be able to handle it quite adequately, since all the major work has been done already.'

Arthur Ainsley ignored her patronizing tone, although he winced. He had been trying to ingratiate himself with Emma Harte for the past year without success, and this infuriated him. Nevertheless, he responded with studied charm. 'I sincerely hope I can, Mrs Harte. I always aim to please, you know.'

'Indeed,' Emma said dismissively. 'When I spoke to your father yesterday morning I did not explain why I wished to see him today, so obviously he was unable to brief you. Let me fill you in. Several weeks ago I started negotiations with Mr William Layton, of Layton's woollen mill in Armley. Mr Layton has wanted to sell for some time. He's getting too old to run the mill efficiently and his business has fallen off drastically. Mostly due to the poor quality of the cloth he has been producing and indifferent selling. In fact, it's my opinion he's only a few steps away from bankruptcy. Mr Layton agreed to sell the mill to me for fifty thousand pounds. I considered this a fairly reasonable figure, although the mill is small, there's virtually no good will to speak of, and his customers are few. He's also stuck with an enormous quantity of shoddy cloth which I will have to practically give away, simply to get rid of it –'

'It doesn't sound like a good proposition to me,' Arthur cut in, hoping to impress her.

Emma frowned and held up her hand. 'Please, Mr Ainsley, let me finish!' Her voice was chilly. 'The machinery is good and the building is sound, if in need of a few renovations. Also, Layton's is carrying huge stocks of raw wool, of major importance to me. Anyway, to come to the point, Mr Layton agreed to my terms, which were fifteen thousand on signing of the purchase agreements, ten thousand after three months, and the final payment of twenty-five thousand pounds at the end of six months. That is approximately the length of time I require to turn the mill around. We were about to go to contract when Mr Layton backed down. His excuse was that he no longer wanted to sell. I found this hard to swallow, but naturally I had to respect his decision.'

'You probably could have held him to that agreement, you know, even though it was verbal,' Arthur interjected. 'I'm sure my father told you that, didn't he?'

'He did indeed,' Emma said. 'However, I decided at the time not to do so. Mr Layton is an old man and I didn't want to back him into a corner. After all, it was his prerogative to change his mind. I told your father I would look around for another suitable mill, since I was anxious to acquire one. Then a few days ago I discovered, through a reliable source of my own, that Mr Layton had received another offer,' Emma explained. 'This offer was not higher than mine, but the terms were seemingly more appealing to Mr Layton. My competitor was prepared to make two payments instead of three, each one of twenty-five thousand pounds. The first on signing, the second after six months. I am not an unreasonable woman, Mr Ainsley, but Mr Layton's duplicity appalled me. After all, we had shaken hands on the deal and then he turned around and reneged. Moreover, he did not have the integrity to inform me of that bid, and so give me the opportunity to match it.'

'I appreciate your feelings, Mrs Harte,' Arthur said with a fawning smile. 'I suppose you want to match this new bid?'

'No, better it, in a sense. I have decided to pay the purchase price in full. On Monday.'

Arthur Ainsley sat up smartly, rubbing his chin nervously. 'But that's not bettering it, is it? You're simply changing the payment schedule, that's all. What makes you think the other party won't do the same thing? Then you'd be faced with an impasse, and Layton still might not sell to *you*. Also, how do you know they haven't concluded the transaction?'

Emma smiled confidently. 'They haven't, and I happen to know that the party in question does not have the ready cash to make payment in full at this moment. He has just modernized the mill he owns and has put in costly machinery. I realize, of course, that he could borrow from the bank to purchase Layton's. That would have been very good business practice a week ago, but today, with the bank rate up to 8 per cent, I think the rival buyer may well have second thoughts about doing that. I've been informed that he's over-extended and well into the bank already. They may not wish to oblige him with further credit. It is my belief that if I move swiftly I can knock him out of the picture completely.'

'Yes, perhaps you can,' Arthur agreed cautiously.

'It is my understanding that Mr Layton does not want protracted negotiations.

His creditors are on his back and he wants a fast sale. And so I am dealing from strength, wouldn't you say?'

Arthur nodded, obviously impressed. She was constantly surprising both him and his father. Then another thought struck him. 'Look here, let's think about this for a second. Are you sure you want to invest fifty thousand in a new business at a time like this? Since we are at war, I'm not so sure this is a moment for taking risks.'

'I'm not taking any risks and, furthermore, this is exactly the right time to buy Layton's, because I intend to obtain government contracts to produce cloth for the armed forces. Cloth for uniforms, Mr Ainsley. With those contracts I can have that mill on its feet and in profit overnight!'

'Well, I must say, you certainly think of everything!' He had no doubts she would get the contracts, yet he felt compelled to say, '*Are you sure*? Really sure you can get them? It occurs to me the established cloth manufacturers in Yorkshire will be after the same contracts. They could beat you to it.'

'I don't think so, Mr Ainsley,' Emma said softly, and with a self-assured smile. '*Naturally* they will go after them, but I have connections in London. And, in any event, the government is going to need plenty of cloth for uniforms, believe me. There will be enough business to go around.'

Dazzled, Arthur said, 'My father has always considered you to have remarkable vision and certainly you seem confident. What would you like me to do, in regard to the Layton mill?'

'Telephone Mr Layton and tender my offer as soon as you get into your office on Monday. Arrange an appointment with him for Monday afternoon. I will go with you and we can sign immediately. And make sure he has his solicitor there. I don't want any procrastination.'

'Yes, I understand,' Arthur said, echoing her businesslike tone.

Emma picked up the papers on her desk and handed them to him. 'These are the original contracts. I have made various changes, those I considered necessary. However, I am sure they are in order. In fact, the changes are so minor you should be able to redraw the contracts by noon.'

She certainly knows how to give her orders, Arthur thought with a stab of resentment, but nodded. 'That's no problem,' he asserted.

'And here is my cheque for the full purchase price.' Emma gave him the envelope and went on, 'I want you to take it today so that you can tell Mr Layton, in all truthfulness, that you have it in your hands when you speak with him.' Emma's green eyes, now brilliant, rested on Arthur. To her amusement he appeared to be dumbfounded. 'I don't think you will have any problems with Mr Layton. I am making him an offer he will find extremely difficult to refuse under the circumstances,' she said. 'I know my rival will not be able to move as rapidly as I can.'

'Oh, I endorse that wholeheartedly!' Arthur then said, with a disarming smile, 'May I invite you to lunch on Monday, before we go to Layton's? It would be my pleasure.'

Emma feigned dismay. 'Oh dear, I can't. It's very kind of you to ask me, but I already have an appointment for lunch that day. I will meet you at your office at two o'clock, if that is convenient, and we can go over the contracts before our appointment with Mr Layton.'

Arthur concealed his disappointment, aware that his charm had no effect on her.

'Yes, that's fine. Is there anything else you wish to discuss?' he asked, anxious to prolong his visit.

Invariably pressed for time and having no use for idle chatter, Emma said, 'No, that's it.' She rose abruptly. Arthur jumped up, reaching for his briefcase. Emma accompanied him to the door. 'Thank you for coming in, Mr Ainsley. And do give my best to your father. I hope he feels better soon.' She stretched out her hand, shook Arthur's quickly, and opened the door. He found himself whisked out of her office with such speed he barely had a chance to take his leave of her courteously.

Emma smiled when she was alone. Arthur Ainsley fancies himself, she thought, and then forgot all about him, turning her attention to the store's business. A few minutes after Ainsley had left the office Joe marched in unexpectedly. Having determined, the night before, to be her most affectionate with him in every way, Emma greeted him warmly, only to be rebuffed by a gruff response. Despite her irritation at this intrusion on her busiest morning, and her bafflement at his obnoxious manner, the smile on Emma's face did not falter. She opened her mouth to ask him why he was upset when he saved her the trouble.

'What the hell was Arthur Ainsley doing here?' he growled, flinging himself into the chair recently vacated by the young man.

'Because he's our solicitor. Don't tell me that has *slipped* your mind, Joe.'

'His *father* is our solicitor,' Joe snapped.

'Frederick Ainsley is ill. I had some urgent business to be dealt with and he sent Arthur in his place.'

'I don't like that chap!' Joe announced.

Joe's tone was so harsh Emma was further startled. 'For goodness' sake, don't be so snappy, dear. Arthur Ainsley is pleasant and also able, I think.'

'He's charming to you, Emma. You wear skirts. That chap's a real womanizer. He's a rake!'

Emma laughed. 'Oh, Joe, don't be so silly. Anyway, his private life is his own affair, I think.'

'Well, I don't like the way he behaves around you, Emma. I've noticed how young Ainsley dances attendance on you, and he positively leers at you. He's too bloody cocksure of his so-called *fatal* charms, if you ask me.'

Emma bit back a smile. Joe was jealous, an emotion he had not hitherto displayed before. But then she never gave him any reason to be jealous, nor did she have any inclination to do so. Men were the last thing on her mind.

'Look here, Joe, you're getting excited about nothing. I don't encourage Arthur Ainsley's attentions. In fact, I've never noticed them, to tell you the truth. It's hardly my fault that Mr Ainsley sends him here on business matters. Come along, love, don't be childish,' she said cajolingly.

Joe felt suddenly foolish and he grinned, looking shamefaced. 'Yes, you're right, but what was so urgent that you had to deal with it on Saturday?'

Emma told him about her decision to buy Layton's mill, explaining some of the ramifications and the necessity for moving with a degree of swiftness. 'Surprise is often the best weapon,' she pointed out. 'Percy Lomax thinks he's got Layton's mill. He thinks he's outsmarted me, but he's wrong. Nobody outsmarts *me*. Ever!'

Joe was staring at her askance. 'Don't you think you're biting off more than you can chew?' he cried.

'What do you mean?' she asked in surprise.

'Between the store, the Gregson Warehouse, and Lady Hamilton Clothes it seems to me that you have enough to keep you busy twenty-four hours a day, without that blasted mill.'

She laughed. 'I'm not going to be running the mill, Joe.'

'Knowing you, Emma, you'll want to take an active interest in the administration. You never leave anything to chance, and you'd have to be involved out of necessity. From what I hear, Layton's needs reorganizing, doesn't it?'

'Yes, it does. But I've thought everything out well in advance. I'll get a good manager.'

'Who? They're hard to come by, you know.'

'Ben Andrews. I've –'

'Ben Andrews! Good God, Emma, he's been at Thompson's mill for donkey's years. You'll never get him to leave.'

'That's where you're mistaken, Joe. I've had several meetings with Ben and he wants to leave Thompson's. I only have to say the word. He hasn't been too happy there since the new owners took over four years ago. He's itching to get out, if you want to know the truth.'

Joe grinned. 'I've got to take my hat off to you, Emma. You certainly know how to pick 'em. Ben is a hell of a good man. The best in the woollen business. He's made Thompson's, that's a certainty.'

Emma nodded. 'I know. And that's the secret of my success. Finding the right people and being willing to delegate authority to those who are capable of handling it. I'm also very generous. I made Ben an offer Thompson's would *never* match, even if he wanted to stay with them!'

Observing her with grudging approbation, Joe saw her delighted smile turn into one of triumph. He could not help laughing. Shaking his head, he said, 'I suppose it tickles you to death to be in a position to employ Ben Andrews, considering he was your boss when you worked at Thompson's. I can't say I blame you.'

'No, it doesn't,' Emma said softly and in all truthfulness. It was the idea of luring Ben Andrews, three top foremen, and twenty of the best weavers away from Thompson's that intoxicated her. Without Ben's superior management and those experienced workers, Thompson's output would be crippled and the mill would be in disastrous trouble. A thrill of pure elation ran through her. She had just made her first move against the Fairleys, owners of J. P. Thompson and Son.

'Congratulations, Emma. You're a millowner at last.'

'Don't congratulate me yet, Joe!' Emma exclaimed. 'I'm superstitious about celebrating before a transaction is final.'

'Oh, it will be, Emma. I don't doubt that for one minute,' he said with an odd smile. 'You always get what you want, don't you? There's no stopping you once you've made up your mind. You rush in, sweeping everybody to one side, so intent on your purpose you don't care who gets trampled underfoot.'

Emma looked at Joe, surprised at his harsh words and the sarcastic edge to his voice. Normally she disregarded his taunts, but now she could not help saying angrily, 'You make me sound ruthless and hard. And I'm not. I'm simply a good businesswoman. Furthermore, nobody has ever handed *me* anything on a plate. I've had to work like a dog for everything I own, Joe.'

'I can't deny that. Work *is* your consuming passion, though, isn't it?' His eyes were as hard as pebbles, and condemning.

Emma sighed. She began to shuffle her papers, impatient for him to leave and in no mood to joust. 'Why are you in town so early this morning?' she asked gently, changing the subject.

'I'm going to the office. I'm behind with some of the ledgers for the properties,' he said offhandedly, and stood up. 'Then I'm meeting Blackie for lunch at the Metropole. I want to talk to him about putting new roofing on the tannery and reinforcing the top floor. He's been too overwhelmed with building contracts to attend to the work before now, but both jobs are long overdue.'

'Give him my love and tell him I'll come to see Laura on Sunday.' Emma's face changed, softening as she spoke of her friend. 'I'm worried about Laura, Joe. She hasn't seemed at all strong since the last miscarriage. She needs building up. I wish there was something I could do to –'

'There's nothing you can do,' Joe exclaimed. 'That's Blackie's problem. He should exercise a little self-control and stop getting her –' He bit off his sentence, flushing.

'In the family way,' Emma finished for him with chilly disdain. 'Look who's talking!'

Joe dismissed this dig with a wave of his hand, although his flush deepened. 'Besides, you do enough for Laura as it is, Emma. Why, the way you dote on that woman anybody would think she's a member of the family.'

'She is!' Emma snapped. 'She's like my sister, my dearest friend. I would do anything for Laura. Anything in this world.'

'That I know!' He strode to the door. 'I'll see you at home, Emma. Bye.'

'Goodbye, Joe.'

After he had left, Emma stared at the door he had so harshly banged behind him, shaking her head. *He's* got a bee in his bonnet this morning, she thought wearily. She did not have time to worry about Joe and his infantile bursts of petulance. She picked up the ledgers and carried them to the safe where she always kept them and locked them away securely. She walked back to her desk, a spring in her step, her head held high. She was about to become a millowner and stick a knife in Gerald Fairley's back at the same time. She laughed aloud. The idea of being able to enhance her business enterprises whilst damaging the Fairleys appealed to her sense of irony. She looked at the photograph of her eight-year-old daughter reposing in a silver frame on her desk. 'That's called poetic justice, Edwina,' she said to the photograph. 'Justice for both of us. And it's just the beginning.'

Emma rested her head against the chair. Once again she contemplated the war, endeavouring to gauge the effect it would have on commerce and industry. Her considered reflections prompted her to make a sudden decision. She would definitely discontinue selling certain types of merchandise to other retailers. She was undoubtedly going to need most of the warehouse stock for Harte's in time, and she had no alternative but to curtail the activities of the two remaining commercial travellers to a degree, and enforce limitations on their supplies. She began to selectively tick off the goods she could readily dispose of in her own store. Good old Gregson's, she muttered under her breath. It's the best investment I ever made.

And indeed it was. In 1910, a few months after her marriage to Joe, Emma had learned that the Gregson Warehouse, a wholesale company acting as the middleman between the manufacturers and the retailers was in trouble and up for sale for a song.

Emma wanted it. More accurately, she craved it passionately. And she determined to have it, recognizing its enormous potential as a moneymaker of no mean proportions. It was also the vehicle she had been seeking, one that would enable her to implement two of her most potent schemes – rapid expansion for a small investment and volume buying from the manufacturers to obtain quality merchandise at low prices. She purchased Gregson's for two thousand pounds and, with her own brand of initiative and expediency, smartly divested herself of its dated and second-rate goods with lightning speed. Her technique was simple but foolproof. She slashed prices drastically and sold everything to local stores that were in constant need of bargains for their semi-annual sales.

As she had shrewdly suspected, she actually made money from the stocks. With this money, and by persuading the manufacturers to give her extended credit, she bought in bulk. Some of the smaller clothing manufacturers even began to produce solely for her; consequently much of her merchandise was exclusive as well as reasonably priced. Utilizing the services of four veteran commercial travellers, who worked on a commission basis, she then became a wholesale vendor to retailers in London, Scotland, and Lancashire. Emma was also now in the enviable position of being able to stock her own three shops at no cost to herself, and by cannily supplying stores located in distant areas she kept her wares select and suffered no competition.

Early in 1911, when Gregson's was operating smoothly, Emma had asked Joe to sell her the three shops she rented from him and the other five he owned. He had not wanted to sell to her, even though she had offered him five thousand pounds. Since he received a trifling annual income of fifty pounds from each shop, she had pointedly remarked he was making an immediate profit, and from his own wife.

'I don't want to make a profit at all,' Joe had rejoined defensively, going on to grouse that he was disinclined to sell, preferring the income.

'But I'm willing to give you the equivalent of ten years' rent for each shop, plus an extra thousand pounds,' Emma had cried, on the verge of losing her temper.

Joe was adamant, being reluctant to diminish his property holdings. But as a compromise, and in order to restore tranquillity to their home life and appease her, he had suggested she could rent the five other shops, leaving ownership in his hands. This was a lacklustre alternative to Emma, who had her own motives for wanting the shops, and she flatly refused to consider the proposition.

The deadlock was broken by Frederick Ainsley, who, to Emma's surprise, became her champion and backed her unstintingly. His remarkably persuasive talents and smooth tongue were fortunately not altogether lost on the recalcitrant Joe. 'It is only because of Emma's unflagging work that the three shops are such a success. They were failures and vacant half the time before she rented them from you, Joe,' Ainsley had adroitly pointed out. 'Under the circumstances, don't you think she deserves to own what she has so assiduously built up? It's her investment for the future. And what do you have to lose, Joe, my boy? She's prepared to pay an excellent price, one that more than recompenses you for the income you would receive, whilst relieving you of the burden of maintenance and repairs. Do be a good chap and at least consider selling her the eight shops, Joe. It's to your advantage. That five thousand could easily be invested in something more lucrative.'

Privately, Frederick Ainsley had expressed surprise that Joe had not offered to give her the deeds to the shops. 'As a wedding present, perhaps,' the courtly solicitor had gallantly murmured. He was much taken with Emma, being aware of her superior brain and her business acumen. Skill with finances and nerve to gamble were a redoubtable combination in his eyes. They added up to business genius.

Emma had shaken her head vigorously. 'No! I want to *buy* them from him. Then I know they're really mine and no one can ever dispute the fact!' she had cried.

Frederick Ainsley, appreciating the sagacity of her comments, and accurately guessing her ultimate goal, had readily concurred. The solicitor had resorted to another tactic to help Emma attain her wish. He had simply presented Joe with several potential investments guaranteed to pay high dividends. 'Think about selling to Emma. It's an opportunity that doesn't present itself every day,' Ainsley had casually remarked. 'And you could have that five thousand working for you most profitably.'

Joe thought and eventually sold, if somewhat reluctantly, feeling vaguely uneasy about the whole affair.

Emma had known she would have to mortgage Gregson's to raise the money for the shops, but this did not deter her. And she wanted to pay Joe the total amount immediately. Six months later she had repaid the mortgage on the warehouse and within another twelve months she was ready to put the second and most ambitious part of her well-conceived plan into operation – the acquisition of a department store in Leeds.

To finance this venture Emma sold her eight shops in Armley for a total price of twenty thousand pounds. Joe, dumbstruck, implied she was guilty of sharp business practice, insisting she had wilfully inflated the price of the shops above their real market value to suit her own ends. He warned of repercussions.

'Nonsense!' Emma had countered icily, infuriated by his accusatory tone. 'I'm not selling the buildings *only*, as you did, Joe. I'm also selling large stocks of quality merchandise and enormous good will. And what about all the renovations I've made? Which I paid for.'

Joe had shrugged, disguising his disapproval behind a façade of studied indifference, and had announced he was washing his hands of the whole questionable business.

With the nerve and monumental self-assurance of a seasoned entrepreneur, Emma had taken out a new and far higher mortgage on the warehouse, borrowed from the bank by pledging the new store as collateral, thrown the twenty thousand into the kitty, and purchased Lister's. She had redeemed her promissory notes from the bank in a relatively short space of time, anxious to have title of the department store free and clear, and the mortgage on the warehouse had been paid off within a year.

A sharp knock on the door interrupted Emma's careful examination of the inventory of Gregson's current stock. She looked up.

Gladys came in. 'It's only me with a cup of nice hot tea. I thought you'd like one before you go down on the floor, Mrs Harte.'

'That was thoughtful of you, Gladys. Thank you.' Emma pushed her chair back, propped her elegantly shod feet on the desk, and sipped her tea, reviewing the Gregson inventory in her head. She could easily keep Harte's well supplied for the duration of the war, she concluded, and with a little of her gambler's luck she would survive without too many losses.

She recommenced her perusal of the last page of the inventory, wanting to complete her assessment before going down into the store. But thoughts of the mill intruded. She could not wait to get her hands on Layton's. It was a potential gold mine. Then she pictured Gerald Fairley's face when his manager, three foremen, and his best weavers walked out.

That bastard's in for a real surprise, she thought, and with not a little vindictiveness.

THIRTY-NINE

Edwin Fairley loitered outside Harte's department store, gazing into one of the windows, trying to summon up enough courage to go inside. It was always like this when he arrived on the doorstep. His nerve inevitably failed him for ten minutes or so, and sometimes altogether.

He pretended to be studying the chic evening gowns in the window, thinking of the first time he had walked past the store on Commercial Street. That had been over a year ago and he had stopped dead in his tracks, instantly struck by the name, staring in astonishment at the silvery metal letters which spelled out E. HARTE against the royal-blue woodwork over the door. Concluding that it was a coincidence, he had proceeded down the street and then suddenly retraced his steps, his curiosity whetted.

Edwin had approached the doorman and inquired about the ownership of this fine new establishment. The doorman had politely informed him that a Mrs Harte was the proprietor. A few more probing questions had supplied some startling answers, and he had hastened off, considerably shaken. There was no question in his mind, from the glowing description of Mrs Harte he had wrung out of the doorman, that this was indeed Emma's store. Within a few hours he had received confirmation from Gerald, who had been unable to resist adding a vulgar warning to keep his trousers buttoned. Edwin had turned away in disgust, concealing his anger and repressing the violent urge to punch his brother on the nose.

And the store had attracted him like a magnet ever since. Whenever he visited Yorkshire he made an excuse to Jane to go into Leeds alone, automatically gravitating to Harte's, propelled by a mixture of emotions. Eventually he had found the nerve to enter the store, and had been overwhelmed by the elegance of the interior and staggered at Emma's singular achievement, which he considered awesome. And he had experienced a curious sense of pride in her. He had returned on several occasions afterwards, nervously walking around, wondering if he would catch sight of Emma. But he never had, and he cursed himself for his juvenile behaviour, always vowing never to torture himself in such a ridiculous manner again.

Still, here he was on this warm August Saturday, a day he should have been at Fairley with Jane and the family, longing to go inside, hoping for a brief glimpse of Emma Harte, yet, conversely, afraid he might bump into her. Fool, he muttered, filled with angry frustration at his own indecisiveness.

After several moments of window gazing Edwin took a deep breath, adjusted his tie, and pushed open the doors. Feeling ill at ease amongst the women shoppers thronging the main floor, he immediately headed for the men's haberdashery.

In his haste and preoccupation he was unconscious of the admiring glances bestowed upon him by some of the ladies who stepped aside to let him pass. At twenty-six Edwin Fairley was a good-looking young man. Tall and firmly built, he had a dashing air and, since he had inherited his father's penchant for elegant clothes, he was always impeccably dressed. But it was his face that caused many women to look twice and speculate. Finely drawn and ascetic, there was, nevertheless, a marked sensuality about his mouth, and his eyes held an indefinable expression that hinted of passion.

Arriving at the haberdashery, Edwin asked to see some silk cravats, examining them whilst surreptitiously glancing over his shoulder, anxiously seeking that one incomparable woman in the crowd. He finally bought a grey silk tie he did not want, because he was embarrassed to walk away after the salesgirl had been so obliging. Declining to have it gift-wrapped, he paid, picked up the package, and moved on.

After making this initial purchase Edwin discovered he was beginning to relax, and he strolled through other departments with a degree of self-assurance, browsing to waste time. He halted at the perfumery counter and bought two bottles of expensive French scent for his wife and his aunt. In order to linger in Harte's he asked to have them individually gift-wrapped. The young woman nodded, smiled, and busied herself with this task. Edwin leaned nonchalantly against the counter, his light grey eyes scanning the main floor. He swung around and looked up at the main staircase.

And it was then that he saw her.

Emma was coming down the stairs. Edwin sucked in his breath. She was more beautiful than ever, fashionably dressed in black silk that fell in fluid lines around her shapely figure. He recognized at once that she had poise and distinction, and in young womanhood her loveliness was in full bloom. She paused at the turn of the stairs to speak to a customer, her face lighting up, full of vivacity. Edwin gazed at her with intensity, mesmerized by that exquisite oval face, unable to pull his eyes away, and his heart twisted inside him.

He had not set eyes on Emma Harte for nine years, but now, to Edwin, it might have only been yesterday that he had held her in his arms in the cave on the moors. He longed to rush over to her, to beg her forgiveness, to ask about their child. He dare not. He knew, with a sickening sense of despair, that she would repudiate him just as surely as he had repudiated her so long ago on that ghastly morning in the rose garden.

Emma continued to the bottom of the stairs and glided across the floor with infinite grace and aplomb, obviously in command of herself and her store. And then, to his immense horror, Edwin realized she was walking directly towards him. He was rooted to the spot, incapable of moving or even turning his head, and his heart was thundering in his chest. To his supreme relief she paused at another counter and became engaged in conversation with a sales assistant. At one moment she looked over her shoulder and stared right at him, or so it seemed. He stiffened. There was an engrossed expression on her face and her eyes swivelled to the jewellery department. She shook her head, leaned forward, and continued her discussion. Had she seen him or not? Or had she simply not recognized him? He dismissed this idea instantly. That was inconceivable. He had not changed very much and, in any case, his resemblance to his father was now so pronounced it was difficult for anyone to mistake his identity.

The salesgirl spoke to him. Startled, he pulled himself together and gave her his attention. She handed him the packages and the bill, all the while chatting to him pleasantly. He heard her voice faintly through the crashing noises reverberating in his head. It required all of his self-control to keep his hands from shaking as he reached for his wallet. From the corner of his eye he saw Emma approaching and he dropped his head, his heart in his mouth.

Emma brushed so close to him he could have touched her. He heard the soft swishing of the silk of her dress and caught the faint whiff of her perfume, something light and fresh like lily of the valley. His anguish was acute, and he had to suppress the urgent desire to reach out and take her arm.

And then she was gone. He watched her disappearing into another department, smiling and nodding graciously to customers.

He completed his business and stumbled out of the store without looking back, feeling sick and undone. He stood in the street experiencing that awful sense of loss again, and the gnawing hollowness in his heart, which never left him, was more chilling than ever.

Edwin walked towards City Square, moving blindly through the crowds, unaware of the traffic or the bustle, seeing nothing but her face. The face he would never forget as long as he lived. It was burned on his brain like a brand stamped on steel. By taking deep breaths Edwin managed at last to steady himself and he struck out determinedly towards the main post office, suddenly intent in his purpose. He had just made a decision and nothing would induce him to reverse it.

Within a short while his business in the post office was completed. He made another stop, attended to the matter at hand with remarkable swiftness, and left. He found the Daimler, parked near the railway station, told the chauffeur to take him home, and fell on to the back seat feeling wretched and depleted.

On the drive back to Fairley, Edwin thought of Emma. The impact of seeing her had been so tremendous he knew at last why he had dreaded it whilst striving towards that goal. She had awakened old longings and also made him painfully conscious of the emptiness of his life. She had rekindled his guilt and shame, never far from the surface anyway.

The memory of her tortured him. Why could he find no satisfaction in the arms of other women? And there had been plenty in the last five years. *Why*, oh God, *why* did he persistently seek out women that resembled her if only vaguely? Searching, always searching for another Emma. Irresistibly drawn to green eyes, russet-brown hair, silken white skin, only to be disappointed, dissatisfied, and torn apart in the end. Awake or asleep, Emma haunted him.

He contemplated their child. He had a compelling yearning to see it. It must be eight years old now, if it had lived. Of course it has lived, he told himself firmly, wanting to believe that part of Emma and himself existed in another human being. Was it a girl or a boy? Did it favour Emma or himself? Or was it a mixture of them both?

A bitter smile slid on to his pale face, gaunt in the dim light of the car. How ironic that Emma had borne him a child out of wedlock, a child forbidden to him, whilst Jane had never conceived and given him the son or daughter he craved. Had she presented him with a child their union might have been more bearable. He pictured Emma, and then Jane. He should never have married her. He should have resisted all that family pressure. His barren, dull, insipid wife. *She* was the cross he had to bear in life. No, that was a dishonourable thought and unfair. He could not condemn poor Jane. She was lovely, and adoring, and it was hardly her fault that he had nothing of himself to give her. He belonged to Emma Harte; that was unalterable and would never change except in death.

Edwin's bleak mood engulfed him all afternoon and well into the evening. He struggled through the family dinner, which seemed more interminable than usual to him, making polite but strained conversation. He was glad when his father suggested they retire to the library. Edwin was also vastly relieved Gerald was absent, for he had been seeking an opportunity to speak to his father alone since his return from Leeds.

Adam poured the drinks and they settled themselves in front of the fire. His father chatted amiably about inconsequential things until finally Edwin could no longer contain himself. 'Father, there's something I must speak to you about,' he announced abruptly.

Adam looked at him closely, frowning. 'You sound serious, Edwin. In fact, you have been very morose all evening. Nothing wrong, I hope.'

'No, Father, everything is fine.' Edwin hesitated and cleared his throat. 'I wanted you to know that I made a decision today. A decision about joining the army. Immediately.'

Adam's face changed radically and he placed the brandy and soda on the table with the utmost care. 'Edwin, I think you are being hasty. These are early days yet. I don't want you rushing off to war until we have more news, see what the developments are. I beg you to reconsider, my boy.'

'I can't, Father. I don't want to upset you, or worry you, but I must go. Please, do try to understand my point of view.'

'Edwin, you don't have to volunteer. Only single men have been asked to go to the front.'

'Yes, I know that, Father. Nevertheless, I have made the decision.' Edwin stood up, reached for the *Yorkshire Morning Gazette* on the library table, and said, 'I don't *have* to read this government bulletin to you, Father. You must be familiar with it. The paper has been running it for several days now. But I *am* going to read it to you.'

'Look here, Edwin –' Adam began.

Edwin held up his hand and looked at the newspaper, reading from it carefully and slowly.

'Your king and Country Need You! Will you answer your country's call? Each day is fraught with the gravest possibilities and at this very moment the Empire is on the brink of the greatest war in the history of the world. In this crisis your country calls on all of her young men to rally round the Flag and enlist in the ranks of the army. If every patriotic young man answers her call, England and Empire will emerge stronger and more united than ever. If you are unmarried and between eighteen and thirty years old, will you answer your country's call and go to the nearest recruiting office, whose address you can get at any post office. AND JOIN THE ARMY TODAY!'

Edwin dropped the newspaper on the chesterfield and sat down, his eyes resting on his father.

Adam shook his head wearily. 'Oh, Edwin, Edwin, don't try to appeal to my own sense of patriotism. I *know* the country is in grave danger, but I am concerned about *you*. That governmental bulletin asks for *single* men. I beg of you, Edwin –'

'It's too late, Father. I joined up this afternoon when I was in Leeds. I have to report on Monday.'

'Oh, my God! Edwin!'

'I'm sorry, Father. Please don't be angry, and please give me your blessing. I don't want to leave here with your disapproval –'

'Good heavens, Edwin, I wouldn't let that happen for the world.' Adam sprang up and joined his son on the sofa. He put his arm around Edwin's shoulder and for a horrible moment he thought he was going to cry. 'Now, my boy, enough of that nonsense. I do wish you had waited, of course. But naturally you have my blessing.'

'Thank you, Father.'

Adam rose and fixed himself another drink. He propped himself against the mantelshelf and gazed down at Edwin, filled with anguish. I've known for days he would do this; none the less, it doesn't make it any easier to bear. 'I imagine I would do the same, if I were your age, and I'm quite certain my father would have felt the way I feel.' Adam shook his head. 'But you're so young, Edwin. So young.'

'So is every other Englishman who's going, Father.'

Adam glanced at Edwin. 'Have you told Jane about this, my boy?'

Edwin nodded. 'I told her when we were dressing for dinner. She was upset, but she understands. There has been a long line of soldiers in her family, you know. Her brother told us that he intends to volunteer this coming week.'

'I see.' Adam said, looking thoughtful. 'Will Jane come and live with us in South Audley Street? We'd like that, you know, and I don't think she should be on her own in Eaton Square. She will be awfully lonely in that big house by herself, with only the servants.'

'Thank you, Father. I appreciate your kindness. However, Jane told me she wants to go to London next week, close up the house, and return to Yorkshire. She would like to be with her father, since her brother will be going. She likes the country and I think that would be the wisest thing, under the circumstances. Don't you?'

'Yes, of course, Edwin. Well, it seems it's all settled,' Adam finished, staring gloomily into the fire.

After a small silence, Edwin said, 'Father, there's something I want to give you. I've had it for years.' He reached into the pocket of his dinner jacket and removed a silk handkerchief. He handed it to Adam, who took it absently.

As his father unwrapped the object in it, Edwin went on, 'I found it years ago. Now I'd like you to have it. I know you painted it, and also that it bears a striking likeness to Aunt Olivia.'

Adam was staring at the round pebble in the silk handkerchief, his eyes resting on that sweet face. The oils were remarkably well preserved. He smoothed one finger over it. 'Did you varnish this again, Edwin?'

'Indeed I did, Father. To protect the paint.'

Adam continued to gaze at the pebble, faded memories returning. He had painted this stone when he had been seventeen or thereabouts. The decades dropped away. He saw her standing under the crags at the Top of the World, her dark hair blowing in the breeze, her eyes as blue as speedwells and radiant with light, and he heard her voice echoing faintly across the years. 'Adam, I'm going to have a baby.'

Edwin was looking up at his father, puzzled by the expression on his face. 'It is Aunt Olivia, isn't it?' he said insistently, shattering Adam's memories.

Adam did not respond. He smiled, remembering. But then he had never really forgotten. He wrapped the stone in the handkerchief, almost with tenderness. He returned it to Edwin. 'You keep it, my boy. You found it. I want you to have it. One day I will tell you the story behind that stone, but not now. This is not the time.' He flashed Edwin a curious look. 'I presume you came across it in that old cave up on the moors by Ramsden Crags.'

Edwin was watching his father intently. 'Yes, I did.' He swallowed and said, 'There's something else, Father. Something I have wanted to tell you for years. Unfortunately my courage has always failed me. It's been on my conscience for so long. I must unburden myself to you before I go off to war.'

Adam sat down in the wing chair, nursing his drink. 'Then unburden yourself, Edwin,' he said gently. 'Perhaps you will feel easier after you have spoken to me. Certainly I shall give you all of my understanding.'

'Well, you see, it was like this,' Edwin began nervously. 'Oh God, I need another drink,' he cried, and leapt up, hurrying across the room.

He not only resembles me in appearance but in every other way as well, Adam said to himself, staring after Edwin. He lit a cigarette and leaned back in the chair, waiting. He's going to tell me about Emma Harte and the child, Adam thought, and his heart went out to his son.

FORTY

Lord Kitchener had been appointed Secretary of State for War and had raised an army of one hundred thousand volunteers with his first appeal. Winston Churchill already had the Fleet on standby and between August 6 and August 20 the first four divisions of the British Expeditionary Force had crossed the Channel and the fifth and sixth divisions followed early in September. Not a ship was sunk, not a life was lost, and it was a triumph for Churchill, militant trustee of the British Royal Navy. The rest of Great Britain mobilized for war with ferocious speed and not one of its citizens was unaffected as the grim days rolled by.

The guns of August roared on through September, October, November, and December of 1914, and into 1915. They wrought slaughter, ruin, and misery. Hundreds of thousands of young men, the hope of a new generation, were felled on the bloody battlefields of France and Belgium.

The stakes were terrifying to the British and their allies: annihilation or survival. They understood this was not a war for the possession of a fortress or a country, but for the inalienable right of any nation to live and develop as it wished.

Like every other intelligent person, Emma Harte Lowther often contemplated the aftermath of the war, the conditions they would be facing, and the future of business, but she did not dwell unduly on the years stretching ahead. Her priorities were all immediate, leaving no room for speculation. She was not blind to the commercial opportunities now presenting themselves, nor was she adverse to accumulating money, and whenever she felt a prick of conscience about making a profit from war she dispelled her discomfiture with logical reasoning: Somebody had to produce the uniforms for the fighting men, and if she did not do it, others would. In fact, were doing it. The majority of the cloth manufacturers of the West Riding were making khaki and navy and air force blue for Great Britain and the Allies, and millions of yards were coming off the looms of Yorkshire to clothe the forces.

Lately it struck Emma that she devoted herself entirely to work these days and shamefully neglected her family. But guilty feelings were swept away by the pressure of her business and the knowledge that she had no choice but to steer the same course. She raced between Harte's, the Gregson Warehouse, Layton's mill, and the clothing factory at breakneck speed, handling everything with her own brand of efficiency, charm, and assertiveness. And yet somehow the days were never long enough for her.

To her relief, Harte's was steady and holding its own. Although business had fallen off to a degree, she did not envision any serious setbacks. The stock housed in Gregson's Warehouse was lasting because she allocated it sparingly and she had also found several new sources of supplies. Layton's, under the skilful management of Ben Andrews, was running smoothly and the mill was meeting the huge government contracts with apparent ease and more promptly than many of her competitors. David and she had temporarily discontinued the line of Lady Hamilton Clothes at the outset of the war, and the factory's entire production had been turned over to the manufacture of uniforms. All in all, everything was under control, her business enterprises were stable, and, in particular, the mill and the factory were operating at a high level of super-efficiency and were flourishing money-makers.

But now, on this cold afternoon in December of 1915, Emma's mind was not preoccupied with business. Sitting next to the driver in one of Harte's vans, on her way to a meeting with David, her mind dwelt on the Christmas holidays. She was determined to make it as festive an occasion as possible, despite shortages and the depressed mood that engulfed everyone.

Frank was coming to stay for several weeks and she was looking forward to it with the excitement of a child, thrilled at the prospect of seeing her brother again. He had been wounded in November, but his injuries were fortunately not serious. He had been hit by a bullet in the right shoulder and had been shipped back to England to recuperate. If only Winston could get home on leave the family would be complete, but she acknowledged realistically that there was not the remotest possibility of that. The navy was in the thick of the fighting and the news was grim on all fronts. Nevertheless, there would be a Christmas tree, and a turkey dinner with a plum pudding and all the traditional trimmings, mulled wine, and presents for everyone. Most importantly, Frank would receive the love and rest he needed so badly, and all the comforts of home she could provide.

The van arrived at the clothing factory in York Road within minutes. Emma told the driver to wait and hurried inside. As she entered David's office she was surprised to see Abraham Kallinski ensconced with David.

Her old friend stood up and embraced her warmly, his bright dark eyes twinkling behind his spectacles. He scrutinized her appraisingly and said, 'Well, Emma, you look wonderful. And it is a pleasure to see you. So long it has been.'

Emma smiled. 'How are you? And how is Mrs Kallinski?'

'She is well. I am well. Janessa is always asking for you. She misses you, Emma. I miss you.'

'I am sorry I have neglected you both lately,' Emma said. A rueful smile touched her lips. 'But business does seem to take up all my time these days.'

'Ah, yes! My little Emma has become the lady tycoon,' Abraham exclaimed, regarding her with affection and pride. She continued to amaze him with her success, which he considered remarkable, and especially since she was a woman.

David was standing behind his desk, obviously in the throes of a mountain of paper work. He laughed. 'Don't sound so surprised, Dad. I always predicted she would go far.' He came around the desk, took her by the shoulders, and kissed her cheek. Her arms automatically went around him. She felt the strength of his hands gripping her tightly as the pressure of her own fingers increased gently. They pulled away without releasing their hold on each other and exchanged a long gaze.

Abraham Kallinski, observing them paternally, thought with an unexpected flash of dismay: My son. My son. He holds her too long. Ach and I know that look in a man's eyes! I pray to God that his wife Rebecca and Joe never notice it. Clearing his throat, Abraham said, 'Come, Emma. Come, sit here next to me.' He indicated the other chair in front of David's desk.

She sat down and said, 'There's nothing wrong, is there? Why did you want to see me so urgently, David?'

David leaned back in his chair, his vivid blue eyes focusing on hers. 'I have a proposal to make and I hope you will approve. And go along with it.'

Emma laughed lightly. 'You know I trust your judgement implicitly. What is it?'

'Dad has been harassed of late. He'd like to ease up a little. Not work so hard.' David lit a cigarette. 'We've been discussing his problems and I think I have a solution that would be beneficial to everyone concerned. It occurred to me that we could merge his company with ours, take over his factory and its management with relatively no problems at all. That would relieve him of running it entirely on his own. He would continue there, of course, but he wouldn't have to work such long hours.' David looked at her expectantly. 'Well, what do you say?'

Instantly recognizing the enormous potential inherent in this proposition and visualizing a means of simple but swift expansion, Emma did not have to think twice. 'It's an excellent suggestion.' She turned to Abraham. 'Would you be happy if we did that, Mr Kallinski?'

'I would, Emma. And so would Janessa. She worries about me. Worries so much I worry about her worrying,' he responded with a wry laugh.

'Then let's combine the two companies, David,' Emma said. 'I'm all for it. And now is certainly the right time to do it.'

'There are a number of details to be worked out, Emma. But before we get into those I would like you to know my personal feelings about the proposed idea,' David said. 'If you're agreeable, I think we ought to purchase Dad's business outright, for a fair price that would give him a decent profit. After all, he has devoted years to building it up. We would make him a director of the parent company and pay him director's fees. I also think he ought to share in the profits, as we do. In addition, he would receive a salary for running his factory. How do you feel about these terms, Emma?'

'I'm in accordance with you, David. Your father should have something to show for all the years he's been in business. Why don't the two of you settle on an equitable price. Whatever you decide will be acceptable to me, I'm quite certain.' She laughed and shook her head, giving David a fond look. 'I can't imagine why you thought I would object. This is basically your business, David. You run it and you're the majority shareholder.'

'You pull your weight and you are my partner.' He smiled, looking relieved. 'Good. Dad and I will thrash it out. You and I can go over the final details later. Then I'll talk to Frederick Ainsley and have him draw up the agreements in a week or so.'

'That's perfect,' Emma said. She shifted in her chair and gave her attention to Abraham, asking him questions about his government contracts, his cloth supplies, his work force, and his output. Whilst they were engaged in this protracted conversation, David sat back, regarding Emma with intensity.

Winter sun was pouring in through the windows, bathing her in its bright light. She really has that special kind of English beauty that looks its best in the daytime, David thought. That inimitable beauty that Gainsborough and Romney immortalized. And yet curiously Emma was unaware that she was a great beauty. Certainly she was devoid of personal vanity and that was also part of her charm. She was so fresh and radiant and filled with a vitality that was almost sensual in nature. No wonder she is irresistible to all men of all ages, David reflected. Funny, but she was not conscious of this either.

'Don't you agree, David?'

Startled, David sat up abruptly. 'Sorry, I was wool gathering.'

'I said I thought we ought to take over immediately. By consolidating our work forces we could probably increase production and operate both places even more efficiently. Your father is willing.'

'That's an excellent thought! I'll have Victor move in there tomorrow.' He looked at his father. 'Is that all right with you, Dad?'

'I shall be glad to have him back,' Abraham said. 'It will put my mind to rest, and your mother's.'

Emma stood up. The men also rose. 'If you'll excuse me, I should be going,' she said. 'I promised Edwina I would be home early today, to help her dress the Christmas tree. She has been looking forward to it. I don't want to disappoint her.'

'No, you must not do that,' Abraham said. 'It is wrong to break a promise to a child.' He gave David a pointed stare. 'Which you so often do to my grandsons,' he said, sighing heavily.

'But only because of the business, Dad,' David rejoined defensively.

'Ah, yes. The business. Always the business. Well, you be off, Emma. Give my best to Joe.'

'And mine to Mrs Kallinski. Tell her I'll stop by soon.'

'I'll see you out,' David said, helping Emma into her coat and taking her arm possessively.

The Christmas tree was just the right size, Emma decided. She had purposely chosen this particular tree, even though grander specimens were available, in order to avoid ostentatious display, which she felt would be inappropriate in wartime. The housekeeper had potted it the previous evening, and now it reposed on a skirted table in a corner of the drawing room, next to the fireplace. Emma stepped back, her head on one side, viewing it with a critical eye. It was a healthy young fir, a rich dark green, and its branches were thick and luxuriant.

'Hello, Emma. You're home early.'

Emma swung around as Joe entered the drawing room and strode to the fire, rubbing his hands together.

'Hello, Joe. Yes, I promised Edwina I would help her to dress the tree.'

'Oh, that's right. I'd forgotten.'

Continuing to unwrap the decorations, Emma told him about her meeting with the Kallinskis. 'I think it's an excellent idea to join forces, don't you?' she finished, glancing at him over her shoulder.

Joe was frowning. 'I'm not so sure. Won't it mean a lot of extra work and worry for you?'

'Why me? David bears the brunt of that business.'

'It strikes me you both have enough on your plates as it is. Particularly you.' Joe sounded grouchy, and as always he was opposed to innovation.

'Don't be so negative, Joe. I don't understand you sometimes,' Emma said quietly. 'And anyway, there's Mr Kallinski to think about. He's not been well lately. The merger is the best solution for him.'

'The old man could have sold his business to someone else,' Joe suggested.

'Yes, he could. But why should he? It was only natural that he would come to David,' Emma explained. 'Besides, Abraham Kallinski has always been good to me. I'm delighted to make his life a little easier.'

'I'm only thinking of you, Emma. However, if you believe it's such a wonderful idea, who am I to criticize? You and David always do what you want with the factory anyhow.'

'We always tell you our plans,' she countered swiftly, detecting that disgruntled tone in his voice.

'Yes, I know. After the fact.'

'Oh, Joe, please don't be sour. It's almost Christmas. Let's not bicker now.'

'Bicker! Who's bickering!' Joe retorted. 'Really, Emma, I can't open my mouth without you accusing me of –' He stopped short and his voice changed, became tender, as he said, 'Hello, sweetheart. Come in. Don't stand there.'

Emma turned around. Edwina was hovering in the doorway. She skipped across the floor. 'Daddy! Daddy!' she cried, flinging herself at Joe. He picked her up and swung her around. Her blue velvet dress billowed out and her waist-length hair, of a blonde so pale it was almost silver, flew out behind her, gleaming in the lamplight. She laughed delightedly and after a few more whirls Joe put her down on the floor, holding her arms to steady her.

'You're not dizzy, are you, angel?'

'No, Daddy.' She smiled up at him, her exquisite little face dimpling prettily.

'Well, there you are, darling,' Emma said. 'I've been waiting for you. I've unpacked all the ornaments and we can start.'

'Hello, Mother,' Edwina said without looking at Emma. She grabbed Joe's hand. 'Daddy, will *you* help me to dress the tree. Please. Please. Oh, do say yes, Daddy.' She fixed her luminous silvery eyes on him appealingly.

Joe laughed and patted her head. 'Of course I will, love.' Edwina dragged him to the tree. She climbed on to the stool Emma had placed next to the table, still clutching Joe's arm.

Emma was holding a silver bell in her hand. 'Where shall I put this, dear?' she asked, smiling at her nine-year-old daughter.

Edwina made no response. She looked up at Joe and flashed him a radiant smile. 'Where do you think it should hang, Daddy?'

'Well, I'm not such an expert at these things. Perhaps here.' He indicated a branch.

'May I have the bell please, Mother.'

Emma handed it to her silently. Edwina immediately gave the bell to Joe. 'You put the bell on the tree, Daddy. Anywhere you want. I think you should be first.'

This little ritual continued for several minutes. Whenever Emma picked up an ornament and suggested a spot for it, Edwina took it from her quickly, ignoring her suggestions, deferring always to Joe. Stunned, Emma stepped away from the tree uncertainly, acutely aware of the slight. She was the interloper, and unwanted. She retreated to the fireplace, watching them laughing happily together. She experienced a small stab of dismay and pushed it away quickly. She should not be envious of their relationship. She should be happy they were so adoring of each other.

Joe and Edwina were so engrossed with each other and the tree they did not notice Emma glide quietly out of the room. She closed the door softly behind her and leaned against it. She swallowed hard, conscious of the prick of tears behind her eyes, the ache in her throat. After a moment she was in control of herself and her step was firm as she walked across the marble-floored hall. She took her coat from the closet, picked up the two baskets standing on the floor, and slipped out of the house quickly.

It was a cold night, dark and without a moon, and snow was falling in light flurries. Fortunately the lamps on the iron gates of each house were burning, and their dim glow lighted her way as she turned up the flagged walk that fronted the mansions in the Towers. The snow was beginning to settle. It would be a white Christmas after all, just as Edwina had so fervently wished. Emma bit her lip. Christmas had suddenly lost its appeal for her. She reflected on Edwina's snubs, filled with regret, her mind fogged by the hurt she was still experiencing.

A few seconds later Emma was pushing open the gate of the last mansion in the row, where the O'Neills lived. Blackie had bought it in 1913, two years after his marriage to Laura. If it was not the fine Georgian edifice he had talked about building years before, it was rather imposing, and he had made many grand improvements.

The little Irish maid greeted her cheerfully. She took Emma's coat and scarf along with the baskets, inquiring politely after her health. Emma was just about to ask her where Mrs O'Neill was when Blackie appeared at the top of the red-carpeted staircase.

At twenty-nine Blackie O'Neill was a commanding figure and the years had treated him generously. He and his Uncle Pat had done well and the building firm had grown into one of the largest in Leeds. Success sat well on him. Not yet the millionaire he had bragged of becoming, he was, however, a rich man and he had certainly turned himself into the 'toff' he had always yearned to be. He dressed elegantly and expensively. After his marriage to Laura she had tactfully persuaded him to curb his predilection for flashy ties, colourful brocade waistcoats, and gaudy jewellery. Most of his rough edges had been smoothed away and he was even sophisticated to a degree. His thick Irish brogue had all but disappeared, except for an almost indiscernible lilting burr. Laura had had a refining and gentling influence on him, yet without destroying his natural ebullience. And there was still quite a lot of the actor in him, a trait he had discovered was an asset in business.

He waved to Emma and ran lightly down the stairs, his face merry. 'Emma, me love. You're a sight for sore eyes,' he cried, sweeping her into his arms so forcefully her feet left the floor. He swung her around, planted her firmly in front of him, and, as was his way, tilted her chin and looked down at her. 'And what kind of a face is this to be making? You look as if you've lost a pound and found sixpence.'

Emma laughed in spite of herself, as always infected by Blackie's good humour. 'I'm all right, Blackie. Just a bit under the weather, that's all.'

'*You* under the weather! That's hard for me to believe.' He looked at her closely. 'Are you sure nothing is upsetting you?' he asked, his eyes surveying her perceptively.

'No, truly not. Where's Laura?'

'In the parlour waiting for you.' He hurried her across the hall. 'She thought you might drop in.'

Laura was sitting by the fire knitting a knaki scarf and she threw it down and flew to Emma, embracing her lovingly. 'Emma, darling. I hoped you would have time to visit us tonight. Do you realize it's been almost a whole week!'

The dismal look on Emma's face lifted at the sight of her dearest friend. 'I know. I've really been up to my neck.' She smiled. 'I brought you the things you wanted from the store. For the Sunday-school Christmas party. The maid took them. Incidentally, I put in a few extra things I'm sure you can use for the needy children.'

'Oh, Emma, you're so good. Thank you.' Laura linked her arm through Emma's and they walked back to the fireplace chatting.

'I can see when a fellow's not wanted,' Blackie teased. 'I'll be leaving the two of you to your female gossipings. But make it brief, me darlin's. I'll be back shortly to have a Christmas drink with you.'

Sitting in the charmingly decorated parlour, listening to Laura's light tinkling voice, Emma discovered that her tension was beginning to slip away. Emma knew these feelings of warmth and ease now enveloping her did not come from the heat of the roaring fire, but from Laura's comforting presence. This gentle woman, so dear to her heart, always managed to soothe her. Laura was talking about the party she had arranged for the children who attended her Sunday-school classes and as Emma listened she observed her friend with mounting pleasure. Laura looked remarkably lovely this night. Since her last miscarriage, two years ago, she had completely regained her strength and was blooming and full of life. In her dark blue dress, with her honey-blonde hair bound in a chignon to reveal that calm and tender face, Emma thought she looked more Madonna-like than ever. Laura was happy with Blackie, and the only thing that marred her joy was her disappointment that she had not given him a child.

'The party seems to have taken up most of my time these past few weeks,' Laura explained. 'Blackie found me a beautiful tree for the church hall. I'm going to decorate it tomorrow.'

Emma stiffened and she knew her face was tightening.

Laura looked up from her knitting. She stopped, staring at Emma. 'Goodness, darling, you look awful. Whatever's the matter?'

Emma shook her head. 'Nothing. Really,' she managed, and glanced quickly at her hands.

'Yes, there is. I know you too well. Please, dear, if you are fretting about something, do confide in me. It might help.'

Emma cleared her throat. 'Well, Edwina was so cutting with me tonight. It really upset me.' Taking a deep breath, Emma recounted the incident with the Christmas tree.

Laura frowned and then said, 'Girls always gravitate to their fathers, Emma. *You* know that. It's nothing unusual. She'll grow out of it. I'm sure it's just a stage she's going through.'

'She's always seemed to prefer Joe to me,' Emma countered softly. 'Not that I mind. I'm happy they're so devoted. It's these occasional displays of coldness which disturb me. I do try so hard to win her affection.'

'I know you do.' Laura sighed and reached out, squeezing Emma's arm. 'Children can be *so* unkind. They don't mean to be cruel. They're simply thoughtless, that's all.'

'Yes, perhaps you're right.'

'And she is a very good child, isn't she?'

'Yes, almost too good in a sense. I've often thought that Edwina was born an adult.' Emma pondered, and continued, 'Sometimes I feel Edwina lives within herself, Laura. She can be very distant. And she always has a faraway look in her eyes.'

Laura laughed, trying to dispel Emma's obvious anxiety. 'Oh, darling, that's only natural. Girls are always daydreaming.'

'I suppose so,' Emma said, wanting to believe this.

'As for being distant, I think she's simply rather reserved by nature. Why, Blackie was saying the other day –'

'What was I saying?' Blackie boomed from the doorway, strolling into the room. He hovered over Laura and Emma, puffing on a cigar.

'I was about to tell Emma that you think Edwina is refined and quite the little lady with charming manners,' Laura told him.

'She is that. And a beauty!' He turned away, moving to the sideboard. 'What can I offer you, ladies?' he asked gaily, pouring himself an Irish whiskey.

'What would you like, Emma? Please do have a little something for once,' Laura urged gently.

'I believe I will!' Emma laughed. 'I think I need a drink tonight. I'll have a sherry, Blackie. Thank you.'

'And the same for you, Laura, me darlin', I presume.'

'Yes, please, Blackie. But only a small one.'

'A Merry Christmas to my best-loved ladies,' Blackie said with his typical show of exaggerated gallantry, lifting his glass.

'Merry Christmas,' they said in unison, and Emma added tartly but in a teasing tone, 'I should hope *we* are your best-loved ladies. We'd be very angry if there were any others.'

Blackie grinned. 'Laura tells me we are joining you on Christmas Day. I'm looking forward to it. We must make the *most* of this one and have a bit of festivity.'

They both stared at him. 'What do you mean by that, Blackie?' Laura asked.

'Oh, nothing, love,' he responded smoothly, regretting the remark.

'Blackie, please don't hedge. Answer me, dear. Do you know something – something about the war that we don't know?' Laura persisted.

'Not at all, at all,' he said, reverting to a thick brogue. 'Come along, no talk of the war tonight, darlin'.' He joined Laura on the sofa and took her hand in his. Glancing carefully at Emma, he said, 'I hear Thompson's mill is in a bad way. Producing poor cloth and falling down on their government orders as well.'

'So I believe,' Emma said dispassionately. Her face was inscrutable and she adroitly changed the subject.

The New Year brought more disastrous news for Britain and her allies. Men were dying in thousands in the trenches, and the overall losses were so monumental the world was horror-struck. On January 4, 1916, Prime Minister Henry Asquith stood up on the floor of the House of Commons and introduced a bill for the compulsory military service of all single men deemed fit for enlistment in the army. The bill met enormous opposition, especially from the diehards and defenders of the old voluntary system of military duty. But on Monday, January 24, the bill passed its third reading by a majority of 347 votes, the opposition having fallen to a mere 36. And so the first Compulsory Service Act came into force on March 2.

Although this measure at first applied only to single men, Emma began to experience a feeling of rising alarm as the days passed. She read the newspapers carefully, analysing the developments in the war, aware that more soldiers were needed, and on a continuing daily basis, because of the toll of Britain's manhood. And she recognized that it was only a question of weeks before married men were called. And she was right.

Reading *The Times* one morning at the beginning of May, she saw that her fears were indeed becoming realities. She quickly scanned the story which reported that the Prime Minister had asked leave to introduce into the House a new Military Service Bill.

'Joe, I think married men are going to be *forced* to enlist,' she said quietly.

He looked at her across the breakfast table, his eyes grave. 'It was bound to come, Emma. Kitchener's been shouting for more men for weeks.'

Emma nodded. 'The new bill lays down the rule that *every* male British subject between eighteen and forty years of age is to be deemed duly enlisted in the regular forces for general service, unless he's exempt for some reason.' She proffered him a weak smile. 'I don't suppose you're exempt, are you?'

'No, love, I'm not.'

A few days later she read with gloomy resignation that although the House divided on the bill, the majority of Members were in favour. Finally, on May 27, the new Military Service Act received royal assent.

That evening Emma sat in the drawing room with Frank, who was staying with them again, discussing the news. 'What exactly does that mean – royal assent?' she asked.

'It means that in the great crisis of its destiny the British nation has reverted to the method of Norman and Saxon times, when the King had the right to take in men, ships, and every available chattel in his dominion for the purpose of defending the nation,' Frank told her solemnly.

She understood. But understanding did not necessarily ease her troubled thoughts.

Emma, having previously always complained, and in the most vociferous voice, of the procrastination and red tape of bureaucracy, now cursed its deadly efficiency. The three men most prominent in her life went with the hordes. First David, with the infantry, and then Joe and Blackie, who left together. At the end of May they had both joined the Seaforth Highlanders, her father's old regiment, and one that was particularly favoured by Yorkshiremen.

'Except that I'm not a Yorkshireman,' Blackie had declared. 'An Irishman living in England, married to a Sassenach, lapsed from the Church, serving in a Scottish regiment and wearing a skirt to boot. Unique, eh?' Laura and Emma had joined in his laughter but their hearts were heavy.

Joe and Blackie had been immediately dispatched to Ripon for field training. This picturesque and ancient garrison town was a place of old memories for Emma. Two weeks later they came home on leave for twenty-four hours, en route to Tilbury for embarkation to France. On a damp June morning Emma accompanied them to the railway station. Laura, who was now pregnant, begged to go along, but Blackie was adamant.

'Not in your condition, darlin',' he said gently, stroking her hair. 'I don't want you getting distraught and upsetting yourself and the baby.'

At the last minute Blackie almost had to forcibly restrain Laura, who clung to his arm fiercely, endeavouring to hold back the tears without success. But her strained white face was filled with immense courage as they took their leave of her. She stood at the window, a pale image against the glass, waving to the three of them as they walked down the garden path and disappeared from view.

It was a silent journey into Leeds. Emma was staggered when they arrived at City Station. Crowds of troops, from many other regiments as well as the Seaforth Highlanders, were filing through the gates. The gloomy grime-coated platforms were jammed with hundreds more, and women and girls of all ages and classes, wives and mothers and sweethearts saying farewell to their men. Blackie took their kit bags on to the train and Emma and Joe stood on the platform holding hands.

'You'll be fine, love,' Joe said, tightening his grip on her fingers. 'Don't worry about me. Just take care of yourself and the children.'

Emma bit her lip, striving for composure. Joe had been surprisingly tender and considerate over the past few months, obviously realizing the time for separation was drawing near, and they had become much closer in many ways. 'It's you who must take care, Joe,' she said softly.

Blackie rejoined them after a few seconds. Emma reached for his hand, pulling him to her. 'And you, too, Blackie.' She attempted to laugh. 'Don't either of you get into any scrapes –' She stopped, her lips shaking.

Joe lifted her face to his gently. 'Now, where's that famous smile of yours, love?'

'I'm sorry.'

The whistles began to hoot and clouds of steam and smoke enveloped them as the trains revved up to roll on their journey south. Blackie put his arm around her. 'Goodbye, mavourneen. Stay well and look after me darlin' Laura for me. See she takes it easy and don't let her fret.' He kissed her cheek, his eyes wet.

Emma swallowed, looking up at Blackie. 'I will. I promise I won't let anything happen to her or the baby.'

Blackie leaped on to the train steps and stood hanging on to the bar, turning away to give them a moment of privacy.

Joe took Emma in his arms. 'You've been the best wife, sweetheart.' Seeing the look of fear cross her face, he added hastily, 'And that's why you can be damned sure I'm coming back to you!'

'I know you will, love. And you've been a good husband, Joe. Be careful over there.'

He nodded, choked and unable to reply. He kissed her again and she felt his tears mingling with her own on her cheeks. Joe released her abruptly and sprang on to the steps to join Blackie. The wheels started to grind with a high-pitched screech against the rails and the train began to pull out. It was moving so slowly Emma was able to walk alongside it, holding on to Joe's hand.

Unexpectedly a lone soldier's voice rang out, sweet yet melancholy. 'Keep the home fires burning, though your hearts are yearning . . .' Another voice joined in and another and another, until the immense station hall reverberated with the song as troops in other trains and many of the women picked up the refrain, and Blackie's baritone rose above them all, as rich and magnificent as always.

The train gathered speed. Joe dropped Emma's hand and she halted on the spot, waving to them. And her luminous valedictory smile was courageous despite her moist eyes. She watched the train until it was lost from sight and then she turned and left, jostled by the crowds, blinded by tears and wondering despairingly if she would ever see either of them again.

FORTY-ONE

They marched through a curtain of shrapnel, ankle-deep in mud, their kilts swinging in the breeze, the skirl of the bagpipes a mournful dirge below the roar of the cannonade. The tornado blasts from the British guns now rose to a fearful and deafening crescendo and the pipes ceased abruptly.

Behind this moving barrage of gunfire came the 51st Division of the Seaforth Highlanders. They had slowly advanced from the Somme Canal, tramping across the sodden and bloody fields ripped apart by shelling, cut deep with trenches and intersected with wire entanglements. Hardecourt was behind them. To the right, Combles and Guillemont. To the left, Mametz. Ahead, Bazentin and Longueval. And the bull's-eye centre of this triangle composed of the six towns was Trônes Wood – their objective.

General von Arnim was entrenched in that wood. Having suffered heavy defeats in Mametz he had tried to redress his losses on his left by a furious drive to his right into Trônes Wood. The wood stretched across a narrow valley along which a stream ran to Fricourt, and the Germans had two railways lines running through it, connecting it with Guillemont and Combles. Trenches extended across the centre of the wood and down the northern and southern sides; wire entanglements reinforced by machine guns protected the western edge against assault. In essence, it was a long, wide wedge of ground, 1,400 yards from north to south, and 400 yards along its base, driven against the enemy's second line at Guillemont and Longueval.

The British had already moved into the wood and the Lancashires had gained a partial grip on this dense green tract. But there was a terrible disadvantage to this new British salient. It was covered on all sides by German infantry. General von Arnim was exerting all his available strength in men and shell to hold and cut off this long strip of woodland. Four times the British had advanced further and been repulsed by von Arnim, who was spending his men's lives in tens of thousands to recover the whole of Trônes Wood, a vital and strategic position in the great Somme Offensive. At night, unperturbed by his incredible losses, von Arnim flung out more divisions to repeat the enveloping assault. For the fifth time, his men utterly failed under a hurricane of shell fire from British guns west of the wood and French guns near Hardecourt. But a sixth desperate attack by the British enabled the German general to regain the greater part of the wood. Meanwhile, Sir Henry Rawlinson's orders had come down to the British field commanders operating below the Bazentin ridges: *Smash through Trônes Wood, destroy the German bulwark and press on and upward to Longueval and Bazentin.*

Now on the afternoon of 13 July the wood was again swept by Allied artillery as the Seaforth Highlanders approached to reinforce the Lancashires. It was a grey day, the overcast sky fiercely illuminated by great arcs of vivid red gunfire and exploding shells, and filled with British aeroplanes strafing German observation balloons.

403

'Fix bayonets!' came the terse command.

Metal hit metal with deadly precision.

'Forward march!'

Rifles drawn and ready, they moved ahead, in perfect step, as though they were one giant body of tartan and khaki, backs straight, eyes sharp, heads held proudly high. They were tall and strapping men, these Seaforth Highlanders, whose fierce indomitable courage and their dark green-and-navy regimental kilts had induced the enemy to name them 'the ladies from hell'.

Into the wood they moved, stalwart and determined in their deadly purpose, seeking a terrible vengeance for their fallen comrades. The battle was atrocious in its ferocity and men were mercilessly cut down in increasing numbers on both sides. After several hours of general ploughing fire, the British guns massed in a single gigantic machine-like effect, tearing up the ground, hurtling mud and rocks, trees and men wantonly into the air. But this massive effort, as terrible and as destructive as it was, enabled the Seaforth Highlanders to drive the enemy back. The British penetrated deeper and deeper into the wooded area, now so smashed and riven apart it looked as if it had been cracked open by an earthquake.

After swaying, hand-to-hand fighting of the most relentless kind, a group of the Seaforths won a small but satisfying victory when they managed to capture the upper portion of the wood. A young captain, who was the only senior officer in the group, set up temporary battalion headquarters with a couple of lieutenants and instructed the men to seek cover in the trenches running on the southern edge of the forest. Their orders: *Hold fast to the last man.*

Blackie O'Neill wearily wiped the mud from his face and glanced around swiftly at the men in his trench, his bloodshot eyes seeking out Joe Lowther. He was not amongst the handful crowded together and Blackie wondered, with numbing dread and the most awful sinking feeling, if he was alive or dead? Had Joe made it to this sector? Or was he out there with the other corpses? Blackie crushed down on this fearful thought, refusing to contemplate such a chilling idea. Perhaps Joe was with the rest of the regiment who had been thrown back with the Lancashires. He prayed to God he was.

Spotting a particular pal, a Yorkshireman called Harry Metcalfe, Blackie edged down past the other men to join him, his boots sinking in to the slime which squelched and sucked around his calves and seeped through his gaiters. His nose curled with distaste. The mire had a peculiar putrid smell of its own and intermingled with it was the gagging stench of urine, vomit and excrement, strong reminders of the previous occupants.

'Jesus, Mary and Joseph! There's so much bleeding mud we're going to drown in it before we get out of here,' Blackie said when he reached Harry.

'Aye, there's summat to that, lad.'

'Have you seen Joe Lowther? We got separated out there.'

'Last I saw of him he was going arse over tit into a trench back yonder. He's safe, mate.'

'Thank God for that. I thought he'd bought it.'

'No, he didn't, but a lot of our lads did. I saw MacDonald and Clarke both go down like ninepins. Poor bloody sods. Mac got blown to smithereens by a shell and Clarkey was shot in the face and chest. Mashed to a pulp he was.'

'Oh sweet Jesus! Clarkey has a young wife and couple of bairns back home. Just babies.' Blackie's eyes closed, his face grim. 'Oh God! This lousy rotten war! This stinking filthy lousy rotten war!'

'Here, take it easy, Irish,' Harry said, throwing him a sympathetic look.

Blackie leaned back against the wall of the trench, resting his head against a sandbag. He was suddenly drained of all strength and filled with a rising nausea caused by the feculent trench, the stink of smoke and explosives polluting the air, and the gamy effluvian of the men. All were fouling his nostrils. The pounding of the cannons still reverberated in his ears and for a moment a dizziness enveloped him.

'You badly, Blackie lad?'

'No, just catching me breath,' Blackie said, opening his eyes. He looked more closely at Harry. His khaki jacket was covered in blood. 'How about you? You didn't get hit, did you, Harry?'

'No, not me. I'm just caked with this pissing mud. And a Jerry's guts.' Harry glanced down at the khaki apron covering his kilt, which all Highland troops were issued with for battle, and made a face. 'And when this muck hardens I'll be as stiff as a board. You too, by the looks of you, me old cock.'

'Don't tempt providence,' Blackie protested, his Celtic hackles rising. And then he laughed, grimly amused at his ridiculous comment. Here they were, engaged in violent warfare, their lives on the line, and he was being superstitious.

Harry gave him a lopsided grin. 'Got a fag-end, mate?'

'Sure and' I do, Harry.' Blackie fumbled for his cigarettes and they each lit one.

'It's no bloody wonder our lads call this Hell Hole Wood. It *was* a sodding inferno out there. We've had a lucky escape, Irish. Aye, we have that.' Harry pushed back his helmet and rubbed his muddy face with his equally muddy hands. 'I'll tell you this, Blackie, I never thought I'd be hankering to get back to Huddersfield to me nagging old woman, but by bleeding hell I wish I was there right at this minute, listening to her nag. And supping a nice warm pint of bitter. I do that. She suddenly seems like Lady Godiva to me – and with bells on!'

Blackie grinned but said nothing. He was thinking of his own sweet Laura. He closed his eyes, drawing on the soothing memory of her loveliness, of her shining immaculate face, to obliterate the visions of death and bloodshed that engulfed his mind.

'Here, mate, don't start copping forty winks!' Harry nudged Blackie in the ribs. 'Got to keep our bleeding wits about us, you knows, at a time like this. We ain't on a flaming day trip to Blackpool, lad.'

Blackie blinked, straightened up to his full height and drew on his cigarette. He and Harry exchanged full and knowing glances and hunched further together, settling in to wait. They did not know what was in store for them or what their inevitable fate would be, and neither of them dwelt on it. For the moment they were relieved to have this small respite from the horrendous fighting. Splattered with slime and blood, their faces ringed with fatigue, their bodies exhausted from the raging battle they had endured, they looked like a couple of defeated, battle-scarred veterans with no fighting spirit left. But this was not the case. Their courage was boundless and their stamina illimitable.

Suddenly Harry grabbed Blackie's arm. 'Do you notice summat right bleeding queer, Irish?'

'No. What do you mean?'

'The sodding guns have stopped, Blackie.'

'Christ, you're right, Harry.'

They stared at each other, and to Blackie and Harry the overwhelming silence was so stunning it seemed more sinister and deadly than the tumult.

'The lull before the next storm?' Blackie suggested, his eyebrows puckering together in a jagged line.

'No,' Harry muttered, shaking his head. 'It'll be dark soon. The Jerries won't waste shells trying to hit what they can't see. You knows what I mean, mate?'

'Sure an' I do.'

Darkness was beginning to fall quickly. Blackie turned and peered over the top of the trench, scanning the landscape. In the dim twilight he saw a half-bent figure running towards their trench. He reacted instantly, reached for his rifle. 'Stand to!' he bellowed. All of the men in the trench scrambled for their guns, immediately alert and ready to defend themselves.

'That you, O'Neill?'

Blackie's tensed muscles relaxed as he recognized the voice. 'Yes, lieutenant, it's me,' he said, staring out into the greying dusk.

'Good lad,' The lieutenant leaned into the trench, his eyes swiftly scanning the men, his face grave. 'Now listen, boys. A piece of bad news. We've been cut off from the rest of our chaps. We're alone up here. About a hundred of us. The captain's orders are simple. We're to bloody well hold this bit of forest, come hell or high water. So dig in, lads. Keep your eyes and ears open, and set up a watch. At once.'

'Yes, sir,' Blackie said. 'Do you think they'll attack in the dark?'

'No way of knowing, laddie. But we've got some Lewis guns and plenty of grenades. We'll have to manage the best way we can.'

'Lieutenant, I'd like to join me mate, Joe Lowther. Metcalfe here says he saw him make it into one of the rear trenches,' Blackie said.

'Right, O'Neill. But make it snappy. And pass the news on to the lads holed up back there.' The lieutenant disappeared into the gloom.

'Mind if I come with you, Irish?'

'No, I don't, Harry. But let's skedaddle,' Blackie replied, clambering up and out over the sandbags.

Blackie and Harry made it to the far trench without incident. 'It's O'Neill, Seaforth Highlanders,' Blackie cried in a low voice as rifles appeared menacingly over the edge.

'Jump in, lads, before you get your friggin' heads blown off by one of me trigger-happy mates,' a gruff voice called back.

Blackie and Harry leaped simultaneously, mud flying as they landed with some force. They struggled up to be greeted by a chorus of highly descriptive but friendly-voiced curses from the men they had just covered in mire. Cigarettes glowed in the darkness, and Blackie squinted at those tired, drawn and grimy faces, hoping to find Joe's amongst them. 'Anybody seen Joe Lowther?' he asked.

'Aye, he's down at the other end,' a voice responded.

Blackie came across Joe sitting smoking nonchalantly, his helmet pushed back, his rifle across his knee, a photograph of Emma in his hand.

'All the comforts of home, I see,' Blackie exclaimed, grabbing Joe's shoulder and punching it with affection.

A look of relief spread across Joe's face. He slipped the photograph back into his tunic pocket, then his hand encircled Blackie's arm tightly. 'Christ, Blackie, have I been worried about you! No damage done, I hope.'

'No. And I can see you're in bloomin' bloody health. And what the hell are you sitting on?'

Joe grinned. 'Cases of corned beef!' He began to laugh at the expression on Blackie's face. 'We found a dugout over there, filled with supplies. The Lancashires were holed up there for a week or so, and they left a load of stuff behind when they retreated. We're lucky it wasn't blown to bits. We don't have time to eat the flaming stuff, but at least we can sit on it. Keep our arses dry, courtesy of Fray Bentos.' Joe edged over to make room for Blackie.

Harry ploughed up to them. 'By bloody hell, some of us have it right cushy,' he remarked, staring at the cases. Another soldier laughed and offered to share his makeshift seat with Harry.

Blackie passed the word down that they were cut off, and repeated the captain's orders. The dozen men in the trench drew around him and Blackie said, 'We'll set up a watch now. One man at each end and two on the look-out on both sides. We'll keep relieving each other every hour. I'll take this end for a start. The rest of you relax while you can. And you lads on guard better keep your bleeding eyes peeled,' he ordered in a firm voice. The men scattered to their posts.

Blackie had only been on watch duty for half an hour when he thought he discerned movement at the edge of a clump of saplings not felled in the onslaught. He narrowed his eyes, straining to see in the gloom, instinctively raising his rifle, every one of his reflexes coming into play. A formation of dark clouds obscuring the moon drifted away from its silvery surface and the dark sky was instantly filled with brilliant light.

'Holy Mother of Jesus!' Blackie exclaimed quietly.

Joe heard him. 'What's wrong?' he demanded, jumping up.

'Look! Over there! Do you see what I see?'

Joe stiffened. '*Holy Christ.*'

'Over the top, boys!' Blackie screamed. 'The bleeding German infantry's right up our backsides!'

Men were scrambling out of the other trenches and milling around on the muddy ground which had been levelled by the shelling. And all eyes were riveted on the grey column advancing. Each man fixed his bayonet automatically. The captain was hastily drawing up formations, and even orderlies and signallers were instructed to arm themselves with rifles and grenades.

Again, it was hand-to-hand fighting of the most bloody kind. Rushing forward into the fray, Blackie prayed silently: *Hail Mary, full of grace. Hail Mary, full of grace. Hail Mary, full of grace.* His face was harshly set and frightening in its terrible ferocity. He killed and killed and went on killing, his rifle spewing forth bullets, his bayonet slashing until it dripped with the blood of the enemy as though it were some horrible living organ. He did not know how many men he killed and he no longer cared. All he knew was that it was his life or a German's, and *he* was going to live. And in the end he simply stopped thinking and charged.

After two hours, the enemy unexpectedly fell back, retreating for cover in the lower part of the wood, and the Seaforths crawled into the trenches, weary but unvanquished. Blackie had lost sight of Joe and Harry during the horrifying slaughter and there was no way of finding them now. He prayed, with all the fervency of his heart and soul, that his friends were safe.

For the next twenty-four hours the Germans attacked this little band of brave men – heroes all. They tried to rush the Lewis gun positions by bombings delivered under the fire of massed machine-guns; they attempted to creep from shell-hole to shell-hole in the darkness, hoping to wear out the Seaforth Highlanders by lobbing grenades at them. But the captain had arranged such lines of fire with his Lewis guns and rifles that each attack was repulsed.

The Seaforth Highlanders went through indescribable strain during these skirmishes, which lasted all night and were in full force when dawn broke. And worse was yet to come. By noon of the next day, Sir Henry Rawlinson was pouring every ounce of power he had on Trônes Wood, believing it had been totally lost and that the British troops holding it had all been struck down. His bombardment was one of unparalleled intensity, for the general was planning to storm the enemy's Bazentin line.

Although much of this heavy bombardment fell on the Seaforth Highlanders, they grimly endured the pounding they were taking, realizing that it was an absolute necessity. It also had its useful side, since it served to interfere with the enemy's movements and crippled their infantry attacks.

At one point, the Germans parleyed and asked the British to surrender to avoid total annihilation. But those fearless Seaforth Highlanders refused, and dug in with relentless determination to hold this part of the wood. The Germans, recognising their stubbornness and indomitability, began to place more field guns in position, readying themselves for another raid.

At the same time, Rawlinson's guns thundered on without cease, and Trônes Wood was slowly but decisively conquered in a brilliant infantry operation, conducted under the double crashing of shell from British and German artillery. It was a pulverizing action stupendous in its magnitude.

And through this awesome hurricane of fire tramped the Sussex and other English county regiments intent on finally destroying the enemy and capturing this strategic zone.

'Hello, lads,' went up the unanimous cry from the glorious Seaforth Highlanders as they were rescued and hobbled out of the trenches to embrace their fellow countrymen, each one of them grinning from ear to ear.

The ground was ripped asunder and stained with the blood of men from both sides. British and German troops lay dead or dying on the crippled earth and in the shell-shocked trenches. The carnage all around them was so terrible it brought tears to the eyes of many of the tommies.

Red Cross ambulances rumbled in and medical officers leaped out, hastening to the wounded. The doctors tried to ease their suffering as best they could in conditions so appalling to behold that one young doctor turned away, vomiting at the sight of such needless butchery. And the dead were slowly carried off and laid at the far end of the wood.

Blackie, dripping with sweat, filthy and blood-stained, his uniform ripped at the shoulder, his helmet dangling around his neck, began his search for Joe and Harry.

A Seaforth Highlander, thrown against a tree like a crumpled rag doll, a jagged wound ripping open his chest, was obviously in the throes of dying. 'Help me, for God's sake, help me,' he moaned through parched lips.

Blackie knelt down and took him in his arms. The boy tried to speak again. 'Don't talk,' Blackie murmured, cradling him like a baby, his eyes urgently seeking a medical officer to no avail.

The boy sighed deeply and shuddered and went limp in his arms. Blackie looked down at him. He was dead, his eyes wide and staring. Blackie closed the lids, gazing at that young face, so tender, so innocent in death. No more than nineteen, Blackie thought, and tears of compassion and hopeless anger dimmed his vision. Blackie released the dead boy and with great gentleness laid him down under the tree, the only one standing for miles.

Filled with a searing pain that seemed to split his chest in half, Blackie flung himself on to a patch of grass miraculously not torn up by the shelling. He pressed his face in to the earth and closed his eyes. The last two days had passed in a haze of blood and killing and pain. He knew he would never forget the screams of the men as they were mowed down with such relentless efficiency, or ever cleanse himself of the stench that clung to his body like another skin. It was compounded of every kind of foul thing on this earth.

How will it end? he asked himself, this war of senseless murder and destruction precipitated by evil men seeking dominion over the world and the enslavement of mankind to satisfy their own greed for power. He did not know the answer. His mind reeled with furious rage, indignation and despair; his sorrow overwhelmed him. He pressed his face deeper into the grass and felt the cool clean sensation of the dew against his skin. And he did not know that the grass was dry or realize that his face was wet with his own tears.

Reality in the shape of a strong arm on his shoulder roused Blackie. He lifted his head. Harry was standing over him. 'Come on, me old cock. We're not at a bleeding Sunday school picnic,' Harry joked. He pulled Blackie to his feet.

'Have you seen Joe?'

Harry shook his head and a dismal look wiped the cheery grin off his face. 'No, I haven't, lad. And I wouldn't know where to begin to look, not in this bloody mess I wouldn't.'

'Help me to find him, Harry. *Please*,' Blackie begged, his voice suddenly cracking.

'Aye, I will that, lad. Don't worry, he must be somewhere hereabouts. Come on then, mate, let's start with that group of wounded tommies over yonder.' Growing increasingly aware of the worried expression on Blackie's face, Harry grinned and punched his arm. 'Joe can't have gone for a bloody hike, now can he!' he asserted, endeavouring to be jocular. 'I bet we'll find the old cocker puffing away on a fag-end, Blackie, and looking as if he don't have a bleeding care in the world.'

FORTY-TWO

Emma sat on the edge of Christopher's bed, the storybook in her hand, the lamp infusing her face with roseate tints and casting an aureole of light around her head. She closed the book and smiled at her son. 'Now, come along, Kit. It's time to go to sleep.'

409

Kit's wide-set hazel eyes regarded her steadfastly and his small round face, covered with a dusting of light freckles, was very intense for a five-year-old. 'Please, Mummy, just *one* more story,' he begged. '*Please*, Mummy. You promised to read to me a bit longer tonight and you never break a promise, do you? At least that's what you're always saying.'

Amused at his unsubtle brand of persuasion but unswayed by it, she laughed and rumpled his hair playfully. 'I *have* read longer to you, Kit. You must go to sleep now. It's well past your bedtime.' She put the book on the table and, leaning forward, kissed his cheek.

His sturdy little arms went around her neck and he nuzzled closer to her. 'You smell so nice, Mummy. Just like a flower. Like a whole bunch of flowers,' he murmured in her ear.

Smiling, Emma drew away and smoothed back his hair. 'Snuggle down, Kit. Good night and sweet dreams.'

'Good night, Mummy.'

Emma turned out the light and closed the door quietly behind her. She paused at Edwina's door, hesitating uncertainly before tapping lightly and entering. Edwina was sitting up in bed reading, her pale blonde hair tumbling in luxuriant waves around her thin shoulders visible through the light cotton nightgown. She lifted her head and focused her cool silver-grey eyes on Emma, looking as if she resented this intrusion on her privacy.

'I just came to kiss you good night,' Emma said carefully, crossing the floor. 'And don't burn the midnight oil for too long, will you, dear?'

'No, Mother,' Edwina said. She placed the book on one side and continued to gaze at Emma, a patient expression on her face.

Emma hovered near the bed. 'Our little nursery dinner *was* fun tonight, wasn't it?' she gaily remarked, wishing to reinforce the rapport, tentative though it was, which had recently sprung up between them.

Edwina nodded. 'Yes.' The child studied her for a moment and then said, 'When is Uncle Winston coming to stay with us, Mother?'

'I'm not quite certain, dear. Very soon, I hope. He said in his last letter he expected to get leave imminently.'

'I'm glad he's coming. I like Uncle Winston,' Edwina volunteered.

Surprised at this unexpected confidence and encouraged by it, Emma lowered herself on to the bed gingerly, always acutely conscious of Edwina's abhorrence of close physical contact. 'I am happy that you do, Edwina. He loves you very much and so does your Uncle Frank.'

'Will Uncle Frank be coming, too? I mean, when Uncle Winston gets his leave?'

'Yes, that was the plan, Edwina. We'll have some jolly evenings together. We'll play charades and have singsongs. You'll like that, won't you?'

'Oh, yes, it will be nice.' Edwina proffered Emma a rare smile, a deliquescent smile that softened her cold young face and brought a hint of warmth to those enormous argent eyes.

Emma, observing Edwina intently, felt her heart miss a beat. There it was again. *That smile.* That melting smile she remembered only too well. She dropped her eyes, aware that a flicker of fear had entered them, and nervously straightened the coverlet. 'We'll make plans for your Uncle Winston's visit tomorrow,' she said in a low voice, and stood up abruptly. Bending down, she kissed Edwina fleetingly, afraid of being repulsed, and went on, 'Good night, darling. Sleep tight.'

'Good night, Mother,' Edwina responded dutifully in a stiff tone, and returned to her book without giving Emma a second glance or a second thought. Her mother, this woman whom everyone claimed was beautiful and charming and clever, hardly existed for the ten-year-old girl. Edwina lived in a world entirely of her own making and she did not permit anything or anyone to penetrate it, and the only two people she loved were Joe and her Cousin Freda in Ripon.

The child was an enigma to Emma. She ran lightly down the stairs, Edwina's smile lingering in her mind as she entered the study. She grows to look more like *her* every day, Emma thought with a stab of acute discomfort. But it's only a *physical* resemblance, she reassured herself, hurriedly dismissing those characteristics which were becoming more pronounced in her daughter and which disturbed her from time to time. The desk was covered with a pile of papers that needed Emma's immediate attention and she sat down, determined to wade through them that evening. After half an hour she realized her powers of concentration had fled and she put down her pen in irritation and leaned back in the chair, wondering what ailed her. Strain? Tiredness? She had felt distracted and restless that morning, feelings unprecedented for her. But they had persisted throughout the day and she had left the store earlier than usual, conscious of need to break loose from the fetters of her business and assailed by a desperate longing to be at home with her children.

It was the housekeeper's day off and Emma had shooed Clara, the devoted nursemaid, out of the kitchen and prepared the dinner herself. Emma had enjoyed the simple pleasure of working with the food and using her hands instead of her brain for once, and this brief domestic sojourn had refreshed her. Later she had joined Clara and the children for their evening meal in the nursery, and she had experienced such a profound sense of serenity in their untroubled world her own cares had disappeared.

It was a lovely interlude, Emma said to herself, and vowed she would stop depriving herself of her children's company as she had done so often lately. She was not going to allow business to interfere so relentlessly with her hours with them. This time in their lives was precious and she wanted to share it. Even Edwina was warmer in disposition and more outgoing than usual during supper, Emma reflected with genuine pleasure, and the child's sudden declaration of her liking for Winston was quite remarkable in view of her dismaying lack of feeling for most people. It had been a revelation to Emma, and she was hopeful that it signalled a change for the better.

Emma's drifting thoughts settled on her daughter. She's a Fairley through and through and there's no mistaking that. Emma had long recognized the striking likeness Edwina bore to her grandmother on the paternal side. She was a faithful reproduction – a mirror image – of Adele. Have Winston and Frank ever detected it? she wondered. They had never passed one comment. Blackie, on the other hand, was a wholly different matter. Emma suspected he had arrived at the truth years ago, although he, too, had been discreetly silent on the subject and had never displayed even the slightest hint of his suspicions, either by a knowing look or by a careless reference.

Emma thought then of Edwin Fairley. Her hatred for him remained constant, yet it had changed in nature and now sprang from her intellect and not from her heart. Consequently, it was deadlier than before, for it had objectivity and thus direction.

Even if she wanted to forget the Fairley family, Emma would have found that virtually impossible, since the *Yorkshire Morning Gazette* consistently reported their activities, social or otherwise. She knew a great deal about Edwin. He was a captain in the army and had been awarded the Victoria Cross 'for bravery above and beyond the call of duty'. Bravery indeed, she thought, her lip curling with contempt. She had also seen the announcement of his son's birth in the paper only yesterday. His wife, the Lady Jane Fairley, daughter of the Earl of Carlesmoor, had been delivered of a seven-pound boy, to be baptized Roderick Adam in honour of his two grandfathers.

But Edwin Fairley's life was of no concern to her – at the present time. Adam and Gerald Fairley were her primary targets and for a simple reason: *they* controlled the Fairley mills and therefore the Fairley fortune. The family's destiny was in *their* hands. Over the years Emma had come to understand that the most potent way to strike back at them was through business. She had already created immense problems for them at Thompson's mill, because they found it practically impossible to replace the work force she had stolen. There was nothing she did not know about their holdings and the general state of their commercial affairs. Her information had been acquired with limitless patience, incalculable diligence, and in the utmost secrecy, and she was already formulating her plans for the future.

They were exposed and vulnerable to her and they did not know it! Adam Fairley, always negligent about business, had become excessively so of late. Olivia Wainright Fairley had recently been struck down by some strange illness and she rarely, if ever, came to Yorkshire. The reins were in Gerald Fairley's hands, and *he* was a bumbling fool. *He* was the weak link in the iron chain which she intended to dismantle and cast to one side, just as her father and her daughter and she herself had been cast aside by them. And it was mainly on Gerald Fairley that her vivid green eyes rested with virulent loathing. No woman ever expunged the terrifying memory of the man who had attempted rape on her and Emma was no exception. Yes, Gerald was the key to their downfall. All she had to do was stick out her foot and trip him and the others would come tumbling behind. There were no doubts in her mind about the final outcome. Once she had set herself a goal nothing could deter her from achieving it.

The doorbell rang, echoing through the silent house. It brought Emma up with a start and pulled her away from her contemplation of the Fairleys. She rose and went into the hall, her silk dress swishing as she moved with her usual rapidity. She opened the front door, wondering who could be calling at this hour, to be confronted by a telegraph boy.

'Evening, missis,' he said, deferentially touching his cap. He handed her the telegram, touched his cap again, and ran down the steps. Emma closed the door and glanced at the yellow envelope. It was undoubtedly from Winston, announcing his arrival.

Emma glided into the centre of the hall and stood under the crystal chandelier where the light was brighter and ripped it open. Her eyes travelled quickly across the top line and they widened and widened, and the smile on her face faded as she read: '*It is with deep regret and the greatest sympathy that the War Office must*

412

inform you that your husband Private Joseph Daniel Lowther of the 1st Battalion of the Seaforth Highlanders was killed in action on July 14 in France . . .'

The remaining words blurred and ran together and, recoiling, Emma sat down on the hall chair with a thud, stunned and for a moment disbelieving. She stared blankly at the opposite wall, the light in her eyes dulled, her mouth trembling. Eventually she brought her reluctant gaze back to the telegram crumpled in a ball between her clenched fingers. She straightened it out and read it again. The devastating words slowly sank in and her heart plunged.

It can't be true! There has been a mistake! A ghastly error! Emma cried inwardly, moving her head from side to side, denying the words. Joe could not be dead. Her throat thickened as reality struck at her, and she sat frozen in the chair, as rigid as stone, held in the grips of the most paralysing shock.

After what seemed like an eternity to Emma she pushed herself up out of the chair, forcing her shaking legs to move forward, blindly making her way to the stairs. She held on to the banister to steady herself, a sensation of fainting weakness trickling through her entire body. She manoeuvred herself up the staircase, dragging one leaden foot after the other, moving with laborious care like an old woman crippled by arthritic pain. She stumbled into her bedroom, collapsed on to the bed, and lay motionless, staring at the ceiling in a trance-like state, her eyes dark pools of sorrow.

Poor Joe. Poor Joe. Struck down after only a brief few weeks at the front. He was too young to die. It was unfair. Unfair. Emma began to weep, the tears streaming down her face unchecked. She would never see Joe again. The children would never see him again. Her mind floundered at the thought of Kit and Edwina sleeping so peacefully in their beds. She could not tell them the news. Not now. Tomorrow would be soon enough.

Her anguished mind began to race. How had Joe died? And where was his body? She wanted Joe's body. Irrational as the idea was under the present circumstances, she wanted to give him a proper burial. The thought of Joe's body lying smashed and neglected somewhere in France haunted her. It was a horrendous image that wobbled in the very centre of her brain.

Emma lay in the bedroom, unaware of the hour, watching the night descend, abandoned and lonely in her misery. And she grieved inconsolably for Joe. He had been honourable, and kind in an infinite number of ways, and now she dismissed all the traits that had irritated her, forgot the revulsion she had experienced in their marital bed. She carefully obliterated everything that had been distressing, remembered only the good and the best.

And she wept all night for the loss of a decent man, for all that he had been and had represented, and for the life they had shared together.

It was a glorious Sunday afternoon in late October, one of those unexpected Indian-summer days, radiant with crystalline light that flooded the periwinkle-blue sky. The garden was bathed in a golden haze and the trees and the shrubs were already turning colour, the autumnal foliage a glowing mixture of yellows and orange running to scarlet and burnt sienna.

Laura O'Neill sat on the garden seat lost in contemplation. Her thoughts as always were with Blackie in France. She had not received a letter for several weeks.

On the other hand, that dreaded telegram had not arrived either. Despite the lack of news of any sort, Laura held the deep conviction that Blackie was safe and would continue to be safe and that he would come home to her when the war was over. Her unwavering faith in Almighty God was the rock upon which her life was built, and she knew with absolute certainty that Blackie was under His divine protection. Laura, always devout, now went every day to mass, disregarding Emma's advice that she stay in bed and rest. She lit innumerable candles for Blackie and Winston and for all of the other fighting men. And her gentle heart overflowed with grief for those who had lost sons and husbands and sweethearts, and most especially for Emma, widowed four months before.

Emma was working at the other end of the garden, filling a basket with magnificent gold and copper winter chrysanthemums. Laura's hazel eyes rested on her dearest friend and her heart tightened with love and sympathy. She's painfully thin, Laura thought. And she's exhausted. She works like a Trojan and her responsibilities would crush anyone else. Even the strongest and most determined of men would stagger under the burden.

It seemed to Laura that Emma had been imbued with an almost inhuman strength since Joe's death. She not only ran her own businesses and managed Joe's properties as well, but played a major administrative role at the Kallinski factories. Yet withal she still found time to devote hours to the children, trying to surround them with love and security. That is Emma's way of coping with her sorrow, Laura decided. The only way she knows how to go on. Her work and the children have become her citadel.

Laura sighed deeply. Death was never final. The person loved was gone but there were always the others, the ones left behind to mourn. The sadness of life is ever present, Laura thought, and yet there is joy in life, too. Joy like the child she was carrying. The child she yearned to give Blackie. She placed her hands across her stomach protectively and with love, and she thanked God she had not miscarried this time. Yes, there was death, but there was also birth. A continual renewal ... the endless cycle that was eternal, that was man's inexorable fate.

Emma having completed her tasks, pulled off her gardening gloves and joined Laura on the seat. 'You're not feeling chilly, are you?' she asked. 'I think we ought to go in shortly. I don't want you to catch a cold. Not now when you've been so well.' Emma eyed Laura lovingly. 'You only have two more months to wait and then you'll be presenting Blackie with that son and heir.'

Laura nodded, her happiness overflowing in her eyes. 'This pregnancy has been so easy, Emma. A miracle. I offer thanks for that every day.'

'So do I, love.'

Laura took Emma's hand in hers and said softly, 'I haven't wanted to upset you by bringing it up before, but is Edwina any better?'

'A little.' Emma's voice was low. 'If only she would cry then perhaps her grief for Joe would be alleviated. As it is, it's all pent up and her self-control frightens me. It's not natural.'

A look of sympathy crossed Laura's face. 'No, it's not healthy to repress that kind of anguish and pain. Poor Edwina, she did adore Joe so much.'

'I've talked to her for hours, tried to give her comfort and understanding, without much success. It's as if she wants to bear it alone. Stoically. I don't know what to do anymore –' Emma stopped. After a moment she added in a dim voice, 'Sometimes I think I misjudged Joe.'

'What do you mean?' Laura asked in puzzlement.

'Well, now when I look back, I realize how kind he was, and so generous in a variety of ways. His will, for instance. I was thunderstruck when Mr Ainsley read it to me and I learned Joe had left all the properties to me. I expected him to make Kit the sole beneficiary, willing him the business and everything. I haven't been able to get over that gesture. After all, Kit is the only son.'

'Joe left all of his money to Kit, dear,' Laura cut in swiftly. 'Except for the annuity for Edwina. Look, Emma, Joe always appreciated your business acumen. He wasn't cheating Kit. He was simply being wise, knowing you would handle everything with efficiency and in doing so provide for the children's future. He trusted you, Emma. He knew you would do the right thing.'

'I suppose so. But I still feel I did Joe many injustices when he was alive.'

Laura squeezed Emma's arm affectionately. 'You were a good wife. Don't start chastising yourself now for things that happened in the past. And don't forget, human relationships are never static. They change from day to day, because they are highly complex and also because people are changeable. And life intrudes. Problems intrude and create tensions. You gave Joe a great deal, even if you did have disagreements occasionally. I know you made him happy. Please, Emma, you must believe that.'

'I hope I did,' Emma murmured.

Noting the sad echo in Emma's voice and wishing to distract her, Laura said briskly, 'Shall we go in, dear? I'm getting cold and I would like some tea.' As she spoke she stood up, pulling the yellow shawl closer around her shoulders.

Emma took Laura's arm as they walked across the lawn. 'What would I do without you, my sweet Laura? You're so wise, and you always make me feel better.'

'I can say the same thing about you, Emma. Why, you're the best friend I ever had.'

FORTY-THREE

'Ah, there you are, Mrs Lowther,' Dr Stalkley said, hurrying through the swinging doors of the waiting room. 'Mrs O'Neill has been asking for you.'

Emma stood up, clutching her handbag tightly. 'Please,' she said anxiously, 'is everything all right? I don't understand what happened so suddenly.'

The doctor gave her an avuncular pat on the shoulder. 'It was a question of operating or going through with the natural childbirth. Because of her religion, Mrs O'Neill was quite adamant about the operation –'

'What do you mean? I'm not following you, Doctor,' Emma interrupted peremptorily.

'Mrs O'Neill would not permit us to operate because there was the possibility – in fact, the great probability – that she would have lost the child. The operation would have been wiser, safer, of course. However, she would not take any chances with the child's life.'

'*But is she all right?*' Emma demanded.

'Weak,' the doctor responded quietly, avoiding Emma's eyes.

'And the baby?'

'A fine boy, Mrs Lowther.'

Emma's stare became more penetrating. 'Mrs O'Neill isn't in any danger, is she?'

'She's tired, naturally. It was a difficult birth,' the doctor said. 'But let's not stand here chattering. She's waiting to see you. Please come this way.'

Emma followed him down the corridor, her mind racing as she tried to assess the gravity of the situation. Instinct told her Dr Stalkley was hedging and this frightened her. When they reached the door of Laura's room the doctor paused and turned to Emma. His face was unreadable as he said, 'We've sent for the priest.'

'Priest! Why?'

'Mrs O'Neill asked for him.' The doctor shook his head. 'She is very weak. Worn out. Please don't excite her.'

Emma clutched his arm. 'She's not –'

The doctor opened the door for her. 'Please, Mrs Lowther, let's not waste time.' He ushered her in and closed the door softly behind him.

Emma hurried to the bed, her eyes sweeping over Laura, who lay propped against the pillows. She was at once aware of Laura's terrible exhaustion. Her lovely face, so wan in the cold light, was etched with lines of extreme fatigue and there were dark smudges under her huge eyes, which lit up at the sight of her friend. Emma's heart sank, for she recognized all the distressing telltale signs, but the smile on her face did not falter for an instant. She bent over Laura and kissed her cheek. Smoothing back the honey-blonde hair that tumbled over the pillows, she said softly, 'How are you feeling, darling?'

Laura smiled. 'So happy. And grateful. It's a boy, Emma.'

Emma sat down on the chair next to the bed. Swallowing hard, she adopted her most cheerful tone. 'Yes, it's wonderful. Blackie will be thrilled.'

Laura nodded, her eyes shining. She reached for Emma's small hand, took it in hers, and squeezed it. 'Have you been waiting long, dear?'

'No,' Emma lied. 'And you mustn't worry about me. You're the one who needs all the care and attention now. I expect you'll be discharged in a week and then you're coming to stay with me and the children. I'm going to look after you like you looked after me when Edwina was born. You will come, won't you, darling?'

A faint smile flickered on Laura's white lips. She said, 'I want him to be called Bryan.'

'That's a lovely name, Laura.'

'And Shane Patrick, after Blackie and Uncle Pat.'

'They will be pleased, love.'

'Come closer to me, Emma,' Laura murmured, 'so that I can see you better. The light seems to have dimmed, doesn't it?'

'Yes, it is getting dark outside,' Emma said, even though the light was still very bright.

Laura's fine eyes searched her face. 'I want Bryan to be brought up as a good

Roman Catholic. You know what Blackie is like. So careless about some things. You'll see to it for me, Emma, won't you?'

Emma's fear flared again. 'What do you mean?'

'I want you to promise me that you'll make sure Uncle Pat does the right thing while Blackie is away, and that you'll take care of Bryan for me until his father comes back from the war.'

'But you'll be doing that, love.'

Laura's brilliant eyes remained unwavering. 'I'm dying, Emma.'

'Don't say that!'

'Emma, listen to me. *Please listen*. I have so little time left,' Laura whispered, her faint voice now vibrating with urgency. 'Promise me that you'll make certain Uncle Pat has Bryan christened in the Roman Catholic Church and that he attends to his religious training as long as Blackie is gone. And promise you'll look after Blackie for me.'

Emma was unable to speak for a moment. 'I promise,' she finally said, her voice thick with emotion and quavering.

Laura lifted her hand weakly and touched Emma's face. She smiled at her. 'I love you, Emma.'

'Oh, Laura, I love you, too.' Emma could no longer suppress the tears and they spilled down her cheeks and splashed on to Laura's hand.

'Don't cry, dear. There's nothing to cry about.'

'Oh, Laura – Laura –'

'Hush, darling. Don't cry.'

Emma took a deep breath and endeavoured to pull herself together. 'Laura, listen to *me* now. You must fight. Try harder, love. Please fight to live,' she implored with great intensity. She gathered Laura's frail body into her strong arms and cradled her close, pressing Laura harder against herself, as if trying to infuse her dying friend with some of her own enormous strength, her own stubborn will, as she had done so long ago with her mother.

A small sigh escaped Laura's lips, a soft fluttering sigh that was hardly audible. 'It's too late,' she said in a fading voice.

Emma placed her back on the pillows, her lips shaking, her face white and strained. 'Please try, love. Try for Blackie. For the baby. For me.'

There was a rustling noise as the priest came in carrying a black bag. He touched Emma on the shoulder lightly. 'She must receive Extreme Unction, Mrs Lowther,' he said.

Emma stood up and moved away with a degree of self-containment, although her knees were buckling. Tears rolled unchecked down her face and then it darkened as she watched the priest bending over Laura. She wanted him to leave. He was a harbinger of death. If he left, then Laura would live. *There is no God! No God, do you hear me!* Emma shouted at him, but the shouts reverberated in her head unuttered.

Emma thought her heart was surely breaking. The room was very quiet; the only sounds were the faint swishing of the priest's cassock as he moved nearer to the bed, the low murmur of his voice and Laura's as she confessed and he absolved her of her sins. *Sins*, Emma thought bitterly. *She* has never sinned. Laura never did anything to hurt anybody. She's only given love to everyone she knows. She's never sinned against God. Never sinned against the world. Never. Ever.

417

The priest administered Holy Communion, made the sign of the cross, and put the wafer in Laura's mouth. He was anointing her. Emma turned away and looked out of the window. It was all so wasteful. Yes, even sinful. The operation would probably have killed the baby, but Laura would have been alive. This dogma of the Catholic Church was barbaric. Insane. Who cared about the baby? It was Laura they knew and loved.

When the priest had finished the last rites he came to Emma. 'Mrs O'Neill wishes to speak with you,' he said dolorously.

Emma brushed past him rudely and flew to the bed. She brought her face close to Laura's. 'I'm here, my darling. What is it?'

Laura's eyelids lifted slowly. 'I'm sorry to keep asking you to promise me things. Just one more favour. Be brave for Uncle Pat. He's so old now and he's going to need your courage, Emma.'

'Oh, Laura, Laura, don't slip away from me!'

Laura smiled and her face was glorious, incandescent, and her eyes, so large they seemed to engulf her face, were steady and full of peace.

'There is no such thing as death in my lexicon, Emma. As long as you live, and Blackie lives, I will live, too, for you will both carry the memory of me in your hearts always. And there will be Bryan for Blackie.'

Emma had no words. She pressed her hands to her mouth, her shoulders heaving.

Laura said, 'Tell Blackie that I love him.'

'Yes, darling.' Emma bit her lip and blinked back the blinding tears. 'Oh, Laura, what will I do without you?' she gasped, choked and grief-stricken.

'You'll be fine, Emma. I'm very sure of you. You're so good; so brave. And remember, God never gives us a burden that is too heavy to bear.'

'Oh, Laura, I can't –'

'And don't forget my Christmas presents for the children, will you? The dog is at the kennel for Kit and the jasmine scent for Edwina is all wrapped. In my bedroom. You'll find it. There's something for you, too, my dearest Emma –' Laura closed her eyes and the smile, so radiant a moment before, was a mere fleeting shadow on her face.

'No, I won't forget, darling.'

Emma felt Laura's hand go slack in hers. 'Laura! Laura!' she cried, pressing the cold hand to her lips.

Dr Stalkley had to forcibly uncurl Emma's fingers from Laura's hand, so tightly was she grasping it. The priest led her out of the room, murmuring words of condolence. Emma closed her ears, drained and numb in her terrible sorrow.

After a few minutes the doctor joined them. 'I think we will be able to discharge the baby in a few days, Mrs Lowther. We'll let you know when you can come and fetch him. That was Mrs O'Neill's wish.'

Emma hardly heard him. 'Yes, I understand,' she responded automatically in a low voice. 'You have my address and telephone number.' She left them abruptly and without saying goodbye.

Emma pushed open the door of St Mary's Hospital and walked along the drive and out through the iron gates, moving like a somnambulist. She turned and headed up over Hill Top, climbing steadily, gazing ahead yet seeing nothing. It was a cold December afternoon and the empty sky was bloated with snow and sunless, and the harsh wind blew hard over the hill and dried the tears coursing down her cheeks.

Emma trod the path of her grief in measured steps – steps that sometimes faltered and often slowed but which never failed completely. She buried her pain deep and the world saw only that face of inscrutability, and as the weeks and months passed she learned to live with her heartbreak and the crushing loneliness of her life.

The baby, Bryan, lived with her and the children. Blackie, who had come home briefly on compassionate leave, had agreed this was the most sensible course to take under the circumstances, recognizing that his son would be in a more normal atmosphere with her than if he was put in charge of a nurse at his Uncle Pat's house. Blackie, unconsolable, and burdened down by his grief, had returned almost at once to the front, and Emma was alone again.

At first Emma had resented the baby, seeing it as the instrument of Laura's death, but one day it struck her, and most powerfully, that she was being unjust and bitter. She came then to understand that she was betraying Laura's love and trust in her and was also negating her own abiding love for Laura with her attitude. This was Laura's son, the child she had yearned for and had died for so that he might live. Emma was seized by remorse and became ashamed of herself and she took the child to her compassionate heart as if he were her own. Bryan had Blackie's dark colouring and jet-black hair, yet his eyes were Laura's, large and limpid and of the same soft hazel. He was a good baby, with Laura's sweet disposition, and when he smiled it was Laura's smile that Emma saw and she would pick Bryan up out of the crib and hold him fiercely to her breast, overcome with love, and she determined to cherish him always.

Sometimes Emma forgot that Laura was dead, and her hand would automatically reach for the telephone whenever she had a special confidence to impart, and then it would fall away and she would sit for a while, lost in memories of the past ten years, her eyes moist, her heart aching. But there were always the children to help dispel her sadness and pain. Emma devoted all of her free time to them, aware that they needed her more than ever now, with Joe gone and in their most formative years, and she gave of herself unstintingly. Winston came home on leave and Frank visited her regularly and she found solace in her family.

PART FIVE

THE PINNACLE
1918–50

He who ascends to mountaintops, shall find
The loftiest peaks most wrapt in clouds and snow;
He who surpasses or subdues mankind
Must look down on the hate of those below.

– LORD BYRON, 'Childe Harold's Pilgrimage'

FORTY-FOUR

'Why are you angry, Frank?' Emma asked, staring at her brother across the dinner table in the Ritz Hotel.

Consternation swept across Frank's sensitive face and he reached out and squeezed her arm. 'I'm not angry, love. Just worried about you, that's all.'

'But I'm feeling so much better, Frank. Truly I am, and I've quite recovered from the pneumonia,' she reassured him with a vivid smile.

'I know, and you look wonderful, Emma. But I do worry about you. Or rather, your life,' he responded quietly.

'My life! What do you mean? What's wrong with my life?' she exclaimed. Frank shook his head regretfully. 'What's wrong with your life? you ask. Oh, Emma, don't you ever stop to think? You're on a treadmill, love. In fact, you're as much a drudge now as you ever were at Fairley Hall –'

'That's ridiculous!' Emma interjected, her face clouding over.

'You're not scrubbing floors, I'll grant you that,' Frank countered quickly, 'but you're still a drudge, albeit in luxury. You've put yourself in bondage with your business, Emma.' He sighed. 'You'll never break free.'

'I don't want to break free, Emma said, suddenly laughing. 'Hasn't it ever occurred to you that I might enjoy my work?'

'*Work*! That's all you do, and that's exactly what I'm getting at. Isn't it about time you had a bit of fun in life? Now, while you're still young.' He threw her a wary look and his tone was cautious as he added, 'Also, you're going to be twenty-nine in a few months. I think you ought to consider remarrying.'

Laughter rippled through Emma. 'Remarry! Frank, you're absolutely crazy. Who would I marry? There are no men around. There's still a war on, you know.'

'Yes, but it's bound to end later this year. When America got in, the situation started to change and the Allies are making great headway. I'm positive armistice will be declared within nine months or so, and men will be coming back.'

'But it's still only January,' Emma gasped, still laughing, her eyes wide. 'All the young men are noticeably absent. You're a little premature, darling.'

'What about Blackie O'Neill, for one thing?' Frank suggested, watching for her reaction. 'He's always adored you. And you're both free now. Not only that, you've been looking after Bryan as if he were one of your own for the past year.' Noting she was not perturbed, he grinned and finished, 'It's not as if you are strangers.'

'Oh, Frank, don't be so silly,' Emma said dismissively, with an airy wave of her hand. 'Blackie is like a brother to me. Besides, I'm not sure I want to remarry. Apart from anything else, I don't think I would like a man interfering with my business.'

'That blasted business, Emma! I don't understand you sometimes.' His eyes were thoughtful when he glanced up at his sister. 'Surely you must feel secure these days. You are a rich woman in your own right and Joe left you well provided for. How much is going to be enough money for you, our Em?'

A small smile flitted across her mouth on hearing this affectionate diminutive from their childhood, and she shrugged casually. 'It's not the money, really. I *do* enjoy business, Frank. Honestly, I get a lot of gratification out of it and I do have the children to think about as well. Their futures. And I can handle my life without any help from anyone, or advice, however well-intentioned.'

Frank held up his hand. 'I simply think you ought to take it a bit easier and relax for once in your life.'

Emma leaned forward. 'Look, Frank, do stop worrying or I shall get awfully cross and take the next train back to Leeds if –' She broke off and dropped her eyes.

'What's wrong?'

'Nothing. Well, it's the two men at the table directly opposite. They keep staring at us. I wondered if you knew them. But don't look now, they'll see you.'

'I noticed them when they came in. The maître d' was bowing and scraping all over the place. However, I don't know them. But I do know that the younger one, the handsome major, is an Australian, from the insignia on his uniform. He's with the 4th Brigade of the Australian Corps.'

'A damned colonial! No wonder!'

Amused at the anger flaring in her eyes, Frank said, 'And what's that supposed to mean?'

'He's been quite insufferable since he sat down. Every time I look up I find his eyes on me. And speculatively so,' she said furiously.

'Come on, Emma. What do you expect? I don't think you realize how beautiful you really are, love.' Frank took in the bottle-green velvet gown, the creamy pearls at her throat and ears, the sleek hair pulled back in a chignon. 'You look about eighteen, Emma. And I'm glad you don't wear all that muck on your face most women have taken to using lately.' He smiled. 'Yes, you're undoubtedly the best-looking woman in this room.'

'There's not much to choose from,' Emma replied pithily, but she smiled and asked in a curiously shy voice, 'Am I really, Frank?'

'You are indeed.'

The waiter approached the table and said deferentially, 'Excuse me, sir, but you're wanted on the telephone.'

Frank nodded and turned to Emma. 'I won't be a minute. Excuse me.' He pushed back his chair and stood up. 'Why don't you look at the menu and decide what you want for a pudding.'

'Yes, all right, dear.' Emma watched Frank cross the floor of the Ritz Hotel dining room. He looked so distinguished and well bred in his dinner jacket, and she was extremely proud of his achievements and the shape his life had taken. He was a dear, and always concerned about her happiness. Emma smiled, wondering what Frank would say if he knew about the Emeremm Company. He'd probably give me another lecture and say I was taking on too much, she mused. But that company's going to be the making of my real fortune. The new business had been a brilliant concept, even if she did say so herself. It was an acquisition and holding company, which she had financed by selling Joe's shoe factory and the tannery for exorbitant prices, and in the eleven months it had existed it was already in the black. The name Emeremm was her invention, a contraction of the words emerald and Emma. One day she intended to call it Harte Enterprises, but for the moment she did not want the world to know she was associated with it. For her own reasons she sought concealed ownership. Although she was the sole shareholder she did not appear on the board, nor was she an officer of the company. Ostensibly it was run by the managing director and the two other directors she had appointed. Men bought by her and therefore owned by her. Men of straw who would do her bidding.

Emma looked around the elegant dining room absently, her mind dwelling on the Emeremm Company and its endless financial possibilities. As her glance swept past the other tables her eyes inadvertently met those of the Australian major, and Emma found to her amazement she was momentarily unable to look away. He's too handsome, too sure of himself, Emma thought with a stab of annoyance. The sleek hair, the thick brows, the clipped moustache above the sensual mouth were too glossily black against the deep tan of the rugged and arresting face. And those eyes were of a blue so deep they were almost violet. Even the cleft in his chin was more deeply indented than was normal. His wide mouth lifted in a tantalizing smile, brought dimples to his cheeks, and his gaze was now so bold and so provocative she flinched. Blushing, she turned away. Why, he's positively indecent, she thought, her cheeks burning. She had the odd feeling he knew exactly what she looked like stark naked. Embarrassed, Emma reached for the glass of wine and in her nervousness she knocked it over. Mortified, she began to dab at the cloth with her serviette.

The waiter promptly came to her rescue, murmuring that he could easily repair the damage, and quickly placed a clean serviette over the stain. He cleared away the dirty dishes and Emma thanked him as he moved away. The major was once again in her direct line of vision and she saw to her indignation that his audacious gaze still rested on her. There was an amused smile playing around his mouth and undisguised challenge in his eyes. Emma picked up the menu angrily and buried her flaming face behind it. She cursed the intolerable fool across the dining room who was so blatantly trying to flirt with her, and doubly cursed Frank and his interminable telephone call.

Bruce McGill's tanned and weather-beaten face was a study in fond amusement and his clear blue eyes twinkled as he said, 'If you can drag your gaze away from that fetching creature for a brief moment, perhaps we can have a little decent conversation with dinner, my boy.'

'Oh, sorry, Dad,' Paul McGill said. He shifted in his chair and gave his father his full attention. 'But she is undoubtedly the most fascinating woman I've ever seen. Don't you agree?'

Bruce nodded. 'I do, my boy. You inherited my taste for the ladies, I'm afraid. Never could resist a beauty. However, I would like to talk to you, Paul. I don't get to see you that often these days.'

'You'll be sick of the sight of me in a few weeks. This blasted wound is taking a hell of a long time to heal.'

Bruce looked concerned. 'Not too painful, I hope.'

'No, just aggravating and especially so in this lousy English weather.' Paul smiled wryly. 'I shouldn't be grumbling, should I? Instead I ought to be thanking my lucky stars. It was a miracle I got through the Gallipoli campaign without a scratch. Then this had to happen in France.'

'Yes, you were lucky.' A sober expression crossed Bruce's face. 'I had hoped you would get out after this, so that you could come back to Coonamble with me. But I suppose there's no chance of that. Will you be going back to France to join Colonel Monash?'

'I expect so. But let's not worry about that tonight. I intend to have a whale of a time while I'm in good old Blighty.'

'Glad to hear that, son. You damn deserve it after the hell you've been through. But take it easy, laddie.' Bruce laughed, his eyes merry again. 'No more little scandals this time. Dolly hasn't let me forget that last romantic encounter you had with her friend.'

'Oh, Jesus, don't remind me, Dad. I swear off women every time I think about that particular mess. When are we supposed to be at Dolly's?'

'Any time after dinner, my boy. You know Dolly and her theatrical friends. Those parties of hers usually last until dawn. Incidentally, I hope you don't mind, but I've decided not to go. You can pop along there alone. You'll enjoy it. Give her my regrets. Afraid I'm not up to it tonight. Also, I would like to drop in at South Audley Street and see Adam Fairley.'

Paul's dark head came up sharply. 'How is he these days?'

'Not well at all, poor chap. Very sad really – that whole business. He was never the same after Olivia's death, and now the stroke. It's hard for me to see him confined to a wheelchair. He was always so active. Olivia's death was a tragedy and he's taken it hard. Leukemia, you know. Such a vivacious, lovely woman. I remember the first night I met her, about fourteen years ago. Rather fancied her myself, to tell you the truth. I can still remember the way she looked. Ravishing. Wearing a kingfisher-blue dress and sapphires.'

At this moment Emma and Frank rose and left the dining room. Paul McGill's eyes were riveted on Emma for every step she took. He observed the proud set of her head, her straight back, her total self-assurance, and her regal bearing as she glided out, and he was further intrigued.

Paul caught the headwaiter's eye and motioned to him. To his father he said, 'I'm going to find out who she is right now ... Charles, who was the gentleman who just left with the lady in the green velvet?'

'That was Frank Harte, sir. *The* Frank Harte of the *Daily Chronicle*. Fine young gentleman. Made quite a name for himself as a war correspondent.'

'And the lady?' Paul asked.

'Forgive me, Major, but I'm afraid I don't know.'

'So Mr Harte is well known, is he?' Bruce interjected.

'Oh yes, indeed, sir. He writes on politics now. I understand he was, and is, quite a favourite of Mr Lloyd George's.'

'Thank you, Charles,' Bruce said. 'You've been most helpful.' He leaned forward and fixed his thoughtful gaze on his son. 'Look here, Paul, I don't want you doing anything foolish. Just watch your step. I'm heavily involved with a number of politicians in this country. I would hate to have problems because of your romantic philanderings. That might easily be the chap's wife, you know, and since he's well connected it could be a dangerous game you're contemplating.'

'Don't worry, Dad. I won't embarrass you. However, I am going to find out who she is if it kills me.' Paul sat back in his chair and took out a gold cigarette case. He lit a cigarette, his mind turning rapidly. His father's immense fortune had opened every door for him, all the right doors, and he began to enumerate his friends, wondering who would be the most suitable candidate to arrange an introduction to Frank Harte.

There were a dozen or so people in Dolly Mosten's drawing room when Emma and Frank entered it later that evening. Emma had only taken three small steps into the room when she halted abruptly and grabbed Frank's arm. Startled, he turned to her quickly.

'Frank, we've got to leave!' she hissed.

Surprise flickered on to his face. 'Leave! But we've only just arrived.'

Her fingers tightened on him and her eyes were pleading. '*Please*, Frank! We've *got* to leave. Immediately!'

'Don't be foolish, Emma. It would seem most odd and I don't want to offend Dolly. That's a fate worse than death. Anyway, apart from the fact that she's London's leading actress and not to be slighted, she's been very helpful to me in the past. She would never forgive me. Why the sudden turnabout? You wanted to come earlier.'

'I feel – sick,' Emma improvised. 'Faint.'

'Sorry, but I'm afraid it's too late, old girl,' Frank muttered. Dolly Mosten was descending upon them, a cloud of yellow chiffon and canary diamonds, her flaming red hair a fiery nimbus around her superb but vacuous face. And in her wake was the Australian major they had seen at the Ritz. *So that's it!* Frank thought. His eyes were teasing as he looked at Emma and said pointedly, 'He won't bite.'

Emma did not have a chance to reply. Dolly was greeting them warmly and making the introductions, her famous bubbling voice ringing with laughter, her theatrical vivaciousness enveloping them in an intimacy Emma found curiously distasteful. She averted her head to avoid the major, who loomed up in front of her, all too predatory. Emma felt cornered, and then she found her hand being tightly grasped by a much larger, stronger one. Emma was in a quandary and she stared down at the fine black hairs spreckling that hand, almost afraid to raise her head.

'I'm most delighted to meet you, Mrs Lowther. It is an undeniable pleasure and one I did not anticipate experiencing quite so soon, although, to be frank, I had determined to make your acquaintance. How fortuitous for us both that I stopped by Dolly's tonight,' the resonant voice drawled, the faint Australian twang hardly discernible.

Why, the impertinent and conceited devil, Emma thought, the embarrassment and discomfiture she had experienced at the Ritz flaring within her again. She had the overwhelming desire to slap his face, but her innate good manners prevented her. Instead, she lifted her head and finally looked up into that face staring with such intensity at hers. Her mouth parted. No words came out. She blinked, conscious of the roguish expression in those stunning eyes, the sardonic smile as he waited for her response.

Emma felt the insistent pressure of Frank's hand on her back and then to her horror, and before she could stop herself, she said coldly, 'I understand you are an Australian, Major McGill. I hope the deplorable manners you so patently displayed earlier this evening are not typical of your nationality, but merely spring from your own lack of upbringing. Otherwise your fellow countrymen will find a frosty reception in this country, where women are treated with respect. This is not the Outback, Major.'

Dolly gasped. Frank cried. 'Emma, you are being ungracious!'

But Major McGill was apparently amused. He threw back his head and roared with laughter, and he held on to her hand all that more firmly, so that Emma winced.

Emma turned to Dolly. 'Forgive me, Dolly. I don't mean to be discourteous to you. Please excuse me. I must leave. I feel perfectly dreadful. *Something definitely disagreed with me at dinner.*' She endeavoured to extract her hand, but the major had tightened his grip like a vice.

The major said, '*Touché*, Mrs Lowther. I deserved that, I do believe.' Paul bent forward, lowered his head, and offered his right cheek to Emma. 'Want to slap it and get it over with?'

Flushing, Emma took a step backwards. The major immediately pulled her forward into the group again. He said, 'I think I had better take Mrs Lowther for a glass of champagne. And I hope I will be able to convince her that even colonials are civilized.' He tucked Emma's arm through his in a proprietary way. Emma tried to disentangle her arm, but he instantly clamped his free hand over it and shook his head slowly. 'Come along, Mrs Lowther,' he said commandingly. She saw that his eyes were irreverent and taunting, and she loathed him more than ever.

'Do excuse us,' Paul said to Dolly and Frank, obviously well pleased with himself as he swept her away.

'A little champagne will cool you off,' Paul said, bowing elaborately to a couple he knew but without slowing his pace.

'You can lead a horse to water but you can't make it drink,' Emma hissed, her blood boiling.

'Even the most stubborn and temperamental fillies eventually get thirsty, Mrs Lowther,' he said in a low voice, his eyes roving over her boldly. 'Depending, of course, when they last quenched their thirst. You look positively parched to me.'

His words, appearing innocent enough on the surface, were full of innuendo and the unconcealed desire flickering in his eyes was revealing of his thoughts and his intentions. Emma's cheeks were scarlet as they walked across the floor, and to her considerable irritation she discovered she was acutely aware of Paul McGill's physical proximity – of his fingers biting into hers, of his arm brushing so intimately against her bare shoulder. He was taller and broader than she had realized at the Ritz, and he seemed to overpower her. He exuded a sheathed strength, an earthy and domineering masculinity that disturbed her. The room swam before her eyes and she was overcome by faintness. A peculiar tingling sensation invaded her entire body and her heart quickened, beating so rapidly underneath the green velvet she thought it was about to burst. She was flustered and unnerved. It's only anger, she told herself, and she truly believed this was the real cause of her sudden distress.

Dolly's drawing room appeared to Emma to have tripled in size and she thought the long stretch of chartreuse carpet would never come to an end. 'Please, I would like to sit down,' she said breathlessly. 'Over there. You can go and find a waiter –'

'Oh no, not on your life! You're not going to escape quite so easily,' Paul cried.

'Where are you taking me?'

Paul stopped in his tracks and swung her to face him. He peered down at her, his violet eyes filled with speculation. 'Well now, I'm not quite sure. There are hundreds of interesting possibilities and alternatives –' Observing the chilly expression on her face, he laughed that bantering laugh and remarked softly, 'Don't look so terrified. I'm not going to abscond with you. I merely wanted to get you away from your brother and Dolly.' He scanned the room and inclined his head to the left. 'Over there perhaps, near the potted palm. That seems a likely place for us. A quiet and secluded spot.'

Emma attempted to break free from him. 'Please let me go.'

'Never.'

He manoeuvred her into the corner with great adeptness. Emma realized, and with mounting dismay, that there was now no opportunity for immediate flight, and she also acknowledged that she owed it to Frank to stay at Dolly's for a respectable interval. She sat down on the sofa, relieved to be released from the major's grip, and grudgingly took the glass of champagne which he whisked off the tray as the waiter glided past.

But she had no intention of pandering to this arrogant devil of a man, nor would she spare his feelings, and so she said icily, 'I suppose this rough and masterful technique you adopt is successful with most women, Major.'

Paul nodded and crossed his legs nonchalantly. 'Generally speaking, I would say,' he said lazily. He looked her over with an insolence that brought a deep flush to her chest and neck.

'Let me assure you it won't be with me!' Emma exclaimed, her face haughty. 'I am different from most women.'

'I am aware of that,' he admitted, the roguish glint still lingering in his eyes. 'In fact, I do believe I detected that characteristic in you at once. I think that's what attracted me to you, apart from your staggering looks.' He grinned. 'You are seemingly staggeringly blunt as well, Mrs Lowther. And strong-minded and sassy to boot. Yes, very different, I would say. Fire and ice perhaps?'

'*All ice*, Major,' Emma parried.

'Ice can melt, you know.'

'It can also be very dangerous. People have been known to have fatal accidents with ice,' Emma snapped.

'Danger has always attracted me, Mrs Lowther. I find it exciting. Challenging. It brings out all my masculine instincts.'

Emma threw him a scathing look, turned away contemptuously, and glanced around the room, her eyes seeking Frank. This man elicited an immediate and direct response from her, and one that both infuriated and baffled her. With his monumental egotism, his astonishing appearance, his swaggering self-assurance, and his flippant tongue, he was quite unlike any man she had ever met. And no man had ever had the temerity to be so brash with her or address her in such a suggestive manner. She detested the major and resented his assumption that she was about to fall swooning at his feet. There was also a ruthlessness about him that oddly enough did not trouble her and she was nonplussed, momentarily not understanding that ruthlessness was a trait she was familiar with and could easily handle.

Paul leaned back in the chair, his eyes reflective as he studied Emma's exquisite profile, and he marvelled at his incredible luck in meeting her quite by accident this very night. He thought: She *is* very different. An original. She must belong to me. I won't rest until I have her for myself. All of her. Not only her body but her heart and her mind as well. He was shaken to his very core, for no woman had evoked such a violent reaction in him before. Paul McGill, at thirty-six, was lusty, adventurous, worldly, and charismatic, with a down-to-earth sexuality that cut across class lines to awaken a fervent response in all women. Shopgirls and upper-class ladies equally found him irresistible and, consequently, his conquests had been all too easy, and so numerous he had long ago lost count of his romantic entanglements. His approach, until this precise moment in his life, had been based on a 'take me or leave me' attitude. Women fell over themselves to take him, and with an eagerness that was almost indecent, before he sauntered out of their lives, the rakish grin intact, his heart untouched.

For all that, and despite the debonair and hedonistic stance he struck, Paul McGill was intelligent and possessed shrewdness and psychological insight. Much smarter than he pretended to be, he now recognized, with a sudden flash of clarity, that Emma was a wholly different proposition. *She* was not going to succumb to his brash charm or his potent virility. This was a women to be conquered only through understanding, honesty, and subtle strategy. Ruefully admitting he was antagonizing her unnecessarily with his raillery, he decided to change his tactics and cease his baiting of her at once.

He leaned forward and said, 'Let's stop this silly bantering. We're spoiling it.'

'Spoiling what?' Emma asked snappishly.

'Our first meeting. Our first evening together.'

'And our last!'

Paul brought his face closer to hers. 'I like a woman with spirit, Mrs Lowther. I presume Mr Lowther has the same preference.'

Taken by surprise, Emma gaped at him. What a blundering imbecile he is, she thought with irritation. Her stare was glacial. 'I am a widow, Major McGill. My husband was killed eighteen months ago. In the Somme offensive.'

Oh, my God, Paul thought. He said quickly, 'Please forgive me. I am so terribly sorry. I had no idea. I am a thoughtless fool.' He swore under his breath and sat very still. Emma was silent and unresponsive.

Paul now said, 'It was very tactless of me. One should be more careful in wartime. I am truly sorry. I hope you will also accept my apologies for my appalling behaviour at the Ritz. It was quite unforgivable.'

Emma heard the sincerity in his voice, detected sympathy in his eyes, saw that the mocking expression had been wiped off his face, and she was amazed at the radical change in his manner.

'Will you accept my apology?'

'Yes,' Emma murmured.

Frank joined them and handed a walking stick to Paul. 'Dolly asked me to give you this.' He turned to Emma. 'How are *you* feeling? Better, I hope.'

'Yes, thank you,' Emma said. 'I am sorry, Frank, I didn't mean to embarrass you.'

'Look here, Frank, it was all my fault,' Paul cut in. 'Let's forget the incident, shall we?'

'Of course, Paul.' He grinned at them and strolled off to join a well-known politician holding court at the far end of the room.

Emma was eyeing the walking stick. Paul said, 'I'm wounded. But you probably didn't notice the limp.' There was a sheepish look in his eyes as he said, 'I have to admit I was trying my hardest to conceal it when we walked across the room.'

'You succeeded very well.' Emma found herself smiling at him and she discovered this small admission of pride on his part induced her to revise her opinion of him. She knew all about self-esteem, and she softened a fraction. She leaned back against the sofa feeling more relaxed. With that grin he looked like the eternal little boy. 'I hope your wound is not too painful, or serious,' she remarked softly.

'No, not at all. In fact, I'll be going back to France shortly.' Paul regarded her thoughtfully, his face serious. He was aware he had gained ground with her, but he hesitated before saying, 'I'm on leave for a few more weeks. Would it be possible for us to meet again? I know you think I'm some sort of scoundrel, but I'm not, really. I have no excuse for my ghastly display at the Ritz, other than to confess I was bowled over by your beauty. Still, I should not have caused you discomfort. Can we lunch tomorrow so that I can make amends?' His eyes twinkled. 'I promise I'll behave – like an officer and a gentleman and not a scallywag from the Outback.'

'I have a luncheon engagement,' Emma said.

'Is it terribly important? Couldn't you break it?'

'I don't think so. It's with Frank and I don't see him very often. He would be disappointed.'

'Yes, I understand.' Paul's face lit up. 'I don't want to seem forward, but could I join you? May I invite you both to be my guests?' He smiled engagingly. 'After all, you would be chaperoned with your brother present.'

Emma smiled. He was quite transparent. 'I would have to ask Frank. I'm not sure how he would feel.'

To Paul's annoyance Dolly sailed up to them and he stood up, offering her his chair. She declined and said, 'I see you two have recovered from your little contretemps.' Her eyes swept over Emma and settled on Paul. 'How is the wounded warrior? I do hope you're enjoying yourself, darling. We must keep our valiant soldiers happy, mustn't we?' She patted his arm playfully. 'I can see you're in good hands. I presume I shall see you at your father's luncheon party tomorrow.'

'No, I'm afraid not. I have a long-standing appointment. With destiny.'

'Destiny?' Dolly's brow puckered in puzzlement. 'I don't think I know her.'

Paul kept his face absolutely straight. 'I don't believe you do, Dolly.'

Dolly shrugged. 'One can't be acquainted with everyone in London, I suppose. Do excuse me. I must circulate, my darlings.'

Paul leaned closer to Emma, his face sober. 'I am, aren't I?'

'You are what?'

'Lunching with destiny.'

She looked up at him and smiled, that unique smile that illuminated her face with incandescent radiance. 'I thought you were lunching with Frank and me,' she said.

Frank said, 'Why are you doing this, Emma?'

'Doing what, dear?'

'You know exactly what I mean. Leaving London so unexpectedly.'

'I only intended to stay in town for a few days. I've been here two weeks. I have to go back to Yorkshire.'

'I never thought I would see my sister running away.'

'I'm not running away.'

'Yes, you are. It's Paul McGill, isn't it?'

Emma looked at him and bit her lip. She sighed. 'Yes, it is.'

'I guessed as much. But I still don't understand why you are rushing off.'

'Because he's getting to be a nuisance and, anyway, I don't particularly like him.'

'Emma! How can you say that! If you don't like him, why have you spent so much time with him? Every night, as far as I can gather. The theatre, dinners, parties, and luncheons, too. I've hardly seen you alone, and I must say you have certainly given the impression you are mesmerized by him.'

'That's not true, Frank Harte!'

Frank shook his head and looked out of the taxi window. He brought his eyes back to Emma. After a moment's reflection he said, 'He's fallen for you like a ton of bricks.'

'Oh, phooey!'

'Yes, he has. I can tell. Everyone who sees the two of you together can tell. He positively devours you with his eyes. And I know *you* like *him*, Emma.'

'Frank, will you please leave me alone.'

'Give me a good reason why you don't want to see him any more.'

'Because he's too charming, too handsome, too fascinating. And too much – for me to handle. Besides –' She broke off, her voice faltering.

'Besides what?'

'I'm afraid I'll get more involved if I stay.'

'I knew it! But surely you mean fall in love with him, don't you?'

'Yes.' Her voice was a whisper.

Frank took her hand. 'Does he know you're leaving?'

'No. There's a note for him at the Ritz. He'll get it tonight when he comes to collect me.'

'That wasn't a very nice thing to do to the poor chap.'

'It was the *only* thing to do. Now, darling, please shut up about Paul McGill. And tell the taxi driver to hurry. I'll miss my train.'

FORTY-FIVE

Calculating of brain though she was, Emma could be impulsive of heart and especially when her deepest emotions were involved, and she had acted on impulse the day she had returned with such abruptness to Yorkshire. Recognizing that she was falling under the spell of the magnetic Paul McGill, she had fled, propelled by panic and fear.

Long ago, Emma had come to the conclusion that she was unlucky where men were concerned. They either hurt her or she hurt them. Her relationships had never been balanced. She doubted that she could ever inflict pain on the self-assured Paul McGill, but he was a terrible threat to *her*. Contentment with her life, such as it was at this moment, was at stake. She could not afford to risk emotional upheaval. Only in business was she prepared to gamble.

But now, after two days, she was beginning to feel perplexed by his total silence. Aren't you also a little disappointed? a small voice nudged at the back of her mind, and she smiled wryly, her eyes straying to the telephone. Perhaps you are, but you're also relieved, she said inwardly, and looked down at the latest report from the Emeremm Company. Almost immediately her attention wandered again, her thoughts returning to Paul.

He had danced attendance on her every day for two weeks. He had been charming, gallant, and amusing, and a gentleman, more or less. He *had* taken her in his arms and his kisses had been sensual and his passions had been fully inflamed. She knew that he was aware that he had aroused the same desire in her, but ultimately he held himself in check. He had made no untoward proposals or attempted to seduce her, and his constraint had baffled her, despite her profound relief at this display of chivalry.

She shivered, recalling his amorous embraces, and instantly crushed down the memory of him. He had apparently forgotten *her* immediately. Or perhaps he was stinging from the blow to his pride. For a proud devil he was and his self-esteem had more than likely been seriously damaged. She was positive no other woman had ever run out on him. So much for Major McGill, she thought. He's dangerous and disturbing. Nevertheless, disappointment flared again and she shook her head, musing on her own inconsistencies, and then brought her eyes back to the papers. Her business needed her undivided attention.

Gladys knocked and came in quietly, looking pink and flustered. 'You have a visitor, Mrs Harte,' she said, hovering in front of the desk.

'I don't have any appointments this morning.' Emma frowned. 'What's the matter, Gladys? You look very fluttery –' Emma paused and her heart missed a beat. She guessed what Gladys would say. Only one person in this world could bring that special look to a woman's eyes.

'It's a Major McGill, Mrs Harte. He said you weren't expecting him but that you would see him anyway.'

Emma nodded, her face inscrutable. 'Yes, of course I will see him, Gladys.'

He strode in, closed the door firmly behind him, and leaned against it. He was wearing a trench coat over his uniform and his cap was pushed rakishly to one side. He was carrying a picnic basket in one hand but he was no longer using the stick.

Paul gave Emma a hard look. 'Coward,' he said.

'What are you doing in Yorkshire?' Emma managed unsteadily. Her heart was pounding and her legs had turned to water.

'I've come to have lunch with you.' He held up his hand and wagged a finger at her. 'I know, don't say it. You always eat lunch in the office.' He glanced down at the basket. 'I anticipated that and brought a picnic. So you have no excuse. I can't answer for the Metropole's food, but the champagne is Dom Pérignon.'

'That's very enterprising of you,' she said quietly, recovering some of her composure.

'Yes, isn't it just!' He put the basket on the chair, threw his cap after it, and limped across the floor. He put both of his hands on the desk and leaned forward, his gaze fixed unwaveringly on her pale face. 'You ran away. You were frightened,' he said.

Unable to deny it, she did not respond.

'Who were you afraid of? Me? Or yourself?' he demanded, his voice unexpectedly harsh.

'I don't know.' She looked down at the desk. 'Of you, I suppose.'

'You silly little fool! Don't you know I'm in love with you!'

He came around the desk and pulled her into his arms, his grip powerful and crushing, his mouth hard and unrelenting on hers. Emma could not resist. Her arms went around him and she returned his kisses, the excitement he aroused in her manifest again, racing through her like fire. Her head swam and she was assailed by a weakness that trickled into her thighs. He pulled away suddenly, as he had done so often in the past, and gazed down at her. He tilted her face to his. His eyes, so darkly violet they looked as black as the brows curving above them, were filled with seriousness.

Paul shook his head. 'Did you think a few hundred miles would discourage me?' He laughed. 'I'm an Australian. Distance means nothing to me. And you haven't learned much else about me, Emma, have you? Or you would know I'm very tenacious.' He put his arm around her, hugging her to him, and laughed again. 'What am I going to do with you, my Emma? My stubborn, wilful, but adorable Emma. Tame you? But I wonder, would a bridle sit well on you, my sweet?'

Emma clung to his trench coat. She was speechless and her mind was chaotic. What had he said? That he was in love with her. Her heart was tight and her legs shook and she dare not open her mouth. If she did she knew she would tell him that she loved him, too.

Paul seemed unconcerned by her silence. He said, 'First of all, we are going to have lunch. Then you are going to show me around your store. After that I want to see Layton's mill.' He grinned that engaging lopsided grin, and said, 'Later I want to meet your children and I hope you will invite me to stay to dinner. You wouldn't abandon a lonely soldier to an evening by himself in this godforsaken city, would you?'

Emma shook her head.

'We're in agreement, then?'

'Yes, Paul,' she whispered, and her voice was surprisingly meek.

Paul McGill stayed in Yorkshire for three days and during that time Emma came to know a very different side of him. In London she had felt there was a deep core of sincerity in him, and although he had often given the impression he lacked the inner conviction to remain serious for very long, she had suspected otherwise. She was not wrong. That thoughtful side was now revealed to her. He was also a gentle man, a characteristic that was displayed most obviously with her children. He listened attentively to Edwina, responding with kindness to her questions about Australia, and he treated Kit like an equal. Kit hung on his every word, and was thrilled when Paul took him sledging down the drive and played with his trains in the nursery.

It seemed to Emma that Paul brought out the very best in her children, and even Edwina, always so distant, emerged from her shell under his vivacious influence. Emma watched Paul closely, revelling in his genuine interest in her family, but she frequently noticed a curiously yearning look flickering in those violet eyes when he believed he was unobserved. She speculated on the reason for it and wondered about this extraordinary man who was so contradictory and compelling.

The day he departed he said, 'I don't have very much time left, Emma. I'll be going back to France shortly. Will you come and visit me in London? Very soon?'

Emma did not think twice. 'Yes,' she said, smiling up at him.

He touched her cheek lightly. 'When?'

'I have a meeting tomorrow morning. But I could come the day after. On Friday.'

'Couldn't you make it tomorrow afternoon? Time is running out.'

'All right, then.'

He tilted her face to his. 'Are you sure about this, Emma?'

'Yes, I am.' As she spoke she knew that she had made a commitment to him.

It was a bitterly cold February evening and drizzling when Emma stepped off the train at King's Cross. She saw him before he saw her. He was standing at the ticket barrier, the cap pushed back at the same jaunty angle, the collar of his trench coat turned up. Her heart leapt and she began to run. It was undignified but she could not help herself. She did not stop until she was in his arms, breathless and laughing, her face resplendent with happiness.

He held her close, told her she looked beautiful, found the porter with her luggage, and bustled her into his father's car, taking command in his usual way. As they drove through the evening traffic Emma became aware of a difference in Paul, and although he held her hand and chatted to her casually, his voice light, she sensed a disquiet under the surface. It was a controlled tension but, nonetheless, quite evident to her.

The Daimler came to a standstill before they reached the Ritz Hotel, where Emma was staying. Paul said, 'I'm going to get out here and walk the rest of the way.'

She stared at him. 'But why?'

He grinned. 'I know how circumspect you are. I would hate to compromise you the moment you arrive. Check in alone and I'll join you for a drink in an hour. Anyway, you need a little privacy. Time to change and bathe.'

'Very well. In an hour, then.'

He nodded, jumped out, and slammed the door. Emma sat back against the seat, touched by his thoughtfulness. And then she suffered such a sharp sense of loss, and acute loneliness, she was jolted. How silly she was being. She would see him very shortly.

The sitting room of the suite overlooked Green Park. A fire blazed in the grate, the lamps had been turned on, and there were masses of flowers everywhere, all of them from Paul, Emma discovered on reading the amusing messages on the white cards, reposing in each arrangement. She smiled with delight but did not pause long to admire. She hurriedly unpacked, hung up her clothes, and took a bath in the huge marble tub.

The bath dispelled the chill in her bones and revitalized her, and Emma slipped into a white silk robe and sat down at the dressing table, humming under her breath, feeling happier than she had in years. She brushed out her long hair until it gleamed in the lamplight and slowly began to coil it on top of her head. She was pushing the last hairpin into the coil when she tensed and remained perfectly still, experiencing the strange sensation that she was not alone. She swung her head slowly and jumped back in the chair. Paul was leaning casually against the door of the bedroom, his legs crossed, a glass in his hand, observing her with great concentration.

'I'm sorry. I didn't mean to frighten you. I should have knocked,' he said. 'You make a very pretty picture, my sweet.'

'How did you get in?' Emma gasped.

'Why, through the door of course.' He strolled over to the dressing table and placed a small jewel case in front of her. 'These are for you,' he said. 'Put them on.'

Emma threw him a quick, puzzled glance and opened the case. The emerald earrings shimmered like pools of green fire against the black velvet and she drew in her breath. 'Oh, Paul! They're beautiful.' She frowned. 'But I can't possibly accept them. They are far too valuable.'

'Put them on,' he ordered.

Emma's hands trembled as she screwed the emeralds into her ears. She gazed at Paul through the mirror. 'They are incredible. How did you know emeralds are my favourite stone?'

He smiled. 'I didn't. But with eyes your colour you should only wear emeralds. See how they echo the light in your eyes.' He put down his drink and cupped his hands underneath her chin and, tilting her head back, he bent forward and kissed her forehead. 'If you don't accept them I'll be terribly offended. I might never speak to you again.'

'In that case I suppose I must. But it was very extravagant of you.' She smiled at him tenderly. 'Thank you, Paul.'

He moved away from her. 'Come into the other room and have a drink,' he said, pausing at the door.

'I'll just put my dress on.'

'No, don't bother. I want to talk to you. You're decent enough.'

Emma pulled the white silk robe around her and followed him, feeling self-conscious, but concerned by his tone and unable to protest. He sounded grave and her heart sank. Was he leaving sooner than expected for France? Was that the reason for his tension? When she walked into the sitting room she saw immediately how he had managed to enter the suite so silently. The door at the far end was open and beyond she could see another identical suite. She faltered, unprepared for such an intimate arrangement and unnerved by the implication.

'So that's how you got in,' she remarked, and there was a hint of anger in her voice.

He ignored the comment. 'I'm drinking scotch, but I know you prefer wine. I'll get you a glass of champagne.'

Her eyes followed him as he strode out, and her resentment spilled over into quiet rage. Paul had assumed too much. Assumed she would be an eager and willing partner in this – this – little game of his. She bit her lip. She was being inconsistent again. Had she not known when she stepped on to the train earlier in the day that there would be no going back. This scene now being enacted should not shock her. It was exactly what he had intended from the beginning, and anticipated once she had agreed to come back to London. And she had probably led him to believe it would be so.

Paul returned with the champagne, interrupting her racing thoughts. He handed her the glass and sat down opposite her, and as if he had read those thoughts, he said, 'I don't blame you for being angry, Emma. I know you're also upset and uncomfortable as well, aren't you?'

She did not answer him, but stared down at the glass and took a fast sip to hide her nervousness.

'I'm a damn fool. It was presumptuous of me and now I apologize for that presumption. I feel quite certain you understood what my intentions were when you saw that open door and the other suite. Seduction, of course. I had planned it all very carefully for weeks.' His mouth lifted in a small self-deprecatory smile. 'I'm not too subtle, am I? However, I realized in the car that I had manoeuvred you into a situation which you would have great difficulty extracting yourself from. So, I am going to do that for you.' Paul went on, 'I am going to finish this drink and then I am going to walk through that door. You will lock it. When you are dressed I will come and fetch you. We will go out to dinner. No obligations. Now, or later. All right?'

Emma stared at him. 'Yes, of course. But why have you changed your mind?'

He laughed ironically. 'Yes, it is out of character, isn't it? The reformed rake doing the honourable thing.' He shrugged. 'I'm amazed at myself.'

'Why do you want to do the honourable thing?'

'Because I love you, and too much to manipulate a situation to suit my own ends, my own advantage, without giving a thought to you and your feelings.'

'I'm not sure I quite understand.'

'You have to love *me* and want *me* as much as I love and want you, Emma. Otherwise there is no point to all this.' He gulped down the drink and stood up. 'Now run along and dress. I'll be waiting for you and we'll go out to dinner.'

He stopped at the door. 'Lock this after me,' he said without glancing back. Emma did as he said and turned the key, her face as grave as his. She sat down on the sofa. She did not know what to do. He loved her. She loved him. She had come to London knowing there was an unspoken commitment between them, and yet now she was acting resentful and outraged. Yes, and being a hypocrite, she reproached herself. Her behaviour did not make sense. She closed her eyes and pictured him behind that closed door, waiting to take her to dinner. But also waiting for her decision, one which would determine the outcome of their relationship. Had he passed the decision over to her to avoid responsibility? No, that was unfair. There was no duplicity in him. Why am I frightened of taking this step? she asked herself. And the answer struck her with such force her head spun. She was not afraid of Paul or of her own emotions. She was afraid of the final act of love, of consummation, because of her distasteful sexual experiences with Joe. And she was afraid of hurting Paul by recoiling from him, afraid of failing him as a woman. Perhaps if she explained . . .

Emma flew across the room, unlocked the door, and stood on the threshold. Paul was hunched over the fireplace, his head bent. He appeared to be in the grips of a terrible anguish.

'Paul –'

His dark head swung around and he stared at her. She walked to him slowly. 'I – I – would like to talk to you.'

He nodded, looking down at her soberly. 'I know I put the burden of the decision on you. But only because I wanted to be absolutely sure of you. I also wanted you to be sure of yourself.'

Emma put out her hand and touched his lapel, her mouth quivering, her eyes darkly green. She had lost all power of speech and she had certainly lost the courage to discuss her feelings.

Paul took her hand in his and kissed the fingertips. 'Such a small, dear hand,' he said.

'Oh, Paul!'

Her face, blazing with her love, told him everything he wanted to know. He pulled her to him and kissed her deeply and then he swept her up in his arms and carried her into the bedroom. He kicked the door shut with his foot and walked over to the bed. He laid her down on it and sat on the edge. 'Say it, darling,' he commanded hoarsely. 'Say it!' His eyes burned into hers.

'I love you, Paul.'

'And?'

'I want you.'

'Oh, Emma, Emma, you always have, my darling. Don't you understand? This was fated to happen from the first moment we set eyes on each other.' He traced a line down her cheek. 'I *knew*. But you had to recognize it, and that is why I would not force the issue tonight. I wanted and needed you to come to me of your own free will.'

He stood up and unbuckled his Sam Browne belt, throwing it to one side. His jacket followed and his tie and his shirt. As he undressed her eyes did not leave his face, and the fear was dissipating, and she thought: I have never seen a man completely naked before. Why, he has a beautiful body. It was tanned and firm. His shoulders were broad, his waist narrow, his legs long, his stomach flat.

'Take your robe off, my love,' he said softly, as he came towards her.

He covered her body with his own and cradled her in his arms, smiling down into her expectant face. 'It's such a pity to ruin this exotic hairdo,' he murmured as he began to pull the pins from her hair. The russet tresses spilled around her shoulders, porcelain fragile and pink in the warm glow of the lamp, and he gasped at her loveliness now so perfectly revealed to him. He ran his hand through the heavy lengths and held her by the nape of her neck, bringing her face up to his own. His lips met hers, savouring their warmth and their sweetness, and they were both engulfed by their longing and the emotions which had been denied release for weeks. He moved his mouth into the hollow of her neck, kissing her shoulders, her breasts, and the deep valley between, and his strong hands smoothed over her firm skin and he caressed every part of her until he knew her fervour matched his own.

Emma was suffused with an unfamiliar warmth, a burning heat that flooded her being. Her whole body arched up, cleaved to him. She ached to be joined to him, to become one with him, and she marvelled at her pleasure in his body and in her own, was astonished at the ease with which her reluctance had fallen away as if it had never existed. And she willingly gave herself to him, receiving his kisses and responding wildly to his demands.

With a stab of surprise he was aware of her lack of sexual sophistication and this touched him, thrilled him further. It was as though he was the first man to possess her. But he also recognized the latent sensuality in her and he drew out that hidden voluptuousness, brought her along the fine edge of desire until she quivered under his touch and called his name, and pledged her love for him.

Paul finally took her to him with flaring passion, his ardour gentled but in no way muted by his tenderness. Silken arms and legs entwined him, fluid and weightless, yet they pulled him down ... down ... down. He was plunging head-long into a warm blue sea filled with slanting sunlight, carrying her with him. Down faster, into darker, greener depths, green the colour of her eyes. Down into a bottomless ocean. Waves crashed around him. His heart thundered in unison. He thought he was losing consciousness as he spiralled into infinity with her. He felt the warm enveloping softness of her flesh, the rise of her thighs and breasts thrusting against him, the velvet strands of her hair entwined in his fingers. His body locked to hers, spasmed, was submerged in hers. Oh, God! Oh, God! This was the only way it should ever be! A man and a woman joined together, the perfect communion of twin bodies, twin souls. His endless quest was over. That ultimate joy which had so long eluded him was surging through him and he was reborn in her. *This* was the secret of life, the ecstasy of life, so fleeting in that final moment of truth, but overpowering in its brief intensity. He was floating up, taking her with him to the surface. Up into that radiant light. She *was* that light. Pure golden light.

He opened his eyes and looked down at her and he saw the flush of unprece-dented pleasure on her face, the pulse beating in her neck, the eyes so wide and green and spilling her adoration. And there was a vulnerability in that face, and perfect innocence, and his eyes unexpectedly filled with tears. He kissed her with tenderness and pulled her to him, vowing never to let her go.

Emma lay with her head on his shoulder, dazed, languorous with euphoria, basking in her love. She was filled with peace and the first real fulfilment she had ever experienced, and there was wonderment in her eyes as she contemplated the mysterious transformation he had wrought in her, the joy he had given her, and her heart crested high with love for him. Her hand rested on his chest, fingers buried deep in the black hair covering it and she thought: He is a man just like any other man, but with him *I* am different.

Paul passed his hand over the crown of her head and kissed her hair. There had been so many other women before her, but just as he had believed he was the first man to take her, now he felt she was the only one who had ever truly possessed him. She was in his blood and he would never be free again. The light in his eyes changed, darkened, became anguished as he stared into space.

'Emma, darling.'

'Yes, Paul?'

'I'm married.'

The hand on his chest did not move and she remained utterly motionless in his arms, but she felt as if she had been struck in the face and her stomach lurched. Finally she said in a small voice, 'You certainly picked an inappropriate time to make your startling announcement.'

He tightened his embrace, resting his head against hers. 'It's not inappropriate. I purposely picked this time.'

'Why?'

'Because I wanted you in my arms when I told you. Intimately, like this. So that I could hold you closer and make you understand how unimportant my marriage is. So that I could love you again and tell you that *you* are the reality.' Emma did not reply and he went on anxiously. 'I wasn't trying to hide the facts, Emma. It's not a secret and it might easily have been mentioned in your presence by any one of my friends. I prayed it wouldn't, of course, because I wanted you to hear it from me. I simply delayed telling you because I was afraid of losing you. I knew you would have disappeared if I'd told you sooner. That you would never have permitted our relationship to go this –'

'You clever devious bastard!'

She struggled to get off the bed. He pulled her back and pinned her under him with roughness, gazing into her cold white face. Emma thought she was being swamped by the startling blueness of those eyes swimming above hers.

'It's not like that, Emma!' Paul cried furiously, his face blazing. 'Please believe me. I know what you're thinking – that I wanted to accomplish my own ends before telling you. But all I wanted to do was make you love me, so that you would be bound to me irrevocably. Once loving me, I knew you would not let the circumstances get in the way. Stand between us. I love you, Emma. You're the only thing of value in my life.'

'And your wife!' she whispered.

'We have not lived together for six years. And we ceased being man and wife a year before that.'

'How long have you been married?' Her voice was almost inaudible.

'Nine years. Emma, it is a meaningless marriage. It's not even a marriage. But right now I am tied to her because of – Tied to her legally. After the war is over I'll sort it all out. I want to spend the rest of my life with you, if you'll have me. You are my life now. Please, darling, you must believe me.' His voice shook.

Emma stared at him, her turbulent thoughts clouding her judgement momentarily, and then her head cleared. She could feel the tension rippling through him. His haunted face was naked in its agony and his sincerity leapt from his eyes, stunning her. 'I believe you,' she said slowly, in a stronger tone, and ran one finger across his lips. 'Yes, Paul, oddly enough I do believe you.'

FORTY-SIX

The weeks that followed were enchanted, endless hours filled with rapture so dreamlike in quality time might have been suspended. Days merged into nights, nights drifted into dawns, and every single moment was spun out, intertwined with desire and joy that bound Emma and Paul inexorably together.

They existed only for each other, wanted only each other, rejoiced in each other. They remained in the two adjoining suites at the Ritz Hotel, rarely venturing out except for walks in Green Park and an occasional quiet dinner in a secluded restaurant off the beaten track of fashionable society. They were so wildly, so passionately in love they could barely contain their feelings for each other, were reluctant to share even a minute with friends and jealously guarded their privacy. Plans were cancelled, invitations declined, Bruce McGill and Frank held at bay, and the world was well lost for them both.

They were so overwhelmed by their sexual attraction and their growing love they were unnerved, and they would stare at each other in wonderment that this miracle had occurred. A mere glance was as devouring as a kiss, a simple gesture as meaningful as an embrace, and every word they uttered to each other was cloaked with its own significance.

Emma was filled with incredulity and overpowered by the intensity of her compelling emotions. But for once she did not pause to analyse. She was ecstatic with happiness. Fulfilment and soaring joy now dislodged the grief and hurt and humiliation of years. Love ripped the mask of inscrutability from her face; love exposed her heart in all its vulnerability; she was brought to life by the touch of love. Paul's adoration, and his deep understanding of her, made dust out of the suspicion and self-protectiveness which were inherent in her nature and which hitherto had ruled her life. She was her true self with him in a way she had never been with another soul. All the guards were finally lowered for the only man she had ever really loved and to whom she had given herself with no reservation.

Paul was a revelation to her. His rakish pose and sardonic manner had long been dropped, but now she was also permitted to know him as no other woman had been allowed before. The reflective and introspective side of him was disclosed and she discovered there was a fine mind behind that handsome and polished façade. She was impressed by his brain and his vast knowledge of the world. She was captivated by his sophistication, and admiring of his savoir-faire that unmistakably sprang from security engendered by old money, the privilege that accompanied great wealth, and an education at Wellington and Oxford. And she was constantly entertained by his swift wit. In short, she was spellbound.

Paul, in turn, was equally besotted, held in the grips of the only genuine love he had experienced in his years of romantic dallying. He believed her to be the most beautiful woman he had ever seen in his wanderings around the world; he also thought she was the most intelligent he had known, and her vividness of mind startled him. But the one thing he marvelled at continually was her incredible presence, that quality of personality that set her apart and made her so unique. It was as though an incandescent glow emanated from her innermost core. He could only compare it to that vitality and indefinable charisma that made an alluring actress a great star. For them both it had been a *coup de foudre* – as though struck by lightning, they had fallen blindingly in love instantaneously.

The days passed in a dreamy haze of passion flaring and assuaged and flaring again with a stronger brighter flame, of animated talk that continued far into the nights, of thoughts and emotions unveiled and shared. They discovered in each other all they had yearned for in a lover and a companion and their communication was a fusion of minds and souls as well as bodies.

One afternoon when they were lying in each other's arms, exhausted by their passion, Paul said, 'You won't mind if I go out for a little while, will you, darling? I have a few things I must attend to.'

'Not if you promise to hurry back,' Emma replied, brushing her lips against his chest.

'Nothing could keep me away from you for longer than an hour. I'll be back by four,' he said, kissing the strands of her hair. He released his hold of her and disappeared into the bathroom. He emerged a few minutes later freshly shaven, his black hair slicked back, a towel wrapped around his waist. From her position on the bed Emma observed him stealthily like a cat, her intent green gaze riveted on him, and she discovered she derived enormous pleasure from watching him occupied in so simple a task as dressing. He picked up his shirt from the chair and the muscles on his wide back rippled and she had to suppress the impulse to run to him and enfold him in her arms. She thought: He has become my whole world.

He buckled the Sam Browne belt on over his army jacket and strode over to the bed. He bent down and kissed her and her arms went around his neck. He removed her arms gently after a moment. 'I have to go, sweetheart.'

'And I wonder just *where* you are going,' Emma said, fluttering her eyelashes coyly. 'Shaved and groomed and scented to high heaven. Why, Major McGill, if you have a rendezvous with another woman I'll scratch your eyes out. I swear I will! And hers, too!'

He grinned and touched the tip of her nose playfully. 'O tiger's heart wrapp'd in a woman's hide!'

'Waxing poetic, Major?' she teased.

'Stolen from Shakespeare, I must confess. *Henry VI.*' Paul kissed her fingertips, his hand tightening, his eyes penetrating. 'And if *you* ever so much as *look* at another man I will kill you.' He stood up. 'Be a good girl. I won't be long.'

After he had left, Emma busied herself with telephone calls to her secretary at the store and to her housekeeper, anxious to reassure herself that all was well in Yorkshire during her absence. Relieved that everything was still under control since yesterday's calls, she then spoke to Frank at the *Chronicle*.

'Good Lord! No wonder it's snowing!' Frank exclaimed on hearing her voice. 'So he's let you out of his clutches long enough for you to ring me.' He laughed. 'I'm only joking. I'm happy for you, Emma.'

'Oh, Frank, I'm happy, too. So very happy I can't believe it. And you're wrong for once. I'm the one who's let Paul out of *my* clutches for an hour.'

'Mmmmm! I see! Well, I must say, he's apparently very good for you. I've never heard you sound better. But why didn't you tell me who he actually is?'

'What do you mean?'

'That he is the only son, the only child, of *the* Bruce McGill. A millionaire and one of the most powerful men in Australia. I suppose you know Paul stands to inherit a fortune. A vast sheep ranch. Mineral rights and mining. Coal fields, and God know what else.'

'He's mentioned the family's various business interests, of course. But how do *you* know so much all of a sudden?'

'I was with Dolly Mosten the other day and she was telling me a few things about Paul —'

'What else did she tell you?' Emma asked suspiciously, her heart sinking.

'Nothing. That was all. She simply remarked that the McGill family was extremely rich and powerful. What's wrong? You sound edgy.'

'No, I don't.' She laughed. 'How are you, Frank? Are you all right, dear?' she inquired, quickly changing the subject.

'Yes, everything is fine. But I'm afraid you've caught me at a bad time, Emma. I can't really talk right now. I have to go into an editorial conference. Can you call me tomorrow so we can chat longer, love?'

'Yes, of course.'

'Take care now. Give my best to Paul. Bye.'

'Goodbye, Frank.'

Emma put the telephone down and stared at it, her face brooding, her thoughts weaving a tortuous web in her head as she contemplated the McGill family, or, more precisely, the mysterious Mrs Paul McGill. The wife he had never referred to again and about whom she had not dared to question him; had not wanted to know about. But now Emma was unexpectedly eaten up with curiosity. What did she look like? Was she beautiful? How old was she? Why had the marriage gone awry? Did they have children? Was that the reason Paul had never divorced, in spite of his long separation? Emma closed her eyes, crushing the questions flaring in her mind. She would not open Pandora's box. He would tell her everything eventually, she was certain of that, and she did not want anything to mar the time they had left together. This very precious time.

She looked at the clock on the mantelshelf and to her surprise she realized Paul had been absent for over two hours. It was already five-thirty. For no logical reason she was seized by panic. This feeling was irrational, but none the less, her nervousness increased, and she had the sudden premonition that Paul would be leaving her imminently. He had carefully refrained from mentioning the date of his departure, but she was aware that two weeks had flown by. In Yorkshire he had told her time was running out. Has it now done so? she asked herself, dismay trickling through her.

To still her disquieting thoughts, Emma hurried into the bathroom and preoccupied herself with her toilet. She took a hot bath, towelled herself dry, sprayed her body with perfume, and went into the bedroom. She put on a long powder-blue panne velvet housecoat she had designed herself and which Paul admired on her. It was in the French Empire style with a high waist, tight bodice, long sleeves, and frogging from the low square neckline to the hem, and it gave her the air of an ingénue. She brushed her long hair and left it hanging loose the way he preferred it, and after she had added a little lip rouge and the emerald earrings she drifted through into the sitting room to wait. By seven o'clock agitation swamped her, and the panic began to disintegrate into real fear. Where was he? Had he had an accident? She clenched her hands in her lap, every muscle tense. And then instinctively she knew. Paul was at the War Office receiving his orders. He was leaving. She was positive this was so. The war! Forgotten for days whilst they had lived blindly in their ecstasy. He might be killed . . . he might never come back . . . She pressed her hands to her aching eyes.

'Here I am, my sweet,' he said, coming through the door that linked his suite to hers.

Emma dropped her hands, jumped up, and ran to him, her face taut. 'I thought something had happened to you!' she gasped, grabbing the lapels of his trench coat.

'Nothing is going to happen to me,' he reassured her. 'I have a guardian angel. And anyway, my time's not up yet. There are all those years earmarked for me. Years to be spent with you. You haven't forgotten that you are my destiny, have you? It hasn't been fulfilled yet, my love.'

Her heart began to beat more normally. She looked up at him, smiled, and pulled away. 'Your coat is wet through,' she said. 'You'd better take your clothes off before you catch your death.'

443

His eyes crinkled at the corners with laughter. 'That's the best proposition I've had in the last four hours, madam.' He winked suggestively.

'Oh, you know what I mean, you wretch!'

'I hope I do,' he said. 'Give me ten minutes. I've already ordered dinner for nine o'clock, and there's a bottle of champagne cooling in my suite. Excuse me, angel, I'll be right back,' he called over his shoulder.

When Paul returned he had changed into civilian clothes. He wore a white silk shirt, a pair of black worsted trousers, and a silk smoking jacket striped in burgundy and black. He looked casually elegant as he carried the champagne bucket to the console. 'I think it's cold enough,' he said, opening the bottle of Dom Pérignon.

Once more Emma watched him alertly. Just as his eyes normally followed her every movement, now hers were concentrated on him, and she saw him afresh. When he had been gone for a period of time, however brief, she was always startled by the impact his looks had on her when he reappeared. It was no one thing in particular but the sum total of the man. And she was inevitably struck by his commanding manner, the panache with which he did everything.

He caught her staring at him and pursed his lips, grinning with fond amusement. He strode over and handed her the glass of champagne. 'I 'ain't bin wiv anover leidy, I swear I 'ain't,' he said, adopting a Cockney accent.

'I 'opes yer 'ain't,' she said, responding in kind. But her eyes were serious, searching his face, and she was afraid to ask where he had been. 'You were gone so long, darling,' she murmured softly.

'I had to see my father about a few things. Business matters to discuss,' Paul said, clinking her glass. 'Here's to you, my lovely Emma.'

'To us.'

Paul leaned back in the chair. 'I'm afraid I've neglected the old man these last few weeks –'

'It's all my fault!'

'No, it's not. It's nobody's fault,' he countered swiftly, and flashed her his boyish grin. 'He has an understanding heart – when it comes to matters of the heart.'

'Nevertheless, I've deprived him of your company at a crucial time, and kept you away from all of your other friends.'

'Ah, but you must think only of the happiness you have given *me* and not be concerned with them. I'm not. It was my choice. I do believe I made the rules, didn't I? Anyway, we could have seen people if I had considered it important. I didn't. There wasn't a soul in the world I wanted to be with but you. Others would have profaned our private world. This special world we have created for ourselves, here in our little cocoon. I didn't want anything to intrude, to shatter the illusion.'

'You make it sound as if what we have exists only here!'

He stared at her and an eyebrow went up in a quirk. 'No, I don't! Good God, Emma, surely you know this is real wherever we are, and wherever we might be in the future. This is no illusion. This is reality. I've told you that before.'

Her heart lifted. 'I'm glad it's not an illusory world we have been living in. I would hate to wake up and discover it has all been a dream –'

Paul saw the smile slip, the cloud cross her face. Acutely in tune with her moods, he leaned forward and touched her knee and asked, 'What is it, Em? Is something troubling you, darling?'

'You were at the War Office. And then you went to see your father, to say goodbye, didn't you? You're going, aren't you, Paul? And very soon.'

'Yes,' he admitted quietly.

'When?'

'Tomorrow.'

'Oh, my God!'

He crossed to the sofa and took the glass of champagne from her shaking hand and placed it on the table. He drew her close to him, looking into her anxious face. 'I read something at Oxford years ago, about lovers who were about to be separated. It has always stayed in my mind. It went something like this: "This parting cannot be for long; for those who love as we do cannot be parted. We shall always be united in thought, and thought is a great magnet. I have often spoken to thee of reason, now I speak to thee of faith."' He saw that her eyes, so steadfastly fixed on his, were filled with tears. He tenderly brushed them away from her long lashes with his fingertips. 'Don't, my darling. Please don't.'

'I'm sorry, Paul. It was those words. They moved me so. Who said them?' she asked tremulously.

'Abélard to Héloïse. They were uttered centuries ago, but they are as true now as they ever were then. Don't forget them, my Emma, and please have faith. And believe that we will always be united in thought and therefore as one. And know, too, that I will carry you in my heart for the rest of my life.'

'Oh, Paul! I love you so much! I cannot bear to be without you!'

His clenched fist came up under her chin, moving against it lightly. 'Come along, sweetheart. You must be brave. And we're not going to talk about my leaving any more. We are going to think only of *now*. There is only *now*. At least until this mess is over.' The roguish smile crossed his wide mouth and his eyes swept over her in the old appraising way. 'And we do have hours of pleasure ahead of us yet. The whole *night*, in fact,' he said. He leered at her theatrically, endeavouring to distract her, wanting to make her laugh. 'And my dear, I must honestly confess that one night with you is worth –'

'Why, you wicked letch! You – you – reprobate,' she exclaimed, smiling lovingly through her tears.

'A fairly accurate description of me, I would say, especially when it comes to you.' He took her in his arms and moved his lips along the soft curve of her cheek and down the line of her neck. He began to speak in a low voice, using expressions of such love and intimacy the blush rose to her cheeks. She clutched at him, her fingers biting into his arm. Her heart raced as he pushed her back on the sofa, pressed his body against hers, and began to unfasten the buttons on her robe. His eyes were so brilliant she was blinded. She closed her eyes as he brought his lips to hers.

FORTY-SEVEN

'Amputate!' Emma cried, her face turning deathly white. 'But he has been so well for the last few days.'

'No, he hasn't. Your brother has been hiding the facts from you, Mrs Lowther. He has also been refusing to have the operation. Despite our warnings he has been fighting us. But you can't fight gangrene. It's virulent, and ultimately deadly.'

Emma sat down abruptly, her eyes pinned on the doctor. 'Isn't there an alternative?'

The doctor shook his head. 'No, there isn't. Unless you want to call death an alternative.' Seeing the fear registering on her face, the doctor seated himself next to her and took her hand. 'I'm so sorry. I don't mean to be brutal. But circumstances necessitate honesty, even bluntness, I'm afraid. Time is of the essence.'

'What happened, Doctor? I thought you had been able to remove all the shrapnel from his foot and calf.'

'We did, but the gangrene set in several days ago and it travels rapidly. It's already above his knee. You *must* sign the papers giving us permission to operate. Otherwise –' He lifted his hands helplessly, his face grave.

Emma swallowed, 'But – but – Winston has to make that decision –'

'Mrs Lowther, don't you understand? Your brother is incapable of making the decision in his present state of mind. *You* must take the responsibility. Now. *Today.* Tomorrow will be too late.'

Emma bit her lip and nodded. Her heart was heavy as she said, 'Give me the papers, please.'

The doctor stepped to his desk, returned with the documents, and handed them to her with the pen. 'You are doing the right thing, Mrs Lowther. The only thing you can do. Your brother will be grateful to you for the rest of his life. Please believe that.'

Emma looked at him sombrely but made no comment. She signed, and although she was quivering inside, her hand was steady. 'May I see my brother now?' she asked dully.

'Yes, of course. I'll take you to him right away,' the doctor said. His face was sympathetic as he led her out of the office.

Winston was in a ward with other sailors who had been wounded. Screens had been placed around him, and as Emma walked past them and approached the bed she saw that his eyes were glazed over with pain and beads of perspiration stood out on his forehead. She leaned down to kiss him and he let out a stifled scream, his eyes febrile. Emma pulled back hurriedly in alarm. 'Whatever is it, Winston, dear?'

'You touched the bed,' he moaned. 'I can't stand the slightest movement. The pain is excruciating.' He drew in his breath sharply and closed his eyes.

Emma watched him with consternation. After a moment she said with the utmost quiet, 'Why didn't you tell me you had gangrene, Winston?'

He opened his eyes and glared at her, the old bravado of childhood momentarily invading his face. 'I'm not having it off, Emma!' he cried vehemently. 'I'm not going to be a cripple for the rest of my life!'

Emma sat down on the chair near the bed and nodded, her heart aching for him. 'I know how you must feel, dear. It's a terrible thing to have to face. But if they don't amputate you'll – you'll die.'

'Then I'll die!' he shouted, defiance now supplanting the feverishness in his blue eyes. 'I might just as well be dead with only one leg! I'm a young man, Emma, and my life will be over. Finished.'

'No, it won't, darling. You will be incapacitated to a certain extent, I realize that. And the prospects must seem terrifying to you right now. But isn't amputation preferable to not being here at all?'

'I'm not having my leg off,' he mumbled in a tired voice.

Emma's tone was pleading as she continued, 'Winston, listen to me. You must have the operation. *You must*, dear. And immediately. If you delay any longer your whole system will be poisoned.' Her voice broke at this thought. 'If you won't do it for yourself, then do it for me. *Please! Please, Winston!*' she begged. 'I love you very much. Apart from the children, you and Frank are the only family I have –' She groped in her bag for a handkerchief, pulled it out, and blew her nose, attempting to control herself. 'I've had too many losses in the last few years, Winston. Mam, Dad, Joe, and Laura. And then Aunt Lily only last week. I don't think I could endure the loss of another loved one. I just couldn't. It would kill me.' Tears filled her eyes, and she finished tremulously, 'I just couldn't stand it if you died, too, love.'

'Don't cry, Emma. Please don't cry, pet.' A spasm of pain streaked through him like a ripping knife and he flinched, his face ashen and sweating more profusely now. He sighed. 'All right, then, let them cut it off. To tell you the truth, I don't think I can take the pain much longer.' A faint smile touched his white lips. 'Half a loaf is better than no bread at all, I suppose. You'd better sign the papers and get it over with, Emma.'

'I already did.'

He mustered a grin. 'I might have known. Old Miss Bossy Knickers.'

Emma smiled weakly. 'It's going to be fine, Winston. I know it is. The doctor is preparing the operating theatre now. In a few minutes the nurses will be coming in to get you ready.' She stood up. 'I have to go. The doctor said I must make it brief. Every minute counts now.'

'Emma –'

'Yes, love?'

'Will you – can you wait?'

'Of course I'll wait, dear. I wouldn't dream of leaving until it's all over.' She blew him a kiss, not daring to approach the bed again.

Emma gazed out of the window of the waiting room of Chapel Allerton Naval Hospital, her thoughts with Winston, now undergoing surgery. How frightening for him to lose a leg. He who had taken such pride in his good looks, and his virility, who had loved sports and dancing and was so physical by nature. She acknowledged that he would indeed have a number of major readjustments to make, and in many ways he would have to start a new life. But, despite the restrictions the amputation of his right leg would impose, she was thankful he was alive.

He had been wounded during a naval battle in the North Sea. His battleship had staggered into Hull half crippled, and it was nothing short of a miracle that the ship had made it to that great Humber port, so fortuitously close to Leeds and the naval hospital. Otherwise he might be dead by now.

Emma leaned her head against the window, closing her eyes. In a few weeks she would be twenty-nine. Only twenty-nine and yet she felt like an old woman, weary and worn out from her responsibilities these days. A nurse thoughtfully brought her a cup of tea and Emma sat down to drink it – and to wait. That seemed to have become one of her chief occupations of late: *waiting*. Mostly she waited for letters from Paul, feeling crushed and apprehensive when she did not receive one, filled with soaring relief when there was a note, however brief and hastily written.

She took Paul's last letter out of her handbag and read it again. It was worn from too much handling and some of the words had blurred from her tears. He had returned to France to rejoin Colonel Monash and the Australian Corps in the middle of February. Now it was the beginning of April. But he was still safe and well. When Paul had left he had taken an essential part of her with him and she felt incomplete, only half alive without him.

The minutes ticked by slowly. Almost two hours had passed since Winston had been wheeled down to the operating room. Had something gone wrong? Had they been too late? Quite unexpectedly, just when she thought she was going to scream from frustration, the doctor strode in. He was nodding and smiling. 'He's fine, Mrs Lowther.'

Emma closed her eyes and exhaled with relief. 'Are you sure?'

'Absolutely! He's a little woozy from the anaesthetic, but he's young, healthy, and strong. He'll mend well.' The doctor's eyes clouded. 'There is just one thing –'

'*What?*'

'We had to amputate very high. The gangrene was well above the knee and we had to cut a good four inches above that, to be certain we got it all.'

'What does that mean exactly?'

'It means there's the possibility he might not be able to wear an artificial limb.'

'My brother's not going to spend the rest of his life on crutches,' Emma cried. 'Or in a wheelchair. He's going to wear an artificial leg if – if I have to damn well design a special one myself! My brother is going to walk, Doctor!'

And walk he did. But it was a gruelling period for Emma. Winston's mood swings were erratic and, not unnaturally, highly emotional. He plunged from relief in being alive to depression, from depression to rage, frustration, and self-pity, and then unexpectedly the euphoria returned, but soon to be replaced by foul black moods. Emma cajoled, threatened, screamed, implored, and challenged, using every ruse she knew to shatter the melancholia that engulfed him and lift him out of it, her only tools her stubborn belief in the indomitability of the human spirit and her conviction that anything was possible in life, *if* the will was strong enough. Slowly she made progress with Winston, badgering him relentlessly, and after several weeks she managed to instil in him the determination to lead a normal life. She gave him strength, and her optimism bolstered his own natural courage.

The Limb Fitting Centre at Chapel Allerton Hospital in Leeds was already renowned throughout England for the remarkable feats of rehabilitation accomplished there since the outset of the Great War. The doctors worked painstakingly with the men, especially those who had lost legs, endeavouring to get them ambulatory in the shortest possible time. Winston was no exception. His flesh healed quickly and within two months the doctors had him moving about on crutches. He was fitted for a leg, released from the hospital, and went to live with Emma during his recuperation period. To Emma's relief, when the leg arrived he was able to wear it, in spite of the shortness of the stump. All that was required were two extra stump socks to cushion the stump against the metal. Three times a week he was driven to Chapel Allerton Hospital in one of the Harte vans, where he underwent physical therapy and wore the leg for half an hour at a stretch. And so he commenced the long and difficult task of adjustment to the artificial leg and learning to walk with it correctly.

One day in October, eight months after the amputation, Winston literally strolled into Emma's office, self-confident, smiling, steady on his feet, and in absolute control of the leg, and it was one of the most gratifying moments of her life. His limp was negligible and he had taken her advice, proffered months before, to make the leg an integral part of him.

'I can't dance, but there's not much else I can't do,' he informed her proudly. He placed his walking stick on a chair, moved across the room without it, and sat down. 'I can certainly move with great speed if I have to and I can climb and descend stairs easily. Believe it or not, I can also swim. And now that I have the final release from the hospital I am going to look for a job.'

'But, Winston, I told you months ago you could come and work for me. Why don't you?'

Winston frowned. 'Here at the store? But what would I do?'

'You've always liked figures. I could put you in bookkeeping until you get used to things, and then I would like you to become my assistant. I need somebody I can trust implicitly. Don't forget, I have other businesses, Winston, as well as the store.' Emma paused, eyeing him carefully, and finished, 'For instance, there's the Emeremm Company.'

'What's that? You've never mentioned it before.' Winston looked at her with alertness.

'It's a holding and acquisition company, which I formed in 1917.' Emma leaned forward. 'I financed it myself and I own one hundred per cent of the shares, but it's run for me by a man called Ted Jones. Apart from Ted, and the other directors, no one else knows I'm behind it. Except for you now. I want to keep it that way, Winston. Not even Frank knows, so don't ever discuss it with him.'

'I would never talk about your business to anyone,' he said quickly. 'But why all the secrecy?'

'Mostly because men don't like doing business with a woman, especially in areas of high finance. There are other reasons, personal reasons, but they are not important for the moment.'

Winston grinned. 'You are a dark horse!' he exclaimed. 'And even more successful than I realized. You know, I think I'd like to work for you, Emma. It sounds challenging.'

'I'm delighted. You can start on Monday if you like. It's up to you. However, there are a few things you should know about me, Winston, if you are going to work here. First of all, I don't like surprises, especially nasty ones. So you must always tell me everything. And if you make any mistakes, don't hide them. As long as I'm informed they can be corrected. Secondly, I want you to understand some-

449

thing else and this is *imperative*. I never deal from a position of fear. Only from strength, and if I don't have that strength I make damned sure the world thinks I do. You will have to learn to do the same if you're going to act on my behalf. Do you think you can?'

'Yes, Emma.'

'Good.' Her eyes focused on him intently. 'I believe the key to success in business is discipline, dedication, concentration, and patience. And I won't tolerate temperament in business. It is immature. I am not suggesting you are temperamental, but I want you to comprehend that you must always keep a cool head and you must never let emotions get in the way.' She smiled. 'Any questions, Winston?'

'Yes, quite a lot.' He grinned engagingly. 'But they can wait until later. Until I start working for you on Monday. Right now I have an appointment.'

'Who with?' she asked in surprise.

'With one of the nurses from the hospital. That pretty brunette – Charlotte. I'm taking her out to tea.'

Emma laughed gaily. 'You don't waste much time, do you? But I'm glad to hear it. Now I know you're really your old self.'

Emma had told Winston only half the truth about her attitude towards business. Over the years she had embraced a merciless philosophy – never show weakness, never lose face, never confide. She had also mastered the art of compromise and this instinct towards accommodation had served her well, permitting her to negotiate and manoeuvre with more flexibility than many of her competitors, who were rigid. Since she had a particular aversion to conflict and confrontation, she preferred always to move in roundabout ways and if necessary with stealth, and she was to acquire much of her power by stealth.

Later that afternoon, when Winston had left, she moved covertly in the direction of the Fairleys and struck a deadly blow at their business enterprises. Her strategy was simple: she manipulated a weak and foolish man, who blithely, if unwittingly, put Gerald Fairley exactly where Emma wanted him – in her clutches.

This development had not occurred by accident. One of the first purchases the Emeremm Company had made in 1917 was Procter and Procter, a wholesale cloth warehouse in Bradford. Emma bought it for several reasons. It was a sound investment, even though it had been mismanaged over the years. Also, the sprawling warehouse sat on a prime piece of land in the centre of Bradford, and Emma knew this land could only increase in value over the years. But aside from the company's potential, Alan Procter, the owner, was a crony of Gerald Fairley's and Emma had recognized that here was a conduit to her sworn enemy, a source of vital information about the latter's activities.

At first Alan Procter had been reluctant to sell, despite the fact that he had run the company into the ground, had innumerable creditors and personal debts, many of them due to his inveterate gambling. However, the Emeremm Company's terms were so appealing they inevitably won Procter. Emma had made the terms irresistible. The purchase price was fair without being so excessive as to create suspicion. More importantly to Procter, he was offered a contract to remain as chairman of the board at a salary he could not afford to dismiss. There was one clause – Procter must not reveal the change of ownership of his company. If he did his contract would be instantly terminated.

Seeing his problems miraculously disappearing before his eyes, the venal and exigent Procter had not bothered to question the necessity for this secrecy. In fact, he had rather welcomed it, envisioning a means of continuing to run his company, at the same time solving his personal and business debts and saving face in Bradford. He sold, signed the employment contract with its secrecy-of-ownership clause, and in so doing became the property of Emma Harte. Emma had instructed Ted Jones to put an Emeremm man inside Procter and Procter. 'Procter is merely a front. I want his hands tied so that he cannot do any further damage to the business. And whoever you put in must ingratiate himself with Procter. Become his confidant.'

Her scheme worked. Procter had a loose tongue, especially after it had been well oiled over splendid luncheons with the new managing director – the Emeremm man. All manner of useful information came filtering in to Emma about Procter's associates in Leeds and Bradford, many of them her competitors, and prominent amongst it was a great deal about the Fairleys. Through Procter Emma learned early in 1918 that Gerald Fairley was in dire straits with Thompson's mill and wanted to sell. 'Buy it for as little as possible,' she coldly told Ted Jones. Using Procter and Procter as the purchaser, the Emeremm Company acquired Thompson's. Believing he was selling to Alan Procter, an old and trusted friend, and because of his strained financial situation, Gerald Fairley had accepted a quarter of the mill's true value, to Emma's immense satisfaction.

Now a piece of new information had landed on Emma's desk that very morning, and it had brought her head up with a jolt. Gerald Fairley had lost heavily at cards and had gone running to Alan Procter. He wanted to borrow two hundred thousand pounds. Procter had blabbed to the Emeremm man and had inquired about the possibility of making a corporate loan to Gerald Fairley.

Emma's vivid eyes rested on the memorandum again and a curious glint entered them. She recognized that here was the opportunity she had been waiting for and she seized it, moving with her usual swiftness. She picked up the telephone and spoke to Ted Jones at the Emeremm Company in London. 'You can inform Alan Procter he can make that corporate loan to Fairley.'

'What are the terms, Mrs Harte?'

'I want a noncontestable one-hundred-eighty-day note. But I want the note collateralized.'

'What kind of collateral, Mrs Harte?'

'The deeds to the Fairley mills in Armley and Stanningley Bottom.'

Ted Jones sucked in his breath. 'Rather steep terms, wouldn't you say?'

'Those are my terms,' Emma said icily. 'Gerald Fairley can take them or leave them. It's no skin off my nose either way. He won't be able to raise the money anywhere else. He's in too deep with the banks. I also happen to know he has borrowed heavily from some of his father's old business associates. He owes Procter money personally as well.' She laughed dryly. 'Where is Mr Gerald Fairley going to go, Ted?'

'You have a point there. I'll pass on the terms to our man at Procter and Procter and he can relay them to Alan. I'll get back to you later this afternoon.'

'I'm in no hurry, Ted. I'm not in trouble. It's Fairley who is sinking.'

'Yes, he is. The damned fool. It takes some sort of genius for ineptness to suffer

451

losses in wartime when every other cloth manufacturer has made a fortune from government contracts.'

'That's very true. Goodbye, Ted,' She hung up.

Emma leaned back in her chair and a gloating smile settled on that beautiful face. It's all happening sooner than I expected, she thought. It struck her then that she did not have to make a serious effort to destroy the Fairleys. Gerald was doing it for her. Ever since Adam Fairley had been felled by a stroke Gerald had been in total control of the mills and without his father's guidance he was floundering. All I have to do now is sit back and watch him dig a pit so deep he will never climb out, Emma said to herself.

Later she acknowledged that Gerald would undoubtedly fight the Procter and Procter terms, but he would have to accept them eventually out of the necessity to save his skin. And he would never be able to raise the money to pay off the note on its due date. But she could afford to be generous. She would extend the note for a few months and thus lull Gerald Fairley into a greater sense of false security. When she was ready she would foreclose on the note and take over the Fairley mills. Emma laughed. She had Gerald Fairley cornered and he was in complete ignorance of the fact.

As she had suspected, Gerald Fairley at first balked at the terms and backed off from the proposition for longer than she had anticipated. To her considerable amusement she heard he was running around endeavouring to raise the money he required. He was miserably unsuccessful. After four days, panic-stricken and dealing from a position of increasing desperation, he finally slunk back to Alan Procter and signed the noncontestable corporate note to which he had been forced to attach the deeds of the two Fairley mills. He did so because, once again, he thought he was dealing with a friend whom he believed would never make a move to endanger the ownership of his mills.

One week later, when Emma placed the note and the deeds in her safe, her triumph was unalloyed.

FORTY-EIGHT

David Kallinski pulled the car to a standstill outside Emma's house, and turned to her. 'Thanks for working this morning, Emma. It was good of you to give up part of your Sunday with the children.'

Emma smiled. 'I didn't mind. Really, I didn't, David. Actually I was glad to get the summer sketches for the Lady Hamilton line out of my hair, and I knew you were anxious to put them into work immediately.' She opened the car door. 'Are you sure you won't come in for a drink?'

'No. Thanks anyway, but I've got to be going. I promised my father I'd stop in to see him.' He caught her arm abruptly. 'Emma, there's something I want to tell you.'

So intense was his voice Emma was alarmed. 'Is there something wrong, David?'

'I'm thinking of getting a divorce.'

Thunderstruck, Emma gaped at him in disbelief. 'A divorce! My God, David!' She hesitated, and then said, 'Aren't things quite right between you and Rebecca?'

'No better than before the war.' He cleared his throat. 'I'm finding life intolerable since I came home. I might as well be honest with you –' He broke off, staring at her closely. 'I'm still in love with you, Emma. I thought if I was free – Well, I had hoped you would marry me.'

Emma stiffened, taken unawares, and shaken by his proposal. 'Oh, David, David.' She touched his hand clenched on the car wheel and said, 'My dear, you know that's not possible. I didn't make that sacrifice nine years ago, when you were single, in order to create a catastrophe now that you are married. It would kill your mother. Besides, you have two young sons and I have two children. There are other people to think about, as well as Rebecca and yourself. I told you years ago that it's not possible to build happiness on other people's misery, and I know I'm right.'

'But what about you and me, Emma?' he asked, his eyes filling with pain.

'There is no you and me, David.' Sharply conscious of his disappointment, she said softly, 'I hope I haven't done anything to encourage you, David. Surely I haven't built up your hopes, have I?'

He grinned ruefully. 'No, of course you haven't. And I haven't spoken out before now because I've been doing a lot of soul searching. Finally, last week, I knew I had to tell you how I felt. Being silent was accomplishing nothing. You see, I always thought you loved me, even after you married Joe. All through the war I believed that. It kept me going, kept me alive, in a sense. My feelings are exactly the same as they were and so I assumed yours were, too. But you don't love me anymore, do you?'

'Oh, David, darling, of course I do. As a dear friend. To be truthful, I *was* still in love with you when I married Joe. Now I have a different kind of love for you, and I am different. The vicissitudes of life do intrude and ultimately feelings change as well. I've come to understand that the only thing that is permanent is change.'

'You're in love with someone else, aren't you?' he exclaimed with a flash of intuition.

Emma did not answer. She dropped her eyes and clutched her handbag tightly and her mouth slipped into a thin line.

David said, 'I know the answer to that, although you are silent. You don't have to spare my feelings,' he announced crisply but without rancour. 'I ought to have guessed. Nine years is a long time. Are you going to marry him?'

'No. He's gone away. He doesn't live in this country. I don't think he will ever come back.' Her voice was muffled.

David detected the sorrow and defeat in her and, despite his own hurt, sympathy surged up in him, for he truly loved her and had her welfare at heart. He put his hand on hers and squeezed it. 'I'm awfully sorry, Emma.'

Emma looked at him through dulled eyes. 'It's all right. My wound is almost healed – I hope.'

'There's no chance for me, is there, Emma? Even with him out of the picture.'

'That's true, David. And I will always tell you the truth, although it is often distressing to hear. I would not intentionally hurt you for the world, and there's very little I can say to comfort you, I suppose. Please forgive me, David.'

'There's nothing to forgive, Emma. I can't condemn you for not being in love with me anymore.' His eyes were soft. 'I hope you find peace yourself, Emma darling.'

'I hope so, too.' She opened the door. 'No, please don't get out.' She kissed him on the cheek. 'Think carefully before you do anything rash about Rebecca and your marriage. She is a good person and she does love you. And remember that you are very special to me, David. I'm your friend and I'm always here if you need me.'

'Thank you for that. And I'm your devoted friend, too, Emma, and if there's anything I can do to make things easier for you, now or later, you know I will.' He smiled. 'It seems we're both crossed in love. If you need a strong shoulder – well, it's here.'

'Thank you for being so kind and understanding.' She attempted to smile. 'I'll see you at the factory as usual next week. Bye.'

'Goodbye, Emma darling.'

Emma walked up the garden path without looking back, her feet crunching on the hard snow, her head bent. She was filled with compassion for David, conscious of his dejection, and his suffering was her own. Her face was stark in the bleak winter light as her thoughts swung abruptly to Paul. She stopped at the front door, and took a deep breath before going inside. She took off her coat and hat in the hall, looked in on Mrs Fenton, who was preparing Sunday lunch in the kitchen, and then wearily climbed the staircase to the nursery.

It was the week before Christmas in the year 1919. Exactly twelve months ago Paul McGill had been in this house with her and the children and her brothers. The Great War had finally ended in November, and Paul had come to stay with them before returning to Australia to be demobilized. It had been a joyous Christmas, full of gaiety and love. Emma had been giddy with happiness, and more deeply in love with Paul than she had believed possible. She had felt as if everything she had always yearned for and desired was hers at last. Hers for ever. But now she had nothing . . . a broken heart and loneliness and despair. How foolish she had been to have believed it could be otherwise. Personal happiness always eluded her. And how different this Christmas would be. Her hand rested on the doorknob of the nursery. She thought: I *must* make an effort and be cheerful for the children's sake.

Kit was seated at the table painting. His eyes lit up and he jumped down and skittered across the floor. He flung himself at Emma. 'Mummy! Mummy! I'm so glad you're home,' he shouted, hugging Emma's legs.

She kissed the top of his head. 'Good gracious, Kit, whatever have you been doing? You seem to have more paint on yourself than there is on the paper. And what are you painting, sweetheart?'

'You can't see it! Not yet. It's a picture. For you, Mummy. A Christmas present.' Kit, who was now eight years old, looked up at Emma, wrinkling his nose and grinning. 'You can have a peek if you want.'

'Not if it's meant to be a surprise.'

'You might not like it, Mumsie. If you don't, I can paint another one. It's bestest you have a look, just in case. Come on.' Kit grabbed Emma's hand and dragged her across the room.

'Best, not bestest, darling,' Emma corrected, and looked down at the painting. It was childlike, awkwardly composed, out of perspective and splashed haphazardly with gaudy colours. It depicted a man in a uniform. Emma held her breath. There was no doubt in her mind who it was meant to be. Not with that thick black smudge across the upper lip and the bright blue eyes. 'It's very good, darling,' Emma said, her face pensive.

'It's Uncle Paul. Can you tell? Does it look like him? Do you really like it, Mummy?'

'I do indeed. Where's your sister?' Emma asked, changing the subject.

'Oh, stuffy old Edwina's in her room, reading or something. She wouldn't play with me this morning. Oh well, who cares! I want to finish this painting, Mummy.' Kit climbed back on to the chair, picked up the brush, and attacked the painting with renewed vigour and enthusiasm. A look of concentration settled on his freckled face. 'I must get it just right for you, Mums. I think I'll put a kangaroo in it. And a polar bear.'

'Don't you mean koala bear, Kit?'

'Well, a *bear*, Mummy. Uncle Paul told me there were bears in Australia.'

'Yes, dear,' Emma said absently. 'Lunch in half an hour, Kit. And don't forget to tidy up before coming down.' She rumpled his hair and hurried out to her own room, feeling the need to be alone to collect her scattered thoughts.

Winter sun was pouring in through the tall windows and the room was awash with rafts of pristine light. The deep peach walls and the matching carpet had taken on a golden hue and the pale green watered silk covering the bed, the sofa, and several small chairs held a faint shimmer as though shot through with silvery grey. Georgian antiques, their patinas mellow, punctuated the room with dark colour and the crystal lamps with their cream silk shades cast a warm glow against the rosy walls. A fire blazed in the white marble fireplace and the ambiance was cheerful. Emma hardly noticed her surroundings. She stood in front of the fire warming her hands, the old iciness of childhood trickling through her limbs. Her head throbbed and she felt more depressed than usual.

David's declaration of his love for her and her subsequent rejection of him had served to underscore the searing torment Paul McGill had caused her. Always prominent in her mind, this feeling was now more rampant than ever, and she felt utterly defeated. After a moment she crossed to the chest of drawers and opened the bottom drawer. She pushed her hands under the silk nightgowns and lifted out the photograph of Paul. She had placed it there weeks ago, no longer able to bear the sight of it on her dressing table. Her eyes rested on that well-loved face, took in the direct gaze of the eyes underneath the thick brows, the smile on the wide mouth, and her lacerated heart ached. Unexpectedly, a furious anger invaded her and she hurled the photograph across the room with great force, her eyes blazing.

The moment it left her hand she regretted her immature action and ran to pick it up. The silver frame had been dented and the glass had shattered, but to her relief the photograph was undamaged. She knelt on the floor, gathering up the broken glass and placing it in the wastepaper basket. She sat down in the chair by the fire, hugging the photograph to her, thinking about Paul. The photograph had been taken the preceding January, just prior to his leaving England, when they were staying at the Ritz together. He was wearing his major's uniform and looked incredibly handsome. She saw him then, in her mind's eye, standing on the platform at Euston, before he boarded the boat train. He had tilted her face to his and looked deeply into her eyes, his own spilling with love. 'I'll come back, my dearest darling. I promise I will be back before you know I'm even gone,' he had said. And she, imbecile that she was, had believed him.

She looked down at the picture. 'Why didn't you come back, Paul? You promised! You vowed nothing could keep you from me!' Her question echoed hollowly around the room, and she had no answer for herself, once more baffled and racked with despair. Paul had written to her twice and she had replied immediately. To her surprise he had never responded to her second letter. At the time, wondering if it had gone astray, she had written again. This letter had also remained unanswered. Finally, swallowing her immense pride, she had penned a circumspect note, and then had waited for word from him. The weeks had turned into months, and the silence had been absolute. In a state of bewilderment and shock, she had done nothing. She had lost her nerve. By October, Emma had miserably resigned herself to the fact that Paul was not man enough to write and tell her that he no longer loved her. That it was over. It was the only conceivable conclusion she could draw in her heartsick state. He simply has no further use for me, she thought. I served a purpose when he was alone in England. He has resumed his old life in Australia. *He is a married man.*

Emma leaned back, staring into space abstractedly, her face cold and set, her eyes wide and tearless. She had cried all the tears she would ever cry for Paul McGill, night after night for months past. Paul McGill did not want her and that was that. There was nothing she could do about it . . .

'Mother, may I come in?' Edwina asked, poking her head around the door.

'Yes, darling,' Emma said, slipping the photograph under the chair and forcing a smile. 'Did you have a nice morning? I'm sorry I had to go to the factory on your day. It was an emergency.'

'You work too hard, Mother,' Edwina said reprovingly. She sat down in the opposite chair and smoothed her tartan kilt.

Emma disregarded the remark and the offensive tone and said cheerfully, 'You haven't told me yet what you would like for Christmas. Perhaps you would like to come to the store with me next week and look around, darling.'

'I don't know what I want for Christmas,' Edwina said, her silvery eyes observing Emma. 'But I would like to have my birth certificate, please, Mother.'

Emma froze in the chair. She kept her face bland. 'Why do you want your birth certificate, Edwina?' she asked, adopting a mild voice.

'Because I need it to get a passport.'

'Good heavens, why do you need a passport?'

'Miss Matthews is taking the class to Switzerland next spring and I am going, too.'

Emma's sweeping brows puckered together. 'I notice you have simply assumed you are going. You haven't asked my permission. I find that quite dismaying, Edwina.'

'May I go, Mother?'

'No, Edwina, you may not,' Emma said firmly. 'You are only thirteen. In my opinion that's far too young for you to be travelling to the Continent without me.'

'But we will be chaperoned. Most of the girls are going. Why can't I?'

'I have *told* you why, dear. You are too young. Furthermore, I find it hard to believe that most of the girls are going. How many exactly will there be in the group?'

'Eight.'

'That's more like it! Eight girls out of a class of twenty-four is merely a third. You are prone to exaggerate sometimes, Edwina.'

'So I can't go?'

'Not this coming year. Perhaps in a couple of years. I will have to give it some careful thought. I'm sorry to disappoint you, but you should have discussed it with me first. And my decision is quite final, Edwina.'

Knowing that it was useless to argue with her iron-willed mother, Edwina sighed theatrically and stood up. *She hated her.* If her father were alive he would have let her go abroad. She smiled at Emma, craftily concealing her dislike. 'It's not that important,' she said, and glided across the room to Emma's dressing table. Picking up the brush, she began to brush her waistlength silver-blonde hair, staring with total absorption in the mirror. Emma watched her with mounting annoyance, her eyes narrowing as she saw the self-gratified smile on her daughter's face revealed in the glass.

'You know, Edwina, for a little girl you are terribly vain. I don't think I've ever seen anyone gaze into a mirror as often as you do.'

'Now *you're* exaggerating, Mother,' Edwina countered haughtily.

'Don't be impertinent,' Emma said crossly. Her patience was worn thin this morning and her nerves were on edge. But regretting her flash of temper, she said in a lighter tone, 'Your Uncle Winston is coming to tea today. You'll enjoy that, won't you, darling?'

'Not particularly. He's not the same since that woman got him.'

Emma suppressed a smile. 'Your Aunt Charlotte hasn't *got* him, Edwina, as you so curiously put it. She's married to him. And she's awfully nice. You know, too, that she is very fond of you.'

'He's still not the same,' Edwina said stubbornly. She stood up. 'I have to finish my homework, Mother. Please excuse me.'

'Yes, dear.'

When Emma was alone she returned Paul's photograph to the drawer, her mind preoccupied with Edwina's request for her birth certificate, a disastrous development she had not anticipated. She ran downstairs to the study, closed the door firmly behind her, and telephoned Blackie in Harrogate.

'Hello, me darlin',' Blackie said.

'Blackie, something perfectly dreadful has happened!'

He heard the fear in her voice. 'What's wrong, Emma?'

'Edwina just asked me for her birth certificate.'

'Jaysus!' He recovered himself swiftly. 'Why does she suddenly want her birth certificate?'

'To get a passport for a school trip to the Continent next year.'

'You refused, I presume.'

'Of course. But the day will come when I can't stall her, Blackie. What am I going to do?'

'You'll have to give it to her. But not until she's old enough to handle the situation, Emma.' He sighed. 'This was bound to happen one day.'

457

'But how will I explain your name on the certificate? She thinks Joe was her father.'

'You could let her think that I really am her father.'

'But that's such a responsibility for you, Blackie.'

He laughed. 'I have a broad back, me darlin'. You should know that by now.' His voice changed perceptibly, and he went on, 'Of course, you could tell her who her real father is. But I don't suppose you want to do that, do you, Emma?'

'No, I definitely do not!' Emma made a decision, drew in her breath, and plunged. 'You know who he is, don't you?'

Blackie sighed softly into the phone. 'I can hazard a guess. She looks too much like Adele Fairley for me to be in doubt any longer. It was Edwin, wasn't it?'

'Yes, Blackie,' Emma responded quietly, and felt a sudden rush of relief that she had finally told him the truth. 'But Edwina will never know. Must never know. I have to protect her from the Fairleys all of her life.'

'Then you will just have to let her believe that I am her true father. I don't object, Emma.' He chuckled quietly. 'Come on, me darlin', relax. I can feel your tension coming over the wire. Forget this little problem for the moment. Delay as long as you can. You're a clever woman. You can skirt the issue for several years. At least until she's seventeen or eighteen.'

'I suppose I can,' Emma said slowly. 'We're never free of the past, are we, darling?'

'No, mavourneen, that's the sad truth, I'm afraid. But let's not dwell on the past. It's fruitless. Now you haven't forgotten me party on Boxing Day, have you?' Blackie went on in an effort to distract her. 'The party for me new house. It's a beauty, Emma, even though I do say so meself.'

'Of course I haven't forgotten. I wouldn't miss it for anything. Frank is coming to Yorkshire for Christmas and he's promised to bring me. And I'm longing to see the house. You've been so secretive about it.'

'Ah, but you'll be recognizing it the minute you see it, Emma. It's exactly the way I described it to you all those years ago on the moors. Me fine Georgian mansion right down to the last detail.'

'I'm so thrilled for you, Blackie. It was always one of your dearest dreams.'

'Aye, that's so. Emma, I must hang up. I can see me beautiful Bryan coming up the drive with Nanny. Now don't you worry about that birth certificate. Forget it for the next year or so. We'll deal with it only when it's absolutely necessary.'

'I'll try. And thank you, Blackie. You're always such a comfort to me.'

'Sure and it's nothing, mavourneen.'

Emma hung up the telephone and sat lost in introspection, her mind dwelling on her daughter. There was something so unapproachable about her, an innate coldness in her nature, and Emma was aware at all times of a curious disapproval in Edwina's manner, and she was often at a loss to deal with it effectively.

How will I ever find the courage to face that child with the truth? she asked herself. How can I tell her without losing the little affection she has for me? She flinched at the thought of a confrontation, however far off it was, and for the first time in months Emma momentarily forgot about Paul McGill and her own misery.

Blackie O'Neill strolled across the magnificent entrance hall of his Georgian mansion in Harrogate, his arm around Winston's shoulders. He ushered him into the library and locked the great double doors behind them.

'Why are you doing that?' Winston asked, looking puzzled. 'I thought we came in here for a quiet brandy.'

'True. True. But I want to talk to you privately and I don't want any interruptions.'

'Who would interrupt us? Everyone's too busy enjoying the party.'

'Emma, for one.'

'Aha! You want to talk about my sister. Is that it?'

'It is indeed.' Blackie busied himself at the console, pouring generous amounts of the Courvoisier into two brandy balloons.

From his stance by the Adam fireplace, Winston watched Blackie, wondering what he had on his mind. He shook his head in bafflement and glanced around with admiration, appreciating the elegance of the furnishings and the beauty of the setting. The bleached pine walls, interspersed with bookshelves, were balanced by forest-green velvet draperies, and a carpet of the same colour covered the centre of the mahogany parquet floor. A number of deep sofas and armchairs were upholstered in lighter green velvet and rose damask, and this warm colour highlighted the cool greenness. Tables, consoles, and a fine desk in the mingled designs of Sheraton and Hepplewhite graced the room, and a spectacular Waterford crystal chandelier dropped down from the soaring ceiling. The library, like the rest of the new house, was a splendid tribute to Blackie's sense of perspective and colour and his knowledge of the decorative style of the Georgian period.

Looking exceptionally handsome and prosperous in his dinner jacket, Blackie handed Winston a balloon of the cognac. 'Cheers, Winston,' he said.

'Cheers, Blackie.'

Blackie selected a cigar, clipped off the end, lit it slowly. He puffed on it for a few seconds and finally fixed his bright black eyes on Winston. 'When is she going to stop all this foolishness?'

'What foolishness?' Winston demanded with a frown.

'Throwing money around. She's gone crazy in the past six months. At least so it seems to me.'

'Emma's not throwing money around. In fact, she's not very extravagant with herself at all.'

Blackie raised a black eyebrow quizzically and a faint smile flitted across his mouth. 'Now, Winston, don't play the innocent with me. You know damn well what I mean. I'm talking about the way she's been plunging into the commodities market. Recklessly so, I might add.'

Winston grinned. 'Not recklessly at all. She's made a fortune, Blackie.'

'Aye, and she can easily lose it! *Overnight*! Speculating in commodities is the most dangerous game there is, and you know it.'

'Yes, I do. And for that matter, so does Emma. She *is* something of a gambler in business, Blackie. We're both aware of that. However, she's also astute and she knows what she's doing –'

'It's all much too chancy for my liking! She could easily be ruined!'

Winston laughed. 'Not my sister. You've got to admit it takes real genius to start out with nothing and build what she has so brilliantly built. Only an idiot would be stupid enough to risk throwing it all away. Emma's nobody's fool and, anyway, she stopped buying and selling commodities several weeks ago.'

'Thank God for that!' Blackie looked relieved, but his tone was worried as he continued, 'Still, I am concerned about all this rapid expansion she's undertaken. The new stores in Bradford and Harrogate were admittedly good buys, but the renovations she insists I make are going to be very costly. And I couldn't believe my ears tonight when she told me she's thinking of building a store in London. As usual, her ideas are pretty grandiose. To be honest, Winston, I was dumb-founded. How the hell is she going to pay for it all? That's what I want to know. It's my opinion she's over-extending herself.'

Winston shook his head adamantly. 'No she's not! She's as smart as a whip and never does anything rashly. How is she going to pay for it? I just told you she made a hell of a lot of money in commodities. And she has been selling off Joe's remaining properties for very high prices. In fact, she's gradually divested herself of all the real estate he left her, except for that plot of land in the centre of Leeds. She's hanging on to that, because she thinks it will increase in worth, and you know she's right. The store in Leeds is in profit and, also, this boom in the cloth trade since the end of the war has turned Layton's into a bigger money-maker than it ever was. Orders are pouring in from all over the world and Ben Andrews has had to put most of the workers on overtime to meet them. The Gregson Warehouse is fully operating again, and don't forget, Emma is David Kallinski's partner –'

Pausing, Winston eyed Blackie with amusement. 'Does that answer your questions about how she intends to pay for everything?'

Blackie had the good grace to laugh. 'Aye, me boyo, it does.' He shook his head wonderingly. 'She's obviously become a very rich woman – richer than I had imagined, from what you tell me.'

Winston nodded, a proud look on his face. 'How much do you think she's worth?' he said with a spontaneity he instantly regretted, since he could not tell the truth.

'I couldn't even hazard a guess.'

Winston took a sip of brandy to hide his hesitation. He could not admit Emma's true worth, because he dare not reveal the existence of the Emeremm Company and her ownership of it. Therefore he selected a conservatively low figure and said, 'A million pounds. That's on paper, of course.'

'Jaysus!' Blackie exclaimed. He knew Winston was not lying or exaggerating and he was immensely impressed. Blackie lifted his glass. 'That deserves a toast. Here's to Emma. She has surpassed us all, I do believe!'

'To Emma.' Winston eyed Blackie thoughtfully. 'Yes, she has. Do you know why? Do you know the secret of my sister's great success?'

'Sure and I do. I attribute it to a number of qualities. Shrewdness, courage, ambition, and drive, to name only a few.'

'*Abnormal* ambition. *Abnormal* drive, Blackie. That's the difference between Emma and most people. She won't allow anything to stop her and she will go for the jugular with a business adversary, especially if her back is against the wall. But those are not the only reasons for her success. Emma has the killer instinct to get to the top.'

'Killer instinct! That's a hell of a thing to say about her. You make her sound ruthless.'

'She is in some ways.' Winston could not help laughing at Blackie's startled expression, and said, 'Don't tell me *you've* never recognized that trait in her!'

Blackie pondered, recalling incidents from the past. 'At times I have thought her capable of ruthlessness,' he murmured slowly.

'Look, Blackie, enough of all this. I hope I've alleviated your worries about her.'

'Yes, you have. I'm glad we had this talk, Winston. I've been concerned about that commodity lark ever since she mentioned it. Scared the hell out of me, if you really want to know. Well, now we've got that out of the way, shall we go back to the party?'

'Whenever you wish. Incidentally, talking of killers, I notice the lady killer is on the prowl tonight. He can't take his eyes off Emma and he's certainly fawning all over her.'

Blackie was alert and interested. 'Who are you talking about?'

'Why, Arthur Ainsley, of course. The great hero of the war – according to him. Conceited bastard.'

'I always thought Emma didn't like him.'

'I wouldn't know about that. I wasn't around, remember? But she did tell me that he'd changed and she seems unperturbed by his attentions tonight.'

'I hadn't really noticed,' Blackie said curtly, and stood up with abruptness. He was preoccupied as they returned to the drawing room. Immediately upon entering, Winston drifted off to join Charlotte and Frank, and Blackie ambled over to the piano. He leaned against it nonchalantly, but his full attention was focused with intensity on Emma, who was engaged in conversation with Frederick Ainsley and his son Arthur.

Blackie thought Emma looked particularly lovely tonight, if a little paler and wistful. Her hair was worked into a coronet of plaits atop her head and the upswept style made her face seem more delicate than ever. She wore a white velvet gown, cut low and off the shoulder, and pinned on to one of the small sleeves was the emerald pin he had given her for her thirtieth birthday. It was the exact replica of the cheap little green-glass bow he had bought for her when she was fifteen, but larger and more exquisitely worked. He had been gratified at her obvious surprise that he had remembered a promise made so long ago, and thrilled at her delight in the costly gift. Now, to him, it looked like a trumpery bauble in comparison to the magnificent emerald earrings that sparkled with such brilliance at her ears.

Automatically his hand went into his pocket, his fingers curling around the jewellery box that reposed there. It contained the diamond ring he had purchased last week. He had intended to ask Emma to marry him tonight. After their recent conversation about Edwina's birth certificate and the dilemma it posed, he had finally made the decision he had been toying with for months. Lately he had come to understand that if he did not love Emma in quite the same worshipful and spiritual way he had loved his Laura, love Emma he did. He had always loved her, ever since she had been an innocent child, his starveling creature of those bleak and misty moors. Her happiness was important to him. He found her physically alluring, she amused him, and he valued her friendship. Apart from his own deep attachment to her, Bryan adored her and his darling Bryan needed a mother. Also, Blackie had concluded, if he married Emma perhaps the sting would be taken out of the blow Edwina would receive when she discovered her illegitimacy. He would be like a father to the child, would try to replace Joe in her affections. If she learned to love him in return, then she might not be so resentful when she saw his name on the birth certificate, and he would willingly give her his name legally.

All in all, he had thought his idea foolproof – until Winston's revelations a few minutes before. Suddenly Blackie saw Emma in a wholly different light, saw her now as a woman of undeniable power and enormous wealth. He had never under-estimated her, for he was too intelligent by far for that. He had simply not realized or, in fact, recognized exactly what she had become, being too subjective to focus on her as a woman of the world and a successful tycoon. He himself had done well, but she had more than outstripped him, and David Kallinski, and in the most staggering manner. Furthermore, he now admitted that she would never be like a normal woman, dedicated to a husband, a family, and a home. She could never be wrested from her business. In many ways it *was* her.

Blackie was no longer sure she would accept him as a husband and, perhaps more cogently, he was uncertain of his ability to handle her. And so Blackie O'Neill, thirty-three years old, charming, rich, and hitherto a man of self-assurance and élan, lost a fraction of his confidence because of Emma's incredible achievements. And he faltered in his determination to propose.

He caught Emma's attention and she excused herself from the Ainsleys and glided over to him. 'It's a lovely party, Blackie, and I can't get over the house. It's superb.' She looked up at him, her eyes glittering vividly in that pale oval. 'And it *is* exactly as you said it would be, with your light greens and blues and fine Georgian furnishings.' She laughed. 'Do you remember when I asked you who Hepplewhite, Chippendale, and Sheraton were?'

'I do. I also remember I told you then that you would be a grand lady one day. My prediction came true.'

She smiled.

Blackie became aware of Arthur Ainsley's eyes on them and he said with a frown, 'I always thought you couldn't stand young Ainsley, but tonight you appear to be quite kindly disposed towards the fellow.'

'Oh, he's not so bad. He's much more intelligent than I thought and amusing. Actually, I find him rather charming as well.'

Blackie's eyes flared. 'Aye, he is. If he weren't a Sassenach I'd swear he'd kissed the Blarney stone,' he pronounced.

Emma laughed at Blackie's sarcastic retort and admitted, 'Yes, I suppose he is a bit too smooth sometimes. But at least he's entertaining and easy to be with.'

'Have you been spending a lot of time with him?' Blackie asked evenly enough, although he experienced a twinge of jealousy.

'No, not at all. I only see Arthur on business matters. Why?' She gave him a puzzled look.

'No particular reason. I just wondered. Incidentally, talking of business, where do you intend to build your store in London?'

'I've found a large piece of land in Knightsbridge, and I can get it for a good price. I would like you to see it.' She touched his arm. 'Could you come to London with me next week, darling?'

'Sure and I'd be delighted. If you go ahead with the purchase I can start the plans immediately. I'll build you a magnificent store, Emma. The best in London.'

They talked for a while about the intended department store. Emma expounded her ideas, which were grandiose, but her enthusiasm was so infectious Blackie found himself growing unexpectedly excited about the challenge she was presenting to him and his talents. After a little further discourse, Blackie seated himself at the piano and began to play. He sang a number of amusing Irish jigs and Emma sat back, as always enjoying his marvellous voice. Many of the guests thronged around the piano, just as they had done in the Mucky Duck, and Emma remembered the old days, and smiled to herself. And then she froze as Blackie's rich baritone rang out again, pure and clear, in the opening strains of 'Danny Boy'. Familiar words invoked in her a terrible yearning and a sadness that was overwhelming.

His voice swelled and filled the room as he commenced the second verse: 'But when ye come, and all the flow'rs are dying –'

Emma could not bear to listen any more. She slipped out of the room, her heart tearing inside her, and her throat was choked as she thought of Paul, and only of him: gone from her for ever.

Frank and Winston exchanged alarmed glances and Frank shook his head as Winston rose. 'I'll go. You stay here with Charlotte.' Frank followed quickly on Emma's heels and caught up with her in the entrance hall. He took her arm and propelled her into the library without saying a word. He closed the door, put his arm around her shoulders, and then said, 'He's not coming back, Emma. You might as well face the facts.'

'I have, Frank,' she responded in a low resigned voice.

'You know I would never interfere in your life, but I can't stand to see your heartbreak any longer, Emma. There are certain things I must tell you. That you must know. I can't hold them back.'

Emma looked at him warily. 'What do you mean?'

'Paul McGill is married.'

'I know, Frank dear. I've always known.'

'I see.' His sensitive mouth settled into a grim line.

'I suppose Dolly Mosten told you,' Emma ventured.

'Yes, she did.'

'Dolly's a gossip! She had no right to –'

'I asked her, Emma. Forced her to tell me, in point of fact. Only out of concern for you, though.'

'Oh,' Emma said, and stared down at her hands miserably.

'So Paul told you he was married. I suppose he also promised to get a divorce.'

'He said he'd sort it all out after the war,' Emma whispered, conscious of the venom in Frank's voice.

She fell silent and Frank went on furiously, 'Did he tell you he's married to the daughter of one of the most prominent men in Australian politics and that her mother is from one of Sydney's first families?'

'No, he never discussed his wife.'

'*I bet he didn't!* I bet he didn't tell you he had a child either.'

Emma gaped at Frank, her lip trembling. 'A child!'

'Yes. A boy. I gather he refrained from passing on that piece of vital information.'

'He did,' Emma confessed, her heart sinking. A wife he was estranged from she might have been able to compete with, but she could not fight a child. A son. Men as wealthy as Paul McGill pinned all of their hopes on the new generation, on the heir to the dynasty. He would never give up his son for her.

'I need a drink,' Frank said, standing up. 'And so do you, by the looks of you.' He poured a glass of champagne for Emma and a brandy for himself, observing his sister closely. By God, she *is* a strong woman, he thought admiringly. He knew she was shocked and distressed, but she was in full control of herself. He said, 'I'm so sorry I had to hurt you, love, but you had to know.'

'I'm glad you told me, Frank.' She laughed bitterly. 'You certainly gave Dolly a grilling, didn't you?'

'You'd be surprised what a woman will confide in her lover, especially in the intimacy of the bedroom.'

'You and Dolly! Frank, I don't believe it!' she cried incredulously.

'Yes, for the moment anyhow.'

'But she's years older than you.'

'Ten to be exact. However, I don't think my relationship with Dolly is the issue right now, is it?'

'No, it's not.' Emma leaned forward intently. 'How does she know so much about the McGills?'

'She used to be Bruce McGill's mistress several years ago.'

'Philandering seems to be a family characteristic!' Emma exclaimed contemptuously. 'What else did she tell you? I might as well know all the details.'

'Not much, really. Mostly Dolly talked about their wealth and their power. Actually, she didn't seem to have much information about Paul's wife or his son. In fact, I rather got the impression there was a bit of a mystery about the wife. Dolly said something about Paul always appearing alone in public, even in Sydney before the war, and she indicated that he is a –' Frank stopped short, and looked down at his drink.

'*A what?*'

Frank cleared his throat. 'Well, if you must know, Dolly implied he is a womanizer.'

'I'm not surprised, Frank. Don't be upset you told me.'

Frank tossed down the brandy. 'I'm not upset. I'm just angry that you have been hurt.' He rose and crossed to the console, returning with the bottles of cognac and champagne. He filled Emma's empty glass and said, 'I always liked Paul. I didn't think he was such a bastard. Just goes to show you how wrong one can be in life. Why don't you tell me about it, Emma? It sometimes helps to unburden yourself.'

Emma smiled grimly. 'I doubt it. But I'll tell you anything you want to know, Frank. Perhaps *you* can explain his behaviour to me.'

As Emma confided in Frank she slowly drank the whole bottle of champagne and for the first time in her life she deliberately got drunk. When Winston appeared in the doorway an hour later he stared at her in surprise. 'You're three sheets to the wind, Emma!' he cried, moving with unusual swiftness across the floor.

Emma lifted the glass and waved it in the air, spilling half of the champagne. 'Splishe the brashemain. I mean splishe the mainbrashe,' she slurred, and hiccuped.

'How could you let her get so pie-eyed, Frank!' Winston exploded in an accusatory tone. He regarded Emma reclining languorously on the sofa, her eyes half closed, her mouth twitching with silent laughter. 'She'll have some head tomorrow,' he muttered crossly.

'So what? Don't be so harsh, Winston,' Frank said quietly. 'For once in her life I think she really needed to let her hair down.'

FORTY-NINE

Edwin Fairley's face was grim and there was a cold anger in his eyes as he said, 'You put the noose around your neck all by yourself, Gerald. There is absolutely nothing I can do to help you.'

Gerald gaped at his brother in stupefaction. His sly black eyes, narrowing in the bloated face, appeared smaller and more evil than ever. 'Are you telling me that Procter and Procter are really within their legal rights? That they can take over the mills just like that?' he asked fearfully.

'Yes, I'm afraid I am, Gerald. A noncontestable note is just that – noncontestable. And since you attached the deeds as collateral you don't have a leg to stand on if you can't pay off the note. That was most foolhardy. Why did you do it?'

'I needed the money,' Gerald muttered, unable to meet Edwin's direct stare.

'To pay off your blasted gambling debts! I *know* that. I mean, why did you hand over the deeds to the mills without seeking legal advice first? If not from me, at least from the family solicitor.'

'There would have been no point to that. I needed the money desperately. I had nowhere else to go and those were the only terms acceptable to Procter and Procter. My talking to the family solicitor wouldn't have changed *their* minds. I had no option, and anyway I thought Alan would be reasonable. Give me time to repay the loan.' A bitter look slid on to Gerald's face. 'As it is, Alan Procter has turned on me. He's a bloody thief! He's stolen my mills!'

'Don't be ridiculous, Gerald,' Edwin countered impatiently, staggered at his brother's lack of business acumen. 'Alan hasn't stolen the mills. You handed them to him on a plate. I'm appalled by your lack of foresight. Furthermore, from what you have just told me, Alan has been very understanding. The note was for six months. It's been extended three times, for an additional period of eight months all together. I would say he has been exceptionally considerate under the circumstances. After all, it was a company loan. Alan has a board of directors to answer to.'

Gerald dropped his head in his hands, overcome as always by self-pity. After a few minutes he looked up and said in a demanding voice, 'You have to lend me the money, Edwin.'

Edwin sat bolt upright on the Chesterfield and stared at Gerald in amazement. 'Are you joking! I don't have two hundred thousand pounds, plus the interest due. You must be mad to think I do.'

'Father left you a trust, Edwin. You *must* have it. You don't want to help me out of a jam,' Gerald whined.

'The income from my trust is meagre and you know it!' Edwin cried, infuriated. 'Father lived lavishly all of his life and spent lavishly, particularly after he married Aunt Olivia. What he left me was negligible compared to what you received, and you've thrown most of it down the drain.' Edwin glared at Gerald with disdain.

He then said, 'Besides, as little as it is, I need the income from the trust. *I* have a wife and son to provide for and a household to maintain.'

'But you're doing well in your law practice –'

'Yes, but not well enough to support your bad habits!' Edwin snapped peremptorily.

'Father left you the majority of his shares in the *Yorkshire Morning Gazette*. You could borrow against them.' Gerald said, scowling at his brother.

'I could, but I have no intentions of doing so. I promised Father I would hold on to them and take an active interest in the newspaper and I will not renege on my promise,' Edwin responded with firmness. 'I can't understand how you could get yourself into such a predicament –'

'Don't start giving me another bloody lecture!' Gerald shouted, lumbering out of the chair. He began to pace up and down the library, his cringing fear palpable.

He is a coward and a fool, Edwin thought, scrutinizing his brother. Gerald's gluttony had only increased over the years and he was now elephantine and gross in his ugliness, and the dissipation of his life was revealed on his ravaged face. To Edwin, Gerald appeared obscene and he looked away in revulsion.

Gerald plodded over to the black-walnut chest and poured himself a large neat whiskey. 'I don't suppose you want a drink, do you?' he mumbled without looking around.

'No, thank you,' Edwin snapped. 'I have to be going.'

Seating himself opposite Edwin, Gerald pinned his crafty eyes on him. 'You believe yourself to be the brain in the family, so you tell me what to do, brother,' he said scornfully.

'Listen to me, Gerald. Things could be worse for you. After all, you still own the mill here in Fairley and the brickyard. I suggest you tighten your belt, cut down on personal expenditures, stop gambling, and retrench in every way. Devote your attention to the one mill you still have. I don't know much about the woollen business, but only a fool could fail to realize the cloth trade is booming. Actually, I don't understand why the Fairley mill isn't going better. Surely you can turn it around.'

Always full of self-justification, Gerald countered in a defensive tone, 'Things are different than they were in Father's day. You don't know the burdens I have to carry. There's a hell of a lot more competition now, Edwin. Thompson's makes the same cloth as us and they've swiped many of my customers of late. So has your bloody Emma Harte. She owns Layton's mill, in case you didn't know, and she's giving me a run for my money as well. If the truth be known, she helped to ruin me. My problems started when she stole Ben Andrews and some of the best workers away from Thompson's in 1914.' Gerald's voice echoed with invective as he declared, 'Yes, your bloody whore has been a thorn in my side for a long time. The bloody little whoring bitch. She's –'

'Don't let me hear you call Emma a whore ever again! Do you hear me, you filthy bastard!' Edwin cried, clenching his hands and leaning forward threateningly. His face had whitened and his eyes blazed.

Gerald grinned derisively. 'Still carrying the torch for the servant girl, eh, Edwin? Whatever would the Lady Jane say if she knew you had an itch in your crotch for that bit of working-class –'

'That's enough, you rotten swine!' Edwin shouted, springing up. It took all of his self-control to restrain himself from hitting Gerald in the face. 'I drove over to Fairley with the best of intentions, hoping to help you with legal advice. I did not come to listen to your obscenities about Emma,' he said furiously. He glowered at Gerald and his contempt was so clearly written on his face Gerald shrank back in the chair. Edwin went on, 'I happen to be very proud of Emma. She's made something of herself and she's a damned sight better than you. You – you – piece of scum!' Edwin stepped away from his brother abruptly, conscious that he was prepared to inflict bodily damage on him if further provoked. 'Goodbye. You won't be seeing me for a long time.'

Gerald taunted, 'You're too transparent, Edwin. So Emma Harte's in your blood, is she? My, my, my! She must have something sweet between *her* legs to hold your interest all these years. Tried to make it with her myself once when I found her living in Armley –'.

'You did what!' Edwin, who was halfway to the door, spun around and shot across the library. He leapt at Gerald, clutched his lapels, and shook him fiercely, his rage exploding. 'If you so much as rest your eyes on Emma I will kill you! Kill you! I swear to God I will!' Edwin's face, so close to his brother's, was twisted with a mixture of loathing and deadly intent, and this registered forcibly with Gerald, who flinched, suddenly afraid.

Edwin let go of Gerald's lapels and wiped his hands on his trouser legs with the utmost distaste, his lip curling. 'I don't want to soil myself by touching you,' he hissed. '*You are a foul specimen of humanity! You are contemptible!*' He turned on his heel and walked out, his limbs shaking, his head spinning with unbridled hatred and disgust.

FIFTY

Emma stepped out of her shoes, took off the tailored black dress she always wore at the store, removed her jewellery, and placed it all on the dressing table. Discarding her underwear, she slipped into the silk robe the maid had put out for her and hurried into her bathroom.

As she stood in front of the oval gilt-framed mirror tying a chiffon scarf around her recently bobbed hair, she smiled as she always did when she entered this particular room in her new mansion. It was too opulent by far, and when Blackie had shown her the original plans for its remodelling she had told him it looked like a cross between the Hall of Mirrors at Versailles and a courtesan's boudoir. Not that she had ever seen anything like the latter – only the former, when she and Arthur Ainsley had gone to Paris on their honeymoon three years before. Over her mild protestations that it was excessively grand, Blackie had insisted on executing the design intact, exhorting her to trust his judgement. To her amazement, she had actually liked the bathroom when he had finally completed the overall décor, deriving a certain sensuous satisfaction from its luxurious appointments.

The walls were lined with shell-pink marble, intersected with wide panels of mirror running from the floor to the ceiling for an infinity of reflections. The domed ceiling was a pale turquoise blue across which cavorted pink dolphins and sea urchins intertwined with delicate green tendrils of seaweed and vivid pink and mauve sea anemones. The turquoise oval tub was sunk into the pink marble floor and two leaping silver dolphins, each one foot in height, stood sentinel at the top and bottom, and the taps were miniature silver dolphins. On a narrow mirrored console table reposed innumerable bottles of French perfumes and Floris bath oils and silver-topped crystal pots for her creams and lotions. Blackie had also included a chaise-longue upholstered in rose silk at one end, along with a mirror-and-glass Art Deco coffee table. At the other side of the chaise a huge garden basket painted pink overflowed with all the latest fashion and illustrated magazines and financial journals. The ambiance was feminine, and this one room in the house had become Emma's haven, a place of repose where she could retreat to unwind after her busy days at the store.

Emma poured Floris gardenia bath oil into the water the maid had already drawn and, removing her robe, she stepped into the tub. She stretched out her long legs, luxuriating in the heavily scented water, her thoughts turning to the supper dance she was giving that evening. Since her marriage to Arthur they had entertained on an increasingly lavish scale, yet this was undoubtedly the most elaborate social event she had planned to date and she was looking forward to it. The dance was to celebrate Frank's engagement to Natalie Stewart, the daughter of a prominent London politician, a match Emma had approved of from the beginning and which she had enthusiastically helped to foster. Apart from the fact that Natalie was a lovely young woman, Emma had been relieved to see her brother released from Dolly Mosten's clutches. Natalie was a lady to the manner born, and if her exquisite blonde beauty seemed somewhat delicate, Emma knew it belied a stalwart heart and a backbone of steel. Increasingly she reminded Emma of her beloved Laura.

Emma had spared no expense on the dance, determined to do justice to Frank's engagement. The house looked magnificent, each one of the spacious reception rooms resplendent with fine antiques and paintings, filled with colour and banked with masses of spring flowers. Since the elegant mansion was three times as large as the house she had formerly owned in Armley, it lent itself to entertaining in the grand manner and Emma had become a charming hostess whose spontaneous grace put her guests at ease.

The catering department of Harte's had provided a superb supper and the dishes had been arranged on a long buffet table in the formal dining room. Emma considered the menu she had chosen. There were two soups, jellied consommé and cream of watercress served in cups, salmon mousse, smoked salmon with capers and lemon wedges, lobster patties, mayonnaise of turbot, beef Wellington, turban of chicken and tongue, quenelles of pheasant, roasted spring lamb with mint sauce, tomatoes à la tartare, French beans, and pomme soufflé. The desserts were baba au rhum, compote of fruit, trifle, parfait, apricot snow, and almond cake, and there was an assortment of drinks, including champagne, claret cup, white and red wines, cider, fruit juices, coffee, and tea. The selection was wide enough to appeal to the most discerning or pernickety of palates, Emma decided, and made a mental note to congratulate the chefs at Harte's, who had surpassed themselves for the occasion.

The one hundred guests would dine at small tables covered with pink cloths and partnered with gold chairs, which had been arranged in the dining room, the library, and the morning room. After supper there would be dancing in the long marble gallery overlooking the gardens, and those who did not wish to dance could enjoy conversation in the two lovely drawing rooms. The band engaged for the evening had already arrived and when she left the gallery the musicians were setting out their instruments. Faintly, wafting up on the night air, came the strains of a popular song as the band warmed up. Everything was in hand. Nothing had escaped her, and there was a small army of waiters and maids, plus her own staff, to look after the guests. Arthur had told her earlier that she had organized everything with the efficiency of a general planning war manoeuvres. Emma closed her eyes, feeling languorous as the tensions of the day slipped away.

Meanwhile, in the adjoining suite of rooms, Arthur Ainsley dressed for the evening, as preoccupied with the details of his appearance as Emma was with the plans for the dance. He stepped back from the cheval mirror and regarded his reflection with immense concentration, well pleased with what he saw.

At thirty-two Arthur still carried the air of a juvenile lead, this impression further emphasized by his dandified dress and elegant mannerisms that often bordered on the effeminate. He shot his cuffs below his jacket sleeves, adjusted the black-onyx-and-diamond dress studs on his shirt, and reached for the comb on the nearby commode. For the fourth time he ran it through his soft blond hair, patted the waves precisely into place, and smoothed one manicured finger over the neat blond moustache he favoured. He then put down the comb and drew himself up to his full height, raptly absorbed with his image.

Regrettably, Arthur Ainsley did not have much to recommend him in his character. All of his life he had been so concerned about his exterior beauty he had made no effort to acquire any inner resources. Consequently, he was a shell of a man, and his very shallowness caused him to put store only on what was readily visible. Not unintelligent, educated at the best schools, Arthur was, however, so indolent and self-involved he was utterly unable to retain any serious thoughts for very long. He was cursed with a singleminded concern for pleasure, and his perpetual need for instant gratification was infantile in nature. Thus, although he loved the outward manifestations of wealth and success, he did not have the ability to acquire them for himself, being averse to hard work, lacking in diligence, and without the power of concentration.

Arthur moved away from the mirror, glancing at his platinum-and-diamond pocket watch. He had dressed too early and now he had an hour to waste before the guests were due to arrive at ten o'clock. He reached into one of the drawers of the commode and took out a bottle of brandy. He started to pour himself a drink and then hesitated, grimacing at the thought of Emma's disapproval.

Arthur Ainsley had been seeking refuge in the bottle for the past eighteen months, ever since he had discovered he was impotent with Emma. He believed he drank because of his impotency but, in point of fact, he drank to excuse it. It was so much easier to blame the liquor than face the real reasons for his inadequacy, which were highly complicated. Critical self-examination was alien to Arthur's vainglorious nature and so he was uncomprehending of the causes. In truth, he had become impotent with Emma because he was a latent homosexual and also because his wife was everything he was not.

Emma had done nothing at all to emasculate him. Simply by being herself she had caused him to suffer damage to his self-esteem. Thus, he now sought out women who bolstered his male pride. Chiefly his targets were shopgirls, waitresses, and barmaids, who, flattered by his attentions, fawned over him.

Arthur's feelings about Emma were continually vacillating. He frequently desired her, yet his constant fear of sexual failure isolated him from her; he needed her strength and her wisdom, whilst resenting these attributes; he boasted of her achievements but was envious and insecure because he did not measure up in his own career. In his way, Arthur loved Emma. Unhappily, he also harboured many grudges against her, at the root of which was his terrible sense of powerlessness. This manifested itself in repressed rage, and sometimes he actually experienced a real hatred for her.

Always drawn to Emma during her marriage to Joe Lowther, he had pursued her unavailingly for months after his return from the war. Then unexpectedly, at Blackie O'Neill's on Boxing Day night of 1919, she had seemed to thaw towards him and, being exceedingly opportunistic, Arthur had pressed his suit with a rare show of determination in the new year, egged on by his ambitious parents. After a whirlwind courtship of three months they had been married in the spring of 1920.

Arthur had believed that Emma was as smitten with him as he was with her, his vanity not permitting him to think otherwise. In all truth, Emma had married him for wholly different reasons. The terrible implications of Paul McGill's silence and continuing absence from England had devastated her and her anguish had become too painful to bear. Her increasing loneliness had prompted her to reassess her life. Plain common sense had led her to conclude that there was no future for her with Paul, and she acknowledged that to yearn for him was not only foolish but inevitably self-destructive. She tried to put Paul out of her mind completely, deciding that she must lead a more normal life for her children's sake as well as her own. Convinced that she would never again experience the same kind of sublime love she had had with Paul, she sought instead a companion, a man who was easy to be with. She also wanted a father for her children and a suitable male head for her household. In short, she was prepared to compromise, to settle for less out of necessity and in the belief that great love was not always a prerequisite for a happy marriage.

At first amused by Arthur's most transparent and eager overtures, Emma had come to view him as the perfect solution to her problems. He was a gentleman and came from a good family. He also had charm and handled himself with a degree of elegance in all situations. He was amusing, attentive to her needs, and enamoured with her. Furthermore, Emma liked beauty and had strong aesthetic instincts, and she found Arthur attractive. If he aroused no great passion in her, he likewise did not repulse her, and she had decided she could easily tolerate the physical aspects married love entailed, concluding that other factors in their relationship were of more vital consideration to her. Emma knew Arthur was weak, yet curiously she turned a blind eye to faults in his character for several fundamental reasons: Arthur did not threaten her; she recognized that he would never interfere with her business or the manner in which she led her life; she instinctively knew that she would always retain the upper hand. These reasons aside, he had a winning way with her children and treated them with a naturalness she appreciated.

Emma wanted to obliterate Paul McGill by involving herself in a new relationship. She was determined to marry quickly, and Arthur appeared to be the most suitable candidate on the horizon. Expedient by nature, she plunged ahead, seeking action and commitment in preference to waiting. Her unprecedented imprudence stunned her brothers and Blackie, who met such icy imperiousness when they tried to interfere they immediately retreated, recognizing it was fruitless to offer advice once she had made up her stubborn mind.

Ruefully Emma acknowledged her error after only a few weeks of marriage, but by then it was too late. She had conceived on their honeymoon. It had not taken her long to discover that Arthur's charm was meretricious, and his wit often as cruel as it was entertaining. He was captious, and his shallowness and indolence appalled her. Also, his sexual appetite was as voracious as Joe Lowther's had been, although Arthur displayed more finesse and he did not induce physical revulsion in her. Nonetheless, Emma soon found their love-making burdensome because it was only Paul she loved and desired.

But she was honest enough to admit that she had made the mistake, and because she took her obligations seriously, Emma endeavoured to maintain a civilized front and simulated passion whenever necessary. In the beginning the union was relatively tranquil, mostly due to Emma's expert dissembling. Arthur, unaware of her feelings, was euphoric at his good fortune in winning this beautiful, accomplished young woman, and he basked in Emma's prestige and enjoyed the privileges that came with her money. He was, for the most part, considerate and acquiescent. Unhappily, after the twins, Robin and Elizabeth, were born in 1921 he grew careless and offhand with Emma, confident that his marriage was secure now that he had fathered two children by her, and convinced of her devotion to him.

During Emma's confinement, Arthur had taken to amorous adventuring, and having acquired a taste for the excitement inherent in illicit relationships, he found them increasingly impossible to forgo. Then when he and Emma resumed their marital intimacy, he was unable to fire up his ardour sufficiently for effective consummation. After several disastrous experiences Arthur had retreated into his own room. To his relief Emma never questioned his absence from her bed. In his vanity he ascribed this to her preoccupation with her business, the children, the demands of a large household, and her nervousness about becoming pregnant again so soon after the birth of the twins. It never occurred to him that she loved another man, and as the months passed his complacency increased, as did his arrogance.

As Arthur contemplated his appearance, Emma climbed out of the bath and dried herself briskly. She stood for a moment in front of one of the mirrored panels, gazing at her body with detached interest. Her full breasts were high and firm, her thighs gently rounded, her stomach flat. She had kept her figure; considering she would be thirty-four next month, and had borne four children, she looked amazingly youthful. There was nothing matronly about her shape, thanks to her busy schedule and her singular distaste for rich foods that sprang from the deprivations of her spartan childhood. Turning away, she put on the silk robe and padded into the bedroom.

Seating herself at the dressing table, Emma picked up a silver monogrammed hairbrush, her head held on one side. She was delighted she had decided to cut off all her hair last week. She liked this new bob that was all the rage. The style suited her and was absolutely perfect with her new haute couture clothes from Vionnet and Chanel. There was a sudden loud knock and Emma swung around as Arthur strode in. Emma stared at her husband, surprised by his unexpected appearance. She pulled the robe around her swiftly and suppressed a stab of impatience, resenting the intrusion. She was finding it increasingly difficult to maintain a cordial front with him these days.

'Really, Arthur, you quite startled me.'

'Did I just!'

Emma's eyes lighted on the drink in his hand. 'You're starting a bit early, aren't you?' she said, striving to hide her annoyance.

'For God's sake, don't start that again!' he cried, walking over to the yellow velvet sofa. He draped himself on it and threw her a scathing look. 'You can be such a crashing bore, my dear. A real kill joy, as a matter of fact.'

Emma sighed, recognizing his mood. 'We are facing a long evening, Arthur. I don't want you to –'

'Get drunk and disgrace you, my pet,' Arthur interjected. 'Emma must never be upset. God forbid that should happen,' he snapped with a flash of arrogance. 'What am I supposed to do all evening? Tread in the Queen's shadow?'

Ignoring the jibe, Emma turned to the dressing table and picked up a bottle of Guerlain's L'Heure Bleu. She dabbed the crystal stopper behind her ears and, not wanting to provoke a quarrel, she changed the subject. 'I had a sweet letter from Kit today. He sends his love. He's enjoying school. I'm so glad I sent him to Rugby. He's in his element.'

'Yes, that was a good idea of *mine*, wasn't it?' Arthur smirked. 'I do have quite a lot of them, you know, if only you would give me half a chance. Instead you treat me like an idiot.'

After a moment's silence, Emma said, 'I have to finish dressing. Did you come in for something in particular, Arthur?'

'Oh yes, I did, by Jove!' Arthur answered, looking up. 'I thought I had better glance at the guest list. Refresh my memory.'

'It's on my desk.' Emma shifted in the chair and took a pair of superb teardrop diamond earrings out of a jewel case and screwed them on absently.

'Rather a distinguished crowd we're having,' Arthur remarked, scanning the list and noting the names of a number of beautiful and possibly acquiescent ladies amongst the guests. Wanting suddenly to make his escape, he threw the list on the desk and edged to the door. 'I think I'll go downstairs and take a look around.' He pulled out his watch. 'It's nine-thirty. I'll leave you now so that you can dress.'

'Thank you. I would appreciate that.' Emma watched him saunter out. She shook her head, pondering on Arthur. If he was a fool, then she was surely a monumental fool. This mess was all her fault. How curious it was that she never made the same mistake twice in business, yet continually repeated them in her personal life. Loving David Kallinski, she had deliberately married Joe ... loving Paul McGill, she had plunged into matrimony with Arthur. But the circumstances were different, she told herself. David had been forbidden to her because of the Orthodoxy of his mother. Paul had abandoned her because he did not want her. Still, it seemed that she had a penchant for picking the wrong men as husbands. Joe was decent, though, she mused, whereas Arthur is worthless. 'Marry in haste, repent at leisure,' she said, remembering her brother's words of warning. Damn my stubbornness, she muttered.

Emma stood up purposefully. She could not dwell on this disastrous marriage tonight. She would think about it later. Tomorrow. She hurried to finish dressing and stood staring at herself in the mirror of the armoire. Her gown was a long slender sheath of turquoise silk encrusted with thousands of tiny bugle beads in shades of pale blue and emerald green. When she moved, however slightly, it undulated and changed colour in the way a summer sea ripples from blue to green to aquamarine. The gown emphasized her svelte figure and brought out the colour of her incomparable eyes. With her diamonds and pearls she was the epitome of elegance. If outward appearances counted for aught, then apparently she had everything. A handsome husband, lovely children, good looks, wealth and power. The world envied her.

The carriage clock on the mantelshelf chimed ten and roused Emma from her reflections. She left her bedroom and stood poised at the top of the curving staircase for a brief moment. And then she picked up one side of her skirt and swept down to greet the first of her guests, who were just arriving. Her famous smile was intact, but her heart was covered with a layer of frost.

FIFTY-ONE

The butler who opened the door of Fairley Hall was a middle-aged man they did not know.

Blackie said, 'Good afternoon. My name is O'Neill. I have an appointment with Mr Gerald Fairley.'

'The Squire's expecting you, sir,' the butler replied, opening the door wider. 'Please come this way.' He led them across the huge gloomy entrance hall and showed them into the library. 'He will be with you in a moment. Please make yourselves comfortable.' He bowed and retreated.

When the door had closed Blackie said, 'Murgatroyd must have retired.'

'He's dead,' Emma said. 'He died two years ago.'

'And Cook?' Blackie asked, remembering Elsie Turner with fondness.

'She's still alive. But she doesn't work here anymore. She's too old. She lives in the village.'

Blackie strolled over to the fireplace and stood with his back to the flames, warming himself. 'Well, how does it feel – being back in this house after all these years?'

Emma threw him a swift glance. 'Rather strange, I must admit.' Her cool green gaze swept around the room and she laughed mirthlessly. 'Do you know how many times I dusted this panelling, beat these carpets, and polished this furniture?' She shook her head wonderingly, and her mouth unconsciously tightened into a grim line.

'So many times I expect you've forgotten by now,' Blackie said.

'I never forget anything,' Emma replied crisply.

She walked slowly around the library, regarding the furnishings with interest. She had once thought this room so impressive, but in comparison to the library in her house in Roundhay it looked dreary and there was an unmistakable air of dejection about it. April sunshine was flooding in through the tall windows and the bright light focused attention on the overall shabbiness. The Persian carpets were threadbare, their once vibrant red-and-blue jewel tones dimmed by time, and the velvet draperies at the windows were faded, the upholstery on the wing chairs badly worn. Even the ruby-coloured chesterfield was dark and muddy, and the leather was cracked. Emma recognized that the antiques were fine and obviously of value, as were the many leather-bound books and hunting prints, but withal the room's dreadful neglect was patently obvious.

Emma shrugged and glided over to a window to look out. In the distance the wild implacable moors soared up before her eyes, a grim black line undulating beneath a clear spring sky, a sky the colour of her mother's eyes. She had a sudden longing to go up to the moors, to climb that familiar path through the Baptist Field that led to Ramsden Crags and the Top of the World. The place her mother had loved the most, up there where the air was cool and bracing and filled with pale lavender tints and misty pinks and greys. That was not possible today. Innumerable memories assailed her, dragging her back into the past. She closed her eyes, and heard the sweet trilling of the larks, could almost smell the scent of the heather after rain, could feel the bracken brushing against her bare legs and the cool wind caressing her face . . .

From his position at the fireplace Blackie scrutinized Emma, held in the grips of his own memories. He thought of the day he had first met her, so long ago now. This imperious and distinguished woman standing before him bore no resemblance to his poverty-stricken colleen of the moors. He shook his head, marvelling at her and all she had become. At thirty-four, Emma Harte Ainsley was undoubtedly at the height of her beauty, a beauty so staggering it startled and bewitched everyone. Today she wore an expensive and fashionable silver-grey wool-crêpe suit trimmed with sable and a smart sable hat. His emerald brooch gleamed on the collar of her grey silk blouse, matchless pearls cascaded from her slender neck, and the magnificent emerald earrings were just visible below her stylishly bobbed hair. She was not only elegant but cultivated and self-assured and she exuded an aura that bespoke undeniable power.

Emma swung around unexpectedly and was immediately aware of Blackie's eyes resting on her with such intensity. She laughed lightly. 'Why are you staring at me? Is my slip showing?'

Blackie grinned. 'No, I'm just admiring you, me darlin'. Just admiring you. And also remembering – so many things.'

'Yes,' Emma said slowly, a thoughtful look drifting on to her face. 'This place does evoke all kinds of memories, doesn't it?' She smiled faintly, stepped to the desk in the corner, and placed her suede bag on it.

'Aye, it does.' Blackie lit a cigarette, drew on it, and shifted his stance. 'Fairley's taking his sweet time. I wonder what he's trying to prove.'

'Oh, who cares.' Emma shrugged. 'Anyway, we're not in a hurry.' She sat down at the desk, the desk which had once been Adam Fairley's, and leaned back in the chair. She pulled off her grey suede gloves slowly, smiling to herself. She examined her hands. Small strong hands and certainly not the most beautiful in the world. But they were white and soft and the nails were polished to a soft pink sheen. They were no longer red and chapped from scrubbing and scouring and polishing . . . no longer the hands of the skivvy who had been in bondage in this grim house.

The door flew open and Gerald Fairley entered, dragging his great weight, his steps lumbering. He did not see Emma, who was in the shadows, and he hurried over to Blackie, his hand outstretched.

'Good afternoon, Mr O'Neill.' He looked Blackie over with unconcealed interest. 'I thought your name was familiar when you made the appointment. Now I remember you. Surely you used to do repairs here when I was a boy.'

'That's correct,' Blackie said, stepping forward and shaking Gerald's hand. 'Pleased to meet you again, Mr Fairley.' Not having set eyes on Gerald for many years, Blackie was astounded at the man's hippopotamic body, his ruined face, and his apparent dissipation. Gerald was so physically repugnant Blackie shuddered with distaste.

'Never forget a face,' Gerald went on. 'Now, may I offer you a drink before we get down to business?'

'No, thank you,' Blackie declined politely.

'I need a brandy myself. Always do after lunch.' Gerald plodded over to the black-walnut chest and poured himself a generous measure of cognac. As he turned around, glass in hand, he spotted Emma seated at the desk. His porcine eyes opened wide and a look of disbelief spread itself across his blubbery face. 'What the hell are *you* doing here?' he bellowed.

'I am with Mr O'Neill,' Emma responded softly. Her face was without expression.

'*You* bloody well know how to make yourself at home, don't you!' Gerald exploded, still incredulous. 'How dare you take such a liberty! Sitting at my desk!'

'I believe it is my desk now,' Emma said in the softest voice, her eyes fixed unwaveringly on Gerald.

'Your desk! What the hell are you talking about?' Gerald stamped into the middle of the room and swung to face Blackie, his manner bellicose. 'What does she mean, O'Neill? What is the explanation for all this! I sold Fairley Hall to Deerfield Estates. You yourself told me on the telephone that you represented them, and had been engaged to do the renovations. So why in God's name is *that* woman in my house? You had no right to bring *her* here.' He did not wait for Blackie's answer, but heaved his monstrous body to face Emma. 'Get out! Get out!' he yelled. 'Get out, do you hear me! I will not tolerate your presence at this private meeting.'

Emma remained perfectly still. Not even an eyelash flickered. She smiled darkly. 'I have no intentions of leaving. And I do have every right to be here, *Mr Fairley*,' she pronounced with cold disdain. 'You see, *I am Deerfield Estates*.'

For a moment Emma's words did not sink into Gerald's befuddled mind. He continued to glare at her uncomprehendingly, and then, as if a veil had been miraculously lifted, he stuttered, 'Y-y-y-you are Deerfield Estates –'

'I am indeed.' Emma opened her purse and took out a piece of paper. She gave it a cursory glance and looked across at Gerald. 'Yes, this desk *is* listed on the inventory, just as I thought. I purchased it along with some of the other contents. And, since you have already cashed the cheque from Deerfield Estates, this is *my* desk, as this is undoubtedly *my* house. I have paid for them.'

Reeling, Gerald fell into one of the wing chairs. What had she said? That she was the owner of Fairley Hall? Emma Harte, the servant girl they had once employed! Never, not in a thousand years! The idea was unthinkable, outrageous. Gerald's eyes swivelled to Blackie, standing calmly at the fireplace, his hands in his pockets, a faint amused smile playing on his mouth.

'Is it true?' Gerald asked, his voice unsure. 'Is she telling the truth?'

'Yes, she is,' Blackie replied, endeavouring to keep his face straight. By God, he would not have missed this scene for the world.

'Why didn't you tell me she was coming with you when you made the appointment?' Gerald now demanded in an accusatory tone.

'It was not my prerogative to do so,' Blackie said, taking out his cigarette case.

Gerald stared at the drink in his hand, all manner of vindictive thoughts flashing through his addled brain. Good Christ, if he had known this little tramp was connected with Deerfield Estates he would not have sold the house to them. He must cancel the sale at once. Yes, that was undoubtedly the right thing to do. And then sickeningly he recalled her words of a moment ago. He *had* cashed the cheque and spent all the money. He had used it to pay off some of his gambling debts. He was trapped. He lifted his shaking hand and tossed down the drink in one gulp.

Emma flashed a glance at Blackie and her green eyes below the curving golden brows sparkled. She rose and walked sedately over to the chesterfield. She sat down, gracefully crossed her legs, and studied Gerald. 'Under the terms of the sales contract you should have vacated this house by now,' she said in a light, clear voice. 'I will give you one more week to do so.'

Gerald blinked and shook his head so vigorously his chins wobbled. 'That's not long enough,' he whined. 'You've got to give me more time.'

'One week,' Emma repeated. She paused and her gleaming eyes narrowed. 'Furthermore, I must insist you remove all of your personal belongings from your office at the Fairley mill immediately. Today. By five o'clock, in fact. Otherwise they will be packed in cardboard boxes and deposited in the mill yard to be retrieved by you at your convenience. By five o'clock today.'

Gerald was jolted upright in the wing chair, and he stared at Emma thunderstruck. He opened his mouth to speak but no words came out, so undone was he. He sat gaping stupidly, paralysed by his spiralling fear.

Emma continued icily, 'I am not wrong in thinking you sold the Fairley mill two weeks ago, am I? To the General Retail Trading Company.'

'What's that got to do with you?' Gerald spluttered, rousing himself. He was obviously perplexed as he added, 'General Retail Trading is a division of Procter and Procter, which is owned by my friend Alan Procter.'

'I am well aware of General Retail Trading's connection with Procter and Procter,' Emma said. 'However, you are slightly misinformed. Procter and Procter is, in turn, a subsidiary of the Emeremm Company. It does not belong to Alan Procter. It has not belonged to him for some years. He is merely an employee of the parent company.' She sat back, watching him.

'Alan Procter never mentioned that to me,' Gerald muttered. A most terrible and unacceptable thought now entered his swimming head. He asked haltingly, 'Who owns the Emeremm Company?'

'I do,' Emma said, smiling thinly and enjoying the expression on Gerald's face. 'Consequently, I control Procter and Procter and the General Retail Trading Company, as well as Deerfield Estates.' She leaned forward, clasping her hands together. 'Therefore, I now own all of your mills, as well as Fairley Hall.'

'You!' Gerald screamed, half rising. 'It was you!' He fell back into the chair, seized by an uncontrollable shaking, and then he experienced a stab of pain in his chest, one so acute it knocked the breath out of him. He clutched his chest and the shaking increased. He thought he might be having a seizure. Suddenly the reality of her revelations overwhelmed him and with dawning horror he recognized the ghastly truth. Emma Harte now possessed all that had been his. Most of the Fairley enterprises were in her hands. And so was his family home. His ancestral home. She had smashed his life. All he had left were a few shares in the *Yorkshire Morning Gazette* and the brickyard, neither of which he gave a damn about. He shuddered and dropped his head into his hands.

Blackie gazed dispassionately at Gerald. He saw a devastated and broken man and yet Blackie felt no sympathy for him. He turned and glanced at Emma, who sat poised and calm on the sofa, in command of herself and the situation, and then he sucked in his breath. Her beautiful face was a bronze mask, her eyes as deadly as steel, and his hackles rose. There was power and stealth in this room, and a ruthlessness so tangible the air seemed to vibrate with it. And it emanated solely from Emma. Blackie swallowed and looked away, finally truly understanding what a force she was to be reckoned with.

Gerald lifted his head slowly and glared at Emma venomously. 'You conniving bloody bitch!' he hissed from between clenched teeth. 'You have been behind all the dreadful things that have happened to me. Why, you deliberately set out to steal my mills. You ruined me!'

Emma laughed sardonically and for the first time that day her virulent loathing for Gerald was fully revealed. 'Did you think I made an idle threat that day, thirteen years ago, when you tried to rape me? I will never forget that day. And now, neither will you. It will haunt you as long as you live, Gerald Fairley.' She gave him a curious icy smile. 'Yes, I set out to ruin you, as I vowed I would when you forced your way into my house and attacked me. But you were my willing ally. You made it very easy for me. If the truth be known, you really ruined yourself. I simply helped you along the way.'

Gerald's monumental fury and humiliation pushed aside all reason. He stood up unsteadily. He wanted to put his hands around her neck and squeeze and squeeze until she had no life left in her. He *must* destroy her. He stepped towards Emma, his hatred blazing, his eyes bulging in his twisted face. He raised his hand as if to strike her.

Blackie, astonished and enraged by what he had just heard, moved with swiftness, catching Gerald's arm as it came down, neatly deflecting the blow. Although Gerald was huge, he was weak and his weight was cumbersome, and so he was no match for Blackie's strength and speed. Blackie spun Gerald around roughly and grabbed him with both hands, pinning his arms to his sides. He increased his vice-like grip and forced Gerald down into the chair.

'Don't try that again, Fairley!' Blackie cried, anger suffusing his face with dark colour. 'If you so much as breathe on her I will give you the worst thrashing of your life!'

Foolishly disregarding Blackie's warning, Gerald struggled upright, mumbling foul imprecations. He heaved himself to his feet, sweating profusely, and glowered at Emma. He seemed about to attack her and then suddenly he changed his mind and lurched at Blackie. Blackie was prepared and stepped aside adroitly, swung his right fist, and caught Gerald a glancing blow on the jaw. A look of stunned surprise crossed Gerald's purple face before he crumpled and collapsed in a heap at their feet, overturning a small mahogany table as he fell.

'Oh my God!' Emma exclaimed, rising.

'That bastard asked for it!' Blackie muttered, and gave her a sharp, puzzled glance. 'Why didn't you tell me he tried to rape you when it happened? I would have knocked the living daylights out of him! He would have been crippled for life, after I'd finished with him!'

'I know. That's why I never mentioned it, Blackie,' Emma said quietly. 'I thought it advisable to keep it to myself. I didn't need any more trouble in those days. My life was difficult enough as it was.' Emma righted the table and smiled wanly. 'But thank you for interceding now. I really think he meant to hit me.'

Blackie looked at her askance, as always surprised at her fearlessness. 'What do you mean, think he did? I know he intended you bodily harm. The nasty piece of work.'

Emma gestured at Gerald. 'What are we going to do with him? We can't just leave him lying there.'

A malicious gleam entered Blackie's eyes. 'I can think of a lot of things I'd like to do with him. But he's not worth going to jail for, I can tell you that.' Blackie spotted a jug of water on the walnut chest. He brought it over to Gerald and threw the contents on him unceremoniously. 'There, that should do it!' he exclaimed, and stood regarding Gerald coldly.

After a moment Gerald struggled into a sitting position, spluttering and wiping the water from his face. Blackie pulled him to his feet. 'No more violence, Fairley. Do you understand me? Otherwise I won't be responsible for my actions,' Blackie said harshly, his manner threatening. He manoeuvred Gerald into the chair with a degree of roughness and hovered over him. 'Now, let's get down to the business at hand. You know why I came. Presumably you are going to permit us to make a tour of inspection. I don't think you have any alternative under the circumstances, do you?'

Gerald ignored Blackie and snarled viciously at Emma, his enmity for her more palpable than ever. 'I'll get you for this!' he shouted, shaking his fist at her. 'You're not going to get off scot-free,' he blustered. 'Or as easily as you think, Emma.'

'Mrs Ainsley to you,' Blackie said as Emma walked over to the desk.

Emma picked up her gloves and handbag and said, 'Please leave us now. I believe you have something to attend to – removing your personal belongings from your office at the mill.'

Gerald stood up uncertainly. He held on to the back of the chair and his tone was venomous as he said, 'I give you fair warning –' His voice broke and tears welled in his eyes. 'I am going to –'

'You can do nothing,' Emma said, and she turned away in disgust.

Blackie said firmly, 'You heard the lady, Fairley. You had better do as she says and be quick about it. I think it would be rather embarrassing to find your stuff dumped in the mill yard.'

Gerald stumbled out of the library, his shoulders hunched in defeat. He slammed the door behind him and the wall sconces rattled in their sockets.

Emma, who abhorred violence, had been alarmed by the altercation, as brief as it was, but she had not lost her composure. She glanced across at Blackie and said dismissively, 'So much for fools. Shall we look around the house?'

'Why not? That's why we're here, isn't it?'

'One of the reasons,' Emma said.

Blackie's eyes rested reflectively on Emma. Revenge generally came at a high price and, whilst he understood her motivations, he wondered, abstractly, if the price had been worth it to her. Superstitious Celt that he was, Blackie shivered unexpectedly. The desire for revenge was not unnatural, but it could curdle and embitter the soul, and it often destroyed the avenger. Was it not perhaps infinitely wiser to abjure the wicked and abandon them to the fates, and trust in God to make retribution in His own good time? He found himself saying, almost inaudibly, 'Vengeance is mine; I will repay, sayeth the Lord.'

Emma gave him a peculiar look, and then she laughed. There was a hint of irony in her voice as she retorted, 'Don't start getting mystical with me. You know I don't believe in God. Besides, even if I did, I would still have taken matters into my own hands. You see, Blackie, I didn't have time to wait for the Lord.'

'And you also wanted the satisfaction of seeing Gerald Fairley's face when he discovered you had been his adversary all these years,' Blackie asserted.

'Do you blame me?' Emma asked, one eyebrow raised.

'I don't suppose I do,' Blackie admitted, and regarded her for a long moment. 'And tell me, Emma, how do you feel, now that you have accomplished what you set out to do?'

'Why, I feel wonderful. Why shouldn't I? I have waited twenty years to see the tables turned on the Fairleys. Twenty years, Blackie! And let me tell you something. Revenge is sweet. Very sweet indeed.'

Blackie did not reply. He put his arm around her shoulders and gazed down at her. To his relief that cold and implacable mask had been discarded, had been replaced by the sweetest of expressions, and the hard glint in her emerald eyes had disappeared. A thought struck him. 'And what of Edwin Fairley?' Blackie asked curiously. 'Do you have something special in store for him?'

'You will have to wait and see,' Emma said cryptically, and smiled. 'Anyway, don't think Edwin won't be upset by all this, because he will. For one thing, he will be mortified by the scandal, the terrible disgrace. Gerald is practically bankrupt and the whole of Yorkshire's business community knows it. Furthermore, Edwin's income is going to be most seriously affected. He had an interest in the Fairley mills, under his father's will. Now that's gone up in a puff of smoke,' she finished triumphantly and with an eloquent wave of her hand.

Blackie said softly, 'Is there anything you don't know about their affairs?'

'Nothing.'

Blackie shook his head. 'You're an amazing woman, Emma.'

'Aren't I, just. I amaze myself sometimes.' Emma laughed. 'Well, let's do what we came here to do and make our grand tour of Fairley Hall.'

They went out into the entrance hall and slowly mounted the great staircase washed in the eerie light sifting in through the huge stained-glass window that soared high above the central landing. They walked down the endless dusky corridors that reeked faintly of wax and gas and dust and that peculiar mustiness that seeped out of the walls, and the wood creaked and the wind moaned in the eaves and the light dimmed, and it seemed to Emma that the ancient house was expiring all around them. They looked in on various rooms where grimy dust sheets draped the furniture and then moved on into the main corridor of bedrooms.

Emma paused at the door of the Blue Suite and glanced back at Blackie standing behind her. 'These were Adele Fairley's rooms,' she remarked, and hesitated, her hand resting on the knob. And then she braced herself, flung open the door, and went in purposefully. Motes of dust rose up from the carpet in eddying whirls and danced in the sunlit air as they disturbed the room, which had obviously been unused for years and held an aura of neglect more pronounced than the library. Although Emma had never liked this room as a child, she had been awed by the quality of the antiques and some of the other furnishings. Now she saw it through the eyes of the connoisseur she had become, and she grimaced. Here poor Adele Fairley had lived out her life in her introverted world, isolated from her family and escaping reality by fleeing down the neck of a bottle. Emma had long ago acknowledged that Adele had been an alcoholic. But was she also mad? She pushed aside the troubling thought of inherited insanity and drifted through into the adjoining bedroom, pausing by the huge four-poster bed swathed in faded green silk. The silence was overwhelming and, in the way the imagination can play queer tricks, Emma heard Adele's tinkling laughter and the rustling of her peignoir, caught a faint whiff of her Jasmine perfume. She blinked rapidly and gooseflesh spreckled her arms. She laughed at herself and then swung around and hurriedly returned to the sitting room.

Blackie followed her, assessing everything as he did. 'These are fine rooms, Emma,' he said, peering about. 'Beautifully proportioned. They have a lot of potential. Of course, you'll have to get rid of most of this junk Adele Fairley collected.'

'Yes, I will,' Emma said, and thought: What a pathetic memorial to Adele Fairley. She who was so beautiful.

Emma inspected the other bedrooms perfunctorily yet with a degree of curiosity. She hovered in front of the dressing table in the Grey Room, once occupied by Olivia Wainright Fairley, musing on her. Unexpectedly, a wave of reluctant affection surfaced in her. Olivia *had* been kind; *had* eased her burdens in this terrible house. She wondered if her empathy for Olivia had been unconsciously engendered by that woman's marked resemblance to her mother. Perhaps. Emma's face softened and she turned and left the Grey Room. But her expression changed radically when she pushed open the door of the Master's Room. Her eyes were stony as she surveyed the austere furnishings, thinking of Adam Fairley. And Emma remembered anew all that had happened to her at Fairley Hall and she felt no compunction about what she had done. Her revenge had had a long gestation period, but it had been surely worth it.

Fifteen minutes later Emma and Blackie descended the main staircase and quickly traversed the reception rooms on the ground floor. All the while Blackie chatted enthusiastically about the renovations he would make, and outlined his plans for transforming Fairley Hall into an elegant home for her. Emma listened and nodded but said little. At one moment, when they were viewing the drawing room, she touched Blackie's arm and asked, 'Why was I so frightened of this house when I was a child?'

Blackie squeezed her hand lovingly. 'You weren't afraid of the house, Emma. You were afraid of the people in it.'

'I suppose you're right,' she replied softly. 'And now those people are just ghosts.'

'Yes, me darlin', just ghosts. And this is only a house, after all. I once told you it could never harm you.'

'I know you did.' Emma took Blackie's arm. 'Let's go outside and look at the grounds. It's chilly in here, and rather depressing.'

Emma blinked when they stepped out into the bright sunlight. 'Do you know, it's warmer out here than it is in there,' she remarked, and stared up at the grim edifice soaring in front of her. Emma's face became introspective as she walked along the flagged terrace, regarding Fairley Hall from time to time. This daunting house was enduring – and inescapable; a bastion of wealth and privilege, a monument to a society long outmoded, to a cruel class system she detested, and it sorely offended her.

Inclining her head towards the house, she murmured, 'My father used to call this Fairley's Folly.'

'And so it is.'

'Tear it down,' Emma said with cool deliberation.

'Tear it down!' Blackie echoed, gazing at her incredulously. 'What do you mean?'

'Exactly what I say. I want you to tear it down. Brick by brick by brick, until there is nothing left standing.'

'But I thought you were going to live in it,' Blackie exclaimed, still flabbergasted.

'To tell you the truth, I don't think I ever really intended to do that. You once said it was a monstrosity and that's a decided understatement. There is no place in this world for monstrosities. I want it wiped off the face of the earth as if it never existed.'

'And the furniture?'

'Sell it. Give it away. Do as you wish. I know I don't want one piece of it. You can take anything you like, Blackie.' She smiled. 'You might consider keeping Adam Fairley's desk. It is quite valuable, you know.'

'Thank you, Emma. I'll think about it.' Blackie rubbed his chin. 'Are you sure about this decision? You did pay a lot for the house.'

'I am very sure.' Emma swivelled and tripped lightly down the terrace steps until she stood at the entrance to the rose garden. In her mind's eye she saw herself as a young and desperate girl, and she recalled the day she had told Edwin she was pregnant, and remembered his repudiation of her as clearly as if it had happened yesterday.

'And destroy this garden,' she said icily. 'Demolish it completely. I don't want one rosebud, one single leaf left growing.'

The villagers were agog at the news that Emma Harte, Big Jack's daughter, was now the owner of Fairley Hall and the mill. It was a reversal of circumstances so unlikely it staggered the imagination, and, in turn, they were stunned, astonished, and finally wryly amused at the ironic justice so inherent in the turn of events, which were quite unexpected. Hidebound as they were by tradition and prejudice, and trapped in a rigid caste system that kept the workers in their place, they nevertheless marvelled at her audacity in daring to defy that system and break all the rules set down by the Establishment for centuries.

The following morning women stood on doorsteps and leaned over garden gates, arms akimbo, shaking their heads and exclaiming about the remarkable success story of one of their own. That night in the White Horse, the men at the bar, most of whom worked at the mill, crowded together, speculating about the future of the mill and chuckling at the demise of the Fairleys' power. Although Adam Fairley had not been particularly liked, because he was not of the same ilk as his bluff and hearty father, being too 'fancy' for their north-country tastes, he *had* been respected since the men recognized his basic integrity and fairness. However, Gerald, who was a tyrant and a fool, was loathed, and no one was unhappy to see his downfall, nor did they have a shred of pity for him. 'Good riddance to bad rubbish' was the phrase most often heard in the ensuing days as the villagers waited eagerly for the arrival of their new employer and the future mistress of Fairley Hall.

But Emma did not come to the village – at least not until Gerald Fairley had vacated Fairley Hall. Two days after his departure her silver-grey Rolls-Royce pulled up into the mill yard and she went into the mill to hold a meeting with the workers. The manager, Josh Wilson, son of Ernest, who had served Adam so well, assembled the men and women in the weaving shed. Emma, wearing a navy-blue tailored dress, a navy cloche, and pearls, cordially greeted some of the men she remembered from her childhood and then addressed the gathering.

She was direct: 'As you are only too well aware, there has been a slump in the cloth business for almost eighteen months, ever since the price of wool hit rock bottom, to be followed by the price of cloth. Due to the inferior management of the previous owner, Fairley mill has been limping along and I know that many men were laid off over the past few months.' Emma paused and cleared her throat. 'I am afraid I cannot reinstate those men.' She held up her hand as loud groans and mutterings rippled through the audience. 'However, I am going to give a small pension to the men who have been laid off and who have not found work in the nearby towns. I would also like to say now, and most definitely, that I have no intention of closing the mill, as I believe many of you thought I would. But under the present circumstances, I must retrench, economize, reorganize, and decrease the staff. Therefore, all men of retiring age and close to it will be retired immediately. Each man will receive a pension. Younger men, especially those who are single, will be offered jobs in my other companies, if they are willing to leave Fairley and carve out a niche for themselves in the cities of Leeds and Bradford. Those who do not wish to take advantage of this offer may remain. Of course, I hope some of you will consider it, so that I can reduce the work force here in order to operate more economically. As I told Josh, I am going to sell the quality cloth we produce to the three Kallinski tailoring factories in Leeds, but even their orders will not be sufficient to keep the mill in full production. I have a solution to that problem. I am going to start making a lower-quality cloth immediately, to be sold at cheaper prices abroad, and I hope there will be a demand for it here, too.'

Emma smiled confidently. 'I am fortunate in that I can afford to ride out this slump, and with a little luck, and your cooperation, I know we can turn this mill around and put it on a paying basis quickly. Let me say again, I am not going to close the mill, so I don't want any of you to worry about your jobs. I don't intend to let this village starve.'

They cheered her rousingly, and one by one, clutching their cloth caps, the men came to shake her hand, to thank her, and to welcome her back to Fairley. 'I knew yer dad, love,' one man told her, and another added, 'By gum, Big Jack'd be right proud of yer, lass.'

After a meeting with Josh Wilson, Emma stepped into her Rolls and told the chauffeur to drive her to Fairley Hall. Blackie O'Neill's workmen were already swarming all over the house, scrambling up ladders and across the roof. Windows were being removed, chimneys dismantled, and slates ripped off. Emma smiled to herself, and returned to Leeds.

At first the villagers believed the Hall was being renovated and they were excited about this development and looked forward to welcoming Emma Harte as the lady of the manor. But within the space of a week, they realized, to their shock, that the house was being slowly demolished, and they were baffled.

In the middle of May, Emma made a second trip to Fairley Hall. She walked along the terrace, which still remained intact, and regarded the great tract of rough bare ground where the house and stables had formerly stood. Not one brick was left and the rose garden, too, had disappeared. Emma felt an enormous surge of relief and an unexpected sense of liberation. Fairley Hall, that house where she had suffered such humiliation and heartache, might never have existed. It could no longer hurt her with the painful memories it evoked. She had exorcized all the ghosts of her childhood. She was free at last of the Fairleys.

Blackie, who arrived a few moments later, put his arm around her shoulders. 'I followed your instructions down to the letter and removed the monstrosity, mavourneen. But like the whole of the village, I am eaten up with curiosity, Emma. Tell me, darlin', what are you going to do with this land?'

Emma looked up at him and smiled. 'I am going to turn it into a park. A beautiful park for the villagers of Fairley, and I am going to name it after my mother.'

FIFTY-TWO

A week later, on a lovely evening at the end of May, Emma stepped out of a taxi at the Savoy Hotel in London and hurried through the lobby to the American Bar. She saw Frank before he saw her. He was seated at a table facing the lobby, and as she mounted the short flight of steps into the bar she noticed that he looked reflective and brooding as he nursed his drink.

'Penny for your thoughts,' she said, coming to a standstill in front of him.

Momentarily startled, Frank raised his head quickly and his eyes lit up. 'There you are!' He rose and pulled out a chair for her. 'And don't you look lovely, our Em.'

'Why, thank you, darling.' She smoothed the skirt of her lime-green silk dress and took off her white kid gloves. 'It is a scorcher, isn't it? I think I'll have a gin fizz, Frank, please. It will refresh me. I had quite a hectic day at the store.'

Frank ordered the drink and lit a cigarette. 'I'm sorry to drag you all the way down to the Strand, but it is closer to Fleet Street and I've got to be back at the paper in a short while.'

'I didn't mind coming here. I rather like this bar. Anyway, why did you want to see me? You sounded urgent when you phoned me at the store. I was a little worried, to tell you the truth.'

'I'm sorry, Emma. I didn't mean to do that. Actually, it's not all that urgent, but I did want to talk to you.'

'What about?'

'Arthur Ainsley.'

Emma's shapely brows shot up. 'Arthur. Good heavens, why do you want to talk about *him*?'

'Winston and I have been worried about you lately. You're sitting in a hopeless marriage and it disturbs us both. In fact, we think you should divorce Arthur. I promised Winston I would broach the idea to you.'

'A divorce!' Emma laughed gaily. 'Whatever for? Arthur doesn't bother me.'

'He's not right for you, Emma, and you know it. There's his terrible drinking, for one thing, and the way he carries on with –' Frank swallowed and drew on his cigarette.

'Other women,' Emma finished for him. She looked amused. 'I realize the wife is always supposed to be the last to know. However, I've been aware of Arthur's activities for a long time. You don't have to spare my feelings.'

'And it doesn't upset you?' Frank asked.

'My monumental lack of interest in Arthur Ainsley and the way he conducts his life must surely negate the idea that I *care* for him. Actually, I have no feelings for Arthur whatsoever.'

'Then why not get a divorce, Emma?'

'Because of the children, mainly.'

'Fiddlesticks! You're using them as an excuse. Edwina and Kit are away at boarding school. They wouldn't be affected –'

'I was thinking of the twins, Frank. They are Arthur's children and they need a father.'

'What kind of father is Arthur?' Frank snorted.

Emma picked up the drink the waiter had placed before her. 'Cheers.'

'Cheers. Now, come on, give me an answer.'

'Well, he is a presence in their lives. He's very fond of them, and quite good with them, really.'

'When he's sober,' Frank pointed out with a degree of acerbity.

Emma sighed. 'There's a grain of truth in what you say, of course. But look here, Frank, I honestly don't want to divorce Arthur, even though I have grounds. At least, not right now. You know I hate upheaval and I really *do* think it's the wrong time. Perhaps when the children are older I'll consider it.' Her voice trailed off and she looked pensive. She cheered. 'I'm reasonably content. Arthur doesn't interfere with me, or the business, and you know how much I love that.'

'You can't take ledgers to bed with you, our Em. They don't keep you warm on a cold night, and they certainly can't cherish and love you as you should be cherished and loved.'

Emma laughed. 'Why is it you men are always thinking of sex?'

'I did say "cherished" and "loved". You're a young woman. You should have some companionship, a relationship with a decent man. My God, you must be bloody lonely!'

A cloud passed over Emma's face and her eyes were briefly sad. She shook her head slowly. 'I don't have time to be lonely. I'm very busy these days, as you well know, constantly travelling between here and Leeds. And I am adamant about the divorce, Frank. Now, let's not waste any more time talking about Arthur. Tell me about the house you found in Hampstead. Does Natalie like it?'

Frank groaned, acknowledging it was useless to pursue the conversation, and said, 'Yes, she does. So do I. It's ideal for us. But I would like you to take a look at it, and give me your opinion. It's quite expensive, you know.'

'I'd be delighted. And don't worry about the price, Frank. If it's more than you can afford, I'll give you the difference.'

'Oh, Emma, I couldn't take it,' Frank protested.

'Don't be ridiculous. Years ago Blackie told me that money was meant to be spent and he was correct. I want you to have a nice house, to start this marriage off on the right foot. I want you to be happy, Frank.' She laughed. 'Whoever said money doesn't buy happiness was misinformed, in my opinion. It buys a lot of happiness, for a lot of people. And frankly, I'd rather be miserable with money than without it.' She squeezed Frank's arm. 'You know anything I have is yours and Winston's. It will be part of my wedding present to you and Natalie.'

'You're so generous, Emma. I really appreciate it. And what can I say but thank you very much.' Frank sipped his drink and continued, 'Can you spare an hour to view it tomorrow?'

'Indeed I can. How is dear Natalie?'

Frank beamed. 'She's marvellous. A treasure. I love that girl, Emma. I really do.'

'I know. You're lucky, Frank. You're going to have a wonderful marriage. She's –' Emma stopped and caught her breath. From her position at the table, a vantage point in the bar, Emma could see a major portion of the lobby and her eyes were now riveted on two men talking together near the reception desk.

Frank, watching Emma carefully, said, 'What's wrong?'

Emma glanced at Frank, white with shock. 'It's Paul McGill!' She looked down the steps again. 'Oh my God! He's coming this way. I think he's heading for the bar. I must leave immediately, before he sees me.'

Frank put a restraining hand on her arm. 'It's perfectly all right, Emma. Don't get excited. And please don't leave,' he implored softly.

Emma's eyes blazed. 'Frank! You knew he was in London, didn't you?'

'Yes.'

'You didn't – you couldn't possibly have asked him to join us?'

Frank did not answer. He looked down at his drink.

Emma hissed, 'My God! You did!'

'Guilty, I'm afraid,' Frank murmured.

'Oh, Frank, how could you?' Emma half rose, and Frank pressed her gently back into the chair.

'Please, Emma. You have to stay.'

She looked at him furiously. 'This sudden desire to talk about Arthur and the house was just a ruse, wasn't it?' she cried accusingly.

'No!' Frank exclaimed. 'It wasn't! I did want to discuss your marriage. I have for a long time. I told you, Winston and I are very perturbed. And I do need your advice about the house. However, I did agree to arrange this meeting.'

'My God! What am I going to do?' Emma whispered hoarsely.

'You are going to be your civilized self and have a drink with Paul.'

'I can't,' she wailed. 'You don't understand. I must go!' As she spoke, Emma knew it was already too late to make a graceful exit. Paul was bounding up the steps and then he was standing at the table, his bulk casting a shadow on them. Emma lifted her eyes slowly and looked at him looking down at her. She was relieved she was seated. Her legs had turned to jelly and her heart was palpitating.

'Hello, Emma,' Paul said, and stretched out his hand.

Automatically she gave him hers. 'Hello, Paul,' she responded in a strangled voice, shaking internally. She felt his strong fingers tighten on hers, felt the bright colour flooding her face. She extracted her hand quickly and gazed blindly at the table.

Paul greeted Frank like an old friend and sat down. He ordered a scotch and soda, leaned back, crossed his legs nonchalantly, and lit a cigarette. He turned his attention to Emma. 'It's good to see you, Emma. You look lovely. You haven't changed a bit. And I must congratulate you. Your store in Knightsbridge bowled me over. It's magnificent. A monumental accomplishment. You should be proud of yourself.'

'Thank you,' she murmured, not daring to look at him.

'I must congratulate you, too, Frank. Your new book is splendid. Thanks for the copy. I was up half the night reading it. Couldn't put it down, in fact.'

Frank grinned with pleasure. 'I'm glad you like it. I'm also happy to say it's doing very well.'

'And so it should. It's one of the best novels I've read in years.' Paul's drink arrived and as he lifted it he said, 'Here's to old and dear friends, and your impending marriage, Frank.'

Emma was silent. She had never thought her brother capable of duplicity, but he had certainly been devious in this instance, and was obviously on cordial terms with Paul.

Frank said, 'I'm delighted you will be here in July. Natalie and I hope you can come to the wedding.'

Emma could not believe her ears. She glared at Frank, who ignored her penetrating look and continued, 'And thanks for the invitation to dine with you later this week. Natalie suggested Friday, if you are free.'

'I am. And I wouldn't miss the wedding for anything.' Paul's eyes rested on Emma. 'Could you join us for dinner on Friday, Emma?'

'I'm quite sure I can't,' she responded, avoiding his eyes.

'Why don't you check your appointment book later?' Frank suggested.

'I don't have to. I am positive I have a dinner engagement,' she enunciated clearly and in a firmer tone, her eyes signalling her displeasure to Frank.

Recognizing the stubborn expression settling on her face, Paul refrained from pressing the point and, turning to Frank, he said, 'Where are you planning to go on your honeymoon?'

'We've been considering the South of France, although we haven't definitely decided yet.'

Emma sat back in the chair, no longer listening to them. Their conversation washed over her as she retreated into herself. She had been utterly thrown off balance by Paul's unexpected arrival and she could, at this moment, have cheerfully killed Frank for his participation in the scheme. She felt dazed, and many mixed emotions, so well controlled over the years, broke free in her. The impact of seeing him was devastating. Paul McGill was sitting *here*, unconcernedly chatting to Frank, smiling, nodding, and behaving as if nothing had happened between them. She felt the enormous power of him, his sheathed strength and virility, and she remembered every detail of the days they had spent together at the Ritz. And then she recalled, with a stab of sadness, how she had yearned for him. Pined for him. Needed him in the past. Now he was only inches away, and she stifled the impulse to reach out and touch him, to reassure herself he was real. Instead she looked at him surreptitiously. He was as immaculate as always, dressed in a dark grey chalk-striped suit and a gleaming white silk shirt. Sapphire-and-gold links glittered in the French cuffs and he wore a deep blue silk tie, and a white handkerchief flared in his breast pocket. She knew he had been forty-two at the beginning of February, but he looked exactly the same as he had in 1919, except that his face was more deeply tanned and there were additional character lines around his eyes. His colouring was as vivid as it had ever been, and his chuckle was deep and throaty. How well she knew that amused, sardonic chuckle. Sudden anger swamped her. How dare he come back here so casually and expect her to treat him with civility after all the pain he had caused her. What audacity. What arrogance. Resentment edged out all other feelings, and she steeled herself against his potent charm.

Dimly, she heard Frank saying goodbye. He was leaving her alone with Paul. The idea terrified her.

'I must go,' she said, picking up her gloves and her purse. 'Please excuse me, Paul. I have to leave with Frank.'

'Don't go, Emma. Please. I would like to talk to you,' Paul said in the softest of voices. It was imperative that he detain her at all costs, yet he dare not exert obvious pressure on her.

Frank threw Paul a conspiratorial glance and addressed Emma. 'I have to get back to Fleet Street. I'm running late.' He kissed her on the cheek perfunctorily and departed before she could protest further, and she knew she was trapped.

Paul summoned the waiter and ordered more drinks, and then he leaned forward intently. His eyes were serious, his face grave. 'Please don't be angry with Frank. I persuaded him to arrange this meeting.'

'Why?' Emma asked, and for the first time she looked at Paul fully and with coldness.

Paul winced. He knew he had a difficult time ahead of him, but he was determined to convince her of his sincerity. 'As I said, I wanted to see you and to talk to you. Very desperately.'

'Desperately!' she echoed, and laughed cynically. 'That's a strange word to use. You can't have been all that desperate, otherwise you would not have let so many years elapse.'

'I understand your feelings only too well, Emma. But it does happen to be the truth. I have been *really* desperate. And for the past four and a half years,' he insisted.

'Then why didn't you write to me?' she demanded, and her voice shook unexpectedly. She took furious control of herself, determined not to show any emotion whatsoever.

'I did write to you a number of times and I also sent you three cablegrams.'

Emma stared at Paul, a look of disbelief crossing her face. 'Don't tell me they all got lost in the post! And that the cablegrams disappeared into thin air! I would find that very hard to swallow.'

'No, they didn't. They were stolen. As your letters to me were stolen,' Paul said, his eyes not leaving her face.

'Stolen by whom?' Emma asked, returning his intense stare.

'By my private secretary.'

'But why would she do a thing like that?'

'It's rather a long story,' Paul said quietly. 'I would like to tell it to you. That was the reason I wanted to see you. Will you at least give me the courtesy of listening, Emma? Please.'

'All right,' she murmured. It would do no harm to hear what he had to say and her curiosity also got the better of her.

'When I returned to Australia in 1919, the only thing on my mind was seeing my father and then returning to you as quickly as possible.'

Paul paused as the waiter appeared with the drinks. When he was out of earshot he went on, 'I walked into quite a mess when I arrived in Sydney, but I won't go into that now. Let me first tell you about the letters. Years ago my father befriended a young girl who worked in our Sydney office. He groomed her to be his private secretary during my absence. After I was demobbed I had to take over the reins of the business at once, because Dad was not at all well, and so I inherited her. Marion Reese was a godsend in those first few weeks. Anyway, for a couple of months I was working very long hours with Marion at my side, guiding me, helping me, and filling me in on most things. My father was gradually getting worse and he was confined to bed. Frankly, Emma, I relied heavily on Marion. I had enormous responsibilities thrust upon me and I was out of touch.' Paul lit a cigarette, inhaled, and continued, 'Marion had been like a member of the family before the war. My father was very fond of her and I looked on her as a friend, as well as a valued employee. She was like an older sister in a sense, since she is about four years my senior. One night, after we had been working rather late, I took her to supper, and I confided in her. I told her about you and my plans for the future, my intention of marrying you, once I had sorted out my marital problems.'

A regretful smile played around Paul's mouth and he shook his head. 'Confiding in Marion was a terrible mistake, as it turned out. A mistake I made when I had had a few drinks too many. Of course, I didn't realize it was a mistake at the time. Marion was most understanding. She promised to help me pull everything back into shape as quickly as possible, so that I could come to London for a few months and –'

'Why was it a mistake?' Emma interrupted, frowning.

'I didn't know it at the time, but Marion Reese was in love with me and had been for many years. There had been nothing between us ever, and I had never done anything to encourage her. Naturally, the last thing she wanted was for me to leave Australia, and especially to go to another woman, although I was not aware of that then. In any event, I went on furiously reorganizing the business and writing to you, not realizing that my devoted secretary was confiscating my letters to you instead of posting them. I was puzzled and unnerved when you didn't reply to my letters, other than the first one. I sent two cablegrams, begging you to at least let me know you were well. Of course, they were never transmitted. Marion destroyed them. Still, in spite of your silence, which I couldn't understand, I was determined to see you and, as soon as I could, sailed for England.'

Emma, who had been listening attentively and digesting his words, knew with absolute certainty that he was speaking the truth. She looked at him alertly. 'When was that?'

'About a year later. In the spring of 1920. I wrote out a cable and gave it to

Marion before I departed, announcing my arrival, and I prayed you would meet the boat. You didn't because you never received the cable. The first person I telephoned was Frank. He told me you were on your honeymoon. That you had married Arthur Ainsley just one week before.'

'Oh my God!' Emma cried, her eyes flaring open. Dismay swamped her. Paul's smile was pained and he nodded his head. 'Yes, I was a week too late to stop that. *Unfortunately.*'

'But why didn't you come before? Why did you wait a whole year?' Emma demanded, her voice rising.

'I simply couldn't get away, Emma. You see, my father was dying of cancer. He passed away about eight months after I had returned to Australia.'

'I'm so sorry, Paul,' Emma murmured, and genuine sympathy was reflected in her eyes.

'Yes, it was sad. And Dad was very dependent on me in those last few months. Well, to continue. I had hoped to leave immediately after Dad's funeral, but then my wife –' Paul hesitated and grimaced slightly. 'My wife, Constance, became very ill, and I was further delayed. Just when I thought I could get away at last, my son fell sick.' Paul eyed Emma carefully. 'I have a son, you know.'

'Yes, so I heard. You could have told me, Paul. I wish you had,' she reproached.

'Yes, I should have, Emma. But Howard, well, he has problems, and I have always found it difficult to talk about him.' Paul sighed heavily and his eyes dulled momentarily. He straightened up in the chair. 'Once Howard recovered I was able to leave for England.'

'And you met with Frank?'

'Not at first. Frank was a little reluctant to see me. I don't believe he thought very highly of me. However, he did know how devastated I was when I learned of your marriage and I suppose he took pity on me, especially since I had told him on the phone that I had been writing to you diligently over the whole of the previous year. When he told me that you had never received my letters, and that you had also been writing to me, I was flabbergasted and baffled.'

'How did you discover the letters had been stolen?' Emma asked, her face as grim as Paul's.

'It struck me immediately, and most forcibly, that someone had been tampering with my mail. Several letters going astray was one thing, but not a dozen or so. It didn't take much to deduce it was Marion. She was the obvious culprit, since she handled my correspondence in both Sydney and at the sheep station in Coonamble. And she also mailed all of my personal letters as well.'

'It's a pity you didn't post them yourself, isn't it?' Emma said quietly, cursing Marion Reese under her breath. Her penetrating eyes focused on Paul.

'Yes, that's true. I admit I was careless. On the other hand, I had no reason not to trust her. Also, I was facing monumental problems. I was overworked and preoccupied.'

'I presume you confronted her when you returned to Sydney,' Emma ventured.

'I did indeed. She denied it at first. But eventually she broke down and confessed. When I asked her why she had done it, she said she had hoped to sabotage our romance, so I would not leave.'

'She succeeded,' Emma said drily, and thought of the wasted years.

'Yes.' Paul searched Emma's face, which was unreadable. He reached into his inside breast pocket and pulled out an envelope. 'This is a letter from her solicitors. In it they acknowledge her guilt, on the understanding that I would not prosecute her, which I had threatened to do. Theft of mail is a felony, you know. I demanded this,' he explained, tapping the envelope, 'because I hoped one day to have the opportunity to show it to you, to prove that I am not the blackguard you undoubtedly think I am.' He handed her the envelope and finished. 'They also returned my letters to you, and yours to me, by the way.'

Emma looked at him askance. 'You mean she kept them! How peculiar!' she exclaimed.

'I thought that, too. Please, Emma, read the letter from her solicitors. The story is so incredible it has occurred to me that you might think I have invented the whole thing.'

Emma was reflective for a moment, and then she took the letter out of the envelope and perused it rapidly. She returned it to Paul, smiling faintly. 'I would have believed you without this letter. Nobody could invent such a yarn. Thank you for showing it to me, though. And what happened to Marion Reese?'

'Naturally I fired her at once. I've no idea where she is today.'

Emma nodded. She pondered, looking down at her hands, and then she lifted her head and met Paul's gaze directly. 'Why didn't you wait for me to return from my honeymoon four years ago, so that you could tell me you had written, Paul?'

Paul gave her a swift glance. 'What would have been the point of that? It was too late, Emma. I didn't want to interfere with your marriage. Besides, you might not have believed me. Remember, I was only speculating on what had happened to the letters. I had no proof until I returned to Sydney.'

'Yes, I understand. However, I am surprised Frank never told me.'

'In all fairness to him, he did want me to stay and meet with you. And he even wanted to tell you himself. I asked him not to do so. I thought it pointless. I felt you were lost to me.' Paul shrugged. 'At the time, it seemed wiser for me to simply disappear, quickly and quietly.'

'And why are you telling me now, after all this time?'

'I have always wanted to explain, Emma. To exonerate myself with you. The knowledge that I caused you suffering has haunted me. I've seen Frank on previous trips to London and he's kept me informed about your life. But I thought it was inappropriate to come to you, under the circumstances, although I longed to. Last week, when I first arrived, I lunched with Frank. Almost at once he said your marriage wasn't working. When I heard you were unhappy with Arthur and spending a lot of time alone in London, I decided I would no longer be upsetting anything if I saw you. I insisted Frank arrange this meeting. I did want the chance to vindicate myself,' he finished, praying fervently that he had.

Paul leaned across the table, his face tensely set. 'I know you were shocked to see me, and perhaps it *was* a little unfair of me to spring myself on you without warning, but quite honestly, I didn't know what else to do. I hope you're not angry with me, or with Frank.'

'No, I'm not. And I'm glad we met.' Emma looked down at the table contemplatively, and when she raised her head to meet Paul's unwavering gaze her face was grave, her eyes moist. 'I was as unnerved and as perplexed as you were, when I didn't hear from you, Paul. And very hurt. Heartbroken, in fact,' she found herself admitting. 'It helps knowing the facts, even now so long afterwards.' Emma smiled wryly. 'I suppose, really, we are both victims of circumstances – and of Marion Reese's possessiveness. How different our lives might have been if she had not interfered.' She shook her head. 'Why is it some people want to play God?' she asked, her face wreathed in sadness.

Paul sighed. 'I don't know, Emma. In her case, I imagine it was a truly sick mind at work. You know the old saying, "Hell hath no fury like a woman scorned." But I will never understand what she hoped to gain. I did not display the slightest interest in her as a woman.'

'People can always hope,' Emma murmured. 'And fantasize.'

'That's so,' Paul acknowledged. He scrutinized Emma closely for a few seconds and then said quietly. 'Do you still hate me, Emma?'

A look of surprise flashed across her face. 'I never hated you, Paul!' She half smiled. 'Well, at least only fleetingly, when my emotions overcame me. You can't blame me for that.'

'I don't blame you at all.' Paul shifted in the chair and lit a cigarette to hide his nervousness. 'I wondered – would it be possible – could we be friends, Emma? Now that the air is cleared between us. Or is that too much to ask?' He held his breath.

Emma dropped her eyes, feeling suddenly wary. Dare she expose herself to him again, if only in friendship? She had been acutely conscious of him as a man from the moment he had arrived. He was just as dangerous to her as he had been in the past. Despite her inherent caution, she finally said slowly, 'Yes, Paul, if you want that.'

'I do,' Paul responded firmly. He looked at her in his old appraising way, his eyes admiring. She was composed and as beautiful as always. Time had not marked her exquisite face, although he detected a certain sadness in her eyes when her face was in repose. He had to curb the compelling desire to take her in his arms and kiss her. He did not even dare to touch her hand. He must be careful if he was to win her back and possess her completely again. He saw her glance at her watch and his heart sank. He said quickly, impulsively, 'Have dinner with me, Emma.'

'Oh, Paul, I can't,' she said, flustered.

'Why not? Do you have another engagement?'

'No, but I –'

'Please, Emma. For old times' sake.' He smiled engagingly and his brilliantly blue eyes danced. 'I'm not afraid. Are you?'

'Why should I be afraid?' Emma countered defensively, staring at him. Her heart missed a beat. He was hard to resist.

'You have no reason at all, I can assure you,' Paul chuckled, relaxing for the first time. As the tension slipped away he took command with his usual panache. 'Then it's settled. Where would you like to go?'

'I don't know,' Emma said, feeling curiously weak and so overpowered she was incapable of declining the invitation again.

'Let's go to Rules across the street in Covent Garden. Do you know it?' She shook her head. 'I've heard of it, but I've never dined there.'

'It's a charming old place. I know you'll like it,' he said, and motioned to the waiter for the bill.

They were halfway through dinner when Paul said, somewhat abruptly, 'Why did your marriage go wrong, Emma?'

Emma was so startled by the unanticipated question she did not answer for a long moment. Because I still loved you, she wanted to say. Instead she murmured, 'Because Arthur and I are incompatible.'

'I see. What's he like?' Paul questioned, riddled with curiosity and not a little jealousy.

Emma said carefully, 'He's handsome, charming, and from a good family. But he's also a little weak. And rather vain.' She glanced back at Paul and said quietly, 'He's not the type of man you would have much in common with.'

Nor you apparently, my love, Paul thought, but said, 'Are you going to get a divorce?'

'Not at the moment. Are you?' she retorted, and caught her breath, regretting the question.

Paul's face changed, settled into harsh lines. 'Well, I asked for that one, I suppose,' he responded quietly. 'I want a divorce, Emma. I have for many years. However, I have some serious difficulties with Constance.' He paused, ruminated briefly, and went on. 'My wife is an alcoholic. She was a heavy drinker before the war. That is one of the reasons the marriage broke up. By the time I returned to Sydney she was a lost cause. I put her in a nursing home at once. She ran away, just after I had buried Dad. It took me five weeks to find her and she was in a pretty ghastly state. Physically debilitated and mentally deranged as well. That was why I couldn't come to England when I wanted to – I had to see her settled first. Believe me, I was infuriated. I don't want to sound callous, but I have tried to help Constance over the years, to no avail. She won't help herself. I lost my patience a long time ago.'

'Yes, I know what you mean,' Emma said grimly. 'I'm sorry, Paul. Truly sorry. It's a terrible situation for anyone to cope with. Is she still in the nursing home?'

'Yes, she is. They have dried her out, but she is very weak in every way and not capable of looking after herself, or functioning normally. She will have to be institutionalized permanently, I imagine. Constance is a Roman Catholic, Emma, so that is another impediment to the divorce. Nonetheless, I haven't given up hope of gaining my freedom one day.' Paul took a sip of Montrachet. After a moment he continued, 'There is something else I must tell you, Emma. It's about my son.' He hesitated. 'Howard is – well, he's retarded, I'm afraid. That's what I meant earlier when I said he had problems.'

Emma was stunned. The pain on his face was raw. 'Oh, Paul! Paul! How awfully tragic. And what a heavy burden for you to carry alone.' Compassion flooded her face and her eyes softened. 'Why ever didn't you tell me years ago? Surely you knew I would have been sympathetic, and talking about your son might have helped you.'

Paul shook his head. 'Perhaps I should have told you, Emma. I think I was a little ashamed, to tell you the truth. Especially after I had met your children. Also, I have always found it hard to discuss Howard. I love him, of course. However, my emotions are mixed. My heart aches for him. I also carry enormous guilt. And sometimes I – ' Paul frowned. 'I am reluctant to admit this, and I never have to another soul, but at times I almost hate him. I know I shouldn't. Yet I can't help it. I hope you don't despise me for that.'

Emma's heart went out to him. 'I don't despise you, Paul. I know that parents of retarded children often do experience hatred. It apparently springs from frustration and despair. Truly, your feelings are not abnormal.' Impulsively she reached out and touched his arm. 'You must feel very helpless. How old is Howard?'

'He's twelve, Emma. And, yes, I do feel absolutely despairing most of the time.' He shook his head. 'Nature plays strange tricks. You know, he is a lovely-looking boy. He has a sweet, almost ethereal face and the most gentle eyes. And the mind of a five-year-old.' Paul ran his hand across his face wearily. 'And he'll never be any different!'

Emma was silent, filled with sorrow, and she did not know how to comfort him. Eventually, she asked, 'Where does he live?'

'Out at the sheep station in Coonamble. He has a male companion-nurse who is devoted to him. My housekeeper is there and quite a large domestic staff. When I'm at Dunoon I spend a great deal of time with him, although I'm quite sure he doesn't really know I'm around. He lives in his own very special world.' Paul lit a cigarette. 'I'm sorry, Emma. I didn't mean to pile all my problems on you tonight. I never discuss them with anyone.' He grimaced. 'I must admit, though, I have felt rather defeated by my personal life in the past few years. It is so arid and unrewarding. Thank you for listening, for being so understanding.'

'I have been far enough down to know what the realities of life are, Paul,' Emma said. 'My life has never been easy. Whatever you might think.'

He looked at her attentively, his eyes narrowed. 'I'm sure it hasn't, Emma.'

'But then life *is* hard, Paul. The important thing is how one copes with the hardships and overcomes them.' She smiled her dauntless smile. 'Let's face it, Paul, neither of us are too badly off. Not when you look around and see other people's problems. We are both successful. Wealthy. In good health. We are also fortunate in that we have our work.'

Paul gazed at her. He thought: She truly is a rare woman. He said, 'Yes, I have buried myself in work these last few years, as I'm sure you have. And you are right, Emma. Our lives are not too bad. We must be grateful for all the good things we do have.' He smiled at her lovingly. 'Thank you again. I'm glad I told you about Constance and Howard. I feel a great sense of relief.'

'I'm glad, too.'

Paul lifted his glass. 'Here's to you, Emma. You are a wise and understanding lady. I'm so happy we are going to be friends again, aren't you?'

Emma touched his glass with hers. 'Yes, I think I am, Paul.'

'Well, enough of all this misery. Let's talk about something more cheerful.'

Emma smiled at him. 'Tell me about your oil fields in Texas, and the Sydney-Texas Oil Company. I was very intrigued when you mentioned your new venture earlier.'

After dinner Paul escorted Emma home to her small house in Wilton Mews, just off Belgrave Square. He helped her out of the cab, told the driver to wait, and saw her inside. He kissed her tentatively on the cheek. 'Thank you for a lovely evening, Emma. May I call you soon?'

'Yes, Paul. And thank you. Good night.'

'Good night, Emma.'

Later, when she was in bed, Emma lay awake for a long time, musing on the evening. Paul McGill's dramatic reappearance in her life was the last thing she had ever anticipated. Life was full of staggering surprises. She dwelt momentarily on Marion Reese. If Paul had not been the man he undoubtedly was, then perhaps that frustrated woman might never have loved him . . . might never have stolen the letters. If Paul had only written to Frank . . . If she had not rushed into marriage with Arthur. If . . . if . . . if. She sighed inwardly. It was such a waste of time dwelling on what might have been. And surely their characters had made their destinies. Her heart filled with sadness as her wandering thoughts settled on the tragic circumstances of Paul's life. He who was so virile, and extraordinarily brilliant, must surely chafe under the burdens he had to carry. His life was as difficult and sterile as her own. She realized then, with a flash of surprise, that she had enjoyed the evening, once she had recovered from her initial shock and anger. She wondered if he had merely wanted to see her to set the record straight, or if he had been motivated by other reasons. Did he still love her? She did not know the answer to that. She shivered. One thing she did know: She was mortally afraid of his persuasive charm and of being engulfed by it again. She endeavoured to push him out of her mind, but when she finally fell asleep she was still thinking about Paul McGill.

FIFTY-THREE

'You look as if you're about to commit murder,' Winston said quietly, drawing to a standstill next to Paul McGill. He followed Paul's gaze, which was resting with loathing on Arthur Ainsley. 'He's asinine,' Winston went on. 'Don't pay any attention to him. Frank and I don't.'

Paul swung to Winston, his expression one of mingled anger and disgust. 'He makes my blood boil! The preposterous fool has embarrassed Emma all through lunch and now he's compounding his execrable behaviour. The bloody imbecile. Apart from the fact that he can't hold his liquor, he can't keep his hands off the other women present. Emma must be mortified.'

Winston smiled thinly, his animosity for Arthur barely concealed. 'I know. You don't have to tell me. He's a dyed-in-the-wool bastard. And furthermore, I'm quite sure he does it on purpose. As for Emma, she appears not to notice. That's sheer defensiveness, of course. You know my sister. She doesn't miss a trick.' Winston shook his head. 'I'll be glad when Frank and Natalie are married next week, and these interminable luncheons and dinners end. Then we won't have to suffer Ainsley's continuing presence.'

'He's a bit of an unsavoury character, isn't he?' Paul probed. Winston was silent, and Paul continued, 'I know a lot of Englishmen of his particular upbringing and education do have somewhat effeminate mannerisms, and that these don't necessarily indicate a lack of masculinity, but, if I didn't know differently, I'd swear to God he was a raving homosexual. Don't you agree, Winston?'

'It's crossed my mind, and more than once lately. I've noticed a change in Arthur over the past few months. Certain tendencies seem to be coming out. Being married to Emma and fathering the twins doesn't necessarily preclude sexual deviation, although I've no evidence to prove that about him. And he does go after women all the time.'

Paul frowned. 'Perhaps he likes both sexes. That's not unheard of, you know – bisexuality.'

'I wish to God my sister had never married him. We all tried to stop her, but she's very stubborn. She was on the rebound, of course.'

'I realize that only too well,' Paul muttered, and looked down at the drink in his hand. 'You don't have to rub it in.'

Winston drew Paul into a secluded corner of Lionel Stewart's drawing room, where the guests had gathered after a prenuptial luncheon. Winston, who had always liked Paul, had discovered that his admiration and empathy for the Australian had only increased over the past ten days when, at various social functions, they had been thrown together and had gravitated to each other. Now he said, in a confidential tone, 'Frank tells me you have been seeing quite a lot of Emma during the last month. I'm happy about that.' Observing the look of astonishment flit across Paul's handsome face, Winston grinned. 'I know you regard me as the protective older brother, so I just wanted you to know that I approve, in spite of the complications in your very complicated lives. Emma needs a man like you, Paul. To be accurate, she needs *you*. You're about the only man I know who is strong enough to handle her on a permanent basis. She can be quite intimidating. Most men can't cope with an independent and brilliant woman – albeit a very alluring one!'

Paul smiled engagingly, a trifle startled, but delighted at this endorsement. 'Thanks, Winston. I'm glad to hear it. And I agree with you.' His eyes crinkled with laughter. 'Do me a favour and tell that to the lady in question. I need all the help I can get.'

'I have told her. So has Frank. But you know Emma. She has to make up her own mind.' Winston regarded Paul keenly. 'Perhaps she thinks you'll take off for Australia at any moment. After all, you do have vast business interests there.'

'True enough. However, I've told her that I intend to be around for a long time. It doesn't seem to make a dent. Actually I've reorganized my business enterprises so well in the last few years I will only need to make an occasional trip to Australia from now on – maybe once a year, twice at the most. Emma is also aware that I expanded my London offices last year and that I'm going to operate from here in the future.' He shook his head. 'I don't say much any more because she always looks sceptical. I can't say I blame her.'

'Maybe you've been *too* subtle,' Winston volunteered. 'You know what women are like. Sometimes you've got to spell everything out for them.'

'Emma's hardly like most women.'

'That's the understatement of the year.' Winston laughed. 'Give her a chance to get used to the idea that you're here on a permanent basis. She'll come around to accepting it eventually.'

Paul nodded and glanced about the spacious, elegantly appointed drawing room, seeking out Emma. He spotted her talking to Frank and Natalie and the latter's parents. It was a scorching July day and everyone was suffering from the heat. The guests looked uncomfortable and a little wilted – except for the incomparable Emma. She was wearing a yellow silk summer frock that was simply styled, crisp and fresh. It gave her a carefree girlish air, as did the gay confection on top of her russet bobbed hair. She looked exceedingly feminine, and the other women paled in comparison. It was not only her beauty that set her apart, but that incandescent glow which emanated from her. It took one hell of a woman to conduct herself so elegantly and with such composure in the light of Ainsley's antics, he conceded. Then he saw, to his surprise, that Emma was leaving. He handed his drink to Winston hastily. 'Look after this, old chap. I'll be back in a minute. Excuse me.'

Paul caught up with Emma in the entrance hall. 'Where are you off to in such a hurry?' he asked, taking her arm possessively and turning her to face him fully. 'Running out? I thought I was the only one who did that.' He chuckled.

Emma could not help laughing. 'I am also fleet of foot when I want to be, Mr McGill,' she said. 'I felt it would be simpler if I made a quiet exit. I didn't want to break up the party, and unfortunately, I have to get back to the store.'

Like hell you do, Paul commented dryly to himself, guessing she wanted to escape her ludicrous husband. 'I'll drive you,' Paul asserted swiftly, taking charge and propelling her to the door.

At first Emma made a little desultory conversation as Paul edged his Rolls-Royce through the Saturday afternoon traffic congesting Mayfair. But after a few moments she fell silent, ruminating on the luncheon. She was seething. Arthur's tasteless display had appalled her. He had not only demeaned himself but her as well. Usually indifferent to him, she had experienced real discomfiture during lunch and afterwards. She had handled it well, concealing her fury behind a dignified façade, yet, nonetheless, Arthur's disregard for the social amenities rankled. She could no longer afford to turn a blind eye. After Frank's wedding she would not expose herself in social situations. In part, her embarrassment sprang from the fact that Paul had witnessed it all. And yet, curiously, his presence had also been comforting.

Emma stole a glance at Paul, wondering what he was thinking. His face revealed nothing. On her recent trips to London she had dined with Paul on a regular basis. He had taken her to the theatre and the opera, and to parties. He had been charming, gallant – and oddly detached. She had half expected him to make overtures after their first few evenings together, but he had not, somewhat to her relief. In all honesty, she had wanted to see him, to spend time with him, and she could not deny he held a fascination for her. On the other hand, her inbred sense of self-preservation still made her wary of him. Her marriage was no marriage at all, yet the rest of her life was orderly. She could not permit anything to jeopardize her tranquil state of mind, acquired at such cost, and Paul could easily do that because he had the ability to hurt her. She was determined never to suffer for love again. An unprecedented feeling of depression swamped her. She looked at her watch.

'Perhaps you had better take me home, Paul,' she said. 'It's a bit late to go to the store. It's almost five o'clock.'

'Of course,' Paul said. 'Anything you want, Emma.' He noticed that her expression was pensive and a wave of tenderness swept through him. As he stopped at the traffic lights he pondered on her, trying to gauge her feelings for him. She was pleasant and gay whenever they met, yet she held herself apart, and he had admitted days ago that she was impervious to his charms. He knew she was riddled with insecurity about him and he had acted accordingly, endeavouring to dispel this, but apparently without success. He wondered if his strategy had been all wrong. As he headed towards Belgrave Square he made a snap decision, drove around the square, bypassed Wilton Mews, and headed back to Mayfair.

'Where are you going?' Emma asked in a puzzled voice. 'I thought you were taking me home.'

'That's exactly where I am taking you. *Home*. With me.'

Emma gasped. 'But –'

'No buts, Emma,' he said forcefully and with a finality that forbade argument.

Emma held herself stiffly in the seat, clutching her bag. A protest rose on her lips, remained unspoken as her mouth went dry. Taken aback at this sudden bold move on his part, she found herself in a quandary. She had never been to his flat and was petrified of being alone with him. A self-deprecatory smile slid on to her face. She, who was afraid of nothing and no one, was actually frightened of Paul McGill! Yet he was only a man. After all, she was a grown woman and perfectly capable of looking after herself. Anyway, was not life full of risks?

His face was rigidly set and determined and he appeared to be perturbed. The tension in his broad shoulders conveyed itself to her, and she shivered involuntarily. Her eyes focused on his strong hands, which gripped the steering wheel so fiercely his knuckles protruded sharply, and, to her consternation, her heart began to beat with unusual rapidity.

Paul brought the car to a stop in Berkeley Square. Silently he helped her out and took hold of her arm firmly, manoeuvring her across the lobby and into the lift. His fingers bit into her flesh, yet she welcomed his support. She thought her legs would buckle at any moment.

He did not release her even after they had entered his flat. He slammed the door shut with ferocity and swung her to face him. He lifted her veil with the other hand, searching her face, and then he pulled her to him roughly. His lips crushed down on hers, hard and insistent. She tried to push him away, but he was too strong for her. He tightened his hold on her, tremors rippling along his arms, and she heard his heart banging like a sledgehammer in his expansive chest. His mouth suddenly softened on hers. He parted her lips gently and found her tongue with his. Emma ceased struggling as a swooning faintness enveloped her. She found herself yielding to him, clinging to him, returning his kisses. Her handbag fell to the floor unheeded. His hands slid down her back and on to her buttocks, and he pressed her body into his so that they were welded together. He shifted his stance slightly and she felt the hardness of his rising passion through the thin silk of her frock and her legs almost gave way, and she was suffused with that old familiar warmth which spread like fire through her body. He pushed her head back against his wide shoulder and covered her breast with one hand, his fingers rubbing against it and playing with the nipple with increasing urgency. She was overwhelmed by him, and filled with exquisite sensations long forgotten but now so well remembered. She was helpless in his arms.

Paul's fervent kisses ceased abruptly, and he looked down into her face. She gazed back at him dizzily, saw the wild desire leaping from his clear blue eyes, took in the burgeoning impatience congesting his face, recognized the physical and emotional pressures driving him beyond endurance, and new tremors swept through her. Her lips opened and a cry strangled in her throat. His face closed in on her, his eyes darkening to brooding violet, and he was kissing her again, ravaging her mouth almost savagely, and she did not want him to stop. Prayed he would not stop. Desire engulfed her, and all of her true feelings surfaced, obliterating her fears, both rational and irrational. Her defences crumbled like a sand castle before an onrushing tide, and she willingly surrendered to him, her sensuality, so long submerged, taking hold of her completely, dazing her.

He placed her away from him, but he did not remove his hands from her shoulders. His mouth curved up in a small challenging smile. He leaned forward, pressing her against the door. 'Now tell me you don't love me!' he whispered hoarsely in her ear. 'Now tell me you don't want me!' His breath was warm and tantalizing against her throat. Before she could respond, he said in a low voice thickened by desire, 'You can't deny either, Emma, because I know you do!' He peered deeply into her burning face and perceived the yearning in her eyes that surely reflected his own, and he finally released her. He took her hand gently in his and led her into the bedroom.

Late-afternoon sunlight was streaming in through the windows and Paul left her to draw the curtains. The room was suddenly cool and dim. Mesmerized, she stood in the middle of the floor watching him. He swung around and strode back to her, moving lithely, like a great panther, and he appeared taller and broader and more domineering in his masculinity than ever. He removed her hat and tossed it on to a chair. He pulled off her gloves slowly. He unbuttoned her dress and slipped it over her shoulders. It fell to the floor, a rippling pool of yellow at her feet. He guided her away from the dress and sat her down on the bottom of the bed, all the while smiling at her faintly, and his eyes did not once leave her face. He discarded his jacket, his tie, and his shirt, and she caught her breath, stunned at the sight of his handsome torso and the sheer physical size and beauty of him.

He knelt before her. He took off her shoes and kissed her feet, and then he buried his head in her lap. Automatically she ran her hands through his crisp black hair and bent to kiss the crown. She smoothed her fingers over his enormous shoulders and down his sunburned back, and she felt his muscles rippling under her touch.

'There hasn't been a day I haven't thought about you, Emma. A day I haven't wanted you. Longed for you. Needed you, my love. Never in all these years,' he cried in a muffled voice. He gripped her thighs, burying his face deeper into her. He finally raised his head and looked up, his eyes brilliant. 'I've never stopped loving you, Emma.'

'And I've never stopped loving you, Paul,' she said softly, and her eyes grew huge, turned dark, and swam with tears.

He stood up and pressed her back on to the bed. He stretched himself on top of her, encircling her with his arms, kissing her face, her throat, and her shoulders. It seemed to Paul that the rest of their clothes just fell away. They were naked and in each other's arms again, and he was blinded by his searing passion, the feverishness of his unendurable desire. He could hardly wait to possess her, to become one with her, but he controlled himself rigorously, leading her along as he always had in the past, arousing her as only he could. He covered her entire body with kisses, and caressed every intimate and erotic part of her until she gasped with delight, and her unbridled excitement only served to inflame him more than ever.

She thought: *There is only him. He is the only thing that matters in my life. He is the only man I have ever truly loved and desired. If he goes away, and I never see him again as long as I live, this moment will have been worth it. It will last me for ever.*

He felt her fingers gripping his shoulders. She stiffened and spasmed and then her body was racked by shudders, and she called his name in a low moaning voice and he knew, with the utmost certainty, that only with him had she experienced this special kind of ecstasy and fulfilment. He lifted his head and trailed his lips up over her smooth flat stomach until they reached her breasts. His mouth lingered there a moment and moved on into the hollow of her neck. She sighed and quivered under him, her arms entwining him, her hands sliding voluptuously down his back. He thought he was going to explode. He arched his body over hers, his arms braced on either side of her, and gazed down into her pleasure-filled eyes. Her deepest emotions were explicit on her face, that best-loved face that haunted him always, and he was moved by the wonder of it all, by the wonder of her, and his heart twisted.

And he took her then, his manhood at full flood, thrusting deeply into the very core of her, to touch her heart, and she responded with a rush of enveloping sweet warmth, spontaneously, wildly giving herself with no reserve. And her need for him was as clamouring as his need for her.

Memory became reality. Pain was transmuted into joy. Anger was diffused by passion. They were fused together in desire and exquisite bliss. Having suffered for each other and their love, there was a new awareness between them, an intensity of feelings heightened, a rare poignancy in their breathless consummation. And as perfect as their lovemaking had been in the past, this time it was more stunning than ever before, and they were devastated by the impact of their reunion.

Much later, when they lay clasped in each other's arms, unable to tear themselves apart, shattered and exhausted, Paul said, 'I will never leave you again, Emma. Never, as long as I live. I know you're afraid I will hurt you. But I won't. You must believe me, my darling.'

'I'm not afraid, Paul,' she said against his chest. 'And I do believe you. I know now you will be with me always.'

He felt her smile. 'What is it?'

'Years ago someone called me Doubting Emma. Perhaps I was. Do you remember when you quoted Abélard to me and told me to have faith, before you went back to the front?'

'Yes, I do, my love.'

'Well, if I had had that faith, when you were absent in Australia in 1919, perhaps all this anguish and torment we have experienced could have been avoided. I'll never doubt you again.'

He smiled and pulled her closer to him and kissed a strand of her hair. 'We'll make up for the lost years,' he said.

FIFTY-FOUR

Emma let herself into her house in Roundhay, shivering slightly from the cold December wind. She slipped out of the sable coat, which Paul had bought for her the previous winter when they had been in New York together, and threw it on to a chair. She walked briskly across the hall, thinking of Paul with a rush of tenderness. She must telephone him immediately to let him know she was arriving in London tomorrow.

She went into the library and stopped dead in her tracks on the threshold, astonishment flashing on to her face. 'Good heavens, Edwina! What are you doing at home? I thought the winter term didn't end until next week.'

'It doesn't,' Edwina snapped, staring coldly at her mother.

Her daughter's face was unusually pale, and the girl's distress instantly communicated itself to her. Upon reaching the sofa Emma made a motion to kiss her, but Edwina swiftly averted her head. Faltering, Emma sat down opposite Edwina. On closer inspection the girl seemed positively ill. Or was it that grey school uniform which drained the colour from her face? Edwina looked almost gaunt in the winter afternoon light.

'Whatever is it, darling?' Emma asked with real concern. 'What are you doing at home? Did something happen to upset you?'

'No, it didn't. I came home because I wanted to see you,' Edwina retorted. 'To talk to you about this.' She pulled an envelope out of her pocket and tossed it to Emma.

'Whatever it is they are teaching you at that expensive boarding school, it certainly isn't manners,' Emma remarked softly, and bent to pick up the paper at her feet.

Edwina cried shrilly, 'You don't have to bother looking inside. It's my birth certificate. You wouldn't give me the original, so I wrote to Somerset House for a copy. You *know* what's on it. And now I know why you have hidden it from me all these years.'

The envelope fluttered in Emma's shaking hand and she stared at it blankly, the blood draining out of her. She looked at Edwina, a feeling of nausea overwhelming her, and her mouth was stiff and white-lipped. She could not speak.

In turn, Edwina regarded Emma fixedly, a scornful expression on her face. 'Why are *you* looking so shocked, *Mother?*' she spat. 'I'm the one who should be shocked. After all, I'm the one who is illegitimate.' She pronounced the word with such harshness, and her contempt was so evident, Emma flinched.

Edwina now leaned forward and her silver-grey eyes were febrile with hatred. 'How could you let me go on believing Joe Lowther was my father all these years, when it was Blackie O'Neill?' She laughed with derision. 'Blackie O'Neill! Your dearest friend. I'll bet he is. Hanging around you like a lovesick dog for as long as I can remember, and through two marriages!' Her eyes narrowed. 'You disgust me, Mother. I grieved for Joe for years after he was killed, and you let me. How cruel of you!'

Emma managed to pull herself together, but her voice shook as she said, 'Would my telling you have helped, Edwina? Would it have assuaged your grief, or lessened it? Joe *was* your father, in the best sense of that word. He loved you as much, if not more than his own child. You loved him, too, and you would still have grieved for him if you had known the truth. Any man can father a child, Edwina. It's what a man does after the child is born that makes him a *real* father, a *good* father. And although you were not of Joe's flesh and blood he certainly treated you as if you were. And that's all that counts.'

'You were just protecting yourself! You – you – lying tramp!'

500

Emma gaped at the eighteen-year-old girl sitting before her and she did not know what to do, or to say, to calm her, to deflect her obvious pain.

'And what am I supposed to call myself, might I ask, Mother *dear*? I don't have a name, do I? Is it O'Neill? Or Harte, perhaps?' Edwina sucked in her breath harshly and her eyes were metallic. 'You are a lying, immoral bitch!'

Emma recoiled as if she had been slapped but she ignored the abusive remarks and took control of herself. 'Your name is Lowther, Edwina. Joe adopted you and gave you his name.'

'Thank you. That's all I wanted to know.' Edwina rose and held out her hand. 'I'll have my birth certificate, since I went to so much trouble to get it.' She grabbed it from Emma rudely. 'I am leaving.'

Emma also rose. She took hold of Edwina's arm, but the girl snatched it away angrily. 'Don't touch me!' she screamed, and darted across the library.

'Edwina, please sit down,' Emma said quietly. 'You are old enough to discuss this with me calmly and intelligently. In a sensible manner.' Her voice took on a pleading note. 'Please, darling. I know you are terribly upset and hurt, but let me explain. Please give me a chance to tell you –'

'Nothing you have to say interests me. I'm leaving,' Edwina rejoined.

'Where are you going?' Emma asked agitatedly, and stepped forward, stretching out her hand imploringly to her daughter. 'Please, Edwina, don't go. Let us talk this out. I want to make you understand, and then perhaps you will forgive me for hiding the truth. I had good reasons. I wanted to protect you. I only had your welfare at heart, my darling. I love you.'

Edwina gave Emma a scathing look and her voice was tinged with bitterness. 'I told you I am not interested in your explanations.' She drew herself up haughtily. 'I am leaving this house and I will never set foot in it again.'

'But, darling, you can't leave! Where will you go?' Emma's throat ached with suppressed tears.

'I am going to stay with Cousin Freda in Ripon for Christmas. After the holidays, I intend to go to finishing school in Switzerland. The one I asked you to send me to, but which you refused to consider. Please make the necessary arrangements now.' Edwina smiled contemptuously. 'You're rich enough to pull all the right strings to get me in at this late date. I presume you will continue to pay my school tuition, Mother. And that you will not stop my allowance.'

'How could you even think that?' Emma cried. 'I have never deprived you of anything and I never will. Please stay.' Emma's eyes brimmed and her voice was unsteady. 'Don't leave like this. Let us discuss –'

'I have said all I want to say to you.' Edwina stepped purposefully to the door. Her hand rested briefly on the knob. She turned and looked at Emma and her delicate face twisted. 'I hate you, Mother! I never want to see you again as long as I live!'

The door slammed behind Edwina. Emma stared at it, her face crumpling, and she staggered into the nearest chair. She dropped her head into her hands and the tears rolled silently down her cheeks. She had dreaded this day for years, had tried to avert this ugly confrontation. And now that it had finally happened she felt incapable of dealing with Edwina, who was so unbending. She had always known her daughter would react violently, just as she had always known she would lose Edwina's affection, scant as it was, when the truth was revealed. Edwina had never had any deep feelings for her. Edwina had loved only Joe and Freda. All the devotion and tenderness she had showered on her firstborn had fallen on stony ground. Edwina had rejected her, even as a small child. She wondered suddenly if she should go and tell Edwina who her real father was. But that would not assuage Edwina's pain and terrible humiliation. She would still be illegitimate. It was better to let matters rest for the moment. A jumble of painful memories and stark images danced around in her head. She thought of her struggles, the sacrifices she had made, the fears and humiliations she had experienced. And she thought, too, of all she had done to shield Edwina. Had it all been for nothing? Surely not. Besides, she had not known what else to do, and she *had* done her best.

Emma wiped the tears from her face, and her inherent optimism surfaced. Perhaps in a few weeks, when Edwina was calmer, there would be a chance for a reconciliation. This new thought cheered her and she hurried upstairs. She would persuade Edwina to meet with her after Christmas, beg her to do so if necessary, and surely somehow they could reach an understanding. But to Emma's dismay the girl was nowhere to be found. Emma stood in the centre of Edwina's room, staring at the open armoire where empty coat hangers told their own story. She crossed to the window, looking down into the driveway. The Rolls had disappeared. Edwina had obviously asked the the chauffeur to take her to the railway station. Emma pressed her throbbing head against the windowpane and she knew, with a terrible sinking feeling, that there never would be a reconciliation. Her daughter was lost to her.

She turned away, her face ashen and troubled, and walked with leaden steps into her own bedroom. She must speak to Blackie. She reached for the phone and then her hand fell away. He was in Ireland until next week, which would be soon enough to break the news. Emma sat down wearily, overcome by a sense of loss. And her heart ached for Edwina, who was suffering such agonies, and she longed to comfort her.

Eventually Emma stood up, pulling herself together with effort, and went into the bathroom. She splashed cold water on to her aching face and her swollen eyes, and redid her makeup. When she was sufficiently composed, Emma telephoned Arthur at the office. 'Are you coming home for dinner tonight?' she asked quietly when he came to the phone.

Arthur was taken aback. 'No. Why?' he asked in his usual peremptory tone.

'I must see you, Arthur. It's rather urgent, actually, since I am leaving for London tomorrow. I won't take up much of your time. Just half an hour at the most.'

'Well – all right,' he acquiesced grudgingly, although more from curiosity than a desire to please her. 'I'll be there in about twenty minutes.'

'Thank you, Arthur.' Emma hung up and went downstairs to wait for her husband.

When Arthur entered the library a little later he gave her a guarded look and said, 'What's ruffled your feathers? You look bloody awful.' He poured himself a drink and carried it to the fireplace. He sat down opposite Emma and scrutinized her with great interest. 'What's wrong?'

Emma said, 'Arthur, I have something important to tell you.'

'Go ahead, my dear. I'm all ears.'

'I'm going to have a baby,' Emma said evenly.

Arthur had the drink in his hand halfway to his mouth and for once in his life it did not reach its destination. He banged it down unsteadily and gawped at her, for a moment nonplussed. And then he threw back his head and laughed. 'Oh my God! That's rich! Little Miss Goody Two-shoes has finally taken a lover. He must be a brave man indeed to want to tango with you!' he cried. 'And who's the lucky fellow?'

'I have no intention of telling you that, Arthur. I merely wanted you to know that I am almost four months pregnant. I am going to have the child, and you will recognize it as yours.'

'You don't think I'm going to give some bastard my name, do you? That's preposterous. I shall divorce you immediately, Emma.'

'I don't think you will, Arthur.' Emma fixed her cool gaze on him and smiled faintly. 'I don't want a divorce. At least, not at this moment. And neither do you.'

'I bloody well do. You're not going to rear your illegitimate brat as mine.'

Emma rose and walked across to the bookshelves. She pressed a button and a panel swung open to reveal a concealed safe. She opened it, removed a pile of documents, and returned to the fireplace. She looked at Arthur thoughtfully and said, 'Your father is a conservative old gentleman, Arthur. And as fond of him as I am, I have to admit he is also narrow-minded and decidedly old-fashioned. If I give him these documents he will cut you out of his will at once, and without the proverbial shilling. And I fully intend to hand them over to him if you make trouble for me, or attempt to divorce me. And these do make fascinating reading.' She smiled her icy smile. 'Your father may not be surprised to learn of your gross infidelities to me over the years, or of your excessive drinking and gambling. However, Arthur, I am quite certain he will be shocked to discover his son, his heir, has questionable relationships with young men of dubious character who are known sexual deviants.'

Arthur looked like a man who had been handed a death sentence. 'That's a damnable lie!' he shouted. 'You're bluffing!'

'No, I'm not, Arthur. You see, I have had a detective on you for several years. There is absolutely nothing I don't know about your private life. Unfortunately you have not been very discreet.'

'I say you are bluffing!' Arthur yelled.

Emma offered him the documents. 'See for yourself.'

He snatched them from her anxiously and shuffled through them, his eyes widening. He paled, and then an embarrassed flush suffused his neck and face. He looked at her, and very deliberately began to tear the papers into shreds, throwing the pieces into the fire.

Emma let him continue without a word and, when he had disposed of them entirely, she laughed. 'Oh, Arthur, you do underestimate me. Those were copies. I have the originals safely locked away. And, furthermore, I won't hesitate to use them if you force my hand. I promise you I *will* go to your father.'

'You bloody cow! That's blackmail!'

'Call it what you will, Arthur.' Emma sat back and folded her hands in her lap.

He stood up unsteadily. 'What a nerve you have! Expecting me to live in this house with you, when you're carrying another man's bastard.' He laughed hollowly. 'I'm not going to tolerate your adultery.'

Emma looked at him coldly. 'Don't be a hypocrite. That's exactly what I've been tolerating for years.'

He stepped away with abruptness, glaring at her with unconcealed animosity. He was shaking now and his face was strained and grey. He looked down at her. 'You bitch!' he hissed. 'You may have won this round, but we'll see about the next.'

Emma remained utterly still, and she was silent. Arthur continued to glower at her for a prolonged moment and then he walked across the room in swift deliberate steps. When he reached the door he swung to face her. He was livid and fuming with rage. He drew in his breath. 'God, how I hate you!' he cried, then he left the library, banging the door behind him with a thunderous crash.

FIFTY-FIVE

Paul McGill paced the floor of Emma's living room in Wilton Mews with restless impatience, his hands plunged deep into his pockets, his shoulders hunched. He stopped at the window and gazed out, and when he eventually turned his head his eyes focused on Emma with intensity. He observed her reflectively, his face troubled.

Finally, he said, 'I don't understand why you didn't ask Arthur for a divorce, Emma. I really don't. I thought we had agreed you would seek your freedom immediately. Why are you procrastinating? Is it because Constance won't divorce me? Don't you trust me? Don't you know that I intend to be with you always? I would like an explanation, Emma.'

'Come and sit down next to me, darling,' Emma said gently.

Paul joined her on the sofa and she took his hand in hers. 'Of course I trust you, Paul. My decision had nothing to do with your situation. I know you are doing everything you can to rectify it. And I *will* divorce Arthur. But not until after the baby has been born, registered, and christened. I want the baby to have a name, Paul. I don't want the birth certificate to show that it is illegitimate.'

'What you are actually saying is that you want *my* child to be brought up as Ainsley's! I don't like that, Emma. I'm not sure I will stand for it!'

Emma stared at him in surprise. This was the first time he had ever spoken harshly to her. She must make him understand her motives. 'I know how you feel,' she placated. 'But we must think about the child, Paul. You see –'

'I *am* thinking about the child. I want it to have the benefit of my love and protection and all the other things I can give it, and I don't want it growing up not knowing *me*. Furthermore, I want my child reared under my influence and not another man's. I won't have it living under Ainsley's roof under any circumstances. You know my opinion of him. I thought I had made myself clear about all this, Emma.'

'Yes, you did, darling. I told you the baby would remain in London. But I must protect the child. It must not carry the stigma of illegitimacy all of its life.'

Paul sighed impatiently. 'My money will protect the child, Emma. Give it immunity from scandal. Besides, I told you I would adopt it immediately. Please, Emma, you must consider naming me as the father on the birth certificate. I wish to acknowledge paternity.'

'No! We can't do that!' Emma cried fiercely, her eyes flaring. Instantly recognizing the hurt flickering on his face, she brought his hand up to her lips and kissed it. She looked at Paul long and hard. She drew a deep breath and very slowly, in a sure voice, she told him.

She told him first of her confrontation with Edwina the preceding day, and of the way she had handled Arthur. She told him about her early life as a servant at Fairley Hall. She told him about Edwin Fairley, her pregnancy, his repudiation of her, and her anguished flight to Leeds as a terrified young girl. She told him about her struggles and her poverty, her deprivations and the punishing days of toil she had endured. She told him of Gerald Fairley's attempted rape of her. She told him everything there was to know, and she spoke with candour and with eloquence, and she neither embellished nor dramatized. Very simply, she gave him the facts without any show of emotion.

Paul listened attentively, his eyes riveted on her face, and he was moved as he had never been before by anyone. When she had finished he took her in his arms and stroked her hair, and pulled her closer to him, overwhelmed by feelings of protectiveness and abiding love.

'Whoever passed around the ridiculous story that this is a civilized world we live in?' he murmured into her hair, and kissed her forehead. He fell silent and then he said softly, 'Oh, Emma, Emma. I have to make up for so much – all the pain you have suffered over the years. And I will. I promise you that.'

Paul held her away from him and looked deeply into her eyes. 'Why ever didn't you tell me all this before?' When she dropped her eyes and did not answer, he continued gently, 'Did you think it would have made any difference to the way I feel about you?' He bent forward and kissed her on the lips. 'You don't know me very well if you think your past matters to me. I love you all the more for what you have made of yourself, what you have become. And for your indomitability and enormous strength. You are a very special woman, Emma.'

'I didn't deliberately avoid telling you,' Emma said quietly. 'There just never seemed to be the right opportunity.'

Paul gazed at her, his heart bursting with his love. He thought: Oh, my darling, what cruelties and humiliations you must have endured and how bravely you have dealt with life.

Emma said, 'You do understand now, don't you, Paul? I mean about my not divorcing Arthur just yet. I don't want our child to turn on me one day. I couldn't bear a repetition of yesterday's scene with Edwina.'

'That would never happen. Not with our child. But yes, I do understand,' he said, 'I will do whatever you want, Emma.'

Their child, a girl, was born early in May of 1925, at a private nursing home in London. It was Paul who paced the waiting-room floor. It was Paul who took Emma in his arms after the delivery. It was Paul who chose the baby's name. She was to be called Daisy after his mother.

The following day Paul visited Emma, his face wreathed in smiles, his arms filled with flowers and gifts. 'Where's my daughter?' he asked.

'The nurse will bring her in momentarily,' Emma said, smiling radiantly.

He settled himself on the edge of the bed and embraced Emma. 'And how's my love?'

'I'm wonderful, Paul. But you must stop spoiling me.'

'You might as well get used to it. That's the way it is going to be from now on.' He took her hand in his and to her amazement he pulled off her wedding ring before she could protest, opened the window, and threw it out.

'Good heavens, Paul, whatever are you doing?'

He did not respond. He reached into his pocket and took out a platinum wedding band. He slipped it on to her finger and then he added the great square-cut McGill emerald which had belonged to his mother and his grandmother before her.

'We may not have had the benefit of clergy, but as far as I'm concerned you are my wife,' he said. 'From this day forward until death do us part.'

Since his return to England in 1923, Paul Mcgill had made his feelings for Emma obvious in every way. He was passionately in love with her and his emotional involvement transcended all else in his life. He admired her as well, and was filled with a sense of pride in her achievements. After the birth of their daughter these feelings were only intensified. She and their child became the core of his life, his reason for living. They gave shape and meaning to everything he did, to the way he ran his life and his enormous business enterprises. Old disappointments and defeats, and the hurts which had accumulated over the years, were swept away and he was filled with burgeoning hopes for the future. Daisy might not bear his name, but she was his child, of his blood, and in her he saw the continuation of the McGill line and the dynasty founded by his grandfather, the Scottish sea captain who had settled in Coonamble in 1852.

In all truth, he worshipped Emma and Daisy and he had no intention of letting either of them out of his sight, or his presence, for very long, despite the complications of their lives and the obstacles presented by their marital entanglements. He took matters firmly into his own hands in the late summer of 1925, when he purchased an unusually beautiful mansion in Belgrave Square, immediately giving the deeds of ownership to Emma. He then set about remodelling it into two flats, sparing no expense. The smaller bachelor quarters on the ground floor he retained for himself. The three floors above became an exquisitely appointed maisonette for Emma, Daisy, a nanny, a housekeeper, and a maid, whom he engaged. To the casual observer the two flats were entirely separate and self-contained, each having its own entrance. But they were linked by a private interior elevator.

They lived together, but discreetly so, with an eye to all the proprieties, for Emma was reluctant to flaunt their relationship in view of her other children and her responsibilities as a mother. Paul was constantly astonished at the duality in her nature. He would tease her, calling her a bundle of contradictions, and point out that she, who was so fearless in business and scorned what the world thought of her, was curiously sensitive about public opinion regarding her personal morals. 'Once I'm divorced I won't give a damn,' she would temporize, and Paul would simply smile, realizing that her self-consciousness about their life sprang from the experiences of her early life.

As it happened, the divorce came sooner than anyone anticipated. In June, acutely aware of Emma's overwhelming desire to protect their child, Paul permitted Emma to take Daisy to Yorkshire, agreeing she could be christened at a local church in Leeds. However, he insisted on being invited and travelled to Yorkshire with Frank and Natalie for the occasion. As a long-standing friend of the family, his presence was not unseemly, and, because of an unexpected turn of events, it actually went almost unnoticed. Several days prior to the christening, Arthur Ainsley's mother collapsed and died of a heart attack. The baptism, following so quickly on the heels of the funeral, was a glum affair and Frederick Ainsley and Arthur were so grief-stricken they were hardly aware of the proceedings or of the other guests, and, also, Arthur had no interest in the event. Daisy was duly christened without incident and the next day Emma took her back to London. Three months later Frederick Ainsley, old, frail, and long in ill health, followed his wife to the grave. Arthur came into his inheritance and, in an unprecedented show of gallantry that stunned Emma's brothers, he allowed her to divorce him on the grounds of adultery. Emma was not stunned. She had cannily bought Arthur's gallantry for ten thousand pounds.

Once the decree nisi was granted, Emma's life changed radically. She brought the twins, Robin and Elizabeth, to live with her in Belgrave Square, and, just as she had guessed, Arthur made no objections. Apart from being happy to be free of him at last, she also welcomed the idea of bringing up the twins without his influence.

Kit, who was at boarding school, spent half terms and vacations with Emma and made no secret of the fact that he approved of Paul and was devoted to him. Nor did he shed any tears about the abrupt disappearance of Arthur Ainsley from his young life. Emma also reorganized her business drastically, so that she could spend most of her time in London. Winston was appointed managing director of the Yorkshire shops and the mills, and Emma supervised her northern industries from her headquarters at the Knightsbridge store, making a monthly trip to Leeds, where she spent five hectic days, working long hours with Winston.

She and Paul were as circumspect as possible, especially in front of the children, but as time passed no one seemed to care about their unusual living arrangements and their rather extraordinary household filled with her diverse children by different fathers. Very early Paul had established himself as the titular head of the household and with his strength, plus his inherent gentleness, he was both respected and adored by the children, and he quickly became the father figure to them all. Slowly Emma began to relax. Paul had patiently explained to her that their combined wealth set them above the usual conventions, making them invulnerable to social censorship, and she admitted the truth in what he said. Her natural self-confidence and courage soon overcame her earlier misgivings.

Paul and Emma were inseparable. He bedecked her in magnificent jewels and furs and lovely gowns. He entertained on a lavish scale with her at his side as his hostess. They went to the theatre, the opera, concerts, dinners, and parties. They mixed with the wealthiest and the most influential people in London and in other cities across the world – politicians, tycoons, socialites, and men and women from the arts and letters on three continents. He took her to the capitals of Europe when he travelled, whether for business or pleasure. She went with him to New York and to Texas, where his oil fields were located, and twice she accompanied him on his annual trips to Australia. Just as she had fallen in love with New York and Texas, so, too, was she captivated by the Antipodes. Paul was still endeavouring to gain his freedom, but continually met implacable opposition from Constance, who would not agree to a divorce. This was the one thing that marred his happiness. Although he had legally adopted Daisy, and had provided for both her and her mother, he desperately wanted to marry Emma and put their lives in order. However, so secure was Emma in their relationship by this time she was unperturbed by the situation and constantly tried to alleviate Paul's anxiety. Now it was she who told *him* to relax and not to fret so much, optimistically remarking that things would work out in the end, reiterating her love for him and reassuring him of her happiness.

The only disturbing factor in Emma's life was Edwina's continued estrangement, for she had not been able to mend the rift between them. Her only tenuous communication with her eldest daughter was through Winston, who took care of Edwina's financial affairs on Emma's behalf. After two years at the finishing school in Switzerland, Edwina had taken a flat in Mayfair and was leading a dizzy social life with her upper-class friends, enjoying her status as the well-heeled daughter of a very rich woman. Emma had not curtailed Edwina's spending, and had set up a trust fund for her which gave the girl an annual income of no mean proportions. Emma longed to see Edwina, to draw her back into the bosom of the family, yet she was wise enough to refrain from making overtures, understanding that the first move must necessarily come from the girl.

And so for the most part Emma was content, more so than ever before. Paul's abiding love, and hers for him, sustained her at all times. Emma also took great consolation in Daisy, who was her particular pride, and even though she was reluctant to admit it even to herself, she loved Daisy more than any of her other children. This was the child of love, the one child she truly carried with joy. There was a closeness between them she had not experienced with those born before, and it only became stronger with time. Sometimes, when she looked at the growing child, Emma's heart would clench with the most overwhelming feelings of tenderness, seeing her beloved Paul so perfectly reflected in her. For Daisy was undoubtedly her father's daughter, favouring him in every way. Being his constant companion, she unconsciously copied many of his mannerisms and when she smiled her face became as mischievous and as endearing to Emma as his. By nature Daisy was sweet and loving, and because of the affection and attentions showered on her by her parents she was a self-confident, outgoing little girl, yet she was utterly unspoiled and natural with everyone. There was much of Emma in her character. She had inherited her mother's sunny disposition, her optimism, and her stubborn will.

When Daisy was five years old, Paul had insisted she accompany him and Emma to Australia. After a week in Sydney he took them up to Coonamble and they spent four weeks at Dunoon. An unusual rapport sprang up between the vivacious little girl and her half brother, Howard, and Emma and Paul were touched by the relationship. Daisy seemed to reach the boy in a way no one else ever had before, and her devotion to him and his dependency on her warmed their hearts. They returned every year thereafter with Paul, who did not want to deprive Howard of the joy his little stepsister so apparently brought to his restricted life.

The years slipped by so quickly Emma often wondered what happened to time. The children were all growing up and leaving the house in Belgrave Square. Kit, a fine-looking young man who much resembled Joe Lowther, went to Leeds University, and the twins departed for their respective boarding schools, bitterly complaining about being separated for the first time. If Daisy was Emma's best-loved child, then Robin was undoubtedly her favourite son, and she missed him more than she had realized she would during school terms. Robin had none of Arthur Ainsley's annoying characteristics or habits, and bore a strong likeness to Winston. He was a thin vital boy, with a vivid intelligence, a quick wit, and inbred charm. Scholarly by inclination, he was a brilliant student and Emma had high expectations for him.

His twin, Elizabeth, also favoured the Harte side of the family. Emma would sometimes look at her and catch her breath, seeing striking echoes of her own mother in the girl, and occasionally she even caught a fleeting glimpse of Olivia Wainwright in Elizabeth's lovely face. She would ponder briefly then on the past, recalling the uncanny resemblance between those two women from such different worlds and which had so startled her as a girl. Of all Emma's children, Elizabeth was the real beauty, willowy, graceful, her exquisite face delicately translucent, surrounded by a thick cloud of dark hair. She too, was blessed with an abundance of charm. Unfortunately, Emma had long detected other traits in her, which she found dismaying. Elizabeth was violent of temper, flighty, and often difficult to control. Paul agreed with Emma that she needed a firm hand, and they hoped that the discipline of boarding school would tone her down without breaking her spirit.

Emma's businesses continued to grow. The Knightsbridge store became world-famous, the Yorkshire stores a household name in the North; the mills flourished, as did the Kallinski clothing factories; the Emeremm Company, now known as Harte Enterprises, blossomed into an enormously rich organization with diverse holdings throughout the world. By following her own shrewd instincts and listening to Paul's advice, Emma invested her money wisely and multiplied her worth three-fold, as well as that of Winston and Frank, whose personal financial affairs she supervised. By the time she was forty-six years old she was a millionairess many times over and a power to be reckoned with, not only in London and the north of England, but in international business circles as well.

Despite her happiness with Paul and her family, and as preoccupied as she was with her gargantuan business enterprises, Emma's interest in the Fairley family had not waned one iota. Their affairs continued to obsess her as they always had. Gerald Fairley, after she had ruined him in 1923, spent the last few miserable years of his life depending on the largesse of Edwin, since the brickyard was not a profitable concern. He died in 1926, 'obviously from the gross excesses of his nature', Emma had remarked to Blackie on hearing the news, and in the ensuing years her icy gaze had rested solely on Edwin. She followed his career with undivided interest. How she had longed for him to be a failure! But he had made a name for himself as a criminal lawyer of great brilliance, and there were constant rumours in the Temple that he would be made a KC, although this had not yet happened. He resided and practised in London, but he had not entirely severed his ties to Yorkshire. He was often in Leeds, where he devoted an unflagging amount of energy to the *Yorkshire Morning Gazette*, just as Adam Fairley had done before him. He was chairman of the board and the majority shareholder, and thus wielded the power on the newspaper.

Emma wanted that paper and she would stop at nothing to get it. Both Winston and Blackie pointed out that she had done enough to cripple the Fairley influence in Yorkshire, and remonstrated with her to drop her vendetta and forget about the newspaper. But Emma, as self-willed as always and still vindictive about the Fairleys, would not listen. She was determined to acquire their only remaining holding.

Gradually she began to buy up the common shares as they came on to the market, moving with her usual stealth, and waiting patiently until she could find the right opportunity to move against Edwin. Although the paper was losing money, Edwin somehow managed to keep it operating and he clung to his shares, much to Emma's frustration. Until she could wrest those shares from him she was powerless to move in and take over. She dreamed about the day she would oust Edwin. Only then would her revenge be complete.

'And I do have the patience of Job,' she told Winston one day in the summer of 1935. 'I won't rest until I own the *Yorkshire Morning Gazette*, and I will own it one day.'

'I know you will,' Winston said, and shifted in his chair. He lit a cigarette and went on, 'I had a call from Joe Fulton yesterday. He's prepared to sell you the remainder of his shares in the *Sheffield Star*. If you buy, you will have control. Do you want them?'

'I do indeed,' Emma declared, and her face brightened. 'I also think you should talk to Harry Metcalfe again. He's been hankering to sell the *Yorkshire Morning Observer* for a long time. I think I'd like to own it, after all. I can certainly use it as a vehicle against Edwin Fairley. Give him a run for his money and a lot of stiff competition. If we do buy the shares in both newspapers, I will really have a foothold in publishing in the North.' Her eyes lit up. 'Let's start a new company, Winston. What shall we call it? How about the Yorkshire Consolidated Newspaper Company?' she suggested, and rushed on, before Winston could reply, 'Yes, that's a strong-sounding name. Let's do it!'

'I can't think of any good reasons why you shouldn't take over both papers, Emma,' Winston said, suddenly infected by her enthusiasm. 'They can easily be turned around. All they need is good management, an infusion of money, and some top-notch journalists to inject new life. Maybe Frank can recommend the right men. I'll get on to it first thing tomorrow.'

'I do wish we'd thought of this before,' Emma exclaimed, hardly able to contain her excitement at the prospect of becoming a publisher, and going into competition with Edwin Fairley.

'Obvious ideas are generally the last ones we think of, you know,' Winston remarked casually, and stood up.

He walked slowly across the lovely upstairs parlour at Pennistone Royal, the great house near Ripon, which Emma had purchased three years before, and stood in front of the oriel window gazing down into the grounds. It was a glorious August Sunday, the sky a blaze of crystal blue above the clipped lawns, fanciful topiary hedges, and luxuriant abundance of trees, so verdant and lush and shimmering in the summer air. The gardens were spectacular, Elizabethan in design and so very English with their overwhelming greenness and profusion of vivid flower beds.

In the distance, he heard the plopping of tennis balls and he wondered how Paul found the energy to play three sets on such a gruelling day. His thoughts now turned to the news he had to impart to Emma, edging out all else as he sought the simplest way of doing it. His common sense told him to be direct. He looked at Emma sitting on the sofa, coolly beautiful in a white shantung dress and with her russet hair falling to her shoulders. Well, he might as well tell her. He said, 'I spoke to Edwina yesterday. She's getting married.'

'Married!' Emma repeated, sitting bolt upright on the sofa. She put down the balance sheet she was reading and gave him her full attention. 'To whom, might I ask?'

Winston cleared his throat. 'To Jeremy Standish.'

Emma stared at him open-mouthed. 'Jeremy Standish? The Earl of Dunvale?'

'That's right. The wedding is in two weeks. In Ireland, of course, at his estate, Clonloughlin.'

'But he's so much older than she is, Winston,' Emma said. 'I'm not so sure about this marriage.' She frowned. 'It's not a very likely match, in my opinion.'

'There's absolutely nothing you can do about it, Emma,' Winston pointed out, relieved her reaction had been so mild. 'After all, she is twenty-nine. Besides, it might just be the stabilizing influence she needs. And he does have pots and pots of money, you know.'

'Perhaps you're right,' Emma mused. She looked at Winston. 'I don't suppose she is inviting any members of the family.'

Winston shook his head. 'No, I'm afraid she's not. But she did ask me to give her away. How do you feel about that? Do you mind, dear?'

Emma leaned forward and clasped her hand over his. 'Oh, darling, of course not. I think it's wonderful of her to ask you. It would please me enormously. She won't seem quite so alone if you're there.' Emma paused and then asked hesitantly, 'Did she mention me?'

'No, Emma, she didn't. I'm sorry.'

'I must send a nice wedding present, of course.' Emma changed the subject, realizing there was nothing further to add, but her eyes were reflective as she continued her business discussion with her brother.

When Winston returned from Ireland, Emma was full of questions about Edwina, the Earl of Dunvale, and the wedding. Winston satisfied her curiosity, and assuaged her anxieties about Edwina's marriage to the man, who was twenty years her senior. It had been apparent to him that Edwina was deliriously happy, although he was not absolutely certain whether this was because she had become the Countess of Dunvale and a member of an ancient and celebrated Anglo-Irish family, or because she truly loved her husband. Dunvale, for his part, was besotted with Edwina, and Winston had no doubts about the bridegroom's feelings in the least.

A year later Emma became a grandmother, when Edwina gave birth to a son, baptized Anthony George Michael. As the first-born he had the courtesy title of Lord Standish and was heir to the earldom. Emma wrote to her daughter congratulating her, and sent a gift, as she had done at the time of the wedding. Emma received a courteous but cool thank-you note from Edwina and she was hopeful that it would lead to a complete reconciliation one day. And she determined to enlist Winston's help to effect this. Kit was not so positive. Feeling slighted at not having been invited to his sister's fancy society wedding, he took to making derogatory remarks about her disregard for family, and her snobbishness, whenever the opportunity presented itself. Paul constantly admonished him and finally, in exasperation, forbade him to discuss Edwina with his mother. He himself encouraged Emma's belief that she would be on friendly terms with her eldest daughter again, knowing that this was the only possibility acceptable to her, and he dare not demolish her hope.

One of Emma's greatest assets was her ability to shelve unsolvable problems, and eventually she managed to put Edwina out of her mind. The present was her first priority, her true imperative. Her own life was as demanding as always. There was her work, her relationship with Paul, and the other children. She had no complaints about them and in general things were harmonious. Kit was working in the mills and learning the woollen business. Robin, in his last year of boarding school, was preparing to go up to Cambridge to study law. Elizabeth had expressed a wish to follow in Edwina's footsteps and was at a fashionable Swiss finishing school. Finally the day came when Daisy left for boarding school, and Emma and Paul were alone in the house in Belgrave Square for the first time.

'I'm afraid you're stuck with me, and only me now,' he teased her one evening when they were having a glass of champagne in the library.

'I miss them all, particularly Daisy, but I'm glad we have our time together at last, Paul. Just the two of us.'

'And we do have lots of time, Emma. Years and years stretching ahead.' He grinned. 'I don't know how you feel, my love, but I rather like the prospect of growing old with you.'

It was the first week of September in 1938. And sitting there in the handsome mellow library, talking quietly as the twilight descended to fill the room with soft drifting shadows, it did not occur to Emma and Paul that anything could happen to destroy their security. They were at peace with themselves and with each other, and still deeply in love. And so they spoke for a long time about their future together, and made plans for the Christmas holidays at Pennistone Royal, and discussed their impending trip to America in the new year. Later they went out to dinner at Quaglino's, laughing and holding hands like young lovers, and it was one of the most carefree evenings they had spent in months.

But the Nazi shadow was spreading itself across Central Europe. Hitler, who gained power in Germany after the burning of the Reichstag in 1933, was on the march. War was inevitable. It was only a question of time.

FIFTY-SIX

'There will be a war in the Pacific, just as surely as there will be a war in Europe,' Paul McGill said quietly. 'The facts are incontrovertible. Japan industrialized late, as Germany did, and their success has shaped them both into arrogant, warlike nations with plans for world domination.' He paused and drew on his cigarette. 'I know I'm not wrong, Dan. America had better be prepared. Europe isn't, unfortunately.'

Daniel P. Nelson, one of the most powerful men in the world, and grandson of the most famous of all the great robber barons, nodded thoughtfully. He smiled but his eyes were worried as he said, 'I don't doubt you, Paul. I've been saying the same thing for months. Told the President, only last week when I was at Hyde Park, that Japan has real aims in the Pacific. Has had since the twenties, to be accurate. Roosevelt's not blind. He's aware of the situation. On the other hand, this country's still recovering from the Depression. Not unnaturally, his thoughts are focused on the domestic scene. There are still ten million unemployed here, Paul.'

'Yes, I know. What worries me is that since Congress passed three neutrality acts a few years ago the prevailing attitude has been isolationist. It still is, I'm afraid. However, America can't possibly remain neutral if Britain goes to war with Germany.'

Dan said, 'But as far as Roosevelt's concerned, I know he's not an isolationist himself. I feel he will come to Britain's aid if the necessity arises. We've been natural allies for more than a century, and he's also aware he can't let the West sink. But – enough of all this depressing talk of war. Emma is looking far too grave.'

'I am concerned,' Emma said, 'as any informed person is today. My brother is a political writer in London, and he believes Hitler seeks global power and will stop at nothing to get it. Unfortunately, like his good friend Winston Churchill, Frank is patently ignored. When will the world open its eyes and see what is going on?'

Dan smiled faintly. 'The prospect of another world war is frightening, my dear. There is a tendency to dismiss those with the vision to foresee onrushing disaster. The public has a bad habit of sticking its collective head in the sand, as do a great number of politicians.'

'I suppose that's human nature – the desire not to face such a terrible reality as war. But some of us must be prepared –' She stopped short, as Paul caught her eye. Aware that he wished to discuss business with Dan Nelson, she murmured, 'Well, I'll leave you. If you will excuse me, I must attend to my other guests.'

The two men watched her glide across the drawing room, the white chiffon evening gown floating out behind her, the magnificent emeralds blazing at her throat and ears, on her arms and hands. Dan said, 'I do believe Emma's the most remarkable woman I've ever met. You're a lucky man.'

'I know,' Paul replied. He turned his attention to Dan Nelson and went on, 'I wanted to talk to you about my oil tankers and a couple of other rather pressing matters. I think we have time before we leave for the opera. Let's step into the library.' They slipped out discreetly.

As Emma circulated amongst the other guests assembled in their luxurious Fifth Avenue apartment, the thought of impending war nagged at the back of her mind. She had, only that morning, received a disturbing letter from Frank, who had just returned from a trip to Berlin. He had been full of dire predictions, and, trusting his judgement as she did, she knew he was not exaggerating. He had said Britain would be at war before the end of the year, and she believed him. She glanced at the three other men in the room. They also wielded immense international influence and their combined wealth added up to hundreds of billions of dollars. She saw that their eyes betrayed their fears, even though they, too, were making a show of conviviality that befitted the occasion. Yes, they knew that the world was on the brink of another holocaust. She thought of her two sons with a stab of apprehension. Both of them were eligible to be called up. Another generation of young men in their prime would be sacrificed to the war machine. Despite the warmth of the room she shivered and she thought then of Joe Lowther, and remembered the Great War and the havoc it had wreaked. Had the past twenty-one years been only an armed truce?

Later, when they were seated in their box at the Metropolitan Opera, Emma was temporarily distracted by the anticipation that pervaded the air. Her eyes swept over the opulent red-and-gold décor, took in the glittering beauty of the bejewelled women and the elegance of the men in their tails. And she thought how normal they all seemed, even carefree, as though they were oblivious to the gathering storm.

Emma glanced down at her programme, determined to enjoy the opera. It was from Blackie O'Neill that she had learned about music, and as the breathtaking theatrical spectacle unfolded on the stage she suddenly wished Blackie was here with them to share the experience. She began to relax, captivated by 'Mignon'. Risë Stevens, the young mezzo-soprano who had made her debut two months before, was magnificent in the title role and at one moment her glorious voice so moved Emma she felt the rush of tears. What a gift that superb voice was. Emma was soon transported into a magical world of make-believe and she let herself be engulfed by the melodic arias, the performances of Risë Stevens and Ezio Pinza, the exquisite sets and costumes, and for several hours her worries were entirely forgotten.

Paul had invited their eight guests to Delmonico's for dinner, and as they settled themselves at the table Emma looked across at Paul, endeavouring to assess his mood. Despite the grave conversation with Dan Nelson earlier, he now appeared to be unconcerned, and as always he was the expansive host, ordering Dom Pérignon and caviar, and beguiling everyone. He is the most brilliant and handsome man here, Emma thought with a flash of possessiveness. It was February 3, 1939. His birthday. He was fifty-nine years old, but he carried his years splendidly, and the wings of white in his black hair only served to emphasize his dashing appearance. His eyes had not lost their vivid blueness and the brows above were still the colour of jet, as was his moustache. There were deep lines around those eyes, but his tanned face was surprisingly free of wrinkles and his body was as firm and as muscular as it had been twenty years ago. Emma was always slightly stunned by the sheer physical size of him, the bulk of those wide shoulders and barrel chest. Tonight, in his white tie and tails, he had an aura of true glamour that was more electrifying than ever.

His eyes met hers and he winked, and then gave her that old appraising look she knew so well. Why, the devil's flirting with me. And after all these years, she thought. She herself would be fifty in April. It hardly seemed possible. She had known Paul for twenty-one years, and they had been together on a permanent basis for sixteen of them. Sixteen incredible years. They had not always been easy years. Paul could be as authoritative and as self-willed as she was herself, and he often felt the need to assert himself forcefully. He was domineering, frequently bossy, and he had made it clear who wore the trousers in their household. She had learned to let him have his way in most things pertaining to their private lives, and he, in turn, was wise enough never to interfere in her business. Paul was also a flirt and he made no secret of the fact that he liked the ladies. Emma suspected he might have had other women when he travelled abroad alone, but he never gave her cause for heartache, or embarrassment, and she never doubted his devotion. Also, since she considered sexual jealousy a useless emotion, she rarely contemplated his infidelities, if indeed there were any. His passion for her had not lessened with time, and she knew she was a lucky woman.

Emma sat back in the chair, and between the champagne, the delicious food, the stimulating conversation, and the gaiety that prevailed amongst their friends, she managed to push aside those troubling thoughts of war that had assailed her at the outset of the evening.

In the following week Paul did not mention the war again and she carefully avoided the subject herself. They went to East Texas to visit the Sydney-Texas Oil Company, recently renamed Sitex at her suggestion, and then proceeded to West Texas, where Paul purchased oil leases in Odessa and Midland, much to Harry Marriott's annoyance. Emma did not particularly like Paul's partner and had not hesitated to say so when she had first met him some years before. It was on their return journey to New York that she reiterated her opinion, and asked Paul why Marriott was so unhappy about the new purchases.

Paul grinned and said, 'Because he always wants to play it safe. He never wants to gamble. He's afraid of losing or diminishing what we've already accumulated over the years. The fool. We're one of the richest oil companies in America today, but expansion is necessary. No, vital. Harry means well, but he lacks imagination. Remember how he fought me when I bought the oil tankers? I proved him wrong about that. They've been an enormous asset to the company and more than earned their money back. I'll prove him wrong again, Emma. I have a nose for oil, and I guarantee you it will be discovered in Odessa and Midland within a few years. I plan to start drilling there before the end of the year.'

'It's a good thing you own the majority of stock in that company, otherwise you might have really insurmountable problems with Marriott,' Emma said.

'You're damned right.' Paul chuckled. 'You don't think I'd be fool enough to spend the millions I invested initially without having control, do you?'

'No,' she conceded, laughing. 'You're far too tough and smart for that.' She hesitated. 'Are you sorry Daisy wasn't a boy?'

'Good Lord, no! Whatever makes you ask that, darling?'

'Well, Howard can't very well follow in your footsteps. And it's often occurred to me you might be disappointed you don't have a son to carry on the business, the McGill dynasty.'

'What makes you think I've dismissed the idea of Daisy doing that? After all, if she takes after her beautiful mother she'll make a hell of a good businesswoman. And she'll marry one day and have children. My grandchildren. Ponder on that one, Emma.'

She did, never once forgetting his words.

One day, at the end of February, Paul came home early from the Sitex offices in New York, and Emma knew at once that something was terribly amiss. He appeared to be unusually preoccupied, kissed her somewhat absently, and fixed himself a drink, which was also rare in that it was only four o'clock.

Never one to hedge, she said immediately, 'You're upset, Paul. What is it?'

'I can never hide anything from you, my love, can I?' He sipped the drink, lit a cigarette, and then he told her, 'I have booked a passage for you to England on the *Queen Elizabeth*. I was lucky enough to get a stateroom for you, even at this late date, so you will be comfortable, darling. You sail on Thursday.'

'Aren't you coming with me?' she asked as evenly as possible, but her throat tightened.

'No, darling, I can't.'

'Why not, Paul? You had planned to return with me.'

'I want to go back to Texas for a few days, to take care of certain matters and to reassure myself that Harry fully understands I want to start drilling in Odessa as soon as possible. And then I'm going to Australia.'

'But you weren't supposed to go there until later in the year!'

'Later in the year might be too *late*, Emma. I must leave as quickly as possible now, to attend to my interests over there and confer with the men who run my companies. You know how I feel about Japan's threat to the Pacific. I can't possibly leave anything to chance.'

Emma's face had paled. 'I don't want you to go!' she cried 'I'm frightened – frightened you'll get stuck in Australia if war breaks out before you can return to England. We could be separated for years.' She rose and went to kneel at his feet. She looked up at him. 'Please don't go, darling. I beg you not to go!' She touched his face lightly, the dearest face in the world to her, and her eyes brimmed.

'You know I must, Emma darling,' he said with the utmost gentleness. He smoothed one hand over her head and his eyes regarded her tenderly. 'But I won't stay for long. Only two months at the most. Things are in relatively good order out there. They have been for years. However, I must be sure everything will run smoothly, should I have to be absent for longer than the usual year. And I might have to be. We don't know how long this war will last when it does come, do we?' He smiled at her confidently. 'I'll get back quickly. I want to be with you in England when the conflict starts. I certainly don't want you to be alone. Now come along, cheer up, sweetheart. I'll only be gone eight weeks. That's not so bad.'

Emma did not argue with Paul or further attempt to dissuade him, knowing it would be fruitless to do so. His holdings were so vast they staggered the imagination, and he could not shrug off the responsibilities they entailed, which were of equal magnitude. Power had its undeniable privileges but it brought crushing burdens as well. It was quite apparent that Paul, in all good conscience, could not ignore the world political situation, and the effect it would have on his business. Because of who and what she was, Emma understood his motives and acknowledged the necessity of his plan, even though she was not enamoured of it.

And so she put up a gay front for the next few days before she sailed. But the idea of being separated from Paul depressed her more than it ever had before, and that awful sense of foreboding stayed with her during the entire voyage to England. Even when she was settled in their house in Belgrave Square it persisted, gnawing at her peace of mind.

FIFTY-SEVEN

Torrential rain was falling when Paul left the nursing home on the outskirts of Sydney. He turned up the collar of his trench coat and made a dash for the Daimler.

He was drenched when he got inside and he shrugged out of his wet coat, tossing it carelessly on to the back seat. He took out a handkerchief and wiped his streaming face before lighting a cigarette. He noticed that his hand shook as he did so. He was in a blinding rage with Constance, so that was not very surprising. He had been on the verge of striking her a few moments before, and it had taken all of his will power to control himself, to take his leave of her with a degree of civility. The violence of his emotions appalled him. He had never struck a woman in his life, had not experienced such overwhelming anger in years.

Paul inserted the key in the ignition, pulled out of the parking area, and turned into the main road leading back into the city. His patience with Constance had entirely evaporated years ago, along with his pity, and now he loathed her. *Loathed her.* Damn it, he wasn't going to be tied to her any longer. He would find a way to get the divorce himself. He would talk to his solicitor. There must be a legal loophole, a means of disentangling himself from this ridiculous marriage, which had not been a marriage for twenty-seven years. It was absurd that a man of his undeniable power should find himself in such an untenable situation, shackled to that demented creature, who surely held on to him only out of sheer perversity. He wondered what he had ever done to Constance to make her want to punish him. He had been a good husband in the early years. It had been her drinking and her promiscuousness which had come between them, and inevitably killed his love for her. *He must have his freedom.* For Emma and Daisy. And he was bloody well going to get it, come hell or high water. He gripped the steering wheel and hit the open road with ferocity.

The etiolated sky, bleached out by lightning, rocked with the deafening booms of thunder and, as if there had been a sudden cloudburst, the rain fell more profusely, sluicing down the windows in streaming sheets, dimming his vision momentarily. He took the turn in the road too fast, saw the approaching lorry too late. Instinctively he swerved and braked, but the car was travelling at such high speed it seemed to move with its own velocity. It went into a slithering skid and spun out of control, careering across the wet road. He fought to regain control but despite his enormous strength he was unable to do so. The car slewed up over the embankment, leapt into the air, somersaulted down into the gully, and impacted against a formation of boulders. He felt himself being crushed against the steering wheel, and then he blacked out.

It was the lorry driver who pulled him out of the wreckage a fraction of a second before the car burst into flames. Paul was still unconscious when the ambulance arrived at the hospital in Sydney two hours later. And he remained unconscious for several days. That he had lived at all was a miracle, the doctors said.

517

Paul manoeuvred himself across his study in the wheelchair until he was directly in front of his desk. He lit a cigarette and then settled down to peruse the pile of legal documents Mel Harrison, his solicitor, had left with him a week ago, just before he had been discharged from the hospital. He had gone over them endlessly, searching for any kind of small omission, or a clause that might lack clarity, and so far he had found none. But to be absolutely certain before he signed them, he went through them for the last time, reading each page slowly, weighing each word scrupulously. At the end of three hours he was satisfied nothing could be misinterpreted. As usual, Mel had drawn the documents with his special brand of brilliance. Every one of them was watertight and would stand up in any court of law, in any country in the world, should they be challenged. He did not expect that to happen. He was mostly concerned that his exact intentions were crystal clear, and indeed they were. Paul smiled for the first time in days. Something had gone right for once.

It was almost six o'clock. Mel was due any moment. What a staunch, supportive, and devoted friend he had been in the last three months since the accident, always there when he was needed, and often when he was not. Preparing legal papers; attending to matters too confidential to hand over to anyone else; visiting the hospital on a daily basis; even neglecting his wife and family at weekends, to sit with him and bolster his courage, to pull him out of the black moods which sometimes engulfed him. Since the bandages had been removed, Paul had not wanted any visitors except Mel and the men who worked for the various McGill corporations. He had certainly not wanted his other friends to see his shattered face. He could not have stomached their sympathy, or their pity.

Despair trickled through him and he closed his eyes, wondering how much longer he could go on. Sometimes he thought he could not tolerate another day of living in this wretched state. What a rotten twist of fate. The accident would never have happened if he had listened to Emma in New York and not returned to Sydney. Now here he was, chained to a wheelchair and dependent on others for almost everything he needed. It was a condition that did not sit easily with him. He had always been in the enviable position of being able to bend life to his will, to reverse circumstances to suit himself. But ever since the crash he had experienced a sense of powerlessness so acute it was devastating. It engendered a monumental frustration that spiralled into blazing anger. Even his money and his influence, always potent weapons in the past, had become quite useless to him.

Smithers, the butler-valet who had been in his employ for years, knocked and entered the study, interrupting Paul's thoughts. 'Mr Harrison has arrived, sir. Shall I show him in here, or do you want to go into the sitting room?'

'In here, Smithers, please.'

A moment later Mel was grasping his hand. 'How are you, Paul?'

'Feeling much better, believe it or not,' Paul said, and motioned to the butler. 'Fix us the usual, Smithers, please.'

'Right away, sir.'

Paul swung the chair away from the desk. 'Let's sit over there by the fire. I always feel chilled to the bone these days.'

When the butler had left, Paul said, 'I should have been more forceful with the

518

doctors weeks ago, and made them discharge me then. I think being in familiar surroundings has helped me a great deal.'

'I'm sure it has,' Mel said brightly. 'Cheers, old chap.'

'Cheers,' Paul responded. They clinked glasses and Paul went on, 'I've spent a lot of time on the papers, Mel. They're in good order now. We can sign them later.'

'Fine, Paul. Incidentally, I told Audrey I wouldn't be home for dinner. If you can stand my company for a second night running I thought I'd foist myself on you. Is that all right?'

'Of course. I'd be delighted to have you dine with me.' He wheeled himself to the bar and poured another scotch. 'How's your drink, Mel? Can I freshen it up?'

'Not right now, thanks. Listen, Paul, I've been thinking a lot about Emma these past few days, since you've been home. I think we ought to send for her. I've discussed it with Audrey, and she agrees with me.'

'No!' Paul spun the wheelchair around. He peered into Mel's face and his eyes blazed. 'I absolutely forbid it!' he exclaimed harshly. 'I don't want her to see me like this. Besides, the news is getting graver every day. We could be at war with Germany tomorrow. I don't want her travelling halfway across the world at such a dangerous time.'

Mel regarded Paul carefully. 'I understand your feelings. But I also dread to think what she'll do to me when she finds out I've lied to her in my letters, just as you have in yours. You also used your considerable influence to keep the details of the accident out of the newspapers, and so she is in the dark about the seriousness of your condition. But isn't it time you wrote and told her the truth? She should know.'

Paul shook his head. *'She's not to know.* Not under any circumstances whatsoever.' He softened his tone. 'Not yet, anyway. I'll decide when it's the right time to tell her.' His face became morose. 'How *does* a man tell a passionate and active woman like Emma that she's tied to a hopeless cripple who is paralysed from the waist down, who has lost half his face and –' He paused and looked at Mel intently. 'And who is impotent. Who will always be impotent. Not easy, my friend. Not easy at all.'

Mel did not know how to respond and such strong feelings of sympathy swept through him he stood up quickly before Paul detected the pity filling his eyes. He stepped to the bar and picked up the bottle of scotch. He said, 'I think you might be underestimating Emma. In fact, I'm damned sure you are. She would want to be with you. To give you all of her support and love. Let's cable her, Paul. Now.'

'No,' Paul said, his voice suddenly tinged with weariness. 'I don't want her to be burdened down with me. I'm no use to her. I'm not much use to myself, if the truth be known.'

Mel walked back to the fireplace, racking his brains for a way to convince Paul to send for Emma. He needed her more than he had ever needed her in his life, but he was an obstinate devil, and proud. 'Emma wouldn't see it that way. She loves you. Why, she worships the ground . . . You,' Mel quickly corrected himself, and cleared his throat. Then his face brightened perceptibly as another thought struck him. He said rapidly, 'Look here, if you don't want Emma travelling, why don't you book a passage to England yourself? You could be there in a month.'

'That's not feasible. I have to go to the hospital almost every day for treatment. There are no medical facilities of the kind *I* need on board a ship.' Paul gulped down the scotch and placed his glass on the table. He brought his gaze back to Mel and his eyes were deadly serious, his tone bleak. 'There is something I haven't told you, Mel. The prognosis is bad. Very bad, actually. The doctors don't know how long they can keep the infection out of my kidneys. That's what usually kills paraplegics – kidney failure.'

Mel stared at Paul and his ruddy face lost most of its colour. 'H-h-how l-l-long?' he stammered, unable to complete the question.

'Nine months – at the most,' Paul replied in a matter-of-fact voice. He had already adjusted to his death sentence. He had no alternative.

Mel said with a desperate urgency, 'I think we ought to call in more specialists, Paul. Surely there must be a way to –'

'No, there isn't,' Paul said. 'If I had broken my spine the doctors could have fused it. But the nerve ends of the spinal cord were crushed. There is no known way to repair those.'

Mel looked away into the fire. He had no words that would comfort Paul. The accident had been a catastrophe, but he had been led to believe Paul had years of life ahead of him, albeit confined to the wheelchair. But now ... Oh, God, what a waste of a rare and brilliant man. Eventually, after a long silence, he said, 'Is there anything I can do, Paul? Anything at all? You only have to ask me.'

Paul smiled gently. 'No, old chap. Thanks, though. Don't take this so hard. And for Christ's sake, don't start getting maudlin on me now. I need that cheery spirit of yours, and your optimism. Also, you've become my right arm and you're going to be around me a great deal. I don't want a glum face staring at me. Now come on, let's have another drink and then we'll dine. I've got some great Chambertin, which my father put down years ago. We'll have a couple of bottles with dinner. Might as well drink it now, while there's still –' Paul bit off his sentence abruptly. He picked up the empty glasses, dropped them into his lap, and rolled over to the bar.

Mel was again unable to respond coherently. He reached for his handkerchief and blew his nose loudly. He looked at Paul's wide shoulders and broad back outlined above the chair, and his eyes dimmed with infinite sorrow. It was heart-breaking to see that splendid body so horribly broken, that extraordinarily handsome face so hideously ruined. And yet how stoically this incredible man bore his afflictions. The admiration Mel had always held for his oldest and dearest friend increased inordinately. Paul's unimpaired courage and his strength of character in the face of defeat were immense. He wondered if he could have been so brave and indomitable in similar circumstances. He was not sure. One thing he did know, Paul needed all the support he could get and he was going to do his damnedest to give it to him without reserve.

Much later that same evening, long after Mel had left, Paul sat in his dimly lit study, nursing a balloon of brandy and chain-smoking. His face was calm, his eyes thoughtful as he mused on the conversation of earlier. Perhaps Mel was right. Perhaps he should write to Emma and tell her the truth. In his previous letters he had underplayed the accident and used business as an excuse for his tardiness in not returning to England. Yes, he owed her that. The truth. For all they had been to each other and still meant to each other. And it must be the absolute truth. Nothing less would do for his Emma. He moved the wheelchair up to the desk, pulled a piece of notepaper towards him, and began the letter.

Sydney, July 24, 1939

My dearest darling Emma:
   You are my life . . .

His eyes lifted and rested on the gold-framed photograph of her on the corner of his desk. He picked it up, gazing at it intently. It had been taken a few years after Daisy's birth and Emma looked radiant and she was smiling that incandescent smile that was so uniquely hers. He thought his heart would burst with his love for her, and unexpected tears welled in his eyes and trickled down his cheeks unchecked. Paul held the photograph to his chest for a long time, hugging it to him as if it were Emma herself he held in his arms, remembering the past, pondering on the future. And he did not write the letter.

FIFTY-EIGHT

Frank Harte left El Vino's bar and walked down Fleet Street towards the *Daily Express*, reflecting on the piece he had written earlier that evening. It still sat on his desk, for he had wanted an hour away from the office to think about the tone of it.

   The hour in El Vino's had not been restful. The bar had been jammed with reporters from all the newspapers, their faces grim, their voices sombre as they had talked about the political situation, which was worsening, and reviewing the depressing news flooding in from all parts of Europe. Now he asked himself if he had been excessive as he considered the piece, written for the Editorial Opinion page. But that fool Neville Chamberlain *should* be kicked out of office. Winston Churchill was, without doubt, the man they needed as Prime Minister, with war an inevitability. He knew the Old Man agreed with him on that issue. Beaverbrook and Churchill were long-time friends.

   Frank crossed Fleet Street and looked up at the *Daily Express*, a shimmering sliver of black glass and steel and blazing lights, the modern architecture incongruous, juxtaposed against the time-worn buildings that flanked it on all sides. It was as if the Old Man had deliberately cocked a snook at tradition when he had built the *Express*, and yet nobody was more traditional than Lord Beaverbrook, tireless defender of the British Empire and all that it entailed. Jealous competitors considered the building to be an eyesore, an offence to the historic Street of Ink, but Frank loved it. He saw it as a tribute to modern journalism and the changing times. The Old Man had been right to build it, for it was certainly the most striking landmark on Fleet Street.

   Pushing through the swinging doors of the *Express*, Frank traversed the lobby and took the lift up to his office. He threw his hat on a chair, sat down, picked up the column, and propped his feet on the desk. He read his words with as critical an eye as possible. It was good, damned good, even though he said so himself. He would let it stand. He jumped up and took it in to Arthur Christiansen.

Chris, young editor of the *Daily Express*, was the boy wonder of Fleet Street. Beaverbrook's star protégé, he was the man responsible for changing the look and tenor of English popular journalism. In his shirt sleeves, his face flushed, his hair rumpled, he looked harassed but was obviously in total control behind the paper-strewn desk. He gave Frank a cheery grin. 'I wondered what had happened to you. I was just about to send a copy boy over to El Vino's to get you.'

Frank handed him the column. 'I wanted time to think this over. I thought I might have been too strong.'

Chris's bright, probing eyes focused on the pages of copy. He read them quickly. 'Good man. It's damned clever, Frank. We'll run it as it stands. No changes necessary. If you tone it down it will lose its impact. The Old Man will like this. You've struck just the right note, as usual.'

'You're sure it's not excessive?'

Chris grinned again. 'I am. It's very balanced, in fact. But then everything you've been writing about the world situation lately has been thoughtful. And damn it all, let's face it, you *are* dealing with facts. Nobody can deny that.' Chris wrote on the first page: *Set as is. No changes.* 'Boy!' he called, motioning to a copy boy loitering near the door of his office. 'Run this down to the chief sub.'

Frank said: 'If you don't need me, I'll get off. My sister's expecting me. You have her number if anything cames up.'

Chris nodded. 'Fine, Frank.' He picked up one of the telephones, which was ringing loudly. 'Christiansen here. Good evening, sir.' He covered the mouthpiece and said to Frank, 'It's Lord Beaverbrook calling from Cherkley. Excuse me, Frank.'

Frank collected his hat from his office and strolled through the newsroom, as always lingering there for a moment. The bustle and activity had reached fever pitch as the deadline for the first edition of Monday's paper approached and the noise was deafening. There was a sense of immediacy in the atmosphere, and the air was pungent with the smell of damp newsprint and wet ink from the page proofs, which always sent a thrill of excitement coursing through Frank's veins. Popular and successful novelist though he had become over the years, he could no more abandon journalism than he could stop breathing. It was in his blood. And there was no other place quite like the offices of a daily newspaper at this hour, just before the giant presses rolled. It was the pulse, the very heartbeat of the world.

Frank paused at the Reuters wire machine and glanced with quickening interest at the stories coming in. The news was ominous, presaging war. A copy boy dodged past him, tore off the latest Reuters dispatches, and raced away. As he did, Frank's eye caught a new story coming over the wire. His attention was riveted on it. He was motionless for a long time, reeling from shock, and disbelieving, and then he roused himself and moved up to the Associated Press machine. After a moment he went to look at the United Press ticker. All the wire services were carrying the identical story and he groaned. There was undoubtedly no mistake. No mistake at all. He tore off the UP story and had a word with the chief sub about it, who acquiesced when Frank asked to take it with him. Pushing the piece of paper in his pocket, Frank walked out of the newsroom, benumbed and sick at heart.

Within seconds he was in the street and hailing a cab. Despite the muggy August weather, he shivered and his hands were unsteady as he lit a cigarette. He wondered how in God's name he was going to find the strength to do what he must do.

Winston was in London on business and he was staying with Emma, as he always did. They were seated in the drawing room, drinking their after-dinner coffee, when the housekeeper showed Frank in a few minutes later.

Emma's face lit up when she saw him, and she rose to embrace him. 'We'd just about given you up!' she exclaimed, hugging him.

'I'm sorry I'm so late,' Frank murmured.

Emma said, 'Let me get you a drink. What would you like, Frank?'

'A brandy, please, Emma.' He turned to Winston. 'How long are you staying?'

'A few days. Do you want to have lunch tomorrow?'

'Yes, I do.'

Emma handed Frank the drink and sat down in the chair opposite. She looked at him intently and then frowned. 'You look awfully pale, Frank dear. You're not sickening with something, are you?'

'No, I'm just tired.' He tossed down the brandy and stood up. 'Mind if I have another? I need it tonight.'

'Of course not.' Emma's eyes swivelled to Winston and one brow shot up quizzically.

Winston noticed his brother's weary stance. 'Are you sure you're not ill, Frank? Emma's quite right, you don't seem to be your usual self.'

Frank swung around and managed a smile. 'I suppose the situation is getting on top of me,' he muttered, and returned to the chair. 'The Nazis are about to move into Poland. We're all convinced of that.'

Winston and Emma plied him with questions, and Frank responded automatically, attempting to sound coherent. Emma had been listening thoughtfully and she turned to face Winston, who was fixing himself a scotch and soda, and she said, 'I expect we ought to start thinking about our various staffs. They will be badly depleted when the men get called up.' She caught her breath and her hand flew to her throat nervously to finger her pearls. 'And my God! What about the boys! Kit and Robin are bound to go. And Randolph, Winston. He's also of age.'

'Yes, he is. In fact, he wants to join the navy. *Immediately*.' Winston's mouth tightened. 'He's determined to do it. I won't be able to stop him.'

Emma gave her older brother an anxious glance. His only son was the apple of his eye. 'Randolph's headstrong, I realize that, and so are my boys. They're not going to listen to us. I don't suppose there is anything we can do. They will ultimately get their papers.' She now addressed Frank. 'Well, at least your Simon is not old enough to be called up.'

'For the moment,' Frank said, and rose. He poured a large brandy and brought it to Emma. 'You had better drink this. I think you are going to need it.'

Emma regarded him with puzzlement. 'Why do you say that?' She frowned. 'And you know I don't like brandy. It gives me heart palpitations.'

'Please drink it,' Frank said quietly.

Emma brought the brandy balloon up to her mouth and took a drop of it, wrinkling her nose with distaste. She put the glass down on the butler's tray table in front of her, and focused her attention on Frank. Once more she noted his extraordinary pallor. And when she saw the apprehension, now so clearly etched on his sensitive face, it alarmed her. A dreadful feeling of impending disaster struck Emma and she clasped her hands tightly together in her lap. 'Something's terribly wrong, isn't it, Frank?'

Frank felt a dryness in his mouth and his voice was hoarse as he finally said, 'I've had some very bad news. Just now, before I left the office.' Despite the iron control he was exercising, his voice shook badly.

'Frank dear, whatever is it?' asked Emma, every one of her instincts alerted for trouble.

Winston said rapidly, 'There's nothing wrong at the paper, is there?'

'No,' Frank responded in a low voice. 'It's . . . it's about Paul, actually.'

'Paul! You've had bad news about Paul! What's wrong with him?' Emma demanded.

'I don't know how to tell you this, Emma –' Frank stopped. After an awful moment of silence he finished in a faltering voice, 'He's – he's – he's passed away.'

Emma stared at her brother with stunned disbelief, and she shook her head in bewilderment. 'What do you mean?' she asked, unable to digest his words. 'I don't understand what you are saying. I just had a letter from him. Yesterday. *What are you saying to me?*' She had turned so deathly pale she looked as if she was going to faint and she was shaking.

Frank went to kneel at her feet. He looked up at her gravely and took her hand in his. He said with great gentleness, 'Paul's dead, Emma. The story came over the wires when I was on my way here.'

'Paul,' Emma whispered incredulously, and her expression was one of blank stupefaction mingled with fear. She cried in a tremulous voice, 'Are you sure there is no mistake? There *must* be a mistake!'

Frank shook his head dismally. 'All the wire services are carrying the same story. I checked them out.'

'Oh my God,' Emma groaned, her blood turning cold.

Winston, as grey as a ghost, managed, 'How did Paul die, Frank?'

Frank gazed at Emma, bleakness washing over his face as he sought the appropriate words. But nothing would soften the blow. Frank found himself incapable of speech.

Now Emma tightened her grip, her fingers biting into his hand. 'Did Paul –? Was it his injuries? Were they more serious than he told me?' She sounded weak.

'Well, yes, I believe they were much worse than he led you to understand –'

The trilling of the doorbell startled them all, and Emma's eyes widened with apprehension and appealed to Winston. He nodded and pulled himself up out of the chair. As he left the drawing room he prayed it wasn't the press wanting a statement. To Winston's relief the housekeeper was admitting Henry Rossiter, a partner in the private merchant bank which handled all of Paul's business in England, and much of Emma's as well. Henry's face was as dolorous as Winston's. He shook Winston's hand and asked, 'Does she know?' Winston inclined his head. 'How is she taking it?' Henry murmured.

Winston said, 'She's stunned. It hasn't really sunk in yet. There will be a horrible delayed reaction, of course, Henry. I dread to contemplate it.'

Henry nodded his understanding. 'Yes. They were so close. What a tragic, tragic thing to happen. How did Emma hear about it?'

Winston quickly explained and motioned to the drawing room. 'We'd better go in, Henry. She needs us.'

Henry entered the living room and sat down next to Emma. 'I'm sorry. So very sorry, my dear. I got here as quickly as I could. As soon as I knew.'

Emma's throat worked and she passed her hand over her throbbing head. She said, 'Did someone in Sydney contact you, Henry?'

'Yes, Mel Harrison. He has been trying to get me all day. I was in the country, unfortunately.'

'Why didn't he attempt to reach me?' she asked in a voice echoing with sorrow.

'He wanted me to break the news to you in person, Emma. He didn't want you to be alone when you heard –'

'When did Paul die?' she interrupted, her heart squeezing.

'His body was found on Sunday night. It's early Monday morning there now. Mel put in a call to me as soon as he arrived at the house. He realized he couldn't hold off the press indefinitely, since the police have to –'

'Police!' Emma exclaimed. 'What do you mean? Why were the police there?'

Henry looked at Frank with dismay. They exchanged worried glances and both men were silent. Frank now contemplated lying to Emma, but there was no point in dissembling. Better to get it over with. He said gently, 'Paul took his own life, Emma.'

'Oh my God! No! No! It's not true! I don't believe you! Paul wouldn't do that. *Never*,' Emma cried.

'I'm afraid it's true, darling,' Frank said, and put his arm around her.

Emma moved her head wildly from side to side, denying Frank. She seemed to shrink in the chair. 'How did he –' She could not continue.

Frank bit his lip. 'He – he – shot himself.' He did not add that Paul had shot himself through the heart. He could not bring himself to tell her that.

'No!' she shrieked, losing control. '*It's not true!*' she gasped. A tearing sob strangled in her throat and she twisted her hands agitatedly. Her eyes, brimming with shock, focused on Henry.

He nodded sadly. 'It is true, Emma.'

'It's not! It's not!' she cried, her voice rising. 'Oh my God! Paul! Paul! Oh, my darling. Why?' Her voice broke and tears welled in her eyes. She pushed Frank aside and stood up, moving to the centre of the room. She stretched out her arms, clutching blindly at the empty air, as if seeking Paul, to hold him to her.

Frank sprang up and took her arm, leading her back to the sofa. 'Sit down, Emma. Please, darling.'

Winston rose unsteadily and walked across the room, anxiety dulling his eyes, and he wondered desperately where she was going to find the strength to bear this tragedy. He picked up the glass of brandy. 'Drink this, our Emma. Drink it, love. We're here. We'll stay with you.'

She took the glass from him with both hands, which were trembling, and she gulped it down quickly. 'I must know everything. Please, Frank, you must tell me everything. I must know it all. For my own sanity.'

Frank was alarmed. 'I have the UP story with me, Emma, but I don't think I should –'

'Yes, you should. You must. *I beg of you.*'

'I think you had better give Emma the facts, Frank,' Winston interceded, adopting

525

a calmness he did not feel. 'She won't rest until she knows all the details. However painful they are to hear, you must tell her.'

Frank nodded and pulled the piece of paper out. In a slow, saddened voice he read:

'*Paul McGill, Australia's most renowned industrialist, was found shot to death on Sunday night at his home in Sydney. Mr McGill, who was fifty-nine years old, was in a serious automobile accident four months ago, which paralysed him from the waist downward. One side of his face was also badly shattered. Mr McGill had been confined to a wheelchair since his release from the hospital and his doctors believe he took his own life in a moment of acute depression, undoubtedly caused by his condition. No note was found. Mr McGill, who had resided mostly in London for the past sixteen years, was the only son of Bruce McGill and the grandson of Andrew McGill, founding father of the famous Australian family, one of the wealthiest and most influential in the country. It was Andrew McGill, a Scottish sea captain, who began the family sheep station, Dunoon, in Coonamble, in 1852. One of the biggest and most prosperous in New South Wales, the sheep station was inherited by Paul McGill upon his father's death in 1919. Mr McGill, believed to be one of the richest men in the world, was chairman of the board of numerous Australian companies, including the McGill Corporation, which operated the sheep station, McGill and Smythson Real Estate, the McGill Mining Corporation, and the McGill Coal Company. He was also chairman of the board of the Sitex Oil Corporation of America, headquartered in Texas, and president and chief executive officer of McGill-Marriott Maritime, which owns and operates one of the world's largest oil-tanker fleets.*'

Frank stopped. 'There's a lot more about the business, the family, Paul's war record, and his education. Do you want to go on, Emma?'

'No,' she whispered. She turned to Henry miserably. 'Why didn't he tell me about the paralysis? His face? I would have gone to him immediately. He should have told me, Henry.' Tears seeped out of the corners of her eyes and trickled silently down her cheeks. 'Did he think his condition would have made any difference to *me*? And I should have been with him.' She began to sob brokenly. 'I loved him.'

Henry's voice was sympathetic. 'Mel wanted him to send for you. But you know how stubborn and proud Paul was. He was adamant, it seems. According to Mel, he didn't want you to see him that way, or know the seriousness of his injuries, or to be burdened with him.'

Emma was speechless. Not to be burdened with him, she thought. But I loved him more than life itself. Oh, Paul, why did you keep me away from you when you needed me the most? She envisaged Paul's pain and the terrible despair which had prompted his action, and an overwhelming sorrow engulfed her.

It seemed to Emma that the whole world had abruptly stopped. There was no sound in the room, except for the faint ticking of the carriage clock on the mantel-shelf. She looked down at the great McGill emerald glittering on her finger, and at the wedding ring Paul had given her when Daisy was born, and her unchecked tears fell on her hands and splashed against the rings. And she remembered the words he had spoken that day: 'Until death do us part,' he had said. Her heart twisted inside her. She lifted her head and glanced about, and a terrible aching numbness entered her body. She felt as though she, too, was paralysed and would be quite unable to move ever again. The pain was beginning, and she understood with a flash of clarity that she would never be free of it. She thought: I cannot live without him. He was my life. There is nothing left now. Only the empty years ahead to endure until I, too, die.

Winston and Frank were helpless in their despair. Winston could not stand to see her suffering, and telephoned the family doctor, who arrived fifteen minutes later. Emma was given a sedative and the housekeeper helped her to bed. But racking sobs continued to convulse her and they did not cease for over two hours, when the sedative finally lulled her into a more tranquil state.

Her two brothers, Henry Rossiter, and the doctor stayed with Emma until she finally fell into a drugged sleep. As they left the bedroom, Winston said, 'Her sorrow is only just beginning.'

Tragedy had struck at Emma many times in her life. It had caused her to falter, but it had never brought her to her knees. Paul's death felled her with one swift blow.

All of her children, except Edwina, came home to be with her. They had loved and admired Paul, and they were aghast and grief-stricken, most especially Daisy, who had been the closest to him. Each one in their own way tried to comfort their mother, but their efforts were in vain.

Frank's wife, Natalie, came immediately; Charlotte, Winston's wife, and their son, Randolph, travelled up to London from Leeds with Blackie and his son Bryan, the four of them accompanied by David Kallinski and his sons, Ronnie and Mark. None of them could reach Emma and, after a brief visit with her in her bedroom, they assembled in the library, their faces clouded with anxiety.

Blackie attempted to alleviate their worry. He said, 'Even the strongest heart can be broken, you know. But a strong heart always mends. I put my money on Emma any day. She's a born survivor and she'll survive this. Also, I think it's much better she gets her grief out. I know she'll be all right.' And he meant every word, for he knew the stern stuff she was made of.

But for days Emma lay prostrate, half crazed and incoherent with grief. She became so debilitated at one point Winston seriously contemplated hospitalizing her. The dawn hours were the worst for Emma. She would lie motionless in her bed, bereft and without hope, watching the cold grey light creeping in, waiting for the beginning of a new endless empty day, staring vacantly into space like a blind woman. But her vivid and active mind was for ever in a turmoil, filled with conflicting and troublesome thoughts. She wondered if she had failed Paul in some way. Failed to properly convey over the years the depth and sincerity of her love for him. She castigated herself for not having gone to Australia when he had first had the accident, believing she could have prevented him from lifting that fateful gun. If she had not listened to him she could have saved his life, of that she was absolutely convinced. The weight of her guilt was heavy to bear, and her despondency and wretchedness only increased.

Henry Rossiter had told her of the doctors' dismal prognosis, and slowly, as the shock receded, she began to dimly understand that a man like Paul, so virile, so powerful, would regard suicide as the only viable solution to his awful predicament, and yet sometimes she felt utterly abandoned and betrayed by him. However, mostly she was able to dismiss these feelings as manifestations of self-pity, a curious anger, which was baffling, and her own sense of powerlessness. It was also incomprehensible to her that Paul had not written, for she was unable to accept the fact that he would kill himself without one last word to her, and every day she looked for a letter, which did not come.

Winston, who had taken charge of the household and the Knightsbridge store, decided to keep Daisy at home from boarding school after the rest of the family departed. It was she who eventually reached Emma and brought her a measure of relief. Emma's youngest child was surprisingly mature for a fourteen-year-old, and understanding beyond her years. Her own sorrow was acute, but she carefully strove to conceal this most of the time, and she finally achieved a real breakthrough with her mother. She persuaded Emma to eat a little every day, and gradually helped to stem the flow of tears with her loving presence. Occasionally Emma would look intently at Daisy and she would see Paul so clearly reflected in the child's face her tears would start afresh, and she would cling to their daughter, calling for Paul. Daisy would wipe away the tears and calm her with soothing words, rocking her in her arms as if she were the mother and Emma the daughter.

One night, after Emma had collapsed again, Daisy tenderly cajoled her into a more peaceful state of mind, and for the first time Emma fell into a natural sleep that was heavy and deep. When she awakened several hours later she felt rested and had even acquired a degree of composure. She at once noticed Daisy curled up on the chaise dozing. And she suddenly saw her daughter objectively. With a flash of insight Emma recognized she had been burdening Daisy with her own grief when the child herself needed love and support. With a supreme effort she roused herself from her lethargy, and some of that strength, always formidable, began to trickle back into her weary body.

Emma got out of bed unaided and moved slowly to the chaise, her legs shaking and unsteady. Daisy woke up instantly and when she saw her mother bending over her she took hold of her hand swiftly, her eyes apprehensive. 'Mummy, what is it? Do you feel ill again?'

'No, darling. In fact, I think I'm a bit better.' Emma took Daisy in her arms and held her close, stroking her glossy black hair. 'I've been very wrong, Daisy, putting the burden of my grief on you. So wrong. Please forgive me, darling. Now, I want you to get ready for bed and have a really good night's sleep. And I don't want you to worry about me any more. I will be fine. And tomorrow I am going to send you back to boarding school.'

Daisy pulled away and stared at Emma in surprise, and her vivid blue eyes were brilliant with tears. 'But I want to stay with you, Mummy. To look after you. Paul would want that. He really would. He wouldn't want you to be alone, Mummy.'

Emma smiled gently. 'You've been looking after me very well, and now it's my turn to look after you. I am going to be all right, darling. Truly I am.'

Daisy began to cry and she buried her head on Emma's breast, sobbing as if her heart would break. 'Hush, darling. Hush,' Emma murmured. 'We must be strong and brave, and help each other in the coming months.'

'I've been so afraid, Mummy.' Daisy sobbed, her tears drenching Emma's crumpled nightgown. 'I thought you were going to die, too.'

Emma said, in a voice that was surprisingly steady, 'I am not going to die, Daisy, I have you to live for now.'

It was a glorious afternoon in late September, sunny and warm and with a cloudless sky that was radiant with light. But Emma shivered as she walked wearily across the drawing room. She huddled in a chair in front of the fire, warming herself, her thoughts on her sons. War had been declared on September 3, and although she had been too bereaved to pay attention then, the situation could no longer be ignored. Britain was mobilizing with the same speed and efficiency it had displayed in her youth, and she knew that they would be in for a long siege.

Feeling warmer, she shifted in the chair. As she did a shaft of bright sunlight illuminated the ravages her grief had wrought. She had shed pounds and looked painfully thin in the simple black wool dress, its severity unrelieved by jewellery. The only pieces she wore were Paul's rings, and a watch. But her hair was bright and crackling with life.

'Here I am, me darlin',' Blackie called from the doorway, startling her. She rose to greet him, managing a smile. 'It's lovely to see you, Blackie dear,' Emma said, embracing him.

He enveloped her in his arms and held her tightly to his broad chest, and he choked up as he felt the fragility of her body. She was a bag of bones. He held her away, looked down into her face, and put his hand under her chin. 'You're a sight for sore eyes, mavourneen. It's grand to see you up and about.'

They sat in front of the fire and talked for a while about the war and the probability that the boys would enlist imminently. 'Bryan is in London with me,' Blackie told her. 'He wanted to come with me today, but I wasn't sure you'd be up to it.'

'Oh, Blackie, I am disappointed. I'd love to see him,' she exclaimed, her face brightening. 'Could he come tomorrow? You know how dear Bryan is to me.'

'Sure and he can. I'll bring him meself.' Blackie now gave her a guarded look. 'When do you think you'll be fit enough to go back to the store?'

'Next week. The doctor was against it, actually. He thinks I should go to Yorkshire for a rest. But I simply can't neglect the business any longer, and it's just not fair to Winston. He's carrying all the responsibility. Besides, he ought to go back to Leeds. We've a lot of reorganizing to do.'

'I know what you mean. I'm facing the same problems. Anyway, Emma, I think it's a good idea for you to get back into the harness again. You must keep your mind occupied, so that you don't dwell on things.'

Her face clouded momentarily. 'Yes, that's true.' The maid knocked and came in with the tea tray. Emma eyed the heavy Georgian teapot warily, wondering if she had the strength to lift it. For days she had been like a woman with the palsy, dropping and spilling things. She lifted it carefully and poured two cups, and to her relief her hands did not tremble for once.

She said, 'I spoke to David yesterday. He sounded very down in the dumps. Ronnie and Mark have already joined up. He's going to miss them terribly. They've been his whole life since Rebecca died.'

He observed the sudden mistiness in her eyes and said swiftly, 'He'll be all right, Emma. Tell you what, I'll take him under my wing when I get back to Leeds. Get him out of that great mausoleum where he lives in such solitary splendour. It'll do him good to start socializing again.'

'I wish you would, darling. I do worry about him.' Emma looked into the fire reflectively, and when she turned back to Blackie her expression was sorrowful. 'How does one go on, Blackie? It's so hard, isn't it?'

'Yes, but not impossible, Emma. Not for someone with your courage.'

'I haven't been very strong these past few weeks,' she said drearily.

'You can't rush it, Emma. You'll have a lot of readjusting to do. You must give yourself time, darlin'.'

'However did you manage after Laura died?' she asked.

'I sometimes wondered that myself at the time.' He smiled faintly. 'After I went back to the front I tried my damnedest to catch a bullet, to get myself killed. But the good Lord protected me from me own foolishness. After the war it took me a long time to forgive myself for being alive, but once I did I started to live again. I looked around and became aware of my responsibilities, my duty to Bryan. He was a great help, Emma. A great source of sustenance. As Daisy will be for you. That child, of all your children, is the most like you in character. She understands you and she worships you, mavourneen.'

'Yes, I know,' Emma responded quietly, and looked away again. 'I just – just – just don't know how I can go on without Paul.'

Blackie took her hand and held it tightly. 'You can, darlin'. *You will*. The human soul has great fortitude.' He paused and his black eyes swept over her piteous face. He said gently, 'Do you remember what Laura said to you when she was dying? I've never forgotten the words since you repeated them to me, and they have helped me many times. Do you remember what she said about death, Emma?'

Emma nodded. 'Yes, I remember her words as if she had spoken them only yesterday. Laura said there was no such thing as death in her lexicon, and that as long as I lived and you lived she would live, too, for we would carry the memory of her in our hearts for ever.'

Blackie said, 'Aye, mavourneen, and she was a wise lady, my Laura. She truly believed that, as I have come to believe it, and as you must. It will help you, I know. And just as I have Bryan, you have Paul's daughter. She is part of his flesh, part of him, and you must cleave to that and take strength from it.'

His words seemed to give her comfort and so he continued. 'You also told me Laura said God doesn't give us a burden that is too heavy to bear. She *was* right, Emma. Think on that.' He sighed under his breath. 'I know you are heartbroken and that you feel lost and alone. But none of us are alone, Emma. We all have God, and God has helped me over the years. Why don't you try Him on for size?'

Emma's eyes widened. 'You know I don't believe in God.'

Observing the look on her face, Blackie refrained from making any further comments and wisely talked of other things.

But later, when he left Emma's house, Blackie walked to the Brompton Oratory. He crossed himself on entering that fine old church, sat down in a pew, and lifted his face to the altar. And he prayed to God to give Emma comfort and courage in her crushing loss, and he prayed for her soul.

Before she went to bed that night, Emma sat at the window in her bedroom for several hours, dwelling on those words of Laura's. The sky was a peculiar cobalt blue, clear yet intense, and shining with hundreds of stars, and a pale silver moon rode high in the heavens. Its beauty was so perfectly revealed to her it made her catch her breath and she suddenly had the most overwhelming sense of the Infinite. It was a feeling she had never experienced before and she was strangely moved as she sat gazing at that incredible night sky. And then it seemed to her that Paul was with her in the room. And she thought: But of course he is, for he is in my heart always. And she drew strength from this knowledge, and that night she slept a deep and untroubled sleep.

Two days later Emma received a letter from Paul. It had been posted the day before his death and it had taken three weeks to arrive. She looked at it for a long time before she finally found the courage to slit open the envelope and take out the letter.

My dearest darling Emma:

You are my life. I cannot live without my life. But I cannot live with you. And so I must end my miserable existence, for there is no future for us together now. Lest you think my suicide an act of weakness, let me reassure you that it is not. It is an act of strength and of will, for by committing it I gratefully take back that control over myself which I have lost in the past few months. It is a final act of power over my own fate.

It is the only way out for me, my love, and I will die with your name on my lips, the image of you before my eyes, my love for you secure in my heart always. We have been lucky, Emma. We have had so many good years together and shared so much, and the happy memories are alive in me, as I know they are in you, and will be as long as you live. I thank you for giving me the best years of my life.

I did not send for you because I did not want you to be tied to a helpless cripple, if only for a few months at the most. Perhaps I was wrong. On the other hand, I want you to remember me as I was, and not what I have become since the accident. Pride? Maybe. But try to understand my reasons, and try, my darling, to find it in your heart to forgive me.

I have great faith in you, my dearest Emma. You are not faint of heart. You are strong and dauntless, and you will go on courageously. You must. For there is our child to consider. She is the embodiment of our love, and I know you will cherish and care for her, and bring her up to be as brave and as stalwart and as loving as you are yourself. I give her into your trust, my darling.

By the time you receive this I will be dead. But I will live on in Daisy. She is your future now, my Emma. And mine.

I love you with all my heart and soul and mind, and I pray to God that one day we will be reunited in Eternity.

I kiss you, my darling.

Paul

Emma was motionless in the chair, clutching the letter, the tears seeping out of her eyes and rolling silently down her pale cheeks. She saw him in her mind's eye, tall and handsome, his deep violet eyes laughing, and she remembered him as he wanted her to remember him. She thought of the years and the joy and love he had given her. And she forgave him, now understanding, and with great compassion, both his dilemma and his motives.

At the beginning of October, Mel Harrison took a four-engined 'C Class' Qantas flying boat from Sydney to Karachi, and there boarded an English aeroplane that provided the link to Great Britain. Several days later he arrived in London. His purpose: to see Emma and present Paul McGill's will to the solicitors who handled the McGill legal work in England and Europe.

Emma, austerely dressed in black, appeared wan and fragile, yet she was composed when she arrived at Price, Ellis, and Watson for the reading of Paul McGill's last will and testament. Winston, Frank, and Henry Rossiter accompanied her.

'Paul made you the executrix of his estate,' Mel informed her as she sat down. She was taken by surprise, but she simply nodded, at a loss for words.

There were bequests to servants, to old and loyal employees, and a two-million-pound trust fund had been created to provide for his wife and son during their lifetimes. Upon their deaths it was to go to charity. His entire estate he had willed to Emma in perpetuity, passing to Daisy upon her death, and from Daisy to her progeny. To Emma's astonishment Paul had left her everything he owned, holdings worth well over two hundred million pounds. He had made her one of the richest women in the world and their daughter the heiress to a great fortune. But the thing that moved Emma the most was the fact that Paul had accorded her the respect and consideration generally reserved for a man's legal widow and not his common-law wife. In death, as in life, Paul had declared his devotion and love for her, had acknowledged her to the whole world. And into her hands had passed the McGill dynasty for safekeeping.

FIFTY-NINE

Emma's grief was a mantle of iron, but slowly she came to grips with her heartache. In all truth, her sorrow did not really lessen and she missed Paul and yearned for him constantly, but she took control of her emotions, and as the weeks passed she began to function like her old self. Also, her anguish was muted by the circumstances of her life and the world crisis which had developed.

She was beset by the most pressing problems as England plunged into the European conflict, and consequently her energies were taxed to the fullest, leaving little time or strength for self-indulgences. Her sons joined the forces, Kit enlisting in the army, Robin in the Royal Air Force.

Elizabeth, who had enrolled at the Royal Academy of Dramatic Art in the summer of 1939, was quietly married to Tony Barkstone during the Christmas holidays. Although Elizabeth was only eighteen and still too flighty to marry, in Emma's opinion, she did not have the heart to object. Everyone had to grasp happiness when they could, especially in these terrible times, and, in spite of her misgivings, she gave her blessing. The young couple were obviously head over heels in love, and Emma approved of Tony, who was a friend of Robin's from Cambridge and also a pilot in the RAF.

Despite the austerity, a spirit of gaiety prevailed at the wedding and all of the family were briefly reunited, with the exception of Edwina, who was still estranged from Emma, and Kit, who was unable to get leave. June, his wife of one year, came up to London for the occasion and stayed with Emma through the New Year. In

January of 1940, Elizabeth dropped out of the Royal Academy to become a Red Cross nurse, much to Emma's amazement. 'But I thought you always dreamed of being a famous actress and seeing your name in lights,' she exclaimed when she heard the news. 'Oh, phooey to all that nonsense,' Elizabeth quickly responded. 'I feel I must be part of the war effort, too, Mummy.' Emma was soon impressed by Elizabeth's seriousness and her dedication to nursing, and she began to think the marriage would be the stabilizing influence her most wayward child needed.

The news grew more distressing by the day, and in March Emma contemplated sending Daisy to America to live with the Nelsons at their Hudson River estate. But the more she thought about it, the more she balked, acknowledging that the transatlantic crossing could be hazardous, and she decided that the child's present location at boarding school in Ascot was probably the safest place.

As the year progressed, Emma threw herself into work with a vengeance, but she welcomed the distraction it offered. Henry Rossiter, who had handled some of her business in the past, became her financial adviser on a full-time basis, since she now had all the McGill holdings to supervise as well as her own. She was in constant touch with Mel Harrison in Sydney and Harry Marriott in Texas, and her days were longer and more arduous than ever before as her responsibilities increased. But she took everything in her stride. She was the dynamo she had been in her youth, and most especially during the First World War when she had also been left to cope single-handedly. If Emma's face grew graver by the day, then so did every other face in England, for the country was held in the grip of fulminating desperation as Hitler's blitzkrieg continued unabated.

Towards the end of May, just after his fifty-fourth birthday, David Kallinski came to London to discuss their mutual business interests with Emma. He was still a good-looking man and those penetrating blue eyes had not dimmed, although his hair was iron grey and he had thickened around the waist. His devotion to Emma had remained constant over the years and he was always concerned about her. To his relief, when she greeted him at the house in Belgrave Square, he immediately saw that her face had lost its gaunt look and her beauty was returning, and she had also put on a little weight. Later they were joined by Blackie, and after a light supper they adjourned to the library for coffee and liqueurs, their conversation revolving around the war.

'Do you think we'll be able to get the boys off the beaches in time?' Emma asked, thinking not only of Kit, and Ronnie and Mark Kallinski, but of the thousands of other British troops stranded in Dunkirk.

'If anybody can do it, by God, Winston Churchill can!' Blackie asserted. He shifted in his chair and went on, 'He's assembled an armada the likes of which the world has never seen, albeit a motley one. But it's united in one goal – getting our boys safely home to Deal and Ramsgate before they are annihilated by the Germans advancing across the Low Countries into France.'

'I read they came from all over England to assist the Royal Navy's destroyers,' David interjected, puffing on his cigar. 'Volunteers from all walks of life, with their rowing boats, sailing boats, fishing trawlers, yachts, pleasure steamers, and even barges. It's the most wonderful display of patriotism and heroism I've ever heard of in my lifetime.'

Blackie nodded. 'Aye, it is, David. Seven hundred vessels of all shapes and sizes, including the destroyers, of course. It seems the volunteers are picking up the men and carrying them out to the bigger ships that can't get close enough to the beaches, while some are even ferrying the boys across the Channel on a round-the-clock basis. Enormously brave men, sure and they are, and indefatigable.'

'How long do you think the evacuation will take?' Emma inquired quietly, looking from Blackie to David with consternation.

David said, 'A few days longer at least. There are hundreds of thousands of British and French troops to lift off, you know.'

'I read today that the Luftwaffe is keeping up a steady bombardment of the beaches,' Emma said. 'I dread to think of the casualties.'

'There are bound to be some, Emma,' Blackie said. 'But the RAF boys are up there in their fighter planes doing their damnedest to –'

'Bryan, Robin, and Tony amongst them, Blackie,' Emma interjected, and she looked away.

'We all feel frustrated and helpless, sitting here in London. But all we can do is pray that our sons will be safe. And we must be cheerful.' Blackie said. 'Now come along, let's have another drink. It will do us good.' As he fixed their drinks Blackie's eyes strayed to the clock on the mantelshelf. 'Do you mind if we turn the radio on, Emma? Winston Churchill's about to speak.'

'No, of course not. I'd like to hear him myself.' She rose and fiddled with the knob, tuning in to the BBC, and a moment later the familiar rhetorical voice rang out: 'Good evening. This is the Prime Minister.' The three old friends, who had shared so much in the past thirty years, sat back to listen, even more strongly joined together by fear for their sons and all the sons of England. When the Prime Minister had finished, Emma's eyes stung and her voice quavered when she said, 'What an inspiration that man is to us all. God help us if we didn't have Churchill.'

The epic of Dunkirk gripped the imagination of England and her allies. Out of hell came back all the little steamers and rowing boats and pleasure steamers, bringing back the living and the wounded. The evacuation had taken eleven days, and 340,000 Allied troops had been rescued by the time the Germans captured the French sea town. Only 40,000, mostly French, were left behind. Emma and David were lucky. Amongst those to land at Ramsgate on June 1 and 2 were Ronnie and Mark, and on June 3 Kit stepped off the barge that had transported him to Deal across a choppy Channel jammed with vessels and wreckage. Kit told Emma later, when he came home on leave, 'I just made it by the skin of my teeth, Mother. I must have a guardian angel watching over me.' He embraced her tightly, and, clinging to him, she choked up, thinking of his father, who had died in France in 1916, apparently in vain.

On June 4 Winston Churchill rose in the House of Commons and made a speech on Dunkirk. At one moment he said, 'We shall fight on the beaches, we shall fight on the landing-grounds, we shall fight in the fields and in the streets, we shall fight in the hills; we shall never surrender.' Six days later the French Government and the Army High Command fled Paris as the Nazi army drew closer. Four days after that the French capital was captured by the Germans, who took it without firing one shot. France had fallen.

Britain stood alone.

That summer was the worst Emma could remember. In July the Battle of Britain began in earnest. Hitler had ordered an all-out offensive against the RAF, specifically Britain's aircraft factories and the fighter bases that ringed London. Day after day, night after night, huge fleets of Dornier and Heinkel bombers swept across the Channel to pulverize Britain, while Messerschmitt fighter planes fought off the RAF Hurricanes and Spitfires that rose up into the sky in swift retaliation.

Awakened at night by the screaming air-raid sirens, Emma would get up and stand by the window in her darkened bedroom, looking out at the night sky starkly illuminated by the searchlights and echoing with the incessant drone of the bombers and fighter planes, her heart in her mouth as she thought of Robin, Tony, and Bryan and the other young pilots up there risking their lives. Some nights she was joined by Elizabeth, who had given up the small flat she had taken during her Royal Academy days, and was again living at home. 'Are you awake, Mummy?' she would invariably whisper, gliding into the room in her nightgown. 'Yes, darling,' Emma would answer, and the two of them would stand together, their arms around each other, watching the planes zooming past.

One night Elizabeth grasped her mother's arm fiercely, and her voice was unusually harsh when she cried out, 'Why, Mummy? Why? Why did this ghastly war have to start? What's the purpose of it? They're all going to be killed! Tony and Robin and Bryan, and all of our other boys!'

Emma had no answers for her daughter, or for herself. Elizabeth became distraught, sobbing uncontrollably. Emma put her arms around Elizabeth's shoulders and led her to the bed. 'They're not going to be killed, darling,' she comforted. 'They're going to be all right. I promise you. We must be brave. Get into my bed and sleep with me tonight. We'll keep each other company.'

'Yes, Mummy, I think I will,' Elizabeth said, crawling under the covers. Emma held her close, as she had done when she was small and frightened of the dark. 'Don't cry and try not to worry, Elizabeth.'

'If Tony gets killed I won't be able to bear it,' Elizabeth said through her tears. 'I love him so much. And if Robin –'

'Hush, darling. Try to sleep now. You must have your rest.'

'Yes, I'll try. Thank you, Mummy. Good night.'

'Good night, dear.'

Emma lay in the darkness, waiting for Elizabeth's tense body to relax and go limp in sleep. But it did not, and Emma knew that her daughter would spend yet another sleepless night worrying about her husband and her twin, as she would herself.

Emma had made a habit of walking to the store in Knightsbridge every day, and as the summer drifted on she did so to the accompanying sounds of anti-aircraft guns, whining sirens, falling rubble, and shattering glass. She would flinch when she saw a favourite landmark demolished, an ancient church in ruins, old haunts she and Paul had frequented flattened to the ground. Yet in spite of London's devastation, its bleak mood, and the weary expressions on the faces she passed in the streets, Emma would nevertheless marvel at the stoicism and indomitability of her fellow countrymen and countrywomen. Often a cheery Cockney voice would break into a song, perhaps a fireman hosing a pile of smoking bricks or a workman clearing away the debris, and a cab driver would have a breezy comment to make, and they lifted her heart with their courage. It was at times like these that she would remember Churchill's words: 'We shall never surrender', and her strength was renewed, a spring returned to her step, her back straightened, and her head flew up proudly. And somehow her burdens seemed all that much lighter to bear.

The summer drew to a close. In September a large portion of the East End docks was destroyed in a massive air attack. The daily raids continued and the RAF pilots were tested to their limits, flying nonstop missions. The usual two- and three-day leaves were cancelled and Emma did not see Robin for weeks. The Royal Air Force was Britain's last defence, and even though they were outnumbered three to one, the boys in blue in their Spitfires and Hurricanes out-performed the Luftwaffe. By October the Fuhrer's plan to destroy the RAF and break English morale in readiness for a full-scale invasion had proved a failure. In fact, Hitler had suffered his first major defeat. But the German bombers still continued night raids on the large cities, levelling many to the ground, and the grim years dragged on endlessly. Years of the Blitz; coupons, ration cards, and queues; shortages and deprivations; sorrow and grief as old friends and the sons and daughters of old friends were killed or named missing in action.

But in the midst of the devastation there was the miraculous renewal of life. In 1942, June, Kit's wife, gave birth to a daughter. Emma was fond of June and delighted at the arrival of a second grandchild, and she went up to Leeds for the baptism of the baby, who was called Sarah. The same year, at the end of the summer term, Daisy left boarding school and came home to live with her mother and Elizabeth in Belgrave Square. Now the house did not seem so lonely and there were even moments of gaiety and laughter, especially when Robin came up from Biggin Hill, where he was stationed. He invariably brought one or two of his RAF friends from the 111th Squadron with him, explaining to Emma, 'The chaps are going to bunk in with us, Ma. You don't mind, do you? All the hotels are jam-packed.' Emma did not mind. In fact, she willingly opened her doors and her heart to those dauntless young pilots.

At Christmas, Robin was fortunate to get a three-day pass at the last minute and he arrived unannounced on Christmas Eve, as usual dragging three friends in his wake. The moment David Amory walked into her living room Emma's heart missed a beat. He was tall and dark, with bright blue eyes and a flashing smile, and there was something about his looks and his engaging manner that reminded her of Paul McGill. David was not as outrageously handsome as Paul had been as a young man, nor did he have his massive size or his audacious personality, yet he struck a chord in her memory of Paul as he had been during the First World War. David was twenty-four, a new arrival at Biggin Hill and already something of a war hero. With an ingenuousness that was quite endearing, he charmed Emma at once.

That Christmas was a particularly merry one and the house rang with peals of laughter, the friendly but unmerciful bantering that went on between the RAF boys and her daughters, the endless sound of the gramophone and the clink of glasses. Emma entertained gaily, taking them all under her wing, enjoying the fun as much as the young people. But whether she was being the gracious hostess or quietly sitting in a corner, looking on and knitting a Balaclava helmet, she was aware of David Amory. Her smile was benign but her eyes were watchful as she observed the seventeen-year-old Daisy, her most beloved child, being bewitched and falling under the fatal spell of the dashing young RAF officer. And David appeared to be as enamoured with Daisy as she was with him, and he was never far from her side. Emma held her breath, knowing they were falling in love and that there was nothing she could do to prevent it. Nor was she certain she wanted to interfere. After the holidays, David Amory became a constant visitor at Belgrave Square, whether he arrived with Robin or came alone, and over the months Emma took him to her heart. He was from an old Gloucestershire family, well bred and well educated, and had been studying law when the war had erupted. Emma quickly discovered he had integrity and a bright mind, as well as a gentleness that she found appealing, and she could not help but approve of him for Daisy. It did not come as a surprise when David asked her permission to marry her youngest child. He did so in May of 1943, just after Daisy's eighteenth birthday. 'But she's so young, David darling,' Emma exclaimed, intending to persuade them to wait. But she found herself saying instead, 'When do you plan to get married?'

Daisy, who had been hovering nervously by the fireplace, hugged her so furiously Emma winced. Daisy's face was radiant and her eyes sparkled. 'Next weekend, Mummy, if that's all right with you.'

The wedding was quiet, just as Elizabeth's had been, because of the war-time conditions and Emma's natural reluctance to display her wealth in such troubled times. Daisy wore a blue silk dress, a matching picture hat, and carried a nosegay of summer flowers. Winston gave her away, Robin was the best man, and Elizabeth the matron of honour. David's parents and younger sister came up from Gloucester-shire for the wedding and there was a small reception at the house afterwards. The young couple had a one-night honeymoon at the Ritz Hotel before David returned to Biggin Hill and Daisy to her mother's house.

And then, almost before Emma could catch her breath, Robin married Valerie Ludden, a nursing friend of Elizabeth's, in January of 1944, and a few weeks later Elizabeth gave birth to a son, whom she named Alexander. Elizabeth, who wanted to be close to Tony, found a small cottage near the airfield and moved there when the baby was a month old.

'It hardly seems possible they are all married now,' Emma said to Winston one day in the spring, when they were lunching together. 'Or that I have three grandchildren. I feel as old as the hills.'

'Nonsense,' Winston declared. 'You're the damnedest-looking grandmother I've ever seen. And you'll never get old, Emma. You have the kind of beauty that is indestructible.' He grinned at her affectionately. 'Furthermore, Frank tells me that the American major you met at his house has taken quite a fancy to you. *You* might find yourself with a suitor before you know it.'

'Don't be foolish, Winston,' Emma snapped, but she smiled as she spoke.

'I'm not being foolish,' Winston responded. 'After all, you'll only be fifty-five next month. Besides, you look years younger.' He paused and eyed her carefully. 'And Paul has been dead for almost five years.'

Emma was silent and Winston changed the subject. He and Frank constantly talked about the possibility of Emma forming a relationship with another man, and they went out of their way to introduce her to their eligible friends. But although she was gracious, she was patently not interested. She would never replace Paul in her life; she did not want to.

The year 1945 began auspiciously for Emma. Daisy gave birth to her first child in January. It was a girl.

'How do you feel, darling?' Emma asked as she walked into Daisy's private room at the London Clinic.

'Thin,' Daisy said, laughing. She hugged Emma. 'I was awfully lucky. It was an easy birth.'

'Yes, I know. The doctor told me.' Emma moved a strand of hair away from Daisy's face and kissed her. 'I just spoke to David at Biggin Hill. He's thrilled to bits. Celebrating with the boys from the squadron, and playing the proud father. He's going to phone you a little later. And good news, darling. He's got a twenty-four-hour pass. He'll be up in town tomorrow.'

'Oh, that's wonderful, Mummy. I can't wait to see him.' Daisy wrinkled her nose. 'I'm not sure who the baby looks like. She's awfully crumpled and red, poor little thing. But she has black hair, and I think she's going to have a widow's peak like yours from the way her hairline is formed. And her eyes are violet. Do you think they'll change colour?'

'They might,' Emma said, sitting down. 'They often do. Still, yours remained blue.'

'I've chosen the baby's first two names, Mummy,' Daisy announced. 'I'm going to call her Paula McGill. After my father.'

Emma's face, normally inscrutable, was only too readable for once in her life, and Daisy burst out laughing. 'Don't look so shocked. Honestly, Mummy, for a woman as sophisticated as you are, you can be awfully naïve sometimes. Did you think I didn't know Paul was my father?'

Emma said, 'I – I –' and stopped.

Daisy laughed again, but it was a gentle laugh and full of love. 'Even when I was quite small I thought he was my father. After all, he was always with us and we travelled everywhere with him. Then, as I grew older, I realized how much I resembled him physically. And let's face it, I never knew Arthur Ainsley, whose name I bear.' Daisy paused and her bright blue eyes were fixed intently on Emma. 'Anyway, when I was twelve Paul told me himself.'

Emma's jaw dropped. 'Paul told you he was your father! I can't believe it!'

Daisy nodded. 'Well, he did. He said he wanted me to know, and that I was old enough to understand. But he said it must be our secret for a few years. He was worried you would be upset. He explained everything to me very directly and carefully, and with so much gentleness. He told me why you and he couldn't be married, but that he hoped to solve the problem one day. He also told me that he had legally adopted me, and he said he loved us both more than anything in the world.' Daisy's eyes were moist. She cleared her throat and finished, 'Actually, it didn't come as much of a surprise to me, Mummy, because by that time I had guessed. I told him so, and he really chuckled. He said he knew his Princess was the smartest girl in the world.'

'Didn't – doesn't it bother you, knowing you are illegitimate?' Emma managed to ask.

'Oh, Mummy, don't be so old-fashioned. Of course it doesn't. I'd rather be Paul McGill's illegitimate daughter than Arthur Ainsley's legitimate daughter any day of the week.'

Tears welled in Emma's eyes and she fumbled for her handkerchief. 'I – I – don't know what to say,' she began falteringly.

Daisy leaned forward and held out her arms to Emma. 'I love you, Mummy. And I loved Paul. I couldn't have had better parents if I'd chosen them myself. And you have been the most wonderful mother in the whole world.'

'But why didn't you tell me you knew before?' Emma asked in a muffled voice, her face pushed against Daisy's shoulder. 'Why didn't you tell me when Paul died?'

'I didn't think it was really the right time. My main concern was trying to alleviate your grief.'

Emma sat back in the chair, blowing her nose. She smiled weakly at Daisy, her face reflecting her love. 'I'm glad you know, darling. I should have told you myself. But I thought you would react like – that you would be upset and that you would hate me and Paul.'

'You are a silly goose, Mummy. I could never hate or criticize you or my father for what you did. You loved each other.' Daisy took hold of Emma's hand and squeezed it. 'I'm proud to be your daughter.' Daisy gave Emma a questioning look. 'Are you sure you don't mind my calling the baby after my father?'

'I'm thrilled,' Emma said.

The nurse came in, interrupting them. Emma held the baby in her arms and her face glowed as she looked down at the small bundle nestling against her shoulder. This is Paul's first grandchild, she thought, and her heart quickened. If only he had been alive to see her. Paula McGill Amory, the first of a new generation in the McGill dynasty.

One week later Daisy came home to Belgrave Square, where her old nursery had been beautifully prepared to receive its new young occupant. Almost immediately the child became the centre of Emma's world, and if she sometimes usurped Daisy's role as mother, Daisy did not seem to mind in the least. She was gratified to see Emma so joyous and smiling. And she enthusiastically encouraged her mother when she talked of her plans for Paula and her future.

And the future in general was beginning to look brighter. 'It's as if Paula's birth was a good omen,' Emma said one morning over breakfast, gesturing to the newspaper she was reading. 'The Allies are really making a breakthrough. I think the war will end soon.'

She was right in this assumption. As the new year eased into spring, the whole of England took heart. In March, the American First Army crossed the Rhine over the bridge at Remagen and established an invasion bridgehead in Germany. Between April 20 and 25, the Russians entered Berlin, and five days later Hitler and Eva Braun committed suicide. The Third Reich, which the Führer had said would last a thousand years, had disintegrated in humiliating defeat. On May 7, the Germans surrendered unconditionally at Reims in France.

Emma was in Leeds on May 8, which was V-E Day in Britain. She dined that night with Winston and Charlotte and they drank two bottles of champagne in celebration. But in spite of the flags hanging out of windows and fluttering on flagpoles all over Leeds, and the festivities going on around them, Emma felt more relieved than jubilant. And she drew her first easy breath in six years. Her sons were safe, and her sons-in-law, and the sons of her brother and her dearest friends, Blackie O'Neill and David Kallinski. There had been no casualties in their families, and for that Emma was deeply grateful.

And slowly they all came home.

'I just stopped by to congratulate you, Emma,' Blackie O'Neill said, striding into the drawing room at Pennistone Royal. 'Winston tells me the Yorkshire Consolidated Newspaper Company has taken control of the *Yorkshire Morning Gazette*. So you've finally won!'

Emma smiled at him faintly. 'Yes, I have. But then you always knew I would, didn't you?'

'Yes, I did.' He threw her a sharp glance and asked, 'How did you do it, Emma? I'm very curious.'

'Patience, really, and a weak adversary.' She folded her hands in her lap, looked down at the McGill emerald and then went on crisply. 'My newspapers are the most successful in Yorkshire and they have slowly eaten up all of the *Gazette*'s circulation. That paper's been losing money since the end of the war. To be honest, I deliberately ran the *Gazette* into the ground, and I did so without compunction. Edwin Fairley is not a good businessman. He should have stuck to law.' She laughed dryly. 'And he's made a few fatal errors, not the least of which was selling a big block of his shares two years ago. He weakened his position. He has not been dealing from strength for a long time.'

'But he stayed on as chairman of the board,' Blackie interjected.

'Yes, he did. But he failed to recognize the tenuousness of his position, and he also underestimated the other shareholders, both the old and the new. He just didn't seem to realize that loyalty flies out of the window when there's a great deal of money at stake. The board has been worried about the failing paper for years, and when Harte Enterprises approached them to buy up their shares they were willing to sell, almost to the last man. I've been acquiring shares in the company for years, and those, coupled with my last purchases, gave me a lot of power. Those shareholders who didn't at first sell to me finally threw their weight behind me when I offered to step in and put new management into the company. Very simply, Edwin Fairley was outvoted at the last board meeting and had to step down as chairman. Harte Enterprises made an offer for the remainder of his shares and, surprisingly, he sold.'

'Quite a coup for you, Emma, eh?' Blackie remarked. 'But I'm surprised you weren't present at that board meeting to witness his demise. Winston said *he* represented you.'

Emma's face changed radically and a cold glint entered her eyes. She said, 'Forty-five years ago I told Edwin Fairley I would never see him again as long as I lived, and I haven't. You don't think I want to set eyes on him now, do you?'

Blackie shrugged. 'I suppose not,' he responded quietly. 'Did Winston say how Edwin reacted when he learned you were behind his fall from power at the *Gazette*?'

Emma nodded. 'Apparently he was poker-faced. All barristers are good actors, you know. Then he said, "I see." But Winston told me Edwin had a peculiar look on his face, which he found hard to fathom.' She paused and stared fully at Blackie. 'Winston said he thought Edwin looked gratified. Odd, wouldn't you say?'

'Yes, I would. I can't imagine why Edwin Fairley would be gratified you had taken over his newspaper.' He shook his head, baffled. 'The paper that's been in his family for three generations.'

'God knows,' Emma said, 'it's a mystery to me. I told Winston it was more than likely sheer relief he witnessed.' She laughed ironically. 'In one way, you might say I've lifted a burden from Edwin's shoulders.'

'Aye, mavourneen,' Blackie said, and his face was unreadable as he lit a cigar. Maybe she's right, he thought. Maybe Edwin Fairley *is* relieved, but not for the reason she thinks.

Emma rose. 'I must go out and look for Paula. It's time for her lunch. I won't be a minute, Blackie. Please excuse me.'

Blackie nodded and followed her out on to the terrace. He stood watching her hurry down into the garden, his eyes trained on her and narrowed against the bright August sunlight. Emma drew to a standstill at the lily pond at the bottom of the garden and bent down to talk to Paula, who was playing with her doll's pram on the lawn. Emma was as lithe as she had ever been, and in the distance, in her light summer frock and with her still luxuriant hair now tinted to the russet-gold shade of her youth, she appeared to be the young girl he had first met on the moors so long ago, and for an instant the decades fell away. He clearly recalled his little servant girl of Fairley Hall, and a slow smile spread itself across his face. Almost half a century had passed and so much had happened, things he had never dreamed possible. How extraordinary life was. And Emma went on for ever, as indomitable now as she had been then. He blinked and shaded his eyes. He saw her smooth her hand over the child's head and then she straightened up and returned to the terrace, walking briskly.

Blackie smiled at her fondly. 'You're undoubtedly the most doting grandmother I've ever seen,' he remarked with a chuckle. 'And as for the wee one, why, she's become your shadow.'

'I suppose we do seem like an odd couple, the old woman and the five-year-old, but we understand each other.' She turned back to look at the child and her face softened. 'All my dreams and hopes and expectations are centred in her, Blackie. She is my future.'

PART SIX

THE VALLEY
1968

And yet, the order of the acts has been schemed and plotted,
And nothing can avert the final curtain's fall.
I stand alone. All else is swamped by Pharisaism.
To live life to the end is not a childish task.

— BORIS PASTERNAK, *Doctor Zhivago*

SIXTY

Emma sat at her desk in the lovely upstairs parlour at Pennistone Royal, going over the legal documents spread out before her, her sharp eyes flicking swiftly across the pages. She eventually nodded with satisfaction, returned the papers to her briefcase, snapped it shut, and placed it on the floor next to the desk. Half smiling, she stood up and glided over to a small Georgian table, where she paused briefly to pour herself a sherry. She carried it to the fireplace and stood as usual with her back to the flames, endeavouring to warm her icy limbs.

Emma Harte Lowther Ainsley was seventy-eight years old. At the end of April, just a month away, she would celebrate her seventy-ninth birthday. And yet in old age, as in youth, her looks were still so arresting they startled with their vividness and clarity. Years before, she had stopped tinting her hair and it was a blaze of pure silver around her oval face, immaculately coiffeured and waved, the prominent widow's peak protruding on to her wide brow as dramatically as always. Those once incomparable green eyes seemed smaller, hooded now by the ancient wrinkled lids, and they were more penetratingly observing than ever, and they missed nothing. Her face was lined and scored by the years, there were folds and creases in her neck, but her excellent bone structure had not blurred with time and her pink-and-white complexion was as translucent as it had been when she was a young woman. Her adherence to a simple diet had enabled her to keep her slender figure: she easily passed for a woman in her early sixties, without consciously wishing to do so, for vanity had never been one of her frailties.

This evening she wore a stunning black chiffon gown by Balmain, cut on loose flowing lines like a kaftan and with long wide sleeves. Emeralds threw off prisms of intense colour at her neck and ears and on her narrow wrists, and the huge square-cut McGill emerald blazed like green fire on her small left hand. In the past ten years she had acquired a different kind of beauty, a beauty that was austere and autocratic, and she looked exactly what she had become – a woman of immense power and substance. She was the true matriarch in every sense, and if she was demanding and imperious, she was also understanding, and even her enemies grudgingly acknowledged she was one of the most extraordinary women of her time. Eleven years older than the century, there was almost nothing she had not seen or experienced. She was a living legend.

She took a sip of the sherry, turned and placed the glass on the mantelshelf, and looked down into the fire reflectively, musing on the evening that stretched ahead. Her children and her grandchildren had all arrived, either last night or earlier that day, summoned by her to Pennistone Royal, ostensibly for a family weekend after her bout of pneumonia, but in actuality for the confrontation she had been planning for several weeks. Her face changed, and the light in her eyes dulled as she thought wearily of her children or, more accurately, of the first four she had borne – Edwina, Kit, Robin, and Elizabeth. The plotters caught red-handed in their scheming, but as yet unaware that she had been apprised of their duplicity and disloyalty, or that she had already circumvented them.

When her secretary, Gaye, had revealed her children's plotting to her in New York in January, Emma had been shocked. But she had not permitted emotions to obscure intelligence, for it was her vivid intelligence which had saved Emma from disaster many times in her life. She had immediately seen everything with objectivity and without sentiment, and she had moved with speed and with consummate resourcefulness, as was her way when she was facing opponents. Whilst they were still fumbling around, inept in their intriguing, she had taken steps to render them powerless against her.

Emma shook her head sadly. She had lost the taste for battle after she had taken over the *Yorkshire Morning Gazette*, and had buried the sword years ago. She found it regrettable that her children had forced her to take it up again to protect all that which she had so doggedly built up over sixty long years of purpose and sacrifice. The scene which would be enacted that evening was one she did not relish, but her business and the dynasty she had founded must be preserved.

The door opened and Paula came in, interrupting Emma's ruminations. Paula halted in the doorway, staring at Emma. She's up to something, Paula thought. Despite Grandy's reassurances to the contrary, this weekend was not planned for the reasons she gave me. She's about to do battle. I know that look in her eyes only too well.

'Why, Grandy, you look absolutely fabulous,' Paula exclaimed. She kissed Emma and stood away, her expression admiring. 'You're really going to knock their eyes out in that gown and with your jewels.'

'I wonder,' Emma said. Her eyes settled on her favourite grandchild, became softer, and the obdurate look disappeared from her face. She nodded approvingly. Paula wore a deep violet-blue silk evening dress that perfectly matched the colour of her eyes and enhanced the translucency of her skin. Her coal-black hair tumbled loosely around her face, giving her a vulnerable quality that touched Emma. She said. 'You look perfectly lovely, Paula. Like a bit of spring sky.'

'Thank you, Grandy.' Paula walked over to the Georgian table and filled a glass with white wine. 'But just wait until you see Emily. She looks gorgeous in your red chiffon dress and diamond earrings. I noticed her mother eyeing those, and quite covetously.'

'Elizabeth always was acquisitive,' Emma said dryly, and picked up her glass of sherry. She took a sip and went on, 'I suppose they have all assembled by now and are waiting for me to come down. Riddled with curiosity to see how the old woman is holding up.' She laughed cynically. 'I really think they thought I was going to kick the bucket this time. But I'm not pushing up daisies yet and it will be a long time before I do.'

Paula said, 'Yes, they're slowly straggling into the drawing room, where Uncle Blackie is holding court. It doesn't seem possible he's eighty-two and still going strong. He's a miracle, isn't he?'

'He is indeed,' Emma said. She was filled with a rush of warmth as she thought of Blackie. They had been friends for sixty-four years and he had always been there when she had needed him. 'My dearest friend,' Emma added almost to herself, and went on, 'Has Jim arrived yet?'

'Yes, he has. The aunts and uncles looked positively flabbergasted to see a *Fairley* in this house, and for a family gathering, no less. Especially Uncle Robin.'

'I'm not surprised. He's not particularly enamoured of Jim, you know. He thinks I've given him too much power in the newspaper company, that I let him have his head. I do, to a certain extent. But I'm not going to engage a man to run my papers and then manacle his hands.' Emma's eyes turned flinty. 'Ever since your Uncle Robin has been Member of Parliament for South-East Leeds he has held the misconception that my papers should be vehicles for his socialistic viewpoints. But I've never espoused his politics and I have no intentions of doing so now. He misguidedly blames Jim for the Tory policy of the papers, not appreciating that I dictate policy. I always have and I always will. Anyway, Robin's opinions don't really interest me,' she finished dismissively. 'He's too damned left-wing for my taste.'

'Robin's political philosophy and his way of life don't quite dovetail, though,' Paula remarked. 'Share and share alike is his motto to his constituents. But that only holds good as long as he doesn't have to share what *he* has. He's a hypocrite and an opportunist, if you want my opinion.'

Emma threw back her head and laughed uproariously. 'Enough of Robin. Has Jim spoken to your father?'

'He's doing that right now. They're in the library together. Jim said he'd like to see you privately before dinner, Grandy. Is that all right?'

'Of course. He can come up shortly. I want to see your Aunt Edwina first, but what I have to say to her won't take long. Now come, darling, sit here with me for a few minutes. There's plenty of time, and anyway I'm in no hurry to go down.' She smiled a trifle maliciously. 'Let them wait.'

Paula joined Emma on the sofa, her violet eyes, so like Paul McGill's, clouding over. 'Is there something wrong, Grandmother? You sound serious.'

'No,' Emma said. 'Don't look so worried.' She took Paula's long tapering hand in her small strong one and her eyes swept over her granddaughter's face searchingly. 'You are happy now, aren't you?'

'Oh yes, Grandy! Very happy.' Paula's face was filled with radiance. 'I do love Jim so much. Thank you for reversing your decision, for giving us permission to marry. You've changed my whole life, given me the one thing I truly want.'

'I'm so glad, so very glad, darling,' Emma murmured. 'Your happiness is more important to me than anything else in this whole world. It was a small gift really, in view of what you mean to me. As I told you last night, I decided it was ridiculous, and yes, even wicked, to let the pride and bitterness of an old woman get in the way of your heart's desire, your future.' She looked deeply into Paula's eyes. 'The Fairley family have touched my life with pain since I was a girl of fourteen. Perhaps now the last of the Fairleys will touch it with joy.' Emma shook her head bemusedly. 'It's odd, when I think about it. I went out of my way to protect my children from the Fairley family, to keep them well out of their orbit, and yet it never occurred to me to protect my grandchildren from them, particularly you. I suppose because there weren't any Fairleys left, except Jim.'

'And yet you gave him a job with the newspaper company, Grandy.'

Emma laughed wryly. 'Yes, that I did. I must admit when he applied for the position I was thrown off balance, and then my curiosity got the better of me. I wanted to see for myself what he was like. When he came up from Fleet Street for the interview I was impressed with his ability, despite my terrible prejudice. I knew he was the right man, the best of all the candidates. It would have been self-defeating to pass him over.' Emma's mouth twitched with amusement. 'I also suspect I derived a great deal of satisfaction at the idea of a Fairley working for me. But in my wildest imaginings I never thought you two would meet, particularly since you have nothing to do with the publishing side of Harte Enterprises.' Now Emma leaned forward. 'How *did* you meet him? I've often wondered.'

'I didn't meet him in Leeds, Grandy, if that makes you feel any better. I met him on a plane coming back from Paris. I'd been covering the fashion shows for the stores, and he'd been on holiday.' Paula grinned. 'Actually he'd been eyeing me at the airport, and he went out of his way to get the seat next to me. I was aware of him and attracted to him at once. But when he told me his name, and who he worked for, I almost had a heart attack. It's no great secret you've always hated the Fairleys, and I knew you wouldn't approve if I went out with him. A Fairley in your employ is one thing, courting your grandchild quite another.'

Emma gave Paula a penetrating look. 'You did go out with him, though, despite your misgivings. But then you're as stubborn and as self-willed as I am, I suppose.'

Paula returned Emma's look steadily. Just as you intended me to be, she thought. Aware of Emma's continuing interest, she said, 'Looking back, I think I fell in love with Jim the second time we met. He asked me to have dinner with him the following evening. I knew I shouldn't, that it was asking for trouble, but I couldn't help myself. I wanted to see him again. And in all fairness to Jim, he didn't know who I was. I had been rather evasive about myself. We dined at the Mirabelle and your favourite waiter, Louis, spotted me. Naturally he made quite a fuss of me and sang your praises to high heaven. He wanted to know when you would be in town and dining at the restaurant again. Jim became inquisitive about you. He wanted to know who my famous grandmother was.'

As she imagined the scene, Emma's eyes twinkled. 'And what did you say?'

Laughter bubbled in Paula. 'I was a bit naughty, really. I couldn't resist saying, "My grandmother is the chairman of the board of the Yorkshire Consolidated Newspaper Company and your boss." Jim almost fell out of the chair. He stared at me dumbfounded and then he remarked about us both having a widow's peak, and said that you must have looked like me when you were young. I know you don't think we resemble each other physically, but I do. I've seen all those old photographs of you, and the likeness *is* there, Grandy.'

'Your Uncle Blackie would agree with you, but I'm not so sure. Perhaps because I have always thought you take after your grandfather in appearance. Anyway, what happened after you had dinner together?'

'I went on seeing Jim, against my better judgement. We couldn't resist each other. When I realized how involved we were becoming, how serious Jim's intentions were, I pulled away. You know the rest.'

Emma looked down at her hands, a thoughtful expression on her face. 'So it was a chance meeting. A meeting that would have happened whether Jim worked for me or not. I suppose not even I can control events. It was meant to be, perhaps.'

'I think it was, Grandy. Jim is my destiny and I am his.'

Emma started and gave Paula a curious look. 'It's strange you should say that. Your grandfather told me I was *his* destiny fifty years ago.'

There was a knock on the door before Paula could respond, and Edwina walked in peremptorily, carrying a glass of scotch. 'You wanted to see me, Mother,' she said coldly, and gave Paula a curt, unsmiling nod.

'I did indeed, Edwina. I see you already have a drink, so come and sit down. Please excuse us, Paula dear. Tell Jim I'll see him shortly.'

'Yes, Grandy,' Paula murmured, and left.

Edwina, Dowager Countess of Dunvale, swept majestically into the parlour and seated herself opposite Emma, her antipathy thinly veiled. She stared at her mother, waiting expectantly, and there was a belligerent look on her face.

Emma regarded Edwina with quickening interest. She thought: If Adele Fairley had lived to be Edwina's age this is exactly how she would have looked. Edwina was sixty-two and she had not worn as well as her mother. Her exquisite blonde beauty had been too delicate to weather the years, and her looks had faded long ago. Her hair was still a shimmering silver-gold, but its colour now came from a bottle, and the once-lovely argent eyes were dimmed and heavily lidded.

'That's a lovely gown, Edwina,' Emma said, and took a sip of her sherry, peering at her eldest daughter above the glass.

'Why did you want to see me, Mother?' Edwina responded with icy disdain. 'I'm quite certain you didn't ask me to come up here to compliment me on my dress.'

'That's perfectly true,' Emma said. She smiled faintly. Edwina had not softened with age. 'Let me ask you a question before I answer yours. Why did you accept my invitation to come here for the weekend?'

'Invitation!' Edwina exclaimed, her eyes filling with hostility. 'It was a command, as usual, Mother. And none of us ever ignores your commands, do we? I was ambivalent about coming. But you said you wanted to see Anthony, too, and when I told him, he insisted we make the trip.' Edwina threw Emma a baleful glance. 'My son adores you. Neither his mother's wishes nor wild horses could have kept him away from this little gathering. He was also worried about your health. And so, since I love my son and wish to please him, I acquiesced. If it had not been for Anthony I would not have come, let me assure you of that.'

Emma sighed audibly. 'When your Uncle Winston effected a reconciliation between us in 1951, I hoped we could become friends. But it's always been an armed truce, hasn't it?'

'Yes, Mother. And if you want to know the truth, it was Jeremy who persuaded me to see you again. My husband always did have great family feelings. He felt we should make peace.'

'Such as it is,' Emma retorted. 'But let us not bicker. I wanted to see you alone because I have something important to tell you. I wish to speak to you about your father.'

Edwina's face stiffened. 'I can't imagine what you could possibly have to say about *him*,' she snapped, deep colour flooding her face. 'He's sitting downstairs at this very moment, behaving like the grand seigneur. Frankly, I don't know how you could be so thoughtless as to have him here in my presence, or in the presence of my son, who is, after all, a peer of the realm. That intolerable man makes me feel uncomfortable. But then I suspect you enjoy making us all squirm, don't you, Mother? You are addicted to manipulating people.'

'You never did know me very well, Edwina,' Emma sighed. 'And there is no reason why Blackie O'Neill should make you feel awkward or cause you discomfiture, because he is not your father.'

549

Edwina's jaw dropped. She gaped at Emma, but said nothing. Recovering her speech, she cried quickly, 'But his name is on my birth certificate!'

'That's true, but for quite different reasons than you believe. Blackie was my only friend when I was sixteen, alone, almost penniless, and carrying you. He asked me to marry him, out of friendship, I think. I refused. He insisted I name him as your father because he thought the phrase "father unknown" would be yet another stigma for you to bear. He also thought it would protect us to a certain extent, and in a way it did,' Emma finished, thinking of how it had given her the courage to deny Edwina's paternity, indeed her existence, to Gerald Fairley.

'Then who was, or is, my father?' Edwina demanded.

'Your father was Edwin Fairley.'

Edwina leaned forward alertly. 'Do you mean Sir Edwin Fairley? The famous criminal lawyer who died last year? One of the Fairleys from Fairley village?'

'Yes, I do,' Emma said quietly.

'Good God!' Edwina sat back in stupefaction and took a long swallow of her drink. After a moment she said, 'Why didn't you tell me this that day I showed you the copy of my birth certificate?'

'You didn't give me an opportunity to explain anything. You fled to Cousin Freda's, if you remember. Besides, I'm not sure I would have revealed his identity then. I might have, but it's doubtful. The Fairley family have caused me a great deal of heartache. I did not want you to suffer or to be exposed. I also –'

'Why *now*? Why are you suddenly telling me *now*? What has prompted this unprecedented display of honesty on your part, and at this late date?'

'Because tonight I am going to announce Paula's engagement to Jim Fairley, your father's only grandson. He will be a member of this family, and also you are his only living blood relative. His parents were killed in a plane crash in 1948. I thought he ought to know you are his aunt. I would also like to wipe the slate clean once and for all.' A reflective look entered Emma's eyes. 'I want Paula and Jim to start their marriage in the right way. No skeletons in the cupboard. No ancient secrets to haunt them. But apart from that, I felt I owed it to you to tell you the truth, Edwina. It's long overdue.'

The understatement of the year, Edwina thought bitterly. Finally, she said slowly, 'Edwin Fairley was a brilliant barrister and renowned throughout the country, and, perhaps more importantly, he was a gentleman. He had breeding and lineage. I'm not ashamed to acknowledge him as my father. You may tell Jim if you want. In fact, I think I would like you to do so.'

'Thank you, Edwina.'

Edwina stood up. 'I wish you had been honest with me years ago, Mother. Things might have been different between us.'

I sincerely doubt that, Emma thought, but said, 'Perhaps they would.'

Edwina walked to the door without another word and Emma was aware of the gratified look in her daughter's eyes. She's such a ridiculous snob, she said to herself. Her illegitimacy doesn't matter to her anymore, now that she knows her father was gentry. Emma called after her, 'Please ask Jim to come upstairs.'

Edwina swung around. 'Yes, Mother.' She hovered and said hesitantly, 'You remarked that the Fairleys had caused you grief, and yet you – you named me after my father . . .'

'A mere slip of the tongue, I'm afraid,' Emma said pithily, 'but then that's another story.'

A few minutes later Jim Fairley walked in and Emma straightened up, smiling pleasantly. Jim, who was thirty, was about six feet one in height, with broad shoulders, a narrow waist, and long legs. He had an attractive, rather sensitive face, although his mouth had a sensuality about it that contrasted markedly with his ascetic features and his soulful bluish-grey eyes. His light brown hair, streaked with blond, was brushed loosely across his shapely head and worn slightly longer than the vogue. His appearance was faultless, for he was always impeccably dressed, and he was the epitome of the perfect English gentleman right down to his hand-made shoes. He wore a flawlessly tailored evening suit, Edwardian in cut, which was the current fashion, and his fine lawn evening shirt was ruffled down the front and punctuated with sapphire studs.

Jim might have stepped right out of another era into the present, and as he strode towards her, smiling engagingly, Emma was carried back in time to the elegant dinner at Fairley Hall which Olivia Wainright had given in 1904. I always believed Jim looked like Edwin, Emma thought. He drew to a standstill and she recognized that it was Adam Fairley who stood before her tonight. James Arthur Fairley, the last of the line, was the reincarnation of his great-grandfather.

Emma felt unnerved for a second, but she brushed aside the peculiar feeling of déjà vu and said in a gracious voice, 'Good evening, Jim.' She rose and stretched out her hand. 'Welcome to my house. Welcome to my family.'

Jim smiled warmly. He revered and almost worshipped this regal old woman grasping his hand, and his admiration was fully revealed on his face. 'Good evening, Mrs Harte. And thank you. I am honoured to become a member of your family, and to be in your home.' He held on to her fingers and looked down into her eyes. 'I love Paula with all my heart. I will be a good husband to her.'

'Yes, I believe you will, Jim,' Emma said, extracting her hand. 'Can I offer you a drink?' As she spoke she moved towards the Georgian table.

Restraining her, Jim said, 'Thank you. I'll have a glass of wine. But I'll get it. Don't trouble yourself.'

Emma watched him stride across the room with that easy grace that sprang from self-confidence engendered by breeding and background, and she saw him yet again through newly objective eyes, wondering why she had never detected his uncanny resemblance to Adam. Perhaps it's more apparent because of the Edwardian evening clothes, she decided, and looked into the fire, filled with remembrances of things past.

Jim returned with his drink.

Emma lifted her glass. 'I understand from Paula you want to speak to me.'

'Yes, I do, Mrs Harte. But first I have something for you.' He put down the drink and reached into his pocket. He took out a small silver cardboard box and handed it to her.

Emma looked up at Jim. 'What is it?'

'Open it,' Jim said.

Emma did so quickly, her curiosity aroused. The box contained a silk handkerchief, its whiteness yellowed by time, and it had been carefully folded so that the initials E.F. were clearly visible. Her hands trembled as she lifted the corners. She caught her breath, staring down at the stone lying on the ancient silk. It was the flat pebble she and Edwin had found in the cave at the Top of the World, and upon which had been painted the miniature portrait of a woman. It was extraordinarily well preserved, the oils almost as vivid as they had been over half a century ago. She picked it up and gazed at it, and then lifted her eyes to Jim's questioningly.

'My grandfather gave it to me the day he died,' Jim told her, watching her face. 'He told me to bring it to you. He wanted you to have it.'

'Why?' Emma asked in a low voice. So Edwin Fairley had not forgotten her, after all. He had remembered her on his deathbed.

'I'll get to that in a moment, Mrs Harte. I'd like to explain something else first. My grandfather knew about my relationship with Paula. You see, I took her to meet him at his house in Harrogate, when we first started seeing each other. At the time I couldn't understand why he looked as if he'd seen a ghost when she walked in. Anyway, over the months he grew to love her and he was enthusiastic about the match. It seemed to give him renewed energy. His dearest wish was that we should marry.'

Jim paused, lit a cigarette, drew on it, and went on, 'Then Paula suddenly broke off with me, explaining that you would never accept a Fairley in the family, that you bore us a hatred she could not understand. She told me she would never do anything to cause you pain, because you had had too much pain and grief in your life. I argued with her, begged her to discuss it with you, or let me talk to you. But she became so hysterical at the mere suggestion of this, I decided to let her calm down, hoping she would have a change of heart. She didn't, as you know.'

Emma nodded. 'And you explained all this to your grandfather?'

'I did. I implored him to enlighten me. Many times, in fact. He refused point-blank. I knew you had wrested control of the *Gazette* from him in 1950, and I asked him if your hatred towards our family sprang from business conflicts. Again he refused to answer me or discuss you. He seemed to go downhill when Paula left me. He brought me up, you know, and we were very close, but not even I could reach him. He grew awfully frail in the last few weeks of his life, and one day last December he sent for me. I think he knew he was dying –'

'And he gave you this stone to give to me,' Emma interrupted. 'And he told you the whole story, didn't he? He told you about me and what had happened between us when we were young,' she finished in a faint voice.

'Yes. He told me everything. He said he hoped you would relent and give us your blessing, but if you did not, I was to come to you with this stone. He said it was imperative that you knew it was a painting of your mother and not Olivia Wainright, as he had believed when he found it.' Jim stopped and gazed at her, trying to gauge her emotions, but Emma's face was a mask of inscrutability.

In point of fact, Emma was not surprised at his revelation. 'I thought it was my mother,' she murmured softly. 'I think I always knew that. Adam Fairley painted it, did he not?'

'That's correct. Grandfather took the stone to his father after Olivia died, thinking he would want to have it for sentimental reasons. Apparently Grandfather had offered it to Adam before, and once again he wouldn't accept it. My great-grandfather then explained why. He said it was a painting of your mother, and he told Grandfather they had been childhood sweethearts.'

Emma nodded her head slowly. 'That was another thing I suspected years ago – that there had been a friendship between them.'

Jim took a deep breath. 'Your mother and my great-grandfather were more than friends, Mrs Harte. They were lovers.'

Emma was jolted upright on the sofa and her fingers tightened on the stone. 'Are you certain of that, Jim?'

'Oh, yes. Great-grandfather explained it all to Grandfather very carefully and in detail. It seems Adam fell in love with your mother, Elizabeth, and she with him. She became pregnant by Adam and ran away from Fairley. He found her some weeks later in Ripon. He had decided to abandon his military career, defy his father, and emigrate to America with your mother. It was too late. She had miscarried. Adam did not know if it was a natural miscarriage or one induced by some quack midwife. Elizabeth was very ill. She almost died. And she would not countenance Adam's idea of elopement. Eventually she recovered, returned to Fairley, and soon after she married your father, Jack Harte. And she never spoke to Adam Fairley again.'

Emma was silent, filled with a terrible aching sadness. I knew it always, she thought. That was probably one of the reasons I hated Adam Fairley with such virulence. But *how* did I know? Did I overhear something as a child? A family quarrel? Recriminations between my parents? Local gossip? She searched her mind and found no answers.

Jim came and sat next to her on the sofa. 'I hope I'm not upsetting you, Mrs Harte, opening old wounds that must be painful for you. However, I felt you ought to know Grandfather had confided in me, and I wanted you to have the stone, even though you had relented about Paula and me of your own accord.'

A wistful look flitted across Emma's face. 'No, you're not upsetting me, Jim. I'm glad you followed your instincts. I loved my mother very much and I don't have a photograph of her. I shall treasure the stone. Now, please continue. I'm sure there is more.'

'Yes, there is. When Grandfather gave me the stone for you, he said that the Harte women had always held a fatal fascination for the Fairley men, but that they had been for ever crossed in love. "Doomed by circumstances of birth" was the phrase he used. He said, "Tell Emma to let it end now. Tell her to let this generation have the happiness she and I were denied, and which her mother and my father were denied. Tell her that in all good conscience she must end it, once and for all. Tell her it is she, and she alone, who can finally join our two families together in holy matrimony." He was very emotional, Mrs Harte. I said I would do as he asked.'

Emma took Jim's hand in hers, and her eyes, so old and wise, were moist. 'Why didn't you come to me before, Jim? Your grandfather has been dead three months.'

'I was going to come to you in January, but then you and Paula left unexpectedly for America. When you returned, you fell ill. I intended to speak to you a few weeks ago, but you were so preoccupied I didn't want to disturb you, particularly so soon after your illness.' He smiled. 'And then out of the blue you approached me and said you would approve of the marriage if we both still felt the same way.'

'I'm glad I made the first move,' Emma said. 'Somehow it makes me feel better.' She shook her head wonderingly. 'It is strange, isn't it, that three generations of Fairley men have fallen in love with Harte women and have always been thwarted until now. Three generations, Jim, spanning almost a hundred years.' She sighed deeply. 'Too long. And there has been too much heartbreak. Your grandfather was right. It must end now.' She smiled. 'Why, it *has* ended, hasn't it, Jim?'

'Yes. Thank God.' To Emma's surprise and astonishment Jim now knelt down on the floor at her feet and took her hands firmly between his. He looked up into her face, his eyes almost beseeching. 'Grandfather asked me to do something else, Mrs Harte. Just before he died, he said, "When you have told Emma all this, I want you to get down on your bended knees and beg that woman's forgiveness for everything the Fairleys have done to her. In particular, ask her to forgive *me*. Tell her I've never stopped loving her all the days of my life, and that without her my life has had no real meaning. A part of me died the day I repudiated Emma in the rose garden, and I have paid dearly for what I did." I promised faithfully to do as he wished, Mrs Harte, but Grandfather suddenly became agitated, and made me promise over and over again. He also said, in the most sorrowing voice, "Jim, it will be an unquiet grave I lie in if Emma does not forgive me. Implore her to do so, Jim, so that my tortured soul can rest in peace." I told him I knew you would forgive him, and eventually I managed to calm him. He fell asleep for a short while. When he opened his eyes he didn't seem to see me. There was a faraway look on his face. He stared out of the window for a long time. When he lay back on the pillows I knew he was slipping away. Quite unexpectedly he smiled, and it was a triumphant, happy smile. He cried in the strongest voice, "Emma! Emma! I'm going back to the Top of the World," and then he died peacefully in my arms.'

Emma blinked back her tears. 'Poor Edwin. Poor Edwin,' she said in a voice that quavered. 'I think perhaps your grandfather suffered more than I did, after all.'

'Yes, I believe he did,' Jim said. His face became intense. 'You do forgive the Fairleys, don't you, Mrs Harte? And Grandfather in particular.'

'I forgive them, Jim. All of them, and most especially Edwin.' She touched Jim's face lightly, and with affection. But it was Edwin she now saw kneeling before her. I've spent a lifetime seeking revenge for what you did to me, she thought. But it wasn't really necessary. Your own conscience did my work for me. If only I had known. What a lot of pain and effort it would have saved. You wanted me to win. It was a salve for your overwhelming guilt. That's why you looked so relieved when I stole the *Gazette* from you. You knew the vendetta was finally over.

'Mrs Harte, are you all right?' Jim asked anxiously.

Emma blinked and stared at him. 'Yes, I'm fine. Now be good enough to lend me your handkerchief. I can't go downstairs to announce your engagement with tears streaming down my face, now can I?'

'As far as I'm concerned you can do anything you want,' Jim said as he handed her his handkerchief.

Emma blew her nose and said, 'I was going to tell you tonight that I had born your grandfather's child, Jim. I wanted you to know. My eldest daughter, the Countess of Dunvale, is your Aunt Edwina. Or rather, your half aunt.'

'I guessed as much when I met her this evening.' Jim grinned. 'She looks like a Fairley, if you don't mind my saying so.'

Emma chuckled. 'She does indeed. She used to be the spitting image of your great-grandmother, Adele, when she was younger. Now, give an old woman your arm and escort me downstairs to greet my family.'

'I will be honoured,' Jim said.

SIXTY-ONE

The dinner had been in progress for some time. Emma sat at the head of the long mahogany table in her splendidly appointed Adam dining room, surrounded by her children, their spouses, and her grandchildren. The food was superb, the wines were excellent, and now a certain conviviality prevailed. Everyone appeared to be relaxed, their jealousies, hatreds, and differences buried or well concealed behind their smiling façades.

All the clowns wear masks, Emma thought, borrowing a line from a poem she had once read, for she detected an undercurrent of tension in the atmosphere, although to a degree it was less pronounced than when she had arrived in the drawing room earlier, on the arm of Jim Fairley. Her grandchildren, who loved her dearly and were fiercely loyal to her, had greeted her with enthusiasm and great affection, the camaraderie they shared most apparent. Her children had been amiable enough, if somewhat reserved, but Emma had been conscious of a cautiousness in some, veiled hostility in others, a wariness in them all, with the exception of Daisy.

She had been sardonically amused to see that the four conspirators had assiduously avoided each other. However, she had not missed the apprehensive glances Kit and Robin had occasionally exchanged when they thought they were unobserved, yet they, too, had remained aloof from one another. Even Elizabeth, who was as close to Robin as ever, had adroitly sidestepped her twin, hovering attentively over Blackie, fawning and flattering him. Edwina had remained by the side of her son all through the cocktail hour. The engagement had been announced, champagne toasts given, congratulations effusively offered, and despite their obvious surprise when they learned she had accepted a Fairley into the bosom of her family, her children's expressions had hardly slipped.

Now, in the flickering candlelight, as she toyed with the dessert on her plate, Emma looked up from time to time, surreptitiously regarding the four culprits, her green eyes watchful beneath the hooded lids. She had the advantage. A lifetime's experience in dealing with people had augmented her natural ability to assess her children's individual capacities and handicaps. She had discovered their flaws long ago and they no longer baffled or surprised her. She could read each one like an open book. After tonight she would not have to bother. The book would be closed.

Her eyes rested briefly on Kit. How like Joe Lowther he had become over the years. Plodding, phlegmatic, and lacking in imagination or initiative. And what a monumental fool he had been to throw his lot in with Robin, who would double-cross him at the drop of a hat. She shifted her glance to the latter. How handsome Robin looks tonight, she thought, and experienced a twinge of pain. Robin had always been her favourite son and the knowledge that he had been the instigator of the plot hurt more than she had realized. He was urbane and suave, the true dyed-in-the-wool politician, facile of tongue, the deal maker. Unfortunately, like his father, Arthur Ainsley, his overweening vanity was his fatal flaw, and it constantly obscured his judgements.

In many ways his twin sister was much shrewder than he, except that she rarely bothered to exercise that capacity. Emma glanced at Elizabeth, swathed in silver lamé and turquoise chiffon and dripping diamonds. *Her* problem was a desire to pursue pleasure to the exclusion of all else. Just like her father, too.

At forty-seven Elizabeth was still stunning, the real beauty of the family, but she was more highly strung than in her youth, brittle, and immature in innumerable ways. Emma thought: She's a dreadfully unhappy woman. But then, when was Elizabeth ever happy? And how many husbands had she had since she divorced Tony Barkstone, father of Alexander and Emily? Emma had almost lost count. There had been Michael Villiers and then Derek Linde, by whom she had had the twins, Amanda and Francesca. After their birth Elizabeth had lost the taste for Englishmen, and had sought out more exotic fare. A Polish prince with an unpronounceable name, to be followed in quick succession by the Italian count, who was a good fifteen years younger. Some count, Emma thought dryly. More like a gigolo.

Emma now observed that the count was being excessively attentive to Edwina, who in turn was playing the role of the Dowager Countess of Dunvale to the hilt, acting condescendingly and with a display of superiority that was nauseating. How transparent Edwina was. After tonight, with the information she now had about her paternity, she would really feel obliged to turn up her snooty nose at the world.

Well, so much for those four, Emma remarked to herself with cold detachment. Little joy or comfort they've offered me in my old age. But they did give me my grandchildren and for that I will be eternally grateful. Emma put down her fork and sat back in her chair, smiling benignly. But her eyes were for ever watchful and if any of them had looked more closely they would have detected a cynical light glittering in their ancient depths. She moved her head and peered down the table at Blackie, who sat in the host's chair, stately and distinguished. His hair was snow white but still abundant and wavy, his skin glowed with ruddy health, and his black eyes were as merry as they had been sixty years ago. He had become a majestic figure of a man, his bulk undiminished, his mind unimpaired, and he carried his old age blithely. He had outlived Winston and Frank, who had both died in the early 1960s within a year of each other, and David Kallinski, who had passed on in the summer of 1967. There are only the two of us left now, Emma thought. And Blackie will go on for ever. He's an old war-horse. But then, so am I.

Emily, who was sitting further down the table, caught Emma's attention, rolling her eyes upward, silently mouthing words Emma could not understand. She frowned and motioned for Emily to come to the head of the table.

'What on earth's the matter with you, Emily? You look as if you're having a fit!'

Emily bent forward and whispered, 'It's Aunt Edwina, Grandy. She's three sheets to the wind, and tilting. As usual. It's all that wine she's guzzled, plus the four scotches and the champagne before dinner. If you ask me, she's got a drinking problem. She's getting awfully snotty with Gianni. I know you don't like him, but he's harmless and he's good to the twins and Mummy. I think she's been abominably rude and he's so uncomfortable. Mummy's bombed, too. Not that that's so unusual these days. Shouldn't Hilda serve coffee?'

Emma patted Emily's arm affectionately. 'Good girl. I'm glad you told me. Now, do me a small favour and run upstairs. You'll find my briefcase in the parlour. Put it behind the desk in the library.'

'I will, Grandy. In just one minute.' Emily returned to her place at the table, reached over, and picked up her glass. She stood behind her chair and cleared her throat loudly. 'Please, be quiet, everyone!' she pronounced in a strong voice. The buzz of conversation stopped abruptly and they all looked at her in surprise.

The self-confident Emily, who was never put out by anything, exclaimed, 'Far be it from me, as a member of the younger generation of this family, to suggest that someone here has been remiss tonight. But I would like to point out that no one has proposed a toast to Grandmother, who has just recovered from a serious illness. I think we should drink to her continuing good health. For we all love her very dearly –'

Emily paused and glared at Robin and Kit, whom she detested. Her green eyes, so like Emma's, were condemning. 'And so *I* am going to propose a toast to her. To Emma Harte. A great lady. To whom we *all* owe so much. May she be with us for a long time to come. To Emma Harte!'

'To Emma Harte!' they said in unison, raising their glasses.

Emma was moved by Emily's gesture. But, perhaps more importantly, she was proud of her twenty-one-year-old granddaughter. She's got guts, that one, Emma thought, and she's not afraid of anyone, least of all her uncles. Emma took in the furious expressions on the faces of her sons, and she concealed a small smile as she rose to her feet.

'Thank you,' she said, inclining her head. 'And now let us adjourn to the library for coffee and liqueurs.' And the last round, she added silently, thinking of the winning cards she had up her sleeve.

SIXTY-TWO

The library was a large room with a high-flung ceiling and mullioned windows looking out on to the grounds. With its western aspect and early eighteenth-century pine panelling, it made a gracious setting for the fine antique tables and cabinets, the grand Chippendale desk, the many books, the comfortable sofas covered in light green floral chintz, the dark green velvet chairs and matching draperies.

Emma walked briskly across the Aubusson carpet that covered the dark wood floor and stood in front of the massive carved stone fireplace, the original that dated back to 1611, when Pennistone Royal had been built. She spread her hands and warmed them in front of the log fire and then looked up at the overmantel that soared to the ceiling. Her eyes settled on the relief in its centre. How appropriate, she thought, with a faint ironic smile. It depicted the Judgement of Solomon.

Emma swung round as Emily hurried in breathlessly. She held up the briefcase, grinned, and deposited it behind the desk, and then flitted over to the fireplace, the red chiffon flaring out behind her. She hugged Emma. 'I do adore this dress, Grandy. Thank you again for giving it to me.'

Smiling affectionately, Emma touched Emily's cheek, the gesture tender. 'You may also keep the earrings, dear.'

Emily gasped. 'Oh, I couldn't! Are you sure?' Emily stared at her grandmother, her eyes sparkling. 'You *do* mean it. I can tell by the look on your face. Oh, you are a darling. Thank you. Oh, gosh!' She broke off and her young face fell. 'Mummy's going to be as mad as hell. She was furious when she saw me wearing them.'

Emma swallowed a smile. 'I think I can dispose of my jewellery any way I like, Emily. It's none of your mother's business, or anybody else's for that matter. Don't give it another thought.'

Sarah, Kit's only child, appeared in the doorway. She made a striking picture in her bottle-green velvet gown, her russet-gold hair tumbling around her freckled face to soften her angular features. Thank God she doesn't take after her father or her grandfather, Joe, Emma thought, as Sarah joined them at the fireplace.

The twenty-six-year-old tucked her arm through Emma's possessively and said with a frown. 'I don't know what's wrong with my father. He's been edgy all evening. I just ran into him in the Stone Hall talking to Uncle Robin. They both looked like thunder and seemed to be having a terrible row. I hope they won't spoil this lovely party with their bickering. They're impossible, as usual.'

'I'm sure it's nothing of any consequence, Sarah. Don't worry,' Emma said. She thought: So, the conspirators are at each other's throats. Not surprising.

Emily volunteered in her breathless voice, 'I think all the oldies have been behaving a bit strange since they got here. Sort of jittery, Grandy. Especially Mummy. But then she's always a bag of nerves. Oh, well, who cares. We're having fun.'

'Indeed we are,' Emma said, and plunged into an animated discussion about business with her granddaughters.

The others began to stroll in gradually. They seated themselves around the room or clustered in groups. Hilda, the housekeeper, served coffee and the butler dispensed after-dinner drinks and cigars. Blackie strolled over to Emma, nursing a brandy and puffing on a cigar.

'A lovely evening, Emma.' He peered down into her face. 'And you look wonderful, mavourneen. If I were two years younger I'd be asking ye to marry me. On the blessed heads of the saints I swear I would,' he laughed, lapsing into his brogue as he was wont to do of late.

'There's no fool like an old fool,' Emma laughed. Her face sobered. 'And talking of fools, don't you think you ought to take it easy with these?' she asked, indicating the drink and cigar.

'I hardly have to worry about my health at my age. I'm living on borrowed time as it is,' he exclaimed, and continued, 'Bryan sends you his love. And I'm happy to announce that Geraldine's expecting me third grandchild.'

'Congratulations, Blackie. That *is* wonderful.'

Elizabeth, who looked feverishly excited, pounced on Blackie and dragged him away, chatting incessantly as she led him over to her husband. Emily and Sarah drifted off and Emma stood alone in front of the fireplace quietly observing the scene. She felt completely at ease with herself and she was enjoying the company of her nine grandchildren, who in their different ways gave her such happiness. One by one, the younger generation gravitated to her. They kept her entertained and warmed her tired heart and she basked in the love that flowed out from them. And her conviction that she had been right in all she had done to preserve her dynasty was more strongly reinforced in her than ever.

Philip, whom she had recalled from Australia earlier that week, recounted anecdotes about happenings at the sheep station, and as she listened she was filled with fond memories of Dunoon and of the happy times she had spent with Paul and Daisy in that lovely old house. Paul would be proud of his grandchildren, she thought. They turned out well. Philip was as straight as a die, intelligent, and a hard worker, and he was proving himself a good businessman. Along with Paula he would ensure the continued success of the McGill enterprises.

Emma glanced over at her granddaughter, who was totally absorbed in Jim Fairley and radiating happiness, and her mind turned automatically to the Fairleys. She had brought ruin to that family and she wondered if it had all been worth it. But regrets were a waste of time. She remembered words uttered years before by Paul. 'Success is the best revenge, Emma,' he had said. Perhaps her own success *would* have been enough in the long run, and yet without her hatred for the Fairleys to goad her on she might not have reached the pinnacle. Revenge had been the spur. Now she was in the valley of her life, and after tonight she could relax, secure in the knowledge that all she had built was intact for this generation, and the ones that followed.

I must get it over with. Be done with it, she said to herself. An hour had already passed and it was time to show her hand. She quietly disengaged herself from the group in front of the fireplace and edged her way around her guests until she was standing in front of her desk at the far end of the room.

'Can I have your attention, please,' Emma said, walking behind the desk. The buzz of conversation continued unabated. She picked up a glass paperweight and banged it hard on the leather blotting pad. There was a lull as they stopped talking and all faces turned to look at her. 'Please make yourselves comfortable. I have a little family business to go over with you.'

Glances were anxiously exchanged by some, and they all did as she asked. When they were settled, Emma sat down at the desk and opened her briefcase. She removed the pile of documents and spread them out before her, taking her time. Her glance caught Jonathan's, who winked and gave her a broad smile. He looks more like Arthur Ainsley than Robin, she mused, shuffling the papers. It's fortuitous his character is more like mine. She smiled at Jonathan. 'Please be good enough to get me a glass of water, dear.' Jonathan sprang up and did as she asked. Emma took a sip, savouring the moment, purposely keeping the plotters on tenterhooks.

Emma picked up a document at last and her voice rang out:

'*I, Emma Harte Lowther Ainsley, of Pennistone Royal, Yorkshire, being of sound mine and body do hereby declare this to be my Last Will and Testament, hereby revoking all wills and codicils heretofore made by me.*'

A collective gasp rose on the air. Emma paused and lifted her silver head. All eyes were on her and the silence in the room was suddenly so acute a pin dropping would have sounded like a clap of thunder. Emma smiled, deriving malicious enjoyment from the astonished expressions on the faces of her children. Only Daisy and the grandchildren seemed unperturbed.

Emma smiled, but her eyes were steely. 'I know it is not the usual practice for a will to be read by the testator, but there is apparently no legal reason why this cannot be done. Unorthodox perhaps, but then, I've never been one to conform to the rules.'

'Isn't this a bit morbid, Mother?' Elizabeth exclaimed unsteadily, her face strained.

'Please don't interrupt me! And no, I don't think it is morbid.' Emma tapped the will and went on, 'This is rather an unwieldy document to read word by word, since it is over a hundred pages long. It is also full of legal terminology. Therefore, I think it will be easier to cut through it all and tell you, in simple language, how I have disposed of my business holdings, properties, and not inconsiderable wealth.'

Emma leaned back in the chair. Her eyes swept around the room, keenly observing. No one uttered one word and the four who had conspired against her looked as if they had been turned to stone images in their chairs.

Placing the will to one side, Emma continued, 'Before I proceed with the disposition of my estate, I would like to clarify something. I think there is probably a misunderstanding about the McGill empire which I inherited. It struck me recently that there might be those amongst you who believe Paul left me everything unconditionally, and that I can therefore dispose of the McGill fortune in any way I see fit. However, this is not the case.'

She took a sip of the water and shifted in her seat. She looked at the gathering at large and said in a solemn tone, 'Under the terms and conditions of Paul McGill's last will and testament, his natural daughter, Daisy Ainsley Amory, automatically inherits the entire estate when I die. From her, the estate passes to her two children, Paula McGill Amory and Philip McGill Amory, to be divided in equal shares between them after their mother's death.'

Low murmurings broke out. Emma held up a silencing hand. 'During her lifetime, Daisy will receive the income from the McGill estate, with the Rossiter Merchant Bank acting as trustees. I have appointed Daisy executrix of the McGill estate and Henry Rossiter as co-executor. Upon my death, Daisy's daughter, Paula, will take my place on the board of the Sitex Oil Corporation and will act on behalf of her mother, as she has been trained by me to do. Also, upon my death, Daisy's son, Philip, will take full control of the McGill holdings in Australia and will run them for his mother, which he has been learning to do under my supervision for the past three years. I assume you all clearly understand that in no way can any of my other children, or grandchildren, inherit one single penny from the McGill estate.'

No one spoke. Emma's narrowed eyes travelled swiftly across the faces staring at her with rapt intensity. Whatever her other children were thinking, they were keeping their feelings to themselves and their faces were unmoving.

She said, 'With the McGill inheritance clarified, I will now commence with the disposition of my own estate.' Emma felt the tension and expectancy increase so palpably it seemed to reach out and touch her in waves. Her gaze settled on Edwina's only child, the thirty-two-year-old Earl of Dunvale, grandson of Edwin Fairley and half cousin to Jim. 'Anthony, please come here and stand by me.'

The young earl, who was rather shy, looked momentarily startled to be singled out, but, none the less, he did as she asked and took up a position to the right of Emma. She flashed him a smile and turned back to face the others. 'My eldest grandson, Anthony, will receive the income from a two-million-pound trust which I have created for him. I also give to Anthony my house in Jamaica, British West Indies, and all furnishings therein, with the exception of the paintings currently hanging in that house.' Emma looked up at Anthony, who was astonished and speechless. She said, 'I have not left you any interest in my business because you have never worked for me, and also because you are fully occupied running your estates in Ireland and the various business ventures you inherited from your father.' She paused and gave him a penetrating stare. 'I hope you understand and do not feel cheated in any way.'

'Good Lord, Grandmother, absolutely not!' he cried, blushing. 'I don't know what to say. I'm overwhelmed. You've been generous beyond belief. Thank you.' He made to return to his seat.

Emma restrained him. 'Stay here with me,' she said. Anthony nodded and stepped back, standing behind Emma's chair at the right. 'Now to come to my two youngest grandchildren, Amanda and Francesca.' She beckoned to the fourteen-year-old twins, daughters of Elizabeth, grandchildren of Arthur Ainsley, who sat on the floor at Blackie's feet. They stood up, looking slightly bewildered, and approached the desk holding hands.

'Stand over there by your cousin, girls,' Emma instructed. 'I have also established a trust of two million pounds for Amanda and the same for Francesca, who will receive the income from said trusts upon reaching the age of eighteen.' She swivelled to regard the twins. 'I know you are a little young to understand these proceedings. I will explain everything to you later.'

'Yes, Grandy,' they said together. Amanda cried tearfully, 'You're not going to die, are you, Grandmother?'

Emma shook her head and smiled reassuringly. 'No, not yet, dear. But I must make proper provision for your futures. That's what this is all about.'

'We can come and live with you, can't we?' Francesca asked plaintively, her face puckering up.

'We'll talk about that tomorrow, dear.'

Emma leaned forward, clasping her hands together, and her voice, always strong, sounded more vibrant than ever. 'I will now discuss the disposition of Harte Enterprises, the company that controls my clothing factories, woollen mills, Deerfield Estates, the Roe Land Development Corporation, as well as the General Retail Trading Company and the Yorkshire Consolidated Newspaper Company. As you know, it is a holding company worth many millions of pounds and I own one hundred per cent of the shares –'

She broke off, took a sip of the water, and leaned back in the chair, her face inscrutable. A faint smile touched her lips fleetingly. As raptly attentive as the four conspirators had been before, they were now mesmerized. She looked pointedly at Robin and then at Kit.

'I bequeath to my grandson Alexander Barkstone, fifty-two per cent of my shares in Harte Enterprises.'

She heard Kit suck in his breath, incredulity spreading across his face. Robin gasped, 'My God!', turned ashen, and half rose. Emma glared. 'To continue. I bequeath to my grandchildren Sarah Lowther, Jonathan Ainsley, and Emily Barkstone the rest of my shares in Harte Enterprises. Said shares to be divided equally between these three, each one receiving sixteen per cent of the remaining shares.'

She motioned to the four beneficiaries to come to the desk. They stood before her, their faces suitably serious. Emma looked at each one of them in turn and said evenly, 'I hope you understand my reasoning behind the disposition of Harte Enterprises. After careful deliberation, I decided the only way to preserve the company, and prevent any dissension or quarrelling later, was to put control of the company into one person's hands. In my considered opinion, Alexander is the best equipped, in knowledge and experience, to run the company. But this is no reflection on your capabilities, which are superior. You will continue to work in the subsidiaries and take control of your own divisions upon my death. And of course, you will derive considerable income from the shares I have given you. I have also established a one-million-pound trust for each one of you, Alexander included. I hope you don't think I've played favourites, or been unfair.'

They reassured her that they fully understood, individually thanked her profusely, and stepped to the left of the desk. Sarah looked fixedly at the stone fireplace, unable to meet Kit's angry gaze. She knew her father had expected to inherit a large chunk of the Harte Enterprises shares. Jonathan looked down at his feet, avoiding Robin's glaring countenance for the same reason. But the saturnine Alexander and his ebullient sister, Emily, seemed unconcerned about Elizabeth. Their mother's reaction was one of bewilderment bordering on stunned disbelief.

Emma continued, 'To digress for a moment from my business holdings. I would like to tell you how I am disposing of my various homes, collections of art, sculpture, and jewellery. To my grandson Philip McGill Amory, I leave the remainder of my art collection and sculpture, with the exception of the paintings here at Pennistone Royal, which currently repose in my various other homes, executive offices in London, Paris, and New York. Philip, please come and join your cousins.'

Philip paused at the desk and thanked her. She said, 'I am not leaving you anything else, Philip, because you are going to be a multi-millionaire under your grandfather's will. I hope you appreciate my motives.'

'I do indeed, Grandy. You have been eminently fair.'

'Now to my other homes. I bequeath the following residences to the following of my grandchildren. To Alexander, the villa at Cap Martin in the South of France. To Sarah, the house in Belgrave Square. To Emily, the Avenue Foch apartment in Paris. To Jonathan, the Fifth Avenue apartment in New York. The same grandchildren will also inherit all the furnishings in said residences. My jewellery, with the exception of my emeralds, is to be divided equally amongst my granddaughters Sarah, Emily, Francesca, and Amanda.'

Emma stopped and signalled to Daisy with her eyes. Her youngest daughter, acutely aware of the antipathy in the room, rose and glided swiftly across the floor, positioning herself next to her son, Philip. Emma said, 'To my daughter Daisy, I give the McGill emerald ring, earrings, and necklace, given to me by her father. I also bequeath to her this house, Pennistone Royal, and all of its contents, to be used by her during her lifetime. Upon Daisy's demise it will pass to her daughter, Paula.'

Mutterings and whisperings rippled in the air. Dresses rustled. Chairs creaked as bodies were shifted angrily. Her four eldest children, seated at the opposite side of the room, were staring at her with open antagonism, but Emma's gaze did not waver, and her face was implacable. Her eyes focused on Jim Fairley. She lifted a document from the pile. 'This is for you, Jim,' she said, putting it in an envelope quickly and holding it out to him.

Jim was taken aback, his eyes widening, and then he hurried to her side. She handed him the envelope. 'This is your new contract, ensuring your employment with the Yorkshire Consolidated Newspaper Company for the next ten years. Peruse it, show it to your solicitors, and return it to me next week. Signed. I am also appointing you managing director of the company, to take effect next month, with an increase in salary.'

'Thank you very much, Mrs Harte. I don't know how to express my gratitude. I will –'

Emma said crisply. 'Later, Jim. And please, stay here with the others.' Emma lifted the glass of water and drank deeply, emptying the glass. She straightened up in the chair, her demeanour imperious, her face glacial. 'I now come to the disposal of the Harte department-store chain. Something I'm quite certain you've all been anxiously waiting to hear about.' She stopped, her eyes becoming reflective. 'I built that chain from nothing, with the toil of these hands.' She lifted them in the air for them all to see. 'A lifetime's work has gone into building that chain into what it is today. One of the biggest in the world. I decided several weeks ago that it must pass into the right hands, that it must go to the one person who would ensure its continuation, who would run it efficiently, in the manner in which I have always run it –' She bit off the end of her sentence dramatically. The silence was overwhelming now, the tension almost unbearable.

'I give and bequeath *all* of my shares in Harte Stores to my granddaughter Paula McGill Amory. I also give to Paula the remainder of my emerald collection.'

Automatically Paula rose, discovering to her dismay that her legs were unsteady as she traversed the long stretch of carpet. But she kept her face expressionless, her eyes pinned solely on Emma. Alerted for trouble though she had been all week, she had not expected anything quite as dramatic, and she dared not think of the repercussions. She stood in front of the desk. 'Thank you for the trust you are showing in me, Grandmother. I promise Harte Stores will be safe always.'

'Do you think I don't know that, darling?' Emma said.

Paula stepped towards the others who ringed Emma like a phalanx. Grandmother's divided the room into two camps, Paula said to herself, and wondered with sharpening interest what was going to happen next.

'Finally, I have appointed my daughter Daisy Amory as executrix of my estate, and Henry Rossiter, of the Rossiter Merchant Bank, as co-executor.'

Edwina, Kit, Robin, and Elizabeth were paralysed with shock, and Emma saw hatred mingled with bitterness and disappointment gleaming on their cold faces. She sat perfectly still, waiting for the furore to begin.

It was Robin who recovered first. He sprang up, his face apoplectic. 'Now look here, Mother. You've been grossly unfair. You have cold-bloodedly cut us out of your will, deprived us of what is rightfully ours. I fully appreciate the ramifications of the McGill estate, but your own fortune and business holdings should have automatically come to your children. *We are your legal heirs*. I don't intend to accept this. I am going to contest the will, and the others will back me. Undue influence has obviously been brought to bear on you. I will prove that you were incompetent when you drew it. You are obviously no longer responsible for your actions. Any court of law will recognize that. Furthermore –'

'Shut up and sit down,' Emma said, her voice cutting through the air. She stood up and gripped the edge of the desk. 'I did indeed cut you out of my will. And for good reason. You see, I know you four plotted to wrest my empire from me, to get everything for yourselves, even at the expense of your own children.' She laughed sardonically. 'I think I might have had a grudging respect for you if you had been subtle in your scheming. I've always admired clever adversaries. But you were inept and obvious.' She sucked in her breath. 'And there was a fatal flaw in your plot. *You underestimated me.*'

She gazed at them, her eyes thin green slits beneath the old lids. 'Henry Rossiter once described you as a nest of vipers. How right he was. You really don't deserve any consideration in view of your unconscionable behaviour. But I am not as vindictive as you might suppose, and as many others would be in my place. And so I have decided not to revoke the trust funds I established for each of you some years ago.' Emma's lip curled with disdain. 'As for contesting my will, well, I expected that. I second-guessed you on that one, Robin. And I am prepared for that contingency.'

Emma picked up an envelope, from which she took four pieces of paper. She held them up in the air and fluttered them between her fingers. 'These are cheques made out to each one of you. The value of each cheque? *One million pounds.* A drop in the bucket to what you would have received if you had not betrayed me, but, nevertheless, a lot of money by anybody's standards.' She smiled cynically. 'Don't think these are outright gifts. They are not. I am simply buying you. And I know you *all* have a price.'

Placing the cheques on the desk, she picked up a sheaf of documents. 'If you each accept your cheque for one million pounds, cashable on Monday, incidentally, you will sign an individual contract with me.' She waved the documents she was holding at them. 'They are already drawn, as you can see. Each contract is a legal agreement between us, stipulating that you will not challenge my will. As a lawyer, Robin, you know that by signing such an agreement and accepting monetary consideration, you cannot ever contest.'

Her eyes flickered from Robin to Kit, Edwina, and Elizabeth. 'Let me warn you now I have made certain my will is irrevocable. Since this is the case, you might wonder why I am prepared to give you each one million pounds. Very simply, to prevent your disturbing my business empire with so much as a single ripple, and to ensure none of you causes trouble for my grandchildren.' She took hold of the cheques again, waving them in the air. 'Let's just say I believe in insurance policies.'

She sat down, gazing at them unemotionally. Kit had slumped in the chair. He was flustered, and he could not meet her eyes. Elizabeth was nervously twisting her hands together, held in the grip of obvious indecision, while Robin, the ringleader, had adopted an expression of false bravado. Of them all, it was Edwina who seemed the calmest, the least concerned.

Emma, who had paid no attention to her daughters-in-law or her son-in-law, the count, during the proceedings, now addressed them. 'Would you like to confer with your better halves?' she asked, and laughed. 'A million pounds is a hell of a lot of money to turn down.' June and Valerie, who had always been fond of Emma and were obviously horror-stricken at the duplicity of their husbands, shook their heads mutely. And the count, aware of his rocky position in the family, also politely declined.

'Come on, make up your minds,' Emma snapped. 'I haven't got all night.' She stood up and briskly began to return the documents to the briefcase. 'Suit yourselves. But I'm warning you for the last time, you won't win if you attempt to contest the will after my death. Never. I will outsmart you from the grave.'

Elizabeth roused herself first. 'Where's the pen?' she cried, standing up, avoiding Robin's furious gaze. Edwina followed her. Robin joined them, bristling with rage. They all signed the contracts and accepted their cheques. Kit was the last. Emma noticed that his hand shook and he was quite unable to look her in the face.

Emma locked the contracts in her briefcase. 'Well, now that this little bit of family business has been completed satisfactorily, I suggest we continue the party.'

There was a moment of absolute silence and everyone gaped at her, and then the pandemonium she had anticipated earlier suddenly broke loose. They all started to speak at once, thronging around her. Emma picked up her briefcase and said, 'Please excuse me for a few moments.' She took hold of Paula's arm. 'Go up to the parlour with Jim. I would like to see you both alone for a moment. And take my briefcase with you, please.'

'Of course, Grandy.'

Emma glided across the room. She tucked her arm through Blackie's. 'Will you come and have a quiet drink with me?'

'I'd be delighted,' Blackie said. He tilted her face to his, as was his way, and looked deeply into her eyes, his own twinkling. 'Quite a performance, Emma. Quite a performance!'

Emma smiled back at him, but she remained silent, and together they left the library, crossed the Stone Hall, and followed Paula and Jim up the great curving staircase. Something prompted Emma to pause at the bend in the stairs. She turned and glanced back. Kit, Edwina, Robin, and Elizabeth were standing in the doorway of the library, watching her ascent, their faces unreadable. But she knew what they were thinking. She straightened up and with one foot she kicked out the back of her chiffon gown in a flippant gesture of disdainful dismissal. And she continued up the stairs, as proud and as regal as ever.

Upon entering the parlour, Emma excused herself and went through into her bedroom. She returned a few minutes later to find Jim and Paula seated on one sofa, Blackie on the other. She stood in front of the fireplace and looked from Jim to Paula. 'Have you told Paula the extraordinary story of the Harte women and the Fairley men?'

Jim said quickly, 'No, I haven't, Mrs Harte. I felt it was up to you to do so.'

'What extraordinary story?' Paula asked curiously.

'I'll let Jim recount it to you. He'll tell you later. This is not the time.' Now Emma uncurled her right hand. 'I found this locket amongst my mother's things after she died. It is engraved "A to E 1885". I know that it was given to my mother, your great-grandmother, by Adam Fairley, Jim's great-grandfather. I want you to have it, Paula.'

Intrigued, Paula took the locket and examined it. 'Thank you,' she said. 'I will keep it always.' She looked at Jim. 'You must tell me the story when we go downstairs. It sounds fascinating.'

Emma now turned to Jim. 'I also found this gentleman's gold stick-pin with the locket. Could it have belonged to your great-grandfather?'

'Why, I believe it did!' Jim exclaimed, turning it over in his hand. 'There was a photograph of Great-grandfather in Grandfather Edwin's desk which I found when I was going through his possessions. Adam was a very young man when it was taken and he was dressed in riding clothes. I'm quite positive he was wearing this in his stock.'

'Please keep it, Jim,' Emma said softly.

'Why, thank you, Mrs Harte. I'm very touched. And thank you for the contract, and the promotion. For everything. I didn't expect –'

'It was the least I could do,' Emma interrupted. 'Now run along, you two, and enjoy yourselves. I want to talk to Blackie for a while. We've hardly exchanged a word all night. We've a lot of gossip to catch up on.'

Jim stood up. He bent down and kissed her on the cheek. 'You are indeed a great lady, Mrs Harte.'

Emma smiled. Paula hugged her grandmother and whispered in her ear, 'I knew you were a foxy old thing, and that you were up to something. But even I was flabbergasted. You're still full of surprises, Grandy. And I do love you.'

Emma watched them leave the parlour together, holding hands and smiling into each other's eyes. They'll be all right, she said to herself.

Blackie regarded her carefully, puffing away on his cigar, his black eyes filled with tenderness. He had loved her for sixty-four years, his wild young colleen of the moors. They had come a long way together, shared so much sorrow and joy, and she never failed to amaze him. Eventually he said, 'So the vendetta has finally ended. You have united the two families at last. Paula will become a Fairley.' He smiled at her gently. 'I'm beginning to think you're a sentimental old woman, after all, Emma Harte.'

'Yes, perhaps I am.' Emma settled back against the sofa and smoothed her gown. 'You know, Blackie, if I live long enough I will have Fairley great-grandchildren to bounce on my lap. Who would ever have believed that!' Her eyes sparkled. 'I'm so glad I relented about Jim and Paula. It's their happiness that counts now. They are the future.'

Blackie said, 'Aye, indeed they are.' He rose and strode across to the Georgian table. 'Would you like a drink, Emma?' he asked, pouring himself a cognac.

'I'll have a Bonnie Prince Charlie, please.'

Blackie returned and sat next to her on the sofa. They clinked glasses. 'Here's to those we've loved and lost, to those we've loved and kept, and to those of ours who are yet to be born, Emma.'

'Yes, to the next generation, Blackie.'

They sat in silence for a while, ruminating, and as at ease with each other as they had always been since the first day they had met on the moors above Fairley village. Suddenly Blackie took her hand in his. He said, 'It's an extraordinary road you've travelled, Emma, in your quest for power and wealth, and I'm curious. Tell me, did you discover anything special along the way that you would like to impart to your old friend?'

'Yes, Blackie, I did. I believe I learned the secret of life.'

Blackie looked at her intently. 'And what is that, mavourneen?'

Emma gazed back at him for a prolonged moment. And then she smiled that incomparable smile which illuminated her face with radiance.

'It is to endure,' she said.

Act of Will

Dedicated with love to the memory
of my parents, Freda and Winston Taylor.
She gave me the greatest gift a mother
can give a child, the desire to excel.
He taught me to be strong of
heart and to stand tall.

It is also for my husband Bob,
whose love and support has equalled
theirs, with all of my love.

Contents

PROLOGUE

Audra, Christina and Kyle

1978

PROLOGUE

Audra Crowther sat on the sofa in the living room of her daughter's Manhattan penthouse. She held herself tensely and clenched her hands together so hard that the knuckles shone white as she looked from her daughter Christina to her granddaughter Kyle.

The two younger women stood in the middle of the room, their faces pale, their eyes blazing as they glared at each other. Their angry words of a few minutes ago still reverberated on the warm afternoon air.

Audra felt helpless. She knew that to remonstrate with them, to attempt to make them see reason, was a waste of time, at least at this moment. Each was convinced she was right, and no amount of persuasion would make them reverse their positions or endeavour to understand the other's point of view.

Even their clothes were like uniforms, underscoring their intrinsic differences, further separating them. Blue jeans and sneakers for Kyle, the white Swiss voile shirt her only concession to style, the combination giving her an oddly vulnerable, childlike look, with her scrubbed face and long hair hanging loose. And for Christina, an expensive, beautifully cut dress and tailored jacket of matching raw silk, without doubt bearing her own couture label; the silver-grey of the silk the perfect foil for her chestnut hair shot through with reddish-gold lights, the grey also emphasizing her lovely smoky eyes which had always been her best feature. She was slender, impeccably groomed, and not showing her forty-seven years in the least.

Tycoon versus student . . . role model versus rebel . . . mother versus daughter, Audra thought, smothering a sigh. Well, it wasn't the first time a mother and daughter were at odds with each other; that was an age-old conflict.

Suddenly Kyle broke the protracted silence when she snapped, 'And there's another thing, Mother. You had no right to drag poor Grandma into this débâcle, drag her all the way from England, especially since –'

'I didn't!' Christina shot back. 'It was your father who telephoned my –'

'Oh yes, go on, blame Dad,' Kyle cut in, her voice scathing.

'But it *was* your father who phoned my mother,' Christina protested. She appealed to Audra. 'Isn't that so, Mummy?'

Audra focused her attention on her granddaughter. 'That's quite true, Kyle.'

Kyle tossed back her mane of black hair, then thrust her hands in the pockets of her jeans, her movements brusque, defiant. Her huge brown eyes, usually doe-like and soft, flashed rebelliously. 'I suppose he thought we needed a mediator. Well, we don't . . . there's nothing to mediate –' She brought herself up short, swung her long-limbed body towards Audra and gave her a wan half-smile. 'Sorry, Grandma, I don't mean to be rude to you, but you shouldn't have been forced to travel half-way around the world just because my parents have discovered they can't *influence* me, or *handle* me any more.' Kyle let out a laugh that was abnormally harsh. 'You see, the trouble is that my parents treat me like a child, Grandma.

Anyone would think I'm nine years old, not *nineteen*, for God's sake, the ridiculous way they're carrying on.'

Before Audra had a chance to comment on these strident assertions, Kyle pivoted to face Christina. Her voice rose shrilly as she rushed on, 'Nothing will induce me to change my mind, Mother. *Nothing*. And *nobody*. Not even Grandma. I'm going to live my life the way I want. It's my life and no one else's. You and Dad can cut me off without a nickel. I don't give a damn. I'll manage somehow. I'll get a job to support myself while I'm studying. I don't need any help from you!'

'Neither your father nor I have ever said anything about cutting you off,' Christina exclaimed, furious that Kyle was even suggesting such a thing. '*Your* problem is your inability to discuss this matter intelligently. And *calmly*. You fly off the handle every time we attempt to have a reasonable conversation with you.'

'Listen who's talking! You're not calm either!'

Christina's mouth tightened in aggravation, but she strove hard to curb her increasing exasperation with her daughter. 'That's not so surprising is it?' she countered in her coldest tone. 'I have built an enormous empire, an international fashion business worth millions and millions of dollars, and you're my only child, my *heir*. It's always been understood that you'd succeed me, one day. Understood by *all* of us. Why, you're being trained with that in mind . . . and now, out of the blue, you announce that you don't want the company. I'm flabber –'

'No, I don't!' Kyle shouted. 'Can't you get that through your head *yet*, Mother? I've been saying it for days! I'm not in the least bit interested in your stupid business empire! It can go to hell, *collapse*, for all I care! It's your problem, not mine!'

Recoiling, Christina drew in her breath sharply. She was as much stunned by Kyle's vehemence as by her words.

Audra, shocked, admonished swiftly, 'Steady on there, Kyle.'

Immediately, Kyle knew she had gone too far, and she bit her lip in embarrassment. Bright hot colour blotched her neck, sped up into her smooth young cheeks. She glanced at her grandmother, so pale and still on the sofa. She saw the sadness and disappointment reflected in Audra's candid blue eyes, saw the gentle reproach on her sweet face. Discomfort tinged with shame swept over her. She recognized she had discredited herself with her grandmother, whom she adored, and this she could not bear. She burst into tears and fled before she disgraced herself further, slamming the door behind her.

Christina stared at the door speechlessly.

She was mortified, enraged, and so taut that her shoulder blades protruded through her thin silk jacket. 'Can you believe it!' she exploded and took a step forward, obviously intent on following Kyle.

'No, no, let her go,' Audra said firmly, pushing herself up, hurrying across the room. She took hold of Christina's arm and led her back to the sofa.

Gently forcing her daughter down next to her, she went on, 'There's no point in continuing this. There's nothing to be gained. You know very well that the things we say when we're angry are difficult to retract later, and you must admit you're both overwrought at the moment.'

'Yes, I suppose we are.' Distractedly, Christina ran a hand through her hair, then slumped against the cushions, feeling miserable and frustrated. But after only a moment she jumped up, restlessly began to pace back and forth in front of the fireplace.

As she watched her, Audra's worry intensified. She had never seen Christina quite like this before, so agitated, with her temper so close to the surface and her patience so tightly stretched. Normally she was calm, in control, no matter what the circumstance. But then her world had never been rocked as it was rocked now; and Audra knew, too, that Kyle's words, thoughtlessly uttered in the heat of the moment and without any real malice, had nevertheless been cruel, hurtful to Christina.

Wishing to assuage that hurt as best she could, Audra said in her most reassuring voice, 'Kyle didn't mean it, Christie. You know, about not caring if the business collapsed. Of course she cares, and she does love you, dear.'

'She has a fine way of showing it,' Christina grumbled without looking at her mother, continuing to pace, her nervousness unabated, her mind still fogged by the pain her daughter had inflicted.

Audra sighed and, understanding everything, remained silent. She settled back in the corner of the sofa, waiting for Christina to calm herself, relieved that the shouting had stopped. There was hardly any sound in the room now, only the faint murmur of silk against silk as Christina moved, the ticking of the brass carriage clock on a chest between the French windows, the muffled rumble of the traffic on Sutton Place spiralling up through those windows, standing wide open on this balmy day in the middle of May. She glanced towards the terrace, mottled with sunlight, blooming with greenery and flowering plants, absently wondering how well the pink azaleas would do out there.

Then she brought her eyes back to the interior, let them roam around. For a split second her anxiousness was diluted as she absorbed the loveliness of the setting awash with tones of peach and apricot and cream, the beauty surrounding her, enveloping her . . . the priceless art on the walls, two Cézannes, a Gauguin . . . the fine English antiques with their dark glossy woods . . . bronze sculpture by Arp . . . the profusion of flowers in tall crystal vases . . . all illuminated by silk-shaded lamps of rare and ancient Chinese porcelains.

What marvellous taste Christina and Alex have, Audra thought, and experienced a burst of motherly pride in her daughter and son-in-law. This was not induced merely by the graciousness they had recently created in this room, but was a genuine pride in what they were as people, for all that they had achieved in their life together. They had a harmonious relationship, and their marriage had only gone from strength to strength over the years, and for that Audra was thankful.

Her thoughts settled on Alex Newman. He was a kind and gentle man, one of the most thoughtful people she had ever met. He had been like a loving son to her. How she wished he were here at this moment. He may not have succeeded in quelling the trouble which had erupted between his wife and daughter, but with his tact and good humour, and worshipping Christina the way he did, he always had a tranquillizing effect on her.

Audra turned her head, looked over at the carriage clock. To her disappointment, it was only ten minutes to five and Alex never got home from work before seven. On the other hand, perhaps he would arrive earlier today, since they were going out to dinner at eight. As she contemplated the evening stretching ahead, her heart sank. Unless there was a radical change in Kyle's disposition in the next few hours it was going to be an awkward evening.

Now, as though she had homed in on Audra's thoughts, Christina said, 'I don't much relish the idea of going to dinner at Jack and Betsy Morgan's, nice though they are, and so fond of you, Mummy. No, not with Kyle in this bolshy frame of mind.'

Drawing to a standstill at last, Christina looked directly at her mother and smiled ruefully, her greyish-blue eyes filled with concern. For the first time she noticed the weariness etched on Audra's face and she bit her lip, frowning.

'You must be bone tired and terribly jet-lagged, darling,' she exclaimed. 'How selfish we've been since you arrived yesterday. We haven't given you a chance to catch your breath. I'd better pack you off for a rest before we go out to dinner.'

'No, not just yet, Christie. I'm all right, really I am,' Audra said.

Christina crossed to the sofa, sat down next to Audra and took her hand. She held it tightly, looked into her mother's lined face, swamped by the deep and abiding love she felt for her. She shook her head and her smoky gaze was tender as she said, 'Kyle's judgement might be cockeyed about some things, but she could easily be right about dragging you all this way, *needlessly –*' Abruptly she stopped. Guilt flooded through her. Her mother was seventy years old, almost seventy-one, and should not be exposed to their problems at this time in her life. She and Alex ought to be capable of dealing with their recalcitrant daughter themselves. Irritated at the thought of their ineptitude, Christina cried, 'We haven't been fair to you, expecting you to cope with us and our mess when you could be at home with Daddy! You could be pottering around in your garden, or going off on your little day trips to the seaside – certainly leading a tranquil life. You must think Alex and I are a couple of imbeciles!'

'Don't be so silly.' Audra squeezed Christina's slender hand, so different from hers, gnarled as it was by arthritis. 'You know what your father always says – that I'd come to you no matter what it entailed if you needed me, and even if I had to walk the three thousand miles to get here. I love you, Christie, and I love that granddaughter of mine, and Alex. I can't bear to see you all so unhappy.'

Christina confided in a low, tense voice, 'It's so wrong of Kyle to abandon her courses at the Fashion Institute and to spurn my business the way she is doing. Having her take over from me one day has always been a cherished dream of mine.' These last few words caught in her throat and she had to steady herself before she could continue, 'Oh Mum, what's it all been *about*? What's all my hard work been *for*, if Kyle walks away?' Christina's eyes welled with tears and she averted her head, blinking.

Audra felt a pang of sympathy, and her heart went out to her daughter. In an effort to comfort her, she murmured, 'But Christie darling, you've derived a great deal of pleasure and satisfaction from your designing, and making a name for yourself in the fashion world has always been important to you, as well as a challenge. What you've accomplished, your staggering achievements and success – why surely these things must be gratifying to you . . .' Audra let her sentence trail off. She was incapable of finishing it. How hollow the words are, she thought.

I, and I alone, know what Christina sacrificed, what it cost her to create the business. She paid a high price, a terrible price, really. That's why she's so emotional about it, why she can't stand Kyle's rejection of it now.

Having regained her composure, Christina was remarking in a more level voice, 'The last two weeks have been sheer purgatory with Kyle, Mother. She's downright stubborn. Her implacability astounds me. Unnerves me, actually. I've never met anyone like her.'

Oh, Audra thought, *haven't you?* She threw her daughter a startled glance but she wisely said nothing. This was not the time to start delving into ancient events; there was already far too much turbulence and emotional upset in this family as it was. And so adopting a positive manner, Audra said, 'Kyle and I have always been such good friends since she was a child, and that's one of the reasons we decided I should come to New York, isn't it? Anyway, I promised to spend the day with her tomorrow. I'm sure she wants to unburden herself to me, and I am more than ready to listen.'

'But you will *talk* to her, won't you? I mean as well as listen.' Without waiting for a reply, Christina plunged on, 'She respects you, pays attention to you, wants to please you. So you will make her see reason, won't you, Mummy?'

Audra nodded, although she had her misgivings, and managed to say encouragingly, 'Yes, I will, and somehow we'll sort this out, Christie.'

For the first time in days Christina felt a little of the heaviness lifting from her and her tired eyes brightened. She leaned into Audra, kissed her wrinkled cheek, very tenderly, then rested her head on her mother's shoulder. 'I'm so glad you're here, Mam. You're such a comfort, and I know you'll make everything come out right, as you always have.'

Mam, Audra repeated silently. For years it had been Mummy or Mum or Mother. *Mam* was the childhood name. Hearing it now, suddenly, after all these years made Audra flinch. It evoked so many memories, not all of them happy ones. Then a rush of warmth and love filled her throat and for a moment she could not speak. Automatically she lifted her hand and stroked Christina's glossy hair. It's true, old habits die hard, Audra thought, bending down, kissing the top of her daughter's head. All that money, all that power, all that fame, but she's still my little girl. I can't stand to see her distressed in this way. But then there is also Kyle. My only grandchild, and *her* unhappiness is insupportable. What a dilemma. Skating on thin ice between the two of them. Oh, dear God, wherever will I find the wisdom and strength to help each one without somehow inflicting hurt on the other.

Growing conscious that her daughter was waiting for a response, Audra clamped down on her worries. 'I can only *try* to make things come out right for you, Christie,' she said softly. 'I told you, when I arrived, that I'm not going to take sides. Anyway, Kyle is correct about it being *her* life. And she does have the right to live it the way she sees fit.'

Straightening up, Christina nodded slowly. 'Yes,' she replied evenly, 'I know what you mean. But she's very young and inexperienced, and she can't possibly know her own mind. Not yet, at any rate.' Rising, Christina walked over to one of the French windows, stood gazing out at the terrace. Then she swung around and gave Audra a penetrating look. 'Rejecting my business out of hand is not only foolish but irresponsible of her, wouldn't you say?'

'Well, yes,' Audra felt bound to agree, yet she had the need to defend her granddaughter, and could not help adding, 'Still, Kyle is intelligent, as well as being a spirited and independent girl. And, you know, I also find her very wise for someone her age.' Audra paused, thinking: Well, in for a penny, in for a pound, and I might as well say it all. Taking a deep breath, she finished in her firmest manner, 'I just want you to give some consideration to *her* needs, *her* desires, as well as your own. Promise me that you will.'

Christina was startled, and there was a brief silence before she muttered, 'All right . . . yes . . . I promise.'

It struck Audra that there was a lingering reluctance in this promise. Slowly and very carefully, she said, 'Once, a long time ago, I told you that a child is only lent to you, Christina. Don't ever forget that.'

Christina stared at Audra and the strangest expression crossed her face. She opened her mouth to speak and then closed it. She swung away, focusing her eyes on the terrace once more, as she reflected on her mother's words.

Absently, Audra pushed a strand of silver hair away from her face, and sat back, watching, waiting. She saw her daughter's shoulders droop in dejection, saw at once the pensive expression settling on her pretty mouth. Yes, she's remembering, Audra thought. And I've said enough for today. Maybe too much, if the truth be known. It would be wiser to let things rest where they are for the present.

Gripping the arm of the sofa, Audra pulled herself to her feet a bit unsteadily, exhaustion finally getting the better of her. 'I think I will have a rest before dinner, perhaps try to get a little sleep,' she said.

'Yes, yes, you should,' Christina responded swiftly. She went quickly to Audra's side, put her arm around her shoulders lovingly, and escorted her out of the room.

Half an hour later Audra was still wide awake, much to her own irritation. Try though she might to sleep, she was unable to do so. Christina had accompanied her to the guest suite at the far end of the penthouse, had closed the curtains, plumped up the bed pillows, and generally fussed solicitously until Audra had impatiently waved her out. Glad to be alone at last, Audra had undressed, slipped on a robe and stretched out on the bed. She had done so gratefully. Every bone in her body ached, she was debilitated by jet-lag and her hands and knees throbbed painfully as her arthritis flared. But the moment her head touched the pillow her mind had started to race.

Mostly Audra was worried that she had made a terrible mistake in coming to New York. Might it not have been more prudent to refuse Alex's request and leave them alone to battle it out between themselves? she wondered. And it *was* going to be a battle, Audra was quite positive of that. It would be a trial of strength. Christie would worry it through, refusing to let go, tenacious to the end; Kyle would dig her heels in, equally stubborn and determined to win no matter what the cost to everyone involved. The stakes were so high neither of them could possibly act in any other way. Where was it all going to end? In disaster, she suspected. They couldn't both win. One of them would have to lose. And the loser would be bitter and resentful.

I have to find a way to help them settle this, Audra told herself, then with a stab of dismay she wondered how. If Alex, who was intelligent, diplomatic and persuasive, had been unable to arbitrate their differences, then surely she would not be able to influence them either. I *must* find a way, she muttered.

With a sigh of weariness, Audra opened her eyes, acknowledging that sleep was going to evade her. The spacious bedroom looked as tranquil as it always did in the gentle light seeping in through the curtains. Usually the blue-and-white colour scheme, elegant furnishings and opulent comfort engendered a sense of well-being in her, soothed her. But these feelings were sadly absent tonight.

Audra shivered. The early evening breeze blowing in through the window was cool now and there was a sharp tinge of dampness in the air; it seemed to penetrate her joints. Shivering again she drew the quilt up over her body and reached for her pills. Putting one in her mouth, she washed it down with a sip of water, reminding herself that this was her third; the doctor had warned her not to take more than four in one day.

Sometimes she wondered about her arthritis, wondered if her hard life, all the gruelling work, had not contributed to her present condition. Doctor Findlay said it hadn't, but when she thought of the endless scrubbing and cleaning and washing and ironing, the terrible drudgery that had been her lot for so many years, she could not help pondering. Well, those days had long since gone. In her old age she had a life of ease.

As she put the tumbler back on the bedside table her glance fell on the photograph standing near the cobalt-blue glass lamp. Audra turned on her side, rested herself on one elbow and gazed at it thoughtfully.

Three faces stared back at her. Christina's, Kyle's and her own.

The picture had been taken last summer, in her rose garden in Yorkshire. What a wonderfully happy day that had been ... her seventieth birthday. The weather had been glorious, as the colour photograph attested.

After a little tea party on the terrace, Alex had insisted on taking this picture. In honour of the occasion and for posterity, he had laughingly said, as he had lined them up near the old stone sundial, a few steps to the right of her best hybrid tea roses.

Vincent had stood next to him, smiling benignly, looking inordinately pleased with himself and his family, but most especially with her. She recalled how she had smiled back at him, thinking that he looked handsome and distinguished at seventy-four, and her love for him had swelled in her.

And at that exact moment Alex had snapped his camera and captured that love as it spilled out of her eyes.

They had come a long way together, she and Vincent Crowther.

They had had their struggles and more than their fair share of trouble. And pain and heartbreak, too. But they had survived it all, and their marriage had survived, which was the most important thing. And they were content with each other. At last, in their old age. Over fifty years they had been married. Funny, it didn't seem that long ... how fast the time had slipped by.

Audra focused her attention on the photograph, studying it more intently.

Three generations, she murmured under her breath. But we don't look as if we're related. We might easily be strangers, as disparate in appearance as any three women could be. And yet we are very much alike deep down within ourselves.

Almost half a century ago Vincent told me that I had an implacable will. He said I was relentless and propelled by a terrible driving force within myself. He was very angry that day. And I was angry, too. And hurt. But he spoke the truth. And they have inherited those characteristics from me ... my daughter, my granddaughter. When Christina was a child I committed an act of will that changed all of our lives irrevocably. And then when she was a young woman Christina repeated the pattern, performed an act of will of her own that was as powerful as mine. Now it is Kyle's turn ... she is on the verge of doing the same. And, as before, our lives won't ever be the same again.

Audra sat up with a jolt, sudden comprehension flickering on her face. 'I am to blame,' she said aloud to the silent room, and then she thought: If I had done things differently, things would be different now. Everything that is happening *now* harks back to me when I was a young woman. *Cause and effect.* Every act we commit, trivial or important, has its inevitable consequences. It's like throwing a pebble into a pool and watching the ripples spread out . . . farther and farther, ever far reaching.

Audra sank back onto the pillows and lay there, allowed herself to drift with her thoughts. They were centred entirely on Kyle.

Slowly the pain in her hands and knees began to ease and her body grew warmer under the quilt. Audra closed her eyes at last.

Nineteen-twenty-six, she mused drowsily . . . such a long time ago . . . but not so long that I can't remember what *I* was like then . . . when *I* was Kyle's age.

Audra

1926–1951

1

Today it was her birthday.

It was the third of June in the year 1926 and she was nineteen years old.

Audra Kenton stood at the window of her room in the Fever Hospital in Ripon, where she worked as a nurse, gazing out at the back garden. She watched the play of light and shadow on the lawn, as the sunlight filtered through the leafy domes of the two great oaks that grew near the old stone wall. There was a gentle breeze and the leaves rustled and trembled under it, and shimmered with green brilliance as they caught the sun. It was radiant and balmy, a pretty day that invited and beckoned.

Matron had given Audra the afternoon off for her birthday. The problem was that she had nowhere to go and no one to spend it with. *She was entirely alone in this world.*

Audra only had one friend, another nurse at the hospital called Gwen Thornton, but Gwen had been summoned home to Horsforth yesterday. Her mother had been taken ill and she was needed. Weeks ago, Gwen had arranged to exchange her day off with one of the other nurses, so that she could be with Audra, celebrate this important occasion with her, and the two of them had planned a very special day. Now their elaborate plans were laid to waste.

Leaning her head against the window frame, Audra sighed, thinking of the empty hours looming ahead. Unexpectedly her throat tightened and she felt the tears gathering behind her eyes as sadness mingled with bitter disappointment trickled through her. But after only a few seconds she blinked and cleared her throat, managed to take hold of herself. Resolutely she pushed aside the negative emotions momentarily invading her, refusing to feel sorry for herself. Audra despised self-pity in others, considered it to be a sign of weakness. *She was strong.* Her mother had always told her that she was, and her mother had rarely been wrong about anything.

Turning away from the window, she walked over to the chair and sat down heavily, wondering what to do with herself.

She could read, of course, or do a little embroidery, or even finish the sketch of the blouse she was designing, and which she intended to make – when she could afford to buy the fabric. On the other hand, none of these occupations had any real appeal for her. Not today. Not on her birthday.

She had been so looking forward to the outing with her friend, to enjoying a few carefree hours of pleasure for once in her life. Audra had little to celebrate these days, and festive occasions were a thing of the past, a rarity indeed. In fact, her life had changed so radically, so harshly, in the last few years, she hardly recognized it as her own.

It suddenly struck her that resorting to one of those mundane hobbies, normally used to pass the time when she was off duty, would be infinitely worse than just sitting in this chair, doing nothing. They're poor substitutes, all of them, for the plans Gwen and I made.

Audra had long since trained herself not to notice this room where she lived in the hospital. But now, seeing it so clearly illuminated in the bright sunshine, she became painfully aware of its ugliness and lack of comfort. Having been born into gentility, albeit somewhat impoverished, Audra was a young woman of breeding and refinement. She possessed taste in abundance, had strong artistic leanings, and the austerity of the spartan furnishings and institutional colour scheme offended her sensibilities, made her wince in dismay.

Confronting her were walls painted a dismal porridge-beige which ran down to a floor covered with dreary grey linoleum that had seen better days. The iron bedstead, rickety night stand and chest of drawers were notable only for their shabbiness and utilitarian design. The room was chillingly bleak, intolerable at any time, but especially on this sunny afternoon. She knew she had to escape its oppressive boundaries for a short while, no matter where she went.

Her gaze fell on the dress lying on the bed, where she had placed it a short time before. It was new. She had saved up for a whole year, putting away a shilling every week, in order to buy herself a present for her birthday.

She and Gwen had gone to Harrogate two Saturdays ago with this in mind. They had wandered around for several hours, mostly window shopping and admiring the beautiful things they saw and which they knew they would never be able to afford. Audra filled with warm and affectionate feelings for Gwen as she thought of that day now.

Gwen was especially attracted to jewellers' shops, and Audra had found herself constantly cupping her hands and dutifully peering through glass at some bauble that had caught Gwen's attention. '*Oh Audra!* Just look at *that*!' Gwen kept crying, pointing to a brooch or a ring or a pendant. At one moment she had clutched Audra's arm fiercely and whispered in awed tones, 'Have you ever seen anything like that gorgeous bangle, Audra! Why, the stones could be *real* the way they sparkle like diamonds. It *would* suit you, Audra. Let's go in . . . it doesn't cost anything just to *look*.'

Audra had half-smiled and shaken her head, not saying a word, and she had thought of her mother's jewellery, which had been much more beautiful than any of these tawdry imitations of the real thing.

Gwen's excited exclamations and urgent proddings continued a bit too long for Audra that afternoon, and she had eventually grown exasperated, had silenced her friend with a stern look and a sharp admonition to be quiet. Immediately regretting her shortness, she had apologized to Gwen. And she had gone on to explain to her, for the umpteenth time, that *she* had no money to spare for frivolous items like brooches and bracelets and nonsensical hats and bottles of Devon Violets scent, which were just a few of the things Gwen constantly craved.

'You *know* I only ever buy clothes for myself,' Audra had said, and had added, with a tiny rueful laugh, 'and usually the most *practical* clothes I can find, at that, Gwen. Things I know will last me for a very long time.'

And then, not ten minutes after she had uttered these fateful words, Audra had seen the dress in the window of Madame Stella's gown shop. She had fallen in love with it instantly. It was a frock destined only to go to parties, a bit of airy, gossamer muslin. Effectively draped on a stand in the centre of the window, it was the one piece of clothing displayed. Next to it, accessories were scattered on the floor; a picture hat of cream leghorn, a parasol of ruffled cream silk, and three long strands of pearls. All had epitomized true elegance to Audra, but most particularly the dress. It was highly impractical, obviously costly and very, very beautiful. She had gazed at it for ages, not knowing when or where she would ever wear it, and yet aching to own it just the same.

Even so she had hung back, would not budge when Gwen, shrewdly observing the expression of longing on her face, had pushed open the door and insisted they go in and ask the price. Despite Audra's reluctance and her adamant refusal to enter the shop, Gwen had obviously had no intention of being thwarted. She had taken Audra's arm in a vice-like grip and frogmarched her into Madame Stella's.

Although both girls had expected the dress to be expensive, the two of them had been stunned, nevertheless, when they had learned that it cost three guineas. Audra had made to leave at once. But the redoubtable Gwen had restrained her, and had somehow managed to manoeuvre her into the fitting room before she could make a graceful escape. Not wanting to create an embarrassing scene in front of the sales lady, Audra had had no option but to try on the dress.

It was the colour that captivated her – a clear bright blue that had reminded her of the delphiniums at High Cleugh. She had not needed Gwen to tell her that it suited her to perfection; she had seen herself in the cheval mirror.

Indeed, Audra had been momentarily taken aback by her own reflection that afternoon. For the first time in some years she had acknowledged to herself that for once she looked quite pretty. Mostly she referred to herself as a 'Plain Jane', which she genuinely believed to be the truth. But in this she did herself an injustice.

Audra Kenton was not beautiful in the strictest sense but neither was she plain. She was in a category somewhere in between. There was a certain stubbornness in her well-defined face. This was reflected in the determined set of her chin and in her firm and resolute mouth, which was quite beautiful when she smiled. Her best features were a faultless, creamy complexion, glossy light brown hair glazed with a golden sheen in the summer, and lovely eyes. These were the most spectacular thing about her. They were large, set wide apart, thickly fringed with golden-brown lashes and accentuated by finely arched brows. But it was their colour that was so memorable and caused people to look at her twice. They were of a blue so deep and so vivid it was startling.

As Audra had stared back at herself in the mirror of the fitting room, she had not failed to notice how the blue of the muslin intensified their depth of colour. She also saw that the 'flapper' style of the dress was flattering and did wonders for her. Audra was small, only five feet two inches, and her lack of height was a constant source of irritation to her. Yet despite her diminutive size she was nicely proportioned, and the simple cut of the frock emphasized her pretty figure, whilst its short skirt, cut on the cross so that it flared out, drew attention to her shapely legs and slender ankles.

And so in the end, after some indecision on her part because of its price, and worried whisperings with Gwen, she had finally bought the dress. To make up the three pounds three shillings needed, Audra had used her entire savings of two pounds twelve shillings, every other penny in her purse – which was all she had in the world – plus one and six borrowed from Gwen.

'Don't look so glum,' Gwen had whispered, whilst they had been waiting for the sales lady to wrap the dress. 'It's worth every penny. Besides, it's about time you treated yourself to something nice.'

There was no question in Audra's mind that the dress was the most beautiful thing she had owned since she was a child. And a memory had stirred, a memory of another time when she had come to Harrogate shopping – with her mother and Uncle Peter. It had been 1919, just after he had returned from the Great War. She had been twelve and he had bought her a pink party frock which had entranced her just as much as the blue muslin.

As they left Madame Stella's, Audra had told Gwen of that particular trip and the pretty pink frock, had confided more about her past life and Gwen had been agog and full of questions. Audra, who was a private person and reserved by nature, had nonetheless answered some of them, not wanting to offend Gwen by appearing secretive. Later, arms linked, they had taken a leisurely stroll along The Stray, the stretch of green common carpeted with lovely flowers which made a natural tapestry of brilliant colour underneath the shady trees. Then Gwen had taken them to Betty's Café, the posh tea-room on The Parade overlooking The Stray, and had generously paid for them both, since Audra had spent all of her cash. She had also loaned her the money for her ticket back to Ripon, just as she had promised she would when Audra had been wavering in Madame Stella's. And Audra had reminded herself yet again how lucky she was to have Gwen for her friend.

At the end of their day's excursion, on the way to the bus stop, they had passed the Arcadian Rooms, where tea dances were held every afternoon in the Palm Court. Everyone knew that this was *the* place to go, the smart spot in town where the local swells foxtrotted and tangoed to the strains of Stan Stanton and His Syncopated Strollers.

Both young women had been itching to visit the Palm Court for weeks, and Gwen, who had learned the Charleston from her brother, had been teaching it to Audra in their off-duty hours. Audra had been astonished and thrilled when Gwen had announced she was taking them to a tea dance at the Palm Court on her birthday. 'It'll be my treat, my birthday present,' Gwen had said, beaming at her. 'And you'll wear your new dress and everyone will admire you in it.' The two of them had been bursting with excitement and anticipation as they had ridden on the bus back to Ripon, and they had been counting the days ever since.

But there would be no trip to Harrogate after all. No tea dance at the Palm Court of the Arcadian Rooms. No one to admire her or the new dress. Audra sighed. Earlier she had planned to wear it just for her own pleasure, although she had not been quite sure where she would *go* in it all by herself. But now she changed her mind.

Audra was nothing if not practical, and it struck her that it would be foolish to risk ruining it, or getting it crumpled and soiled. Far wiser to save the frock for another special occasion, she reasoned. And there's bound to be one in the future, now that I have a friend like Gwen. Perhaps we'll go to the church Garden Fête in August, and then there's Gwen's birthday in September. We must celebrate that. Yes, something's bound to come up, she reassured herself, her natural optimism surfacing as it invariably did.

Audra was blessed with a sunny disposition and a cheerful personality, and it was these traits, coupled with her strong will and intelligence, which had saved her in the past. They helped her to cope with her problems in the most positive way. She never let her troubles burden her for very long, sought always to solve them with expediency. And if this was not feasible, she tried not to dwell on them unnecessarily.

Now she roused herself, took the blue frock off the bed and returned it to the wardrobe in the corner of the room.

After she had slipped out of her blue-and-white-striped nurse's uniform and put it away, she peered at the other garments hanging there, wondering what to wear for her walk in the country.

Although she did not have an extensive wardrobe, the clothes she did own were of good quality, and because she was fastidious they were never anything but immaculate. For economic reasons, Audra made all of her summer clothes herself, and these were mostly light-weight dresses in the darker spectrum of colours; to her practical turn of mind these were guaranteed to wear better than the paler shades. Finally her hand came to rest on a navy cotton dress with a dropped waistline and a sailor collar trimmed with white. She pulled it out, found her black leather walking shoes with flat heels, and began to dress.

Suddenly Audra thought of Gwen. How self-centred I'm being, she chastised herself. Here am I, concerned about my birthday, when Gwen has a sick mother to nurse. Audra wished she could go to Horsforth today, to help Gwen, but it was much too far to travel with only an afternoon free. Poor Gwen must be run off her feet, not to mention dreadfully worried, she thought. Then her face brightened as she adjusted the collar of her dress, pivoted to look at herself in the small mirror standing on the chest of drawers. Gwen's father was a doctor, and her brother Charlie was a medical student at Leeds University. Mrs Thornton was in good hands. She would soon be well again, and Gwen would be returning to the hospital in no time at all.

As she left her room and hurried down the corridor, it struck Audra how truly attached she had become to her friend. Ever since Gwen had come to work at the hospital a year ago, her life had changed for the better and it was much more bearable now. Until then none of the other nurses had ever attempted to be friends with her. Audra knew that this was mainly because of her background, her manners and her cultured way of speaking.

The other nurses thought she was a snob, that she was stuck up and unapproachable. But this was not true at all. It was her shyness that held her somewhat apart, prevented her from making the first gesture.

As if she had instinctively understood this, happy, laughing, gregarious Gwen had paid not the slightest attention to her reserve. Having singled Audra out as the one girl she wanted as her friend, she had persisted, and had broken down the protective walls Audra had built around herself. Within the first week of knowing each other they had become inseparable.

I don't know what I'd do without Gwen, Audra thought, banging the front door of the hospital behind her. She's the only person I have in the world.

2

She had not intended to go to High Cleugh.

But before she realized it she was almost there.

When she had set out from the hospital, Audra had had no particular destination in mind. She had taken the road that led to Sharow and Copt Hewick, both small villages on the outskirts of Ripon.

There was no special reason for her to go there, other than that they were pleasant little spots; also, the route was picturesque, the surrounding landscape pastoral and unusually pretty at this time of year.

Arriving at Copt Hewick, Audra wandered slowly up the cobbled main street, thinking how well-kept everything looked on this hot June afternoon. The dainty gardens in front of the neat cottages were bright with lupins and poppies and delphiniums; lace curtains glowed whitely behind sparkling windows; every doorstep was newly scrubbed, each step outlined with yellow scouring stone.

Glancing up ahead at the Blackamoor Inn, Audra noticed that it, too, was spruced up. Its white walls and black shutters had been treated to fresh coats of paint, and even the sign swinging over the front door appeared to have been artistically embellished with a few colourful daubs from somebody's paintbox.

Audra hesitated at the Blackamoor Inn, which was the juncture of several roads, wondering whether to take the main thoroughfare to Boroughbridge or the secondary side road that led to Newby Hall and Skelton. She chose the latter, although she did not follow the road to its end. Instead she veered off to her right when she was half way down, favouring a narrow lane flanked on either side by drystone walls.

After only a few steps along the lane she stopped dead in her tracks, immediately understanding exactly where her feet were leading her. She half turned, wanting to go back the way she had come. She discovered she could not.

High Cleugh drew her towards it like a powerful magnet.

With every step she took Audra Kenton told herself she was making a mistake, exposing herself to heartache, especially today of all days, yet still she continued to walk, almost against her own volition.

By the time she came to the bottom of the long, twisting lane she no longer cared whether she was being foolish or not. She was conscious only of her yearning to see the one place she loved above all others on this earth. She had stayed away far too long.

She climbed over the stile set in the wall, jumped down into the long pasture and ran through the tall grass. It rippled and swayed like an undulating sea of green under the light breeze which had blown up. Unexpectedly, a couple of cows lazily lumbered across her path, and she dodged around them, plunging ahead, her young face taut with anticipation, her long hair flying out behind her as she ran.

Audra did not break her pace until she came to the huge sycamore tree at the end of the pasture. Upon reaching it she stooped down and stepped under its spreading branches which formed a canopy of green, shutting out the sky. She leaned her body against the tree, pressed her face to its trunk and closed her eyes. She was out of breath and panting with exertion.

After only a few moments she began to breathe more evenly. Slowly, she smoothed her hand over the tree, felt the rough texture of the bark under her fingertips, and she smiled to herself. This was her tree. Her place.

She had named it the Memory Place in her mind. For that was exactly what it was – the place to remember *them*, to relive the past, to recall the happiness and joy that had once been hers and was no more.

Frequently they had come here together. Her mother. Her brothers, Frederick and William. And Uncle Peter. And when she was here at the tree they were with her again, and her misery was vanquished for a brief while.

Audra opened her eyes, blinking in the cool green darkness of the sycamore's shade, and then she moved out from underneath its branches. Circling the tree, she came to a standstill at the edge of the little slope that fell away to the banks of the River Ure just a few feet below her. Finally she lifted her head and gazed out across that narrow band of swift-running water to the wooded valley on the opposite side of the river. There it was, nestled in the palm of a natural dell set amidst the trees.

High Cleugh: the small but lovely old manor where she had been born nineteen years ago today. The house where she had grown up, had lived for the best part of her life. Her beloved home until five years ago.

She feasted her eyes on it, struck as always by its simplicity and gentleness which, to her, were the things that made it compellingly beautiful.

High Cleugh was an eighteenth-century house, long and low, with a fine symmetry that gave it an incomparable gracefulness. It was built of local grey stone and had many leaded windows that winked and glinted now in the bright sunlight. These faced out onto a terrace made of the same ancient stone; running the length of the house, the terrace was broken in the centre by a very long flight of steps that sliced its way through lawns tilting to the river. Herbaceous borders, wide, rambling, grew beneath the terrace walls, splashed vivid hues against the dark stone and verdant grass.

But it was the massed delphiniums which caught the eye, entranced. These flourished in great abundance at the bottom of the lawns near the river's edge, their blossoms blanketing the ground with a breathtaking mixture of blues. Cobalt bled into a powder blue so delicate it was almost white, this tint giving way to cornflower, then a luscious violet-blue that in turn brushed up against lavender and the purple tones of belladonna.

Her mother's delphiniums . . . planted with such care and nurtured so lovingly by her over the years. Audra's heart clenched with a bittersweet mixture of pleasure and pain. Oh, how she longed to be in those gardens once again. It would be so easy for her to slip over to the other side of the river. All she had to do was follow the path along the bank until she came to the stepping stones. These giant flat slabs, worn smooth by running water and time, stretched across the shallowest part, led directly to the copse adjoining the manor.

But she could not go to High Cleugh. If she did she would be trespassing. Another family lived there now.

She sat down on the springy grass, pulled her knees up to her chest, rested her chin on them and clasped her arms around her legs.

For the longest time Audra stared at High Cleugh.

There was no sign of life. It appeared to slumber in the brilliant sunshine as if it were not inhabited at all. A peacefulness lay over the motionless gardens. Not a blade of grass, not a single leaf stirred. The wind had dropped and the air was warm and languid. There was no sound except for the faint buzzing of a bee somewhere nearby and the gurgle and splash of water rushing over dappled stones as the Ure wended its way below her.

Audra's gaze became more intense than ever. She saw beyond the exterior walls to the inner core of the house. She closed her eyes, let herself sink down into her imagination, remembering, remembering . . .

She was inside the house.

She stood in the hall with its apricot-coloured walls and worn green velvet bench and the palm in the pitted brass pot. All was shadowy, quiescent. She listened for a while to the stillness. Then she stepped forward, her footsteps echoing with a metallic ring against the marble. Slowly she climbed the staircase. It twisted upward in a graceful curve. She paused on the first landing. Her room was here. She went inside, closed the door, sighed with pleasure.

Familiar walls of the palest green surrounded her, reminded her as always of a summer sea on a misty Yorkshire morning. The polished wood floor gleamed like glass under her feet as she stepped up to her four-poster bed. She reached out, touched the tulips printed on the worn coverlet, traced a finger around their once-red petals long since washed-out to the colour of old rust. Burnt sienna it was called in her paintbox. She glided to the window, looked out across the Dales, heard the rustle of the curtains as they flapped about in the breeze. The scent of carnations filled the summer air. She turned her head, saw a cloud of pink petals in the blue willow-patterned bowl that stood on the oak chest. Their perfume drifted away, was replaced by a sweeter, headier fragrance. October roses lifted full-blown heads from the bowl, shining yellows against the blue. It was Autumn now. The time of the harvest.

How well she knew the changing seasons of this house.

The air had grown chillier. The fire crackled in the grate. She felt the warmth of the flames on her face. Snowflakes fluttered against the window pane. The gardens were made of white icing sugar.

She was no longer alone in the house.

She caught the sound of her mother's laughter, the swish of her silk gown as she joined her by the fire. The Beautiful Edith Kenton. That was how they always spoke of her hereabouts.

Sapphires blazed at her throat, on her cool white arms. Blue fire against that translucent skin. Hair the colour of new pennies, an aureole of burnished copper light around the pale heart-shaped face. Warm and loving lips were pressed down to her young cheek. The smell of gardenias and Coty powder enveloped her. A slender, elegant hand took hold of hers, guided her out of the room.

Frederick and William waited in the hall, sang carols as they descended the stairs. Rowdy, loving brothers and devoted sons. Uncle Peter stood behind them in the entrance to the drawing room. He embraced her with his smile and ushered them all into the room.

She stood transfixed.

The room had acquired a magical quality this Christmas night. Its faded elegance had taken on a curious new beauty in the muted, golden light. Candles glowed on a sturdy little fir. Logs hissed and spurted up the chimney. Sprigs of holly decorated the paintings, draped the mantle, hung in great beribboned swags in front of the windows. Mistletoe fell from the cut-glass chandelier. Paper chains were inverted rainbows looped across the ceiling. The air was redolent with new aromas that assailed her senses. She smelled pine cones and wood smoke and eggnog, and succulent goose cooking and chestnuts roasting on the fire.

They crowded around the fireplace.

They sang carols and drank the eggnog from little crystal cups and lifted the steaming chestnuts from their bursting shells. And their laughter reverberated through the house.

Three red felt stockings hung from the mantelpiece. They opened them . . . she and Frederick and William. In hers there was a treasure trove. An orange, an apple, a bag of nuts and a new penny tied in a scrap of silk; a sachet of potpourri, Pears soap and yards of silk ribbons for her hair plus a box of Egyptian dates, lavender water and a book of verse with the name Edith Kenton written on the flyleaf in her mother's flowing script. Little things which had cost nothing but whose value was priceless to her.

Snowdrifts were banked outside the house.

Sleet and bitter winds rattled against the window panes and heralded the new year. The Christmas decorations had disappeared. The house was hushed and desolate without her mother's laughter. It was the time for Uncle Peter to go away again. She saw the sadness on his face, and her mother's eyes, blue like the sapphires she wore, were filled with tears . . .

Audra's face was wet with tears . . . she had not realized she had begun to cry. She straightened up and brushed her eyes with her fingertips, tearing her gaze away from High Cleugh.

She lay down and buried her face in the cool, sweet-smelling grass, then squeezed her eyes tightly shut as she felt the sharp prick of tears once more. But now she did not bother to suppress them; instead, she allowed herself the luxury of weeping.

And she wept for those she had lost and for the past and for the way things had once been.

Eventually her tears ceased. She lay there quietly, staring up at the china-blue sky, watching the drift of the scudding clouds, ruminating on her beloved family and all of the things which had happened in the last few years.

3

Audra's father was a shadowy figure in her mind.

He had died in 1909, when she was only two years old, and her memories of him were smudged and indistinct.

But the images of her mother, and of Frederick and William, were potent and fresh, so very vivid to her the three of them might have been standing there, looking down at her lying on the grass. And Uncle Peter was as indelibly imprinted on her heart as the other three were.

How inexorably their lives and their destinies had been bound up with his.

Peter Lacey had died in 1920 whilst still a young man. He had been an officer in the British Army during the Great War, and had fought in the trenches of France, where he had been badly gassed in the Battle of the Somme. His lungs had been so seriously damaged his health had never been the same, and that was why he had died. Or so they said at the time.

Audra's mother, the Beautiful Edith Kenton, had been inconsolable. She had followed him to the grave less than a year later, in July of 1921. She had been thirty-seven.

Frederick, Audra's eldest brother, had told her that their mother's death was due to heart failure, but she had recently substituted *heartbreak* for the latter. Audra had come to believe that their mother really *had* died of a broken heart as she had pined away for Peter Lacey; since Audra had grown to young womanhood she had come to understand their relationship so much better. They had been lovers, of course. There was no longer any doubt in her mind about that.

As a child Audra had never questioned his presence. He was their Uncle Peter, a distant relative of their father's, a third cousin, she had been led to believe, and he had been there for as long as she could remember.

After Adrian Kenton had died of consumption, Uncle Peter had become an even more frequent visitor, staying with them at High Cleugh for a week or two at a time. Because of his business interests and financial affairs he had returned to London at regular intervals, but he was never absent for very long. And whether he came for an extended visit or a brief few days he never came empty handed. There were usually presents for them all.

'Isn't it wonderful the way Uncle Peter looks after us,' her mother had said once to Audra. 'I am a great burden to him, I fear. He is such a busy man . . . but very kind and generous, and most uncommonly thoughtful. He *wishes* to take care of me, and of you and your brothers. He insists, and will not have it any other way.' Edith had sighed, then smiled her shimmering smile. 'He was devoted to your father, of course. That is the reason why he has made *us* his responsibility, Audra.'

But it was not devotion to their father at all, Audra had come to realize. It had been adoration of their mother that had caused Peter Lacey to become their benefactor and protector.

Once she had come to understand the reality of their life together, Audra had accepted the truth about them, and she had never blamed or censored her mother and her uncle in her heart. They had been very much in love. He had also loved Edith's fatherless children, and behaved as a father would towards them; he had taken care of the Kenton family to the best of his ability and his financial means. There had been a wife somewhere in the background, and two children, a boy and a girl, otherwise Edith Kenton and Peter Lacey would have married.

Audra and William had not understood the situation when Edith and Peter were alive, but Audra had lately come to wonder if Frederick had ever had his suspicions. After all, he *was* the eldest. He had been seventeen when Edith had died, and William fifteen, and Audra had just celebrated her fourteenth birthday the month before.

The Kenton children had been stunned and heartbroken at the unexpected death of their mother, disbelieving. It had been so sudden. And then, only a short hour after her coffin had been lowered into the ground, they had suffered another terrible blow.

They were dazed, so shocked they were unable to speak, when they learned that Edith had died penniless, and that they were not only destitute but without a roof over their heads. High Cleugh was not their property as they had always believed. It had never belonged to their father, in fact. He had merely rented it from the owner – Peter Lacey. Peter had permitted Edith to live on at High Cleugh, without paying rent, since 1909.

Apparently a codicil in his will had protected Edith after his death – but not them. High Cleugh was to remain her home for as long as she lived; after her death it must revert to his estate. The annuity he had left her also ceased when she died.

There was no separate provision for them, most probably because Peter Lacey had not anticipated that their mother would die at such an early age. Obviously neither had she, despite her great sorrow at his passing, since she had not left a will.

The three orphans were told all this by their mother's cousin, Alicia Drummond. She had taken them back to her house, The Grange, after the funeral service at St Nicholas's Church and the burial in the adjoining cemetery in the village of West Tanfield. She had hurried them into the library, a cheerless room filled with gloomy shadows, dolorous paintings and ponderous Victorian furniture, where tea was to be served later. Aunt Alicia's husband, Uncle Percival, her daughter, Cousin Winifred, and her mother, Great-Aunt Frances Reynolds, had attended the funeral and had joined them for tea afterwards.

Although the Kenton children disliked the Drummonds intensely, they held a certain affection for their great-aunt, who had always shown a particular fondness for Edith, her only niece, and the Kentons. And so they automatically gravitated to the Chesterfield sofa next to her chair. Here they aligned themselves in a row. They were a staunch little trio, wearing their best Sunday clothes and black arm-bands of mourning, sitting stiff-backed and controlled. Somehow they managed to hide their sorrow behind expressionless faces, and, amazingly, not one of them showed their nervousness.

Aunt Alicia had poured tea from a Georgian silver pot, and the maid had passed around the delicate china cups, then offered them plates of watercress sandwiches and carraway-seed cake. They were not able to eat a thing.

Audra was the first one to speak up, after Aunt Alicia had delivered her devastating news about their impecunious state. 'What's going to happen to us? Are we to be sent to the workhouse?' she asked in a small but curiously steady voice, fixing Alicia Drummond with a penetrating stare.

Great-Aunt Frances, shocked, exclaimed. 'Of course not, dear child!' and then she reached out and patted Audra's hand. She was a much nicer person than her daughter, and she continued in a kindly tone, 'I'm too old to take you in, I'm afraid. However, you will all come and live here at The Grange. Your Aunt Alicia and Uncle Percival have very generously offered to provide a good home for the three of you.'

The Kenton children, with no other living relatives, had been obliged to accept this offer, dubious though they were about moving in with the Drummonds. After only a few days at The Grange they realized just how much they were going to detest living there.

The large Victorian mansion, situated between West Tanfield and Ripon, was as cold and as forbidding as Alicia Drummond herself, who was also a snobbish, bigoted, avaricious and crafty woman. The house was run on ludicrous timetables; the rules were rigid; the atmosphere was depressing and unpleasant; the food mediocre at best. The Kenton children had been brought up with a great deal of love, understanding and freedom by a woman who was also an excellent cook, and they were shocked by life at The Grange.

A week after Edith Kenton's funeral, some of her furniture and other possessions from High Cleugh were sold at the auction rooms in Ripon, to pay for her funeral expenses and settle her debts. At least, this is what her children were told by their aunt. The best pieces of furniture, a number of good paintings, and choice items of silver were removed to The Grange by Alicia Drummond. 'I shall be happy to store these things for you until you are old enough to have them,' she had explained to the three young Kentons.

Despite the fact that this sounded reasonable enough to Frederick and William, Audra, who was far brighter than her brothers, did not trust the woman. And her distrust only increased when, several days later, she noticed her mother's things appearing in various rooms of her aunt's house. And so that night, when everyone was asleep, she had crept down the corridor to the room which Frederick and William shared. She had awakened her brothers, and, curling up at the bottom of Frederick's bed, she expressed her concern to them both, whispered that they must make an inventory of all of their mother's possessions which were now in this house.

William, who knew Audra was much cleverer than he or his brother, nodded in agreement. But Frederick blanched in alarm, afraid that they would be thrown out if they so much as put one foot wrong. 'She'll take offence,' he whispered back, frowning. 'We can't do it, Audra. It would be throwing aspersions on her character – as if we think she's dishonest.'

Sweeping aside his protestations, Audra hissed, 'I'm sure she is, so we *must* do it. To protect ourselves. And what about Mother's jewellery? The sapphires in particular? Does *she* have those too, Frederick?'

Frederick shook his head vehemently. 'No, she doesn't, and that I know for an absolute fact. But they *have* disappeared. I looked everywhere for them the day after Mother died, and to no avail. When I was searching her drawers I suddenly remembered that I hadn't seen her wear them since Uncle Peter's death. She must have sold them, Audra, and used the money to help support us over the past year. It's the only possible solution.'

'Why didn't you tell me about the sapphires before now?' Audra demanded in a low but fierce voice, throwing him a reproachful look.

'Because I didn't want to worry you,' Frederick hissed back, and then his voice sank as he added, 'But Aunt Alicia does have Mother's other jewellery. She took the box away from me . . . for safekeeping, she said.'

Although she had faithfully promised Frederick she would not do anything rash, and so risk incurring their aunt's disfavour, Audra was determined, nevertheless, to have her own way about the inventory. Alicia Drummond did not intimidate her, but after thinking it through she wisely decided to bide her time, to wait for the right moment to introduce the subject to her aunt. This had presented itself much sooner than Audra had anticipated.

At the end of that same week, on Sunday, Great-Aunt Frances returned with them for lunch after church services. And it was the old lady herself who inadvertently gave Audra the perfect opportunity. They were all seated in the dark and depressing library, where Uncle Percival proceeded to pour careful glasses of sherry for the adults, when unexpectedly their great-aunt brought up the matter of Edith Kenton's jewellery.

Out of the blue, she said, 'I think Audra is old enough to have something of dear Edith's, a memento of her mother. Perhaps the cameo brooch. Please be kind enough to fetch me Edith's jewellery box, Alicia.' Aunt Alicia, tight-lipped and sheathing her annoyance, did so.

Smiling at Audra warmly, the old lady took out the cameo and pinned it on the front of her summer frock. 'Take care of it, child, it was a favourite of your mother's,' she said.

Audra promised that she would, and thanked her great-aunt for allowing her to have it now. Then she shrewdly seized the moment. 'Frederick, William, come and look at Mother's jewellery. You must have your share of it when we grow up.'

As her two brothers joined her at their great-aunt's side, Audra exclaimed to Frederick, 'Perhaps I ought to make a list of these things, so that we can talk about them later, and decide what we'd each like to have. That's only fair, isn't it, Frederick?'

There was a startled silence.

Frederick gaped at her, aghast, and bit his lip worriedly, knowing full well what she next had in mind. William tried to hide his delight in her audacity without succeeding; his eyes danced mischievously.

And then, before anyone could make a comment, Audra ran to the desk, found a pencil and scrap paper, and returned to her great-aunt's chair, where she pored over the box. At one moment, as she scribbled away, Audra looked up at the silver-haired old lady, and remarked in an off-hand manner, 'Great-Aunt Frances, do *you* think I should also list Mother's furniture and her possessions which Aunt Alicia is storing for us here? You know, so that my brothers and I can divide everything else properly.'

Great-Aunt Frances gave her a surprised look and then she smiled slightly. 'Well, Audra, you are a practical child, it seems. I think that's an excellent idea, especially since poor dear Edith did not think to make a will. This way the three of you can discuss the division of your mother's property at leisure, and make your decisions. Why don't you take an inventory next week, my dear.'

Audra nodded solemnly, camouflaging her triumph behind a bland expression. 'Yes, I think I will, Great-Aunt.'

In the days which followed this conversation, Frederick, quaking in his boots, had warned Audra that there were bound to be repercussions. *He* had noticed the calculating look in Aunt Alicia Drummond's mean little black eyes when they had all been in the library, even if his brother and sister had not.

But nothing untoward had happened in the end, and the long, hot summer had slithered into a cool autumn; then winter had come finally, and life at The Grange had continued uneventfully. And as miserable as the Kentons were in the cold and unloving environment of their aunt's home, even Audra felt bound to agree with William, her favourite, that they were fortunate in one respect: the three of them were together, they had each other to love, and for companionship and consolation.

It was the week before Christmas when Audra chanced to hear a strange remark, one that worried her briefly; its true meaning was to baffle her for some time thereafter.

Late one afternoon, knowing that Great-Aunt Frances had come to visit, Audra went looking for her.

She was about to push open the drawing-room door, which was already ajar, when she heard Aunt Alicia mention her mother's name in the most scathing manner. She did not catch what her aunt said next because Alicia lowered her voice. But Audra stiffened as Great-Aunt Frances suddenly exclaimed in a horrified tone, 'You cannot punish the children for the sins of the mother, Alicia!'

Instantly, Audra's hand dropped from the knob and she quickly backed away, not wishing to hear any more, and knowing that it was wrong to eavesdrop anyway.

She crept down the dark passage to the back parlour, where she sat for a while, pondering her great-aunt's odd remark. Audra knew that it had to do with them – that much was patently obvious. But she could not fathom its meaning. *How* had her mother sinned? At once she told herself that her mother had not committed a single sin in her entire life. As young as she was, Audra was perceptive and she had long known that Alicia Drummond had always been jealous of her mother's classical beauty, her charm and her refinement. So much so, she had never lost a chance to demean Edith Kenton during her lifetime. Seemingly she could not resist doing the same thing after her death.

For the next few days Audra continued to wonder why Alicia wanted to punish them, but eventually she managed to curb her worry. She consoled herself with the knowledge that whatever punishment *she* had had in mind for them, their great-aunt had obviously found a way to put a stop to it.

But as it turned out, Frances Reynolds's words had apparently meant little or nothing. Certainly they had not been a deterrent to her daughter.

For in the end they had been punished.

Two months later, in February of 1922, Frederick and William were dispatched to Australia as emigrants, and Audra was sent to work at the Fever Hospital for Children in Ripon.

Their fierce protestations and anguished pleadings to stay together had made no impression. They were helpless in the face of their aunt's determination. And so, against their wishes, and those of their Great-Aunt Frances, they had been forced to do as Alicia Drummond said.

It was a wrenching moment for the three young Kentons when Frederick and William took leave of their sister on that bitter winter morning. Before setting out for London and the boat to Sydney, they had huddled together in the front hall, saying their goodbyes, fighting back their tears.

Audra clung to William. Emotion welled up in her, and her throat was so tight she could barely speak. Finally she managed, 'You won't forget about me, will you, William?' And then she started to sob brokenly and her eyes streamed.

Swallowing his own tears, trying to be brave, William tightened his arms around his adored little sister. She looked so young and vulnerable at this moment. 'No,

I won't. *We* won't,' he said reassuringly. 'And we'll send for you as soon as we can. *I promise*, Audra.'

Frederick, equally emotional, stroked the top of Audra's head lovingly, and reiterated this promise. Then her brothers stepped away from her, picked up their suitcases and left the house without uttering another word.

Audra snatched her coat from the hall cupboard and ran out. She flew down the drive, calling their names, needing to prolong these last few minutes with them. They stopped, turned, waited for her, and the three of them linked arms and walked on in silence, too heartbroken to speak. When they arrived at the gates the two boys silently kissed Audra for the last time, and tore themselves from her clinging arms before they lost control completely.

Holding one hand to her trembling mouth, stifling her sobs, Audra watched them stride courageously along the main road to Ripon until they were just small specks in the distance. She wanted to run after them, to shout, *'Wait for me! Don't leave me behind! Take me with you!'* But Audra knew this would be useless. They could not take her with them. It was not her brothers' fault they were being separated from each other. Alicia Drummond was to blame. She wanted to rid herself of Edith Kenton's children and she did not care how she did it.

Only when her brothers had finally disappeared from sight did Audra drag her gaze away from the empty road at last. She turned back into the driveway and wondered, with a sinking heart and a sickening feeling of despair, if she would ever see her brothers again. Australia was at the other end of the world, as far away as any place could possibly be. They had promised faithfully to send for her, but how long would it take them to save up the money for her passage? A whole year, perhaps.

As this dismaying thought wedged itself into Audra's mind she looked up at that bleak, grim house and shivered involuntarily. And at that precise moment her dislike for her mother's cousin hardened into a terrible and bitter hatred that would remain with her for the rest of her life. Audra Kenton would not ever find it in her heart to forgive Alicia Drummond for her cold and deliberate cruelty to them. And the memory of the day her brothers had been sent away would stay with Audra always.

The following afternoon, white-faced and trembling, and fretting for her brothers, Audra had gone to live and work at the Fever Hospital. Since there were no vacancies that year for student nurses she had been taken on as a ward maid.

Audra Kenton's life of drudgery had begun. She was still only fourteen years old.

She had been awakened at dawn the next morning. After a breakfast of porridge, dripping and bread, and tea, eaten with the other little ward maids, the daily routine had commenced. Audra was appalled at the hardship of it, and she, who had never done a domestic chore in her entire life, had found that first day unspeakable. Balking at the tasks assigned to her, she had asked herself despairingly how she would manage. Yet she had not dared complain to her superiors. Being intelligent, and alert, she had understood within the space of a few hours that they were not interested in the likes of her. She was inconsequential in the hierarchy of the hospital, where everyone – doctors and nurses alike – worked extremely hard, and with conscientiousness.

On her second morning she had gritted her teeth and attacked her chores with renewed vigour, and she had learned the best way she could, mainly by observing the other maids at work. At the end of the first month she was as efficient as any of them, and had become expert at scrubbing floors, scouring bathtubs, washing and ironing sheets, making beds, emptying bed pans, cleaning lavatories, disinfecting the surgical ward and sterilizing instruments.

Every night she had fallen into her hard little cot in the maids' dormitory, so bone tired that she had not noticed her surroundings or the uncomfortable bed. She was usually so exhausted in these first weeks she did not even have the strength to weep. And when she did cry into her pillow it was not for her state of being or for her mean and cheerless life. Audra wept out of longing for her brothers, who were as lost to her now as her mother and Uncle Peter lying in their graves.

There were times, as she scrubbed and polished and toiled in the wards, that Audra worriedly asked herself if *she* had brought this disastrous state upon her brothers and herself. Guilt trickled through her when she remembered how insistent she had been about taking those inventories of her mother's possessions. But generally her common sense quickly surfaced and Audra recognized that they would have been punished no matter what. In fact, she had come to believe that Alicia Drummond had callously determined their fate on the very day their mother had died.

When Audra had been pushed out of The Grange and sent to the hospital, Aunt Alicia had told her that she could visit them every month, on one of her two weekends off, and spend special holidays with them. But Audra had only ever ventured there twice, and then merely to collect the remainder of her clothes and a few other belongings. For as far back as she could remember, she had never felt anything but uncomfortable in that appalling house; she understood she was not welcome.

The second time she went to fetch the last of her things she had had to steel herself to enter The Grange, and she had made a solemn vow to herself. She had sworn she would never set foot in that mausoleum of a place again, not until the day she went back to claim her mother's property. And so, over those early months of 1922, as she had learned to stand on her own two feet, she had kept herself to herself. She had continued to do her work diligently, and she had stayed out of trouble at the hospital.

If her daily life was dreary, and lacked the normal small pleasures enjoyed by most girls of her age, she nevertheless managed to buoy herself up with dreams of a pleasanter future. Hope was her constant companion. No one could take *that* away from her. Nor could anyone diminish her faith in her brothers. She was absolutely convinced that they would send for her, that she would be with them in Australia soon. Three months after Frederick and William had left England their letters had started to arrive, and these had continued to come fairly regularly. They were always full of news, good cheer, and promises, and the pages had soon grown tattered from her constant reading of them. Audra treasured her letters; they were her greatest comfort and joy in those days.

The hospital routine had scarcely varied during Audra's first year. The work was hard, even for the strongest of the girls. Some of them had left because their daily chores had worn them down and inevitably demolished their interest in nursing. Only the truly dedicated remained. Audra, with nowhere else to go, stayed out of sheer necessity.

However, there was also something very special in Audra Kenton, call it stubbornness, that made her stick it out until she could graduate to nurse's training. Small though she was, she had unusual physical stamina, as well as a mental energy and toughness of mind that were remarkable in one so young. Despite her youth, she possessed inner resources which she was able to draw on for courage and strength. And so she had valiantly continued to scrub and clean and polish endlessly ... run up and down endless stairs and along endless wards ... forever on her feet or on her knees.

The toil and monotonous grind of her days quite apart, Audra could not complain that she was ill treated in any way, for she was not. Everyone at the hospital was kind to her and the other little ward maids, and if the food was plain, even stodgy at times, at least there was plenty of it. No one ever went hungry. Audra, plodding along and braced by her stoicism, would tell herself that hard work and plain food never killed anybody.

But by the end of the year she was looking to better herself. Her eyes were focused on the day she would take a step forward and start climbing the ladder. She had been sent to work at the hospital against her will, but slowly, as she had mastered her chores, she had had a chance to look up, to observe and absorb. Gradually she had begun to realize that nursing appealed to her.

Audra knew she would have to earn a living, even if she went out to join her brothers in Sydney; she wanted to do so as a nurse. According to William, she would have no trouble finding a position in a hospital. He had written to tell her that there was a shortage of nurses Down Under, and this knowledge had fired her ambition even more.

It was in the spring of 1923, not long after Audra had started her second year at the hospital, that her chance came. Matron retired and a successor was appointed. Her name was Margaret Lennox and she was of a new breed of woman, very modern in her way of thinking, some said even radical. She was well known in the North of England for her passionate espousal of reforms in woman and child welfare, and for her dedication to the advancement of women's rights in general.

With the announcement of her appointment there was a flurry of excitement and everyone wondered if the daily routine would be affected. It was. For, as was usually the way, a new broom swept clean and a new regime, in this instance the Lennox Regime, was swiftly instituted.

Audra, observing everything with her usual perspicacity, decided that she must waste no time in applying for nurse's training at once. From what she had heard, Margaret Lennox favoured young and ambitious girls who wanted to get on; apparently she went out of her way to give them her unstinting support and encouragement.

Two weeks after Matron Lennox had taken up her duties, Audra sat down and wrote a letter to her. She thought this was the wisest tactic to use, rather than to approach her personally. Matron Lennox had been in a whirlwind of activity and surrounded by a phalanx of hospital staff since her arrival.

Less than a week after Audra had left the letter in Matron's office she was summoned for an interview. This was brisk, brief and very much to the point. Ten minutes after she had walked in, Audra Kenton walked out, smiling broadly, her application approved.

With her superior intelligence, her ability to learn quickly, Audra swiftly became one of the best student nurses on the hospital staff, and earned a reputation for being dedicated. She found the new work and her studies challenging; also, she discovered she had a desire to heal, and therefore, a real aptitude for nursing. And the young patients, with whom she had a genuine affinity, became the focus of the love she had bottled up inside her since her brothers had gone away . . .

Now, remembering all of this, as she lay in the grass on the crest of the slope above the River Ure, Audra thought not of her diplomas and nursing achievements over the past four years, but of Frederick and William.

Her brothers had not sent for her in the end.

They had not been able to save up the money for her passage to Australia. Things had not gone well for the Kenton boys. Frederick had had two serious bouts with pneumonia and seemed to be in a state of physical debilitation a great deal of the time. Apart from the problems with his health, he and William were unskilled and untrained. They had had a hard time scraping a living together.

She sighed and bestirred herself, then sat up, blinking as she opened her eyes and adjusted them to the brightness. Poor Frederick and William had had nothing but bad luck really. Their letters, which arrived less frequently these days, were permeated with defeat. Audra had all but given up hope of going out to join them in Sydney. She continued to fret and to miss them, and she supposed she always would. They were her only family, after all, and she loved them very much.

Her work at the hospital gave her satisfaction, and for this she was grateful, but it was not enough. Her sense of isolation, of not belonging to anyone, or more precisely of not being part of a family, and her dreadful loneliness, all contributed to the aridness of her life. Sometimes she found it unbearable, despite her treasured friendship with the devoted Gwen.

Audra stood up, then cast her gaze to the other side of the river.

The light had changed in the last few hours and High Cleugh now looked as if it had been built from polished bronze stones. It was bathed in a golden glow, appeared to shimmer like a mirage in the distance, and even the gardens had a burnished sheen in the rosy sunset. All of her life thus far, at least the best, the happiest parts of it, and her dearest memories, were bound up with that old house. A rush of feeling swept over Audra and she suddenly knew that she would never cease to yearn for High Cleugh and all the things it represented.

4

Here they were, sitting in the Copper Kettle in Harrogate. She and Gwen.

Audra could hardly believe they were finally meeting after all these weeks. The two girls had not seen each other since the beginning of June. On this hot and muggy Saturday it was already the end of August, the end of the summer, and the first time Gwen had been able to travel from Horsforth for a visit with her best friend.

Even so, Gwen had not been able to make it as far as Ripon, and in her letter she had asked Audra to meet her half way. Audra had agreed to this request immediately, and had sent off a note by return post.

Now, flushed with happiness, Audra looked across the table and broke into a smile. 'It's lovely to see you, Gwen. I've really missed you.'

'So have I – missed you, I mean.' Gwen's cherubic face, covered with freckles and vividly alive, was filled with laughter; it signalled her own pleasure at their reunion. 'I still feel ever so *awful* about not being able to spend your birthday with you –' Gwen broke off, reached down for the fabric shopping bag at her feet and proceeded to rummage around in it. She pulled out a package wrapped in royal blue paper and tied with scarlet ribbon.

With a flourish and a little grin, Gwen handed it across the table to Audra. 'Anyway, this is your birthday present, lovey. I never did get to take you to one of the fancy tea dances at the Arcadian Rooms, so here, I bought you something instead.'

'You didn't have to, you shouldn't have!' Audra protested, but it was easy to see she was thrilled to receive the gift. It had been a long time since she had been given a present, and there had been nothing on her birthday. Her face lit up and her bright blue eyes danced as she tore off the ribbon and paper with the excitement of a small child.

'Oh Gwen! *A paintbox!*' Audra looked up and beamed at the other girl. 'How lovely. And how clever of you. I really needed a new one. Thank you so much.' She reached out and took hold of Gwen's hand lying on the table and squeezed it affectionately.

It was Gwen's turn to look pleased. 'I wracked my brains, trying to think of something ... something ... well, *just right.* You being ever so particular as you are. As it happened, I was looking at that watercolour you painted for my mother last Christmas ... the tree reflected in the pond, and it suddenly occurred to me. The paintbox, I mean. I thought to myself, that's exactly the thing for Audra. It'll appeal to her practical side, but it'll give her pleasure as well.'

Gwen sat back and wrinkled her pert, very freckled nose. Her gaze did not leave Audra's face as she asked, 'It will, won't it?'

'Oh yes, Gwen, lots and lots of pleasure.' Audra's smile widened. Then she lifted the shiny black lid of the paintbox and looked inside at the small blocks of bright colour. She repeated some of the familiar names under her breath: *Chrome yellow ... rose madder ... cobalt blue ... jade green ... burnt sienna ... crimson lake ... Saxe blue ... royal purple ... burnt umber ... Malaga red.* Audra loved the sound of the names almost as much as she loved to paint.

It had been her favourite pastime since her childhood. Her father had been a gifted artist and his paintings had sold fairly well, but then he had fallen gravely ill just as he was becoming known. Adrian Kenton had not really had a chance to make a name for himself before he had died. She had inherited his talent – or so her mother had always told her.

Audra closed the lid of the paintbox and raised her eyes to meet Gwen's soft hazel-amber gaze. How pretty she looks, Audra thought, so blonde and golden from the sun. Gwen's fair colouring and her flaxen hair, cut short in a halo of curls around her head, added to the angelic impression she gave; so did the pale blue frock with its big white Quaker collar, which she had chosen to wear today. She

601

reminds me of a sweet young choirboy, Audra thought, and smiled at this analogy. With her beautiful bosom and lovely figure, there was nothing very boyish about Gwen Thornton.

Audra noticed that for once Gwen looked very restrained. Usually she glowed and glittered with all kinds of jewellery: necklaces and beads, earrings and bangles and rings. Obviously she had made a big effort to be both understated and dignified for this trip to Harrogate. She wants to please me, Audra decided, and her warm feelings for Gwen soared.

Leaning forward, Audra said, 'I'm going to paint a very special picture for you, Gwenny. For your room at home. Would you like a scene – the kind I did for your mother? Or a still life, such as a bowl of flowers? Oh, I *know* what I'll paint for you. The Valley Gardens here in Harrogate. You've always said that's your favourite spot when all the flowers are in bloom. Would you like that?'

'Yes, that'd be ever so nice. Thanks very much, Audra. I'd treasure one of your paintings – Mum says they're masterpieces. The Valley Gardens would look lovely on my wall. So I'd –'

'Can I take your order, miss?' the waitress interrupted rather peremptorily. She looked first at Gwen, then at Audra, her pencil poised impatiently above her pad.

'We'd like to have tea,' Audra said pleasantly, ignoring her huffy manner and angry stance. 'For two, please.'

'A pot? Or the set tea?' the waitress asked in the same snippy tone and licked the end of her pencil.

Gwen said, 'You oughtn't to do that. I hope that pencil's not indelible. You'll get a purple tongue, and probably lead poisoning.'

'Get on with you, I won't get no such thing!' the waitress scoffed disbelievingly, then gave the two of them a worried glance. 'Will I?' she muttered and carefully examined the tip of her pencil. 'Oooh bloomin' heck! It *is* indelible.'

Gwen nodded solemnly. 'I thought it would be. You'd better go and see a doctor immediately if you develop peculiar symptoms tonight, especially if they're at all like convulsions.'

'*Convulsions!*' the waitress repeated in a shrill voice and turned as white as her apron. 'Are you having me on, like?'

Audra, taking pity on the young woman, said, 'No, we're not. We're nurses and we know about these things. But I'm sure you won't get lead poisoning from licking that pencil a few times. My friend tends to be a bit of an alarmist.'

The waitress, appearing slightly relieved, nodded her head. 'I wouldn't want to be getting poorly . . .'

'You'll be perfectly all right,' Audra reassured, and went on briskly, 'Now about our order, I think we'd better have the *set* tea. I suppose that means it includes everything . . . sandwiches, scones, jam, clotted cream, cakes – all of the usual things?'

'Yes,' the waitress said laconically. She brought the pencil up to her mouth, then dropped her hand quickly. She scribbled on her pad and edged away from their table.

When she was out of earshot, Audra stared at the merry-faced Gwen and shook her head a bit reprovingly. However, she could not help grinning at Gwen's gleeful expression. 'You're incorrigible, Miss Thornton. And that really *was* a little mean of you. Why, you've gone and ruined that poor young woman's day.'

'I jolly well hope I have!' Gwen cried with a show of indignation. 'She's a right tartar, that one, Audra.'

'Perhaps she has bad feet – or a bad love life.'

'I don't know what she's got. Yes, I do – a nasty manner, that's a certainty. I remember *her* from past experience. Oh yes I do, very well, Audra. She's always snotty-nosed with the customers, especially the older folk. I noticed her giving that grey-haired lady over there a hard time before you arrived. So it *does* serve her right.'

'I suppose it does,' Audra agreed. Like Gwen, she loathed unkindness, the small unnecessary cruelties inflicted on the weak by the strong. Besides, the waitress had been extremely short with them, to the point of rudeness.

There was a small silence, and then Audra reached for her handbag, took out some coins and placed them on the table in front of Gwen. 'Before I forget, this is what I owe you. The one and six I borrowed when I bought the blue dress.'

Gwen was about to say it didn't matter, to refuse the coins, then she thought better of it. Audra was very proud and she would be insulted; she might even take umbrage and that Gwen could not bear. And so she picked up the money and said, 'Thanks very much, lovey.'

'I *am* glad your mother has recovered her health at long last,' Audra said with genuine feeling. 'I know these last few months have been very worrying for you, and such hard work as well.'

Gwen let out a tiny sigh. 'Yes, Mum's out of the woods, thank goodness. But I don't mind telling you, she's been a trying patient, Audra. Hard to keep in bed. The minute she felt stronger she wanted to be up and about.' Gwen pursed her lips and sighed again. 'Well, you know what Mum's like, a typical Yorkshire-woman, very tough, who believes it's a crime to be ill. My father has finally convinced her she must take it easy, so that's all right then. But listen, Audra, enough of this . . . tell me *your* news. You didn't say much in your letters, except for boring bits and pieces about the *boring* hospital.'

'There wasn't anything special to tell,' Audra replied, amused at the eager and expectant expression which had suddenly appeared on Gwen's dimpled face. 'Certainly nothing startling. It hasn't taken *you* very long to forget that Ripon's a sleepy old backwater, not a great big metropolis like Leeds.'

Gwen giggled. ' 'Course I haven't forgotten, silly. But what I meant was how're your brothers? What've you heard recently?'

'Frederick's health has seemingly improved – at long last. At least, so William wrote and told me. I was very upset with them both in June, though.' Audra's face changed slightly and the light in her eyes dulled. 'I thought they had forgotten all about me . . . and my birthday, but then their card finally did arrive . . . two weeks late.'

'That's brothers for you, Audra, they're a bit daft at times,' Gwen said swiftly, wanting to make her friend feel better. It struck her once more how sad Audra's nineteenth birthday had been. She vowed to make it up to her on her birthday next year.

Audra said, 'Anyway, how are your brothers?'

'In top form. Jem's got himself a job as a copy boy on the *Leeds Mercury*, Harry's going to be apprenticed to one of the leading architects in Leeds, and our Charlie's flying high, feeling very chuffed with himself.' A huge grin spread across Gwen's face.

Audra looked at her curiously. 'Why is Charlie so pleased?'

'Because he got *very* high marks in his exams, Audra. Dad's really proud of him, and so am I. Anyway, old Charlie can't wait to get back to medical school now that the summer hols are just about over. Oh, and that reminds me, he asked to be remembered to you.' Gwen's eyes took on a wicked twinkle and she brought her fair head closer to Audra's, whispered in a conspiratorial manner, 'As I keep telling you, I think our Charlie really fancies you, Audra. And quite a bit, at that.'

Audra blushed furiously. 'Don't be so silly, Gwen, of course he doesn't.'

'He does too! He's always asking questions about you!' Gwen shot back with unprecedented fierceness, giving her friend a stern glare. 'He's *definitely* interested in you, I just know he is.'

'Oh,' was the only thing Audra could think of to say, feeling flustered all of a sudden.

'Well, you could do worse, you know.'

'Yes,' Audra murmured, and then clamped her mouth shut as the waitress hove in view.

Much to Audra's relief the young woman headed straight for their table, carrying a laden tray. She began to unload the tea things with a great deal of fuss and clattering, and this curtailed their conversation for a few moments. Gwen threw Audra a disgusted look and made a face, indicating her disapproval of the noisy waitress, who seemed hell bent on irritating them.

Audra bit back a smile and glanced away. Once the waitress had departed, she picked up the large brown pot and began to pour tea into Gwen's cup, remarking, 'I suppose I could say *she's* just had the last word.'

'Oh no she hasn't, not by a long shot,' Gwen said with a sly little smile. 'Wait until it's time for her tip.'

5

Gwen Thornton was a sweet affectionate girl, open hearted and generous of nature, and she genuinely cared for Audra Kenton.

From the first moment she had met her, Gwen had been drawn to Audra. She had recognized there was something very special about the small, delicate-looking girl with the extraordinary blue eyes and the shy smile that could dazzle at times.

Gwen had quickly come to understand what it actually was that made Audra stand out in a crowd. It was her background and upbringing. Coming from an ordinary, though solid, middle-class family as she did, Gwen knew that Audra's air of breeding was downright impossible to imitate. You either had it or you didn't. It simply could not be acquired. And it not only gave Audra distinction, but explained her aristocratic aloofness, her manners and her self-assurance, which were bred in the bone.

However, Gwen admired and loved Audra for a variety of other reasons, all of which added to her uniqueness. Audra was a superior young woman in every way, one who was inordinately loyal and loving; she was also the most indomitable person Gwen had ever met.

Yet, despite these commendable traits, Gwen could not help worrying about Audra sometimes. She chiefly worried because Audra was without a family. Gwen knew more than anyone how much this bothered Audra. She sorely missed her brothers, yearned to *belong* in the way she had when her mother had been alive. This was why Gwen went out of her way to make her best friend feel like a real member of the Thornton clan, to make her truly understand she was as much loved as her baby sister Jenny-Rosalie, and her brothers, Charles, Jeremy and Harry.

Ever since Charlie, the eldest, had shown an interest in Audra, Gwen had been encouraging him, endeavouring to foster a relationship between them, to fan the flames. But from time to time Gwen had had to admit to herself that the interest was a trifle one-sided thus far; and she sometimes wondered if her sweet but rather dull brother was the right match for Audra. Inevitably, Gwen managed to convince herself that he really was ideal. Certainly there was no question in her mind that Charlie was a good catch, since he was such an admirable young man, and one with an assured future, after all. He would not stay a bachelor for very long, once he had qualified as a doctor, and he would make a wonderful husband and father. Gwen had always known in her bones that Charlie was cut out to be a family man.

And in Gwen's mind, the crucial word was indeed *family*. This was what Audra longed for the most and so she was going to help her dearest friend acquire a family of her very own. And, of course, Charlie was the key.

All of these thoughts, which had frequently preoccupied Gwen during the past few weeks, had started to swirl around in her head again this afternoon.

She and Audra were now strolling through the beautiful Valley Gardens. Both girls were glad to be out in the open air, after being cooped up inside the noisy café.

Gwen cast a glance at Audra as they headed down the sloping path. She decided she would be very hard pressed indeed to find a sweeter or prettier candidate for a sister-in-law. Audra looked particularly attractive today, wearing a primrose-yellow print dress patterned with primroses, and a straw boater with a yellow silk band and matching ribbons fluttering down at the back. The boater gave her a jaunty air, whilst the simple cut of the frock and its sunny colour were flattering to her.

She might be small, Gwen thought, but she's quality through and through. And then before she could stop herself she said out loud, 'Yes, good stuff in a little room.' Gwen could have bitten her tongue off, instantly regretted repeating this comment Charlie had made about Audra, who hated any reference to her height, or lack of it. She cleared her throat nervously.

Audra said, with a puzzled look, 'Excuse me, I don't quite understand what you're referring to, Gwen.'

Deciding it would be better not to mention Charlie, Gwen explained, 'Oh it was just something my mother said about you – good stuff in a little room means that a small person often has a lot of wonderful qualities. Haven't you heard the expression before? It's very Yorkshire.'

Audra shook her head. 'No, I haven't, but it's a nice compliment.'

'Yes,' Gwen said, delighted that she had taken it so well, and tucked her arm through Audra's companionably. 'And talking of Mum, she says I can have a party for my birthday, so I hope you'll come and stay with us at The Meadow, the third weekend in September. There'll be Charlie, Jem and Harry, of course, and I can invite a *few* friends. But only a few. 'Cos Mum couldn't cope with a big crowd after her illness. You *will* come, Audra, won't you? It wouldn't be the same without you.'

'Of course I'll come. It'll be a lovely treat for me, and I always enjoy staying at your house. Thank you for inviting me.'

Gwen laughed gaily. 'You'll get to wear your gorgeous blue dress. *Finally*. Why, Audra, you'll be the belle of the ball. All the boys will be after you.' Especially our Charlie, Gwen added to herself, and hoped he wouldn't be rejected.

Audra glanced up at Gwen, who was a few inches taller, and joined in her laughter. '*You'll* be the belle, after all it's your birthday party. But I must admit, I am dying to wear my new dress. And what frock are you going to wear, Gwenny?'

'Oh I don't know. I'll find something suitable, I expect. Now, who else do you think I should invite?' Not giving Audra a chance to reply, Gwen hurried on, 'I'll tell you what, let's go and sit over there on that form and talk about the party. You're so clever, Audra, I'd like your advice about a few things. You know . . . such as what kind of food and drinks to serve and your suggestions in general. Come on, lovey.'

Gwen steered Audra in the direction of a park seat positioned under one of the lovely weeping willows which were planted throughout the Valley Gardens. Here the two girls sat themselves down and brought their heads together. They chatted animatedly about Gwen's twentieth birthday party for the next half hour, covering all the different aspects of it, planning the menu and the guest list.

Finally Gwen said, 'Thanks Audra, you've been a great help, and I appreciate your ideas, I really do. It'll be a nice party . . .' Gwen left her sentence unfinished as she began to fan herself with one hand, then fished around in her fabric shopping bag for her hankie. She patted her face with it, exclaimed, '*Phew!* I am hot. It's still close even though the sun's gone down.'

'There's no breeze at all.' Audra lolled back against the seat. She glanced up at the sky, hoped it would not rain.

They fell silent for a while.

Audra turned her attention to the passers-by, thinking how smart some of the women looked, dressed in their finery, and out for a stroll before dinner at one of the swanky hotels. They were obviously from London, judging by their clothes, and visiting Harrogate to 'take the cure'. It had been a renowned spa since Victorian times, and people came from all over the world to drink the different waters available in the Pump Room, and visit the hydros at the Royal Baths. Her mother had always loved Harrogate for its elegance and the Beautiful Edith Kenton had called it a throwback to Victorian times and a more civilized age.

Their mother had often brought them here for the day. Audra recalled a memorable afternoon in 1911 when they had come to get a glimpse of the queens of England, Russia and Poland, who had all been visiting Harrogate on the same day. Their Uncle Peter had been with them, and he had lifted her up on his shoulders so that she could see above the crowds. There had been lots of excitement and flags waving and a band playing . . . Audra drifted along with her remembrances of things past.

Gwen, however, was thinking of the future, and wondering how to break her awful news to Audra. Earlier, she had toyed with the idea of not saying anything, of writing a letter at a later date. But Gwen knew that Audra, who had so much integrity and was such a fair person, deserved better from her than that. She decided there really was only one way to do it, and that was to jump right in, both feet first.

Reaching out, she touched Audra's arm tentatively, and said in an unusually subdued voice, 'There's something I want to tell you before we go to the bus station for our buses . . .'

Audra looked at her, instantly coming back to the present. 'You sound very serious all of a sudden, Gwenny. Is there something wrong?'

Gwen swallowed and cleared her throat. 'I've wanted to tell you this all afternoon, but I haven't known how to begin. Well . . . look, it's like this, Audra . . . I won't be coming back to work at the Fever Hospital. I'm ever so sorry.'

Audra gaped at her friend, flabbergasted at this announcement. It was a bomb-shell, the last thing she had expected to hear. 'Oh Gwen,' she murmured so softly it was a whisper.

Observing her closely, detecting the misery now flooding her bright blue eyes, Gwen cried, anxiously, 'Please, oh *please* don't be upset, Audra. *I'm* not going to *Australia.* I'll only be a couple of hours away, either in Leeds or Horsforth. We can see each other all the time, and listen, Mum wants you to come and stay for Christmas, like you did last year. And we'll be together on my birthday next month.'

Audra, considerably shaken by Gwen's news, was only able to nod mutely.

'You see, it's like this, Audra. Dad wants me to be nearer home, because of Mum's weak heart. He says I have to apply for a position at the Infirmary or St James's Hospital, and until I get something at either place I've got to stay at home with Mum. Dad's ever so set on it, Audra, I can't make him change his mind.'

Audra heard the distress in Gwen's voice, and she smiled faintly, and nodded. 'I understand, Gwenny,' she said. But her heart sank at the prospect of being all alone in Ripon. She felt as though she was being abandoned, left behind once more.

Gwen, who was watching her intently, had a sudden idea. She exclaimed, 'Look, Audra, why don't you apply too? For a hospital job in Leeds, I mean.' She drew closer, took hold of Audra's small hand and was surprised how cold it was on this muggy day. She clutched it tightly, begged, 'Say you will. Please, lovey.'

'I'm not sure whether I should –'

'*Why not?*' Gwen demanded, her voice rising. 'There's not one good reason for you to stay in Ripon.'

Audra blinked and returned Gwen's hard stare, realizing immediately that her friend was absolutely right. She began to nod her head emphatically. 'Yes, I'll do it, Gwenny!' And a smile broke through at last, expunged the sadness which had darkened her lovely eyes.

Gwen threw her arms around Audra. She hugged her tightly, bursting with happiness and filled with relief. The thought of leaving her friend behind at the Fever Hospital had been more than the girl could bear.

6

'Matron wants to see you, Kenton,' Sister Rogers said, drawing to a standstill, fixing a stern eye on Audra. 'She did say *immediately*, so you'd better look sharp.'

Audra, who had just finished taking a child's temperature, nodded. 'Thanks. I'll go up at once.'

Moving away from the bed, Audra glanced around at her young patients with her usual concern. The small isolation ward was occupied by children suffering from whooping cough and she was worried about each of them on this icy December morning.

As she and the head nurse walked down the ward towards the door, Audra dropped her voice and said, 'They're all a bit restless, especially little John Martin over there by the window. He's exhausted from the whoop, and he's not been able to keep his breakfast down because of his coughing. Or anything else since, for that matter, and Doctor Parkinson is a bit concerned about him. Can you send a junior nurse in to keep an eye on him? And on the others, of course?'

'Don't worry about it, I'll stay here myself until you get back. I'm sure you won't be very long with Matron.' A slight smile touched the head nurse's mouth and there was a sudden softening in her attitude towards Audra, and she remarked in a quiet tone, 'Your diligence really is most commendable, Kenton. You've turned out to be a good nurse.'

These were words of praise indeed, coming from this most senior member of the nursing staff who had worked herself up from ward maid, and who was renowned as a disciplinarian. Audra, surprised, returned her smile and with a little burst of pride, she drew herself up to her full height. 'Thank you, Sister,' she said. 'I do try.'

Sister Rogers inclined her head and turned away.

It was a dismissal of sorts, and Audra crossed the front hall and ran up the wide main staircase, hoping against hope that Matron had good news for her at long last. After making the decision to leave Ripon and find a nursing job in Leeds, Audra had confided her intentions in the head of the hospital and had asked for her advice. Matron had given it, and had generously offered to do everything she could to help Audra secure a position elsewhere. Unfortunately, they had not been successful so far. It seemed there were no vacancies in any of the hospitals in Leeds or the surrounding districts.

Audra, however, was not overly dismayed about this situation, since Gwen herself had only just managed to find a place at Leeds General Infirmary. Lonely though she was at the hospital without her dearest friend for companionship in her off-duty hours, Audra remained cheerful and optimistic as she went about her duties.

For the past three months, Audra had held the firm conviction that something would turn up eventually, and now, as she came to a stop outside Matron's office, she wondered if it finally had materialized. She tugged at her cuffs to straighten them, smoothed her hands over her starched white apron, then knocked on the frosted-glass panel of the door. At Matron's bidding she went in.

Margaret Lennox sat behind her large, paper-strewn desk.

She was wearing the navy-blue tailored dress and small white muslin cap that signified the highest nursing rank in the hierarchy of every hospital, and she seemed more formidable than ever. But Audra knew from experience that this stern-looking woman had generosity and warmth and the kindest of hearts.

Matron raised her eyes. She smiled at the sight of Audra, who was a particular favourite of hers, for whom she had a great deal of respect and not a little admiration. She was fully aware of Audra's history from the hospital files, and she never ceased to marvel at this girl's strength of character.

'Ah Audra,' she began pleasantly, 'do come in and sit down. I have a matter to discuss with you.'

'Yes, Matron.' Audra stepped up to the desk briskly, and lowered herself onto the wooden chair where she sat straight-backed as always, her hands clasped in her lap. Her wide blue eyes were riveted on the matron's face.

Margaret Lennox glanced at the letter in her hand, then put it down on the desk. 'Well, Audra, I think I might have a position for you in Leeds.'

A look of delight flew onto Audra's face and she opened her mouth to speak.

But before she could say anything, Matron lifted her hand, exclaimed, 'Just a moment! Don't get too excited ... at least not yet. I must explain that this is not the type of nursing job you've been looking for, Audra. It's not in a hospital, I'm afraid.'

'Oh,' Audra said. 'I see,' and her face fell.

'I know you're disappointed that I have not been able to get you situated somewhere appropriate,' Matron went on in a sympathetic way. 'However, I do think you should consider this private position, especially since you are so very anxious to move to Leeds.'

'Of course I will, Matron.'

'Good girl. Now, Audra, I have had a letter from a Mrs Irène Bell, who is the wife of a well-known Leeds solicitor. She's looking for a nanny, and has contacted me about finding a suitable candidate here at the hospital. Naturally, Audra, I thought of you at once.'

Matron Lennox then went on to explain that she had originally met Mrs Bell through her work with the suffragette movement before the Great War, and that they had remained friendly over the years. Then she continued, 'I cannot speak highly enough of Mrs Bell. She is a unique woman and I have a strong feeling you and she would be most compatible. In any event, from what she says in her letter, it's not a difficult job. There is only one child to look after, a little boy of five years. The other three children are grown up, away at school I believe.' Matron's brow lifted questioningly. 'What do you think, Audra? Are you interested?'

Audra had been listening avidly, and she knew she would be foolish if she turned down this opportunity without investigating it further. So she immediately said, 'Yes, I am, Matron.'

Matron nodded, as though confirming something to herself, and said, 'I am confident you can handle a job such as this with the greatest of ease.' She sat back, brought her hands together and steepled her fingers, contemplated Audra over them for a few moments, before remarking: 'You have such a wonderful way with children, I know you will do well as a nanny. But you are an *extraordinary* nurse, Audra, a true healer, and that's rare. Don't ever forget that you have this remarkable ability . . . one might even call it a gift.'

'No, I won't,' Audra said, flushing with pleasure. She murmured her thanks to Matron for her kind words and the confidence she expressed in her.

Margaret Lennox went on, 'I did have special plans for you here at the hospital, Audra, and I had envisaged promotions coming your way quickly.' She smiled at the young woman with obvious fondness, then lifted her shoulders in a small resigned shrug. 'Well, there we are . . . I for one shall be *most* sorry to see you go, if you *do* decide to leave, Audra. But, as I've told you all along, I would never presume to stand in your way.'

'Yes, I know that, Matron, and I do appreciate everything you've done for me.'

Matron half-smiled, finished in a more businesslike tone, 'I will call Mrs Bell today, and arrange for you to go over to Leeds for an interview. I'll let you know the details as soon as I have them. In the meantime, you had better return to your duties on the ward, Audra.'

'Yes, Matron,' Audra said, standing up. 'Thank you again.'

She was on her way to Leeds.

To meet Mrs Irène Bell of Calpher House, Upper Armley.

Audra had the feeling that this was going to be an auspicious occasion. She laughed at herself under her breath. It was only an interview for a job after all. On the other hand, if everything went well there would be big changes in her life at long last. It might even be the beginning of a brand new life.

This thought brought an extra spring to her step as she crossed the Market Place in Ripon, making her way towards the small country railway station on North Road. Audra's eyes sparkled with such radiant light, and there was such a glow on her fresh young face this morning, several people turned to look at her as she passed them by. But she did not notice this. Nor was she conscious of the weather. It was a harsh day, exceptionally cold, and the sky was sullen, laden with snow. But it might have been the middle of spring for all she knew, or cared, so intent was she in her purpose. She was also filled with anticipation and excitement. A week ago she had never heard of the Bell family, and now, here she was, journeying half-way across Yorkshire to seek a post with them.

What if she did not like the Bells?

At this thought her step faltered, but only for a split second. Stepping out as briskly as before, she told herself she would make a polite excuse and leave at once if the people at Calpher House did not appear to be suitable employers.

The ticket collector at the station gave Audra a cheerful greeting as he punched her ticket and handed her the return stub. He touched his cap politely, and she nodded in acknowledgement, then hurried down the platform where the Leeds-bound train was already standing, puffing out steam and hooting. She boarded it swiftly and went into the first empty First Class carriage she saw. She took a corner seat near the window with only a few minutes to spare before the guard blew his whistle and the train shunted out.

Audra soon began to realize that it was warmer in the carriage than she had anticipated. She pulled off her grey woollen gloves and unbuttoned her coat, then settled back, making herself comfortable for the journey.

Audra knew she looked smart today.

For her trip to Leeds she had chosen to wear her best grey Melton topcoat. Although it had been purchased in a sale and was already two years old, it was still fashionable, a wrap-around style with long, rolled lapels fastening at the hip with a huge button. Underneath the coat she had on a straight skirt made of grey wool and a matching grey jumper that came down over her hips. Together they created a slender tube-like effect, and she believed that this long line and her black court shoes with Cuban heels made her look taller; this pleased Audra who was always trying to gain a few inches. Her only jewellery was her mother's cameo brooch, which she had pinned onto the front of her jumper, and her treasured watch.

When Audra had been visiting Gwen in September, her friend had given her a cloche made of plum-coloured brushed felt. 'My worst buy ever!' Gwen had said when she had shown the hat to Audra. 'It's like a pea on a drum. I look awful in it, but I bet it suits you to a T, lovey.' Gwen had been quite correct. The cloche *was* perfect on Audra, and she had been happy and grateful to accept it, had treasured the hat for a special occasion such as this.

But now she wondered if the hat was too frivolous for the interview with Mrs Bell, and she opened her bag, took out her mirror. Her reflection reassured her at once. The cloche, which was very much the rage, gave her a stylish up-to-date look, and the rich plum tone of the felt added just the right touch of necessary colour to her all-grey ensemble. Her clothes were sober and dignified, and she felt sure she would make a good impression on Mrs Irène Bell.

As the train rumbled on through the Dales towards Leeds, Audra's thoughts stayed with the woman she was going to see; she began to review the few things she had gleaned about her from Matron, turning them over in her mind.

It was Audra's understanding that Irène Bell was a successful business woman who had a strong intellectual bent and was something of a blue stocking. She was devoted to furthering the cause of women's rights, and had always been a staunch disciple of the Pankhurst women who had done so much for female emancipation. According to Matron, Mrs Bell was also a great admirer of Nancy Astor, the American married to Lord Astor who was the first woman to sit in Parliament. Actively involved in politics herself, Mrs Bell was seemingly a tireless worker for the Tory Party in Leeds, with many of her own political ambitions – especially regarding Parliament.

There was no doubt in Audra's mind that she was obviously an unusual and interesting woman, and one who was quite different from any *she* had ever met. Except for Margaret Lennox, of course, who was a true original, and whom Audra revered, even idealized.

Gazing out of the train window, hardly aware of the fields and hedges speeding by, Audra attempted to visualize Mrs Bell in her mind's eye. Since she had been a friend of Matron's for many years and had grown-up children, Audra reasoned she must be a woman in her middle forties. Instantly she was confronted by the image of a stern and somewhat severe person, perhaps resembling Matron, and one who was a model of organization and efficiency.

Audra arrived at this last conclusion because of the tone of the letter she had received from Mrs Bell earlier in the week. It was detailed and explicit, and her instructions for getting to Calpher House, Upper Armley, left nothing whatsoever to chance. It struck Audra, and for the second time in the last few days, that Mrs Bell must be an exceptionally thoughtful woman, since she had sent her a First Class rail ticket instead of a cheaper one, as might have been expected under the circumstances. This was a truly considerate gesture, and one which certainly seemed to augur well for the future, at least to Audra's way of thinking. She suddenly realized how curious she was about Irène Bell, and just how much she was looking forward to meeting her.

Punctuality was one of Audra's strong suits, and she always became agitated if she was late. Throughout the journey, she had glanced at her watch, praying that the train would be on time. Much to her relief it was. It pulled into Leeds City Station at exactly one minute to two, early, in point of fact, by sixty seconds.

Once she had left the bleak and grimy railway station, Audra was plunged into a whirl of traffic and pedestrians hurrying about their business. For a second or two the strident noise and the feverish bustle of the greatest industrial city in the North of England startled and overwhelmed her. The cacophony of sounds was a deafening contrast to the bucolic calm of sleepy, rural Ripon.

But since nothing ever fazed Audra Kenton for very long she adjusted relatively quickly to her surroundings. After only a brief pause, she sucked in her breath, threw her shoulders back and brought her head up to a proud angle, ready and set to brave anything in this exciting new world awaiting her.

Tucking her handbag tightly under her arm, she walked purposefully across the road to City Square, where the statue of the Black Prince on his charger dominated the scene. She found the tram stop she wanted without any difficulty, and after a ten-minute wait in a small queue she followed the people ahead of her onto a tramcar going to Whingate. This was the terminus in Upper Armley where the tram turned around to go back to the city. Mrs Bell had told her to stay on the car all the way to the end of the line.

Half an hour later, Audra alighted from the double-decker tram, which she had thoroughly enjoyed riding on, and she stood for a moment, looking around her with burgeoning interest. After all, she might soon be living here.

To her right was the tiny wedge of a park enclosed by spike-topped black iron railings and a neatly-clipped privet hedge; Mrs Bell had said that it had the curious name of Charlie Cake Park. To her left was a huge red brick building, sprawling out behind a low brick wall, and she assumed this to be West Leeds Boys' High School.

Audra knew exactly which way she had to go now.

She began to walk ahead at a brisk pace, glancing at the scenery and taking everything in with keenly observing eyes. She saw at once that the village of Upper Armley was picturesque and that it had a quaint Victorian charm. And despite the darkly-mottled sky, sombre and presaging snow, and a landscape bereft of greenery, it was easy to see how pretty it must be in the summer weather.

Following Mrs Bell's instructions, which she had committed to memory days ago, Audra hurried up Greenhill Road in the direction of Hill-Top, the area where the Bell home was located.

It was a nippy afternoon, very blustery, and she had to hold onto her little cloche as she struggled forward, buffeted by the wind that whistled down over the hill with icy ferocity. Audra was shivering when she reached the crest of the hill and drew to a stop in front of a pair of tall and imposing wrought-iron gates upon which hung a large lozenge-shaped plaque. This was made of brass that had been rubbed up to a glittering sheen. It was inscribed with the name *Calpher House* in fancy scroll letters and it told her she had reached her destination.

7

Mrs Irène Bell bore no resemblance to the image Audra had conjured up in her mind. The woman who walked towards her down the long stretch of luxurious Turkey carpet was tall, lissom, very smart, and she had the brightest, reddest of auburn hair. This had been cut in a sleek and fashionable bob, then shaped into a fringe above pencilled brows and velvety brown eyes that shone with great brilliance. High cheekbones and a slender aristocratic nose were peppered with freckles; a rather wide mouth was outlined in scarlet lipstick.

Irène Bell was stunning; and she had an arresting personal style that was highly dramatic.

She took swift strides through the handsome blue-and-white living room, filled with antiques, where Audra stood waiting, and there was something reminiscent of the bold tomboy in her manner, the way she moved. In fact, her looks had a marked hoydenish quality; she also appeared to be much younger than a woman in her mid-forties. The red wool-jersey dress she wore underscored her intrinsic youthfulness with its long, loose-fitting bodice and pleated skirt, rather short, that swung around her splendid legs.

Audra, sharp eyed, recognized the dress at once. She had seen a photograph of it only last week in an old summer issue of *Harper's Bazaar*, which she had bought at the second-hand bookstall in Ripon market. It had been designed by a young French *couturière* called Gabrielle Chanel, who was currently all the vogue.

'Hello! Hello!' Mrs Bell exclaimed, gliding to a stop, thrusting her hand towards her visitor. 'So *very* pleased to meet you, Miss Kenton.'

Audra took the proffered hand, then found her own being squeezed in the tightest of grips. 'Good afternoon, Mrs Bell. I'm happy to meet you, too.'

Giving her a warm and winning smile, continuing to hold her hand, Irène Bell drew Audra forward to the two huge sofas which were positioned opposite each other in front of the fireplace. 'So very good of you to travel all this way, Miss Kenton. And in this frightful weather. Yes, so very *good* of you indeed. Do, *do* sit here. Yes, *yes*, next to the fire. Warm yourself after your journey. Cook is preparing hot chocolate. Cora will bring it up shortly. I *do* hope you like hot chocolate. Would you prefer tea? Or coffee, perhaps?'

'The chocolate would be lovely, thank you very much,' Audra said, seating herself tentatively on the edge of the blue velvet sofa. Her keen eyes rested on Mrs Bell, who sat down on the other one.

Now that she was seeing her close up, Audra realized that she had not been wrong about Irène Bell's age after all. She was definitely a woman in her mid-forties, but very well preserved and exquisitely groomed. Although there were tell-tale lines of age around her eyes and her mouth, these were fine, hardly discernible; she had kept her figure and there was no visible grey in her fiery hair, which was quite obviously natural, not dyed. And her vivacity, her energetic way of moving and speaking with intensity and swiftness, somehow added to the impression of youthfulness she projected.

Intuitively, Audra knew that she was going to like this woman, even though she had only been in her presence for a few minutes. There was something open and easy, honest and down-to-earth about Mrs Bell, and Audra found herself responding to her on a variety of levels. She sat back, instantly relaxing, feeling suddenly comfortable here at Calpher House. And she, who was usually so shy, so reserved with strangers, was perfectly at ease with Mrs Bell.

Irène Bell crossed her long and elegant legs, and focused her dark intelligent eyes on Audra, assessing her, yet without really appearing to do so.

She said in her light, gay voice, 'In some ways I do feel rather foolish, Miss Kenton. Asking you to come for an interview like this. Matron Lennox spoke so highly about you, gave you such a wonderful reference, I actually thought of engaging you over the telephone. Without even bothering to meet you personally.'

Laughing as though at herself, her velvet eyes glowed with humour as she added, 'But then I realized how unfair that would be to you, Miss Kenton. After all, it is important for *you* to like *us*. For you to *want* to live and work here at Calpher House. I knew I must give you the opportunity to come here and look *us* over.'

Irène Bell laughed again, leaned back, rested one elbow on the pile of silk cushions, and continued to study Audra discreetly, not wishing to embarrass her. She was intrigued by the young woman who sat before her, who handled herself with such grace and dignity. Margaret Lennox had painted a charming verbal picture of her, and the Matron had obviously not exaggerated. Audra Kenton was smaller than she had expected her to be, even delicate looking, but she was not terribly concerned about physical stamina. Strength of character, refinement, morality and a pleasant personality were her chief considerations when it came to selecting and engaging a nanny. This girl had every one of these qualities, and more, according to Margaret, whose judgement she trusted.

'Matron Lennox told me that she thought you and I would be most compatible, Mrs Bell, and she felt sure that I could handle the job here easily.' Audra levelled her blue eyes at the other woman, and ventured, 'But she *was* vague about it. Perhaps you would be kind enough to give me a few more details, Mrs Bell.'

'Good Lord, of course! I must fill you in, mustn't I? Well now, let me see. As you know from Matron, you would be entirely responsible for our youngest child, Theo. Our only son. Our three daughters are almost grown up. The eldest, Pandora, lives at home. The younger two, Felicity and Antonia, are away at boarding school. Let me explain something, Miss Kenton. I go to business every day. I run the woollen mill I inherited from my father, I also have an exclusive ladies' gown salon in Leeds. *Paris Modes*. I'm quite certain you must know it.'

Audra shook her head, looking regretful. 'I'm sorry, I'm afraid I don't, Mrs Bell. The only store I know in Leeds is Harte's Emporium. I went there once with my friend Gwen.'

Mrs Bell said, 'My dress shop is not as large as Emma Harte's store. But my imported French gowns *are* beginning to rival those she sells in her Model Room at Harte's. Even if I do say so myself. But to continue. Obviously, because I am out most of the day, I need a responsible person in charge of the nursery and the baby. A person such as yourself. As to your accommodation here, there is a lovely bedroom, large and comfortable, which overlooks the gardens. It's on the nursery floor, has its own private bathroom. You would have one day off during the week, and every other Sunday. One week's holiday a year. I would provide you with three cotton uniforms for summer, plus a summer coat and hat. The same amount of clothing for winter. Now, regarding the wages –'

Mrs Bell broke off at the sound of a knock, and glanced towards the door. It opened to admit a plump young maid, who rushed forward rather too quickly, pushing a laden tea trolley in front of her with great gusto.

'Ah Cora, there you are at last!' Mrs Bell exclaimed. *'Do*, please, be *careful*. Bring the trolley over here by the fire. This is Miss Kenton, Cora. Whom I sincerely hope will be joining us at Calpher House. As the new nanny.'

Cora and the tea trolley came to an abrupt stop with a rattling jolt. She stared at Audra, narrowing her eyes, squinting at her. Then, as if she had decided she liked the look of her, she smiled broadly, bobbed a half-curtsy. 'Please ter meet yer, Miss,' she said, and proceeded down the long stretch of Turkey carpet, handling the trolley with a kind of dangerous abandon.

Audra inclined her head graciously, and returned the maid's smile. 'Good afternoon, Cora,' she replied, and cringed as she watched Cora's perilous progress towards them. She hoped that nothing would go crashing to the floor, for the maid's sake.

After coming to a shuddering halt, Cora positioned the trolley next to Mrs Bell, gave it a final little jiggle to straighten it, asked, 'Do yer want me ter pour the 'ot chocolate then, ma'am?'

'No, no, Cora, that's all right, I can manage,' Irène Bell replied swiftly, wincing at the thought. She dismissed Cora with a smile and a nod, lifted the silver jug and carefully filled two large breakfast cups, remarking, 'We have a wonderful cook, Mrs Jackson, and the butler is Mr Agiter. I believe you saw Dodie, the other housemaid, when you arrived? Did she not open the door to you?'

'Yes, she did, Mrs Bell.' Audra rose and went over to the tea trolley, took the cup of hot chocolate which was being offered to her.

Irène Bell exclaimed, 'Do, but *do*, try one of Cook's hot Cornish pasties, Miss Kenton. They're delicious. And quite renowned hereabouts.'

'Thank you.' Audra placed the cup of steamy, frothing chocolate on the antique mahogany table next to the sofa, put one of the meat turnovers on a plate and returned to her place.

Taking a sip of chocolate, Mrs Bell continued, 'As I was about to say when Cora came in, your wages would be sixty pounds a year. This is an increase of ten pounds above what I paid the last nanny. Matron Lennox said it would not be fair of me to offer you anything less than sixty pounds. In view of your superior training at the hospital.' Irène Bell now leaned forward intently. 'Well, Miss Kenton, are you interested in taking the position, do you think?' A perfect, pencilled brow lifted eloquently.

Audra was both startled and delighted at the amount of money she would be paid. She said, 'I am interested, Mrs Bell, very much so. However, I would like to meet your little boy before I finally say yes.' Audra gave her a forthright look, and her sudden smile was one of sweetness and sincerity. 'I'm quite positive I will like him, but I do want to be sure *he* likes *me*.'

'What a lovely sentiment, Miss Kenton. And I'm overjoyed, simply *overjoyed*, that you're going to join our little family.' Irène Bell's face, always mobile and expressive, now filled with a mixture of relief and pleasure. Her merry laugh echoed around the room. 'I know the baby will take to you. How could he not? He's having his afternoon nap at the moment, but you shall meet him later. And before you leave I shall show you around Calpher House. And introduce you to the staff.'

The motor car slid to a standstill in front of the General Post Office in City Square.

A moment later the uniformed chauffeur was opening the rear door and helping Audra to alight. 'Thank you so much, Robertson,' she said, giving him an appreciative little smile.

'It's a pleasure, Miss. Good afternoon, Miss.' He touched the neb of his peaked cap and hurried back to the driver's seat.

Audra swung around and took a step towards Gwen, who was standing near the steps of the Post Office where they had arranged to meet.

Gwen's eyes were out on stalks. Instantly recovering herself, she rushed forward to meet Audra. Grasping hold of her hands, she cried in a shrill, excited voice, 'Well, aren't *we* posh then! Rolling up in a fancy motor car. Imagine that!'

Audra could not help laughing at Gwen's incredulity. Then she explained, 'Mrs Bell kept me at Calpher House rather longer than I expected. I started to get a little nervous in the end. I didn't want to be late, to have you standing waiting outside in the cold. So she sent me in the car.'

'That was nice of her!' Gwen exclaimed, obviously impressed not only by the car but by Mrs Bell as well. She peered into Audra's face, and demanded, 'Well, did you take the job then?'

'Yes, Gwen, I did.'

'Oh, lovey, I *am* glad!' Gwen threw her arms around Audra, hugged her tightly. Audra hugged her back and the two of them clung to each other, did a happy little jig, and then began to laugh uproariously.

Their frivolity was interrupted by a masculine voice, which said, 'They'll be sending the wagon for you two next, the way you're carrying on like a couple of lunatics, and in the middle of City Square, no less.'

'Oh hello, Charlie,' Gwen said, pulling away from Audra, looking up at her brother, who stood with his hands in his pockets, towering over them both, surveying them through amused eyes. 'You're right on time, I see.'

'Aren't I always?' Charles Thornton grinned at his sister, then gave Audra a shy smile. 'Hello, Audra,' he said, unable to keep the look of adoration off his face. He thrust his hand at her.

Audra's heart sank at the sight of Charlie, whom she had not expected to join them for the evening, as he no doubt had. She had wanted to be alone with Gwen. They hadn't seen each other for several weeks and they had a number of things to talk about, especially now that she had taken the job with the Bells.

'Hello,' Audra responded in her quiet way, taking his hand, glad she was wearing her gloves. Charlie always had such clammy hands, even in the cold weather. Audra found this unfortunate physical trait dismaying and distasteful. She liked Charlie well enough as a person but she had no wish to have him as her boyfriend. This was Gwen's hope though, and she was forever pushing Charlie at her. Audra fervently wished she would stop doing it. Charlie Thornton was not her type at all. It was not that he was unattractive, because he wasn't. He was tall, well built, with broad shoulders, very masculine really, although Audra suspected he would become flabby as he grew older. He had blond hair, a fair complexion and friendly grey eyes. His face, like his personality, was bland. Audra could not help thinking that he was soppy in certain ways, and most of the time she found him dreadfully dull. She supposed he was a good person, very worthy, and yet instinctively she knew he was a weak man.

Gwen volunteered, 'Charlie's taking us to the pictures later, Audra. He's treating us. We're going to the Rialto in Briggate to see the new Mary Pickford picture. Isn't that nice of him?'

'Oh yes it is,' Audra was quick to agree and forced a smile.

Taking charge as usual, Gwen rushed on, 'Well, don't let's stand here like three sucking ducks gawping at each other. We've an hour to waste before we go to the pictures, so let's toddle along to Betty's and have a nice cup of tea.'

Audra and Charlie readily agreed.

It had turned even chillier and the snow that had threatened throughout the day began to fall in small fluttering flakes, settling on the ground. The light was being squeezed out of the lowering sky as dusk descended rapidly. Charlie took hold of the girls' arms and hurried them across City Square in the direction of Commercial Street where the café was located. As they turned into the street they all three stopped abruptly, staring into the windows of Harte's department store, captivated by what they saw. The windows had been dressed for Christmas and they were dazzling in the gathering twilight, filled with twinkling coloured lights and glittering scenes depicting different fairy tales. One window was devoted to Cinderella, showed her arriving at the ball in her shimmering glass coach, another to Hansel and Gretel, who stood outside the gingerbread house, and yet a third paid tribute to The Snow Queen in all her icy glory.

'How beautiful they are,' Audra murmured, lingering a moment longer than the other two, thinking of High Cleugh and the glorious Christmases of her childhood.

'Yes, aren't they just,' Gwen said, tugging at her. 'Come on, lovey, the snow's really coming down now. We're going to be soaked before we know it.'

Gwen tucked her arm through Audra's and kept up a continual stream of conversation as they walked down Commercial Street, living up to her reputation as a chatterbox. Charlie, trudging along on the other side of Audra, interjected a few comments, but Audra remained silent – and reflective.

She was suddenly feeling mean and uncharitable for having had such unkind thoughts about Charlie, who was harmless really, and meant well. *All* of the Thorntons meant well, and they had *all* been very good to her. Mrs Thornton was forever telling her to consider The Meadow her home, and she had even turned the little box room at the end of the second-floor landing into a bedroom for her. Mrs Thornton had insisted she keep a few clothes there, and when she had visited Gwen in November she had left behind some toilet articles and a nightgown, which she would be able to use tonight.

Next week she was coming back to Horsforth to spend Christmas with Gwen, and she was well aware that the Thorntons would make her feel like a part of the family, truly one of them, as they always did. They had such a wealth of generosity and kindness in them. *And I'm very ungrateful*, Audra chastised herself. She knew how much it would please Gwen if she were nice to Charlie, and so she resolved to be pleasant to him, but without leading him on, giving him the wrong impression. *He must not misunderstand.* That would be disastrous. And after the holidays she was going to explain to Gwen, in the gentlest and kindest possible way, that she was not looking for a husband.

8

It was a very cold morning. *Icy.*

Perhaps it *would* turn out to be the coldest day of the winter after all, Audra thought, just as the gardener had warned yesterday when she had been returning from her walk. He had put down his wheelbarrow and looked up at the sky, narrowing his eyes and sniffing, as if he had a way of divining such things in this arcane manner.

And then he had made his prediction. 'Yer'll be nithered ter death termorra, Miss Audra. T'weather's coming in bad from t'North Sea. Arctic weather, mark my words, lass.'

She had never been to the Arctic Circle, but she did not imagine it could be any colder than her bedroom at this moment. It was freezing, and it seemed to Audra that her nose, peeping over the bedcovers, had turned into an icicle. An Arctic icicle.

She slithered further down in the bed, hunching the covers up over her shoulders, almost obscuring her face entirely, revelling in the warmth of the quilt. It was filled with the down of the eider duck; Mr and Mrs Bell had purchased a baker's dozen of these quilts when they had been on holiday in Munich several years before.

Mrs Bell had told Audra this when she had come to work at Calpher House, had gone on to explain that the sheet under the quilt was the only other piece of bed linen required. Irène Bell had also cautioned Audra not to wear her thick flannel nightgown, but to discard it in favour of a cotton garment. Although she had nodded her understanding, she had not been absolutely certain that she really understood at all. But later that night, at bed time, she had done as she had been bidden earlier in the day, and within ten minutes of being in bed she had begun to feel a lovely sensation of warmth permeating her whole body. The heat generated by the quilt was extraordinary, something quite amazing to Audra, and she realized that Mrs Bell had been correct about the cotton nightie. Anything else would have been far too hot.

She smiled to herself now, remembering her first night here, and then swivelled her eyes to the clock on the mahogany chest as it began to chime. It was only six but this did not surprise her in the least. She was accustomed to awakening at this hour. It was an old habit left over from her years at the hospital in Ripon. Fortunately the routine was not so rigorous here at Calpher House, and she could stay in bed until seven, even a bit later if she wished.

Audra had truly come to cherish this dawn hour when all the family were asleep and no one was about except for the servants downstairs. She thought of it as her own special and private time, enjoyed the luxury of lingering in her downy cocoon, without having the need to rush, idly drifting with her diverse thoughts ... and sometimes day-dreaming about the future.

And the future seemed decidedly rosy to Audra on this December morning of 1927.

Certainly the years stretching ahead could not be any worse than the five years which had preceded her arrival at Calpher House, she frequently told herself these days. Naturally optimistic, she always looked at things in the most positive way, anticipating the best. She also expected the best from people, despite her distressing experiences with her Aunt Alicia Drummond. Burying the dreadful hurt she had suffered at the hands of that inhuman woman, she would remind herself that not everyone was cruel, selfish or dishonest, that the world *did* have its ample share of kindly folk. And the Bells and their staff at Calpher House had helped to reinforce this belief in Audra. She had been made to feel welcome from the very first day, and she never once forgot how fortunate she had been to find such a congenial place to work.

It was exactly one year ago today that she had started here as the nanny.

From the first moment she had stepped into this house Audra had felt as if she belonged here. It was as if she had returned after a long journey to a place she had always known. In a way it had been like coming home ... home to High Cleugh. It was not that Calpher House resembled her beloved former home; as houses they were entirely different in architecture and furnishings. What she had found so familiar, had recognized with such clarity, was the presence of love within these walls.

For the most part, it was the happiest year that Audra had spent since her mother had died and tragedy had struck their little family.

She fitted in well at Calpher House.

Because of her upbringing, her disposition and personality, everyone found her a pleasure to be around, and she was popular upstairs and downstairs. The Bells were kind and considerate; the servants treated her with a deference and respect that was marked by friendliness.

After years of frugality and spartan living at the hospital, she was now surrounded by enormous luxury and comfort, the likes of which she had never known even at High Cleugh, where money for anything other than the real essentials had been fairly scarce most of the time. All of their pleasant little extras had come from Uncle Peter.

The Bells were successful, affluent people and they could afford the very best. And because of Mrs Bell's generous nature there was an overabundance of everything.

Wonderfully delicious meals emerged from Mrs Jackson's amazing kitchen. She was a gourmet cook, and Audra also got a chance to taste such delicacies as *pâté de foie gras*, caviar and smoked salmon. Crystal dishes of bon-bons and nuts and Turkish Delight were scattered across small occasional tables in the elegant blue living room, for anyone to nibble on who wished, and even the everyday nursery

619

meals could hardly be called *everyday* because of the way they tasted. Such things as steak-and-kidney pudding, apple dumplings, bacon-and-egg pie, Irish stew, and pork, beef and lamb roasts all had the most distinctive, mouth-watering flavours. As far as Audra was concerned, Cook was the first person to rival her mother in a kitchen; Mrs Jackson was forever coming up with something extra-special to tempt their palates. Audra's favourites were Little Pigs of Heaven, a warm chocolate dessert that literally melted in the mouth, and Bandit's Joy, a hot potato dish flavoured with honey and nutmeg that made a perfect accompaniment to saddle of mutton, and she had asked Mrs Jackson for the recipes for these dishes. On very special occasions, Mr Agiter, the butler, had been instructed by Mr Bell to serve her a glass of sparkling, ice-cold champagne. But she was already familiar with this wine, since it had not been out of the ordinary for her Uncle Peter to bring a bottle to celebrate her mother's birthday, or for Christmas Day at High Cleugh. She and Frederick and William had always been allowed one small glass by their mother.

Apart from the wonderful food and vintage wines which seemed to flow without cease at Calpher House, there was a plethora of other things which added their distinctive touches to the sense of opulence that prevailed throughout.

Innumerable bowls and vases of flowers and exotic plants punctuated every room downstairs; the latest magazines and newspapers, current novels and other books spilled over large circular tables in the library, in Mrs Bell's study and most especially in the family parlour where everyone seemed to congregate at night. Sofas and chairs were plump and inviting with piles of soft cushions, or they had their arms draped with fluffy mohair throws from Scotland, to be used on colder evenings wrapped around legs and shoulders.

Startled at first though she had been, and even a bit overwhelmed by all this luxury in one house, Audra had grown accustomed to it. Whilst it would be true to say that she enjoyed the comfort and the cosseting, she nonetheless did not consider it of any great importance in her life. The real reason she was happy at Calpher House was because her employers and the staff were all so nice, really good people who cared about others and their well-being.

These aspects of her job aside, it had been a fine year for Audra Kenton in other respects.

The letters which came from her brothers were much more positive these days, and were written in the same optimistic vein that had enhanced their earliest epistles to her. Frederick was growing stronger in health every week, and things had improved immeasurably for them. They both had good jobs in Sydney at long last. William was working in the circulation department of the Sydney *Morning Herald*; Frederick had become private secretary to an industrialist, a Mr Roland Matheson, and Audra was happy for them, and proud of the way they had coped with their initial bad luck and daunting set-backs. And knowing they were no longer in difficult straits made her own continuing sense of loss and yearning for them that much easier to bear.

Then again, she and Gwen had been able to spend a great deal of their free time together. Mrs Bell had kindly given her permission to invite Gwen to stay overnight at Calpher House on numerous occasions; she herself frequently travelled across to Horsforth to spend her day off with Gwen. Sometimes they took the tramcar into Leeds to browse in the stores and window shop, and she was beginning to know the city well. Quite often they went to the picture house, and recently they had seen their first talking picture, *The Jazz Singer*, starring Al Jolson.

June had been a particularly happy month for Audra, mostly because of the attention everyone paid to her twentieth birthday. How different it had been from the previous year, when she had spent that very special day in her life entirely alone. Her brothers' cards had arrived from Australia not only in time but two days early; on the third, a small celebration was held in the nursery, with presents from the Bells and the staff at Calpher House.

And later that week, on Saturday, Mrs Thornton and Gwen had given a party for her at The Meadow. There had been a splendid summer tea on the lawn. The table, covered in a white cloth, had groaned under the weight of all manner of lovely things – cucumber-and-tomato sandwiches, a Yorkshire pork pie, trifle, strawberries and cream, big pots of hot tea, plus an iced cake with the message *Happy Birthday, Audra* written on it in pink icing sugar and twenty pink candles encircling the edge. And each member of her friend's family had given her a small but significant gift. After tea they had trooped inside for dancing to the latest records, which they had played on Gwen's new gramophone. They had done the Charleston to the strains of 'Black Bottom', 'Aint She Sweet', and 'Yes, Sir, That's My Baby', fox-trotted slowly to 'Blue Skies' and 'Among My Souvenirs', and everyone had thoroughly enjoyed themselves that night.

Charlie had been present, along with his brothers, Jem and Harry, Mike Lesley, his best friend, and a couple of his chums from medical school. He was still attentive to her whenever he got the opportunity, even though she did her level best to discourage him.

Once she had moved to Leeds the previous December and settled in with the Bells, Audra had spoken to Gwen about her brother. She had explained to her friend in the sweetest way that, as nice as Charlie was, he was not for her. She had asked Gwen not to encourage Charlie any more. Gwen had said she understood and agreed at once to stop 'fanning the flames', as she so aptly called it. But Audra had seen the hurt in her friend's eyes and she had quickly added that it had nothing to do with Charlie *per se*, that men in general did not interest her for the time being. She had then announced, and in a very firm voice, that she had no intention of getting married, of settling down, until she was thirty at least.

Gwen had looked at her askance on hearing this, had eyed Audra with a degree of scepticism, but she had refrained from making any sort of comment. At least until last month – November the fifth to be exact – when she had come to Upper Armley to join in their celebrations on Bonfire Night.

Mrs Bell had told Audra she could invite Gwen to spend the night at Calpher House, since they were both off duty the following day. After one of Cook's extra-special nursery teas, and as soon as it grew dark, they had gone outside for the lighting of the bonfire that Fipps, the gardener, had made in the grounds. They had shared the family's fun, watching the fireworks, waving the sparklers which Mr Bell had produced, and eating piping hot chestnuts and roasted potatoes pulled from the embers of the fire. And then the two of them had gone off to the Guy Fawkes Day party and dance at Christ Church Parish Hall in Ridge Road.

Audra first saw the young man when everyone was crowding around the huge bonfire outside the hall, gathered to watch the burning of the effigy of Guy Fawkes. He was alone, standing near the porch, leaning against the wall, smoking a cigarette. As he nonchalantly tossed it to the ground, then stubbed his toe on it, he glanced across at the commotion around the bonfire, noticed her, smiled.

Audra looked back at him and experienced a queer sensation, one that was unfamiliar to her. She felt suddenly faint and a little breathless, as if she had been punched.

His face was clearly illuminated in the glow from the fire and she saw that he was most arresting in appearance.

His dark hair, which came to a widow's peak above a wide brow, was brushed to one side, parted on the left, and he had dark brows, light-coloured eyes. His face was sensitive, but it was the purity reflected in it that struck her so forcibly, made such a strong and lasting impression.

Their eyes connected. And locked. He gave her a hard, penetrating stare.

She flushed to her roots, looked quickly away.

A moment later, when she and Gwen turned around to go into the parochial hall, Audra noticed immediately that he was no longer propping up the wall, and she filled with disappointment.

Once they were inside her eyes searched for him, but in vain. He seemed to have disappeared. She waited for him to come back, but he did not, and the dance fell flat for her after that. As the evening progressed, Audra found it impossible to tear her eyes away from the door for very long, and she silently prayed that he would return. There was something about him that intrigued her.

Although she was asked to dance several times, and accepted these invitations, for most of the evening Audra sat it out on the long bench with the other wallflowers. She was quite content to be an observer, watching the dancers, in particular Gwen, who twirled around the floor with various young bucks from the neighbourhood, obviously enjoying herself immensely. But Audra thought that none of Gwen's partners looked half as handsome or as fascinating as the dark young man who had so engaged her interest earlier.

Audra had almost given up hope that he would make an appearance again when he came barrelling through the door, looking slightly flushed and out of breath, and stood at the far side of the hall, glancing about. At the exact moment that the band leader announced the last waltz he spotted her. His eyes lit up, and he walked directly across the floor to her and, with a faint smile, he asked her if she would care to dance.

Gripped by a sudden internal shaking, unable to speak, Audra nodded and rose.

He was taller than she had realized, at least five feet nine, perhaps six feet, with long legs; lean and slenderly built though he was, he had broad shoulders. There was an easy, natural way about him that communicated itself to her instantly, and he moved with great confidence and panache. He led her on to the floor, took her in his arms masterfully, and swept her away as the band struck up 'The Blue Danube'.

During the course of the dance he made several casual remarks, but Audra, tongue-tied, remained mute, knowing she was unable to respond coherently. He said, at one moment, 'What's up then, cat got your tongue?'

She managed to whisper, 'No.'

Glancing down at her with curiosity, he frowned, but he did not bother to say anything further, appeared to be lost in his thoughts, or concentrating on the dance.

When the music stopped he thanked her politely, escorted her back to the bench, inclined his head, strolled off.

Her eyes followed him all the way to the front door. And as he walked out into the dark winter night she wondered who he was and if she would ever see him again. She desperately hoped she would.

Later when she and Gwen were hurrying up Town Street, making their way back to Calpher House, Gwen suddenly blurted out: 'Well, I must say, for someone who protests they're not interested in men, you were certainly mesmerized by that chap you had the last dance with. But I can tell you this, Audra, he's bad news. Oh yes, definitely, lovey.'

Audra, startled, asked, 'How can you say he's bad news? You don't even *know* him.'

Gwen took hold of Audra's arm in her usual possessive way, slipped her own through it. She said, 'I can tell just by looking at him that he's a real devil. I'm always suspicious of the pretty ones. *Very wary.* They generally end up breaking some poor woman's heart, lovey, maybe even two or three hearts, for that matter. You'd be much better off with somebody like our Charlie. And you know how *he* feels about *you*, lovey. *He hasn't changed.*'

Audra said nothing. Gwen's remarks about the young man irritated and annoyed her. She considered them to be unwarranted and just a shade preposterous under the circumstances. Presumptuous, in fact, and for the first time in their friendship she was put out with Gwen. The next morning, still rankling somewhat, Audra scrupulously avoided referring to the evening before, and she and Gwen did not discuss the young man again.

But Audra could not help thinking about him.

In the days which immediately followed the encounter, she kept recalling certain things about that night and about him ... the way he had looked down at her, narrowly, speculatively, through the greenest eyes she had ever seen ... the turbulent emotions he had aroused in her, feelings she had not believed really existed except in the novels on Mrs Bell's shelves ... his ineffable grace as he had moved them around the dance floor ... the true classical beauty of his face, so unusual in a man.

Now, nearly two months afterwards, Audra was still asking herself why she never ran across him in Upper Armley. Ever since the dance she had expected to do so, and she looked for him when she went out and about with the child who was in her charge. She was convinced the young man came from these parts for she could recognize the local accent when she heard it.

As Audra focused her thoughts on him, an echo of his voice reverberated clearly in her head, and an image of his face leapt before her eyes. And despite the warmth of the quilt, she shivered unexpectedly and goose flesh speckled her skin. She wrapped her arms around her body, hugging herself. She pictured his face close to hers on the pillow, tried to imagine what it would be like to be kissed by him, touched by him, held by him. Since their brief encounter, the mysterious dark young man had haunted her, intruded on her thoughts at the oddest times.

Presently Audra opened her eyes and endeavoured to quench the unfamiliar longings stirring within her. Until she had met *him*, danced with *him*, Audra had never known sexual desire, and of late some of the strange, new feelings she was experiencing confused and frightened her, yet excited her at the same time. She pressed her face into the pillow, wanting to block out the memory of him, and discovered, as she had so often in the past few weeks, that she was unable to expunge the image of his face, his unbelievable eyes. She knew she wanted him.

Turning onto her back, she lay very still, staring up at the ceiling, her eyes wide, unblinking, and she wondered what she would do if she did not run into him again. Dismay gripped her, then instantly dissipated. Audra believed that they *would* meet and that they would come to know each other well. Very well indeed. She felt this in her bones.

A sudden clattering in the corridor outside her bedroom pierced the early morning silence.

Audra started in surprise, then cocked her head, listened. She heard a stifled exclamation, then low unintelligible mutterings, followed by the sound of feet clomping into the adjoining day nursery.

Audra knew that it was Cora going about her morning chores. She suspected that the housemaid had dropped the coal scuttle, which was not an unusual occurrence by any means. Cora, who was perpetually cheerful, had turned out to be a friendly soul, but she was also the clumsiest person Audra had ever met. A day did not go by without a breakage of one kind or another, and the culprit, sadly, was always poor Cora.

There was a loud knock on the door and Cora's scrubbed and shining face appeared around it. 'Mornin', Miss Audra.'

'Good morning, Cora,' Audra said, pushing herself up on one elbow, smiling in the half light.

'Is it all right if I comes in then, Miss Audra? Ter make t'fire for yer?'

'Yes, of course, Cora.'

Cora's plump little body, encased in her pink-striped morning uniform, rotated across the room like a fast-spinning top. She dumped the coal scuttle and the ashpan down on the hearth unceremoniously, then spun over to the huge window. Pulling back the curtains with a great flourish, flooding the room with brilliant sunshine, she exclaimed, 'It's ever so cold out this mornin', Miss. Arctic weather, so Fipps says. Aye, he says it's cold enough ter freeze t'balls off a brass monkey, that he does.'

'Really, Cora!'

'That's what he said ter me, Miss.'

'But you shouldn't repeat something vulgar like that, Cora,' Audra reprimanded softly.

'No, I don't expects I should, least ways not in yer presence, Miss Audra.' This was said somewhat apologetically, but, nevertheless, Cora threw her a cheeky grin as she hurried back to the fireplace. Crouching in front of the grate, she proceeded to take out the ashes. After a short pause, she asked, 'And what are yer doin' termorra night then, Miss Audra?'

'Nothing special, Cora. My friend Miss Thornton is on night duty at the Infirmary for the next two weeks, so I won't be going to any New Year's Eve parties. I'll be staying here at Calpher House.'

'Oh but Mr Agiter allus has a party for t'staff yer knows.' Cora glanced over her shoulder, smiled with her usual engaging cheerfulness, added, 'Yer were ever so shy last December, when yer first started here, and yer wouldn't come downstairs, but I hopes yer'll be with us this year, ooh I *do*, Miss Audra, ever so much.'

'Yes, I will, Cora. Mr Agiter has already invited me, and I'm looking forward to joining you all for a glass of champagne around midnight . . . to toast in 1928.'

Audra had grown to love Theophilus, Theo for short, in the year she had been taking care of him.

He was an odd-looking little boy, not exactly plain, but then neither was he fancy.

The first time she had set eyes on him she decided that he was highly individualistic. This turned out to be true – and in many more ways than merely his appearance. Theophilus had a plump, perfectly round little face, not unlike a suet pudding, but his skin was pink and white rather than doughy or pasty in colour. His fair hair, soft, silky, straight, had a way of flopping down over two very sharply-observing black eyes that resembled bright little chips of coal, and he was forever pushing it away with an impatient gesture.

It often struck Audra that these very dark eyes and the pale blond hair didn't quite go together, but then that was Theophilus. He seemed to be made up entirely of spare parts, each bit individually attractive if not specifically designed to go with the others.

Not matched up, are you, my little love? Audra murmured under her breath as she brushed his hair. His appearance usually preoccupied her for a few minutes before they went out, and this morning was no exception. She put the brush down, stepped away, regarded him critically, her head on one side. Reaching out, she straightened his tie, nodded in satisfaction, then bending over, she planted a kiss on his cheek.

'There you are, all ready!' she exclaimed, taking his hands in hers, helping him to jump down off the table. 'And you're as bright as a new penny today, Theo.'

He looked up at her through solemn eyes which were curiously wise and knowing for a six-year-old. 'I hope the doctor also thinks that.'

She bit back a smile of amusement, said, 'I'm sure he will. Now, run along to see your mother, whilst I get my things together, and then we can be off.'

'Oh yes, I had better do that. Before she leaves for Leeds. My spending money is due today.' He set his face determinedly, marched towards the door in small but purposeful strides and disappeared into the corridor.

Audra watched him go, turned away, laughing to herself as she crossed the spacious and comfortably furnished day nursery. She had a few minutes to spare before following the boy downstairs and she stood with her back to the fire, warming herself, thinking of her young charge.

Theophilus Bell never ceased to amaze and amuse Audra. He was a precocious child, although his precocity was not offensive. Cook said he was 'old-fashioned' and this description fitted him perfectly. Audra was not a bit surprised he was the way he was – so serious and self-possessed. He had spent most of his young life with adults; even his sisters were much older than he. Pandora, who had married in the spring and moved out of Calpher House, was twenty-two. Antonia and Felicity, both now attending finishing school in Switzerland, were nineteen and eighteen respectively; all three happened to be sophisticated young women who were well educated, well travelled and had been exposed to a variety of people and a great deal of radical thought in this house. And so they also were much older than their years and, not unnaturally, they had had an influence on their small brother. The girls called Theo 'the afterthought', and although Audra disliked this term, considered it to be rather unkind, she realized that there was a degree of truth in it. He had been born to Mrs Bell when she was forty-two, long after she had expected to bear any more children, and, as she had said to Audra, 'Theo just missed being a change-of-life baby, thank heavens.'

Audra considered it a small miracle that the Bells had not fallen into the usual trap of pampering and spoiling Theo, which so often happened to an only son who came to his parents later in life and who was their pride and joy. He *was* indulged occasionally, but this seemed to have little or no effect on him, and he was not given to making excessive demands on anyone, nor was he a temperamental child.

In actuality, Theo was a lot like his mother. Certainly he had inherited Irène Bell's quick-wittedness, her intelligence and her studious nature. And if he was sometimes unnerving in his forthrightness, he was, nevertheless, a good child, very obedient; he had never given Audra one moment's trouble in the past twelve months.

Ten loud chimes, echoing through from the bedroom, suddenly alerted Audra to the hour. Theo had been suffering with a sore throat, and although he was better she was taking him to the doctor this morning for a check-up.

Hurrying through into the other room, she glanced at herself in the glass, smoothed one hand over her hair, newly bobbed that summer, then went to the wardrobe in the corner. She took out her heavy winter coat and hat, and a thick woollen scarf and gloves in anticipation of the Arctic weather which had apparently descended on them, just as the gardener had predicted it would yesterday.

9

His name was Vincent Crowther and he was something of a rebel.

He was born in the year 1903, at five minutes to midnight on the twelfth day of June, in the middle of the worst thunderstorm the new century had witnessed.

A lusty, robust nine-pound baby, he came screaming into the world, fists flailing, face red and contorted, and giving vent to such a fierce and angry display of temperament the doctor told the midwife that the baby's tantrums were only out-matched by the violence of the weather outside.

His mother secretly called him her Stormy Petrel thereafter, and she was the least surprised of anyone when her rebellious child grew up to be an equally rebellious man, one who was a maverick, who always stood out in a crowd.

He was a natural star, one who drew others to him by sheer force of personality, dashing looks and more than his fair share of a most beguiling charm. Further, it did him no harm that he had what his father called 'the gift of the gab'.

The first born of Eliza and Alfred Crowther's eight children, Vincent boasted an almost feminine beauty as a child, but this turned into a masculine type of handsomeness as he matured to manhood. And there never was any question about his virility. It was like a gloss on him. In consequence, women fell at his feet swooning and they had done so since he was sixteen. He was well versed in their ways and in love and sex; he was master of these games at a very tender age, had broken many a heart. He was twenty-four.

His looks dazzled.

It was his colouring that was so sensational. The gleaming black hair and the black brows were in marked contrast to a light, creamy complexion and cheeks that held a tinge of pink like the bloom on a peach; he had cool green eyes, the colour of light, clear tourmalines, fringed with thick black lashes. His eyes and his skin were the envy of his sisters – and most other women.

Matched to the striking colouring and handsome profile was a superb athletic body. He was exactly five feet nine and a half inches tall, well muscled, firm and taut and without one ounce of fat or flab on him.

Immaculate at all times, Vincent considered himself to be a bit of a dandy, loved clothes, wore them with flair and elegance. He cut quite a swathe wherever he went, especially on the dance floor, where his easy grace and good looks showed to such advantage.

He was his mother's favourite.

His siblings were aware of this. They did not care. Neither were they jealous. In fact, they shared their mother's feelings about him. His brothers admired or hero-worshipped him; his sisters adored him.

Only his father treated him like a normal, ordinary person.

Alfred Crowther loved his first-born child, but he had no illusions about him. A former sergeant-major in the Seaforth Highlanders, Alfred was a veteran of two great wars, having fought the Boers on the African veldt and the Germans on the fields of Flanders. Subsequently, he knew men and their motivations, could read them well, and his own son was no exception. He had a great deal of insight into Vincent.

Alfred recognized there was a lot of devilishness in the boy, not to mention temperament, stubbornness and a good measure of vanity. He thought Vincent was too handsome by far for his own good. But, being a realist, Alfred knew there was not much point in worrying about this eldest child of his who had been born with the looks of a matinée idol. Fretting would not alter these facts nor accomplish anything. The elder Crowther believed that what was meant to happen eventually happened. His fatalistic attitude could be ascribed to his Irish mother, Martha, who, when he was growing up, had constantly told him, 'What will be, will be, Alf, sure an' it will. 'Tis *preordained*, I am thinkin', this life each one of us poor souls be livin' in this hard and cruel world.'

Father and son were good friends. They enjoyed sharing a pint of beer, usually stopped off at the pub together at weekends, and often they went to race meetings in Doncaster and York, especially in the summer weather. However, despite a certain masculine camaraderie, there was not as much intimacy between them as might have been expected. It was his mother who was Vincent's confidante and friend. She always had been. She always would be – until the day she died.

His manifest physical attributes and pleasant demeanour aside, Vincent Crowther was no dunce. He was quick, bright, and intelligent; he had powerful analytical ability, and a retentive memory.

But coming from the working class as he did, he had left Armley Council School when he was fourteen and had found himself a job in one of the tailoring shops in Armley. He had quickly grown bored, mainly because his interests lay elsewhere. He was particularly drawn to building and construction and frequently wished he could have studied architecture.

After leaving the tailoring shop, he had a short spell labouring in the local brickyard, before finally finding an opening with a building firm. He was currently learning his trade; he liked working in the open air, drew pleasure and satisfaction from seeing each building take shape and grow and so fulfil the architect's original vision.

Sometimes Vincent told himself he was going to enrol in night school in Leeds, to learn draughtsmanship, but he put this off, was always sidetracked and distracted by other more pleasurable activities. He was partial to dancing and he had been a voracious reader when a boy, but otherwise he had no real hobbies to speak of. For the most part, he spent his free time drinking with his cronies and could usually be found propping up the bar in the tap room of one of the local pubs, quaffing down pints or studying a *tissue*, the pink racing sheet that was published every week day and was his bible.

He was engrossed in his *tissue* on this cold Saturday morning in late December, wondering which horses to back at today's Doncaster races. In particular he was concentrating on the runners in the one o'clock race, turning the salient facts over in his clever mind, considering the virtues and the weaknesses of the trainers and the jockeys as well as those of the different horses, and carefully weighing the odds.

Vincent was seated at the table in the centre of the basement kitchen in the Crowther home in Armley, a tall, Victorian terrace house with two upper floors and huge attics under the eaves. The kitchen, with a big window fronting onto a patch of garden and yard, was a large yet cosy room; eminently inviting, it was comfortably furnished in the manner of a parlour, which was the custom in these parts.

The focal point in the room was the fireplace. This was actually a Yorkshire range, so called because it combined an open fire with an adjoining oven. The range also boasted an arm for supporting a kettle or a stew pot over the fire, and a boiler for heating water. All of these elements were built into the one unit which was about four and a half feet in height and the same in width.

The black iron range was surmounted by a heavy polished wood mantelpiece. On this stood a fancy chiming clock, two brass candlesticks, a tobacco jar, a rack holding Alfred's pipes and a container of spills. The hearth was encircled by a heavy brass fender that was cleaned with Brasso by one of the girls every Friday, and it glittered like gold in the dancing flames of the fire, banked high up the chimney back. Two green-moquette wing chairs flanked the fireplace, faced each other across a large broadloom rug patterned with blood red roses on a deep green background.

In point of fact, roses abounded in this kitchen. They were Eliza's favourite flowers. Pink and white cabbage roses entwined into garlands flowed down the wallpaper to meet scarlet rambler roses scattered all over the green linoleum; rose-patterned white china filled the shelves of a Welsh dresser positioned in a corner; pillows embroidered with yellow rosebuds marched across the dark green leather sofa set against the far wall.

It was a cheerful room with a gay and welcoming ambience, and it was generally the centre of activity, the heart of the family's home life. But this morning it was strangely silent and deserted.

Vincent was alone.

He was glad to have peace and quiet for once, to be able to pursue the serious work of picking out his potential winners in absolute tranquillity, without the distracting racket often created by some of his brothers and sisters.

Taking a sip of tea, he continued to peer at the racing newspaper, frowning to himself in his concentration. He had been at this task for almost an hour, and at last he made several selections, wrote down the names of his horses on a scrap of paper, sat staring at the list for a moment. Slowly he nodded his head, satisfied he had made the best choices, then he reached for the packet of Woodbines.

He leaned back in his chair, sat smoking reflectively.

For no reason at all he suddenly thought of the girl. *Again.* She had a way of popping into his head when he least expected. He had met her only once in his life, but when he closed his eyes he could see her face so clearly, and in such detail, he might have known her forever.

When he had first noticed her standing near the bonfire in the grounds of the Parish Hall, he had instantly and instinctively understood, and without the benefit of knowing her, that she was not the type of young woman whom a man played around with. *She was serious business.*

And since he was not interested in being serious with any girl, or of starting a relationship that would lead to the terrible bondage of marriage, he had fled, rushed to the White Horse for a game of darts and a drink with the lads. But just before ten o'clock he had run all the way back to the hall, hoping to have the last waltz with her.

How shy she had been, so stiff and unbending. Her manner and her attitude had put him off, and he had wandered out of the hall, discouraged, and also baffled by her, asking himself why she had bothered to dance with him in the first place. She could have so easily declined his invitation.

But he had been unable to forget her.

Vincent sighed, took a long drag on his cigarette, blew smoke rings up into the air, watched them float away and evaporate as they did. And he decided that thinking about the diminutive Venus de Milo of the bright blue eyes and gorgeous legs was a hopeless waste of time. For one thing, she had apparently evaporated – just like the smoke rings. Ever since bonfire night, he had made a point of popping down to the church dances for a few minutes, looking for her, and he had kept his eyes peeled when he had gone about his business in Armley. He had never once run into her. Furthermore, none of the regulars who attended the church dances every Wednesday and Saturday seemed to know who she was. He had made innumerable inquiries about her for the past two months. The only bit of information he had been able to garner was that her busty blonde girlfriend, also nameless it seemed, was a nurse at the Infirmary. Some good that did him. He knew he had about as much chance of ever meeting Blue Eyes again as a snowball in hell.

Perhaps that's just as well, he muttered under his breath. All I need is a *steady* . . . not bloody likely I don't.

At this moment the front door flew open so unexpectedly and with such force Vincent sat up with a jerk, looking startled. An icy blast of air blew right through the kitchen, chilling him. It brought with it Laurette and Maggie, two of his three sisters.

They had been to the Co-op to do the weekend shopping and each carried two bags filled to overflowing. They were bundled up in navy-blue winter topcoats, green-and-black tartan tam o'shanters and matching long woollen scarves. The cold wind had given them polished apple cheeks, turned their noses into bright red cherries. Their eyes sparkled and there was such a gaiety and liveliness about them they brought a delighted smile to his face.

'Hello, Vincent,' they chorused, grinning at him.

'Hello, you two beauties,' he responded, then exclaimed, 'For God's sake close that door, Maggie.'

'Oh, sorry,' the twelve-year-old girl said, and pushed it with her foot. It banged so hard the frosted-glass panel rattled.

'Watch that glass!' Vincent cautioned and shook his head, mildy exasperated with her.

Maggie mumbled, 'Sorry,' and followed her elder sister to the counter near the sink, where she deposited her bags of groceries.

Turning to face her brother, starting to unbutton her coat, Laurette said, 'It's very quiet in here, Vincent. Where is everybody then?'

'Upstairs. Or out.'

'Who's upstairs?' Maggie asked, always inquisitive. Shedding her coat she flung it down on the sofa.

'Hang that up, young lady,' Laurette instructed, giving her a sharp look.

Maggie pulled a face but she did as she was told. She pressed, 'Who's upstairs then?'

'Our Mam. She's dusting the front rooms. And Jack, who's reading to Danny. Mam says he's got to stay in bed today – because of his bad cold,' Vincent explained.

'I knew it! I just knew he wouldn't be any better!' Maggie cried shrilly, rolling her eyes dramatically, showing exaggerated alarm. 'I *told* Mam that. He coughed and coughed all night. Poor little Danny, he's always badly. But what can you expect, he's the runt of the litter.' She continued to cluck sympathetically like a middle-aged matron of vast experience, then finished in a superior, knowing tone, 'Change-of-life babies are often weak in health.'

Vincent averted his head, biting down on his laughter. Maggie was a card. None of them ever knew what she would come out with next. His father said she was as old as the hills.

Laurette, however, was not in the least amused and the look she gave her young sister was stern, disapproving. She thought Maggie was impertinent at times, that the girl saw and heard far too much for her age. But Laurette said nothing. She walked over to the cupboard and put her own things away. Then she took a cup and saucer out of the cupboard above the sink, joined Vincent at the table. She lifted the cosy, felt the pot, poured herself a cup of tea, added milk and sugar.

Vincent watched her all the while, his expression loving, caring. He was concerned about Laurette's well-being at the moment. Just over a year ago she had married their first cousin Jimmy, but it had not worked out. She had come back home to live three months ago, much to his relief. He had believed that particular union to be doomed right from the outset, had never had much time for his cousin, whom he considered to be a bit of a wet rag.

Laurette was a sweet-natured girl, and at twenty-two she was the nearest to Vincent in age. They had always been very close. She was lovely looking with fair, wavy hair, a sensitive face and grey eyes that were enigmatic and soulful. Tall, slender, she had a frame and a build similar to her brother's, but it was young Maggie who truly resembled him, with her gypsy-dark hair, widow's peak and large green eyes that were a reflection of his. Olive, the middle sister, was more like Laurette to look at, but she too had dark hair, and she had inherited her mother's pale blue eyes. Olive, who was twenty, had married her childhood sweetheart when she was eighteen and she and her husband Hal lived near by.

Maggie joined Vincent and Laurette at the kitchen table.

She stood next to her favourite brother, rested one hand on his shoulder and with the other she slapped a packet of Woodbines down in front of him, along with some loose change.

'Here's your cigs, our Vincent. And don't smoke 'em all at once either. Because I'm not going out again today. Not for nobody I'm not. Not even you. So there!' Flopping down on the chair next to him she threw him a challenging look, added, 'If you want to know, I'm fed up being everybody's blinking errand boy!'

He threw back his head and roared. 'Aren't you the tough little tiddler this morning. But thanks for getting my cigs, love.'

Laurette said, 'I can't believe everybody went out . . . on a cruel day like this . . . why, it's blue murder out there, Vincent. Where on earth have they all gone?'

'Dad went to the barber's to get a hair cut. Our Frank, the aspiring equestrian, is at Hardcastle's stables, helping to exercise the horses. And the learned Bill took his books back to the library.'

'I see.' Laurette sipped her tea. There was a short pause. Then she asked, 'Olive's not been up this morning, has she?'

'No, not yet.'

'Oh I am glad I haven't missed her. We're supposed to be going to the old-time dancing tonight, and I want to make my arrangements with her.' Laurette paused and smiled at her brother as an idea struck her. 'Would you like to come with us, Vincent?'

'I would!' Maggie interjected eagerly, swinging her eyes to her sister. 'Let me come with you and Olive, Laurette. *Please*.'

'No, you can't, you're too young,' Laurette said. 'Well, Vincent, what about it?'

He shook his head. 'No, thanks for asking, though.'

'But why not?' Laurette demanded. 'You'd enjoy it. Come on, say you'll come with us.'

He shook his head more vehemently.

Maggie cried, 'Oh he doesn't want to go *there*, Laurette! It's too tame. He always goes to the *pub* on Saturday nights. But first he goes down to the Parish Hall and has a look round . . . giving all the girls the once over, that's what I've heard. I bet that's why he stands in front of that there mirror over there, titivating himself for hours on end. I'm not surprised it drives our dad bats. He's vain, our Vincent is, and he fancies himself. Anybody would think he's a girl the way he looks in the glass all the time.'

Vincent flushed, glared at her. 'You're getting to be a right cheeky little bugger, do you know that, our Maggie?'

Maggie stiffened in her chair, shrieked, 'You'd better not let me dad hear you call me that, our Vincent! Or he'll land you a clout that'll send you right into the middle of next week!'

'Huh! Fat chance of that!' Vincent shot back.

'Now you two, quieten down,' Laurette hushed, scowling at them. She wagged a finger at Maggie. 'You *are* getting too big for your breeches, and so you'd better watch it from now on. As for you, Vincent, you ought to know better than to swear at her. Mam doesn't like that either, you know.'

'Aye,' Vincent muttered, annoyed with himself for letting the girl get his goat in the way that she had.

Maggie, genuinely regretting that she had teased him, leaned across the table, peered into his handsome face, saw that it was cold and closed. She filled with chagrin, said softly, 'I'm ever so sorry, Vincent, really I am.' She reached out, squeezed his arm. 'Let's be friends again. Oh and by the by, you said you'd give me something, for going for your Woodbines.'

'If you're not careful it'll be a thick ear,' he growled.

'Well, I never!' Maggie gasped. 'It's the last time I'll do an errand for you, Vincent Crowther. You don't keep your promises.'

For a reason he couldn't explain he began to laugh. His eyes twinkled as he reached out, rumpled his little sister's hair. Then he pushed a sixpence towards her. 'There you are, love, that's for your money box.'

Maggie beamed at him. 'Oh no, I'm going to spend it immediately. Thanks.'

Vincent gave Laurette a curious glance, asked, 'And who's taking you to the old time-dancing? Allan Turner?'

Laurette's eyes glowed. She broke into smiles, nodded. 'Yes.'

Vincent was thoughtful. After lighting a cigarette he murmured in a low tone, 'Don't you think it's about time you settled things with Jimmy? Went to see a solicitor in Leeds . . . about a divorce?'

'Yes, it is, and, as a matter of fact, I have an appointment with a solicitor next Saturday. Jimmy's agreed to everything.'

'Dad's going to be ever so pleased to hear *that*!' Maggie announced before Vincent had a chance to say a word. 'He never did think much of that marriage of yours, Laurette. He says that's how idiots get born . . . first cousins marrying and having babies, I mean.'

Laurette gaped at her. She paled and her soft grey eyes suddenly swam. She stood up unsteadily, rushed over to the door leading to the staircase, yanked it open. 'I think I'll go and help Mam,' she whispered in a hoarse voice and flew up the stairs.

Vincent was furious with Maggie and he turned on her angrily. 'Will you never learn, lass? Your mouth's always open and your foot's always in it, for Christ's sake!'

'What have I said *wrong* then?' Maggie wailed. 'And anyway, our dad *didn't* like her marrying Jimmy Wells.'

Vincent sprang up, his anger spiralling. He looked down at his youngest sister in dismay. It took all of his self-control to keep his hands off her. He wanted to shake her until she rattled. Finally he said, 'You know as well as I do how upset Laurette's been because she didn't get pregnant.'

Her defiance fully intact, Maggie declared, 'Well, if what Dad says is true, it's a good job she didn't, and that's a fact!'

Vincent lifted his eyes to the ceiling, groaned out loud. 'Old wives' tales . . . our dad's out of date, living in Dick's days.' He strode across to the cupboard, took out his overcoat.

Maggie cried, 'Where are you going, Vincent?'

'Anywhere to escape you.'

10

Vincent saw her through the window of the pet shop.

For a moment he could not believe his eyes, could not believe it was really her.

He stood staring, transfixed. And then he cupped his hands around his face, pressed closer to the glass. Oh yes, it was her all right. As large as life, looking at budgies. Then he noticed the child standing next to her.

Vincent's heart took a dip to his boots.

Was she a married woman? No, that was not possible. She had not been wearing a ring at the dance. And she was certainly too young to have a child as big as the one accompanying her. No, the boy was most likely her brother. And she was probably buying him a budgie, just as he himself had decided to buy his little brother Danny a pet of some sort. That was the reason he had directed his steps towards the shop in the first place.

Well, Vincent thought, standing here isn't going to get me anywhere, so I might as well go inside. His hand went to his tie automatically, and he straightened the knot, then, taking a deep breath, he opened the shop door.

The tinkling of the bell caused the girl to glance over her shoulder. At the sight of him her eyes widened. Seemingly she was as astonished as he had been a moment before.

Vincent smiled at her.

She smiled back, her face dimpling.

He thought her smile was quite the most dazzling he had seen in a long time. Encouraged, he strode across the shop, very determined.

She turned around to face him, watched his progress in her direction with quickening interest.

As he drew to a standstill in front of her, Vincent saw the expectant look in her eyes. He took off his hat, stood holding it in his hands. He smiled again, said, 'Excuse me . . . I wonder if you remember me?'

'Why yes, of course I do. We had the last waltz at the Parish Hall . . . on Bonfire Night. And I must apologize for not thanking you for asking me to dance that evening. You must have thought me very ungracious.'

She was a lady. He stared at her, startled, and momentarily flustered. His voice fled and so did his nerve. Why would a girl of her obvious breeding be interested in the likes of him? he wondered, clutching his hat all that much tighter. A feeling of enormous disappointment trickled through him. *She* was beyond *his* reach. Oh yes, most assuredly she was. And just as she had been tongue-tied at the dance, now it was his turn to be struck dumb, and he felt like a ninny.

There was an awkward silence.

It was the child who broke it. He asked, in a shrill little voice, 'What's *your* name?'

The girl exclaimed sharply, but in a low tone, 'Now, now, that's most rude of you. Mind your manners, young man.'

'It's Vincent Crowther,' Vincent said, swiftly, grabbing this opportunity. He was surprised that his voice sounded so normal and this helped to restore his diminished confidence. He glanced down at the boy and grinned at him, thankful for his presence.

The child turned his small bright face up to Vincent's, thrust his hand towards him, announced, 'And I'm Theophilus Bell of Calpher House, Upper Armley.'

Vincent shook his hand, endeavouring to match the child's enormous solemnity as he said, 'I'm very pleased to meet you. And if you don't mind me saying so, that's quite a mouthful of a name you've got, by gum it is, lad.'

'It means *beloved of God* in Greek,' Theophilus explained, puffing out his little chest importantly. He gave Vincent a shimmering smile and added, 'But you can call me Theo for short.'

'That's right nice of you. Thanks very much, I will.' Raising his head, Vincent now directed his gaze at the young woman. He cleared his throat, and having entirely regained his composure, not to mention his cool cheek, he gave her his most engaging smile. 'Well,' he said, 'you know my name. Can I have the honour of knowing yours?'

'Yes, of course you may, Mr Crowther. It's Audra Kenton.' Her smile was warm, and as friendly as his had been, and she offered him her hand.

Vincent took it in his, was surprised at the firmness of her grip, the strength in her hand as she shook his. Such a small hand it was too, just as she herself was small and delicate. He held onto her hand for longer than was necessary, unable to release it as he gazed into her clear, very bright blue eyes which reminded him of cornflowers. Unexpectedly, he thought: *I cannot let this woman go. Never. Ever. I want her for the rest of my life.*

He was appalled at his thoughts.

He blinked, finally let go of her hand, glanced away, and he was struck at once by the irrationality of his feelings. The mere idea of marriage was absurd, and to this woman it was positively ludicrous. She was different. Special. A lady. And one who would hardly be interested in *him*, a bricklayer learning his trade. She was obviously a relation of the Bells, who were local gentry, posh folk with pots and pots of brass and lots of clout in the neighbourhood. These facts aside, marriage was not part of his present plans; he had a lot of living to do before tying himself to a woman's apron strings. That was a mug's game. Why, he wouldn't even be twenty-five until June.

All of this had flashed through Vincent's head in a matter of seconds and now he wanted to run out of the shop immediately, to escape before it was too late. But to his own irritation he discovered he could not move. He was rooted to the spot. Suddenly he felt uncomfortable, ill at ease with himself and, therefore, with her, and he began to twist the brim of his trilby in his hands.

Theophilus tugged at Vincent's coat, piped up, '*We're* looking for a budgerigar, Mr Crowther. What've *you* come to buy?'

Thank God for the boy, Vincent thought. He said, 'Well, I don't rightly know, if you want the honest truth.' Giving his entire attention to the child, he stooped down, confided, 'You see, Theo, I came to get something for my little brother. He's four. But I didn't think to ask him what he'd like before I left the house. So now I'm stuck, sort of. You look like an experienced young man when it comes to pets. Maybe you could make a suggestion or two.'

'Mmmm. Let me think a minute.' Theo nodded his head sagely, pursed his lips, adopted an expression of great concentration. He swung his observant eyes around the pet shop, leaned into Vincent and said, 'It's a bit difficult really, making a proper suggestion, I mean. There's not much to choose from, you see.'

Vincent burst out laughing at the boy's pithiness, his blunt words. 'You'd better not let Mr Harrison hear you say that. He thinks he owns the best pet shop in Armley.'

'And he does, since it's the only one,' Theo replied, grinning, looking inordinately pleased with himself.

'Little boys are meant to be seen and not heard,' Audra remarked. But this was the mildest of chastisements. Laughter bubbled up in her throat and her eyes danced. She glanced at Vincent, then shrugged. She murmured, 'What can you do?'

Vincent said, 'He's a right rum 'un, he is that.'

Theo's beady black eyes, swivelling between the two of them, settled on Vincent, who obviously fascinated him. He said, 'I think you should buy your brother a budgie. At least Mr Harrison has a big lot of those to choose from. Come on, Mr Crowther, let me show you.' He plucked at Vincent's sleeve. 'What's his name? Your brother, I mean.'

'Danny.' Vincent allowed himself to be led over to the many bird cages which lined one wall of the shop. He and the boy stood regarding them with interest, and after a moment Vincent said, and with some admiration, 'I'll say this, Theo, they are beautiful.'

Now Audra joined them. Vincent was instantly conscious of her coming to a stop next to him. He was troubled by the emotions she evoked in him, by the strong physical attraction he felt for her. He wanted to take hold of her hand, lead her out of this shop, go with her somewhere so that they could be alone. He wanted to crush her in his arms, to make love to her. His longing stirred within him and he felt the heat rise up into his face. He swallowed hard, tried to concentrate on the birds.

Presently, Audra said, 'Theo wants that one over there, on the right, Mr Crowther. The one in the green cage. What do you think? Do you like it?'

Vincent could only nod.

Theo said, 'Audra's buying it for me, Mr Crowther.'

'Aren't you the lucky little lad,' he managed to mutter.

'Yes, I am. Go on, Mr Crowther, pick a budgie for Danny. They're easy to look after. You don't have to walk them like a dog and they don't cost a lot to keep in food. They don't eat much.'

'True,' Vincent agreed. He was in control again, and he exchanged an amused look with Audra.

Theo pressed on relentlessly. 'Now just look at this one! What a pretty bird. I bet Danny would like it. And it's a lovely example of the Australian parakeet . . .

635

greenish-yellow body, bright blue on the cheeks and tail feathers, and brown stripes down the wings.'

'*Parakeet*,' Vincent repeated, sounding baffled. He frowned at Theo. 'I thought these were budgies.'

'They are. But the budgerigar comes from the parrot family, and there are three hundred and fifteen species of colourful birds in that family,' Theo told him proudly, enjoying airing his knowledge. 'Lovebirds, lories, cockatoos, cockatiels and macaws, to name a few. I wanted a parrot. I was going to teach it to talk. To say rude words. But you have to be careful when you buy parrots. Because of psittacosis. That's parrot fever, and it's an infectious disease that *people* can catch. It's a bit like pneumonia. Anyway, Mr Harrison doesn't have any parrots in stock. That's why I'm getting a budgie instead. But one day I *will* own a parrot.'

Looking at the child in amazement, shaking his head, Vincent said, 'For a little nipper you're certainly a mine of information, Theo. That you are. You sound as if you've swallowed an encyclopedia. *Is* that where you get all of your facts from then?'

'Oh no, I get them from Audra,' Theo explained. 'She's very clever, you know, and she's taught me a lot since she's been with me. My mother says she's the best nanny I've ever had. If you don't wish to get Danny a budgie, you could buy him one of those canaries over there. *They're* from the finch family.' Theo drew Vincent's attention to the other birds, continued, 'They're pretty too, but the best thing about them is that they actually *sing*. I know Danny would like to own a canary. You'd have to teach him to sing, though. The canary, I mean, not Danny.'

'Yes, I understand,' Vincent said absently. *Nanny*, he repeated to himself. She was the boy's *nanny*, for God's sake, not a posh relative of the Bells after all. She was one of their employees. Of course, that did not alter the facts one iota. Audra Kenton was still a lady. But a lady who worked for a living. Impoverished gentility, he decided.

Perhaps she was not beyond his reach after all. Vincent's hopes soared. His heart leapt.

The three of them walked up Town Street together.

Vincent carried the birdcage for Audra. They had bought similar budgerigars in the end, but Vincent had told Joe Harrison to hold his until he returned for it a bit later in the day. And then he had asked Audra if he could escort her and the boy back to Calpher House. She had said yes. Hoisting the birdcage in one hand, he had opened the shop door with the other and ushered her out, grinning from ear to ear, and congratulating himself on his luck this morning.

Now they walked along at a steady pace, side by side and in step, not speaking but comfortable in the silence drifting between them. Theo frisked ahead like a happy little puppy.

Although it was almost noon it was still quite raw, but the wind had died away and it was a shimmering kind of day, crystal clear. The sky, so high and vast above them, was cerulean blue, cloudless, pristine, and bathed in the silver light of a cold winter sun.

It's turned out to be magnificent, Audra thought, looking about, smiling with pleasure. A tiny burst of joy surged through her, filled her with a lovely inner warmth. A day like this made you realize that anything was possible in life. Anything at all.

Vincent breathed deeply, took a lungful or two of icy air, feeling healthy and robust, as he always did in this type of bright and bracing weather. He stole a surreptitious glance at Audra, thinking how smart she looked, and then he realized how proud he was to be with her – and to be seen with her in Town Street, the main thoroughfare in Armley and as busy today as it usually was on Saturdays.

Before they reached Calpher House he was going to invite her out, Vincent now decided, even though he was a bit nervous about doing so. If she refused him he would feel like a damned fool; on the other hand, if he didn't ask her he would never know. He wondered where to take her if she did accept. That was a problem. Perhaps he should bring her to their New Year's Eve party tomorrow. No, that wouldn't work. The poor girl would be overwhelmed by his boisterous family. Besides, on their first date he wanted to have her all to himself. He began to wrack his brains for a suitable place to go.

Audra, also lost in her private musings, felt as though she was floating, so buoyed up was she. For two months she had held onto the belief that they would meet again one day, but when he had walked into the pet shop she had been completely taken aback. Initially. And then, within minutes, it had all seemed so natural. She knew it was meant to be. The awkwardness she had experienced at the dance was no longer in evidence, and she did not feel in the least shy with him. Quite the contrary, in fact.

He was even more handsome than she remembered, immaculate in his appearance, and as well dressed as he had been at the dance. He was a charming young man with a pleasant personality, and the way he had behaved with the child had only made her like him all the more. Audra smiled. *Like* was a funny word to use. It hardly described her feelings. She had fallen in love with him in the pet shop.

She looked up at him through the corner of her eye. He was the only man for her. The only man she would ever want.

Vincent glanced down as she was looking up.

Their eyes met and held for a brief moment. He smiled at her, lovingly. She smiled back, a little tremulously. A very intimate communication passed between them at this precise moment, and they both caught their breath, staring at each other. And then fully understanding what had been conveyed without benefit of words, they instantly averted their faces, stared ahead, walked on in silence.

After a short while, Vincent finally spoke. He said, 'I hope you don't think I'm being nosy, but how long have you worked for the Bells then?'

'A year,' Audra replied. 'As a matter of fact, Mr Crowther, it's exactly one year ago today that I started my job at Calpher House. That's why I bought Theo the bird. As an anniversary gift.'

'They should be giving you presents,' he said gruffly before he could stop himself. And then for a reason he could not fathom he experienced a small stab of resentment towards the Bell family.

Audra had caught the odd, disgruntled tone, and she eyed him curiously, for a moment puzzled. But then she smiled at him prettily and said, 'They did, Mr Crowther. At breakfast this morning.'

'Well, that's good then, isn't it. I'm glad.' He cleared his throat rather loudly and went on, 'You don't come from these parts, I can tell that by your voice. You don't speak with a Leeds accent. So where are you from?'

'Ripon's my home town, and that's where I lived until last year. Have you ever been there, Mr Crowther?'

'Yes, I have, to the races. It's a lovely spot.' His green eyes gleamed with mischief. 'And lucky for me, I don't mind telling you. I've always managed to win a bob or two at Ripon races, and there are some nice pubs there too.'

Audra nodded. 'Yes. And you're from this area, aren't you, Mr Crowther?'

'Oh aye, I am that. Armley born and bred, that's me. And listen a minute, would you mind calling me Vincent? I keep thinking you're addressing me dad every time you say Mr Crowther.'

Audra laughed. 'Of course I will, and you must call me Audra.'

'Done,' he cried and came to a sudden and abrupt stop. He took hold of her arm and gently broke her stride.

She stared up at him, frowning.

Vincent said, in a rush of words, 'Will you go out with me tonight, Audra? I'd like to take you somewhere nice. Maybe into Leeds, to go dancing. Say you will. *Please*.' He flashed her his most winning smile and held her with his eyes.

She said, 'I'm afraid I can't. You see I have –'

'You don't have to bother explaining,' he cut in, sounding huffy and hurt. 'I understand.' A tinge of pink crept up into his face.

'No, you *don't* understand, Vincent,' Audra said firmly. 'I was about to say that I'm working tonight. But I would like to go out with you on my next evening off. Really I would.'

'Oh,' he said, momentarily thrown off balance. He recovered himself instantly, beamed at her. 'That's all right then. And when *is* your next night off?'

'This coming Wednesday.'

His face fell. 'Not 'til then. Oh dear. Well, never mind. But it'll have to be the church dance that night. How do you feel about going there?'

'I'll enjoy it . . . with you.' She offered him a small smile, suddenly feeling shy.

Vincent gave her a long, knowing look. 'Yes,' he said, 'so will I, Audra.'

They began to walk again.

Within seconds they were at the gates of Calpher House where Theo stood waiting for them. When they came to a standstill, Vincent turned to Audra and said, 'I'll meet you here at the gates on Wednesday, at seven sharp.'

'But you don't have to trouble yourself, Vincent. Really. I can find my own way to the Parish Hall.'

'*No.* I wouldn't want you walking down there alone.'

'Very well then,' she said.

He handed her the birdcage.

Theophilus said, 'Goodbye, Mr Crowther. I hope I see you soon. Then you can tell me if Danny liked his budgie.'

'I'll do that, Theo. Ta'rar, lad.'

Vincent swung to Audra. With a faint smile he raised his hat and was gone.

Audra watched him walk down the hill in long, brisk strides. He turned once, saw her and waved. She waved back. And then she took hold of Theo's hand and led him up the drive, only vaguely listening to the child as he chattered away.

As they drew closer to the house, Audra lifted her eyes and looked at it, thinking of the happy times she had spent here in the past year. And then some deep instinct told her she would not be living at Calpher House for much longer.

Today is the beginning, she thought. The beginning of my life with Vincent Crowther.

He is my destiny. I am his.

They were married five months later.

Some people were astonished; others were not.

The wedding took place at Christ Church in Upper Armley on a sunny June Saturday, a couple of days after Audra's birthday and one week before Vincent would celebrate his.

The bride wore blue. It was a simple yet elegant afternoon dress of crêpe de Chine, which she had designed herself, cut and sewn with the help of a seamstress from *Paris Modes*, Mrs Bell's exclusive gown shop in Leeds. Her cloche was of blue silk swathed in chiffon, her court shoes with Louis heels were of grey suede as were her elbow-length gloves. She carried a bouquet of pink roses, lily-of-the-valley and stephanotis.

Gwen Thornton was Audra's bridesmaid and Laurette Crowther her matron of honour.

They were dressed in identical frocks of dove-grey crêpe georgette overprinted with yellow roses, cloche hats of stitched grey silk and their posies were of yellow roses.

As they fussed and hovered around her in the entrance hall of Calpher House, Audra thought how truly lovely they looked, both so tall and fair, so young and fresh, and she was proud to have them as her attendants.

Mr Bell had graciously offered to give her away, and so it was on his arm that Audra walked down the aisle of the beautiful old Anglican church with its Norman architecture and magnificent stained-glass windows.

It was when the organ music swelled and the strains of the hymn 'O Perfect Love' reverberated through the high rafters that Audra's throat tightened. Her eyes filled with tears and she ached for her brothers. But knowing she could not let herself break down, she took control of herself, blinked hard. She lifted her head higher, looked towards the altar where Vincent was waiting with his brother Frank, who was his best man.

The love illuminating his face, the genuine admiration in his eyes, were comforting, reassuring, and she thought how wonderful he looked in his dark blue suit, which was brand new, the crisp white shirt and silver-grey silk tie.

Within seconds of drawing to a standstill at the altar, Mr Bell stepped aside. Vincent took his place. His presence and the vicar's kindly expression instantly dispelled the feelings of loneliness she had experienced a second before.

The Reverend Baxter's words seemed to wash over Audra . . . for better or for worse . . . for richer or for poorer . . . in sickness and in health . . . forsaking all others. Of course she forsook all others. How could she ever want anyone but Vincent. The idea was quite unthinkable.

Before she realized it the ceremony was over.

They were married. She was Mrs Vincent Crowther.

She walked back down the aisle, this time clinging to the arm of her husband as the organist pumped away enthusiastically and Mendelssohn's wedding march, joyful, thunderous, filled the church.

She and Vincent lingered on the church steps for only a few minutes, to have their photographs taken, greet his family, friends, the Bells, and Matron Lennox, who had travelled over from Ripon for the occasion.

And then, amidst lots of laughter and a deluge of confetti and rice, they dashed to the car waiting at the church gates. Vincent's Uncle Phil drove them to Calpher House, where the champagne wedding breakfast was being given by Mr and Mrs Thomas Bell.

Sitting very close to him in the back of the motor car, Audra smiled up at her young husband and then glanced down at the gold band on her finger. She had not thought it possible she could ever be so happy.

11

The moonlight had transformed her into a silver statue.

She stood near the window, motionless, staring out towards the sea, one arm resting on the sill, her body held at an oblique angle, turned inward to the room, her face in profile. It was the white satin nightgown, a mere wisp of a thing, that caught and held the light from the full moon, and in the duskiness of the room it had taken on the sheen and colour of pure silver.

There was something ethereal and illusory about her as she stood there, so still and unmoving. Unobserved, Vincent regarded her from the doorway, unable to tear his eyes away from her, wanting to prolong this moment, to etch this image of her on his mind and his memory.

She did not seem real to him at all; it was as if she was part of some dream he had dreamed long ago and was dreaming again. He felt that if he moved, or spoke, the scene would shatter and then evaporate, as all dreams did, and that she would be lost to him for all time.

As he gazed at her his longing shot through him, and in the same sharp and urgent way that it always did when she was near him. He had never wanted a woman as much as he wanted her. When they had arrived here at the Victoria Hotel in Robin Hood's Bay late on Saturday afternoon he had been unable to restrain himself. The pent up emotions, the desire constantly suppressed and held in check for the past five months, had exploded the minute they were alone in the suite. He had taken her to bed at once, before they had even unpacked.

In five days they had hardly left the suite.

He had become the inspired and skilful teacher, enjoying and revelling in this role, she the attentive and ardent pupil, eager, so ready to please. After the first couple of days she had begun to overcome her modesty and her shyness with him, and now she was very much at ease with him in their lovemaking. She accepted everything without question, her adoration of him written all over her face. He had been overjoyed to discover that his tender and blushing virgin had a deeply ingrained sensuality, just as he did himself, was thrilled that her ardour was now beginning to match his.

Oh how he loved her, this warm, loving, willing young woman who was his now . . . and forever. His woman. His lover. His wife.

The knowledge that he possessed her in every way was like an aphrodisiac, and just looking at her brought him to searing heat. He fastened his eyes on her slender yet shapely figure, so fully revealed to him through the flimsy texture of the satin that clung to her body in such a provocative way. She was small boned and finely wrought – but beautifully curvaceous. Her breasts were young, high, taut under the satin. He could see her nipples standing out sharply.

Heat raged through his loins, and in his groin there was a dull ache. Suddenly he had an enormous erection. He could not remember being as hard as this ever before, not even in the past five days and nights with her, she who charged him up more than any other woman ever had.

He took a step forward. His movement disturbed the air.

She swung her head towards the door, saw him, faintly smiled.

When he reached her side, Vincent took her face in his hands tenderly, looked deeply into her eyes. They were inky black in the dim light. He bent forward, kissed her brow, her eyes, her cheeks and tasted the salt of her tears.

Startled, he drew back, stared at her in bafflement. 'Audra, whatever is it, love? Aren't you happy with me?' His erection went down.

'Oh Vincent, yes, I am. Of course I am.' She drew closer to him, put her arms around his back, rested her head against his smooth, bare chest. A deep sigh rippled through her.

'Then what is it? Why are you so upset?'

'I'm not upset, truly I'm not.' She nestled closer, hoping her body movements would reassure him. She loved this man so very much, with all of her heart and soul and mind. She did not want him to misunderstand her tears.

Slowly, she said, 'I was standing here, waiting for you, admiring the beauty of the sea in the moonlight, when all at once I thought of the endless, endless miles of ocean stretching from here to Australia. And quite suddenly I did miss William and Frederick so, it was like a tight pain in my chest, a terrible constriction. I felt very sad, and I longed for them to be here in England. Somewhere. Anywhere. It didn't really matter where, so long as they were under the same sky as me . . . and then I thought of my wedding, and that's when I started to cry. Oh I do wish they'd been there, Vincent, that they had seen us get married.' She sighed again, but it was a light sigh and one that was barely audible. 'There was a moment in the church, just before the vicar married us, that I felt utterly and completely alone. It was awful.'

'Yes, I understand,' he murmured gently, stroking her hair, pressing her closer to him. 'Of course you missed your brothers, wanted them at your wedding, it's only natural.' He kissed the top of her head. 'But the instant we were married you were no longer alone, Audra. And you'll never be alone again. You have me now.'

'I know I do, Vincent. And you have me.'

'I'll never forget the way you looked on Saturday morning in the church, Audra. Not as long as I live, I won't. You were so bonny in your blue frock. You should always wear blue, it does suit you, love.'

He felt her smile against his chest. He knew that her sadness was trickling away, and he was glad of that.

She said, 'Vincent . . . tell me again . . . you know, the things you said last night.'

He chuckled softly. 'I said a lot of things last night. What *things* in particular do you mean?'

'Why you married me.'

'Because I love you.'

'And why do you love me?'

'Fishing, are we?' He laughed, very quietly.

'Tell me,' she persisted in a low, whispery voice, and she trailed her fingers across his shoulder blades.

This made him shiver. Instantly he wanted her.

'Because I love the look of you, the sound of you, the touch of your hands. I love the way you feel under my hands. I love every part of you. Oh Audra . . . *love*.' He tilted her head back, kissed her throat, her soft yielding mouth. The blood rushed through him. His desire for her was rampant.

She responded to his kisses ardently. When he moved his lips against hers she opened her mouth slightly so that his warm, loving, probing tongue could enter, rest against hers. His embrace tightened perceptibly and he kissed her more deeply, passionately, and their teeth grazed.

Audra shifted slightly so that their bodies melded together. Moving closer to him, she felt his hardness against her stomach through the thin fabric of the satin nightgown and she shivered involuntarily. A fierce and sudden heat began to throb at the core of her, and the shivering intensified as she anticipated what would happen next, thought of the way it felt when he took her to him. The first time they had made love, on their wedding night, she had been apprehensive when she had seen him standing naked before her. But he had loved her with such care and tenderness, and so exquisitely, the pain had only been a few moments of sharp discomfort; now they fitted each other perfectly.

Unexpectedly his kisses ceased.

Stepping back, Vincent slipped the thin straps of her nightgown over her shoulders, pulled it down past her breasts. It slithered to the floor unaided, lay like a gleaming pool at her feet.

Again Vincent gazed deeply into Audra's eyes, his love for her spilling out. He lifted his hand, stroked her cheek. After a long moment he dropped his eyes and kneeling down in front of her, he rested his head against her stomach and his arms went around her. Pressing his hands into the small of her back, he slowly smoothed them over her buttocks, moved her body slightly, adjusted her stance to suit him.

She trembled under his touch, and her desire for him swept through her. Her blood raced, her heart beat rapidly and her skin tingled in anticipation. Reaching out, she stroked his hair, then let her hands fall onto his shoulders, where they rested.

Covering her stomach with light, fluttering kisses, he continued to stroke her back, her buttocks and her thighs. Then he leaned away from her ever so slightly, rested on his heels, brought his hands around onto her stomach, still smoothing and stroking her skin. Finally, his hands came to a stop in the soft silky coils of fair hair that covered the mound between her legs. Slowly, with infinite care, he parted the tender petals, touched the tiny folds of warm, moist skin that protected her womanhood.

He kissed her navel and her stomach. They were long, slow, lingering kisses, and all the while his hands played amongst the musky folds, touching and seeking. At last he brought his tongue to join the quest. He began to nuzzle her, kiss her, and as he did he heard the soft moans in her throat. She gripped his shoulders, straining towards him, and he brought her to the edge of ecstasy.

He stopped abruptly, pulled away from her.

She caught her breath. Her eyes flew open. She gaped at him.

He took hold of her wrist quickly, firmly, pulled her down onto the floor with him. Impatiently, he kicked off his pyjama bottoms, stretched out next to her on the carpet, wrapped his body around hers, held her close to him. Wanting to possess her though he was, he wished to prolong their loving for a short while.

Lifting himself up on one elbow, he glanced down. Their eyes locked in a gaze so filled with passion, so intense, so searching in its depth of feeling it seemed to sear them both. Vincent thought he was seeing into her very soul. Her face overflowed with her abiding love for him and her yearning. And looking into those clear green eyes, Audra saw the burning desire in them, and the wonderment, and the glitter of bright tears, and her heart clenched as she reached up to touch his face.

It was Vincent who finally broke the contact. He found it unbearable, suddenly, to look at her in this manner, so moved was he by her and so choked up with feeling.

Now his glance swept over her body stretched out before him.

How pale and translucent she looked in the moonlight streaming in through the open window. She resembled a piece of perfectly sculpted marble, except that no cold stone was she. He sighed. She was warm and desirable flesh and blood. How lovely her breasts were, pearly-tinted, rounded and smooth, and her nipples were upright and hard like little bursting May buds, deep rose in colour.

'Oh Audra,' he breathed. 'My Audra. You're so beautiful.'

She half smiled, lifted her hand, smoothed one finger along his lips, then traced an outline around his mouth in the shape of a bow.

He caught hold of her hand, kissed the palm, then bent over her, brought his mouth to the cleft between her breasts and kissed her, enjoying the fragrant smell of her young sweet skin. Presently, he cupped his hand around her breast, began to fondle the nipple. It sprang up, grew more taut and erect than ever under his caressing fingers. Audra let out a little gasp of joy as his mouth came down on her other breast.

She cleaved to him, ran her hands over his back, then up onto his neck, and she twined her fingers in his crisp dark hair.

'Oh Vincent, Vincent, I love you so much,' she whispered.

On hearing his name, this endearment, he pulled away from her, moved rapidly. He braced himself above her on his hands.

There was no reason to wait now. He could not wait.

He took her urgently, needing to be joined to her, needing to make them as one. He shafted deeper and deeper, luxuriating in her total embrace, one that enfolded him in warmth and love and made him feel complete in a way that he had never felt except with her.

Oh yes, how he did love her ... this lovely girl he held in his arms ... his beautiful wife. She was his. They were made for each other, belonged together. And oh, how he fitted into her so well.

Slipping his hands under her body, he lifted her closer to him, clasping her tightly, plunging in and out. And she thrust herself up to meet his long and thrusting strokes. Her arms clung to him and she matched his fervent loving with an urgency of her own.

He cried out in his rapture, called her name over and over, all the time clutching her to him as though never to let her go. He knew he could not control himself much longer, that he was on the verge of exploding. He thought he might be blacking out. He seemed to be pitching forward from a great height ... falling, falling, falling.

'Oh, I'm ready,' he gasped against her burning cheek. 'Oh Audra. Take all of me. *Now*.'

'Oh Vincent!'

She arched her body towards his, meeting his passion, accepting it with love, offering him her passion in return, showing no restraint.

Wave upon wave of pure joy washed over her and she thought she was drowning in her pleasure and his. Suddenly she was gripped by an uncontrollable trembling and she crested up on the soaring waves and as she did she felt an immense shuddering pass through him, and they were united in their shattering release. And then he fell against her, lay exhausted in her arms and she stroked his hair, rested her head on his, feeling exhausted too, and overwhelmed by her emotions.

Eventually Vincent roused himself. 'I'm too heavy,' he murmured against her throat.

'No, it's all right. Anyway, I like to feel the weight of you on me,' she whispered. Then she shook her head. 'Why on earth am I whispering?' she wondered out loud, speaking in her normal voice.

'I've no idea. And God knows why we're lying here on the floor.' He began to chuckle.

'What's so amusing?'

'I am, love. For months and months all I could think about was making love to you in a nice comfy bed and now that we have one in the very next room I ignore it, choose the floor instead. Can you beat that!' He pushed himself up on one elbow, moved a strand of hair away from her face. 'Anyway, it's all your fault.'

'Why?'

'Because you're a little temptress, that's why. There you were, standing by the window in the moonlight and my heart did somersaults. I couldn't resist you. I had to have you. Right here on the floor, no less.' He chuckled again. 'There's no two ways about it, you do get me going, make me feel hot, love.'

Audra made no response, glanced away.

Vincent sensed her sudden shyness, her embarrassment.

That was the curious thing about her ... she was a mass of contradictions, he had discovered. From the moment he had made her his on the first night of their honeymoon, she had been a generous and giving partner, questioning nothing, doing as he wished. Yet in the aftermath of their lovemaking she never wanted to discuss the pleasure they had just shared; nor did she like it when he made mention of it. He had noticed that she invariably fell into an extraordinary reticence. A veil went down, shutting him out. He supposed her attitude sprang from her upbringing, her breeding. It was all right to do it, but not to talk about doing it, when you were a lady. Well, no matter. Such things were not really very important in the long run. She was his and he did love her so.

Pushing himself up off the floor, Vincent gave Audra his hand, hoisted her to her feet. After smothering her in a huge bear hug, he found her nightgown for her, slipped it on over her head, then pulled on his pyjamas.

'I don't know about you, but I'm famished all of a sudden. Let's have a picnic on that bowl of fruit.' As he spoke he went over to the table and picked it up.

'What a good idea,' Audra agreed. 'I'm a bit hungry myself.'

Wrapping his other arm around her, Vincent walked her into the bedroom. They installed themselves in the middle of the large double bed, where they sat cross-legged, munching on big red juicy apples. A minute or two later, Vincent returned to the adjoining sitting room and retrieved the half-finished bottle of wine he had ordered from room service with their dinner. He carried it back to the bedroom with two glasses, which he filled. Handing one to Audra, he joined her on the bed once more.

After propping a pillow behind his back, making himself comfortable, he lit a cigarette, said, 'Tell me some more about High Cleugh, about when you were little.'

'Goodness, you are insatiable, and my past is not especially interesting,' she replied with a light laugh. 'Besides, it's your turn.'

He made a face. 'There's not much left to tell . . . you know all about my boyish adventures with my friend Redvers Buller.' He winked at her. 'I can't believe you want to hear about them again, and the scrapes we got into, the canings we got from Mr Alford, the headmaster. It's boring stuff.'

'But you're such a good raconteur, Vincent.'

'Well, I don't know about that, love.' He drew on his Woodbine, blew a smoke ring, flashed her one of his very cheeky boyish grins. His dancing green eyes glistened as he leaned forward, pinned them on her. He cajoled, 'Go on, Audra, let's hear about your mother and your Uncle Peter . . . the Beautiful Edith Kenton and the dashing army captain. I must admit, the two of them intrigue me.'

'Aha, you're a true romantic, Vincent Crowther.'

'I am?' He sounded doubtful.

'Yes.' Audra smiled. 'I could tell you about the mystery of my mother's vanishing sapphires, if you like?'

'Your eyes are like sapphires, do you know that?' He gave her a soulful look and blew her a kiss.

'Do you want to hear this story or not?'

'Yes.'

As she began to speak he settled back, sipped his wine, listening to her attentively. Vincent was as fascinated and as impressed by Audra's background and family as he was enamoured of her. And so not unnaturally he loved hearing about her childhood, and in particular he loved the sound of her melodious voice as she spoke of those days with such love.

12

'Close your eyes,' Audra said, 'and keep them closed until I tell you to open them.'

'Okay,' Vincent said, promptly doing as he was told.

Audra looked up at him adoringly, smiling to herself. Her happiness knew no bounds today and she was almost bursting with joy. She reached for her husband's hand, drew him across the grass, saying, as she did, 'It's all right, there's nothing in your way, just walk normally.'

'That's what I *am* doing.' He stopped suddenly, swung his head to her, opened his eyes and winked. Then he snapped them shut before she had a chance to admonish him. 'All right, lead on, MacDuff!' he cried, gaiety echoing in his voice.

Audra smiled in amusement. 'It's just a few more steps,' she said, guiding him forward. She gripped his hand a little tighter as she told him, 'Turn your head towards me, to the left a bit more.'

Vincent did as she said.

'Now!' Audra exclaimed.

He lifted his lids, blinked for a second or two in the bright morning sunlight, then brought his hand up to shade his eyes. He squinted slightly against the brilliance, trying to focus.

'Look, over there, near the trees . . . in that dell,' Audra was saying.

He followed the direction of her outstretched arm. His breath caught in his throat. '*That's* High Cleugh,' he said in the strangest of voices, and stared in astonishment at the old manor house.

'Yes.' Audra glanced up at him, frowning in concern. 'You sound so surprised. Are you disappointed? Don't you think it's as beautiful as I made it sound, as I described it?'

'Oh, I do, I do,' he was quick to reassure her. 'But it's so big, Audra, and it looks ever so grand. I'd no idea. I mean I just never imagined it was that kind of house, you know, a *mansion*.' He was unable to disguise the awe in his voice. It was obvious he was impressed.

Audra squeezed his fingers. 'It looks a lot larger than it actually is, Vincent.'

'Maybe so, but it's bigger than anything I've ever been used to, lass. And those gardens, Audra. Why, they fair take my breath away, they do that.'

Audra beamed at him. 'My mother planned and planted them, and those are her delphiniums down near the edge of the river. Whenever I see delphiniums I always think of her and of High Cleugh.'

'I can certainly understand why, love.'

'If you look down the river a little bit, over there to your right, you'll see the stepping stones I told you about. That's where we used to cross the river to come up here for our picnics . . . to the Memory Place. Of course, it wasn't called that then. I only gave it that name afterwards –' She broke off, glanced away and there was a hint of sadness in her voice as she finished, 'You know, after *they* died, and after my brothers were sent away from me.'

'Yes,' he said, putting his arm around her shoulder comfortingly.

She looked up into his face, gave him a small smile.

He smiled back, all the while scrutinizing her closely, hoping that coming here had not upset her unduly. Days ago, when he had asked her to show him High Cleugh on their way back to Leeds from Robin Hood's Bay, he had not stopped to think that this might stir up memories that would make her sorrowful. After all, she had agreed so readily, even eagerly. But now Vincent could not help wondering if his forcefulness had been misplaced; perhaps he had been thoughtless. Her vivid cornflower eyes looked suspiciously moist to him.

Vincent cleared his throat. 'Are you sure you want to have our picnic here, Audra love?'

'That's what I'd thought. It's so pretty, and there's such a lovely view for miles around. Don't you want to stay?' she asked, sounding worried, as always wishing to please him.

'Yes. Anything you say is all right by me.'

Leaning forward, he kissed her cheek, then strode over to the sycamore tree. A few minutes before he had deposited two brown-paper shopping bags under the spreading branches; he carried these back to the top of the slope above the River Ure, where Audra had remained standing. Taking a large tartan blanket out of one of them, he shook it out, spread it at her feet.

And then, with a great flourish, pretending to take off a non-existent hat, he did a sweeping bow in front of her, bending low in the manner of an old-fashioned cavalier.

'My cloak for your comfort, m'lady, and pray do be seated so that we can partake of our repast,' he said, adopting an exaggerated upper-class accent.

Laughing, her eyes sparkling with delight, Audra offered him a small curtsy in return. 'Why, Sir Galahad, my grateful thanks indeed.' She lowered herself onto the car rug with her usual grace of movement.

Joining in her laughter, Vincent flopped down next to her and remarked, 'I must say, it was nice of the hall porter at the Victoria Hotel to arrange this food for us, wasn't it?' As he spoke he began to take small packages out of the other shopping bag.

'Yes, most kind,' Audra agreed, helping him in his task. 'Oh look, the hotel chef put in some lovely Scotch eggs,' she exclaimed, unwrapping the grease-proof paper.

Vincent eyed them. 'Well, they look as tasty as anything me mam could make,' he said, his mouth watering. 'And I've just come across a little bag of pickled onions and a slab of fine Wensleydale cheese.' He flashed her a huge grin. 'We might as well dig in, Audra. Oh, and here's your bottle of milk, pet.'

'Thank you, Vincent.'

They were both hungry after their long drive from Robin Hood's Bay on the East Coast, across the sprawling North Yorkshire Moors and down to Ripon. They said very little as they munched on the delicious tid-bits in the picnic lunch which had been provided by the hotel.

It was an exceptional June day.

The sky was bright blue and filled with sunshine. The lightest of balmy breezes rustled through the trees, but there were no other sounds except for the faint tinkle of running water, the occasional trilling of the wild birds and the rushing and fluttering of their wings as they flew up into the sparkling summer air.

Neither Audra nor Vincent ever minded these silences which frequently fell between them. In fact, they found them companionable, enjoyed them as much as everything else they did together. They were content simply to be in each other's company, knowing that they did not always have the need to talk, to make forced conversation. There was an ease between them; it had been thus since the beginning of their relationship in January.

Audra studied him surreptitiously.

It was the twelfth of June and he was twenty-five today. But he looked much younger to her. Perhaps this was because of his fresh complexion, the tan he had acquired in the last few days. Although they had been ensconced in the hotel suite for a good part of their honeymoon, the time they had spent outdoors had been put to good use. They had walked a lot, and when she had ventured up onto the precipitous cliffs to paint watercolours of Robin Hood's Bay from that vantage point, he had insisted on accompanying her. He had read his newspaper, studied his racing form, and then stretched out next to her, sunning himself.

Suddenly Audra wondered what Vincent would say if she told him that she had not enjoyed her wedding day very much. In point of fact, she would not have enjoyed it at all if he had not been present. Audra laughed under her breath at the ridiculousness of this thought. Obviously, without Vincent Crowther there would have been no marriage in the first place.

He had enjoyed his wedding, though. All aspects of it, too. Smiling, laughing, shaking hands, he had been at home with everyone. So much so, she had been struck quite strongly by his carefree manner. He was nonchalant; he might have been the lord of the manor at Calpher House. Not that his behaviour had been offensive to the Bells or anyone else for that matter – only enviable, as far as she was concerned. For she had experienced great unease most of the time, although she had tried to hide this behind a gracious demeanour, a bright smile carefully glued into place.

From the outset, she had sensed strange undercurrents at the reception. Vincent had been unaware of them.

To begin with, there had been a certain awkwardness between the Thorntons and the Crowthers, and she had watched this develop into veiled antipathy within the first hour. Her internal discomfort had spiralled into distress, and she had found herself growing quieter and quieter with everyone; Vincent, full of bonhomie, had simply grown more expansive.

At one moment, she had gone into the Bells' elegant dining room looking for Vincent. Here Mr Agiter, Cora and Dodie had been serving the breakfast buffet, a wonderful selection of good Yorkshire fare and other tempting delicacies from Mrs Jackson's well stocked larder. Instantly, she had noticed Gwen and Charlie huddled in one corner, heads together, looking conspiratorial. Just as she was about to turn away she had observed them fasten their eyes on Vincent, who was on the far side of the room talking to Irène Bell. They had stared at him daggers drawn.

If looks could kill he'd drop dead this very minute, Audra had thought, and gooseflesh had sprung up on her arms. Averting her face, she had hurried over to join her husband, taken hold of his arm almost protectively.

After chatting with Mrs Bell for a moment or two, she had then excused them both to her former employer, explaining that she wanted Vincent to become better acquainted with Matron Lennox. Still holding onto his arm, she had led him out into the hall. She had felt sick inside. And dreadfully hurt.

She had been relieved, even glad, to leave for their honeymoon as soon as it was possible to do so politely without giving offence to the Bells. They had been kind, exceedingly generous, and she did not wish them to think she was unappreciative. Naturally, Vincent had wanted to stay longer, he being the social animal that he was.

Audra shifted slightly on the tartan rug, stretched out her legs in front of her and reached for a piece of the Wensleydale cheese, nibbling on it absently, trying to dismiss thoughts of Gwen. She found she could not.

Her best friend disliked her husband.

That was the sad truth, and it troubled Audra a great deal. Unfortunately, Gwen had taken a dislike to Vincent months before she had actually met him – her words on Bonfire Night still echoed in Audra's ears. It was all because of Charlie, of course. Gwen had condemned Vincent without bothering to get to know him, simply because he had been chosen instead of her brother.

How immature Gwen is being, Audra thought. She was disappointed in Gwen; she had certainly expected better of her friend. Having cherished their friendship from the day it had begun, she was upset that it was threatened. But it was Gwen, not she, who was putting it in jeopardy. She loved Gwen; she did not want to lose her. But she also loved her husband. If she and Gwen were going to continue to see each other, Gwen would have to be more amiable with Vincent. He came first now. And Vincent, being oblivious to the girl's dislike of him, was always friendly and cordial to her. In Audra's opinion, he should have received better treatment from her friend.

Swallowing a sigh, Audra leaned back on her elbows, thinking hard. She must find a way to show her how unfair she was being. Audra did not want Gwen to be a casualty of her marriage. She was going to see Gwen as soon as possible, talk to her about this. I shall have to be diplomatic, Audra thought, and immediately began to rehearse what she would say.

For his part, Vincent was ruminating on High Cleugh.

Ever since they had arrived on the slope he had been stealing glances at it. The old house was now in his direct line of vision across the river, and he felt a compulsion to bring his gaze back to it time and again. And as he did he could not help thinking of the little cottage he and Audra had found in Upper Armley and which they had rented a month ago.

When they had stumbled on it, quite by accident one day, he had considered them most fortunate. The cottage was sturdy, in good repair, and convenient for his work. But suddenly it had lost its appeal. How small and insignificant it was in comparison to High Cleugh where his wife had been born and brought up. What he was offering her was so much less.

He gazed at her appraisingly and with a flash of unprecedented objectivity. How pretty she was in her buttercup-yellow dress, fresh and sweet and desirable in every way. She had so many different and laudable attributes. He was convinced she was going to make him the very best wife. Although he was never given to much introspection, Vincent sank down into his thoughts, contemplating Audra.

If the circumstances of her life had been different she would never have been permitted to marry him.

This unanticipated thought shook Vincent to the core. The fact that *her* family would have objected to her marrying *him* had never occurred to him before, but now that it had he knew he was absolutely correct in this assumption, and this knowledge depressed him. He remembered his mother's dire words. 'Asking for trouble, that's what you are, my lad,' she had said. 'If you marry her you'll rue the day.' Laurette had been against their marriage too, even though she liked Audra a lot. 'You're from two different worlds,' his sister had said when he had challenged her about her views. 'It's not going to work. She's a lady born and bred.'

In an effort to convince Laurette that this did not matter he had told her about Audra's hard life as a ward maid, the drudgery of her demanding work as a nurse at the Fever Hospital. She had gaped at him, incredulous. 'Don't be such a fool, Vincent, what's that got to do with anything! Her breeding and her gentility will always be part of her. She's different from you and me, from *us*, and believe me, that *difference* makes a big difference.'

Always quick to flare up at the slightest thing, he had flown into a temper and stormed out, bristling with anger. And he had been put out with his favourite sister for weeks. Vincent had a strong mind of his own, and so he had gone about his business, done as he had seen fit. And he had seen fit to marry Audra despite the opposition from his family, which she knew nothing about.

Vincent was still convinced that his mother and his sister were wrong. Surely it was of no great consequence that he and Audra were from different backgrounds. They loved each other. That was all that counted, wasn't it?

Audra, her eyes on Vincent, sensed a change in him. She said, 'Are you all right? You look a bit funny.'

'Oh I'm fine, love,' he said, then laughed somewhat shakily.

'You looked quite troubled a moment ago. Are you sure nothing's bothering you, Vincent?'

He forced a bright smile. 'Never felt better,' he exclaimed and thought to add, 'I'm sorry that this is the last day of our honeymoon, that it's over.'

'Not quite.' She kissed his cheek, gazed into his face, loving him with her eyes. 'We've still got the whole of today, and this evening in Harrogate. We'll have a lovely dinner for your birthday at the White Swan. It's a pretty hotel, you'll enjoy staying there.'

Audra sat back, tipped her head to one side, went on, 'Even though our honeymoon will come to an end tomorrow, our life together is only just beginning, Vincent. Think about that ... and I know we're going to have a wonderful life, you and I.'

'Yes,' he said, relaxing.

Audra suddenly grew animated and talkative, and there was a new vivacity about her as they finished their picnic. She spoke to Vincent at length about their future, and was full of enthusiasm for all the good things she believed it held in store for them.

13

'Do you see anything that belongs to you, Audra?' Vincent asked, swinging his green gaze around the drawing room of The Grange.

'Those two oil paintings on either side of the French windows and the watercolour on that side wall,' she said. 'They're by my father. If you look at them closely you'll find they're signed Adrian Kenton.'

Vincent strode across the floor, peered at the two beautiful landscapes and then at the still life, and nodded his head. He pivoted to face Audra, who hovered near the fireplace. 'What else is yours?'

'Most of the wood pieces in here ... the inlaid chest next to the door, these two small Sheraton tables, and the console over there, oh, and the Meissen clock on it. There are two Chippendale-style chairs, but those must be in another room. She also has my mother's Georgian silver tea service, some smaller pieces of silver and three more paintings, but only one of those is by my father.' A confident smile struck Audra's mouth and she patted her handbag. 'I have my inventory in here, and the one for the jewellery, so I'm well armed –' Audra stopped, focused on the door as it opened.

Vincent did the same. He was riddled with curiosity about the woman he was going to meet. He had heard a few things about her from Audra, and he did not like what he had heard.

Alicia Drummond paused on the threshold.

Vincent, observing the middle-aged woman with quickening interest, thought: *Narrow*. Everything about her is narrow. Eyes, nose, mouth, face and body. He did not even question that she was narrow-minded as well; he had already surmised *that* from Audra's comments about her.

Audra, who had not seen her relative for almost six years, was startled. She decided that Alicia Drummond had not only aged considerably in this time, but looked as if she were ill. The woman was drawn, haggard even, and excessively thin; her stony black eyes were sunken into their sockets. Wispy grey hair was pulled back into a bun, and she wore a drab brown silk dress that was unbecoming.

Closing the door behind her, Alicia walked into the room with her usual sedate stiffness. She said fretfully, in her high-pitched voice, 'Hello, Audra. When you wrote to me two weeks ago you didn't say you'd be bringing someone with you. I expected you to be alone. I was most surprised when the maid told me you were accompanied by –' She surveyed Vincent, her eyes filling with curiosity and speculation, and finished, 'Your young man.' It came out sounding more like a question than a statement of fact.

Audra said briskly, 'Good afternoon, Aunt Alicia. I would like to introduce my husband to you. This is Vincent Crowther. Vincent, this is my mother's first cousin, Alicia Drummond.'

Alicia, rarely at a loss for words, was momentarily speechless. *Husband*, she thought, utterly amazed. This smartly dressed, good-looking young man was married to dull, insignificant little Audra. It hardly seemed possible.

Stepping forward, Vincent thrust out his hand. 'Pleased to meet you, Mrs Drummond.'

'How do you do,' Alicia responded, her cold eyes weighing him up. Vincent spoke nicely and there was only the merest trace of the broad Yorkshire accent in his vowels, but Alicia caught it. Working-class, more than likely, she commented to herself. Well, that explained everything.

Waving a hand airily, in the direction of the sofa, Alicia murmured, 'Do sit down, both of you.' She herself perched on the edge of a chair and gave her attention to Audra. 'Why didn't you let us know you were getting married?'

Ignoring the question, which she considered to be ridiculous under the circumstances, Audra said, 'We spent our honeymoon at Robin Hood's Bay, and as I knew we'd be passing close by on our return to Leeds, I thought it would be a good idea to come and see you. I wanted Vincent to meet you, since –'

'I'm glad you did.'

'Since he'll be coming back next Saturday. With a van, to –'

'*A van.*' Alicia sounded perplexed.

'Yes. He'll be coming to collect my things.'

'*Things?*'

'Yes, my things, Aunt Alicia. Or perhaps I should say my mother's things, which have belonged to me since her death and which you have been . . . *storing* here, shall we say?'

'Gracious me, Audra, don't tell me you're planning to go to the expense of hiring a van to come all this way – from Leeds, you say? – to pick up a few odd bits of valueless furniture.'

'Valueless,' Audra echoed, giving her a sharp stare. 'I wouldn't say that.'

'Oh, *I* would. They're not worth much.'

'Whatever they're worth I want them. I wish to have my mother's things around me. Besides, they belong to me – and have for a long time.'

'It seems to me that a couple of old tables hardly merit such enormous effort,' Alicia scoffed. Adopting a scornful expression, she swung to Vincent. 'Imagine hiring a van to come and pick up a few sticks of worthless furniture. Audra is being quite ridiculous, in my opinion. What a waste of money. I'm sure you agree.'

'Audra wants her things,' Vincent said quietly, but with great firmness. 'And anything Audra wants I'm going to make sure she gets.'

'Quite,' Alicia sniffed, looking down her nose at him.

'There's the matter of the jewellery, Aunt Alicia. I will take that with me today,' Audra announced.

Alicia opened her mouth, immediately closed it, conscious of the grim determination glittering in Audra's eyes, the implacable curve of her mouth. 'I'm not sure the jewellery is here,' she improvised. 'If I remember correctly, my mother took it to her house for safekeeping.'

'You're not *sure*,' Audra repeated. Her expression hardened. 'I would think you'd be scrupulously careful with other people's possessions. I'm also rather surprised you didn't get in touch with me yourself weeks ago. You knew I'd be twenty-one at the beginning of this month, that I was coming of age, and was therefore legally entitled to what's mine.' Audra's laugh was soft but knowing. 'Actually, there was no good reason why I shouldn't have had my mother's things years ago. My –'

'You weren't married years ago,' Alicia cut in, sounding defensive. 'What would you have done with the furniture? Where would you have put it?'

'I'm talking about my mother's jewellery,' Audra exclaimed. 'And I was about to say that my former employer, Mrs Irène Bell, said exactly the same thing only a couple of weeks ago. Both she and Mr Bell were amazed you hadn't been in touch with me early in May, to find out what I wanted to do about my possessions. Mr Bell's a solicitor, extremely well known in Leeds, and he's very conscious of legalities, all that sort of thing.' Audra let her narrowed blue gaze linger on the other woman pointedly.

Alicia flushed, grew uncomfortable under this fixed and probing scrutiny. Ever since she had received Audra's letter she had been put out. She was reluctant to relinquish the girl's valuables and she had been scheming to keep them. But now she was reconsidering her moves. She had no desire to become entangled with a solicitor, or with this husband, who looked as if he could turn difficult at the slightest provocation. Striving to hide her irritation, Alicia stood up. Clearing her throat, she muttered, 'There is the possibility that my mother spoke about removing the jewellery to her house, to look after it for you, but that she never got around to doing so. My memory's not what it used to be, I'm afraid. It could still be here. Perhaps I had better go upstairs and check.'

'Yes, that would be wise,' Audra said.

Alicia hurried out, cursing Audra under her breath. She had not bargained for solicitors and husbands. The girl had caught her off guard.

The minute they were alone, Vincent said in a quiet voice, 'She's a right crafty devil, that one.'

'I know, and she's trying to steal my things,' Audra murmured, also keeping her voice low.

'Don't worry, I won't let her. Anyway, I bet she's afraid you'll bring Mr Bell down on her if she does anything wrong. I noticed the way her face changed when you mentioned he was a noted Leeds solicitor.'

'Yes.'

Audra sat back on the sofa, glanced around, disliking this room as much as she disliked the entire house and those who lived in it. She thought of the cruel things Alicia Drummond had done to her in the past and a coldness settled over her heart like a hoarfrost. Unexpectedly, an image of her brothers saying goodbye to her as they set out for Australia leapt into her mind and with such vividness she stiffened. Then that awful sense of loss gripped her. She snapped her eyes shut, wondering if she would ever be free of this distressing feeling. Surely she would. After all, she was no longer alone. She had Vincent. He was her family now. Opening her eyes, she swung her head to look at him.

He met her gaze, noticed the bright blueness of her eyes dulling as a sadness crept into them. He squeezed her hand, said, 'This place upsets you and it gives me the willies. Let's scram as soon as you've finished your business with the old battle-axe.'

Audra nodded.

The two of them sat together on the sofa in silence, holding hands, waiting.

It was not very long before Alicia Drummond returned, carrying the wooden jewellery box. She brought it straight to Audra, thrust it at her rudely. 'Here it is,' she snapped. 'No doubt you want to check, to make sure nothing is missing. And quite frankly, I would prefer you to do so. I don't want to be accused of misappropriating your property – at a later date.'

There was no response from Audra.

She sat staring down at the box on her lap. How familiar it was. It had always stood on the dresser in her mother's bedroom at High Cleugh. Sometimes, when she had been a child and playing at dressing up in her mother's clothes, she had been allowed to dip into it, to take out a pin or a brooch or a pendant to wear for a while.

After a moment, she raised the lid, filling with relief now that she had these most personal things of her mother's in her hands at last. She began to sort through the items in the box, fingering each one lovingly. She thought of her mother's elegance and grace, smiled to herself as innumerable memories flooded her, touched off as they were by the different pieces.

She picked up her mother's engagement ring set with three tiny diamonds and gazed at it. My mother wore this for most of her life, Audra thought, and now I shall wear it. She slipped it on the third finger of her right hand and as she did she experienced a sense of deep satisfaction. She felt as though the ring brought her mother closer; it was like a link to the past. And this pleased her.

Audra had no need to refer to the inventory, since she knew it by heart. The jewellery was intact. Nothing had been taken. And whether or not Alicia Drummond had been wearing it all these years was suddenly beside the point. The box and its contents were now hers, and rightfully so, and this was the only thing of any importance.

Placing the box on the sofa between her and Vincent, Audra opened her handbag and took out the other inventory. Directing her gaze at Alicia, she said, 'This is the list of my mother's furniture and silver and paintings which are in this house. I'll leave it for you to look over later. Vincent will come back with two of his brothers next Saturday morning to collect everything. At about ten o'clock. I hope that's convenient?'

Mortified, Alicia could only nod.

Audra placed the piece of paper on one of the Sheraton occasional tables, and went on, 'In the meantime, I thought we could take my father's paintings with us today. We have the motor car and they'll fit nicely in the back.'

Wanting to be finished with the business, and get Audra away from this depressing house, Vincent sprang up, interjected, 'I'd better start taking them off the walls.' He glanced at Alicia, explained, 'I know which pictures were painted by Audra's father, she already pointed them out to me.'

Alicia Drummond thought she had turned to stone.

She could neither speak nor move. She simply gaped at Vincent, watched transfixed as he removed one of the oils, leaned it against a chair, then walked over to the other one, reached his hands up for it.

It was then that something cracked in Alicia Drummond. Years of rigid self-control fell away. 'Don't touch my paintings! Don't you dare touch it!' she cried, leaping up, rushing across the room, all semblance of dignity evaporating. She grabbed Vincent's arm roughly, peered into his face, shouted with mounting rage, 'Don't you dare touch any of my paintings!'

He was flabbergasted at her words and her behaviour. He shrugged off her hand, stepped back, turned his eyes to Audra on the sofa. They exchanged looks of astonishment.

Audra was on her feet swiftly and hurried across the floor. 'They're not your paintings, Aunt Alicia. They're mine,' she said in a firm but reasonable voice. She wondered if the woman had lost her senses. 'Unless you've forgotten, my father painted them. And they always hung at High Cleugh. They are part of my legacy from my father and my mother, and I –'

'Your mother!' Alicia screamed, whirling on her. 'Don't you mention your mother to me. She was nothing but a whore!'

Audra gasped, recoiled.

Vincent could not believe he had heard correctly.

'Here, watch it,' he exclaimed. 'Don't you talk like that to my wife. I won't stand for it.' He drew closer to Audra, slipped his arm around her and glared at Alicia. 'Where do you get off, calling Audra's mother such a terrible thing?'

'Don't you like the word *whore*? Then pick any name you prefer . . . trollop, slut, harlot, strumpet! They all fit her. Because that's what she *was*. She took him away from me, she stole my darling Adrian.' Alicia's shrill voice now turned into a wail. Near tears, she rushed on, 'He belonged to me. We had an understanding. We were to be married. Until she set her cap at him, turned his head, inveigled him into her bed with her wiles and her fancy ways.' The words choked in her throat. Alicia began to take gasping breaths, holding her hand to her chest as if in pain.

Audra was so appalled, so sickened by what she had heard, she could only stare at her relative in horror. 'So that's what it's been about all these years,' she said finally, shaking her head in disbelief. '*Oh my God!* My brothers and I were punished merely because you were *jealous*. How despicable – to tear us apart when we were children just because of something as ridiculous and futile as that. And when my parents were already dead, when the past no longer mattered. You are a foul woman, Alicia Drummond, foul. As for you and my father being involved –' Audra paused, took a deep breath. 'I hardly knew my father, but from what I've heard about him, Adrian Kenton was a fine and sensitive man. I don't believe for one minute that he could have ever been interested in the likes of *you*. That's a figment of your imagination.'

Filling with disgust, Audra turned away from the woman. She said to Vincent, 'Please take down the other paintings by my father and then we can go.'

Vincent did as she asked.

Audra walked over to the sofa, picked up her handbag and the jewellery box.

Additional restraints, self-imposed over the years, began to snap inside Alicia Drummond. And all of the ancient hatred she had harboured for Edith Kenton, and which had not abated even in death, rose up in her. It seemed to congeal in her face, which was contorted into an ugly mask.

She scurried across the carpet to Audra, leaned close to her and hissed in her face, 'Adrian Kenton was not your father! Not your father, do you hear? You're a bastard. *Peter Lacey's bastard.* She was carrying on with him when Adrian was still alive. My poor Adrian, my poor darling Adrian, having to bear witness to that.'

Audra took a rapid step back, shaking her head from side to side frantically, denying the woman's words. 'It's not true! It's not true!' she cried.

'Yes, it is,' Alicia snarled, 'your mother was a whore and an adulteress and you are a bastard!'

'And you are a liar, Alicia Drummond!'

Vincent knew he must act immediately.

He seized hold of Audra's arm and almost dragged her into the entrance hall. Pivoting on his heels, he sped back to the drawing room, grabbed the three paintings he had taken off the walls, then swung to Alicia Drummond.

She stood in the middle of the room, twisting her hands together in agitation. There was a febrile look on her face and a wildness in her eyes. He thought she had gone quite mad.

He said, 'I'll be back next Saturday for the rest of Audra's stuff, and everything had better be in good condition – *or else.*'

'How dare you threaten me!'

'I'm not threatening you, I just want you to know that I mean business. And the law is on our side; think on, Mrs Drummond.'

Audra was standing where he had left her in the hall, clutching the jewellery box to her chest. Her face was white and she trembled.

'Come on,' he cried, 'and open the door please, love, my hands are full.'

'Yes,' she said, trying to throw off the sense of shock she was feeling, hurrying after him to the front door.

Once they were inside his Uncle Phil's motor car and driving away from the house, Vincent breathed a lot easier. As he came to the gates at the end of the long driveway he slowed, eased the car out onto the main road to Ripon. He drove in this direction for a few minutes, wanting to put a bit of distance between themselves and The Grange; soon he brought the car to a standstill, parked under a tall hedge.

Audra and he turned to face each other at precisely the same moment.

Vincent had never seen her looking so pale. She hugged the wooden box as if she was afraid someone was going to wrest it from her. But at least she had stopped shaking. His heart went out to her as he stared into her eyes. They were awash with hurt. He wanted to make her feel better but he was not sure how to do so.

He said softly, 'It's all right now, love. And you don't have to set foot in that bloody awful house ever again.'

Audra nodded. 'Yes,' she said.

There was a small silence as they continued to look at each other.

Eventually, she asked in a low voice, 'You don't think it's true, do you, Vincent? You don't think that I'm . . . illegitimate, do you?' Her lip began to quiver and her eyes brimmed.

'Oh I don't! I don't!' he exclaimed, his vehemence echoing loudly in the confines of the small car, 'you said it yourself and right to her face . . . she's a liar.'

'But why would she make up something so awful, something as despicable as that?'

Startled by these questions, Vincent now looked askance at his young wife, and said, 'Audra . . . *love* . . . you're not daft, you *know* why. She spelled it out to you.'

656

His voice changed, grew much harder and sharper. 'She's a bloody old cow, bitter and spiteful. Not only that, she's crackers, if you ask me. Off her rocker, that one. I wouldn't be surprised if they cart her off one day, put her away in a padded cell . . .'

'Yes, perhaps you're right,' Audra said slowly, wondering if he really was. Her eyes turned reflective as she ruminated on Alicia Drummond. The woman was wicked, wasn't she? *Evil.* Madness might not be involved at all. Audra's mind automatically swung to her brothers and she sighed as she thought of them, remembering their years of hardship and worry in Australia, and her own problems and loneliness after they had been sent away. The shocking thing was that none of it need ever have happened. It had all been so unnecessary.

'Are you all right?' Vincent asked.

'Oh yes,' she murmured, 'I was just thinking . . . people can be rotten, can't they?'

'Aye, lass, they can,' he agreed, then reached out, touched her arm lightly. 'Try and relax . . . nobody's going to steal the jewellery box.'

Audra half-smiled. She loosened her tenacious grip on it, let it rest on her knee, and after a moment or two she remarked, 'Well, I suppose we'd better be getting along. We can't sit here all day.'

'Okay . . . but where to, Audra? Do you still want to go and see your great-aunt? Or shall we forget it and make tracks for Harrogate instead?'

There was a fractional hesitation on Audra's part, then she said, 'I think we should go and see her. She *is* expecting me, and I want you to meet her.' Audra gave him a reassuring look. 'She's nicer than her dreadful daughter, I promise you.'

'I'll have to take your word for it,' he said with a grin and turned on the ignition. 'Just point me in the right direction.'

'We're not very far away, as a matter of fact. Drive down this road, for about ten minutes, until we come to Cobbler's Green on the right-hand side. That's where we turn off, Bedelia Cottage is at the bottom.'

Neither of them spoke as Vincent drove along at a steady speed, and it was only after they had turned into Cobbler's Green that Audra said, 'It *could* be true, you know.'

Instantly understanding what she meant, he answered quickly, 'Maybe it could, but I wouldn't spend any time worrying over it, if I were you.'

'Why not?'

'Because you'll never know the answer. Your mother is the only person who could have told you the truth, and she's dead.'

'She might have confided in Great-Aunt Frances. I told you before, they were close.'

'You're not going to ask the old lady, are you?'

'Well . . . well, yes, I may.'

But in the end, Audra did not ask her great-aunt anything at all.

From the moment they arrived at Bedelia Cottage it was easy to see that the old lady was very frail indeed. Even though it was late afternoon, it was still a lovely day, sunny and warm. Nevertheless, the windows were tightly closed and she sat in front of a huge fire in her cluttered parlour, a silk shawl draped around her withered shoulders, her hands outstretched to the warming flames.

Audra led Vincent through the maze of Victorian furniture and bric-à-brac, the long-forgotten smell of the room immediately assailing her. The dry, dusty air held a hint of over-ripe apples, furniture polish and potpourri, as it had for all the years Audra had been coming here as a child. And when she bent to kiss the wrinkled cheek she caught a faint whiff of moth balls mingled with lavender water and peppermints and she felt a rush of affection for Frances Reynolds. Sudden nostalgia took a grip on her, held her in its spell for a few moments.

Her great-aunt was overjoyed to see Audra after such a long time, and to meet Vincent. Surprised though she was that Audra had appeared with a husband, whom *she* had heard nothing about, she took to him at once, or so it seemed to Audra. She chirped away like a small bright bird, smiling at them benevolently. From time to time she nodded her head and patted Audra's hand and as she did she plied her with innumerable questions about her life.

Audra, equally glad to see her great-aunt, answered her as best she could, all the while observing the octogenarian closely. She looked as delicate and as translucent as the paper-thin china cups they were drinking tea from, and Audra thought that if she breathed too heavily on her the old woman would shatter. Silver-haired and slight of build for as long as Audra could remember, there was a new fragility, a brittleness, about her; Audra wanted to wrap her in cotton wool.

Old bones, old flesh, soon to turn to dust, Audra commented silently, and a little shiver ran down her arms despite the warmth of the room. Audra's intuitiveness told her that she was probably seeing her aunt for the last time. Frances Reynolds was very, very old now; her life on this earth was coming to an end. It was then that Audra also knew that it would be quite wrong to start probing into her mother's past. That would be too upsetting to this gentle old lady, who had so adored her mother, who was always so affectionate towards her, and who had made Vincent feel so welcome.

And Vincent is correct in what he said, Audra now thought. Only my mother knew the truth and she has taken it to the grave with her. It suddenly struck Audra that it would besmirch her mother's memory to start talking about adultery and questioning her own legitimacy.

And so she remained silent.

They spent almost two hours at Bedelia Cottage and it was only when they made motions to leave that her great-aunt mentioned Edith Kenton.

Peering at Audra through ancient eyes, she said in her whispery voice, 'When my darling Edith died Alicia removed all of her papers from High Cleugh. But I took them away from her, because I wanted to keep them for you, Audra, until you were grown up.'

Frances Reynolds paused, smiled slightly and shook her silvered head. 'Ah, dear child, you are looking so eager, but I'm afraid there is nothing of great importance amongst your mother's papers. Some old letters, her birth certificate, her marriage lines, a few old photographs, nothing much else.'

Audra's face fell, then she said, 'But I want them anyway.'

'Of course you do, my dear, and that is why I kept them safe for you all these years.' She glanced at Vincent. 'The papers are in that case over there on the floor. Could you bring it here, please?'

'Right away,' he said, leaping to his feet. He was back in a moment, offered it to the old lady.

'No, no, give it to Audra, the papers belong to her, Vincent.'

'Thanks,' Audra said, taking the case from him. She noticed that her mother's initials, EWK, were stamped in gold on the front between the locks. She snapped these open, peeped inside, touched the papers on the top, then decided to examine everything later, in the privacy of their room, after they arrived at the White Swan Hotel in Harrogate.

'Thank you very much for keeping the papers for me, Great-Aunt Frances, I'm most appreciative.'

The old lady smiled and nodded. 'I know you were going to see Alicia,' she said in her weak voice that slightly quavered. 'I presume that you did so and that you collected your mother's jewellery.'

'Yes,' Audra said and paused awkwardly, afraid to say anything more than this. She glanced across at her husband.

Vincent came to her rescue. 'Everything was fine, and I'll be driving over with my brothers and a van next week, to get the furniture and the rest of Audra's things.'

The old lady beamed at him and a satisfied, almost triumphant look entered her eyes. She reached for her cane. 'Come along the two of you, let us go into the dining room. I want you to choose a piece of silver for your first home.'

14

'Please, Vincent, you have to get up,' Audra said, shaking his shoulder.

He shifted his position in the bed, turned on his back and opened his eyes, blinking in the filtered light coming in through the filmy curtains. 'Why?'

'Vincent, you know very well why,' Audra exclaimed as lightly as possible, trying to sheath her annoyance with him. 'Gwen's coming to supper.'

'*If* she shows up.'

'It was my fault last Sunday,' Audra said hastily, 'I got the dates mixed up.'

He threw her a sceptical look, said nothing.

'*Please*, Vincent,' she begged, her voice rising, 'please get up.'

His answer was to reach out and catch hold of her wrist. He pulled her down next to him, wrapped his arms around her and hugged her. He whispered against her cheek, 'Come to bed with me for half an hour.'

Audra struggled against him. 'I can't, you know very well I can't, there isn't time.'

'You mean you don't want to,' he said and let go of her at once.

Rising quickly, Audra stepped away from the bed and looked down at him, pursing her lips. 'You're being terribly unfair.'

'Oh no I'm not. You've turned cold on me lately.'

She flushed. 'I haven't. You always pick the wrong time!'

He looked at the alarm clock on the bamboo night stand. 'What's wrong with four-thirty on a Sunday afternoon. It strikes me it's the perfect time.'

'We're expecting a guest.'

'Ah yes. La-di-da Miss Gwen Thornton.' He pronounced the name with acerbity, added, 'I don't know what you see in her, why you run after her.'

'I don't run after her!'

'Yes, you do. I'm beginning to think you prefer her to me.'

'Don't be so ridiculous,' Audra exclaimed, staring at him in total astonishment, 'you know that's not true.' She felt a sudden surge of anger towards him and went on crossly, 'Anyway, I'm not in the mood to . . . come to bed, to make love, not after your behaviour these past few weeks.'

'*My* behaviour! What the bloody hell are you talking about?' He sat bolt upright in the bed and glared at her, his brilliant green eyes flashing as his temper flared.

Audra shook her head, very slowly, swallowing her exasperation with him, suddenly comprehending. 'You just don't *know* what you *do*, Vincent, do you?'

'What do you mean?'

'Oh Vincent, *Vincent*, you're impossible. And you make me so cross at times. For one thing, I'm getting impatient with your performance every Sunday at lunch time. You go off to the pub with your brothers, think nothing about strolling in well after two o'clock, having promised to be back by one at the latest, and then you turn nasty on me because lunch is spoiled . . . as if that were my fault.'

'I didn't turn nasty today.'

'Yes, you did. Actually, alcohol doesn't agree with you at all, it brings the worst out in you, makes you belligerent and touchy.'

He was about to ignore these criticisms, since she had lately developed a habit of carping, but changed his mind. 'Don't start giving *me* a lecture,' he snapped, 'I don't like it. I'm a man not a kid. I've always gone to the pub on Sundays, ever since I was eighteen, and I'm not going to stop now. Not for you or anybody else. And anyway, everybody goes to the pub on Sundays, it's an old English tradition.'

Only with the working class, she thought, and instantly hated herself for even thinking this; she despised any kind of prejudice in others. She said, 'There's something else . . . you left me alone to mark time at your mother's *again* last night, whilst you went off carousing in the pubs with your brothers –'

'It was our Bill's birthday,' he cut in indignantly, all of his defences going up.

'That's true, and I don't begrudge it when you celebrate a special occasion of that kind. But it wasn't Bill's birthday last Saturday, or the Saturday before, *or* the one before that, when you also went off on your own.'

'You didn't have to stay at my mother's last night, you could have gone to the old-time dancing with Laurette. After all, she invited you.'

'I'm not married to Laurette, I'm married to you.'

He sighed heavily and his mouth tightened in aggravation. 'I hope that doesn't mean that I've got to be tied to your apron strings twenty-four hours a day for the rest of my life, because believe you me, I won't be.'

Audra bit back the retort on the tip of her tongue, asking herself why she was bothering to argue with him at this particular time. Gwen was due to arrive within the hour and she wanted the atmosphere in the house to be tranquil. All she needed was for Gwen to think there was some sort of trouble between them.

And so she walked to the bedroom door, said softly, 'I still have a few chores,' and ran downstairs before he could say another word.

Pushing aside her worries about the recent changes in their relationship, she busied herself in the parlour-kitchen of their four-room cottage in Pot Lane. After covering the deal table in the centre of the floor with her best lace cloth, she took out several pieces of the beautiful china dinner service the Bells had given them as a wedding present, and went about setting the table for supper.

Once she had finished she glanced at the grate in the centre of the Yorkshire range, wondering whether or not to light the fire yet; these September nights soon turned cool. On the other hand, it was still sunny. Thinking of the weather reminded Audra that she needed fresh flowers for the table and for the console in the tiny sitting room next door. She hurried across to the work table next to the sink under the window, found the scissors in the drawer, took the flower basket off the set-pot and went outside.

The cottage did not have a name, only the number thirty-eight painted in white on its green door; it was one of three in a cul-de-sac behind The Towers in Upper Armley. Each house had a small garden, but Audra's was the most flourishing and resplendent because the previous tenants had cultivated it well over the years. Also, she had tended it diligently herself since they had moved into the cottage in June, and had made some new plantings and other improvements.

The last of the summer roses were full blown, tipped heavy and luxuriant heads down to the dark earth, and as Audra bent over the bushes she breathed deeply of their scent. It was rich and sweet, and just a little heady, and it made her feel slightly dizzy. She began to cut the roses with great care, not wanting to destroy the fragile blossoms by knocking any of the petals off. She selected mostly from the pale yellow and pink blooms, since these seemed to be fading faster than the others.

'You've no idea how bonny you look, love,' Vincent said from the doorway of the cottage.

She glanced up.

He flashed her one of his most beautiful and winning smiles.

She smiled back, understanding that he now wished to make up. 'Thank you,' she murmured. Rising, she picked up the flower basket, walked towards him down the flagged garden path.

His eyes did not leave her face. When she came to a standstill in front of him, he put his arm around her affectionately and led her inside. After closing the door and taking the basket out of her hands, he drew her into his arms, kissed her deeply and with growing passion.

Audra responded, held onto him tightly, returned his kisses. And she did so willingly now, all of the resentment which had been building up falling away from her suddenly, unexpectedly. She thought: I love him, he loves me, and that's all that matters really. We'll work out our differences. Somehow we will.

After a moment he stopped kissing her, tilted her face up to his, looked down into her startling eyes. It seemed to him that their bright cornflower blue had turned to the deeper hue of the violet, and as always they reflected her innermost emotions. His own gaze was intense, searching. 'Do you have any idea how much I want you at times?' he asked finally, in a hoarse voice.

'Yes.' She hesitated, then whispered, 'I feel the same way.'

Vincent smiled to himself, knowing how difficult it was for her to talk about such

661

things. Trailing a finger down her cheek, he said, 'Perhaps Gwen won't stay too late?' A dark brow lifted hopefully.

'No, I don't think she will. It's Monday tomorrow.'

Vincent leaned closer, murmured in her ear, 'Let's make a date to have an early night, Mrs Crowther.'

'Yes, let's.'

He hugged her to him, then released her. Swinging away, Vincent walked over to the front door. 'I'll be back in time for supper.'

Surprised, she asked, 'Where are you going?'

'To my mother's.'

But why?

'I promised Frank I would help him to fill in his military papers . . . Dad's finally given him permission to join the army, and he's very excited, our Frank is. You know how badly he wants to get into a cavalry regiment and go out to India. Can't say I blame him, either. Not the way things are in this bloody country right now.' He made a face. 'So many men on the dole and more being laid off work every day.'

Audra held herself very still. 'You're all right at Varley's, aren't you? They're not having problems too, are they, Vincent?'

'No, no, of course not.' He smiled reassuringly. 'We're in the middle of building that ruddy great house for old man Pinfold and his missus. Anyway, don't *you* worry your little head about such things, that's my job, as the man of the house.' He blew her a kiss, flashed his cheeky grin. 'Ta'rar, love, I'll see you a bit later.'

15

'So you did get a sofa. *Finally*,' Gwen said, stepping into the little sitting room from the parlour-kitchen.

'Yes,' Audra replied, following sharply on her heels, frowning at her friend's back.

Gwen marched up to this piece of furniture, which stood in the centre of the room facing the fireplace, and promptly sat down on it. She crossed her legs, settled against the cushions and made herself comfortable.

Audra hovered in front of her, studying her face intently. It was bland, as always, and innocent enough. And Audra knew at once that Gwen had not meant anything mean or unkind by the remark, even though the way she had said finally had sounded a trifle catty, as if she thought they hadn't been able to afford one before.

'We bought the sofa two weeks ago,' Audra volunteered in her usual quiet way. 'We'd been looking for that particular style for quite a while, since before we were married, actually.'

'Oh, had you,' Gwen said and swung around, brought her face closer to the back of the sofa, the three strands of cheap beads rattling as she moved. She sniffed the material. 'Mmmm. *Leather*. Very nice too, Audra. I must admit, I do like the genuine thing. Nothing imitation for me, either.'

Audra bit back a smile, walked over to the fireplace. She was amused by the incongruity of this last remark, in view of Gwen's penchant for fake jewellery. Always dripping in it, and a walking advertisement for Woolworth's, she had really outdone herself today. She was bedecked in a curious assortment of coloured rhinestones and paste; none of it matched and she glittered like an out-of-season Christmas tree. But that's my Gwenny, Audra thought with a rush of real warmth, her deep affection for her friend surfacing. She just wouldn't be the same without her beads and bracelets and dangling earrings; they're her trademark, and I don't suppose I would change her, even if I could.

Smiling, Audra reached for the Swan Vestas on the mantelpiece. 'It seems to have turned a little chilly,' she said, crouching in front of the grate, striking a match. She brought the flame to the paper and wood chips and went on, 'Are you sure I can't get you a cardigan, Gwen?'

'No, thanks very much, lovey, I'm all right. At least I will be now that you're getting the fire going.' Gwen smoothed her hand over the skirt of her brilliant red silk dress, explained, 'I should have worn something warmer than this, I suppose, but it's brand new and I wanted you to see it. Do you like it, Audra?'

'It's a lovely frock and it really does suit you,' Audra answered truthfully. She stood up, glanced approvingly at her friend.

Gwen preened; she patted her blonde hair. 'And what do you think of my new marcel wave?'

'I like it, and as a matter of fact I'm considering having one myself next week. Now, shall I make us a cup of tea? Or would you prefer a drink perhaps?'

'I wouldn't say no to a glass of sherry.'

'I think I'll join you.' Audra went to the hutch cupboard in the corner of the room, took out a bottle of Amontillado and two glasses, carried them to the mahogany console table which stood against the back wall.

Looking over the back of the sofa at Audra, Gwen remarked, 'And while we're handing out compliments, let me pay you one. You've made this room look really nice, you have that, Audra. Your father's paintings are beautiful, especially that one over the fireplace, and this furniture of your mother's – well, it looks ever so handsome in here. The place does you proud, lovey.'

Audra beamed at her. 'Thanks, Gwen, and I am glad you like it. The room's small, of course, but that makes it cosy and comfortable, don't you think?'

Gwen nodded, then let her eyes roam around. 'And what did you say the name of this funny green on the wall is?'

Audra laughed. '*Eau-de-Nil.*'

'What a strange name.' Gwen made a face.

'It means water of the Nile in French, and it's a very popular colour at the moment . . . in fashion, I mean.'

'Oh is it. Fancy that. Well, you always did keep up with the latest trends in clothes, lovey, didn't you? I keep telling Mum that you're *the* expert on fashion and styles and fabrics and all that kind of thing. I hope you realize how much I value your advice. Yes, you've got the best taste of anybody I know.' Gwen accepted the drink from Audra. 'Thanks, lovey,' she said.

The two women clinked glasses and Audra stepped up to the fireside, sat down in one of the Chippendale-style chairs which had belonged to her mother. 'I'm glad you think so – that I have taste, I mean.'

Gwen smiled at her. 'And where's Vincent then?'

'He went to his mother's, to help his brother fill out some papers. But he'll be back in time to have supper with us.'

Gwen took a sip of sherry, not trusting herself to speak.

It seemed to her that Vincent was always rushing off to his mother's house, on some pretext or another, but she did not dare say this to Audra. Ever since their tense discussion on the subject of Vincent in July, Gwen had been scrupulously careful not to make any critical remarks about him. She had soon realized, on that hot summer day when they went to tea at Betty's Café in Leeds, that she was perilously close to losing Audra's friendship, and this had both distressed and alarmed her.

Audra was extremely important to Gwen and so nowadays she kept a tight rein on her tongue at all times. But privately she believed that Vincent Crowther was not good enough for her friend, and nothing would make her change her mind. There was something about him that did not sit right with Gwen Thornton, although she would have been hard pressed to pinpoint what this was, if asked. She thought of him as being emotionally dangerous, and her instinct told her he would make Audra extremely unhappy one day.

She wondered, yet again, why he was constantly trotting off to his mother's, if that was where he really had gone, and then dropped this thought. She was delighted he was not at home. This afternoon she wanted Audra to herself for a while. She had something important to tell her and she preferred to do so without Vincent being present. He could be very opinionated. And he expressed those opinions without being asked.

Conscious of the growing silence, Audra leaned forward, peered across the dusky room. The twilight had come down early today, and the only light emanated from the fire. 'You're very quiet, Gwen,' she remarked. 'Are you troubled about something?'

'No, no, nothing's wrong,' Gwen was quick to say. She too drew closer, and let her voice sink low as she added, 'I don't want you to tell anyone, not even Vincent, but I'm thinking of getting married.'

'How wonderful, Gwen dear!' Audra cried, and then her brow furrowed in puzzlement. 'But I thought Mike had another two years of medical school? You told me in the spring that he wouldn't be able to afford a wife for a few years.'

'Oh, but it's not Mike I'm thinking of marrying.'

In the dimming light Audra could see that Gwen looked very pleased with herself, and this further perplexed her. 'But you told me you were in love with Mike Lesley, and certainly the two of you have behaved as if you were in the past year . . . you've been like a couple of love birds in fact,' Audra said, 'so what's suddenly happened to change all that?'

'Don't be so dense, Audra,' Gwen said with a light laugh, 'obviously I've met someone else.'

'Who?'

'It's someone you know – well sort of – but you'll never guess in a million years,' Gwen declared, her voice echoing with glee.

'No, I'm sure I won't, so you'd better tell me.'

'*Geoffrey Freemantle.*'

Audra was flabbergasted.

She opened her mouth, then closed it without uttering one single word. She simply gaped at Gwen in disbelief. Taking a deep breath, she said at last, 'You don't mean *Doctor* Freemantle? The one who was at the Fever Hospital for a while ... you couldn't possibly mean *him*.'

'Why couldn't I?' Gwen asked with sudden huffiness, 'of course I mean him.'

'*Oh.*' Audra put her glass down on the Sheraton table a little unsteadily. She was staggered. If ever a man was wrong for Gwen Thornton it was Geoffrey Freemantle. He was cold, arrogant, sarcastic and a snob. Good-looking yes, in a stiff, formal sort of way, and from a wealthy family, too, but he was a pompous and disdainful man, older than Gwen by about fourteen years. Audra found herself filling with genuine dismay and concern. It was hard for her to visualize the gay, laughing, fun-loving Gwen with such a stuffed shirt who believed himself to be superior to the rest of the human race.

'Is that all you're going to say? Just *oh* and nothing else?' Gwen's voice held a new tremulous quality and her feelings were obviously hurt.

'No, of course it isn't,' Audra said, reaching out, squeezing Gwen's arm. Pushing an enthusiasm into her voice which she did not feel, she added, 'I'm very, very happy for you, Gwen, really and truly I am. But I must admit to being a bit taken aback, since this was the last thing I expected to hear today. How did it all happen? Do tell, Gwen.'

Mollified to a certain extent, Gwen said in a cheerier voice, 'Well, after Geoffrey left Ripon, he went up to Northallerton, but he wasn't particularly happy there, so he transferred back to the General Infirmary in Leeds, this past spring. Anyway, we kept running into each other in the corridors, and we remembered each other from Ripon. He was always very friendly with me –' Gwen broke off and giggled. 'He finally asked me out at the beginning of July. And after one date it happened – just like that!' She snapped her thumb and fingers together and the glass rings flashed in the firelight.

'It's been a bit fast,' Audra commented, very softly.

'Yes, it has ... just like you and Vincent.'

Well, she's had the last word there, Audra thought and said, 'How do your parents feel about it?'

Gwen's face immediately underwent a radical change and she bit her lip, looking worried and troubled. 'To tell you the truth, Audra, I'm ever so upset with Mum and Dad. They don't seem to have taken to Geoffrey one little bit, and they're not pleased. Course, I think that's because Mike has been such a close chum of our Charlie's for years and they always hoped I'd marry him. But what can I do? Geoffrey's the one for me, oh yes, he *is*, lovey.'

'So you've made up your mind, Gwen?'

'Oh yes, I think so ... no, I *know* so. And he's quite a catch for me, really he is.' Her face began to glow again, reflecting the imitation jewels around her neck and she appeared to swell with pride. 'We've been looking at houses in Headingley, and I think we've found just the right one. It has a dining room, a lounge, a study, and five bedrooms, perfect for when we start a family. Next week, Geoffrey's taking me to Greenwood's in Leeds, to pick out an engagement ring, a *diamond* engagement ring, and the announcement will be in the *Yorkshire Post*.'

'Have you fixed a definite date?' Audra asked. She forced a bright smile.

'Not exactly, but Geoffrey wants us to be married in the spring, because he's taking me to Paris for our honeymoon and he says you should only ever see Paris in the spring – for the first time, that is. He's going to fit me out with lots of new clothes too, in Paris, and we're to stay at the Ritz. Can you imagine *that*! And then we'll go down to the Riviera. Geoffrey says mimosa time in the south of France is very beautiful and not to be missed and we'll be spending a whole week at the Negresco in Nice. It's a very posh place, you know, but then, so is the Ritz.'

Gwen finally paused, leaned forward eagerly, fixing her eyes on Audra's face, seeking a reaction.

Audra simply smiled.

Clasping her hands together tightly, Gwen's expression of excitement now changed to one of awe at the glamorous prospects facing her in the future.

'Once we've settled in the house in Headingley, which I'm *certain* we'll buy, Geoffrey is going to leave the Infirmary and set up in private practice. But not in Headingley. That's too suburban, Geoffrey says. He's going to take consulting rooms in Park Place in Leeds. He aims to be a fashionable doctor, treating the local gentry and society women, and he'll be very successful and rich and I'm going to help him all I can. We'll entertain a lot, for one thing, give elegant dinner parties and luncheons, and that's why I need lots of new clothes, Geoffrey wants me to look very smart.'

Audra could only nod, since her dismay was increasing and she did not know what to say. The fake stones Gwen was wearing, glittering so brilliantly in the lambent flames of the fire, held her attention. For a split-second they seemed real, looked like emeralds and rubies and sapphires and not bits of Woolworth glass. The jewellery will be the first to go, she suddenly thought. He'll make her get rid of it the minute they're married. Audra felt a stab of sadness as she pictured Gwen stripped of all her silly garish baubles which were quite worthless, yet had always meant so much to her.

Poor little Gwenny, Audra thought, trying to visualize her friend after *he* had worked his transformation on her, after *he* had dressed her and groomed her and turned her into the kind of Mrs Geoffrey Freemantle *he* wanted. In her mind's eye she saw a curiously stiff, cold woman, an image that had nothing to do with *her* Gwen Thornton. But then none of the things Gwen had been saying had much to do with the girl she knew so well and cared so much about.

Getting to her feet, Audra went and snapped on the small lamps standing on the Sheraton side tables flanking the fireplace. Then she hurried over to the console, brought back the bottle of sherry and refilled their glasses.

Knowing Gwen was waiting for some sort of comment after her graphic recital, Audra murmured, 'Well, it all sounds wonderful, very wonderful indeed.'

After this statement there was no holding Gwen.

Audra realized this when she returned to her chair and offered her friend the warmest of smiles – and her undivided attention.

Always a chatterbox, Gwen talked non-stop about her impending wedding, Geoffrey, his parents, the honeymoon, and the life they would lead afterwards, all without drawing breath.

Leaning back, sipping her sherry, Audra merely nodded occasionally, aware that she would not be allowed to get a word in edgewise. But she did not really want to; neither was she listening very closely.

Her thoughts were centred on Geoffrey Freemantle. It was patently obvious to Audra why he wished to marry Gwen Thornton. She was much younger than he, and was a beautiful blonde with a curvaceous figure; she had a vivacious, outgoing personality and a very loving nature. So all in all she was most desirable in every way; she would be to any man. Also, since she was a nurse and the daughter of a doctor, her background was ideal for an ambitious physician, and unquestionably Geoffrey Freemantle was that. Yes, Gwen could not be anything but an asset to him.

What truly bothered Audra was Gwen herself. Why on earth would she want to become *his* wife? He was the antithesis of Mike Lesley, and whatever Gwen now thought about Mike, Audra was well aware that she had been genuinely smitten with Charlie's closest chum. There was only one answer. Gwen wanted Geoffrey Freemantle for everything he represented and all the things he could give her – prestige, position, money.

Instantly, Audra tried to dismiss these uncharitable thoughts. Yet deep down inside herself she was convinced she was right. Not once in the entire time Gwen had been speaking about Geoffrey Freemantle had she mentioned that most crucial word *love*. How can a marriage work without love? Audra wondered. Perhaps she ought to talk to Gwen about that. Immediately she decided against doing so, remembering how much *she* had resented Gwen's gratuitous comments about her own marriage.

Anyway, perhaps I'm wrong, Audra told herself. Maybe she does love him. And then, much to her astonishment, she thought: but loving a man doesn't necessarily make for happiness, does it?

16

Later that evening, towards the end of supper, Gwen flashed Audra a conspiratorial look. 'Shall I tell Vincent my news?'

'Why not?' Audra said, laughing, well aware that her friend had been bursting to let him in on her secret all night.

'What news?' Vincent asked, glancing from one to the other.

'I'm getting engaged next week,' Gwen announced, then sat back in the chair, beaming and looking pleased with herself.

'Well I can't say I'm surprised.' Vincent leaned over and kissed her cheek. 'Congratulations, Gwen, and you ought to have brought Mike with you to supper. I like him, he's a straight bloke, and you've made a good choice for yourself.'

There was a small silence.

Gwen said quickly, 'Oh, but it's not Mike I'm marrying.'

'*Not Mike,*' Vincent echoed, sounding startled. He wrinkled his brow. 'Well, I'm blowed! And I thought you two were as thick as thieves. So you've found somebody else then.'

'Yes.'

'Cut up, Mike is, I'll bet.'

Gwen's throat tightened and she discovered she could not speak. She simply nodded.

'Yes, I can well imagine how he's feeling.' Vincent gave Gwen a very hard stare. 'Mike thought a lot about you, Gwen, he did that.'

Gwen said, 'I know he did and I cared for him too, but obviously not enough, if I could fall for another man.'

'And who's the lucky chap then?' Vincent asked, wondering how she could pass Mike Lesley up for someone else. Mike was very special, and now that he thought about it, the kind of man he would like for his sister Laurette.

'His name's Geoffrey Freemantle,' Gwen was saying, giving him a bright, confident smile, 'and he's a doctor at Leeds Infirmary. But he's originally from Harrogate and that's where his parents live.'

'And when did all this happen? I mean, we were all together with Mike at the end of June, so it must've been in the last couple of months, right?'

'Yes, Geoffrey first asked me out at the beginning of July, but I've –'

'All a bit *quick*, Gwen, isn't it?' Vincent broke in peremptorily, and not giving her a chance to respond, he hurried on, 'Marriage is a tricky business, you know, so I hope you're really sure about this chap. What I mean is that I *know* for a fact that Mike is the genuine thing, a really fine upstanding man, so I hope this new bloke is just as . . . *okay*. I wouldn't want you to be making a big mistake – a *terrible* mistake, Gwen.'

Gwen's mouth tightened in annoyance and she glared at Vincent, bristling. How like him to express his unwanted and unasked-for opinions. She exclaimed coldly, 'It just so happens that I've known Geoffrey for a long time – since I worked in Ripon. And as I pointed out to Audra earlier, you and she hardly had what I would call a lengthy courtship, so just think on, Vincent Crowther, people in glass houses shouldn't throw stones. Besides, it's none of your business, so there!' She sat back in a huff, still glaring at him.

'Oh excuse me, I'm sorry I spoke,' he muttered and puffed hard on his cigarette, looking annoyed.

Audra could see they were heading for one of their little tiffs and she exclaimed, 'Now you two, stop this, don't spoil a lovely evening. Anyway, I have something to tell you both – a little news of my own.'

Vincent swung to her, his brow lifting quizzically. 'What news, love?'

'I've taken a job and I start in two weeks.'

Vincent's jaw dropped and he stared at her in astonishment.

Gwen, equally surprised, cried, 'What *kind* of job? *Where?*'

'At St Mary's Hospital, here in Armley,' Audra explained. It was her turn to look pleased with herself, and she rushed on enthusiastically, 'And as a nurse, of course. Mrs Bell introduced me to the matron there, and I'm looking forward to it immensely. It's a challenge, since I'm going to be on the Maternity Ward.'

'Whatever made you *do* such a *stupid* thing?' Vincent demanded furiously, his green eyes blazing, an angry flush spreading up from his neck into his face. 'I don't believe I'm hearing you right!'

Audra was so taken aback at his extraordinary outburst, she was momentarily thrown off balance. And then she sat up straighter and retorted, 'I don't think it's stupid! I think it's very *clever* of me! After all, I've had a very good training and it's a pity to waste it. Matron Lennox has always said that nursing is a real gift with me, so why shouldn't I put it to good use? Not only that, I *want* to work.'

'Well, you can forget it! No wife of mine is going out to work and that's that!'

His temper was boiling very near to the surface and he shook his head with vehemence. 'My God, Audra, what are you thinking about? How could you do such a thing? I can just hear my mates talking, sniggering behind my back because my wife has to work to help support the household.'

'But that's not the reason I want to work!' Audra exclaimed.

'Maybe not, but that's what they'll think. Just you remember that I'm the man in this house and the bread winner and that *I* wear the trousers, and make the decisions, not you.' Glancing at Gwen, he appealed to her by saying, 'I bet *you're* not going to work after you're married, are you? Will *you* continue to be a nurse at the Infirmary?'

'No, I won't,' Gwen answered softly. She looked at Audra apologetically, reached out, touched her arm. 'I'm sorry, lovey, but I'm afraid I *have* to agree with Vincent. He's right, really he is. Anyway, why would you want to go back to nursing in a hospital? It's such demanding work and the money's not much.'

'Look, I want to use my skills, and be *useful*.' Determined to stand her ground with Vincent, Audra threw him a fierce look. 'And why does it matter what people think? You're being absurd –'

'I refuse to discuss this any further, Audra!' he interjected. 'The matter's closed!' He brought his fist down on the table much harder than he had intended and the dishes rattled.

'Vincent, don't be so stubborn!' Audra was so infuriated by his attitude and his behaviour she could barely contain herself. 'Being married to you doesn't mean that you can control me, make me do as you say. I would like to have a career in nursing, and it's my right to –'

'There you go again, Audra.' Vincent laughed sarcastically. 'It's Mrs Irène bloody Bell talking, not you. I don't want any of her women's rights and suffragette nonsense in my house, lass, and you'd better not forget that!'

Audra sucked in her breath, took a hold of herself. 'Oh Vincent, you're being so very unfair,' she murmured, softening both her voice and her manner. She took hold of his hand, hoping to placate him, wanting to get her own way ultimately. 'You're misunderstanding everything I've said.'

He gave her a cold sulky little glance, made no response.

Laughing somewhat self-consciously, Gwen looked from Audra to Vincent, then said, 'I don't like to see the two of you quarrelling in this way. Come along, kiss and make up.'

Knowing that Vincent would do no such thing, and wishing to curtail the quarrel because of Gwen's presence, Audra pushed back her chair and rose. Putting her arm around his shoulder, she brought her face down to his and kissed him on the cheek.

'All right, you win,' she said softly. 'I'll go to the hospital next week and tell them that I can't take the job.' But she was merely making a gesture for the sake of peace and quiet. She did not mean one word she said and she had no intention of giving in to him.

17

The marriage that had begun with an intense physical passion in the heat of the summer had a winter frost on it by December. And the passion had cooled considerably.

Vincent and Audra were frequently at loggerheads in the latter part of 1928, and certainly the tranquillity that had initially reigned in the little cottage in Pot Lane had given way to constant bickering and stormy quarrels.

The odd thing was that they were very alike in many respects, and this was actually part of the problem. Both were stubborn, strong-willed and independent minded. In consequence, they were forever locking horns. Then again, each believed the other was wrong and therefore at fault. They were young and immature and unable to make allowances for normal human frailties; neither could they compromise, which might have helped to lessen the tension between them.

Vincent, who was too self-involved at this time in his life to see much beyond his own desires and interests, had very little real understanding of Audra.

Surprisingly, she, who usually had so much insight into others, was rarely able to read him accurately because she was so subjective. In fact, Audra's view of Vincent Crowther would always be blurred and off-centre, influenced as she was by emotions of the most powerful kind.

Audra was generally in a turmoil about him and filled with conflicting feelings. There were times when she believed she loved him to distraction, others when she was convinced she had nothing but hatred for him. Vincent, as it happened, felt exactly the same way, and he was often as confused about Audra as she was about him.

Another stumbling block in their relationship was their newly-acquired habit of arguing violently about almost everything. They were suddenly incapable of discussing their problems in a quiet and rational way, so that neither of them ever really knew what the other *truly* thought or felt. And their mutual ambivalence about their marriage, and their dissatisfaction with each other, simply grew.

Sometimes they were able to make up in the darkness of their bedroom, drawn to each other – almost against their own volition – by the strong physical attraction they shared. But these occasions were growing rarer because their problems intruded more and more, and also because Audra, in particular, brought her anger to bed with her.

She had been holding a number of grudges against Vincent since September, and the one thing which truly rankled the most was his adamant refusal to let her return to nursing. She had reasoned, cajoled, argued and pleaded, in an effort to bring him around to her way of thinking. But Vincent had refused to budge, had remained as cold and unbending as he had been on the night of the supper with Gwen.

In the end, Audra had been the one to give in, suddenly understanding that if she defied him, and took the job at the hospital, he would leave her. And very simply put, life without Vincent Crowther was quite inconceivable to her, whatever their difficulties might be. Therefore, she had allowed his wishes to come before her own, telling herself that her marriage was far more important to her than a job. Somehow she had managed to wear a cheerful expression most of the time, one that did nothing to betray her feelings of disappointment and frustration at his obstinacy.

But when Audra had gone to Calpher House to tell Mrs Bell what had happened, her eyes had filled with tears and her unhappiness had tumbled out unexpectedly.

Irène Bell had been warm and sympathetic, as she always was towards Audra, and she had done her level best to comfort her. And whatever Mrs Bell had thought privately about Vincent's attitudes she had wisely kept her opinions to herself. 'Perhaps he'll come around, change his mind at a later date,' Mrs Bell had said encouragingly, giving her a hopeful smile.

But Audra knew he would not do so. It was not in Vincent's nature to admit that he was wrong. Similar though they were in some ways, Audra did not share these particular characteristics with him. She was always able to recognize when her judgement was flawed or when she had made an error.

As she hurried down Pot Lane, on this raw afternoon early in December, she was telling herself just how wrong she had been. Wrong to marry him in the first place, and certainly wrong to stay with him as she had, forever wavering about what to do, forever indecisive. She should have packed and left the minute everything had started to go askew in August.

Well, she had done that now. There was no turning back.

She tightened her grip on the small suitcase she was carrying and clenched her teeth, thrusting out her small determined chin. The decision had been made. *Finally*. She had walked out on Vincent Crowther and she had no intention of returning.

Deep down inside herself Audra knew that she still loved Vincent. She supposed she would always love him. But she had come to the realization that love was not necessarily enough to sustain a relationship. A couple had to be able to live together in harmony if a marriage was going to be successful. Seemingly she and Vincent could not do that. They were constantly at each other's throats these days, tearing each other apart with angry, hurtful words that were sometimes hard to retract later.

Last night they had had a particularly violent quarrel, their worst yet, and one that had left her shaken and despairing.

An hour earlier she had been ironing the last of his shirts in the parlour-kitchen when suddenly she had put the flatiron down on the trivet with a bang, instantly understanding what she must do. She had quickly tidied away the ironing things, changed her clothes, packed a suitcase, then taken her meagre savings and left the cottage.

As she had turned the key in the lock her eye had caught the number thirty-eight painted on the green door and she had stared at it, had felt a strange pain in her chest. And then an immense sadness had fallen over her and she had leaned her head against the door, closing her eyes, thinking of the past few months here. Simple and ordinary though it was, this humble little house was a palace to her. It was her first home of her own, and it contained not only all of the things she owned in life but her very life itself. Certainly her dreams and expectations for the future were sheltered within its walls. She had believed that these would come to flower here with Vincent; that they would start a family of their own, build a good life together. But that was not meant to be apparently – or so it seemed to her.

Audra had cut off these thoughts, not daring to let her mind run on in this manner. After slipping the key under the doormat, she had picked up her suitcase and almost run out of the cul-de-sac and into the lane.

And now as she headed in the direction of Whingate tram terminal she was still trying to push aside that sadness, as well as the awful depression that had descended on her. But the feelings lingered. Her dreams were shattered, her hopes were flattened; the sense of loss she had lived with for years loomed enormous in her. She had lost again. Lost her husband, lost their life together, lost her future.

Audra's step faltered and for a split-second, as she hesitated, she almost changed her mind and went back to the cottage. But something inside her said *no*. She plunged ahead determinedly.

The weather, which had been nasty all through the day, had turned ominous.

There was a pewter-coloured glaze on the sky and the surrounding landscape was bleak and bereft, without a single spot of colour. It reminded Audra of a painting in *grisaille* with its many tints of grey, and the stark and blackened trees stood out in relief, were like pieces of metal sculpture silhouetted against the lowering sky.

It had begun to drizzle. There was the low boom of distant thunder echoing like cannon across the nearby fields which stretched in a long, flowing line down to Old Farnley. A storm threatened and the wind was gusting over Hill-Top.

Audra huddled against the railings of Charlie Cake Park, sheltering as best she could as she waited for the tramcar from Leeds to arrive at the terminal. It was long overdue.

Shivering, she tightened the thick wollen scarf around her neck and stamped her feet in an effort to keep them warm. The kitchen of the cottage, with its fire banked up the chimney back, had been so cosy and comfortable she had not realized earlier just how bad it was outside. She stepped forward, glanced down Town Street. The street was strangely empty and deserted; the few pedestrians who were out and about were obviously in a hurry to get home before the storm broke.

What miserable weather it is, Audra thought; it matches my mood exactly. She drew back into the niche between the park's railings and the policeman's booth, sighing. She had chosen to leave Vincent and yet she was already missing him. How perverse I am, she muttered, not understanding herself. And then she thought: I'm stupidly ambivalent about him still. But I'm doing the right thing. I know I am. *Oh am I? Am I?*

Wrapping her arms around her body, Audra tried not to think about him or to envision his face when he walked in tonight and found that she had gone, found her note. She pushed her hands under her armpits for additional warmth and went on stamping her feet. She was chilled to the bone now, and she could feel the dampness seeping through her Melton coat and the plum-coloured cloche.

About twenty minutes later she heard the tram rumbling to a stop at the other side of the tiny wedge-shaped park and then the sound of voices and footsteps as people alighted. Filling with relief, she hoisted her suitcase and hurried forward –

and collided bodily with a young woman who came hurtling around the corner at breakneck speed.

They both recovered their balance, started to apologize, stopped mid-sentence as they recognized each other in the murky, late afternoon light. Audra found herself staring into the pretty face of the sister-in-law who was her closest friend in the Crowther clan. Her heart dropped.

'Audra! For heaven's sake, what are you doing here?' Laurette demanded and broke into warm and affectionate smiles.

'Catching a tram,' Audra mumbled and began to edge away.

Spotting the suitcase, Laurette frowned. 'Where are you going?'

'I don't know,' Audra responded in all truthfulness, then found herself saying, 'anywhere, I suppose, as long as it's far away from Vincent.'

'What do you mean?' Laurette looked at her intently, her eyes filling with alarm.

'I'm leaving him.'

Sucking in her breath, Laurette exclaimed, 'Audra, *no*, don't say that. You *can't* leave him.'

'Oh yes, I can.'

'But where will you *go*? You know full well you have *nowhere* to go. We're the only family you have.'

Ignoring this remark, Audra improvised swiftly, saying, 'I can always go to the Fever Hospital in Ripon.' She nodded to herself, realizing that this was quite true. 'Matron Lennox will find a place for me. I just know she will.'

'Audra, listen to me! Please don't be hasty, don't do something that you may live to regret. Reconsider . . . at least about leaving today. It's getting late, it's almost four and the weather's worse. Anyway, by the time you reach Leeds you'll have missed the last train to Ripon. Come on, love, let's go back to the cottage and talk about this,' Laurette pleaded, taking hold of Audra's arm.

'Please let go of me, Laurette.' Audra tried to shake off her sister-in-law's hand but Laurette's grip was firm. 'Laurette, *please*! This is ridiculous. And I certainly don't want to go back to the cottage.'

'Then let's go to my mother's . . . we're only five minutes away, come on, Audra, don't be stubborn. You're shivering, your face is blue with cold and you're going to catch your death of cold out here.'

'What's the point of going to your mother's house? I have nothing to discuss with her, or with you, for that matter. I'm not being rude, but it's true. I've made up my mind and I won't change it. *I'm leaving Vincent.*'

Laurette drew closer and put her arm around Audra's shoulders, lovingly, almost protectively. She confided softly, 'Look, I'm the first to admit I was against your marriage initially, but now that you are married I do think you and our Vincent should attempt to solve your problems and –'

'How can *you* of all people say that to me!' Audra exploded in amazement, looking askance at Laurette. 'Let's not forget that *you* are in the middle of a divorce.'

'Yes, I know, but that's different. You and Vincent love each other. Jimmy and I didn't, not really, not deep down.'

'Love is not always enough.'

'But it's a foundation to build a life on, Audra, really it is.'

'I've thought about this for weeks and I'm not going to be persuaded to do something against my will –' Audra broke off as a bell clanged and the tram rolled away down the tracks to Leeds.

Audra stared after it in dismay, then she swung to Laurette angrily. 'Now look what you've done! You've made me miss my tram! And there won't be another one for half an hour at least,' she wailed, then burst into tears of aggravation and frustration.

The profusion of roses on the walls, underfoot and patterning the china on the Welsh dresser looked more glorious than ever on this cold winter's afternoon. They seemed to glow with the vividness of real flowers in the blaze from the fire that roared in the hearth like a furnace, and threw off tremendous heat.

All was welcoming warmth and cheeriness in Eliza Crowther's kitchen. The air was fragrant with the smell of freshly baked bread and mince pies and tea cakes cooling on the set-pot, the sharper aromas of cloves, cinnamon, nutmeg and other spices from the Indies mingling with the fruity tang of candied peel, sultanas and Egyptian dates.

Eliza Crowther had been baking, which she usually did on Friday afternoons, come winter or summer. But today she had been busier than normal. Christmas was only three weeks away and she had been making holiday fare for her large family. She moved with agility between the table under the window and the sink, where she was now placing her dirty mixing bowls and spoons, cleaning up after herself. In a short while she would have to prepare tea for those members of her family who still lived at home, and she always preferred everything to be spic and span in her kitchen before she started.

A woman of medium height and build, Eliza looked all of her forty-nine years. This was mainly because of her plain way of dressing, her severe hairdo pulled straight back in a bun, and her stocky body, which had thickened since the birth of her last child, Danny. But she had an attractive, pleasant face, good bones, and her pale blue eyes were bright, lively – and coolly appraising.

And just as there was no artifice in her appearance, neither was there a jot of it in her manner. She stood no nonsense from anyone and prided herself on being a hard-working Yorkshirewoman who had her feet firmly planted on the ground. She spoke plainly and to the point, was even a little blunt at times; she had a saying, a maxim, or an old adage for almost everything in life and liberally peppered her speech with them.

After washing and drying all of her cooking utensils, Eliza went to the oven to check her Christmas cakes, date loaves and the huge bacon-and-egg pie she was baking for tea. Satisfied that they were coming along nicely, she returned to the table under the window; she stood screwing down the lids on the jars of the dried fruits she had just used in her cakes.

Since she was not expecting anyone at this hour she glanced up in surprise when the front door suddenly opened.

Laurette walked in, followed by Audra. They looked pinched and cold and they were shivering.

'You're home early, love,' Eliza said to Laurette. 'Nothing wrong at work, I hope?'

'No, Mam, it's my early Friday. Have you forgotten?'

'Oh, I had that.' Eliza looked at her daughter-in-law. 'Hello, Audra.'

'Hello, Mrs Crowther.'

Eliza turned back to her jars, finished replacing the last few lids. She had noticed the suitcase Audra was carrying but she decided not to make any comment. Laurette was now pushing it into the cupboard quickly, as if to hide it. There's trouble brewing for Vincent, Eliza thought, but she said, 'When you've taken your coat off, Laurette, you can mash a pot of tea, please, and you, Audra, come over to the fire and get yourself warm. You look nithered to death.'

Both young women did as she said in silence.

Laurette was pleased that she had succeeded in persuading Audra to come home with her. Although she had not intended to make her miss the tram, this had served a good purpose in the end. A tender-hearted girl, Laurette had grown to care deeply for Audra. The idea of her sister-in-law wandering the streets of Leeds in this bitter weather had been more than she could stomach. If she won't go home to Pot Lane tonight she can share my bedroom, Laurette thought, busying herself with the tea caddy. And I'm going to have a few strong words with that brother of mine at the first opportunity I get. We've spoiled him, Mam and Olive and I. And even little Maggie has always done his bidding. I bet he's not easy as a husband, or easy to live with, for that matter.

Audra, for her part, sat hunched in one of the green-moquette wing chairs, staring gloomily into the fire. She had been furious with herself for giving into Laurette, but now she had to admit that she was glad to be inside in the warmth. The dampness had penetrated her bones and she still felt terribly cold despite the huge fire.

The kettle was hissing and steaming on the hob, as it always was in winter, and Laurette filled the large brown teapot with boiling water then turned and put it on the table in the centre of the room.

Seating herself at the table, she looked across at her mother and said, 'Where're Maggie and Danny? It's well turned four and they should be home from school by now, shouldn't they?'

'No, not today. They've gone to the Parish Hall to see about the Sunday School pantomime. They both want to be in it so badly, I said they could go to try out for the parts. It's *Cinderella* they're doing this year.'

'Knowing Maggie, she'll want to play the leading role and nothing else,' Laurette said with a laugh. 'Come on, Mam, have this cup of tea before it gets cold.'

Eliza joined the two of them in front of the fire.

She took the other wing chair and, after a sip of tea, focused her attention on her daughter-in-law. 'Now then, Audra lass, what's all this about? I saw the suitcase, you know. Are you running off somewhere, or moving in here?'

Audra flushed and bit her lip. But she did not reply, since she had no wish to confide in Vincent's mother.

Laurette volunteered, 'I met Audra at the tram stop, Mam. She looked ever so upset and she said she was leaving Vincent, going back to work at the hospital in Ripon. But she missed her tram to Leeds when we were talking, so I made her come home with me.'

'I see.' Eliza sat up straighter and stared hard at Audra, frowning to herself. 'What kind of silliness is this then, lass?'

'It's not *silliness*!' Audra protested indignantly, and before she could stop herself she rushed on with some fierceness, 'Vincent's been behaving very *badly* in the past few months! He's not treating me properly, and there's no good reason why I should stay with him any longer!'

'He can't have been hitting you!' Eliza asserted swiftly, secure in the knowledge that her son would never strike a woman, even if severely provoked. 'So what *do* you mean? Explain yourself, lass.'

Knowing that she was trapped, Audra took a deep breath, said in a more even tone, 'He leaves me alone a great deal these days, and you *know* he does, Mrs Crowther. In fact, he's always out at the pub with his brothers and his friends, or at the bookie's office betting, and I don't think that's very fair of him. We might as well not be married, for all we see of each other, the little time we spend together.'

Eliza sighed heavily and shook her head. 'But that's the way it *is* with us, the way it *is* in our working-class world, Audra. Our men toil hard, and their way of relaxing, of enjoying themselves, is to go to the pub for a pint, a game of darts, a few laughs with their mates. And what's the harm if they put a few coppers on a horse, have a bit of a flutter once in a while? Surely you don't begrudge Vincent his bit of harmless pleasure?'

'No, of course I don't. It's just that I would like to see more of him, share his leisure hours. After all, I am his wife. But he goes out alone to the White Horse several nights a week, and he always disappears at weekends. He leaves me to my own devices and I'm lonely.'

'Aye, I know, but as I said, that's the way it is and the way it'll always be now that the two of your are married, settled down. It's different when you're courting, it's all sweetness and light like. But once he's got the wedding band on your finger, a man's attitude changes, Audra, and you'd better accept that. Oh aye, you had, lass. All marriages are the same and you won't notice things so much when you have a few bairns tugging at your skirts. *They'll* occupy your time, mark my words, and you'll be glad to have Vincent out from under your feet, you'll see.'

Audra's mouth tightened in annoyance. 'I'm not planning on having children just *yet*, Mrs Crowther. What I would like to do is to return to nursing but that's another problem between us, because Vincent won't hear of me working.'

Eliza was aghast. 'I should think he won't!' she exclaimed in a horrified voice, 'how could you ever suggest such a thing to him? It would make him feel *small*, much *less* of a man, if his wife went out to work. Whatever would people think? And what would his mates say?'

'I don't know and I don't care! Furthermore, we could really use the money I'd be earning as a nurse,' Audra shot back, unable to suppress her irritation any longer. 'Vincent and I had the worst quarrel we've ever had last night, it was very nasty really, almost violent. And it was about *money*. I've discovered that we're in serious debt, yes, *deeply* in debt, Mrs Crowther, and it's Vincent's fault, not *mine*, so don't look so disapprovingly at *me*. He went off and bought things on hire purchase at Wigfalls in Leeds without telling me. He had no right to do that.'

'What things?'

'The leather sofa, the wardrobe and the bed.'

'And why are you acting so surprised? You knew you had those things, they're in your home, lass, aren't they?'

'Yes, but I didn't know he'd bought them on hire purchase, I thought he'd paid for them outright, paid cash. And the reason I know he didn't do so is because Vincent has missed some payments, and Wigfalls have written a nasty letter, which I opened when it came in the post yesterday. And apparently it's not the first letter they've sent him either.' Audra shook her head, her expression baffled. 'We need the money so badly and yet Vincent goes out drinking and gambling as if he doesn't have a care in the world. And he refuses to let me go back to nursing. It doesn't make sense . . . his pride gets in the way of everything, and that's very stupid of him.'

'I'm sure there's a right good explanation why he missed a payment,' Eliza replied, instantly defending her favourite child, her Stormy Petrel. 'Vincent has money in the bank, I know that for a fact.'

'No, he doesn't, Mrs Crowther. He spent his savings on new clothes for the wedding, our honeymoon in Robin Hood's Bay and on other things for the cottage. I offered him my savings, and I said I would willingly sell a piece of my mother's jewellery to help clear up our debts, but he won't let me do anything to help.'

'That's because he doesn't need your help,' Eliza exclaimed huffily. 'He probably has a nest egg tucked away somewhere, and knowing my son he'll only get angrier if you try to cut the legs out from under him. Let *him* deal with these matters, Audra, in his own way, and don't interfere. He *is* the man of the house, after all.' Eliza's eyes narrowed slightly, and she went on in a sterner voice, 'Anyway, I'm sure you're making a mountain out of a molehill, it's usually six of one and half a dozen of another in any marriage, and yours can't be much different from anybody else's. At least he's not chasing after other women, and you ought to be grateful for *that*. Take my advice, try a bit harder, try to understand Vincent better.'

Audra stared at her mother-in-law in utter astonishment. The woman was apparently blaming her for all of their troubles and exonerating Vincent completely. She felt suddenly defeated, worn down and totally misunderstood. 'I *have* tried . . . I know you don't like me, but I'm not a bad person –' Audra's mouth trembled and she turned her head to one side as scalding tears stung the back of her eyes.

Eliza, startled by this statement, exclaimed, 'Nay, Audra lass, don't say a thing like that! I *do* like you, I always have, and I think you're a fine young woman.'

'*Do you?*' Audra swallowed down the incipient tears. 'But you haven't acted as if you like me, really you haven't, Mrs Crowther. You didn't want us to get married, did you?' Audra asked, stabbing in the dark now.

'No, that's true, I didn't,' Eliza admitted quietly. 'But only because you're from a different world to us. I was convinced you and our Vincent would end up wanting different things in life, and I wasn't so far wrong was I?'

Audra bit her lip. 'I don't know, I'm a little confused.'

Eliza nodded. 'Aye, you are, and that's why you shouldn't be doing owt hasty, like leaving Vincent.'

'But if you feel our marriage won't work, why do you want me to stay with him?'

'We're respectable people, and one divorce in this family is enough,' Eliza muttered and looked through the corner of her eye at Laurette. She cleared her throat. 'Marry in haste, repent at leisure, that's what I told our Vincent. But he wouldn't listen, and I don't suppose you did either, to your friends, I mean. Well, there we are, the two of you have made your bed so you must lie in it, regardless of whether the mattress is lumpy or not.' Leaning forward, giving Audra a sharper look, she finished, 'It's always the woman who makes a marriage work, never the man. Just you be remembering that, lass.'

'But that's not fair!' Audra cried, her indignation surfacing.

Eliza laughed hollowly. 'Whoever said a woman's life was fair? Certainly not women from my walk of life, at any rate.' She laughed again, shaking her head. 'Anyway, Audra, I expect things'll get better between you and Vincent once the babies start coming along and you have the little ones to love and look after.'

'But I want to do something more with my life, to achieve things, and I want to be happy –'

'*Happy*,' Eliza spluttered, looking at Audra as if she had uttered an obscenity. 'That's a word you'd better erase from your vocabulary, my girl, and right sharpish. Just you be thankful you've got a roof over your head, food in your stomach and a good husband to provide for you. Happiness is not for the likes of us, Audra, it's for the gentry, for the rich, them as have time for happiness and can afford it. We can't.'

What a bleak outlook she has, Audra thought, and turned to Laurette. They exchanged knowing glances and Laurette shrugged her shoulders. Then she stiffened slightly and sniffed. 'Mam, is there something burning?'

'Oh my God, the Christmas cakes and the pie for your dad's tea!' Eliza leapt to her feet, grabbed the oven towel and yanked open the oven door. She began pulling out her baking tins, exclaiming to Laurette over her shoulder, 'Well, don't sit there gawping, lass, get another towel and help me. And Audra, make a bit of space on the set-pot, please.'

Laurette and Audra sprang to her assistance and within seconds the Christmas cakes, the date loaves and the bacon-and-egg pie had been spread out to cool. Eliza's critical eyes roved over them and she nodded happily when she saw none of them had been ruined. 'We saved them in the nick of time,' she murmured, sounding relieved.

'It's only me, Mam!' The door burst open and Vincent came barging in, pulling off his cap as he did. When he saw Audra his brows shot up in surprise. 'What are you doing here, love?' he asked in the pleasantest of voices, smiling at her warmly.

Last night might never have happened, Audra thought, staring back at him mutely, marvelling at his ability to shrug everything off. His nonchalance at this moment was quite remarkable. It annoyed her.

'She's having a cup of tea,' Laurette said quickly. 'We ran into each other in Town Street and I invited her back to visit for a little bit.'

'Oh, I see.' He started to shrug out of his coat, swung to the cupboard.

Laurette hurried over to him. 'Here let me hang this up for you, Vincent,' she said, taking his overcoat. 'You get over to the fire and warm yourself up. You look frozen.'

She doesn't want him to see the suitcase, Eliza thought, watching her children closely. But he's bound to see it sooner or later. She sighed, turned back to her cakes.

'Thanks, Laurette,' Vincent said, rubbing his cold hands together, striding across the room. 'I wouldn't mind a spot of tea meself.'

'Coming right up,' his sister said, and went to the Welsh dresser. Bringing a cup and saucer to the table, she lifted the teapot and poured for him.

A moment later the door again flew open and Danny ran into the kitchen, followed more sedately by Maggie, who was feeling very grown up and important this afternoon.

'We got the parts! We got the parts!' Danny cried to the room at large, throwing his cap and scarf onto the sofa. His overcoat followed, and then he scurried over to the birdcage in the corner. 'I'm home, Flyaway,' he cooed to the budgie sitting on its perch. 'Come on, sing a song for me.' He gazed lovingly at the little bird, which Vincent had bought for him and also named.

'Danny, hang up your things at once,' Eliza called to her youngest.

'I will, Mam, in a tick.'

Maggie, who was taking off her own coat, said, 'Oh, I'll do it, Mother.'

'And what part have you got, Tiddler?' Vincent asked when the little boy came and stood at his knee a moment later.

Danny looked up at his handsome eldest brother and smiled sweetly. 'I'm going to be a page boy. I don't get to say owt, but I do get to carry a luvely red velvet cushion with the glass slipper on it.'

Vincent rumpled his hair. 'That's grand, lad.'

Maggie joined Laurette and Vincent at the table, sat down between them and grinned. '*I* have a speaking part though, a big part too. I'm going to be one of the Ugly Sisters.'

'What perfect casting!' Vincent cried and laughed uproariously.

'You are awful our Vincent!' Maggie screeched, punching him hard on the arm. 'And if I'm ugly then so are you, 'cos everybody says we look exactly alike.' She punched him again.

He grabbed hold of her wrist, held her tightly.

'Now then, you two, stop all this rough housing!' Eliza cried, 'your dad'll be home any minute and he'll be wanting a bit of peace and quiet after his hard day at work.'

Eliza walked over to the Welsh dresser and took down two of the largest serving platters. 'And you'd better stop to your teas, Audra and Vincent. There's plenty for all of us. There's the bacon-and-egg pie, and I made a lovely jellied tongue yesterday.' She peered at Audra over her shoulder. 'You will stay?'

'That's up to Vincent,' Audra murmured.

'Yes, of course we'll stay, Mam, why not?' He pulled out his Woodbines and lit one.

Audra sank back into the wing chair gratefully and gazed into the fire, her face abstracted.

She preferred to be here rather than alone with him at the cottage, where they were bound to quarrel. In a few minutes his brothers Jack and Bill would return from work and the atmosphere would probably turn boisterous, as it usually did when they were all together. But as rough-and-ready as the Crowther clan sometimes were, she knew they were good-hearted.

Often Audra did feel overwhelmed by them, and occasionally she saw them looking at her oddly. She sensed they thought she was standoffish and a snob, and frequently they seemed wary with her. But not Laurette and Mr Crowther. *They* were her real friends in this family and she was quite certain they truly cared about her, just as she cared about them. They were the ones she would miss when she

679

was back in Ripon. Despite what his mother had said, Audra was still planning to leave Vincent. She would go tomorrow.

'How could you do it? How could you go blabbing to our Laurette and me Mam?' Vincent demanded furiously, the minute they arrived at the cottage in Pot Lane.

Glaring at Audra, he went on heatedly, 'I couldn't believe it when Laurette took me up to the sitting room after tea, and told me how she'd stopped you from running off and leaving me. It's bloody *embarrassing*, that's what it is!'

'I didn't go blabbing to them, as you put it,' Audra said evenly, holding herself very still. She was determined not to let him goad her into losing her temper as he had last night. 'Laurette told you what happened. If I hadn't run into her at the tram terminal, and quite by accident, neither she nor your mother would know anything.'

'Well, they *do* know, and you've gone and humiliated me again!'

'What on earth do you mean?' she demanded, drawing herself up to her full height and glaring back at him.

'First you diminish me in front of Gwen, what with all your talk of getting a job, going out to work and behaving as if I can't support you, and now you've been complaining about me to my mother and sister. Anybody would think that I'm the devil incarnate the way *you* bloody well carry on.' His sudden laughter was harsh and there was a sarcastic edge to his voice as he added, 'And I thought *I'd* be the one to embarrass *you*, seeing as how you're so very much the lady. But the boot's on t'other foot it seems to me.'

'Please don't worry, Vincent, I won't embarrass you any more. I won't be around to do so. I'm leaving you tomorrow. For good.'

'Suit yourself.' He marched across the little parlour-kitchen to the front door and picked up his cloth cap.

'Where are you going?' Audra demanded.

'To the pub,' he replied and slammed out of the cottage without uttering another word. The door crashed behind him.

But Audra did not leave the following morning as she had threatened to do. She could not even leave their bed. Her throat was sore, her eyes were watering and she had a raging fever.

By eleven o'clock Vincent was so worried about her he sent for Doctor Stalkley, the local physician who had brought him into the world.

'Influenza, I'm afraid, Vincent,' the old doctor pronounced, after he had examined Audra. 'There's a lot of it going around in Armley just now. See that she stays in bed and give her plenty of liquids. Not much else you can do, my boy, it has to take its course.'

18

Irène Bell paused on the threshold of the dining room at Calpher House, catching her breath in surprise.

Always a handsome room, with its cranberry-coloured wallpaper of flocked velvet and English Regency antiques, it had a special kind of beauty this afternoon. This was due in no small measure to the Christmas decorations which were now in place, and which had been created by Audra in her absence.

Mrs Bell had just returned from a two-day business trip to London and she stood for a moment longer, taking in the details of the seasonal décor.

She saw that Audra had eschewed tinsel and glitter, instead had turned to nature for her decorative theme. Garlands and branches of evergreens and mistletoe and the traditional hawthorn were much in evidence, tied and swagged with burgundy velvet or gold lamé ribbons. Crystal compotes held miniature pyramids of fruit and fir cones and nuts, and had been trimmed with brightly-coloured bows; there were masses of white candles everywhere and two small fir trees stood guard on either side of the fireplace. These were covered with bows and ribbon streamers in rainbow hues, and the tubs were wrapped with gold lamé fabric in the Victorian manner.

In fact, the entire theme had an old-fashioned, Victorian air about it, and it was one which Irène found charming. As always she was impressed and admiring of Audra's artistic talents.

I wonder how best to compensate her for this marvellous work? Irène asked herself, giving the room a final glance before turning away. I cannot offer her money, she'll be insulted. She's such a proud young woman. I must find her a very special gift tomorrow, quite aside from her Christmas present from us.

Crossing the hall in her usual energetic way, Irène Bell mounted the stairs, knowing that her child's former nanny would be in the day nursery with him, unless she had already gone home to Pot Lane.

They were sitting at the table near the fire, with a paintbox and sketching pad spread out in front of them, and they both looked up as Irène walked in saying, 'Hello, hello,' to them.

Theophilus cried, 'Mummy! Mummy! You're home!'

He ran across the floor and flung himself at her joyously. Irène bent down and kissed the top of his head and hugged him to her, then she raised her face and smiled across at Audra.

'Good afternoon, Mrs Bell,' Audra said, smiling back.

'I'm so glad you're still here, Audra. I just saw the dining room and I must thank you for the wonderful decorations. The room looks beautiful, just *beautiful*. You're to be congratulated.'

A look of gratification flitted across Audra's pale face. 'Thank you, but I did have a few willing helpers, you know.'

Irène's brow puckered. 'You did?'

'Oh yes, Mrs Bell. Theo and Dodie, not to mention Cora.'

'*Cora*. Gracious me, you are brave.' Irène shook her bright auburn head. 'I don't mean to be unkind, but oh dear, that poor girl does seem to get clumsier every day. And how kind of you to include her, yes, so *very* kind of you, Audra.'

Irène walked over to the table with Theo, where they both sat down.

Audra explained, 'Cora's enthusiasm is worth a lot, Mrs Bell, and she would have been heartbroken if I hadn't asked her to do something. She helped Theo to make the garlands, actually.'

'That was a safe job, Mummy,' Theo volunteered, earnestly gazing up at his mother. 'Audra said there was no risk involved, since all Cora could break was a twig or a bit of wire. Anyway, I kept an eye on her.'

'I'm sure you did, darling,' Irène murmured, biting back a smile of amusement. She turned to Audra, remarked, 'I just can't begin to tell you how much I appreciate your efforts. What with Cook under the weather, Mr Agiter coming down with influenza, and the unexpected trip to London, I was quite at my wits end earlier this week. I don't know what I would have done, if you hadn't been able to help me out with the dining room décor, Audra. We have so many dinners planned, and I must admit I can't help wondering how on earth we'll manage without a butler at Christmas. *Oh dear.*' Irène's gay, freckled face clouded. Instantly, it cleared. 'Well, never mind, *never mind*. One can't worry about such things. I shall cope somehow.' Irène peered at Audra in the firelight. 'How inconsiderate of me, I haven't even asked you about your health, my dear. Are you feeling better?'

'Oh yes, thank you, Mrs Bell.'

'But you look as peaked as you did on Monday, when I came down to the cottage to see you.'

'I'm perfectly fine, honestly I am, Mrs Bell.'

Theo said, 'Look, Mummy, Audra's been showing me how to paint a scene.' He pushed the sketching pad towards her.

Glancing down at it, Irène nodded. 'Very good, darling, very good indeed.' Her eyes strayed to the left-hand page where Audra had painted a simple landscape for him to copy. But in its very simplicity it was absolute perfection. Irène looked at it for the longest moment, struck by its delicate beauty, the reflection of light she had captured on paper. Finally lifting her eyes to Audra's, Irène said, 'This is lovely . . . haven't I seen something similar before?'

'Yes, I did a larger version several years ago and it was hanging in my room when I worked here.'

'Of course. And you had given it an unusual name, as I recall.'

'The Memory Place,' Audra said very softly. 'The painting is of the sycamore tree on the slope opposite High Cleugh . . . where my family and I used to picnic.'

'Yes, I remember now.' Leaning forward, Irène said in her emphatic voice, 'You are a remarkably talented artist, Audra, and I can't understand why you don't pursue your painting.'

'Oh, but I'm not very good, Mrs Bell, really I'm not,' Audra replied with an odd laugh that was at once both dismissive and self-deprecating. 'It's just a hobby, after all.'

'It could be your profession.'

'Oh no, Mrs Bell, *nursing* is my forte. You know that Matron Lennox said I was truly gifted as a nurse, a real healer.'

'Yes,' Irène said, very slowly. Her eyes grew thoughtful and, after a short pause, one of her perfectly-pencilled brows lifted inquiringly. 'I presume Vincent did not change his mind and that he is still against your going back to nursing?'

'Yes, he's adamant, I'm afraid.' Audra lowered her eyes, then glanced away.

'I see.' Irène decided to let the subject drop immediately, understanding that she was treading on dangerous ground. She wondered if there was some sort of trouble between Audra and Vincent, other than their differences about her nursing career. The girl had seemed strangely quiet and withdrawn at the beginning of the week. But then perhaps that was due to her recent bout with 'flu. Perhaps she was merely a little rundown.

Audra was saying, 'And speaking of my husband, I really ought to be going in a few minutes, if you'll excuse me, Mrs Bell.' She took a peek at the nursery clock. 'Oh goodness, it's already five-thirty. Vincent will be home from York at seven.'

'*Why* has he been to York? What's he been *doing* there?' Theo demanded, as always insatiably curious about Vincent, who totally fascinated him.

'Really, Theophilus,' his mother chastised, 'you know it's rude to ask such personal questions.'

'Oh that's perfectly all right, Mrs Bell,' Audra said, then explained to the child, 'he went with Mr Varley, you know, the man who owns the building firm, and they were going to have a meeting with Mr Rowntree ... something about building an extension onto one of the chocolate factories.'

'Ooooh! How *scrumptious*! I wish I could go to a chocolate factory. Do you think Vincent will bring you back a box of Black Magic? They're my favourite, Audra.' Theo looked at her hopefully.

'I know they are, but I don't think Mr Rowntree gives his chocolates away, Theophilus,' she responded with a small smile and stood up.

'Oh Audra, please don't go,' Theo pleaded, 'I hardly ever get to see you these days.'

Audra reached out, stroked his fair head with tenderness, filling with love for him. He was such a dear. 'That's not strictly true,' she said gently, 'and besides, now that you're a big boy and going to preparatory school, you don't need a nanny. After all, you are seven years old.'

'I know – but you *promised* we'd be extra special chums.'

'And so we are.' Audra bent forward, kissed his cheek. Theo put his arms around her neck, clung to her for a moment.

Irène Bell said, 'Don't behave like a *baby*, Theophilus, you know very well Audra has other responsibilities now that she's married.'

'Yes,' he mumbled and let go of Audra, although he did so somewhat reluctantly.

'Shouldn't you be getting ready for the pantomime at the Grand Theatre in Leeds?' Irène now suggested, her eyes sparkling with merriment.

'Oh Mummy! *That's* my surprise! And I've been wracking my brains for days!' the child shouted excitedly, jumping down off the chair. 'I've been longing to see *Jack and the Beanstalk*.'

'Then run along and wash your hands and face. And Theo, please change your shirt, the one you're wearing is splattered with paint,' his mother pointed out.

'Goodbye, Theo,' Audra said, blowing a kiss from the doorway.

''Bye, Audra. Don't forget my party tomorrow and please, *please* make Vincent come with you. You will, won't you?'

'I'll do my very best.'

As they went down the staircase together, Irène said to Audra, 'Theo does have a soft spot for Vincent, doesn't he?'

'Yes, and the feeling is mutual, I believe.'

'He seems to be doing awfully well at Varley's, and that must please you.'

'Oh yes, it does. Mr Varley likes him and, of course, Vincent does have a great eye and a marvellous sense of perspective when it comes to architecture. I've told him many times that he's a born builder.'

'I think it's most commendable that he's started going to night school,' Irène said, turning to face Audra as they drew to a standstill in the hall. 'Is he enjoying studying draughtsmanship?'

'Yes,' Audra murmured, not wishing to admit that Vincent had only *talked* about enrolling in the course, had never actually done so.

Studying her face closely, Irène Bell saw a flicker of something at the back of Audra's startlingly blue eyes. It was a peculiar look and it alarmed her. She's a very troubled young woman, Irène thought, with a flash of intuition. Reaching out, she touched Audra's arm lightly. Her voice was low and warm as she asked, 'Is everything all right with you, my dear?'

Audra hesitated.

For a fraction of a second she was on the verge of confiding in Irène Bell, and then she changed her mind. Apart from the fact that her pride and her strong sense of privacy got in the way, her intelligence told her that Mrs Bell could not help her. Nobody could help her now.

Audra forced a bright smile onto her face. 'Oh no, nothing's wrong, Mrs Bell. Thank you for asking, but everything is fine.'

'And your health *really* is all right?' Irène pressed, still not convinced.

There was a small silence before Audra nodded, and almost too emphatically.

'You do look *awfully* pale suddenly,' Irène insisted, frowning at her.

'It's just the aftermath of the 'flu, and I am also feeling a little tired now.' Audra gently extricated her arm, hurried over to the coat stand. She took down her grey Melton coat and the plum-coloured cloche, put them on, glancing in the hall mirror at herself as she adjusted the hat.

A moment later, as she wrapped her woollen scarf around her neck and pulled on her gloves, she asked, 'Would you like me to come a little earlier on Christmas Eve? Perhaps there's something I could do to help at Theo's party, Mrs Bell.'

Irène chuckled softly, 'Indeed there is, Audra, I'd be most grateful if you would keep an eye on Theophilus and nine other little terrors, at least until the Punch-and-Judy show starts.'

No sooner had the door closed behind Audra, than it sprang open again within the space of minutes.

Irène was half way up the staircase.

She turned and her face lit up at the sight of her husband.

'Thomas darling!' she cried, 'you're home early, how lovely.' She sped swiftly down the stairs, across the marble hall and into his welcoming arms.

After hugging her tightly, kissing her cheek, he looked down into her face. His own filled with pleasure. 'Did you have a pleasant journey back?'

'Oh yes, thank you, Thomas. All my news over a nice cosy drink shortly, before we go to the Grand. But first, take off your coat, and then I'll show you the decorations Audra has created in the dining room.'

'I saw her leaving the house as we turned into the drive,' Thomas remarked, removing his scarf. 'I had Robertson stop the motorcar, and I told her he would run her home if she waited a moment, but she wouldn't hear of it. She's always been an independent little thing, though, hasn't she?'

'Yes,' Irène agreed.

She linked her arm through her husband's and led him across the floor in the direction of the dining room. 'Audra doesn't look terribly well to me, and I have a feeling she and Vincent are not as happy as she would like to have me believe.'

'Mmmmm. Handsome chap, Vincent Crowther. Probably ruined too, by his mother and those doting sisters of his, not to mention women – women in the past tense, of course. No, Irène, I don't imagine that that young whippersnapper is easy to live with. And then of course, he is from a different class.'

'Thomas!' Irène exclaimed, drawing away, looking up at him sharply. Her eyes were dismayed. 'You know I detest that sort of thing – class prejudice absolutely *incenses* me.'

'Yes, but you're not going to change the nature of the English . . . it's endemic. Besides, the lower classes are just as bad as the aristocracy when it comes to that sort of thing. Snobs too, in their own way.' He smiled at her somewhat wryly. 'And whatever you say, background *does* make a devil of a difference, darling. Audra is a lady, and breeding will out – why, it's obvious in everything she does. And unfortunately Vincent will always hold her back, hold her down, you'll see.' Thomas Bell shrugged. 'But they are married, and it isn't actually any of our business.'

'No, but I'm so fond of her, Thomas.'

'Yes,' he said.

The Bells paused on the threshold of the dining room. '*Voilà!*' Irène exclaimed, waving her hand towards the room.

For a moment Thomas Bell was startled. 'Why, it looks exquisite,' he managed at last, obviously as impressed as his wife had been earlier.

'Very original, and quite breathtaking,' Irène said, and then sighed so heavily that Thomas eyed her curiously.

Irène met his direct gaze. She shook her head, and a look of perplexity washed over her expressive face. 'Audra thinks she's especially gifted as a nurse, but she's not, she's simply very good and that's all. Of course, she would never believe me if I told her this, since Margaret Lennox has expressed entirely different views to her.'

Swinging her eyes towards the dining room, Irène waved her hand at it again. 'No, this is where her gift truly lies – in her artistic endeavours. She is an extraordinary painter, Thomas, but she can't see it, and I don't understand why she's so blind.' Once again Irène sighed. 'Oh Thomas, what a *waste* of talent. That's the saddest part of all.'

'Perhaps it is. Poor Audra, she never had much of a chance, really. Life sort of came charging at her full tilt, and when she was so young . . .'

19

Why ever did I tell Mrs Bell that I'm fine? I'm not fine at all. And I'm trapped. Whatever am I going to do?

These thoughts pushed all others to the back of Audra's mind as she busied herself in the parlour-kitchen of the cottage in Pot Lane, not long after she had left Calpher House.

I *should* have confided in Irène Bell, she told herself, unexpectedly regretful that she had kept her worries bottled up inside. It helped to air problems, especially if the listener was a sympathetic and understanding person like Mrs Bell. But she had remained silent when the opportunity had presented itself, and now it was too late.

I really am on my own, Audra thought, just as I've always been on my own since I was fourteen. I have nowhere to go. No one to turn to . . . I only ever did have Matron Lennox, but even she can't help me. She can't possibly give me a job as a nurse now that I'm pregnant.

The despair that Audra had been carrying around with her for days spiralled into sudden panic, and as she put the cups and saucers on the table she saw that her hands shook slightly. Standing absolutely still in the middle of the kitchen, she took rigid control of herself. *Be calm, be calm*, she kept repeating, breathing deeply, reminding herself that panic never accomplished anything.

When Audra felt more composed, she went to look at the lamb stew for Vincent's dinner, which had been simmering in the oven of the Yorkshire range all afternoon. Satisfied that it was slowly cooking to perfection, she made a cup of tea and carried it to the fire, where she sat for a while, mulling over her predicament.

During the two weeks she had been ill with influenza she had begun to suspect that she was pregnant. For the last few days she had been absolutely certain; a variety of changes in her body could no longer be ignored. When the cold facts had sunk in at the beginning of the week, her first thought had been of flight. She had intended to stick to her plans to leave Vincent.

But this evening, walking home from Calpher House, she had come to realize that this would be a foolish move to make when she was with child. She had no money, no job – and nowhere to run, anyway. Laurette had put it most succinctly when she had said, 'We're the only family you have.' *It was true.*

But to stay with Vincent? How could she? They only ever argued and bickered. Well, that was not strictly true. At least, not at the moment. He had been solicitous of her well-being whilst she had been in bed with the 'flu, and exceptionally kind to her, and there hadn't been a cross word between them since she had recovered.

A few days ago, he had asked her, unexpectedly and in a subdued voice, if she still intended to leave him. And she had said *yes*, as soon as she was well enough to do so. There had been such an odd look on his face when he had turned away, and thinking about it now she realized, suddenly, that it had been a look of genuine sadness. And she was certain there had been a hint of regret in his eyes, and that he was sorry for all of their angry words, their virulent rows that served no purpose. After all, they had started out with so much. *Oh why can't it be the way it was in the beginning?* she asked herself, and leaning back in the chair she closed her eyes, thinking of the happy days of their courtship, fervently wishing they would come back.

A little while later, Audra sat up with a jerk, roused from her ruminations by the sound of footsteps on the flagstone path outside. The door flew open and Vincent hurried in, carrying a large bunch of holly dangling from a string.

His face brightened. He was relieved to see her sitting by the fire. These days he never knew for certain whether he was coming home to an empty house or not.

'Hello, love,' he said, putting the holly on the floor, taking off his scarf and trilby hat.

'Hello,' Audra responded, and she could not help thinking how handsome he looked tonight. The cold wind had brought fresh colour to his cheeks and his green eyes were alive and sparkling under the black brows. She asked, in her usual quiet way, 'How was your trip to York?'

'Oh it was grand, and ever so successful, I'm happy to report. It looks as if we'll get the contract, oh yes, very definitely. Mr Varley is right chuffed and so am I ... it means all of our jobs are safe, well, for a bit, at least. Which is saying a lot when you look around and see what's going on in the country. Mr Varley says we're heading for an economic crisis ...' He let his sentence trail off, but as he struggled out of his coat and hung it up, he added, 'oh and by the by, you can congratulate me.'

Audra's brow lifted. 'Why? What's happened?'

'I've been promoted. Mr Varley made me the new foreman this afternoon. There hasn't been one, you know, since old Harry Watkins retired.'

'Congratulations *are* in order, Vincent, and I am pleased for you,' Audra said enthusiastically, meaning her words. 'You certainly deserve it, you've worked hard enough.'

'Thanks for that, love.' He cleared his throat, picked up the holly and walked across the floor. 'I bought this from a farm cart on one of the country roads on the way back. What shall I do with it? Shouldn't it be in water?'

'It'll be all right for a while. Put it on the set-pot. Would you like a cup of tea?'

'Er, no thanks, love.' He hesitated, as if uncertain of his next move, and then he walked over to her chair, bent down and kissed her cheek. But he quickly moved away, stood with his back to the fire, warming himself.

'Thank you for the holly, Vincent,' Audra murmured, looking up at him with a half smile. 'It was nice of you ...'

'Oh, it was nothing ... do we have any beer left?'

'Yes, there are several bottles in the pantry.'

He went to get one, asking, as he strode across the floor, 'How's the lad, then?'

'Excited about his Christmas party, and the last thing he said to me, as I was leaving, was to be sure to make you come with me tomorrow.'

'Oh I don't know about that ...' Returning to the fireside. Vincent sat down in the chair opposite her, his expression reflective.

'Theophilus will be disappointed if you don't go.'

Vincent stared at her in surprise, frowning, and there was a hint of bafflement in his voice as he asked, 'Would you *mind* if I went? I mean, do you *want* me to go with you.'

'Yes, and anyway, Theo has his heart set on it. You know the boy hero-worships you.'

He nodded, took a sip of beer, said hesitantly, 'Well . . . I do get off work early. Mr Varley always shuts down at twelve on Christmas Eve.'

'Yes.' Audra glanced away, sat looking into the fire.

Vincent fumbled in his jacket pocket, searching for his cigarettes.

A silence fell between them.

It was the kind of companionable silence they had so often shared in the early days of their relationship, and tonight they seemed to be at ease with each other in a way that they had not been for months. Quite suddenly Audra felt his eyes on her and she brought her gaze to meet his. She held her breath. There was a look of such tenderness and love on his face it was heart stopping.

She opened her mouth to speak and then closed it without uttering a word, incapable of saying anything at this moment, filled with a bewildering array of emotions. She glanced down at her hands. Her wedding band glinted in the firelight, so burnished, so bright, a symbol of her dreams – and hope for the future. She thought of the baby she was carrying. The child *was* the future . . . just as it was part of the past, their *past*, created out of their love and their passionate feelings and their need for each other. Deep in the inner recesses of her heart Audra understood that in spite of everything her love for Vincent remained intact and unchanged; that was an inescapable fact.

Almost as if he were reading her mind, Vincent threw his cigarette into the fire and rose. He went and knelt next to her chair, and taking her hands in his he looked deeply into her eyes, which were huge tonight, bright and vividly blue in her wan face.

He swallowed, said tremulously, 'Don't leave me, Audra, please don't leave me. On my way home tonight I didn't know whether you'd be here or not, and my heart was in my mouth. It's always in my mouth these days . . . not knowing what to expect. And I thought, what will I do if she's not there? How can I live without her?' He paused, attempted a smile, but it faltered. 'The truth is, I can't live without you, and I don't want to anyway. You see, Audra, I love you, I really do.'

She knew he meant every word. There was not only a ring of sincerity in his voice, but a desperateness too, and as she returned his penetrating gaze steadily she saw the glitter of tears at the back of his green eyes.

For a moment she could not speak.

'Please don't leave me,' he begged again, his voice low and emotional.

Audra touched his face gently, and then to her own surprise, she blurted out, 'I'm going to have a baby.'

Vincent drew back, his eyes widening as he stared at her, and then grabbed her in his arms and hugged her to him. 'Oh Audra, what wonderful news!' Immediately he pulled away from her. All the anxiety had been wiped off his face and he was grinning boyishly. 'You can't leave me now, you know you can't! Besides, I won't *let* you. You need me to look after you, to take care of you and the baby.'

'Yes,' she acknowledged, knowing this was the truth.

'We'll have a better life together, I promise,' he said with genuine feeling. 'And I promise I'll be a better husband, I really will, Audra.'

At first he was true to his word.

The kindness he had shown during her bout with influenza continued, and he was more considerate than he had ever been to her, or anyone else, for that matter. At night he rushed home from work to be with her, and he never left her side in his free time, not even at weekends when he was accustomed to going off on his own with his friends. He fussed over her, cosseted her, and was a model husband and expectant father.

Tranquillity descended on the little house in Pot Lane.

Audra was content in a way she had never been in her entire life, and grateful to have peace and quiet – and also rest. Her pregnancy was turning out to be a difficult one. The morning sickness was unusually severe, and the nausea often continued during the day; she felt out of sorts in her general health and was constantly debilitated.

In the beginning, Vincent was concerned for her and sympathetic about her condition. But it was not very long before his patience gave way to irritability and, worst of all, boredom.

Just before Christmas, when they had reconciled, they had done so lovingly and had assumed their marital relationship. But once again this had ceased. Vincent more or less understood Audra's physical withdrawal from him, since he thought that an expectant woman might not be overcome by sexual desire for her husband. What truly troubled him was her lack of real interest in him and his daily life. He found her attitude strange, disconcerting – and very hurtful.

And so not unnaturally, given his nature, he soon began to find domesticity stifling. He did love Audra, and he did want to be married to her, but he also craved the life of a bachelor. This was not because he needed to chase after other women, for indeed he did not, but rather because he missed the camaraderie of masculine company, of roistering around with his friends in the pubs and betting at the bookie's office and the race track. He had done these things all of his adult life and he saw no reason to change his habits.

He also resumed his constant visits to his mother's house: he missed the hurly-burly atmosphere and the joviality of being part of a big family, particularly one filled with affection and warmth for each other as the Crowthers were.

And he did not feel guilty about his behaviour in any way, mainly because Audra had become completely absorbed in the baby. It seemed to Vincent that her entire being was concentrated on the child she was carrying, to the exclusion of all else.

He was not mistaken in this belief.

The baby represented so much to her, perhaps more than he could truly understand. To Audra, the baby was not only the fruit of their love and their first child, but the beginning of that family of her very own which she had so craved for so many years.

Terrified of endangering the baby in any way, she took care of her health so scrupulously and so obsessively that even Laurette grew impatient with her on occasions; and when she was not fussing over herself, her health and her diet, she was preparing for the great event as if this was the first child that had ever been born.

The second bedroom at number thirty-eight was turned into a nursery, with great attention paid to the smallest detail, both decoratively and hygienically. She involved almost every member of the Crowther clan, insisting that they help with the scrubbing, cleaning, wallpapering and painting of the room. And then, after she had sold a small diamond bar pin of her mother's, she went to Harte's in Leeds, where she purchased a set of nursery furniture that was beautifully made.

Vincent's sister Olive was renowned in the family, and amongst her friends, for the exquisite garments she knitted and in the past year she had been teaching this practical hobby to Laurette. Audra asked Olive to help her with her own knitting, and within a short space of time she had cunningly pressed both Olive and Laurette into making clothes for the baby. The three young women knitted as if their lives depended on it. They were a comical sight when they were together, their needles clicking, their eyes glazed in concentration on their patterns, oblivious to everything. Bonnets, bootees, leggings, cardigans, jackets, and blankets for the cot and the pram were the result of their diligence. Later Audra sewed and embroidered a variety of other baby clothes and she crocheted two beautiful lacy shawls; it was not long before a superb layette had been created. As Audra put the tiny garments away in the bedroom chest she carefully placed tissue paper between the layers of finely worked handmade things, feeling very proud of this exquisite wardrobe of clothes for her unborn child.

Yet with all of her domestic activities and despite being surrounded by innumerable, and often boisterous, Crowthers, there were times when Audra felt more isolated and alone than ever. This was due, in part, to Vincent's defection, and because she had no real kin of her own. Try though she had to become closer to Eliza, she had been unable to do so. She was still wary of her mother-in-law, and cautious in her presence. She believed that Eliza had blamed her for all of their problems months before, and continued to hold her responsible, whilst exonerating Vincent. Although this was not true, nothing would have convinced her to the contrary.

On the other hand, Laurette and Audra were warm and loving with each other, and Audra enjoyed a good relationship with Alfred Crowther, who considered his son extremely fortunate to have such a fine young woman for a wife. In fact, Alfred was disapproving of Vincent's behaviour, and minced no words when telling him so, which he did with increasing frequency. It was Vincent's father and his favourite sister who helped Audra through some difficult moments and trying situations at this time in her life.

Oddly enough, there were no rancorous feelings between Audra and Vincent during her pregnancy, even though they were in a sense leading quite separate lives. They no longer quarrelled bitterly, and even their bickering had ceased. It was as if a truce had been declared between them. They were civil, even cordial with each other – and totally preoccupied with their own problems and with themselves.

Time passed.

The harsh winter gave way to the most glorious spring anyone had seen in years. Blue skies and bright sunshine lifted everybody's spirits. So did the trees bursting with green buds and the appearance of the first daffodils and crocuses, shooting up early to sprinkle the dark earth with brilliant yellow and purple.

And then suddenly it was the occasion of Gwen's marriage to Geoffrey Freemantle. Audra had had to decline Gwen's request to be matron-of-honour, because she felt she would look ungainly in her condition.

But she and Vincent did attend the wedding at St Margaret's Church in Horsforth on a sunny, breezy Saturday afternoon in the first week of April in 1929.

Audra had made herself a new maternity dress and matching loose coat of navy blue bouclé wool, and had bought herself a gay little hat made of straw and trimmed with midnight lace and deep blue roses. When Vincent saw her in the outfit he exclaimed at her prettiness, but Audra looked at him sceptically as she followed him out of the cottage. She felt like a small rather rotund whale, and there was no question in her mind that she looked it.

As they drove over to Horsforth in his Uncle Phil's car, borrowed for the occasion, Audra thought of Gwen, and of the way their friendship had begun to drift during the winter months. Between her work at the Infirmary, furnishing and decorating the house in Headingley and planning her wedding, Gwen had had little time for her, or for anyone else, it seemed. Also, the circumstances of their very different lives these days were slowly coming between them.

There was another problem too, in that Vincent had become friendlier than ever with Mike Lesley, Gwen's former boyfriend. In consequence, Vincent did not want to make friends with Geoffrey Freemantle, whom he persisted in referring to as 'the usurper', and even if he had, Audra knew that the snobbish doctor would have looked down on Vincent.

I'm going to lose Gwen eventually and all because of Geoffrey Freemantle, Audra thought, as she sat staring out of the car window, and she filled with sadness.

Not much later, as she stood in the pew with Vincent, watching Gwen walk slowly down the aisle on the arm of her father, the sadness seemed to intensify, as did a sense of separateness and distance. Gwen looked so beautiful, more beautiful than she had ever been, and Audra was momentarily stunned. This was a different Gwen from the one she had known.

She wore a crinoline gown of cream lace over cream satin, a veil and a long train of Alençon lace; the veil was held in place by a coronet of waxy orange blossoms. She carried a bouquet of white roses whose petals were tinged with the palest of pinks. A diamond heart on a strand of pearls glittered at her throat and there were diamonds in her ears. Gwen was a radiant bride, blonde and blue-eyed and everybody's idea of the typical English rose; there was no question that on this very special day in her life she was absolutely breathtaking.

And I've already lost her, Audra thought wistfully. She's gone from me. Gwen's entered a new world, one *I* shall never know. Suddenly she was choked with tears and there was an odd ache in the region of her heart.

There was a time in my life when I had absolutely nothing and no one. All I had was Gwen, Audra thought. *And she was so good to me. I'll never forget her for that. I'll always love her and she'll always be my best friend. Not even Laurette can take her place, dear though she is, and so loving and loyal.*

As Gwen drew level with Audra she smiled with warmth and radiance.

Audra smiled back, looked fleetingly, but deeply, into that pretty, open, honest face and she said goodbye to her friend in the silence of her heart. But she wished Gwen nothing but happiness and joy all the days of her life.

Even though her sense of loss enveloped her, Audra did manage to seem carefree at the reception. This was held at The Meadow, and Audra experienced a little spurt of pleasure to be back in that house where she had spent so many happy hours. But whereas she was able to put up a good front, she noticed that the Thorntons were not so successful at this bit of deception. Audra decided she had never seen a family looking so glum.

She had not been in the drawing room long before Mrs Thornton led her into a quiet corner, to speak to her alone. Phyllis Thornton immediately confided, without any preamble, that none of the family cared very much for Doctor Freemantle. Audra tried to cheer her up by saying positive things and smiling a lot, but Mrs Thornton was not deceived. She shook her head mournfully. 'He's an odious man, and you don't like him either, Audra, whatever you say ... poor Gwenny, whatever has she done?' Mrs Thornton sighed heavily before gliding off to greet some wedding guests who had just arrived.

Audra's eyes followed her. She was filled with sympathy for Mrs Thornton, who had always been kind to her. Vincent joined her and they went over to the buffet, where they took a selection of sandwiches, then moved away. Charlie found them a few minutes later, and he brought over his fiancée to meet them. She was a petite, dainty girl called Rowena, who, Audra immediately noticed, was moulded from the same clay as she was. She smiled. Perhaps it was true that men always fell for the same type of woman. But she was glad that Charlie had found someone he so obviously cared about. That he was indeed smitten with Rowena was written all over his face.

After the introductions had been made, Charlie lowered his voice and pronounced Gwen's marriage to be a horrible mistake. 'My parents are heartbroken, and so am I,' he confided. He and Vincent were soon picking the doctor apart, and agreeing that Gwenny should have married the devoted, and desirable, Mike Lesley.

Why are people always so dreadful at weddings? Audra wondered. She had no ready answers for herself.

Gwen's marriage was the highlight of the spring and the early months of summer. Audra and Vincent plodded along in much the same way, absorbed and preoccupied with themselves.

Audra was on her own a lot more than ever, since Vincent was now spending two and three days a week in York. Varley's had won the contract for building the small extension onto Rowntree's chocolate factory, and Mr Varley had put him in charge of the project. But neither Audra nor Vincent minded too much about these absences; they were both far too relieved that he still had a job.

More and more men were on the dole. When Audra went to Calpher House she would see them standing outside the Labour Exchange at Hill-Top and her heart went out to them. They looked so without hope. She thanked God that Vincent was not one of them.

By the end of June the building job in York was completed, and Vincent was again working locally and living at home all the time. It was a scorching Saturday morning at the beginning of July that Audra experienced her first contractions. Vincent rushed her to St Mary's Hospital in his Uncle Phil's car and several hours later their first child was born. It was a boy.

They had chosen his names weeks before. He was to be baptized Adrian Alfred, after their respective fathers. But right from the beginning Vincent called him Alfie and the name stuck.

Everybody loved Alfie.

He was a happy, laughing, easy-going baby with bright green eyes, dark silky hair, and a cherubic face. He hardly ever cried and his disposition was so sweet that Vincent and Audra considered themselves to be the most fortunate of parents. All of the Crowthers petted and spoiled Alfie, most especially Eliza and Alfred, who doted on their first grandchild. But his aunts adored him too, and Audra knew there would never be a shortage of baby sitters, whenever they were required.

As the months passed, Alfie only became sweeter and happier. He gurgled and laughed and kicked his legs a lot, whether lying in his cot or his pram, and when Audra wheeled him out down Town Street total strangers would stop her to go into raptures over 'the beautiful child'. He was the kind of cuddly baby that everyone wanted to pick up and hug and squeeze and kiss. Audra soon learned to be on guard about this, forever trying to prevent it, afraid as she was of Alfie being exposed to germs.

She loved her child to distraction. Sometimes she would stop her work and go out into the little garden to look at him. As she peered down into the pram she was certain his face lit up at the sight of her, that there was recognition in his dancing green eyes, and this made her heart leap with happiness. She had never known such happiness as this tiny person gave her.

It was obvious to Audra and everyone else that Alfie was going to favour Vincent in his looks – certainly his vivid colouring echoed his father's perfectly. Vincent loved his son as much as Audra did, and both parents were aware that their infant boy was unusually alert and bright. He was already showing signs of exceptional intelligence by the time he was six months old, and they took great delight in little Alfie and were proud of him.

In a way, the child had brought them together again.

Their relationship had improved and there was a peaceful atmosphere in the cottage in Pot Lane. Vincent stayed home more during the week now, and when he went out on Saturday nights Audra accompanied him more often than not. This latter development was due in no small measure to Laurette, whose own circumstances had changed – and for the better.

Vincent had played matchmaker successfully.

His favourite sister and Mike Lesley were courting. Laurette was constantly issuing invitations to Audra, and these were readily accepted. Vincent had become close to Mike, after Gwen had broken off with him the previous year; the two men enjoyed each other's company and Vincent was quite happy to forgo his Saturday nights at the pub to take his wife out with them.

These four shared a love of music, in particular the popular operettas of Sigmund Romberg and Victor Herbert. Since these were currently all the rage, touring companies from London came regularly to the Grand Theatre in Leeds and Mike was the first to buy tickets for such hit shows as *Naughty Marietta*, *The Desert Song*, and *The Student Prince*. Sometimes they went dancing to the Mecca, or to see the latest talking pictures, but whatever they did they generally had fun together.

The foursome became a regular thing during the summer and autumn of 1929, and they were all looking forward to spending Christmas together. Audra, for one, was especially happy this year. Her marriage was suddenly steady, she had a family of her own, and there was harmony in her home.

20

Audra and Laurette walked slowly up Pot Lane in the gathering twilight of the January day.

It was the first week of 1930. The beginning of a new year and of a new decade.

Both young women were full of good spirits and happier than they had been in years. Despite the worsening conditions in England, and the world economic crisis, their own futures seemed rosy – and secure at last.

Audra was content with her life, and with Vincent. And, of course, there was Alfie, her darling little baby, who grew more beautiful by the day, who was the joy of her life. Vincent continued to do well at Varley's; he had had an increase in pay and they were finally out of debt. Things had never looked better.

As for Laurette, she was filled with a marvellous sense of euphoria. She was deeply in love with Mike Lesley, and he with her, and last night they had become engaged; they planned to be married in the summer.

Although Mike was still studying medicine at Leeds University, his bachelor uncle had recently died and left him a small inheritance. This unexpected and welcome little windfall had enabled them to speed up their marital plans, since it would enable Mike to support a wife until he qualified as a doctor at the end of the year. And so her head was teeming with thoughts of her wedding, her trousseau, finding a house in Upper Armley, where they wanted to live, and making a comfortable home for this man whom she so adored.

Earlier in the day, the two young women had celebrated Laurette's engagement.

Audra had insisted on treating her sister-in-law to lunch on this very special occasion. Since they only ever went to Betty's Café in Leeds, she had decided that a change was definitely in order, and she had been happy to splurge. It had been worth it just to see the look of surprise and delight on Laurette's face when she had led her into Turkish Delight, the charming café with an oriental theme in Harte's.

After lunch they had wandered around the elegant department store for a while, playing their favourite game of pretend shopping. They had looked at the exquisite couture dresses and evening gowns in the Model Room; exclaimed over fox and beaver and ermine coats in the Fur Salon; tried on chic hats in the Millinery Box; doused themselves with a variety of expensive French scents at the perfumery counter. And, all in all, they had enjoyed this harmless bit of fantasy, this brief escape from their everyday lives.

Later they had gone to Leeds Market in Kirkgate, as they usually did every Saturday afternoon. 'Down to earth with a bang,' Laurette had said with a wry laugh, as they had trudged around the produce stalls, looking for good buys.

Audra had also laughed as she had picked up a cauliflower and examined it.

She had murmured, 'Everyone's looking at us, or I should say *sniffing* us. We must really and truly *pong* after all that perfume we sprayed on ourselves.'

'We probably smell like a Chinese whore house, as our Vincent would say.'

Giggling and laughing like a couple of giddy, carefree schoolgirls, they had plunged through the throngs of shoppers, found their bargains and left the huge market with laden shopping bags, making their way to Upper Armley on the tram.

Now, as they headed along the darkening lane in the direction of the cottage, they were both shivering in the chill wind that had blown up. During the week it had rained a lot and the wind carried with it the pungent odour of dripping foliage, wet earth and mouldering leaves. There was a dampness on the air and a mist was coming down which presaged rain again.

'These wet leaves are treacherous on the path,' Audra exclaimed, 'so do watch your step, Laurette.'

'Yes, I will. Listen, Audra, thank you for a lovely day. I've really enjoyed myself, especially our lunch and browsing in Harte's. Now I'm looking forward to a nice cup of tea. I suddenly feel jiggered.'

'I'm a little tired myself,' Audra confessed. 'All those people in the Market, I've never seen it so busy.'

'I've had enough of crowds for one day . . . I'm certainly relieved we're not going dancing tonight, I don't think I'd last very long.'

'I know what you mean, my feet are killing me too,' Audra said, as they went down the steps into the cul-de-sac.

Before they reached the end of the flagstone path, the door of number thirty-eight flew open and Maggie stood in a circle of light, peering out into the gloomy night. *'Audra? Laurette?'*

'Yes, it's us,' Audra responded, hurrying forward. She had caught an odd note in the fourteen-year-old's voice, and a warning signal went off in her head. 'Is everything all right?'

'It's our Alfie,' Maggie said tensely, opening the door wider, stepping aside to let them enter. 'I think he's right badly, Audra.'

Audra dumped her shopping bags on the floor and flew across the room without bothering to remove her coat. She bent over the bassinet in the corner of the kitchen, staring anxiously at Alfie.

She saw at once that her baby was not well. His eyes were glazed and he was obviously feverish. Her throat tightened. Pulling off her gloves, she reached out, touched his flushed cheek lightly with the tip of one finger. His little face was burning. Instantly, she became alarmed. But it was not in Audra's nature to panic; also, because of her training as a nurse, plus Matron Lennox's belief that she was a gifted healer, she felt confident, and certainly capable of looking after her own child when he was ill.

Straightening up, she struggled out of her coat, tossed it on a chair, hurried to the kitchen sink to wash her hands.

She said to Laurette, 'Please get me the thermometer out of the medicine chest in the cupboard near the pantry. Then clear the tea things away and put a clean towel on the table, please. I want to examine Alfie under the light and sponge him down, to cool him. Could you also bring his toilet basket, oh, and dampen his flannel for me, would you please, whilst you're at it?'

'Right away.' Laurette bustled around the kitchen, doing as Audra requested.

After Audra had washed and dried her hands, she rinsed the thermometer in cold water, placed it on the kitchen table, then went to get her child. She lifted him out of his bassinet carefully and carried him to the table, where she slipped off his cardigan and romper suit, and removed his vest and his nappy. There was gentleness and tenderness in her every movement as she handled the infant.

She took Alfie's temperature, looked up at Laurette and shook her head. 'It's a hundred and four, but I'm not really surprised, he's awfully feverish. Give me the flannel would you please, Laurette?'

'What do you think he's got?' Laurette asked, sounding worried as she brought the face cloth to Audra.

'I don't know, it could be any one of a number of children's ailments – measles, chicken pox, scarlet fever. On the other hand, I don't see any sign of a rash or spots . . .' She let her sentence trail off, finished sponging his fat little legs, his plump little feet, then dusted him down with Fuller's Earth Powder. As she began to dress him again, she said to Laurette, without looking up, 'But he does have such a high temperature. I wonder if I ought to give him a Fenning's Fever Powder? Or some gripe water? No, I'd better not. I think I have to send for the doctor.'

Laurette nodded. 'Yes, perhaps you should.' She glanced at the clock. 'If only Mike were here he could examine Alfie. I can't imagine what's keeping him and Vincent.'

'I can run down for Doctor Stalkley,' Maggie volunteered, her voice shrill and anxious.

'Yes, I think you'd better,' Audra murmured, lifting Alfie in her arms, taking him back to his bassinet. Turning to face Maggie, she said, 'But before you do, tell me everything you can about the way Alfie acted this afternoon, what time you realized he wasn't well, and any symptoms you noticed – anything odd about him.'

Maggie had been worried out of her wits for hours. She had been afraid to take Alfie to the doctor's surgery, for fear of endangering him further; for the same reason, she had not dared to leave him alone whilst she went to fetch the doctor. Now she was not only nervous but on the verge of tears.

She said, with a tremor, 'Vincent and Mike went off to the football match at about one. Just after that, our Alfie started to cry, and he kept crying off an' on for ages, and he was ever so fratchy and that's not like him, he's allus so good. I kept going to check on him, Audra, honest I did, to see if he was all right, to see if he was wet. But his nappy was dry and there was no pin sticking in him. Then a bit later, it must've been three or so, I saw how red he was getting. It was ever so hot in here and I took him into the sitting room to cool him down. We sat there a bit. I was nursing him on my lap, singing to him, and he started to vomit, and in ever such a funny way, Aud –'

'Describe the vomiting,' Audra interjected, stiffening.

'I don't know how to, it's difficult to describe,' Maggie wailed and looked at Audra, conscious of the sudden change in her sister-in-law. Audra's acute anxiety had instantly transmitted itself to Maggie.

'Try.'

Maggie gulped, remained mute, wracking her brains for the right words.

'Please try.'

Maggie nodded. She took a deep breath, said, 'The vomit sort of came straight out of him. It was like somebody gave him a big *thump* on his back and knocked it out. I don't know how to explain it proper like, Audra, I don't really. What was funny was that Alfie didn't heave, or do owt like that.'

Maggie shook her head. 'It must sound ever so strange, and it *was* queer, but that's what happened. Oh the poor little mite, whatever can be the matter with him?' Projectile vomiting, Audra thought, with a stab of dread. That is what Maggie had tried so hard to describe. Oh my God. *Meningitis*. It simply can't be. Audra stood very still, knowing that it was imperative she keep a firm hold on herself, that she stay absolutely calm and clear-headed. For her baby's sake she must not permit emotion to cloud intelligence and judgement.

Swallowing her apprehension, Audra turned to the crib and peered down at Alfie. He looked so listless, and he was as flushed as before.

'Hurry to the doctor's, Maggie,' Audra instructed. 'Tell Doctor Stalkley that Alfie is ill, and that he must come immediately.'

Maggie shot across the kitchen and snatched her coat from the cupboard. 'What do you think's wrong with our little 'un then, Audra? It's not summat serious, is it?'

'I can't be certain, but the vomiting and the high fever do worry me.'

'I'll tell t'doctor about both them things,' Maggie said, pivoting at the front door. 'And I'll run all the way there, and as fast as me legs'll carry me, so don't you worry.'

The moment they were alone, Laurette asked anxiously, 'Audra, whatever is it? You've turned as white as a sheet. What on earth *is* wrong with Alfie? You must have some idea.'

'I'm not sure, really I'm not,' Audra replied, striving to keep her voice steady, not daring to say the name of that most ghastly illness. She had seen two children die of it when she had been a nurse at the Fever Hospital and their suffering had been pitiful to witness.

Laurette stood up. 'Well, you look awful, and I'm going to make us a pot of tea.' She hurried to the sink to fill the kettle, glad to keep busy. She wished Mike were here. His presence was always comforting; Audra trusted him, had faith in his judgement.

Audra sat up slightly in the easy chair, thinking hard. She had committed a great deal of medical information to memory in the past. Suddenly, in her mind's eye, she pictured the page of her hospital text book which dealt with meningitis. She sat staring into space, saw every word on that page quite clearly, as though someone held the book in front of her. *Meningitis: Acute inflammation of the membranes of the brain and spinal cord, or both. Also called 'spotted fever', due to extensive spotting of the skin in severe cases. Symptoms: Severe headache, high fever, frequently neck and back rigidity; also twitching or convulsions. Severe vomiting is common; known as projectile vomiting due to sudden ejection of vomit to some distance; spotting of skin in severe cases; delirium, coma.*

Once more, Audra leapt to her feet and rushed over to the bassinet. Her eyes flicked over Alfie, seeking signs of the symptoms she now so clearly recalled. But she saw nothing unusual. The child remained flushed, but there was no evidence of twitching or convulsions, or neck rigidity, and certainly there had been no rash on his body when she had examined him a few minutes earlier.

She let out a sigh of relief. Of course it's not meningitis, she told herself. How could it be? Anyway, Alfie's probably coming down with a winter cold, or influenza at the worst. *But his high fever, what about his high fever?* a small voice nagged at the back of her mind.

Alfie began to cry, wiping this thought right out of her head. She bent over the bassinet, reaching for him.

'Hush, sweetheart, hush, my little darling,' she murmured, holding him tenderly against her breast. She smoothed her hand over his dark head and across his small back, hushing him softly. Immediately, Alfie stopped crying and nestled into her. Audra walked up and down, soothing him, murmuring to him gently, and she was filled with such love for her child she thought her heart was going to burst.

And as she continued to pace back and forth in front of the fire, desperately trying to give comfort to her tiny son, she began to pray. *Oh please, God, don't let anything happen to my baby. Protect my little Alfie, please keep him safe and make him well again*, she entreated silently. And she kept repeating the words over and over again as she waited for the doctor to come.

21

Alfie died.

His death was so unexpected, so swift, that everyone was stunned and disbelieving. One minute he was a healthy, robust baby, laughing and gurgling in his crib, the next he was gone from them.

On that fateful Saturday evening, Doctor Stalkley had come to the cottage at once, following sharply on the heels of Vincent and Mike, who had walked in from the football match a few minutes before.

After examining Alfie, neither the doctor nor Mike believed that he had meningitis. Despite the peculiar vomiting in the afternoon, which had not recurred, his only symptoms were the feverishness and the high temperature. 'Not enough to go on,' Doctor Stalkley had said. 'I'll come back tomorrow morning, but meanwhile keep a close eye on him, Audra.' Picking up his Gladstone bag, striding to the coat closet, he had motioned to Maggie. 'Now, lassie,' the old Scotsman had said, 'you'd best be coming back to my surgery with me, and I'll give you a drop of medicine for the wee bairn.'

Because the doctor and Mike had been so hopeful for Alfie's recovery from whatever it was that ailed him, Audra and Vincent had taken heart. Following the doctor's instructions explicitly, they had watched over Alfie all weekend, had not left him alone for one moment.

Audra had sponged him down frequently, to keep him cool and refreshed; she had given him the fever medicine at the prescribed times and had generally tended to him with all the skills of the professional nurse that she was. And she had hardly closed her eyes during that time.

But Audra did not care about sleep. Alfie was the only thing that mattered to her and Vincent. By Sunday night the entire Crowther family believed that Alfie was over the worst of his mysterious ailment. The febrile look had vanished from his eyes and the scarlet flush had disappeared from his plump cheeks.

But on Monday morning, just before noon, the child had a relapse.

Audra's worst fears had been confirmed.

Alfie had started to have convulsions and the tiny spots, which looked like bright red pin pricks, had begun to appear on his milky skin. Endeavouring to control her terrible fear for her child, Audra had wrapped him in several woollen shawls and rushed to the doctor's surgery.

Doctor Stalkley had taken one look at Alfie and shaken his head. After a rapid examination he had dispatched Audra to St Mary's Hospital, just a short distance away. He promised to visit Alfie as soon as his morning surgery was over, when he started his daily rounds in the district.

Whilst she had waited for Alfie to be admitted to the children's ward, Audra had cradled him in her arms, cooing to him softly, fighting back her tears. It had been wrenching to leave him, but she had no choice. And she had fervently wished that she was a nurse at St Mary's, so that she could care for her beloved child herself.

Four days later Alfie came home to them in a small pine coffin.

Burdened with sorrow, Vincent dragged himself to every window in the cottage, closing the curtains to shut out the light until after the funeral, as was the custom in the North.

And then he went to comfort his wife.

Audra was inconsolable.

'Why couldn't I make him better?' she kept asking Vincent as she stood by the side of the open coffin, blinded by her scalding tears. 'Matron Lennox says I'm an exceptional nurse,' she sobbed, 'so why couldn't I make our baby get well?'

'Audra . . . *Audra love*, nobody could have helped our poor little Alfie. It's not your fault, it's nobody's fault. Meningitis is generally fatal in small babies. Mike told me so,' Vincent said quietly, 'and you know that yourself, lovey.'

'I should have kept him at home, nursed him myself, not left him to strangers,' she cried, clutching Vincent's arm, staring at him wildly. 'If I hadn't let Alfie go into the hospital, he'd be alive. He would, I just know he would!'

'No, love, that's not true,' Vincent said gently, drawing her to him, smoothing her hair away from her ravaged face. 'They did their very best up at St Mary's, more than their best; they fought hard for Alfie's life. It just wasn't meant to be, Audra love.'

Vincent led her out of the sitting room where the coffin stood, and took her back to the kitchen. He held her in his arms and tried to give her solace and her tears drenched the front of his shirt as they wept together for the child whom they so loved.

Eliza and Alfred came to see their dead grandchild, to share the grief of their son and daughter-in-law, to offer condolences and do what they could to help.

Alfred, the ex-sergeant-major of the Seaforth Highlanders, who considered himself to be so tough, broke down and sobbed quite openly at the coffin. He was profoundly moved at the sight of Alfie, his namesake. In death, the child's beauty seemed more potent than ever and perfect in its wax-like state. For a moment Alfie looked as if he was merely sleeping. But when Alfred bent over and kissed the delicate cheek its immense coldness struck him like a knife in the chest and he clutched at Eliza's arm. She tried to comfort him as best she could, though her own sorrow was enormous.

When they joined Vincent and Audra in the kitchen a while later, Alfred looked around him, as if dazed, and asked in a shaken voice, '*Why? Why* has our little Alfie's life been snuffed out? He was only a baby, and nothing but pure joy and innocence . . . tell me why he has been taken from us so cruelly.'

No one had an answer for Alfred: there was no answer.

22

It was a golden day in late October, one of those especially glorious Indian Summer days that so often occur in the autumn, just before the harsh winter sets in. The sky was the colour of speedwells, luminous in the sunlight, and the breeze was light, almost warm.

What a grand afternoon it is, Vincent thought, lifting his eyes, enjoying the radiance of the day. I hope this weather lasts 'til the weekend. Turning off Town Street, he increased his pace as he heard the church clock strike three. He was heading down Ridge Road in the direction of H. E. Varley and Son, Builders, and he did not want to be late for his appointment with Mr Fred Varley.

It was a Thursday, almost the end of a week that had been exceptionally hard. He had pushed his men relentlessly to finish the warehouse they were building onto Pinfold's woollen mill, and by noon tomorrow the job would be completed. No doubt that was why Mr Varley wanted to see him, to congratulate him, and there was bound to be a nice bonus for himself and his crew.

At the thought of a little extra money, Vincent began to whistle and he stepped out jauntily. He touched his cap, smiled and nodded as he passed the vicar's wife near Christ Church Vicarage, and then crossed the road. A few seconds later he was entering the builder's office and greeting Maureen, Mr Varley's secretary.

'Hello, love,' he said, taking off his cap, giving her a broad smile. 'Mr Varley sent for me.'

'Good afternoon, Vincent,' Maureen replied and nodded her head towards the door. 'You can go in, he's waiting for you.'

Mr Varley was speaking on the telephone, but as Vincent hove in view in the doorway, he immediately said goodbye, hung up and beckoned for Vincent to enter. 'There you are, lad, come in, come in, and sit yourself down.'

'Thanks, Mr Varley.' Vincent lowered himself into the chair facing the desk. 'The Pinfold job will be finished tomorrow at noon,' he went on. 'The lads have done right well, Mr Varley, and I know you'll be pleased when you see the warehouse. It's a bit of good building work, even though I do say so myself.'

'Aye, I'm sure it is, lad, you're a good worker, and a good foreman, the best I've ever had, in fact.' Fred Varley cleared his throat. 'That's why it's so hard for me to tell you this . . . I've got some right bad news for you, I'm afraid, Vincent, I do that. I'm going to have to shut up shop.'

Vincent stared at him, for a moment uncomprehending. 'Close down?' he said swiftly, raising his brows. '*Close* Varley's?'

'Aye lad – as of tomorrow.'

'Oh my God!' Vincent was shocked. 'I don't understand,' he began, and then faltered, as all of the implications sank in.

'I'm going to have to go into bankruptcy, I've no alternative,' Varley said.

'But why? We've had a lot of jobs in the last few months –'

'Aye, I knows we have, lad,' Mr Varley cut in, 'but some of the buggers haven't paid up yet, and I've no bloody idea when they will. I've been operating on credit for a hell of a long time, Vincent, and I'm so heavily into the bank I don't dare borrow more, and I doubt that they'd lend it to me now, anyway. I'm mortgaged up to the hilt.' Shaking his head sadly, he finished, 'There's no two ways about it, I've got to cut my losses. Only one way to do that ... *close down.*'

'I can see what you mean,' Vincent mumbled, his eyes troubled as he looked across the desk at his employer. He was thinking not only of himself but of the other men who would be thrown out of work tomorrow. They were all married men, too, except for Billie Johnson, the plumber's mate.

Varley said, 'Naturally, I'll tell the lads meself. Tomorrow. I wouldn't be leaving owt like that to you, shirking me duty, so to speak. I shall be able to meet this week's pay roll, but that's about it. No severance pay, no bonuses, nowt like that, I'm sorry to say.' Fred Varley leaned over his desk, and added, concerned, 'When you get your cards tomorrow, Vincent, I should go up and sign on at once at the Public Assistance Board, if I was you. Better start drawing the dole as soon as you can.'

Vincent nodded grimly.

'I'm hoping I'll be able to sort out this mess,' Mr Varley remarked, rising, obviously wanting to terminate this difficult conversation. 'And things are bound to turn around in the country right soon. The Depression can't last forever. I intend to start afresh you knows, and in the not too distant future, and what I want to say is this – when I do open up again, there'll be a job for you, Vincent. I do hope you'd come back to me.'

Vincent also stood up. 'Thanks, Mr Varley, and yes, I would. You've always been very decent with me, very fair indeed. And I'm sorry your business has gone down the drain, really sorry.'

'Aye, lad, so am I. And I'm doubly sorry for you and the rest of the men. I know how rough it's going to be on all of you.'

'I'll see you tomorrow then, Mr Varley. Ta'rar.'

'Ta'rar, lad.'

23

Vincent Crowther sat in the recreation grounds, behind the park in Moorfield Road, smoking a Woodbine.

He was no longer aware of the beautiful Indian Summer afternoon, and all of his earlier jauntiness had dissipated. He was engulfed in his worries about earning a living in order to support himself and Audra.

Only the other day he had read in the *Yorkshire Post* that there were one million nine hundred thousand men out of work in England. Plus one, he muttered under his breath, now that I'm about to join them. The idea of going on the dole appalled him. But he would have to do so, since there was nothing else he *could* do until he found another job.

When he had left Varley's office he had felt as if he had been kicked in the stomach and the feeling persisted. He had wandered into the little park twenty minutes ago, hoping to clear his befuddled head, marshal his swimming senses before he went home. But he was still stunned, and just a bit bewildered. He had believed Fred Varley to be shrewd and successful, had never once imagined that the firm could go out of business, that Fred Varley, of all people, would go down. Just goes to show, he thought, you never really know about anybody.

Vincent had no idea where to begin to find work, for the simple reason that there weren't any jobs to be had. Nor did he have any idea how he was going to break this terrible news to Audra.

What a blow it'll be for her, he thought, and just when she was on her feet again after little Alfie's death. He groaned out loud, then took a long, satisfying drag on his cigarette. He suddenly held it away, looked at it with a frown, asking himself how long he would be able to afford his Woodbines. And his pint of bitter. And a bet on the ponies on Saturday afternoons. A grimness settled over him. The prospects looked bleak. Bloody bleak indeed.

Rubbing his hand over his forehead, he closed his eyes, thinking about the money he had in the Yorkshire Penny Bank. Not much really. His savings would only tide them over for a month, at the most. And all he could expect to get on the dole was something like a pound a week for the two of them, perhaps a shilling or two more. Obviously he was going to have to do his damnedest to get a job, no matter what it was, or where it was, for that matter. He might well have to try other areas of Leeds, such as Bramley, Stanningley or Wortley, or go even farther afield to Pudsey and Farsley.

'Well, well, well, if it's not the gentleman of leisure! I wish I had time to sit on a park bench in the *rec* and idly fritter away the afternoon – *and* in the middle of the week no less!'

Vincent recognized the deep, masculine voice of his friend and brother-in-law. He opened his eyes, stared into Mike Lesley's warm and friendly face peering down into his. 'Yes, that's what I am, Mike,' he said with a weak laugh, 'a gentleman of leisure ... as of about half an hour ago. Yes, I've joined the ranks of the unemployed, like the rest of me mates, and half the bleeding country.'

Mike sat down heavily and frowned at his friend. 'I know you're not joking, Vince, I know you *wouldn't* joke about anything as serious as this, but what happened? I thought Varley's was the one building firm in these parts that was doing well.'

'So did *I*, so did *everybody*. But old man Varley just broke the news to me himself, about half an hour ago. He's going into bankruptcy.'

Mike shook his sandy head slowly, his expression immediately turning dismal. 'The situation's dreadful. I heard of three other companies that have gone down in the last month and God knows where it's all going to end. But look here, Vincent, you're a skilled man, surely you'll be able to find something fairly soon –'

'Not bloody likely!' Vincent interrupted. 'Even Mr Varley has seen the writing on the wall, as far as I'm concerned, that is. He suggested that I sign on at the Labour Exchange at once.'

Mike was silent. He shrugged further into his tweed overcoat and his compassionate hazel eyes filled with concern for his best friend. He wondered if there was anything he could do to help Vincent find a job. He doubted it.

There was a momentary silence between these two young men who had gravitated to each other from the first moment they had met. They had grown even closer in the last couple of years and were like brothers now that Mike was married to Laurette. He was younger than Vincent, but he was blessed with great insight. If anyone understood the unusually complex man who was Vincent Crowther, then it was Mike Lesley.

Suddenly Vincent said, 'However will I tell Audra that I've lost my job?'

Mike's sandy brows drew together in a puzzled frown. 'You'll tell her in the same way that you've told me, very directly,' Mike said.

'She's going to be upset, to put it mildly . . . I couldn't stand it if she fell back into that awful depression. When I think of this spring, when she was so ill after Alfie died, I tremble in me boots, I do that, Mike. Audra was so odd, she was like a stranger to me.'

'Yes, she *was* in a bad way,' Mike conceded, 'but a lot of women react as she did when they lose a child, especially when it's the first baby. They're demented for a while. And her loss was a terrible one, in that she's had so many other losses in her life already.'

'Yes, she has. Poor Audra.'

'Look here, Vince, my money is on your wife. She's an indomitable young woman. Why, she's got more character in her little finger that most people have in their entire bodies. She's plucky, a fighter, and she's full of Yorkshire grit and determination. I have a strong feeling that that wife of yours will take this news without flinching.'

'I hope to God you're right, Mike, I do that.' Vincent pushed himself up off the park bench. 'Well, there's no point putting it off, I'd better get on home and tell her.'

'I think you should.' Mike rose and the two of them walked across the recreation grounds together.

'Do you still want to go to the City Varieties on Saturday night?'

'Of course I do!' Vincent exclaimed. 'I can see no reason to change our plans. Anyway, Audra and Laurette have been looking forward to going, I wouldn't want them to be disappointed.'

'Neither would I,' Mike agreed.

The moment he strode into the cottage in Pot Lane, Vincent knew that something had happened – something special.

There was a record playing on the gramophone in the sitting room, filling the house with the strains of a Gilbert and Sullivan song from *The Mikado*. A vase of bronze and yellow autumnal chrysanthemums stood in the centre of the table, which had been covered with a lace cloth and laid for supper with their best china. He surveyed the table, wondering if someone had been invited, but saw at once that it was set only for two. Glancing around the parlour-kitchen with quickening interest, Vincent next noticed the bottle of red wine on the set-pot; then he sniffed. His mouth began to water as he recognized the faint aroma of his favourite lamb stew coming through the oven door, which was slightly ajar. Pursing his lips, he wondered what was afoot, his curiosity truly fired now.

He had just taken off his coat and cap and hung them in the closet when the staircase door opened and Audra stepped into the kitchen. She wore a pretty, delphinium-blue blouse that matched her eyes and a dark skirt – plus the biggest smile he had seen on her face in ages.

'You look nice, love,' he said, observing her appreciatively through his narrowed green gaze, half smiling as he spoke. He waved his hand around the room. 'What are we celebrating then? Have you come into some sort of windfall?'

'You might say we've had two windfalls, in a sense . . .' She left her sentence dangling and ran to kiss his cheek. Then she stood away from him, gave him a queer, almost smug, smile and led him by the arm to the fireside. She took an envelope off the mantelpiece, waved it in front of his eyes. 'First, there's this! It's a letter from that firm of solicitors in Ripon, you know, the ones who wrote to me in June to tell me that Great-Aunt Frances Reynolds had died and that she had left me something in her will. You thought it was going to be another piece of silver, or that china teapot I admired, but it isn't either. It's *fifty pounds*, Vincent! Wasn't that lovely of her?'

'Aye, lass, it certainly was,' he said with a grin, thinking that Audra's little legacy could not have come at a more propitious time. He was about to say so, wanting to tell her that he had lost his job, get the unpleasant task over with, when she prevented this. She flung herself at him and hugged him so tightly he was taken aback.

But he hugged her in return, stared down into her face.

He saw that it was filled with laughter and her bright eyes were more brilliantly blue than ever: there was a radiance about her. 'What is it, Audra? You look like the cat that's swallowed the canary. Right chuffed with yourself, my girl, that's what you are!'

'Yes, I am, Vincent. I went to see Doctor Stalkley this morning and he's confirmed it to me. I'm two months pregnant. We're going to have a baby . . . next May.'

It seemed to Vincent that his heart did a tiny somersault of joy. He had been praying that she would get pregnant. Another child would fill the terrible void Alfie had left, and for both of them, not just her. His grief had been as acute as hers, and he still thought about his dead son with sorrow.

Vincent drew her closer, pressed her head against his chest, stroked the crown of her burnished head. 'You couldn't have told me anything better, love,' he said, 'I've been hoping to hear this for months, I really have. No wonder you're chuffed . . . so am I.'

'I thought you would be, Vincent.'

His response was to tighten his arms around her. And he decided not to spoil the special evening she had planned for them by giving her his bad news. He would tell her about Varley's going bankrupt tomorrow. That was soon enough.

Unexpectedly, and much to his astonishment, he suddenly felt optimistic about finding a job. The baby was a lucky omen.

24

'Oh, Audra, what a bonny little girl!' Gwen cried, her face lighting up as she bent over the hospital bed to look at the new-born infant in Audra's arms. 'She's just perfect.'

'Thank you, Gwen, I think so, too, but then I'm her mother, so I suppose that's natural.' Audra smiled up at her friend, who had dropped in unexpectedly to visit her at St Mary's Hospital, then turned her eyes to the bedside table. She let them rest on the lavish bouquet Gwen had placed there a moment before. 'And thank you for the flowers, they're lovely.'

'Well, you always did like yellow roses, lovey. There's also this . . .' Gwen placed a package on the bed. 'It's for –' She stopped, glanced at the baby and laughed. 'You haven't told me her name.'

'Goodness, how stupid I am. We're going to call her Christina. Do you like it?'

'Oh I do, it's ever such a pretty name.' Seating herself on the chair next to the bed, Gwen leaned forward and touched the gift. 'Shall I open this for you . . . and Christina?'

Audra laughed. 'Please.'

'I hope you like it,' Gwen murmured as she untied the ribbon around the fancy box and took off the lid. She lifted out a shell-pink dress with deeper, rose-pink smocking across the front, and held it up for Audra to see. 'It's silk and it's handmade.' She looked at Audra expectantly.

'Oh Gwen, it's exquisite and I love it! Christina will look so pretty in it, but you *are* extravagant.' Audra reached out and squeezed Gwen's hand.

Gwen beamed with pleasure. She leaned back in her chair and regarded Audra thoughtfully. 'I must say, you do look well. Certainly a lot better than you did after you'd had Alfie –' Her voice quavered as she said his name, and she stopped, chagrined. 'Oh, I'm sorry . . .'

'Don't be so silly, Gwenny, we can't avoid mentioning Alfie's name occasionally, and it doesn't upset me, truly it doesn't.' Audra smiled at her reassuringly. 'I've recovered from his death now, in the sense that my grief *has* lessened. It's not too painful any more. Of course, I shall never forget Alfie and I shall always love him, hold him dear in my heart. But there's Christina now.'

Audra dropped her eyes to the child in her arms and smiled down at her, then glanced at Gwen. 'I feel quite wonderful, really. It was an easy birth, just as it was an easy pregnancy. It's odd, isn't it, that I had such a bad time with Alfie. But I hardly knew I was carrying Christina and the delivery was over before I could blink – well, almost.'

Gwen nodded her stylishly-bobbed blonde head. 'Yes, it often happens that way.' She gazed out of the window almost absently, and a wistful expression flitted across her face. 'You are lucky . . . I wish I could get pregnant.'

'Oh you will, just give it time.'

'*Time!*' Gwen laughed softly. 'It's May 1931. I've been married exactly two years and one month.' She gave a little shrug of her shoulders, added, 'But then again, Geoffrey says I'm too anxious, too tense, and that I must relax about having a baby.'

'Perhaps he's correct, after all he is a doctor. And how is Geoffrey?'

'Oh he's all right.' Gwen jumped up abruptly. 'The nurses on this ward seem to be very careless in the execution of their duties. These roses will be half dead by the time one of them decides to bring a vase.' She reached for the bunch of flowers. 'I'll put them in water . . . be back in a jiffy.'

Audra's eyes followed Gwen as she walked up the ward. She had changed a lot in the last two years, as Audra had known she would. *He* had changed her . . . changed the way she dressed and spoke and walked and perhaps even the way she thought. And she had changed yet again since the last time they had met. There was definitely something odd about Gwen today, something that Audra could not quite put her finger on. They saw each other infrequently these days, since their friendship had continued to drift after their marriages. And so the slightest difference in Gwen was most apparent to Audra, the shrewd observer, when they did meet. It has to do with her appearance, Audra now thought, frowning. Was it her outfit? Certainly the black linen dress and jacket were rather dowdy, and stark with their lack of adornment. Also, the sombre colour drained the life from her face. But no, it was not her clothes. It was something else, something indefinable.

Puzzled, Audra let her eyes rest on Gwen as she marched back to the bed, carrying the vase of roses. And as she drew nearer, Audra knew, suddenly, what it was that was so different about her friend today. *All of the light in her eyes had died.* She's no longer happy with him, Audra thought, if she ever was. That's why she doesn't want to talk about him, the reason she leapt up and rushed to put the roses in water. Oh poor Gwenny, she expected so much from this marriage, envisioned such a wonderful life for herself with Geoffrey, and I bet it's pure hell.

'Thank you,' Audra murmured when Gwen placed the vase on the night stand. She scrutinized her surreptitiously. Yes, there *was* a sadness behind those pretty pale blue eyes and a funny little droop to Gwen's mouth which had not been there before.

Gwen interrupted her thoughts, when she announced, 'I just want you to know that I gave that young nurse a good ticking off.'

'I bet you did . . . you see how it is, Gwen, when you're back on a ward you want to take charge . . . old habits die hard, don't they?'

'Yes, perhaps they do.' Gwen sat down, went on, 'Whilst we're on the subject of nursing, are you going back to work for that woman in The Towers when you get out of hospital?'

'You mean Mrs Jarvis . . . oh yes, I *promised* her, and I can't let her down. She's not at all well, and besides, we need the money.'

A sympathetic look flashed across Gwen's face as she remarked, 'It must be awful for you, lovey, Vincent *still* being out of work.'

'Well, it's worse for him, really,' Audra said softly, eyeing Gwen carefully, detecting criticism in her tone. 'The frustration of not being able to find a job is dreadful for him, as I'm sure you can appreciate. Vincent's not a lay-about, or a lazy man, you know, and –'

'I wasn't suggesting anything like that!' Gwen cried, flushing slightly.

Ignoring this comment, Audra continued speaking in an even voice, 'He's out again this afternoon, doing the rounds. He's very responsible. He follows up on every lead.'

'It must rankle with him a bit,' Gwen murmured, 'I mean, he was always dead set against you going out to work.'

'Yes, he was, and don't think he's changed his mind, because he hasn't. However, that's the way it has to be just now.'

'Yes, I realize that, lovey. The last time we saw each other, in March I think it was, you told me that your William had written to suggest that you and Vincent join him in Australia. Didn't that idea come to anything, then?'

'No, it didn't, and I never expected it would. Vincent might give lip service to the idea of emigrating, Gwen, but he wouldn't leave England. He grumbles, of course, about the Depression, the present conditions, and he calls the Government and the politicians every nasty name he can think of, but he loves this country.'

Audra shook her head slowly. 'No, he wouldn't leave his mother and father and the rest of the family – they're a very close knit family, you know, the Crowthers. And there was another reason – I didn't really want to go myself. Of course, I'd love to see William and Frederick again, but I don't think I'd want to live in Australia. Not any more. It's *so* far away.'

Gwen grimaced. 'Yes, I know what you mean, it does seem like the back of beyond.' Waving her hand up and down in front of her face, Gwen now exclaimed, 'Phew! It's hot in here all of a sudden, but then it's very warm for May, isn't it?' She slipped off her jacket and hung it on the back of the chair. 'Didn't you tell me that your Frederick got engaged? Is he married yet?'

Audra did not respond.

Gwen looked at her curiously. 'What's the matter? Why are you staring at me like that?'

'What on earth have you done to your arm?' Audra asked, unable to take her eyes off Gwen. The dress she was wearing was sleeveless, revealing an arm that was badly swollen and dark brown with fading bruises.

With a small, embarrassed laugh, Gwen said, 'Doesn't it look awful! I fell down the cellar steps the other day. Geoffrey was furious with me for being such a clumsy thing. We were going to a dance that night, and I wasn't able to wear my new dress with cap sleeves and I paid such a lot for it in the Model Room at Harte's. Geoffrey said I could have killed myself, and he was ever so cross that I was anywhere near the cellar steps to begin with.' She laughed a little nervously.

'I'm not surprised that he was angry, and you *could* have killed yourself. I remember thinking how steep the cellar steps were, when I first came to see the house. You must be more careful,' Audra cautioned.

'Yes, I know.' Gwen stood up, appeared restless all of a sudden and strolled over to the window in the corner, looked out. After only a split second she stiffened, peered again through the glass, then swung to Audra. 'Mike and Laurette are coming through the hospital gates with Vincent. I'd better be going.'

'But they'd all love to see you and say hello to you.'

Gwen laughed awkwardly. 'I don't really want to see Mike, to tell you the truth.'

'Oh, you're being silly. Now that you're both married there's no reason for you to feel self-conscious.'

'I know, but they're your family and I'd only be in the way. And I really should be getting back to Headingley. I've things to do . . . we're having another dinner party tonight, and that maid of mine bears watching.'

'I wish you'd stay.'

Gwen shook her head with a faint smile. 'No, I must be off.' She lightly touched the top of Christina's head, bent to kiss Audra's cheek. 'Bye-bye, lovey, I'll see you again soon.'

'Goodbye, Gwenny,' Audra said, very quietly, knowing it would be many months before she set eyes on her again. 'Thanks for coming to see me.'

Audra watched her dear old friend hurrying off down the ward and she thought: Oh Gwenny, you're being so silly. You'll run right into Mike on the front steps of the hospital.

'How're my girls?' Vincent asked, bending over, kissing Audra on the cheek, then peeping at his daughter in her arms.

'We're both blooming,' Audra said, smiling, glancing up at him quickly. She knew from his expression that he had not found any work.

Laurette came forward to greet her with great affection and warmth, then said, 'Mam's sent this small fruit pie, she thought you'd enjoy it.'

'I shall, and please thank her for me, Laurette.'

Vincent perched on the edge of the bed, said, 'We just ran into Gwen, and she skittered off down the path as if we were carrying the Black Death.'

'She had to get home,' Audra told him. 'She said something about a dinner party.'

'I had a feeling she didn't want to talk to Mike,' Laurette volunteered, looking from one to the other.

'Aye, maybe you're right,' Vincent said, nodding his head. 'And I'm sure the feeling's mutual. What could he possibly have to say to *her*?'

Audra asked, 'Where is he, anyway?'

'He stopped in to see a patient in another ward, he'll be here in a second,' Laurette told her, then said, 'can I hold Christina for a few minutes, Audra?'

'Of course you may, here, come along, take her from me, dear.'

Audra was glad to change her position in the bed, stretch a little. For a few seconds there was a quietness between the three of them, and Audra watched Laurette rocking the baby, cooing to her softly, holding her so tenderly. She suddenly said, 'Vincent and I wondered – hoped actually – that you would be her godmother, Laurette, and that Mike would be her godfather.'

'Oh I'd love to be!' Laurette exclaimed excitedly, 'and I know Mike will too.' She hesitated, then asked, 'But who's the other godmother going to be? Gwen, I suppose.'

'No, I have a feeling that wouldn't work somehow,' Audra replied, looking at Vincent. 'Do you?'

'I never did, and I'm certainly glad you've changed your mind.' He grinned, glanced along the ward and added, 'And here comes Mike now.'

Mike made a beeline for Audra.

After kissing her cheek and squeezing her shoulder gently, he said, 'No need to ask how you're feeling. For a woman who had a baby only two days ago, you look marvellous . . . I presume everything's all right, no problems of any sort?'

'No, none.' Audra returned his smile, thinking yet again that he was the kindest man she had ever met. The compassion in his soul was reflected in those clear, caring eyes of his, and she knew he would become a successful doctor. His presence, his deep, warm voice, his concern engendered confidence; all were comforting. It's a gift, she thought, that sweetness of his. No wonder all of his patients love him.

Realizing that Mike was still hovering over her, looking down at her as if waiting for her to say something further, Audra remarked, 'Doctor Stalkley was here earlier, and he says I can go home in a few days.'

'He knows best, of course – just don't rush it,' Mike warned, and strode over to his wife. Resting his hand on Laurette's shoulder, he looked down at the baby in her arms and said, 'She's going to be a bonny child.'

'We'd like you to be Christina's godfather, Mike,' Vincent announced, 'Laurette's already agreed to be her godmother. So, what do you say?'

'I say yes.' Mike grinned at them all. 'You've just got yourself a godfather, and who's the other godmother?'

Vincent and Audra exchanged glances and Vincent said, 'I was thinking about our Olive, Audra, how do you feel about her?'

'She'd be perfect . . . yes, do let's keep it in the family.'

Laurette said, 'Olive will take her responsibilities as a godparent very seriously, as we will, naturally.'

'Yes,' Vincent agreed, 'I know you'll all do your duty.' He rose, went to his sister, stretched out his arms. 'Can I borrow my little girl from you for a minute or two, Laurette? I haven't held her today.'

Laurette gave the child to him and he stood looking down at her as he settled her comfortably in the crook of his arm, adjusted her shawl. Her face was not red and crumpled as Alfie's had been at birth. Her skin was smooth and clear, her features well defined. A feeling of awe crept over him as he continued to gaze at Christina and his heart twisted with love for her. He said, at last, 'From the minute I heard from Audra that she was expecting, I felt this baby was a lucky omen. And she is. She's going to turn out to be special.'

'Very, very special,' Audra added. 'I am going to give her the world.'

They all looked at her in surprise.

There was a curious silence. Her words seemed to hang there in the air.

Laurette smiled, then bit her lip, not sure how to properly respond to this extraordinary statement.

Vincent walked towards the window with the baby, stood looking out, his silence pointed.

Mike's worried eyes followed him. From the tense set of his shoulders, he knew that Vincent was angered by Audra's comment. Well, it *had* sounded . . . possessive, to say the least. Couldn't she have said *we*? he thought.

Clearing his throat, wanting to bridge the awkward moment, Mike said, 'That's a lovely sentiment, Audra.'

'Oh, but I mean it very seriously!' she shot back, quite sharply, in the strongest of voices, and pinned him with her eyes.

He had always known she had determination and guts, but now Mike saw something he had never seen before. There was a cold implacability in the set of the mouth and the thrust of the jaw, a terrible relentlessness in those extraordinary cornflower blue eyes. She not only *means* it by God, he thought, but she's going to make it a crusade. And God help anyone who gets in her way; and that includes Vincent.

25

And so it became a driving force in Audra Crowther's life – the desire to give Christina the world.

It was all she thought about from this moment on, and the struggle towards this goal, one which would last for over twenty years, began that summer of 1931.

The moment she came out of the hospital, Audra went back to work for Mrs Jarvis, whom she had nursed for four months before Christina's birth. She had promised the old lady she would resume her duties after the confinement; this aside, they desperately needed the money. Vincent only received twenty-five shillings on the dole, a two-shilling increase per week now that they had a child. It was hardly enough to support the three of them.

The job with Mrs Jarvis was neither difficult nor complex; it was convenient, in that the invalid lived in The Towers, only a few minutes away from the cottage in Pot Lane.

But Audra preferred hospital work to private nursing. After only a month of looking after Mrs Jarvis again she made it clear to the old lady that she was going to apply for work at St Mary's. She did so at the beginning of July.

There was a vacancy at the hospital in November and Audra got the job. To her enormous delight she was assigned to the children's ward.

Audra was well aware that she had been favoured, had been given this most coveted position because of the strings Matron Lennox had pulled, the influence Mrs Bell had exerted on Matron Fox. But this did not trouble her in the least. She had the job and that was all that mattered.

By the spring of 1932, Audra was well settled at the hospital and enjoying it. Matron Fox had taken a liking to her, she was popular with the doctors, and she envisioned promotions coming her way soon. She never thought of these promotions, which she *knew* would be forthcoming, in terms of self-aggrandizement; very simply they would bring her more money, and that was why she wanted them. Money for Christina . . . for her clothes, her education, her future.

Although she could not save a single penny for Christina at the moment, she had every intention of doing so within the next couple of years. Audra had made long-term plans, since she believed this was the only way she would succeed, given her resources. She already had an idea for earning extra money, and she was going to put it into operation once she felt she was truly entrenched at the hospital. She was going to become a dressmaker in her free time.

Nursing gave Audra a sense of gratification, and she threw herself into it with her usual enthusiasm and energy; as she went about the wards there was a new spring in her step, a smile on her face.

But things were not happy at home.

There was trouble between Audra and Vincent yet again, and their curious marriage was once more on a rocky footing.

In a way, the rift that had recently developed between them was mostly Audra's fault this time. Her entire attention was focused on Christina, whom she loved with an almost abnormal ferocity, perhaps because she had already lost one child in death.

Vincent also loved his little girl, but he had overwhelming problems of his own to contend with and, being a young and virile man, he had urgent needs as well. He wanted a relationship with his wife that was normal on every level. Sadly, Audra was not merely preoccupied with Christina and her work; she now had no interest whatsoever in Vincent sexually.

She had stopped sleeping with him some months earlier, and this rankled. He was filled with frustration at being jobless and relegated to looking after the child. Audra's physical coldness and rejection were beginning to aggravate his growing bitterness.

One Saturday evening in April, after Christina had been put to bed in her room upstairs, he decided to have it out with Audra once and for all.

He bided his time until she had cleared the table and washed the dishes. But once she had settled herself in front of the fire and picked up her darning, he switched off the wireless and took the chair opposite her.

'Why did you do that?' she asked without looking up, intent on mending the hole in his sock.

'Do what?' he asked, knowing full well what she meant.

She lifted her head. 'Turn the wireless off . . . I was listening to the –'

'I want to talk to you, Audra. Seriously,' Vincent said, leaning forward, fastening his eyes on hers.

'Oh,' she said, and dropped the darning into her lap, instantly aware of his stern tone. She sat back, gave him her undivided attention.

This is exactly what he had intended. He said, 'We have *very* serious problems, you and I, Audra, and it's about time we got them out in the open. No more shoving them under the rug because you –'

'Problems?' she cut in, looking at him oddly. 'What do you mean, Vincent?'

'Come on, Audra, don't play daft with me. You know very well what I'm talking about. Our problems in bed, that's what. You forever turn away from me, spurn me. Don't you love me any more?'

As usual when he spoke about sex, a faint blush touched her cheeks. She exclaimed, with some indignation, 'Of course I love you.'

'Strange way you have of showing it. An iceberg has nothing on you.'

'Oh Vincent, how unfair you are! Please don't be like this. I do care for you, I do love you. But . . . well . . . I'm fearful of getting pregnant again. Look, you know as well as I do that another child would stretch our resources to the limit. We hardly have enough money as it is –'

'It's not my fault that the bloody country is in such a mess!' he hissed, interrupting her, throwing her an irate look. 'You can blame Ramsey MacDonald and his blasted Government for that! I'm not the only man out of work. There are two million eight hundred thousand of us now. And we're not simply jobless but desperate, and diminished as men because we're reduced to being on the dole –'

'You're misunderstanding me! I *wasn't* pointing a finger, Vincent. I would never

711

do that. I *know* it's not your fault and I also know how hard you try every day to find something. However, if we had another child it would jeopardize Christina's chances . . . don't you agree? Don't you *see* that?'

'Oh yes, I bloody well see it all right. You're planning this glittering future for her and she's not yet one year old. I sometimes wonder about you, Audra, wonder about your sanity.'

He jumped up, his anger getting the better of him, and strode to the coat cupboard, grabbed his sports jacket off the hook and threw it on.

'Where are you going?' she asked, surprised that he was suddenly curtailing their important discussion, yet relieved at the same time.

'To my mother's.'

'Naturally. And after she's sympathized with you, fussed over you, she'll give you more money to go to the pub, as she always does.'

'What goes on between my mother and me is none of your bloody business,' he exclaimed, glaring. 'I've never asked you for a single penny and I never will.'

She made no response.

He flung himself out of the house, but resisted slamming the door behind him. He did not want to awaken his child.

As he walked down Town Street ten minutes later, Vincent's temper began to cool. Nonetheless, he did not excuse Audra's attitude towards him, nor did he forgive her in his heart. If anything, he held a bigger grudge against her than before. He was not sure why, although she *had* managed to really get his goat tonight.

If I were a rich man, he mused, married to a cold, indifferent woman like Audra, I would take myself a mistress. She would be beautiful, accessible and very loving, and I would keep her in great style. Unfortunately I'm not rich, so I can't afford a mistress.

A thought struck him. He *could* afford Millicent Arnold, who would not cost him anything except a few good manners, some sweet talking and a little of his persuasive charm. Millie was not especially beautiful, but she had a pleasant face and a gentle nature. Most importantly, she had always had a soft spot for him, a crush on him, and for a number of years, now that he thought about it.

There's nothing like a woman who truly yearns after you, he thought. Instantly Vincent changed his plans.

He did not go to his mother's house. Nor did he stop off at the White Horse, where he knew his brothers Jack and Bill would be playing darts and waiting for him.

Instead he went to visit Millicent Arnold, a widow woman at only thirty-five and childless, who, he was quite certain, would give him a very warm welcome indeed.

Hurrying up Moorfield Road, he almost ran across the recreation grounds and through the gate at the far side, then sped up the ginnel that led to Rose Cottage. This was where Millie lived alone, now that Ted was dead these past two years. The house was in a tucked-away corner of Armley, and this pleased him. If he was lucky enough to become a frequent visitor, it was better that no one saw him coming and going.

After knocking several times, and getting no answer, he turned away, disappointment filling him.

Then the door sprang open and Millie was exclaiming, 'Why, Vincent, whatever brings you to *my* doorstep on a Saturday evening?'

'Well, it's like this,' he said, pivoting, smiling down into the warm velvet-brown eyes upturned to his, 'I was walking across the rec when I remembered what you said to me last week, you know, when we ran into each other near the library. You told me you were getting more lonesome and blue by the day. Know something strange, Millie? So am I . . . so am I . . .'

'Are you really, Vincent?'

He nodded, smiled his most engaging smile and leaned against the door jamb, let his eyes roam over her provocatively. He had not realized what a voluptuous figure she had. Suddenly he began to chuckle in a way he had not chuckled for years and his vivid green eyes danced.

'I was heading for the pub to meet my brothers, when I thought of you Millicent, thought of how lonely you are, of how lonely I am.' He paused. 'It struck me that you might like a bit of company, and that you might be kind enough to offer a very thirsty man a beer.'

Millicent swallowed, hardly daring to believe her good fortune that he had stopped by to see her. She had wanted him for years, for as long as she could remember, even when Ted was alive. She parted her moist lips, but said nothing. She simply took him by the arm and gently pulled him inside.

'Several beers, if you can drink them,' she said at last, allowing her breast to brush against him, propelling him across the entrance hall.

Millie stopped abruptly, squeezed his arm and peered up into the handsome face which was now staring down at hers. A slow and languorous smile touched her lips. 'And perhaps a spot of supper, too? You *can* stay to supper, can't you, Vincent?' Her eyes were inviting.

'I can indeed,' he said, throwing his shoulders back, standing up straighter, feeling like a man again.

He put his arm around her slender waist and escorted her into the sitting room. And as she nestled closer to him he knew he had nothing to worry about tonight.

Vincent's daily routine did not change, even though he had plunged into an affair with Millicent Arnold.

He was discreet.

He liked Millie, enjoyed her company, basked in her affection for him, enjoyed the way she spoiled him, catered to his every need. And they found a great deal of pleasure and release in their long hours of lovemaking in her large and comfortable bed at Rose Cottage.

But it was a physical liaison, nothing more than that.

Vincent knew the relationship would not last very long, as did Millie herself, and they agreed to simply let it run its course. They had also agreed there would be no recriminations on either side when one of them ended it.

All of this apart, Vincent was too responsible a man to neglect the child he adored, or to curtail his search for work simply because of a dalliance. He only visited Millie once a week, wanting to be disciplined about seeing her, and he was circumspect: he only went to Rose Cottage at night.

He continued to plod along as he had these many months.

He looked after Christina in the morning, wheeled her down to his mother's house around noon, where he had a lunchtime snack with her and Danny. And usually he left Christina in his mother's care for the remainder of the day, returning for her around four o'clock.

Almost every afternoon, and without fail, Vincent scoured the city and the outlying districts, looking for work. Sometimes he was fortunate enough to stumble on an odd job, but it was only ever for a day or two at the most. Nothing permanent came his way.

And as the spring and summer slipped by, and autumn gave way to the winter months, Vincent Crowther began to acknowledge that nothing *was* going to turn up. The Government was in the deepest and most prolonged depression ever known. England was truly on the edge of disaster, as was the entire world, since by now the economic crisis was global. In his bones, Vincent felt they were in for a long siege, and certainly there was trouble brewing everywhere; riots and hunger marches were becoming the norm.

Leeds, like the other great industrial cities, was acutely hit. The Salvation Army opened soup kitchens, other charitable organizations provided clothing and boots for the children who needed them, and also helped those who wished to leave the depressed areas to do so.

Vincent had never seen so many men on the streets – queuing up at the Labour Exchanges, loitering outside the bookies' offices and the pubs, or simply standing about in groups on street corners, looking glum and disgruntled, commiserating with each other. And there was an air of doom hanging over them all. As he looked around him, Vincent shoved aside the feelings of hopelessness that frequently invaded him these days, and dug deeper into himself for inner strength. He knew he had to keep going no matter what, that he must not let his problems eat away at him like a canker, that he must keep his spirits up as best he could.

Although Vincent had never wanted Audra to go to work, he now thanked God that she was a nurse at St Mary's. He was also grateful that other members of the Crowther clan were still working; it was a consolation to know that his parents were better off than most.

His father was with the transportation department of Leeds Industrial Co-operative Society, where he had worked for a number of years, and his job appeared to be secure. Bill was a librarian at one of the public libraries, and Jack, who was studying landscape gardening at night, had a job with the Leeds City Parks Department. Even Maggie had managed to find work in a tailoring shop in Armley, doing buttonholes on men's jackets.

These three did not earn as much as their father by any means, but their combined wages added up to more than most people had to live on. And so there was always plenty of good nourishing food on his mother's table, and coal in her cellar, and Vincent knew that whatever happened Audra and Christina would never go cold or hungry as many folk did in these terrible days.

As Christmas of 1932 approached, Vincent doubled his efforts to find employment, desperately wanting – and needing – to provide something for his little family over the holidays. He wanted to be able to buy a gift, however small, for Audra, a toy for Christina, and put a few luxuries on their table.

There were several big snowstorms in the early part of December and the snow settled. Many of the driveways were blocked, and late one Friday afternoon Vincent finally hit it lucky and got himself a job shovelling snow at one of the big houses nearby. Since it was already growing dark, the housekeeper told him to come back the following day at nine o'clock.

Saturday morning dawned bright but bitterly cold and there was a biting wind. But Vincent did not care. He was so excited about earning a bit of money, nothing was going to deter him. Audra, who had the weekend off from the hospital, insisted he wrap up well. She made him put on two pullovers under his sports jacket, and, as he buttoned his overcoat, she tied a thick woollen scarf around his neck, handed him his woollen gloves.

He kissed her cheek, then said, 'It shouldn't take me more than three hours at the most to clear the drive at Fell House, so I'll be back in time for lunch, love.'

'I think I'll make a large pot of soup today, you'll be needing something like that after being outside in this weather,' she remarked, walking with him to the door. The icy blast hit her in the face as he stepped out, and she shivered. 'I'm not going to take Christina for a walk this morning, it's far too cold.'

'No, I wouldn't, if I were you. Ta'rar, love, see you later.' He strode off down the path, turned and waved. His mood was jubilant.

Audra was very busy all that morning, looking after Christina, making the vegetable soup, doing her household chores. The time sped by.

Before she knew it, the clock was striking twelve. After setting the table for lunch, she turned on the wireless, took Christina in her arms and sat down by the fire to feed her.

When Vincent had not returned by one o'clock Audra began to wonder what had happened to him; by two she was truly concerned. He could be tardy when he went to the pub with his brothers and friends, but never when he was working. He always came straight home from work for a cup of tea or a snack, and to change his clothes if he was going out later.

After putting Christina back in the small cot she kept in the parlour-kitchen, Audra poured herself a cup of soup, but discovered she was not very hungry.

From time to time she went to the window, parted the curtains and peered out, but there was no sign of him.

It was almost three o'clock when she heard the sharp, metallic ring of his boots on the path outside.

'I was getting dreadfully worried,' she said, as he walked in and closed the door behind him. 'I couldn't imagine what had happened to you.'

'There was a lot of snow to shovel,' he said, pulling off his cap, unwinding his scarf, slowly removing his gloves, which were hard with frozen snow. 'More than I'd bargained for . . . the front driveway, two long terraces, the path down between the lawns, and the back yard.'

'You must be exhausted, Vincent, and you're blue with cold. Come to the fire and get warm.'

'They didn't even offer me a cup of tea at twelve –'

'My God, what kind of people are they!' She stared at him aghast, sat down heavily in the chair.

He did not answer her.

As he came towards the fire, Audra saw something in his face that alarmed her.

'Vincent,' she began and hesitated. 'Are you all right?' she asked, watching him carefully.

He remained silent, stood with his back to the fire, warming himself. After a moment he put his hand in his pocket, brought something out. He turned a pinched and tired face towards her and opened his trembling hand.

'This is what they paid me,' he said in a voice that rang with bitterness, showing her the coin in his palm.

For a moment Audra could not believe her eyes. 'Sixpence!' She was horrified. 'They paid you *sixpence* for *six hours' work*. But that's outrageous ... those people ...' She could not go on; her anger choked her.

'Yes ...'

Audra took a deep breath, steadying herself. 'Oh, Vincent, Vincent dear ...' She leapt to her feet and hurried to him, her face grave with concern. She took hold of his arm in the most loving way. 'I'm never going to let you do anything like this again. Never.'

He shook his head, glanced away, blinked. After a minute or two, he turned to her. His eyes were bleak.

'There's a blight on this land,' he said.

26

'Happy birthday to you, happy birthday to you, happy birthday dear Mam, happy birthday to you.'

The second she had finished singing, Christina flew across the room, hurled herself bodily against Audra, almost knocking her over, and hugged her tightly.

Then she looked up at her mother, said, 'We're giving you a birthday party, Mam, we planned it all by ourselves, and it's just for the three of us. It's a surprise.'

Audra smiled down into the small, bright, eager face lifted up to hers. 'Why, how lovely, darling,' she said, brushing a strand of hair away from the six-year-old's forehead, thinking how much she looked like her father today.

Although Christina had her hair and her colouring in general, she had inherited Vincent's finely-chiselled features, Laurette's smoky grey eyes. She's certainly more of a Crowther than a Kenton, at least in her appearance, Audra thought yet again. This resemblance had always been marked, but it seemed more pronounced than ever lately. Christina had recently shot up, and she was going to be tall; this was another Crowther characteristic.

'Happy birthday, love,' Vincent said, walking over to her, kissing her on the cheek.

Audra said, with a faint laugh, 'And I thought you'd forgotten it.'

He grinned, took a puff on his Woodbine. 'How could we? You've dropped enough hints lately,' he teased.

'Mam, please ... come on, come *on*! In here!' Christina cried, catching hold of her hand, pulling her away from the front door of the cottage in Pot Lane. 'You've got to come in here, into the sitting room, you too, Daddy. Oh please come *on*!'

Laughing, Audra placed her handbag on the small table near the door, allowed herself to be dragged across the floor and into the next room by the surprisingly strong and determined little girl.

'There,' Christina said, giving her a very gentle push, 'sit there, Mam, on the sofa, and you, Dad –' she glanced over her shoulder at Vincent, added, 'can sit in that chair.'

'Right you are.' As an aside to Audra, he said, 'I think we've got the makings of an army general in this one.'

Audra nodded, amused. She sat back, smoothed the skirt of her summer cotton frock and looked across at Vincent, expectantly.

He gazed back at her poker faced; his expression revealed nothing.

Christina darted to the antique chest in the corner and returned with a number of envelopes. 'Here are your birthday cards, Mam, the postman brought them just after you'd gone to the hospital this morning. I'll give them to you one by one.' She handed Audra a card, then leaned forward slightly, peering at her mother, trying to see the card she held. Unable to conceal her curiosity any further, Christina asked, 'Who's it from?'

'Auntie Laurette and Uncle Mike.' Audra showed her the card. 'Bluebirds sitting on a branch. Isn't it pretty?'

Christina nodded. 'If you give it to me, I'll put it on the mantelshelf . . . oh thank you, Mam.' She offered Audra another envelope. 'Open this *next* . . .'

Audra noted the Australian postmark, recognized William's handwriting. 'Well, we *all* know exactly *who* it's from, don't we?' she exclaimed with a little laugh.

'May I see it?' Christina came to Audra, stood with one small hand resting on her mother's shoulder, looking at the card with her. 'This one's pretty too, Mam, but there's lots more yet.'

The cards were slowly handed over, opened, exclaimed about and lined up with care on the mantelpiece. There was another one from Sydney, from her brother Frederick and his wife Marion; others from various members of the Crowther clan, and one from Gwen.

The last of the pile was presented with something of a flourish by the solemn child who was so intent on making this a special day for her mother. 'It's from us,' she whispered leaning closer to Audra, touching her cheek lovingly. 'Dad picked it really, but he took me to the shop with him and I helped.'

Audra ripped open the envelope and pulled out the birthday card. It was the most expensive of the lot, made of glossy paper, with a yellow silk cord slotted through it and tied around the spine. The picture on the front was a bowl of yellow roses standing on a table near an open window, and fluttering above the bowl was a red butterfly.

'It's just beautiful,' Audra said, before looking inside the card and reading the short, printed verse. Vincent had written underneath this: *Wishing you many happy returns of the day, with lots of love from your dearest husband and daughter*, and he had signed his name, and Christina had added her own signature. 'Thank you, it's the loveliest birthday card I've *ever* had in my whole life,' she told them, looking up, smiling first at Christina, then at Vincent.

They beamed back at her.

Christina said, 'I'll get your present, Mam.'

She flew to the chest, took a package from a drawer and carried it back to her mother. 'This is from Dad and me,' she said, smiling gravely, handing Audra the gift.

Audra slipped off the ribbon and paper, wondering what they had bought for her, filled with swelling happiness that they were making such a fuss over her birthday. She was so very touched she could hardly speak for a moment.

She found herself holding a framed watercolour. As she turned it slightly, the better to see it, her eyes widened and she caught her breath in surprise and delight. The painting was of a summer garden at sunset, and the scene was filled with golden light and there were raindrops caught on a cluster of leaves, as if there had been a brief shower before the artist had picked up the paintbrush.

The watercolour was small, but quite lovely, even though it was flawed in parts and needed much more work; one side of it was unfinished and amateurish, and yet there was something distinctive about the scene, something that caught and held the attention. How fascinating, Audra thought, her eyes narrowing as they lingered on the painting. It looks curiously like my father's work.

But Audra knew that Vincent had not managed to find a very early watercolour by Adrian Kenton.

Christina's name was boldly and clearly written in one corner, but even if it had not been, she would have recognized this as her daughter's creation. As awkward as certain aspects of the painting were, and child-like, Christina had managed to do one thing – capture light on paper. She had sometimes shown this ability in the past and it was no mean feat. With this new piece of work she had demonstrated just how much she had developed lately. The girl had displayed a remarkable talent for drawing and painting since she was four years old, but her latest endeavour proved that she was much more than merely talented. She was extraordinarily gifted. Audra felt a sudden tingle of excitement at this discovery, and she filled with immense pride in her child.

Lifting her head, she found herself staring into a pair of large grey eyes worriedly fixed on her face.

'Don't you like it, Mam?' The child's lip quivered.

'Oh Christie, I do! I really do! It's simply beautiful, darling. Thank you so much.' Audra brought the little girl into her arms and held her close. 'I'm sorry I didn't say so immediately, I was far too busy admiring it, I'm afraid.'

Christina looked into her mother's eyes, her own shining with joy. 'I painted it specially for your birthday, Mam, and Dad took it to Mr Cox's shop in Town Street and had it framed. That's why it's from the two of us . . . 'cos Daddy paid for the frame.'

Giving her husband a radiant smile, Audra said, 'Thank you . . . it's the best present you could have given me, really it is. I shall treasure it always.' Her bright blue eyes held his with keenness. 'And it *was* worth framing, Vincent, wasn't it?'

'Aye, it was that. I recognized the beauty of it the minute our Christina showed it to me.' There was a proud expression on his face as he added, 'You're a right clever little lass, love.'

Christina looked pleased, wrinkled her nose at him, then she turned to her mother, asked, 'Where shall you put it, Mummy?'

'Well, let's see . . . I know *one* thing, it's going to take pride of place in *this* house,' Audra declared. 'What about here, on the mantelpiece? For the moment, anyway.'

Audra rose as she spoke, crossed to the fireplace and propped the painting on the shelf in the midst of the birthday cards.

Turning, she asked her daughter, 'And whose garden is it? Where did you go to paint it?'

'Calpher House . . . I went up to see Mrs Bell to ask her if I could . . . and I went all by myself. And she said yes I could paint her garden for you, and so I picked that sweet little corner near her roses . . . she kept coming out to see how I was doing. She was ever so interested. It was last week that I did it, Mam, and she made me come inside when it rained and she gave me a glass of milk and a Cadbury's chocolate finger, no *two*, and after it stopped raining I went out and I started all over again. I liked the garden better then . . . it sort of glistened after the rain.'

Audra nodded. 'You certainly captured that feeling beautifully, Christina. It's the best work you've done so far . . . you've made leaps and bounds.'

The child glowed.

Vincent said to his daughter, 'Now, Christie love, what about the tea party then? Isn't it about time.'

'Oh yes! Mam, come on, and you too, Dad!'

27

It was the most splendid tea party.

Audra was not allowed to do anything.

And so she sat at the table in the parlour-kitchen, watching her husband and her child bustle around, getting everything ready. She had noticed earlier how they had both dressed up; they had turned her birthday into a truly special occasion, one of importance, and she could not help but feel happy and flattered. She just wished she had had time to change out of the cotton frock she had worn to work that day, to put on something more attractive herself, but Christina had not given her the chance.

How handsome Vincent looks, Audra thought, watching her husband as he moved around the parlour-kitchen. He wore a dazzling white shirt, a burgundy tie and dark grey slacks, and he had obviously rushed home from work to shave again and to change his clothes for the tea party. She could see that he was freshly barbered and his black hair, brushed sleekly back to reveal his widow's peak, was still damp with water.

As for Christina, she looks adorable, Audra thought. Yes, she's the prettiest thing imaginable today.

Her little daughter had donned her best party frock of pale-blue silk trimmed with narrow bands of white lace down the bodice and on the skirt. She had put on clean white ankle socks and her Sunday-best shoes with ankle straps, made of shiny black patent leather. A blue silk ribbon was tied around her head and finished in a bow on her crown. Audra smiled to herself. Vincent had done quite a decent job of fixing the bow.

Audra sat back in her chair, now eyeing the table with interest. It was covered with their good linen cloth and set with their best china, which only came out for visitors. She saw that a linen serviette had been placed on each plate and there was a posy of yellow roses from the garden in a glass vase in the centre. Again she smiled. She fancied these were her daughter's touches.

Vincent went to the set-pot and turned off the kettle, which was whistling on the gas ring. He made a big pot of tea in the silver pot from High Cleugh; Christina brought out plates of food from the pantry.

She explained, in her piping child's voice, 'The teeny-tweeny sandwiches are made the way you like them, Mam, and they're all your favourites . . . potted-meat spread, tomato and cucumber and Dad bought a tin of salmon at the Co-op and we made lots of sandwiches with it.'

'They all look delicious,' Audra said, 'you have been working hard, haven't you?'

'Dad helped,' Christina said and made several more trips to the pantry, returning with chocolate biscuits, currant buns with white, icing-sugar tops, scones and raspberry jam. 'Grandma made the buns and the scones for me,' she explained to Audra, and ran back to the pantry one more time. 'Strawberries, Mam!' she announced depositing the dish in front of her mother. 'Oh, and the cream! I forgot the cream!'

'Come on, Christina love, sit yourself down now,' Vincent called, bringing the teapot to the table, pouring for the three of them. 'I don't know about my two girls, but I'm famished.'

During tea, Audra and Vincent chatted happily.

She spoke of her busy day at St Mary's Hospital, where she was now a sister and in charge of the two children's wards as well as the maternity ward.

He spoke about the temporary job he and Fred Varley had, building stables onto the Pinfold mansion in Old Farnley. They were doing it together, working side by side, since Fred Varley had not been able to open up again after his bankruptcy, at least not in a big way. Varley took on small building jobs, when he could get them, and usually it was Vincent he employed to help him.

'But he'll open up shop again soon, and permanently,' Vincent said, 'he will that, never fear.' And Audra nodded her head, and crossed her fingers under the table, praying that this was true. Vincent loved his work and things were a lot easier between them when he had a job and was earning money and supporting them himself. She had slowly come to understand that it was his frustration and resentment when he was out of work that caused some of their greatest problems.

Vincent started to talk about his brother Frank, who was in the Ninth Lancers – a cavalry regiment – and with the British Army in India. He was coming home on leave and Vincent had decided that the entire Crowther clan should give a party for Frank's homecoming: this was now the chief topic of conversation.

Christina kept her ears cocked as she always did when she was with her parents, looking from one to the other, her large grey eyes wider than ever, interested, missing nothing.

She was attentive to their every word as she munched on her sandwiches. Occasionally she made a remark of her own, but mostly she listened. They were both so clever, her mam and her dad. She loved to hear them talk. Her mam had such a lovely voice, so soft and musical.

She always enjoyed times like this when they were so friendly with each other and her mother smiled a lot and her eyes got very, very blue and very bright; she didn't like it when they squabbled. Then her father went out, banging the door behind him with a crash and didn't come home until ever so late at night when *they* were fast asleep. Her mother was always cross with him for days after and looked at him in a queer way through the corner of her eye and tightened her lips.

Once, last year when she had been little and not grown up like now, her mam had waited up for her dad to come home after a row. They had shouted at each other and her mam had screamed, 'If that's the way you feel about it, then go back to your fancy woman.' She had heard it all, because she had been so surprised to hear her mam shouting that she had crept out of her room, had hung over the banisters to listen.

And for days afterwards she had worried that her dad was going to go away and live with the woman who was fancy. She had wondered if *they* weren't fancy enough for him. Perhaps if they made themselves fancy he would stay, she had thought, but she hadn't been sure how to do this.

Finally she had asked her grandma what a fancy woman looked like. Her grandma had sucked in her breath, had stared hard at her, had asked where she had heard something like that, and she had fibbed, had said, 'at school'. She didn't know, even now, why she had fibbed to Grandma, except that somehow she knew she should not talk about things that happened at home. Her mam never did when *she* went to Grandma's. She hardly said anything at all, and she wasn't a bit like *her mam* when she was at Grandma's house. She was different, somehow.

But in the end they hadn't had to get themselves all fancy, because her dad had not gone away. A short while after the terrible quarrel her mam and her dad had been all smiles again, and loving, and forever kissing each other on the cheek and hugging. It was always like that with them.

Her father's sudden laughter brought Christina out of her reverie.

She looked at him alertly.

His expression was merry and his green eyes were all sparkly like the necklace Auntie Gwen wore when they went to tea at her house in Headingley, except that they didn't go to Auntie Gwen's any more. And her mother was laughing too; her eyes danced and danced with blue lights and she knew her mother was happy today.

Christina did not understand why her parents were laughing in this way; she had missed what her mother had just said. But she began to laugh too, wanting to be part of it, part of *them*, part of their happiness and gaiety.

Vincent, still chuckling, said, 'Oh and by the way, Audra, Mike's bought tickets for the Grand Theatre on Saturday . . . it's Noel Coward's *Cavalcade*. He's invited us, so that's another nice birthday treat for you, love.'

'How sweet he is, so thoughtful.'

Christina asked, 'Will Auntie Maggie be looking after me when you go out on Saturday night?'

'She will that, love.'

'Oh goody, Dad. We have such fun and she always lets me stay up late.'

'She does!' Audra exclaimed.

'It's time for the strawberries, Mam, I'll serve,' Christina cried, jumping down off her chair. 'And you get to get the most, 'cos it's your birthday.'

'Don't be so silly,' Audra demurred, 'we'll all have exactly the same amount, it's share and share alike in this family.'

'No, *you* have to have the most,' Christina insisted as she carefully spooned the fruit into the small glass dishes she had brought from the sideboard.

They had not had strawberries for a long time, because they were so expensive and such a special treat. And so none of them spoke as they ate them slowly, savouring every bite, but their eyes shone and they smiled at each other with their eyes. And when they had finished they all three agreed that these were the *best* strawberries they had ever eaten ... sweet, succulent and juicy.

But the highlight of the tea party was the birthday cake.

Christina and Vincent fussed over it in the pantry, before the child walked out, slowly, sedately, carrying it high in front of her.

And father and daughter cried in unison, 'Happy birthday! Happy birthday!'

Drawing to a standstill in front of her mother, Christina said, 'I'm sorry there's only one candle, Mam, but that's all that was left from my birthday cake. The others were ever so burned down.'

'I don't mind, Christie, one candle is certainly better than none.'

'That's what I told her,' Vincent remarked, sitting down opposite Audra. 'And I also said you'd probably prefer one candle to thirty.'

Audra gave him a small, rueful smile. 'I can't believe that I'm actually thirty years old today. Vincent ... where have all the years gone?'

Vincent shook his head, smiled faintly. 'Don't ask me, lass. I've no idea. And I'll be thirty-four in nine days ... or had you forgotten?'

Before Audra had a chance to answer, Christina cried, 'We have to have a party for you too, Dad!'

Christina knelt to say her prayers.

Audra sat in the rocking chair and listened.

Once she had finished the long ritual of blessing her uncles in Australia and every member of the Crowther clan, Christina clambered up onto her bed and slid down between the sheets.

Rising, Audra went over to her, tucked in the covers and straightened the quilt, then sat on the edge of the bed. She smoothed her hand along her child's innocent cheek and smiled at her. 'It was a lovely birthday party, Christie, thank you.'

Christina smiled back. Then she asked anxiously, 'We can have a party for Daddy, can't we?'

'Of course we can. It wouldn't be fair if we didn't ... you had yours last month and there was mine today – so it's his turn next.' Audra leaned forward, kissed her daughter.

Plump little arms reached out and went around Audra's neck. Christina nuzzled against her mother, filling with pleasure at the familiar smell of her cool fresh skin and the scent of Gardenia Flower Essence behind her ears. She whispered, 'I love you, Mam.'

'Oh darling, I love you, too. So very much. Come on, curl up and go to sleep. It's very late now. Sweet dreams, honeybunch.'

'Yes, Mam. 'Night, Mam.'

Christina did not fall asleep immediately.

She lay in bed watching the sky through the window. They had let her stay up way past her bedtime tonight since it was a special occasion, and now it was very dark outside.

The sky was inky black and filled with glittering stars oh so far away and the moon was as round as a silver half crown and just as shiny. A full moon, her father had said, just before she had been packed off to bed.

Oh how she loved her dad. And her mam. She liked it the best when it was just the three of them . . . her mam and her dad and her. Her dad had invited Auntie Laurette and Uncle Mike to the tea party. She was ever so glad they hadn't been able to come. It wasn't that she didn't love them. She did. She loved all of her aunts and uncles and her grandma. And Grandpa. Especially Grandpa. She liked the way he smelled of leather and Gentleman's Hair Pommade and eucalyptus pastilles that he sometimes gave to her, secretly when no one was looking, and he took her up on his knee and told her stories of many wonderous things. She didn't mind that his big white curly moustache tickled her when he kissed her, or that he puffed away on a pipe that filled Grandma's parlour-kitchen with smoke and made her eyes water. He called it, 'My fine Calabash,' and he wouldn't let anybody touch that pipe of his, not even Auntie Maggie, who he thought the world of, so her dad said.

But she loved her mam and her dad the most. More than the whole world put together. They belonged to her. And she belonged to them. She wouldn't want any other mam and dad. Hers were special. She just knew they were.

She snuggled down in the bed and closed her eyes, slowly drifting off to sleep. She could hear the murmur of their voices floating up the staircase . . . soft, warm, loving voices . . . she always felt so safe when she heard their voices . . .

'She's a very special child, Vincent,' Audra said, settling back against the sofa in the sitting room.

'Yes, she's clever.'

'What she has is more than cleverness, more than talent even . . . she's gifted, Vincent, exceptionally gifted.' Audra let her eyes rest on the mantelpiece where the painting stood, propped up in the middle of the birthday cards. 'Before tea, you said you were struck by the watercolour, so much so you decided to have it framed.'

'Aye, no two ways about it, I was impressed.' Vincent glanced at the painting Audra had done years before of The Memory Place, then let his eyes wander to the back wall where a landscape by Adrian Kenton hung. 'Our Christina gets it from you and your father, Audra, her artistic talent, I mean.'

'Yes, she does. But she's going to be a much better artist than I am when she grows up . . . and she'll probably be better than my father too. The indications are already there.'

'There shouldn't be any doubt in your mind any more about who your father really was, Audra.' He gave her a slow smile.

'Oh, there isn't, and I don't suppose there ever was actually. I knew my mother would never do anything to hurt my father whilst he was alive. It was not in her nature to do anything shoddy. I think I've always known, deep down, that she and Uncle Peter only ever became involved later, much later, after she was widowed.'

Vincent nodded and reached for his glass of beer. He was glad that they had laid that old ghost finally.

They were both silent for a while, lost in their own thoughts.

The June evening had turned coolish and Vincent had put a match to the fire whilst Audra had been putting Christina to bed. Now she sat staring into the flames, thinking of the child who lay asleep upstairs. The gifted child, the child she had always known was going to have a glittering future.

Suddenly, Audra leaned forward, startling Vincent as she exclaimed, 'Yes, we must do it!'

'Do what?' he asked, looking at her curiously.

She did not answer this question directly; instead she said, 'I've been teaching her art for the last couple of years, and I'll continue to do so, but there's only so much knowledge *I* can impart.'

'Yes,' he said, crinkling his eyes, staring harder.

'She'll go to art school –'

'When?' he interrupted.

'When she's sixteen. They won't accept her at Leeds College of Art before then. Later she'll have to go to London. To study at the Slade, no, better still, at the Royal College of Art.'

'How are we going to pay for all this?' he demanded, his voice rising sharply. 'We'll never be able to afford an education like that for her, not even if the Depression ends and I get a permanent job. It'll cost *thousands*.'

'Yes, I know, but we'll do it,' she replied, very firmly. 'We must, Vincent, we must!' There was an eagerness in her voice, an excitement he had not heard for a long time. 'Christina must be given every chance, every opportunity,' Audra rushed on, 'I won't have her cheated just because of a lack of money. She has a gift . . . it must be trained. She's going to be a brilliant painter, a great artist, Vincent.'

'Well,' he said slowly, his voice sinking, 'I just don't know . . .'

Audra sat up straighter and gave him one of her penetrating stares. 'There can be no hesitation on our parts, Vincent, none whatsoever, do you hear! We must strive towards this goal, whatever the cost, whatever the sacrifice. Christina must have that chance. And I, for one, am going to make sure she gets it!'

28

'I don't know what to do about Audra any more, Mike, I don't really. I'm at the end of my tether,' Vincent said in a shaky voice.

He jumped up, and strode over to the window, where he stood looking out, narrowing his eyes against the bright April sunlight.

Mike said, 'Yes, I'm aware how worried you've been – and for quite a while.' The young doctor frowned, conscious of his friend's anxiety, his frustration at being jobless. Vincent's emotions were close to the surface these days, and the set of his shoulders indicated to Mike just how tense and distressed he was this morning.

'What can I do to help –' Mike began, but broke off as the sitting-room door swung open.

Laurette backed herself into the room, carrying a tray. She turned and marched over to the fireplace. 'Sorry I took so long with the tea,' she said brightly, 'but I had to check on the Sunday joint and the roast potatoes first. I brought myself a cup ...' Laurette paused in mid-sentence, suddenly noticing Mike's troubled face, Vincent's rigid stance near the window.

'Oh,' she said quickly, 'am I interrupting something? Were you having a private talk? I'd better take my tea back to the kitchen and leave you both in peace.'

'No, don't be ridiculous,' Vincent said, spinning around on his heels, coming back to the fireplace. 'It's not anything you can't hear.' Lowering himself into a chair, he took out his cigarettes, lit one.

Laurette passed around the cups, then sat down, looking at Vincent expectantly, waiting for him to continue. For a moment or two Laurette observed her brother.

Vincent sat staring into the fire morosely, his face brooding as he smoked his cigarette.

Finally, hoping to draw him out, she asked, 'Where did you say Audra and Christina have gone today?'

'To Fountains Abbey,' he said without looking up. 'Another painting lesson in the country, a field trip as Audra calls it.' At last he turned his face to Laurette, and added, 'But you know she always takes Christie out to paint on her Sundays off from the hospital.'

'Yes, and I think it's admirable the way she's teaching her everything *she* knows, schooling her in art, showing her paintings in the big houses like Temple Newsam and Harewood. Audra's giving Christie a good grounding, Vincent, and she'll be well prepared for art school.'

Vincent nodded, but made no comment.

Mike remarked, 'You said you didn't know what to do about Audra any more. Let's talk about it ... it does help to get it off your chest, and that's really why you came to see us this morning, isn't it?'

'Yes, that's true, Mike.' Vincent cleared his throat. 'It's Audra's health that I'm worried about. She's pushing herself harder than ever these days, stretching her strength to the limit. You both know what her schedule's like ... she's working damned hard at the hospital and taking on additional duty, whenever she gets the chance, for the extra money. Then when she comes home she's looking after us, cooking, cleaning, washing and ironing. *And* she's tutoring Christie in art. And when she's not doing that, she's toiling at that bloody sewing machine Mrs Bell gave her, doing alterations and making clothes for people. The work aside, she scrimps and scrapes, does without herself, in order to save every penny she can for Christina's education.'

They both looked at him attentively, saying nothing, their faces sympathetic.

Vincent shook his head slowly. 'It's this relentless pursuit of money that troubles me, and I'm powerless to stop it. Helpless, really.' Unexpectedly, Vincent's voice shook again. 'I daren't interfere, daren't say a word ... when I have in the past she's bitten my head off ... I was hoping *you'd* talk to her, Mike, you know, as a doctor. She'd listen to you.'

'I doubt that, Vince,' Mike answered, his tone gloomy. 'Of course I'd be willing to try, but I'd be wasting my breath. And so would Laurette, as close as she is to Audra. No one, nothing, is going to stop Audra. She's single-minded, and she's stubborn. *Implacable.*'

'Aye, I know that only too well,' Vincent muttered. 'All this started years ago when Christina was first born. I told Audra at the time that she was propelled by a terrible driving force within herself, and I was right.' He ran his hand over his weary face. 'There's nothing wrong with being ambitious, wanting the best for a child, I realize that. But what Audra's been doing these past few years – well, it's bloody abnormal if you ask me.'

Laurette said, 'I'm not sure if abnormal is quite the right word, Vincent –' She hesitated, searching for the correct expression to convey the sudden thought that had struck her. Then she said, slowly, carefully, 'What we're witnessing is an act of will, and one so selfless, so powerfully motivated it's ... well, it's just *awesome* to watch.'

'Bloody frightening, you mean,' Vincent said harshly. He took a deep breath, tried to soften his voice. 'Look, Laurette, I want the best for our Christie, I really do. But there's a limit to what people in our circumstances can do. Audra's reaching too high, reaching for too much for the lass. I love Audra ...' He paused, cleared his throat. 'I don't want her to collapse, to get sick. I'm only trying to protect her.'

'I don't think she'll pay any attention to any of us, as I said, but I *will* have a talk to her tomorrow, Vince,' Mike promised. 'I'll be up at the hospital to see patients and I'll find an opportunity to say something to her. I'll insist she has a general check-up, just as a matter of routine. At least that might ease your mind.'

'Oh it will, Mike, it will. Thanks ever so much.'

Laurette smiled at her brother, patted his arm. 'Try and relax a bit, love, it'll be all right.'

Vincent nodded, put another cigarette in his mouth, struck a match.

'Will you stay for Sunday lunch?' Laurette asked. 'It's roast lamb, new potatoes and spring cabbage – all the things you like.'

'No, thanks though. I said I'd meet our Bill and Jack for a drink at the Traveller's Rest at Hill-Top, then I'll probably walk back to our mam's with them, have a spot of lunch there.' Vincent eyed his sister, said in a careful tone, 'I don't want you to say anything to Mam, but our Bill is thinking of joining up, going into the Merchant Navy.'

Laurette stared at him, her eyes widening. 'She's not going to like that! Not with our Frank already in the army.'

'I know she won't.' Vincent turned to his brother-in-law. 'There's going to be a war, Mike. The writing's on the wall, what with Hitler on the march, invading parts of Czechoslovakia in March and now, just last week, the man was making impossible demands on Poland –'

'I was reading about that in the *Sunday Express* before you came in,' Mike interrupted. 'The man's a maniac, getting greedier than ever, demanding that the Free City of Danzig be ceded to Germany. It seems we've pledged to support Poland in this new crisis; so has France.'

Their troubled eyes locked.

'It's an uneasy peace we have at the moment, Mike, and it won't last long ... we'll be at war with Germany before the end of the year, mark my words.'

'Don't say that!' Laurette exclaimed, looking from her brother to her husband. Her voice quavered slightly as she asked, 'Will you ... will you both have to go if there's a war?'

'Yes,' Mike said, very quietly.

29

'What a lovely morning it is,' Audra said, walking to the open door of the cottage in Pot Lane, standing on the doorstep, looking out.

'Yes, it *is* a bonny day,' Vincent agreed, joining her in the doorway. He followed her gaze. It was directed to the bottom of the small garden where Christina sat sketching, and he smiled with pleasure at the sight of his child. 'And much too nice to stay inside ... I think I'll come with you this afternoon, if you'll have me, that is.'

Audra looked at him in astonishment. 'But you always go to the White Horse on Sunday lunchtimes –' She broke off as the laughter bubbled up inside her and her eyes grew bright with happiness. 'But we'd love it if you came with us. We're not going far, only to Temple Newsam. I want Christie to study some of the paintings there, in particular the Old Masters.'

Vincent put his arm around her, squeezed her shoulder, stared down into her face. He saw the tiredness behind the sudden radiance filling her face at this moment, and his heart tightened. She was still pushing herself too hard, despite Mike's friendly lecture in the spring, and she worried him a lot. But she would not listen to him; his words seemed to make no impression on her. She continued to toil as she always had.

Vincent said, in a rush, 'Listen, love, I've got an idea, a wonderful idea. Let's get ready and go to Temple Newsam *now*. Well, in about half an hour or so. You know, make a day of it, Audra. We could take a picnic with us ... that'd save you struggling over a hot stove, cooking Sunday lunch before we go. Come on, what do you say?'

Audra nodded her head, smiling. It was not often that he ventured out with them on these Sunday art excursions, when they went to the country or the seaside, or to visit stately homes, and she was delighted. She looked over her shoulder at the clock on the mantelpiece. 'It's ten past eleven already ... but oh *yes*, why not!' Swinging to face the garden, shading her eyes against the sunlight, she called, 'Christie, Christie, come inside, please.'

The girl looked up. 'In a minute, Mam, I'm trying to get this tree exactly right.'

'Very well, but don't be *too* long. Your daddy's coming with us to Temple Newsam, and we're going to leave this morning instead of this afternoon. We're taking a picnic lunch with us and I need you to help me.'

'Oh!' Christina cried and leapt to her feet, excited that her father was going too. 'I'm coming in now, Mam.'

A split-second later she was hurrying into the parlour-kitchen carrying her folding stool and sketching things. After putting them away, she asked, 'What do you want me to do, Mam?'

'Let's start making the sandwiches first, and once we have the lunch packed, we'll get ready,' Audra said, bustling over to the pantry.

'Can I do anything to help?' Vincent asked.

'Not really, but you might put the wireless on, it would be nice to have a bit of music this morning.'

'Done,' he said, striding to the set, twiddling the nob. 'Ah, here's a nice bit of music ... why it's the *Blue Danube*, Audra. Fancy that – the first dance we had together at the Parish Hall, all those years ago, when I asked you to have the last waltz with me. Do you remember?'

'Of course I remember,' she said, turning her head, giving him the sweetest of smiles, then she frowned as the music stopped abruptly, was cut off in mid-stream. 'Oh dear, don't tell me that the wireless is broken again. Vincent, we'll just have to buy a –'

'We interrupt this programme to bring you an important message from the Prime Minister,' a BBC announcer was saying.

Vincent and Audra stared at each other, neither of them moving as the voice of Neville Chamberlain flowed out of the set, told them and the rest of the country that England was now at war with Germany. He spoke of the Polish situation, and explained that the British Government had done everything possible to establish peace and had a clear conscience.

'Now may God bless you all and may He defend the right.' The Prime Minister's voice, so grave and sombre, then faded away with these words, was replaced by the national anthem, and the familiar strains of *God Save The King* reverberated around the kitchen.

'It's September the third today,' Vincent muttered, glancing at Audra through troubled eyes. 'I've been expecting a war, but it came sooner than I thought it would.'

'Yes.' Audra put the knife she was holding down on the set-pot and lowered herself into the nearest chair, feeling strangely weak in the legs as the implications of the Prime Minister's message sank in.

Christina looked from her mother to her father, her eyes puzzled. 'What does it mean? What's going to happen, Dad?'

'We're going to be fighting the Germans, but don't you worry, pet, everything's going to turn out all right in the end.'

'What shall we do about Temple Newsam?' Audra suddenly said, 'perhaps we'd better not go today, after all.'

'Oh Mam, don't say that,' Christina cried. 'Not when Daddy said he'd come with us.'

Christina's face was so crestfallen and she sounded so let down, Vincent could not help exclaiming, 'Oh what the hell, let's go, Audra. It'll probably be the last chance we get to do something together like this for a long time.'

'That's true.' Audra hesitated.

Eagerly, Christina asked, 'Can we go then, Mam?'

Audra half-smiled at her. 'Yes – run upstairs and change your frock. Your daddy will help me to finish preparing the picnic.'

'Shall I wear my yellow cotton frock with the primrose pattern?'

'If you like, dear.'

When they were alone, Vincent said, 'I don't know when the recruiting offices will open, tomorrow or Tuesday, I expect.' He paused. 'But I'm going to volunteer as soon as they *are* open for business.'

'Yes,' she said, 'yes, I knew you would, if war came. As much as you've ranted and raved about the Government and the Depression, you're very patriotic at heart.'

'Aye, I am that, lass, like every Englishman worth his salt. Besides, the Government's not the country. And anyway, if *we* don't do the fighting, who *is* going to do it? Who's going to defend what we believe in? Oh yes, I must go and fight for my King and country, Audra. God knows, I don't wish war on any of us, it's going to be hell on earth, but maybe I can now stand up and be a man.'

She stared at him in amazement. 'You've always been a man to me, Vincent.'

Vincent Crowther joined the Royal Navy on Tuesday, and by the end of the week he had been sent to the big naval barracks at Harwich to start his basic training.

The cottage in Pot Lane seemed quiet and empty without him. It was the first time they had been separated since their marriage and Audra soon began to realize just how much she missed him.

They had an odd marriage in some ways, she was the first to admit that, but in spite of their quarrels and differences, they loved each other. They had this glittering prize who was their daughter Christina, and it was she who bound them together irrevocably.

And so as she went about her work at the hospital and at home, Audra thought about Vincent and worried about him and wondered how he was getting on in the Royal Navy.

Soon his letters started to come on a regular weekly basis and she and Christina sat and pored over them and re-read them and talked about him lovingly; they could not wait for his first leave.

Because of his absence, Christina had to look after herself during the day when Audra was working at St Mary's. 'I don't mind, Mam, I can manage, honestly I can,' the girl kept telling her, and this was the truth. Christina was exceptionally grown up for an eight-year-old, mostly because of her own intelligence and the practical domestic training she had been given by her mother; but also because she had been surrounded by adults all of her life.

In particular, she was close to her Auntie Laurette, and when Audra was on night duty Christina now began to sleep at her aunt's house. Mike Lesley had enlisted in the Medical Corps, and since she was alone Laurette was happy to have her niece for company. With Mike's departure, Laurette had gone back to work. Wanting to do her bit for the war effort, she had taken a job with an engineering firm in Armley which was now making bombs; she was secretary to the managing director.

Every day, when her mother was at work, Christina went to her grandmother's for lunch, as she had done since she was a baby and had been taken there by her father in her pram. Eliza's cheerful kitchen with its plethora of roses had always rung with laughter and the jollity of her boisterous family. But now it was deathly quiet.

Bill had joined the Merchant Navy, Jack had gone into the army, and Maggie had enlisted in the ATS – the Auxiliary Territorial Service. She had first gone to a training centre near Reading for a month's basic army training, then on to a huge camp in Shropshire where she was learning to use anti-aircraft instruments. Hal, Olive's husband, was in the Royal Air Force, and only Alfred and Danny, who was just sixteen, remained at home.

The Crowthers were suddenly a family of women, except of course for Alf and his youngest son, whom they all knew would go when he was old enough, and they drew closer as England mobilized for war.

Barrage balloons and searchlights, air-raid sirens and the 'All Clear' signal, blackout curtains at every window, identity cards, air-raid shelters and gas masks – all became quite commonplace. So did food rationing, clothing coupons, petrol rationing and shortages of every kind. And air-raid drill. This was conducted by members of the Civil Defence, and Mr Trotter, the local air-raid warden for Pot Lane, became a familiar and friendly face to Audra and Christina.

As trying and as difficult as these times were, Audra kept to her regular routine of years standing, and she insisted that Christina do the same. Aside from her school work, the tutoring in art continued and Christina was expected to work at it with dedication every day.

But they had their little pleasures too, and in particular they loved going to the pictures to see the latest films from America, as well as those made at home. They were also rabid fans of the radio, and listened to everything from the news to comedy and musical programmes. It was the cinema that always won out, though, and they went once a week, sometimes twice, usually accompanied by Laurette.

One Saturday afternoon in late October of 1939, Audra, Laurette and Christina were having tea in the kitchen of the cottage, before going to the Picturedrome to see the latest Robert Donat picture, *Goodbye, Mr Chips*.

Laurette, who was a real fan of films and film stars, had been telling them about the Donat movie, relating something of the story.

'Don't tell us any more,' Audra exclaimed, 'otherwise you'll spoil it for us.'

'Oh sorry,' Laurette apologized, and, changing the subject, she went on, 'What *I* can't wait to see is *Gone With The Wind*. I've been reading about it in *Picturegoer Magazine* and it sounds wonderful. Vivien Leigh looked so beautiful in last week's issue, and Clark Gable! *He's* just gorgeous.'

Audra grinned. 'If Mike heard you, he'd be jealous –' She glanced over her shoulder at the sound of knocking on the front door.

'I'll go,' Christina cried, slipping off the chair, excusing herself from the table, running to open the door. 'Oh hello, Mr Trotter,' she said, staring up at the air-raid warden.

'Hello, love, is your mam in?'

'Yes, Mr Trotter.' Christina opened the door wider. 'Please come in.'

Jim Trotter took off his metal helmet, stepped into the house, and adjusted the canvas gas-mask case on his shoulder as he did.

'Good evening, Mrs Crowther,' he said, smiling warmly at Audra, nodding politely to Laurette. 'I'm ever so sorry to trouble you, just when you're having your teas, but I stopped by to have a word with you about Miss Dobbs in the corner cottage.'

'Don't stand there in the doorway, Mr Trotter, please come in,' Audra said, rising. 'Would you like a cup of tea?'

'No, ta ever so much, though.'

'What about Miss Dobbs?' Audra asked, standing with her hand resting on the chair back, regarding the older man curiously.

'Well, you see, it's like this, Mrs Crowther, she never comes to the air-raid drills, and I don't know what's going to happen to her when there's a real air-raid, I don't really.'

Audra frowned. 'She'll join us in the bomb shelter at the bottom of the garden, Mr Trotter. My father-in-law built it for us and Christina and I have made it relatively comfortable and –'

'Oh but she won't *go* into the air-raid shelter, Mrs Crowther,' Jim Trotter exclaimed, interrupting her. 'I've just had a word with Miss Dobbs about that and I got a real flea in me ear for me trouble, I can tell you.'

'Oh,' Audra said, giving him a baffled look.

'You'll never believe what she said to me,' Mr Trotter went on, staring hard at Audra.

'No, I don't suppose I will,' she said. 'What did Miss Dobbs say?'

'Well, she sort of looked at me funny like, as if I'd landed from another planet, and shouted, "Go and sit in that hole, yonder down the garden, sit *under* the ground. Not likely, lad. I'm going to be in the ground a long time when I'm dead, so I'll be staying up here as long as I'm alive, and if I get hit by a bomb I get hit by a bomb." Them's her exact words, Mrs Crowther.'

Audra tried hard, but there was no way she could keep her face straight. Her mouth twitched and she burst out laughing. Christina and Laurette also began to laugh.

Jim Trotter looked at them all askance, then addressed Audra. 'It's no laughing matter, Mrs Crowther,' he said indignantly.

'No, I know it's not,' Audra gasped, striving unsuccessfully to swallow her laughter. 'She is a strange old lady and I can just hear her saying that to you ... I'm sorry, I don't mean to treat this lightly, but one does have to keep a sense of humour, Mr Trotter. And in a way I sort of share her sentiments – about sitting in a hole under the ground.'

'I sincerely hope you don't, Mrs Crowther!' There was sudden alarm on Jim Trotter's face and he shook his head in dismay. 'I'd be very upset indeed if I had two of you in this yard being *difficult*.'

Audra nodded, biting her lip, unable to speak. She was finding it difficult to suppress her laughter.

Trotter went on, 'What am I going to do about Miss Dobbs? I mean, I'm responsible for everyone in these houses in Pot Lane.'

Understanding, all of a sudden, why he had come, Audra said as soberly as she could, 'I'll do my best to get Miss Dobbs to come into the shelter with us when there's a raid, Mr Trotter. But I can only try, I can't force someone against their will.'

'Thank you very much, Mrs Crowther, I'm grateful for your cooperation. Good evening.' The warden took his leave quickly.

As his footsteps faded away down the path Audra let out a great guffaw, unable to restrain herself any longer. Laurette and Christina also rocked with laughter, for they too had been hard pressed to control themselves during Mr Trotter's visit.

Eventually Audra managed to compose herself and she shook her head slowly, remarked to Laurette. 'Poor Mr Trotter . . . he always seemed to like me, but I don't think he's going to feel quite the same way about me ever again. Oh dear . . .'

'Don't be silly,' Laurette said. 'Anyway, he does take himself a bit seriously. And you were right when you said we had to keep a sense of humour in these awful times. If we didn't, I think we'd all go mad.'

The English had mobilized for war and then nothing very much had happened on the home front.

In fact, there was such inactivity in the air and on the land that this period soon became known as the 'twilight war' or the 'phony war'.

At sea, though, war had started almost at once in September; in October the *Royal Oak* was torpedoed as she lay in Scapa Flow, supposedly in safe harbour and secure from German attack. And by the middle of November something like 60,000 tons of British shipping had been sunk by the dreaded and deadly magnetic mines.

Every time Audra picked up a paper or listened to the wireless, her heart filled with fear. The news of the war at sea was never anything but disastrous; not unnaturally, she worried about Vincent all the time now that he had been assigned to a destroyer and was somewhere out there at sea. Every letter she received from him brought a sigh of relief, as did his letters to his mother.

Although he did not get leave for Christmas of 1939, he did come home in January of 1940 on a seventy-two-hour pass from Hull, where his ship was docked after a stretch patrolling the North Sea.

Audra had asked for time off from the hospital, so that she could be with him for his entire stay, and Matron Fox had been happy to give it to her. And so she was waiting for him at the cottage on that cold and drizzly Thursday afternoon, wearing the delphinium-blue blouse he liked so much and a dark grey skirt.

The moment he walked through the door she saw how proud he was to be in the Royal Navy, to be wearing the uniform. He held himself very straight, with his shoulders thrown back, and looked taller than ever, and there was a new air of assurance about him, a confident look in his bright green eyes.

Audra flew across the floor to him, and he hugged her tightly, held her away, looked deeply into her eyes and then gave her a long and loving kiss on the mouth.

'It's nice to be home, love,' he said, finally releasing her.

'And it's nice to have you back! I've missed you, *we've* missed you.'

'Yes, I know what you mean. It's been the same for me.'

'The kettle's hot . . . would you like a cup of tea, or something else?'

'Tea'll be fine, love,' he said, joining her by the fire, taking a chair, lighting a Woodbine.

A few minutes later, as they sat drinking their cups of tea, Audra gave him all the news about the Crowther clan and his brothers and Maggie, who were away in the service. Then in a soft voice she told him how worried she had been for months on end.

'All I read about are naval disasters, Vincent. Aren't we ever going to have a victory?'

'We did have one, in December, Audra!' he exclaimed fiercely. 'Don't tell me you've already forgotten that three British cruisers scuttled the German battleship *Graf Spee* during the Battle of the River Plate?'

'No, I haven't, but I was thinking of something closer to home –'

'The *Graf Spee* had eluded the British Navy for months, and sinking her was a tremendous feather in our caps . . . don't think it hasn't had a demoralizing effect on the Jerries, because it has.' Vincent's face glowed. 'Winston's right pleased, I can tell you that.'

Audra smiled indulgently. 'Don't tell me you're on a first name basis with the First Lord of the Admiralty,' she teased. 'Does Mr Churchill *know* that you are?'

Vincent grinned. 'We all call him Winston, behind his back, of course. We all love him – that's why.' He leaned forward with a certain eagerness. 'Do you know how the Admiralty announced his return last September? I mean, announced it to the entire British Fleet.'

Audra shook her head. 'How could I?'

After taking a long draw on his cigarette, he said, 'In a way, you might think it was just a signal that the Admiralty sent, just the words *Winston is back*! But it was a hell of a bloody compliment to him . . . a joyful salute. Aye, he's a great man, Churchill is, lass. He ought to be Prime Minister. He probably will be too, *everybody's* dissatisfied with Chamberlain.'

'Wouldn't you be upset to lose . . . *Winston* as First Sea Lord?'

'Yes, but I'd rather have him at the helm of this country than anybody else, I bloody would –' Vincent broke off, glanced around as he heard the door open.

'Daddy!' Christina dropped her satchel and sped across to him without taking off her coat and hat. She flung herself into his outstretched arms. They hugged and hugged each other and then Vincent pulled away and asked, 'How's my little poppet?'

Christina stared up into his familiar, much-loved face, and burst into tears.

'Now then, what's all this, love?' Vincent asked, pulling her back into his enfolding arms, smoothing his hand over her hair gently.

Christina's shoulders shook and she gasped for breath as she clung to him. 'I – I – thought I'd never – never – see you again,' she sobbed. 'I've been so worried, Daddy, I thought your ship would get sunk.'

'Aren't you the silly duck egg!' Vincent laughed and chucked her under the chin. 'Nothing's ever going to happen to me, Little Miss Muffett. Come on, take your coat off and let's go to the table and have the nice tea your mam's made. Then later we'll walk down to see your grandma.' He leaned into her, his eyes twinkling, and said in a half-whisper, 'And tomorrow I'm taking you and Mam to the pictures in Leeds. You'll like that, won't you?'

Christina nodded her head, her eyes shining.

Audra smiled as she watched the two of them together. He had always been a loving father to Christina; she could never take that away from him.

Vincent's leave came to an end all too quickly.

Audra got up at five o'clock on Sunday morning, to make breakfast for him whilst he shaved and dressed.

Eggs were a precious commodity, very scarce, but Audra had managed to get hold of two. She had cooked one for Christina's tea the day before, and now she fried the second for Vincent, along with a tomato and a small piece of bacon which Eliza had given her.

When Vincent saw the egg on his plate he was upset. 'Oh you shouldn't have,' he said, frowning at her. 'You should have kept it for yourself. Come on, take half of it to eat with your toast.'

Audra prevented him from dividing the egg by taking hold of his arm firmly, restraining him. 'Thanks, but I'm not very hungry. Please eat it, Vincent, you won't get anything else for hours and hours. You told me the troop trains are running slowly, and you've no idea what time you'll get back to Hull today.'

'That's true.' Nevertheless, he ate the egg reluctantly, and he wished she had kept it for Christina, if she did not want it for herself.

Neither of them said much during breakfast. They were both aware that he was going back to fight a war, and they had no idea when they would see each other again. It could be months on end, maybe years.

As the clock struck six, Vincent stood up. 'I'd better be going. My train's at seven.'

'Yes.'

As he put on his regulation navy topcoat, picked up his sailor hat and brought his kit bag to the door, he said, 'I kissed Christie before I came down for breakfast . . . I don't want to go upstairs again, I might wake her. Say goodbye to her for me.'

Audra nodded, too choked to speak. She came to him in the doorway, stood on tiptoe to kiss him. He kissed her in return, held her tightly for a moment longer.

'Please be careful, Vincent,' she managed to say in a tight voice.

'I will, don't fret, love. I'll write . . .'

A second later he was gone.

Suddenly she was standing alone in the kitchen.

She ran to the window, parted the curtains, watched him hurrying down the path in the cold, remote light of the January dawn.

Instinctively her hand came up to her heart, fearing for him, fearing for his safety. Come back to me, she whispered in the silence of the empty room. And Audra stood there for a long time after he had disappeared from sight, facing an irrefutable fact. Her love for Vincent Crowther was undiminished, despite all of their troubles and problems over the years. It existed, therefore it had to be.

30

The spring came, bringing with it an end to the 'phony war'.

Audra sat glued to her wireless in the evening, whilst Christina did her homework or sketched and painted. And the more Audra heard, the more she became alarmed for her husband and the rest of the family, and friends, who were fighting the enemy.

Events were moving so rapidly she could scarcely keep track of them. On 9 April Hitler invaded Denmark and Norway. Denmark fell at once, but the valiant Norwegians fought back heroically, and appealed to Britain for help. Immediately naval and military forces were dispatched.

For the next three weeks Audra walked around like a sleepwalker, doing everything automatically, as if by rote. She was worried that Vincent's destroyer might be amongst those ships which had sailed to assist the Norwegians. She was frozen with fear and for once her optimism seemed to desert her completely.

The news grew more grim by the day; and every time she picked up a newspaper her heart lurched.

The Luftwaffe all but demolished the British forces as they tried in vain to help the Norwegians, but by the end of the month most of the British had been evacuated. Vincent's ship finally limped back into British territorial waters; miraculously he was safe. The losses to the forces were enormous and it soon became clear to Audra, and the rest of the country, that the failure to heed Winston Churchill's warnings in the past had been disastrous.

'Thank God he's finally been made Prime Minister,' Audra said to Laurette as they sat close to the wireless on the evening of 13 May. That morning, three days after accepting the premiership from the King on 10 May, Churchill had given his first speech as Prime Minister to the House of Commons. In a few minutes he was to address the nation.

'Vincent has always said that Churchill is the only man to lead us out of this mess and I know he's right,' Audra said.

Laurette nodded. 'I agree, but even so, I think we're in for a long siege.'

'Still, we have a *real* leader now –' Audra stopped, tapped Christina on her shoulder and motioned to the radio, then brought her finger to her lips.

The three of them sat perfectly still, straining to hear every word, mesmerized by the extraordinary voice and rhetoric of Winston Churchill bringing hope and courage and inspiration to the English people.

Audra and Laurette were buoyed up that evening, but as the days passed Audra knew that her sister-in-law had been correct. They *were* in for a siege and it would be both long and deadly.

First there was the hell of Dunkirk.

Thousands upon thousands of British and Allied troops were stranded on the beaches of France, cruelly caught between the sea and the advancing German army. England held its breath. And then only through acts of desperate heroism were they rescued by a motley armada of British destroyers and cruisers, pleasure launches, rowboats, fishing trawlers, yachts and even barges. Civilians had answered Winston Churchill's plea for everyone who had a vessel to pitch in and help the Royal Navy get the boys off the beaches. In doing so they saved lives by the hundreds of thousands – and gripped the imagination of the whole of England and her allies with their extraordinary valour.

The great epic of Dunkirk was an inspiration to everyone and when Audra went around the general adult wards in the hospital, which she was now supervising, she saw how high morale was amongst her patients. Men and women alike took hold of her hand, and with tears in their eyes they spoke of their pride and their patriotism, and mentioned Churchill with reverence and love.

Audra herself had immense faith in Winston Churchill, this man who had said to them only a few weeks before: '*I have nothing to offer but blood, toil, tears and sweat.*' She understood words like that only too well, and she also understood that Dunkirk was only the beginning ... Churchill had warned the British people on

4 June that a terrible storm would soon break over them to test them all. And it did.
France fell.

Suddenly England stood alone.

And then the might of the German Luftwaffe was flung against the country in bombardments that were to continue for many months to come.

The Battle of Britain had begun.

At first the bombings were centred on London and the southern counties, but they soon became more widespread and many of the great industrial cities and airfields in the Midlands and the North became prime targets.

Audra was cutting roses in her garden one Saturday afternoon when the drone of planes and the harsh and relentless rattle of machine-gun fire broke the silence of the sultry day.

Her head flew up. As she squinted against the sun, she saw something she had never imagined she would see – desperate aerial combat raging in the blue summer sky immediately above her house and her precious little world.

To Audra it was a horrifying and shocking sight, this dog fight between the Air Force and the Luftwaffe. That it could happen in the middle of the day over England stunned her. She was momentarily rooted to the spot as she continued to stare up into the sky. Then one of the planes exploded in a great burst of flames and began to fall.

'Mam! Mam!' Christina cried, flinging down her brush and palette, running up the flagstone path.

The girl's voice roused Audra, galvanized her into action. Grasping Christina's hand, she raced her child back along the path and into the air-raid shelter. Audra blinked in the darkness, trying to adjust her eyes as she groped for the matches to light the candle. When she had done so, she carried it over to the orange crate that served as a table, and sat down next to Christina on a bunk bed.

'I thought we'd better come in here for a few minutes, just in case of falling debris,' Audra said, giving her nine-year-old child a reassuring look. She forced a bright smile. 'I suppose we could have gone into the house, but I seem to run for the shelter these days.'

'Everybody does, Mam.' Christina's brow furrowed. 'It was one of the German planes that came down. Do you think it crashed near here, Mam?'

'It's hard to tell, darling . . . I'm not sure.'

'It was such a lovely afternoon, and it happened so suddenly, Mam, didn't it?'

'Yes.' Audra stared at the corrugated-iron wall of the shelter, an abstracted look crossing her face as she murmured in a saddened voice, 'Hearts at peace, under an English heaven.'

'That's from the book your mother gave you long ago, isn't it, Mam?'

Audra nodded. 'Yes, it is. Rupert Brooke. I looked up into our lovely English sky a few minutes ago, Christina, and saw those planes going at each other hammer and tongs, and that line of verse flashed through my mind. I couldn't help wondering just when our hearts *would* be at peace again.'

A flicker of fear touched Audra's blue eyes, and she added, 'It might easily have been Theo up there . . . he is so young, only nineteen. But then all of our Air Force boys are young. Oh, I pray that Theo is safe, Christie, I pray for him every day.'

'Yes, Mam, so do I, when I pray for Daddy and Auntie Maggie and Uncle Mike, and all of my uncles and everybody who's fighting for us.'

It was not long after this incident that the Germans stepped up their bombing raids on England and although London was the chief target, Leeds was one of the northern cities that came in for heavy pummelling.

Audra and Christina now found themselves virtually living in the air-raid shelter at night. But they were the only occupants. Try though she had, Audra had been unable to persuade old Miss Dobbs to join them; the other family in the third cottage in the cul-de-sac had closed it up for the duration, and moved to the country to stay with friends.

If Laurette was visiting them when the banshee wailing of the sirens started, Audra insisted that she spend the night with them in the shelter. She would not allow Laurette to walk home to Moorfield Road during a raid, even though the sky was brilliant with searchlights. Audra believed in following rules and regulations and they had been warned by the Civil Defence to stay inside.

The shelter was by now quite well equipped with cots, blankets and pillows, candles, paraffin lamps, a kerosene stove for heat, and a first-aid kit. Audra had stacked up tins of food, and every day she and Christina carried bottles of fresh water down to the shelter in case of emergency.

But in spite of the bombings, the perpetual fear, the worry about Vincent and the rest of their family and friends, and the hardships in general, life somehow went on.

The newspapers were full of talk about the German invasion of England in late August, but the English seemed to take this with a pinch of salt.

Audra's attitude seemed to sum up the universal feeling when she said to Christina one day in late August, 'Invasion or no invasion, you're starting at Miss Mellor's Private School for Girls when the winter term begins in September. You've got to have an education, whether the Germans land here or not. Besides, as Winston Churchill said, we'll fight them in the hedges, if we have to, and demolish them to a man.'

'You mean I *am* going to Miss Mellor's School after all!' Christina cried excitedly, breaking into smiles.

The two of them sat on the upper deck of the tram car going into Leeds and Audra turned to look at her. 'Of course you are, why do you sound so surprised?'

'Well, you haven't mentioned it lately, even though I passed the entrance exam. I thought you'd changed your mind.'

'Now why on earth would I change my mind, dear?'

'I thought Grandma might have said something to you, Mam.'

'*Grandma?*'

'Yes. I heard her telling Grandpa that you oughtn't to be sending me to a private school, that Christ Church was good enough. She said you had big ideas for me and that they'd only lead to trouble. I thought she'd said the same to you and that you'd listened to her.'

'That'll be the day,' Audra replied with a hint of acerbity. 'And just as a matter of interest, what did Grandpa say in response to Grandma's comments?'

'He said you were wise to reach for the stars, that he admired you for it, and then he told her I was going to be a great artist one day.'

Audra smiled to herself. Alfred Crowther had always been her friend. 'Your grandfather is quite right, Christie.'

Christina tucked her arm through her mother's companionably. 'Is that why we're going to town, Mam? To buy my school uniform?'

'Yes, it is, and I'm thrilled you're going to start at Miss Mellor's, Christie. They have an excellent Fine Arts programme, and I've had several long chats with Miss Leatherson, the art teacher. She knows all about our plans, and she'll prepare you well for Leeds College of Art.'

'And then after that I'll go to the Royal College of Art in London, won't I, Mother?' Christina looked into Audra's face, her grey eyes bright with anticipation.

Audra could not help laughing. 'Of course, I promised, didn't I? But they won't accept you until you're twenty, you know. We've a long way to go yet.'

Christina and Audra had always been close, but they drew closer than ever during the war years. With Vincent away at sea it was just the two of them, and although they saw Laurette at least once a week, they were mostly on their own.

The glittering future she had planned for her child occupied Audra most of the time. When she wasn't working like a Trojan and scrimping and scraping to pay for Christina's education, she was imparting knowledge to her, finding ways to expand the child's mind in other areas as well as in art.

Wartime conditions being what they were, there were not many plays coming to the theatre in Leeds. But when something new did open, Audra always tried to get tickets for them; she took Christina to classical music concerts and to the opera whenever a company came to Leeds. Books, too, especially the English classics, were also part of Audra's cultural programme for her daughter, and Christina acquired a love of reading early in her life.

As always, films were the mainstay of their entertainment during the forties and they both derived a great deal of pleasure from their Saturday night jaunts to the local cinema. Usually Laurette accompanied them, for she and Audra had become dearer friends than ever, bound by so many common bonds and family ties, but mostly because of their deep and genuine love for each other.

As the war years dragged on, leaves were few and far between and neither Vincent nor Mike came home more than once between the summer of 1941 and the winter of 1942.

Both women worried a lot about their husbands who were away fighting, and about the rest of the Crowther family who were in the services. But they were women of strong character, and they learned to live with constant air raids, life in the shelters, rationing, shortages and hardships, and the terrible fear of losing loved ones. They did so without complaint, always endeavouring to look to the future, to the day when Britain would win the war and life would return to normal.

In October of 1944 Audra had a wonderful piece of good luck. Margaret Lennox, whom she had always idolized since her days in Ripon, was appointed matron of Leeds Infirmary. And almost immediately she telephoned Audra at St Mary's to offer her the position of sister in charge of the main surgical ward. Audra accepted the job over the telephone, without having to think twice. Although it would mean travelling to Leeds every day, the money was much more than she was earning and the job itself was a challenge. Also, Audra had always dreamed of working with Matron Lennox again.

It did not take Audra long to settle into life at Leeds General Infirmary, even though it was a vast and hectic hospital and not as cosy and intimate as St Mary's had been. But she found the work stimulating and satisfying; as she plunged into it with her usual energy and concentration she realized that it was helping to keep fear at bay.

Christmas of 1944 was the best one Audra and Christina had had since the beginning of the war, even though Vincent was not with them and was sorely missed. Maggie was the only member of the family who came home on leave, and she managed to keep all of them in peals of laughter with her wit and funny anecdotes about life in the women's army.

To Audra's vast relief the new year brought good news of allied breakthroughs all over Europe. The tide was turning and there was no longer any question who was going to win the war. It was only a matter of time.

Soon Audra was reaching for the newspapers and switching on the radio with eagerness and excitement rather than dread. By the spring she had started to take heart, as had the whole of Britain. In March her spirits truly lifted when she read that the American First Army had crossed the Rhine over the bridge at Remagen and had established a bridgehead for the invasion of Germany. And then between 20 and 25 April the Russians entered Berlin and five days later the Third Reich collapsed. On 7 May the Germans surrendered unconditionally at Reims in France.

Suddenly the war in Europe was over.

Audra and Christina could hardly believe it. They laughed and they wept and they laughed again, and they wept some more as they embraced each other fiercely in the cottage in Pot Lane.

Two days earlier, Christina had celebrated her fourteenth birthday and now she said to Audra, 'But this is my best birthday present, Mam, knowing that it's over and that Daddy's safe.'

'Yes, it is, darling,' Audra replied, wiping her eyes with her handkerchief. She glanced at the collection of framed photographs lined up on the sideboard: Vincent, her brother William in the Australian Forces, Mike, Theo Bell, Maggie and Vincent's brothers Frank, Jack, Bill and Danny, and Olive's husband Hal. How smart they looked and so proud in their different uniforms of the armed forces.

She turned to Christina and said, softly, 'They're all safe, thank God! How lucky we've been ... luckier than most.'

31

Audra Crowther so concentrated on what she was doing in the next few years she hardly ever had time to pause, except to look at her lovely and gifted daughter.

But one day she found herself staring into the mirror on her dressing table – and taking stock.

It was a warm day in July of 1951, and later that afternoon Christina was graduating with honours from Leeds College of Art. It was a most important occasion in her daughter's life, as well as her own and Vincent's, and so not unnaturally she wanted to look her best.

Audra leaned closer to the glass, inspecting her face.

There were a few faint tell-tale lines around her eyes, and the stubbornness and resoluteness that had always marked her face seemed more pronounced than ever.

But aside from these little flaws, if they could be called that, and a hint of grey at her temples, she decided she did not look too bad for forty-four.

Her light brown hair, cut short and framing her face in a flattering style, was still thick and luxuriant; her creamy complexion was as flawless as it had always been, and the blueness of her eyes had not dimmed over the years.

She reached for the bottle of foundation lotion. Usually she only had time to dab a powder puff on her nose and put on a trace of lipstick, before dashing off to Leeds Infirmary, where she still worked and was now a senior member of the staff. But today she was going to take her time and do a proper job of making herself up, and to this end she had borrowed some of Christina's cosmetics.

After smoothing on the foundation, she powdered her face, dusted off the excess, added rouge to emphasize her high cheekbones, then used brown mascara on her lashes, before outlining her mouth with pink lipstick.

Satisfied that she had done the best she could, Audra sat back and regarded herself. She was momentarily startled by her own reflection. The makeup had brought out her best features and highlighted her eyes and her skin. Her face had taken on a fresh look, seemed more vibrant and alive. Pleased with the effect she had created, she brushed her hair, smoothed it into place with the comb and then, as a final touch, she added a dab of her favourite gardenia perfume behind her ears.

Standing up, Audra walked across the bedroom to the wardrobe, and took out the tailored navy-blue silk dress she had made for herself last week. It was a perfect copy of a Christian Dior afternoon dress she had seen in *Vogue* magazine earlier in the year, and she had clipped out the photograph, as she always did when she saw a style she liked, whether it was for herself or for Christina.

After placing the dress on the bed, she took out her navy bag, white fabric gloves, the small navy straw trimmed with a single white rose and the pair of navy court shoes she had bought yesterday.

Once she had slipped on the dress and shoes, Audra returned to the dressing table and sat down again. She put on her hat, added the marquisite earrings Vincent had given her for Christmas, her mother's engagement ring, and her watch, and then she slid open the drawer and took out the box containing Laurette's pearls.

Lifting the lid, Audra stared at them, admiring them. There was only one single strand, but the pearls were beautiful, of good quality. Mike had bought them for Laurette at Greenwood's, the finest jewellers in Leeds, not long after the end of the war, and her sister-in-law had so loved them.

Audra sighed, touched by a sudden fleeting sadness for her darling Laurette, who had died three years ago. It had been sudden; she still hadn't quite recovered from the shock. None of them had. Laurette had looked so well in the spring of 1948, but she had fallen sick that summer and by November they were burying her. It had been cancer. She was thankful that Laurette had gone quickly, that her suffering had not been prolonged. She missed her so very much. There would always be a void without Laurette – and for all of them.

Remembering the time, Audra sat up straighter in her chair. She took the pearls from the box and fastened them around her neck, looking in the mirror again, touching the necklace, smiling softly to herself. And she let go of the sadness, let go of the painful memories of Laurette's passing. The last thing *she* would have wanted was for her to be sorrowful on a day like this. Laurette had always been so terribly proud of Christina.

Rising, Audra went to the bed, picked up her gloves and bag and hurried down the stairs. She dropped her things on the hall table next to the telephone, and paused, glanced at the grandfather clock, wondering what had happened to Vincent. He had said he would be home by one-thirty and it was already one-forty-five. He'll probably want a cup of tea, she thought. He usually does. I'd better go and put the kettle on.

Apart from the shock and anguish they had suffered with Laurette's death, the last few years had been quite good to the Crowthers. They no longer lived in the cottage in Pot Lane. They had moved into this much larger house in Upper Armley in 1949. It was not far from Charlie Cake Park, and it had three bedrooms, a dining room, a sitting room, and a big, family-style kitchen-parlour, where, as usual, everyone seemed to congregate. The rooms were spacious and there was a light, airy feeling about the house in general: it had a happy atmosphere.

In particular, Audra loved the long back garden. She had planted it with rose bushes and delphiniums and a variety of other flowers, and with its smooth green lawn stretching down to two shady trees at the bottom, it was a little paradise in the summer weather. Audra derived much enjoyment from it, and from her flowers and the small vegetable plot she had started near the high back fence beyond the trees.

Vincent was more prosperous. Immediately after he was demobilized, at the end of the war, he had gone into partnership with Fred Varley and his son, Harry. And finally, after talking about it for so many years, he had enrolled in night school in Leeds, to study architecture and draughtsmanship. He no longer worked outdoors on the building sites, but ran the business with Fred; he did most of the planning, drawing and paperwork. Varley and Crowther was a small company, but they were kept busy with local building projects and Vincent was earning a decent living; he was able to support his family himself. The money Audra earned at the Infirmary went into the bank for Christina's education and her clothes.

The war had changed Vincent Crowther.

His turbulent character and wayfaring ways had been somewhat tempered by the death and destruction he had witnessed in the Navy. He still liked to go to the pub at weekends, and he continued to bet on the horses, but he no longer indulged himself in romantic flings with other women.

Not that his relationship with Audra had changed. But after twenty-three years together they were used to each other. It was an enduring marriage, it seemed, and they shared a common bond, one that truly welded them together: their immense pride in their daughter, who had turned out to be very special indeed.

Audra was thinking about Christina and the clothes she still had to make for her as she filled the teapot and carried it over to the table. There were only ten days left before they went to London to get Christie settled in the little studio flat. Well, she would have time to cut and sew at least one more dress in that time, and the remainder of her clothes for college would have to be sent by parcel post.

'Sorry I'm late,' Vincent said, barging in through the back door in a great rush. 'There was such a lot of traffic between here and Pudsey, I thought I'd never get here –' He cut himself short, stared at her through narrowed eyes. 'What have you done to yourself, Audra?'

'I haven't done anything,' she exclaimed, stiffening, giving him a defensive look. His tone had sounded critical.

741

He held his head on one side and studied her thoughtfully. 'It must be the hat, or maybe it's the new dress –'

'Oh for heaven's sake it's the makeup,' she muttered. 'I'm wearing some of Christie's foundation lotion and rouge.'

'I like it,' he said, grinning at her. 'You look nice. Ever so nice, love. You should wear makeup more often.'

Audra half smiled, and then glanced away quickly. She felt suddenly self-conscious under his unexpected scrutiny. Vincent had not looked at her like that in years . . . She said, 'Do you want a cup of tea now? Or later, after you've changed your shirt and suit?'

'Later. I won't be but a few minutes.' He hurried out.

Audra remained standing near the kitchen table, staring after him, thinking how well he looked.

Vincent had hardly changed over the years, hardly aged at all. Last month he had celebrated his forty-eighth birthday, but he appeared to be so much younger. There wasn't a grey hair on his head and his face had retained a certain boyishness, and the smoothness of his cheeks and brow, along with his fresh complexion, only underscored his youthfulness.

She took a chair, sat waiting for him to return, thinking about him, wondering if he ever had love affairs these days. Years ago she had suspected that he saw other women, even though there had never been gossip, nor had she had any proof. But their relationship had been so bad at times she had supposed he found solace for his woes in more welcoming arms than hers.

A deep sigh escaped her, and she shook her head, mildly irritated with herself. She was having such strange thoughts today. First she had been on the verge of tears, dwelling on Laurette, missing her, and now here she was brooding over all sorts of imponderables about Vincent. As if it made any difference now.

'Let's have that cup of tea, Audra,' Vincent exclaimed, coming back into the kitchen. 'We haven't got much time to waste.'

As he spoke he sat down opposite her and reached for the teapot. 'Did our Christie get off all right?'

'Yes,' Audra said. 'She left at noon. She said she had several things to check in the college gallery – the exhibition, I expect. She always fusses about having the proper kind of light on her paintings, you know what a perfectionist she is, everything has to be exactly right.'

'Just like her mother,' he said with a laugh. 'Come on, love, get your bits and pieces together and let's be off, we don't want to miss the ceremony, it's something you've been looking forward to for the last twenty years.'

Audra smiled. 'That's absolutely true. And so have you.'

'Yes.'

Later, as they were driving into town, Audra suddenly put her hand on Vincent's knee and squeezed it.

He glanced at her through the corner of his eye. 'What?'

'I *know* that one day Christina will be as famous as those other two great Leeds College art students, Barbara Hepworth and Henry Moore.'

Vincent nodded. Who was he to argue with her. She had always been right about their daughter thus far.

Christina

1951–1965

32

Christina loved the little flat in London.

It was in a tall, narrow house in Chester Street, not far from Belgrave Square. The house had belonged to Irène Bell for years, and Christina and her mother had stayed at the flat several times in the past when they had come to London on their art educational trips, to visit the many galleries and museums. She already knew it well.

Irène Bell was renting the flat to Audra for four guineas a week. Audra thought it was a bargain at the price, and indeed it was, but Christina knew that Mrs Bell hated charging her mother rent. She would have much preferred to let her have it for nothing. But as she had explained privately to Christina, that was not Audra's way of doing things. 'Your mother's too shrewd,' Irène Bell had said. 'If the rent doesn't seem right to her she'll be suspicious.' Christina had agreed, and together they had arrived at a suitable figure.

The flat was on the top floor of the house, was, in fact, converted attics with a living room, bedroom, bathroom and kitchen. It had its own front door and was a self-contained little dwelling within the house.

Originally, Irène Bell had created the studio flat at the top of her house for her daughters to live in at different stages of their lives. It had been a *pied-à-terre* for them, and later for Theo, when he had been studying law at Cambridge and came to London on weekends occasionally. Theo, who was thirty and a barrister with chambers in the Temple, had recently married, and he and his wife Angela occupied the town house. Sometimes Irène Bell came to stay with her son and daughter-in-law, but only rarely. She was in her seventies now, and since Thomas Bell's death three years before she rarely ventured far afield. She liked to hold court at Calpher House, and have her children and many grandchildren visit her there.

On the day that Christina and Audra had arrived from Leeds, the Bells' house in Belgravia was deserted. Theo and Angela were away on holiday in France, but Mrs Bell had given Audra a set of keys and told her they should make themselves at home.

This they had done and now, at the end of the first week in London, Christina was well and truly settled in the studio under the eaves. Her easel, spare canvases, paints and brushes had been unpacked and put away, as had her books, her other possessions and her clothes.

These filled the large closet in the bedroom and every time Christina looked inside she was impressed with the spectacular selection of outfits her mother had made for her.

The measuring, cutting, pinning, sewing and pressing had gone on for the last eight months, but it was only when she saw everything hanging there together that she realized what an extraordinary undertaking creating this stylish wardrobe had been for her mother.

'I'm going to be the best dressed girl at the Royal College of Art,' Christina said to Audra late on Friday afternoon as she took a pearl-grey silk dress from the wardrobe, held it against herself, stared in the mirror.

'I should hope so,' Audra said with a light laugh, watching her from the doorway of the bedroom. 'I certainly worked hard enough.'

'Oh Mummy, you did! I *know* you did. Thank you for all of my lovely clothes, for all the time and effort you put into them, and the money you've spent. You're a wonder, Mother, you truly are.'

'I don't know about that,' Audra said, hastily brushing aside the thanks and the compliment. But nevertheless she looked pleased as she came in to the bedroom and sat down on one of the twin beds.

Christina swung around, still holding the silk dress pressed close to her lithe body. 'What do you think about this for the theatre tonight, Mummy?'

Audra nodded her approval.

Christina flashed her a vivid smile, hung the dress on the top of the cupboard door and said, 'I'd better find the right shoes and bag . . . the black patent, I think. And perhaps I'll take the grey silk Dior shawl Grandma gave me for my birthday, just in case it gets cool later.'

'I doubt that's going to happen,' Audra said, 'it's been awfully hot today. In fact, I think we're in for a heat wave this weekend.'

'Don't say that, Mother!' Christina made a face. 'Not when we've planned to go to Windsor Castle for the day on Sunday. I don't fancy the idea of sweltering in the scorching August sun all day, as we tramp around the grounds.'

Audra smiled as she leaned back against the pillows, watching her daughter take out her accessories for the evening, thinking how striking she was to look at.

Christina's light brown hair of childhood had turned years ago to a deeper, richer chestnut, and in the summer it was always shot through with reddish-golden streaks from the sun. Her resemblance to her father was marked, and although she was not strictly beautiful, she had an arresting face with clear, chiselled features and a lovely complexion like Audra's. Her huge grey eyes, so soft, so smoky, were Laurette's eyes, and Christina had inherited the Crowther height, stood five feet seven in her stockinged feet. This pleased Audra. She had always hated being only five feet two inches tall.

Her attractive appearance and her obvious artistic gifts to one side, Christina had turned out to be an exceptional young woman in other ways. Everyone agreed on that. Despite Grandma Crowther's dire predictions that the private school and Audra's big ideas would lead to trouble, this had not been the case. Christina had not grown up to be difficult, rebellious or a snob; nor had she turned on her parents, preferring her college friends to them. Quite the contrary, in fact. She was a loving and caring daughter, who adored Audra and Vincent in much the same way as they adored her, and, as she had done when she was a child, she enjoyed their company, believed *them* to be special.

Audra Crowther had done her job well.

Apart from providing Christina with the best of everything within her power, she had given the girl the best of herself. She had taught Christina the proper human values, instilled in her a sense of honour, duty and purpose. Drawing on her own genteel upbringing, Audra had reared her to have consideration for others. But perhaps most importantly of all, Audra had given Christina something else of incalculable value – a feeling of self-worth. And so she was remarkably secure.

Frequently uncommunicative and undemonstrative with Vincent, which had always been at the root of the trouble between them, Audra had been able to express her love for her child verbally, and with a show of physical affection. Yet with this unconditional love had come discipline, from both her parents. Vincent, in particular, had been very strict with Christina when she had been a teenager.

Yes, she does have a certain kind of grace, Audra commented to herself, continuing to observe her daughter as she moved around the bedroom. But she's not perfect by any means, and of course who is? Christie does have Vincent's quick, rather violent temper, and his expensive tastes, his love of clothes and the finer things of life. And she can be impetuous. But, withal, she's not a spoilt girl. Audra smiled. How many times had Eliza said, 'You're spoiling that girl, Audra, and so is Vincent. You'll both live to regret it ... oh yes, spare the rod and spoil the child.' An echo of her mother-in-law's voice reverberated in her head.

'You're looking pensive, Mummy, is something wrong?'

Audra sat up with a start. 'No.' She laughed wryly. 'To tell you the truth I was thinking of your grandma. She always said my plans for you were far too elaborate and high flown. And la-di-da ... That was her favourite expression for anything that had to do with me when you were little.'

'Don't I know it. She's old-fashioned and so class-bound, poor old thing. But she means well, Mummy, and she's always been very loving with me.' Christina grinned. 'But then I'm the only child of her darling Stormy Petrel.'

'*Stormy Petrel?*'

'Yes, that's what she called Daddy when he was first born, and when he was a little boy. Didn't she ever tell you that?'

'No. But then your grandma and I have never been close, never seen eye-to-eye on anything much, and certainly her ideas about a woman's place in the world have always gone against the grain with me.'

'What do you mean?'

'Your grandma has always believed that women should ... well, be subservient to men. Long before you were born, she was horrified when I said I wanted a nursing career. She told me it was my duty to settle down and have babies and toe the line and cater to your father.'

'I can understand her saying that, Mother. I don't think she approves of my coming to London and attending the Royal College of Art at all. She seems to think it's a waste of money. When I went to say goodbye to her and Grandpa the other day she clucked and said something about it being a terrible expense, when I was bound to give up my art to get married and have babies the moment I met the first suitable young man.'

Audra smiled faintly. 'That sounds like Eliza ...' She paused reflectively, and then after a moment she fixed her bright blue eyes on Christina. 'You know, Christie, I am glad you're ambitious, that you want a career for yourself, as well as those other things in life. You can have them all, you know, you really can. In fact, there's nothing you can't have if you try hard enough, work hard enough and strive towards a goal. And never, never limit yourself –'

'I shall always reach for the stars,' Christina interrupted, smiling at Audra. 'Just as you've taught me to ... and I remember very well when Grandpa said that about you, that September you sent me to Miss Mellor's, when Grandma was doing her usual bit of grousing about you to him. He gave her such a nasty look and told her you were right to *reach for the stars*. He's always admired you for that, Mummy, and –' Christina swung to the small desk and reached for the shrilling telephone.

'Oh hello, Daddy. How are you?' There was a short pause as she listened carefully, then she looked across at Audra, nodding and smiling. 'Yes, Daddy, I understand.' There was another pause. 'Yes, we've had a very nice day. We went to lunch at Fortnum's and then we spent the afternoon at the Tate looking at the Turners.' Christina laughed at a remark of her father's, listened briefly, then finished, 'Yes, I will. Let me get Mummy for you now.'

Audra rose and went to take the telephone from her daughter. 'Hello, Vincent. Is everything all right?' she asked and immediately fell silent as Vincent spoke to her in a rush of words.

Christina slipped out, smiling to herself. She crossed the minuscule hall and went into the kitchen that adjoined the living room; after putting the kettle on the gas, she took endive, lettuce and tomatoes from the refrigerator and began to wash them.

A few minutes later, Audra joined her in the small galley-style kitchen. 'Let me help you,' she said.

'There's not much to do, really.' Christina glanced over her shoulder and remarked, 'Honestly, Daddy's getting to be such an old fuss pot. I can't have a conversation with him at the moment without him telling me to watch my step, and he keeps saying, "think on, love, think on." I don't know what's got into him lately.'

'Well, you're *still* his little girl in many ways, and he's a bit worried about you being out on your own, I suppose. And you'd better not let him hear you call him *old*, he wouldn't like that.'

'Mmmmm,' was Christina's only response as she began to peel a tomato. Suddenly she giggled, swung to her mother and said, 'Gosh, you're going to have a *huge* phone bill, Mum, when you get home. Daddy's hardly been off it this week.' She began to giggle, and her eyes were mischievous. 'I do believe he's courting you again.'

'Don't be so ridiculous!' Audra exclaimed.

That evening Christina took Audra to see her favourite actress and actor – Vivien Leigh and Laurence Olivier.

They were starring in the Festival of Britain production of Shaw's *Caesar and Cleopatra* and Shakespeare's *Antony and Cleopatra*, each play being performed back to back on successive nights.

This was Christina's big surprise for her mother.

Audra knew they were going to the theatre, but she had no idea what they were going to see and she was thrilled when Christina told her their destination as they sat on the bus.

'There's no point in seeing one play without the other, so I bought tickets for both nights, Mummy, and we'll be coming back tomorrow.'

'Oh darling, how extravagant you are, just like your Daddy,' Audra said, but her face glowed with happiness.

'This is a theatrical *first*, Mum, I know we're in for a splendid evening in the theatre, one we're not likely to forget,' Christina remarked, filled with pleasure that she could do something nice for her mother.

Audra could hardly contain her excitement as they took their seats in the theatre, and she reached out and squeezed her daughter's hand, whispered, 'Thank you, Christie, for thinking of this very special treat for me . . . I know I'll never forget it.'

From the moment the curtain rose on the great sphinx that opened the Shaw play and would close Shakespeare's the following night, they were captivated by this most famous of all husband-and-wife acting teams and all of the other actors and actresses.

Audra and Christina talked about the performances and the costumes and the scenery for hours afterwards, both on the bus returning to the flat, and when they were having a cup of tea together before going to bed.

'Vivien Leigh is simply beautiful,' Audra said. 'And as for her coronation robes – why I've never seen anything more magnificent. And Sir Laurence Olivier is the consummate actor, the greatest on the stage today, isn't he?'

'He certainly is, Mummy,' Christina agreed. 'I can't wait for tomorrow night.'

Before either of them realized it, Audra's second week in London came to an end.

It had been a wonderful time for them both. Apart from getting Christina settled in the flat before she started her courses at the Royal College of Art in September, they had been able to share some happy days together. They had been to see other plays and to the pictures, which they always enjoyed; they had visited museums and as many art galleries as they could cram in.

Vincent had given Audra some money before they had left Leeds and told her to take themselves out to dinner on him, and this they had done. There had been days when they had simply pottered around the little flat and gone for walks through Green Park and down The Mall, or window shopped in Bond Street and browsed around Hatchard's, Audra's favourite bookstore. But every minute had been precious to mother and daughter, and Audra would never forget her two weeks with Christina at this time in her daughter's life.

'My stay in London has been so special,' Audra said as they sat in the taxi going to King's Cross, on Friday morning at the end of her stay.

'And for me too, Mummy,' Christina replied, and instantly became silent. She suddenly realized how much she was going to miss her mother and it also registered, forcibly, that from today she was going to be on her own.

They were both a little sad as they walked down the platform towards the train for Leeds, and just before Audra boarded, Christina hugged her, said in a tremulous voice, 'I'll never be able to thank you enough, or repay you for everything you've done for me, Mummy. You've been the best, the most wonderful mother in the world.'

Audra stared at Christina, a look of surprise crossing her face. 'But I only did my duty,' she said.

Audra had told Vincent not to meet her at Leeds City station and being as frugal as always she took a tram back home to Upper Armley.

From the moment she let herself into the house she was conscious of the quietness; she was stunned by it, really. As she put her suitcase down in the hall and took off her hat she felt the tears she had suppressed throughout the day begin to brim in her eyes. All of the sunshine has gone out of my life, she thought, groping in her pocket for her handkerchief.

Vincent also felt Christina's absence when he came home from work that evening. But he did not say anything to Audra, aware of her sadness. Instead he chatted about her trip, endeavoured to draw her out about it, believing this would cheer her up, lift her out of herself. And it did for a while.

But after supper, as they sat drinking their coffee in front of the fire, she retreated into herself. So did he, and they were lost in their own thoughts for a short while.

Suddenly, Vincent felt that he had to talk to her about his feelings, and he looked across at her and murmured, 'It's odd, isn't it, not having our Christie around? So quiet, Audra.'

'Yes.'

Vincent sighed softly. 'Well, lass, she's gone from us now. I don't suppose she'll ever come back here – to live, I mean.'

Audra frowned at him. 'I don't want her to, Vincent. If she did that, what would it have all been about?'

'Aye, that's true. You said you'd give her the world when she was a baby in St Mary's Hospital, and you have, love.'

'I only did my duty as a mother,' she said.

Vincent made no comment, merely sipped his coffee, then took out his packet of cigarettes. He toyed with them for a few minutes, before putting them down on the coffee table. He fixed his eyes on her. 'We've been through a lot, Audra, you and I.'

'Yes, we have.' She met his gaze. A curious thought struck her and before she could stop herself, she said, 'We've been tested, I think.'

He stared at her intently.

'But we've come through all right. We have, haven't we, Vincent?'

He nodded, then cleared his throat. 'I was thinking that you might like to go away with me next weekend . . . now that we're alone there's no reason why we can't do that, is there?'

Audra was flabbergasted. 'Where to? Where would we go?'

'Robin Hood's Bay?'

'Why?'

'Because that's where we went on our honeymoon –' Vincent paused, took a deep breath. 'It's not too late for us, is it, Audra? Couldn't we start all over again, as if this was the beginning?'

'Perhaps it is,' she said.

33

Although she missed her parents and was frequently homesick, Christina soon settled into her new life of independence.

She was exhilarated by the excitement of London and all of the attractions it offered, but because she was aware of the supreme effort which had been expended by Audra, to bring her to this point in her life, she was an assiduous student.

Christina had no intention of falling into bad ways, neglecting her studies and so risk disappointing her mother. This aside, she was a hard worker by nature, and ambitious.

From the first day she started in September, her classes at the Royal College of Art in Kensington were challenging and stimulating, and she threw herself into her work with enthusiasm, diligence and dedication.

It was at this time – the early fifties – that the college was starting to be known as the art mecca of the world, and it was teeming with gifted people, tutors and students alike, and in all departments – from figurative and landscape painting and sculpture to textile, costume and scenic design.

From the day she had applied for entry into the college earlier that year, had submitted her best work, then been interviewed and accepted, the tutors at the college had been aware of her extraordinary gifts as a landscape painter. Since her childhood, Christina had seen everything in terms of light, and her paintings seemed drenched with it, whether it was the golden light of a sunlit summer day, the cold, pewter-coloured light of a Yorkshire sea in a winter storm or the brilliant luminous light that suffused the Dales in spring. Because of the quality of her work and her dedication to it, Christina was soon a favourite with her tutor, as well as other members of the staff, who all saw in her the ideal student.

Being an open, outgoing and friendly young woman, Christina was also popular with her contemporaries and within her first couple of weeks at college she quickly made a number of friends of both sexes. But the one she gravitated to the most, and who was her special favourite, was a girl of her own age called Jane Sedgewick.

Jane was ebullient, good-natured and full of fun. Pretty and dashing, with flaxen hair and eyes the colour of pansies, she was one of the most engaging girls Christina had ever met.

They were painting together in one of the big studios on a particular afternoon in September when she completely endeared herself to Christina.

Unexpectedly, Jane began to camp it up. Adopting the stance of a tragedienne, she cried dramatically, in a voice of mock despair, 'My work looks like the devil's brew compared to yours. Alas, alack, woe is me.' She paused, brought her clenched fist up to her chest and rolled her eyes to the ceiling. 'I have no alternative but to kill myself. But before I put an end to this sweet young life . . . grant me one last favour.'

'Of course, what is it?' Christina asked, playing along with her, laughing at her histrionics.

'Come and have coffee with me after class.'

Still laughing, Christina accepted the invitation. A little later they wandered off down by the side of the Victoria and Albert Museum, chatting animatedly on their way to a coffee shop nearby. And neither girl knew that this was the beginning of an extraordinary friendship, one which was to last all of their lives.

Over several cups of *espresso* they learned more about each other. After Christina had told Jane something about herself it was her turn to listen and she did so attentively. She was startled to discover that Jane was the eldest daughter of Dulcie Manville and Ralph Sedgewick, a husband-and-wife acting team equally as famous as the Oliviers, in their own way. And then she thought: but that explains her theatricality.

The Sedgewicks had appeared in countless films made by Gainsborough Pictures in the forties, and Christina and Audra had seen all of them at the Picturedrome in Armley.

She told Jane, 'Gosh, my mother will be *thrilled* to hear that I know you. She's a great fan of your parents, and so am I. In fact, when she was here in August, we went to see them in *Lovers' Quarrel* at the Haymarket. We laughed our heads off, it was simply marvellous, the best comedy we've seen in years.'

'How would you like to meet the old folks in person?' Jane asked. 'Do come and stay with us this weekend. We'd love to have you.'

Christina stared at her in surprise. 'But are you sure it's all right? It is a bit last minute, isn't it? I mean for them. Today's Thursday, Jane.'

'Oh that's no problem, we have a jolly old crazy household. Come on, *do* say yes. We'll have some fun, and the grounds are pretty, so you can paint if you want to. Mind you, there's only one problem –' Jane made a sour face. 'My siblings, the little monsters, are positively *revolting*, but I suppose we don't have to bother with them. So, will you come?'

'Why yes, I will, thank you very much,' Christina said smiling. 'It's a lovely invitation.'

Christina and Jane drove down to Kent the following afternoon in Jane's beaten-up MG sports car painted a vivid yellow.

The Sedgewicks owned an old country house called Hadley Court in the pretty village of Aldington. Not long after they had left the village behind, Jane slowed down and pointed to a beautiful Tudor manor, long and low with leaded windows, set behind large iron gates and just visible from the road.

'That's Goldenhurst, Uncle Noël's house,' Jane explained. 'He's my godfather, and quite a dear. On Sunday morning we'll be going over to his house for drinks and a slap-up Sunday lunch. It'll be quite mad, of course, he always has the most scandalous and outrageous people as house guests. But at least we'll have a giggle and escape the *revolting* monsters for a while.'

Christina gave her a puzzled look. 'What's wrong with your brothers and sister?'

'They're little beasts. You'll soon see.'

'And when do your parents come down to the country?'

'After the Saturday night performance. They flee the theatre still wearing their makeup and race down here at breakneck speed, arrive at midnight. That's when you'll meet them, *if* you can stay awake to have sandwiches and coffee with them at that hour. Oh here we are, Christie.'

Jane swung the MG into a long driveway that twisted and turned up to the house, and Christina fell in love with it the minute she saw it. In a way, the architecture reminded her of High Cleugh, which her mother had often taken her to see when she was a child. They had had picnics on the slope near The Memory Place and her mother had told her about the house where she had grown up. And later she had gone back to the slope above the River Ure and painted High Cleugh as a gift for Audra.

Hadley Court was a rambling old place with odd-shaped rooms, great fireplaces, flaring windows and lots and lots of character. The grounds were pastoral and romantic-looking, with weeping willows and a lily pond and randomly-planted flowers that gave it an old-world air. Later when Christina strolled around the gardens her fingers itched to put their misty green beauty and the soft southern light of Kent on the canvas she had brought with her.

As Jane had promised her, the weekend was a lot of fun.

But Christina did have a few surprises, and she soon discovered that her new friend had a tendency to exaggerate.

The revolting siblings, as Jane called them, were not revolting at all, nor were they little beasts. Hadley and Lyndon, the eleven-year-old twins, were tow-headed, freckled-faced boys who were cherubic and well behaved. Jane insisted that this was because she had terrified them into toeing the line that weekend, by making all manner of dire threats against them. Their sister, nine-year-old Poppy Louise, was an enchantress with huge pansy-coloured eyes like Jane's and bright red-gold hair. She captivated Christina with her winning smiles and fanciful child's chatter.

As for Dulcie and Ralph Sedgewick, they were gracious and charming to her and made her feel like a member of the family immediately. They were not a bit like she had expected them to be, not at all theatrical or showy. They were both soft spoken, cultivated and witty. Ralph, in particular, was most amusing. Christina quickly decided that it was Jane who had all the flamboyance and theatricality in this family.

Uncle Noël turned out to be Noël Coward, and Christina was rendered speechless when she walked into the living room at Goldenhurst on Sunday and found herself being introduced to Laurence Olivier, and, shortly thereafter, to Vivien Leigh.

When she finally managed to get Jane into a corner, Christina whispered, 'What do you mean outrageous and scandalous house guests! You might have warned me!'

Jane giggled and rolled her eyes. 'But it wouldn't have been any fun if you'd known Larry and Viv were coming.' Her face sobered, and she took hold of Christina's arm, stared anxiously into her face. 'You're not angry with me, are you? I couldn't bear it if you were.'

Christina said, 'No, of course I'm not, Janey,' and gave her a reassuring smile.

After this first weekend, Christina became a regular guest at Hadley Court, and a constant visitor to the Sedgewicks' flat in Mayfair. Dulcie Manville Sedgewick had taken a great liking to Christina and thought her to be a wonderful influence on her rather scatter-brained daughter.

Being an only child, Christina revelled at being in the midst of the loving and amusing Sedgewick family, and enjoyed meeting the celebrated personalities who populated their parties – show-business folk, writers, journalists and politicians.

Yet this exciting and glittering world, as captivating as it was, did not unduly dazzle Christina, and her feet were always planted firmly on the ground, her dedication to her art intact.

And as always she was devoted to her parents, most especially Audra. During the next nine months her mother came twice to stay at the little studio flat in Chester Street and Christina often went up to Yorkshire for weekends, and always during the holidays when the college was in recess.

Christina knew that her mother lived for these times when they were together and that she derived enormous vicarious pleasure as she listened to anecdotes about the Sedgewicks and her other friends, the parties and elegant dinners she attended.

Audra's pride in her daughter knew no bounds. Christina's record at the Royal College of Art was brilliant, and her popularity and success in social circles was gratifying, another reason for Audra to rejoice. She knew, at last, that she had kept the vow she had made to herself years ago. She had given her daughter a far better life than she herself had known. And she was satisfied that her own life, and everything she had done for Christina, had been justified.

Christina's first and second years in London were full of numerous challenges and new experiences, and were productive periods for her. Only one thing marred her happiness – the knowledge that her mother was still working.

Although Vincent was a partner in Varley and Crowther and doing quite well, he was still not earning enough to carry *all* of the family's financial burdens. Audra had continued nursing at the Infirmary essentially to support Christina's life in London. It was she who paid Christina's tuition, rent, and gave her an allowance, bought the fabrics for her clothes, and other clothing. Christina was acutely aware that without these commitments her mother would be able to cease her endless toil and have a much easier life.

And so at the end of her second year at college, Christina cautiously suggested getting a part-time job to help out. Audra was furious, adamant in her refusal to even consider such a thing, believing it would distract Christina and interfere with her studies. But she had not bargained for her daughter's stubbornness and determination. Christina was as strong-willed as Audra, and she resolutely set out to curtail the flow of money from Leeds to London.

She did not dare get a job, but she did adopt a more frugal way of living; and she cut down on overheads by moving in with Jane. Her best friend had been asking her to share her flat in Walton Street for ages, and since it was owned by Jane's Aunt Elspeth, who lived in Monte Carlo since her marriage, the rent was nominal. 'Oh, just give me a pound a week,' Jane had said when Christina had asked her what her share would be.

Christina also decided she must start making her own clothes. Whilst this step might not save money exactly, it would take the job off her mother's back. She was egged on by Jane, who knew she had a great flair for designing. In fact, Christina had inherited Audra's cleverness with scissors and a needle; also, she had stood at her mother's knee for years, watching her make beautiful garments for themselves as well as for other people, and her technique had brushed off. In no time at all she had revamped some of her old dresses and created a couple of new ones, and she was inordinately pleased with herself.

Audra was not.

However, she finally came to admit that the sewing was not injuring her daughter's work at the Royal College of Art. Grudgingly, she agreed that the hand-painted dresses and jackets, and the starkly tailored suits, had elegance and originality.

Christina found time to make a hand-painted blouse for her mother in the autumn of 1953, and she took it with her when she went to Leeds for the winter holidays.

Audra was thrilled when she opened the box on Christmas Day, and immediately exclaimed over its beauty and the wonderful mingling of the blue delphiniums on the paler blue silk.

'But you shouldn't have,' she chastised mildly. 'All this sewing is taking you away from your studies.'

'No, it isn't,' Christina said with a laugh, hugging her. 'I wanted you to have something beautiful, something that I had painted and made for you, Mummy.'

That particular December was a happy time for the Crowthers. They had a simple family Christmas and in January Christina returned to London to resume her classes at the Royal College of Art.

She launched herself into her final courses with the immense enthusiasm and the extraordinary dedication she had previously shown, knowing that she would be graduating in August. She wanted to do well not only because of her own sense of pride, but for her mother.

34

Vincent saw Christina before she saw him.

She had alighted from the London train at the far end of the platform and he caught flashes of her as she dodged in and out between the other passengers now hurrying towards the exit turnstile.

How young and lovely she looked in the belted camel coat and the very high-heeled court shoes she always wore. She stepped out briskly, her shoulders thrown back, her head held erect, and there was something very confident about her and this pleased him.

She would be twenty-three next month. He could hardly believe it. Why, it seemed like only yesterday that he had been pushing her around in her pram. She had grown up to be a good girl, with a good head on her shoulders. He trusted her implicitly. When she had first gone to live in London he had worried about her, been concerned about her judgement of situations and people – and particularly men. And then one day he had wondered why he was fretting. They had brought her up properly, she knew the difference between right and wrong. He had stopped worrying that instant. Yes, their daughter was a credit to them.

Suddenly Christina caught sight of him, waved, increased her pace, her face illuminated by the brightest of smiles.

Vincent hurried forward, smiling and waving himself.

They came to a standstill in front of each other.

'Hello, Daddy,' she cried, dropping her suitcase.

'Hello, pet,' he said, beaming at her, reaching for her.

They embraced, laughing, then stepped away, staring into each other's faces. It was Good Friday afternoon and they had not met since Christmas; as they usually did after an absence, they took stock of each other.

He looks a bit tired, older, Christina thought, surprised. Her father rarely showed his age.

She's more radiant than ever, Vincent thought, and his heart tightened imperceptibly. He knew she was going to be upset when he told her about Audra and that her radiance would be diluted. He wondered when he should tell her. Well, certainly before they got home.

'Come on, love,' he said, lifting her suitcase, taking her arm, hurrying along the platform with her. 'Your mam's waiting for you, and as anxiously as always.'

'I can't wait to see her either. Where are you parked, Dad?'

'Just outside the station. I'll have you home in no time at all.'

As Vincent drove them up Stanningley Road in the direction of Upper Armley, Christina chatted to her father about her plans for the Easter holidays. 'I thought I'd spend the weekend at home with you and Mummy, and then if it's all right with the two of you, I'd like to go off on one of my field trips to paint for a few days.'

'That's fine, Christie. Where were you thinking of going?'

'Originally I had the Lake District in mind, but I want to do a seascape and I was toying with the idea of going to the East Coast ... Whitby, Scarborough, Flamborough Head, somewhere around there. What do you think?'

'All of your childhood haunts, eh? Well, you could do worse to pick one of them, but what about up near Ravenscar? There are some very dramatic views from the cliffs, and there's a nice hotel nearby. We like you to be comfortable when you're off on these field trips, you know.'

'You both spoil me,' she said, laughing. 'I wish Mummy could get a couple of days off from the Infirmary to come with me. It'd do her good, don't you think, Daddy?'

Vincent was silent. He pulled the car into the side of the road and braked, turned to face his daughter. 'There's something I have to tell you –'

'What is it?' she cried, cutting him off, knowing at once that something was terribly wrong from the tone of his voice, the concern in his vivid green eyes. 'It's Mummy, isn't it?'

Vincent nodded. 'I'm afraid it is, love.'

She reached out, clutched at his arm, stared at him, anxiety filling her face. 'What's the matter?' she demanded.

'Your mam's been ill, gravely ill, Christie. She collapsed three weeks ago with viral pneumonia. She was in the Infirmary for over two weeks ... there were complications at first, the doctors were worried about her lungs. Don't look so frightened, love, she's fine now. She's recuperating at home.'

Christina was momentarily stunned.

She sat staring at her father for a few seconds, and then she exclaimed, with a flash of anger, 'Why didn't you let me know? How unfair of you, Dad, to keep me in the dark. I should have been with her, been here, and most certainly last week I should, once she was at home.' Her angry stare intensified, and she added furiously, 'You should have told me!'

'I didn't dare go against your mother's wishes, Christie love,' Vincent said quietly. 'I didn't dare upset her, and I would have if I'd sent for you. She didn't want you to be worried. You know what your mam's like.'

'I don't understand you, I don't really,' Christina cried, shaking her head in perplexity. 'I can't imagine why you listened to Mummy. And anyway, who *has* been looking after her since she's been at home?'

'I have,' Vincent said, turning on the ignition, glancing behind him before pulling out. 'I took a week off from work. We're not very busy at the moment, and I had some holiday time due me, anyway.'

'I could have come up last week,' Christina snapped, her annoyance unabated. 'I was just marking time in London, waiting to come home, I didn't have any special classes at the college.'

Vincent realized that it would be wiser to remain silent. With their similar temperaments they could quarrel very easily and that was the last thing he wanted today. He put his foot down on the accelerator and concentrated on his driving.

Half way up Ridge Road, he glanced at her quickly out of the corner of his eye and said in the softest but firmest of voices, 'I hope you've calmed down, our Christie. I don't want you barging into the house full of belligerence and upsetting your mother.'

'God, Dad, you're impossible at times! How could you even think I would do such a thing?'

Audra's eyes looked bigger and bluer than ever in her face, which was drawn and chalky in colour and reflected her suffering of the last few weeks. It lit up at the sight of Christina standing in the doorway.

'Hello, darling,' Audra said in a weak voice, half pushing herself up on her elbows as Christina sped to her bedside.

'Oh Mummy, Mummy darling,' Christina whispered, kneeling down, taking Audra in her arms tenderly, embracing her. 'You should have let Daddy send for me,' she murmured against her mother's hair, 'you really should have.' Releasing her, she sat back, regarding her carefully, wanting to assess her true condition, full of troubled concern.

Audra lifted her hand, touched Christina's face. 'You have your studies and they're more important than anything else right now.'

Although Christina did not agree with this, believing that her mother's health came first, she nodded her head. Rising, she went to the bay window, pulled a chair closer to Audra, sat down.

Vincent came in, hovered near the foot of the bed. He said to Audra, 'How do you feel, love? Are you all right? Comfortable?'

'Yes, thank you, Vincent.'

'I'll go and put the kettle on,' he said.

Christina leaned forward after her father had left the room, said in a cheery tone, 'Well anyway, I'm here now, Mummy, and for the next week I'm going to look after you. I'm going to pamper and spoil you in the way you deserve.'

A frown creased Audra's brow. 'At Christmas you told me you were thinking of going off on a field trip to the Lake District. I hope you haven't changed your mind because of me.'

'No, no,' Christina said quickly. 'My tutor doesn't think it's necessary, I have plenty of finished paintings in hand.'

'It'll be nice to have you here for the whole week,' Audra murmured, settling back against the pillows, her face suffused with sudden contentment. 'How's Jane?'

'As sweet as always, Mummy, and she sends you her love.'

'I'm glad you have her for a friend, and that you're happy sharing the flat in Walton Street with her. It's such a charming, cosy place.' Another smile flitted across Audra's thin face. 'Tell me everything you've been doing . . . you know how I love to hear about your exciting life in London.'

'Yes, I will, but first I'm going downstairs to help Daddy . . . would you like to have something to eat with your cup of tea?'

'No, I'm not hungry, darling, but thank you.'

Christina ran downstairs, wanting to alert her father that she had changed her plans before he blurted something out in front of her mother.

She found him in the kitchen unwrapping a slab of butter. He looked up as she came in. 'Oh there you are, love. I bought some hot-cross buns at the baker's earlier. I thought I'd butter one for your mam.'

'She said she's not hungry, Dad.'

'Oh but she'll eat this,' he said confidently. 'She always likes a hot-cross bun at Easter, you know that. It's sort of a tradition with her, from her childhood at High Cleugh . . . having one on Good Friday.' He sliced the bun in half and began to spread the butter on it. 'You may think your mother looks haggard, but she's a lot better, Christie, she really is, and very much on the mend now.'

Christina nodded. 'Look, I just wanted to warn you not to say anything to her about my field trip to the East Coast. I'm not going now, I'm staying here to look after Mummy for the entire week.'

'Oh, but she won't like that, it'll upset her –'

'I've already told her, Dad!' Christina interjected firmly, giving him a hard stare. 'So *please* don't say anything. It was never very definite anyway, and she knows that. I just told her my tutor didn't think it was necessary.'

'Very well then.' He glanced up and his eyes filled with love for his only child. 'You're a good lass, Christie, and it'll be a real tonic for your mother to have you here for a while. Better than any medicine.'

It was a busy week for Christina.

She took over the running of the house; she cleaned and shopped and cooked and ironed and looked after her mother with efficiency, tenderness and the greatest devotion.

When the Easter weekend was over she insisted that her father return to work, and he did so, although he protested vociferously about her bossiness to her mother. She heard him say to Audra as she passed their bedroom one morning, 'I always warned you we had the makings of an army general in that one, and I knew I was

758

right. She's just proved it to me. And I'll tell you something else, I wouldn't like to work for *her*.'

Christina had smiled as she had gone about her chores. She knew very well from whom she had inherited her bossy nature: her father.

Nursing her mother, pampering her and catering to her every need gave Christina a great deal of satisfaction. But as the week progressed it struck her that her mother had been making a stupendous effort to be bright and lively for her benefit.

It was now becoming obvious that this effort had been a terrible strain. Towards the end of the week Audra looked drained of all strength, listless and debilitated, and Christina's concern grew.

On Friday, her last morning at home, she was upset when she saw that her mother had only picked at the breakfast she had made for her. The scrambled eggs and bacon were untouched, the toast only half eaten, the peach unpeeled.

'Mummy, you've got an appetite like a sparrow! I shall be sick with worry once I've left.'

'Don't be so silly, dear. I'm not hungry at the moment, that's all it is, and don't forget, I have been quite ill, Christie. My appetite will improve when I get my energy back, when I'm up and about again.'

'I think I'd better stay at home another week.'

'Absolutely not, I won't hear of it. There are your studies to think about. You mustn't neglect them, and this *is* your last term.'

Christina sighed and lifted the tray, placed it on a nearby chest. She came to the bed and sat down, took hold of her mother's hand. 'Can't you try and eat the peach if I peel it for you?'

'No, but thank you.' Audra squeezed her hand. 'It's been lovely to have you here, darling, but now you must get back to your life in London, the college, your friends,' she said, smiling deeply at her daughter.

Christina smiled back, then the smile slipped.

In the bright sunlight of the April morning her mother's face was clearly illuminated, and for the first time in years she saw Audra with stunning objectivity. And as her eyes remained fixed on that wan tired face that was so very dear to her, Christina was appalled.

She thought: how she's aged in the last three years. She's not quite forty-seven but she looks like an old woman today.

Her mother's life of sacrifice and struggle flashed through her mind with such breathtaking clarity Christina was suddenly filled with an aching sorrow. And then her heart clenched with feelings of tenderness and compassion for this small, fragile-looking woman who stood ten feet tall in her eyes.

Christina leaned forward and embraced her mother, not wishing her to see the emotions unexpectedly overwhelming her.

And as she clung to Audra it became clear to Christina that she could not permit her to continue living her life in this way. I can't, I simply can't, she said to herself. All of this work and sacrifice and struggle for *me* must come to an end.

I myself will end it.

35

Later that day, as she sat on the train going back to London, Christina could not expunge the image of her mother's worn face from her mind.

She knew deep within herself that it would continue to haunt her for a very long time.

As she sat morosely staring out of the train window, she asked herself what she was going to do.

One thing was certain ... she could not allow her mother to go on supporting her after she had graduated from the Royal College of Art later that summer.

Christina sighed heavily and leaned her head against the window. It would take her years to establish herself as a landscape painter, to make a name for herself, to start selling her work and so earn a living. She was well aware of that, as every young artist was these days.

And so was Audra. How many times had she said in the last couple of years: 'Don't be concerned, Christie. You just continue to paint your beautiful pictures and let me worry about the money and where it's coming from.'

Remembering these words sent a coldness trickling through Christina, and she shivered involuntarily. That was the crux of the problem – well at least part of it – her mother's determination to support *her* until she was famous and her paintings were in great demand.

Christina shivered again and goose bumps speckled her arms. It was as if somebody had walked over her grave. Was her mother going to have to continue working at Leeds Infirmary until she was a very old woman, in order to pay *her* rent, buy *her* clothes, put food on *her* table, pay for everything she needed in *her* life?

No, Christina said under her breath. *No*. I won't let her work like a slave, be a drudge any more, to earn money for *me*. I won't. I will end it, just as I vowed I would this morning. But how? And what am I going to do? She huddled in the corner of the seat and closed her eyes.

The wheels of the train turned and turned and they seemed to pound this question into her brain relentlessly. By the time the Pullman was pulling into King's Cross Station she had a splitting headache and she felt slightly faint. She wondered if she was coming down with the 'flu.

And it would be raining, Christina thought miserably as she glanced out of the window, then pulled her suitcase down off the rack above her head when the train came to a final shuddering halt.

A few seconds later, as she hurried along the platform, she decided to take a taxi home to Walton Street, even though being careful with money was now uppermost in her mind. It was absolutely imperative to Christina that she get back to the flat quickly. She needed to be enveloped in its peacefulness and solitude. She had some hard thinking to do tonight, some hard choices to make.

In the past when she had come back from Yorkshire after the holidays, Christina had been disappointed if Jane was not already ensconced in Walton Street and waiting for her. But as she let herself in tonight she was pleased that her friend was not returning from Hadley Court until Sunday evening.

Christina needed to be alone, to wrestle with her problems, to find a solution to each one of them. Before she settled down to do this, she rang her father in Leeds to tell him she had arrived safely. 'Don't disturb Mummy,' she said, after a brief chat with him. 'Just give her a big hug and a kiss from me.' After hanging up the phone, she unpacked her suitcase, then ran a bath.

She soaked for a good fifteen minutes, emptying her head of everything, trying to relax, and as soon as she felt a little of the tension easing out of her aching muscles, she stepped out of the bath and dried herself hard.

Later, wrapped in a towelling robe, she sat curled up on her bed, drinking a cup of Nescafé with cream and sugar. Slowly her eyes began to roam around her room . . . there was one of her paintings on each wall, and her gaze finally settled on her latest which she had called *Lily at Hadley*. It was an oil of the lily pond at Hadley Court, and it abounded with many different shades of green . . . the murky green-blue of the pond water, the lighter, softer green of the spongy moss trailing over the edge of the pond, the polished, glossy green of the floating lily pads. The only other colours were the sharp, pure white of the single lily, its petals beautifully defined and glistening with drops of crystal dew, and the colour of the light, a narrow corridor of radiance that filtered through the jungle-like foliage in the background of the painting. This light held a hint of yellow, appeared to shimmer with sunlight as it touched the water, then spread out in a spray-like effect, became diffused over the lily itself.

Christina put down the cup of coffee on the bedside table and turned on her side, pressed her face into the pillow. She found it unbearable to look upon that painting, or on any of her paintings for that matter. All of her joy in her art had been suddenly snuffed out, extinguished by her immense pain.

Too high a price had been paid for it.

Audra's years of punishing, brutal toil . . . her health . . . all the little luxuries and comforts she might have bought for herself . . . a holiday occasionally . . . a new outfit.

A lump formed in Christina's throat. How long had she seen her mother wearing the same navy blue reefer coat? Winter after winter, for years and years. The tears came then, pouring out of her eyes, and she wept for her mother and for all of those lost years in Audra's life when she had been slaving away in order to give *her* a future. And she cried until there seemed to be no tears left inside her, and finally she dozed.

Christina felt as if she was falling . . . falling through dark space, and she snapped her eyes open, half sat up with a start, coming awake. She wondered where she was for a moment, feeling disoriented, and then she realized she was lying on her bed in the Walton Street flat. She glanced at the alarm clock. It was almost one in the morning. She had slept for hours, an exhausted sleep.

She turned out the light, fell back against the pillows and closed her eyes. Her mind turned on her dilemma yet again. It struck her that getting a job to support herself whilst she painted would be easy enough, but that was not relevant, not the real issue. *What was crucial was the debt she owed her mother.*

This sudden revelation was so enlightening it brought her upright in bed again. And as she stared out into the darkness of the room she understood then what had been troubling her for hours. *The debt she owed her mother.* That was it. She must repay it.

If I do not it will weigh heavy on my conscience all the days of my life, she thought. And that I could not bear.

36

'Listen, Crowther, I know something's been troubling you for weeks, and tonight we're going to talk,' Jane announced aggressively, pouncing on Christina the moment she walked into the flat.

Christina stared at her, closed the door, then allowed Jane to take her arm, to propel her into their living room.

After gently pushing her dearest friend down onto the sofa, Jane took the chair opposite. 'I am right, aren't I, Christie?' Jane pressed, a blonde brow lifting questioningly. 'Something *is* terribly wrong, isn't it?'

'Yes,' Christina admitted. 'I *have* been wrestling with a problem, a number of problems really, and I've wanted to talk to you, to unburden myself, but . . .' Christina paused, shook her head slowly, looked out of the window, a faraway expression touching her lovely eyes.

Jane sat watching her, waiting patiently now, understanding that Christina was finally going to confide in her. She was filled with relief. Her friend had not been at all like herself for the past two months, ever since she had returned from Yorkshire after the Easter holidays. She had been subdued, distracted, depressed, irritable and gloomy by turn, but every time Jane had approached her she had denied there was anything amiss.

Finally, Christina spoke. 'First, I must apologize, Jane,' she said, giving her a loving look. 'I know I haven't been easy to live with, and that I've been very short and snappy at times. I'm sorry . . . forgive me?'

'Don't be so silly, there's nothing to forgive. But if it makes you feel any better, yes, I do forgive you.'

A fleeting smile crossed Christina's face. She went on, 'I've been struggling to make some decisions and I didn't want to talk to you until I had.'

Jane returned Christina's long thoughtful look but made no comment, merely nodded her understanding.

'I've decided to give up my painting,' Christina said softly.

'You can't be serious!' Jane shouted, sitting bolt upright.

'Yes, I am.'

'I won't let you!' Jane bellowed.

Christina shook her head vehemently. 'You can't stop me. And anyway, listen who's talking. *You* told me six months ago that *you* were going to give up *your* art to become a scenic designer. I distinctly remember you telling me that you had no intention of starving in a garret in the faint hope that somebody would buy one of your paintings one day. In fact, you went on to add that art lovers who had money

762

to spend bought only big name artists, such as Renoir, Van Gogh, Monet, Manet, Utrillo, Chagall, Picasso etcetera, etcetera, etcetera.'

'But you're better than I am!'

Christina ignored this remark. She said, 'Rob Petrie, Jamie Angers, Danielle Forbes and Patricia Smith, to name only a few of our classmates, are all going into other areas of art – textile design, interior design, costume and scenic design, like you are.'

Jane repeated, 'But *you* are better than *we* are.' Her deep-violet eyes swept the room, and she waved her hand at two of Christina's paintings hanging on the walls. 'Look! Just look! How can you give *that* up?'

'Very easily,' Christina said, her voice so low it was hardly audible. 'Since it's costing a woman's life.'

'What on earth do you mean?' Jane cried in astonishment.' *Whose life?*'

'My mother's.'

Christina did not give Jane a chance to respond to this. She began to speak slowly and carefully; with great eloquence she explained everything to Jane, recounting the history of Audra's background, the years of hard work, struggle and sacrifice on her behalf. And when Christina had finally finished Jane had tears in her eyes. She could only nod, so touched was she by the story.

Christina continued, 'You see, Jane, I don't believe I could convince her to stop working, even after I graduate later in the summer. She'll insist on supporting me until my paintings start selling. She's stubborn, implacable really. I could get a job, earn a living whilst I paint, and send the money she sends me back to her. And I suppose I could eventually convince her that I can stand on my own two feet, and so put an end to her toiling. But none of that is quite good enough for me, Janey.'

'I don't think I'm following you, Christie.'

'It's simply not enough for me to just say to her: *Thank you, I can look after myself now, Mother.*' Christina shook her head. 'No. I have a terrible need, a compelling need, to bring ease and comfort to her life. I want to give her the kind of luxuries she's never known. And the kind of luxuries I'm thinking about cost money . . . oodles and oodles of money. As a struggling artist it would take me years and years to earn enough to give her those things. I don't have time to wait. I want her to have them as quickly as possible, whilst she's still young enough to enjoy them.'

'But how are you going to make your pots and pots of money?' Jane asked, looking at her, baffled.

'I'm going into business, that's where the money is . . . and I mean *business* with a capital B. I'm going to become a fashion designer, but I aim to be a rich and famous fashion designer, and very, very quickly.'

'But how are you going to get started?'

'Actually, with your help.'

'My help.'

'Your mother's really, if you'll give me your permission to talk to her about this project.'

'Of course you can talk to her. But how can Mummy help?'

Christina leaned forward, sudden enthusiasm filling her eyes, extinguishing the worry of earlier. 'She's constantly after me to make her one of my hand-painted silk dresses, and she told me only a few weeks ago that she could sell them to her friends like hot cakes, if only I had a secret hoard of them tucked away somewhere.

She was laughing when she said that, about her friends, I mean, but I bet some of them would be interested in buying from me. You know, at that party your mother gave for her American agent, both Polly Lamb and Lady Buckley were admiring my hand-painted silk jacket. They both wanted to know where I'd bought it. Don't you see, Janey, my hand-painted evening clothes are very original, my *exclusive* design, and they *would* be a beginning. Later on, I could make my tailored suits . . . everyone so admires those.'

'You're right!' Jane exclaimed. 'You *must* talk to Mummy, get her measurements, and then design the dress for her. And I'm sure she won't mind if you approach her friends, especially those who were so interested at the cocktail party.'

'Oh, I am glad you agree! However, there's a slight problem.' Christina threw Jane a worried glance, plunged in. 'Do you think your mother would give me half the money in advance? You know, pay half the price of the dress before I deliver it? And get her friends who order dresses to do the same? If they did, it would help me immensely. I could use the money to buy the fabrics and the special paint I need.'

'Of course Mummy will pay up front, and she'll jolly well make sure her friends do too.' Jane sat back, looking confident, then she frowned, screwed up her mouth in a thoughtful way. 'But that's not the real solution, Christie. If you're going into the fashion business, and want it to become *big* business, then you must have working capital.'

Christina laughed hollowly. 'Don't I know it . . . however, I'm afraid I don't have a bean to my name.'

'Oh but I do!' Jane announced gleefully. 'I have the five thousand pounds that Granny Manville left me, and the money's just sitting there in the bank earning a bit of interest that's worth tiddly winks. I'm going to lend you my five thousand pounds!'

'Jane, that's truly a wonderful gesture, but I couldn't possibly borrow money from you,' Christina protested.

'You're going to take it . . . I shall *force* you to take it. If you have a bit of decent capital behind you, the business will grow much faster, and things will run better. You could take on a seamstress, maybe even two, and also find small premises.'

'Yes, you're right. As a matter of fact, I had made those sort of plans, thought everything through,' Christina remarked, standing up, walking over to the fireplace. She ran her hand over her mouth, pondering for a moment. 'Of course, I hadn't intended to branch out like that until next year, when I'd already made a little money.' Christina directed her steady, smoky gaze at Jane. 'If you lend me your five thousand pounds, I could do it sooner, that's true. So – thank you, I accept your offer, and I'm very grateful, Janey darling.' She went over to Jane's chair, bent down and hugged her.

Jane immediately sprang to her feet, hugged Christina in return, her face wreathed in smiles. Then she thrust out her hand. 'Shake, partner. I'll draw the money out of my savings account tomorrow morning first thing, and *voilà* you'll be in business!'

They stood in the centre of the floor, grinning broadly at each other.

Jane said, 'And I'll help you any other way I can, rustle up business, do whatever you want me to –' Jane broke off and her face fell.

'What's the matter?' Christina asked.

'I just thought of something . . . how on earth will you break this news to your mother? She'll be devastated when you tell her that you're giving up painting. Oh my God, Christie, she'll be dreadfully upset.'

'Yes, I know,' Christina agreed, sounding suddenly gloomy. 'Don't think I haven't wrestled with that problem for weeks, because I have. And I've come to the conclusion that it's better I don't tell her anything at all now. Once I've graduated in August, I shall let her think that I'm painting away, and about four or five months after that, let's say around Christmas, I'll tell her I've sold some of my work and that I can start supporting myself.'

'Do you think she'll believe you?' Jane asked.

'I hope so, Janey, I sincerely hope so.'

37

Artistic talent was not the only thing that Christina had inherited from Audra.

She had her mother's penchant for hard work, her physical stamina and energy, her stubbornness, and her determination to succeed at whatever she did.

And all of these characteristics came into play in the first six months she was in business; they were fundamental to her extraordinary success in this relatively short period of time.

Christina also discovered that she had a good head for business, something she had not hitherto realized she possessed, and this too played a large role in her rise to stardom in the world of haute couture.

Even so, perhaps her greatest strength was her gift for translating art into fashion, in the form of the exquisite, elaborately painted evening gowns and coats and jackets which were to become her lasting trademark, and which would forever be in demand throughout her career.

Jane said to her one afternoon, 'Fortuny became renowned for his pleated silk Delphos gowns, Chanel for her cardigan suits, Dior for his New Look, and Balenciaga for his perfect cutting. *You* are going to be known for your translation of art into couture, for your incredible paintings on silk. Those gowns will soon become classics, just like Poiret's beaded evening gowns. People are going to keep your dresses for years and years to come, Christie my pet.'

Christina accepted this compliment from her friend and partner, knowing that she was speaking from the heart. Then she suddenly broke into laughter and exclaimed, 'I shall also be remembered for my ability to work eighteen hours a day, seven days a week, for weeks and weeks and weeks on end.'

'Yes, that's true,' Jane admitted, grinning at her. 'You *have* worked like a galley slave these last few months, but let's face it, the effort was worth it. We're inundated with orders –' Jane gave Christina an amused look, then went on, 'When I told Mummy you were toiling in the salt mines these days, she said that surely I must mean the gold mines! And listen, talking of the orders piling up, shouldn't we do something about finding another seamstress?'

Christina nodded. 'Yes, and the word is already out. Elise and Germaine are asking around amongst their friends in the French community, and I'm sure they'll dig somebody up pretty quickly.'

'I hope they do, otherwise *we'll* be the ones sitting at the sewing machines making the underslips for the dresses, not to mention the hand sewing. Which would be all we need after painting the damn things!'

Christina said, 'Listen, I'm very grateful to you for helping with those mandarin sleeves on the two chiffons for Mrs Bolton. Thanks, Janey.' She eyed her friend with amusement. 'You've got pink paint all over your nose . . . still, you really do do the best butterflies in town.'

Jane giggled, felt her nose. 'I'll wash the paint off in a minute, anyway, I'm glad to be of assistance, Christie. I just wish I could do more in the business for you. I'm merely puttering around, helping with bits and pieces, not making much of a contribution. I feel sort of useless to you most of the time . . .' Her voice trailed off and she stared at Christina helplessly.

'Don't be so silly, you're invaluable, Jane! You work on the accounts, do a bit of everything really, and furthermore, without you there would be no business. Don't let's forget your five thousand pounds.'

'It's a good investment, Crowther. Aren't I the shrewd one, backing *you*.' Jane rolled her eyes, then reached for the coffee pot. 'Do you want another cup or shall I dump this?'

'Ugh, no more for me, I'm swimming in it, thanks.'

Jane went to empty the coffee pot in the small kitchen adjoining the office, whistling under her breath.

Christina leapt to her feet, stretched and walked over to the window, stood looking out into the back yard behind 'the factory', as she called their premises. She had found these in August, not long after graduating from the Painting School of the Royal College of Art. Previously a greengrocer's shop and living quarters, the building was located at the far end of the King's Road, and, apart from its reasonable rent, she considered it to be perfect for her needs for several reasons.

There was a great deal of natural light coming in through the windows, which was essential for the painting of the fabrics and the sewing of the garments; then again, the space was more than adequate, even allowed for growth, since the living quarters attached offered plenty of room for additional staff if and when they were required.

The shop part, where vegetables had been sold until very recently, had been transformed into a small reception area. Here clients could wait to be measured and fitted. Christina and Jane had painted all of the interiors white, except for the reception area; they had used soft pearl-grey paint on the walls here and had hung a café curtain of grey watered silk across the window fronting onto the street. It prevented pedestrians from looking inside, offered a degree of privacy to the waiting clients. Dulcie had given them an oriental rug, several chairs, a table and a lamp, all cast-offs from Hadley Court, and with the addition of a couple of potted plants and some of their own drawings on the walls, the girls had created a cheerful decorative effect.

The living room behind the shop had been turned into a general office; upstairs, one bedroom had become the sewing room, a second smaller bedroom was the fitting room, while the third and largest bedroom was the studio where Christina worked. It was here that she painted the fabrics for the evening clothes, and where

Jane and a couple of their former classmates helped her out at times by painting sleeves. Since the major art work on the gowns and coats was signed by Christina she would permit no one else to do this.

Now, as she stood staring out of the window on this grey March afternoon in 1955, the hand-painted fabrics were very much on her mind. She swung to face Jane and said, 'Listen, I know we're making a great deal of money with the evening clothes, but I do think I have to start designing other garments and expand the line.'

'I've been expecting you to say that ... the painting is very time-consuming, Christie. I think you *must* always make the hand-painted clothes, they are your trademark after all, but perhaps you can cut down on them a little.'

'Yes, and I'll start designing the tailored suits and dresses your mother admires so much ... she's a good judge of what will sell, Janey.'

'That's true, and talking of my mama, I had better love you and leave you,' Jane murmured, rising to her feet. 'She'll be cross if I'm late for my appointment with her and Gregory Joynson, and I do have to dash home and change first. So, Crowther, aren't you going to wish me luck?'

'Of course I am, and I know he'll like your preliminary costume designs ... they are out of this world.'

Jane gave her a sly wink as she picked up her handbag and coat. 'It's a good job the star likes them, isn't it? Thank God for my mother, the actress, who is such an advocate of nepotism.' Pausing at the door, Jane added, 'And don't stay here burning the midnight oil, Crowther, you're starting to look tired.'

'No, I won't. See you back at Walton Street later.'

Once she was alone, Christina went upstairs and turned on all of the powerful overhead lights which she had had installed in the big studio so that she could work at night. She looked at the fabric she had finished painting that morning and nodded her head in satisfaction.

The painting was of white calla lilies on black chiffon, and she had worked on the large piece of fabric before she had started to design the actual dress. This she planned to do tomorrow, and she would design and cut the dress to fit the painted motif. She often adopted this method; other times, she would create the style of the dress or gown or coat, make the *toile*, cut the front and back panels, and then paint her flowers within the framework of the garment. She never limited herself, always left herself open to her art, and in a sense she let the art dictate the style of the piece of clothing. For this reason none of her hand-painted clothes were ever alike.

Christina checked several other fabrics, then returned to her office downstairs, where she seated herself at her desk. Pulling a piece of writing paper towards her, she started a letter to her parents. She always wrote to them once a week, and phoned every Sunday without fail, and her weekly letter was due today.

She sighed to herself as she filled the pages with lies ... lies about the paintings she was selling ... lies about her social activities ... lies about her life in general. She had to invent because she had no personal life at all at the moment, and no boyfriend either, since she had quarrelled violently with Rob Petrie. He had been put out with her for ages, because she spent most of her days and nights working, and their relationship had been terminated by him just after Christmas. Oh well,

Christina thought, I don't really have time for men at this juncture in my life. I'm far too busy carving out a career for myself.

Putting her elbows on the desk, resting her head on her hand, Christina racked her brains for something exciting to make up, to recount to her mother. Audra so loved hearing about her dazzling social life with Jane and the Sedgewicks and the other celebrated people she met at their parties.

Leaning back in the chair, she put down the pen, thinking suddenly of Dulcie Manville. What a good friend she had been to her, and how sweet she had been to her parents when they had come to London for her graduation. Jane had moved out of the Walton Street flat, had gone back to her parents' Mayfair home for a few days, so that Vincent and Audra could stay with her. They had enjoyed being with her, and their trip had been an enormous success all around.

The Sedgewicks had given a party for Jane and her, to celebrate their graduation. Dulcie had seemed taken aback when she had met her father, and now Christina smiled to herself as she remembered Dulcie's reaction. She had taken her to one side, and remarked, 'You might have told me your father looked like Robert Taylor, Christie. My goodness, if he were an actor his face would be his fortune, my dear.' Later that evening when she had repeated the comment to her parents, her father had looked tickled to death but her mother had seemed put out, even irritated; she had known then that her mother was terribly jealous of Vincent.

Those two, Christina muttered under her breath, reaching for the pen again. I'm always on a roller coaster ride with them; they're either at each other's throats or in each other's arms. She thought of her parents with a sudden rush of warmth and affection. She loved them both very much, and she had always tried to walk a line between them, doing a balancing act in a sense, endeavouring not to take sides, not wishing to hurt either one. And I think I've succeeded, she added to herself, as she attempted to finish her letter of lies. But they're only white lies, she thought.

It was nine o'clock when Christina finally left 'the factory' and headed up the King's Road towards Sloane Square. Her thoughts still lingered on her mother as she walked along at a brisk pace. She had managed to convince Audra not to send any more money, by vehemently insisting her work was now selling well. But what troubled Christina was that Audra was still working at Leeds Infirmary. 'She won't listen to me, lass,' her father had said when she had tackled him about it during the Christmas holidays. 'Your mother's always had a mind of her own, and I'd be the last one to make her change it.' Audra had not listened to her either, and she had eventually let the matter drop, hoping that her mother would decide to retire from nursing soon.

Well, at least I have the satisfaction of knowing she is keeping the money she earns for herself, Christina thought, dropping the letter in the box at the Post Office in Sloane Square. It's a huge relief to know she's no longer working simply to support me.

Ever since she had given up her art, Christina had not thought too much about this move. As far as she was concerned, her decision was irrevocable, and she religiously refused to dwell on her disappointment, nor did she harbour any regrets. Carving a niche for herself in the world of high fashion, and in a big, big way, had now become the most powerful motivating force in her life. Christina believed that only by making money, vast amounts of it, could she repay her immense debt to her mother by surrounding her with comfort and every luxury imaginable. And she hoped soon to be able to do this; she could not wait for the day.

Now, as she hurried along Sloane Street, tightening her headscarf against the March wind, Christina thought of the large order for clothes she had received from the actress Miranda Fowler. The star was leaving in three months for New York, where she was to appear in a Broadway play, and had asked Christina to make as many evening clothes as she could for her.

However will I get them finished in time, Christina wondered, as she let herself into the flat in Walton Street. And over a sandwich and a glass of milk she started to make notes that night, focusing on the designs with her usual concentration.

In the next few days it seemed to Christina that inspiration dwelt in her fingertips.

Her sketch pad was soon overflowing with the first early sketches for the Miranda Fowler wardrobe and ideas flowed out of her without cease as she visualized the clothes in her fertile imagination. Forms, shapes, styles, colours, flower formations, fabrics, embroideries . . . all jostled for prominence in her head. Within ten days she had edited her initial ideas and sketches, selected her favourites, completed the drawings and started to pick the materials she would use.

For several days chiffons, silks, satins, brocades, crêpes and georgettes swirled around her in a dizzying array of colours. Slowly these, too, were edited down until she had settled on silk, chiffon and georgette for the evening dresses, heavy satin for evening pyjamas and a long evening coat, brocade for two jackets to wear with silk pants.

When the actress came to have her measurements taken she was delighted with the drawings and fabrics; Christina explained that if she was to create a full wardrobe of evening clothes for her not all of them could be hand-painted. The new client said this was acceptable.

Christina worked around the clock, whilst the two French seamstresses sewed like demons to finish the wardrobe for the celebrated musical comedy star. Several weeks after she had started work on the clothes, Christina hired another Frenchwoman, a friend of Germaine's, called Lucie James. Lucie came highly recommended; apart from being an excellent needlewoman she had a fine reputation as a cutter, and had worked at the Balenciaga salon before the war and her marriage to an Englishman in 1938. Lucie had previously been working for Mr Michael, the couturier with a salon in Carlos Place. It did not take Christina long to realize that she had a real find in Lucie. She knew Lucie would take some of the burdens of cutting the garments off her back, which meant she could devote herself to the painting.

It had been a supreme effort on all of their parts, and a monumental achievement to have the clothes ready by the date Miranda Fowler had specified. In point of fact, Christina was a little ahead of time, and early one warm evening towards the end of May, she took Jane upstairs to see the rack of clothes in the studio.

Flipping the switch, flooding the studio with light, she pulled the sheet off the rack and cried, 'The unveiling . . . ta-da ta-da! And before I show you each elegant and exquisite creation, let me just say this . . . once Miranda Fowler has paid me I'll be able to finally repay you your five thousand pounds. Isn't that wonderful news, Janey?'

'Yes, it is, but there's no real hurry,' Jane said, and then she went into raptures over the stunningly beautiful outfits.

When the two girls had returned to the office, Christina said, 'Look, I'm taking my three lovely women to dinner tonight, a special treat for them, for all the hard work they've put in. Why don't you come with us, Janey? After all, you're part of the family.'

'Oh that's lovely of you, but I really am whacked,' Jane said. 'I've been pushing myself hard on those costumes for the play, and I've got to solve the problem with those blasted ruffs tonight. They won't stay stiff and starch is so scratchy against the actors' necks. Oh God, why does my mother have the urge to play Elizabeth Tudor?'

Christina laughed at the look on her face, and pointed out, 'It might do you good to come with us . . . it would take your mind off those ruffs.'

Jane shook her head. 'Thanks, but no thanks. I shall do some work, make a fried egg sandwich and go to bed early.' She eyed Christina dourly and her pretty young mouth twisted in a grimace. 'Romantic life we both lead these days, isn't it?'

'We'll make up for it when we're both rich and famous.'

'You bet we will,' Jane said, with a leer. 'And listen, Crowther, don't come banging and clattering into the flat tonight, I really meant it when I said I intend to go to bed early.'

'You can sleep late tomorrow – it's Saturday.'

'Fat chance of that.' Jane picked up her briefcase. 'Have a lovely meal, darling . . . oh, and where are you going?'

'I'm not sure, Janey, maybe to that seafood bistro – in Elizabeth Street. You know, Le Matelot.'

'Well, have fun.'

It was a few minutes after eleven when Christina walked down Walton Street later that night, after taking her three employees to dinner.

She was suddenly feeling weary.

It had been a hard few months and for the first time in ages she had relaxed during the evening, had finally let go; the rich meal at Ox on the Roof restaurant and the red wine had also had an enervating effect on her. She could not wait to get undressed and climb into bed.

Remembering that Jane had said she was going to sleep early, Christina could not help wondering why all of their living-room lights were blazing. As she drew to a stop in front of the house where they lived on the top floor, she looked up at the windows, frowning to herself.

I expect she's forgotten to turn them off, she muttered, unlocking the street door, climbing the steep flight of stairs to their landing.

Christina was fumbling with her key chain, standing outside the door of the flat when it suddenly flew open.

Surprised, she jumped and glared at Jane. 'Honestly, you scared me –' she began and stopped when Jane grabbed her arm.

Jane hissed, 'Your parents are here. And your mother is absolutely *furious* . . . she can't take her eyes off your paintings hanging on our walls.'

'Oh my God,' Christina whispered back, blanching. 'How stupid I am.'

38

The coldness in her mother's startling blue eyes blinded her.

She hesitated in the doorway. All of her strength ebbed out of her and she was gripped by a terrible internal shaking.

Her parents sat together on the sofa. They both looked as if they had turned to granite.

No one spoke.

Somewhere behind her in the hall, Jane hovered nervously.

She could move neither forward nor backward. She had turned to stone like her parents.

At last she found her voice. 'Hello, Mummy, Daddy ... this is a surprise.'

'Apparently so,' Audra responded in an icy tone that matched her eyes.

Christina swallowed.

Vincent glared.

The silence became protracted, overwhelmed her.

Audra suddenly sprang up, startling them.

She began to move around the room rapidly, pausing briefly at each one of Christina's paintings, saying their names in a clipped, cold voice, '*Elms in Winter ... Sky at Gunnerside ... Houghley Beck ... Edith's Delphiniums*, and through the open door of your bedroom –' She snapped off the end of her sentence, pivoted to face Christina, and glaring at her, she finished, 'I can see *Lily at Hadley*. You told me you had *sold* all of these paintings. You lied to me, Christina. *Why*? And how are you managing to live? How are you paying your bills? Something is wrong, very, very wrong here. I demand to know what's going on at once! *At once, do you hear me!*'

Christina moved forward, galvanized by her mother's angry words, knowing she had to get this over with once and for all.

She drew to a stop next to Audra. She took a deep breath. 'Mummy, I have something to tell you, something I've been wanting to tell you for ages ...' She looked down at her mother, so small, so fragile, and she was instantly intimidated by the sheer force of Audra's personality, the indomitability reflected in her face. She could not go on. Her nerve failed her.

Audra's bright blue eyes impaled hers. 'I'm waiting, Christina.'

In a great rush of words, Christina blurted out, 'I've given up my painting. I've become a fashion designer. I decided it wasn't worth it, being a struggling artist. You see, I wanted to make money. My clothes are lovely, beautiful really, I know you'll like them –'

'You gave up your art to become a *dressmaker*!' Audra gasped, stunned. She gaped at Christina. All of the colour drained out of her face and her eyes were stark with incredulity. 'You gave up your art!' she repeated. 'You threw away your great gift for creating beauty for ... a *commercial* venture. I can't believe it! I just can't believe it!'

Audra shook her head from side to side as if denying this awful knowledge.

She suddenly cried, 'And after all I did to give you your art! Oh my God, when I think of all my years of gruelling work and sacrifice and scrimping and scraping, and going without to give to you, and giving and giving of myself until I had nothing left to give, and always putting you first, always putting you before your father, neglecting him –'

Audra was unable to continue.

She turned to Vincent. A look of excruciating pain mingled with overwhelming sorrow settled on her face and her eyes, dark with hurt, filled with sudden tears. 'Oh Vincent –' She reached out for him blindly, the tears falling unchecked, blurring her vision.

He was by her side in a flash.

His arms went around her and he held her protectively against his body, one hand patting her shoulder, gentle, loving, comforting. He looked down at her and he sighed, ever so lightly, and then he lifted his head.

Vincent levelled his gaze at his daughter. He stared as if seeing her for the first time.

Christina flinched under his hard, cold scrutiny. Her mouth began to tremble.

Disdain flashed onto Vincent's handsome face and his eyes were steely green, uncompromising. 'You've just broken your mother's heart,' he said in a voice that shook.

Without another word he turned his back on Christina and led the weeping Audra from the room.

Christina stared after her parents speechlessly. And then she ran forward, caught up with them in the hall. 'Daddy ... wait,' she cried, reaching out, grasping his sleeve.

He shook her hand off, a certain harshness in his movements, and glanced over his shoulder. 'Don't *you* Daddy me,' he snapped, 'I've had enough of *you* for one night, Christina. I never thought I'd live to see this day, live to see you hurt your mother ... so cruelly.'

Christina recoiled at his words, and she remained rooted in the doorway of the flat as her mother and father crossed the landing and went down the stairs together.

From behind her, Jane whispered, 'Oh God, Christie, that was awful, simply ghastly. Are you all right?'

When Christina did not respond, Jane put her arm around her dearest friend and drew her inside. She pushed the front door closed with her other hand, walked Christina through the hall and into the living room, pressed her down onto the sofa.

Christina began to shake uncontrollably and she looked at Jane helplessly. 'I must go after them,' she began and immediately burst into tears as she attempted to rise.

'Oh darling, don't, don't,' Jane murmured, her voice consoling as she lowered herself onto the sofa and took Christina's hand in hers. 'You can't go after them and it wouldn't do any good, not tonight.' Jane gave her a quick hug and rose, hurried out.

She returned a moment later with a large handkerchief. 'Here wipe your eyes,' she said, giving it to Christina, 'and I'll get us a drink, I think we could both use a brandy.'

After mopping her eyes and blowing her nose, Christina accepted the cognac from Jane, took a long swallow. She said, 'Perhaps I'd better ring them in a little while. They must be staying in the studio flat at Theo's – he so adores Mummy, and Dad is a great favourite of his . . . they have *carte blanche* to stay there any time they –'

'Oh no, they're at a hotel,' Jane interjected, and grimaced. 'Oh botheration, what an idiot *I* am! I should have asked your father which hotel, when he mentioned it.'

'Oh Jane . . .' She fell back against the sofa, her misery growing more acute by the moment. 'I simply assumed they were at the house in Chester Street, now I'll *never* find them this weekend.'

'Perhaps they'll phone you tomorrow,' Jane said, her face brightening at this thought. 'Oh yes, I'm sure they will.'

'I doubt it very much. Mummy is devastated and my father's furious with me – on her behalf.' Christina rubbed her hand over her weary eyes and asked in a low, gloomy voice, 'Tell me what happened this evening, I mean, when did they arrive? What did they say?'

'They arrived at about ten fifteen. I'd gone to bed earlier, but the phone kept ringing. The calls were stupid too . . . first Gregory Joynson called to complain that one of my costumes for Mummy clashed with a pillow on the stage – he's such a nit. Then she rang up, worrying about those damned Elizabethan ruffs. I'd no sooner hung up on her, when Harry Manderville phoned to invite us to some stupid arts ball next month. In sheer desperation I finally took the phone off the hook. I promptly fell fast asleep. The next thing I knew, the intercom was buzzing for all it was worth. It was your father, telling me they were downstairs. Naturally, I asked them to come up, what else *could* I do? Besides, I was half asleep, and I didn't even think of the paintings.'

'Oh Jane, I don't blame *you* for anything!' Christina exclaimed. 'Of course you had to ask them upstairs. But did they say why they were in London? They don't usually take it into their heads to come up to town, not just like that.'

'Your father apparently had the brilliant idea of bringing your mother to London to see you – as a special treat. They wanted to surprise you, that's why they didn't let you know they were coming.'

'If only they had . . . we could have taken the paintings down, stored them at the factory, and they would never have been any the wiser.'

'Only too true,' Jane agreed and threw Christina an apologetic look. 'I must admit, I do feel a bit responsible. If I hadn't had the phone off the hook they would have got through to me . . . you see, they had been trying earlier. When it was constantly busy they went to have supper somewhere, tried to ring us again later. They were worried, and decided to come over when the operator told them the line was out of order. Oh hell, if only I'd spoken to them I could have reassured them that everything was all right, prevented them from coming here until tomorrow, and certainly I could have done the necessary with the paintings.'

'Oh Jane, please don't feel responsible. *Please.* If I hadn't taken the women out to dinner I would have been here myself. Life is always full of *if onlys* and *buts* and *maybes*. You know that as well as I do.'

'Incidentally, where *did* you have dinner? I tried Le Matelot, wanting to alert you about your parents, but the head waiter said you weren't there.'

'No, I couldn't get a table for the time I needed it, so we went to Ox on the

Roof.' Christina's eyes roamed around the living room, and she remarked quietly, 'I suppose my mother spotted the paintings right away.'

'Do you have to ask! Of course she did, you know she doesn't miss a trick and who *could* miss these? They're larger than life. I realized immediately what a couple of fools we'd been, and I rushed to the kitchen, put the kettle on . . . I felt violently sick, and the only thing I could think of doing was making them a cup of tea. It was a jolly strained hour too, being here with them, waiting for you to return.'

'Did she ask you a lot of questions – about what I was doing?'

'Not one, and neither did your father.'

Christina looked at her watch. 'I keep telling myself they'll ring, but that's just wishful thinking on my part. I know they won't.'

'They will tomorrow, you'll see.'

Christina nodded, knowing Jane was only trying to make her feel better. She also knew her friend was wrong.

Christina could not sleep.

She did not even try. She lay in bed thinking about her mother and waited for the morning to come.

At seven o'clock she snapped on the bedside lamp, drew her telephone book towards her and found Mike Lesley's number. During the dawn hours it had struck her that if anyone knew where her parents were staying it would be Uncle Mike. She dialled the Leeds number quickly, now that it was a reasonable hour to telephone him.

'Doctor Lesley here,' he said, answering immediately, sounding wide awake.

'Hello, Uncle Mike. It's Christie.'

'Yes, I know. Good morning, dear.'

'I'm sorry to disturb you so early, but I thought you might know which hotel Mummy and Daddy are staying at. We had a bit of an upset last night and –'

'Yes, your father told me all about it a short while ago.'

'*Oh.* So you must know which hotel they're at then.'

'Yes, they were staying at Brown's, Christie. But your father called me about half an hour ago, and they were just checking out to drive back to Yorkshire. You won't reach them now.'

'Oh damn,' she exclaimed, 'and I was hoping to see them this morning, to explain . . .' Her disappointment choked her, and she left her sentence dangling.

Mike said, 'Perhaps it's just as well they've left, Christie dear. I think you'll be far better off talking to your mother later. In a few weeks, when she has calmed down.'

'A few weeks!' Christina cried, her voice rising shrilly. 'Oh no, I don't think so, Uncle Mike. I have to talk to her in the next *day* or two. She was so distressed last night and terribly hurt. Didn't Daddy explain everything to you?'

'Yes, he did, Christie.'

'So you know that I've given up my painting, that I've become a designer?'

'Yes.'

'And you don't approve either?'

'It's your life, Christina, and you must live it as you see fit . . . and I'm sure you have your reasons for doing what you've done, good reasons.'

'Oh Uncle Mike, I do, I do. And I must make Mummy understand them. You see, I couldn't let her go on supporting me, I really couldn't. I have to take care of myself from now on. The fact that she was still working, slaving at the Infirmary to give me financial help, was just intolerable to me. I have a real talent for fashion designing, and I saw a chance to make a success out of it, to make money. Not only money for me, but money for my mother. I do want to repay my great debt to her.'

'Oh Christie . . .' There was a silence at the other end of the telephone and Mike sighed heavily. He said softly, 'Your mother didn't do what she did looking for a reward, Christie. Her reward is her pride in you.'

'That may be enough for Mummy, but it certainly isn't enough for me, not by a long shot. I want her to have so much more – I want her to have the best of everything money can buy actually, and I won't rest until she has it!'

'No, I don't suppose you will,' he said with dawning comprehension. 'There's too much of Audra in you. But I wonder if *she* will ever understand that you are repeating the pattern.'

'What do you mean?' Christina asked, tightening her grip on the receiver. 'I'm not following you . . . what pattern are you talking about, Uncle Mike?'

Mike Lesley did not answer this in a direct way. Instead he said, 'Years ago your father came to talk to me about your mother, he was worried about her health you see, worried about the way she was working, pushing herself to the limit. It was the spring of 1939, I remember the year very well, because war broke out that September. Anyway, your father said that what your mother was doing to ensure that you had a glittering future was abnormal. Laurette said she didn't think that abnormal was quite the right word. And then she told your father and me that we were witnessing an act of will. Yes, an act of will so extraordinary, so powerfully motivated and so selfless it was awesome to witness.'

Tears sprang into Christina's eyes and she blinked, brushed them away with her fingertips. She said, 'And it was exactly that, wasn't it?'

'Yes, my dear. And now you are committing your own act of will, and your mother won't be able to stop you, just as your father was never able to stop her.'

'But why do you say she won't understand, Uncle Mike?'

'Because she'll never accept the fact that you've given up your art in order to pay your debt to her. She would find that absolutely preposterous. And if you tell her that this is the reason why you have gone into business, her answer will be very simple, Christie. She'll insist you go back to painting pictures because she doesn't want the best that money can buy.'

Christina was silent. 'Yes,' she said after a short pause, 'perhaps you're right. But I have to do what I believe I have to do.'

It was his turn to be silent.

Waiting, Christina heard him sigh deeply at the other end of the phone.

'So be it,' he said at last. 'And God bless you, Christie.'

'I want to go big, and I really mean *big*,' Christina said. 'And I want to do it at once. *Now!*'

Startled, Jane stared at her, removed a couple of pins from her mouth and waved them at Christina. 'I do wish you wouldn't make your important announcements when I have these between my teeth. I almost swallowed them.'

'Oh sorry.'

Jane grinned. 'Okay, so you want to go big, I'm all ears, tell me more, Crowther.'

'I fully intend to in a minute,' Christina replied, walking across the studio to the corner where Jane was working on a costume for Dulcie.

It was a scorching hot July afternoon, and in an effort to beat the heat Jane had tied her pink cotton skirt under her bust to reveal a bare midriff, exchanged her skirt for a pair of white cotton shorts, discarded her shoes and stockings, and swept her long, wheat-coloured hair on top of her head.

Christina could not help thinking how pretty her friend looked, despite the somewhat messy hairdo, makeup that had streaked and lipstick that had been chewed off. Her admiration and deep affection for Jane Sedgewick welled up in her. How lucky she was to have her friendship.

'How about a glass of lemonade?' Christina asked, putting the tray she was carrying down on the table, unscrewing the cap of the bottle. 'You must be parched, Jane, it's sweltering in here.'

'I know, I think we have to buy another fan. And thanks, I will have some of that stuff.' Jane stepped away from the dressmaker's dummy, eyed the Tudor-style theatrical costume she was working on, then swung around, sat down on a stool nearby and took the glass of lemonade from Christina. 'So go on,' she said, 'tell me about your plans. Knowing you, I bet you've got them all worked out.'

'Sort of,' Christina admitted and perched on the end of the table. 'We've been in business for ten months and we've done extremely well. But we could sell twice as many clothes if we could produce them. I think we should expand, go big, as I just said.'

'How?'

'Hire more cutters and seamstresses, as well as office staff, and take showrooms in the West End.'

'That'll cost money. Even if you keep my five thousand pounds in the business, that won't be enough, Christie.'

'I know. I need about fifty thousand actually.'

Jane whistled. 'As much as that! *Gosh!* But yes, I think you're right.'

'I know I am,' Christina asserted. 'I've worked it all out on paper. Aside from the salaries, we'd have to carry plenty of stock – fabrics, other supplies, and then of course there would be the rent of the showroom. I've looked at several in the last week and they're expensive, especially those in Mayfair, which is where I feel we should be.'

'You do mean *big* when you say big, don't you?'

'Yes, and *fancy*. About the fifty thousand, Jane, I think we could borrow it from the bank, even though neither of us has any collateral, if your mother would be our guarantor, you know, guarantee the loan, or the overdraft, if that's what it's going to be.'

Jane shook her head, frowned hard, and bit her lip. 'No, I don't think that's a good idea – going to the bank, I mean. I'd rather borrow the money from Mummy, and I think she'd give us at least half. I know Aunt Elspeth would cough up the rest, because she once asked me if you needed money for the business. It was when I was telling her that I'd invested Granny Manville's five thousand, and she made some remark about coming to her if you ever needed additional capital. So I know she'd go for it, and she is a great fan of you and your clothes.'

'Jane, that would be wonderful if they would do it . . . do you honestly think they'd take a gamble on me?'

'Yes, I do. Besides, backing you is hardly a gamble, we all know that.'

'I'd prefer to make it a loan, repayable with interest, of course, if that'd be all right with them. We don't need too many partners, do we?'

'No, you're right there. Not that Mummy or Aunt Elspeth would interfere, but still, I agree with you, I prefer they lend us the money.' Jane jumped off the stool. 'Let's go down to the office and phone Mummy now,' she cried, full of tremendous enthusiasm for Christina's latest scheme. 'I know she's at home learning her lines, and once we've spoken to her I'll call Aunt Elspeth in Monte Carlo. Oh this *is* exciting, Christie, and I know they'll jump at it. You'll see . . . by next week we'll really be rolling. Rolling in a *big* way, just like you want, heading for the *big* time.'

Jane skipped and danced across the studio, did a Highland Fling when she reached the doorway, and then tripped down the stairs singing, 'We're heading for the big time, the big time, the big time, we're heading for the big time, tra-la, tra-la, tra-la.'

Christina followed more sedately, laughing at her friend's exuberance, and keeping her fingers crossed, praying that Jane was right.

She was.

Dulcie Manville and her sister Elspeth D'Langer provided the extra working capital Christina Crowther needed to expand her haute couture business and move to the West End.

Elspeth flew from France four days after receiving Jane's phone call. She and her sister and the girls had several meetings with Dulcie's solicitors. It was during these meetings that Dulcie and Elspeth decided that Christina needed more cushioning in case of unforeseen emergencies. And so they increased their loan to one hundred thousand pounds, by putting up fifty thousand each.

This was the amount Christina finally deposited in her business account at the bank before the month of July was out, after the necessary papers had been drawn and duly signed by everyone.

In a sense the hard part started *after* this.

Christina found she had to split herself in two.

By day she was the businesswoman. She interviewed office staff; she saw seamstresses, cutters, needlewomen who did only hand sewing and embroidered work, and hand pressers, and as always she hired only the very best in every area. Lucie James, whom she had promoted to head of the workrooms, had good advice and suggestions to make. Lucie had a great many friends in the French community in London, and it was she who introduced Giselle Roux to Christina, suggested she be taken on as head *vendeuse* in charge of the showroom. Giselle, like Lucie, was married to an Englishman, and had lived in London since 1952. An elegant and sophisticated woman in her thirties, she had been a *vendeuse* at the Pierre Balmain salon in Paris, and was experienced and responsible. Christina left the hiring of the other sales women to Giselle, trusting her judgement completely. And when she wasn't interviewing and hiring staff, Christina was looking at possible showrooms, tramping through buildings throughout the West End of London, and growing more and more discouraged.

Just when she had given up hope of ever finding the right building she stumbled on a small but elegant town house in Bruton Street in Mayfair.

The estate agent showed her around the house on a muggy, drizzly Saturday morning late in August, but despite the weather, Christina saw at once how airy the rooms were, especially on the upper floors.

She rented it immediately, knowing it was ideal, that she would never better this place. The house was in good condition, needed little work.

There was plenty of space, on six floors, for offices, workrooms, and a studio for herself, plus two large reception rooms which opened off a central hall and would be perfect for the showrooms.

These were on the second floor of the house, had high ceilings, fireplaces, tall French windows opening onto little balconies, and their dimensions were spacious. As she walked between the two, light-filled rooms, Christina visualized how charming and elegant they would look, decorated entirely in her favourite soft shades of grey and white, with thick carpeting and shimmering crystal chandeliers dropping from the ceilings.

By night she shed the role of businesswoman, became the creative artist.

Long after everyone had left the factory in the King's Road, Christina worked on her designs for her first collection under the *Christina* label. It was a summer collection and she planned to present it to the public and the press at the beginning of 1956. She had only five months to create the sixty-five outfits she wanted to show, and so she knew she had her work cut out for her. This was her first collection proper, since in the past ten months of being in business she had simply shown clients sketches and fabrics, and then made the garments to measure for them.

Designing an entire line of clothes with a distinctive underlying theme was tremendously challenging to Christina; it was the excitement, the sheer exhilaration of such a huge creative effort that fed her natural energy, kept her going at an extraordinary pace. For apart from designing the outfits themselves, she had to design or select the accessories to go with them. To her, each dress or suit or coat was not finished until it had been properly accessorized down to the last detail. She saw it as an entity.

Although Christina was thrilled that she was now being launched in the way she wanted and was deriving a great deal of artistic satisfaction from her work, one thing marred her happiness. This was her estrangement from her mother and father.

After their terrible upset in May, she had telephoned them constantly, been up to Yorkshire to see them and she had written regularly. She still phoned every Sunday, and wrote once a week. Her father had warmed up a little, but her mother was still remote and cold, so distant that Christina had decided to take Mike Lesley's advice. In consequence, she did not divulge her real reason for giving up her life as an artist – her overwhelming desire, her genuine need, to give her mother a life of total comfort and ease as a way of repaying her debt to her.

Christina harboured the belief that she and her mother would be reconciled one day soon. She knew Audra loved her far too much to remain angry with her for very long. She also hoped that her father was already exerting some influence.

In the meantime, she was going to do her damnedest to make them proud of her.

40

Christina stood in the hallway that linked the two reception rooms, looked first to her right and then to her left.

Each room was a replica of the other: pearl grey walls and matching carpet, white-painted fireplaces, French crystal chandeliers and wall sconces, and antique Venetian mirrors.

The two rooms flowed into each other beautifully, just the way she had planned. She nodded in approval, appreciating the cool, calm feeling produced by the pearl grey and the hint of white. This essentially monochromatic scheme was unrelieved by any other colour – and purposely so. Christina did not want anything to distract from her clothes, or compete with them. Even flowers were barred from these two rooms, appeared only in hallways of the Bruton Street house.

Turning, Christina glanced at the floral arrangement on the Louis XVI console in the hall. It was composed entirely of white flowers, and once again she nodded, knowing it was exactly right, perfect in this particular spot.

Moving forward she hurried into the larger of the two rooms and looked around for the umpteenth time on this cold January day, checking every detail.

A runway now divided the room in half, and on either side of it stood rows of little gilt chairs. Christina experienced a tingle of excitement, feeling the thrill of it all. In less than an hour her first couture collection was going to be unveiled, presented to the world. She took a deep breath and clasped her hands together, sudden apprehension tugging at her as she thought of the clothes she had designed, worrying about them . . .

'Mademoiselle –'

She swung around to see her head *vendeuse* hovering in the doorway that led out to the dressing rooms in the back, where the models were getting ready for the show which was due to start at three.

'Giselle!' she exclaimed and glided down the room.

'I came to wish you *bonne chance*, Mademoiselle,' the Frenchwoman said, smiling at her warmly.

'Thank you, Giselle,' Christina replied, also smiling, then her face changed. 'The collection *is* all right, isn't it?'

The head *vendeuse* brought her fingertips to her lips and kissed them, then blew the kiss into the air. 'Not all right, Mademoiselle, superb, simply *superb*. When I was at the House of Balmain I always told Monsieur that when there was the great excitement in the workrooms there would be the thunder in the chairs –' She paused, waved her hand at the golden rows, and added confidently, 'And at the House of Christina we have the excitement in the workrooms – so be assured there *will* be the great applause out here.'

A young assistant dresser poked her head around the door at the far end of the room. 'Sorry to interrupt, Miss Christina, but Madame Roux is needed.'

'Excuse me, Mademoiselle,' the head *vendeuse* said and hurried out.

Christina walked over to the fireplace and stood with her back to it. She looked down the entire room, through the hallway and into the adjoining room, her eyes following the first runway and then the second. And in her imagination she visualized the models walking, turning, swirling, halting, posing, showing off her clothes to their best advantage. She loved each garment she had designed and she could only pray that everyone else would. She asked herself how she had done it, how she had finished this collection in so short a time, and she had absolutely no idea whatsoever. Blood, toil, tears and sweat, she said under her breath, thinking of Winston Churchill's memorable line from the war years when she had been a child.

Turning around, she stared at herself in the Venetian mirror above the fireplace. She had thought she looked tired and pinched earlier, and she had put on more rouge than she normally wore. But it seemed to have been absorbed into her skin. She was pale again. Perhaps it was the black suit that was pulling the colour from her face. She always needed more make-up when she wore black.

Christina stepped back, regarded herself, holding her head slightly on one side, studying the suit. Beautifully cut and tailored, it was a masterpiece of engineering. Its only adornment was a white gardenia pinned on one shoulder – the white gardenia that she had chosen to become her own special motif, her trademark.

Lifting her hand, Christina smoothed her hair.

It was then that she saw them reflected in the mirror, standing in the doorway, looking uncertain, hesitant.

For a split second she thought it was her imagination playing tricks. But of course it was not. She turned slowly, opened her mouth to say something. No words came out. She simply stood there, staring, unable to move.

Her mother took a few steps forward and then stopped abruptly. Audra said, 'We had to come . . . we couldn't stay away. Not today.'

'Oh Mummy –'

'Christie darling –'

Both women moved at the same time. They met in the middle of the floor.

Audra looked up at Christina and her bright blue eyes filled with tears. 'I've missed you so much . . .'

Christina reached out, put her arms around Audra, hugged her mother to her as if never to let her go. 'Oh Mam, I've missed you too, you'll never know how much.'

Suddenly Vincent joined them, and he put his arms around them both, and they all three cried a little, then laughed. And finally Christina stepped away and looked at her parents, and her happiness was reflected in her shining eyes, her joyous smile.

'I'm so glad you came, so very, *very* glad. It means so much to have you here. Thank you, thank you –' She broke off, then looked deeply into Audra's face and asked, very softly, almost in a whisper, 'Have you forgiven me, Mother?'

'There's nothing to forgive, Christie,' Audra answered, her voice gentle, loving. 'I was angry and upset with you, and dreadfully, dreadfully hurt. But I realize now that I was wrong to cut you off in the way that I did. As your Uncle Mike said to your Daddy and me quite recently, you had to do what you had to do.' A lovely smile touched Audra's mouth. 'I may have given you the chance to have a better life, but I cannot live that life for you. I came to realize this, and I knew that I had to make my peace with you, darling.'

Christina bent forward and kissed Audra's cheek. 'Today is going to be the best day for me, now that you and Daddy are here.'

Turning to Vincent, she took his arm, squeezed it affectionately, reached up and kissed his cheek. 'Thank you for bringing her, Daddy, and for being here yourself. I love you both very much.'

Vincent put his arm around Christina's shoulders. He said, 'We love you too, Christie, and when your invitation came with your little note, I told your mother we couldn't miss this very special and important day in your life.'

41

Christina Crowther became a superstar in the international fashion firmament overnight.

Success was so instantaneous, orders so overwhelming, she knew within the first twenty-four hours that additional space had to be found, extra help hired, more fabric ordered – and at once. There was no time to waste.

Elise, Germaine and Lucie handled all of these details, with speed and efficiency, whilst Giselle Roux and her small showroom staff coped with clients who came flooding in through the doors of the Bruton Street house.

Christina's private clientele bought extensively from the collection, as did innumerable new customers, but there were some gigantic orders from stores which not only staggered Christina but also the more experienced Giselle.

The buyer from Bergdorf Goodman in New York was so dazzled by the clothes she took practically the entire collection, as did the buyer from the Haute Couture Salon at Harte's in Knightsbridge. It was she who announced to everyone that Christina was the fashion discovery of the decade, and pointed out that there hadn't been such a sensational success and a stampede like this since Christian Dior opened his own salon in 1947 and introduced his now-famous New Look. Giselle concurred, said: 'It *is* the same *vraiment*, Mademoiselle, truly, it is.' Christina believed her.

These orders represented hundreds and hundreds of thousands of pounds.

Christina had become very big business in one leap from the former greengrocer's shop in the King's Road to the elegant town house in Mayfair. It was a gigantic leap.

The cause of all the excitement and furore was the collection Christina had called The Flower Line. And indeed it was exactly that, with the theme of the flower running throughout.

The evening clothes were exquisite and extraordinary, featuring all manner of flowers from the exotic orchid to the simplest kind of blooms. When her first big collection had been conceived months before, Christina had realized she could not paint every evening garment personally. It was far too time-consuming. And so she had hired several clever artists to copy her paintings, insisting on perfect duplication.

But she had also had some of her own flower paintings handscreened onto fabrics, and these prints on romantic, floating chiffons and georgettes were as much of a sensation as the hand-painted garments. Evening and cocktail dresses made from these prints would become huge sellers and remain popular forever, earning her millions of pounds and millions of dollars over the years.

Other evening gowns of heavier-weight silk had a single but dominant flower motif. This might be on the skirt at the back and front; on the bodice and the one shoulder; sometimes it was repeated on the skirt and the bodice. But this single flower was always heavily encrusted with jewelled embroidery and was like an enormous piece of jewellery. These evening gowns were also snapped up instantly, with no questions asked about the price.

All of Christina's evening clothes in The Flower Line were lavish and very feminine, and they caused most people to gasp in delight when they first set eyes on them. Colours ranged from white and delicate pastels to vivid red, yellow, sapphire and summer black, which Christina had always advocated.

The flower theme was preserved all the way and reappeared in the day wear, this time in the actual contour of the clothes.

Suits, coats and dresses boasted a slender skirt, but from the waist up the tops were slightly over-sized, as were the shoulders, but these were softly rounded not squared-off. The shape of all these garments suggested a flower on a delicate stem.

The day wear was austere in some instances, immaculately cut and tailored, often with an architectural feeling, and it was undeniably chic.

Fabrics were light and feminine, included silks, cottons, linens and light wool crêpes. Colours were clear, often sharp, with many pinks and mauves and lovely English blues, and greens that ran from bright emerald to the softer lime. And each garment, whether for day or evening, was perfectly accessorized for the total look Christina insisted on presenting.

Apart from her acceptance by the public, Christina had become the darling of the press. They loved her, showered accolades on her personally and in print.

The fashion editors from *Vogue, Harper's Bazaar* and *Queen* were all smart, sophisticated women who had seen it all. None of them was readily fooled and they could as easily spot a phony as they could recognize and applaud genuine talent. They knew at once that Christina was no flash in the pan, that she would go from strength to strength.

As for the popular newspapers, they adored her too.

She was wonderful copy for them, after all: a new discovery who was all the rage, young, immensely talented, good looking – and from an ordinary background, girl from the provinces. The latter made her specially attractive to them, since their readers could identify with her, and certainly with Vincent and Audra, who had been much photographed with her at the unveiling of her collection in January.

Christina enjoyed her success, basked in it a bit. But her feet continued to be firmly planted on the ground, and she understood deep in her heart that the best part of it all was the pride her parents had in her. She would never forget the expressions on their faces as *she* had watched *them* watching the gorgeous models parading down the runway, to the sound of the thunderous applause, under the glittering lights.

And as Jane said later that evening, after the three Crowthers had been to dinner with the three Sedgewicks, 'They were beside themselves with happiness and pride, Christie. I thought they were going to burst at the seams during the show, and I do believe your father had tears in his eyes at one moment.' Christina had smiled and nodded, and then she had repeated her mother's lovely words to Jane.

The words continued to echo in Christina's head weeks later. Audra had come up to her at the champagne reception after the show, had given her a knowing, half-apologetic smile, and had murmured, 'This is a lot more than dressmaking, Christie. *This is art.*'

Those had been words of praise indeed, coming from her mother. And slowly Christina had come to realize that they had also been words of exoneration.

Although Christina had promised to go with Jane to the French Alps for a winter vacation in February, in the end she was only able to have a long weekend with her at the ski resort. There was too much activity at the fashion house and she could not neglect her flourishing business.

But the four days she did spend in Alpes d'Huez with Jane were relaxing and the two girls had great fun. There were plenty of attractive and charming admirers around to take them for cocktails in the evening or fondue suppers and sometimes dancing afterwards at one of the rustic Alpine bars.

Christina did not ski and she had no intention of even trying, but she enjoyed watching the athletic Jane whiz down the slopes. Her friend was a crack skier and an expert skater. And on the Sunday afternoon, as Christina sat at the open-air rink, her eyes were glued to Jane in admiration as she floated and pirouetted across the ice.

It was then that a thought struck Christina . . . the thought that women needed clothes that were relaxed and loose, to allow for ease of movement and comfort. And several new ideas for her winter collection began to germinate in her fertile brain. This prescience to see ahead, to visualize what women would want, to forecast in her own mind coming trends, would prove to be another secret of her success. For it was her great vision that lifted Christina Crowther from the ranks of the merely talented designers into the stratosphere of the truly brilliant.

The ideas which had come to her at the ice rink in the Alps immediately went onto the drawing boards in her studio at the top of the Bruton Street house, when she returned to London. Christina was aware that her winter collection had to be in production by May, if it was to be ready for showing in September of that year. And so she kept her head down working hard all through the remainder of February and into March, as did Jane.

Jane's career as a costume designer was flourishing.

The clothes she had designed for her mother and the rest of the cast in *Elizabet. Regina* had been highly acclaimed; she had gone on to design the costumes fo another West End production. During the spring of 1956 she was busy at work or the entire wardrobe for a film soon to be shot at Elstree Studios, and once thi was completed she was planning to go to New York for several months. She ha recently signed a contract to design the costumes for a Broadway show, a musica that was apparently going to be spectacular. Not unnaturally, she considered thi to be a great challenge and was looking forward to her sojourn on the other sid of the Atlantic.

But in spite of all their work, the two friends managed to have a busy social life and in many ways this was the most hectic spring and summer either of them ha ever experienced.

At the beginning of May, Ralph Sedgewick invited them to come and sta at the villa he and Dulcie had rented in the South of France for the month o June.

'Do let's go,' Jane said. 'We both need a holiday, but especially you, and Beaulieu sur-Mer is such a pretty place. And listen, Crowther, after we've had a few day of rest and recuperation we can take a car and drive up to Grasse, so you ca investigate that perfume idea.'

'Of course!' Christina exclaimed, 'what a wonderful suggestion that is, Janey And I'd love to come. I'll ring your father tomorrow, to thank him and accept.'

She did so, and for the next few weeks Christina turned her attention to th perfume she wished to market under the Christina label. Her name had already acquired cachet on both sides of the Atlantic, and she knew that a perfume woul do well.

This had actually been the brainstorm of Giselle Roux, immediately after th immense success in January. 'You must have the *parfum*, Mademoiselle,' the hea *vendeuse* had told Christina. 'That has always been the tradition with the gran *couturiers* ... Dior, Chanel, Balmain, Balenciaga, Givenchy. Yes, yes, you must d it, you must, it is *important*, Mademoiselle.'

'But how would I go about it?' Christina had asked, her face alive with burgeoning interest. She had seized on the idea at once, seeing its tremendous possibilities.

'First, Mademoiselle, you must consider the fragrances ... the ones that giv you pleasure ... the special scent of *les fleurs*, your favourite flowers. Perhaps th rose ... the lily of the valley ... the jasmine. Then you must go to Grasse Mademoiselle. Here is the centre of the French *parfumerie* industry, and here the will create for you the special Christina *parfum*, Mademoiselle.'

Christina had thanked her head *vendeuse*, and had promised to look into it. Sh had been far too busy designing her winter collection to follow through immediately although she had mentioned it in passing to Jane. But she had put it at the top o her list of important future projects.

Now with the trip to the South of France coming up in June, Christina asked Giselle to make arrangements for her to visit some of the men who created th scents, who were working in Grasse. The head *vendeuse* had written off to a contac in Paris at once.

'*Gardenia!*' Christina said to Jane as they sat in the rented car driving to Grasse, during the latter part of June. 'It must be gardenia. That's the one fragrance that I keep coming back to ... it's very evocative ... perhaps because my mother always wore gardenia scent when I was a child. It was called Gardenia Flower Essence and Mrs Bell used to buy it for her at Harrods as a gift.'

'I like the smell of gardenias too,' Jane replied, 'but you've got to come up with a better name. You can't call it just *gardenia*. That's far too mundane. You must find a fancier name.'

'*Blue Gardenia,*' Christina suggested.

'No, there was a movie with Alan Ladd called –'

'That was *The Blue Dahlia*,' Christina shot back, grinning. 'Listen, Janey, I *do* like *Blue Gardenia*. It has a nice ring to it, and my mother does have the bluest of eyes ...'

Jane smiled. 'Then *Blue Gardenia* it must be. Actually, I like it, too, especially since you're naming it for your lovely Mum.' Jane suddenly began to sniff the air blowing in through the car windows. 'Gosh, I can smell the flowers already. We must be nearly there,' she said, slowing the car.

'Yes, we are,' Christina exclaimed, 'look, there's Grasse in the distance. I'd better keep my eyes open for the hotel when we get into the town ... we're staying at a place Giselle recommended – La Regent.'

Christina and Jane spent three days in the lovely little town of Grasse, which was situated in the Alpes Maritimes high above Cannes. It was a charming spot, ancient, and totally surrounded by field upon glorious field of flowers and magnificent rose gardens. Fragonard, the great French painter, had been born here, and there was a Fragonard Museum, which of course the girls gravitated to the first chance they had. They also spent time going around the splendid Gothic cathedral, and visiting the many famous gardens.

But mostly they were ensconced within the walls of the perfumeries, sniffing scents and talking to the chemists. In the end, Christina settled on two fragrances which would be created specially for her, to be marketed the following year. One would have gardenia as its base, the other roses, and their names would be *Blue Gardenia* and *Christina* respectively.

42

'I don't think I've seen Hadley Court ever looking quite as beautiful as it does tonight,' Christina said, turning to Jane's father, smiling at him. 'The flowers and candlelight inside the house create such a magical effect, and the gardens out here ... why they are *ethereal* in the reflected light from the house.'

The famous actor, tall, rangy, with the look of the professor about him, followed her gaze across the lawns of his country manor house in Aldington in Kent.

'Yes, the gardens do have a special quality, especially when viewed from this terrace ... they're like a backcloth on the stage tonight, almost too perfect to be real. But I don't suppose there is anything quite as lovely as an English summer evening, after a day of truly glorious weather,' Ralph said, his mellifluous voice echoing on the warm air.

His was one of the most celebrated voices on the English stage and Christina never tired of listening to it.

Ralph continued, 'You said *magical*, Christie, and I do believe the entire evening has had a touch of magic to it, everything has gone so beautifully. And out here, now, it's so gentle and balmy, and there's not a whisper of that frightful wind we often get down here. Yes, we've been lucky, it's been perfect July weather for Janey's party.'

Turning to look at Christina, Ralph Sedgewick adopted a fatherly manner towards her, asked, 'Have you enjoyed yourself, my dear?'

'Oh yes, I have, Ralph, thank you very much. It's been a simply gorgeous evening, but I am a little sad that Jane's going off to New York for four or five months – I'm going to miss her terribly. Oh gosh, that sounded so selfish! I know you and Dulcie are going to feel it too, when she's gone.'

'Yes, we are,' he admitted, 'but I'm hoping we might be lucky enough to do a play on Broadway whilst she's there. David Merrick wants us for a new comedy, so our American agent tells us. Anyway, Christie, aren't you planning to go over to the States for a visit in October? At least I think that's what Dulcie said to me?' He made this sound like a question. 'Or am I mistaken?'

Christina suppressed a smile of amusement. Ralph's absentmindedness was an old joke within the Sedgewick family and Jane was forever saying the only thing her father could remember was his part in a play.

'No, no you're not wrong, Ralph. I do hope to be going over to America then,' Christie told him. 'My clothes have done well in New York, and Bergdorf Goodman have invited me to show my winter collection, after it's opened here in London, of course.'

'Congratulations, Christie, that's wonderful.' He squeezed her arm, smiled at her through warm hazel eyes. 'I must admit, I am extraordinarily proud of you and my little Janey ... you've both done wonderfully well since you graduated from the Royal College and –'

'There you are!' Jane cried.

Christina and Ralph swung to face her.

She glided through the French doors and out onto the terrace, her feet barely touching the ground. She was exceptionally happy tonight and she looked ravishing. Her *Christina* gown was made of tulle and lace, and it had a bouffant skirt decorated with lover's knots picked out in silver and pearl sequins, and it floated around her like a soft hazy pink cloud shot through with iridescent lights.

'I've been looking all over for the two of you. What a couple of fuddy-duddys you are, standing there, nursing your drinks ... and *gossiping*, I've no doubt,' Jane said. 'What am I missing? No, don't bother to tell me. You should both be inside, dancing and whirling around the floor.'

She grinned at them, tucked her arm through her father's. 'I must say, Daddy, that's a really super band you found. They've got a fabulous beat, and they've got everybody really going at it, jiving it up. Come on, let's go inside and shake a leg,' she finished gaily, her voice and her face filled with her infectious girlish laughter.

Ralph gave her a loving, indulgent look. 'I'm afraid I'm a little too old for that sort of thing,' he announced. 'And it's jolly warm indoors, that's why Christina and I came out here in the first place, to get a breath of fresh air.'

He swung to face the gardens again, put his brandy glass down on the stone wall of the terrace, reached into the pocket of his dinner jacket and took out a gold cigarette case.

After lighting a cigarette, he asked, 'Where's your mother, by the way? Don't tell me she's jumping up and down like a mad thing . . . not in this heat, I hope, at her age.'

Jane giggled. 'Honestly, father mine, you do make Mummy sound old. She's only fifty-one, for God's sake. But no, she's not dancing, she's talking to Miles, who arrived a little while ago. And all on his little *own* too –' Jane paused dramatically, rolled her eyes and made an ugly face.

'Miles is here!' Ralph sounded and looked extremely pleased.

'He certainly is,' a light, faintly amused voice said from the direction of the French doors.

'Miles, old chap! How wonderful that you could make it after all!' Ralph hurried forward, his hand outstretched.

The two men clasped hands, beamed at each other. They had only recently become friends, but they had liked each other immediately.

Miles said, 'So sorry I wasn't able to get here in time for supper, Ralph, but I got caught up in town . . . nothing I could do about it really . . . *you* know how it is . . . in my position . . .' He allowed his voice to trail off, as if suggesting he had been detained by important Government business that could not be discussed. Top secret sort of stuff. Miles knew he had no need to explain his tardiness. Politicians were generally excused for this little social sin, if not for anything else they did.

Now he glanced at Jane, whom he had already greeted inside the house, and acknowledged her again with a slight nod, a half-smile.

Ralph asked, 'Are you quite positive you don't want something to eat . . . a spot of cold supper? I know the buffet is still being served, Miles. And I must get you a drink. What would you like? A glass of –' Ralph came to a stop as he realized that Miles was not really listening to him, that the other man's attention was focused behind him.

Ralph swung around, apologetic. 'How frightfully rude of me, Christina, my dear. Don't hang back there. Do come and meet Miles.'

'Yes, you must meet Miles,' Miles said, stepping out into the middle of the terrace.

Jane said, 'Excuse me, I'm going to get myself a glass of the old bubbly.' She disappeared through the door, saying over her shoulder, 'I'll be back in a minute.'

Christina moved forward slowly, conscious of the blue radiance of the eyes fixed so intently on her. There was a sudden constriction in her chest.

As he watched her approach, Miles Sutherland thought he had never seen such a lovely young woman. Her chestnut hair was swept up on top of her head to form a crown of curls. It was an odd style, reminiscent of the 1940s, and yet it suited her. She was dressed in a simple gown. Chiffon. Pale grey, Grecian in style. One shoulder bare. She wore a choker of beads and earrings that matched. Grey stones, resembling those huge grey luminous eyes that seemed to fill her face. Opals? Moonstones? He wasn't sure.

He smiled, sensing a certain shyness in her, wanting to put her at ease.

Ralph cleared his throat, 'Christina, may I present Miles Sutherland, one of our most brilliant politicians, as I'm sure you're aware. And Miles, this is Christina Crowther, Jane's dearest friend and flat mate, whom we consider to be a member of the family, actually.'

'How do you do,' Christina said.

Miles took the cool, tapering hand in his and held it tightly. Slowly he increased the pressure of his fingers, not wishing to let go of it. He knew at once that he wanted her. He aimed to have her.

'I'm very pleased to meet you,' Miles said finally, and reluctantly released her hand, adding, 'I've heard a great deal about you – from my sister. She wears your clothes.'

'Your sister?' she repeated, feeling like an imbecile for not knowing who his sister was.

He said, 'Yes, Susan Radley.'

'Lady Radley?' she asked and felt even more foolish.

He smiled, as if amused. 'Yes.' He glanced at Ralph, said, 'I wouldn't mind that drink, old chap, if you would show me where the bar is I'll –'

'No, no, stay where you are, Miles,' Ralph insisted. 'What would you like?'

'Scotch, I think, with a splash of soda. Thanks, Ralph.'

Ralph Sedgewick looked at Christina. 'You haven't touched your cognac, my dear. Would you prefer something else perhaps?'

'Please . . . a glass of champagne would be nice.' She suddenly wished Ralph would not go away and leave her alone with this man who continued to stare at her with his curiously hypnotic eyes.

They were alone on the terrace.

Miles smiled a lazy sort of smile, gave her a long, searching look, as if answering a question in his own mind, then took out a packet of cigarettes. He offered her one silently. She shook her head.

After striking a match, drawing on the cigarette, he said in that same amused, superior voice, 'Your newspaper photographs don't do you justice, don't you know . . . they make you look much older too . . . and tell me, how do you manage to cope with our national press? I find them a bit pesky myself, at times.'

Christina ignored the backhanded compliment he had paid her, said carefully, '*I* find the press – wonderfully well, thank you very much. They're certainly extremely decent to me, but then I'm not a brilliant politician who's always making national news.'

'Touché.' He laughed, moved closer to her and leaned against the stone balustrade, his posture nonchalant. He said, 'That choker you're wearing . . . are those moonstones?'

Startled that *he* would ask a question about clothes, she said, 'No, they're just grey glass beads, but I liked the milky effect they have, that's why I bought them.'

'Do you ever wear opals?'

She shook her head.

He stared at her, his gaze speculative, appraising, bold.

She found herself returning his stare unblinkingly.

He said at last in a low, quick voice, 'You should, you know. Opals would look lovely against that extraordinary skin . . . with those extraordinary eyes . . .'

Christina was startled. She could not answer him. Her legs needed support. She sat down on the balustrade.

Miles Sutherland could not tear his eyes away from her. She touched him in a way that he had not been touched in years and he felt curious stirrings within himself. His physical desire for her was hot and urgent.

To Christina's immense relief Ralph walked out onto the terrace carrying their drinks.

She sat sipping her champagne, listening to the murmur of their voices as they spoke at length about British politics. But she was not really hearing anything at all. She was studying Miles Sutherland, wondering what it was about the man that so unnerved her. Was it his great presence? Force of personality? Charisma? She was not certain. He was not the most handsome man she had ever met, but he did have an attractive face, lean, intelligent, composed of uneven planes and angles. His hair was a dark blondish-brown that had a hint of grey at the sides. Slim and lean in build, he was not much taller than she was, only about an inch or so in fact.

It was his eyes, of course, that so mesmerized, had a spellbinding effect. They were a lovely clear blue that reminded her of an English sky on a summer day.

The two men continued to talk for a while, and she listened, let his voice roll over her, absorbing it, committing it to memory. It was full of shadings and nuances and inflections. She pictured him speaking in the Commons.

And suddenly Miles was standing in front of her, saying goodnight.

'It was so nice to meet you,' he said in a distant voice.

Christina slid off the balustrade, took his hand, shook it briskly. 'I enjoyed meeting you,' she said, forcing cheerfulness, and followed him into the house, her arm tucked through Ralph's companionably.

Later, when she was in bed, she wondered why she was feeling so disappointed and let down.

43

Jane exclaimed, 'What a nerve he's got, strolling in here, trying to seduce you!'

'He didn't stroll in,' Christina corrected. 'He phoned me at Bruton Street. And he's not trying to seduce me.'

'Oh yes he is.'

'Don't be so silly, Janey ... over lunch?' Christina began to laugh.

'*After* lunch,' Jane cried fiercely. 'The French call it a *matinée.*'

'This is London, not Paris, remember?'

Jane chewed her inner lip nervously. 'My God, Mummy would have a fit – she'd be absolutely furious if she knew. After all, you met him through us down at Hadley.'

'You're not going to tell her?' Christina sounded horrified.

'Of course I'm not.' Jane looked at her askance. 'God, you can be stupid at times, Crowther ... and you'll certainly be *bloody* stupid if you go out with Miles Sutherland.'

'*Why?*'

'Because he's dangerous. Emotionally dangerous. I just know it in my bones.'

'You're the one who's being stupid now, and far-fetched. How can he possibly be dangerous to me?' Christina demanded.

'He's married, for one thing.'

'Estranged, separated. Everybody knows that. It was all over the newspapers ages ago.'

'But he's not *divorced*, Christie.'

'I don't know why you're acting this way, Jane, I really don't. Miles seems to be a nice man, and I'm sure he's decent and honourable too.'

Jane let out a guffaw. 'I bet he's a cad.'

Christina gaped at her. 'I don't know what's got into you today, making such sweeping statements.'

Jane stared at her dearest friend. 'Okay, let's go over a few facts. Miles Sutherland is good-looking and charming and he cuts quite a swathe at parties, I'll grant you that. But let's not forget that he also cuts quite a swathe in the House of Commons and that he is a brilliant and ambitious politician.'

'I'm not sure I understand what you're getting at, Janey.'

'Oh for God's sake, Christina, don't be so bloody dense! There happens to be a woman in his life already, a woman called Candida Sutherland, who is his wife and the mother of his three brats. Who just happens to be the daughter – actually the only child – of one of Britain's foremost industrialists. She's got pots and pots and *pots* of money, and if –'

'I *know* all that.'

'And you can be damned sure that Miles Sutherland *knows* which side *his* bread is buttered on, my darling. Oh yes. When a man's a Member of Parliament and a leading light in the Labour Party, with a spectacular career unfolding, his wife's money comes in very useful indeed. Do you think he's going to jeopardize all that –'

'Jane, stop this!' Christina spluttered. 'You're being absolutely preposterous.' She let out a funny little laugh and eyed Jane curiously. 'The way *you're* talking, anybody would think we're having a wild affair when –'

'I bet he'd love that! Miles Sutherland looks very randy to me.'

'– when I hardly know the man. Besides, he's only invited me to lunch.'

Jane looked at her through narrowed violet eyes. 'When a man like Miles Sutherland invites a woman like you to lunch, he has only *one thing* on his mind and it's certainly not buying you a decent meal.'

'I am going to have lunch with him, Jane, no matter what you say,' Christina asserted in a firm tone.

'I wish you wouldn't ... You just won't be able to cope with it.'

'With *what?*'

'His bloody fatal charm and sophistication and smooth talk and all that sort of codswallop. Don't forget, he's a politician.'

'I can take care of myself, Jane.'

'No, you can't.'

Christina said slowly, almost reflectively, 'My mother had a friend once – Gwen.

Auntie Gwen I used to call her when I was little. They were very close when they were young women, nurses at Ripon Fever Hospital. They really cared rather deeply for each other. But Gwen never did like Daddy much, which naturally made Mummy furious, and then Gwen married some awful twerp called Geoffrey Freemantle. Anyway, Geoffrey sort of came between them too, as my father had, in a way.'

Christina paused, took a deep breath. 'And I just don't want that to happen to *us*, Janey, I really don't. So let's make a pact right now. Let's agree that men will *never* come between us. Let's try and be above all that sort of thing. What do you think?'

'Oh Christie darling, of course I agree with you completely! We mustn't let the men we get involved with make one single ripple between us.'

Later that evening Christina and Jane went to Le Matelot in Belgravia for dinner.

They both liked the little bistro. It reminded them of their trip to the South of France the month before.

As they sipped their glasses of white wine, waiting for the first course, Jane asked, 'What happened to her?'

'Who?' Christina looked puzzled.

'Your mother's friend – Gwen.'

'Oh gosh, Janey, that's quite a sad story really. Her life wasn't very happy with the Geoffrey person. He turned out to be a wife beater, for one thing.'

'My God, how awful!' Jane exclaimed, looking horror-struck.

'Yes, it was.' Christina leaned her elbows on the table, said, 'When I was small Mummy began to suspect there was something odd going on there, at least that's what she told me when I was grown up. You see, poor Auntie Gwen was always having these terrible accidents ... falling down the staircase, or the cellar steps, or some such thing, and it began to worry my mother. At first she thought Gwen had an illness, you know a brain tumour or something like that, and then it finally dawned on her. And she tackled Gwen about it, but of course Gwen denied it, and that's when we stopped going to see her.'

'And what happened to Gwen in the end?' Janey asked.

'During the war she came to see us. Unexpectedly. I remember it very well because she brought me some pretty glass beads. I must have been about ten or eleven at the time. Anyway, she came for tea and stayed the evening, and after I'd gone to bed she apparently told my mother everything. I think she must have been at the end of her tether by then. Eventually Mummy persuaded her to move back to live with her parents, although I believe *that* took a lot of doing.' Christina sat back, took a sip of wine.

Jane said, 'Go on ... I'll kill you if you don't finish the story.'

'My mother talked to Gwen's brother, Charlie,' Christina explained, 'and he told the husband that he'd better not come near Gwen again. Not ever. And he didn't.'

'And she got a divorce.'

'No, but the Geoffrey fellow was killed during the war. He wasn't in the forces, but he was here in London on some business, in 1944 I think it was, and he was killed during a bombing raid.'

'And where's Gwen now? What happened to her in the end?'

Christina smiled, and her eyes lit up. 'Her story had a happy ending really, Janey. She married my Uncle Mike in 1952. He was a widower by then and he'd been inconsolable after my Aunt Laurette died in 1948, and very lonely. It was my mother who persuaded him to join them for dinner with Gwen. You see, years before *they'd* gone out together. I suppose you could say they picked up where they left off.'

'Hardly that,' Jane said with a laugh. 'But I *am* glad her life finally turned around . . . poor woman.' After a short pause, she said, 'Christie, about Miles –'

'What about him?'

'When are you having lunch with him?'

'Friday – the day after tomorrow,' Christina said.

Jane sat back and grimaced, eyeing her friend in concern. 'That's the day I leave for New York, and since I'm booked on the ten o'clock flight, you'd better call me later in the day and tell me what happens. I shall be all ears!'

Christina burst out laughing. 'Oh Jane, you are impossible. Nothing's going to happen . . . but I'll phone you anyway to make sure *you're* all right, that you've arrived safely in little old Manhattan.'

'Do you find Miles so irresistible, Christie? I mean, are you madly attracted to him?' Jane probed.

'He's quite attractive,' Christina murmured, wanting to sound as noncommittal as possible, not daring to confide her true feelings in Jane.

He cancelled the lunch at the last minute.

'I'm so frightfully sorry to do this,' he said in an apologetic voice when he telephoned her on Friday morning, 'but I can't meet you today as we arranged. Something's come up . . . it's all become *rather* complicated. Do forgive me, Christina. Another time perhaps?'

'Oh,' Christina said, gripping the receiver much tighter, sitting down behind the desk in her studio at the Bruton Street house.

'I say, I have a much better idea!' Miles exclaimed, as if something brilliant had just struck him. 'Why don't we have *dinner* next week? Instead of lunch. I see from my calendar that I'm awfully jammed with luncheon engagements . . . what about having dinner with me on Tuesday evening?'

'I'd love to Miles, but I can't,' Christina said genuinely regretful. 'You see I'm going to Paris on Monday.'

Disbelief echoed in his laughter. 'Paris in July. You're going to find that all the Parisians have fled. There'll be no one there but American tourists.'

'I'm going on business,' she explained softly, feeling her disappointment about the cancelled lunch so acutely that her throat was tight.

'Business or pleasure, it's still one of my favourite cities. When do you plan to return?'

'In about ten days.'

'Then I shall give you a ring in . . . let's say two weeks? Is that all right, Christina?'

'Yes, that'll be lovely, Miles.'

After she had hung up she stared at the phone for a long time. It troubled her that he aroused such strong feelings in her.

44

Although she no longer painted landscapes, Christina still saw everything in terms of light.

And the first week she was in Paris it seemed to her that every day was filled with a luminous light that was glorious. As she went from the Ritz Hotel, where she was staying, to her various appointments, she would look up and marvel at the shining sky flung high like a canopy of pale blue silk above this most beautiful of cities.

The weather was perfect, mild, sunny and without the mugginess that had made London so unbearable before she had left. Yet despite her appreciation of the radiant skies, the sunlight shimmering on the River Seine and leaking through the leafy green cupolas of the trees, and casting its golden glow on the wide boulevards and ancient buildings, Christina had no desire to put what she saw on canvas.

The day she had given up her painting she had vowed she would not hanker after it, or have regrets, and she had not.

In some ways, it was a relief for her not to have to strive to top the world's most renowned painters, which was something her mother had somehow always believed she could do. It would be impossible for anyone to better Turner, that greatest of all the nineteenth-century English landscape artists, who had captured light on canvas with such genius and brilliance; or Van Gogh or Renoir or Monet.

And in all truth, Christina had really come to enjoy her work as a fashion designer. It was a constant challenge and more rewarding every day; she was savouring the business side as well as the creative endeavour it involved.

And, not unnaturally, the extraordinary acclaim she was receiving also gave her great pleasure, whilst the money she was earning was more than gratifying – it was thrilling. She knew that by the end of the year she would be able to repay her loans to Dulcie and Elspeth. But most important of all, her mother had finally retired from Leeds General Infirmary and had agreed to accept a cheque every month from her. It had been a battle, but *she* had won in the end, thanks in no small measure to her father, who had run a great deal of interference for her. He had understood how much it meant to her.

This week, as she had gone from her appointments with the perfume manufacturer to meetings at the fabric houses, and generally attended to her business, she had managed to find time to go shopping for gifts for her parents. For her mother she had found butter-soft kid gloves and a silk scarf and several blouses; for her father, silk ties and voile shirts and an elegant cigarette lighter. Jane had not been left out; she had bought her dearest friend a glamorous silk evening shawl from Hermès in a mixture of the pretty pinks Jane loved.

Christina thought of Jane now, as she walked slowly across the Place Vendôme towards the Ritz Hotel early on Friday evening at the end of her first week in Paris. It didn't seem possible that Jane had left for New York only last Friday. It felt so much longer.

She missed her a lot, but then they had been inseparable for the last five years, so that was only natural, she supposed. Jane was the best friend she had ever had, and the only close friend really. Her mother had kept her so busy with her painting when she was growing up there hadn't been much time for playmates when she was little, or chums when she was a teenager. It had always been painting lessons and field trips and museums and galleries and being force-fed art, art, art. Now that she looked back, she realized that she had spent most of her growing-up years with Audra, until she had left for the Royal College of Art.

Christina smiled to herself as she went through the doors of the Ritz, remembering with some affection the little Hôtel des Deux Continents where she and Jane had stayed on several trips to Paris in their college days. It had been a far cry from this elegant edifice where Hemingway had once hung out and movie stars and princes and the rich and famous stayed. She wished Jane were here with her on *this* trip, staying *here* . . . what fun they would have together.

Her suite was in the other wing of the Ritz, at the rue Cambon side of the hotel, and she had to traverse a long gallery of shops to reach the smaller of the two lobbies. But she did not stop to browse as she usually did; she was far too anxious to get up to her suite, take off her shoes and order a pot of tea. It had been a hectic day and she had walked a lot, since most of her appointments had been close to each other.

The *concièrge* smiled pleasantly as he handed her the key to her suite, and told her no, there were no messages, in answer to her question. Smiling back, murmuring her thanks, she swung around, took a step towards the lift.

It was then that she saw him.

She stopped dead in her tracks, staring.

His eyes were riveted on her. He rose from the chair, walked towards her in easy, graceful strides.

She was dazzled by the blue radiance of his eyes.

As he drew level with her, he said, '*Hello.*'

'Miles.' After a pause, finally finding her voice, she managed, 'What are *you* doing here?'

The small, amused smile she remembered so well tugged at one corner of his mouth. 'I'm staying here,' he said. 'I always stay at the Ritz when I'm in Paris.'

'Oh.'

He put his hand under her elbow purposefully and escorted her to the lift. They did not speak riding up, and he followed her out at her floor; when they reached the door of her suite she fumbled with the key and, in her nervousness, dropped it.

He picked it up, put it in the lock, turned it, held the door open for her, then stepped inside after her. He leaned against the door watching her move ahead of him, so willowy and lithe. She had the most gorgeous legs. Why hadn't he noticed before now? But how could he have known? She had been wearing the long grey Grecian gown at Hadley. He knew one thing, though. The heat was in him again, as it had been the night he had first set eyes on her at the beginning of the month. He wondered why this so surprised him. That was why he was here, wasn't it?

Strolling across the foyer towards the sitting room, Miles leaned against the door jamb, still watching her, fascinated by her. He couldn't wait to take her in his arms, to make love to her. He would like to do that now, at this very moment. Yet he knew he could never make a move like that. He was a gentleman and he did not want to frighten her by pouncing on her. She struck him as being an innocent, naïve, and inexperienced, at least where men were concerned. Beyond all of these things, though, he wanted to get to know her a little better, to savour her and enjoy the anticipation of his ultimate possession of her.

Christina placed her handbag and document case on a chair and pivoted so suddenly she startled him.

She said, 'It's not a coincidence, is it?'

'Of course it isn't, Christina.'

He moved into the room, came to a stop next to her and took her hand in his, held onto it tightly, crushing it between his fingers. He looked at her deeply, his face close to hers, their eyes on a level. He said, 'I decided I didn't want to wait two weeks to take you out to dinner. That's why I'm here . . . to have dinner with you. Tonight – I hope. You are free, I trust?'

'Yes.' She was not sure if she believed him. She searched his face, her brows drawing together in a pucker. 'Don't you have business here too? I mean, you didn't fly from London to Paris simply to have dinner with me . . . surely not?'

'I most certainly did.'

'Oh.' She felt the sudden rush of heat to her face and there was that tight feeling in her chest again. She wanted to look away but she found she could not. His eyes held hers in the same mesmerizing way they had at Hadley Court.

Miles smiled an odd little smile and let go of her hand, walked over to the window and parted the curtain, looked down into the gardens below. Swinging to face her he said lightly, 'If it weren't July and the tourist season I'd take you to Maxim's tonight, but since it is, and since I didn't bring a dinner jacket which is obligatory masculine dress on Fridays, shall we dine in the gardens here at the hotel?'

'Anywhere you wish. Yes, here would be lovely, Miles.'

'Then I'll meet you downstairs in the American Bar at –' He pushed up his cuff, glanced at his watch. 'Eight o'clock? Is that all right with you? It does give you an hour to change and dress.'

'That's plenty of time, thank you.'

He came across the room, paused as he drew alongside her and looked deeply into her face for the second time in a few minutes. He took her hand, kissed her finger tips, then said, 'Of course I came to Paris because of you. Believe it – it's true. You see, I haven't been able to get you off my mind since we met at Hadley.'

He was gone before she could say a word in response, striding across the sitting room, through the foyer and out of the suite. He did not look back as she somehow thought he might.

The door clicked softly behind him.

She was standing alone in the middle of the floor.

She blinked, for a moment unable to absorb everything that had happened in the space of . . . what? Fifteen minutes, at the most? He had followed her to Paris as soon as he could get away . . . he had been in the lobby waiting for her to return this evening . . . and of course he had more on his mind than buying her a decent meal, as Jane had so succinctly put it. But then, so did she.

She had not been able to stop thinking about Miles Sutherland for the past two weeks, and her disappointment over the cancelled lunch had been so acute it had lingered for days. Walking through into the bedroom, unbuttoning her black linen dress, Christina let her mind rest on Miles.

He was unlike any man she had ever met. And he was a man. Not a boy like Robin Petrie. Poor Rob. Their abortive little love affair had gone awry very quickly. And how ridiculous their fumbled lovemaking had been.

It would be different with Miles Sutherland.

He was, after all, a sophisticated man of the world. A little shiver ran through her as she slipped out of her dress and went to the armoire, thinking about Miles. She shuddered, remembering how intensely and passionately he had looked at her as he had held her hand, then kissed her fingers. She had thought, for a moment, that he was going to take her in his arms, and she had felt weak with desire for him. Her excitement and anticipation about the evening accelerated. And as she gave her attention to the clothes hanging in front of her she could not help wondering what sort of evening it would turn out to be.

Her hand settled on a cocktail dress made of a chiffon that was striated in a mélange of lilacs and mauves that bled into each other and faded to the softest of greys. Sleeveless, it had a ruched bodice and a very low vee neckline at the front and the back, and a full gathered skirt.

She knew how alluring she looked in it. She wanted to be as irresistible to Miles Sutherland as he was to her.

A few minutes later, as she pinned up her hair before taking a bath, she peered at herself in the bathroom mirror. She saw his face in her mind's eye so vividly and felt his presence so strongly he might have been standing behind her looking at her in the glass.

'Oh Miles,' she said out loud. 'I haven't been able to get you out of my mind either.'

45

His heart quickened at the sight of her.

She stood poised at the entrance to the bar, wearing a dress the colour of lilacs in the spring, and the choker of milky-grey glass beads encircled her throat; her hair was upswept in a coronet of curls as it had been on the night he had first met her in Kent.

He was on his feet at once and half way across the small bar before she saw him, and when she did a smile struck her face and she came forward in a rush. As they met he caught a faint whiff of her perfume, something light and fresh and green-smelling which evoked sunny summer meadows.

Neither of them spoke. They looked at each other, their eyes locking for a split second.

And then he took hold of her arm and drew her towards the table in the far corner, where the bottle of Dom Pérignon sat in a bucket of ice and his cigarette was smouldering in an ashtray next to the glass of good Scotch whisky he had been fortifying himself with before she arrived.

They sat down opposite each other and he stubbed out the cigarette, lifted his head and smiled at her, very deeply, and she smiled back at him.

In one sense, he was glad to have the table between them. It was a welcome barrier since it prevented him from doing something foolish, like taking her in his arms and kissing her and so making a spectacle of himself in public. And anyway, he wanted to look at her, study her face, reinforce the image of her that was already etched in his mind: it had been for several weeks.

'You were drinking champagne at Hadley, so I ordered a bottle,' he said. As he spoke he heard the tightness in his voice and he was amazed. The tension had been building up in him since he had decided to come here to Paris, and the last hour of waiting for her to change and join him had become unbearable. 'Is that all right with you?' he went on, trying to relax, motioning to the waiter to come and open the bottle.

'Why yes, thank you, Miles, it's lovely,' she said, 'and I only ever drink white wine or champagne, never hard liquor. Anyway, champagne *is* so festive and this *is* a special occasion, after all.'

'It is?' He looked at her alertly.

'Absolutely.'

'Why?' he asked, fishing. He leaned over the table ever so slightly.

'Because it's not often that I get taken out to dinner by a celebrated English politician . . . and one who flies across the English Channel, no less, in order to do so.'

He saw the merriment in her eyes, the laughter bubbling under the surface, and he felt the sudden, unexpected laughter in himself, realizing that she was teasing him, and he thought: Thank God she has a sense of humour.

'The flight was well worth it,' Miles replied, letting his eyes rest on her appreciatively, 'just to have the view from where I'm sitting – it's quite lovely.'

'Thank you.'

The waiter poured the champagne and Miles tasted it and nodded, and the waiter filled their flutes. Miles raised his glass. Clinking it against hers, he said, 'To our first evening together.'

'Yes – and to our dinner. It's probably the most expensive you've ever had to buy, if you include your air fare and the hotel room here. Unless, of course, you do this kind of thing frequently, then I realize it must be very run-of-the-mill for you, nothing exceptional at all.'

He stared at her intently, wondering if she was insinuating something about other women, but he saw at once there was no innuendo behind her words. Her expression was guileless.

Then her laughter rippled on the air between them, light, amused.

Miles took in her merry face and dancing grey eyes and he burst out laughing too. The laughter helped to ease his tension, though not much. He had wanted her for two weeks, had fantasized about making love to her so many times he had worked himself up into a terrible state. Now that he was finally with her he was focused entirely on her, and his whole body was taut with his desire to possess her. He thought he was ready to explode, and he knew that he would before the night was out if he did not make love to her.

Christina sipped her champagne, eyed him quizzically, asked, 'Miles, what would you have done if I'd had another date tonight?'

He sat back, took a cigarette, struck a match, the bright blue eyes still crinkling at the corners with laughter. 'That possibility had occurred to me, I must confess. I did have contingency plans –'

He leaned across the table in an intimate manner, explained, 'I would have invited you to dine tomorrow or Sunday, and if you'd had engagements for those evenings, I would have asked you out to lunch or suggested that we have drinks on one of those days. And in the end, I would have probably settled for a cup of tea, or breakfast, or a walk in the *bois* or whatever you'd agreed to do with me. You see, I did want to get better acquainted with you, Christina, and I can be very, very persistent.'

'Yes, I know.'

'You do?' He raised an eyebrow. '*How?*'

'From what I've read about you in the newspapers over the past few years. You seem to have a reputation for stubbornness and determination ... you certainly keep going after the Tories, keep *them* on their toes in the House of Commons, don't you?'

He grinned, drew on his cigarette. 'That's the duty of members of the shadow cabinet ... to keep the opposition unnerved, off-balance, you know.'

Miles leaned back in the chair, studied her face thoughtfully. 'I meant what I said at Hadley – those photographs I've seen of you in the papers and magazines definitely do *not* do you justice. Far too grainy in the papers particularly, and they make you look older.' He paused, then asked, 'How old *are* you, Christina?'

'I was twenty-five in May.'

He was surprised. He had thought she was about twenty-seven or twenty-eight. Not that she looked it, but there was her enormous success as a *couturière* to consider; also, she had a certain reserve in her manner, a caution, a prudence almost, and these things suggested maturity to him somehow. *Twenty-five.* She was so young really, just a girl.

Miles said, 'I'm much older than you – I'm thirty-eight.'

'Forty.'

He threw back his head and roared.

Christina sat back, gazing at him, her eyes filled with mischief.

'Well, well, well, how's that for a small display of male vanity? And how did you know my real age? I don't think I've ever seen it mentioned in the newspapers, at least not lately.'

She had gone to the library and looked him up in one of the political reference books, but she had no intention of admitting this. So she lied, 'I think Jane must have told me.'

'Oh yes, of course, my sister is very friendly with Dulcie. But then you know that, since it was Dulcie who introduced Susan to you – and your gorgeous clothes.' He poured more champagne into their glasses, continued, 'You've done awfully well in your career as a fashion designer and become quite a celebrity too – and all in a very short few years. I admire women of accomplishment and brains ... I want to know all about you and how you did it, Christina. Will you tell me?'

'Yes, if you really want to hear.'

'I most certainly do.'

She kept her recital succinct, recounting her years of growing up in Yorkshire, meeting Jane at the Royal College of Art, and then she told him about her decision to become a *couturière*. But she did not reveal her real reason for giving up painting, preferred to let him think that she had done so because fashion-designing was her first love.

Fifteen minutes later she finished, 'There, you have it all in a nutshell.' She reached for her glass, took a long swallow of champagne.

'It's been a meteoric rise. I salute you,' he said, giving her a look of sincere admiration. He had enjoyed listening to her. She had a pleasant, well-modulated voice, and suddenly he was feeling curiously soothed. Perhaps this was because he knew she was his captive for the next few hours, and a lot could happen in that time.

Christina smiled at him, said, 'Now it's *your* turn to tell me all about *you*, Miles.' What she had read in reference books had been scanty at best, and she wanted to know as much as possible about him.

'There's nothing very exciting to tell,' Miles said, with a shrug, a small smile. 'I was born in London. Grew up there and in Suffolk. Went to Eton, Oxford, studied law, practised as a barrister for a short while. Preferred politics, you know. Won my first election when I was twenty-seven. Became a Member of Parliament, and have managed to keep my constituency in Manchester over the years. Very loyal voters, fortunately. My parents are still alive, thank God, and I have just the one sister. No hobbies, no interests really, other than politics. I love it, it's my life, actually.' He stubbed out his cigarette, lifted his glass. 'That's *my* potted biography. Rather a dull chap, wouldn't you say?'

She shook her head. 'Quite the contrary,' Christina answered and thought: But he didn't mention his wife.

As if he had read her mind Miles brought his head closer to hers, fixed her with a hard stare and his voice was low, suddenly intense, when he said, 'Oh, and by the way, I'm separated from my wife.'

'I know you are.'

'Jane told you?'

'No, I saw an item in William Hickey's column in the *Daily Express* – when you became estranged.'

'But that was two years ago.' He gave her an astonished look. 'Isn't that odd – we've both read so much about each other and remembered it.' He stopped; his mouth twitched with hidden amusement. 'Do you think it signifies something special?' he asked in a teasing tone.

'Yes, that we both have excellent memories for the rubbish we read in the gossip columns.'

Miles grinned, enjoying her more than ever, then reached out and took her hand in both of his. 'Oh, I think it's more than that,' he said.

'What do you mean?'

'I'll tell you later.' He motioned to the waiter, reached inside his jacket for his wallet. 'I think perhaps we ought to go out to the garden for dinner. I don't want to lose the table.'

46

The tension that had eased out of him in the bar took hold of him again during dinner.

It happened so unexpectedly he was startled, and to his amazement he thought his hand was going to shake. He put down his fork, sat back, looked across at her.

There was a hurricane lamp on the table between them and in the flickering light of the candle her face had taken on a mysterious cast; as she moved slightly a shadow obscured her mouth. He wanted to kiss that mouth, crush it under his own, take her to him, love her with all the strength of his body. He wondered why they were squandering their time here in the restaurant.

Christina reached for her glass of Montrachet, took a sip, regarded Miles over the rim, feeling the potency of his presence more than ever. Apart from being charismatic and charming, he was an elegantly dressed man and this pleased her. She studied him surreptitiously, thinking how well he looked in the chalk-stripe grey suit and the pale blue shirt that emphasized the colour of his eyes.

Suddenly she saw those mesmeric eyes change, darken, as if he was troubled, and a fretful expression flicked onto his narrow, intelligent face; his mouth tightened noticeably.

What was wrong? Did he now regret his actions? Was he sorry he had flown to Paris after all? Dismay lodged in the pit of her stomach. What if he said a polite goodnight to her at the end of the evening and left it at that? Perhaps she had imagined that look in his eyes at Hadley Court and earlier this evening in the bar. Perhaps it was all wishful thinking on her part. She didn't want him to leave her alone after dinner. She wanted to be with him. *She wanted him.*

Before she could stop herself, she leaned forward, asked, 'Is there something wrong, Miles?'

'No, of course not,' he exclaimed, rousing himself, pushing aside his erotic thoughts of her. He picked up his glass, drank, then asked, 'Whatever made you think there was?'

'You looked distressed –' she blurted out and stopped, stared at him, saw the amusement crossing his face.

'Did I?' He put his glass down, took a packet of cigarettes out of his pocket. 'Do you mind if I smoke?' He looked at her inquiringly, then went on, 'I'm afraid I'm not very hungry.'

'Neither am I.'

'So I notice,' he murmured as he glanced at her plate. She had merely toyed with the veal medallions as he had himself; she had barely eaten a mouthful.

Now Miles lifted his head. His eyes settled on her eyes. And he saw something in them that brought him up with a start. There was a new awareness of him in them and a sexuality reflected there as well. He had always known she was interested in him. He had seen that quickening curiosity mixed with speculation illuminate

800

her face at Hadley Court. But was she feeling exactly what he was feeling? Could it be that she desired him as much as he desired her?

Miles bent forward and said in the quietest of voices, without preamble, 'When you get to know me better, you'll soon discover that I can be brutally frank, but at least you'll always know exactly where you stand with me. I want to be frank now, to say this to you . . . let's not be juvenile about tonight. We're both adults and you know as well as I do why I came to see you in Paris.' He reached across the table, gripped her hand tightly. 'I want to be with you, Christie, to hold you in my arms, to make love *to* you and *with* you. Do you want me in that way?'

'Yes, Miles, I do,' she whispered.

'Then I don't think we should torture ourselves any longer. Let me get the bill and we'll get out of here.'

He took her in his arms the moment they entered her suite, pushing the door closed with his foot.

Drawing her to him roughly, he brought his mouth down hard on hers and kissed her passionately, parted her lips, pushed his tongue in her mouth, began to savour hers. Then he tightened his hold so that she was welded against the hardness of his growing erection and ran his hand over her shoulders and her back and onto her buttocks.

Her arms were around his neck. She was returning his kisses with an ardour that was as fervent as his, and she let her tongue slip under his. She felt a shiver run through him as she did.

Christina thought she was dissolving into Miles, becoming part of him, and she held onto him tightly, afraid that her legs were going to buckle. And then unexpectedly he broke away from her and lifted her up in his arms and carried her into the bedroom.

The bed was huge and the sheets gleamed whitely in the corridor of light streaming in from the sitting room. He laid her on it, took off his jacket, flung it on a chair, kicked off his shoes.

As he took a step towards the bed she opened her arms to him and he saw the intensity and longing on her face and his heart leapt with anticipation and excitement. He lay down on the bed next to her. Again she opened her arms to him and he came into them, embracing her, pressing her tightly to his chest.

'Christie, oh Christie,' he said against her neck. 'I want you so much. I've ached for you since the night I saw you on Ralph's terrace.'

'Oh Miles, I know, I want *you*, I've longed for *you* . . .'

He raised himself on one elbow, looked down into her face, touched her cheek gently. He gave her a searching look, murmured, 'Oh darling, if only you knew how much you've haunted me.' He kissed her. It was a long, slow, melting kiss. She yielded her mouth up to his demands. He sucked her tongue into his mouth and he felt the ecstasy of their prolonged kiss shoot down to the pit of his stomach. Every one of his senses strained towards her. Possession of her was the only thing that mattered to him at this moment.

With one hand, he caressed her face and her throat, then slid his fingers down the vee of her dress to touch her breast; and he experienced a thrilling sensation as he realized she was not wearing a bra.

He bent his head over her, parted the neckline, slipped his hand under her breast, lifted it out of the dress, took the hardening nipple in his mouth. He drew up her chiffon skirt, trailing one hand along her leg, finding the silky feel of her stocking erotic, exciting, and when his hand came to rest on the bare flesh of her thigh, he raised his head, sighed deeply, then put his mouth very gently on hers. His fingers came to their final resting place between her legs and as they crept inside the silken pants he felt the moistness of her, knew that she truly yearned for him as passionately and as anxiously as he yearned for her.

Against her ear, he whispered, 'Take your dress off, darling,' and immediately he stood, began to shed his clothes.

Christina did the same, feeling quite unselfconscious in front of him. She was undressed first. She lay down on the bed, let her eyes rest on him as he came towards her. Miles had a lean, taut body, without an extra ounce of flesh on it, and she felt that athletic hardness, the strength of it, as he took her firmly in his arms and wrapped his long legs around her.

His hands went up into her hair, pulling out the pins, and once her hair was flowing freely around her face he slipped both his hands up into it, held her head very tightly between them, started to kiss her face and her neck and her mouth.

But he stopped abruptly, said in an urgent voice that was low and thick with desire, 'I've got to have you now, I can't help it. I'm sorry. I've got to be inside you, Christie.'

'Yes, yes, I know.'

He braced himself above her on his hands, looked down into her face, experiencing the most overwhelming feelings for her. And instantly he saw the radiance that filled her face, saw the joy and desire for him in her marvellous eyes, and he knew everything he needed or ever wanted to know.

Christina reached up to touch his hair, then smoothed her hand along his tense cheek, looked up into his eyes, her gaze penetrating. 'Oh Miles,' she sighed, 'Oh Miles.'

He lowered himself on top of her, pushing his hands under her buttocks and drew her closer to him. And as he entered her he felt a rush of intense heat searing through his whole body, reaching up to touch his heart and then his mind. He plunged deeper into her, quickly, expertly, and she moved against him and they found their own rhythm immediately, their entwined bodies rising and falling together. And he thought triumphantly: *I knew it. I knew it would be perfect with her, that we were meant for each other, that we would be as one.*

And Christina, clinging to him, thought: *I never realized it could be like this. I want all of him, every part of him, I want to be bound to him always, to be in his arms always. I belong to him now. He has made me his tonight. Irrevocably and completely his.*

Suddenly Miles felt a great wave of strength and passion surging through him unchecked, and he could no longer restrain himself, and unable to hold back he cried against her tumbled hair, 'Oh my darling, my darling I'm so sorry I can't help it I'm coming oh please come to me my darling.'

'I will, I will, Miles! Oh Miles!'

'Christie, *now.* Oh my Christie! Oh my God!'

The match flared in the semi-darkness of the room as he lit a cigarette, inhaled deeply, then turned to her and said softly, 'I'm sorry, that was too quick. It'll be better next time.'

'Don't be so silly Miles . . . it was wonderful, you're wonderful.'

'Ah, but you're prejudiced, my love.'

'Well yes, I am, but nevertheless what I just said *is* true.' She smiled at him.

Miles smiled back. It was a tender smile, and he put his arm around her, pulled her closer, so that her head rested against his chest.

'May I ask you a question, Miles?'

'Of course.'

'What did you mean when you said that our reading things about each other in the newspapers and remembering them signified something special?'

'It suddenly struck me in the bar earlier that perhaps we'd been unconsciously drawn to each other before we actually met at Jane's party.'

She smiled against his chest. 'I think I was.'

'So was I . . . I do believe,' he admitted.

Christina confessed, 'When I saw you come out onto the terrace at Hadley I got a terrible pain in my chest, a tightness that was really quite awful, and I felt very wobbly all of a sudden.'

Miles smiled. She was so open and guileless. Relatively few women would have told him something so revealing at this stage in the relationship. But he was glad she had. She was straightforward, an innocent, despite her sophisticated circle of friends. He liked this about her. He was pleased she was untarnished by other men.

'If it makes you feel any better, Christie, I had a strong reaction to you, too. I knew I had to see you again.' He drew on his cigarette, flicked ash in the ashtray on the bedside table. 'And I really was most frightfully annoyed when I had to cancel lunch at the last minute.'

'So was I . . . well, disappointed really, Miles . . . When did you decide to come to Paris?'

'Earlier in the week. Fridays are generally quiet in the Commons. They're usually devoted to uncontroversial issues and private bills, and I knew I could get away early, so I booked a flight –'

'And obviously rang up Bruton Street to ask where I was staying.'

'I did.'

'I'm surprised my secretary didn't tell me.'

Miles chuckled. 'I said I was calling for Susan Radley, that she wished to send you flowers and needed the name of your hotel in Paris. I explained you weren't to be told, since the flowers were meant to be a surprise. And I thought to add that I was the florist.'

Christina laughed. 'Aren't you the crafty one,' she teased. 'And why didn't you want me to know you were coming to Paris? Obviously you *didn't*, from what you've just said.'

'I wanted to surprise you.'

'How did you know I wasn't meeting someone here? A special man? A lover?'

'I hoped and prayed you weren't.' Stubbing out the cigarette, Miles bent over her, kissed her brow, whispered, 'Are you glad I decided to hop over?'

'Yes, Miles, very glad.' Her arms went around him and they kissed quietly and then Christina placed her hands on his bare chest and gently pushed him away, looked up at him. 'Are you going to stay through tomorrow too?'

'Oh yes, indeed I am. In fact, I'm going to stay all weekend. I'm not leaving until early on Monday morning, my sweet.' The lazy smile touched his mouth and he took hold of her shoulders, forced her down onto the pillows. Kneeling over her he began to stroke her breasts and then her stomach, murmuring, 'Now lie still, don't say a word, I want to make love to you in a very special way . . .'

They got up at midnight and went out.

Miles loved jazz and he took her to one of his favourite old haunts, the Mars Club, just off the Champs Elysées. It was dark and smoky and intimate. They sat squashed close together on a red plush banquette, holding hands, and he drank slightly warm Scotch and she sipped icy white wine. And between sets he talked jazz, told her about Bix Beiderbecke and Charlie Parker and Fats Waller and Django Rhinehardt and Louis Armstrong. And from time to time he would kiss her cheek unexpectedly, or squeeze her knee, and smile into her eyes, and as the minutes ticked by Christina fell more and more in love with Miles Sutherland.

Later they went off to Les Halles, the old market, to have the famous onion soup at one of the little cafés, and as they spooned it up hungrily, and ate the toasted French bread and runny cheese that floated on top, he spoke of his childhood, of growing up in the rambling old country house in Suffolk that had been his family's home for centuries. And she listened attentively, relishing every word, enjoying hearing about his youth and his father and mother, and it was almost six in the morning when they returned to the Ritz, holding hands and laughing, still wide awake and excited about discovering each other.

Miles opened the door of her suite and followed her inside.

'You're not going to throw me out?' he asked, removing his jacket, loosening his tie, slipping off his shoes. 'I *can* sleep here with you, can't I? Please don't banish me . . .'

Her answer was a smile at him, a long, slow smile, and her hand. He took it in his and together they walked into the bedroom.

Miles closed the door and locked it. He took her in his arms, whispering her name over and over again as he lifted her in his arms and carried her to the bed. And they made love once more and slept, and made love, and that's that way it was for the rest of the weekend.

47

'No two ways about it,' Miles said to Christina on Sunday night, 'I've got a really horrendous week ahead of me.'

They were having dinner at La Coupole on the Left Bank and she looked at him, put her fork down on her plate. He hadn't sounded serious at all during the weekend. Now he did. 'What do you mean?' she asked, reaching for her glass of wine.

Miles leaned closer. 'Hugh Gaitskell is going to be coming down hard on Anthony Eden because of the trouble with Nasser and the Suez Canal. I'm going to be really slogging it out with my opposition, especially as one of Hugh's protégés. But then I suppose the entire shadow cabinet is going to be on the attack. It's such a terrible mess.'

'You don't really think there's going to be a war in the Middle East, do you?'

Miles nodded and his face became instantly grave. 'I'm afraid so – Egypt – because of the Canal problems. But let's not discuss it tonight. When will you be coming back to London, Christie?'

'Not until Saturday. My lawyer Maître Bitoun needs me here to conclude everything with the perfume manufacturer.'

Miles took hold of her hand and he gave her a mischievous look. 'Shall I come back next weekend ... to be with you here?'

'Oh Miles, could you?' Her face flushed, grew intensely bright and her eyes sparkled. 'That would be wonderful, wouldn't it?'

'That's what I think,' he said and grinned.

After dinner they walked for a while and then they took a rackety old cab, the only one they could find, back to the hotel. 'I swear to God he's three sheets to the wind,' Miles muttered in her ear as they sat on the back seat holding hands while the driver weaved his way across Paris somewhat perilously.

Later that night, as he held her in his arms in bed, Miles said in his low, intense voice, 'I'm afraid I'm getting rather entangled with you, Christie.'

'And I with you, Miles.'

'I know I shouldn't, that we shouldn't, but I just can't seem to stop myself, or *you*, I suppose.'

'Why shouldn't we get involved?' Christie asked, drawing closer, wrapping one leg over his body, tightening her arms around him.

A deep sigh rippled through Miles and for a moment he did not respond, then he said, very quietly, 'I've nothing to offer ... she'll never divorce me ...'

'I don't care.'

'You might one day, Christina.'

'Why won't she? Divorce you, I mean?'

'I've not been able to fathom it, actually. You see, she doesn't want me, but she doesn't want anyone else to have me either.'

'Do I? Have you, I mean? Do I have just a tiny little half inch of you?'

He smiled. Now it was her turn to fish. He had been doing that almost the entire weekend in a variety of different ways, at times feeling as foolish as a lovesick schoolboy.

Miles said, 'Yes, you do ... just a tiny little half inch of me, as you said.' He bent over her, kissed her hair. 'However, I think too much of you to play games with you, darling. I want this, want us, want you. Yes, I *damn well* do want what we've started this weekend to continue ... selfishly I want it. But if we do continue, it would have to be a clandestine affair. That's not fair to you. If Candida ever found out she would create a frightful scandal. I couldn't afford that ... there's my political career – don't you see?'

'I do. But *I* want *us* too, Miles. *I want you.* Look, we can be careful. We don't have to go out ... be in public. I don't mind it being secret.'

'You'll mind one day, Christie.'

'Oh no, I won't, Miles.'

He made no response. He held her close in his arms and eventually they both fell into an exhausted sleep.

Miles left for London the following morning.

He thought about this last conversation a lot in the ensuing week, as he went from his flat in Knightsbridge to the House of Commons, and about his other business. And over and over again he asked himself if he ought not to take matters into his own hands and simply terminate their relationship. Miles Sutherland was a responsible man and bore no resemblance to the cad Jane Sedgewick had conjured up in her girlish imagination. He was honest, caring and decent, a man of honour, a man of commitment. He longed to be free of his neurotic wife; he had no interest in her money or her father's money, since he was a man of private wealth himself.

End it now, before it gets out of hand, he kept saying to himself, but then he would telephone Christie at the Ritz in the evening, as he had said he would, and the sound of her voice drove any thoughts of rational action right out of his head. He wanted this woman in a way he had never wanted a woman before. He was hopelessly involved with her whether he wanted to be or not. *He could not change the way he felt.*

And so on Friday afternoon he flew back to Paris.

The minute Miles walked into her suite and saw Christina, he felt his heart skip a beat and his spirits lift, and he knew that *he* would never be the one to put an end to their love affair. She was like air and light and sun to him.

Christina had second-guessed him. Before he even got a chance to say he did not wish to go out to a restaurant to dine, she informed him she had ordered some smoked salmon, brie, French bread and fresh fruit, and that they were about to have a picnic. 'In bed,' she said gaily, laughing as she brought him a glass of Scotch with ice and a splash of soda, mixed exactly the way he liked it.

After they had sipped their drinks, Miles put his hand in his pocket and brought out a small red leather jewel case. 'These are for you, Christie. Opals ... remember how I said you should always wear opals the night we met?'

'Oh Miles, they're so beautiful!' she exclaimed, 'exquisite.' She glanced up at him, her eyes shining. 'I've never seen anything with such fire ...'

'Yes, and they're going to look superb on you. Come, let's see.'

He led her to the mirror and she fastened the earrings on, and admired them, and he admired her wearing them and they laughed, enjoying being together again. And then she ran into the bedroom and returned with a package.

'This is for you,' she said.

He was grinning with pleasure as he tore off the paper. 'Oh my God, you *really* shouldn't have!' He shook his head, looking down at the Cartier gold cigarette case in his hand.

Much, much later when they made love, it seemed to Miles that he had never touched her before. Every part of her body seemed fresh and new to him, and more beautiful than ever. And at one moment, at the height of his passion, as he soared above her in ecstasy, he cried out, 'I love you, Christie! I've fallen in love with you!'

'And I love you, Miles! Oh my darling, I love you so much!'

They were ecstatic when they were together, obsessed with each other. This was not a question of one loving the other more. They were crazy about each other. They were deeply and intensely involved on every level. It was her first real love affair; although Miles was worldly, experienced sexually, and had had other affairs, he realized that this was the first time he had ever been truly in love.

At one point that weekend, Miles had the brilliant idea of coming to Paris every Friday. He felt safer here, free from prying eyes. And so they made their regular weekend trips through August.

'But we must start going to another hotel,' Christie said at the end of the month, looking at him worriedly. 'We can't stay at the Ritz . . . we're becoming a couple, in quotes, and people are beginning to notice us.'

And so they stayed at the George V and the Prince des Galles and the Lancaster and the Raphael. It became a joke for a while, but then Miles decided they had better stop flying in and out of Paris anyway, because that was becoming noticeable too.

'We're going to have to find a little hideaway somewhere in England,' he said to Christie on their last trip to Paris. 'Why don't you get onto it next week, my sweet?'

48

It was pouring with rain.

There was a high wind that blew the rain against the windows and the sound was like hundreds of nail heads striking the glass.

But in the library of the small country house in the Cotswolds all was warmth and muted light and tranquillity on this cold day in early November.

Christina was stretched out on the sofa, listening to the rain. It was oddly soothing and she felt herself drifting with her thoughts, enjoying the aimlessness of this lazy Sunday afternoon.

She stole a secret look at Miles, as she constantly found herself doing. She loved him so much, more than she had ever believed it was possible to love a man. He had become her life. Her career mattered to her and she enjoyed her work and worked hard. But he was her whole reason for being now.

She existed for these weekends. These were the best times . . . being alone together in this charming and secluded house just outside Cirencester, which she had found quite by accident at the beginning of October. It was available for six months, and since it was furnished they had had nothing to do but buy groceries and move in.

They were involved in an extremely clandestine affair.

It had to be so because of his political career. But she didn't care. She didn't need other people, only Miles. They were together whenever he was free during the week; they couldn't go out in case they were seen, so they usually stayed in at the Walton Street flat. And also, since he was often preoccupied with the goings-on in the Commons, the weekends were the most relaxed. They did very little . . . read and talked . . . and went for walks . . . she loved cooking for him, taking care of him, sharing his thoughts, his feelings, his extraordinary passion and his vibrant sexuality. And his tenderness. He was such a mixture.

He sat opposite her in a chair by the fire, engrossed in the *Observer*. The rest of the Sunday papers were scattered at his feet, discarded after he had ploughed through them doggedly, muttering and cursing under his breath, sometimes laughing out loud, or exclaiming '*Damnation!*' and then grinning at her sheepishly, and explaining and sharing. Always sharing everything.

His face was tense at this moment. She knew he was worried about the situation in the Middle East. They were engaged in hostilities with Egypt because President Nasser had nationalized the Suez Canal. Britain and France and Israel had bombed Cairo and Miles was still fuming in private, and driving points home in the Commons.

As if he suddenly became aware of her eyes on him, he looked across at her over the top of the paper, asked, 'What is it, Christie?'

'Nothing, darling,' she replied, sitting up, swinging her legs to the floor. 'Just admiring you.'

'Aha!' he exclaimed and eyed her wickedly. 'In that case, if you so admire me, shall we climb the stairs together for a little sweet dalliance on this quiet Sunday afternoon? What better thing is there to do than make love on a wet day?'

'Honestly, Miles, you are impossible!'

'That's not what you said to me last night . . . you were full of compliments last night.'

Her response was to walk over to him, take the paper out of his hands and sit down on his knee. She leaned into him, kissed him on the cheek. 'Well, you were terrific last night.'

He smiled his faintly amused little smile, took off his horn-rimmed glasses and rubbed his eyes. 'I think I've had it with the papers . . . I wouldn't mind some air. Shall we go for a walk? You're the only person I know, other than myself, and apparently the Queen, who likes to walk in the country in the rain.'

'Yes, come on, let's go, Miles.' Christina jumped up, then offered him her hand.

Miles held her in his arms, looking down at her, watching the play of light on her face. He loved her so much. Far too much, he sometimes thought.

Christina opened her eyes and stared up at him. Then she smiled. 'You're spoiling me . . . you're always making love to *me*, Miles . . .' She touched his cheek lingeringly.

'Mmmm, that's quite true,' he said, and pushed her further down in the bed, and wrapped his legs around her. 'I *am* turning into an unselfish sort of bloke, aren't I? But we can always correct that; or rather, you can, you know. I'm very available right now.'

He brought his mouth to hers, kissed her slowly, sweetly, until the heat began to flow through him, charging him up, making his heart race, his passion soar. He felt her hands in his hair, on the back of his neck, smoothing down over his shoulders. He wanted her. He seemed to want her more and more every day. He could never get enough of her.

His voice was low and thick with emotion as he said, 'Kiss me, Christie, oh please kiss me, my darling.'

She sat up and knelt over him and his eyes locked to hers. She stared into his face intently. She had grown to so love that face. It could block out everything, the image of it filling her mind absolutely until she was lost in it, overwhelmed by it.

She ran her hands over his chest and down onto his flat hard stomach. His skin was as smooth and as dry as polished marble, glistening pale gold here and there where the half light shone on the fine blond hair on his lithe body. She moved to kneel between his legs and felt an involuntary quiver run through him as she put her hands on his thighs.

Christina looked down at Miles and saw that he was gazing up at her, his eyes a reflection of her own, awash with desire and love. Her throat tightened and her heart was clattering as she bent towards him, her mouth anxiously searching out the centre of his passion just as his own had searched for hers a short while before.

He groaned as her mouth made contact with his body. 'Oh God, Christie, what do you do to me?'

She filled her mouth with his sex, her lips lingering lovingly on him.

Now Miles was truly hers, spread out before her, immobile and breathless, offering himself up to her, a gift of love. And she was possessing the very core of him, his life's essence, his soul; at that moment he belonged entirely to her.

He ran his fingers through her thick and tumbled hair, and caressed her shoulders, then brought his hands down to clasp hers gently resting on his stomach. He clenched his fingers around hers in a tenacious hold. An aching moan trickled from his throat.

She lifted her eyes and saw a fleeting flash of anguish smudge out the bright blue of his eyes, so that they became dark and flaring.

Suddenly Miles moved, put his hands around her face, lifted it up. He leaned down to her, kissed her sweetly, and then gently pulled her up the bed to him. He said, 'I want you, Christie, want to be inside you. I must be enveloped in that lovely warmth that is you, my darling.'

Suddenly he was on top of her, floating over her, and she was drowning in the midnight blueness of his eyes. He entered her almost roughly, and she began to quiver as she felt the rock-hard thrust of him. It was as if they ignited each other, moving in a rhythm that soon began to attain great intensity. His passion seemed to spiral up and up, and she met its flight, rising higher and higher with him, at one with him. There was no separation any more.

Miles opened his eyes and looked at her and cried harshly, 'Oh God! Oh you! Oh I –' He crushed his mouth on her; devoured her lips, her tongue.

'I want all of you,' he whispered against the hollow of her neck. 'All of your essence, all of your breath, all of you!' And he began to move against her with a sudden burst of strength.

Christina felt as if he had reached up and touched her heart. And then, as if from a long distance, she heard his name being called. But it was she who was shouting, 'Miles! Miles! I love you!'

They clung to each other with a kind of desperateness, were welded together in an embrace that was primal and full of need. His mouth sought hers briefly, and as he drew all of her strength into him he rushed headlong into the core of her.

And she heard him cry, 'Christie! Christie! I love you I love you I can't live without you don't ever leave oh my God I'm coming come to me my love.'

He lay motionless with his head on her shoulder.

Christina felt dazed. She looked down at his translucent face and her tears welled up. What was it about his face? That face that so moved her, touched some inner spring of memory so poignant it made her want to cry at times.

Miles moved, opened his eyes. 'What happens to us when we're together like this?'

'I don't know. I think we float off somewhere. At least I do. Haven't you noticed that in me, Miles?'

'No, but then I'm wherever it is you are, Christie.'

'Have you ever been there before? With anyone else?'

'No.' He cleared his throat, said softly, 'I think I know what happens to *us*, darling ... when the sex act is so perfect, as it is with us, then that combination of the most intense physical pleasure and ecstasy along with complete mental and emotional connection makes the experience transcendental. We're transported to a higher level of consciousness.'

'Yes, Miles, I think we are.'

He stroked her hair, turned her face to his, murmured, '*Set me as a seal upon thine heart, as a seal upon thine arm, for love is strong as death –*' He paused and frowned. 'Now I've gone and ruined it because I can't remember any more.'

'*Jealousy is cruel as the grave,*' Christina supplied.

'Yes, that's it. What comes next?'

'I can't remember either, but I know a bit of the next verse. *Many waters cannot quench love, neither can the floods drown it.* You see, I know my Bible too.'

'Yes ...' Miles was hesitant and then he said, 'Christie, there's something I haven't told you ... I did something when you were in New York for your show a couple of weeks ago ...'

When he did not finish his sentence and because he sounded so serious, grave, she sat up swiftly, stared at him. 'What did you do?'

Miles also sat, reached for a cigarette on the bedside table, and lit it. He took a long draw, and then looked at her, said slowly, carefully, 'I did something I vowed I would never do ever again. I went to see Candida. To ask for a divorce.'

'And?'

'The answer was *no*. Many *nos* were flung at me, along with a variety of threats about creating a scandal if I broach it again.' He exhaled. 'I went to see her because I want to marry you, Christie. I don't want this creeping around corners, being unable to take you out with me. I want you as my wife.' He shook his head sadly. 'But it seems that's not to be.'

'I don't care,' she exclaimed, coming into his arms. 'It doesn't matter. Nothing matters, Miles, as long as we can be together.'

49

'What's the matter darling?' Miles asked, walking across the living room of the Walton Street flat. 'Don't you like the necklace?' He looked down at her, narrowing his eyes, trying to ascertain why she appeared to be so upset.

Christina's hand went up to her neck and she touched the lacy cobweb of delicate gold chains set with diamonds and opals, then lowered her eyes to look at it. 'Miles, it's the most beautiful gift I've ever had. I love it.'

'Then why such a long face, Christie?' He lowered himself onto the sofa next to her and took her slender, tapering hand in his. 'Is it because I can't spend Christmas with you? Because if it is, I'll try to do something about cutting the holiday short. Look, I have an idea, I'll spend the day with you on Christmas Eve,' he said, improvising rapidly. 'Then that evening I'll drive down to Suffolk in order to have dinner with the boys and my parents. I'll spend Christmas Day with them, come back to town for Boxing Day with you, and –'

'Miles, no, I won't let you cut yourself in two like that, or change your plans at this late date. Besides, it would be impossible for me to change mine. My parents would be so unhappy if I didn't go to Yorkshire, they've been looking forward to it, and I haven't seen much of them lately, you know that.'

'Candida isn't going to be there, if that's what you're thinking. She really is going to take Monica up to Scotland. They're to stay at her father's shooting lodge with him.' Miles shook his head in puzzlement. 'I'll never know why she suddenly said I could have the boys, I really won't.'

Christina sat staring ahead at the fireplace.

Miles lifted his hand, turned her face to his. 'That is the God's honest truth, darling. Candida won't be at Broxley Hall.' When she remained silent, he exclaimed, 'You do believe me, don't you, Christina?'

She heard the anxiety in his voice and saw the alarm on his face, and she squeezed his hand. 'Oh Miles, I know very well you'd never lie to me, it's not in your nature.'

Miles looked deeply into her face. Her emotions were always explicit in her eyes. They usually told him everything. He saw that she was still perturbed but decided not to press her for the moment. They would not be seeing each other for a whole week, the longest they had been apart in the last six months. He had wanted it to be a very special night and he had no intention of spoiling it.

Almost as if he had telegraphed this thought to her, Christina pushed a bright smile onto her face and jumped to her feet. 'Darling, fling a couple of logs on the fire and open the champagne, and let's settle in for a really gorgeous evening. I'm going to get your presents ... after all, this *is* our Christmas tonight.'

'Righto,' he said, standing, smiling at her. He pulled her to him, kissed the hollow in her neck. 'I do love you so much.'

She extricated herself gently and ran to the bedroom, turned in the doorway. He was standing watching her intently. She blew him a kiss.

Miles was fiddling with the cork in the champagne bottle when she came floating back into the room, her arms full of packages. 'Those are not all for me, are they?'

She grinned at him and carried them over to the fireplace. 'One more trip, and that's it.'

He shook his head, laughing with her, and his heart was full of love. There was no woman in this world quite like his Christie.

'You've always hankered after this,' she said, walking towards him, carrying a large parcel wrapped in brown paper. 'And I especially want you to have it. And it's with all of my love, my darling.'

He took the parcel, knowing it was one of her paintings. Since he had admired them all he did not know which one this was. He smiled at her. 'Thank you, Christie. It's one of your paintings from the shape . . . which one is it?'

'Open it and see for yourself.' She stood with her back to the fire watching him as he carried the package to the sofa and tore off the paper. When he had the painting in his hands he held it up and exclaimed, 'Oh Christie, *Lily at Hadley* . . . oh Christie, how generous of you to give me this particular one. I know it's your favourite. Thank you.' He put the painting against the sofa, came over and hugged her tightly.

Christina saw he was pleased, and this pleased her. She said, 'It only became my favourite *after* we met at Hadley Court . . . and that's why I want you to have it, because it will always remind you of me.'

His smile slipped, and he frowned at her. 'Are you going away?'

'No, silly. Why do you ask that?'

'It was the way you said *remind me of you* . . . as if I'd need reminding of you when you're always going to be with me, by my side, come what may.'

'Of course I am, Miles. You just took it the wrong way. Now how about a glass of champagne before you open the rest of your presents.'

'Coming right up.' He went to pour the drinks, remarking, 'I had a Christmas card and a scribbled note from Ralph and Dulcie. I understand they're going to stay in New York for a while, what with that picture coming up in Hollywood and the possibility of a Broadway play. And what have you heard from Jane lately?'

'She was grumbling about the little monsters going over to New York for Christmas when she called me yesterday at the office. But otherwise she doesn't have much news. She's going to do the costumes for the new Hal Prince play on Broadway and she said she'd be staying on for another six months.'

'Good for her. Jane's a talented girl.' Miles brought their drinks and they clinked glasses. 'Happy Christmas, my sweet.'

'Happy Christmas, Miles.'

They sat in front of the fire, slowly demolishing the bottle of Dom Pérignon whilst Miles opened his gifts one by one, thanking her profusely, exclaiming over the books and jazz records, the ties and the silk dressing gown.

But it was the pair of sapphire cuff links that stunned him. 'They're quite extraordinary,' he exclaimed at last, holding them in his hand, admiring them. 'You're far too extravagant.'

'Listen who's talking,' she said, coming to kneel next to his chair, looking up at him adoringly. 'Do you really like them?'

'You know I do.'

'So do I . . . they match your eyes.'

He smiled and put his hand in his pocket, brought out a small gift-wrapped box. 'And this is another Christmas present from me.'

It was a ring: a large opal ring surrounded by diamonds. It matched the necklace he had given her earlier, and the ring was just as exquisite.

'Thank you so much, Miles. How lovely it is.' She slipped it on her right hand, held her hand out, looking at it.

Miles said, 'Wrong hand, darling.' He pulled the ring off and put it on her left hand. 'Let's just say I prefer to see it there –' He broke off, staring at her. Tears swam in her lovely grey eyes and her lip trembled. 'Christie, whatever is it?'

She shook her head, brushed her eyes with her hand, swallowed. 'Miles . . .'

'Yes, darling, what is it? Whatever's wrong?'

Christina looked at him carefully. Her eyes held his. 'I'm pregnant.'

She saw the instant flash of happiness and pride in his eyes, the sudden delighted smile he couldn't suppress and which revealed so much. And then his face was wiped clean like an empty slate. 'Oh Christie,' he said and shook his head slowly. 'Oh Christie . . .'

And she could not fail to miss the dismal tone, the misery in his eyes, the worry which was now enveloping him. She knew him far too well. 'But you were pleased a second ago!' she cried, taking his hand. 'I know you were!'

'Of course I was, but –' He was unable to continue. Miles swallowed, and deep within himself he knew that he had never loved her so much as he did at this moment.

She said, 'I wasn't going to tell you tonight. If you hadn't taken the ring off my right hand and put on the other, I wouldn't have.'

'I'm glad you did . . . we're in this together. You can't carry such a burden all alone, Christie.'

'I didn't want to worry you, not with Christmas just around the corner. I didn't want to spoil it for you . . . you don't get to see the boys enough as it is.'

He touched her cheek. 'You're always so thoughtful, my lovely Christie.' He sat back in the chair, then said, 'Well, this does present us with a problem, doesn't it, darling?'

She nodded. 'Miles, I don't want to have . . . an abortion, I just don't. I realize a baby would be difficult for you to handle, but I was thinking –'

'Christie, a baby wouldn't be difficult it would be *impossible*. I don't want you to have an abortion either.' His brow furrowed. 'I just don't know what the solution is right at this minute.'

'Why couldn't I have the baby, Miles? Who would know it was yours. Only you and I . . . I'm healthy financially, I can take care of everything, and –'

'I'm not sure that would work,' he interrupted swiftly. 'What if something leaked out . . . my political career . . .'

'Yes, I know, there are so many things to consider, aren't there?'

'When did you find out?'

'Four days ago.'

'You should have told me before. I can't bear to think how dreadfully worried you must have been, Christie. It was wrong of you not to confide in me.'

'I didn't want to upset you before Christmas. And now I suppose I have.'

'Not at all. How pregnant are you?'

'Six weeks.'

He brought her into his arms and held her close, stroked her head. 'We'll think of the proper solution,' Miles murmured. 'Try not to worry, darling. We'll cope with everything after the holidays.'

50

Although Miles had told her not to worry, Christina did little else for the next twenty-four hours as she prepared to go to Yorkshire to spend Christmas with her parents.

She worried about Miles. She worried about herself. She worried about the baby. Or more precisely, she worried about what to do about the baby.

Christina knew Miles Sutherland loved her with all of his heart and that he did not want her to have an abortion. She also knew deep within herself that he wanted the baby, wanted *their* child. Yet she was too pragmatical a woman not to understand that there was his political career looming over their heads.

He had once said to her, not in the heat of passion, but quietly on one of their long walks in the country: 'You're my life, Christie.' But this was not strictly true. His political career was his life. And she could never ask him to give it up for her. To live openly with her. To have their baby.

If she did ask him, he would consider it, might even do it. But one day he would regret it, and she would regret it even more. To ask this man whom she loved so desperately to sacrifice his career would mean that she did not love him at all.

Politics and Miles Sutherland were too intertwined ever to be separated. Miles would wither away and die without his constituency, his political cronies, the House of Commons and his life in that combative and exciting arena. Winston Churchill had once said he was a child of the House of Commons. So was Miles Sutherland.

And I am on the horns of a dilemma, I really am, Christina thought the following evening as she walked in from the Bruton Street fashion house at eight o'clock. Miles had left for Broxley Hall in Suffolk that morning, as loving and as warm and as concerned as he had been when she had broken the news. She had finished her Christmas shopping and then gone to her office to sign cheques, give out Christmas gifts, and to attend the Christmas party Giselle had given for the staff.

Now here she was with nothing to do but worry until tomorrow morning, when she was taking the Pullman to Leeds. After hanging up her coat, she went and put a match to the fire that Mrs Green, the char, had laid earlier, then hurried into the kitchen. She was not particularly hungry but she knew she ought to eat something, so she opened a can of tomato soup. As she waited for it to heat on the gas ring, she made herself a smoked salmon sandwich from the remnants left over from last night's dinner.

Ten minutes later Christina took her light supper into the living room, and ate it in front of the now blazing fire. Her mind turned over various possibilities. She could have the baby and perhaps risk losing Miles. She could have an abortion. She could disappear into oblivion, move to a foreign country, have the baby and live abroad for the rest of her life. Miles could visit her from time to time.

She jumped up and began to walk up and down the room. How stupid I am, she thought. None of those possibilities would work. There is only *one* solution. Miles has to force Candida to give him a divorce so that we can be married. Of course! Why hadn't she and Miles thought of it last night. Only because they were now both brainwashed into believing there never would be a divorce. But perhaps something could be worked out after all. Christina returned to the chair by the fireside and relaxed for the first time in several days.

Resting her hands on her stomach, she thought about the baby. *Their* baby. *His* baby. It thrilled her to think that part of Miles was now growing inside her. Oh, she wanted the baby so much because it *was* Miles's child. She was going to have the baby. She was going to marry Miles. It was going to work out.

The shrilling telephone made her jump in surprise. She went to answer it.

He said, 'Hello, my love, how are you?'

'Miles, I'm wonderful. I've just had a brilliant idea.'

He laughed into the telephone. 'So have I. But tell me yours first.'

'You've got to go to you know who again and make her give you your freedom.'

'Well, I always knew I loved you for a reason, and it's obviously your brains! And great minds do think alike, it seems. I thought of the same thing this evening, and I couldn't wait to get through dinner to ring you. I *will* see Candida again, Christie, as soon as she's back from Scotland. We'll sort this out, you'll see. Everything's going to be all right.'

'Oh Miles, I feel that too. Where are you phoning from?'

'Broxley Hall, why?'

'Can anybody hear you? I mean it is rather a revealing conversation, isn't it?'

'I'm alone in my father's study, and the door's closed. And certainly no one is going to pick up the phone and listen in.'

'I feel so much better suddenly. Christmas isn't going to be so difficult after all.'

'No, and we'll be together next week. Listen, darling, are you sure you don't want me to ring you in Leeds?'

'Perhaps you'd better not. I don't want to have to start explaining who you are. You know what parents are like.'

'I do, my sweet. I love you, Christie.'

'I love you, Miles.'

'Where to, miss?' the cabbie asked, after he had stowed her suitcase in the cab.

'King's Cross, please.'

'Right you are, Miss.'

Christina sat back, smoothed the skirt of her coat and glanced out of the window. It had started to snow. Just small flurries but it seemed to be settling. She wondered if it would be a white Christmas, whether it was snowing in Yorkshire.

She looked at her watch. She had plenty of time to catch the ten-thirty restaurant car going to Doncaster, Leeds and Harrogate. The best morning train on the Northern run, it went on up to Edinburgh. Scotland, she thought, her mind turning to Candida. Miles would get his freedom. They would marry. She would have their baby. She let her hand stray onto her stomach. It was flat. Nothing showed yet. But in a few months she would look pregnant. She would have to start thinking about designing herself a wardrobe of maternity clothes . . .

Neither the cab driver nor Christina saw the huge truck go into a skid on the slippery road which was wet with snow and drizzle. The first they knew about it was at the point of impact. The truck slammed hard into the passenger door of the cab and sent the vehicle spinning across the road and into a lamp post.

Christina was flung off the seat. She hit her head on the glass partition in front of her and landed on the floor in a crumpled heap. She was unconscious when they got her out of the mangled cab and put her in an ambulance bound for the Middlesex Hospital. Miraculously her injuries were minor, mostly a light concussion and bruises. But an hour after being admitted to the emergency room she lost the baby.

51

Christina felt empty and desolated for weeks after she lost the baby. Miles was devastated too; he was kind and loving to her, but it took her a long time to heal.

Slowly she began to pick up the threads of her life, put aside her sadness about the miscarriage. Her work was demanding and it helped to keep her going. It wasn't just the loss of the baby which troubled Christina in the early part of 1957. She was also coming to believe that she and Miles would always be hampered by a wife who refused to divorce him. Under normal circumstances they could have lived openly together, but a politician was far too vulnerable, especially a man like Miles, and they would never be able to take that step.

He had gone to Candida again in February and asked for a divorce. Once more he had been refused. And he had come back to Walton Street looking defeated and humiliated. Christina's heart had gone out to him that night.

As he had sipped the Scotch and soda she had handed him, he had said, 'I literally went down on my bended knees and begged. But to no avail. That woman's made of stone.'

And then at the end of the month the bombshell had dropped. His sister had told him that they had been seen together in the Cotswolds. Even their weekends, always so comforting and reinforcing for them both, suddenly became nerveracking. The clandestine nature of their relationship seemed to grow, become more secretive and restrictive than ever.

For the first time since they had fallen in love, she and Miles began to quarrel. Small, insignificant quarrels admittedly, but nevertheless the harmony, the tranquillity they had always enjoyed in their relationship was suddenly disrupted.

In April Christina was sure of only three things: Miles would never be able to rid himself of Candida, except perhaps through death; his political career came first; and she could no longer support the way she herself was living. Her life was built around him, his needs, and the circumstances of his work and the life he had had before they had met. It was impossible for her to continue.

It became clear to Christina in July of that year that there was only one solution to her predicament. She had to leave England for an extended stay in the United States. Only by putting distance between herself and Miles could she ever hope to break off the relationship. She loved him so much she knew that if she stayed in London she would never have the strength or the will to give him up. And she had to give him up to save her own life. The pain she was experiencing was now too great a price to pay for stolen moments. Also she wanted all of the things he had always said she would want one day: a normal life, a husband, children . . . and dignity. She could no longer bear to crawl around corners with Miles. And having to hide in the country had become the last straw.

She did not consult him about her plans, nor did she confide in him. She knew he would never let her go. It would have to be a *fait accompli* when she told him. Her first step was to make Giselle Roux head of the House of Christina on a temporary basis for the next year. She gave her parents the keys to the Walton Street flat and told them to use it once a month. Her secretary Liz was given another set of keys to deal with the post and other day-to-day matters, since Christina did not want to give up the flat and neither did Jane. And she put plans in operation to start up a New York branch of the House of Christina. She had plenty of money to finance this project and a long list of American clients who were loyal and would welcome her with open arms. And finally, she had her dearest friend Jane who was waiting impatiently for her to come. Christina had confided in Jane long ago, and when she had decided to break with Miles she had taken her close friend into her confidence again.

The last person she told was Miles.

'You look so beautiful tonight, Christie,' Miles said, as he sat down in the Walton Street flat and took the glass of white wine from her. 'Cool as the proverbial cucumber,' he said, giving her a glance that was both loving and appraising.

'Thank you,' she said, 'you don't look so bad yourself.' She hurried into the kitchen on the pretence of getting ice, suddenly overcome by her love for him. It was true, he did look good tonight, dressed in a light beige summer suit. Pale colours always sat well on him. She understood, as she filled the ice bucket, that she could not spend the evening with him as she had planned. She had to tell him at once. Immediately. It was too unnerving for her to be with him.

He said, as she went back into the sitting room, 'I've always liked you in lime green, Christie, but you should be wearing my opals with that dress.' He frowned. 'I haven't seen them on you lately, don't you like them any more?'

'Yes, I do, Miles, I love them. But they are so valuable, I keep them locked away.' She cleared her throat, sat down on the edge of the chair and looked across at him. She said as steadily as she could, 'Miles, there's something that I have to tell you.'

He was instantly aware of her grave tone, and knew at once that something was dreadfully amiss.

'I'm going away, Miles. I can't live here in England any longer,' Christina said. He tried to interrupt her, but she held up her hand. 'No, Miles, you must let me finish, you really must. *You* can't go away, after all you're a Member of Parliament, but *I* can and I'm going to New York. Tomorrow. For at least a year.'

'But darling, why, for God's sake *why*?' he demanded furiously, his face as white as a sheet, his eyes stark with shock.

'Because our life together is insupportable, Miles. I love you, I love you so very,

very much, my darling, but I can't continue. I must put distance between us in order to start a new life for myself, don't you see?'

'I'll go and ask Candida again!'

'It won't work, Miles. You know that as well as I do. She'll never divorce you. I must go to save my own life.'

He was on his feet and across the room, pulling her up and off the chair and into his arms. 'I love you, I can't live without you, Christie. You're my life. For God's sake, please don't leave me.'

'I'm not your *whole* life, Miles . . . only a part of it. You have your political career and you have your children, but mostly you have your career. It won't be easy for you, but you'll be all right –' She could not continue. She slipped out of his arms, moved towards the fireplace.

He stared at her. He thought the world had just come to an end. His world had.

Christie said, 'Miles, if you love me, you'll let me go, you'll set me free . . .' Tears came to her eyes. She couldn't control them. 'If you love me as much as you say you do, you'll give me this chance, you'll never try to find me, never get in touch with me, never see me again. You'll let me be in peace.'

'Christie,' he cried desperately, 'please, my darling, this is utter madness. We'll find a way, we'll find a solution.'

She shook her head. 'There is only one way for us now, Miles. *You must let me go.*'

A million thoughts rushed through his head. So many things he had never told her, never shared, so many loving words he had never spoken, so much he still had to give her. He loved her with every fibre of his being. And because he did, he had to give her this chance she asked for. Too late now to do it all differently. Too late now with her.

Miles took a step towards her shakily and then stopped. He could not go and kiss her. He did not dare.

'Goodbye, my darling,' he said, and stumbled out of the room. And as he ran down the stairs he was blinded by his tears: he knew he would never love like this again.

She wept all the way across the Atlantic.

Jane met her at the airport, took one look at her and bundled her into the waiting limousine.

'Thank God they invented dark glasses,' Christie said, trying to be light and normal with Jane, and then promptly burst into tears again.

Jane took her in her arms, patted her back and told her to cry it all out, and Christina sobbed all the way into Manhattan as Jane made sympathetic and loving noises.

The tears were endless. But somehow she managed to go about her business, to lose herself in her work. It was work she loved and it helped to keep grief at bay. And she *was* grieving for Miles, she knew that. She also understood somewhere in the hidden regions of her heart that she would always grieve for him. He had been her first real love and they had loved each other so very much.

But as the weeks turned into months she became more controlled, and one night she actually fell asleep without shedding a single tear.

The next morning at breakfast, she said to Jane, 'I think I'm on the mend. I didn't cry myself to sleep last night.'

'I'm glad, Christie,' Jane said quietly. She had understood from the beginning that Christie was truly suffering, and that she was broken hearted, and so she had been kind, supportive, and continued to be so. Nor had she ever said one mean thing about Miles. Now she murmured, 'But it *has* been a long time, you know.'

'What do you mean?' Christie asked, stirring her cup of tea, giving Jane an inquiring look.

'It is the first week of December, you know, and you arrived here in July. Six months of tears! My God! That must be some record.'

Christina began to laugh.

So did Jane, and she said, 'Now I know you're really on the mend, Crowther. And perhaps you'll help me plan my Christmas party . . . our Christmas party.'

'Are we having one?'

'We are . . . I want you to meet this actor chap, Simon. You'll approve I hope, because I'm actually thinking of marrying him.'

'How long has *that* been going on?' Christina cried. 'Haven't I noticed the actor chap around here or what?'

'Oh no, he's new . . . and adorable.'

'Actors make lousy husbands, Janey.'

'Are you throwing aspersions on my father?' Jane demanded a little indignantly. 'Mummy wouldn't like that.'

'Ralph is different,' Christina said.

'So is Alex Newman.'

'I thought you said his name was Simon.'

'It is, Christie. Alex Newman is for you.'

Christina held up her hand. 'Oh no . . . I'm not ready for men yet!'

But she had not bargained for Alex Newman.

She realized that he was different from the moment she met him. He had a distinction that set him apart, and which had nothing to do with his dark good looks or his charm.

Jane brought him over to be introduced. Christina had no idea as she shook his hand that he had already decided to marry her as he had looked at her from across the room.

He was charming to her all evening, and attentive to her needs throughout the party. He made her laugh a lot and she enjoyed his dry wit and found herself taking to him. But when he asked her out the following evening she shook her head. 'Thank you so much, but I don't think so.'

'Aren't you ready yet?' he asked quietly.

She drew back slightly. 'What do you mean?' She wondered if Jane had told him something about her problems, her unhappiness, and then realized her friend would not have done a thing like that.

'Don't look so affronted,' Alex said, smiling. 'Instinctively I feel that you've been hurt recently. By a man. And I thought that perhaps explained your reluctance to accept my invitation to dinner.' He grinned at her rather boyishly. 'Obviously it's me you don't like.'

'Oh but I do like you, Alex, a lot,' Christina said. 'And yes, I will come out with you tomorrow night.'

He smiled and went to fetch them both an after-dinner drink, and they sat by the fire for a long time, chatting about innumerable things, found they had common interests.

Alex said, 'I understand from Jane that the House of Christina is ready to be launched early next year, so I guess that means you'll be living here permanently?'

'Oh no, I don't suppose so,' Christina said quickly. 'The London house needs me, and so I imagine I'll commute back and forth across the Atlantic. I gave myself a year to get everything rolling properly here.'

'I see. But your business will be bigger here, won't it? Eventually. I would have thought that you could sell twice as much in New York as you do in London.'

Christina looked at him with interest, knowing that he was a banker, and for the rest of the evening they talked about business. And later, after everyone had left and she was helping Jane to clear away the glasses and plates, she found herself thinking about Alex Newman and his fascinating marketing ideas.

As she and Jane washed the crystal glasses, Christina suddenly said, 'I did like Alex, you were right. He is a lovely man, and different.'

'And rich,' Jane said, grinning at her. 'Not that that makes any difference to you.'

'No, it doesn't. And don't get any ideas, Janey Sedgewick, I'm only interested in him as a friend. I liked his ideas about business and he says he'll be happy to help me any time.'

'I'll bet he will,' Jane cried, rolling her eyes and laughing. 'And apart from being charming, good looking, rich and intelligent, he's also single.'

'He sounds like Mr Perfect,' Christina remarked. 'So why isn't he married?'

'I believe he's divorced.'

Christina shook her head and seemed to shrink into the wall, and she turned away, walked back into the living room.

Jane ran after her at once. 'Oh Christie, darling, I'm so sorry. I didn't mean to upset you.'

'You didn't, Janey, really. I don't think I'm ready for other men yet.'

'But go out with Alex tomorrow, he's so nice, and I know he's taken to you. Please, for me.'

And so Christina met Alex Newman for dinner at Le Pavillon the following evening. She did not know then that he would be the one to heal her wounds and make her whole again.

52

'Mommy, why won't you tell me what we've bought Grandma for her birthday? I want to know!'

Christina looked down at her six-year-old daughter and said, 'Ssshhh, Kyle, don't shout in the middle of the street.'

'But why won't you tell me?' Kyle wailed.

'Because you can't keep a secret, and Daddy and I daren't risk confiding in you, since it is such a special gift. We're afraid you'll blurt it out and then it won't be a lovely surprise for Gran.'

'Oh Mommy, I won't,' Kyle protested indignantly. 'I'm not a baby like Auntie Janey's Clarissa.'

Taking hold of the child's hand firmly, Christina walked her across Grosvenor Square in the direction of South Audley Street. It was a bright June day in 1965 and Audra would be fifty-eight years old this week. She and Alex were giving a small dinner for her tonight at their flat in Eaton Square, and Kyle had been a pest for days, badgering her about the gift.

'Please tell me, Mommy!'

'I'll make a deal with you, Kyle,' Christina murmured, curbing her exasperation. 'If you don't mention it again in the street I'll tell you when we get home. Is that agreed?'

'Oh yes, it is.'

They walked on in silence, much to Christina's relief. She was preoccupied with her business and wondered whether to stop in at Bruton Street for a few minutes to talk to Alex and Giselle about the winter collection now being produced. She decided against it. Her parents, Janey and her husband Simon, and the Sedgewicks would be arriving around six thirty, and it was already four. Better perhaps to get back to Eaton Square.

She was thinking about her dress for the evening when she saw him getting out of a chauffeur-driven car ahead.

Her step faltered for a split second but she went on walking at the snail's pace Kyle always adopted.

He swung away from the car, made to go up the steps into a house when something made him turn his head, look down the street in her direction. He saw her immediately. He stopped in the middle of the pavement, staring at her, amazement flooding his face. He stood stock still, as if immobilized by shock, and she realized he was waiting for her.

And then he began to walk, very slowly, towards her, his eyes riveted on her face.

How extraordinary, he hasn't changed at all in eight years, Christina thought. A little greyer at the temples, but he looks exactly the same as he always did. He was a very famous man now. The Labour Party had won the last general election in 1964 and he was a minister – very important in the British Government. Some said he would rise to be Prime Minister one day. Candida had divorced him six years ago to marry some impoverished Frenchman with a grand title, a duke or a count, she wasn't sure. Occasionally she saw his name linked to various women in the columns but he had never remarried.

As they drew closer Christina's heart began to thunder and her mouth went dry.

'Hello, Christina,' he said softly when they finally stood in front of each other.

'Miles –' She could not say anything else for a moment. She was blinded by the blue radiance of his eyes, deafened by the noise in her chest. At last she managed, 'It's lovely to see you after all these years.'

'Yes ... eight years, Christie, a long time.'

'Yes. Congratulations, Miles ... on all of your wonderful successes, becoming a cabinet minister.'

'And yours, Christina. I see your name wherever I look – perfume, clothes, sunglasses, lingerie, hats –' Miles was overcome. He held himself still, afraid that he would grasp her arm, drag her with him to some place, any place, where they could be alone, where he could take her in his arms and tell her how much he still loved her.

Neither of them could move on, or tear their eyes from each other. Time stood still for them both.

A thousand memories flooded her mind and as she looked at him she knew he was remembering so many things himself.

'Mommy.'

The child's voice broke the spell.

Miles looked down. He cleared his throat. 'I'm Miles. What's your name?' he asked in his resonant voice, offering her his hand.

She took it, smiled up at him, her little cheeks dimpling. 'I'm Kyle.'

'How old are you, Kyle?'

'I'm six.'

He lifted his head. 'Oh Christie –'

She saw the pain in his eyes and the sudden glitter of tears. And there was such yearning on his lean, intelligent face she knew then that he had never stopped loving her and that he was thinking of their child, the one she had lost. And she knew too that he had never remarried because of her.

Christina's eyes brimmed. 'Miles, oh Miles,' she said and her voice trembled.

'Don't,' he said, sounding as shaky as she, putting his hand on her arm. 'Oh please don't, my dear, it's hard enough for me to bear. Take care of yourself, Christie ... goodbye, Kyle.'

He pivoted and walked back to the house where his car was parked, and sprang up the steps. And she waited until the door had closed behind him before she started to walk again.

'Why are you crying, Mommy?'

'I'm not.'

'Yes, you are.'

'It's the wind in my eyes.'

'There isn't a wind, Mommy.'

'I'm taller than you, and up here there's a wind.'

'Oh.'

'Let's find a taxi,' Christina exclaimed, brushing her wet cheeks with her finger-tips, hurrying her daughter forward.

'You promised to tell me about Grandma's present when we got home,' Kyle said immediately they entered the flat in Eaton Square.

Christina looked down at her, nodded. 'Yes, Kyle, that's quite true, I did. However, I didn't say what *time* I would tell you. You'll know when Grandma knows – later this evening.'

'That's not fair!'

At this moment, Nanny Fraser, the lovely Scotswoman who looked after Kyle, appeared in the entrance foyer and scooped Kyle up and off to the nursery.

Christina went down the hall and through into her bedroom, dropped her handbag on the bed, and crossed to the adjoining bathroom. She locked the door, turned on the taps in the washbasin, found a hand towel and buried her face in it. And then she leaned against the wall and sobbed and sobbed until there were no tears left inside her. She wept for the child she had lost, the love she had lost. And she wept for Miles, whom she had once loved with all of her heart, for his loneliness and for the tragedy of his life and for all that he had missed with her.

Eventually, when she was calm, she washed her face and pulled herself together, and went out to the bedroom to re-do her make-up and dress for her mother's birthday dinner. Earlier that day she had selected a mauve silk dress and matching mauve silk shoes, and all of the opals that Miles had given her. They went so well with the lilac colours. And now as she held them in her hands she thought how odd it was that she had chosen to wear them tonight, had taken them out of the safe that very morning. She had never bumped into Miles in all the years she had been travelling back and forth between London and New York.

Once she was dressed, Christina left the bedroom, hurried in the direction of the living room to inspect it before their guests arrived. In the entrance hall she heard Kyle's shrill voice echoing from Alex's study and she walked across to it, stood in the doorway. And Kyle was saying, 'And after he left us, Mommy started to cry.'

Alex looked up, smiled. But his eyes were momentarily perplexed as he came towards her. 'Hello, my Chris-Chris,' he said. 'You're looking beautiful tonight. Very beautiful.'

She met him half way, stretched out her hands to his, looked up into his face, loving him with her eyes. She was so glad she was married to this man.

He kissed her cheek, turned to his child. 'Hey, little poppet, shouldn't you run along and get changed? Grandpa and Grandma will be here any minute.'

Once they were alone, Alex took her in his arms and held her very tightly. He said against her luxuriant hair, 'So you finally ran into Miles Sutherland, after all these years.'

'Yes.' There was a small silence. She said, 'I felt so sad for him, Alex. That's why I cried after he left, it was for no other reason.'

'I realize that, Christie. I suspect he's a lonely man, in spite of all the glory and the power.'

'Yes.' And then she murmured, 'It really is the only reason, you know.'

Alex held her away from him, smiled and shook his head. 'Do you think I don't know where I stand with you after seven years of marriage?'

'Was it Miles?' Jane asked, looking at her intently. 'The man who you ran into this afternoon?'

Christina nodded and pursed her lips. 'So she's told you as well, the little monkey . . . she's told your parents too, I think.'

Jane squeezed her arm. 'Don't be annoyed with her, Christie darling. You know what children are like, and anyway, no one's paid any attention.'

Christina laughed hollowly. 'Want to bet?' She drew Jane closer to the window and edged her out onto the terrace of the penthouse. 'My mother came up to me a little while ago, and asked me who we ran into this afternoon. Then she had the nerve to ask me if I was happy with Alex.'

'You are, aren't you?' Jane suddenly looked worried. 'You don't still hanker after Miles, do you?'

'Oh Christ, Janey, how can you of all people ask a question like that. You know how much I adore Alex. I have the best marriage in the world, the best of everything.' Christina took a sip of champagne, eyed Jane carefully and said, 'Now it's my turn to ask you a question, one that's been on the tip of my tongue for years . . . what did you ever have against poor Miles. You were always so down on him.'

Jane gave her a small shamefaced smile. 'I think I was rather attracted to him and furious because he never paid me a blind bit of notice. And then when he started chasing after you I was worried, Christie. I really thought you were going to be hurt.' Jane dropped her voice. 'And you were.'

'Not irreparably, I wasn't.'

'Thank God.' Jane walked to the edge of the terrace, looked down at the leafy gardens in the centre of Eaton Square, then turned, leaned against the terrace railing. 'Everything's all right with Simon and me again, Christie. It was all a storm in a tea cup last week . . . well, you were forever cautioning me about marrying an actor.'

Christina smiled, took hold of her arm, drew her back towards the French windows. 'I knew it would be fine. Now I think we'd better go inside. I know Alex wants me to say my little piece to Mummy, and then we'll give her our present, so that we can pack Miss Tattle Tale off to bedibyes.'

Alex cleared his throat, and said, 'Could we possibly have a little quiet please? Christie has something to say.'

Everyone stopped talking and Christina walked into the centre of the room, leading Kyle by the hand. The child, wearing one of her best party frocks, was carrying a gift-wrapped box.

Christina smiled at her guests and then her eyes settled on Audra. She said, 'I had an idea last year, Mummy, and I confided it to Alex. He loved it as much as I did . . . it was an idea for this year's birthday present for you . . . from us three. It comes with all of our love, and we hope you're going to enjoy it as much as we believed you would when we bought it for you a few months ago.'

Kyle looked up at her mother and Christina nodded. 'Yes, go along, Kyle, give our gift to Grandma.'

'Here you are, Gran,' the child said, offering her the box, and then she put her arms around Audra's neck and kissed her cheek. She leaned against her grandmother, said, 'Please hurry up and open it, Gran, 'cos they didn't tell me what it is . . . Mummy says I can't keep secrets.'

Everyone laughed.

Audra, her face flushed with happiness, untied the blue ribbon, pulled off the crinkly silver paper, and lifted the lid. She stared inside the box and then frowned. 'What is it?' she asked, throwing Alex and her daughter a puzzled stare as she took out the old iron key. She glanced at Vincent sitting next to her. 'Do you know what this key's for?' she asked her husband.

Vincent shook his head, although he knew very well. He had been in on the secret right from the outset and was very much a part of it all.

Christina said, 'It's the key to your new house, Mummy . . . yours and Daddy's. Alex and I have bought High Cleugh for you. That's your birthday present . . . your childhood home.'

Audra opened her mouth. No sound came out. She looked at the key in her hand, then at Vincent, and she pushed herself up off the sofa unsteadily. She had paled and her eyes were exceptionally bright as she went to her daughter and son-in-law. She shook her head, glanced once more at the key.

'I never thought I would ever hold this key in my hand again . . . thank you, Christie and Alex, thank you so much for giving me back that house . . . it has always meant so much to me.' She reached out and took hold of Christina's arm, afraid that her legs were about to give way under her. And then she smiled at her daughter and the tears welled up and she leaned into her and whispered, 'Oh darling, thank you, thank you.' And then Audra smiled and she went on smiling all night.

Christina rested her head against Alex's bare chest and listened to him breathing lightly, smoothing her hand along his arm.

'Do you think Mummy enjoyed her birthday dinner, and that she's excited about owning High Cleugh?'

Alex smiled. 'Yes, to both of those questions. In fact, I think excited is far too mild a word . . . how about ecstatic or overwhelmed?'

Christina laughed, wrapped her legs around him. 'Oh Alex, it was a lovely evening, thanks for helping to make it possible.'

He said nothing, stroked her hair, held her head against him tenderly. He loved his wife so very much. He had from the first moment he had set eyes on her in New York, at that party of Janey's. He had looked across the room at her and his heart had jumped and he had known he was going to marry her. She was so good and decent and open and honest: there wasn't a bad bone in her body. Suddenly he wished his child had not carried home tales about this afternoon's encounter. He would have preferred not to know that Christina had run into Miles Sutherland. All that had been over so long ago, but he hated the thought that she had set eyes on him again. Miles had caused her so much pain in the past. Then he chastised himself for being so selfish. It was better he knew, just in case Christie wanted to talk, to spill out her thoughts. She had never told him much about Miles, but he had known in Paris on their honeymoon that the man had had a deep effect on her and that she had loved Miles. But then he had loved another woman before he had married Christie. Everyone came with a history and a past. But he didn't suppose Christie would say much to him about the British politician. She was secretive about Miles, and yet she shared her thoughts and feelings on everything else. They communicated, *shared*, that was one of the reasons they had such a good marriage; it was also the reason why they worked so well in business together. They were a good team, the best team. He had taken the House of Christina and made it into an international business worth billions. She had the artistic talent, he had the business acumen, and by licensing her name she had become bigger than ever. He didn't care about that ... he cared that Christie was happy ... that they had a good relationship, a good marriage ...

'Are you happy with me?'

'You know I am, my Chris-Chris.'

'Are you sorry I can't have any more children? Would you have liked another child, Alex?'

'No, Kyle is quite enough,' he said, and then groaned in mock horror. 'Imagine two like her.'

'Be serious.'

'I am ... it's fine the way it is, darling. As long as you're happy, Christie. You are, aren't you?'

'Yes, I am. Are you sorry we never had a son? You know, a son as in son and heir ...'

'No, and anyway, we have a daughter and heir and that's sufficient for me.' He sensed her smile and he bent over her, moved her head slightly, brought his face down to hers.

He found her mouth with his and kissed her gently. And slowly and gently he began to make love to her, touching her breasts and stroking her body, letting her know how much he loved her and telling her in a thousand different silent ways that *he* would never hurt her.

And with precision and delicacy and great expertise he brought her to new heights of passion; as she stiffened he took her to him, entered her swiftly, and made her his. Not only for tonight, but for always.

EPILOGUE

Kyle, Audra and Christina

1978

'I don't want to paint dresses like she does, I want to paint pictures,' Kyle said, staring hard at her grandmother.

Audra flinched at these words. There's nothing like getting to the heart of the matter, she thought, but oh, the brutality of the young. She said, 'I know you've wanted to paint, to be an artist, for the last couple of years, Kyle dear, but I'm not sure you've gone about this in *exactly* the right way – with your parents, I mean.'

'It's not Daddy, he doesn't care whether I go into the stupid business or not. It's *her*!'

'Now look here, Kyle, I won't allow you to speak about your mother in that tone of voice. You *are* being unfair, you know.'

Kyle threw Audra a half-apologetic look, but her mouth settled into sulky lines. 'Anyway, I can't imagine why I'm defending Daddy, he's always on her side. He always has been. For as long as I can remember it's been the two of them against me . . . even when I was little I felt left out. They were the best team. That's what they always said, and it *was* just the two of them, Gran. I wasn't included.'

Audra looked at Kyle in astonishment and sighed heavily. She wanted to shake her granddaughter and if they hadn't been in the restaurant of the Carlyle Hotel, having coffee after lunch, she would have done so. 'You're quite wrong, Kyle, in that assumption. I can distinctly remember when you came to England in 1965 . . . you were walking around, singing, "we're the best team, the best team Mommy and Daddy and me, we're the best team." I remember it so well because it was the year your parents bought High Cleugh for me. You were six. And your parents have never shut you out. *Never.* You've been included in everything. They've been wonderful parents and they love you very much.'

'They love each other more than they love me.'

'Don't be so ridiculous,' Audra snapped, genuine anger surfacing. 'Of course they love each other – they've never been anything *else* but very much *in* love, as a matter of fact. And you should thank your lucky stars they have, Kyle. What do you want to be? The child of a broken marriage?'

'I didn't mean it that way,' Kyle answered swiftly, a chagrined expression flickering on her face. 'It's just that I'm so upset, Grandma. I hate the fashion business and everything about it. I don't want to design clothes and sit behind a desk and do shows and cope with imbecilic models who starve themselves to anorexic death and primp and pile ten pounds of icky goo on their faces every day. I want to paint what I see.'

Her young face suddenly became gloriously alive, lost its petulant look, and all of her rebelliousness seemed to fall away from her. Kyle sat forward eagerly, and her dark eyes shone. 'I want to paint landscapes and seascapes, like I did last summer when I was in Yorkshire with you, Gran. Oh it was lovely, being there at High Cleugh with you, going to Robin Hood's Bay and the Dales, and sitting with my easel and being quiet and putting beauty down on canvas, as I saw it my particular way ... through my own special angle of vision. I was so happy last summer with you, Grandma. Happier than I've ever been. And then I had to come back here to New York and go out with Mom on the road. Stupid trunk shows! I detest them. And I detest the Fashion Institute.'

Audra reached out and took the girl's hand. 'I know things have been difficult lately, dear.'

'I'm getting so that I can't function properly any more, I'm so frustrated and unhappy.' Kyle took a deep breath. 'All it would take to make me happy is to be allowed to go to the Royal College of Art in London for a couple of years and then become a landscape painter. But she'll never understand *that*. All she's interested in is making money.'

Audra's eyes welled with tears. 'Oh Kyle, that's not true,' she said and stopped, found her bag on the banquette, opened it, groped for her handkerchief.

Kyle was distressed and she squeezed her grandmother's arm. 'I'm sorry, Gran, I didn't mean to sound nasty. I'm sorry too if I've hurt your feelings. After all she is your daughter.'

'And she's your mother, Kyle, and the best mother in the world,' Audra exclaimed. 'Take my word for it. She only wants the best for you. Why, she'd give her life for you. I've been on your side all along, but I'm not going to be much longer if you play the spoiled child, and speak of your mother in this unkind and disrespectful way.' Audra fixed her piercing blue eyes on Kyle. 'Do I make myself clear?' she asked in a stern and reprimanding voice.

'Yes, Gran,' Kyle replied meekly. She had always been a bit afraid of Audra.

'Very well. Now listen to me, and you'd better listen very carefully ... and perhaps when I've finished you'll understand your mother's motivations, understand her, understand why she loves her business so much. All right?'

Kyle nodded.

'Your mother was a landscape painter, and she sacrificed her art for the business. She once had what you want so badly right in the palm of her hand. And she was talented, Kyle, gifted, brilliant. But she gave it all up for *me* ... to make money for *me* ... to give *me* the comforts and luxuries she thought I was entitled to have.' Audra grasped Kyle's hand, held onto it tightly. 'I'll tell you about it ... Christie should have told you but she hasn't ... so I shall tell you now.'

Kyle gave her grandmother her entire attention and as Audra continued to speak much of the anger and irritation with her mother which had been building for the past year dissolved. And when Audra had finished Kyle's eyes were moist too. 'What an extraordinary thing Mom did for you, Gran. I wish she'd told me.' Kyle bit her lip. 'Do you think she misses painting? Do you think that's why she doesn't have much of her own work around in the New York apartment and the house in Connecticut? I mean, you have most of it at High Cleugh, and Aunt Janey has some. Perhaps she doesn't want to be reminded too much about what she gave up.'

Audra winced. Kyle's excruciating honesty was unnerving at times. 'Perhaps she misses it . . . I don't really know. We never speak of it. We never have actually, not even in the beginning. But I've been wrong, Kyle. We should have talked, she and I.' Audra settled back against the banquette, looking reflective. I was always afraid of saying the wrong thing, of upsetting her, Audra thought. Yes, I was wrong and in so many ways.

'I don't know what to do, Grandmother,' Kyle muttered. 'I feel awful. I've been mean to Mom for months and months. I must have hurt her dreadfully.'

Audra patted her hand. 'You won't have any problems with your mother . . . I know my daughter very well. She loves you so much. You're her only child, and she'll accept your apology and forgive you at once.'

'Do you think so, Gran?'

'I *know* so.' Leaning closer, Audra smiled for the first time in days. 'I think I've come up with a compromise for the two of you. I've been wracking my brains all week, and I think I have the solution, Kyle darling.'

'Oh God I hope so, Grandma. What is it?'

'I'm going to talk to your mother again when we get back to the apartment. If she's still insistent that you go into the business, I'm going to ask her to give you a sabbatical. Mind you, Kyle, you've got to promise to give her three years in the business later, if she gives you three years now, allows you to come back to London with me next week. We'll apply at once to the Royal College, and in the meantime, until you're accepted, you can live with me at High Cleugh and paint to your heart's content. So . . . what do you think?'

'Gran, it's brilliant! Brilliant!'

'Do you agree to keep your end of the bargain?'

'Yep. I do! I do!' Kyle's face glowed.

When they left the Carlyle Hotel they walked down Madison Avenue a short way.

It was a pretty Saturday afternoon at the end of May and the lovely weather had brought many people out to gaze in the windows of the elegant boutiques and browse in the art galleries.

'I think I'd like to go up to Park Avenue and take a cab back to the apartment,' Audra said, reaching for Kyle's arm. 'There are too many people about now.'

'Are you all right?' Kyle looked at her grandmother worriedly.

'I feel a bit tired suddenly.'

Kyle hailed a taxi on Park Avenue and helped Audra inside, and within ten minutes they were alighting in front of the apartment building on Sutton Place where the Newmans lived.

'Now let me do the talking,' Audra insisted firmly as they went up in the lift. 'Keep that busy tongue of yours still for once. And when I've said my piece, you can apologize to your mother for your recent behaviour. And you must do that, Kyle, whatever happens. Understand?'

'Yes.'

Audra was disappointed when they let themselves into the hall.

The huge apartment was deathly quiet and seemed deserted. She knew Alex had had a luncheon engagement to keep, but she had expected her daughter to be home. Then Audra heard footsteps echoing in the marble gallery adjoining the foyer.

Suddenly Christina was standing there, smiling at them, looking impossibly young in a pair of blue jeans and a white silk shirt and lots of heavy gold jewellery. She was positively radiant. The worry and anxiety and rage which had been etched on her face for the past week had completely washed away. She was like a new person. Or rather, like her old self.

'Hello, you two,' Christina said brightly, coming forward eagerly, smiling. 'Did you have a nice lunch? A good talk?'

'Yes, thank you, we did, Christie.' Audra narrowed her eyes, wondering what had wrought the change in her daughter.

'I am glad, Mummy,' Christina said.

'I'd like to talk to you,' Audra announced rather abruptly.

'Then let's go into my study.' Christina spun around and walked down the long gallery in the direction of her den.

Kyle looked at her grandmother and raised a brow. Audra shrugged in answer to the unasked but obvious question. They were both puzzled by the marked difference in Christina and hurried after her, riddled with curiosity.

She stood in the centre of the study, waiting for them. 'What do you want to talk to me about, Mother?' she asked.

Kyle went and perched on the arm of the sofa, and Audra sat down in a chair. She said, 'Christie, I think I've come up with a solution to Kyle's –'

'Just a minute,' Christina exclaimed, holding up her hand. 'Before we go into that, I want to tell you about the plans I've made for your birthday next week, Mummy. Your seventy-first birthday –'

'Really, Christie,' Audra interjected crossly. 'I'm not interested in my birthday. I've better fish to fry this afternoon. Kyle is much more important than –'

'I *insist* on discussing this first, Mother,' Christina cut in, her voice strong and firm. 'And I also want to give you two of your gifts today.'

Audra was furious and her mouth tightened. But she knew better than to interrupt.

Kyle was also annoyed but controlled her own flaring temper, watching, waiting. Whatever her grandma said to the contrary, her mother *was* impossible.

Christina walked to the fireplace, and stood next to it, resting one hand on the mantel. She said slowly, carefully, 'My first gift to you, Mummy, is the thing I know you truly want the most in your deepest heart . . . a granddaughter living in England and studying at the Royal College.'

Audra and Kyle stared at Christina and then at each other. They were stunned.

'I've done a lot of soul searching in the last few days, and I know how wrong I've been about Kyle –' Christina glanced at her daughter, smiled warmly. 'Kyle must have her chance to follow her own lodestar. As you put it to me years ago, and then again the other day, a child is only ever lent to you. And so I want her to do whatever she wants with her life . . . it *is* hers, after all.'

Audra stared speechlessly at her daughter.

'Mom! Mom! Do you really mean it?' Kyle shrieked, jumping off the sofa, running to Christina, grasping her arm.

'Yes, darling, I do. I shouldn't have tried to push you into the business against your will.'

'Oh Mom, I've been rude and cruel and impossible. I'm so very *sorry*. Can you ever forgive me, Mom?'

'There's nothing to forgive, Kyle. I simply want us to be friends again and I want you to have what makes you happy.'

'Mom!' Kyle flung her arms around Christina and kissed her, and they pulled away and looked at each other and laughed and hugged again.

Audra watching them both, thought: Thank God, thank God. Everything's going to be all right after all.

Christina exclaimed, 'And now for your second birthday present, Mother, I'll just go and get it for you.' She hurried across the floor.

'Why do *you* think she changed her mind, Gran?' Kyle asked the minute they were alone. She was flushed, excited, could hardly contain herself.

'I've no idea. But your mother's always had her feet on the ground, had a lot of common sense, and perhaps she finally realized as I once did, that you can't live somebody else's life for –'

'Hello, Audra love.'

Audra turned her head sharply at the sound of the familiar voice, and surprise widened her eyes. She pushed herself to her feet and went to him, saying, 'Vincent. My goodness! However did you get here?'

'By Concorde,' he said, and swung his handsome silver head to Alex, who stood behind him beaming. 'This son-in-law of ours arranged everything. He came to meet me at the airport early this morning, sneaked me in here while you were alseep, then took me out to lunch after you'd gone off with Kyle.' Vincent smiled at her, 'Alex and Christie wanted to surprise you. I've come for your birthday, love.'

'And it *is* a surprise,' Audra exclaimed, standing on her tiptoes, kissing his cheek. He smiled at her and as he put his arm around her, drew her closer, Audra murmured, 'Oh it's so good to see you, I've missed you this past week, Vincent, I really have.'

'And I've missed you, Audra.' Vincent glanced across at Kyle. 'Now, love, what about a kiss for your grandfather?'

She flew to him. They embraced in the middle of the floor and then, arms linked, they walked over to the sofa and sat down. They had always been the best of friends, and had spent a lot of time together when she had come to England as a child.

Audra turned to Alex. 'Thank you for bringing Vincent here, Alex, it was such a lovely gesture. And now that I think about it, my birthday wouldn't have been the same without him, it really wouldn't . . . why, we've always spent it together – for fifty years.'

Alex put his arm around his mother-in-law, the other around his wife. 'It was Christie's idea,' he said.

'No, it wasn't, it was yours,' Christina contradicted, smiling up at him, her luminous grey eyes shining with love.

Alex bent down, kissed Christina's brow, said, 'It doesn't matter who thought about it – as long as it makes everyone happy.'

'Yes, that's true,' Audra agreed.

She looked across at Vincent and Kyle sitting on the sofa, allowed her eyes to rest on her granddaughter. Then she turned to Christina. 'Kyle is the fulfilment of life's purpose . . . my life and yours. *She* reaps the benefit of all that we sacrificed for each other, and that's not such a bad thing, is it?'

Christina looked down at Audra. 'No, it's not, Mother, it's really quite wonderful.'

Reaching out, Audra took Christina's hand in hers and her bright blue eyes were radiant with happiness as she added, 'And in letting her go you have kept her for always.'